ALSO IN *THE NEW YORKER* CENTENNIAL SERIES

A Century of Poetry in *The New Yorker:* 1925–2025

A CENTURY OF FICTION IN
THE NEW YORKER

A CENTURY OF FICTION IN

THE NEW YORKER

1925–2025

EDITED BY

Deborah Treisman

ALFRED A. KNOPF
NEW YORK
2025

THIS IS A BORZOI BOOK
PUBLISHED BY ALFRED A. KNOPF

aaknopf.com

Library of Congress Cataloging-in-Publication Data
Names: Treisman, Deborah, [date] editor.
Title: A century of fiction in the New Yorker : 1925–2025 / edited by Deborah Treisman.
Other titles: New Yorker (New York, N.Y. : 1925)
Description: First edition. | New York : Alfred A. Knopf, 2025. |
Identifiers: LCCN 2024030474 (print) | LCCN 2024030475 (ebook) |
ISBN 9780593801918 (hardcover) | ISBN 9780593688052 (trade paperback) |
ISBN 9780593801925 (ebook)
Subjects: LCSH: Short stories, American. | American fiction. |
LCGFT: Short stories.
Classification: LCC PS648.S5 C45 2025 (print) | LCC PS648.S5 (ebook) |
DDC 813/.0108—dc23/eng/20240711
LC record available at https://lccn.loc.gov/2024030474
LC ebook record available at https://lccn.loc.gov/2024030475

Jacket illustration by R. Kikuo Johnson
Jacket art direction and design by Chip Kidd

Manufactured in Canada
First Edition

CONTENTS

INTRODUCTION

The New Yorker—which was founded in 1925 by the journalist and editor Harold Ross, who headed the magazine for its first twenty-six years, and his wife, Jane Grant, a *New York Times* reporter—was first envisioned as a humor magazine (a "fifteen-cent comic paper" was how Ross described it). The fiction that appeared in the magazine in its first three years was lighthearted, bantering, parodic, or satirical, in most cases indistinguishable from the humor writing or "casuals." In 1928, Katharine Angell (later Katharine White), who had been hired as a manuscript reader in 1925, wrote to a number of short-story writers soliciting more "serious" fiction, and by 1939 she was putting together the magazine's first fiction anthology—a volume that, she wrote to Ross, would be "a distinguished collection of short stories which, though we didn't set out to do it, we seem to have amassed during the years. It would be mostly savage, serious, moving, or just well written fiction with some that are funny in part."

Reading through *New Yorker* fiction from the first century of the magazine is like watching a time-lapse film in which what a story is, or intends to be, changes slightly with each frame. The stories from the first fifteen years of the magazine's life are, for the most part, what we'd now call sketches—each a pithy short scene, bound to one setting, that ends with a punchline of sorts, not necessarily a funny one, but a telling moment in which the protagonist (not always but most often male) confronts a new reality. Or, as James Thurber complained to White in 1938, "We've had an awful lot of the sad drifting little men, muddling gently through the most trivial and impalpable of situations, ending up on a faint and, to me, usually evasive note of resignation to it all, whatever it all is." In the thirties, plot was frowned upon, as was indirection, and a failure to divulge location, time period, and other salient data in the first paragraph. (It would have been difficult to accommodate very involved plots at a time when White was warning new contributors, according to Ben Yagoda's history of *The New Yorker*, *About Town*, that stories generally ran "three thousand words or less.") White had a low tolerance for autobiographical fiction, as well. "For the purposes of this anthology," the foreword to *Short Stories from "The New Yorker," 1925–1940* noted, "reminiscence was ruled out. . . . Parable, prophecy, fable, fantasy, satire, burlesque, parody, nonsense tales . . . were also omitted."

In the forties, things got a bit snappier. As Zadie Smith writes in the *New Yorker* anthology *The 40s: The Story of a Decade*, "Dialogue was the thing. . . . Many of the writers . . . did some work in Hollywood." Also a thing, she adds, was "a robust sense of morality." Lionel Trilling writing, in *The Nation* in 1942, agrees: "*The New Yorker* publishes . . . a kind of short story the main characteristic of which is its great moral intensity. Every week, at the barber's or the dentist's or on the commuting train, a representative part of the middle class learns about the horrors of snobbery, ignorance, and insensitivity and about the sufferings of children, servants, the superannuated, and the subordinate." These stories have a neatness to them, sharp edges, right angles, clearly defined conceits; only occasionally do they spill out a little and hint at something more. It was a neatness that some of the writers themselves rebelled against. Irwin Shaw, writing to the fiction editor Gus Lobrano in 1943, complained about "the patronizing sniffing of critics when they call my stories '*New Yorker* stories,' meaning thereby something pallid and cold that is inexplicably used to pad out the space between cartoons and the Talk of the Town. . . . There is no reason for losing urbanity, but there is place for emotion, place for personal writing, too." *The New York Times*, reviewing a story collection by John Cheever in the same year, noted, "There are thirty sketches in this volume; all of them are worth at least five minutes of your time, even though the majority are exercises in marital frustration, hag-ridden dipsomania, poverty, or plain and fancy jitters. Most of them appeared between the covers of The New Yorker. Perhaps this accounts for their peculiar epicene detachment, and facile despair."

The fifties offer neatness of another kind. A retreat, presumably, from the trauma of war into the safety of domesticity, the clarity of family relationships—though that clarity is often blurred by straying husbands or the consequences of divorce. Along with that, a return perhaps to that note of resignation. In these years, according to Jonathan Franzen, writing in the *New Yorker* anthology *The 50s: The Story of a Decade*, "What made a story *New Yorker* was its carefully wrought, many-comma'd prose; its long passages of physical description, the precision and the sobriety of which created a kind of negative emotional space, a suggestion of feeling without the naming of it; . . . and, above all, its signature style of ending, which was either elegantly oblique or frustratingly coy, depending on your taste." By the fifties, *The New Yorker*'s resistance to autobiographical fiction had returned. "Narrative writers of the present generation have so often drawn upon the material of their own past that there is no longer a hard and fast line between fiction and autobiography, but we have included here autobiographical stories only where the facts are dealt with freely and imaginatively," the editors of *Short Stories from "The New Yorker," 1950–1960* wrote. In other words, elements of these stories had to be provably untrue. Of course, in the first sixty-seven years of *The New Yorker*'s century, there was no rubric in the magazine for fiction—no banner above a story's title (or on the table of contents) classifying it as a short story, as opposed to memoir, reporting, or criticism. One simply had to figure it out as one read.

By the time we get to the sixties and seventies, messiness prevails. Some stories meander and sprawl, one paragraph doesn't always lead to the next, meaning is in the moment, not in the conclusion. Other pieces, whose authors were perhaps reeling from wars that felt more ambiguous—wars in which there was far more question as to whether one side was right and the other wrong—dive deep into absurdity, the fantastical. In 1963, the thirty-one-year-old Donald Barthelme first appeared in the magazine, with number one of a hundred and twenty explosively strange yet unforgettable nonnarratives. It was a time of change, a time of toying with the narrative line, a time of meaning and deliberate avoidance of meaning, a time of colloquialism, ridiculousness, and desperation, all in crazy coexistence with the more traditional strands of fiction. Read Barthelme's iconoclastic prose poems alongside the sly shtetl fables of Isaac Bashevis Singer or Jorge Luis Borges's multilayered allegorical teases, both of which were first published in *The New Yorker* in 1967, or Ann Beattie's playful, sad comedies of misconnection, which began to appear in the magazine in 1974, and you have a sense of the literary disjunctions, as well as the writers' common goal: to pull us all into the political, cultural, emotional maelstrom of the era.

This period sees also an influx of voices from elsewhere. Although Irish and British writers had found regular representation in *The New Yorker*'s fiction section in earlier years, along with the occasional Canadian, with the exception of Vladimir Nabokov, who began publishing fiction in the magazine in 1945, and Nadine Gordimer, who published her first story in the magazine in 1951, writers of other nationalities were rare until the late fifties. In the sixties, Singer and Borges, along with the Austrian-born Lore Segal, the Australian Shirley Hazzard, and others begin to make frequent contributions. The late seventies bring fiction by Jamaica Kincaid, from Antigua, Stanisław Lem, from Poland, Milan Kundera, from Czechoslovakia, and more.

If there is a shift in the eighties and nineties, it represents perhaps an urge to capture something more sociological in the changing world, and also a new exuberance—a new kind of thrill at breaking the rules of voice in storytelling, if they ever existed. Still, under the editorship of William Shawn, from 1952 to 1987, the magazine eschewed vulgarity, profanity, and sexual imagery. In the mid-eighties, when Alice Munro wanted to publish a story in which a woman's pubic hair was described as "the rat between Dina's legs," she was prevailed upon to rewrite the phrase as the "dark, silky pelt of some unlucky rodent." The prohibition was slowly lifted: the word "fuck" first appeared in the magazine in 1985, and not just "rat" as a synonym for female genitalia but "pussy" in 1993. Throughout the decade and into the nineties, there is a loosening of language, an openness to oddness in voice or in pacing, an influx of styles as varied as those of George Saunders, Haruki Murakami, Lorrie Moore, Junot Díaz, David Foster Wallace, Zadie Smith, and even Samuel Beckett. By this point, stories have evolved from the sketches of the thirties to full-blown narratives, almost mini-novels. Lifetimes—or multiple generations—can be encapsulated, single moments viewed through many eyes, long stretches of time leaped. Change occurs frequently in the space of a narrative; the reader ends somewhere quite far from where she began.

These are generalizations, of course, and there were many stories in the magazine—and some in this anthology—that do not fit into these delineations. About the last two decades it's almost impossible for me to opine. I cannot see the forest for the trees; the root systems are still buried, and will, I presume, be dug up by whoever comes next.

To say that it was a daunting task to choose seventy-eight stories from a hundred years of *The New Yorker*, a century in which more than thirteen thousand pieces of fiction were published in the magazine, is beyond an understatement. The question wasn't just which those seventy-eight stories should be, but what, if anything, they should represent: Did they need to be the "best" stories published in the magazine (as if there were a way of quantifying quality)? Did they need to feature work by the writers whose names had historically been most associated with *The New Yorker*—the Johns (O'Hara, Updike, Cheever), say, or the Irish (Edna O'Brien, William Trevor, and others)? Should they include the stories that had become famous, been reprinted in generations of textbooks and anthologies, or turned into celebrated movies—Shirley Jackson's "The Lottery," say, or Annie Proulx's "Brokeback Mountain"? Should they be chosen to represent the work of *writers* who had been important in the magazine's history, or was the goal to showcase *stories*, stories that had held up in memory, in the culture, in the popular imagination, regardless of their byline? Should I jettison stories that were beloved in their time but now felt a little dusty, a little too *of* their time? Or stories that, although they had literary merit, presented opinions and attitudes—toward people of color or toward women, for instance—that were perhaps thought "acceptable" when the stories were published but are definitely not so today? Should I consider the choices of previous *New Yorker* anthologists? Should there be surprises? Would there conceivably be room for surprises? How could I possibly judge the long-term impact of stories published in recent years that had not yet had time to settle solidly in our imaginations and in their cultural context? What could I do about the glaring omissions, since there would inevitably, for space reasons, be many?

There was no perfect answer to these questions, and I had to proceed instinctively, taking the questions into account, but also simply feeling around for the stories, the scenes, the lines, the fictional worlds that kept returning to my thoughts. The only hard rule I set for myself was not to include material that had come to us as part of a novel or a longer work. (A few pieces here were written as freestanding stories and later incorporated into novels.) The anthology of my dreams would be at least twice as long.

The stories appear in chronological order. Some years go unplumbed; other, banner years for fiction are represented by several stories. The book cannot, of course, be read as a complete record of the short story's transformative journey from 1925 to 2025. But, if that journey is a road, I hope that the stories included here can serve as signposts along the way, with a detour here, a scenic overlook there. Happy travels!

—*Deborah Treisman*

A CENTURY OF FICTION IN
THE NEW YORKER

LIFE CYCLE OF A LITERARY GENIUS

BY E. B. WHITE (1926)

I

Shows precocity at six years of age. Writes poem entitled, "To a Little Mouse," beginning, "Last night I heard a noise in my scrap-basket." His mother likes poem and shows it to Aunt Susie.

II

At fourteen years of age, encouraged by former success, writes short essay entitled, "The Woods in Winter," beginning, "I whistled to my dog Don and he raced and romped as we set out together." Sends this to *St. Nicholas Magazine* and wins silver badge.

III

At eighteen years of age, encouraged by success, writes sonnet entitled, "To ——" and sends it to newspaper column. Columnist rewrites thirteen lines and publishes it on dull day.

IV

Encouraged by success, at twenty-four years of age writes whimsical article on "Sex Above 138th Street," which he sends to popular magazine. The article refers incidentally to seventeen-year locusts. Editor of magazine marks it *Use When Timely* and publishes it sixteen years later when the locusts appear.

V

At forty, encouraged by success, accepts invitation to have lunch with editor of the popular magazine. Editor orders exotic dishes and mentions an opening "on the staff!"

VI

Encouraged by success, dies of nervous indigestion right after lunch, leaving an illegitimate son who grows up in obscurity and writes the great American novel.

OVER THE RIVER AND THROUGH THE WOOD

BY JOHN O'HARA (1934)

Mr. Winfield's hat and coat and bag were in the hall of his flat, and when the man downstairs phoned to tell him the car was waiting, he was all ready. He went downstairs and said hello to Robert, the giant Negro chauffeur, and handed Robert the bag, and followed him out to the car. For the first time he knew that he and his granddaughter were not to make the trip alone, for there were two girls with Sheila, and she introduced them: "Grandfather, I'd like to have you meet my friends. This is Helen Wales, and this is Kay Farnsworth. My grandfather, Mr. Winfield." The names meant nothing to Mr. Winfield. What did mean something was that he was going to have to sit on the strapontin, or else sit outside with Robert, which was no good. Not that Robert wasn't all right, as chauffeurs go, but Robert was wearing a raccoon coat, and Mr. Winfield had no raccoon coat. So it was sit outside and freeze, or sit on the little seat inside.

Apparently it made no difference to Sheila. He got inside, and when he closed the door behind him, she said, "I wonder what's keeping Robert?"

"He's strapping my bag on that thing in the back," said Mr. Winfield. Sheila obviously was not pleased by the delay, but in a minute or two they got under way, and Mr. Winfield rather admired the way Sheila carried on her conversation with her two friends and at the same time routed and rerouted Robert so that they were out of the city in no time. To Mr. Winfield it was pleasant and a little like old times to have the direction and the driving done for you. Not that he ever drove himself any more, but when he hired a car, he always had to tell the driver just where to turn and where to go straight. Sheila knew.

The girls were of an age, and the people they talked about were referred to by first names only. Ted, Bob, Gwen, Jean, Mary, Liz. Listening with some care, Mr. Winfield discovered that school acquaintances and boys whom they knew slightly were mentioned by their last names.

Sitting where he was, he could not watch the girls' faces, but he formed his opinions of the Misses Wales and Farnsworth. Miss Wales supplied every other word when Sheila was talking. She was the smallest of the three girls, and the peppy kind. Miss Farnsworth looked out of the window most of the time, and said hardly anything. Mr. Winfield could see more of her face, and he found himself asking, "I wonder if that child really likes anybody." Well, that was one way to be. Make the world show *you*. You could get away with it, too, if you were as attractive as Miss Farnsworth. The miles streamed by and the weather got colder, and Mr. Winfield listened and soon understood that he was not expected to contribute to the conversation.

"We stop here," said Sheila. It was Danbury, and they came to a halt in front of the old hotel. "Wouldn't you like to stop here, Grandfather?" He understood then that his daughter had told Sheila to stop here; obediently and with no dignity he got out. When he returned to the car, the three girls were finishing their cigarettes, and as he climbed back in the car, he noticed how Miss Farnsworth had been looking at him and continued to look at him, almost as though she were making a point of not helping him—although he wanted no help. He wasn't really an *old* man, an *old man*. Sixty-five.

The interior of the car was filled with cigarette smoke, and Miss Farnsworth asked Mr. Winfield if he'd mind opening a window. He opened it. Then Sheila said one window didn't make any difference; open both windows, just long enough to let the smoke get out. "My! That air feels good," said Miss Wales. Then: "But what about you, Mr. Winfield? You're in a terrible draught there." He replied, for the first use of his voice thus far, that he did not mind. And at that moment the girls thought they saw a car belonging to a boy they knew, and they were in Sheffield, just over the Massachusetts line, before Miss Farnsworth realized that the windows were open and creating a terrible draught. She realized it when the robe slipped off her leg, and she asked Mr. Winfield if he would mind closing the window. But he was unable to get the crank started; his hands were so cold there was no strength in them. "We'll be there soon," said Sheila. Nevertheless, she closed the windows, not even acknowledging Mr. Winfield's shamed apologies.

He had to be first out of the car when they arrived at the house in Lenox, and it was then that he regretted having chosen the strapontin. He started to get out of the car, but when his feet touched the ground, the hard-packed frozen cinders of the driveway flew up at him. His knees had no strength in them, and he stayed there on the ground for a second or two, trying to smile it off. Helpful Robert—almost too helpful; Mr. Winfield wasn't that old—jumped out of the car and put his hands in Mr. Winfield's armpits. The girls were frightened, but it seemed to Mr. Winfield that they kept looking toward the library window, as though they were afraid Sheila's mother would be there and blaming them for his fall. If they only knew . . .

"You go on in, Grandfather, if you're sure you're all right," said Sheila. "I have to tell Robert about the bags."

"I'm all right," said Mr. Winfield. He went in, and hung up his coat and hat in the clothes closet under the stairs. A telephone was there, and in front of the telephone a yellow card of numbers frequently called. Mr. Winfield recognized only a few of the names, but he guessed there was an altogether different crowd of people coming up here these days. Fifteen years make a difference, even in a place like Lenox. Yes, it was fifteen years since he had been up here in the summertime. These trips, these annual trips for Thanksgiving, you couldn't tell anything about the character of the place from these trips. You never saw anybody but your own family and, like today, their guests.

He went out to the darkened hall and Ula, the maid, jumped in fright. "Ugh. Oh. It's you, Mr. Winfield. You like to scare me."

"Hello, Ula. Glad to see you're still holding the fort. Where's Mrs. Day?"

"Upstairs, I think . . . Here she is now," said Ula.

His daughter came down the steps; her hand on the banister was all he could see at first. "Is that you, Father? I thought I heard the car."

"Hello, Mary," he said. At the foot of the stairs they went through the travesty of a kiss that both knew so well. He leaned forward so that his head was above her shoulder. To Ula, a good Catholic, it must have looked like the kiss of peace. "*Pax tibi*," Mr. Winfield felt like saying, but he said, "Where have you—"

"Father! You're freezing!" Mrs. Day tried very hard to keep the vexation out of her tone.

"It was a cold ride," he said. "This time of year. We had snow flurries between Danbury and Sheffield, but the girls enjoyed it."

"You go right upstairs and have a bath, and I'll send up—what would you like? Tea? Chocolate? Coffee?"

He was amused. The obvious thing would be to offer him a drink, and it was so apparent that she was talking fast to avoid that. "I think cocoa would be fine, but you'd better have a real drink for Sheila and her friends."

"Now, why do you take that tone, Father? You could have a drink if you wanted it, but you're on the wagon, aren't you?"

"Still on it. Up there with the driver."

"Well, and besides, liquor doesn't warm you up the same way something hot does. I'll send up some chocolate. I've put you in your old room, of course. You'll have to share the bathroom with one of Sheila's friends, but that's the best I could do. Sheila wasn't even sure she was coming till the very last minute."

"I'll be all right. It sounds like—I didn't bring evening clothes."

"We're not dressing."

He went upstairs. His room, the room itself, was just about the same; but the furniture was rearranged, his favorite chair not where he liked it best, but it was a good house; you could tell it was being lived in, *this year*, today, tomorrow. Little touches, ashtrays, flowers. It seemed young and white, cool with a warm breath, comfortable—and absolutely strange to him and, more especially, he to it. Whatever of the past this house had held, it was gone now. He sat in the chair and lit a cigarette. In a wave, in a lump, in a gust, the old thoughts came to him. Most of the year they were in the back of his mind, but up here Mr. Winfield held a sort of annual review of far-off, but never-out-of-sight regrets. This house, it used to be his until Mary's husband bought it. A good price, and in 1921 he certainly needed the money. He needed everything, and, today he had an income from the money he got for this house, and that was about all. He remembered the day Mary's husband came to him and said, "Mr. Winfield, I hate to have to be the one to do this, but Mary—Mary doesn't—well, she thinks you weren't very nice to Mrs. Winfield. I don't know anything about it myself, of course, but that's what Mary thinks. I expected, naturally, I thought you'd come and live with us now that Mrs. Winfield has died, but—well, the point is, I know you've lost a lot of money, and also I happen to know about Mrs. Winfield's will. So I'm prepared to make you a pretty good offer, strictly legitimate based on current values, for the house in Lenox. I'll pay the delinquent taxes myself and give you a hundred and fifty thousand dollars for the house and grounds. That ought to be enough to pay off your debts and give you a fairly decent income. And, uh, I happen to have a friend who knows Mr. Harding quite well. Fact, he sees the President informally one night a week, and I know he'd be only too glad, if you were interested . . ."

He remembered how that had tempted him. Harding might have fixed it so he could go to London, where Enid Walter was. But even then it was too late. Enid had gone back to London because he didn't have the guts to divorce his wife, and the reason he wouldn't divorce his wife was that he wanted to "protect" Mary, and Mary's standing, and Mary's husband's standing, and Mary's little daughter's standing; and now he was "protecting" them all over again, by selling his house so that he would not become a family charge—protecting the very same people from the embarrassment of a poor relation. "You can have the house," he told Day. "It's worth that much, but no more, and I'm grateful to you for not offering me more. About a political job, I think I might like to go to California this winter. I have some friends out there I haven't seen in years." He had known that that was exactly what Mary and her husband wanted, so he'd gone.

There was a knock on the door. It was Ula with a tray. "Why two cups, Ula?" he said.

"Oh. Di put two cups? So I did. I'm just so used to putting two cups." She had left the door open behind her, and as she arranged the things on the marble-topped table he saw Sheila and the two girls, standing and moving in the hall.

"This is your room, Farnie," said Sheila. "You're down this way, Helen. Remember what I told you, Farnie. Come on, Helen."

"Thank you, Ula," he said. She went out and closed the door, and he stood for a moment, contemplating the chocolate, then poured out a cup and drank it. It made him a little thirsty, but it was good and warming, and Mary was right; it was better than a drink. He poured out another cup and nibbled on a biscuit. He had an idea: Miss Farnsworth might like some. He admired that girl. She had spunk. He bet she knew what she wanted, or seemed to, and no matter how unimportant were the things she wanted, they were the things she wanted, and not someone else. She could damn well thank the Lord, too, that she was young enough to have a whack at whatever she wanted, and not have to wait the way he had. That girl would make up her mind about a man or a fortune or a career, and by God she would attain whatever it was. If she found, as she surely would find, that nothing ever was enough, she'd at least find it out in time; and early disillusionment carried a compensatory philosophical attitude, which in a hard girl like this one would take nothing from her charm. Mr. Winfield felt her charm, and began regarding her as the most interesting person he had met in many dull years. It would be fun to talk to her, to sound her out and see how far she had progressed toward, say, ambition or disillusionment. It would be fun to do, and it would be just plain nice of him, as former master of this house, to invite her to have a cup of cocoa with him. Good cocoa.

He made his choice between going out in the hall and knocking on her door, and knocking on her door to the bathroom. He decided on the second procedure because he didn't want anyone to see him knocking on her door. So he entered the bathroom and tapped on the door that led to her room. "In a minute," he thought he heard her say. But then he knew he must have been wrong. It sounded more like "Come in." He hated people who knocked on doors and had to be told two or three times to come in, and it would make a bad impression if he started the friendship that way.

He opened the door, and immediately he saw how right he had

been in thinking she had said "In a minute." For Miss Farnsworth was standing in the middle of the room, standing there all but nude. Mr. Winfield instantly knew that this was the end of any worthwhile life he had left. There was cold murder in the girl's eyes, and loathing and contempt and the promise of the thought his name forever would evoke. She spoke to him: "Get out of here you dirty old man."

He returned to his room and his chair. Slowly he took a cigarette out of his case, and did not light it. He did everything slowly. There was all the time in the world, too much of it, for him. He knew it would be hours before he would begin to hate himself. For a while he would just sit there and plan his own terror.

THE SECRET LIFE OF WALTER MITTY

BY JAMES THURBER (1939)

"We're going through!" The Commander's voice was like thin ice breaking. He wore his full-dress uniform, with the heavily braided white cap pulled down rakishly over one cold gray eye. "We can't make it, sir. It's spoiling for a hurricane, if you ask me." "I'm not asking you, Lieutenant Berg," said the Commander. "Throw on the power lights! Rev her up to 8,500! We're going through!" The pounding of the cylinders increased: ta-pocketa-pocketa-pocketa-*pocketa-pocketa*. The Commander stared at the ice forming on the pilot window. He walked over and twisted a row of complicated dials. "Switch on No. 8 auxiliary!" he shouted. "Switch on No. 8 auxiliary!" repeated Lieutenant Berg. "Full strength in No. 3 turret!" shouted the Commander. "Full strength in No. 3 turret!" The crew, bending to their various tasks in the huge, hurtling eight-engined Navy hydroplane, looked at each other and grinned. "The Old Man'll get us through," they said to one another. "The Old Man ain't afraid of Hell!" . . .

"Not so fast! You're driving too fast!" said Mrs. Mitty. "What are you driving so fast for?"

"Hmm?" said Walter Mitty. He looked at his wife, in the seat beside him, with shocked astonishment. She seemed grossly unfamiliar, like a strange woman who had yelled at him in a crowd. "You were up to fifty-five," she said. "You know I don't like to go more than forty. You were up to fifty-five." Walter Mitty drove on toward

Waterbury in silence, the roaring of the SN202 through the worst storm in twenty years of Navy flying fading in the remote, intimate airways of his mind. "You're tensed up again," said Mrs. Mitty. "It's one of your days. I wish you'd let Dr. Renshaw look you over."

Walter Mitty stopped the car in front of the building where his wife went to have her hair done. "Remember to get those overshoes while I'm having my hair done," she said. "I don't need overshoes," said Mitty. She put her mirror back into her bag. "We've been all through that," she said, getting out of the car. "You're not a young man any longer." He raced the engine a little. "Why don't you wear your gloves? Have you lost your gloves?" Walter Mitty reached in a pocket and brought out the gloves. He put them on, but after she had turned and gone into the building and he had driven on to a red light, he took them off again. "Pick it up, brother!" snapped a cop as the light changed, and Mitty hastily pulled on his gloves and lurched ahead. He drove around the streets aimlessly for a time, and then he drove past the hospital on his way to the parking lot.

. . . "It's the millionaire banker, Wellington McMillan," said the pretty nurse. "Yes?" said Walter Mitty, removing his gloves slowly. "Who has the case?" "Dr. Renshaw and Dr. Benbow, but there are two specialists here, Dr. Remington from New York and Dr. Pritchard-Mitford from London. He flew over." A door opened down a long, cool corridor and Dr. Renshaw came out. He looked distraught and haggard. "Hello, Mitty," he said. "We're having the devil's own time with McMillan, the millionaire banker and close personal friend of Roosevelt. Obstreosis of the ductal tract. Tertiary. Wish you'd take a look at him." "Glad to," said Mitty.

In the operating room there were whispered introductions: "Dr. Remington, Dr. Mitty. Dr. Pritchard-Mitford, Dr. Mitty." "I've read your book on streptothricosis," said Pritchard-Mitford, shaking hands. "A brilliant performance, sir." "Thank you," said Walter Mitty. "Didn't know you were in the States, Mitty," grumbled Remington. "Coals to Newcastle, bringing Mitford and me up here for a tertiary." "You are very kind," said Mitty. A huge, complicated machine, connected to the operating table, with many tubes and wires, began at this moment to go pocketa-pocketa-pocketa. "The new anaesthetizer is giving way!" shouted an interne. "There is no one in the East who knows how to fix it!" "Quiet, man!" said Mitty, in a low, cool voice. He sprang to the machine, which was now going pocketa-pocketa-queep-pocketa-queep. He began fingering delicately a row of glistening dials. "Give me a fountain pen!" he snapped. Someone handed him a fountain pen. He pulled a faulty piston out of the machine and inserted the pen in its place. "That will hold for ten minutes," he said. "Get on with the operation." A nurse hurried over and whispered to Renshaw, and Mitty saw the man turn pale. "Coreopsis has set in," said Renshaw nervously. "If you would take over, Mitty?" Mitty looked at him and at the craven figure of Benbow, who drank, and at the grave, uncertain faces of the two great specialists. "If you wish," he said. They slipped a white gown on him; he adjusted a mask and drew on thin gloves; nurses handed him shining . . .

"Back it up, Mac! Look out for that Buick!" Walter Mitty jammed on the brakes. "Wrong lane, Mac," said the parking-lot attendant, looking at Mitty closely. "Gee. Yeh," muttered Mitty. He began cautiously to back out of the lane marked "Exit Only." "Leave her sit there," said the attendant. "I'll put her away." Mitty got out of the car. "Hey, better leave the key." "Oh," said Mitty, handing the man the ignition key. The attendant vaulted into the car, backed it up with insolent skill, and put it where it belonged.

They're so damn cocky, thought Walter Mitty, walking along Main Street; they think they know everything. Once he had tried to take his chains off, outside New Milford, and he had got them wound around the axles. A man had had to come out in a wrecking car and unwind them, a young, grinning garageman. Since then Mrs. Mitty always made him drive to a garage to have the chains taken off. The next time, he thought, I'll wear my right arm in a sling; they won't grin at me then. I'll have my right arm in a sling and they'll see I couldn't possibly take the chains off myself. He kicked at the slush on the sidewalk. "Overshoes," he said to himself, and he began looking for a shoe store.

When he came out into the street again, with the overshoes in a box under his arm, Walter Mitty began to wonder what the other thing was his wife had told him to get. She had told him, twice, before they set out from their house for Waterbury. In a way he hated these weekly trips to town—he was always getting something wrong. Kleenex, he thought, Squibb's, razor blades? No.

Toothpaste, toothbrush, bicarbonate, carborundum, initiative and referendum? He gave it up. But she would remember it. "Where's the what's-its-name?" she would ask. "Don't tell me you forgot the what's-its-name." A newsboy went by shouting something about the Waterbury trial.

. . . "Perhaps this will refresh your memory." The District Attorney suddenly thrust a heavy automatic at the quiet figure on the witness stand. "Have you ever seen this before?" Walter Mitty took the gun and examined it expertly. "This is my Webley-Vickers 50.80," he said calmly. An excited buzz ran around the courtroom. The Judge rapped for order. "You are a crack shot with any sort of firearms, I believe?" said the District Attorney, insinuatingly. "Objection!" shouted Mitty's attorney. "We have shown that the defendant could not have fired the shot. We have shown that he wore his right arm in a sling on the night of the fourteenth of July." Walter Mitty raised his hand briefly and the bickering attorneys were stilled. "With any known make of gun," he said evenly, "I could have killed Gregory Fitzhurst at three hundred feet *with my left hand.*" Pandemonium broke loose in the courtroom. A woman's scream rose above the bedlam and suddenly a lovely, dark-haired girl was in Walter Mitty's arms. The District Attorney struck at her savagely. Without rising from his chair, Mitty let the man have it on the point of the chin. "You miserable cur!" . . .

"Puppy biscuit," said Walter Mitty. He stopped walking and the buildings of Waterbury rose up out of the misty courtroom and surrounded him again. A woman who was passing laughed. "He said 'Puppy biscuit,'" she said to her companion. "That man said 'Puppy biscuit' to himself." Walter Mitty hurried on. He went into an A. & P., not the first one he came to but a smaller one farther up the street. "I want some biscuit for small, young dogs," he said to the clerk. "Any special brand, sir?" The greatest pistol shot in the world thought a moment. "It says 'Puppies Bark for It' on the box," said Walter Mitty.

His wife would be through at the hairdresser's in fifteen minutes, Mitty saw in looking at his watch, unless they had trouble drying it; sometimes they had trouble drying it. She didn't like to get to the hotel first; she would want him to be there waiting for her as usual.

He found a big leather chair in the lobby, facing a window, and he put the overshoes and the puppy biscuit on the floor beside it. He picked up an old copy of *Liberty* and sank down into the chair. "Can Germany Conquer the World Through the Air?" Walter Mitty looked at the pictures of bombing planes and of ruined streets.

. . . "The cannonading has got the wind up in young Raleigh, sir," said the sergeant. Captain Mitty looked up at him through tousellled hair. "Get him to bed," he said wearily. "With the others. I'll fly alone." "But you can't, sir," said the sergeant anxiously. "It takes two men to handle that bomber and the Archies are pounding hell out of the air. Von Richtman's circus is between here and Saulier." "Somebody's got to get that ammunition dump," said Mitty. "I'm going over. Spot of brandy?" He poured a drink for the sergeant and one for himself. War thundered and whined around the dugout and battered at the door. There was a rending of wood and splinters flew through the room. "A bit of a near thing," said Captain Mitty carelessly. "The box barrage is closing in," said the sergeant. "We only live once, Sergeant," said Mitty, with his faint, fleeting smile. "Or do we?" He poured another brandy and tossed it off. "I never see a man could hold his brandy like you, sir," said the sergeant. "Begging your pardon, sir." Captain Mitty stood up and strapped on his huge Webley-Vickers automatic. "It's forty kilometres through hell, sir," said the sergeant. Mitty finished one last brandy. "After all," he said softly, "what isn't?" The pounding of the cannon increased; there was the rat-tat-tatting of machine guns, and from somewhere came the menacing pocketa-pocketa-pocketa of the new flame-throwers. Walter Mitty walked to the door of the dugout humming "Auprès de Ma Blonde." He turned and waved to the sergeant. "Cheerio!" he said. . . .

Something struck his shoulder. "I've been looking all over this hotel for you," said Mrs. Mitty. "Why do you have to hide in this old chair? How did you expect me to find you?" "Things close in," said Walter Mitty vaguely. "What?" Mrs. Mitty said. "Did you get the what's-its-name? The puppy biscuit? What's in that box?" "Overshoes," said Mitty. "Couldn't you have put them on in the store?" "I was thinking," said Walter Mitty. "Does it ever occur to you that I am sometimes thinking?" She looked at him. "I'm going to take your temperature when I get you home," she said.

. . .

They went out through the revolving doors that made a faintly derisive whistling sound when you pushed them. It was two blocks to the parking lot. At the drugstore on the corner she said, "Wait here for me. I forgot something. I won't be a minute." She was more than a minute. Walter Mitty lighted a cigarette. It began to rain, rain with sleet in it. He stood up against the wall of the drugstore, smoking. . . . He put his shoulders back and his heels together. "To hell with the handkerchief," said Walter Mitty scornfully. He took one last drag on his cigarette and snapped it away. Then, with that faint, fleeting smile playing about his lips, he faced the firing squad; erect and motionless, proud and disdainful, Walter Mitty the Undefeated, inscrutable to the last.

SUCH A PRETTY DAY

BY DAWN POWELL (1939)

As soon as Dave had put the pen in the yard and waved goodbye to the baby, Sylvia got on the phone.

"Hello, Barbs. Scotty gone yet? . . . Listen, Barbs, Dave says they're working overtime this noon, so he won't be home for lunch. . . . Scotty, too, eh? Listen, Barbs, it's such a pretty day, I thought we might go to the city. You bring the kids over and I'll get Frieda. . . . Yes, I know she's a brat and she'll tell the whole neighborhood, but she's good with the kids. Listen, don't say anything. My God, Dave'd kill me. You heard what he said last Sunday—if he caught me thumbing again he'd get a divorce? Listen, he means it. You come on over, Barbs. . . . O.K., Barbs. . . . Oh, I'm goin' to wear my play suit. . . . Your linen? Why don't you wear your play suit? It looks kinda cute on you. . . . Oh, come on, Barbs, I'm going to. . . . O.K., Barbs. The baby's yelling. 'Bye."

Sylvia ran into the bedroom and whisked up the beds. She snatched up newspapers, toys, Dave's pajamas, a ten-cent double boiler with some petrified oatmeal in it, and tossed them all in the closet. That was one thing about having your own house; your mother couldn't be nagging at you to do things her way all the time. Sylvia couldn't get over the thrill of her own house. Five whole rooms, just for her and Dave and the baby. Never had even one room to herself before she was married. Darn it all, she was happy. Let 'em talk. Her own mother was married at sixteen, too, wasn't she? Supposing she'd sat around and finished school, what then? She could have a job in the factory and get up every morning at six-thirty like Gladys Chalk, instead of lying around her own house all day in a nightgown. She could sit around waiting for some guy to call her up, and God knows there weren't enough boys in town to go around, instead of having a nice fellow like Dave all sewed up permanently. So maybe Sylvia wasn't so dumb as her folks said. So what?

Mrs. Peters was in the back yard fooling with the baby when Sylvia went out, and that was all right, because she could ask her about Frieda.

"You look about ten years old in those overalls," said Mrs. Peters. "I should think youda put on more weight being married two years already. I wouldn't take you for more'n twelve at the most."

"No cracks," said Sylvia coldly. "I was nineteen last Tuesday. Did you see the toaster Dave got me? We don't eat much toast, but I have to make a lot 'cause it makes the baby laugh so the way the toast jumps out."

"I don't think that installment plan is good for young folks," said Mrs. Peters, as if it was any of her business, but Sylvia took it because she wanted Frieda.

"How else you going to get anything on eighteen a week, Mrs. Peters?" she merely asked. "Look, Mrs. Peters, could Frieda come over today and look after Davie? I got a chance to go to the city—there's a picture I want to see at the Majestic."

Mrs. Peters blew out her cheeks, and Davie laughed and squealed with joy. He was a good baby. Even Mrs. Peters had to say so.

"I couldn't run around the way you do when I was raising a family," said Mrs. Peters. "If it wasn't washing, it was canning or berrying or helping in Mr. Peters' store."

All right, we'll go into that, then. The trouble with those old married women was they thought they had a racket all to themselves and they didn't like pretty young girls breaking into it.

"Tell Frieda she can make a cake if she wants, too," Sylvia conceded. "There's flour and chocolate, and she can run the radio for a while."

"If it's that Barbara friend of yours you're going with," said Mrs. Peters, "I wouldn't let any daughter of mine run around with her. Her folks are nothing but trash. There hasn't ever been a Moller that amounted to a stick in this town. Frieda says she saw six beer bottles in the sink there one morning."

"Barbs and Scotty are Dave's and my best friends," said Sylvia in her best missus voice, and was that a lie, with Dave half the time saying just what Mrs. Peters was saying! "Tell Frieda to come about eleven. We want to get a good start."

Barbs walked in, wheeling the twins. They were not quite a year old but were big babies, like Davie, and made Barbs look like a school kid, which she probably should have been, but keeping house was a lot more fun. You could say what you liked about Barbs, maybe she did run wild until Scotty and the twins kinda settled her, but you had to hand it to her—she kept that dinky apartment of hers spick-and-span. "Maybe," Sylvia always said, looking around the trim little suite over the butcher shop, "if I only had three rooms instead of a whole house I could get interested, too."

Frieda came over at ten minutes to eleven. She wore thick glasses over her slightly crossed eyes and her former pigtails had been miraculously transformed into a kinky, tangled mass.

"I got a permanent," she said proudly.

Both Barbs and Sylvia were crazy for permanents, so they were silent for a moment in envious awe.

"I don't like permanents on kids," said Barbs haughtily.

"Everybody in my Sunday-school class has one," said Frieda, unperturbed. "My mother says it's a hundred-per-cent improvement. My mother's making me a play suit too. Where you going? To the city? I thought Dave told you not to thumb any more, Sylvia."

"Listen to the brat," said Barbs. "Do you run this town, Miss Wisie?"

"You better be careful or I won't take care of your old twins," said Frieda. "Can I really make a cake, Sylvia?"

Sylvia motioned Barbs into the house, and they went in to whisper ways of getting out to the turnpike without Frieda's being able to tell. Scotty didn't like Barbs' hitching any more than Dave liked Sylvia's, because everybody in the town talked enough anyway, and she was a married woman now and ought to know better.

At first Sylvia thought it was because Scotty was older—he was twenty-seven—and more settled—he'd worked in the factory since he was twelve—but then Dave, who was just twenty, got to talking that way, too. They didn't want their wives hiking around the state like a couple of tramps, they both said. You didn't see the Hull girls doing it, did you? Or Dody Crane?

"The Hull girls and Dody Crane! Can you imagine?" Sylvia repeated in indignation. "Why should they? They got their own cars, and Dody's dad is rich."

At that, Sylvia had nothing against Dody. The Hull girls were snobs because they'd gone away to boarding school while Sylvia and Barbs were plugging through public school, but Dody was all right; she always spoke to Sylvia, and once Dave had taken her to a dance. She wouldn't let him kiss her, so he married Sylvia instead and promoted Dody to be his ideal. Sylvia got kind of sick always being pecked at to do things the way Dody would do them. That was the only thing. But Dody was all right. She sent the baby a cute blanket once.

Barbs stuck the twins' bottles in the icebox and Frieda put all the babies in the pen. She was a fat little girl, but that wasn't the only reason nobody loved her. She pulled out a campstool from behind the tool shed and sat down on it on the grass with a book.

"I'll read to them for a while," she said, "from the Bible."

The three fat little babies, clad in nothing but their G-strings, stared at Frieda, rather pleased with her glasses.

"They'll love that," said Sylvia, and she and Barbs sneaked out the front way, past the garage, to the pike.

They walked sedately enough past the straggling houses, and tried not to look up at tempting cars shooting past, because you couldn't tell yet; it might be somebody from the factory, who would tell the boys. A roadster with two men in it slowed up and one of them yelled, "Hi, Crawford," but the girls dared not look up yet.

"You know, Sylvia, you do look kinda like Joan Crawford," said Barbs, studying Sylvia critically. "Somebody else, I forget who, said so. Me, I'm more the Merle Oberon type."

"You got freckles, too, if that's what you mean," said Sylvia.

A blue sedan drove slowly past, and Barbs nudged Sylvia. It was the Hull sisters on their way to the country club. They stared at the two girls and Barbs and Sylvia stared insolently back. Then Dody Crane's car came along, Dody driving with her mother, two golf bags sticking out of the side. Dody nodded and Sylvia nodded back.

"Imagine a girl that old running around all the time with her old lady," said Barbs, who after all had been ignored by Dody.

Now they were past the club road and on the main highway. They stopped and began working. It never took them long, because they were a couple of good-looking girls, as they well knew, and even women weren't afraid of being held up by such a nice little pair. This time it was a woman in a big Cadillac. She was a thin, browned woman with iron-gray hair, and she drove like a house afire. Some fun! They were in the heart of the city in less than an hour.

"Let's go to the show right away," suggested Sylvia.

Everybody looked at the two bareheaded girls, in their red play suits, wandering through the business section. Barbs stopped short suddenly.

"Listen, Sylvia, I only got fifteen cents."

"But I told you we would go to the Majestic," said Sylvia, annoyed. "You know it's twenty."

"Well, I just don't have it," said Barbs, doggedly. "I guess you wouldn't have it, either, if you had two kids instead of one and your husband had to fork over two bucks a week to his mother."

"Why don't she get on relief?" complained Sylvia. "Dave's mother did."

"Dave's mother is in another town," said Barbs. "And anyway Scotty don't like the idea. So I only got fifteen cents."

Sylvia was furious.

"I go to work and get Frieda for us and let her mess up my kitchen baking a cake, and now you don't have twenty cents for a show. Barbs, honestly, you're a lousy sport. Why didn't you tell me?"

Barbs was sullen.

"I wanted to get outa town for five minutes, show or no show."

Sylvia counted her money. Thirty-seven cents.

"You go alone, and I'll look around the stores," said Barbs.

It ended with their each buying a Frojoy at a corner stand for lunch and then going on a shopping tour. They went through Schwab's because Barbs dared Sylvia to go in. This was a large, cool, dark, swanky store, and so snooty that Barbs and Sylvia clutched each other's hand to keep up their courage before the hostile clerks.

"This is where Dody gets all her clothes," said Sylvia. "Except the ones she gets in New York."

"A lot of good it does her," said Barbs. "I'll bet she'd give her eye-teeth to be married and have kids like we have. She played with dolls longer than any of us. She had the first mamma doll in town."

"I wish I had a little girl," said Sylvia. "I'd get her a mamma doll."

"I'd get her a Quint Set doll," said Barbs, and that reminded her they must go to the Variety store next.

Schwab's doors swung thankfully behind them.

"Even if I had money, I wouldn't buy clothes in that lousy store," said Barbs. "Their styles are all hick. They've got braid on everything. Look!"

A window display of garden furniture, complete with sand, pool, umbrellas, and mint juleps, held them spellbound. Life-size velvety-lashed ladies in garden frocks sat in swings and deck chairs in attitudes of rigid enjoyment. A rosy, wall-eyed athlete in shorts relaxed on a tennis roller. Two beaming little boys in bathing suits sat stiffly on a rubber dolphin in the pool.

"I could get the twins bathing suits and one of those false fish," said Barbs. "I'd fill the old tank on the roof with water."

"Like a penthouse," said Sylvia.

They walked on silently to the big Variety store, Sylvia busy putting the fish and Davie in a bathing suit somewhere around her own premises, and Barbs thinking about the tank. The Variety store was more hospitable than Schwab's. A radio was on, and a girl at the piano counter, in a pink sharkskin sports dress, was playing and singing "I Never Knew Heaven Could Speak."

"Say, if I couldn't sing better than that," muttered Barbs.

"It's my favorite song, too," said Sylvia. "But don't she ruin it?"

They hummed it softly, looking over the counters.

"I'll bet we could sing over the radio if we practiced more," said Sylvia. "Honestly, Barbs, even Dave thinks we're good."

"Ah, nuts!" said Barbs. "Nobody's going to let us do anything ever. Wish I had my hands on that two bucks we sent off to Scotty's Mom right now."

"I could let you have ten cents, maybe," said Sylvia, relenting, but just then her eye caught something and she added, "Still, you got ten of your own, haven't you?"

Barbs saw what Sylvia saw. It was a baby's bathing suit for twenty-nine cents. Probably it was only fair. After all, Sylvia did have thirty-two cents and only one baby.

"Now, you only got three cents," was all Barbs said when the girl gave Sylvia the package. Sylvia unwrapped it right away and held it up. It was bright red, with a little white belt. It was the cutest thing.

"I'd rather have had the striped ones like the ones in the window," said Barbs, but Sylvia read the envy in her voice and grinned.

At the next counter were spades and beach pails, and here Barbs was as lost as Sylvia, because she had to buy two or nothing, so ten cents was no good. At the foot of the counter were rubber floats, and one was a dolphin almost like the one in the window. It was a dollar ninety-eight and it came in a box; you blew it up. Sylvia and Barbs stared at it.

"Kids don't need bathing suits on a roof," said Barbs. "I can fill that old tank anyway."

"Sure," said Sylvia.

"You can bring Davie up to play in it, too," said Barbs, generously. "But he won't need that suit."

"That'll be fun," said Sylvia. Twenty-nine cents wasted.

They could not take their eyes off the sample dolphin.

"He'd hold two, wouldn't he?" said Barbs.

"Sure—three, even," giggled Sylvia.

She almost knew what Barbs was going to do, and yet in a way you could have knocked her down with a feather. The minute the clerk walked off to the next counter, Barbs had snitched one of the rubber things out of its box and stuffed it down her front. Nothing happened. Nobody screamed. Nobody grabbed them. Barbs looked at Sylvia, and Sylvia's mouth moved helplessly.

"W-w-w-well," said Barbs, "I g-g-g-uess we'd b-b-etter be g-g-g-going to the M-m-m-ajestic."

They walked slowly out of the store. A man in a Panama hat watched them from the radio counter, but he couldn't be anything but a customer. The girl at the bathing-suit counter watched them.

"She saw," gasped Barbs. "Just as I popped it in, I saw her looking, but it was too late to yank it out then. Look—I'm afraid to—is anybody following?"

Sylvia was afraid, too. They walked in slow agony down the street. Someone was behind them. Out of the corner of her eye Sylvia saw it was the man in the Panama hat. He grinned. Sylvia grew red. Barbs clutched her arm frantically.

"Let's get a hitch, quick," she whispered. "We got to go home now."

"But it's only two o'clock," said Sylvia. "Anyway, if somebody's watching from the store, they'll see us."

"Oh—oh, what'll we do," whispered Barbs. "Does it show?"

Sylvia giggled.

"No, you only look like Aunt Jemima, that's all."

Barbs was looking up and down the street for a possible hitch. The man in the Panama hat was getting into a Chevrolet coupé. He grinned again, and imperceptibly winked. Barbs and Sylvia walked up to him. Before they spoke, two men in shirtsleeves from the Variety came out on the sidewalk, and with one accord the girls climbed into his car. He slammed the door and drove quickly around the corner.

"Oh, gee!" breathed Barbs. "Oh thanks!"

The man was a swarthy, foreign-looking fellow, with a candy-striped shirt and a diamond ring.

"I got the idea," he said.

Nobody said anything more till they were outside the city limits, and then Sylvia noticed they were not going in the direction of home.

"Albany's my next stop," said the driver. He turned to Barbs. "That wasn't your first job there in the store, was it, sugar?"

Barbs looked blank.

"Don't act so innocent," he said, laughing. "I knew what you girls were up to as soon as I saw those red outfits. But you'd better not work that store again. They've got you down now. For that matter, you'd better leave that town alone a while."

"I don't know what you're talking about," said Sylvia, with dignity, "and anyway we're not going in this direction."

"What do you say going to Albany with me and then on to New York? A couple of girls like you could clean up a thousand dollars a week—just the big stores, understand, nice merchandise, not ordinary snatching. I could send you straight up to a friend of mine on 135th Street and you'd be treated right. A couple of nice kids like you could get away with murder. What do you want to waste your time stealing bathing suits and rubber gadgets?"

"I bought this bathing suit," said Sylvia angrily.

"Why," gasped Barbs, "you don't think we're thieves?"

The girls looked at each other in growing horror at his sardonic laugh.

"Of course you're not thieves, honey," he chuckled. "You was just taking what you liked, that was all. Don't kid me, sister, you're a smart girl—both of you, for that matter. You got talent; you could do big stuff, I'm telling you. I did you a favor today. Why don't you do me a favor now and try out the big time? You could wire your folks."

"We're married women," said Sylvia. "Our husbands would come after us."

"Think it over," said the driver, good-humoredly. "You might give me your names and I'll drop you a card, reminding you where to get in touch if you change your mind." He pulled a silver pencil out of his pocket and a card.

"Dody Crane," said Sylvia.

"Teresa Hull," quavered Barbs.

"Well, Dody and Terry, you'll hear from me," he said, and slowed up near a filling station. "You're the best talent I've seen in these parts. All you need is training and a little protection."

At the filling station, he got out and went inside. Without a word Sylvia and Barbs slipped out and ran to the road, hiding in the bushes along the way. They saw him come back out, look for them briefly, and question the mechanic. Then, with a shake of his head, he got in and drove off. Barbs and Sylvia looked at each other and drew a great breath of relief.

"I never was so scared," said Barbs. "Believe me, I'll never swipe anything again."

"I should hope not," said Sylvia.

Barbs pulled the rubber out of her dress and began to blow it up. Sylvia watched. Barbs' face grew redder and redder, and the fish grew bigger and bigger. It was bigger than the one in the window.

It would easily seat the twins and Davie, all three. Then Barbs' face grew worried; she took the fish away from her mouth.

"I forgot to take the darned stopper," she panted, and tears stood in her eyes. "Oh, darn! Oh, Sylvia!"

"Maybe a piece of paper," suggested Sylvia, but the fish collapsed, dwindled to nothing. Barbs looked down at it in the middle of the ditch in disgust.

"I *would* forget the stopper," she said. "I'd *have* to forget the most important thing."

"Honestly, Barbs, you may keep your house better than I do, but you're dumb about lots of things," said Sylvia. "This is the last I go with her," she thought. "I didn't even get to see 'Dark Victory.' "

An empty ice truck drove along, and Sylvia and Barbs jerked their thumbs. The car slowed down and they climbed in among the burlap bags in the back, where a young man in a bathing suit and dirty white slacks sat, fiddling with a harmonica. The girls settled themselves in the corner opposite him.

"I still got ten cents," Barbs said.

The car jolted them along the country roads, past cornfields and waving wheat.

"Hi, Crawford!" the boy said to Sylvia.

The girls looked at each other and laughed.

"What's that you're chewing?" he asked.

"Bubble gum," said Sylvia, and snapped it.

He said nothing more, but stared at them as he played his harmonica. Barbs and Sylvia sang while he played their favorite piece, "I Never Knew Heaven Could Speak." They sang all the way home. The boy and the truck-driver both said they ought to be on the radio or, at the very least, the stage.

THE WEEDS

BY MARY McCARTHY (1944)

She would leave him, she thought, as soon as the petunias had bloomed. With a decisive feeling of happiness, she set down her trowel and sank back on her heels to rest. Around her lay the brown earth of the converted vegetable garden, a slightly lopsided rectangle, across which careened the flower seedlings in rows that were both neat and unsteady, so that the whole planting, seen from a distance, looked like a letter written by a child who has lost his ruler. If only, she reflected, she had done it the way the book said and marked out the rows with stakes and string. Next year . . . Her heart turned over with horror as she perceived the destination of her thought. She had done it again. Next year, *of course*, she would not be here. She had been telling herself this for five weeks, yet she could not seem to remember it. Left to itself, her idle mind reached out lazily, unthinkingly, for a plan, as doubtless Persephone's hand had strayed toward a pomegranate seed.

She remembered all the times she had thought of leaving him before. But there had always been something—the party Saturday night that she did not want to miss, the grapes blue on the vines waiting to be made into jelly, the new sofa for the living room that Macy's would deliver next week, the man to see about the hot-water heater. And by the time the sofa had come, the man had gone, the jelly had been made, she would no longer be angry with him, or at any rate her anger would have lost its cutting edge and she would have only the dull stone of discontent to turn over and over in her palm.

Now, however, it was settled, this problem that had been agitating her since April, since the morning she had planted the sweet peas instead of packing her suitcase, as she ought of course to have done when he had uttered the unspeakable sentence. Now she had actually set a date for her departure, a date on a real calendar, and not simply on the calendar of her heart, where the years were written as days and it seemed always a matter of a few weeks at most before she would be back with her friends, a returned traveller with a fresh slice of life in her hands and many stories to tell. She had been trying since April to do it, all the while that she went on with her digging and watering and weeding, trying to imagine the flowers in their places in August and herself not there to see them, herself in New York in a hot furnished room. It was a little like imagining her own death, but there had been mornings when she had been almost able to do it, and then she would set down her tools and say to herself in surprise, Why, I can leave tomorrow. There is nothing to keep me here. Always, however, she would have forgotten the petunias, which were growing in flats inside the house and had therefore not fallen under her eye. Suddenly they would flash into her mind, white, ruffled, with yellow throats, blocked out in squares, alternating with squares of blackish red zinnias, with the heavenly blue of the scabiosa making a backdrop of false sky behind them; her heart would contract with love and despair as she saw that she could not leave them—she was in bondage unless they should die.

But to acknowledge this was to feel panic. Speaking to her of time and the seasons, the garden urged her to hurry, to go now, before it was too late, before the wheel, turning, should carry her once again on its slow journey through birth, reproduction, and death. Now for the first time she began to count the weeks. Her sensibility quivered in a continual anticipation of change; she took offense readily, pushed everything to extremes, and, in her mind, renounced her friends, her house, her china, a dozen times a day. Desperate measures occurred to her: if she were to kill the petunias . . . ? *Petunias are peculiarly subject to the damping-off sickness. Water cautiously*, warned the gardening book. She would stare at the pitcher of ice water on the luncheon table as the heir stares at the bottle of sleeping medicine by the bedside of his aging relative. But always her resolution softened; the grotesque temptation passed, and, trembling, she would slip out of the house, quietly, lest her husband hear her and detain her on some pretext (for he considered that she was working too hard, complained that he never saw her, that her temper was being ruined); she would collect the trowel, the spading fork, the hand cultivator, and let herself into her enclosure, fenced off against rabbits and woodchucks, and there begin once again her penitential exercise, her agony in the garden.

"Why do you do it if it gives you no pleasure?" her husband would ask. "Don't pretend you are doing it for me." She knew no answer to this; only once she had turned on him, saying, "Ah, you hate it because it is mine. You would like to see it all go to ruin." And truly she did not understand why she was doing it, unless it was somehow *against* him. It was as though she owed these plants some extra and conspicuous loyalty to make up to them for his jealous hostility, which was always waiting its chance, alleging urgent business, sexual desire, anything, to keep her within doors. Sometimes it seemed to her that she stayed on simply as the guardian and defender of these plants, to which she stood in a maternal relation, having brought them into existence. At other times it was cruder. She would not, she would tell herself grimly, give him the satisfaction of seeing her lose the investment of work and love she had made in this rich but difficult soil. She had made a mistake, she knew it; the nurseryman had warned her, "You're biting off more than you can chew." Now she would pause occasionally to look out at the weeds swaying in the light spring wind, pressing up against the fence of her enclosure, where they grew taller, fiercer, more luxuriant than they did in the field itself. It was as if the field were a hostile sea which billowed and swelled in the distance with a sort of menacing calm and spent itself vindictively in that last breast-high green wave which it launched upon her rectangular island. At such moments, dread would seize her; she would shudder and turn back to her task, knowing that every minute must be made to count, lest she be inundated, her work and tools be lost in this watery jungle of nature. And always it was as if *he* were the ally of the weeds—he was fond of telling her, pedantically, that there was no botanical distinction between a weed and a flower. On mornings when she would hurry out after a rainy spell to find her brown space green with a two-day crop of wild mustard, she would feel him to be nearly victorious; tears of injury and defiance would stand in her eyes as she scratched the ground with the claw.

She could remember a time when it had not been so, when her borders had been gay with simple clear colors, pink and scarlet, lemon yellow and cornflower blue, when her husband had stood by in admiration, saying, "You have green thumbs, my dear." Then she had been ready enough to lay down her tools, to greet a friend, to go on a picnic, to give an order to her maid; then there had been summer afternoons when he sat on a bench with a drink while she let the hose play gently over the flower beds and stopped from time to time to take the glass from him and sip.

Later, kneeling out in the garden, she would try to decide at what moment the change had come. When she had declined to go with him to the city because there was no one to water the flowers? When he had bought the dog that rooted up the tulips? Ah no, she thought. It had been inevitable from the beginning that the garden should have become suffused with suffering, like a flower that is reverting to its original lenten magenta, for everything returns to itself and a marriage made out of loneliness and despair will be lonely and desperate. And if I have a garden to console me, you will have a dog, and your dog will destroy my garden, and so it will go, until all good has turned to evil, and there is not a corner of life that has not been flooded with hatred. It had become meaningless to draw up lists of grievances (her picture torn across the middle and thrown in the kitchen wastebasket), for to have a grievance is to assert that some human treaty has been violated, and they were past treaties, past reparations, past forgiveness; to invoke love, morality, public opinion was pure simony—in every belligerent country the priests are praying for victory.

How far it had gone she had never perceived until yesterday. She was repeating the flower names to herself: black boy, black ruby, scabiosa mourning bride (ah yes, she murmured, that is I, that is I), snowstorm, purity, and last of all the free package thrown in by the seedsman which was designated Peace. Dear God, she had exclaimed, it's as if I were growing flowers for a funeral blanket. Is it possible that I wish him dead? And at once the vision of herself as a young widow slipped into her fancy, like a view into an old stereopticon. She saw herself pale and beautiful in black, murmuring repentant phrases to some intimate woman friend. (It's true that we didn't get along, but I couldn't have wished this to happen. I am sorry now for everything, and I would like to be able to tell him so. If only he could have known that I loved him after all.) Yes, she thought, if he were dead, I could love him sincerely. And how practical it would be! She would not have to give up anything—the Spode salad plates, the garden, the candy-striped wallpaper in the living room. And she would not have to decide whether to take the roasting pan or leave it (it had belonged to her in the first place). All the objects she had nearly determined to relinquish if she were to leave him, all these things she considered already lost, would be restored to her. And she could move about among them alone; she could have everything the way she wanted it, there would be no one to stop her, no one to say, "Why do we have to have a soup *and* a salad course? You are spending too much money."

That was the queer thing, she thought; it was not a question of money. If he died, he would leave her nothing; the commissions would stop automatically, there would not even be any insurance. What he would do for her by dying would be to relieve her of the necessity of decision. How many women, she wondered, had poisoned their husbands, not for gain or for another man, but out of sheer inability to leave them. The extreme solution is always the simplest. The weed-killer is in the soup; the man is in his coffin. One regrets, but now it is too late; the matter is out of one's hands. Murder is more civilized than divorce; the Victorians, as usual, were wiser.

Really, she said to herself, I will have to get away if I am going to have such thoughts. And a dreadful presentiment flicked her heart, lightly at first, like the stroke of a lady's riding whip. What if I were to go in now and find him dead by his work table with the blueprints spread out before him? She saw, as if by second sight, what her remorse would be and knew that she could not bear it. In a moment she was stiff with fright. Clearly, she would have to go and look for him, but she could not move. Look, she said to herself, if he is dead the maid will come to tell me sooner or later. I do not have to find him. I can just stay here. But it was useless. By now she was certain that he was dead; one last hope, however, remained. If she were to get there quickly enough . . . She found herself running down the driveway. Outside his window she stopped. It was too high for her to see in. See, she said to herself, almost happily, perceiving the difficulty, there is nothing you can do. But a stratagem occurred to her. By a supreme effort of will she made herself pull up an orange crate and climb onto it. She looked in. There he was at his table, motionless; she could not make out whether he was breathing. For the first time, she saw him with detachment, a man in a brown suit slumped over some papers, like a figure drawn by a painter and left there, a figure unknown, without history, and yet intensely itself. He moved, and was human again; she knew him, she disliked him; it was all right, he was alive. She drew a deep breath and slipped quickly down from the orange crate, before he should turn his head and see her. All afternoon in the garden she kept congratulating herself, fondly, hysterically, as people do when they have had, or believe they have had, a narrow escape. Yet when he came out at five to call her and startled her by approaching quietly, she gave a long, piercing, terrible scream, a scream that seemed to linger in the air long after she had left the garden. In some way, he had caught her red-handed.

This morning, in the garden, the scream was still there. Overnight, delay had become dangerous. A break must be made. The part of her that put up preserves, built terraces, laid in oil for the winter, would have to come to terms at last with the part that knew the train schedules by heart and kept a ten-dollar bill hidden in its jewelry box. A path would have to be cleared through the thicket of obligations with which she had surrounded herself, and it was not, after all, essential that she should choose the thorniest way. If she could not renounce the petunias, she would have them and then go. The important thing was that she should not make a single plan that would carry her beyond the first of August. Resolutely, she picked up her trowel and stabbed it into the ground, next to a clump of nut grass with its bright, spearlike leaves. Probing carefully, she lifted the plant and saw with satisfaction that the nut was there, dangling from the long root. The point about nut grass was that you must be sure to get the nut; otherwise your pains were wasted—within a week the plant would be up again. Hoeing was out of the question; you had to dig, with a spading fork or a trowel. "Why don't you give it up?" her husband had asked, indifferently, when she had showed him the thousands of green spears of the grass pricking the ground she had just cultivated. "Oh, go away," she had answered, and yet, often, this was what she most wanted to do, to give up and lie down on her bed and never make another effort, to sleep and have her meals brought up and live like a weed herself, silent and parasitic. But always the flowers pressed their claims; she would picture a few starved cosmos plants waving their thin heads among the tall grasses, and she would feel her heart wrung, as if squeezed out by those strong inimical brown roots. Ah well, she said to herself now, next year will be another matter. Next year nature can have her way. Thank God, at any rate, I did not put in any perennials.

All the rest of the morning she worked along cheerfully. When her maid's voice called her in to lunch, she got up with docility. Walking along the lane, she noticed that the wild lilies of the valley were nearly in bloom. There was a shady space along the veranda that could easily accommodate them. With fertilizer and cultivation, the blossoms should, by next year, double in size. . . . Some plants with a good chunk of earth were already in her hands when she perceived what she was doing. "My God," she murmured, "my God," and dropped the plants back into the hole her trowel had cut. She pressed the earth down around them and trod on it with her foot. It had been a close shave, and the beating of her heart informed her, bluntly, that she must run no more risks. The whole property was pitted with traps for her; she walked in danger and there was no time to lose.

In the hotel, the door had not closed behind the bellboy when she picked up the telephone. She had no plans. Her imagination, working (how long?) in secret, had carried her only this far; she had conceived of the future, simply, as a hand, still wearing its glove, reaching out for a hotel phone. To her first five calls there was no answer. This was a possibility she had not counted on. In all her calculations, it was she who had been the doubtful element, she the expected, the long-overdue relation whose homecoming was hourly anticipated, she the beloved sister whose room had been kept just as she left it; and throughout the term of her marriage, the thought of her friends had jabbed at her conscience: they were waiting and could not understand what could be keeping her so long. Now, at the fifth attempt, she put down the receiver peremptorily, to cut off the drilling, importunate sound that her call, unanswered, was making. For a diversion, she drew a bath, saying to herself that it was still too early, that people were out of town for the summer, that one could not expect, et cetera. Yet, after the bath was over, she did not know what to put on, for she both counted and did not count on an invitation to dinner. To her sixth call she got an answer. How nice, said her friend, that she was in town; could she come Thursday for dinner? Thursday was four days off, and she fumbled a little in accepting. Her great news had become suddenly undeliverable. The context was wrong, yet the news remained, almost sensibly, in her mouth, thickening her tongue. She hung up in haste, lest her disappointment be audible on the other end of the wire. On her seventh call, she was informed that the party had moved to Connecticut; on her eighth, she made a date for lunch on the following day. She was conscious of her own folly in withholding her announcement; she needed help, a job, money, reassurance, but she could not break through the fence of social forms she found erected against intimacy. In these five years, she perceived, she had become a visitor, the old friend from out of town who is at the Biltmore for a few days; in her absence, the circle had closed; the hands she had once clasped now clasped each other and would not part to readmit her to the dance. They had forgotten her, forgotten, that is, her former self, which remained green only in her own memory; for her alone, time had stood still.

She left the telephone and began, reluctantly, to dress. Half an hour later, in the hotel dining room, a man eyed her, and though she bent her head strictly over her dinner, her mind vacillated, wondering whether a stranger might not . . . Discretion, however, warned her that she could pay too high a price for a listener. I must be strong, she said to herself, and, slightly reassured by this small victory, yet shaken by the need she saw in herself that had exposed her to so commonplace a temptation, she paid her check. Back in her room, her magazines exhausted, she picked up the Gideon Bible and read doggedly through Kings and Chronicles, and at last fell asleep.

When she woke, it was too early to telephone anyone at an office. She had breakfast and read the help-wanted columns. There was nothing there for her. By ten o'clock her sense of flatness and embarrassment had grown so large that she could not bring herself to telephone anyone who might be able to get her a job. The inevitable question, the Why, stood ahead of her, bristling with condolence and curiosity; she was not ready for it. Better, she said to herself suddenly, to go to an agency, where no personal explanations were required. In ten minutes she was at Rockefeller Plaza, with the list of her qualifications ready on her tongue. But the sight of the Victory garden, the rows of young radishes, made her own garden take shape before her, like a sin she had forgotten to confess. Oh God, oh God, she said to herself, I am unfit—who will hire me? And it seemed to her that she had not gone far enough; she must discard her whole identity. An inspiration seized her: she might hire herself out as a cook. She saw herself, anonymous, in a maid's room in the third story of a house in Pelham, saw the bed with the thin blankets and the lumpy mattress, the bath shared with the baby, or the lavatory in the basement. All the wretched paraphernalia of domestic service became invested with glamour for her—she might lose herself and be saved. If she were to go down to Fourteenth Street now and buy herself a cheap dress and some shoes, by tonight she might have a situation. She could leave her own clothes in the hotel room, and when he came to find her, he would find merely Bonwit Teller, Mark Cross, hat by John-Frederics, fragrance by Schiaparelli. She was already, in her mind, selecting the shoes for her new life (patent leather with bows which would do for her day out, or sensible, flat-heeled black?), when some part of her, her conscience or her good sense, warned her that it would not do. It was a child's dream of revenge (see to what lengths you have driven me), vicious and narcissistic. Regretfully, she relinquished the adventure.

Yet, she said to herself, I must do *something*; by tomorrow I shall be out of money. In her handbag were the few pieces of jewelry she had inherited from her mother. It occurred to her that this was perhaps the moment to sell them; after lunch, with cash in her pocket, she could approach the agencies with more assurance. She walked briskly up toward Fifty-ninth Street, feeling herself lifted once again by that wave of exaltation that had brought her down from the country. She was free again, if only for a few hours; all decisions, commitments, were postponed. It was as though the old-gold and diamond shop which she entered presently were the last station in her flight; passing the jewelry over the counter, she divested herself of her last possession; the appraiser counted her out a hundred dollars, and she no longer had anything to lose. She stuffed the money into her pocketbook and hurried back to the hotel.

At the desk, however, she found a message, breaking her lunch date and asking her to call back. At once, her elation vanished. The day stretched empty ahead of her. She turned quickly back to the street and found a Hamburger Heaven, where she ate lunch. Afterward, she went to the movies, and when she returned to her room she did not telephone anyone, but lay on her bed reading the Gospel according to St. Matthew until she felt it to be late enough to go to sleep. She had eaten no dinner. The third day passed off in much the same way: again the movies, and at night the Bible.

On the morning of the fourth the telephone waked her, and she knew at once that it would be he. "Well," he said, "I found you." "Yes," she said. "It wasn't so hard." "No," he replied shortly. "Will you come down and have breakfast with me?" "No." "Oh go to hell," he retorted, and hung up. When he called up that night, he was not sober, and it was she who hung up. She had seen nobody since her arrival. Since the first night she had eaten nothing but hamburgers, and sandwiches at drugstore counters. Notice of any sort had become painful to her: she was unequal to a headwaiter or a desk clerk; she passed in and out without leaving her key; she felt both conspicuous and obscure. She had gone to a single employment agency and filled out an application. Outside the door, she realized that she had forgotten to note down her previous experience, but she could not go back. She was hiding and waiting, both for him and for someone else, some friend or stranger who would come to help her in response to an appeal she had never made. She was living in a state of peculiar expectation, as though she had put an ad in the newspaper, an ad of the most total purport, which God perhaps might answer, and the message she daily expected to find, written out in the hotel's violet ink and shoved under her door, was not of an ordinary social nature.

Yet this sense of expectancy, of extravagant, unreasonable hope, had for its corollary during these days a strange will-lessness, an attitude of resignation and despair. She knew that it was absolutely necessary that she should bestir herself; her money would soon run out and she would be locked out of her hotel room. Yet she found that she actually looked forward to this catastrophe as a means of release; the credit manager might yet be the Saviour, who, as holy legend tells us, appears in strange disguises. She was, it seemed to her now, utterly at the mercy of chance: a notice of eviction might precipitate her future out of the solution in which it was suspended—she herself was powerless. In her present state, even her flight appeared to her to have been an act of supreme daring; she could not imagine how she could have summoned up the firmness of character to do it. In fact, she said to herself, if she could have foreseen the outcome, she would never have taken the last drastic step, but held it forever in reserve, a threat and a promise—and died, after thirty years of marriage, thinking how different her life might have been had she left him. What folly, she cried, what madness! She had exchanged the prison of the oppressor for the prison of the self, and from this prison there was not even the hope of escape. At six o'clock Thursday evening, she had not decided what to wear for dinner, a long dress or a short. She put two dresses on the bed, but the arguments for each were unanswerable, and at six-thirty she went out and walked until she found a Western Union office, where she sent a telegram of excuse to her hostess, knowing, as she did so, that she was cutting her last line of communication to the world, to the past, to the future.

Yet when he had not called her again by the morning of the sixth day, a faint hope began to ruffle her spirit, like a sea breeze on an August afternoon. If he had given up and returned to the country, something might still be salvaged. She had seen her resolve melt away in these long mornings in the hotel room, and she knew that she was no longer proof against him; if he were to summon, she would obey. With the dissolution of her belief in herself, her case against him had collapsed. Yet, if he were to abandon her, she knew that she would endure, simply because, physically, she was alive and possessed of a certain negative fortitude. Eventually she would go out, she would telephone, get a job, and gradually circumstances would knit a new web around her, as scar tissue will form over a wound, even if the surgeon has not been called to take the proper stitches.

On this sixth day, as the morning passed on and the telephone still did not ring, she felt her spirits rise and an almost forgotten gaiety take possession of her. Surely he must be gone, she said to herself, and now I am really up against it and perhaps it will be fun after all. The sense of being under surveillance was passing off, and she dressed quickly, in her best white dress, black shoes, and large black cartwheel hat. Nothing, she told herself confidently, is more urban than black and white in summer. It was three o'clock and she had had nothing to eat, but the emptiness of her stomach only added to her fine sense of lightness and bravery. The sound of her heels on the stone floor near the elevator was brisk and pleasing, she let her handbag swing gallantly on her bare, tanned arm. For the first time, on pressing the button, she knew precisely where she was going—to call on an old friend who had an important job in an advertising office—and she knew, furthermore, that it was going to be all right, that he would compliment her and take her out to cocktails at a nice place, and that there, over the second drink, an opening would come which would allow her to tell him, quite naturally, quite easily, that she had left her husband. When he would press her—gently—for a reason, it would be merely a question of finding the right formula, of avoiding vindictiveness on the one hand and piety on the other, of packing the truth into some assimilable capsule which her companion could swallow without any noticeable discomfort. As the elevator descended, a sentence spoke itself for her (I would have left him long ago if it hadn't been for those damned petunias). This was the right note, she recognized at once, seeing in advance the effect it would make in her friend's face, where the struggle between incredulity and belief would resolve itself in laughter. She foresaw a whole train, a lifetime, of these sentences. (But you say you left him five days ago; what have you been doing ever since? I've been lying in my hotel room reading the Gideon Bible.) She smiled, feeling herself on home territory. She was back at her port of embarkation, which she had set forth from five years before, back to her native patois, where jest masks truth but does not deny it.

The elevator doors opened and she saw her husband sitting in the lobby.

· · ·

Two days later, he unlocked the door of the house and gave her a slight shove forward, as though she were a dog or a truant child. Her first impression was that the house had in a week grown older and shabbier. She stood in the doorway of the living room, looking about her with the eyes of an observant stranger. She noted the paint peeling on the window frames, the place where the wallpaper had been patched and the stripes did not quite meet, the blue chair that had never belonged there in the first place, the stain where her own head had rested on the back of the sofa. Two rather tacky-looking bouquets of bridal wreath stood on the marble-topped coffee table which she had cut down from an old piece; very plainly, they said Welcome Home in the floral language of her maid. Generally, when this kind of thing happened to her, when a room or the face of a lover did not measure up to memory, she would narrow her eyes, as she did to look at herself in the mirror, till the focus had changed and the image become a little blurred; then, with the quick hand of fancy, she would bestow a few decorations on the object—a bowl of flowers, a glass cigarette box—a look of irony, or a smile; and in a few moments all would be well, the face or the room would have subsided, and her eyes, now wide open, could run over it with love. This time, however, though she narrowed her eyes out of force of habit, nothing of the sort happened; the room became dimmer but it did not reassemble itself. "Well," said her husband, rather heartily, in his business-as-usual tone, "everything looks the same." This statement came in so patly that she made the mistake, fatal in marriage, of speaking to him as an intimate. "Does it?" she asked. "Really? It looks queer to me. The colors look as if somebody had mixed black in them. Do you suppose she has changed the light bulbs?" "Don't be silly," he said, sweeping her ahead of him toward the staircase. "Why should she do that?" "Let's have dinner right away," he added, pushing her slightly again, as though he had expected her to express some morbid and contradictory wish. She obeyed him, mechanically, as she had done ever since she had seen him sitting in the hotel lobby. Her defeat seemed to her shameful and absolute. Fortunately, however, her feelings had died in her; there was no rebelliousness, no resentment—in the conquered country, the officials conferred quietly with the captors and the underground movement slept.

What troubled her all evening was merely the notion that something had happened to the lighting. Across the table in the dining room, she could barely see her husband's face, though the customary twelve candles were burning. In the middle of the meal, she excused herself and got up to turn on the electricity. This was not an improvement; now her husband's face appeared to be unnaturally white. The food also seemed to her to have been tampered with. Her husband was eating with apparent relish; still, she could not disabuse herself of the idea that there was something wrong—perhaps the maid had forgotten to put the sherry in the stew? "You are tired," said her husband warningly, and she accepted this explanation with gratitude. After dinner, nevertheless, she could not restrain herself from going around to each of the lamps to see if there might be dust on the bulbs. But her finger came off clean.

In the morning, the visual derangement persisted. Her eye was caught, on waking, by a window shade which had been white when she had gone to New York; this morning it was certainly ivory. Slightly frightened, she closed her eyes and took refuge in sleep. When she woke, it was to the light sound of the glass bell calling her to lunch, and to an instant conviction of disaster. There was something wrong, something she had forgotten, something more than the persistent queerness of the light or the fact of her being back once again in her husband's bed. But her memory would not yield it up until, during a pause in the lunchtime conversation, she happened to glance out the window and saw on the sill the boxes containing the dead petunias. Her husband heard her gasp and his eyes followed hers. "What's the matter?" he said. "Nothing," she replied. "Something I remembered." He did not pursue the topic, and later, when he asked the question ("Have you been out yet to look at your garden?"), she perceived, with relief, that he was unaware of its significance. For him the question was a mere token of politeness, a bone tossed to the idiosyncrasies of her taste. He was still going through the motions of treating her, rather nervously, as a guest, but his heart was plainly not in it, for he did not trouble to wait for her answer.

For her, however, the question had a more fateful sound. She knew at once that she ought at least to go out and look, yet she put it off, for a day, for two days, while she did nothing but lie on her bed, declining to go to the market, plan the meals, make the French dressing, sleeping from time to time, as she had done in the hotel, and waking always with that terrible start of knowledge that tells us, as we come out of ether or alcohol, that something has changed in our lives, though we are not yet sure what it is. If her husband's question had not been repeated a second and a third time, she might never, she told herself, have made the nearly unbearable effort that took her into the toolshed for her trowel and cultivator and sent her slowly down the garden path to the enclosure in the fields. But the third time his question had had an anxious perplexity in it. Her avoidance of the garden had begun to seem to him abnormal; his mind must be set at rest. For (it had become more and more apparent) he had no comprehension at all of the events of the past week. He imagined that the whole affair was a sort of triumph, that he, the conqueror, guardian of the hearth, had pursued the fugitive nymph and wooed and bullied her home by the sheer force of his will. It had not occurred to him for an instant that the collapse was interior, that, like France, she had fallen, limp, corrupt, disgraced, into the arms of the victor, and so long as he did not perceive this, she had a little bargaining power left. But for the preservation of the illusion, it was necessary that he should believe her unchanged, should have no suspicion of the docility that placed her, not only at his mercy, but at the mercy of every event. Her long hours in her room she had excused on the grounds of emotional exhaustion, but this could hardly be expected to last forever. Already he had begun to look a little critically at the meals, to run a finger over a table that had not been dusted—the holiday, his voice indicated, was over. And now, as she passed his window, she knew that the sound of her footsteps was reassuring to him; it signified the return to normalcy, the resumption of hostilities.

The garden had waited too long, she warned herself; she was too late. Common sense alone could tell you what you might expect to find if you left a garden alone for ten moist days in June. She was prepared for the worst. Yet halfway down the path apprehension gave place to hope, and she began to run, as though this final burst of speed could make up for a long tardiness, as though she might catch the garden in the moment of transformation, effect a last-minute rescue in the very teeth of probability. The garden, however, was gone. Her first impression was that it had disappeared without a trace. In ten days the weeds had swallowed it. The brown enclosure had turned green; the very markers that indicated the rows had vanished, and of the whole enterprise only the fence remained, an absurd testimonial to the fact that this rectangle had been, at one time, the scene of human endeavor. With the first shock, she closed her eyes: this was the nightmare vision she had wrestled with all spring, a ferocious tableau vivant entitled The Triumph of the Weeds, which had appeared again and again to halt her on the road to freedom, to harrow her susceptibilities and appeal to her pity and love. She had turned back before it a hundred times, and when at length she had hardened her heart, she had told herself, I will not be there to see it. Now, however, it was all as she had imagined it, except that the season was not so far advanced and she was here in the midst of it, while the hot furnished room was distant beyond desire. When she opened her eyes again, it was not with the hope of finding some mitigating circumstance, but rather with a kind of morbid appetite to embrace the full details of her disaster. Now she made out the individual weeds, and she saw that while in the field outside there were buttercups and a few daisies already open, here, in her enclosure, flourished only the most virile, the most virid, the most weedlike weeds, the coarse growers—burdock, thistle, milkweed, Queen Anne's lace; the crawlers—carrotweed, Jill-run-over-the-ground, and especially the choking nut grass, which crawled beneath the earth's surface and sprouted fiercely above it. No doubt, she said to herself, there was some natural explanation for this—the rankest weeds were perhaps the strongest and their seeds had a longer viability—yet common sense would not prevail; her heart accepted the phenomenon as a judgment and a curse.

It is hopeless, she murmured to herself, leaning against the fence, hopeless; and for the first time her spirit made an acknowledgment of defeat that was not provisional in character. Up to this moment there had been in her mind small recesses of hope to which her thoughts had fled secretly, unavowedly; in her contract with reality, an escape clause which permitted her to believe that what had been done was not irretrievable, that—in this case—dry weather might have retarded the weeds or some magic helper hoed for her (her maid, a thoughtful neighbor, a small boy employed by her husband?); now solidly before her lay the brutal *fait accompli*, the lost garden, irrecoverable, for though something might still be salvaged (a few gray cornflower plants could be made out in the mat of vegetation at her feet), the original design, the mirror of absolute beauty in which she had glimpsed her own image, was shattered. She sank listlessly to the ground and sat looking about her. Quite simply a sentence came to her and she spoke it aloud: "Now," she said, "I have nothing to live for."

The patent absurdity of these words acted as an astringent. The voice of common sense spoke again, saying, After all, you have a life expectation of at least forty years and you have got to do something with your time, you cannot just go to pieces, and in any case people do not live for gardens, but for ideals, principles, persons. This particular garden is ruined, but it is still possible to transplant. A second-best garden can be made out of the cornflowers, the zinnias, the cosmos, perhaps even the scabiosa. You can move the stronger plants and in August you will have flowers on the table. She presented this idea to her emotions and waited for the familiar bustle of activity, the rolling back of the sleeves, which turned her heart on such occasions into a large and hospitable house that is being made ready for an evening party. But the motors of anticipation remained cold. The second-best garden could not, even momentarily, command her belief. Like an adopted child, or a second husband, it could never make up to her. The weeds had finished all that. The weeds were, in fact, her garden, the end product of her activities, and the white foam that children call spit, which she saw clinging to the young grasses, was the outward mark of her disease. She remained sitting on the warm ground, idle, without thought or feeling, but ashamed to go back to the house.

This time she heard her husband's footsteps approaching, but out of pride she would not look up, even when she felt him stop just behind her at the entrance to the garden. "Gosh!" he said. "What an awful situation!" "Yes," she answered defiantly. "It's ruined." There was a silence during which she imagined him to be shrugging his shoulders. Anger began to boil up in her again, and she spun around to face him. The language of their old quarrels rose to her lips, the classical formulae of accusation and outrage. (See what you have made me do, you wanted this to happen, you are glad), but she was arrested by the expression of his face, which was neither jubilant nor indifferent, but full of simple curiosity and wonder. The weeds had finally made their impression on him; never before had he really believed in them; he had considered them to be a chimera of her dark imagination. Now he stood awestruck by this fearful demonstration of their authenticity, and for the first time the two of them shared in silence a single emotion. "What is that awful stuff?" he asked at length, bending down to pull up a spear of nut grass. The root broke off in his inexperienced hands. "Not that way," she said. "Look." Her trowel came up with the nut secure. "This is the weed I've been talking about all spring." He examined it, turning it over between his fingers in his methodical way. "Why, it's a little bulb," he said. It was not worthwhile to correct this statement; to make the botanical distinction between a bulb and a tuber might simply provide a distraction from the mood of repugnance and terror that had brought them close for a moment. She longed to rush him ahead with her into the particulars of her loss, to say, See what I have been up against, see the sorrel, the field grass, the carrotweed, see where the sweet peas would have been, see where I dug the trench and strewed it with manure, think of the liming and the watering and weeding; she was filled with a kind of wild excitement and joy that he, who had never acknowledged the garden in life, should meet it, as it were, posthumously, and pay his respects. Yet prudence or tact restrained her. The work of initiation could not be hurried. He stood on the brink of her agony in the garden; his wide feet in their brown shoes were planted on one of the surviving cornflowers, as though to illustrate the text of his inculpation—but he must not be pushed. It was enough that he should share, however vaguely, her burden of loss, that her bereavement should to some measure be accepted as his. She waited, half-frightened, half-exalted, for what he would say next.

"Gosh!" he repeated, with intensified feeling, and now she was sure it was coming, the miracle she expected, which might take the form of an embrace, a cry, an apology, but which would be in essence a lament not so much for the garden as for her, for the dead young lady he had brought back from New York, whom he kept propped up in bed, at the breakfast table, on the sofa, in the odor of corruption.

"You have your work cut out for you," he said. For an instant she believed that she had not heard him properly.

"Maybe we can get a boy to help you," he continued in a matter-of-fact tone.

It was over, she knew it at once, yet she made a last appeal. "The garden is ruined," she said in a stubborn, hostile voice, but speaking slowly and emphatically as though to direct his attention to the importance of this statement.

"Nonsense," he replied briskly. "You are always so extreme. I'll call up Mr. Jenkins tomorrow and see if he can send . . ."

At the mention of the neighboring farmer, her mouth opened and she began to scream. "I'll kill you if you do!" she shouted. Picking up the spading fork, she plunged it wildly into the ground, tossing sods and plants into the air in a frenzy of destruction. The loose earth fell on her hair, on her face, down which tears were running. She was aware that she cut a grotesque and even repulsive figure, that her husband was shocked by the sight and the sound of her, but the gasping sobs gave her pleasure, for she saw that this was the only punishment she had left for him, that the witchlike aspect of her form and the visible decay of her spirit would constitute, in the end, her revenge. She continued to lay about her with the spading fork, though the original fury had already passed off, until his solid, uneasy figure had disappeared from view, until his last words no longer sounded in her ears.

It was late in August when he came into the living room with a heterogeneous bouquet in which she recognized some of the stubborner flowers of her garden, cosmos and cornflowers and a few blackish red miniature zinnias. Mixed in with these were some weeds, pinkish sprays of bouncing Bet and the greenish-white clusters of Queen Anne's lace. There was no doubt of it, he had been visiting her garden, and this was not the first time. Toward the end of June she had heard him outside the window, swearing, as he tied up rambler roses; in July, he had brought in raspberries, saying, "Can't we have these for dinner?" The berries were soft and broken—he had been too late in the harvest. She lay now on the sofa, reading a detective story, watching him as he brought in a vase too tall for his bouquet and crammed the flowers into it. She felt no impulse to correct him; his clumsiness, in fact, pleased her, the ugliness of the bouquet pleased her, just as the stain on the coffee table had pleased her, the spot on her maid's uniform at lunch. She basked, as she had been doing all summer, in a sly private satisfaction. She was broken but she was also irreplaceable, and her continued physical existence must be, she thought, an unending reminder to him of everything he had lost. She was enjoying in real life the delight that is generally experienced only in daydreams, the sense of *when I am dead, how they will mourn for me, how valuable I shall become to them when I am no longer theirs.*

She could see her own case now with the detachment of a historian. Between them, he and she had killed off the part of her that had always excited his anxiety and irritation, the part of her which regarded nothing as final, which was continually planning, contriving, hoping, which lived in the future and slept, like a fireman, fully dressed for an emergency. It was this part of her which had dreamed of flight and deliverance, but it was also this part which had created for itself the small mirages of duty and pleasure which had held her to him for five years. These were not, as she had thought, antithetical selves, but the same thing, the creative, constructive principle which, in its restless anticipation of change, built structures of semi-permanency—a series of overnight cabins that in their extension formed, not precisely a city, but at least a road, a *via vitae*.

It was this part of her which had incurred his jealousy, for it was obliged to live slightly estranged, to make large investments of passion in private enterprises; yet it was this part of her he now wished back, for he saw that this had been the nerve, and he now longed for a recurrence of the very symptoms whose presence, three months ago, he had detested. Now, by a hundred spells, he was attempting to bring about a resurrection. He appealed to her housekeeping instinct, to her aesthetic sense, to her vanity, to her pity; his very clumsiness was an appeal for help, and it was not that she did not hear these appeals; she heard, but, as in a dream, she was incapable of action. What it was all leading up to she understood plainly: a moment ought to come when she would rise miraculously from the sofa, sweep the absurd bouquet from his hands, shake it lightly into form, call for a new bowl, and enshrine the product on the mantelpiece, while he stood by, awkward and grateful, as at a religious ceremony, a secular Easter mass. Yet now she could only lie back and watch, with lowered eyelids, pretending to take no notice, enjoying her poor-man's pie of irony and contempt.

For the pleasure she took in her untended house, in her careless and unsupervised maid, in her neglected garden (which, however, she had never, since June, seen) was purely negative in character, a compensation for disability. The discomfort inflicted on her husband by the loss of her imaginative faculty could never atone to her for the joy she had once had in the exercise of it. Lying on the sofa, looking about at the dusty bare room, she would feel excruciating stabs of remorse, like the pains in an amputated limb. She would get up and start at some task, but before the candlesticks were half polished, her interest would have died and she would leave them in the sink for her maid to finish. It could not, it seemed to her, go on much longer, and she prayed for him to abandon her. (Her going, on her own initiative, had become utterly out of the question.) On him her life now depended; where renunciation, the withdrawal of love, had blackened the loved objects as frost blackens the flowers in an autumn garden, he alone had survived, evergreen, sturdily perennial, in the season of death. Disliking him as she did, she had never bothered to renounce him, and now her eyes would come to rest on him with a kind of relief—the familiar detested object in surroundings grown strange and terrible. Her glance held in it also an element of calculation: how long, she asked herself, will he be able to stand me? Her own endurance had become infinite, for she no longer lived in time, but he, being real, being alive, might reach in measurable stages the threshold of domestic suffering.

He set the vase down on the table, took his handkerchief, and dusted the surface in a rather bustling way, like a woman who rattles dishes in the kitchen to awaken a sleeper whom she does not wish to be so rude as to call. He cleared his throat.

"You have some beautiful flowers out back."

She sat up at last to look at him directly, but made no reply.

"You ought to go out and see them."

She watched him hesitate and then think better of what was in his mind to say. He is afraid of me, she thought, with a touch of pity.

"We ought to have some more of them in the house," he continued, enthusiastically. "You have got all sorts of things back there. Even your weeds are wonderful," and he went rattling on nervously, describing the scene in the fields, suggesting improvements—a professional tree surgeon to come for the old apple trees, a wattled fence along the lane, plans she had once proposed and he rejected. She was only half listening; the very idea of these improvements now seemed to her preposterous; one might as well paint a mural in a condemned house.

Seeing that she would not reply, he halted and tried a new tack. He came up to her and took her hand. "I miss the way this room used to look," he said in a voice that was quite new with him, wistful and childlike in its directness. "Those yellow things you used to have on the coffee table." For a moment now, she saw it all through his eyes, saw a vision which was less precise and accurate than hers, a rather smeary vision in which the pale, clear, lemon yellow he was thinking of (African marigold, carnation-flowered, yellow supreme) was likely to be confused with the orange of French marigold or of cosmos orange flare, a vision in which energy and whopping good intentions counted for more than anything else and the bigger a flower the better—but nevertheless a vision, an ideal of beauty, of love and the lavish hand; and the sense of his loss, his large, vague loss, overwhelmed and engulfed her own.

She pressed his hand lightly, murmuring, "Yes, I remember," and then let his fingers drop. He regained her hand, however, and squeezed it. She felt, as once before in the fields, that he was on the verge of some fine avowal. She herself, only now, had made the great leap from pity to sympathy; she grieved for his predicament, of which she herself was the determining factor; could he likewise grieve for hers, whose existence he had never acknowledged, weep with her at last because she could not leave him, because the courage, the more attractive alternative, whatever it was that might separate them, was lacking?

"I've always loved your flowers," he said, his voice blurred and high with emotion. "You know that."

As her ears admitted this lie, this tearful, sentimental, brazen lie, her whole nature rose weakly in rebellion. How dare you, her heart muttered, how dare you say it? Nothing could have been—and at such a moment!—more dishonest; she could have cited him fifty instances which would have controverted him utterly. But the heartfelt insincerity of these words went beyond contradiction, beyond hypocrisy, into regions of spiritual obstinacy and opacity impenetrable to reason, where reason, in fact, and conscience had been cruelly blinded by the will, the will which demanded that everything should be always all right, which had, as it were, legislated the bouquet on the mantelpiece by a kind of brutal denial of color, of tonal values, of the harmony of textures, and which was now enforcing its myth of a harmonious marriage, of tastes and occupations shared, by dictatorial fiat.

And yet there had been the tears in the voice. . . . What the tears meant, she perceived, was that he did love the flowers, now that she had not got them, now that they were no longer dangerous; they had passed, for him and for her, out of experience into memory, and here in this twilight world he could possess them—and her—with a terrible dumb rapacity. She saw also that her pity had been wasted, that he had got her where he wanted her; she had been translated, bodily, into that realm of shadows where the will was all-powerful, the city of the dead. She herself was no more to him now than an oak leaf pressed in a schoolbook, a tendril of blond hair, a garter kept in a drawer. But this was, for him, everything: it was love and idolatry. The lie was a necessity to him, a cardinal article of faith. To protest was useless. He could not be shaken in his conviction, but only be annoyed, confused, thrown off. And in a final burst of generosity, she yielded, conceding him everything—her flowers, her principles, her truths. Let him put them to work for him; she had failed them and would do so again and again. With him, they would see service.

She tightened her clasp on his hand.

"Yes," she said gently, "I know."

It came easier than she would ever have suspected.

A PERFECT DAY FOR BANANAFISH

BY J. D. SALINGER (1948)

There were ninety-seven New York advertising men in the hotel, and, the way they were monopolizing the long-distance lines, the girl in 507 had to wait from noon till almost two-thirty to get her call through. She used the time, though. She read an article in a women's pocket-size magazine, called "Sex Is Fun—or Hell." She washed her comb and brush. She took the spot out of the skirt of her beige suit. She moved the button on her Saks blouse. She tweezed out two freshly surfaced hairs in her mole. When the operator finally rang her room, she was sitting on the window seat and had almost finished putting lacquer on the nails of her left hand.

She was a girl who for a ringing phone dropped exactly nothing. She looked as if her phone had been ringing continually ever since she had reached puberty.

With her little lacquer brush, while the phone was ringing, she went over the nail of her little finger, accentuating the line of the moon. She then replaced the cap on the bottle of lacquer and, standing up, passed her left—the wet—hand back and forth through the air. With her dry hand, she picked up a congested ashtray from the window seat and carried it with her over to the night table, on which the phone stood. She sat down on one of the made-up twin beds and—it was the fifth or sixth ring—picked up the phone.

"Hello," she said, keeping the fingers of her left hand outstretched and away from her white silk dressing gown, which was all that she was wearing, except mules—her rings were in the bathroom.

"I have your call to New York now, Mrs. Glass," the operator said.

"Thank you," said the girl, and made room on the night table for the ashtray.

A woman's voice came through. "Muriel? Is that you?"

The girl turned the receiver slightly away from her ear. "Yes, Mother. How are you?" she said.

"I've been worried to death about you. Why haven't you phoned? Are you all right?"

"I tried to get you last night and the night before. The phone here's been—"

"Are you all right, Muriel?"

The girl increased the angle between the receiver and her ear. "I'm fine. I'm hot. This is the hottest day they've had in Florida in—"

"Why haven't you called me? I've been worried to—"

"Mother, darling, don't yell at me. I can hear you beautifully," said the girl. "I called you twice last night. Once just after—"

"I *told* your father you'd probably call last night. But, no, he had to— Are you all right, Muriel? Tell me the truth."

"I'm fine. Stop asking me that, please."

"When did you get there?"

"I don't know. Wednesday morning, early."

"Who drove?"

"He did," said the girl. "And don't get excited. He drove very nicely. I was amazed."

"*He* drove? Muriel, you gave me your word of—"

"Mother," the girl interrupted, "I just told you. He drove *very* nicely. Under fifty the whole way, as a matter of fact."

"Did he try any of that funny business with the trees?"

"I *said* he drove very nicely, Mother. Now, please. I asked him to stay close to the white line, and all, and he knew what I meant, and he did. He was even trying not to look at the trees—you could tell. Did Daddy get the car fixed, incidentally?"

"Not yet. They want four hundred dollars, just to—"

"Mother, Seymour *told* Daddy that he'd pay for it. There's no reason for—"

"Well, we'll see. How did he behave—in the car and all?"

"All right," said the girl.

"Did he keep calling you that awful—"

"No. He has something new now."

"What?"

"Oh, what's the *dif*ference, Mother?"

"Muriel, I want to *know*. Your father—"

"All right, all right. He calls me Miss Spiritual Tramp of 1948," the girl said, and giggled.

"It isn't funny, Muriel. It isn't funny at all. It's horrible. It's *sad*, actually. When I think how—"

"Mother," the girl interrupted, "listen to me. You remember that book he sent me from Germany? You know—those German poems. What'd I *do* with it? I've been racking my—"

"You have it."

"Are you *sure*?" said the girl.

"Certainly. That is, I have it. It's in Freddy's room. You left it here and I didn't have room for it in the— Why? Does he want it?"

"No. Only, he *asked* me about it, when we were driving down. He wanted to know if I'd read it."

"It was in German!"

"Yes, dear. That doesn't make any difference," said the girl, crossing her legs. "He said that the poems happen to be written by the *only great poet of the century*. He said I should've bought a translation or something. Or *learned the language*, if you please."

"Awful. Awful. It's *sad*, actually, is what it is. Your father said last night—"

"Just a second, Mother," the girl said. She went over to the window seat for her cigarettes, lit one, and returned to her seat on the bed. "Mother?" she said, exhaling smoke.

"Muriel. Now, listen to me."

"I'm listening."

"Your father talked to Dr. Sivetski."

"Oh?" said the girl.

"He told him *ev*erything. At least, he said he did—you know your father. The trees. That business with the window. Those horrible things he said to Granny about her plans for passing away. What he did with all those lovely pictures from Bermuda—*ev*erything."

"Well?" said the girl.

"Well. In the first place, he said it was a perfect *crime* the Army released him from the hospital—my word of honor. He very *def*initely told your father there's a chance—a very *great* chance, he said—that Seymour may com*plete*ly lose control of himself. My word of honor."

"There's a psychiatrist here at the hotel," said the girl.

"*Who?* What's his name?"

"I don't know. Rieser or something. He's supposed to be very good."

"Never heard of him."

"Well, he's supposed to be very good, anyway."

"Muriel, don't be fresh, please. We're *very* worried about you. Your father wanted to wire you *last night* to come home, as a matter of f—"

"I'm not coming home right now, Mother. So relax."

"Muriel. My word of honor. Dr. Sivetski said Seymour may com*plete*ly lose contr—"

"I just *got* here, Mother. This is the first vacation I've had in years, and I'm not going to just *pack* everything and come home," said the girl. "I couldn't travel now anyway. I'm so sunburned I can hardly move."

"You're badly sunburned? Didn't you use that jar of Bronze I put in your bag? I put it right—"

"I used it. I'm burned anyway."

"That's terrible. Where are you burned?"

"All over, dear, all over."

"That's terrible."

"I'll live."

"Tell me, did you talk to this psychiatrist?"

"Well, sort of," said the girl.

"What'd he say? Where was Seymour when you talked to him?"

"In the Ocean Room, playing the piano. He's played the piano both nights we've been here."

"Well, what'd he say?"

"Oh, nothing much. He spoke to me first. I was sitting next to him at Bingo last night, and he asked me if that wasn't my husband playing the piano in the other room. I said yes, it was, and he asked me if Seymour'd been sick or something. So I said—"

"Why'd he ask that?"

"*I* don't know, Mother. I guess because he's so pale and all," said the girl. "Anyway, after Bingo he and his wife asked me if I wouldn't like to join them for a drink. So I did. His wife was horrible. You remember that awful dinner dress we saw in Bonwit's window? The one you said you'd have to have a tiny, tiny—"

"The green?"

"She had it on. And all hips. She kept asking me if Seymour's related to that Suzanne Glass that has that place on Madison Avenue—the millinery."

"What'd he say, though? The doctor."

"Oh. Well, nothing much, really. I mean we were in the bar and all. It was terribly noisy."

"Yes, but did—did you tell him what he tried to do with Granny's chair?"

"*No*, Mother. I didn't go into details very much," said the girl. "I'll probably get a chance to talk to him again. He's in the bar *all* day long."

"Did he say he thought there was a chance he might get—you know—funny or anything? Do something to you?"

"Not exactly," said the girl. "He had to have more facts, Mother. They have to know about your childhood—all that stuff. I told you, we could hardly talk, it was so noisy in there."

"Well. How's your blue coat?"

"All right. I had some of the padding taken out."

"How *are* the clothes this year?"

"Terrible. But out of this world. You see sequins—everything," said the girl.

"How's your room?"

"All right. *Just* all right, though. We couldn't get the room we had before the war," said the girl. "The people are awful this year. You should see what sits next to us in the dining room. At the next table. They look as if they drove down in a truck."

"Well, it's that way all over. How's your ballerina?"

"It's too long. I *told* you it was too long."

"Muriel, I'm only going to ask you once more—are you really all right?"

"*Yes*, Mother," said the girl. "For the ninetieth time."

"And you don't want to come home?"

"*No*, Mother."

"Your father said last night that he'd be more than willing to pay for it if you'd go away someplace by yourself and think things over. You could take a lovely cruise. We both thought—"

"No, thanks," said the girl, and uncrossed her legs. "Mother, this call is costing a for—"

"When I think of how you waited for that boy *all* through the war—I mean when you think of all those crazy little wives who—"

"Mother," said the girl, "we'd better hang up. Seymour may come in any minute."

"Where is he?"

"On the beach."

"On the beach? By himself? Does he behave himself on the beach?"

"Mother," said the girl, "you talk about him as though he were a raving *maniac*—"

"I said nothing of the kind, Muriel."

"Well, you *sound* that way. I mean all he does is lie there. He won't take his bathrobe off."

"He won't take his bathrobe off? Why not?"

"*I* don't know. I guess because he's so pale."

"My goodness, he *needs* the sun. Can't you make him?"

"You know Seymour," said the girl, and crossed her legs again. "He says he doesn't want a lot of fools looking at his tattoo."

"He doesn't have any tattoo! Did he get one in the Army?"

"No, Mother. No, dear," said the girl, and stood up. "Listen, I'll call you tomorrow, maybe."

"Muriel. Now, listen to me."

"Yes, Mother," said the girl, putting her weight on her right leg.

"Call me the *instant* he does, or *says*, anything at all funny—you know what I mean. Do you hear me?"

"Mother, I'm not afraid of Seymour."

"Muriel, I want you to promise me."

"All right, I promise. Goodbye, Mother," said the girl. "My love to Daddy." She hung up.

"See more glass," said Sybil Carpenter, who was staying at the hotel with her mother. "Did you see more glass?"

"Pussycat, stop saying that. It's driving Mommy absolutely crazy. Hold still, please."

Mrs. Carpenter was putting sun-tan oil on Sybil's shoulders, spreading it down over the delicate, winglike blades of her back. Sybil was sitting insecurely on a huge, inflated beach ball, facing the ocean. She was wearing a canary-yellow two-piece bathing suit, one piece of which she would not actually be needing for another nine or ten years.

"It was really just an ordinary silk handkerchief—you could see when you got up close," said the woman in the beach chair beside Mrs. Carpenter's. "I wish I knew how she tied it. It was really darling."

"It sounds darling," Mrs. Carpenter agreed. "Sybil, *hold still*, pussy."

"Did you see more glass?" said Sybil.

Mrs. Carpenter sighed. "All right," she said. She replaced the cap on the sun-tan-oil bottle. "Now run and play, pussy. Mommy's going up to the hotel and have a Martini with Mrs. Hubbel. I'll bring you the olive."

Set loose, Sybil immediately ran down to the flat part of the beach and began to walk in the direction of Fisherman's Pavilion. Stopping only to sink a foot in a soggy, collapsed castle, she was soon out of the area reserved for guests of the hotel.

She walked for about a quarter of a mile and then suddenly broke into an oblique run up the soft part of the beach. She stopped short when she reached the place where a young man was lying on his back.

"Are you going in the water, see more glass?" she said.

The young man started, his right hand going to the lapels of his terry-cloth robe. He turned over on his stomach, letting a sausaged towel fall away from his eyes, and squinted up at Sybil.

"Hey. Hello, Sybil."

"Are you going in the water?"

"I was waiting for *you*," said the young man. "What's new?"

"What?" said Sybil.

"What's new? What's on the program?"

"My daddy's coming tomorrow on a nairiplane," Sybil said, kicking sand.

"Not in my face, baby," the young man said, putting his hand on Sybil's ankle. "Well, it's about time he got here, your daddy. I've been expecting him hourly. Hourly."

"Where's the lady?" Sybil said.

"The lady?" The young man brushed some sand out of his thin hair. "That's hard to say, Sybil. She may be in any one of a thousand places. At the hairdresser's. Having her hair dyed mink. Or making dolls for poor children, in her room." Lying prone now, he made two fists, set one on top of the other, and rested his chin on the top one. "Ask me something else, Sybil," he said. "That's a fine bathing suit you have on. If there's one thing I like, it's a blue bathing suit."

Sybil stared at him, then looked down at her protruding stomach. "This is a *yellow*," she said. "This is a *yellow*."

"It is? Come a little closer."

Sybil took a step forward.

"You're absolutely right. What a fool I am."

"Are you going in the water?" Sybil said.

"I'm seriously considering it. I'm giving it plenty of thought, Sybil, you'll be glad to know."

Sybil prodded the rubber float that the young man sometimes used as a headrest. "It needs *air*," she said.

"You're right. It needs more air than I'm willing to admit." He took away his fists and let his chin rest on the sand. "Sybil," he said, "you're looking fine. It's good to see you. Tell me about yourself." He reached in front of him and took both of Sybil's ankles in his hands. "I'm Capricorn," he said. "What are you?"

"Sharon Lipschutz said you let her sit on the piano seat with you," Sybil said.

"Sharon Lipschutz said that?"

Sybil nodded vigorously.

He let go of her ankles, drew in his hands, and laid the side of his face on his right forearm. "Well," he said, "you know how those things happen, Sybil. I was sitting there, playing. And you were nowhere in sight. And Sharon Lipschutz came over and sat down next to me. I couldn't push her off, could I?"

"Yes."

"Oh, no. No. I couldn't do that," said the young man. "I'll tell you what I did do, though."

"What?"

"I pretended she was you."

Sybil immediately stooped and began to dig in the sand. "Let's go in the water," she said.

"All right," said the young man. "I think I can work it in."

"Next time, push her off," Sybil said.

"Push who off?"

"Sharon Lipschutz."

"Ah, Sharon Lipschutz," said the young man. "How that name comes up. Mixing memory and desire." He suddenly got to his feet. He looked at the ocean. "Sybil," he said, "I'll tell you what we'll do. We'll see if we can catch a bananafish."

"A what?"

"A bananafish," he said, and undid the belt of his robe. He took off the robe. His shoulders were white and narrow, and his trunks were royal blue. He folded the robe, first lengthwise, then in thirds. He unrolled the towel he had used over his eyes, spread it out on the sand, and then laid the folded robe on top of it. He bent over, picked up the float, and secured it under his right arm. Then, with his left hand, he took Sybil's hand.

The two started to walk down to the ocean.

"I imagine you've seen quite a few bananafish in your day," the young man said.

Sybil shook her head.

"You haven't? Where do you *live*, anyway?"

"I don't know," said Sybil.

"Sure you know. You must know. Sharon Lipschutz knows where *she* lives and *she's* only *three and a half.*"

Sybil stopped walking and yanked her hand away from him. She picked up an ordinary beach shell and looked at it with elaborate interest. She threw it down. "Whirly Wood, Connecticut," she said, and resumed walking, stomach foremost.

"Whirly Wood, Connecticut," said the young man. "Is that anywhere near Whirly Wood, Connecticut, by any chance?"

Sybil looked at him. "That's where I *live*," she said impatiently. "I *live* in Whirly Wood, Connecticut." She ran a few steps ahead of him, caught up her left foot in her left hand, and hopped two or three times.

"You have no idea how clear that makes everything," the young man said.

Sybil released her foot. "Did you read 'Little Black Sambo'?" she said.

"It's very funny you ask me that," he said. "It so happens I just finished reading it last night." He reached down and took back Sybil's hand. "What did you think of it?" he asked her.

"Did the tigers run all around that tree?"

"I thought they'd never stop. I never saw so many tigers."

"There were only six," Sybil said.

"*Only* six!" said the young man. "Do you call that *only*?"

"Do you like wax?" Sybil asked.

"Do I like what?" asked the young man.

"Wax."

"Very much. Don't you?"

Sybil nodded. "Do you like olives?" she asked.

"Olives—yes. Olives and wax. I never go anyplace without 'em."

"Do you like Sharon Lipschutz?" Sybil asked.

"Yes. Yes, I do," said the young man. "What I like par*tic*ularly about her is that she never does anything mean to little dogs in the lobby of the hotel. That little toy bull that belongs to that lady from Canada, for instance. You probably won't believe this, but *some* little girls like to poke that little dog with balloon sticks. Sharon doesn't. She's never mean or unkind. That's why I like her so much."

Sybil was silent.

"I like to chew candles," she said finally.

"Who doesn't?" said the young man, getting his feet wet. "Wow! It's cold." He dropped the rubber float on its back. "No, wait just a second, Sybil. Wait'll we get out a little bit."

They waded out till the water was up to Sybil's waist. Then the young man picked her up and laid her down on her stomach on the float.

"Don't you ever wear a bathing cap or anything?" he asked.

"Don't let go," Sybil ordered. "You hold me, now."

"Miss Carpenter. Please. I know my business," the young man said. "You just keep your eyes open for any bananafish. This is a *perfect* day for bananafish."

"I don't see any," Sybil said.

"That's understandable. Their habits are very peculiar. *Very* peculiar." He kept pushing the float. The water was not quite up to his chest. "They lead a very tragic life," he said. "You know what they do, Sybil?"

She shook her head.

"Well, they swim into a hole where there's a lot of bananas. They're very ordinary-looking fish when they swim *in*. But once they get in, they behave like pigs. Why, I've known some bananafish to swim into a banana hole and eat as many as seventy-eight bananas." He edged the float and its passenger a foot closer to the horizon. "Naturally, after that they're so fat they can't get out of the hole again. Can't fit through the door."

"Not too far out," Sybil said. "What happens to them?"

"What happens to who?"

"The bananafish."

"Oh, you mean after they eat so many bananas they can't get out of the banana hole?"

"Yes," said Sybil.

"Well, I hate to tell you, Sybil. They die."

"Why?" asked Sybil.

"Well, they get banana fever. It's a terrible disease."

"Here comes a *wave*," Sybil said nervously.

"We'll ignore it. We'll snub it," said the young man. "Two snobs." He took Sybil's ankles in his hands and pressed down and forward. The float nosed over the top of the wave. The water soaked Sybil's blond hair, but her scream was full of pleasure.

With her hand, when the float was level again, she wiped away a flat, wet band of hair from her eyes, and reported, "I just saw one."

"Saw what, my love?"

"A bananafish."

"My God, no!" said the young man. "Did he have any bananas in his mouth?"

"Yes," said Sybil. "Six."

The young man suddenly picked up one of Sybil's wet feet, which were drooping over the end of the float, and kissed the arch.

"Hey!" said the owner of the foot, turning around.

"Hey, yourself! We're going in now. You had enough?"

"No!"

"Sorry," he said, and pushed the float toward shore until Sybil got off it. He carried it the rest of the way.

"Goodbye," said Sybil, and ran without regret in the direction of the hotel.

The young man put on his robe, closed the lapels tight, and jammed his towel into his pocket. He picked up the slimy wet, cumbersome float and put it under his arm. He plodded alone through the soft, hot sand toward the hotel.

On the sub-main floor of the hotel, which the management directed bathers to use, a woman with zinc salve on her nose got into the elevator with the young man.

"I see you're looking at my feet," he said to her when the car was in motion.

"I beg your pardon?" said the woman.

"I said I see you're looking at my feet."

"I *beg* your pardon. I happened to be looking at the floor," said the woman, and faced the doors of the car.

"If you want to look at my feet, say so," said the young man. "But don't be a God-damned sneak about it."

"Let me out here, please," the woman said quickly to the girl operating the car.

The car doors opened and the woman got off without looking back.

"I have two normal feet and I can't see the slightest God-damned reason why anybody should stare at them," said the young man. "Five, please." He took his room key out of his robe pocket.

He got off at the fifth floor, walked down the hall, and let himself into 507. The room smelled of new calfskin luggage and nail-lacquer remover.

He glanced at the girl lying asleep on one of the twin beds. Then he went over to one of the pieces of luggage, opened it, and from under a pile of shorts and undershirts he took out an Ortgies calibre 7.65 automatic. He released the magazine, looked at it, then reinserted it. He cocked the piece. Then he went over and sat down on the unoccupied twin bed, looked at the girl, aimed the pistol, and fired a bullet through his right temple.

CHILDREN ARE BORED ON SUNDAY

BY JEAN STAFFORD (1948)

Through the wide doorway between two of the painting galleries, Emma saw Alfred Eisenburg standing before "The Three Miracles of Zenobius," his lean, equine face ashen and sorrowing, his gaunt frame looking undernourished, and dressed in a way that showed he was poorer this year than he had been last. Emma herself had been hunting for the Botticelli all afternoon, sidetracked first by a Mantegna she had forgotten, and then by a follower of Hieronymus Bosch, and distracted, in an English room as she was passing through, by the hot invective of two ladies who were lodged (so they bitterly reminded one another) in an outrageous and expensive mare's-nest at a hotel on Madison. Emma liked Alfred, and once, at a party in some other year, she had flirted with him slightly for seven or eight minutes. It had been spring, and even into that modern apartment, wherever it had been, while the cunning guests, on their guard and highly civilized, learnedly disputed on aesthetic and political subjects, the feeling of spring had boldly invaded, adding its nameless, sentimental sensations to all the others of the buffeted heart; one did not know and never had, even in the devouring raptures of adolescence, whether this was a feeling of tension or of solution—whether one flew or drowned.

In another year, she would have been pleased to run into Alfred here in the Metropolitan on a cold Sunday, when the galleries were thronged with out-of-towners and with people who dutifully did something self-educating on the day of rest. But this year she was hiding from just such people as Alfred Eisenburg, and she turned quickly to go back the way she had come, past the Constables and Raeburns. As she turned, she came face to face with Salvador Dalí, whose sudden countenance, with its unlikely mustache and its histrionic eyes, familiar from the photographs in public places, momentarily stopped her dead, for she did not immediately recognize him and, still surprised by seeing Eisenburg, took him also to be someone she knew. She shuddered and then realized that he was merely famous, and she penetrated the heart of a guided tour and proceeded safely through the rooms until she came to the balcony that overlooks the medieval armor, and there she paused, watching two youths of high-school age examine the joints of an equestrian's shell.

She paused because she could not decide what to look at now that she had been denied the Botticelli. She wondered, rather crossly, why Alfred Eisenburg was looking at it and why, indeed, he was here at all. She feared that her afternoon, begun in such a burst of courage, would not be what it might have been; for this second's glimpse of him—who had no bearing on her life—might very well divert her from the pictures, not only because she was reminded of her ignorance of painting by the presence of someone who was (she assumed) versed in it but because her eyesight was now bound to be impaired by memory and conjecture, by the irrelevant mind-portraits of innumerable people who belonged to Eisenburg's milieu. And almost at once, as she had predicted, the air separating her from the schoolboys below was populated with the images of composers, of painters, of writers who pronounced judgments, in their individual argot, on Hindemith, Ernst, Sartre, on Beethoven, Rubens, Baudelaire, on Stalin and Freud and Kierkegaard, on Toynbee, Frazer, Thoreau, Franco, Salazar, Roosevelt, Maimonides, Racine, Wallace, Picasso, Henry Luce, Monsignor Sheen, the Atomic Energy Commission, and the movie industry. And she saw herself moving, shaky with apprehensions and Martinis, and with the belligerence of a child who feels himself laughed at, through the apartments of Alfred Eisenburg's friends, where the shelves were filled with everyone from Aristophanes to Ring Lardner, where the walls were hung with reproductions of Seurat, Titian, Vermeer, and Klee, and where the record cabinets began with Palestrina and ended with Copland.

These cocktail parties were a *modus vivendi* in themselves for which a new philosophy, a new ethic, and a new etiquette had had to be devised. They were neither work nor play, and yet they were not at all beside the point but were, on the contrary, quite indispensable to the spiritual life of the artists who went to them. It was possible for Emma to see these occasions objectively, after these many months of abstention from them, but it was still not possible to understand them, for they were so special a case, and so unlike any parties she had known at home. The gossip was different, for one thing, because it was stylized, creative (integrating the whole of the garrotted, absent friend), and all its details were precise and all its conceits were Jamesian, and all its practitioners sorrowfully saw themselves in the role of Pontius Pilate, that hero of the untoward circumstance. (It has to be done, though we don't want to do it; 'tis a pity she's a whore, when no one writes more intelligent verse than she.) There was, too, the matter of the drinks, which were much worse than those served by anyone else, and much more plentiful. They dispensed with the fripperies of olives in Martinis and cherries in Manhattans (God forbid! They had no sweet teeth), and half the time there was no ice, and when there was, it was as likely as not to be suspect shavings got from a bed for shad at the corner fish store. Other species, so one heard, went off to dinner after cocktail parties certainly no later than half past eight, but no one ever left a party given by an Olympian until ten, at the earliest, and then groups went out together, stalling and squabbling at the door, angrily unable to come to a decision about where to eat, although they seldom ate once they got there but, with the greatest formality imaginable, ordered several rounds of cocktails, as if they had not had a drink in a month of Sundays. But the most surprising thing of all about these parties was that every now and again, in the middle of the urgent, general conversation, this cream of the enlightened was horribly curdled, and an argument would end, quite literally, in a bloody nose or a black eye. Emma was always astounded when this happened and continued to think that these outbursts did not arise out of hatred or jealousy but out of some quite unaccountable quirk, almost a reflex, almost something physical. She never quite believed her eyes—that is, was never altogether convinced that they were really beating one another up. It seemed, rather, that this was only a deliberate and perfectly honest demonstration of what might have happened often if they had not so diligently dedicated themselves to their intellects. Although she had seen them do it, she did not and could not believe that city people clipped each other's jaws, for, to Emma, urban equalled urbane, and ichor ran in these Augustans' veins.

As she looked down now from her balcony at the atrocious iron clothes below, it occurred to her that Alfred Eisenburg had been just such a first-generation metropolitan boy as these two who half knelt in lithe and eager attitudes to study the glittering splints of a knight's skirt. It was a kind of childhood she could not imagine and from the thought of which she turned away in secret, shameful pity. She had been really stunned when she first came to New York to find that almost no one she met had gluttonously read Dickens, as she had, beginning at the age of ten, and because she was only twenty when she arrived in the city and unacquainted with the varieties of cultural experience, she had acquired the idea, which she was never able to shake entirely loose, that these New York natives had been deprived of this and many other innocent pleasures because they had lived in apartments and not in two- or three-story houses. (In the early years in New York, she had known someone who had not heard a cat purr until he was twenty-five and went to a houseparty on Fire Island.) They had played hide-and-seek dodging behind ash cans instead of lilac bushes and in and out of the entries of apartment houses instead of up alleys densely lined with hollyhocks. But who was she to patronize and pity them? Her own childhood, rich as it seemed to her on reflection, had not equipped her to read, or to see, or to listen, as theirs had done; she envied them and despised them at the same time, and at the same time she feared and admired them. As their attitude implicitly accused her, before she beat her retreat, she never looked for meanings, she never saw the literary-historical symbolism of the cocktail party but went on, despite all testimony to the contrary, believing it to be an occasion for getting drunk.

She never listened, their manner delicately explained, and when she talked she was always lamentably off key; often and often she had been stared at and had been told, "It's not the same thing at all."

Emma shuddered, scrutinizing this nature of hers, which they all had scorned, as if it were some harmless but sickening reptile. Noticing how cold the marble railing was under her hands, she felt that her self-blame was surely justified; she came to the Metropolitan Museum not to attend to the masterpieces but to remember cocktail parties where she had drunk too much and had seen Alfred Eisenburg, and to watch schoolboys, and to make experience out of the accidental contact of the palms of her hands with a cold bit of marble. What was there to do? One thing, anyhow, was clear and that was that today's excursion into the world had been premature; her solitude must continue for a while, and perhaps it would never end. If the sight of someone so peripheral, so uninvolving as Alfred Eisenburg could scare her so badly, what would a cocktail party do? She almost fainted at the thought of it, she almost fell headlong, and the boys, abandoning the coat of mail, dizzied her by their progress toward an emblazoned tabard.

In so many words, she wasn't fit to be seen. Although she was no longer mutilated, she was still unkempt; her pretensions needed brushing; her ambiguities needed to be cleaned; her evasions would have to be completely overhauled before she could face again the terrifying learning of someone like Alfred Eisenburg, a learning whose components cohered into a central personality that was called "intellectual." She imagined that even the boys down there had opinions on everything political and artistic and metaphysical and scientific, and because she remained, in spite of all her opportunities, as green as grass, she was certain they had got their head start because they had grown up in apartments, where there was nothing else to do but educate themselves. This being an intellectual was not the same thing as dilettantism; it was a calling in itself. Emma, for example, did not even know whether Eisenburg was a painter, a writer, a composer, a sculptor, or something entirely different. When, seeing him with the composers, she had thought he was one of them; when, the next time she met him, at a studio party, she decided he must be a painter; and when, on subsequent occasions, everything had pointed toward his being a writer, she had relied altogether on circumstantial evidence and not on anything he had said or done. There was no reason to suppose that he had not looked upon her as the same sort of variable and it made their anonymity to one another complete. Without the testimony of an impartial third person, neither she nor Eisenburg would ever know the other's actual trade. But his specialty did not matter, for his larger designation was that of "the intellectual," just as the man who confines his talents to the nose and throat is still a doctor. It was, in the light of this, all the more extraordinary that they had had that lightning-paced flirtation at a party.

Extraordinary, because Emma could not look upon herself as an intellectual. Her private antonym of this noun was "rube," and to her regret—the regret that had caused her finally to disappear from Alfred's group—she was not even a bona-fide rube. In her store clothes, so to speak, she was often taken for an intellectual, for she had, poor girl, gone to college and had never been quite the same since. She would not dare, for instance, go up to Eisenburg now and say that what she most liked in the Botticelli were the human and compassionate eyes of the centurions' horses, which reminded her of the eyes of her own Great-Uncle Graham, whom she had adored as a child. Nor would she admit that she was delighted with a Crivelli Madonna because the peaches in the background looked exactly like marzipan, or that Goya's little red boy inspired in her only the pressing desire to go out immediately in search of a plump cat to stroke. While she knew that feelings like these were not really punishable, she had not perfected the art of tossing them off; she was no flirt. She was a bounty jumper in the war between Great-Uncle Graham's farm and New York City, and liable to court-martial on one side and death on the other. Neither staunchly primitive nor confidently *au courant*, she rarely knew where she was at. And this was her Achilles' heel: her identity was always mistaken, and she was thought to be an intellectual who, however, had not made the grade. It was no use now to cry that she was not, that she was a simon-pure rube; not a soul would believe her. She knew, deeply and with horror, that she was thought merely stupid.

It was possible to be highly successful as a rube among the Olympians, and she had seen it done. Someone calling himself Nahum Mothersill had done it brilliantly, but she often wondered whether his name had not helped him, and, in fact, she had sometimes wondered whether that had been his real name. If she had been called, let us say, Hyacinth Derryberry, she believed she might have been able, as Mothersill had been, to ask who Ezra Pound was. (This struck her suddenly as a very important point; it was endearing, really, not to know who Pound was, but it was only embarrassing to know who he was but not to have read the "Cantos.") How different it would have been if education had not meddled with her rustic nature! Her education had never dissuaded her from her convictions, but certainly it had ruined the looks of her mind—painted the poor thing up until it looked like a mean, hypocritical, promiscuous malcontent, a craven and apologetic fancy woman. Thus she continued secretly to believe (but never to confess) that the apple Eve had eaten tasted exactly like those she had eaten when she was a child visiting on her Great-Uncle Graham's farm, and that Newton's observation was no news in spite of all the hue and cry. Half the apples she had eaten had fallen out of the tree, whose branches she had shaken for this very purpose, and the Apple Experience included both the descent of the fruit and the consumption of it, and Eve and Newton and Emma understood one another perfectly in this particular of reality.

Emma started. The Metropolitan boys, who, however bright they were, would be boys, now caused some steely article of dress to clank, and she instantly quit the balcony, as if this unseemly noise would attract the crowd's attention and bring everyone, including Eisenburg, to see what had happened. She scuttered like a quarry through the sightseers until she found an empty seat in front of Rembrandt's famous frump, "The Noble Slav"—it was this kind of thing, this fundamental apathy to most of Rembrandt, that made life in New York such hell for Emma—and there, upon the plum velours, she realized with surprise that Alfred Eisenburg's had been the last familiar face she had seen before she had closed the door of her tomb.

In September, it had been her custom to spend several hours of each day walking in a straight line, stopping only for traffic lights and outlaw taxicabs, in the hope that she would be tired enough to sleep at night. At five o'clock—and gradually it became more often four o'clock and then half past three—she would go into a bar, where, while she drank, she seemed to be reading the information offered by the Sun on "Where to Dine." Actually she had ceased to dine long since; every few days, with effort, she inserted thin wafers of food into her repelled mouth, flushing the frightful stuff down with enormous drafts of magical, purifying, fulfilling applejack diluted with tepid water from the tap. One weighty day, under a sky that grimly withheld the rain, as if to punish the whole city, she had started out from Ninetieth Street and had kept going down Madison and was thinking, as she passed the chancery of St. Patrick's, that it must be nearly time and that she needed only to turn east on Fiftieth Street to the New Weston, where the bar was cool, and dark to an almost absurd degree. And then she was hailed. She turned quickly, looking in all directions until she saw Eisenburg approaching, removing a gray pellet of gum from his mouth as he came. They were both remarkably shy and, at the time, she had thought they were so because this was the first time they had met since their brief and blameless flirtation. (How curious it was that she could scrape off the accretions of the months that had followed and could remember how she had felt on that spring night—as trembling, as expectant, as altogether young as if they had sat together underneath a blooming apple tree.) But now, knowing that her own embarrassment had come from something else, she thought that perhaps his had, too, and she connected his awkwardness on that September day with a report she had had, embedded in a bulletin on everyone, from her sole communicant, since her retreat, with the Olympian world. This informant had run into Alfred at a party and had said that he was having a very bad time of it with a divorce, with poverty, with a tempest that had carried off his job, and, at last, with a psychoanalyst, whose fees he could not possibly afford. Perhaps the nightmare had been well under way when they had met beside the chancery. Without alcohol and without the company of other people, they had had to be shy or their suffering would have shown in all its humiliating dishabille. Would it be true still if they should inescapably meet this afternoon in an Early Flemish room?

Suddenly, on this common level, in this state of social displacement, Emma wished to hunt for Alfred and urgently tell him that she hoped it had not been as bad for him as it had been for her. But naturally she was not so naïve, and she got up and went purposefully to look at two Holbeins. They pleased her, as Holbeins always did. The damage, though, was done, and she did not really see the pictures; Eisenburg's hypothetical suffering and her own real suffering blurred the clean lines and muddied the lucid colors. Between herself and the canvases swam the months of spreading, cancerous distrust, of anger that made her seasick, of grief that shook her like an influenza chill, of the physical afflictions by which the poor victimized spirit sought vainly to wreck the arrogantly healthy flesh.

Even that one glance at his face, seen from a distance through the lowing crowd, told her, now that she had repeated it to her mind's eye, that his cheeks were drawn and his skin was gray (no soap and water can ever clean away the grimy look of the sick at heart) and his stance was tired. She wanted them to go together to some hopelessly disreputable bar and to console one another in the most maudlin fashion over a lengthy succession of powerful drinks of whiskey, to compare their illnesses, to marry their invalid souls for these few hours of painful communion, and to babble with rapture that they were at last, for a little while, no longer alone. Only thus, as sick people, could they marry. In any other terms, it would be a mésalliance, doomed to divorce from the start, for rubes and intellectuals must stick to their own class. If only it could take place—this honeymoon of the cripples, this nuptial consummation of the abandoned—while drinking the delicious amber whiskey in a joint with a juke box, a stout barkeep, and a handful of tottering derelicts; if it could take place, would it be possible to prevent him from marring it all by talking of secondary matters? That is, of art and neurosis, art and politics, art and science, art and religion? Could he lay off the fashions of the day and leave his learning in his private entrepôt? Could he, that is, see the apple fall and not run madly to break the news to Newton and ask him what on earth it was all about? Could he, for her sake (for the sake of this pathetic rube all but weeping for her own pathos in the Metropolitan Museum), forget the whole dispute and, believing his eyes for a change, admit that the earth was flat?

It was useless for her now to try to see the paintings. She went, full of intentions, to the Van Eyck diptych and looked for a long time at the souls in Hell, kept there by the implacable, impartial, and genderless angel who stood upon its closing mouth. She looked, in renewed astonishment, at Jo Davidson's pink, wrinkled, embalmed head of Jules Bache, which sat, a trinket on a fluted pedestal, before a Flemish tapestry. But she was really conscious of nothing but her desire to leave the museum in the company of Alfred Eisenburg, her cousin-german in the territory of despair.

So she had to give up, two hours before the closing time, although she had meant to stay until the end, and she made her way to the central stairs, which she descended slowly, in disappointment, enviously observing the people who were going up, carrying collapsible canvas stools on which they would sit, losing themselves in their contemplation of the pictures. Salvador Dalí passed her, going quickly down. At the telephone booths, she hesitated, so sharply lonely that she almost looked for her address book, and she did take out a nickel, but she put it back and pressed forlornly forward against the incoming tide. Suddenly, at the storm doors, she heard a whistle and she turned sharply, knowing that it would be Eisenburg, as, of course, it was, and he wore an incongruous smile upon his long, El Greco face. He took her hand and gravely asked her where she had been all this year and how she happened to be here, of all places, of all days. Emma replied distractedly, looking at his seedy clothes, his shaggy hair, the green cast of his white skin, his deep black eyes, in which all the feelings were dishevelled, tattered, and held together only by the merest faith that change had to come. His hand was warm and her own seemed to cling to it and all their mutual necessity seemed centered here in their clasped hands. And there was no doubt about it; he had heard of her collapse and he saw in her face that she had heard of his. Their recognition of each other was instantaneous and absolute, for they cunningly saw that they were children and that, if they wished, they were free for the rest of this winter Sunday to play together, quite naked, quite innocent. "What a day it is! What a place!" said Alfred Eisenburg. "Can I buy you a drink, Emma? Have you time?"

She did not accept at once; she guardedly inquired where they could go from here, for it was an unlikely neighborhood for the sort of place she wanted. But they were *en rapport*, and he, wanting to avoid the grownups as much as she, said they would go across to Lexington. He needed a drink after an afternoon like this—didn't she? Oh, Lord, yes, she did, and she did not question what he meant by "an afternoon like this" but said that she would be delighted to go, even though they would have to walk on eggs all the way from the Museum to the place where the bottle was, the peace pipe on Lexington. Actually, there was nothing to fear; even if they had heard catcalls, or if someone had hooted at them, "Intellectual loves Rube!," they would have been impervious, for the heart carved in the bark of the apple tree would contain the names Emma and Alfred, and there were no perquisites to such a conjugation. To her own heart, which was shaped exactly like a valentine, there came a winglike palpitation, a delicate exigency, and all the fragrance of all the flowery springtime love affairs that ever were seemed waiting for them in the whiskey bottle. To mingle their pain, their handshake had promised them, was to produce a separate entity, like a child that could shift for itself, and they scrambled hastily toward this profound and pastoral experience.

SYMBOLS AND SIGNS

BY VLADIMIR NABOKOV (1948)

For the fourth time in as many years, they were confronted with the problem of what birthday present to take to a young man who was incurably deranged in his mind. Desires he had none. Man-made objects were to him either hives of evil, vibrant with a malignant activity that he alone could perceive, or gross comforts for which no use could be found in his abstract world. After eliminating a number of articles that might offend him or frighten him (anything in the gadget line, for instance, was taboo), his parents chose a dainty and innocent trifle—a basket with ten different fruit jellies in ten little jars.

At the time of his birth, they had already been married for a long time; a score of years had elapsed, and now they were quite old. Her drab gray hair was pinned up carelessly. She wore cheap black dresses. Unlike other women of her age (such as Mrs. Sol, their next-door neighbor, whose face was all pink and mauve with paint and whose hat was a cluster of brookside flowers), she presented a naked white countenance to the faultfinding light of spring. Her husband, who in the old country had been a fairly successful businessman, was now, in New York, wholly dependent on his brother Isaac, a real American of almost forty years' standing. They seldom saw Isaac and had nicknamed him the Prince.

That Friday, their son's birthday, everything went wrong. The subway train lost its life current between two stations and for a quarter of an hour they could hear nothing but the dutiful beating of their hearts and the rustling of newspapers. The bus they had to take next was late and kept them waiting a long time on a street corner, and when it did come, it was crammed with garrulous high-school children. It began to rain as they walked up the brown path leading to the sanitarium. There they waited again, and instead of their boy, shuffling into the room, as he usually did (his poor face sullen, confused, ill-shaven, and blotched with acne), a nurse they knew and did not care for appeared at last and brightly explained that he had again attempted to take his life. He was all right, she said, but a visit from his parents might disturb him. The place was so miserably understaffed, and things got mislaid or mixed up so easily, that they decided not to leave their present in the office but to bring it to him next time they came.

Outside the building, she waited for her husband to open his umbrella and then took his arm. He kept clearing his throat, as he always did when he was upset. They reached the bus-stop shelter on the other side of the street and he closed his umbrella. A few feet away, under a swaying and dripping tree, a tiny unfledged bird was helplessly twitching in a puddle.

During the long ride to the subway station, she and her husband did not exchange a word, and every time she glanced at his old hands, clasped and twitching upon the handle of his umbrella, and saw their swollen veins and brown-spotted skin, she felt the mounting pressure of tears. As she looked around, trying to hook her mind onto something, it gave her a kind of soft shock, a mixture of compassion and wonder, to notice that one of the passengers—a girl with dark hair and grubby red toenails—was weeping on the shoulder of an older woman. Whom did that woman resemble? She resembled Rebecca Borisovna, whose daughter had married one of the Soloveichiks—in Minsk, years ago.

The last time the boy had tried to do it, his method had been, in the doctor's words, a masterpiece of inventiveness; he would have succeeded had not an envious fellow-patient thought he was learning to fly and stopped him just in time. What he had really wanted to do was to tear a hole in his world and escape.

The system of his delusions had been the subject of an elaborate paper in a scientific monthly, which the doctor at the sanitarium had given to them to read. But long before that, she and her husband had puzzled it out for themselves. "Referential mania," the article had called it. In these very rare cases, the patient imagines that everything happening around him is a veiled reference to his personality and existence. He excludes real people from the conspiracy, because he considers himself to be so much more intelligent than other men. Phenomenal nature shadows him wherever he goes. Clouds in the staring sky transmit to each other, by means of slow signs, incredibly detailed information regarding him. His inmost thoughts are discussed at nightfall, in manual alphabet, by darkly gesticulating trees. Pebbles or stains or sun flecks form patterns representing, in some awful way, messages that he must intercept. Everything is a cipher and of everything he is the theme. All around him, there are spies. Some of them are detached observers, like glass surfaces and still pools; others, such as coats in store windows, are prejudiced witnesses, lynchers at heart; others, again (running water, storms), are hysterical to the point of insanity, have a distorted opinion of him, and grotesquely misinterpret his actions. He must be always on his guard and devote every minute and module of life to the decoding of the undulation of things. The very air he exhales is indexed and filed away. If only the interest he provokes were limited to his immediate surroundings, but, alas, it is not! With distance, the torrents of wild scandal increase in volume and volubility. The silhouettes of his blood corpuscles, magnified a million times, flit over vast plains; and still farther away, great mountains of unbearable solidity and height sum up, in terms of granite and groaning firs, the ultimate truth of his being.

When they emerged from the thunder and foul air of the subway, the last dregs of the day were mixed with the street lights. She wanted to buy some fish for supper, so she handed him the basket of jelly jars, telling him to go home. Accordingly, he returned to their tenement house, walked up to the third landing, and then remembered he had given her his keys earlier in the day.

In silence he sat down on the steps and in silence rose when, some ten minutes later, she came trudging heavily up the stairs, smiling wanly and shaking her head in deprecation of her silliness. They entered their two-room flat and he at once went to the mirror.

Straining the corners of his mouth apart by means of his thumbs, with a horrible, mask-like grimace, he removed his new, hopelessly uncomfortable dental plate. He read his Russian-language newspaper while she laid the table. Still reading, he ate the pale victuals that needed no teeth. She knew his moods and was also silent.

When he had gone to bed, she remained in the living room with her pack of soiled playing cards and her old photograph albums. Across the narrow courtyard, where the rain tinkled in the dark against some ash cans, windows were blandly alight, and in one of them a black-trousered man, with his hands clasped under his head and his elbows raised, could he seen lying supine on an untidy bed. She pulled the blind down and examined the photographs. As a baby, he looked more surprised than most babies. A photograph of a German maid they had had in Leipzig and her fat-faced fiancé fell out of a fold of the album. She turned the pages of the book: Minsk, the Revolution, Leipzig, Berlin, Leipzig again, a slanting house front, badly out of focus. Here was the boy when he was four years old, in a park, shyly, with puckered forehead, looking away from an eager squirrel, as he would have from any other stranger. Here was Aunt Rosa, a fussy, angular, wild-eyed old lady, who had lived in a tremulous world of bad news, bankruptcies, train accidents, and cancerous growths until the Germans put her to death, together with all the people she had worried about. The boy, aged six—that was when he drew wonderful birds with human hands and feet, and suffered from insomnia like a grown-up man. His cousin, now a famous chess player. The boy again, aged about eight, already hard to understand, afraid of the wallpaper in the passage, afraid of a certain picture in a book, which merely showed an idyllic landscape with rocks on a hillside and an old cart wheel hanging from the one branch of a leafless tree. Here he was at ten—the year they left Europe. She remembered the shame, the pity, the humiliating difficulties of the journey, and the ugly, vicious, backward children he was with in the special school where he had been placed after they arrived in America. And then came a time in his life, coinciding with a long convalescence after pneumonia, when those little phobias of his, which his parents had stubbornly regarded as the eccentricities of a prodigiously gifted child, hardened, as it were, into a dense tangle of logically interacting illusions, making them totally inaccessible to normal minds.

All this, and much more, she had accepted, for, after all, living does mean accepting the loss of one joy after another, not even joys in her case, mere possibilities of improvement. She thought of the recurrent waves of pain that for some reason or other she and her husband had had to endure; of the invisible giants hurting her boy in some unimaginable fashion; of the incalculable amount of tenderness contained in the world; of the fate of this tenderness, which is either crushed or wasted, or transformed into madness; of neglected children humming to themselves in unswept corners; of beautiful weeds that cannot hide from the farmer.

It was nearly midnight when, from the living room, she heard her husband moan, and presently he staggered in, wearing over his nightgown the old overcoat with the astrakhan collar that he much preferred to his nice blue bathrobe.

"I can't sleep!" he cried.

"Why can't you sleep?" she asked. "You were so tired."

"I can't sleep because I am dying," he said, and lay down on the couch.

"Is it your stomach? Do you want me to call Dr. Solov?"

"No doctors, no doctors," he moaned. "To the devil with doctors! We must get him out of there quick. Otherwise, we'll be responsible. . . . Responsible!" He hurled himself into a sitting position, both feet on the floor, thumping his forehead with his clenched fist.

"All right," she said quietly. "We will bring him home tomorrow morning."

"I would like some tea," said her husband and went out to the bathroom.

Bending with difficulty, she retrieved some playing cards and a photograph or two that had slipped to the floor—the knave of hearts, the nine of spades, the ace of spades, the maid Elsa and her bestial beau. He returned in high spirits, saying in a loud voice, "I have it all figured out. We will give him the bedroom. Each of us will spend part of the night near him and the other part on this couch. We will have the doctor see him at least twice a week. It does not matter what the Prince says. He won't have much to say anyway, because it will come out cheaper."

The telephone rang. It was an unusual hour for it to ring. He stood in the middle of the room, groping with his foot for one slipper that had come off, and childishly, toothlessly, gaped at his wife. Since she knew more English than he, she always attended to the calls.

"Can I speak to Charlie?" a girl's dull little voice said to her now.

"What number do you want? . . . No. You have the wrong number."

She put the receiver down gently and her hand went to her heart. "It frightened me," she said.

He smiled a quick smile and immediately resumed his excited monologue. They would fetch him as soon as it was day. For his own protection, they would keep all the knives in a locked drawer. Even at his worst, he presented no danger to other people.

The telephone rang a second time.

The same toneless, anxious young voice asked for Charlie.

"You have the incorrect number. I will tell you what you are doing. You are turning the letter 'o' instead of the zero." She hung up again.

They sat down to their unexpected, festive midnight tea. He sipped noisily; his face was flushed; every now and then he raised his glass with a circular motion, so as to make the sugar dissolve more thoroughly. The vein on the side of his bald head stood out conspicuously, and silvery bristles showed on his chin. The birthday present stood on the table. While she poured him another glass of tea, he put on his spectacles and reëxamined with pleasure the luminous yellow, green, and red little jars. His clumsy, moist lips spelled out their eloquent labels—apricot, grape, beach plum, quince. He had got to crab apple when the telephone rang again.

THE LOTTERY

BY SHIRLEY JACKSON (1948)

The morning of June 27th was clear and sunny, with the fresh warmth of a full-summer day; the flowers were blossoming profusely and the grass was richly green. The people of the village began to gather in the square, between the post office and the bank, around ten o'clock; in some towns there were so many people that the lottery took two days and had to be started on June 26th, but in this village, where there were only about three hundred people, the whole lottery took only about two hours, so it could begin at ten o'clock in the morning and still be through in time to allow the villagers to get home for noon dinner.

The children assembled first, of course. School was recently over for the summer, and the feeling of liberty sat uneasily on most of them; they tended to gather together quietly for a while before they broke into boisterous play, and their talk was still of the classroom and the teacher, of books and reprimands. Bobby Martin had already stuffed his pockets full of stones, and the other boys soon followed his example, selecting the smoothest and roundest stones; Bobby and Harry Jones and Dickie Delacroix—the villagers pronounced this name "Dellacroy"—eventually made a great pile of stones in one corner of the square and guarded it against the raids of the other boys. The girls stood aside, talking among themselves, looking over their shoulders at the boys, and the very small children rolled in the dust or clung to the hands of their older brothers or sisters.

Soon the men began to gather, surveying their own children, speaking of planting and rain, tractors and taxes. They stood together, away from the pile of stones in the corner, and their jokes were quiet and they smiled rather than laughed. The women, wearing faded house dresses and sweaters, came shortly after their menfolk. They greeted one another and exchanged bits of gossip as they went to join their husbands. Soon the women, standing by their husbands, began to call to their children, and the children came reluctantly, having to be called four or five times. Bobby Martin ducked under his mother's grasping hand and ran, laughing, back to the pile of stones. His father spoke up sharply, and Bobby came quickly and took his place between his father and his oldest brother.

The lottery was conducted—as were the square dances, the teen-age club, the Halloween program—by Mr. Summers, who had time and energy to devote to civic activities. He was a round-faced, jovial man and he ran the coal business, and people were sorry for him, because he had no children and his wife was a scold. When he arrived in the square, carrying the black wooden box, there was a murmur of conversation among the villagers, and he waved and called, "Little late today, folks." The postmaster, Mr. Graves, followed him, carrying a three-legged stool, and the stool was put in the center of the square and Mr. Summers set the black box down on it. The villagers kept their distance, leaving a space between themselves and the stool, and when Mr. Summers said, "Some of you fellows want to give me a hand?," there was a hesitation before two men, Mr. Martin and his oldest son, Baxter, came forward to hold the box steady on the stool while Mr. Summers stirred up the papers inside it.

The original paraphernalia for the lottery had been lost long ago, and the black box now resting on the stool had been put into use even before Old Man Warner, the oldest man in town, was born. Mr. Summers spoke frequently to the villagers about making a new box, but no one liked to upset even as much tradition as was represented by the black box. There was a story that the present box had been made with some pieces of the box that had preceded it, the one that had been constructed when the first people settled down to make a village here. Every year, after the lottery, Mr. Summers began talking again about a new box, but every year the subject was allowed to fade off without anything's being done. The black box grew shabbier each year; by now it was no longer completely black but splintered badly along one side to show the original wood color, and in some places faded or stained.

Mr. Martin and his oldest son, Baxter, held the black box securely on the stool until Mr. Summers had stirred the papers thoroughly with his hand. Because so much of the ritual had been forgotten or discarded, Mr. Summers had been successful in having slips of paper substituted for the chips of wood that had been used for generations. Chips of wood, Mr. Summers had argued, had been all very well when the village was tiny, but now that the population was more than three hundred and likely to keep on growing, it was necessary to use something that would fit more easily into the black box. The night before the lottery, Mr. Summers and Mr. Graves made up the slips of paper and put them into the box, and it was then taken to the safe of Mr. Summers' coal company and locked up until Mr. Summers was ready to take it to the square next morning. The rest of the year, the box was put away, sometimes one place, sometimes another; it had spent one year in Mr. Graves' barn and another year underfoot in the post office, and sometimes it was set on a shelf in the Martin grocery and left there.

There was a great deal of fussing to be done before Mr. Summers declared the lottery open. There were the lists to make up—of heads of families, heads of households in each family, members of each household in each family. There was the proper swearing-in of Mr. Summers by the postmaster, as the official of the lottery; at one time, some people remembered, there had been a recital of some sort, performed by the official of the lottery, a perfunctory, tuneless chant that had been rattled off duly each year; some people believed that the official of the lottery used to stand just so when he said or sang it, others believed that he was supposed to walk among the people, but years and years ago this part of the ritual had been allowed to lapse. There had been, also, a ritual salute, which the official of the lottery had had to use in addressing each person who came up to draw from the box, but this also had changed with time, until now it was felt necessary only for the official to speak to each person approaching. Mr. Summers was very good at all this; in his clean white shirt and blue jeans, with one hand resting carelessly on the black box, he seemed very proper and important as he talked interminably to Mr. Graves and the Martins.

Just as Mr. Summers finally left off talking and turned to the assembled villagers, Mrs. Hutchinson came hurriedly along the path to the square, her sweater thrown over her shoulders, and slid into place in the back of the crowd. "Clean forgot what day it was," she said to Mrs. Delacroix, who stood next to her, and they both laughed softly. "Thought my old man was out back stacking wood," Mrs. Hutchinson went on, "and then I looked out the window and the kids was gone, and then I remembered it was the twenty-seventh and came a-running." She dried her hands on her apron, and Mrs. Delacroix said, "You're in time, though. They're still talking away up there."

Mrs. Hutchinson craned her neck to see through the crowd and found her husband and children standing near the front. She tapped Mrs. Delacroix on the arm as a farewell and began to make her way through the crowd. The people separated good-humoredly to let her through; two or three people said, in voices just loud enough to be heard across the crowd, "Here comes your Mrs., Hutchinson," and "Bill, she made it after all." Mrs. Hutchinson reached her husband, and Mr. Summers, who had been waiting, said cheerfully, "Thought we were going to have to get on without you, Tessie." Mrs. Hutchinson said, grinning, "Wouldn't have me leave m'dishes in the sink, now, would you, Joe?," and soft laughter ran through the crowd as the people stirred back into position after Mrs. Hutchinson's arrival.

"Well, now," Mr. Summers said soberly, "guess we better get started, get this over with, so's we can go back to work. Anybody ain't here?"

"Dunbar," several people said. "Dunbar, Dunbar."

Mr. Summers consulted his list. "Clyde Dunbar," he said. "That's right. He's broke his leg, hasn't he? Who's drawing for him?"

"Me, I guess," a woman said, and Mr. Summers turned to look at her. "Wife draws for her husband," Mr. Summers said. "Don't you have a grown boy to do it for you, Janey?" Although Mr. Summers and everyone else in the village knew the answer perfectly well, it was the business of the official of the lottery to ask such questions formally. Mr. Summers waited with an expression of polite interest while Mrs. Dunbar answered.

"Horace's not but sixteen yet," Mrs. Dunbar said regretfully. "Guess I gotta fill in for the old man this year."

"Right," Mr. Summers said. He made a note on the list he was holding. Then he asked, "Watson boy drawing this year?"

A tall boy in the crowd raised his hand. "Here," he said. "I'm drawing for m'mother and me." He blinked his eyes nervously and ducked his head as several voices in the crowd said things like "Good fellow, Jack," and "Glad to see your mother's got a man to do it."

"Well," Mr. Summers said, "guess that's everyone. Old Man Warner make it?"

"Here," a voice said, and Mr. Summers nodded.

A sudden hush fell on the crowd as Mr. Summers cleared his throat and looked at the list. "All ready?" he called. "Now, I'll read the names—heads of families first—and the men come up and take a paper out of the box. Keep the paper folded in your hand without looking at it until everyone has had a turn. Everything clear?"

The people had done it so many times that they only half listened to the directions; most of them were quiet, wetting their lips, not looking around. Then Mr. Summers raised one hand high and said, "Adams." A man disengaged himself from the crowd and came forward. "Hi, Steve," Mr. Summers said, and Mr. Adams said, "Hi, Joe." They grinned at one another humorlessly and nervously. Then Mr. Adams reached into the black box and took out a folded paper. He held it firmly by one corner as he turned and went hastily back to his place in the crowd, where he stood a little apart from his family, not looking down at his hand.

"Allen," Mr. Summers said. "Anderson. . . . Bentham."

"Seems like there's no time at all between lotteries any more," Mrs. Delacroix said to Mrs. Graves in the back row. "Seems like we got through with the last one only last week."

"Time sure goes fast," Mrs. Graves said.

"Clark. . . . Delacroix."

"There goes my old man," Mrs. Delacroix said. She held her breath while her husband went forward.

"Dunbar," Mr. Summers said, and Mrs. Dunbar went steadily to the box while one of the women said, "Go on, Janey," and another said, "There she goes."

"We're next," Mrs. Graves said. She watched while Mr. Graves came around from the side of the box, greeted Mr. Summers gravely, and selected a slip of paper from the box. By now, all through the crowd there were men holding the small folded papers in their large hands, turning them over and over nervously. Mrs. Dunbar and her two sons stood together, Mrs. Dunbar holding the slip of paper.

"Harburt. . . . Hutchinson."

"Get up there, Bill," Mrs. Hutchinson said, and the people near her laughed.

"Jones."

"They do say," Mr. Adams said to Old Man Warner, who stood next to him, "that over in the north village they're talking of giving up the lottery."

Old Man Warner snorted. "Pack of crazy fools," he said. "Listening to the young folks, nothing's good enough for them. Next thing you know, they'll be wanting to go back to living in caves, nobody work any more, live that way for a while. Used to be a saying about 'Lottery in June, corn be heavy soon.' First thing you know, we'd all be eating stewed chickweed and acorns. There's always been a lottery," he added petulantly. "Bad enough to see young Joe Summers up there joking with everybody."

"Some places have already quit lotteries," Mrs. Adams said.

"Nothing but trouble in that," Old Man Warner said stoutly. "Pack of young fools."

"Martin." And Bobby Martin watched his father go forward. "Overdyke. . . . Percy."

"I wish they'd hurry," Mrs. Dunbar said to her older son. "I wish they'd hurry."

"They're almost through," her son said.

"You get ready to run tell Dad," Mrs. Dunbar said.

Mr. Summers called his own name and then stepped forward precisely and selected a slip from the box. Then he called, "Warner."

"Seventy-seventh year I been in the lottery," Old Man Warner said as he went through the crowd. "Seventy-seventh time."

"Watson." The tall boy came awkwardly through the crowd. Someone said, "Don't be nervous, Jack," and Mr. Summers said, "Take your time, son."

"Zanini."

. . .

After that, there was a long pause, a breathless pause, until Mr. Summers, holding his slip of paper in the air, said, "All right, fellows." For a minute, no one moved, and then all the slips of paper were opened. Suddenly, all the women began to speak at once, saying, "Who is it?," "Who's got it?," "Is it the Dunbars?," "Is it the Watsons?" Then the voices began to say, "It's Hutchinson. It's Bill," "Bill Hutchinson's got it."

"Go tell your father," Mrs. Dunbar said to her older son.

People began to look around to see the Hutchinsons. Bill Hutchinson was standing quiet, staring down at the paper in his hand. Suddenly, Tessie Hutchinson shouted to Mr. Summers, "You didn't give him time enough to take any paper he wanted. I saw you. It wasn't fair!"

"Be a good sport, Tessie," Mrs. Delacroix called, and Mrs. Graves said, "All of us took the same chance."

"Shut up, Tessie," Bill Hutchinson said.

"Well, everyone," Mr. Summers said, "that was done pretty fast, and now we've got to be hurrying a little more to get done in time." He consulted his next list. "Bill," he said, "you draw for the Hutchinson family. You got any other households in the Hutchinsons?"

"There's Don and Eva," Mrs. Hutchinson yelled. "Make them take their chance!"

"Daughters draw with their husbands' families, Tessie," Mr. Summers said gently. "You know that as well as anyone else."

"It wasn't fair," Tessie said.

"I guess not, Joe," Bill Hutchinson said regretfully. "My daughter draws with her husband's family, that's only fair. And I've got no other family except the kids."

"Then, as far as drawing for families is concerned, it's you," Mr. Summers said in explanation, "and as far as drawing for households is concerned, that's you, too. Right?"

"Right," Bill Hutchinson said.

"How many kids, Bill?" Mr. Summers asked formally.

"Three," Bill Hutchinson said. "There's Bill, Jr., and Nancy, and little Dave. And Tessie and me."

"All right, then," Mr. Summers said. "Harry, you got their tickets back?"

Mr. Graves nodded and held up the slips of paper. "Put them in the box, then," Mr. Summers directed. "Take Bill's and put it in."

"I think we ought to start over," Mrs. Hutchinson said, as quietly as she could. "I tell you it wasn't fair. You didn't give him time enough to choose. Everybody saw that."

Mr. Graves had selected the five slips and put them in the box, and he dropped all the papers but those onto the ground, where the breeze caught them and lifted them off.

"Listen, everybody," Mrs. Hutchinson was saying to the people around her.

"Ready, Bill?" Mr. Summers asked, and Bill Hutchinson, with one quick glance around at his wife and children, nodded.

"Remember," Mr. Summers said, "take the slips and keep them folded until each person has taken one. Harry, you help little Dave." Mr. Graves took the hand of the little boy, who came willingly with him up to the box. "Take a paper out of the box, Davy," Mr. Summers said. Davy put his hand into the box and laughed. "Take just one paper," Mr. Summers said. "Harry, you hold it for him." Mr. Graves took the child's hand and removed the folded paper from the tight fist and held it while little Dave stood next to him and looked up at him wonderingly.

"Nancy next," Mr. Summers said. Nancy was twelve, and her school friends breathed heavily as she went forward, switching her skirt, and took a slip daintily from the box. "Bill, Jr.," Mr. Summers said, and Billy, his face red and his feet overlarge, nearly knocked the box over as he got a paper out. "Tessie," Mr. Summers said. She hesitated for a minute, looking around defiantly, and then set her lips and went up to the box. She snatched a paper out and held it behind her.

"Bill," Mr. Summers said, and Bill Hutchinson reached into the box and felt around, bringing his hand out at last with the slip of paper in it.

The crowd was quiet. A girl whispered, "I hope it's not Nancy," and the sound of the whisper reached the edges of the crowd.

"It's not the way it used to be," Old Man Warner said clearly. "People ain't the way they used to be."

"All right," Mr. Summers said. "Open the papers. Harry, you open little Dave's."

Mr. Graves opened the slip of paper and there was a general sigh through the crowd as he held it up and everyone could see that it was blank. Nancy and Bill, Jr., opened theirs at the same time, and both beamed and laughed, turning around to the crowd and holding their slips of paper above their heads.

"Tessie," Mr. Summers said. There was a pause, and then Mr. Summers looked at Bill Hutchinson, and Bill unfolded his paper and showed it. It was blank.

"It's Tessie," Mr. Summers said, and his voice was hushed. "Show us her paper, Bill."

Bill Hutchinson went over to his wife and forced the slip of paper out of her hand. It had a black spot on it, the black spot Mr. Summers had made the night before with the heavy pencil in the coal-company office. Bill Hutchinson held it up, and there was a stir in the crowd.

"All right, folks," Mr. Summers said. "Let's finish quickly."

Although the villagers had forgotten the ritual and lost the original black box, they still remembered to use stones. The pile of stones the boys had made earlier was ready; there were stones on the ground with the blowing scraps of paper that had come out of the box. Mrs. Delacroix selected a stone so large she had to pick it up with both hands and turned to Mrs. Dunbar. "Come on," she said. "Hurry up."

Mrs. Dunbar had small stones in both hands, and she said, gasping for breath. "I can't run at all. You'll have to go ahead and I'll catch up with you."

The children had stones already, and someone gave little Davy Hutchinson a few pebbles.

Tessie Hutchinson was in the center of a cleared space by now, and she held her hands out desperately as the villagers moved in on her. "It isn't fair," she said. A stone hit her on the side of the head.

Old Man Warner was saying, "Come on, come on, everyone." Steve Adams was in the front of the crowd of villagers, with Mrs. Graves beside him.

"It isn't fair, it isn't right," Mrs. Hutchinson screamed, and then they were upon her.

THE LADDER

BY V. S. PRITCHETT (1949)

"We had the builders in at the time," my father says in his accurate way, if he ever mentions his second marriage, the one that so quickly went wrong. "And," he says, clearing a small apology from his throat, as though preparing to say something immodest, "we happened to be without stairs."

It is true. I remember that summer. I was fifteen years old. I came home from Miss Compton's School at the end of the term, and when I got to our place in Devonshire not only had my mother gone but the stairs had gone, too. There was no staircase in the house.

We lived in an old crab-colored cottage, with long windows under the eaves that looked like eyes half closed against the sun. Now, when I got out of the car, I saw scaffolding over the front door and two heaps of sand and mortar on the crazy paving, which my father asked me not to tread in, because it would "make work for Janey." (This was the name he called his second wife.) I went inside. Imagine my astonishment. The little hall had vanished, the ceiling had gone; you could see up to the roof; the wall on one side had been stripped to the brick, and on the other hung a long curtain of builder's sheets. "Where are the stairs?" I said. "What have you done with the stairs?" I was at the laughing age.

A mild, trim voice spoke above our heads. "Ah, I know that laugh," the voice said sweetly and archly. There was Miss Richards, or, I should say, my father's second wife, standing behind a builder's rope on what used to be the landing, which now stuck out precariously without banisters, like the portion of a ship's deck. The floor appeared to have been sawed off. She used to be my father's secretary before the divorce, and I had often seen her in my father's office, but now she had changed. Her fair hair was now fluffed out, and she wore a fussed and shiny brown dress that was quite unsuitable for the country. The only definite idea of what marriage would be like must have come to her from magazines; my father was a successful man, and she supposed she would always be going to cocktail parties, and at twelve in the morning on went the dress.

I remember how odd they both looked, she up above and my father down below, and both apologizing to me. The builders had taken the old staircase out two days before, they said, and had promised to put the new one in against the far wall of the room, behind the dust sheets, before I got back from school. But they had not kept their promise.

"We go up by the ladder," said my father, cutting his wife short, for she was apologizing too much, as if she were speaking to one of his customers.

He pointed. At that moment, his wife was stepping to the end of the landing, where a short ladder, with a post to hold on to at the top as one stepped on the first rung, sloped to the ground.

"It's horrible!" called my stepmother.

My father and I watched her come down. She came to the post and turned round, not sure whether she ought to come down the ladder frontward or backward.

"Backward!" called my father . . . "No, the other hand on the post!" My stepmother blushed fondly and gave him a look of fear. She put one foot on the top rung and then took her foot back and put the other one there, and then pouted. It was only eight feet from the ground; at school, we climbed halfway up the gym walls on the bars. I remembered her as a quick and practical woman at the office; she was now, I was sure, playing at being weak and dependent.

"My hands," she said a moment later, looking at the dust on her hands as she grasped the top rung.

My father and I stopped where we were and watched her. She put one leg out too high, as if, artlessly, she were showing us the leg first. And she was; she was a plain woman, and her legs (she used to say) were her "nicest thing." This was the only coquetry she had. She looked like one of those insects that try the air around them with their feelers before they move. I was surprised that my father (who had always been formally attentive to my mother, especially when he was angry, and had almost bowed to me when he met me at the station and helped me in and out of the car) did not go to help her. I saw an expression of obstinacy on his face.

"You're at the bottom," he said at last. "Only two more steps."

"Oh dear," said my stepmother, getting off the last rung onto the floor, and she turned with her small chin raised, offering us her helplessness for admiration. She came to me and kissed me and said, "Doesn't she look lovely? You are growing into a woman."

"Nonsense," said my father.

And, in fear of being a woman and yet pleased by what she said, I took my father's arm. "Is that what we have to do? Is that how we get to bed?" I said.

"It's only until Monday," my father said.

They both of them looked ashamed, as though by having the stairs removed they had done something foolish. My father tried to conceal this by an air of modest importance. They seemed a very modest couple. Both of them looked shorter to me since their marriage; I was rather shocked by this. *She* seemed to have made him shorter. I had always thought of my father as a dark, vain, terse man, very logical and never giving in to anyone. He seemed much less important now his secretary was in the house.

"It is easy," I said, and I went to the ladder and was up it in a moment.

"Mind!" called my stepmother.

But in a moment I was down again, laughing. While I was coming down, I heard my stepmother say quietly to my father, "What legs. She is growing."

My legs and my laugh! I did not think that my father's secretary had the right to say anything about me. She was not my mother.

After this, my father took me around the house. I looked behind me once or twice as I walked. On one of my shoes was some of the sand he had warned me about. I don't know how it got on my shoe. It was rather funny seeing this one sandy footmark making work for Janey wherever I went.

My father took me through the dust curtains into the dining room and then to the far wall, where the staircase was going to be.

"Why have you done it?" I asked. He and I were alone.

"The house has wanted it for years," he said. "It ought to have been done years ago."

I did not say anything. When my mother was there, she was always complaining about the house, saying it was poky, barbarous—I can hear her voice now saying "Barbarous," as if it were the name of some terrifying and savage queen—and my father had always refused to alter anything. Barbarous—I used to think of that word as my mother's name.

"Does Janey like it?" I asked.

My father hardened at this question. He seemed to be saying, "What has it got to do with Janey?" But what he said was—and he spoke with amusement, with a look of quiet scorn—"She liked it as it was."

"I did, too," I said.

I then saw—but, no, I did not really understand this at the time; it is something I understand now I am older—that my father was not altering the house for Janey's sake. She hated the whole place, because my mother had been there, but was too tired by her earlier life in his office, fifteen years of it, too unsure of herself, to say anything. It was an act of amends to my mother. He was punishing Janey by getting in builders and making everyone uncomfortable and miserable; he was creating an emotional scene with himself. He was annoying Janey with what my mother had so maddeningly wanted and he would not give her.

After my father had shown me the house, I said I would go and see Janey getting lunch ready.

"I shouldn't do that," he said. "It will delay her. Lunch is just ready. Or should be." He looked at his watch.

We went to the sitting room, and while we waited, I sat in the green chair and he asked me questions about school and we went on to talk about the holidays. But when I answered, I could see he was not listening to me but trying to catch sounds of Janey moving in the kitchen. Occasionally there were sounds; something gave an explosive fizz in a hot pan, and a saucepan lid fell. This made a loud noise and the lid spun a long time on the stone floor. The sound stopped our talk.

"Janey is not used to the kitchen," said my father. I smiled very close to my lips. I did not want my father to see it, but he looked at me and he smiled by accident, too. There was a sudden understanding between us.

"I will go and see," I said.

He raised his hand to stop me, but I went.

It was natural. For fifteen years, Janey had been my father's secretary. She had worked in an office. I remember when I went there when I was young she used to come into the room with an earnest and hushed air, leaning her head a little sidewise and turning three-quarter face toward my father, at his desk, leaning forward to guess at what he wanted. I admired the great knowledge she had of his affairs, the way she carried letters, how quickly she picked up the telephone when it rang, the authority of her voice. Her strength had been that she was impersonal. She had lost that in her marriage. As his wife, she had no behavior. When we were talking, she raised her low bosom, which had become round and ducklike, with a sigh and smiled at my father with a tentative, expectant fondness. After fifteen years, a life had ended; she was resting.

But Janey had not lost her office behavior; that she now kept for the kitchen. The moment I went to the kitchen, I saw her walking to the stove, where the saucepans were throbbing too hard. She was walking exactly as she had walked toward my father at his desk. The stove had taken my father's place. She went up to it with impersonal inquiry, as if to anticipate what it wanted; she appeared to be offering a pile of plates to be warmed as if they were a pile of letters. She seemed baffled because it could not speak. When one of the saucepans boiled over, she ran to it and lifted it off, suddenly and too high, in her telephone movement; the water spilled at once. On the table beside the stove were basins and pans she was using, and she had them all spread out in an orderly way, like typing; she went from one to the other with the careful look of inquiry she used to give to the things she was filing. It was not a method suitable to a kitchen.

When I came in, she put down the pan she was holding and stopped everything—as she would have done in the office—to talk to me about what she was doing. She was very nice about my hair, which I had had cut; it made me look older and I liked it better. But blue smoke rose behind her as we talked. She did not notice it.

No, it was not the way to cook a meal.

I went back to my father.

"I didn't want to be in the way," I said.

"Extraordinary," he said, looking at his watch. "I must just go and hurry Janey up."

He was astonished that a woman so brisk in an office should be languid and dependent in a house.

"She is just bringing it in," I said. "The potatoes are ready. They are on the table. I saw them."

"On the table?" he said. "Getting cold?"

"On the kitchen table," I said.

"That doesn't prevent them getting cold," he said. My father was a sarcastic man.

I walked about the room humming. My father's exasperation did not last. It gave way to a new thing in his voice—resignation.

"We will wait, if you do not mind," he said to me. "Janey is slow. And by the way," he said, lowering his voice a little, "I shouldn't mention we passed the Leonards in the road when I brought you up from the station."

I was surprised. "Not the Leonards?" I said.

"They were friends of your mother's," he said. "You are old enough to understand. One has to be sometimes a little tactful. Janey sometimes feels . . ."

I looked at my father. He had altered in many ways. Giving me this secret, his small, brown eyes gave a brilliant flash, and I opened my blue eyes very wide and gravely to receive it. He had changed. His rough, black hair was clipped closer at the ears, and he had that too-young look that middle-aged men sometimes have, for by certain lines it can be seen that they are not as young as their faces. Marks like minutes on the face of a clock showed at the corners of his eyes, his nose, his mouth; he was much thinner; his face had hardened. He had often been angry and sarcastic, sulking and abrupt, when my mother was with us, but I had never seen him before, as he was now, blank-faced, ironical, and set in impatient boredom. After he spoke, he had actually been hissing a tune privately through his teeth at the corner of his mouth.

At this moment, Janey came in smiling too much and said lunch was ready.

"Oh," I laughed when we got into the dining room, "it is like—it is like France."

"France?" they said together, smiling at me.

"Like when we all went to France before the war and you took the car," I said. I had chosen France because that seemed as far as I could get from the Leonards.

"What on earth are you talking about?" said my father, looking embarrassed. "You were only five before the war."

"I remember every bit of it. You and Mummie on the boat."

"Yes, yes," said my stepmother with melancholy importance. "I got the tickets for you all."

My father looked as though he were going to hit me. Then he gave a tolerant laugh across the table to my stepmother.

"I remember perfectly well," she said. "I'm afraid I couldn't get the peas to boil. Oh, I've forgotten the potatoes."

She looked as though she were going to cry. I went to get them. When I came back, I could see she had been crying. She was one of those very fair women, and even two or three tears brought a pinkness to her nose. My father had said something to her sharply, for his face was shut and hard and she was leaning over the dishes, a spoon in her hand, to conceal a wound.

After lunch, I took my suitcase and went up the ladder. It was not easy to go up carrying a suitcase, but I enjoyed it. I wished we could always have a ladder in the house. It was like being on a ship. I stood at the top thinking of my mother leaning on the rail of the ship with her new husband, going to America. I was glad she had gone, because sometimes she sent me lovely things and she had promised me that I should go to America, too.

Then I went to my room and I unpacked my case. At the bottom, when I took my pajamas out—they were the last thing—there was the photograph of my mother, face downward, where it had been lying all the term. I forgot to say that I had been in trouble the last week at school. I don't know why. I was longing to be home. I felt I had to *do* something. One afternoon, I went into the rooms in our passage when no one was there, and I put the snap of Kitty's father into Mary's room—I took it out of the frame—and I put Mary's brother into Olga's, and I took Maeve's mother and put her into the silver frame where Jessie's mother was; that photograph was too big and I bent the mount all the way down to get it in. Maeve cried and reported me to Miss Compton. "It was only a joke," I said. "A joke in very poor teeste," Miss Compton said to me in her voice. "How would you like it if anyone took the photograph of *your* mother?" "I haven't got one," I said. Well, it was not a lie. Everyone wanted to know why I had an empty frame on my chest of drawers. I had punished my mother by leaving her photograph in my suitcase.

But now the punishment was over. I took out her picture and put it in the frame on my chest, and every time I bent up from the drawers, I looked at her, then at myself in the mirror. In the middle of this, my stepmother came in to ask if she could help me.

"You are getting very pretty," she said.

I hated her for admiring me. I do not deny it; I hated her. She was a foolish woman. She either behaved as if the house, my father, and myself were too much hers or as if she were an outsider. Most of the time, she sat there like a visitor, waiting for attention.

I thought: There is my mother, thousands of miles away, leaving us to this and treating us like dirt, and we are left with Miss Richards, of all people.

That night, after I had gone to bed, I heard my father and my stepmother having a quarrel. "It is perfectly natural for the child to have a photograph of her mother," I heard my father say.

A door closed. Someone was wandering about on the landing. When whoever it was had gone, I opened my door and crept out, barefoot, to listen. Every step I made seemed to start a loud creak in the boards, and I was so concerned with this that I did not notice I had walked to the edge of the landing. The rope was there, but in the dark I could not see it. I knew I was on the edge of the drop into the hall and that with one more step I would have gone through. I went back to my room feeling sick. And then the thought struck me and I could not get it out of my head all night. I dreamed it, I tried not to dream it; I turned on the light, but I dreamed it again—that Miss Richards fell over the edge of the landing. She hated me for being like my mother. I was very glad when the morning came.

The moment I was downstairs, I laughed at myself. It was only eight feet. Anyone could jump it. I worked out how I could jump from the top and land on my feet. I moved the ladder—it was not heavy to lift—to see what you would feel like if there was no ladder there and the house was on fire and you *had* to jump. To make amends for my wicked dreams in the night, I saw myself rescuing Miss Richards—I should say my stepmother—as flames teased her to the edge.

My father came out of his room and saw me standing there. "What are you pulling such faces for?" he asked, and he imitated my expressions.

"I was thinking," I said, "of Miss Compton at our school."

He had not foreseen the change in Miss Richards—how she would sit in the house in her best clothes, like a visitor, expectant, forgetful, stunned by leisure, watchful, wronged and jealous to the point of tears.

Perhaps if the builders had come, as they had promised, on the Monday, my stepmother's story would have been different.

"I am so sorry we are in such a mess," she said to me that morning at breakfast. She had said it many times, as if she thought I regarded the ladder as her failure.

"It's fun," I said. "It's like being on a ship."

"You keep on saying that," my stepmother said, looking at me in a very worried way, as if trying to work out the hidden meaning of my remark. "You've never been on a ship."

"To France," I said. "When I was a child."

"Oh, yes," said my stepmother.

"I hate mess," said my stepmother to both of us, getting up. In a prosaic person emotion looks grotesque, like clothes suddenly become too large.

"Do leave us alone," my father said.

There was a small scene after this. My father did not mean by "us" himself and me, as she chose to think; he was simply speaking of himself and he had spoken very mildly. My stepmother marched out of the room. Presently, we heard her upstairs. She must have been very upset to have faced going up the ladder.

"Come on," said my father. "I suppose there's nothing for it. I'll get the car out. We will go to the builders'."

He called up to her that we were going and asked if she'd like to go with us.

Oh, it was a terrible holiday. When I grew up and was myself married, my father said, "It was a very difficult summer. You didn't realize. You were only a schoolgirl. It was a mistake." And then he corrected himself. I mean that. My father was always making himself more correct; it was his chief vanity that he understood his own behavior.

"I happened," he said—this was the correction—"to make a very foolish mistake." Whenever he used the phrase "I happened," my father's face seemed to dry up and become distant; he was congratulating himself. Not on the mistake, of course, but on being the first to put his finger on it. "I happen to know," "I happen to have seen"—it was this incidental rightness, the footnote of inside knowledge on innumerable minor issues, and his fatal wrongness, in a large, obstinate, principled way, about anything important, that, I think, made my beautiful and dishonest mother leave him. She was a tall woman, taller than he, with the eyes of a cat, shrugging her shoulders, curving her long, graceful back to be stroked, and with a wide, champagne laugh.

My father had a clipped-back, monkeyish appearance and that faint grin of the bounder one sees in the harder-looking monkeys that are without melancholy or sensibility; this had attracted my mother, but very soon his youthful bounce gave place to a kind of meddling honesty and she found him dull. And, of course, ruthless. The promptness of his second marriage, perhaps, was to teach her a lesson. I imagine him putting his divorce papers away one evening at his office and realizing, when Miss Richards came in to ask if "there is anything more tonight," that here was a woman who was reliable, trained, and, like himself, "happened" to have a lot of inside knowledge.

To get out of the house with my father, to be alone with him! My heart came alive. It seemed to me that this house was not my home any more. If only we could go away, he and I; the country outside seemed to me far more like home than this grotesque divorced house. I stood longing for her not to answer, dreading that she would come down.

My father was not a man to beg her to change her mind. He went out to the garage. My fear of her coming made me stay for a moment. And then (I do not know how the thought came into my head) I went to the ladder and I lifted it away. It was easy to move a short distance, but it began to swing when I tried to lay it down, and I was afraid it would crash. I could not put it on the floor, so I turned it over and over against the other wall, out of reach. Breathlessly, I left the house.

"You've got white on your tunic," said my father as we drove off. "What have you been doing?"

"I rubbed against something," I said.

"Oh, how I love motoring." I laughed beside my father.

"Oh, look at those lovely little rabbits," I said.

"Their little white tails." I laughed.

We passed some hurdles in a field.

"Jumps." I laughed. "I wish I had a pony."

"What would you do?" asked my father.

"Jump," I said to my father.

And then my terrible dreams came back to me. I was frightened. I tried to think of something else, but I could not. I could only see my stepmother on the edge of the landing. I could only hear her giving a scream and going over headfirst. We got into the town and I felt sick. We arrived at the builders' and my father stopped there. Only a girl was in the office, and I heard my father say in his coldest voice, "I happen to have an appointment."

My father came out and we drove off. He was cross.

"Where are we going?" I said when I saw we were not going home.

"To Longwood," he said. "They're working over there."

I thought I would faint. "I—I—" I began.

"What?" my father said.

I could not speak. I began to get red and hot. And then I remembered. I could pray.

It is seven miles to Longwood. My father was a man who enjoyed talking to builders; he planned and replanned with them, built imaginary houses, talked about people. Builders have a large acquaintance with the way people live; my father liked inside knowledge, as I have said. Well, I thought, she is over. She is dead by now. I saw visits to the hospital. I saw my trial.

"She is like you," said the builder, nodding to me. All my life I shall remember his mustache.

"She is like my wife," said my father. "My first wife. I happen to have married twice." He liked puzzling and embarrassing people. "Do you happen to know a tea place near here?" he asked.

"Oh, no," I said. "I don't feel hungry."

But we had tea at Gilling. The river is across the road from the teashop and we stood afterward on the bridge. I surprised my father by climbing the parapet.

"If you jumped," I said to my father, "would you hurt?"

"You'd break your legs," said my father.

Her "nicest thing"!

I shall not describe our drive back to the house, but my father did say, "Janey will be worried. We've been nearly three hours. I'll put the car in afterward."

When we got back, my father jumped out and went down the path. I got out slowly. I could hardly walk down the path. It is a long path leading across a small lawn, then between two lime trees; there are a few steps down into where the roses are, and across another piece of grass you are at the door. I stopped to listen to the bees in the limes, but I could not wait any longer. I went into the house.

There was my stepmother standing on the landing above the hall. Her face was dark red, her eyes were long and violent, her dress was dusty, and her hands were black with dust. She had just finished screaming something at my father, and her mouth had stayed open after her scream. I thought I could *smell* her anger and her fear the moment I came into the house, but it was really the smell of a burned-out saucepan coming from the kitchen.

"You moved the ladder! Six hours I've been up here. The telephone has been ringing, something has burned on the stove. I might have burned to death. Get me down, get me down! I might have killed myself. Get me down!" She came to the gap where the ladder ought to have been.

"Don't be silly, Janey," said my father. "I didn't move the ladder. Don't be such a fool. You're still alive."

"Get me down!" Janey cried out. "You liar, you liar, you liar! You did move it!"

My father lifted the ladder, and as he did so, he said, "The builder must have been."

"No one has been!" screamed my stepmother. "I've been alone! Up here!"

"Daddy *isn't* a liar," I said, taking my father's arm.

"Come down," said my father when he had got the ladder in place. "I'm holding it."

And he went up a step or two toward her.

"No!" shrieked Janey.

"Now, come on. Calm yourself," said my father.

"No, no, I tell you!" said Janey.

"All right, you must stay," said my father, and stepped down.

That brought her, of course.

"*I* moved the ladder," I said when she had come down.

"Oh," said Janey, swinging her arm to hit me, but she fainted instead.

That night, my father came to my room when I was in bed. I had moved my mother's photograph to the bedside table. He was not angry. He was tired out.

"Why did you do it?" he asked.

I did not answer.

"Did you know she was upstairs?" he asked.

I did not reply.

"Stop playing with the sheet," he said. "Look at me. Did you know she was upstairs?"

"Yes," I said.

"You little cat!" he said.

I smiled.

"It was very wrong," he said.

I smiled. Presently he smiled. I laughed.

"It is nothing to laugh at," he said. And suddenly he could not stop himself; he laughed. The door opened and my stepmother looked in while we were both shaking with laughter. My father laughed as if he were laughing for the first time in many years; his bounderish look, sly and bumptious and so delicious, came back to him. The door closed.

He stopped laughing.

"She might have been killed," he said, severe again. And then he remembered what I had asked him on the bridge at Gilling.

I lowered my head.

"You wanted—" he said.

"No, no, no!" I cried, and tears came to my eyes. He put his arm around me.

My mother was a cat, they said, a wicked woman, leaving us like that. I longed for my mother.

Three days later, I went to camp. I apologized to my stepmother and she forgave me. I never saw her again.

THE FIVE-FORTY-EIGHT

BY JOHN CHEEVER (1954)

When Blake stepped out of the elevator, he saw her. A few people, mostly men waiting for girls, stood in the lobby watching the elevator doors. She was among them. As he saw her, her face took on a look of such loathing and purpose that he realized she had been waiting for him. He did not approach her. She had no legitimate business with him. They had nothing to say. He turned and walked toward the glass doors at the end of the lobby, feeling that faint guilt and bewilderment we experience when we bypass some old friend or classmate who seems threadbare, or sick, or miserable in some other way. It was five-eighteen by the clock in the Western Union office. He could catch the express. As he waited his turn at the revolving doors, he saw that it was still raining. It had been raining all day, and he noticed now how much louder the rain made the noises of the street. Outside, he started walking briskly east toward Madison Avenue. Traffic was tied up, and horns were blowing urgently on a crosstown street in the distance. The sidewalk was crowded. He wondered what she had hoped to gain by a glimpse of him coming out of the office building at the end of the day. Then he wondered if she was following him.

Walking in the city, we seldom turn and look back. The habit restrained Blake. He listened for a minute—foolishly—as he walked, as if he could distinguish her footsteps from the worlds of sound in the city at the end of a rainy day. Then he noticed, ahead of him on the other side of the street, a break in the wall of buildings. Something had been torn down; something was being put up, but the steel structure had only just risen above the sidewalk fence and daylight poured through the gap. Blake stopped opposite here and looked into a store window. It was a decorator's or an auctioneer's. The window was arranged like a room in which people live and entertain their friends. There were cups on the coffee table, magazines to read, and flowers in the vases, but the flowers were dead and the cups were empty and the guests had not come. In the plate glass, Blake saw a clear reflection of himself and the crowds that were passing, like shadows, at his back. Then he saw her image—so close to him that it shocked him. She was standing only a foot or two behind him. He could have turned then and asked her what she wanted, but instead of recognizing her, he shied away abruptly from the reflection of her contorted face and went along the street. She might be meaning to do him harm—she might be meaning to kill him.

The suddenness with which he moved when he saw the reflection of her face tipped the water out of his hatbrim in such a way that some of it ran down his neck. It felt unpleasantly like the sweat of fear. Then the cold water falling into his face and onto his bare hands, the rancid smell of the wet gutters and pavings, the knowledge that his feet were beginning to get wet and that he might catch cold—all the common discomforts of walking in the rain—seemed to heighten the menace of his pursuer and to give him a morbid consciousness of his own physicalness and of the ease with which he could be hurt. He could see ahead of him the corner of Madison Avenue, where the lights were brighter. He felt that if he could get to Madison Avenue he would be all right. At the corner, there was a bakery shop with two entrances, and he went in by the door on the crosstown street, bought a coffee ring, like any other commuter, and went out the Madison Avenue door. As he started down Madison Avenue, he saw her waiting for him by a hut where newspapers were sold.

She was not clever. She would be easy to shake. He could get into a taxi by one door and leave by the other. He could speak to a policeman. He could run—although he was afraid that if he did run, it might precipitate the violence he now felt sure she had planned.

He was approaching a part of the city that he knew well and where the maze of street-level and underground passages, elevator banks, and crowded lobbies made it easy for a man to lose a pursuer. The thought of this, and a whiff of sugary warmth from the coffee ring, cheered him. It was absurd to imagine being harmed on a crowded street. She was foolish, misled, lonely perhaps—that was all it could amount to. He was an insignificant man, and there was no point in anyone's following him from his office to the station. He knew no secrets of any consequence. The reports in his briefcase had no bearing on war, peace, the dope traffic, the hydrogen bomb, or any of the other international skulduggeries that he associated with pursuers, men in trench coats, and wet sidewalks. Then he saw ahead of him the door of a men's bar. Oh, it was so simple!

He ordered a Gibson and shouldered his way in between two other men at the bar, so that if she should be watching from the window she would lose sight of him. The place was crowded with commuters putting down a drink before the ride home. They had brought in on their clothes—on their shoes and umbrellas—the rancid smell of the wet dusk outside, but Blake began to relax as soon as he tasted his Gibson and looked around at the common, mostly not-young faces that surrounded him and that were worried, if they were worried at all, about tax rates and who would be put in charge of merchandising. He tried to remember her name—Miss Dent, Miss Bent, Miss Lent—and he was surprised to find that he could not remember it, although he was proud of the retentiveness and reach of his memory and it had only been six months ago.

Personnel had sent her up one afternoon—he was looking for a secretary. He saw a dark woman—in her twenties, perhaps—who was slender and shy. Her dress was simple, her figure was not much, one of her stockings was crooked, but her voice was soft and he had been willing to try her out. After she had been working for him a few days, she told him that she had been in the hospital for eight months and that it had been hard after this for her to find work, and she wanted to thank him for giving her a chance. Her hair was dark, her eyes were dark; she left with him a pleasant impression of darkness. As he got to know her better, he felt that she was oversensitive and, as a consequence, lonely. Once, when she was speaking to him of what she imagined his life to be—full of friendships, money, and a large and loving family—he had thought he recognized a peculiar feeling of deprivation. She seemed to imagine the lives of the rest of the world to be more brilliant than they were. Once, she had put a rose on his desk, and he had dropped it into the wastebasket. "I don't like roses," he told her.

She had been competent, punctual, and a good typist, and he had found only one thing in her that he could object to—her handwriting. He could not associate the crudeness of her handwriting with her appearance. He would have expected her to write a rounded backhand, and in her writing there were intermittent traces of this, mixed with clumsy printing. Her writing gave him the feeling that she had been the victim of some inner—some emotional—conflict that had in its violence broken the continuity of the lines she was able to make on paper. When she had been working for him three weeks—no longer—they stayed late one night and he offered, after work, to buy her a drink. "If you really want a drink," she said, "I have some whiskey at my place."

She lived in a room that seemed to him like a closet. There were suit boxes and hatboxes piled in a corner, and although the room seemed hardly big enough to hold the bed, the dresser, and the chair he sat in, there was an upright piano against one wall, with a book of Beethoven sonatas on the rack. She gave him a drink and said that she was going to put on something more comfortable. He urged her to; that was, after all, what he had come for. If he had had any qualms, they would have been practical. Her diffidence, the feeling of deprivation in her point of view, promised to protect him from any consequences. Most of the many women he had known had been picked for their lack of self-esteem.

When he put on his clothes again, an hour or so later, she was weeping. He felt too contented and warm and sleepy to worry much about her tears. As he was dressing, he noticed on the dresser a note she had written to a cleaning woman. The only light came from the bathroom—the door was ajar—and in this half light the hideously scrawled letters again seemed entirely wrong for her, and as if they must be the handwriting of some other and very gross woman. The next day, he did what he felt was the only sensible thing. When she was out for lunch, he called personnel and asked them to fire her. Then he took the afternoon off. A few days later, she came to the office, asking to see him. He told the switchboard girl not to let her in. He had not seen her again until this evening.

Blake drank a second Gibson and saw by the clock that he had missed the express. He would get the local—the five-forty-eight. When he left the bar the sky was still light; it was still raining. He looked carefully up and down the street and saw that the poor woman had gone. Once or twice, he looked over his shoulder, walking to the station, but he seemed to be safe. He was still not quite himself, he realized, because he had left his coffee ring at the bar, and he was not a man who forgot things. This lapse of memory pained him.

He bought a paper. The local was only half full when he boarded it, and he got a seat on the river side and took off his raincoat. He was a slender man with brown hair—undistinguished in every way, unless you could have divined in his pallor or his gray eyes his unpleasant tastes. He dressed—like the rest of us—as if he admitted the existence of sumptuary laws. His raincoat was the pale, buff color of a mushroom. His hat was dark brown; so was his suit. Except for the few bright threads in his necktie, there was a scrupulous lack of color in his clothing that seemed protective.

He looked around the car for neighbors. Mrs. Compton was several seats in front of him, to the right. She smiled, but her smile was fleeting. It died swiftly and horribly. Mr. Watkins was directly in front of Blake. Mr. Watkins needed a haircut, and he had broken the sumptuary laws; he was wearing a corduroy jacket. He and Blake had quarrelled, so they did not speak.

The swift death of Mrs. Compton's smile did not affect Blake at all. The Comptons lived in the house next to the Blakes, and Mrs. Compton had never understood the importance of minding her own business. Louise Blake took her troubles to Mrs. Compton, Blake knew, and instead of discouraging her crying jags, Mrs. Compton had come to imagine herself a sort of confessor and had developed a lively curiosity about the Blakes' intimate affairs. She had probably been given an account of their most recent quarrel. Blake had come home one night, overworked and tired, and had found that Louise had done nothing about getting supper. The gin bottle was half emptied, and the first three glasses he took from the bar were smeared with lipstick grease. He had gone into the kitchen, followed by Louise, and he had pointed out to her that the date was the fifth. He had drawn a circle around the date on the kitchen calendar. "One week is the twelfth," he had said. "Two weeks will be the nineteenth." He drew a circle around the nineteenth. "I'm not going to speak to you for two weeks," he had said. "That will be the nineteenth." She had wept, she had protested, but it had been eight or ten years since she had been able to touch him with her entreaties. Louise had got old. Now the lines in her face were ineradicable, and when she clapped her glasses onto her nose to read the evening paper she looked to him like an unpleasant stranger. The physical charms that had been her only attraction were gone. It had been nine years since Blake had built a bookshelf in the doorway that connected their rooms and had fitted into the bookshelf wooden doors that could be locked, since he did not want the children to see his books. But their prolonged estrangement didn't seem remarkable to Blake. He had quarrelled with his wife, but so did every other man born of woman. It was human nature. In any place where you can hear their voices—a hotel courtyard, an air shaft, a street on a summer evening—you will hear harsh words.

The hard feeling between Blake and Mr. Watkins also had to do with Blake's family, but it was not as serious or as troublesome as what lay behind Mrs. Compton's fleeting smile. The Watkinses rented. Mr. Watkins broke the sumptuary laws day after day—he once went to the eight-fourteen in a pair of sandals—and he made his living as a commercial artist. Blake's oldest son—Charlie was fourteen—had made friends with the Watkins boy. He had spent a lot of time in the sloppy rented house where the Watkinses lived. The friendship had affected his manners and his neatness. Then he had begun to take some meals with the Watkinses, and to spend Saturday nights there. When he had moved most of his possessions over to the Watkinses' and had begun to spend more than half his nights there, Blake had been forced to act. He had spoken not to Charlie but to Mr. Watkins, and had, of necessity, said a number of things that must have sounded critical. Mr. Watkins' long and dirty hair and his corduroy jacket reassured Blake that he had been in the right.

But Mrs. Compton's dying smile and Mr. Watkins' dirty hair did not lessen the pleasure Blake took in settling himself in an uncomfortable seat on the five-forty-eight deep underground. The coach was old and smelled oddly like a bomb shelter in which whole families had spent the night. The light that spread from the ceiling down onto their heads and shoulders was dim. The filth on the window glass was streaked with rain from some other journey, and clouds of rank pipe and cigarette smoke had begun to rise from behind each newspaper, but it was a scene that meant to Blake that he was on a safe path, and after his brush with danger he even felt a little warmth toward Mrs. Compton and Mr. Watkins.

The train travelled up from underground into the weak daylight, and the slums and the city reminded Blake vaguely of the woman who had followed him. To avoid speculation or remorse about her, he turned his attention to the evening paper. Out of the corner of his eye he could see the landscape. It was industrial and, at that hour, sad. There were machine sheds and warehouses, and above these he saw a break in the clouds—a piece of yellow light. "Mr. Blake," someone said. He looked up. It was she. She was standing there holding one hand on the back of the seat to steady herself in the swaying coach. He remembered her name then—Miss Dent. "Hello, Miss Dent," he said.

"Do you mind if I sit here?"

"I guess not."

"Thank you. It's very kind of you. I don't like to inconvenience you like this. I don't want to . . ." He had been frightened when he looked up and saw her, but her timid voice rapidly reassured him. He shifted his hams—that futile and reflexive gesture of hospitality—and she sat down. She sighed. He smelled her wet clothing. She wore a formless black hat with a cheap crest stitched onto it. Her coat was thin cloth, he saw, and she wore gloves and carried a large pocketbook.

"Are you living out in this direction now, Miss Dent?"

"No."

She opened her purse and reached for her handkerchief. She had begun to cry. He turned his head to see if anyone in the car was looking, but no one was. He had sat beside a thousand passengers on the evening train. He had noticed their clothes, the holes in their gloves; and if they fell asleep and mumbled he had wondered what their worries were. He had classified almost all of them briefly before he buried his nose in the paper. He had marked them as rich, poor, brilliant or dull, neighbors or strangers, but no one of the thousands had ever wept. When she opened her purse, he remembered her perfume. It had clung to his skin the night he went to her place for a drink.

"I've been very sick," she said. "This is the first time I've been out of bed in two weeks. I've been terribly sick."

"I'm sorry that you've been sick, Miss Dent," he said in a voice loud enough to be heard by Mr. Watkins and Mrs. Compton. "Where are you working now?"

"What?"

"Where are you working now?"

"Oh don't make me laugh," she said softly.

"I don't understand."

"You poisoned their minds."

He straightened his back and braced his shoulders. These wrenching movements expressed a brief—and hopeless—longing to be in some other place. She meant trouble. He took a breath. He looked with deep feeling at the half-filled, half-lighted coach to affirm his sense of actuality, of a world in which there was not very much bad trouble after all. He was conscious of her heavy breathing and the smell of her rain-soaked coat. The train stopped. A nun and a man in overalls got off. When it started again, Blake put on his hat and reached for his raincoat.

"Where are you going?" she said.

"I'm going up to the next car."

"Oh, no," she said. "No, no, no." She put her white face so close to his ear that he could feel her warm breath on his cheek. "Don't do that," she whispered. "Don't try and escape me. I have a pistol and I'll have to kill you and I don't want to. All I want to do is to talk with you. Don't move or I'll kill you. Don't, don't, don't!"

Blake sat back abruptly in his seat. If he had wanted to stand and shout for help, he would not have been able to. His tongue had swelled to twice its size, and when he tried to move it, it stuck horribly to the roof of his mouth. His legs were limp. All he could think of to do then was to wait for his heart to stop its hysterical beating, so that he could judge the extent of his danger. She was sitting a little sidewise, and in her pocketbook was the pistol, aimed at his belly.

"You understand me now, don't you?" she said. "You understand that I'm serious?" He tried to speak but he was still mute. He nodded his head. "Now we'll sit quietly for a little while," she said. "I got so excited that my thoughts are all confused. We'll sit quietly for a little while, until I can get my thoughts in order again."

Help would come, Blake thought. It was only a question of minutes. Someone, noticing the look on his face or her peculiar posture, would stop and interfere, and it would all be over. All he had to do was to wait until someone noticed his predicament. Out of the window he saw the river and the sky. The rain clouds were rolling down like a shutter, and while he watched, a streak of orange light on the horizon became brilliant. Its brilliance spread—he could see it move—across the waves until it raked the banks of the river with a dim firelight. Then it was put out. Help would come in a minute, he thought. Help would come before they stopped again; but the train stopped, there were some comings and goings, and Blake still lived on, at the mercy of the woman beside him. The possibility that help might not come was one that he could not face. The possibility that his predicament was not noticeable, that Mrs. Compton would guess that he was taking a poor relation out to dinner at Shady Hill, was something he would think about later. Then the saliva came back into his mouth and he was able to speak.

"Miss Dent?"

"Yes."

"What do you want?"

"I want to talk with you."

"You can come to my office."

"Oh, no. I went there every day for two weeks."

"You could make an appointment."

"No," she said. "I think we can talk here. I wrote you a letter but I've been too sick to go out and mail it. I've put down all my thoughts. I like to travel. I like trains. One of my troubles has always been that I could never afford to travel. I suppose you see this scenery every night and don't notice it any more, but it's nice for someone who's been in bed a long time. They say that He's not in the river and the hills but I think He is. 'Where shall wisdom be found,' it says. 'Where is the place of understanding? The depth saith it is not in me; the sea saith it is not with me. Destruction and death say we have heard the force with our ears.'

"Oh, I know what you're thinking," she said. "You're thinking that I'm crazy, and I have been very sick again but I'm going to be better. It's going to make me better to talk with you. I was in the hospital all the time before I came to work for you but they never tried to cure me, they only wanted to take away my self-respect. I haven't had any work now for three months. Even if I did have to kill you, they wouldn't be able to do anything to me except put me back in the hospital, so you see I'm not afraid. But let's sit quietly for a little while longer. I have to be calm."

The train continued its halting progress up the bank of the river, and Blake tried to force himself to make some plans for escape, but the immediate threat to his life made this difficult, and instead of planning sensibly, he thought of the many ways in which he could have avoided her in the first place. As soon as he had felt these regrets, he realized their futility. It was like regretting his lack of suspicion when she first mentioned her months in the hospital. It was like regretting his failure to have been warned by her shyness, her diffidence, and the handwriting that looked like the marks of a claw. There was no way now of rectifying his mistakes, and he felt—for perhaps the first time in his mature life—the full force of regret. Out of the window, he saw some men fishing on the nearly dark river, and then a ramshackle boat club that seemed to have been nailed together out of scraps of wood that had been washed up on the shore.

Mr. Watkins had fallen asleep. He was snoring. Mrs. Compton read her paper. The train creaked, slowed, and halted infirmly at another station. Blake could see the southbound platform, where a few passengers were waiting to go into the city. There was a workman with a lunch pail, a dressed-up woman, and a man with a suitcase. They stood apart from one another. Some advertisements were posted on the wall behind them. There was a picture of a couple drinking a toast in wine, a picture of a Cat's Paw rubber heel, and a picture of a Hawaiian dancer. Their cheerful intent seemed to go no farther than the puddles of water on the platform and to expire there. The platform and the people on it looked lonely. The train drew away from the station into the scattered lights of a slum and then into the darkness of the country and the river.

"I want you to read my letter before we get to Shady Hill," she said. "It's on the seat. Pick it up. I would have mailed it to you, but I've been too sick to go out. I haven't gone out for two weeks. I haven't had any work for three months. I haven't spoken to anybody but the landlady. Please read my letter."

He picked up the letter from the seat where she had put it. The cheap paper felt abhorrent and filthy to his fingers. It was folded and refolded. "Dear Husband," she had written, in that crazy, wandering hand, "they say that human love leads us to divine love, but is this true? I dream about you every night. I have such terrible desires. I have always had a gift for dreams. I dreamed on Tuesday of a volcano erupting with blood. When I was in the hospital they said they wanted to cure me but they only wanted to take away my self-respect. They only wanted me to dream about sewing and basketwork but I protected my gift for dreams. I'm clairvoyant. I can tell when the telephone is going to ring. I've never had a true friend in my whole life. . . ."

The train stopped again. There was another platform, another picture of the couple drinking a toast, the rubber heel, and the Hawaiian dancer. Suddenly she pressed her face close to Blake's again and whispered in his ear. "I know what you're thinking. I can see it in your face. You're thinking you can get away from me in Shady Hill, aren't you? Oh, I've been planning this for weeks. It's all I've had to think about. I won't harm you if you'll let me talk. I've been thinking about devils. I mean if there are devils in the world, if there are people in the world who represent evil, is it our duty to exterminate them? I know that you always prey on weak people. I can tell. Oh, sometimes I think that I ought to kill you. Sometimes I think you're the only obstacle between me and my happiness. Sometimes . . ."

She touched Blake with the pistol. He felt the muzzle against his belly. The bullet, at that distance, would make a small hole where it entered, but it would rip out of his back a place as big as a soccer ball. He remembered the unburied dead he had seen in the war. The memory came in a rush: entrails, yes, shattered bone, ordure, and other filth.

"All I've ever wanted in life is a little love," she said. She lightened the pressure of the gun. Mr. Watkins still slept. Mrs. Compton was sitting calmly with her hands folded in her lap. The coach rocked gently, and the coats and mushroom-colored raincoats that hung between the windows swayed a little as the car moved. Blake's elbow was on the window sill and his left shoe was on the guard above the steampipe. The car smelled like some dismal classroom. The passengers seemed asleep and apart, and Blake felt that he might never escape the smell of heat and wet clothing and the dimness of the light. He tried to summon the calculated self-deceptions with which he sometimes cheered himself, but he was left without any energy for hope or self-deception.

The conductor put his head in the door and said "Shady Hill, next, Shady Hill."

"Now," she said. "Now you get out ahead of me."

Mr. Watkins waked suddenly, put on his coat and hat, and smiled at Mrs. Compton, who was gathering her parcels to her in a series of maternal gestures. They went to the door. Blake joined them, but neither of them spoke to him or seemed to notice the woman at his back. The conductor threw open the door, and Blake saw on the platform of the next car a few other neighbors who had missed the express, waiting patiently and tiredly in the wan light for their trip to end. He raised his head to see through the open door the abandoned mansion outside of town, a no-trespassing sign nailed to a tree, and then the oil tanks. The concrete abutments of the bridge passed, so close to the open door that he could have touched them. Then he saw the first of the lampposts on the northbound platform, the sign "SHADY HILL" in black and gold, and the little lawn and flower bed kept up by the Improvement Association, and then the cab stand and a corner of the old-fashioned depot. It was raining again; it was pouring. He could hear the splash of water and see the lights reflected in puddles and in the shining pavement, and the idle sound of splashing and dripping formed in his mind a conception of shelter, so light and strange that it seemed to belong to a time of his life that he could not remember.

He went down the steps with her at his back. A dozen or so cars were waiting by the station with their motors running. A few people got off from each of the other coaches; he recognized most of them, but none of them offered to give him a ride. They walked separately or in pairs—purposefully out of the rain to the shelter of the platform, where the car horns called to them. It was time to go home, time for a drink, time for love, time for supper, and he could see the lights on the hill—lights by which children were being bathed, meat cooked, dishes washed—shining in the rain. One by one, the cars picked up the heads of families, until there were only four left. Two of the stranded passengers drove off in the only taxi the village had. "I'm sorry, darling," a woman said tenderly to her husband when she drove up a few minutes later. "All our clocks are slow." The last man looked at his watch, looked at the rain, and then walked off into it, and Blake saw him go as if they had some reason to say goodbye—not as we say goodbye to friends after a party but as we say goodbye when we are faced with an inexorable and unwanted parting of the spirit and the heart. The man's footsteps sounded as he crossed the parking lot to the sidewalk, and then they were lost. In the station, a telephone began to ring. The ringing was loud, plaintive, evenly spaced, and unanswered. Someone wanted to know about the next train to Albany, but Mr. Flannagan, the stationmaster, had gone home an hour ago. He had turned on all his lights before he went away. They burned in the empty waiting room. They burned, tin-shaded, at intervals up and down the platform. and with the peculiar sadness of dim and purposeless light. They lighted the Hawaiian dancer, the couple drinking a toast, the rubber heel.

"I've never been here before," she said. "I thought it would look different. I didn't think it would look so shabby. Let's get out of the light. Go over there."

His legs felt sore. All his strength was gone. "Go on," she said.

North of the station there was a freight house and a coalyard and an inlet where the butcher and the baker and the man who ran the service station moored the dinghies from which they fished on Sundays, sunk now to the gunwales with the rain. As he walked toward the freight house, he saw a movement on the ground and heard a scraping sound, and then he saw a rat take its head out of a paper bag and regard him. The rat seized the bag in its teeth and dragged it into a culvert.

"Stop," she said. "Turn around. Oh, I ought to feel sorry for you. Look at your poor face. But you don't know what I've been through.

I'm afraid to go out in the daylight. I'm afraid the blue sky will fall down on me. I'm like poor Chicken-Licken. I only feel like myself when it begins to get dark. But still and all I'm better than you. I still have good dreams sometimes. I dream about picnics and Heaven and the brotherhood of man, and about castles in the moonlight and a river with willow trees all along the edge of it and foreign cities, and after all I know more about love than you."

He heard from off the dark river the drone of an outboard motor, a sound that drew slowly behind it across the dark water such a burden of clear, sweet memories of gone summers and gone pleasures that it made his flesh crawl, and he thought of dark in the mountains and the children singing. "They never wanted to cure me," she said. "They . . ." The noise of a train coming down from the north drowned out her voice, but she went on talking. The noise filled his ears, and the windows where people ate, drank, slept, and read flew past. When the train had passed beyond the bridge, the noise grew distant, and he heard her screaming at him, "*Kneel down!* Kneel down! Do what I say. *Kneel down!*"

He got to his knees. He bent his head. "There," she said. "You see, if you do what I say, I won't harm you, because I really don't want to harm you, I want to help you, but when I see your face it sometimes seems to me that I can't help you. Sometimes it seems to me that if I were good and loving and sane—oh, much better than I am—sometimes it seems to me that if I were all these things and young and beautiful, too, and if I called to show you the right way, you wouldn't heed me. Oh, I'm better than you, I'm better than you, and I shouldn't waste my time or spoil my life like this. Put your face in the dirt. *Put your face in the dirt!* Do what I say. Put your face in the dirt."

He fell forward in the filth. The coal skinned his face. He stretched out on the ground, weeping. "Now I feel better," she said. "Now I can wash my hands of you, I can wash my hands of all this, because you see there is some kindness, some saneness in me that I can find again and use. I can wash my hands." Then he heard her footsteps go away from him, over the rubble. He heard the clearer and more distant sound they made on the hard surface of the platform. He heard them diminish. He raised his head. He saw her climb the stairs of the wooden footbridge and cross it and go down to the other platform, where her figure in the dim light looked small, common, and harmless. He raised himself out of the dust—warily at first, until he saw by her attitude, her looks, that she had forgotten him; that she had completed what she had wanted to do, and that he was safe. He got to his feet and picked up his hat from the ground where it had fallen and walked home.

THE STATE OF GRACE

BY HAROLD BRODKEY (1954)

There is a certain shade of red brick—a dark, almost melodious red, sombre and riddled with blue—that is my childhood in St. Louis. Not the real childhood, but the false one that extends from the dawning of consciousness until the day that one leaves home for college and manhood. That one shade of red brick and green foliage is St. Louis in the summer (the winter is just a gray sky and a crowded school bus and the wet footprints on the brown linoleum floor at school), and that brick and a pale sky is spring. It's also heartbreak and loneliness and the queer, self-pitying wonder that children whose families are having catastrophes feel.

I can remember that brick best on the back of our apartment house; it was on all the apartment houses on that block, and also on the apartment house where Edward lived. Edward was a small boy I took care of on the evenings when his parents went out. As I came up the street from school, past the boulevard and its ugliness (the vista of shoe-repair shops, dime stores, hairdressers', pet shops, the Tivoli Theatre, and the closed Piggly Wiggly, about to be converted into a Kroger's), past the place where I could see the Masonic Temple, built in the shape of some Egyptian relic, and the two huge concrete pedestals flanking the boulevard (what they supported I can't remember, but on both of them, in brown paint, was a large heart and the information that someone named Erica loved someone named Peter), past the post office, built in W.P.A. days of yellow brick and chrome, I hurried toward the moment when at last, on the other side, past the driveway of the garage of the Castlereagh Apartments, I would be at the place where the trees began, the apartment houses of dark-red brick, and the empty stillness.

In the middle of that stillness and red brick was my neighborhood, the terribly familiar place where I was more comfortably an exile than anywhere else. There were two locust trees that were beautiful to me—I think because they were small and I could encompass them (not only with my mind and heart but with my hands as well). Then came an apartment house of red brick (but not quite the true shade) where a boy I knew lived, and two amazingly handsome brothers, who were also strong and kind, but much older than I and totally uninterested in me. Then came an alley of black macadam and another vista, which I found shameful but drearily comfortable, of garages and ash pits and telephone poles and the backs of apartment houses—including ours—on one side, the backs of houses on the other. I knew many people in the apartments but none in the houses, and this was the ultimate proof, of course, to me of how miserably degraded I was and how far sunken beneath the surface of the sea. I was on the bottom, looking up through the waters, through the shifting bands of light—through, oh, innumerably more complexities than I could stand—at a sailboat driven by the wind, some boy who had a family and a home like other people.

I was thirteen, and six feet tall, and I weighed a hundred and twenty-five pounds. Though I fretted wildly about my looks (my ears stuck out and my hair was like wire), I also knew I was attractive; girls had smiled at me, but none whom I might love and certainly none of the seven or eight goddesses in the junior high school I attended. Starting in about second grade, I always had the highest grades—higher than anybody who had ever attended the schools I went to—and I terrified my classmates. What terrified them was that so far as they could see, it never took any effort; it was like legerdemain. I was never teased, I was never tormented; I was merely isolated. But I was known as "the walking encyclopedia," and the only way I could deal with this was to withdraw. Looking back, I'm almost certain I could have had friends if I'd made the right overtures, and that it was not my situation but my forbidding pride that kept them off; I'm not sure. I had very few clothes, and all that I had

had been passed to me from an elder cousin. I never was able to wear what the other boys wore.

Our apartment was on the third floor. I usually walked up the back stairs, which were mounted outside the building in a steel framework. I preferred the back stairs—it was a form of rubbing at a hurt to make sure it was still there—because they were steep and ugly and had garbage cans on the landings and wash hanging out, while the front door opened off a court where rosebushes grew, and the front stairs were made of some faintly yellow local marble that was cool and pleasant to the touch and to the eye. When I came to our back door, I would open the screen and call out to see if my mother was home. If she was not home, it usually meant that she was visiting my father, who had been dying in the hospital for four years and would linger two more before he would come to terms with death. As far as I know, that was the only sign of character he ever showed in his entire life, and I suppose it was considerable, but I hoped, and even sometimes prayed, that he would die—not only because I wouldn't have to visit the hospital again, where the white-walled rooms were filled with odors and sick old men (and a tangible fear that made me feel a falling away inside, like the plunge into the unconscious when the anesthetic is given), but because my mother might marry again and make us all rich and happy once more. She was still lovely then, still alight with the curious incandescence of physical beauty. There was a man who had loved her for twenty years and who loved her yet and wanted to marry her. I wished so hard my father would die, but he just wouldn't. If my mother was home, I braced myself for unpleasantness, because she didn't like me to sit and read; she hated me to read. She wanted to drive me outdoors, where I would become an athlete and be like other boys and be popular. It filled her with rage when I ignored her advice and opened a book; once, she rushed up to me, her face suffused with anger, took the book (I think it was "Pride and Prejudice"), and hurled it out the third-story window. At the time, I sat and tried to sneer, thinking she was half mad, with her exaggerated rage, and so foolish not to realize that I could be none of the things she thought I ought to be. But now I think—perhaps wistfully—that she was merely desperate, driven to extremes in her anxiety to save me. She felt—she knew, in fact—that there was going to come a moment when, like an acrobat, I was going to have to climb on her shoulders and on the shoulders of all the things she had done for me, and leap out into a life she couldn't imagine (and which I am leading now), and if she wanted to send me out wrapped in platitudes, in an athletic body, with a respect for money, it was because she thought that was the warmest covering.

But when I was thirteen, I only wondered how anyone so lovely could be so impossible. She somehow managed it so that I hated her far more than I loved her, even though in the moments before sleep I would think of her face, letting my memory begin with the curving gentleness of her eyelid and circle through all the subtle interplay of shadows and hollows and bones, and the half-remembered warmth of her chest, and it would seem to me that this vision of her, always standing in half light (as probably I had seen her once when I was younger, and sick, perhaps, though I don't really remember), was only as beautiful to me as the pattern in an immeasurably ancient and faded Persian rug. In the vision, as in the rug, I could trace the lines in and out and experience some unnamed pleasure, but it had almost no meaning, numbed as I was by the problems of my sonhood.

Being Jewish also disturbed me, because it meant I could never be one of the golden people—the blond athletes, with their easy charm. If my family had been well off, I might have felt otherwise, but I doubt it.

My mother had a cousin whom I called Aunt Rachel, and we used to go and see her three or four times a year. I hated it. She lived in what was called the Ghetto, which was a section of old houses in downtown St. Louis with tiny front porches and two doors, one to the upstairs and one to the downstairs. Most people lived in them only until they could move to something better; no one had ever liked living there. And because of that, the neighborhood had the quality of being blurred; the grass was never neat, the window frames were never painted, no one cared about or loved the place. It was where the immigrants lived when they arrived by train from New York and before they could move uptown to the apartments near Delmar Boulevard, and eventually to the suburbs—to Clayton, Laclede, and Ladue. Aunt Rachel lived downstairs. Her living room was very small and had dark-yellow wallpaper, which she never changed. She never cleaned it, either, because once I made a mark on it, to see if she would, and she didn't. The furniture was alive and frightening. It was like that part of the nightmare where it gets so bad that you decide to wake up. I always had to sit on it. It bulged in great curves of horsehair and mohair, and it was dark purple and maroon and dark green, and the room had no light in it anywhere. Somewhere on the other side of the old, threadbare satin draperies that had been bought out of an old house was fresh air and sunshine, but you'd never know it. It was as much like a peasant's hut as Aunt Rachel could manage, buying furniture in cut-rate furniture stores. And always there were the smells—the smell of onion soup and garlic and beets. It was the only place where I was ever rude to my mother in public. It was always full of people whom I hardly ever knew, but who knew me, and I had to perform. My mother would say, "Tell the people what your last report card was," or "Recite them the poem that Miss Huntington liked so well." That was when the feeling of unreality was strongest. Looking back now, I think that what frightened me was their fierce urgency; I was to be rich and famous and make all their tribulations worth while. But I didn't want that responsibility. Anyway, if I were going to be what they wanted me to be, and if I had to be what I was, then it was too much to expect me to take them as they were. I had to go beyond them and despise them, but first I had to be with them—and it wasn't fair.

It was as if my eyelids had been propped open, and I had to see these things I didn't want to see. I felt as if I had taken part in something shameful, and therefore I wasn't a nice person. It was like my first sexual experiences: What if anyone knew? What if everyone found out? . . . How in hell could I ever be gallant and carefree, like the blond athletes?

I had read too many books by Englishmen and New Englanders to want to know anything but graceful things and erudite things and the look of white frame houses on green lawns. I could always console myself by thinking my brains would make me famous (brains were good for something, weren't they?), but then my children would have good childhoods—not me. I was irrevocably deprived, and it was the irrevocableness that hurt, that finally drove me away from any sensible adjustment with life to the position that dreams had to come true or there was no point in living at all. If dreams came true, then I would have my childhood in one form or another, someday.

If my mother was home when I came in from school, she might say that Mrs. Leinberg had called and wanted me to baby-sit, and I would be plunged into yet another of the dilemmas of those years. I had to baby-sit to earn money to buy my lunch at school, and there were times, considering the dilemma I faced at the Leinbergs', when I preferred not eating, or eating very little, to baby-sitting. But there wasn't any choice; Mother would have accepted for me, and made Mrs. Leinberg promise not to stay out too late and deprive me of my sleep. She would have a sandwich ready for me to eat, so that I could rush over in time to let Mr. and Mrs. Leinberg go out to dinner. Anyway, I would eat my sandwich reading a book, to get my own back, and then I would set out. As I walked down the back stairs on my way to the Leinbergs', usually swinging on the railings by my arms to build up my muscles, I would think forlornly of what it was to be me, and wish things were otherwise, and I did not understand myself or my loneliness or the cruel deprivation the vista down the alley meant.

There was a short cut across the back yards to the apartment house where the Leinbergs lived, but I always walked by my two locust trees and spent a few moments loving them; so far as I knew, I loved nothing else.

Then I turned right and crossed the street and walked past an apartment house that had been built at right angles to the street, facing a strange declivity that had once been an excavation for still another apartment house, which had never been built, because of the depression. On the other side of the declivity was a block of three apartment houses, and the third was the Leinbergs'. Every apartment in it had at least eight rooms, and the back staircase was enclosed, and the building had its own garages. All this made it special and expensive, and a landmark in the neighborhood.

Mr. Leinberg was a cosmetics manufacturer and very successful. I thought he was a smart man, but I don't remember him at all well (I never looked at men closely in those days but always averted my head in shyness and embarrassment; they might guess how fiercely I wanted to belong to them) and I could have been wrong. Certainly the atmosphere then, during the war years—it was 1943—was that everyone was getting rich; everyone who could work, that is. At any rate, he was getting rich, and it was only a matter of time before the Leinbergs moved from that apartment house to Laclede or Ladue and had a forty-thousand-dollar house with grounds.

Mrs. Leinberg was very pretty; she was dark, like my mother, but not as beautiful. For one thing, she was too small; she was barely five feet tall, and I towered over her. For another, she was not at all regal. But her lipstick was never on her teeth, and her dresses were usually new, and her eyes were kind. (My mother's eyes were incomprehensible; they were dark stages where dimly seen mob scenes were staged and all one ever sensed was tumult and drama, and no matter how long one waited, the lights never went up and the scene never was explained.) Mrs. Leinberg would invite me to help myself in the icebox, and then she would write down the telephone number of the place where she was going to be. "Keep Edward in the back of the apartment, where he won't disturb the baby," she would tell me. "If the baby does wake up, pick her up right away. That's very important. I didn't pick Edward up, and I'll always regret it." She said that every time, even though Edward was lurking in the back hallway, waiting for his parents to leave so he could run out and jump on me and our world could come alive again. He would listen, his small face—he was seven—quite blank with hurt and the effort to pierce the hurt with understanding.

Mrs. Leinberg would say, "Call me if she wakes up." And then, placatingly, to her husband, "I'll just come home to put her back to sleep, and then I'll go right back to the party—" Then, to me, "But she almost always sleeps, so don't worry about it."

"Come on, Greta. He knows what to do," Mr. Leinberg would say impatiently.

I always imagined contempt in his voice—contempt for us both. I would be standing by the icebox looking down on the two little married people. Mr. Leinberg had a very red mouth. "Come on, Greta," it would say. "We'll be back by eleven," it would say to me.

"Edward goes to bed at nine," Mrs. Leinberg would say, her voice high and birdlike, but tremulous with confusion and vagueness. Then she would be swept out the front door, so much prettily dressed matchwood, in her husband's wake. When the door closed,

Edward would come hurtling down the hall and tackle my knees if I was staring after his parents, or, if I was facing him, leap onto my chest and into my arms.

"What shall we play tonight?"

He would ask that and I would have to think. He trembled with excitement, because I could always make the games wonderful to him—like his daydreams, in fact. Because he was a child, he trusted me almost totally, and I could do anything with him. I had that power with children until I was in college and began at last to be like other people.

In Edward's bedroom was a large closet; it had a rack for clothes, a washstand, a built-in table, and fifteen or twenty shelves. The table and shelves were crowded with toys and games and sports equipment. I owned a Monopoly board I had inherited from my older sister, an old baseball glove (which was so cheap I never dared use it in front of my classmates, who had real gloves signed by real players), and a collection of postcards. The first time I saw that closet, I practically exploded with pleasure; I took down each of the games and toys and played with them, one after another, with Edward. Edward loved the fact that we never played a game to its conclusion but would leap from game to game after only a few moves, until the leaping became the real game and the atmosphere of laughter the real sport.

It was comfortable for me in the back room, alone in the apartment with Edward, because at last I was chief; and not only that, I was not being seen. There was no one there thinking of me or what I should be or how I should behave; and I have always been terrified of what people thought of me, as if what they thought was a hulking creature that would confront me if I should turn a corner.

There were no corners. Edward and I would take his toy pistols and stalk each other around the bed. Other times, we were on the bed, the front gun turret of a battleship sailing to battle the Japanese fleet in the Indian Ocean. Edward would close his eyes and roll with pleasure when I went "Boom! Boom! BOOOOM!"

"It's sinking! It's sinking, isn't it?"

"No, stupid. We only hit its funnel. We have to shoot again. Boom, Boom—"

Edward's fingers would press his eyelids in a spasm of ecstasy;

his delirious, taut, little boy's body would fall backward on the soft pillows and bounce, and his back would curve; the excited breathy laughter would pour out like so many leaves spilling into spring, so many lilacs thrusting into bloom.

Under the bed, in a foxhole (Edward had a Cub Scout hat and I had his plastic soldier helmet), we turned back the yellow hordes from Guadalcanal. Edward dearly loved to be wounded. "I'm hit!" he'd shriek. "I'm hit!" He'd press his hand against his stomach and writhe on the wooden floor. "They shot me in the guts—"

I didn't approve of his getting wounded so soon, because then the scene was over; both his and my sense of verisimilitude didn't allow someone to be wounded and then get up. I remember how pleased he was when I invented the idea that after he got wounded, he could be someone else; so, when we crawled under the bed, we would decide to be eight or twelve or twenty Marines, ten each to get wounded, killed, or maimed as we saw fit, provided enough survived so that when we crawled out from under the bed we could charge the Japanese position under the dining-room table and leave it strewn with corpses.

Edward was particularly good at the detective game, which was a lot more involved and difficult. In that, we would walk into the kitchen, and I would tell him that we had received a call about a murder. Except when we played Tarzan, we never found it necessary to be characters. However, we always had names. In the detective game, we were usually Sam and Fred. We'd get a call telling us who was murdered, and then we'd go back to the bedroom and examine the corpse and question the suspects. I'd fire questions at an empty chair. Sometimes Edward would get tired of being my sidekick and he'd slip into the chair and be the quaking suspect. Other times, he would prowl around the room on his hands and knees with a magnifying glass while I stormed and shouted at the perpetually shifty suspect: "Where were you, Mrs. Eggnogghead [giggles from Edward], at ten o'clock, when Mr. Eggnogghead [laughter, helpless with pleasure, from Edward] was slain with the cake knife?"

"Hey, Fred! *I found bloodstains.*" Edward's voice would quiver with a creditable imitation of the excitement of radio detectives.

"Bloodstains! Where, Sam? Where? This may be the clue that breaks the case."

Edward could sustain the *commedia dell'arte* for hours if I wanted him to. He was a precocious and delicate little boy, quivering with the malaise of being unloved. When we played, his child's heart would come into its own, and the troubled world where his vague hungers went unfed and mothers and fathers were dim and far away—too far away ever to reach in and touch the sore place and make it heal—would disappear, along with the world where I was not sufficiently muscled or sufficiently gallant to earn my own regard. (What ever had induced my mother to marry that silly man, who'd been unable to hang on to his money? I could remember when we'd had a larger house and I'd had toys; why had she let it get away?) It angered me that Edward's mother had so little love for him and so much for her daughter, and that Edward's father should not appreciate the boy's intelligence—he thought Edward was a queer duck, and effeminate. I could have taught Edward the manly postures. But his father didn't think highly of me: I was only a baby-sitter, and effeminate, too. Why, then, should Edward be more highly regarded by his father than I myself was? I wouldn't love him or explain to him.

That, of course, was my terrible dilemma. His apartment house, though larger than mine, was made of the same dark-red brick, and I wouldn't love him. He wasn't as smart as I'd been at his age, or as fierce. At his age, I'd already seen the evil in people's eyes, and I'd begun the construction of my defenses even then. But Edward's family was more prosperous, and the cold winds of insecurity (*Where will the money come from?*) hadn't shredded the dreamy chrysalis of his childhood. He was still immersed in the dim, wet wonder of the folded wings that might open if someone loved him; he still hoped, probably, in a butterfly's unthinking way, for spring and warmth. How the wings ache, folded so, waiting; that is, they ache until they atrophy.

So I was thirteen and Edward was seven and he wanted me to love him, but he was not old enough or strong enough to help me. He could not make his parents share their wealth and comfort with me, or force them to give me a place in their home. He was like most of the people I knew—eager and needful of my love; for I was quite remarkable and made incredible games, which were better than movies or than the heart could hope for. I was a dream come true. I was smart and virtuous (no one knew that I occasionally stole from the dime store) and fairly attractive, maybe even very attractive. I was often funny and always interesting. I had read everything and knew everything and got unbelievable grades. Of course I was someone whose love was desired. Mother, my teachers, my sister, girls at school, other boys—they all wanted me to love them.

But I wanted them to love me first.

None of them did. I was fierce and solitary and acrid, marching off the little mile from school, past the post office, all yellow brick and chrome, and my two locust trees (water, water everywhere and not a drop to drink), and there was no one who loved me first. I could see a hundred cravennesses in the people I knew, a thousand flaws, a million weaknesses. If I had to love first, I would love only perfection. Of course, I could help heal the people I knew if I loved them. No, I said to myself, why should I give them everything when they give me nothing?

How many hurts and shynesses and times of walking up the back stairs had made me that way? I don't know. All I know is that Edward needed my love and I wouldn't give it to him. I was only thirteen. Many sins can be forgiven a boy of thirteen, but I'm not thinking of the sin; I'm thinking of all the years that might have been—if I'd only known then what I know now. The waste, the God-awful waste.

Really, that's all there is to this story. The boy I was, the child Edward was. That and the terrible desire to suddenly turn and run shouting back through the corridors of time, screaming at the boy I was, searching him out, and pounding on his chest: Love him, you damn fool, love him.

I LIVE ON YOUR VISITS

BY DOROTHY PARKER (1955)

The boy came into the hotel room and immediately it seemed even smaller.

"Hey, it's cool in here," he said. This was not meant as a comment on the temperature. "Cool," for reasons possibly known in some department of Heaven, was a term then in use among many of those of his age to express approbation.

It was indeed cool in the room, after the hard gray rain in the streets. It was warm, and it was so bright. The many-watted electric bulbs his mother insisted upon were undimmed by the thin frilled shades she had set on the hotel lamps, and there were shiny things everywhere: sheets of mirror along the walls; a square of mirror backing the mirror-plated knob on the door that led to the bedroom; cigarette boxes made of tiny bits of mirror and matchboxes slipped into little mirror jackets placed all about; and, on consoles and desk and table, photographs of himself at two and a half and five and seven and nine framed in broad mirror bands. Whenever his mother settled in a new domicile, and she removed often, those photographs were the first things out of the luggage. The boy hated them. He had had to pass his fifteenth birthday before his body had caught up with his head; there was that head, in those presentments of his former selves, that pale, enormous blob. Once he had asked his mother to put the pictures somewhere else—preferably some small, dark place that could be locked. But he had had the bad fortune to make his request on one of the occasions when she was given to weeping suddenly and long. So the photographs stood out on parade, with their frames twinkling away.

There were twinklings, too, from the silver top of the fat crystal cocktail shaker, but the liquid low within the crystal was pale and dull. There was no shine, either, to the glass his mother held. It was cloudy from the clutch of her hand, and on the inside there were oily dribbles of what it had contained.

His mother shut the door by which she had admitted him, and followed him into the room. She looked at him with her head tilted to the side.

"Well, aren't you going to kiss me?" she said in a charming, wheedling voice, the voice of a little, little girl. "Aren't you, you beautiful big ox, you?"

"Sure," he said. He bent down toward her, but she stepped suddenly away. A sharp change came over her. She drew herself tall, with her shoulders back and her head flung high. Her upper lip lifted over her teeth, and her gaze came cold beneath lowered lids. So does one who has refused the white handkerchief regard the firing squad.

"Of course," she said in a deep, iced voice that gave each word its full due, "if you do not wish to kiss me, let it be recognized that there is no need for you to do so. I had not meant to overstep. I apologize. *Je vous demande pardon*. I had no desire to force you. I have never forced you. There is none to say I have."

"Ah, Mom," he said. He went to her, bent again, and this time kissed her cheek.

There was no change in her, save in the slow, somehow offended lifting of her eyelids. The brows arched as if they drew the lids up with them. "Thank you," she said. "That was gracious of you. I value graciousness. I rank it high. *Mille grazie*."

"Ah, Mom," he said.

For the past week, up at his school, he had hoped—and coming down in the train he had hoped so hard that it became prayer—that his mother would not be what he thought of only as "like that." His prayer had gone unanswered. He knew by the two voices, by the head first tilted then held high, by the eyelids lowered in disdain then raised in outrage, by the little lisped words and then the elegant enunciation and the lofty diction. He knew.

He stood there and said, "Ah, Mom."

"Perhaps," she said, "you will award yourself the privilege of meeting a friend of mine. She is a true friend. I am proud that I may say it."

There was someone else in the room. It was preposterous that he had not seen her, for she was so big. Perhaps his eyes had been dazzled, after the dim-lit hotel corridor; perhaps his attention had been all for his mother. At any rate, there she sat, the true friend, on the sofa covered with embossed cotton fabric of the sickened green that is peculiar to hotel upholsteries. There she sat, at one end of the sofa, and it seemed as if the other end must fly up into the air.

"I can give you but little," his mother said, "yet life is still kind enough to let me give you something you will always remember. Through me, you will meet a human being."

Yes, oh, yes. The voices, the stances, the eyelids—those were the signs. But when his mother divided the race into people and human beings—that was the certainty.

He followed her the little way across the room, trying not to tread on the train of her velvet tea gown that slid along the floor after her and slapped at the heels of her gilt slippers. Fog seemed to rise from his raincoat and his shoes cheeped. He turned out to avoid the coffee table in front of the sofa, came in again too sharply and bumped it.

"Mme. Marah," his mother said, "may I present my son?"

"Christ, he's a big bastard, isn't he?" the true friend said.

She was a fine one to talk about anybody's being big. Had she risen, she would have stood shoulder against shoulder with him, and she must have outweighed him by sixty pounds. She was dressed in quantities of tweedlike stuff ornamented, surprisingly, with black sequins set on in patterns of little bunches of grapes. On her massive wrists were bands and chains of dull silver, from some of which hung amulets of discolored ivory, like rotted fangs. Over her head and neck was a sort of caul of crisscrossed mauve veiling, splattered with fuzzy black balls. The caul caused her no inconvenience. Puffs of smoke issued sporadically from behind it, and, though the veiling was crisp elsewhere, around the mouth it was of a marshy texture, where drink had passed through it.

His mother became the little girl again. "Isn't he wonderful?" she said. "This is my baby. This is Crissy-wiss."

"*What* is his name?" the true friend said.

"Why, Christopher, of course," his mother said.

Christopher, of course. Had he been born earlier, it would have been Peter; earlier again, Michael; he had been not much too late for Jonathan. In the lower forms of his school, there were various Nicholases, several Robins, and here and there a Jeremy coming up. But the members of his own class were in the main Christophers.

"Christopher," the true friend said. "Well, that's not too bad. Of course, that downward stroke of the 'p' is bound to give him trouble, and I'm never really happy about an 'r' and an 'i' together. But it's not too bad. Not too. When's your birthday?" she asked the boy.

"The fifteenth of August," he said.

His mother was no longer the little girl. "The heat," she said, "the cruel August heat. And the stitches. Oh, God, the stitches!"

"So he's a Leo," the true friend said. "Awfully big for a Leo. You want to be pretty careful, young man, from October 22nd to November 13th. Keep away from anything electrical."

"I will," the boy said. "Thank you," he added.

"Let me see your hand," the true friend said.

The boy gave her his hand.

"Mm," she said, scanning the palm. "M-hmm, m-hmm, m-hmm. Oh. Well—*that* can't be helped. Well, you'll have pretty good health, if you just watch that chest of yours. There's a long sickness in your twenties and a bad accident some time around forty-five, but that's about all. There's going to be an unhappy love affair, but you'll get over it. You'll marry and— I can't see if there's two or three children. Probably two and one born dead, or something like that. I don't see much money, any time. Well, you watch your chest." She gave him back his hand.

"Thank you," he said.

The little girl came back to his mother. "Isn't he going to be famous?" she said.

The true friend shrugged. "It's not in his hand," she said.

"I always thought he'd write," his mother said. "When he was so small you could hardly see him, he used to write little verses. Crissy, what was the one about the bumpety bunny?"

"Oh, Mother!" he said. "I don't remember!"

"Oh, you do so, too!" she said. "You're just being modest. It was all about how the bunny went bumpety, bumpety all day long. Of course you remember. Well, you don't seem to write verses any more—at least none you show to *me*. And your letters—they're like telegrams. When you write at all, that is. Oh, Marah, why do they have to grow up? And now he's going to be married and have all those children."

"Two, anyway," the true friend said. "I'm not too happy about that third one."

"I suppose I'll never see him then," his mother said. "A lonely old woman, sick and trembling, and no one to take care of me."

She picked up the true friend's empty glass from the coffee table, filled it and her own from the cocktail shaker, and returned the friend's. She sat down near the sofa.

"Well, sit down, Crissy," she said. "And why don't you take off your coat?"

"Why, I don't think I'd better, Mom," he said. "You see—"

"He wants to keep his wet coat on," the true friend said. "He likes to smell like low tide."

"Well, you see," the boy said, "I can stay just a minute. You see, the train was late and everything, and I told Dad I'd be sure to be there early."

"Oh?" his mother said. The little girl ran off abruptly. The eyelids came into play.

"It's because the train was late," he said. "If it had been on time, I could have stayed awhile. But it had to go and be late, and they're having dinner awfully early tonight."

"I see," his mother said. "I see. I had thought that you would have dinner with me. With your mother. Her only son. But no, that is not to be. I have only an egg, but I would have shared it with you so gladly. So happily. But you are wise, of course. You must think first of your own comfort. Go and fill your stomach with your father. Go eat stalled ox with him."

"Mother, don't you see?" he said. "We have to have dinner early because we have to go to bed early. We've got to get up at daybreak because we're driving to the country. You know. I wrote you."

"Driving?" she said. "Your father has a new car, I presume."

"It's the same old heap," he said. "Nearly eight years old."

"Really?" she said. "Naturally, the buses in which I am obliged to ride are all this year's models."

"Ah, Mom," he said.

"Is your father well?" she said.

"He's fine," he said.

"Why not?" she said. "What is there could pierce that heart? And how is Mrs. Tennant? As I suppose she calls herself."

"Let's not do this again, will you, Mom?" he said. "She's Mrs. Tennant. You know that. She and Dad have been married for six years."

"To me," she said, "there is only one woman who may rightfully wear a man's name; the one whose son he has sired. But that is only my humble opinion. Who is to listen to it?"

"You get along all right with your stepmother?" the true friend said.

As always, it took him a moment before he could connect the term. It seemed to have nothing to do with Whitey, with her gay little monkey's face and her flying straw-colored hair.

A laugh fell from his mother's lips, hard, like a pellet of ice. "Such women are sly," she said. "They have ways."

"Well, born on a cusp," the true friend said. "You've got to keep considering that."

His mother turned to the boy. "I am going to do something that you will agree, in any honesty, that I have never done before," she said. "I am going to ask a favor of you. I am going to ask you to take off your coat and sit down, so that for just a few poor minutes it will seem as if you were not going to leave me. Will you let me have that illusion? Do not do it out of affection or gratitude or consideration. Just in simple pity."

"Yes, sit down, for God's sake," the true friend said. "You make people nervous."

"All right, sure," the boy said. He took off his raincoat, hung it over his arm, and sat on a small, straight chair.

"He's the biggest damn thing I ever saw," the true friend said.

"Thank you," his mother said. "If you think I ask too much, I plead guilty. *Mea culpa*. Well, now that we are cozy, let us talk, shall we? I see so little of you—I know so little about you. Tell me some things. Tell me what there is about this Mrs. Tennant that causes you to rank her so high above me. Is she more beautiful than I am?"

"Mom, please," he said. "You know Whitey isn't beautiful. She's just sort of funny-looking. Nice funny."

"Nice funny," she said. "Oh, I'm afraid I could never compete with that. Well, looks aren't everything, I suppose. Tell me, do you consider her a human being?"

"Mother, I don't know," he said. "I can't do that kind of talk."

"Let it pass," she said. "Let it be forgotten. Is your father's country place attractive at this time of year?"

"It isn't a place," he said. "You know—it's just a big sort of shack. There isn't even any heat. Just fireplaces."

"Ironic," she said. "Bitterly, cruelly ironic. I, who so love an open fire; I, who could sit all day looking into its leaping golds and purples and dreaming happy dreams. And I haven't even a gas log. Well. And who is going to this shack, to share the lovely, glowing fires?"

"Just Dad and Whitey and me," he said. "Oh, and the other Whitey, of course."

His mother looked at the true friend. "Is it growing dark in here?" she said. "Or is it just that I think I am going to faint?" She looked again at the boy. "The *other* Whitey?"

"It's a little dog," he said. "Not any particular kind. It's a nice little dog. Whitey saw it out in the street, when it was snowing, and it followed her home, and so they kept it. And whenever Dad—whenever anybody called Whitey, the dog would come, too. So Dad said well, if he thought that was his name, then that was going to *be* his name. So that was why."

"I am afraid," his mother said, "that your father is not aging with dignity. To me, whimsey after forty-five is a matter of nausea."

"It's an awfully nice little dog," he said.

"The management does not allow dogs here," she said. "I suppose that will be held against me. Marah—this drink. It is as weak as the beating of my heart."

"Why doesn't he make us some fresh ones?" the true friend said.

"I'm sorry," the boy said. "I don't know how to make cocktails."

"What do they teach you, anyway, in that fancy school of yours?" the true friend said.

His mother tilted her head at the boy. "Crissy," she said, "want to be a big, brave man? Take the bowl and get some nice, cold ice out of the kitchen."

He took the ice bowl, went into the minuscule kitchen, and took a tray of ice cubes from the tiny refrigerator. When he replaced the tray, he could hardly close the refrigerator door, the shelves were so crowded. There were a cardboard box of eggs, a packet of butter, a cluster of glossy French rolls, three artichokes, two avocados, a plate of tomatoes, a bowl of shelled peas, a grapefruit, a tin of vegetable juices, a glass of red caviar, a cream cheese, an assortment of sliced Italian sausages, and a plump little roasted Cornish Rock hen.

When he returned, his mother was busied with bottles and shaker. He set the bowl of cubes beside them.

"Look, Mom," he said, "honestly I've got to—"

His mother looked at him and her lip trembled. "Just two more minutes," she whispered. "Please, oh, please."

He went and sat again.

She made the drinks, gave one to the true friend, and kept one. She sank into her chair; her head drooped and her body looked as boneless as a skein of yarn.

"Don't you want a drink?" the true friend said.

"No, thanks," the boy said.

"Might do you good," the true friend said. "Might stunt your growth. How long are you going to stay up in this country where you're going?"

"Oh, just over tomorrow night," he said. "I have to be back at school Sunday evening."

His mother stiffened and straightened. Her former coldnesses were as tropical heat to that which took her now.

"Do I understand you to say that you will not be coming in to see me again?" she said. "Do I understand you aright?"

"I can't, Mom," he said. "I won't have a chance. We've got to drive back, and then I have to get the train."

"I quite comprehend," she said. "I had thought, in my tenderness, I would see you again before your return to your school. I had thought, of course, that if you must rush away like a mad thing today, then I would see you again, to make up for it. Disappointments—I thought I had had them all, I thought life could bring forth no new ones. But this—this. That you will not take a little bit of your time from your relatives, who have so much of it, to give to me, your mother. How it must please them that you do not want to see me. How they must laugh together. What a triumph. How they must howl in merriment."

"Mother, don't say things like that," he said. "You shouldn't, even when you're—"

"Please!" she said. "The subject is closed. I will say no more about your father, poor, weak man, and that woman with the dog's name. But you—you. Have you no heart, no bowels, no natural instincts? No. You have not. I must face the fact. Here, in the presence of my friend, I must say what I had thought never, never to say. My son is not a human being!"

The true friend shook her caul and sighed. The boy sat still.

"Your father," his mother said. "Does he still see his old friends? *Our* old friends?"

"Why, I don't know, Mom," he said. "Yes, they see a lot of people, I guess. There's almost always somebody there. But they're alone a lot of the time. They like it that way."

"How fortunate," she said. "They like being alone. Smug, content, no need— Yes. And the old friends. They do not see me. They are all in twos, they have lives, they know what they're going to be doing six months from now. Why should they see me? Why should they have memories, kindnesses?"

"Probably most of them Pisces," the true friend said.

"Well, you must go," the boy's mother said. "It is late. Late—when is it ever late for me, when my son is with me? But you have told me. I know. I understand, and so I bow my head. Go, Christopher. Go."

"I'm terribly sorry, Mom," the boy said. "But I told you how it is." He rose and put on his coat.

"Christ, he gets bigger and bigger," the true friend said.

This time, the eyelids of the boy's mother were lowered at her friend. "I have always admired tall men," she said. She turned again to the boy. "You must go," she said. "It is so written. But take happiness with you. Take sweet memories of our little time together. See—I shall show you that I bear no vengefulness. I shall show you that I wish only well to those who have wrought but evil to me. I shall give you a present to take one of them."

She rose, moved about the room, touched boxes and tables fruitlessly. Then she went to the desk, moved papers and inkstands, and brought forth a small, square box, on top of which was a little plaster poodle, sitting on its hind legs, its front paws curved endearingly, begging.

"This is a souvenir of happier times," she said. "But I need no reminders. Take this dear, happy thing to one you love. See! See what it is!"

She touched a spring at the back of the box and the "Marseillaise" tinkled forth, hesitantly.

"My little music box," she said. "That moonlit night, the ship so brilliant, the ocean so still and beckoning."

"Hey, that's cool, Mom," he said. "Thanks ever so much. Whitey'll love it. She loves things like that."

"Things like that?" she said. "There are no other things like that, when one gives from one's heart." She stopped and seemed to ponder. "*Whitey* will love it?" she said. "Are you telling me that you propose giving it to that so-called Mrs. Tennant?" She touched the box; the tinkling ceased.

"I thought you said—" the boy said.

She shook her head at him, slowly. "Curious," she said. "Extraordinary. That my son should have so little perception. This gift, from my poor little store, is not for her. It is for the little dog. The little dog that I may not have."

"Why, thanks, Mom," he said. "Thanks."

"So go," she said. "I would not hold you. Take with you my wishes for your joy, among your loved ones. And when you can, when they will release you for a little while—come to me again. I wait for you. I light a lamp for you. My son, my only child, there are but desert sands for me between your comings. I live on your visits—Chris, I live on your visits."

A FATHER-TO-BE

BY SAUL BELLOW (1955)

The strangest notions had a way of forcing themselves into Rogin's mind. Just thirty-one and passable-looking, with short black hair, small eyes, but a high, open forehead, he was a research chemist, and his mind was generally serious and dependable. But on a snowy Sunday evening while this stocky man, buttoned to the chin in a Burberry coat and walking in his preposterous gait—feet turned outward—was going toward the subway, he fell into a peculiar state.

He was on his way to have supper with his fiancée. She had phoned him a short while ago and said, "You'd better pick up a few things on the way."

"What do we need?"

"Some roast beef, for one thing. I bought a quarter of a pound coming home from my aunt's."

"Why a quarter of a pound, Joan?" said Rogin, deeply annoyed. "That's just about enough for one good sandwich."

"So you have to stop at a delicatessen. I had no more money."

He was about to ask, "What happened to the thirty dollars I gave you on Wednesday?," but he knew that would not be right.

"I had to give Phyllis money for the cleaning woman," said Joan.

Phyllis, Joan's cousin, was a young divorcée, extremely wealthy. The two women shared an apartment.

"Roast beef," he said, "and what else?"

"Some shampoo, sweetheart. We've used up all the shampoo. And hurry, darling, I've missed you all day."

"And I've missed you," said Rogin, but to tell the truth he had been worrying most of the time. He had a younger brother whom he was putting through college. And his mother, whose annuity wasn't quite enough in these days of inflation and high taxes, needed money, too. Joan had debts he was helping her to pay, for she wasn't working. She was looking for something suitable to do. Beautiful, well-educated, aristocratic in her attitude, she couldn't clerk in a dime store; she couldn't model clothes (Rogin thought this made girls vain and stiff, and he didn't want her to); she couldn't be a waitress or a cashier. What could she be? Well, something would turn up, and meantime Rogin hesitated to complain. He paid her bills—the dentist, the department store, the osteopath, the doctor, the psychiatrist. At Christmas, Rogin almost went mad. Joan bought him a velvet smoking jacket with frog fasteners, a beautiful pipe, and a pouch. She bought Phyllis a garnet brooch, an Italian silk umbrella, and a gold cigarette holder. For other friends, she bought Dutch pewter and Swedish glassware. Before she was through, she had spent five hundred dollars of Rogin's money. He loved her too much to show his suffering. He believed she had a far better nature than his. She didn't worry about money. She had a marvellous character, always cheerful, and she really didn't need a psychiatrist at all. She went to one because Phyllis did and it made her curious. She tried too much to keep up with her cousin, whose father had made millions in the rug business.

While the woman in the drugstore was wrapping the shampoo bottle, a clear idea suddenly arose in Rogin's thoughts: Money surrounds you in life as the earth does in death. Superimposition is the universal law. Who is free? No one is free. Who has no burdens? Everyone is under pressure. The very rocks, the waters of the earth, beasts, men, children—everyone has some weight to carry. This idea was extremely clear to him at first. Soon it became rather vague, but it had a great effect nevertheless, as if someone had given him a valuable gift. (Not like the velvet smoking jacket he couldn't bring himself to wear, or the pipe it choked him to smoke.) The notion that all were under pressure and affliction, instead of saddening him, had the opposite influence. It put him in a wonderful mood. It was extraordinary how happy he became and, in addition, clear-sighted. His eyes all at once were opened to what was around him. He saw with delight how the druggist and the woman who wrapped the shampoo bottle were smiling and flirting, how the lines of worry in her face went over into lines of cheer and the druggist's receding gums did not hinder his kidding and friendliness. And in the delicatessen, also, it was amazing how much Rogin noted and what happiness it gave him simply to be there.

Delicatessens on Sunday night, when all other stores are shut, will overcharge you ferociously, and Rogin would normally have been on guard, but he was not tonight, or scarcely so. Smells of pickle, sausage, mustard, and smoked fish overjoyed him. He pitied the people who would buy the chicken salad and chopped herring; they could do it only because their sight was too dim to see what they were getting—the fat flakes of pepper on the chicken, the soppy herring, mostly vinegar-soaked stale bread. Who would buy them? Late risers, people living alone, waking up in the darkness of the afternoon, finding their refrigerators empty, or people whose gaze was turned inward. The roast beef looked not bad, and Rogin ordered a pound.

While the storekeeper was slicing the meat, he yelled at a Puerto Rican kid who was reaching for a bag of chocolate cookies, "Hey, you want to pull me down the whole display on yourself? You, *chico*, wait a half a minute." This storekeeper, though he looked like one of Pancho Villa's bandits, the kind that smeared their enemies with syrup and staked them down on anthills, a man with toadlike eyes and stout hands made to clasp pistols hung around his belly, was not so bad. He was a New York man, thought Rogin—who was from Albany himself—a New York man toughened by every abuse of the city, trained to suspect everyone. But in his own realm, on the board behind the counter, there was justice. Even clemency.

The Puerto Rican kid wore a complete cowboy outfit—a green hat with white braid, guns, chaps, spurs, boots, and gauntlets—but he couldn't speak any English. Rogin unhooked the cellophane bag of hard circular cookies and gave it to him. The boy tore the cellophane with his teeth and began to chew one of those dry chocolate discs. Rogin recognized his state—the energetic dream of childhood. Once, he, too, had found these dry biscuits delicious. It would have bored him now to eat one.

What else would Joan like? Rogin thought fondly. Some strawberries? "Give me some frozen strawberries. No, raspberries, she likes those better. And heavy cream. And some rolls, cream cheese, and some of those rubber-looking gherkins."

"What rubber?"

"Those, deep green, with eyes. Some ice cream might be in order, too."

He tried to think of a compliment, a good comparison, an endearment, for Joan when she'd open the door. What about her complexion? There was really nothing to compare her sweet, small, daring, shapely, timid, defiant, loving face to. How difficult she was, and how beautiful!

As Rogin went down into the stony, odorous, metallic, captive air of the subway, he was diverted by an unusual confession made by a man to his friend. These were two very tall men, shapeless in their winter clothes, as if their coats concealed suits of chain mail.

"So, how long have you known me?" said one.

"Twelve years."

"Well, I have an admission to make," he said. "I've decided that I might as well. For years I've been a heavy drinker. You didn't know. Practically an alcoholic."

But his friend was not surprised, and he answered immediately, "Yes, I did know."

"You knew? Impossible! How could you?"

Why, thought Rogin, as if it could be a secret! Look at that long, austere, alcohol-washed face, that drink-ruined nose, the skin by his ears like turkey wattles, and those whiskey-saddened eyes.

"Well, I did know, though."

"You couldn't have. I can't believe it." He was upset, and his friend didn't seem to want to soothe him. "But it's all right now," he said. "I've been going to a doctor and taking pills, a new revolutionary Danish discovery. It's a miracle. I'm beginning to believe they can cure you of anything and everything. You can't beat the Danes in science. They do everything. They turned a man into a woman."

"That isn't how they stop you from drinking, is it?"

"No. I hope not. This is only like aspirin. It's super-aspirin. They call it the aspirin of the future. But if you use it, you have to stop drinking."

Rogin's illuminated mind asked of itself while the human tides of the subway swayed back and forth, and cars linked and transparent like fish bladders raced under the streets: How come he thought nobody would know what everybody couldn't help knowing? And, as a chemist, he asked himself what kind of compound this new Danish drug might be, and started thinking about various inventions of his own, synthetic albumen, a cigarette that lit itself, a cheaper motor fuel. Ye gods, but he needed money! As never before. What was to be done? His mother was growing more and more difficult. On Friday night, she had neglected to cut up his meat for him, and he was hurt. She had sat at the table motionless, with her long-suffering face, severe, and let him cut his own meat, a thing she almost never did. She had always spoiled him and made his brother envy him. But what she expected now! Oh, Lord, how he had to pay, and it had never even occurred to him formerly that these things might have a price.

Seated, one of the passengers, Rogin recovered his calm, happy, even clairvoyant state of mind. To think of money was to think as the world wanted you to think; then you'd never be your own master. When people said they wouldn't do something for love or money, they meant that love and money were opposite passions and one the enemy of the other. He went on to reflect how little people knew about this, how they slept through life, how small a light the light of consciousness was. Rogin's clean, snub-nosed face shone while his heart was torn with joy at these deeper thoughts of our ignorance. You might take this drunkard as an example, who for long years thought his closest friends never suspected he drank. Rogin looked up and down the aisle for this remarkable knightly symbol, but he was gone.

However, there was no lack of things to see. There was a small girl with a new white muff; into the muff a doll's head was sewn, and the child was happy and affectionately vain of it, while her old man, stout and grim, with a huge scowling nose, kept picking her up and resettling her in the seat, as if he were trying to change her into something else. Then another child, led by her mother, boarded the car, and this other child carried the very same doll-faced muff, and this greatly annoyed both parents. The woman, who looked like a difficult, contentious woman, took her daughter away. It seemed to Rogin that each child was in love with its own muff and didn't even see the other, but it was one of his foibles to think he understood the hearts of little children.

A foreign family next engaged his attention. They looked like Central Americans to him. On one side the mother, quite old, dark-faced, white-haired, and worn out; on the other a son with the whitened, porous hands of a dishwasher. But what was the dwarf who sat between them—a son or a daughter? The hair was long and wavy and the cheeks smooth, but the shirt and tie were masculine. The overcoat was feminine, but the shoes—the shoes were a puzzle. A pair of brown oxfords with an outer seam like a man's, but Baby Louis heels like a woman's—a plain toe like a man's, but a strap across the instep like a woman's. No stockings. That didn't help much. The dwarf's fingers were beringed, but without a wedding band. There were small grim dents in the cheeks. The eyes were puffy and concealed, but Rogin did not doubt that they could reveal strange things if they chose and that this was a creature of remarkable understanding. He had for many years owned De la Mare's "Memoirs of a Midget." Now he took a resolve; he would read it. As soon as he had decided, he was free from his consuming curiosity as to the dwarf's sex and was able to look at the person who sat beside him.

Thoughts very often grow fertile in the subway, because of the motion, the great company, the subtlety of the rider's state as he rattles under streets and rivers, under the foundations of great buildings, and Rogin's mind had already been strangely stimulated. Clasping the bag of groceries from which there rose odors of bread and pickle spice, he was following a train of reflections, first about the chemistry of sex determination, the X and Y chromosomes, hereditary linkages, the uterus, afterward about his brother as a tax exemption. He recalled two dreams of the night before. In one, an undertaker had offered to cut his hair, and he had refused. In another, he had been carrying a woman on his head. Sad dreams, both! Very sad! Which was the woman—Joan or Mother? And the undertaker—his lawyer? He gave a deep sigh, and by force of habit began to put together his synthetic albumen that was to revolutionize the entire egg industry.

Meanwhile, he had not interrupted his examination of the passengers and had fallen into a study of the man next to him. This was a man whom he had never in his life seen before but with whom he now suddenly felt linked through all existence. He was middle-aged, sturdy, with clear skin and blue eyes. His hands were clean, well-formed, but Rogin did not approve of them. The coat he wore was a fairly expensive blue check such as Rogin would never have chosen for himself. He would not have worn blue suède shoes, either, or such a faultless hat, a cumbersome felt animal of a hat encircled by a high, fat ribbon. There are all kinds of dandies, not all of them are of the flaunting kind; some are dandies of respectability, and Rogin's fellow-passenger was one of these. His straight-nosed profile was handsome, yet he had betrayed his gift, for he was flat-looking. But in his flat way he seemed to warn people that he wanted no difficulties with them, he wanted nothing to do with them. Wearing such blue suède shoes, he could not afford to have people treading on his feet, and he seemed to draw about himself a circle of privilege, notifying all others to mind their own business and let him read his paper. He was holding a *Tribune*, and perhaps it would be overstatement to say that he was reading. He was holding it.

His clear skin and blue eyes, his straight and purely Roman nose—even the way he sat—all strongly suggested one person to Rogin: Joan. He tried to escape the comparison, but it couldn't be helped. This man not only looked like Joan's father, whom Rogin detested; he looked like Joan herself. Forty years hence, a son of hers, provided she had one, might be like this. A son of hers? Of such a son, he himself, Rogin, would be the father. Lacking in dominant traits as compared with Joan, his heritage would not appear. Probably the children would resemble her. Yes, think forty years ahead, and a man like this, who sat by him knee to knee in the hurtling car among their fellow-creatures, unconscious participants in a sort of great carnival of transit—such a man would carry forward what had been Rogin.

This was why he felt bound to him through all existence. What were forty years reckoned against eternity! Forty years were gone, and he was gazing at his own son. Here he was. Rogin was frightened and moved. "My son! My son!" he said to himself, and the pity of it almost made him burst into tears. The holy and frightful work of the masters of life and death brought this about. We were their instruments. We worked toward ends we thought were our own. But no! The whole thing was so unjust. To suffer, to labor, to toil and force your way through the spikes of life, to crawl through its darkest caverns, to push through the worst, to struggle under the weight of economy, to make money—only to become the father of a fourth-rate man of the world like this, so flat-looking, with his ordinary, clean, rosy, uninteresting, self-satisfied, fundamentally bourgeois face. What a curse to have a dull son! A son like this, who could never understand his father. They had absolutely nothing, but nothing in common, he and this neat, chubby, blue-eyed man. He was so pleased, thought Rogin, with all he owned and all he did and all he was that he could hardly unfasten his lip. Look at that lip, sticking up at the tip like a little thorn or egg tooth. He wouldn't give anyone the time of day. Would this perhaps be general forty years from now? Would personalities be chillier as the world aged and grew colder? The inhumanity of the next generation incensed Rogin. Father and son had no sign to make to each other. Terrible! Inhuman! What a vision of existence it gave him. Man's personal aims were nothing, illusion. The life force occupied each of us in turn in its progress toward its own fulfillment, trampling on our individual humanity, using us for its own ends like mere dinosaurs or bees, exploiting love heartlessly, making us engage in the social process, labor, struggle for money, and submit to the law of pressure, the universal law of layers, superimposition!

What the blazes am I getting into? Rogin thought. To be the father of a throwback to *her* father. The image of this white-haired, gross, peevish old man with his ugly selfish blue eyes revolted Rogin. This was how his grandson would look. Joan, with whom Rogin was now more and more displeased, could not help that. For her, it was inevitable. But did it have to be inevitable for him? Well, then, Rogin, you fool, don't be a damned instrument. Get out of the way!

But it was too late for this, because he had already experienced the sensation of sitting next to his own son, his son and Joan's. He kept staring at him, waiting for him to say something, but the presumptive son remained coldly silent though he must have been aware of Rogin's scrutiny. They even got out at the same stop—Sheridan Square. When they stepped to the platform, the man, without even looking at Rogin, went away in a different direction in his detestable blue-checked coat, with his rosy, nasty face.

The whole thing upset Rogin very badly. When he approached Joan's door and heard Phyllis's little dog Henri barking even before he could knock, his face was very tense. "I won't be used," he declared to himself. "I have my own right to exist." Joan had better watch out. She had a light way of bypassing grave questions he had given earnest thought to. She always assumed no really disturbing thing would happen. He could not afford the luxury of such a carefree, debonair attitude himself, because he had to work hard and earn money so that disturbing things would *not* happen. Well, at the moment this situation could not be helped, and he really did not mind the money if he could feel that she was not necessarily the mother of such a son as his subway son or entirely the daughter of that awful, obscene father of hers. After all, Rogin was not himself so much like either of his parents, and quite different from his brother.

Joan came to the door, wearing one of Phyllis's expensive housecoats. It suited her very well. At first sight of her happy face, Rogin was brushed by the shadow of resemblance; the touch of it was extremely light, almost figmentary, but it made his flesh tremble.

She began to kiss him, saying, "Oh, my baby. You're covered with snow. Why didn't you wear your hat? It's all over its little head"—her favorite third-person endearment.

"Well, let me put down this bag of stuff. Let me take off my coat," grumbled Rogin, and escaped from her embrace. Why couldn't she wait making up to him? "It's so hot in here. My face is burning. Why do you keep the place at this temperature? And that damned dog keeps barking. If you didn't keep it cooped up, it wouldn't be so spoiled and noisy. Why doesn't anybody ever walk him?"

"Oh, it's not really so hot here! You've just come in from the cold. Don't you think this housecoat fits me better than Phyllis? Especially across the hips. She thinks so, too. She may sell it to me."

"I hope not," Rogin almost exclaimed.

She brought a towel to dry the melting snow from his short,

black hair. The flurry of rubbing excited Henri intolerably, and Joan locked him up in the bedroom, where he jumped persistently against the door with a rhythmic sound of claws on the wood.

Joan said, "Did you bring the shampoo?"

"Here it is."

"Then I'll wash your hair before dinner. Come."

"I don't want it washed."

"Oh, come on," she said, laughing.

Her lack of consciousness of guilt amazed him. He did not see how it could be. And the carpeted, furnished, lamplit, curtained room seemed to stand against his vision. So that he felt accusing and angry, his spirit sore and bitter, but it did not seem fitting to say why. Indeed, he began to worry lest the reason for it all slip away from him.

They took off his coat and his shirt in the bathroom, and she filled the sink. Rogin was full of his troubled emotions; now that his chest was bare, he could feel them even more distinctly inside, and he said to himself, "I'll have a thing or two to tell her pretty soon. I'm not letting them get away with it. 'Do you think,' he was going to tell her, 'that I alone was made to carry the burden of the whole world on me? Do you think I was born just to be taken advantage of and sacrificed? Do you think I'm just a natural resource, like a coal mine, or oil well, or fishery, or the like? Remember, that I'm a man is no reason why I should be loaded down. I have a soul in me no bigger or stronger than yours. Take away the externals, like the muscles, deeper voice, and so forth, and what remains? A pair of spirits, practically alike. So why shouldn't there also be equality? I can't always be the strong one.' "

"Sit here," said Joan, bringing up a kitchen stool to the sink. "Your hair's gotten all matted."

He sat with his breast against the cool enamel, his chin on the edge of the basin, the green, hot, radiant water reflecting the glass and the tile, and the sweet, cool, fragrant juice of the shampoo poured on his head. She began to wash him.

"You have the healthiest-looking scalp," she said. "It's all pink."

He answered, "Well, it should be white. There must be something wrong with me."

"But there's absolutely nothing wrong with you," she said, and pressed against him from behind, surrounding him, pouring the water gently over him until it seemed to him that the water came from within him, it was the warm fluid of his own secret loving spirit overflowing into the sink, green and foaming, and the words he had rehearsed he forgot, and his anger at his son-to-be disappeared altogether, and he sighed, and said to her from the water-filled hollow of the sink, "You always have such wonderful ideas, Joan. You know? You have a kind of instinct, a regular gift."

A SUMMER'S READING

BY BERNARD MALAMUD (1956)

George Stoyonovich was a neighborhood boy who had quit high school on an impulse when he was sixteen, and though he was ashamed whenever he went looking for a job and people asked him if he had finished school, he never went back. This particular summer was a hard time for jobs, and he had none. Having so much time on his hands, George thought of going to summer school, but he decided the kids in his classes would be too young. He also considered registering in a night high school, but he didn't like the idea of the teachers telling him what to do. He felt they had never respected him. The result was he stayed in his room most of the day. He was close to twenty and had needs with the neighborhood girls, but no money of his own to spend, and he couldn't get much, either, because his father was poor, and his sister Sophie—a tall, bony girl of twenty-three, who resembled George—earned very little, and what she had she kept for herself. Their mother was dead, and Sophie had to take care of the house and work at her job as well.

George's father got up very early in the morning to go to work in a fish market. Sophie left at about eight for a long ride in the subway. She worked in a cafeteria in the Bronx. George had his coffee by himself, then hung around in the house. When the house, a five-room railroad flat above a butcher store on the lower East Side, got on his nerves, he cleaned it up—mopped the floors with a wet mop and put things away. But most of the time he sat in his room.

In the afternoons, he usually listened to the ball games. Otherwise, he had a couple of old copies of the *World Almanac*, which he had bought long ago, and he liked to read in them, and also to read the magazines and newspapers Sophie brought home, which had been left on the tables in the cafeteria. The magazines were mostly picture magazines about movie stars and sports figures, and the papers were generally the *News* and *Mirror*. Sophie herself read whatever fell into her hands, although she sometimes read good books.

She once asked George what he did in his room all day, and he answered that he read a lot, too.

"What besides what I bring home?" she asked. "Do you ever read any worth-while books?"

"Some," George answered, although he really didn't. He had tried to read a book or two that Sophie had in the house, but he'd found he was in no mood for them. Lately he couldn't stand made-up stories; they got on his nerves.

He wished he had some hobby to work at; as a kid he had been good in carpentry, but where could he work at it? Sometimes he went for walks during the day, but mostly he did his walking after the sun had gone down, when it was cooler in the streets.

In the evenings, after supper, George left the house and wandered in the neighborhood. During the sultry spells, some of the storekeepers and their wives sat in chairs on the thick, cracked sidewalks in front of their shops, fanning themselves, and George walked past them, and past the guys hanging out on the candy-store corner. A couple of the guys he had known his whole life, but he and they never recognized each other. He had no place special to go, but usually—saving it for the last—he left the neighborhood and walked till he came to a darkly lit little park with benches and trees and a low iron railing, giving it a feeling of privacy. He stepped over the railing and sat on a bench, looking at the leafy trees and the flowers blooming inside the railing, and thinking of a better life for himself. He thought of the jobs he had had since he quit school—delivery boy, stock clerk, runner, odd jobs in a factory—and he was dissatisfied with all of them. He felt he would someday like to have a good job and live in a private house with a porch, on a street with trees. He wanted to have dough in his pocket to buy things with, and a girl, so as not to be so lonely, especially on Saturday nights. He wanted people to like and respect him. He thought about these things often, and mostly when he was alone at night. Around midnight, he would get up and drift back to his hot and stony neighborhood.

One time, on his walk, George met Mr. Cattanzara coming home very late from work. He wondered if Mr. Cattanzara was drunk, and then saw that he wasn't. Mr. Cattanzara, a stocky, bald-headed man who worked in the change booth of an I.R.T. station, lived on the block next to George's, above a shoe-repair store. Nights, during the hot weather, he sat on his stoop in an undershirt, reading the *Times* in the light from the shoemaker's window. He read it from the first page to the last, then went up to his flat to sleep. And all evening, while he was reading the paper, his wife, a fat woman with a white face, leaned out of the window above, looking into the street, her thick arms folded under her loose breasts, on the window ledge.

Once in a while, Mr. Cattanzara came home drunk, but it was always a quiet drunk. He never made any trouble; he just walked stiffly up the street and slowly climbed the stoop and went into his doorway. He looked the same as always, except for the stiff walk and the fact that his eyes were sad. George liked him, because he remembered Mr. Cattanzara giving him nickels to buy lemon ice with when he was a squirt. Mr. Cattanzara was different from most of the people in the neighborhood. He asked different questions when he met you, and he seemed to know what went on in all the newspapers.

"What are you doing with yourself this summer, George?" Mr. Cattanzara asked that evening when they met. "I see you walkin' around at nights."

George felt embarrassed. "I like to walk," he said.

"What are you doin' in the day now?"

"Nothing much just right now. I'm waiting for a job." Then, since it shamed him to admit he wasn't working, George said, "I'm staying home, but I'm reading a lot to pick up my education."

Mr. Cattanzara looked interested. He mopped his hot face with a red handkerchief.

"What are you readin'?"

George hesitated, then said, "I got a list of books in the library, once, and now I decided to read them this summer." He felt strange and a little unhappy saying this, but he wanted Mr. Cattanzara to respect him.

"How many books are on it?" Mr. Cattanzara asked.

"I never counted them. Maybe around a hundred."

Mr. Cattanzara whistled.

"I figured if I did that, it would help me in my education," George went on earnestly. "I don't mean the kind they give you in high school. I want to know different things than you learn there, if you know what I mean."

Mr. Cattanzara nodded. "Still and all, one hundred books is a big load, just for one summer," he said.

"It might take longer."

"After you've finished with some, maybe you and I can have a nice talk about them," said Mr. Cattanzara.

"When I'm finished," George answered.

Mr. Cattanzara went home and George continued on his walk. After that night, George still did nothing different from the usual, though he had the urge to. He just took his walks at night, ending up in the little park. But one evening the shoemaker from the next block stopped George and said he was a good boy, and George figured that Mr. Cattanzara had told him about all the books he was supposed to be reading. From the shoemaker, the report must have gone on down the street, because in the next few days George saw a couple of people smiling kindly at him, though nobody spoke to him personally. He felt a little better around the neighborhood, and liked it more, though not so much that he would want to live in it forever. He had never exactly disliked the people in it, yet he had never liked them very much, either.

Soon, to his surprise, George found that his father and Sophie had learned about his reading, too. His father was too shy to say anything about it—he had never been much of a talker in his whole life—but Sophie was softer to George now, and she showed him in other ways that she was proud of him.

As the summer went on, George felt in a good mood about things. He cleaned the house every day, as a favor to Sophie, and he enjoyed the ball games more. Sophie gave him a dollar a week allowance, and though it still wasn't enough and he had to use it carefully, it was a lot better than the occasional two bits he'd had before. He got a big kick out of what he bought with the money—cigarettes mostly, an occasional beer, or a movie ticket. Life wasn't so bad if you knew how to appreciate it. Once in a while, he bought a paperback book from a newsstand, but he never got around to reading it, though he was glad to have it and a couple of others in his room. He still read Sophie's magazines and newspapers thoroughly.

Night was the most enjoyable time now, because when he passed the storekeepers sitting out on the sidewalk, he could tell how highly they and their wives regarded him. He walked erect, and though he did not say much to them, or they to him, he could feel approval on all sides. A couple of nights, he felt so good that he skipped the park at the end of the walk. He just wandered in the neighborhood, where people had known him from the time he was a kid playing punchball; he wandered there, then came home and got undressed for bed, feeling fine.

In the next few weeks, after that one encounter, George talked only once with Mr. Cattanzara. The change-maker said nothing more about the books, and asked no questions, but the fact that he didn't made George a little uneasy. For a while, George didn't pass in front of Mr. Cattanzara's house any more. Then, one night, forgetting himself, he approached it. The time was already past midnight. The street, except for one or two people, was deserted, and George was surprised when he saw Mr. Cattanzara still reading his newspaper. George's impulse was to go up and talk to him; he wasn't sure what he wanted to say, but he felt the words would come when he began to talk. Yet the more he thought about it, the more the idea scared him, and he decided he'd better not. He even considered turning around and running home another way, but he was already too near Mr. Cattanzara, and the change-maker might see him and get annoyed. So George unobtrusively crossed the street, trying to make it seem that he had to look in a store window on the other side, and then went on, uncomfortable at what he was doing. He feared Mr. Cattanzara would glance up from his paper and call him a dirty rat for walking on the other side of the street, but all the change-maker did was sit there in his undershirt, his bald head shining in the dim light, while he read his *Times* and upstairs his fat wife leaned out of the window, seeming to read the paper along with him. George thought she would spy him and yell out to Mr. Cattanzara, but she never moved her eyes from her husband.

George made up his mind to stay away from Mr. Cattanzara until he had got some of his paperback books read, but when he started to read them and found that they were all storybooks, he lost interest in them. He lost interest in reading other things, too. Sophie's magazines and newspapers went unread. She saw them piled up on a chair in his room and asked why he was no longer looking at them, and George told her it was because of all the other reading he had to do. Sophie said she had guessed that was it. So for most of the day George had the radio on, turning to music when he was sick of the human voice. He kept the house fairly neat, and Sophie said nothing on the days when he neglected it. She was still kind and gave him his dollar, but now things were not so good for him as they had been for a while.

But things were good enough, considering. Also, George's night walks invariably picked him up, no matter how bad the day had been. Then, one night, George saw Mr. Cattanzara coming down the street toward him. George was about to turn and run, but he recognized from Mr. Cattanzara's walk that he was drunk, and thought that he would probably not even notice him. So George kept on walking until he and Mr. Cattanzara passed each other, and though George felt wound up enough to pop into the sky, he was not surprised when Mr. Cattanzara went on by without a word, walking slowly, his face and body stiff. George drew a breath in relief at his escape, and then he heard his name called, and he stopped, and there stood Mr. Cattanzara at his elbow, smelling like a bar. His eyes were sad, and George felt so intensely uncomfortable that he was tempted to shove him aside and continue on his walk. But he couldn't act that way, and besides Mr. Cattanzara took a nickel out of his pants pocket and handed it to him. "Go buy yourself a lemon ice, Georgie," he said.

"It's not that time any more, Mr. Cattanzara," George said. "I'm a big guy now."

"No, you ain't," said Mr. Cattanzara, and to this George made no reply. "How are all your books comin' along now?" Mr. Cattanzara asked. Though he tried to stand steady, he swayed a little.

"Fine, I guess," said George, feeling redness crawl up his face.

"You ain't sure?" The change-maker smiled slyly, in a way George had never seen him smile when he was sober.

"Sure I'm sure," George said. "They're fine."

Mr. Cattanzara's head swayed in little arcs, but his eyes were steady. He had small blue eyes that hurt if you looked at them too long.

"George," he said, "name me one book on that list that you read this summer, and I will drink to your health."

"I don't want anyone drinking to me," George said.

"Name me one, so I can ask you a question on it. Who can tell—if it's a good book, maybe I might wanna read it myself?"

George knew he looked the same as ever on the outside, but inside he was crumbling. Unable to reply, he shut his eyes. When—years later—he opened them, he saw that Mr. Cattanzara had, out of pity, gone away, but still in George's ears were the words he had said as he left: "George, don't do what I did."

The next night, George was afraid to leave his room, and though Sophie argued with him, he wouldn't open his door.

"What are you doing in there?" she asked.

"Nothing."

"Aren't you reading?"

"No."

She was silent a minute, then asked, "Where do you keep the books you read? I never see any in your room, outside a few cheap trashy ones."

He wouldn't tell her.

"In that case, you're not worth a buck of my hard-earned money," she said. "Why should I break my poor back for you? Go out, you bum, and get a job."

He stayed in his room for almost a week, except to eat. Sophie railed at him, then begged him to come out, and his old father wept, but George wouldn't budge, though the weather was terrible and his small room stifling. He found it very hard to breathe. One night, unable to stand the heat any more, he burst into the street at 1 A.M. He hoped to sneak to the park without being seen, but there were people all over the block, wilted and listless, waiting for a breeze.

George lowered his eyes and walked, in disgrace, past them, but before long he discovered they were still friendly to him. He figured Mr. Cattanzara hadn't told. Maybe, when he woke up out of his drunk the next morning, he had forgotten all about their meeting. George felt his confidence come back.

A little later, a man on a street corner asked him if it was true that he had finished reading so many books, and George admitted that he had. The man said it was a wonderful thing for a boy his age to read so much.

"Yeah," George said.

He felt relieved, but he hurried away. He hoped nobody would mention the books anymore, and when, a couple of nights later, he accidentally met Mr. Cattanzara again, *he* didn't.

One evening early in the fall, George ran out of the house and all the way to the library, where he hadn't been in years. There were books all over, wherever he looked, and though he was struggling to control an invisible trembling, as well as an impulse to run home, he stayed and counted off a hundred.

THE HAPPIEST I'VE BEEN

BY JOHN UPDIKE (1959)

Neil Hovey came for me wearing a good suit. He parked his father's blue Chrysler on the dirt ramp by our barn and got out and stood by the open car door in a double-breasted tan gabardine suit, his hands in his pockets and his hair combed with water, squinting up at a lightning rod an old hurricane had knocked crooked. We were driving to Chicago, so I had packed my good clothes and dressed in worn-out slacks and an outgrown corduroy shirt. But Neil, though not my closest friend, was the one I had always been most relaxed with, so I wasn't very disturbed. My parents and I walked out from the house, across the low stretch of lawn that was mostly mud after the thaw that had come on Christmas Day, and my grandmother, though I had kissed her goodbye inside the house, came out onto the porch, stooped and rather angry-looking, her head haloed by wild old woman's white hair and the hand more severely afflicted by arthritis waggling at her breast in a worried way. It was growing dark, and my grandfather had gone to bed. "Nev-er trust the man who wears the red necktie and parts his hair in the middle" had been his final advice to me.

We had expected Neil since the middle of the afternoon. Nineteen almost twenty, I was a college sophomore home on vacation; that fall I had met in a fine-arts course a girl I had decided I loved, and she had invited me to the New Year's party her parents always gave and to stay at her house a few days. She lived in Chicago and so did Neil now, though he had gone to our high school. His father did something—sold steel was my impression, a huge man opening a briefcase and saying "The I-beams are very good this year"—that required him to be always on the move, so that at about thirteen Neil had been left with Mrs. Hovey's parents. They had lived in Olinger since the town was incorporated; indeed, old Jesse Lancaster, whose sick larynx whistled when he breathed to us boys his shocking and uproarious thoughts on the girls that walked by his porch all day long, had twice been burgess. Meanwhile Neil's father got a stationary job, in Chicago, but he let Neil stay in Olinger until he finished high school. From Chicago to this part of Pennsylvania was a drive of seventeen hours. In the twenty months Neil had been gone, he had come east fairly often; he loved driving, and Olinger was the one thing he had that was close to a childhood home. In Chicago he was working in a garage and getting his teeth straightened by the Army so they could draft him. The Korean War was on. He had to go back, and I wanted to go to Chicago, so it was a happy arrangement. "You're all dressed up," I accused him immediately.

"I've been saying goodbye."

The knot of his necktie was low and the corners of his mouth were rubbed with pink. Years later my mother recalled how that evening his breath stank so strongly of beer she was frightened to let me go with him. "*Your* grandfather always thought *his* grandfather was a very dubious character," she said.

My father and Neil put my suitcases into the trunk; they contained all the clothes I had brought with me from school, for the girl and I were going back to college on the train together, and I would not see my home again until spring.

"Well, goodbye, boys," my mother said. "I think you're both very brave." In regard to me she meant the girl as much as the roads.

"Don't you worry, Mrs. Nordholm," Neil told her quickly. "He'll be safer than in his own bed. I bet he sleeps from here to Indiana." He looked at me with an irritating imitation of her own fond gaze. When they shook hands goodbye it was with an equality established on the base of my helplessness. His being so slick startled me, but you can have a friend for years and never see how he operates with adults.

I embraced my mother and over her shoulder with the camera

of my head tried to take a snapshot I could keep of the house, the woods behind it and the sunset behind them, the bench beneath the walnut tree where my grandfather cut apples into skinless bits and fed them to himself, and the ruts the bakery truck had made in the soft lawn that morning.

We started down the half mile of dirt road to the highway that, one way, went through Olinger to the city of Alton and, the other way, led through farmland to the Turnpike. It was luxurious after the stress of farewell to finger a cigarette out of the pack squaring my shirt pocket. My family knew I smoked but I didn't do it in front of them; we were all too sensitive to bear the awkwardness. I lit mine and held the match for Hovey. It was a relaxed friendship. We were about the same height and had the same degree of athletic incompetence and the same curious lack of whatever force it was that aroused loyalty and compliance in beautiful girls. There was his bad teeth and my skin allergy; these were being remedied now, when they mattered less. But it seemed to me that the most important thing—about both our friendship and our failures to become, for all the love we felt for women, actual lovers—was that he and I lived with grandparents. This improved both our backward and forward vistas; we knew about the midnight coughing fits and bedside commodes that awaited most men, and we had a sense of childhoods before 1900, when the farmer ruled the land and America faced west. We had gained a humane dimension that made us gentle and humorous among peers but diffident at dances and hesitant in cars. Girls hate boys' doubts; they amount to insults. Gentleness is for married women to appreciate. (This is my thinking then.) A girl who has received out of nowhere a gift worth all Africa's ivory and Asia's gold wants more than just humanity to bestow it on.

When he came to the highway Neil turned right, toward Olinger, instead of left, toward the Turnpike. My reaction was to twist and assure myself through the rear window that, though a pink triangle of sandstone stared through the bare treetops, nobody at my house could possibly see.

When he was again in third gear, Neil asked, "Are you in a hurry?"

"No. Not especially."

"Schuman's having his New Year's party two days early so we can go. I thought we'd go for a couple hours and miss the Friday-night stuff on the Pike." His mouth moved and closed carefully over the dull, silver, painful braces.

"Sure," I said. "I don't care." In everything that followed there was this sensation of my being picked up and carried somewhere.

It was four miles from the farm to Olinger; we entered by Buchanan Road, driving past the tall white brick house I had lived in until I was fifteen. My grandfather had bought it before I was born and his stocks went bad, which had happened in the same year. The new owners had strung colored bulbs all along the front doorframe and the edges of the porch roof. Downtown the cardboard Santa Claus still nodded in the drugstore window, but the loudspeaker on the undertaker's lawn had stopped broadcasting carols. It was quite dark now, so the arches of red and green lights above Grand Avenue seemed miracles of lift; in daylight you saw the bulbs were just hung from a straight cable by cords of different lengths. Larry Schuman lived on the other side of town, the newer side. Lights ran all the way up the front edges of his house and across the rain gutter. The next-door neighbor had a plywood reindeer-and-sleigh floodlit on his front lawn and a snowman of papier-mâché leaning tipsily (his eyes were x's) against the corner of the house. No real snow had fallen yet that winter. The air this evening, though, hinted that harder weather was coming.

The Schumans' living room felt warm. In one corner a blue spruce drenched with tinsel reached to the ceiling; around its pot surged a drift of wrapping paper and ribbon and boxes, a few still containing presents—gloves and diaries and other small properties that hadn't yet been absorbed into the main stream of affluence. The ornamental balls were big as baseballs and all either crimson or indigo; the tree was so well dressed I felt self-conscious in the same room with it, without a coat or tie and wearing an old green shirt too short in the sleeves. Everyone else was dressed for a party. Then Mr. Schuman stamped in comfortingly, crushing us all into one underneath his welcome—Neil and me and the three other boys who had shown up so far. He was dressed to go out on the town, in a vanilla topcoat and silvery silk muffler, and smoking a cigar with the band still on. You could see, in Mr. Schuman, where

Larry got the red hair and pale eyelashes and the self-confidence, but what in the son was smirking and pushy was in the father shrewd and masterful. What the one used to make you nervous the other used to put you at ease. While Mr. was jollying us, Zoe Loessner, Larry's probable fiancée and the only girl at the party so far, was talking nicely to Mrs., nodding with her entire neck and fingering her Kresge pearls and blowing cigarette smoke through the corners of her mouth, to keep it away from the middle-aged woman's face. Each time Zoe spat out a plume, the shelf of blond hair overhanging her temple lifted slightly, so emphatic was her politeness. Mrs. Schuman beamed serenely above her fur coat and rhinestone pocketbook. It was odd to see her dressed in the trappings of the prosperity which usually supported her good nature invisibly, like a firm mattress under a homely bright quilt. She was a prime product of the country, a Pennsylvania Dutch woman, who loved feeding her sons, and imagined that the entire world, like her life, was going well. I never saw her not smile, except at her husband. At last she moved him into the outdoors. He turned at the threshold and did a trick with his knees and called in to us, "Be good and if you can't be good, be careful."

With them out of the way, the next item was getting liquor. It was a familiar business. Did anybody have a forged driver's license? If not, who would dare to make one? Larry could provide India ink. Then again, Larry's older brother Dale might be home and would go if it didn't take too much time. However, on weekends he often went straight from work to his fiancée's apartment and stayed until Sunday. If worst came to worst, Larry knew an illegal place in Alton, but they really soaked you. The problem was solved strangely. More people were arriving all the time, and one of them, Cookie Behn, who had been held back one year and hence was deposited in our grade, announced that last November he had become in honest fact twenty-one. I, at least, gave Cookie my share of the money feeling a little queasy, vice had become so handy.

The party was the party I had been going to all my life, beginning with Ann Mahlon's first Halloween party, that I attended as a hot, lumbering, breathless, and blind Donald Duck. My mother had made the costume, and the eyes kept slipping, and were farther apart than my eyes, so that even when the clouds of gauze parted, it was to reveal the frustrating depthless world seen with one eye. Ann, who because her mother loved her so much as a child had remained somewhat childish, and I and another boy and girl who were not involved in any romantic crisis went down into the Schumans' basement to play circular ping-pong. Armed with paddles, we stood each at a side of the table and when the ball was stroked ran around it counterclockwise, slapping the ball and laughing. To run better the girls took off their high-heeled shoes and ruined their stockings on the cement floor. Their faces and arms and shoulder sections became flushed, and when either of the girls lunged forward toward the net the stiff neckline of her semi-formal dress dropped away and the white cups of her brassière could be glimpsed holding in fat, and when one of them reached high her shaved armpit gleamed like a bit of chicken skin. An earring of Ann's flew off and the two connected rhinestones skidded to lie near the wall, among the Schumans' power mower and badminton poles and empty bronze motor-oil cans twice punctured by triangles. All these images were immediately lost in the whirl of our running; we were dizzy before we stopped. Ann leaned on me getting back into her shoes.

When we pushed the cellar door open it banged against the newel post of the carpeted stairs going to the second floor; a third of the way up, a couple sat discussing. The girl, Jacky Iselin, cried without emotion—the tears and nothing else, like water flowing over wood. Some people were in the kitchen, mixing drinks and making noise. In the living room others danced to records: 78s then—stiff discs stacked in a ponderous leaning cylinder on the spindle of the Schumans' console. Every three minutes, with a click and a crash, another dropped and the mood abruptly changed. One moment it would be "Stay As Sweet As You Are": Clarence Lang with the absolute expression of an idiot standing and rocking monotonously with June Kaufmann's boneless sad brown hand trapped in his and their faces, staring in the same direction, pasted together like the facets of an idol. The music stopped; when they parted, a big squarish dark patch stained the cheek of each. Then the next moment it would be Goodman's "Loch Lomond" or "Cherokee" and nobody but Margaret Lento wanted to jitterbug. Mad, she danced by herself, swinging her head recklessly and snapping her backside; a corner of her skirt flipped a Christmas ball onto the rug, where it collapsed into a hundred convex reflectors. Female shoes were scattered in innocent pairs about the room. Some were flats, resting under the sofa shyly toed in; others were high heels lying askew, the spike of one thrust into its mate. Sitting alone and ignored in a great armchair, I experienced within a warm keen dishevelment, as if there were real tears in my eyes. Had things been less unchanged, they would have seemed less tragic. But the girls who had stepped out of these shoes were, with few exceptions, the ones who had attended my life's party. The alterations were so small: a haircut, an engagement ring, a tendency toward plumpness more frankly confessed. While they wheeled above me I sometimes caught from their faces an unfamiliar glint, off of a hardness I did not remember, as if beneath their skins these girls were growing more dense. The brutality added to the features of the boys I knew seemed a more willed effect, more desired and so less grievous. Considering that there was a war, surprisingly many were present—4-F or at college or simply waiting to be called. Shortly before midnight the door rattled, and there, under the porch light, looking forlorn and chilled in their brief athletic jackets, stood three members of the class ahead of ours who in the old days always tried to crash Schuman's parties. At Olinger High they had been sports stars, and they still stood with that well-coördinated looseness, a look of dangling from strings. The three of them had enrolled together at Melanchthon, a small Lutheran college on the edge of Alton, and in this season played on the Melanchthon basketball team. That is, two did; the third hadn't been good enough. Schuman, out of cowardice more than mercy, let them in, and they hid immediately in the basement, and didn't bother us, having brought their own bottle.

There was one novel awkwardness. Darryl Bechtel had married Emmy Johnson, and the couple came. Darryl had worked in his father's greenhouse and had been considered dull; it was Emmy that we knew. At first no one danced with her, and Darryl didn't know how, but then Schuman, perhaps as host, dared. Others followed, but Schuman had her in his arms most often, and at midnight, when we were pretending the new year began, he kissed her; a wave of kissing swept the room now, and everyone struggled to kiss Emmy. Even I did. There was something about her being married that made it extraordinary. Her cheeks burning, she kept glancing around for rescue, but Darryl, embarrassed to see his wife dance, had gone into old man Schuman's den, where Neil sat brooding, sunk in mysterious sorrow.

When the kissing subsided and Darryl emerged, I went in to see Neil. He was holding his face in his hands and tapping his foot to a record playing on Mr. Schuman's private phonograph: Krupa's "Dark Eyes." The arrangement was droning and circular and Neil had kept the record going for hours. He loved saxophones; most of us children of that depression vintage did. I asked him, "Do you think the traffic on the Turnpike has died down by now?"

He took down the tall glass on the cabinet beside him and took a studied swallow. From the side, his face seemed lean and somewhat blue. "Maybe," he said, staring at the ice cubes submerged in the ochre liquid. "The girl in Chicago's expecting you?"

"Well, yeah, but we can call and let her know, once *we* know."

"You think she'll spoil?"

"How do you mean?"

"I mean, won't you be seeing her all the time after we get there? Aren't you going to marry her?"

"I have no idea. I might."

"Well then you'll have the rest of Kingdom Come to see her." He looked directly at me, and it was plain in the blur of his eyes that he was sick-drunk. "The trouble with you guys that have all the luck," he said slowly, "is that you don't give a damn about us that don't have any." Such melodramatic rudeness, coming from Neil, surprised me, as had his blarney with my mother hours before. In trying to evade his steady, wounded stare, I discovered there was another person in the room: a girl sitting with her shoes on, reading *Holiday*. Though she held the magazine in front of her face, I knew from the gaudy air of her clothes and from her unfamiliar legs that she was the girl friend Margaret Lento had brought.

Margaret didn't come from Olinger but from Riverside, a section of Alton. She had met Larry Schuman at a summer job in a restaurant, and for the rest of high school they had more or less gone together. Since then, though, it had dawned on Mr. and Mrs. Schuman that even in a democracy distinctions exist: probably welcome news to Larry. In the cruelest and most prolonged way he could manage, he had been breaking off with her throughout the year now nearly ended. I had been surprised to find her at this party. Obviously she had felt shaky about attending and had brought the friend as the only kind of protection she could afford. The other girl was acting just like a guard.

There being no answer to Neil, I went into the living room, where Margaret, insanely drunk, was throwing herself around as if wanting to break a bone. Somewhat in time to the music she would run a few steps, then snap her body like a whip, her chin striking her chest and her hands flying backward, fingers fanned, as her shoulders pitched forward. In her state her body was childishly plastic; unharmed, she would bounce back from this jolt and begin to clap and kick and hum. Schuman stayed away from her. Margaret was small, not more than five three, with the smallness ripeness comes to early. She had bleached a section of her black hair platinum, cropped her head all over, and trained the stubble into short hyacinthine curls like those on antique statues of boys. Her face seemed quite coarse from the front, so her profile was classical unexpectedly. She might have been Portia. When she was not putting on her savage, pointless dance, she was in the bathroom being sick. The pity and the vulgarity of her exhibition made everyone who was sober uncomfortable; our common guilt in witnessing this girl's rites brought us so close together in that room that it seemed never, not in all time, could we be parted. I myself was perfectly sober. I had the impression people only drank to stop being unhappy and I nearly always felt at least fairly happy.

Luckily, Margaret was in a sick phase around one o'clock, when the elder Schumans came home. They looked in at us briefly. It was a pleasant joke to see in their smiles that, however corrupt and unwinking we felt, to them we looked young and sleepy: Larry's friends. Things quieted after they went up the stairs. In half an hour, people began coming out of the kitchen balancing cups of coffee. By two o'clock, four girls stood in aprons at Mrs. Schuman's sink, and others were padding back and forth carrying glasses and ashtrays. Another blameless racket pierced the clatter in the kitchen. Out on the cold grass the three Melanchthon athletes had set up the badminton net and in the faint glow given off by the house were playing. The bird, ascending and descending through uneven bars of light, glimmered like a firefly. Now that the party was dying, Neil's apathy seemed deliberately exasperating, even vindictive. For at least another hour, he persisted in hearing "Dark Eyes" over and over again, holding his head and tapping his foot. The entire scene in the den had developed a fixity that was uncanny; the girl remained in the chair and read magazines, *Holiday* and *Esquire*, one after another. In the meantime, cars came and went and raced their motors out front; Schuman took Ann Mahlon home and didn't come back; and the athletes carried the neighbor's artificial snowman into the center of the street and disappeared. Somehow in the arrangements shuffled together at the end, Neil had agreed to take Margaret and the other girl home. Margaret convalesced in the downstairs bathroom for most of that hour. I unlocked a little glass bookcase ornamenting a desk in the dark dining room and removed a volume of Thackeray's Works. It turned out to be Volume II of "Henry Esmond." I began it, rather than break another book out of the set, which had been squeezed in there so long the bindings had sort of interpenetrated.

Esmond was going off to war again when Neil appeared in the archway and said, "O.K., Norseman. Let's go to Chicago." "Norseman" was a variant of my name he used only when he was feeling special affection.

We turned off all the lamps and left the hall bulb burning against Larry's return. Margaret Lento seemed chastened. Neil gave her his arm and helped her into the back seat of his father's car; I stood aside to let the other girl get in with her, but Neil indicated that I should. I supposed he realized this left only the mute den-girl to go up front with him. She sat well over on her side, was all I noticed. Neil backed into the street and with unusual care steered past the snowman. Our headlights made vivid the fact that the snowman's back was a hollow right-angled gash; he had been built up against the corner of the house.

From Olinger, Riverside was diagonally across Alton. The city was sleeping as we drove through it. Most of the stop lights were blinking green. Among cities Alton had a bad reputation; its graft and gambling and easy juries and bawdyhouses were supposedly notorious throughout the Middle Atlantic states. But to me it always presented an innocent face: row after row of houses built of a local dusty-red brick, the color of flowerpots, each house fortified with a tiny, intimate, balustraded porch, and nothing but the wealth of movie houses and beer signs along its main street to suggest that its citizens loved pleasure more than the run of mankind. Indeed, as we moved at moderate speed down these hushed streets bordered with parked cars, a limestone church bulking at every corner and the hooded street lamps keeping watch from above, Alton seemed less the ultimate center of an urban region than itself a suburb of some vast mythical metropolis, like Pandemonium or Paradise. I was conscious of evergreen wreaths on door after door and of fanlights of stained glass in which the house number was embedded. I was also conscious that every block was one block farther from the Turnpike.

Riverside, fitted into the bends of the Schuylkill, was not so regularly laid out. Margaret's house was one of a short row, composition-shingled, which we approached from the rear, down a tiny cement alley speckled with drains. The porches were a few inches higher than the narrow pavement. Margaret asked us if we wanted to come in for a cup of coffee, since we were going to Chicago; Neil accepted by getting out of the car and slamming his door. The noise filled the alley, alarming me. I wondered at the easy social life that evidently existed among my friends at three-thirty in the morning. Margaret did, however, lead us in stealthily, and she turned on only the kitchen switch. The kitchen was divided from the living room by a large sofa, which faced into littered gloom where distant light from beyond the alley spilled over a window sill and across the spines of a radiator. In one corner the glass of a television set showed; the screen would seem absurdly small now, but then it seemed disproportionately elegant. The shabbiness everywhere would not have struck me so much if I hadn't just come from Schuman's place. Neil and the other girl sat on the sofa; Margaret held a match to a gas burner and, as the blue flame licked an old kettle, doled instant coffee into four flowered cups.

By the kitchen's solitary window, overlooking a drab Alton street, someone who had once lived in this house had built a breakfast nook like a luncheonette booth, a yellow table between two high-backed benches. I sat in it and read all the words I could see: "Salt," "Pepper," "Have Some LUMPS," "December," "Mohn's Milk Inc.—A Very Merry Christmas and Joyous New Year—Mohn's Milk is *Safe* Milk—'Mommy, Make It Mohn's!,'" "Matches," "Hotpoint,"

"PRESS," "Magee Stove FEDERAL & Furnace Corp.," "God Is in This House," "Ave Maria Gratia Plena," "SHREDDED WHEAT Benefits—Exciting New Pattern KUNGSHOLM." After serving the two on the sofa, Margaret came to me with coffee and sat down opposite me in the booth. Fatigue had raised two blue welts beneath her eyes.

"Well," I asked her, "did you have a good time?"

She smiled and glanced down and made the small sound "Ch," vestigial of "Jesus." With absent-minded delicacy she stirred her coffee, lifting and replacing the spoon without a ripple.

"Rather odd at the end," I said. "Not even the host there."

"He took Ann Mahlon home."

"I know." I was surprised that she did, having been sick in the bathroom for that hour.

"You sound jealous," she added.

"Who does? I do? I don't."

"You like her, John, don't you?" Her using my first name and the quality of the question did not, though we had really—not counting parties—just met, seem forward, considering the hour and that she had brought me coffee. There is little further to go with a girl who has brought you coffee.

"Oh, I like everybody," I told her, "and the longer I've known them the more I like them, because the more they're me. The only people I like better are ones I've just met. Now Ann Mahlon I've known since kindergarten. Every day her mother used to bring her to the edge of the schoolyard for months after all the other mothers had stopped." I wanted to cut a figure in Margaret's eyes, but they were too dark. Stoically she had got on top of her weariness, but it was growing bigger under her.

"Did you like her then?"

"I felt sorry for her being embarrassed by her mother."

She asked me, "What was Larry like when he was little?"

"Oh, bright. Kind of mean."

"Was he mean?"

"I'd say so. Yes. In some grade or other he and I began to play chess together. I always won until secretly he took lessons from a man his parents knew and read strategy books."

Margaret laughed, genuinely pleased. "Then did he win?"

"Once. After that I really tried, and after *that* he decided chess was kid stuff. Besides, he'd used me up. He'd have these runs on people where you'd be down at his house every afternoon, then in a couple months he'd get a new pet and that'd be that."

"He's funny," she said. "He has a kind of cold mind. He decides on what he wants, then he does what he has to do, you know, and nothing anybody says can change him."

"He does tend to get what he wants," I told her guardedly, realizing that to her this meant her. Poor bruised little girl, in her mind he was all the time cleaving with rare cunning through his parents' objections straight to her.

My coffee was nearly gone, so I glanced toward the sofa in the other room. Neil and the girl had sunk out of sight behind its back. Before this it had honestly not occurred to me that they had a relationship, but now that I saw, it seemed plausible, and, at this time of night, good news, though it meant we would not be going to Chicago quite yet.

So I talked to Margaret about Larry, and she responded, showing really quite an acute sense of him. To me, considering the personality of a childhood friend so seriously, as if overnight he had become a factor in the world, seemed absurd; I couldn't even deeply believe that in her world he mattered much. Larry Schuman, in little more than a year, had become nothing to me. The important thing, rather than the subject, was the conversation itself, the quick agreements, the slow nods, the weave of different memories; it was like one of those Panama baskets shaped underwater around a worthless stone.

She offered me more coffee. When she returned with it, she sat down not opposite but beside me, lifting me to such a pitch of gratitude and affection that the only way I could think to express it was by *not* kissing her, as if a kiss were another piece of abuse women suffered. She said, "Cold. Cheap bastard turns the thermostat down to sixty," meaning her father. She drew my arm around her shoulders and folded my hand about her bare forearm, to warm it. The back of my thumb fitted against the curve of one breast. Her head went into the hollow where my arm and chest joined; she was terribly small, measured against your own body. Perhaps she weighed a hundred pounds. Her lids lowered and I kissed her two beautiful eyebrows and then the spaces of skin between the rough curls, some black and some bleached, that fringed her forehead. Other than this

I tried to keep as still as a bed would be. It *had* grown cold. A shiver starting on the side away from her would twitch my shoulders when I tried to repress it; she would frown and unconsciously draw my arm tighter. No one had switched the kitchen light off. On Margaret's foreshortened upper lip there seemed to be two pencil marks; the length of wrist my badly fitting sleeve exposed looked pale and naked against the spiralling down of the smaller arm held beneath it.

Outside on the street the house faced there was no motion. Only once did a car go by—around five o'clock, with twin mufflers, the radio on, and a boy yelling. Neil and the girl murmured together incessantly; some of what they said I could overhear.

"No. Which?" she asked.

"I don't care."

"Wouldn't you want a boy?"

"I'd be happy whatever I got."

"I know, but which would you *rather* have? Don't men want boys?"

"I don't care. You."

Somewhat later, Mohn's truck passed on the other side of the street. The milkman, well bundled, sat behind headlights in a warm orange volume the size of a phone booth, steering one-handed and smoking a cigar that he set on the edge of the dashboard when, his wire carrier vibrant, he ran out of the truck with bottles. His passing led Neil to decide the time had come. Margaret woke up frightened of her father; we hissed our farewells and thanks to her quickly. Neil dropped the other girl off at her house a few blocks away; he knew where it was. Sometime during that night I must have seen this girl's face, but I have no memory of it. She is always behind a magazine or in the dark or with her back turned. Neil married her years later, I know, but after we arrived in Chicago I never saw him again, either.

Red dawn light touched the clouds above the black slate roofs as, with a few other cars, we drove through Alton. The moon-sized clock of a beer billboard said ten after six. Olinger was deathly still. The air brightened as we moved along the highway; the glowing wall of my home hung above the woods as we rounded the long curve by the Mennonite dairy. With a .22 I could have had a pane of my parents' bedroom window, and they were dreaming I was in Indiana. My grandfather would be up, stamping around in the kitchen for my grandmother to make him breakfast, or outside walking to see if any ice had formed on the brook. For an instant I genuinely feared he might hail me from the peak of the barn roof. Then trees interceded and we were safe in a landscape where no one cared.

At the entrance to the Turnpike Neil did a strange thing; he stopped the car and had me take the wheel. He had never trusted me to drive his father's car before; he had believed my not knowing where the crankshaft or fuel pump was handicapped my competence to steer. But now he was quite complacent. He hunched under an old mackinaw and leaned his head against the metal of the window frame and soon was asleep. We crossed the Susquehanna on a long smooth bridge below Harrisburg, then began climbing toward the Alleghenies. In the mountains there was snow, a dry dusting like sand that waved back and forth on the road surface. Farther along, there had been a fresh fall that night, about two inches, and the plows had not yet cleared all the lanes. I was passing a Sunoco truck on a high curve when without warning the scraped section gave out and I realized I might skid into the fence, if not over the edge. The radio was singing "Carpets of clover, I'll lay right at your feet," and the speedometer said 81. Nothing happened; the car stayed firm in the snow, and Neil slept through the danger, his face turned skyward and his breath struggling in his nose. It was the first time I heard a contemporary of mine snore.

When we came into tunnel country, the flicker and hollow amplification stirred Neil awake. He sat up, the mackinaw dropping to his lap, and lit a cigarette. A second after the scratch of his match the moment occurred of which each following moment was a slight diminution, as we made the long irregular descent toward Pittsburgh. There were many reasons for my feeling so happy. We were on our way. I had seen a dawn. This far, Neil could appreciate, I had brought us safely. Ahead, a girl waited who, if I asked, would marry me, but first there was a long trip; many hours and towns interceded between me and that encounter. There was the quality of the 10 A.M. sunlight as it existed in the air ahead of the windshield, filtered by the thin overcast, blessing irresponsibility—you felt you could slice forever through such a cool pure element—and springing, by implying how high these hills had become, a widespreading pride: Pennsylvania, your state—as if you had made your life. And there was knowing that twice since midnight a person had trusted me enough to fall asleep beside me.

DEFENDER OF THE FAITH

BY PHILIP ROTH (1959)

In May of 1945, only a few weeks after the fighting had ended in Europe, I was rotated back to the States, where I spent the remainder of the war with a training company at Camp Crowder, Missouri. Along with the rest of the Ninth Army, I had been racing across Germany so swiftly during the late winter and spring that when I boarded the plane, I couldn't believe its destination lay to the west. My mind might inform me otherwise, but there was an inertia of the spirit that told me we were flying to a new front, where we would disembark and continue our push eastward—eastward until we'd circled the globe, marching through villages along whose twisting, cobbled streets crowds of the enemy would watch us take possession of what, up till then, they'd considered their own. I had changed enough in two years not to mind the trembling of the old people, the crying of the very young, the uncertainty and fear in the eyes of the once arrogant. I had been fortunate enough to develop an infantryman's heart, which, like his feet, at first aches and swells but finally grows horny enough for him to travel the weirdest paths without feeling a thing.

Captain Paul Barrett was my C.O. in Camp Crowder. The day I reported for duty, he came out of his office to shake my hand. He was short, gruff, and fiery, and—indoors or out—he wore his polished helmet liner pulled down to his little eyes. In Europe, he had received a battlefield commission and a serious chest wound, and he'd been returned to the States only a few months before. He spoke easily to me, and at the evening formation he introduced me to the troops. "Gentlemen," he said, "Sergeant Thurston, as you know, is no longer with this company. Your new first sergeant is Sergeant Nathan Marx, here. He is a veteran of the European theatre, and consequently will expect to find a company of soldiers here, and not a company of boys."

I sat up late in the orderly room that evening, trying halfheartedly to solve the riddle of duty rosters, personnel forms, and morning reports. The Charge of Quarters slept with his mouth open on a mattress on the floor. A trainee stood reading the next day's duty roster, which was posted on the bulletin board just inside the screen door. It was a warm evening, and I could hear radios playing dance music over in the barracks. The trainee, who had been staring at me whenever he thought I wouldn't notice, finally took a step in my direction.

"Hey, Sarge—we having a G.I. party tomorrow night?" he asked. A G.I. party is a barracks cleaning.

"You usually have them on Friday nights?" I asked him.

"Yes," he said, and then he added, mysteriously, "That's the whole thing."

"Then you'll have a G.I. party."

He turned away, and I heard him mumbling. His shoulders were moving, and I wondered if he was crying.

"What's your name, soldier?" I asked.

He turned, not crying at all. Instead, his green-speckled eyes, long and narrow, flashed like fish in the sun He walked over to me and sat on the edge of my desk. He reached out a hand. "Sheldon," he said.

"Stand on your feet, Sheldon."

Getting off the desk, he said, "Sheldon Grossbart." He smiled at the familiarity into which he'd led me.

"You against cleaning the barracks Friday night, Grossbart?" I said. "Maybe we shouldn't have G.I. parties. Maybe we should get a maid." My tone startled me. I felt I sounded like every top sergeant I had ever known.

"No, Sergeant." He grew serious, but with a seriousness that seemed to be only the stifling of a smile. "It's just—G.I. parties on Friday night, of all nights."

He slipped up onto the corner of the desk again—not quite sitting, but not quite standing, either. He looked at me with those speckled eyes flashing, and then made a gesture with his hand. It was very slight—no more than a movement back and forth of the wrist—and yet it managed to exclude from our affairs everything else in the orderly room, to make the two of us the center of the world. It seemed, in fact, to exclude everything even about the two of us except our hearts.

"Sergeant Thurston was one thing," he whispered, glancing at the sleeping C.Q., "but we thought that with you here things might be a little different."

"We?"

"The Jewish personnel."

"Why?" I asked, harshly. "What's on your mind?" Whether I was still angry at the "Sheldon" business, or now at something else, I hadn't time to tell, but clearly I was angry.

"We thought you—Marx, you know, like Karl Marx. The Marx Brothers. Those guys are all—M-a-r-x. Isn't that how *you* spell it, Sergeant?"

"M-a-r-x."

"Fishbein said—" He stopped. "What I mean to say, Sergeant—" His face and neck were red, and his mouth moved but no words came out. In a moment, he raised himself to attention, gazing down at me. It was as though he had suddenly decided he could expect no more sympathy from me than from Thurston, the reason being that I was of Thurston's faith, and not his. The young man had managed to confuse himself as to what my faith really was, but I felt no desire to straighten him out. Very simply, I didn't like him.

When I did nothing but return his gaze, he spoke, in an altered tone. "You see, Sergeant," he explained to me, "Friday nights, Jews are supposed to go to services."

"Did Sergeant Thurston tell you you couldn't go to them when there was a G.I. party?"

"No."

"Did he say you had to stay and scrub the floors?"

"No, Sergeant."

"Did the Captain say you had to stay and scrub the floors?"

"That isn't it, Sergeant. It's the other guys in the barracks." He leaned toward me. "They think we're goofing off. But we're not. That's when Jews go to services, Friday night. We have to."

"Then go."

"But the other guys make accusations. They have no right."

"That's not the Army's problem, Grossbart. It's a personal problem you'll have to work out yourself."

"But it's un*fair*."

I got up to leave. "There's nothing I can do about it," I said.

Grossbart stiffened and stood in front of me. "But this is a matter of *religion*, sir."

"Sergeant," I said.

"I mean 'Sergeant,'" he said, almost snarling.

"Look, go see the chaplain. You want to see Captain Barrett, I'll arrange an appointment."

"No, no, I don't want to make trouble, Sergeant. That's the first thing they throw up to you. I just want my rights!"

"Damn it, Grossbart, stop whining. You have your rights. You can stay and scrub floors or you can go to shul—"

The smile swam in again. Spittle gleamed at the corners of his mouth. "You mean church, Sergeant."

"I mean shul, Grossbart!"

I walked past him and went outside. Near me, I heard the scrunching of a guard's boots on gravel. Beyond the lighted windows of the barracks, young men in T-shirts and fatigue pants were sitting on their bunks, polishing their rifles. Suddenly there was a light rustling behind me. I turned and saw Grossbart's dark frame fleeing back to the barracks, racing to tell his Jewish friends that they were right—that, like Karl and Harpo, I was one of them.

The next morning, while chatting with Captain Barrett, I recounted the incident of the previous evening. Somehow, in the telling, it must have seemed to the Captain that I was not so much explaining Grossbart's position as defending it. "Marx, I'd fight side by side with a nigger if the fella proved to me he was a man. I pride myself," he said, looking out the window, "that I've got an open mind. Consequently, Sergeant, nobody gets special treatment here, for the good *or* the bad. All a man's got to do is prove himself. A man fires well on the range, I give him a weekend pass. He scores high in P.T., he gets a weekend pass. He *earns* it." He turned from the window and pointed a finger at me. "You're a Jewish fella, am I right, Marx?"

"Yes, sir."

"And I admire you. I admire you because of the ribbons on your chest. I judge a man by what he shows me on the field of battle, Sergeant. It's what he's got *here*," he said, and then, though I expected he would point to his heart, he jerked a thumb toward the buttons straining to hold his blouse across his belly. "Guts," he said.

"O.K., sir. I only wanted to pass on to you how the men felt."

"Mr. Marx, you're going to be old before your time if you worry about how the men feel. Leave that stuff to the chaplain—that's his business, not yours. Let's us train these fellas to shoot straight. If the Jewish personnel feels the other men are accusing them of goldbricking—well, I just don't know. Seems awful funny that suddenly the Lord is calling so loud in Private Grossman's ear he's just got to run to church."

"Synagogue," I said.

"Synagogue is right, Sergeant. I'll write that down for handy reference. Thank you for stopping by."

That evening, a few minutes before the company gathered outside the orderly room for the chow formation, I called the C.Q., Corporal Robert LaHill, in to see me. LaHill was a dark, burly fellow whose hair curled out of his clothes wherever it could. He had a glaze in his eyes that made one think of caves and dinosaurs. "LaHill," I said, "when you take the formation, remind the men that they're free to attend church services *whenever* they are held, provided they report to the orderly room before they leave the area."

LaHill scratched his wrist, but gave no indication that he'd heard or understood.

"LaHill," I said, "*church*. You remember? Church, priest, Mass, confession."

He curled one lip into a kind of smile; I took it for a signal that for a second he had flickered back up into the human race.

"Jewish personnel who want to attend services this evening are to fall out in front of the orderly room at 1900," I said. Then, as an afterthought, I added, "By order of Captain Barrett."

A little while later, as the day's last light—softer than any I had seen that year—began to drop over Camp Crowder, I heard LaHill's thick, inflectionless voice outside my window: "Give me your ears, troopers. Toppie says for me to tell you that at 1900 hours all Jewish personnel is to fall out in front, here, if they want to attend the Jewish Mass."

At seven o'clock, I looked out the orderly-room window and saw three soldiers in starched khakis standing on the dusty quadrangle. They looked at their watches and fidgeted while they whispered back and forth. It was getting dimmer, and, alone on the otherwise deserted field, they looked tiny. When I opened the door, I heard the noises of the G.I. party coming from the surrounding barracks—bunks being pushed to the walls, faucets pounding water into buckets, brooms whisking at the wooden floors, cleaning the dirt away for Saturday's inspection. Big puffs of cloth moved round and round on the windowpanes. I walked outside, and the moment my foot hit the ground I thought I heard Grossbart call to the others, "'Ten-*hut!*" Or maybe, when they all three jumped to attention, I imagined I heard the command.

Grossbart stepped forward. "Thank you, sir," he said.

"'Sergeant,' Grossbart," I reminded him. "You call officers 'sir.' I'm not an officer. You've been in the Army three weeks—you know that."

He turned his palms out at his sides to indicate that, in truth, he and I lived beyond convention. "Thank you, anyway," he said.

"Yes," a tall boy behind him said. "Thanks a lot."

And the third boy whispered, "Thank you," but his mouth barely fluttered, so that he did not alter by more than a lip's movement his posture of attention.

"For what?" I asked. Grossbart snorted happily. "For the announcement. The Corporal's announcement. It helped. It made it—"

"Fancier." The tall boy finished Grossbart's sentence.

Grossbart smiled. "He means formal, sir. Public," he said to me.

"Now it won't seem as though we're just taking off—goldbricking because the work has begun."

"It was by order of Captain Barrett," I said.

"Aaah, but you pull a little weight," Grossbart said. "So we thank you." Then he turned to his companions. "Sergeant Marx, I want you to meet Larry Fishbein." The tall boy stepped forward and extended his hand. I shook it. "You from New York?" he asked.

"Yes."

"Me, too." He had a cadaverous face that collapsed inward from his cheekbone to his jaw, and when he smiled—as he did at the news of our communal attachment—revealed a mouthful of bad teeth. He was blinking his eyes a good deal, as though he were fighting back tears. "What borough?" he asked.

I turned to Grossbart. "It's five after seven. What time are services?"

"Shul," he said, smiling, "is in ten minutes. I want you to meet Mickey Halpern. This is Nathan Marx, our sergeant."

The third boy hopped forward. "Private Michael Halpern." He saluted.

"Salute officers, Halpern," I said. The boy dropped his hand, and, on its way down, in his nervousness, checked to see if his shirt pockets were buttoned.

"Shall I march them over, sir?" Grossbart asked. "Or are you coming along?"

From behind Grossbart, Fishbein piped up. "Afterward, they're having refreshments. A ladies' auxiliary from St. Louis, the rabbi told us last week."

"The chaplain," Halpern whispered.

"You're welcome to come along," Grossbart said.

To avoid his plea, I looked away, and saw, in the windows of the barracks, a cloud of faces staring out at the four of us. "Hurry along, Grossbart," I said.

"O.K., then," he said. He turned to the others. "Double time, *march!*"

They started off, but ten feet away Grossbart spun around and, running backward, called to me, "Good *shabbus*, sir!" And then the three of them were swallowed into the alien Missouri dusk.

Even after they had disappeared over the parade ground, whose green was now a deep blue, I could hear Grossbart singing the double-time cadence, and as it grew dimmer and dimmer, it suddenly touched a deep memory—as did the slant of the light—and I was remembering the shrill sounds of a Bronx playground where, years ago, beside the Grand Concourse, I had played on long spring evenings such as this. It was a pleasant memory for a young man so far from peace and home, and it brought so many recollections with it that I began to grow exceedingly tender about myself. In fact, I indulged myself in a reverie so strong that I felt as though a hand were reaching down inside me. It had to reach so very far to touch me! It had to reach past those days in the forests of Belgium, and past the dying I'd refused to weep over; past the nights in German farmhouses whose books we'd burned to warm us; past endless stretches when I had shut off all softness I might feel for my fellows, and had managed even to deny myself the posture of a conqueror—the swagger that I, as a Jew, might well have worn as my boots whacked against the rubble of Wesel, Münster, and Braunschweig.

But now one night noise, one rumor of home and time past, and memory plunged down through all I had anesthetized, and came to what I suddenly remembered was myself. So it was not altogether curious that, in search of more of me, I found myself following Grossbart's tracks to Chapel No. 3, where the Jewish services were being held.

I took a seat in the last row, which was empty. Two rows in front of me sat Grossbart, Fishbein, and Halpern, holding little white Dixie cups. Each row of seats was raised higher than the one in front of it, and I could see clearly what was going on. Fishbein was pouring the contents of his cup into Grossbart's, and Grossbart looked mirthful as the liquid made a purple arc between Fishbein's hand and his. In the glaring yellow light, I saw the chaplain standing on the platform at the front; he was chanting the first line of the responsive reading. Grossbart's prayer book remained closed on his lap; he was swishing the cup around. Only Halpern responded to the chant by praying. The fingers of his right hand were spread wide across the cover of his open book. His cap was pulled down low onto his brow, which made it round, like a yarmulke. From time to time, Grossbart wet his lips at the cup's edge; Fishbein, his long yellow face a dying light bulb, looked from here to there, craning forward to catch sight of the faces down the row, then of those in front of him, then behind. He saw me, and his eyelids beat a tattoo. His elbow slid into Grossbart's side, his neck inclined toward his friend, he whispered something, and then, when the congregation next responded to the chant, Grossbart's voice was among the others. Fishbein looked into his book now, too; his lips, however, didn't move.

Finally, it was time to drink the wine. The chaplain smiled down at them as Grossbart swigged his in one long gulp, Halpern sipped, meditating, and Fishbein faked devotion with an empty cup. "As I look down amongst the congregation"—the chaplain grinned at the word—"this night, I see many new faces, and I want to welcome you to Friday-night services here at Camp Crowder. I am Major Leo Ben Ezra, your chaplain." Though an American, the chaplain spoke deliberately—syllable by syllable, almost—as though to communicate, above all, with the lip readers in his audience. "I have only a few words to say before we adjourn to the refreshment room, where the kind ladies of the Temple Sinai, St. Louis, Missouri, have a nice setting for you."

Applause and whistling broke out. After another momentary grin, the chaplain raised his hands, palms out, his eyes flicking upward a moment, as if to remind the troops where they were and Who Else might be in attendance. In the sudden silence that followed, I thought I heard Grossbart cackle, "Let the goyim clean the floors!" Were those the words? I wasn't sure, but Fishbein, grinning, nudged Halpern. Halpern looked dumbly at him, then went back to his prayer book, which had been occupying him all through the rabbi's talk. One hand tugged at the black kinky hair that stuck out under his cap. His lips moved.

The rabbi continued. "It is about the food that I want to speak to you for a moment. I know, I know, I know," he intoned, wearily, "how in the mouths of most of you the *trafe* food tastes like ashes. I know how you gag, some of you, and how your parents suffer to think of their children eating foods unclean and offensive to the palate. What can I tell you? I can only say, close your eyes and swallow as best you can. Eat what you must to live, and throw away the rest. I wish I could help more. For those of you who find this impossible, may I ask that you try and try, but then come to see me in private. If your revulsion is so great, we will have to seek aid from those higher up."

A round of chatter rose and subsided. Then everyone sang "Ain Kelohainu;" after all those years, I discovered, I still knew the words. Then, suddenly, the service over, Grossbart was upon me. "Higher up? He means the General?"

"Hey, Shelly," Fishbein said, "he means God." He smacked his face and looked at Halpern. "How high can you go!"

"Sh-h-h!" Grossbart said. "What do you think, Sergeant?"

"I don't know," I said. "You better ask the chaplain."

"I'm going to. I'm making an appointment to see him in private. So is Mickey."

Halpern shook his head. "No, no, Sheldon—"

"You have rights, Mickey," Grossbart said. "They can't push us around."

"It's O.K.," said Halpern. "It bothers my mother, not me."

Grossbart looked at me. "Yesterday he threw up. From the hash. It was all ham and God knows what else."

"I have a cold—that was why," Halpern said. He pushed his yarmulke back into a cap.

"What about you, Fishbein?" I asked. "You kosher, too?"

He flushed. "A little. But I'll let it ride. I have a very strong stomach, and I don't eat a lot anyway." I continued to look at him, and he held up his wrist to reinforce what he'd just said; his watch strap was tightened to the last hole, and he pointed that out to me.

"But services are important to you?" I asked him.

He looked at Grossbart. "Sure, sir."

"'Sergeant.'"

"Not so much at home," said Grossbart, stepping between us, "but away from home it gives one a sense of his Jewishness."

"We have to stick together," Fishbein said.

I started to walk toward the door; Halpern stepped back to make way for me.

"That's what happened in Germany," Grossbart was saying, loud enough for me to hear. "They didn't stick together. They let themselves get pushed around."

I turned. "Look, Grossbart. This is the Army, not summer camp."

He smiled. "So?"

Halpern tried to sneak off, but Grossbart held his arm.

"Grossbart, how old are you?" I asked.

"Nineteen."

"And you?" I said to Fishbein.

"The same. The same month, even."

"And what about him?" I pointed to Halpern, who had by now made it safely to the door.

"Eighteen," Grossbart whispered. "But like he can't tie his shoes or brush his teeth himself. I feel sorry for him."

"I feel sorry for all of us, Grossbart," I said, "but just act like a man. Just don't overdo it."

"Overdo what, sir?"

"The 'sir' business, for one thing. Don't overdo that," I said.

I left him standing there. I passed by Halpern, but he did not look at me. Then I was outside, but, behind, I heard Grossbart call, "Hey, Mickey, my *leben*, come on back. Refreshments!"

"*Leben!*" My grandmother's word for me!

One morning a week later, while I was working at my desk, Captain Barrett shouted for me to come into his office. When I entered, he had his helmet liner squashed down so far on his head that I couldn't even see his eyes. He was on the phone, and when he spoke to me, he cupped one hand over the mouthpiece. "Who the hell is Grossbart?"

"Third platoon, Captain," I said. "A trainee."

"What's all this stink about food? His mother called a goddam congressman about the food." He uncovered the mouthpiece and slid his helmet up until I could see his bottom eyelashes. "Yes, sir," he said into the phone. "Yes, sir. I'm still here, sir. I'm asking Marx, here, right now—"

He covered the mouthpiece again and turned his head back toward me. "Lightfoot Harry's on the phone," he said, between his teeth. "This congressman calls General Lyman, who calls Colonel Sousa, who calls the Major, who calls me. They're just dying to stick this thing on me. Whatsa matter?" He shook the phone at me. "I don't feed the troops? What the hell is this?"

"Sir, Grossbart is strange—" Barrett greeted that with a mockingly indulgent smile. I altered my approach. "Captain, he's a very orthodox Jew, and so he's only allowed to eat certain foods."

"He throws up, the congressman said. Every time he eats something, his mother says, he throws up!"

"He's accustomed to observing the dietary laws, Captain."

"So why's his old lady have to call the White House?"

"Jewish parents, sir—they're apt to be more protective than you expect. I mean, Jews have a very close family life. A boy goes away from home, sometimes the mother is liable to get very upset. Probably the boy mentioned something in a letter, and his mother misinterpreted."

"I'd like to punch him one right in the mouth," the Captain said. "There's a goddam war on, and he wants a silver platter!"

"I don't think the boy's to blame, sir. I'm sure we can straighten it out by just asking him. Jewish parents worry—"

"*All* parents worry, for Christ's sake. But they don't get on their high horse and start pulling strings—"

I interrupted, my voice higher, tighter than before. "The home life, Captain, is very important—but you're right, it may sometimes get out of hand. It's a very wonderful thing, Captain, but because it's so close, this kind of thing . . ."

He didn't listen any longer to my attempt to present both myself and Lightfoot Harry with an explanation for the letter. He turned back to the phone. "Sir?" he said. "Sir—Marx, here, tells me Jews have a tendency to be pushy. He says he thinks we can settle it right here in the company. . . . Yes, sir. . . . I *will* call back, sir, soon as I can." He hung up. "Where are the men, Sergeant?"

"On the range."

With a whack on the top of his helmet, he crushed it down over his eyes again, and charged out of his chair. "We're going for a ride," he said.

The Captain drove, and I sat beside him. It was a hot spring day, and under my newly starched fatigues I felt as though my armpits were melting down onto my sides and chest. The roads were dry, and by the time we reached the firing range, my teeth felt gritty with dust, though my mouth had been shut the whole trip. The

Captain slammed the brakes on and told me to get the hell out and find Grossbart.

I found him on his belly, firing wildly at the five-hundred-feet target. Waiting their turns behind him were Halpern and Fishbein. Fishbein, wearing a pair of rimless G.I. glasses I hadn't seen on him before, had the appearance of an old peddler who would gladly have sold you his rifle and the cartridges that were slung all over him. I stood back by the ammo boxes, waiting for Grossbart to finish spraying the distant targets. Fishbein straggled back to stand near me.

"Hello, Sergeant Marx," he said.

"How are you?" I mumbled

"Fine, thank you. Sheldon's really a good shot."

"I didn't notice."

"I'm not so good, but I think I'm getting the hang of it now. Sergeant, I don't mean to, you know, ask what I shouldn't—" The boy stopped. He was trying to speak intimately, but the noise of the shooting forced him to shout at me.

"What is it?" I asked. Down the range, I saw Captain Barrett standing up in the jeep, scanning the line for me and Grossbart.

"My parents keep asking and asking where we're going," Fishbein said. "Everybody says the Pacific. I don't care, but my parents— If I could relieve their minds, I think I could concentrate more on my shooting."

"I don't know where, Fishbein. Try to concentrate anyway."

"Sheldon says you might be able to find out."

"I don't know a thing, Fishbein. You just take it easy, and don't let Sheldon—"

"*I'm* taking it easy, Sergeant. It's at home—"

Grossbart had finished on the line, and was dusting his fatigues with one hand. I called to him. "Grossbart, the Captain wants to see you."

He came toward us. His eyes blazed and twinkled. "Hi!"

"Don't point that goddam rifle!" I said.

"I wouldn't shoot you, Sarge." He gave me a smile as wide as a pumpkin, and turned the barrel aside.

"Damn you, Grossbart, this is no joke! Follow me."

I walked ahead of him, and had the awful suspicion that, behind me, Grossbart was marching, his rifle on his shoulder, as though he were a one-man detachment. At the jeep, he gave the Captain a rifle salute. "Private Sheldon Grossbart, sir."

"At ease, Grossman." The Captain sat down, slid over into the empty seat, and, crooking a finger, invited Grossbart closer.

"Bart, sir. Sheldon Gross*bart*. It's a common error." Grossbart nodded at me; *I* understood, he indicated. I looked away just as the mess truck pulled up to the range, disgorging a half-dozen K.P.s with rolled-up sleeves. The mess sergeant screamed at them while they set up the chow-line equipment.

"Grossbart, your mama wrote some congressman that we don't feed you right. Do you know that?" the Captain said.

"It was my father, sir. He wrote to Representative Franconi that my religion forbids me to eat certain foods."

"What religion is that, Grossbart?"

"Jewish."

"'Jewish, *sir*,'" I said to Grossbart.

"Excuse me, sir. Jewish, sir."

"What have you been living on?" the Captain asked. "You've been in the Army a month already. You don't look to me like you're falling to pieces."

"I eat because I have to, sir. But Sergeant Marx will testify to the fact that I don't eat one mouthful more than I need to in order to survive."

"Is that so, Marx?" Barrett asked.

"I've never seen Grossbart eat, sir," I said.

"But you heard the rabbi," Grossbart said. "He told us what to do, and I listened."

The Captain looked at me. "Well, Marx?"

"I still don't know what he eats and doesn't eat, sir."

Grossbart raised his arms to plead with me, and it looked for a moment as though he were going to hand me his weapon to hold. "But, Sergeant—"

"Look, Grossbart, just answer the Captain's questions," I said sharply.

Barrett smiled at me, and I resented it. "All right, Grossbart," he said. "What is it you want? The little piece of paper? You want out?"

"No, sir. Only to be allowed to live as a Jew. And for the others, too."

"What others?"

"Fishbein, sir, and Halpern."

"They don't like the way we serve, either?"

"Halpern throws up, sir. I've seen it."

"I thought *you* throw up."

"Just once, sir. I didn't know the sausage was sausage."

"We'll give menus, Grossbart. We'll show training films about the food, so you can identify when we're trying to poison you."

Grossbart did not answer. The men had been organized into two long chow lines. At the tail end of one, I spotted Fishbein—or, rather, his glasses spotted me. They winked sunlight back at me. Halpern stood next to him, patting the inside of his collar with a khaki handkerchief. They moved with the line as it began to edge up toward the food. The mess sergeant was still screaming at the K.P.s. For a moment, I was actually terrified by the thought that somehow the mess sergeant was going to become involved in Grossbart's problem.

"Marx," the Captain said, "you're a Jewish fella—am I right?"

I played straight man. "Yes, sir."

"How long you been in the Army? Tell this boy."

"Three years and two months."

"A year in combat, Grossbart. Twelve goddam months in combat all through Europe. I admire this man." The Captain snapped a wrist against my chest. "Do you hear him peeping about the food? Do you? I want an answer, Grossbart. Yes or no."

"No, sir."

"And why not? He's a Jewish fella."

"Some things are more important to some Jews than other things to other Jews."

Barrett blew up. "Look, Grossbart. Marx, here, is a good man—a goddam hero. When you were in high school, Sergeant Marx was killing Germans. Who does more for the Jews—you, by throwing up over a lousy piece of sausage, a piece of first-cut meat, or Marx, by killing those Nazi bastards? If I was a Jew, Grossbart, I'd kiss this man's feet. He's a goddam hero, and *he* eats what we give him. Why do you have to cause trouble is what I want to know! What is it you're buckin' for—a discharge?"

"No, sir."

"I'm talking to a wall! Sergeant, get him out of my way." Barrett swung himself back into the driver's seat. "I'm going to see the chaplain." The engine roared, the jeep spun around in a whirl of dust, and the Captain was headed back to camp.

For a moment, Grossbart and I stood side by side, watching the jeep. Then he looked at me and said, "I don't want to start trouble. That's the first thing they toss up to us."

When he spoke, I saw that his teeth were white and straight, and the sight of them suddenly made me understand that Grossbart actually did have parents—that once upon a time someone had taken little Sheldon to the dentist. He was their son. Despite all the talk about his parents, it was hard to believe in Grossbart as a child, an heir—as related by blood to anyone, mother, father, or, above all, to me. This realization led me to another.

"What does your father do, Grossbart?" I asked as we started to walk back toward the chow line.

"He's a tailor"

"An American?"

"Now, yes. A son in the Army," he said, jokingly.

"And your mother?" I asked.

He winked. "A *ballabusta*. She practically sleeps with a dustcloth in her hand."

"She's also an immigrant?"

"All she talks is Yiddish, still."

"And your father, too?"

"A little English. 'Clean,' 'Press,' 'Take the pants in.' That's the extent of it. But they're good to me."

"Then, Grossbart—" I reached out and stopped him. He turned toward me, and when our eyes met, his seemed to jump back, to shiver in their sockets. "Grossbart—you were the one who wrote that letter, weren't you?"

It took only a second or two for his eyes to flash happy again. "Yes." He walked on, and I kept pace. "It's what my father *would* have written if he had known how. It was his name, though. *He* signed it. He even mailed it. I sent it home. For the New York postmark."

I was astonished, and he saw it. With complete seriousness, he thrust his right arm in front of me. "Blood is blood, Sergeant," he said, pinching the blue vein in his wrist.

"What the hell *are* you trying to do, Grossbart?" I asked. "I've seen you eat. Do you know that? I told the Captain I don't know what you eat, but I've seen you eat like a hound at chow."

"We work hard, Sergeant. We're in training. For a furnace to work, you've got to feed it coal."

"Why did you say in the letter that you threw up all the time?"

"I was really talking about Mickey there. I was talking *for* him. He would never write, Sergeant, though I pleaded with him. He'll waste away to nothing if I don't help. Sergeant, I used my name—my father's name—but it's Mickey, and Fishbein, too, I'm watching out for."

"You're a regular Messiah, aren't you?"

We were at the chow line now.

"That's a good one, Sergeant," he said, smiling. "But who knows? Who can tell? Maybe you're the Messiah a little bit. What Mickey says is the Messiah is a collective idea. He went to Yeshiva, Mickey, for a while. He says *together* we're the Messiah. Me a little bit, you a little bit. You should hear that kid talk, Sergeant, when he gets going."

"Me a little bit, you a little bit," I said. "You'd like to believe that, wouldn't you, Grossbart? That would make everything so clean for you."

"It doesn't seem too bad a thing to believe, Sergeant. It only means we should all *give* a little, is all."

I walked off to eat my rations with the other noncoms.

Two days later, a letter addressed to Captain Barrett passed over my desk. It had come through the chain of command—from the office of Congressman Franconi, where it had been received, to General Lyman, to Colonel Sousa, to Major Lamont, now to Captain Barrett. I read it over twice. It was dated May 14th, the day Barrett had spoken with Grossbart on the rifle range.

Dear Congressman:

First let me thank you for your interest in behalf of my son, Private Sheldon Grossbart. Fortunately, I was able to speak with

Sheldon on the phone the other night, and I think I've been able to solve our problem. He is, as I mentioned in my last letter, a very religious boy, and it was only with the greatest difficulty that I could persuade him that the religious thing to do—what God Himself would want Sheldon to do—would be to suffer the pangs of religious remorse for the good of his country and all mankind. It took some doing, Congressman, but finally he saw the light. In fact, what he said (and I wrote down the words on a scratch pad so as never to forget), what he said was "I guess you're right, Dad. So many millions of my fellow-Jews gave up their lives to the enemy, the least I can do is live for a while minus a bit of my heritage so as to help end this struggle and regain for all the children of God dignity and humanity." That, Congressman, would make any father proud.

By the way, Sheldon wanted me to know—and to pass on to you—the name of a soldier who helped him reach this decision: SERGEANT NATHAN MARX. Sergeant Marx is a combat veteran who is Sheldon's first sergeant. This man has helped Sheldon over some of the first hurdles he's had to face in the Army, and is in part responsible for Sheldon's changing his mind about the dietary laws. I know Sheldon would appreciate any recognition Marx could receive.

Thank you and good luck. I look forward to seeing your name on the next election ballot.

Respectfully,
Samuel E. Grossbart

Attached to the Grossbart communiqué was another, addressed to General Marshall Lyman, the post commander, and signed by Representative Charles E. Franconi, of the House of Representatives. The communiqué informed General Lyman that Sergeant Nathan Marx was a credit to the U.S. Army and the Jewish people.

What was Grossbart's motive in recanting? Did he feel he'd gone too far? Was the letter a strategic retreat—a crafty attempt to strengthen what he considered our alliance? Or had he actually changed his mind, via an imaginary dialogue between Grossbart *père* and Grossbart *fils?* I was puzzled, but only for a few days—that is, only until I realized that, whatever his reasons, he had actually decided to disappear from my life; he was going to allow himself to become just another trainee. I saw him at inspection, but he never winked; at chow formations, but he never flashed me a sign. On Sundays, with the other trainees, he would sit around watching the noncoms' softball team, for which I pitched, but not once did he speak an unnecessary word to me. Fishbein and Halpern retreated, too—at Grossbart's command, I was sure. Apparently he had seen that wisdom lay in turning back before he plunged over into the ugliness of privilege undeserved. Our separation allowed me to forgive him our past encounters, and, finally, to admire him for his good sense.

Meanwhile, free of Grossbart, I grew used to my job and my administrative tasks. I stepped on a scale one day, and discovered I had truly become a noncombatant; I had gained seven pounds. I found patience to get past the first three pages of a book. I thought about the future more and more, and wrote letters to girls I'd known before the war. I even got a few answers. I sent away to Columbia for a Law School catalogue. I continued to follow the war in the Pacific, but it was not my war. I thought I could see the end, and sometimes, at night, I dreamed that I was walking on the streets of Manhattan—Broadway, Third Avenue, 116th Street, where I had lived the three years I attended Columbia. I curled myself around these dreams and I began to be happy.

And then, one Saturday, when everybody was away and I was alone in the orderly room reading a month-old copy of the *Sporting News*, Grossbart reappeared.

"You a baseball fan, Sergeant?"

I looked up. "How are you?"

"Fine," Grossbart said. "They're making a soldier out of me."

"How are Fishbein and Halpern?"

"Coming along," he said. "We've got no training this afternoon. They're at the movies."

"How come you're not with them?"

"I wanted to come over and say hello."

He smiled—a shy, regular-guy smile, as though he and I well knew that our friendship drew its sustenance from unexpected visits, remembered birthdays, and borrowed lawnmowers. At first it offended me, and then the feeling was swallowed by the general uneasiness I felt at the thought that everyone on the post was locked away in a dark movie theatre and I was here alone with Grossbart. I folded up my paper.

"Sergeant," he said, "I'd like to ask a favor. It is a favor, and I'm making no bones about it."

He stopped, allowing me to refuse him a hearing—which, of course, forced me into a courtesy I did not intend. "Go ahead."

"Well, actually it's two favors."

I said nothing.

"The first one's about these rumors. Everybody says we're going to the Pacific."

"As I told your friend Fishbein, I don't know," I said. "You'll just have to wait to find out. Like everybody else."

"You think there's a chance of any of us going East?"

"Germany?" I said. "Maybe."

"I meant New York."

"I don't think so, Grossbart. Offhand."

"Thanks for the information, Sergeant," he said.

"It's not information, Grossbart. Just what I surmise."

"It certainly would be good to be near home. My parents—you know." He took a step toward the door and then turned back. "Oh, the other thing. May I ask the other?"

"What is it?"

"The other thing is—I've got relatives in St. Louis, and they say they'll give me a whole Passover dinner if I can get down there. God, Sergeant, that'd mean an awful lot to me."

I stood up. "No passes during basic, Grossbart."

"But we're off from now till Monday morning, Sergeant. I could leave the post and no one would even know."

"I'd know. You'd know."

"But that's all. Just the two of us. Last night, I called my aunt, and you should have heard her. 'Come—come,' she said. 'I got gefilte fish, *chrain*—the works!' Just a day, Sergeant. I'd take the blame if anything happened."

"The Captain isn't here to sign a pass."

"You could sign."

"Look, Grossbart—"

"Sergeant, for two months, practically, I've been eating *trafe* till I want to die."

"I thought you'd made up your mind to live with it. To be minus a little bit of heritage."

He pointed a finger at me. "You!" he said. "That wasn't for you to read."

"I read it. So what?"

"That letter was addressed to a congressman."

"Grossbart, don't feed me any baloney. You *wanted* me to read it."

"Why are you persecuting me, Sergeant?"

"Are you kidding!"

"I've run into this before," he said, "but never from my own!"

"Get out of here, Grossbart! Get the hell out of my sight!"

He did not move. "Ashamed, that's what you are," he said. "So you take it out on the rest of us. They say Hitler himself was half a Jew. Hearing you, I wouldn't doubt it."

"What are you trying to do with me, Grossbart?" I asked him. "What are you after? You want me to give you special privileges, to change the food, to find out about your orders, to give you weekend passes."

"You even talk like a goy!" Grossbart shook his fist. "Is this just a weekend pass I'm asking for? Is a Seder sacred, or not?"

Seder! It suddenly occurred to me that Passover had been celebrated weeks before. I said so.

"That's right," he replied. "Who says no? A month ago—and I was in the field eating hash! And now all I ask is a simple favor. A Jewish boy I thought would understand. My aunt's willing to go out of her way—to make a Seder a month later. . . ." He turned to go, mumbling.

"Come back here!" I called. He stopped and looked at me. "Grossbart, why can't you be like the rest? Why do you have to stick out like a sore thumb?"

"Because I'm a Jew, Sergeant. I am different. Better, maybe not. But different."

"This is a war, Grossbart. For the time being *be* the same."

"I refuse."

"What?"

"I refuse. I can't stop being me, that's all there is to it." Tears came to his eyes. "It's a hard thing to be a Jew. But now I understand what Mickey says—it's a harder thing to stay one." He raised a hand sadly toward me. "Look at *you*."

"Stop crying!"

"Stop this, stop that, stop the other thing! *You* stop, Sergeant. Stop closing your heart to your own!" And, wiping his face with his sleeve, he ran out the door. "The least we can do for one another—the least . . ."

An hour later, looking out of the window, I saw Grossbart headed across the field. He wore a pair of starched khakis and carried a little leather ditty bag. I went out into the heat of the day. It was quiet; not a soul was in sight except, over by the mess hall, four K.P.s sitting around a pan, sloped forward from their waists, gabbing and peeling potatoes in the sun.

"Grossbart!" I called.

He looked toward me and continued walking.

"Grossbart, get over here!"

He turned and came across the field. Finally, he stood before me.

"Where are you going?" I asked.

"St. Louis. I don't care."

"You'll get caught without a pass."

"So I'll get caught without a pass."

"You'll go to the stockade."

"I'm *in* the stockade." He made an about-face and headed off.

I let him go only a step or two. "Come back here," I said, and he followed me into the office, where I typed out a pass and signed the Captain's name, and my own initials after it.

He took the pass and then, a moment later, reached out and grabbed my hand. "Sergeant, you don't know how much this means to me."

"O.K.," I said. "Don't get in any trouble."

"I wish I could show you how much this means to me."

"Don't do me any favors. Don't write any more congressmen for citations."

He smiled. "You're right. I won't. But let me do something."

"Bring me a piece of that gefilte fish. Just get out of here."

"I will!" he said. "With a slice of carrot and a little horseradish. I won't forget."

"All right. Just show your pass at the gate. And don't tell *anybody*."

"I won't. It's a month late, but a good Yom Tov to you."

"Good Yom Tov, Grossbart," I said.

"You're a good Jew, Sergeant. You like to think you have a hard heart, but underneath you're a fine, decent man. I mean that."

Those last three words touched me more than any words from Grossbart's mouth had the right to. "All right, Grossbart," I said. "Now call me 'sir,' and get the hell out of here."

He ran out the door and was gone. I felt very pleased with myself; it was a great relief to stop fighting Grossbart, and it had cost me nothing. Barrett would never find out, and if he did, I could manage to invent some excuse. For a while, I sat at my desk, comfortable in my decision. Then the screen door flew back and Grossbart burst in again. "Sergeant!" he said. Behind him I saw Fishbein and Halpern, both in starched khakis, both carrying ditty bags like Grossbart's.

"Sergeant, I caught Mickey and Larry coming out of the movies. I almost missed them."

"Grossbart—did I say tell no one?" I said.

"But my aunt said I could bring friends. That I should, in fact."

"*I'm* the Sergeant, Grossbart—not your aunt!"

Grossbart looked at me in disbelief. He pulled Halpern up by his sleeve. "Mickey, tell the Sergeant what this would mean to you."

Halpern looked at me and, shrugging, said, "A lot."

Fishbein stepped forward without prompting. "This would mean a great deal to me and my parents, Sergeant Marx."

"No!" I shouted.

Grossbart was shaking his head. "Sergeant, I could see you denying me, but how you can deny Mickey, a Yeshiva boy—that's beyond me."

"I'm not denying Mickey anything," I said. "You just pushed a little too hard, Grossbart. *You* denied him."

"I'll give him my pass, then," Grossbart said. "I'll give him my aunt's address and a little note. At least let him go."

In a second, he had crammed the pass into Halpern's pants pocket. Halpern looked at me, and so did Fishbein. Grossbart was at the door, pushing it open. "Mickey, bring me a piece of gefilte fish, at least," he said, and then he was outside again.

The three of us looked at one another, and then I said, "Halpern, hand that pass over."

He took it from his pocket and gave it to me. Fishbein had now moved to the doorway, where he lingered. He stood there for a moment with his mouth slightly open, and then he pointed to himself. "And me?" he asked.

His utter ridiculousness exhausted me. I slumped down in my seat and felt pulses knocking at the back of my eyes. "Fishbein," I said, "you understand I'm not trying to deny you anything, don't you? If it was my Army, I'd serve gefilte fish in the mess hall. I'd sell *kugel* in the PX, honest to God."

Halpern smiled.

"You understand, don't you, Halpern?"

"Yes, Sergeant."

"And you, Fishbein? I don't want enemies. I'm just like you—I want to serve my time and go home. I miss the same things you miss."

"Then, Sergeant," Fishbein said, "why don't you come, too?"

"Where?"

"To St. Louis. To Shelly's aunt. We'll have a regular Seder. Play hide-the-matzo." He gave me a broad, black-toothed smile.

I saw Grossbart again, on the other side of the screen.

"Pst!" He waved a piece of paper. "Mickey, here's the address. Tell her I couldn't get away."

Halpern did not move. He looked at me, and I saw the shrug moving up his arms into his shoulders again. I took the cover off my typewriter and made out passes for him and Fishbein. "Go," I said. "The three of you."

I thought Halpern was going to kiss my hand.

That afternoon, in a bar in Joplin, I drank beer and listened with half an ear to the Cardinal game. I tried to look squarely at what I'd become involved in, and began to wonder if perhaps the struggle with Grossbart wasn't as much my fault as his. What was I that I had to *muster* generous feelings? Who was I to have been feeling so grudging, so tight-hearted? After all, I wasn't being asked to move the world. Had I a right, then, or a reason, to clamp down on Grossbart, when that meant clamping down on Halpern, too? And Fishbein—that ugly, agreeable soul? Out of the many recollections of my childhood that had tumbled over me these past few days, I heard my grandmother's voice: "What are you making a *tsimmes*?" It was what she would ask my mother when, say, I had cut myself while doing something I shouldn't have done, and her daughter was busy bawling me out. I needed a hug and a kiss, and my mother would moralize. But my grandmother knew—mercy overrides justice. I should have known it, too. Who was Nathan Marx to be such a penny pincher with kindness? Surely, I thought, the Messiah himself—if He should ever come—won't niggle over nickels and dimes. God willing, he'll hug and kiss.

The next day, while I was playing softball over on the parade ground, I decided to ask Bob Wright, who was noncom in charge of Classification and Assignment, where he thought our trainees would be sent when their cycle ended, in two weeks. I asked casually, between innings, and he said, "They're pushing them all into the Pacific. Shulman cut the orders on your boys the other day."

The news shocked me, as though I were the father of Halpern, Fishbein, and Grossbart.

That night, I was just sliding into sleep when someone tapped on my door. "Who is it?" I asked.

"Sheldon."

He opened the door and came in. For a moment, I felt his presence without being able to see him. "How was it?" I asked.

He popped into sight in the near-darkness before me. "Great, Sergeant." Then he was sitting on the edge of the bed. I sat up.

"How about you?" he asked. "Have a nice weekend?"

"Yes."

"The others went to sleep." He took a deep, paternal breath. We sat silent for a while, and a homey feeling invaded my ugly little cubicle; the door was locked, the cat was out, the children were safely in bed.

"Sergeant, can I tell you something? Personal?"

I did not answer, and he seemed to know why. "Not about me. About Mickey. Sergeant, I never felt for anybody like I feel for him. Last night I heard Mickey in the bed next to me. He was crying so, it could have broken your heart. Real sobs."

"I'm sorry to hear that."

"I had to talk to him to stop him. He held my hand, Sergeant—he wouldn't let it go. He was almost hysterical. He kept saying if he only knew where we were going. Even if he knew it was the Pacific, that would be better than nothing. Just to know."

Long ago, someone had taught Grossbart the sad rule that only lies can get the truth. Not that I couldn't believe in the fact of Halpern's crying; his eyes *always* seemed red-rimmed. But, fact or not, it became a lie when Grossbart uttered it. He was entirely strategic. But then—it came with the force of indictment—so was I! There are strategies of aggression, but there are strategies of retreat as well. And so, recognizing that I myself had not been without craft and guile, I told him what I knew. "It is the Pacific."

He let out a small gasp, which was not a lie. "I'll tell him. I wish it was otherwise."

"So do I."

He jumped on my words. "You mean you think you could do something? A change, maybe?"

"No, I couldn't do a thing."

"Don't you know anybody over at C. and A.?"

"Grossbart, there's nothing I can do," I said. "If your orders are for the Pacific, then it's the Pacific."

"But Mickey—"

"Mickey, you, me—everybody, Grossbart. There's nothing to be done. Maybe the war'll end before you go. Pray for a miracle."

"But—"

"Good night, Grossbart." I settled back, and was relieved to feel the springs unbend as Grossbart rose to leave. I could see him clearly now; his jaw had dropped, and he looked like a dazed prizefighter. I noticed for the first time a little paper bag in his hand.

"Grossbart." I smiled. "My gift?"

"Oh, yes, Sergeant. Here—from all of us." He handed me the bag. "It's egg roll."

"Egg roll?" I accepted the bag and felt a damp grease spot on the bottom. I opened it, sure that Grossbart was joking.

"We thought you'd probably like it. You know—Chinese egg roll. We thought you'd probably have a taste for—"

"Your aunt served egg roll?"

"She wasn't home."

"Grossbart, she invited you. You told me she invited you and your friends."

"I know," he said. "I just reread the letter. *Next* week."

I got out of bed and walked to the window. "Grossbart," I said. But I was not calling to him.

"What?"

"What are you, Grossbart? Honest to God, what are you?"

I think it was the first time I'd asked him a question for which he didn't have an immediate answer.

"How can you do this to people?" I went on.

"Sergeant, the day away did us all a world of good. Fishbein, you should see him, he *loves* Chinese food."

"But the Seder," I said.

"We took second best, Sergeant."

Rage came charging at me. I didn't sidestep. "Grossbart, you're a liar!" I said. "You're a schemer and a crook. You've got no respect for anything. Nothing at all. Not for me, for the truth—not even for poor Halpern! You use us all—"

"Sergeant, Sergeant, I feel for Mickey. Honest to God, I do. I *love* Mickey. I try—"

"You try! You feel!" I lurched toward him and grabbed his shirt front. I shook him furiously. "Grossbart, get out! Get out and stay the hell away from me. Because if I see you, I'll make your life miserable *You understand that?*"

"Yes."

I let him free, and when he walked from the room, I wanted to spit on the floor where he had stood. I couldn't stop the fury. It engulfed me, owned me, till it seemed I could only rid myself of it with tears or an act of violence. I snatched from the bed the bag Grossbart had given me and, with all my strength, threw it out the window. And the next morning, as the men policed the area around the barracks, I heard a great cry go up from one of the trainees, who had been anticipating only his morning handful of cigarette butts and candy wrappers. "Egg roll!" he shouted. "Holy Christ, Chinese goddam egg roll!"

A week later, when I read the orders that had come down from C. and A., I couldn't believe my eyes. Every single trainee was to be shipped to Camp Stoneman, California, and from there to the Pacific—every trainee but one. Private Sheldon Grossbart. He was to be sent to Fort Monmouth, New Jersey. I read the mimeographed sheet several times. Dee, Farrell, Fishbein, Fuselli, Fylypowycz, Glinicki, Gromke, Gucwa, Halpern, Hardy, Helebrandt, right down to Anton Zygadlo—all were to be headed West before the month was out. All except Grossbart. He had pulled a string, and I wasn't it.

I lifted the phone and called C. and A.

The voice on the other end said smartly, "Corporal Shulman, sir."

"Let me speak to Sergeant Wright."

"Who is this calling, sir?"

"Sergeant Marx."

And, to my surprise, the voice said, "*Oh!*" Then, "Just a minute, Sergeant."

Shulman's "*Oh!*" stayed with me while I waited for Wright to come to the phone. Why "*Oh!*"? Who was Shulman? And then, so simply, I knew I'd discovered the string that Grossbart had pulled. In fact, I could hear Grossbart the day he'd discovered Shulman in the PX, or in the bowling alley, or maybe even at services. "Glad to meet you. Where you from? Bronx? Me, too. Do you know So-and-So? And So-and-So? Me, too! You work at C. and A.? Really? Hey, how's chances of getting East? Could you do something? Change something? Swindle, cheat, lie? We gotta help each other, you know. If the Jews in Germany . . ."

Bob Wright answered the phone. "How are you, Nate? How's the pitching arm?"

"Good. Bob, I wonder if you could do me a favor." I heard clearly my own words, and they so reminded me of Grossbart that I dropped more easily than I could have imagined into what I had planned. "This may sound crazy, Bob, but I got a kid here on orders to Monmouth who wants them changed. He had a brother killed in Europe, and he's hot to go to the Pacific. Says he'd feel like a coward if he wound up Stateside. I don't know, Bob—can anything be done? Put somebody else in the Monmouth slot?"

"Who?" he asked cagily.

"Anybody. First guy in the alphabet. I don't care. The kid just asked if something could be done."

"What's his name?"

"Grossbart, Sheldon."

Wright didn't answer.

"Yeah," I said. "He's a Jewish kid, so he thought I could help him out. You know."

"I guess I can do something," he finally said. "The Major hasn't been around here for weeks. Temporary duty to the golf course. I'll try, Nate, that's all I can say."

"I'd appreciate it, Bob. See you Sunday." And I hung up, perspiring.

The following day, the corrected orders appeared: Fishbein, Fuselli, Fylypowycz, Glinicki, Gromke, Grossbart, Gucwa, Halpern, Hardy . . . Lucky Private Harley Alton was to go to Fort Monmouth, New Jersey, where, for some reason or other, they wanted an enlisted man with infantry training.

After chow that night, I stopped back at the orderly room to straighten out the guard-duty roster. Grossbart was waiting for me. He spoke first.

"You son of a bitch!"

I sat down at my desk, and while he glared at me, I began to make the necessary alterations in the duty roster.

"What do you have against me?" he cried. "Against my family? Would it kill you for me to be near my father, God knows how many months he has left to him?"

"Why so?"

"His heart," Grosshart said. "He hasn't had enough troubles in a lifetime, you've got to add to them. I curse the day I ever met you, Marx! Shulman told me what happened over there. There's no limit to your anti-Semitism, is there? The damage you've done here isn't enough. You have to make a special phone call! You really want me dead!"

I made the last few notations in the duty roster and got up to leave. "Good night, Grossbart."

"You owe me an explanation!" He stood in my path.

"Sheldon, you're the one who owes explanations."

He scowled. "To *you*?"

"To me, I think so—yes. Mostly to Fishbein and Halpern."

"That's right, twist things around. I owe nobody nothing, I've done all I could do for them. Now I think I've got the right to watch out for myself."

"For each other we have to learn to watch out, Sheldon. You told me yourself."

"You call this watching out for me—what you did?"

"No. For all of us."

I pushed him aside and started for the door. I heard his furious breathing behind me, and it sounded like steam rushing from an engine of terrible strength.

"You'll be all right," I said from the door. And, I thought, so would Fishbein and Halpern be all right, even in the Pacific, if only Grossbart continued to see—in the obsequiousness of the one, the soft spirituality of the other—some profit for himself.

I stood outside the orderly room, and I heard Grossbart weeping behind me. Over in the barracks, in the lighted windows, I could see the boys in their T-shirts sitting on their bunks talking about their orders, as they'd been doing for the past two days. With a kind of quiet nervousness, they polished shoes, shined belt buckles, squared away underwear, trying as best they could to accept their fate. Behind me, Grossbart swallowed hard, accepting his. And then, resisting with all my will an impulse to turn and seek pardon for my vindictiveness, I accepted my own.

WHERE IS THE VOICE COMING FROM?

BY EUDORA WELTY (1963)

I says to my wife, "You can reach and turn it off. You don't have to set and look at a black nigger face no longer than you want to, or listen to what you don't want to hear. It's still a free country."

I reckon that's how I give myself the idea.

I says, I could find right exactly where in Thermopylae that nigger's living that's asking for equal time. And without a bit of trouble to me.

And I ain't saying it might not be because that's pretty close to where *I* live. The other hand, there could be reasons you might have yourself for knowing how to get there in the dark. It's where you all go for the thing you want when you want it the most. Ain't that right?

The Branch Bank sign tells you in lights, all night long even, what time it is and how hot. When it was quarter to four, and 92, that was me going by in my brother-in-law's truck. He don't deliver nothing at that hour of the morning.

So you leave Four Corners and head west on Nathan B. Forrest Road, past the Surplus & Salvage, not much beyond the Kum Back Drive-In and Trailer Camp, not as far as where the signs starts saying "Live Bait," "Used Parts," "Fireworks," "Peaches," and "Sister Peebles Reader and Adviser." Turn before you hit the city limits and duck back towards the I.C. tracks. And his street's been paved.

And there was his light on, waiting for me. In his garage, if you please. His car's gone. He's out planning still some other ways to do what we tell 'em they can't. I *thought* I'd beat him home. All I had to do was pick my tree and walk in close behind it.

I didn't come expecting not to wait. But it was so hot, all I did was hope and pray one or the other of us wouldn't melt before it was over.

Now, it wasn't no bargain I'd struck.

I've heard what you've heard about Goat Dykeman, in Mississippi. Sure, everybody knows about Goat Dykeman. Goat he got word to the Governor's Mansion he'd go up yonder and shoot that nigger Meredith clean out of school, if he's let out of the pen to do it. Old Ross turned *that* over in his mind before saying him nay, it stands to reason.

I ain't no Goat Dykeman, I ain't in no pen, and I ain't ask no Governor Barnett to give me one thing. Unless he wants to give me a pat on the back for the trouble I took this morning. But he don't have to if he don't want to. I done what I done for my own pure-D satisfaction.

As soon as I heard wheels, I knowed who was coming. That was him and bound to be him. It was the right nigger heading in a new white car up his driveway towards his garage with the light shining, but stopping before he got there, maybe not to wake 'em. That was him. I knowed it when he cut off the car lights and put his foot out and I knowed him standing dark against the light. I knowed him then like I know me now. I knowed him even by his still, listening back.

Never seen him before, never seen him since, never seen anything of his black face but his picture, never seen his face alive, any time at all, or anywheres, and didn't want to, need to, never hope to see that face and never will. As long as there was no question in my mind.

He had to be the one. He stood right still and waited against the light, his back was fixed, fixed on me like a preacher's eyeballs when he's yelling "Are you saved?" He's the one.

I'd already brought up my rifle, I'd already taken my sights. And I'd already got him, because it was too late then for him or me to turn by one hair.

Something darker than him, like the wings of a bird, spread on his back and pulled him down. He climbed up once, like a man under bad claws, and like just blood could weigh a ton he walked with it on his back to better light. Didn't get no further than his door. And fell to stay.

He was down. He was down, and a ton load of bricks on his back wouldn't have laid any heavier. There on his paved driveway, yes sir.

And it wasn't till the minute before, that the mockingbird had quit singing. He'd been singing up my sassafras tree. Either he was up early, or he hadn't never gone to bed, he was like me. And the mocker he'd stayed right with me, filling the air till come the crack, till I turned loose of my load. I was like him. I was on top of the world myself. For once.

I stepped to the edge of his light there, where he's laying flat. I says, "Roland? There was one way left, for me to be ahead of you and stay ahead of you, by Dad, and I just taken it. Now I'm alive and you ain't. We ain't never now, never going to be equals and you know why? One of us is dead. What about that, Roland?" I said. "Well, you seen to it, didn't you?"

I stood a minute—just to see would somebody inside come out long enough to pick him up. And there she comes, the woman. I doubt she'd been to sleep. Because it seemed to me she'd been in there keeping awake all along.

It was mighty green where I skint over the yard getting back. That nigger wife of his, she wanted nice grass! I bet my wife would hate to pay her water bill. And for burning her electricity. And there's my brother-in-law's truck, still waiting with the door open.

"No Riders"—that didn't mean me.

There wasn't a thing I been able to think of since would have made it to go any nicer. Except a chair to my back while I was putting in my waiting. But going home, I seen what little time it takes after all to get a thing done like you really want it. It was 4:34, and while I was looking it moved to 35. And the temperature stuck where it was. All that night I guarantee you it had stood without dropping, a good 92.

My wife says, "What? Didn't the skeeters bite you?" She said, "Well, they been asking that—why somebody didn't trouble to load a rifle and get some of these agitators out of Thermopylae. Didn't the fella keep drumming it in, what a good idea? The one that writes a column ever'day?"

I says to my wife, "Find *some* way I don't get the credit."

"He says do it for Thermopylae," she says. "Don't you ever skim the paper?"

I says, "Thermopylae never done nothing for me. And I don't owe nothing to Thermopylae. Didn't do it for you. Hell, any more'n I'd do something or other for them Kennedys! I done it for my own pure-D satisfaction."

"It's going to get him right back on TV," says my wife. "You watch for the funeral."

I says, "You didn't even leave a light burning when you went to bed. So how was I supposed to even get me home or pull Buddy's truck up safe in our front yard?"

"Well, hear another good joke on you," my wife says next. "Didn't you hear the news? The N. double A. C. P. is fixing to send somebody to Thermopylae. Why couldn't you waited? You might could have got you somebody better. Listen and hear 'em say so."

I ain't but one. I reckon you have to tell *somebody*.

"Where's the gun, then?" my wife says. "What did you do with our protection?"

I says, "It was scorching! It was scorching!" I told her, "It's laying out on the ground in rank weeds, trying to cool off, that's what it's doing now."

"You dropped it," she says. "Back there."

And I told her, "Because I'm so tired of ever'thing in the world being just that hot to the touch! The keys to the truck, the doorknob, the bedsheet, ever'thing, it's all like a stove lid. There just ain't much going that's worth holding onto it no more," I says, "when it's a hundred and two in the shade by day and by night not too much difference. I wish *you'd* laid *your* finger to that gun."

"Trust you to come off and leave it," my wife says.

"Is that how no-'count I am?" she makes me ask. "*You* want to go back and get it?"

"You're the one they'll catch. I say it's so hot that even if you get to sleep you wake up feeling like you cried all night!" says my wife. "Cheer up, here's one more joke before time to get up. Heard what

Caroline said? Caroline said, 'Daddy, I just can't wait to grow up big, so I can marry *James Meredith*. I heard that where I work. One rich-bitch to another one, to make her cackle."

"At least I kept some dern teen-ager from North Thermopylae getting there and doing it first," I says. "Driving his own car."

On TV and in the paper, they don't know but half of it. They know who Roland Summers was without knowing who I am. His face was in front of the public before I got rid of him, and after I got rid of him there it is again—the same picture. And none of me. I ain't ever had one made. Not ever! The best that newspaper could do for me was offer a five-hundred-dollar reward for finding out who I am. For as long as they don't know who that is, whoever shot Roland is worth a good deal more right now than Roland is.

But by the time I was moving around uptown, it was hotter still. That pavement in the middle of Main Street was so hot to my feet I might've been walking the barrel of my gun. If the whole world could've just felt Main Street this morning through the soles of my shoes, maybe it would've helped some.

Then the first thing I heard 'em say was the N. double A. C. P. done it themselves, killed Roland Summers, and proved it by saying the shooting was done by an expert (I hope to tell you it was!) and at just the right hour and minute to get the whites in trouble.

You can't win.

"They'll never find him," the old man trying to sell roasted peanuts tells me to my face.

And it's so hot.

It looks like the town's on fire already, whichever ways you turn, ever' street you strike, because there's those trees hanging them pones of bloom like split watermelon. And a thousand cops crowding ever'where you go, half of 'em too young to start shaving, but all streaming sweat alike. I'm getting tired of 'em.

I was already tired of seeing a hundred cops getting us white people nowheres. Back at the beginning, I stood on the corner and I watched them new babyface cops loading nothing but nigger children into the paddy wagon and they come marching out of a little parade and into the paddy wagon singing. And they got in and sat down without providing a speck of trouble, and their hands held little new American flags, and all the cops could do was knock them flagsticks a-loose from their hands, and not let 'em pick 'em up, that was all, and give 'em a free ride. And children can just get 'em more flags.

Everybody: It don't get you nowhere to take nothing from nobody unless you make sure it's for keeps, for good and all, for ever and amen.

I won't be sorry to see them brickbats hail down on us for a change. Pop bottles too, they can come flying whenever they want to. Hundreds, all to smash, like Birmingham. I'm waiting on 'em to bring out them switchblade knives, like Harlem and Chicago. Watch TV long enough and you'll see it all to happen on Deacon Street in Thermopylae. What's holding it back, that's all?—Because it's *in* 'em.

I'm ready myself for that funeral.

Oh, they may find me. May catch me one day in spite of 'em-selves. (But I grew up in the country.) May try to railroad me into the electric chair, and what that amounts to is something hotter than yesterday and today put together.

But I advise 'em to go careful. Ain't it about time us taxpayers starts to calling the moves? Starts to telling the teachers *and* the preachers *and* the judges of our so-called courts how far they can go?

Even the President so far, he can't walk in my house without being invited, like he's my daddy, just to say whoa. Not yet!

Once, I run away from my home. And there was a ad for me, come to be printed in our county weekly. My mother paid for it. It was from her. It says: "SON: You are not being hunted for anything but to find you." That time, I come on back home.

But people are dead now.

And it's so hot. Without it even being August yet.

Anyways, I seen him fall. I was evermore the one.

So I reach me down my old guitar off the nail in the wall. 'Cause I've got my guitar, what I've held onto from way back when, and I never dropped that, never lost or forgot it, never hocked it but to get it again, never give it away, and I set in my chair, with nobody home but me, and I start to play, and sing a-Down. And sing a-down, down, down, down. Sing a-down, down, down, down. Down.

THE INDIAN UPRISING

BY DONALD BARTHELME (1965)

We defended the city as best we could. The arrows of the Comanches came in clouds. The war clubs of the Comanches clattered on the soft, yellow pavements. There were earthworks along the Boulevard Mark Clark and the hedges had been laced with sparkling wire. People were trying to understand. I spoke to Sylvia. "Do you think this is a good life?" The table held apples, books, long playing records. She looked up. "No."

Patrols of paras and volunteers with armbands guarded the tall, flat buildings. We interrogated the captured Comanche. Two of us forced his head back while another poured water into his nostrils. His body jerked, he choked and wept. Not believing a hurried, careless, and exaggerated report of the number of casualties in the outer districts where trees, lamps, swans had been reduced to clear fields of fire we issued entrenching tools to those who seemed trustworthy and turned the heavy-weapons companies so that we could not be surprised from that direction. And I sat there getting drunker and drunker and more in love and more in love. We talked.

"Do you know Fauré's 'Dolly'?"

"Would that be Gabriel Fauré?"

"It would."

"Then I know it," she said. "May I say that I play it myself at certain times, when I am sad, or happy, although it requires four hands."

"How is that managed?"

"I accelerate," she said, "ignoring the time signature."

And when they shot the scene in the bed I wondered how you felt under the eyes of the cameramen, grips, juicers, men in the mixing booth: excited? stimulated? And when they shot the scene in the shower I sanded a hollow-core door working carefully against the illustrations in texts and whispered instructions from one who had already solved the problem. I had made after all other tables, one while living with Nancy, one while living with Alice, one while living with Eunice, one while living with Marianne.

Red men in waves like people scattering in a square startled by something tragic or a sudden, loud noise accumulated against the barricades we had made of window dummies, silk, thoughtfully planned job descriptions (including scales for the orderly progress of other colors), wine in demijohns, and robes. I analyzed the composition of the barricade nearest me and found two ashtrays, ceramic, one dark brown and one dark brown with an orange blur at the lip; a tin frying pan; two-litre bottles of red wine; three quarter-litre bottles of Black & White, aquavit, cognac, vodka, gin, Fad #6 sherry; a hollow-core door in birch veneer on black wrought-iron legs; a blanket, red-orange with faint blue stripes; a red pillow and a blue pillow; a woven straw wastebasket; two glass jars for flowers; corkscrews and can openers; two plates and two cups, ceramic, dark brown; a yellow-and-purple poster; a Yugoslavian carved flute, wood, dark brown; and other items. I decided I knew nothing.

The hospitals dusted wounds with powders the worth of which was not quite established, other supplies having been exhausted early in the first day. I decided I knew nothing. Friends put me in touch with a Miss R., a teacher, unorthodox they said, excellent they said, successful with difficult cases, steel shutters on the windows made her house safe. I had just learned via an International Distress Coupon that Jane had been beaten up by a dwarf in a bar in Tenerife but Miss R. did not allow me to speak of it. "You know nothing," she said, "you feel nothing, you are locked in a most savage and terrible ignorance, I despise you, my boy, *mon cher*, my heart. You may attend but you must not attend now, you must attend later, a day or a week or an hour, you are making me ill . . ." I nonevaluated these remarks as Korzybski instructed. But it was difficult. Then they pulled back in a feint near the river and we rushed into that sector with a reinforced battalion hastily formed among the Zouaves and cab drivers. This unit was crushed in the afternoon of a day that began with spoons and letters in hallways and under windows where men tasted the history of the heart, cone-shaped muscular organ that maintains *circulation of the blood.*

But it is you I want now, here in the middle of this Uprising, with the streets yellow and threatening, short, ugly lances with fur at the throat and inexplicable shell money lying in the grass. It is when I am with you that I am happiest, and it is for you that I am making this hollow-core door table with black wrought-iron legs. I held Sylvia by her bear-claw necklace. "Call off your braves," I said. "We have many years left to live." There was a sort of muck running in the gutters, yellowish, filthy stream suggesting excrement, or nervousness, a city that does not know what it has done to deserve baldness, errors, infidelity. "With luck you will survive until matins," Sylvia said. She ran off down the Rue Chester Nimitz, uttering shrill cries.

Then it was learned that they had infiltrated our ghetto and that the people of the ghetto instead of offering resistance had joined the smooth, well coordinated attack with zip guns, telegrams, lockets, causing that portion of the line held by the I.R.A. to swell and collapse. We sent more heroin into the ghetto, and hyacinths, ordering another hundred thousand of the pale, delicate flowers. On the map we considered the situation with its strung-out inhabitants and merely personal emotions. Our parts were blue and their parts were green. I showed the blue-and-green map to Sylvia. "Your parts are green," I said. "You gave me heroin first a year ago," Sylvia said. She ran off down George C. Marshall Allée, uttering shrill cries. Miss R. pushed me into a large room painted white (jolting and dancing in the soft light, and I was excited! and there were people watching!) in which there were two chairs. I sat in one chair and Miss R. sat in the other. She wore a blue dress containing a red figure. There was nothing exceptional about her. I was disappointed by her plainness, by the bareness of the room, by the absence of books.

The girls of my quarter wore long blue mufflers that reached to their knees. Sometimes the girls hid Comanches in their rooms, the blue mufflers together in a room creating a great blue fog. Block opened the door. He was carrying weapons, flowers, and loaves of bread. And he was friendly, kind, enthusiastic, so I related a little of the history of torture, reviewing the technical literature quoting the best modern sources, French, German, and American, and pointing out the flies which had gathered in anticipation of some new, cool color.

"What is the situation?" I asked.

"The situation is liquid," he said. "We hold the south quarter and they hold the north quarter. The rest is silence."

"And Kenneth?"

"That girl is not in love with Kenneth," Block said frankly. "She is in love with his coat. When she is not wearing it she is huddling under it. Once I caught it going down the stairs by itself. I looked inside. Sylvia."

Once I caught Kenneth's coat going down the stairs by itself but the coat was a trap and inside a Comanche who made a thrust with his short, ugly knife at my leg which buckled and tossed me over the balustrade through a window and into another situation. Not believing that your body brilliant as it was and your fat, liquid spirit distinguished and angry as it was were stable quantities to which one could return on wires more than once, twice, or another number of times I said: "See the table?"

In Skinny Wainwright Square the forces of green and blue swayed and struggled. The referees ran out on the field trailing chains. And then the blue part would be enlarged, the green diminished. Miss R. began to speak. "A former king of Spain, a Bonaparte, lived for a time in Bordentown, New Jersey. But that's no good." She paused. "The ardor aroused in men by the beauty of women can only be satisfied by God.

That is *very* good (it is Valéry) but it is not what I have to teach you, goat, muck, filth, heart of my heart." I showed the table to Nancy. "See the table?" She stuck out her tongue red as a cardinal's hat. "I made such a table once," Block said frankly. "People all over America have made such tables. I doubt very much whether one can enter an American home without finding at least one such table, or traces of its having been there, such as faded places in the carpet." And afterward in the garden the men of the 7th Cavalry played Gabrieli, Albinoni, Marcello, Vivaldi, Boccherini. I saw Sylvia. She wore a yellow ribbon, under a long blue muffler. "Which side are you on," I cried, "after all?"

"The only form of discourse of which I approve," Miss R. said in her dry, sack voice, "is the litany. I believe our masters and teachers as well as plain citizens should confine themselves to what can safely be said. Thus when I hear the words *pewter, snake, tea, Fad #6 sherry, serviette, fenestration, crown, blue* coming from the mouth of some public official, or some raw youth, I am not disappointed. Vertical organization is also possible," Miss R. said, "as in

pewter
snake
tea
Fad #6 sherry
serviette
fenestration
crown
blue.

I run to liquids and colors," she said, "but you, you may run to something else, my virgin, my darling, my thistle, my poppet, my own. Young people," Miss R. said, "run to more and more unpleasant combinations as they sense the nature of our society. Some people," Miss R. said, "run to conceits or wisdom but I hold to the hard, brown, nutlike word. I might point out that there is enough aesthetic excitement here to satisfy anyone but a damned fool." I sat in solemn silence.

Fire arrows lit my way to the post office in Patton Place where members of the Abraham Lincoln Brigade offered their last, exhausted letters, postcards, calendars. I opened a letter but inside was a Comanche flint arrowhead played by Frank Wedekind in an elegant gold chain and congratulations. Your earring rattled against my spectacles when I leaned forward to touch the soft, ruined place where the hearing aid had been. "Pack it up! Pack it up!" I urged, but the men in charge of the Uprising refused to listen to reason or to understand that it was real and that our water supply had evaporated and that our credit was no longer what it had been, once.

We attached wires to the testicles of the captured Comanche. And I sat there getting drunker and drunker and more in love and more in love. When we threw the switch he spoke. His name, he said, was Gustave Aschenbach. He was born at L——, a country town in the province of Silesia. He was the son of an upper official in the judicature, and his forebears had all been officers, judges, departmental functionaries. . . . And you can never touch a girl in the same way more than once, twice, or another number of times however much you may wish to hold, wrap, or otherwise fix her hand, or look, or some other quality, or incident, known to you previously. In Sweden the little Swedish children cheered when we managed nothing more remarkable than getting off a bus burdened with packages, bread and liver paste and beer. We went to an old church and sat in the royal box. The organist was practicing. And then into the graveyard next to the church. *Here lies Anna Pedersen, a good woman*. I threw a mushroom on the grave. The officer commanding the garbage dump reported by radio that the garbage had begun to move.

Jane! I heard via an International Distress Coupon that you were beaten up by a dwarf in a bar in Tenerife. That doesn't sound like you, Jane. Mostly you kick the dwarf in his little dwarf groin before he can get his teeth into your tasty and nice-looking leg, don't you, Jane? Your affair with Harold is reprehensible, you know that, don't you, Jane? Harold is married to Nancy. And there is Paula to think about (Harold's kid), and Billy (Harold's other kid). I think your values are peculiar, Jane! Strings of language extend in every direction to bind the world into a rushing, seamless whole.

And you can never return to felicities in the same way, the brilliant body, the distinguished spirit recapitulating moments that occur once, twice, or another number of times in rebellions, or water. The rolling consensus of the Comanche nation smashed our inner defenses on three sides. Block was firing a grease gun from the upper floor of a building designed by Emery Roth & Sons. "See the table?" "Oh, pack it up with your bloody table!" The city officials were tied to trees. Dusky warriors padded with their forest tread into the mouth of the mayor. "Who do you want to be?" I asked Kenneth and he said he wanted to be Jean-Luc Godard but later when time permitted conversations in large, lighted rooms, whispering galleries with black-and-white Spanish rugs and problematic sculptures on calm, red catafalques. The sickness of the quarrel lay thick in the bed. I touched your back, the white, raised scars.

We killed a great many in the south suddenly with helicopters and rockets but we found that those we had killed were children and more came from the north and from the east and from other places where there are children preparing to live. "Skin," Miss R. said softly in the white, yellow room. "This is the Clemency Committee. And would you remove your belt and shoelaces." I removed my belt and shoelaces and looked (rain shattering from a great height the prospects of silence and clear, neat rows of houses in the subdivisions) into their savage black eyes, paint, feathers, beads.

THE HOUSE OF THE FAMOUS POET

BY MURIEL SPARK (1966)

In the summer of 1944, when it was nothing for trains from the provinces to be five or six hours late, I travelled to London on the night train from Edinburgh, which, at York, was already three hours late. There were ten people in the compartment, only two of whom I remember well, and for good reason.

I have the impression, looking back on it, of a row of people opposite me, dozing untidily with heads askew, and, as it often seems when we look at sleeping strangers, their features had assumed extra emphasis and individuality, sometimes disturbing to watch. It was as if they had rendered up their daytime talent for obliterating the outward traces of themselves in exchange for mental obliteration. In this way, they resembled a twelfth-century fresco; there was a look of medieval unself-consciousness about these people, all except one.

This was a private soldier, who was awake to a greater degree than most people are when they are not sleeping. He was smoking cigarettes one after the other with long, calm puffs. I thought he looked excessively evil—an atavistic type. His forehead must have been less than two inches high above dark, thick eyebrows, which met. His jaw was not large, but it was apelike; so was his small nose and so were his deep, close-set eyes. I thought there must have been some consanguinity in the parents. He was quite a throwback.

As it turned out, he was extremely gentle and kind. When I ran out of cigarettes, he fished about in his haversack and produced a packet for me and one for a girl sitting next me. We both tried, with a flutter of small change, to pay him. Nothing would please him at all but that we should accept his cigarettes, whereupon he returned to his silent, reflective smoking.

I felt a sort of pity for him then, rather as we feel toward animals we know to be harmless, such as monkeys. But I realized that, like the pity we expend on monkeys merely because they are not human beings, this pity was not needed.

Receiving the cigarettes gave the girl and myself common ground, and we conversed quietly for the rest of the journey. She told me she had a job in London as a domestic helper and nursemaid. She looked as if she had come from a country district—her very blond hair, red face, and large bones gave the impression of power, as if she was used to carrying heavy things, perhaps great scuttlesful of coal, or two children at a time. But what made me curious about her was her voice, which was cultivated, melodious, and restrained.

Toward the end of the journey, when the people were beginning to jerk themselves straight and the rushing to and fro in the corridor had started, this girl, Elise, asked me to come with her to the house where she worked. The master, who was something in a university, was away with his wife and family.

I agreed to this, because at that time I was in the way of thinking that the discovery of an educated servant girl was valuable and something to be gone deeper into. It had the element of experience—perhaps even of truth, and I believed, in those days, that truth is stranger than fiction. Besides, I wanted to spend that Sunday in London. I was due back the next day at my job in a branch of the Civil Service which had been evacuated to the country, and, for a reason that is another story, I didn't want to return too soon. I had some telephoning to do. I wanted to wash and change. I wanted to know more about the girl. So I thanked Elise and accepted her invitation.

I regretted it as soon as we got out of the train at King's Cross, some minutes after ten. Standing up tall on the platform, Elise looked unbearably tired, as if not only the last night's journey but every fragment of her unknown life was suddenly heaping up on top of her. The power I had noticed in the train was no longer there. As she called, in her beautiful voice, for a porter, I saw that on the side of her head that had been away from me in the train her hair was parted in a dark streak, which, by contrast with the yellow, looked navy blue. I had thought, when I first saw her, that possibly her hair was bleached, but now, seeing it so badly done, seeing this navy-blue parting pointing like an arrow to the weighted weariness of her face, I, too, got the sensation of great tiredness. And it was not only the strain of the journey that I felt but the foreknowledge of boredom that comes upon us unaccountably at the beginning of a quest, and that checks, perhaps mercifully, our curiosity.

And, as it happened, there really wasn't much to learn about Elise. The explanation of her that I had been prompted to seek I got in the taxi between King's Cross and the house at Swiss Cottage. She came of a good family, who thought her a pity, and she them. Having no training for anything else, she had taken a domestic job on leaving home. She was engaged to an Australian soldier billeted also at Swiss Cottage.

Perhaps it was the anticipation of a day's boredom, maybe it was the effect of no sleep or the fact that the V-1 sirens were sounding, but I felt some sourness when I saw the house. The garden was growing all over the place. Elise opened the front door, and we entered a darkish room almost wholly taken up with a long, plain wood worktable. On this were a half-empty marmalade jar, a pile of papers, and a dried-up ink bottle. There was a steel-canopied bed, known as a Morrison shelter, in one corner and some photographs on the mantelpiece—one of a schoolboy wearing glasses. Everything was tainted with Elise's weariness and my own distaste. But Elise didn't seem to be aware of the exhaustion so plainly revealed on her face. She did not even bother to take her coat off, and as it was too tight for her, I wondered how she could move about so quickly with this restriction added to the weight of her tiredness. But, with her coat still buttoned tight, Elise phoned her boy friend and made breakfast, while I washed in a dim blue cracked bathroom upstairs.

When I found that she had opened my holdall without asking me and had taken out my rations, I was a little pleased. It seemed a friendly action, with some measure of reality about it, and I felt better. But I was still irritated by the house. I felt there was no justification for the positive lack of consequence, which was lying about here and there. I asked no questions about the owner who was something in a university, for fear of getting the answer I expected—that he was away visiting his grandchildren, at some family gathering in the home counties. The owners of the house had no reality for me, and I looked upon the place as belonging to, and permeated with, Elise.

I went with her to a nearby public house, where she met her boy friend and one or two other Australian soldiers, who had with them a thin Cockney girl with bad teeth. Elise was very happy, and insisted in her lovely voice that they should all come along to a party at the house that evening. In a fine aristocratic tone, she demanded that each should bring a bottle of beer.

During the afternoon, Elise said she was going to have a bath, and she showed me a room where I could use the phone and sleep if I wanted. This was a large, light room with several windows, much more orderly than the rest of the house, and lined with books. There was only one unusual thing about it: beside one of the windows was a bed, but this bed was only a fairly thick mattress made up neatly on the floor. It was obviously a bed on the floor with some purpose, and again I was angered to think of the futile crankiness of the elderly professor who had thought of it.

I did my telephoning, and decided to rest. But first I wanted to find something to read. The books puzzled me. None of them seemed to be automatically part of a scholar's library. An inscription in one book was signed by the author, a well-known novelist. I found another inscribed copy, and this had the name of the recipient. On a sudden idea, I went to the desk, where while I had been telephoning I had noticed a pile of unopened letters. For the first time, I looked at the name of the owner of the house.

I ran to the bathroom and shouted through the door to Elise, "Is this the house of the famous poet?"

"Yes," she called. "I *told* you."

She had told me nothing of the kind. I felt I had no right at all to be there, for it wasn't, now, the house of Elise acting by proxy for some unknown couple. It was the house of a famous modern poet. The thought that at any moment he and his family might walk in and find me there terrified me. I insisted that Elise should open the bathroom door and tell me to my face that there was no possible chance of their returning for many days to come.

Then I began to think about the house itself, which Elise was no longer accountable for. Its new definition, as the house of a poet whose work I knew well, many of whose poems I knew by heart, gave it altogether a fresh appearance.

To confirm this, I went outside and stood exactly where I had been when I first saw the garden from the door of the taxi. I wanted to get my first impression for a second time. And this time I saw an absolute purpose in the overgrown garden, which, since then, I have come to believe existed in the eye of the beholder. But, at the time, the room we had first entered, and which had riled me, now began to give back a meaning, and whatever was was right. The caked-up bottle of ink, which Elise had put on the mantelpiece, I replaced on the table to make sure. I saw a photograph I hadn't noticed before, and I recognized the famous poet.

It was the same with the upstairs room where Elise had put me, and I handled the books again, not so much with the sense that they belonged to the famous poet but with some curiosity about how they had been made. The sort of question that occurred to me was where the paper had come from and from what sort of vegetation was manufactured the black print, and these things have not troubled me since.

The Australians and the Cockney girl came around about seven. I had planned to catch an eight-thirty train to the country, but when I telephoned to confirm the time I found there were no Sunday trains running. Elise, in her friendly and exhausted way, begged me to stay without attempting to be too serious about it. The sirens were starting up again. I asked Elise once more to repeat that the poet and his family could by no means return that night. But I asked this question more abstractedly than before, as I was thinking of the sirens and of the exact proportions of the noise they made. I wondered, as well, what sinister genius of the Home Office could have invented so ominous a wail, and why. And I was thinking of the word "siren." The sound then became comical, for I imagined some maniac sea nymph from centuries past belching into the year 1944. Actually, the sirens frightened me.

Most of all, I wondered about Elise's party. Everyone roamed about the place as if it were nobody's house in particular, with Elise the best-behaved of the lot. The Cockney girl sat on the long table and gave of her best to the skies every time a bomb exploded. I had the feeling that the house had been requisitioned for an evening by the military. It was so hugely and everywhere occupied that it became not the house I had first entered, nor the house of the famous poet, but a third house—the one I had vaguely prefigured when I stood, bored, on the platform at King's Cross station. I saw a great amount of tiredness among these people, and heard, from the loud noise they made, that they were all lacking sleep. When the beer was finished and they were gone, some to their billets, some to pubs, and the Cockney girl to her Underground shelter where she had slept for weeks past, I asked Elise, "Don't you feel tired?"

"No," she said with agonizing weariness, "I never feel tired."

I fell asleep myself, as soon as I had got into the bed on the floor in the upstairs room, and overslept until Elise woke me at eight. I had wanted to get up early to catch a nine-o'clock train, so I hadn't much time to speak to her. I did notice, though, that she had lost some of her tired look.

I was pushing my things into my holdall while Elise went up the street to catch a taxi when I heard someone coming upstairs. I thought it was Elise come back, and I looked out of the open door. I saw a man in uniform carrying an enormous parcel in both hands. He looked down as he climbed, and had a cigarette in his mouth.

"Do you want Elise?" I called, thinking it was one of her friends.

He looked up, and I recognized the soldier, the throwback, who had given us cigarettes in the train.

"Well, anyone will do," he said. "The thing is, I've got to get back to camp and I'm stuck for the fare—eight and sixpence."

I told him I could manage it, and was finding the money when he said, putting his parcel on the floor, "I don't want to borrow it. I wouldn't think of borrowing it. I've got something for sale."

"What's that?" I said.

"A funeral," said the soldier. "I've got it here."

This alarmed me, and I went to the window. No hearse, no coffin stood below. I saw only the avenue of trees.

The soldier smiled, "It's an abstract funeral," he explained, opening the parcel.

He took it out and I examined it carefully, greatly comforted. It was very much the sort of thing I had wanted—rather more purple in parts than I would have liked, for I was not in favor of this color of mourning. Still, I thought I could tone it down a bit.

Delighted with the bargain, I handed over the eight shillings and sixpence. There was a great deal of this abstract funeral. Hastily, I packed some of it into the holdall. Some I stuffed in my pockets, and there was still some left over. Elise had returned with a cab and I hadn't much time. So I ran for it, out of the door and out of the gate of the house of the famous poet, with the rest of my funeral trailing behind me.

You will complain that I am withholding evidence. Indeed, you may wonder if there is any evidence at all. "An abstract funeral," you will say, "is neither here nor there. It is only a notion. You cannot pack a notion into your bag. You cannot see the color of a notion."

You will insinuate that what I have just told you is pure fiction.

Hear me to the end.

I caught the train. Imagine my surprise when I found sitting opposite me my friend the soldier, of whose existence you are so skeptical.

"As a matter of interest," I said, "how would you describe all this funeral you sold me?"

"Describe it?" he said. "Nobody describes an abstract funeral. You just conceive it."

"There is much in what you say," I replied. "Still, describe it I must, because it is not every day one comes by an abstract funeral."

"I am glad you appreciate that," said the soldier.

"And after the war," I continued, "when I am no longer a civil servant, I hope, in a few deftly turned phrases, to write of my experiences at the house of the famous poet, which have culminated like this. But, of course," I added, "I will need to say what it looks like."

The soldier did not reply.

“If it were an okapi or a sea cow,” I said, “I would have to say what it looked like. No one would believe me otherwise.”

“Do you want your money back?” asked the soldier. “Because if so, you can’t have it. I spent it on my ticket.”

“Don’t misunderstand me,” I hastened to say. “The funeral is a delightful abstraction. Only I wish to put it down in writing.”

I felt a great pity for the soldier on seeing his worried look. The apelike head seemed the saddest thing in the world.

“I make them by hand,” he said,”these abstract funerals.”

A siren sounded somewhere, far away.

“Elise bought one of them last month. She hadn’t any complaints. I change at the next stop,” he said, getting down his kit from the rack. “And what’s more,” he said, “your famous poet bought one.”

“Oh, did he?” I said.

“Yes,” he said. “No complaints. It was just what he wanted—the idea of a funeral.”

The train pulled up. The soldier leaped down and waved. As the train started again, I unpacked my abstract funeral and looked at it for a few moments.

“To hell with the idea,” I said. “It’s a real funeral I want.”

“All in good time,” said a voice from the corridor.

“*You* again,” I said. It was the soldier.

“No,” he said, “I got off at the last station. I’m only a notion of myself.”

“Look here,” I said, “would you be offended if I throw all this away?”

“Of course not,” said the soldier. “You can’t offend a notion.”

“I want a real funeral,” I explained. “One of my own.”

“That’s right,” said the soldier.

“And then I’ll be able to write about it and go into all the details,” I said.

“Your own funeral?” he said. “You want to write it up?”

“Yes,” I said.

“But,” said he, “you’re only human. Nobody reports on their own funeral. It’s got to be abstract.”

“You see my predicament?” I said.

“I see it,” he replied. “I get off at this stop.”

This notion of a soldier alighted. Once more the train put on speed. Out of the window I chucked all my eight-and-sixpence worth of abstract funeral. I watched it fluttering over the fields and around the tops of camouflaged factories with sun glittering richly upon it, until it was out of sight.

In the summer of 1944, a great many people were harshly and suddenly killed. The papers reported, in due course, those whose names were known to the public. One of those, the famous poet, had returned unexpectedly to his home at Swiss Cottage a few moments before it was hit direct by a flying bomb. Fortunately, he had left his wife and children in the country.

When I got to the place where my job was, I had some time to spare before going on duty. I decided to ring Elise and thank her properly, as I had left in such a hurry. But the lines were out of order, and the operator could not find words enough to express her annoyance with me. Behind this overworked, quarrelsome voice from the exchange I heard the high, long hoot that means that the telephone at the other end is not functioning, and the sound made me infinitely depressed and weary; it was more intolerable to me than the sirens, and I replaced the receiver; and, in fact, Elise had already perished under the house of the famous poet.

The blue cracked bathroom, the bed on the floor, the caked ink bottle, the neglected garden, and the neat rows of books—I try to gather them together in my mind whenever I am enraged by the thought that Elise and the poet were killed outright. The angels of the Resurrection will invoke the dead man and the dead woman, but who will care to restore the fallen house of the famous poet if not myself? Who else will tell its story?

When I reflect how Elise and the poet were taken in—how they calmly allowed a well-meaning soldier to sell them the notion of a funeral—I remind myself that one day I will accept, and so will you, an abstract funeral, and make no complaints.

THE CAFETERIA

BY ISAAC BASHEVIS SINGER (1968)

Even though I have reached the point where a great part of my earnings is given away in taxes, I still have the habit of eating in cafeterias when I am by myself. I like to take a tray with a tin knife, fork, spoon, and paper napkin and to choose at the counter the food I enjoy. Besides, I meet there the *landsleit* from Poland, as well as all kinds of literary beginners and readers who know Yiddish. The moment I sit down at a table, they come over. "Hello, Aaron!" They greet me, and we talk about Yiddish literature, the Holocaust, the state of Israel, and often about acquaintances who were eating rice pudding or stewed prunes the last time I was here and are already in their graves. Since I seldom read a paper, I learn this news only later. Each time, I am startled, but at my age one has to be ready for such tidings. The food sticks in the throat; we look at one another in confusion, and our eyes ask mutely, Whose turn is next? Soon we begin to chew again. I am often reminded of a scene in a film about Africa. A lion attacks a herd of zebras and kills one. The frightened zebras run for a while and then they stop and start to graze again. Do they have a choice?

I cannot spend too long with these Yiddishists, because I am always busy. I am writing a novel, a story, an article. I have to lecture today or tomorrow; my datebook is crowded with all kinds of appointments for weeks and months in advance. It can happen that an hour after I leave the cafeteria I am on a train to Chicago or flying to California. But meanwhile we converse in the mother language and I hear of intrigues and pettiness about which, from a moral point of view, it would be better not to be informed. Everyone tries in his own way with all his means to grab as many honors and as much love and prestige as he can. None of us learns from all these deaths. Old age does not cleanse us. We don't repent at the gate of Hell.

I have been moving around in this neighborhood for over thirty years—as long as I lived in Poland. I know each block, each house. There has been little building here on uptown Broadway in the last decades, and I have the illusion of having put down roots here. I have spoken in most of the synagogues. They know me in some of the stores and in the vegetarian restaurants. Women with whom I have had affairs live on the side streets. Even the pigeons know me; the moment I come out with a bag of feed, they begin to fly toward me from blocks away. It is an area that stretches from Ninety-sixth Street to Seventy-second Street and from Central Park to Riverside Drive. Almost every day on my walk after lunch, I pass the funeral parlor that waits for us and all our ambitions and illusions. Sometimes I imagine that the funeral parlor is also a kind of cafeteria where one gets a quick eulogy or *Kaddish* on the way to eternity.

The cafeteria people I meet are mostly men: old bachelors like myself, would-be writers, retired teachers, some with dubious doctorate titles, a rabbi without a congregation, a painter of Jewish themes, a few translators—all immigrants from Poland or Russia. I seldom know their names. One of them disappears and I think he is already in the next world; suddenly he reappears and he tells me that he has tried to settle in Tel Aviv or Los Angeles. Again he eats his rice pudding, sweetens his coffee with saccharin. He has a few more wrinkles, but he tells the same stories and makes the same gestures. It may happen that he takes a paper from his pocket and reads me a poem he has written.

It was in the fifties that a woman appeared in the group who looked younger than the rest of us. She must have been in her early thirties; she was short, slim, with a girlish face, brown hair that she wore in a bun, a short nose, and dimples in her cheeks. Her eyes were hazel—actually, of an indefinite color. She dressed in a modest

European way. She spoke Polish, Russian, and an idiomatic Yiddish. She always carried Yiddish newspapers and magazines. She had been in a prison camp in Russia and had spent some time in the camps in Germany before she obtained a visa for the United States. The men all hovered around her. They didn't let her pay the check. They gallantly brought her coffee and cheesecake. They listened to her talk and jokes. She had returned from the devastation still gay. She was introduced to me. Her name was Esther. I didn't know if she was unmarried, a widow, a divorcée. She told me she was working in a factory, where she sorted buttons. This fresh young woman did not fit into the group of elderly has-beens. It was also hard to understand why she couldn't find a better job than sorting buttons in New Jersey. But I didn't ask too many questions. She told me that she had read my writing while still in Poland, and later in the camps in Germany after the war. She said to me, "You are my writer."

The moment she uttered those words I imagined I was in love with her. We were sitting alone (the other man at our table had gone to make a telephone call), and I said, "For such words I must kiss you."

"Well, what are you waiting for?"

She gave me both a kiss and a bite.

I said, "You are a ball of fire."

"Yes, fire from Gehenna."

A few days later, she invited me to her home. She lived on a street between Broadway and Riverside Drive with her father, who had no legs and sat in a wheelchair. His legs had been frozen in Siberia. He had tried to run away from one of Stalin's slave camps in the winter of 1944. He looked like a strong man, had a head of thick white hair, a ruddy face, and eyes full of energy. He spoke in a swaggering fashion, with boyish boastfulness and a cheerful laugh. In an hour, he told me his story. He was born in White Russia but he had lived long years in Warsaw, Lodz, and Vilna. In the beginning of the thirties, he became a Communist and soon afterward a functionary in the Party. In 1939 he escaped to Russia with his daughter. His wife and the other children remained in Nazi-occupied Warsaw. In Russia, somebody denounced him as a Trotskyite and he was sent to mine gold in the north. The G.P.U. sent people there to die. Even the strongest could not survive the cold and hunger for more than a year. They were exiled without a sentence. They died together: Zionists, Bundists, members of the Polish Socialist Party, Ukrainian Nationalists, and just refugees, all caught because of the labor shortage. They often died of scurvy or beriberi. Boris Merkin, Esther's father, spoke about this as if it were a big joke. He called the Stalinists outcasts, bandits, sycophants. He assured me that had it not been for the United States Hitler would have overrun all of Russia. He told how prisoners tricked the guards to get an extra piece of bread or a double portion of watery soup, and what methods were used in picking lice.

Esther called out, "Father, enough!"

"What's the matter—am I lying?"

"One can have enough even of *kreplach*."

"Daughter, you did it yourself."

When Esther went to the kitchen to make tea, I learned from her father that she had had a husband in Russia—a Polish Jew who had volunteered in the Red Army and perished in the war. Here in New York she was courted by a refugee, a former smuggler in Germany who had opened a bookbinding factory and become rich. "Persuade her to marry him," Boris Merkin said to me. "It would be good for me, too."

"Maybe she doesn't love him."

"There is no such thing as love. Give me a cigarette. In the camp, people climbed on one another like worms."

I had invited Esther to supper, but she called to say she had the grippe and must remain in bed. Then in a few days' time a situation arose that made me leave for Israel. On the way back, I stopped over in London and Paris. I wanted to write to Esther, but I had lost her address. When I returned to New York, I tried to call her, but there was no telephone listing for Boris Merkin or Esther Merkin—father and daughter must have been boarders in somebody else's apartment. Weeks passed and she did not show up in the cafeteria. I asked the group about her; nobody knew where she was. "She has most probably married that bookbinder," I said to myself. One evening, I went to the cafeteria with the premonition that I would find Esther there. I saw a black wall and boarded windows—the cafeteria had burned. The old bachelors were no doubt meeting in another cafeteria, or an Automat. But where? To search is not in my nature. I had plenty of complications without Esther.

The summer passed; it was winter. Late one day, I walked by the cafeteria and again saw lights, a counter, guests. The owners had rebuilt. I entered, took a check, and saw Esther sitting alone at a table reading a Yiddish newspaper. She did not notice me, and I observed her for a while. She wore a man's fur fez and a jacket trimmed with a faded fur collar. She looked pale, as though recuperating from a sickness. Could that grippe have been the start of a serious illness? I went over to her table and asked, "What's new in buttons?"

She started and smiled. Then she called out, "Miracles do happen!"

"Where have you been?"

"Where did you disappear to?" she replied. "I thought you were still abroad."

"Where are our *cafeterianiks?*"

"They now go to the cafeteria on Fifty-seventh Street and Eighth Avenue. They only reopened this place yesterday."

"May I bring you a cup of coffee?"

"I drink too much coffee. All right."

I went to get her coffee and a large egg cookie. While I stood at the counter, I turned my head and looked at her. Esther had taken off her mannish fur hat and smoothed her hair. She folded the newspaper, which meant that she was ready to talk. She got up and tilted the other chair against the table as a sign that the seat was taken. When I sat down, Esther said, "You left without saying goodbye, and there I was about to knock at the pearly gates of Heaven."

"What happened?"

"Oh, the grippe became pneumonia. They gave me penicillin, and I am one of those who cannot take it. I got a rash all over my body. My father, too, is not well."

"What's the matter with your father?"

"High blood pressure. He had a kind of stroke and his mouth became all crooked."

"Oh, I'm sorry. Do you still work with buttons?"

"Yes, with buttons. At least I don't have to use my head, only my hands. I can think my own thoughts."

"What do you think about?"

"What not. The other workers are all Puerto Ricans. They rattle away in Spanish from morning to night."

"Who takes care of your father?"

"Who? Nobody. I come home in the evening to make supper. He has one desire—to marry me off for my own good and, perhaps, for his comfort, but I can't marry a man I don't love."

"What is love?"

"You ask me! You write novels about it. But you're a man—I assume you really don't know what it is. A woman is a piece of merchandise to you. To me a man who talks nonsense or smiles like an idiot is repulsive. I would rather die than live with him. And a man who goes from one woman to another is not for me. I don't want to share with anybody."

"I'm afraid a time is coming when everybody will."

"That is not for me."

"What kind of person was your husband?"

"How did you know I had a husband? My father, I suppose. The minute I leave the room, he prattles. My husband believed in things and was ready to die for them. He was not exactly my type but I respected him and loved him, too. He wanted to die and he died like a hero. What else can I say?"

"And the others?"

"There were no others. Men were after me. The way people behaved in the war—you will never know. They lost all shame. On the bunks near me one time, a mother lay with one man and her daughter with another. People were like beasts—worse than beasts. In the middle of it all, I dreamed about love. Now I have even stopped dreaming. The men who come here are terrible bores. Most of them are half mad, too. One of them tried to read me a forty-page poem. I almost fainted."

"I wouldn't read you anything I'd written."

"I've been told how you behave—no!"

"No is no. Drink your coffee."

"You don't even try to persuade me. Most men around here plague you and you can't get rid of them. In Russia people suffered, but I have never met as many maniacs there as in New York City. The building where I live is a madhouse. My neighbors are lunatics.

They accuse each other of all kinds of things. They sing, cry, break dishes. One of them jumped out of the window and killed herself. She was having an affair with a boy twenty years younger. In Russia the problem was to escape the lice; here you're surrounded by insanity."

We drank coffee and shared the egg cookie. Esther put down her cup. "I can't believe that I'm sitting with you at this table. I read all your articles under all your pen names. You tell so much about yourself I have the feeling I've known you for years. Still, you are a riddle to me."

"Men and women can never understand one another."

"No—I cannot understand my own father. Sometimes he is a complete stranger to me. He won't live long."

"Is he so sick?"

"It's everything together. He's lost the will to live. Why live without legs, without friends, without a family? They have all perished. He sits and reads the newspapers all day long. He acts as though he were interested in what's going on in the world. His ideals are gone, but he still hopes for a just revolution. How can a revolution help him? I myself never put my hopes in any movement or party. How can we hope when everything ends in death?"

"Hope in itself is a proof that there is no death."

"Yes, I know you often write about this. For me, death is the only comfort. What do the dead do? They continue to drink coffee and eat egg cookies? They still read newspapers? A life after death would be nothing but a joke."

Some of the *cafeterianiks* came back to the rebuilt cafeteria. New people appeared—all of them Europeans. They launched into long discussions in Yiddish, Polish, Russian, even Hebrew. Some of those who came from Hungary mixed German, Hungarian, Yiddish-German—then all of a sudden they began to speak plain Galician Yiddish. They asked to have their coffee in glasses, and held lumps of sugar between their teeth when they drank. Many of them were my readers. They introduced themselves and reproached me for all kinds of literary errors: I contradicted myself, went too far in descriptions of sex, described Jews in such a way that anti-Semites could use it for propaganda. They told me their experiences in the ghettos, in the Nazi concentration camps, in Russia. They pointed out one another. "Do you see that fellow—in Russia he immediately became a Stalinist. He denounced his own friends. Here in America he has switched to anti-Bolshevism." The one who was spoken about seemed to sense that he was being maligned, because the moment my informant left he took his cup of coffee and his rice pudding, sat down at my table, and said, "Don't believe a word of what you are told. They invent all kinds of lies. What could you do in a country where the rope was always around your neck? You had to adjust yourself if you wanted to live and not perish somewhere in Kazakhstan. To get a bowl of soup or a place to stay you had to sell your soul."

There was a table with a group of refugees who ignored me. They were not interested in literature and journalism but strictly in business. In Germany they had been smugglers. They seemed to be doing some shady business here, too; they whispered to one another and winked, counted their money, wrote long lists of numbers. Somebody pointed out one of them. "He had a store in Auschwitz."

"What do you mean, a store?"

"God help us. He kept his merchandise in the straw where he slept—a rotten potato, sometimes a piece of soap, a tin spoon, a little fat. Still, he did business. Later, in Germany, he became such a big smuggler they once took forty thousand dollars away from him."

Sometimes months passed between my visits to the cafeteria. A year or two had gone by (perhaps three or four; I lost count), and Esther did not show up. I asked about her a few times. Someone said that she was going to the cafeteria on Forty-second Street; another had heard that she was married. I learned that some of the *cafeterianiks* had died. They were beginning to settle down in the United States, had remarried, opened businesses, workshops, even had children again. Then came cancer or a heart attack. The result of the Hitler and Stalin years, it was said.

One day, I entered the cafeteria and saw Esther. She was sitting alone at a table. It was the same Esther. She was even wearing the same fur hat, but a strand of gray hair fell over her forehead. How strange—the fur hat, too, seemed to have grayed. The other *cafeterianiks* did not appear to be interested in her anymore, or they did not know her. Her face told of the time that had passed. There were shadows under her eyes. Her gaze was no longer so clear. Around her mouth was an expression that could be called bitterness, disenchantment. I greeted her. She smiled, but her smile immediately faded away. I asked, "What happened to you?"

"Oh, I'm still alive."

"May I sit down?"

"Please—certainly."

"May I bring you a cup of coffee?"

"No. Well, if you insist."

I noticed that she was smoking, and also that she was reading not the newspaper to which I contribute but a competition paper. She had gone over to the enemy. I brought her coffee and for myself stewed prunes—a remedy for constipation. I sat down. "Where were you all this time? I have asked for you."

"Really? Thank you."

"What happened?"

"Nothing good." She looked at me. I knew that she saw in me what I saw in her: the slow wilting of the flesh. She said, "You have no hair but you are white."

For a while we were silent. Then I said, "Your father—" and as I said it I knew that her father was not alive.

Esther said, "He has been dead for almost two years."

"Do you still sort buttons?"

"No, I became an operator in a dress shop."

"What happened to you personally, may I ask?"

"Oh nothing—absolutely nothing. You will not believe it, but I was sitting here thinking about you. I have fallen into some kind of trap. I don't know what to call it. I thought perhaps you could advise me. Do you still have the patience to listen to the troubles of little people like me? No, I didn't mean to insult you. I even doubted you would remember me. To make it short, I work but work is growing more difficult for me. I suffer from arthritis. I feel as if my bones would crack. I wake up in the morning and can't sit up. One doctor tells me that it's a disc in my back, others try to cure my nerves. One took X-rays and says that I have a tumor. He wanted me to go to the hospital for a few weeks, but I'm in no hurry for an operation. Suddenly a little lawyer showed up. He is a refugee himself and is connected with the German government. You know they're now giving reparation money. It's true that I escaped to Russia, but I'm a victim of the Nazis just the same. Besides, they don't know my biography so exactly. I could get a pension plus a few thousand dollars, but my dislocated disc is no good for the purpose because I got it later—after the camps. This lawyer says my only chance is to convince them that I am ruined psychically. It's the bitter truth, but how can you prove it? The German doctors, the neurologists, the psychiatrists require proof. Everything has to be according to the textbooks—just so and no different. The lawyer wants me to play insane. Naturally, he gets twenty per cent of the reparation money—maybe more. Why he needs so much money I don't understand. He's already in his seventies, an old bachelor. He tried to make love to me and whatnot. He's half *meshuga* himself. But how can I play insane when actually I *am* insane? The whole thing revolts me and I'm afraid it will really drive me crazy. I hate swindle. But this shyster pursues me. I don't sleep. When the alarm rings in the morning, I wake up as shattered as I used to be in Russia when I had to walk to the forest and saw logs at four in the morning. Naturally, I take sleeping pills—if I didn't, I couldn't sleep at all. That is more or less the situation."

"Why don't you get married? You are still a good-looking woman."

"Well, the old question—there is nobody. It's too late. If you knew how I felt, you wouldn't ask such a question."

A few weeks passed. Snow had been falling. After the snow came rain, then frost. I stood at my window and looked out at Broadway. The passersby half walked, half slipped. Cars moved slowly. The sky above the roofs shone violet, without a moon, without stars, and even though it was eight o'clock in the evening the light and the emptiness reminded me of dawn. The stores were deserted. For a moment, I had the feeling I was in Warsaw. The telephone rang and I rushed to answer it as I did ten, twenty, thirty years ago—still expecting the good tidings that a telephone call was about to bring me. I said hello, but there was no answer and I was seized by the fear that some evil power was trying to keep back the good news at the last minute. Then I heard a stammering. A woman's voice muttered my name.

"Yes, it is I."

"Excuse me for disturbing you. My name is Esther. We met a few weeks ago in the cafeteria—"

"Esther!" I exclaimed.

"I don't know how I got the courage to phone you. I need to talk to you about something. Naturally, if you have the time and—please forgive my presumption."

"No presumption. Would you like to come to my apartment?"

"If I will not be interrupting. It's difficult to talk in the cafeteria. It's noisy and there are eavesdroppers. What I want to tell you is a secret I wouldn't trust to anyone else."

"Please, come up."

I gave Esther directions. Then I tried to make order in my apartment, but I soon realized this was impossible. Letters, manuscripts lay around on tables and chairs. In the corners books and magazines were piled high. I opened the closets and threw inside whatever was under my hand: jackets, pants, shirts, shoes, slippers. I picked up an envelope and saw to my amazement that it had never been opened. I tore it open and found a check. "What's the matter with me—have I lost my mind?" I said out loud. I tried to read the letter that came with the check, but I had misplaced my glasses; my fountain pen was gone, too. Well—and where were my keys? I heard a bell ring and I didn't know whether it was the door or the telephone. I opened the door and saw Esther. It must have been snowing again, because her hat and the shoulders of her coat were trimmed with white. I asked her in, and my neighbor, the divorcée, who spied on me openly with no shame—and, God knows, with no sense of purpose—opened her door and stared at my new guest.

Esther removed her boots and I took her coat and put it on the case of the Encyclopaedia Britannica. I shoved a few manuscripts off the sofa so she could sit down. I said, "In my house there is sheer chaos."

"It doesn't matter."

I sat in an armchair strewn with socks and handkerchiefs. For a while we spoke about the weather, about the danger of being out in New York at night—even early in the evening. Then Esther said, "Do you remember the time I spoke to you about my lawyer—that I had to go to a psychiatrist because of the reparation money?"

"Yes, I remember."

"I didn't tell you everything. It was too wild. It still seems unbelievable, even to me. Don't interrupt me, I implore you. I'm not completely healthy—I may even say that I'm sick—but I know the difference between fact and illusion. I haven't slept for nights, and I kept wondering whether I should call you or not. I decided not to—but this evening it occurred to me that if I couldn't trust you with a thing like this then there is no one I could talk to. I read you and I know that you have a sense of the great mysteries—" Esther said all this stammering and with pauses. For a moment her eyes smiled, and then they became deeply sad and wavering.

I said, "You can tell me everything."

"I am afraid that you'll think me insane."

"I swear I will not."

Esther bit her lower lip. "I want you to know that I saw Hitler," she said.

Even though I was prepared for something unusual, my throat constricted. "When—where?"

"You see, you are frightened already. It happened three years ago—almost four. I saw him here on Broadway."

"On the street?"

"In the cafeteria."

I tried to swallow the lump in my throat. "Most probably someone resembling him," I said finally.

"I knew you would say that. But remember, you've promised to listen. You recall the fire in the cafeteria?"

"Yes, certainly."

"The fire has to do with it. Since you don't believe me anyhow, why draw it out? It happened this way. That night I didn't sleep. Usually when I can't sleep, I get up and make tea, or I try to read a book, but this time some power commanded me to get dressed and go out. I can't explain to you how I dared walk on Broadway at that late hour. It must have been two or three o'clock. I reached the cafeteria, thinking perhaps it stays open all night. I tried to look in, but the large window was covered by a curtain. There was a pale glow inside. I tried the revolving door and it turned. I went in and saw a scene I will not forget to the last day of my life. The tables were shoved together and around them sat men in white robes, like doctors or orderlies, all with swastikas on their sleeves. At the head sat Hitler. I beg you to hear me out—even a deranged person sometimes deserves to be listened to. They all spoke German. They didn't see me. They were busy with the Führer. It grew quiet and he started to talk. That abominable voice—I heard it many times on the radio. I didn't make out exactly what he said. I was too terrified to take it in. Suddenly one of his henchmen looked back at me and jumped up from his chair. How I came out alive I will never know. I ran with all my strength, and I was trembling all over. When I got home, I said to myself, 'Esther, you are not right in the head.' I still don't know how I lived through that night. The next morning, I didn't go straight to work but walked to the cafeteria to see if it was really there. Such an experience makes a person doubt his own senses. When I arrived, I found the place had burned down. When I saw this, I knew it had to do with what I had seen. Those who were there wanted all traces erased. These are the plain facts. I have no reason to fabricate such queer things."

We were both silent. Then I said, "You had a vision."

"What do you mean, a vision?"

"The past is not lost. An image from years ago remained present somewhere in the fourth dimension and it reached you just at that moment."

"As far as I know, Hitler never wore a long white robe."

"Perhaps he did."

"Why did the cafeteria burn down just that night?" Esther asked.

"It could be that the fire evoked the vision."

"There was no fire then. Somehow I foresaw that you would give me this kind of explanation. If this was a vision, my sitting here with you is also a vision."

"It couldn't have been anything else. Even if Hitler is living and is hiding out in the United States, he is not likely to meet his cronies at a cafeteria on Broadway. Besides, the cafeteria belongs to a Jew."

"I saw him as I am seeing you now."

"You had a glimpse back in time."

"Well, let it be so. But since then I have had no rest. I keep thinking about it. If I am destined to lose my mind, this will drive me to it."

The telephone rang and I jumped up with a start. It was a wrong number. I sat down again. "What about the psychiatrist your lawyer sent you to? Tell it to him and you'll get full compensation."

Esther looked at me sidewise and unfriendly. "I know what you mean. I haven't fallen that low yet."

I was afraid that Esther would continue to call me. I even planned to change my telephone number. But weeks and months passed and I never heard from her or saw her. I didn't go to the cafeteria. But I often thought about her. How can the brain produce such nightmares? What goes on in that little marrow behind the skull? And what guarantee do I have that the same sort of thing will not happen to me? And how do we know that the human species will not end like this? I have played with the idea that all of humanity suffers from schizophrenia. Along with the atom, the personality of *Homo sapiens* has been splitting. When it comes to technology, the brain still functions, but in everything else degeneration has begun. They are all insane: the Communists, the Fascists, the preachers of democracy, the writers, the painters, the clergy, the atheists. Soon technology, too, will disintegrate. Buildings will collapse, power plants will stop generating electricity. Generals will drop atomic bombs on their own populations. Mad revolutionaries will run in the streets, crying fantastic slogans. I have often thought that it would begin in New York. This metropolis has all the symptoms of a mind gone berserk.

But since insanity has not yet taken over altogether, one has to act as though there were still order—according to Vaihinger's principle of "as if." I continued with my scribbling. I delivered manuscripts to the publisher. I lectured. Four times a year, I sent checks to the federal government, the state. What was left after my expenses I put in the savings bank. A teller entered some numbers in my bankbook and this meant that I was provided for. Somebody printed a few lines in a magazine or newspaper, and this signified that my value as a writer had gone up. I saw with amazement that all my efforts turned into paper. My apartment was one big wastepaper basket. From day to day, all this paper was getting drier and more parched. I woke up at night fearful that it would ignite. There was not an hour when I did not hear the sirens of fire engines.

A year after I had last seen Esther, I was going to Toronto to read a paper about Yiddish in the second half of the nineteenth century. I put a few shirts in my valise as well as papers of all kinds, among them one that made me a citizen of the United States. I had enough paper money in my pocket to pay for a taxi to Grand Central. But the taxis seemed to be taken. Those that were not refused to stop. Didn't the drivers see me? Had I suddenly become one of those who see and are not seen? I decided to take the subway. On my way, I saw Esther. She was not alone but with someone I had known years ago, soon after I arrived in the United States. He was a frequenter of a cafeteria on East Broadway. He used to sit at a table, express opinions, criticize, grumble. He was a small man, with sunken cheeks the color of brick, and bulging eyes. He was angry at the new writers. He belittled the old ones. He rolled his own cigarettes and dropped ashes into the plates from which we ate. Almost two decades had passed since I had last seen him. Suddenly he appears with Esther. He was even holding her arm. I had never seen Esther look so well. She was wearing a new coat, a new hat. She smiled at me and nodded. I wanted to stop her, but my watch showed that it was late. I barely managed to catch the train. In my bedroom, the bed was already made. I undressed and went to sleep.

In the middle of the night, I awoke. My car was being switched, and I almost fell out of bed. I could not sleep anymore and I tried to remember the name of the little man I had seen with Esther. But I was unable to. The thing I did remember was that even thirty years ago he had been far from young. He had come to the United States in 1905 after the revolution in Russia. In Europe, he had a reputation as a speaker and public figure. How old must he be now? According to my calculations, he had to be in the late eighties—perhaps even ninety. Is it possible that Esther could be intimate with such an old man? But this evening he had not looked old. The longer I brooded about it in the darkness the stranger the encounter seemed to me. I even imagined that I had read somewhere in a newspaper that he had died. Do corpses walk around on Broadway? This would mean that Esther, too, was not living. I raised the window shade and sat up and looked out into the night—black, impenetrable, without a moon. A few stars ran along with the train for a while and then they disappeared. A lighted factory emerged; I saw machines but no operators. Then it was swallowed in the darkness and another group of stars began to follow the train. I felt confused and shaken. I was turning with the earth on its axis. I was circling with it around the sun and moving in the direction of a constellation whose name I had forgotten. Is there no death? Or is there no life?

I thought about what Esther had told me of seeing Hitler in the cafeteria. It had seemed utter nonsense, but now I began to reappraise the idea. If time and space are nothing more than forms of perception, as Kant argues, and quality, quantity, causality are only categories of thinking, why shouldn't Hitler confer with his Nazis in a cafeteria on Broadway? Esther didn't sound insane. She had seen a piece of reality that the heavenly censorship prohibits as a rule. She had caught a glimpse behind the curtain of the phenomena. I regretted that I had not asked for more details.

In Toronto, I had little time to ponder these matters, but when I returned to New York I went to the cafeteria for some private investigation. I met only one man I knew: a rabbi who had become an agnostic and given up his job. I asked him about Esther. He said, "The pretty little woman who used to come here?"

"Yes."

"I heard that she committed suicide."

"When—how?"

"I don't know. Perhaps we are not speaking about the same person."

No matter how many questions I asked and how much I described Esther, everything remained vague. Some young woman who used to come here had turned on the gas and made an end of herself—that was all the ex-rabbi could tell me.

I decided not to rest until I knew for certain what had happened to Esther and also to that half writer, half politician I remembered from East Broadway. But I grew busier from day to day. The cafeteria closed. The neighborhood changed. Years have passed and I have never seen Esther again. Yes, corpses do walk on Broadway. But why did Esther choose that particular corpse? She could have got a better bargain even in this world.

Translated, from the Yiddish, by the author and Dorothea Straus

CITY LOVERS

BY NADINE GORDIMER (1975)

Dr. Franz-Josef von Leinsdorf is a geologist absorbed in his work—wrapped up in it, as the saying goes. Year after year, the experience of this work enfolds him, swaddling him away from the landscapes, the cities, and the people of Peru, New Zealand, the United States, or wherever else he may live. He's always been like that, his mother could confirm from their native Austria. Even as a small boy, he seemed to present only his profile to her: turned away to his bits of rock and stone. His few relaxations have not changed much since then—an occasional skiing trip, listening to music, reading poetry. Rainer Maria Rilke once stayed in his grandmother's hunting lodge in the forests of Styria, and the boy was introduced to Rilke's poems while very young.

Now he has been in Africa for almost seven years, first on the Côte d'Ivoire, and then, for the past five years, in South Africa. A shortage of skilled manpower brought about his recruitment here. He has no interest in the politics of the countries he works in. His private preoccupation, within the preoccupation of his work, has been research into underground watercourses, but the mining company that employs him in a senior capacity is interested only in mineral discovery. He is much out in the field—"the veld," here—seeking new gold, copper, platinum, and uranium deposits. When he is at home, on this particular job, he lives in a three-room flat in a suburban block with a landscaped central garden, and does his shopping at a supermarket across the street. He is not married—yet. That is how his colleagues, and the typists and secretaries at the mining company's head office, would define his situation. Both men and women would describe him as a good-looking man, in a foreign way. The lower half of his face is dark and middle-aged (his mouth is thin and curving, and no matter how closely he shaves his beard shows like fine shot embedded in the skin around his mouth and chin), and the upper half contradictorily young. He has deep-set eyes (some would say gray, some black) and thick eyelashes and brows. A tangled gaze, through which concentration and thoughtfulness perhaps appear as languor. The women in his office say that he's "not unattractive." Although the gaze seems to contain promise, he has never invited any of them to go out with him. There is a general assumption he probably has a girl who's been picked for him, back home in Europe, where he comes from—that he's bespoken by one of his own kind. It is understood that many of these well-educated Europeans have no intention of becoming permanent immigrants; colonial life doesn't appeal to them.

One advantage, at least, of living in underdeveloped or half-developed countries is that most flats are serviced—resident cleaners come in every day. All Dr. von Leinsdorf has to do for himself is buy his own supplies and cook an evening meal if he doesn't want to go to a restaurant. He simply drops in to the supermarket on his way from his car to his flat after work in the afternoon, and wheels a shopping cart down the aisles. At the cashiers' counters, there are racks of small, uncategorized items for last-minute purchase. Here, as a Colored girl cashier punches the register (he has quickly accustomed himself to South African use of "Colored" to distinguish people of mixed blood from those of pure African descent), he sometimes picks up cigarettes and perhaps a packet of salted nuts or a bar of nougat. One evening in winter, he saw that the cardboard display board was empty of the brand of razor blades he preferred, and he drew the cashier's attention to this. These young Colored girls were usually unhelpful, taking money and punching their machines in a manner that asserted, with the timeserving obstinacy of the half-literate, a limit of any responsibility toward customers, but this particular girl glanced over the selection of razor blades, explained that she was not allowed to leave her post, and said she would see that the stock was replenished "next time." A day or two later, she recognized him as he took his turn before her counter. "I ahssed them," she said gravely, "but it's out of stock. You can't get it. I did ahss about it." He said it didn't matter. "When it comes in," she said, "I can keep a few packets for you." He thanked her.

He was away with the prospectors the whole of the next week. He arrived back in town just before nightfall on Friday, and was on the way from his car to his flat, arms filled with briefcase, suitcase, and two canvas bags, when someone stopped him by standing timidly in his path. He was about to dodge round unseeingly on the pavement, but she spoke. "We got the blades in now. I didn't see you in the shop this week, but I kept some for when you come. So . . ."

He recognized her. He had never seen her outdoors before, and she was wearing a coat. She was rather small and finely made, for one of them. The coat was skimpy, but she did not show a typical big backside. The cold brought a graining of warm color to her cheekbones, beneath which her very small face was quite delicately hollowed. Her skin was smooth, the subdued satiny color of certain yellow wood. She had crêpey hair, but it was drawn back flat into a little knot and pushed into one of the cheap wool nets that he recognized as being among the miscellany of small goods (along with the razor blades) on sale at the supermarket. He said thanks, he was in a hurry—he'd only just got back from a trip. He shifted the burdens he was carrying, to demonstrate. She said, "But if you want, I can run in and get the blades for you quickly. If you want."

He saw at once that all the girl meant was that she would go back to the supermarket, buy the blades, and bring the packet to him there where he stood, on the pavement. It was this certainty that made him say, in the kindly tone used for an obliging underling, "I live just across there. Atlantis—that flat building. Could you drop them by, for me—No. 718, seventh floor?" He gave her a one-rand note.

She had never been inside one of these big flat buildings. She lived a bus-and-train ride away, to the west of the city but this side of the black townships, in a township reserved for people her tint. In the entrance of the building called Atlantis there was a pool with real ferns, not plastic, and even a little waterfall pumping over rocks. She didn't wait for the lift marked "Goods" but took the one for whites. A white woman with one of those sausage dogs on a leash got in with her but did not pay her any attention. The corridors leading to the flats were nicely glassed in, not drafty.

He decided he should give her a twenty-cent piece for her trouble—ten cents would be right for a black—but she said, "Oh, no . . . please," standing outside his open door and awkwardly pushing back into his hand the change from the money he'd given her. She was smiling, for the first time, in the dignity of refusing a tip. It was difficult to know how to treat these people, in this country, difficult to know what they expected. In spite of her embarrassing refusal of the tip, she still stood there, unassuming, with her fists thrust down the pockets of her cheap coat. Her rather pretty thin legs were neatly aligned, knee to knee, ankle to ankle.

"Would you like a cup of coffee or something?" he said.

He couldn't very well take her into his living room and offer her a drink. She followed him to his kitchen, but at the sight of her pulling out the single chair there to drink her cup of coffee at the kitchen table he said, "No, bring it in here," and led the way into the big room, where, among his books and his papers, his files of scientific correspondence (and the cigar boxes of stamps from the envelopes), his racks of records, and his specimens of minerals and rocks, he lived alone.

It was no trouble to her. She saved him the trips to the supermarket and brought him his groceries two or three times a week. All he had to do was leave a list and the key under the doormat, and she would come up in her lunch hour to collect them, returning after work to put away his supplies in the flat. Sometimes he was home and sometimes not. He bought a box of chocolates and left it, with a note, for her to find. That was acceptable, apparently, as a gratuity.

When they were there together, he saw that her eyes went over everything in the flat, although her body seemed to try to conceal its sense of being out of place by remaining as still as possible. Sitting in a chair, she was like a coat laid there until its owner takes it up to go.

"You collect?" she said one day, looking at the stones and bits of rock that took the place of the pretty ornaments she would have expected in such a setting.

"Well, these are specimens—connected with my work."

"My brother used to collect. Miniatures. With brandy and whiskey and that in them. From all over. Different countries."

The second time they had coffee together, she watched him grinding the beans and said, "You always do that? Always when you make coffee?"

"But of course. Is it no good, for you? Do I make it too strong?"

"Oh, it's just I'm not used to it. We buy it ready—you know, coffee essence, it's in a bottle; you just add a bit to the milk or water."

He laughed. "That's not coffee," he said. "That's a liquid synthetically flavored. In my country we drink only real coffee, fresh, from the beans. You smell how good it is as it's being ground?"

One day, she was stopped by the caretaker and asked what she wanted in the building. Heavy with the *bona fides* of groceries clutched to her body, she said she was working at No. 718, on the seventh floor. The caretaker did not tell her not to use the whites' lift. After all, she was not black; her family was very light-skinned.

One day, there was the item "gray button for trousers" on one of his shopping lists. As she unpacked the shopping basket in the flat, she said, "Give me the pants, then," and spread them on her lap as she sat on his sofa, which was always gritty with fragments of pipe tobacco. She sewed swiftly in and out through the four holes of the button with firm, fluent movements of the right hand, her gestures supplying an articulacy missing from her talk. She had a little gap—a peasant's gap, he thought of it—between her two front teeth when she smiled. He didn't much like this, but when her face was turned away to a three-quarter angle, with her eyes cast down in concentration and her soft lips almost closed, it didn't matter. Watching her sew, he said, "You're a good girl;" and touched her.

She remade the bed every late afternoon when they left it and she dressed again before she went home. After a week, there was a day when late afternoon became evening and they were still in the bed.

"Can't you stay the night?"

"My mother," she said.

"Phone her. Make an excuse." He was a foreigner. He had been in the country five years, but he didn't yet understand that where she lived people didn't have telephones in their houses. She got up to dress. He didn't want that tender body to go out in the night cold, and kept hindering her with his hands, saying nothing. Before she put on her coat, when the body had already disappeared, he spoke. "But you must make some arrangement."

"Oh, my mother!"

Her face showed a fear and vacancy he could not read. Did the mother still think of her daughter as some pure and unsullied virgin?

"Why?" he said.

The girl said, "S'e'll be scared. S'e'll be scared we get caught."

"Don't tell her anything," he said. "Say I'm employing you." In his building there were rooms on the roof for tenants' servants.

She said, "That's what I told the caretaker."

She ground fresh coffee beans whenever he wanted a cup while he was working at night. She never attempted to cook anything until she had watched him do it the way he liked, and she learned to reproduce exactly the simple dishes he preferred. Sometimes she handled his pieces of rock and stone, at first admiring the colors: "It'd make a beautiful ring or a necklace, ay." Then he showed her the striations, the formation of each piece, and explained what each stone was, and how, in the long life of the earth, it had been formed. He named the mineral it yielded and what that was used for. He worked at his papers, writing, writing, every night, so it did not matter that they could not go out together to public places. On Sundays, she got into his car in the basement garage, and they drove to the country and picnicked away up in the Magaliesberg, where there was no one. He read or poked about among the rocks; they climbed together to the mountain pools. He taught her to swim. She squealed and shrieked in the water, showing the gap between her teeth as—it crossed his mind—she must when among her own people.

Occasionally, he had to go out to dinner at the houses of colleagues from the mining company. She sewed and listened to the radio in the flat, and he found her in the bed, warm and already asleep, by the time he came in. He made his way into her body without speaking; she made him welcome without a word. Once, he put on evening clothes for a dinner at his country's consulate. Watching him brush one or two fallen hairs from the shoulders of the dark jacket that sat so well on him, she saw a huge room, all chandeliers, and people dancing some dance from a costume film—stately, hand in hand. She supposed he was going to fetch a partner for the evening, to sit in her place in the car. They never kissed when either of them left the flat. Suddenly, kindly, pausing as he picked up cigarettes and keys, he said, "Don't be lonely." And added, "Wouldn't you like to visit your family sometimes, when I have to go out?"

He had told her that after Christmas he was going home to his mother in the forests and mountains of his country, near the Italian border (he showed her on the map). She had not told him how her mother, not knowing there was any other variety, assumed he was a medical doctor, or how she had talked to her mother about the doctor's children and the doctor's wife, who was a very kind lady, glad to have someone who could help out in the surgery as well as the flat.

She remarked wonderingly on his ability to work until midnight or later, after a day at work. When she came home from her cash register at the supermarket, she was so tired that once dinner was eaten she could scarcely keep awake. He explained, in a way she could understand, that while the work she did was repetitive, requiring little mental or physical effort, and therefore unrewarding, his work was his greatest interest; it taxed his mental capacities to their limit, exercised all his concentration, and rewarded him constantly, as much with the excitement of a problem presented as with the satisfaction of a problem solved. Later, putting away his papers, speaking out of a silence, he said, "Have you done other kinds of work?" She said, "I was in a clothing factory before. Sportbeau Shirts—you know? But the pay's better in the shop."

Of course. Being a conscientious newspaper reader, he was aware that it was only recently that the retail trade here had been allowed to employ Coloreds as shop assistants; even punching a cash register represented advancement. With the continuing shortage of semi-skilled whites, a girl like this might be able to edge a little further into the white-collar category. He began to teach her to type. He was aware that her English was poor, but because he was a foreigner her pronunciation did not offend him, nor categorize her. He corrected her grammatical mistakes but missed the less obvious ones because of his own sometimes unusual English usage. She continued to use the singular "it" for the plural "they." Because he was a foreigner (although so clever, she saw), she was less inhibited than she might have been by the words she knew she misspelled in her typing. While she sat at the typewriter, she thought how one day she would type notes for him, as well as making coffee the way he liked it and taking him inside her body without saying anything and sitting (even if only through the empty streets of quiet Sundays) beside him in his car, like a wife.

On a summer night near Christmas—he had already bought and hidden a slightly showy but good watch he thought she would like—there was a knocking at the door that brought her out of the bathroom and him to his feet, at his worktable. During the day, it might have been a canvasser or a hawker, but no one ever came to the flat at night; he was not at home to friends. The summons was an imperious banging that clearly would not stop until the door was opened.

Wearing a big bath towel, she stood in the bathroom doorway, gazing at him across the passage into the living room; her feet and shoulders were bare. She said nothing, did not even whisper. The flat seemed to shake with the strong, unhurried blows.

He made as if to go to the door at last, but now she ran and clutched him by both arms. She shook her head wildly. Her lips drew back, but her teeth were clenched. She didn't speak. She pulled him into the bedroom, snatched some clothes from the clean laundry laid out on the bed, and got into the built-in wardrobe, thrusting the key at his hand. His arms and calves felt weak and cold, but he was distastefully embarrassed at the sight of her crouching there under his suits and coats; it was horrible and ridiculous. "*Come out!*" he whispered. "*No! Come out!*"

"Where?" she said. "Where can I go?"

"*Never mind! Get out of there!*"

He put out his hand to grasp her. At bay, baring the gap in her teeth, she said in a terrible whisper, "*I'll throw myself out the window!*" She forced the key into his hand like the handle of a knife. He closed the door on her face and drove the key home in the lock, then dropped it among the coins in his trouser pocket.

He unslotted the chain that was looped across the entrance door of the flat. He turned the serrated knob of the Yale lock. Three policemen, two in plain clothes, stood there without impatience, although they had been banging on the door for several minutes.

One of the plainclothesmen—a big, dark man with an elaborate mustache—held out, in a hand wearing a plaited gilt ring, some sort of identity card.

"What is it?" Dr. von Leinsdorf said quietly, the blood coming strangely back to legs and arms.

The sergeant told him they knew there was a Colored girl in the flat. They had had information. "I been watching this flat three months," he said. "I know."

"I am alone here." Dr. von Leinsdorf did not raise his voice.

"I know, I know who is here. Come." And the sergeant and his two assistants passed him and moved systematically through the living room, the kitchen, the bathroom (the sergeant picked up a bottle of after-shave cologne and seemed to study the French label), and entered the bedroom. The assistants removed the clean laundry that was laid upon the bed and then turned back the bedding, carrying the sheets over to be examined by the sergeant under the lamp. They talked to one another in Afrikaans, which the doctor did not understand. The sergeant himself looked under the bed and lifted the long curtains at the window. The built-in wardrobe was of the kind that has no knobs; he saw that it was closed, and began to ask in Afrikaans, then politely changed to English, "Give us the key."

Dr. von Leinsdorf said, "I'm sorry, I left it at my office. I always lock up and take my keys with me in the mornings."

"It's no good, man. You better give me the key."

He smiled a little, reasonably. "It's on my office desk."

The assistants produced a screwdriver, and he watched while they inserted it where the wardrobe doors met and gave it a quick leverage. He heard the lock give.

She had been naked, it was true, when he had locked her in, but now she was wearing a long-sleeved shirt with an appliquéd butterfly motif on one breast, and a pair of jeans. Her feet were still bare. In the dark, she had managed to get into some of the clothing she had snatched from the bed, but she had no shoes. She had perhaps been weeping behind the door (her cheeks looked stained), but now her face was sullen and she was breathing heavily, her diaphragm contracting and expanding exaggeratedly and her breasts pushing against the cloth. She looked angry, but it might simply have been that she was half suffocated in the wardrobe and needed air. She did not look at Dr. von Leinsdorf. She would not reply to the sergeant's questions.

They were taken to the police station, where they were at once separated and led in turn for examination by the district surgeon. The man's underwear was taken away and examined, as the sheets had been, for signs of his seed. When the girl was undressed, it was discovered that beneath her jeans she was wearing a pair of men's briefs, with his name on the neatly sewn laundry tag. In her haste, she had taken the wrong garment to her hiding place.

Now she cried, standing there before the district surgeon in a man's underwear. He courteously pretended not to notice. He handed the briefs, jeans, and shirt to someone outside the door, and motioned her to lie on a white-sheeted high table, where he placed her legs apart, resting in stirrups, and put into her where the other had made his way so warmly a cold, hard instrument that expanded wider and wider. Her body opened. Her thighs and knees trembled uncontrollably while the doctor looked into her and touched her deep inside with other hard instruments carrying wafers of gauze.

When she came out of the examining room, back to the charge office, Dr. von Leinsdorf was not there; they must have taken him somewhere else. She spent what was left of the night in a cell, but early in the morning she was released and taken home to her mother's house in the Colored township. She was driven by a white man who explained he was the clerk of the lawyer who had been engaged for her by Dr. von Leinsdorf. The clerk said Dr. von Leinsdorf had also been bailed out that morning. She was not told when or if she would see him again.

A statement made by the girl to the police was handed in to the court when she and the man appeared to meet charges of contravening the Immorality Act in a Johannesburg flat. "I lived with the white man in his flat," it read. "He had intercourse with me sometimes. He gave me tablets to take to prevent me becoming pregnant."

Interviewed by the Sunday papers, the girl said, "I'm sorry for the sadness brought to my mother." She said she was one of nine children of a female laundry worker. She had left school in Standard Three because there was no money at home for gym clothes or a school blazer. She had worked as a machinist in a factory and a cashier in a supermarket. Dr. von Leinsdorf taught her to type his notes.

Dr. Franz-Josef von Leinsdorf, described in the newspaper as the grandson of a baroness—a cultured man engaged in international mineralogical research—said he accepted social distinctions between people but didn't think they should be legally imposed. "Even in my own country it's difficult for a person from a higher class to marry one from a lower class," he said.

The two accused gave no evidence. They did not greet or speak to each other in court. The defense argued that the sergeant's evidence that they had been living together as man and wife was hearsay. (The woman with dachshund had reported suspicions, perhaps, or maybe it was the caretaker.) The magistrate acquitted them because the state failed to prove that carnal intercourse had taken place on the stated night.

In the Sunday papers there was a photograph of the girl's mother, who was quoted as saying, "I won't let my daughter work as a servant for a white man again."

VOICES LOST IN SNOW

BY MAVIS GALLANT (1976)

Halfway between our two great wars, parents whose own early years had been shaped with Edwardian firmness were apt to lend a tone of finality to quite simple remarks: "Because I say so" was the answer to "Why?," and a child's response to "What did I just tell you?" could seldom be anything but "Not to"—not to say, do, touch, remove, go out, argue, reject, eat, pick up, open, shout, appear to sulk, appear to be cross. Dark riddles filled the corners of life because no enlightenment was thought required. Asking questions was "being tiresome," while persistent curiosity got one nowhere, at least nowhere of interest. How much has changed? Observe the drift of words descending from adult to child—the fall of personal questions, observations, unnecessary instructions. Before long the listener seems blanketed. He must hear the voice as authority muffled, a hum through snow. The tone has changed—it may be coaxing, even plaintive—but the words have barely altered. They still claim the ancient right-of-way through a young life.

"Well, old cock," said my father's friend Archie McEwen, meeting him one Saturday in Montreal. "How's Charlotte taking life in the country?" Apparently no one had expected my mother to accept the country in winter.

"Well, old cock," I repeated to a country neighbor, Mr. Bainwood. "How's life?" What do you suppose it meant to me, other than a kind of weathervane? Mr. Bainwood thought it over, then came round to our house and complained to my mother.

"It isn't blasphemy," she said, not letting him have much satisfaction from the complaint. Still, I had to apologize. "I'm sorry" was a ritual habit with even less meaning than "old cock." "Never say that again," my mother said after he had gone.

"Why not?"

"Because I've just told you not to."

"What does it mean?"

"Nothing."

It must have been after yet another "nothing" that one summer's day I ran screaming around a garden, tore the heads off tulips, and—no, let another voice finish it; the only authentic voices I have belong to the dead: ". . . then she *ate* them."

It was my father's custom if he took me with him to visit a friend on Saturdays not to say where we were going. He was more taciturn than any man I have known since, but that wasn't all of it; being young, I was the last person to whom anyone owed an explanation. These Saturdays have turned into one whitish afternoon, a windless snowfall, a steep street. Two persons descend the street, stepping carefully. The child, reminded every day to keep her hands still, gesticulates wildly—there is the flash of a red mitten. I will never overtake this pair. Their voices are lost in snow.

We were living in what used to be called the country and is now a suburb of Montreal. On Saturdays my father and I came in together by train. I went to the doctor, the dentist, to my German lesson. After that I had to get back to Windsor Station by myself and on time. My father gave me a boy's watch so that the dial would be good and large. I remember the No. 83 streetcar trundling downhill and myself, wondering if the watch was slow, asking strangers to tell me the hour. Inevitably—how could it have been otherwise?—after his death, which would not be long in coming, I would dream that someone important had taken a train without me. My route to the meeting place—deviated, betrayed by stopped clocks—was always downhill. As soon as I was old enough to understand from my reading of myths and legends that this journey was a pursuit of darkness, its terminal point a sunless underworld, the dream vanished.

Sometimes I would be taken along to lunch with one or another of my father's friends. He would meet the friend at Pauzé's for oysters or at Drury's or the Windsor Grill. The friend would more often than not be Scottish- or English-sounding, and they would talk as if I were invisible, as Archie McEwen had done, and eat what I thought of as English food—grilled kidneys, sweetbreads—which I was too finicky to touch. Both my parents had been made wretched as children by having food forced on them and so that particular torture was never inflicted on me. However, the manner in which I ate was subject to precise attention. My father disapproved of the North American custom that he called "spearing" (knife laid on the plate, fork in the right hand). My mother's eye was out for a straight back, invisible chewing, small mouthfuls, immobile silence during the interminable adult loafing over dessert. My mother did not care for food. If we were alone together, she would sit smoking and reading, sipping black coffee, her elbows used as props—a posture that would have called for instant banishment had I so much as tried it. Being constantly observed and corrected was like having a fly buzzing around one's plate. At Pauzé's, the only child, perhaps the only female, I sat up to an oak counter and ate oysters quite neatly, not knowing exactly what they were and certainly not that they were alive. They were served as in "The Walrus and the Carpenter," with bread and butter, pepper and vinegar. Dessert was a chocolate biscuit—plates of them stood at intervals along the counter. When my father and I ate alone, I was not required to say much, nor could I expect a great deal in the way of response. After I had been addressing him for minutes, sometimes he would suddenly come to life and I would know he had been elsewhere. "Of course I've been listening," he would protest, and he would repeat by way of proof the last few words of whatever it was I'd been saying. He was seldom present. I don't know where my father spent his waking life: just elsewhere.

What was he doing alone with a child? Where was his wife? In the country, reading. She read one book after another without looking up, without scraping away the frost on the windows. "The Russians, you know, the Russians," she said to her mother and me, glancing around in the drugged way adolescent readers have. "They put salt on the windowsills in winter." Yes, so they did, in the nineteenth century, in the boyhood of Turgenev, of Tolstoy. The salt absorbed the moisture between two sets of windows sealed shut for half the year. She must have been in a Russian country house at that moment, surrounded by a large Russian family, living out vast Russian complications. The flat white fields beyond her imaginary windows were like the flat white fields she would have observed if only she had looked out. She was myopic; the pupil when she had been reading seemed to be the whole of the eye. What age was she then? Twenty-seven, twenty-eight. Her husband had removed her to the country; now that they were there he seldom spoke. How young she seems to me now—half twenty-eight in perception and feeling, but with a husband, a child, a house, a life, an illiterate maid from the village whose life she confidently interfered with and mismanaged, a small zoo of animals she alternately cherished and forgot; and she was the daughter of such a sensible, truthful, pessimistic woman—pessimistic in the way women become when they settle for what actually exists.

Our rooms were not Russian—they were aired every day and the salt became a great nuisance, blowing in on the floor.

"There, Charlotte, what did I tell you?" my grandmother said. This grandmother did not care for dreams or for children. If I sensed the first, I had no hint of the latter. Out of decency she kept it quiet, at least in a child's presence. She had the reputation, shared with a long-vanished nurse named Olivia, of being able to "do anything" with me, which merely meant an ability to provoke from a child behavior convenient for adults. It was she who taught me to eat in the Continental way, with both hands in sight at all times upon the table, and who made me sit at meals with books under my arms so I would learn not to stick out my elbows. I remember having accepted this nonsense from her without a trace of resentment. Like Olivia, she could make the most pointless sort of training seem a natural way of life. (I think that as discipline goes this must be the most dangerous form of all.) She was one of three godparents I had—the important one. It is impossible for me to enter the mind of this agnostic who taught me prayers, who had already shed every remnant of belief when she committed me at the font. I know that she married late and reluctantly; she would have preferred a life of solitude and independence, next to impossible for a woman in her time. She had the positive voice of the born teacher, sharp manners, quick blue eyes, and the square, massive figure common to both lines of her ancestry—the West of France, the North of Germany. When she said "There, Charlotte, what did I tell you?" without obtaining an answer, it summed up mother and daughter both.

My father's friend Malcolm Whitmore was the second godparent. He quarreled with my mother when she said something flippant about Mussolini, disappeared, died in Europe some years later, though perhaps not fighting for Franco, as my mother had it. She often rewrote other people's lives, providing them with suitable and harmonious endings. In her version of events you were supposed to die as you'd lived. He would write sometimes, asking me, "Have you been confirmed yet?" He had never really held a place and could not by dying leave a gap. The third godparent was a young woman named Georgie Henderson. She was my mother's choice, for a long time her confidante, partisan, and close sympathizer. Something happened, and they stopped seeing each other. Georgie was not her real name—it was Edna May. One of the reasons she had fallen out with my mother was that I had not been called Edna May too. Apparently, this had been promised.

Without saying where we were going, my father took me along to visit Georgie one Saturday afternoon.

"You didn't say you were bringing Linnet" was how she greeted him. We stood in the passage of a long, hot, high-ceilinged apartment, treading snow water into the rug.

He said, "Well, she is your godchild, and she has been ill."

My godmother shut the front door and leaned her back against it. It is in this surprisingly dramatic pose that I recall her. It would be unfair to repeat what I think I saw then, for she and I were to meet again once, only once, many years after this, and I might substitute a lined face for a smooth one and tough, large-knuckled hands for fingers that may have been delicate. One has to allow elbowroom in the account of a rival: "She must have had something" is how it generally goes, long after the initial "What can he see in her? He must be deaf and blind." Georgie, explained by my mother as being the natural daughter of Sarah Bernhardt and a stork, is only a shadow, a tracing, with long arms and legs and one of those slightly puggy faces with pulled-up eyes.

Her voice remains—the husky Virginia-tobacco whisper I associate with so many women of that generation, my parents' friends; it must have come of age in English Montreal around 1920, when girls began to cut their hair and to smoke. In middle life the voice would slide from low to harsh, and develop a chronic cough. For the moment it was fascinating to me—opposite in pitch and speed from my mother's, which was slightly too high and apt to break off, like that of a singer unable to sustain a long note.

It was true that I had been ill, but I don't think my godmother made much of it that afternoon, other than saying, "It's all very well to talk about that now, but I was certainly never told much, and as for that doctor, you ought to just hear what Ward thinks." Out of this whispered jumble my mother stood accused—of many transgressions, certainly, but chiefly of having discarded Dr. Ward Mackey, everyone's doctor and a family friend. At the time of my birth my mother had all at once decided she liked Ward Mackey better than anyone else and had asked him to choose a name for me. He could not think of one, or, rather, thought of too many, and finally consulted his own mother. She had always longed for a daughter, so that she could call her after the heroine of a novel by, I believe, Marie Corelli. The legend so often repeated to me goes on to tell that when I was seven weeks old my father suddenly asked, "What did you say her name was?"

"*Votre fille a frôlé la phtisie*," the new doctor had said, the one who had now replaced Dr. Mackey. The new doctor was known to me as Uncle Raoul, though we were not related. This manner of declaring my brush with consumption was worlds away from Ward Mackey's "subject to bilious attacks." Mackey's objections to Uncle Raoul were neither envious nor personal, for Mackey was the sort of bachelor who could console himself with golf. The Protestant in him truly believed those other doctors to be poorly trained and superstitious, capable of recommending the pulling of teeth to cure tonsillitis, and of letting their patients cough to death or perish from septicemia just through Catholic fatalism.

What parent could fail to gasp and marvel at Uncle Raoul's

announcement? Any but either of mine. My mother could invent and produce better dramas any day; as for my father, his French wasn't all that good and he had to have it explained. Once he understood that I had grazed the edge of tuberculosis, he made his decision to remove us all to the country, which he had been wanting a reason to do for some time. He was, I think, attempting to isolate his wife, but by taking her out of the city he exposed her to a danger that, being English, he had never dreamed of: this was the heart-stopping cry of the steam train at night, sweeping across a frozen river, clattering on the ties of a wooden bridge. From our separate rooms my mother and I heard the unrivaled summons, the long, urgent, uniquely North American beckoning. She would follow and so would I, but separately, years and desires and destinations apart. I think that women once pledged in such a manner are more steadfast than men.

"*Frôler*" was the charmed word in that winter's story; it was a hand brushing the edge of folded silk, a leaf escaping a spiderweb. Being caught in the web would have meant staying in bed day and night in a place even worse than a convent school. Charlotte and Angus, whose lives had once seemed so enchanted, so fortunate and free that I could not imagine lesser persons so much as eating the same kind of toast for breakfast, had to share their lives with me, whether they wanted to or not—thanks to Uncle Raoul, who always supposed me to be their principal delight. I had been standing on one foot for months now, midway between *frôler* and *falling into*, propped up by a psychosomatic guardian angel. Of course I could not stand that way forever; inevitably my health improved and before long I was declared out of danger and then restored—to the relief and pleasure of all except the patient.

"I'd like to see more of you than eyes and nose," said my godmother. "Take off your things." I offer this as an example of unnecessary instruction. Would anyone over the age of three prepare to spend the afternoon in a stifling room wrapped like a mummy in outdoor clothes? "She's smaller than she looks," Georgie remarked, as I began to emerge. This authentic godmother observation drives me to my only refuge, the insistence that she must have had something—he could not have been completely deaf and blind. Divested of hat, scarf, coat, overshoes, and leggings, grasping the handkerchief pressed in my hand so I would not interrupt later by asking for one, responding to my father's muttered "Fix your hair," struck by the command because it was he who had told me not to use "fix" in that sense, I was finally able to sit down next to him on a white sofa. My godmother occupied its twin. A low table stood between, bearing a decanter and glasses and a pile of magazines and, of course, Georgie's ashtrays; I think she smoked even more than my mother did.

On one of these sofas, during an earlier visit with my mother and father, the backs of my dangling feet had left a smudge of shoe polish. It may have been the last occasion when my mother and Georgie were ever together. Directed to stop humming and kicking, and perhaps bored with the conversation in which I was not expected to join, I had soon started up again.

"It doesn't matter," my godmother said, though you could tell she minded.

"Sit up," my father said to me.

"I am sitting up. What do you think I'm doing?" This was not answering but answering back; it is not an expression I ever heard from my father, but I am certain it stood like a stalled truck in Georgie's mind. She wore the look people put on when they are thinking, Now what are you spineless parents going to do about that?

"Oh, for God's sake, she's only a child," said my mother, as though that had ever been an excuse for anything.

Soon after the sofa-kicking incident she and Georgie moved into the hibernation known as "not speaking." This, the lingering condition of half my mother's friendships, usually followed her having said the very thing no one wanted to hear, such as "Who wants to be called Edna May, anyway?"

Once more in the hot pale room where there was nothing to do and nothing for children, I offended my godmother again, by pretending I had never seen her before. The spot I had kicked was pointed out to me, though, owing to new slipcovers, real evidence was missing. My father was proud of my quite surprising memory, of its long backward reach and the minutiae of detail I could describe. My failure now to shine in a domain where I was naturally gifted, that did not require lessons or create litter and noise, must have annoyed him. I also see that my guileless-seeming needling of my godmother was a close adaptation of how my mother could be, and I attribute it to a child's instinctive loyalty to the absent one. Giving me up, my godmother placed a silver dish of mint wafers where I could reach them—white, pink, and green, overlapping—and suggested I look at a magazine. Whatever the magazine was, I had probably seen it, for my mother subscribed to everything then. I may have turned the pages anyway, in case at home something had been censored for children. I felt and am certain I have not invented Georgie's disappointment at not seeing Angus alone. She disliked Charlotte now, and so I supposed he came to call by himself, having no quarrel of his own; he was still close to the slighted Ward Mackey.

My father and Georgie talked for a while—she using people's initials instead of their names, which my mother would not have done—and they drank what must have been sherry, if I think of the shape of the decanter. Then we left and went down to the street in a wood-paneled elevator that had sconce lights, as in a room. The end of the afternoon had a particular shade of color then, which is not tinted by distance or enhancement but has to do with how streets were lighted. Lamps were still gas, and their soft gradual blooming at dusk made the sky turn a peacock blue that slowly deepened to marine, then indigo. This uneven light falling in blurred pools gave the snow it touched a quality of phosphorescence, beyond which were night shadows in which no one lurked. There were few cars, little sound. A fresh snowfall would lie in the streets in a way that seemed natural. Sidewalks were dangerous, casually sanded; even on busy streets you found traces of the icy slides children's feet had made. The reddish brown of the stone houses, the curve and slope of the streets, the constantly changing sky were satisfactory in a way that I now realize must have been aesthetically comfortable. This is what I saw when I read "city" in a book; I had no means of knowing that "city" one day would also mean drab, filthy, flat, or that city blocks could turn into dull squares without mystery.

We crossed Sherbrooke Street, starting down to catch our train. My father walked everywhere in all weathers. Already mined, colonized by an enemy prepared to destroy what it fed on, fighting it with every wrong weapon, squandering strength he should have been storing, stifling pain in silence rather than speaking up while there might have been time, he gave an impression of sternness that was a shield against suffering. One day we heard a mob roaring four syllables over and over, and we turned and went down a different street. That sound was starkly terrifying, something a child might liken to the baying of wolves.

"What is it?"

"Howie Morenz."

"Who is it? Are they chasing him?"

"No, they like him," he said of the hockey player admired to the point of dementia. He seemed to stretch, as if trying to keep every bone in his body from touching a nerve; a look of helplessness such as I had never seen on a grown person gripped his face and he said this strange thing: "Crowds eat me. Noise eats me." The kind of physical pain that makes one seem rat's prey is summed up in my memory of this.

When we came abreast of the Ritz-Carlton after leaving Georgie's apartment, my father paused. The lights within at that time of day were golden and warm. If I barely knew what "hotel" meant, never having stayed in one, I connected the lights with other snowy afternoons, with stupefying adult conversation (Oh, those shut-in velvet-draped unaired low-voice problems!) compensated for by creamy bitter hot chocolate poured out of a pink-and-white china pot.

"You missed your gootay," he suddenly remembered. Established by my grandmother, "*goûter*" was the family word for tea. He often transformed French words, like putty, into shapes he could grasp. No, Georgie had not provided a *goûter*, other than the mint wafers, but it was not her fault—I had not been announced. Perhaps if I had not been so disagreeable with her, he might have proposed hot chocolate now, though I knew better than to ask. He merely pulled my scarf up over my nose and mouth, as if recalling something Uncle Raoul had advised. Breathing inside knitted wool was delicious—warm, moist, pungent when one had been sucking on mint candies, as now. He said, "You didn't enjoy your visit much."

"Not very," through red wool.

"No matter," he said. "You needn't see Georgie again unless you want to," and we walked on. He must have been smarting, for he liked me to be admired. When I was not being admired I was supposed to keep quiet. "You needn't see Georgie again" was also a private decision about himself. He was barely thirty-one and had a full winter to live after this one—little more. Why? "Because I say so." The answer seems to speak out of the lights, the stones, the snow; out of the crucial second when inner and outer forces join, and the environment becomes part of the enemy too.

Ward Mackey used to mention me as "Angus's precocious pain in the neck," which is better than nothing. Long after that afternoon, when I was about twenty, Mackey said to me, "Georgie didn't play her cards well where he was concerned. There was a point where if she had just made one smart move she could have had him. Not for long, of course, but none of us knew that."

What cards, I wonder. The cards have another meaning for me—they mean a trip, a death, a letter, tomorrow, next year. I saw only one move that Saturday: my father placed a card face up on the table and watched to see what Georgie made of it. She shrugged, let it rest. There she sits, looking puggy but capable, Angus waiting, the precocious pain in the neck turning pages, hoping to find something in the *National Geographic* harmful for children. I brush in memory against the spiderweb: what if she had picked it up, remarking in her smoky voice, "Yes, I can use that"? It was a low card, the kind that only a born gambler would risk as part of a long-term strategy. She would never have weakened a hand that way; she was not gambling but building. He took the card back and dropped his hand, and their long intermittent game came to an end. The card must have been the eight of clubs—"a female child."

THE BOOK OF SAND

BY JORGE LUIS BORGES (1976)

Thy rope of sands . . .
—GEORGE HERBERT

The line is made up of an infinite number of points; the plane of an infinite number of lines; the volume of an infinite number of planes; the hypervolume of an infinite number of volumes. . . . No, unquestionably this is not—*more geometrico*—the best way of beginning my story. To claim that it is true is nowadays the convention of every made-up story. Mine, however, *is* true.

I live alone in a fourth-floor apartment on Belgrano Street, in Buenos Aires. Late one evening, a few months back, I heard a knock at my door. I opened it and a stranger stood there. He was a tall man, with nondescript features—or perhaps it was my myopia that made them seem that way. Dressed in gray and carrying a gray suitcase in his hand, he had an unassuming look about him. I saw at once that he was a foreigner. At first, he struck me as old; only later did I realize that I had been misled by his thin blond hair, which was, in a Scandinavian sort of way, almost white. During the course of our conversation, which was not to last an hour, I found out that he came from the Orkneys.

I invited him in, pointing to a chair. He paused awhile before speaking. A kind of gloom emanated from him—as it does now from me.

"I sell Bibles," he said.

Somewhat pedantically, I replied, "In this house are several English Bibles, including the first—John Wiclif's. I also have Cipriano de Valera's, Luther's—which, from a literary viewpoint, is the worst—and a Latin copy of the Vulgate. As you see, it's not exactly Bibles I stand in need of."

After a few moments of silence, he said, "I don't only sell Bibles. I can show you a holy book I came across on the outskirts of Bikaner. It may interest you."

He opened the suitcase and lay the book on a table. It was an octavo volume, bound in cloth. There was no doubt that it had passed through many hands. Examining it, I was surprised by its unusual weight. On the spine were the words "Holy Writ" and, below them, "Bombay."

"Nineteenth-century, probably," I remarked.

"I don't know," he said. "I've never found out."

I opened the book at random. The script was strange to me. The pages, which were worn and typographically poor, were laid out in double columns, as in a Bible. The text was closely printed, and it was ordered in versicles. In the upper corners of the pages were Arabic numbers. I noticed that one left-hand page bore the number (let us say) 40,514 and the facing right-hand page 999. I turned the leaf; it was numbered with eight digits. It also bore a small illustration, like the kind used in dictionaries—an anchor drawn with pen and ink, as if by a schoolboy's clumsy hand.

It was at this point that the stranger said, "Look at the illustration closely. You'll never see it again."

I noted my place and closed the book. At once, I reopened it. Page by page, in vain, I looked for the illustration of the anchor. "It seems to be a version of Scriptures in some Indian language, is it not?" I said to hide my dismay.

"No," he replied. Then, as if confiding a secret, he lowered his voice. "I acquired the book in a town out on the plain in exchange for a handful of rupees and a Bible. Its owner did not know how to read. I suspect that he saw the Book of Books as a talisman. He was of the lowest caste; nobody but other untouchables could tread his shadow without contamination. He told me his book was called the Book of Sand, because neither the book nor the sand has any beginning or end."

The stranger asked me to find the first page.

I lay my left hand on the cover and, trying to put my thumb on the flyleaf, I opened the book. It was useless. Every time I tried, a number of pages came between the cover and my thumb. It was as if they kept growing from the book.

"Now find the last page."

Again I failed. In a voice that was not mine, I barely managed to stammer, "This can't be."

Still speaking in a low voice, the stranger said, "It can't be, but it *is*. The number of pages in this book is no more or less than infinite. None is the first page, none the last. I don't know why they're numbered in this arbitrary way. Perhaps to suggest that the terms of an infinite series admit any number."

Then, as if he were thinking aloud, he said, "If space is infinite, we may be at any point in space. If time is infinite, we may be at any point in time."

His speculations irritated me. "You are religious, no doubt?" I asked him.

"Yes, I'm a Presbyterian. My conscience is clear. I am reasonably sure of not having cheated the native when I gave him the Word of God in exchange for his devilish book."

I assured him that he had nothing to reproach himself for, and I asked if he were just passing through this part of the world. He replied that he planned to return to his country in a few days. It was then that I learned that he was a Scot from the Orkney Islands. I told him I had a great personal affection for Scotland, through my love of Stevenson and Hume.

"You mean Stevenson and Robbie Burns," he corrected.

While we spoke, I kept exploring the infinite book. With feigned indifference, I asked, "Do you intend to offer this curiosity to the British Museum?"

"No. I'm offering it to you," he said, and he stipulated a rather high sum for the book.

I answered, in all truthfulness, that such a sum was out of my reach, and I began thinking. After a minute or two, I came up with a scheme.

"I propose a swap," I said. "You got this book for a handful of rupees and a copy of the Bible. I'll offer you the amount of my pension check, which I've just collected, and my black-letter Wiclif Bible. I inherited it from my ancestors."

"A black-letter Wiclif!" he murmured.

I went to my bedroom and brought him the money and the book. He turned the leaves and studied the title page with all the fervor of a true bibliophile.

"It's a deal," he said.

It amazed me that he did not haggle. Only later was I to realize that he had entered my house with his mind made up to sell the book. Without counting the money, he put it away.

We talked about India, about Orkney, and about the Norwegian jarls who once ruled it. It was night when the man left. I have not seen him again, nor do I know his name.

I thought of keeping the Book of Sand in the space left on the shelf by the Wiclif, but in the end I decided to hide it behind the volumes of a broken set of "The Thousand and One Nights." I went to bed and did not sleep. At three or four in the morning, I turned on the light. I got down the impossible book and leafed through its pages. On one of them I saw engraved a mask. The upper corner of the page carried a number, which I no longer recall, elevated to the ninth power.

I showed no one my treasure. To the luck of owning it was added the fear of having it stolen, and then the misgiving that it might not truly be infinite. These twin preoccupations intensified my old misanthropy. I had only a few friends left; I now stopped seeing even them. A prisoner of the book, I almost never went out anymore. After studying its frayed spine and covers with a magnifying glass, I rejected the possibility of a contrivance of any sort. The small illustrations, I verified, came two thousand pages apart. I set about listing them alphabetically in a notebook, which I was not long in filling up. Never once was an illustration repeated. At night, in the meagre intervals my insomnia granted, I dreamed of the book.

Summer came and went, and I realized that the book was monstrous. What good did it do me to think that I, who looked upon the volume with my eyes, who held it in my hands, was any less monstrous? I felt that the book was a nightmarish object, an obscene thing that affronted and tainted reality itself.

I thought of fire, but I feared that the burning of an infinite book might likewise prove infinite and suffocate the planet with smoke. Somewhere I recalled reading that the best place to hide a leaf is in a forest. Before retirement, I worked on Mexico Street, at the Argentine National Library, which contains nine hundred thousand volumes. I knew that to the right of the entrance a curved staircase leads down into the basement, where books and maps and periodicals are kept. One day I went there and, slipping past a member of the staff and trying not to notice at what height or distance from the door, I lost the Book of Sand on one of the basement's musty shelves.

Translated, from the Spanish, by Norman Thomas di Giovanni

FATHER'S LAST ESCAPE

BY BRUNO SCHULZ (1978)

It happened in the late and forlorn period of complete disruption, at the time of the liquidation of our business. The signboard had been removed from over our shop, the shutters were halfway down, and inside the shop my mother was conducting an unauthorized trade in remnants. Adela, our servant girl, had gone to America, and it was said that the boat on which she had sailed had sunk and that all the passengers had lost their lives. We were unable to verify this rumor, but all trace of the girl was lost and we never heard of her again.

A new age began—empty, sober, and joyless, like a sheet of white paper. A new servant girl, Genya, anemic, pale, and boneless, mooned about the rooms. When one patted her on the back, she wriggled, stretched like a snake, or purred like a cat. She had a dull white complexion, and even the insides of her eyelids were white. She was so absent-minded that she sometimes made a white sauce from old letters and invoices: it was sickly and inedible.

At that time, my father was definitely dead. He had been dying a number of times, always with some reservations that forced us to revise our attitude toward the fact of his death. This had its advantages. By dividing his death into installments, Father had familiarized us with his demise. We became gradually indifferent to his returns—each one shorter, each one more pitiful. His features were already dispersed throughout the room in which he had lived, and were sprouting in it, creating at some points strange knots of likeness that were most expressive. The wallpaper began in certain places to imitate his habitual nervous tic; the flower designs arranged themselves into the doleful elements of his smile, symmetrical as the fossilized imprint of a trilobite. For a time, we gave a wide berth to his fur coat lined with polecat skins. The fur coat breathed. The panic of small animals sewn together and biting into one another passed through it in helpless currents and lost itself in the folds of the fur. Putting one's ear against it, one could hear the melodious purring unison of the animals' sleep. In this well-tanned form, amid the faint smell of polecat, murder, and night-time matings, my father might have lasted for many years. But he did not last.

One day, Mother returned home from town with a preoccupied face.

"Look, Joseph," she said, "what a lucky coincidence. I caught him on the stairs, jumping from step to step"—and she lifted a handkerchief that covered something on a plate. I recognized him at once. The resemblance was striking, although now he was a crab or a large scorpion. Mother and I exchanged looks: in spite of the metamorphosis, the resemblance was incredible.

"Is he alive?" I asked.

"Of course. I can hardly hold him," Mother said. "Shall I place him on the floor?"

She put the plate down, and, leaning over him, we observed him closely. There was a hollow place between his numerous curved legs, which he was moving slightly. His uplifted pincers and feelers seemed to be listening. I tipped the plate, and Father moved cautiously and with a certain hesitation onto the floor. Upon touching the flat surface under him, he gave a sudden start with all of his legs, while his hard arthropod joints made a clacking sound. I barred his way. He hesitated, investigated the obstacle with his feelers, then lifted his pincers and turned aside. We let him run in his chosen direction, where there was no furniture to give him shelter. Running in wavy jerks on his many legs, he reached the wall and, before we could stop him, ran lightly up it, not pausing anywhere. I shuddered with instinctive revulsion as I watched his progress up the wallpaper.

Meanwhile, Father reached a small built-in kitchen cupboard, hung for a moment on its edge, testing the terrain with his pincers, and then crawled into it.

He was discovering the apartment afresh from the point of view of a crab; evidently, he perceived all objects by his sense of smell, for, in spite of careful checking, I could not find on him any organ of sight. He seemed to consider carefully the objects he encountered in his path, stopping and feeling them with his antennae, then embracing them with his pincers, as if to test them and make their acquaintance; after a time, he left them and continued on his run, pulling his abdomen behind him, lifted slightly from the floor. He acted the same way with the pieces of bread and meat that we threw on the floor for him, hoping he would eat them. He gave them a perfunctory examination and ran on, not recognizing that they were edible.

Watching these patient surveys of the room, one could assume that he was obstinately and indefatigably looking for something. From time to time, he ran to a corner of the kitchen, crept under a barrel of water that was leaking, and, upon reaching the puddle, seemed to drink.

Sometimes he disappeared for days on end. He seemed to manage perfectly well without food, but this did not seem to affect his vitality. With mixed feelings of shame and repugnance, we concealed by day our secret fear that he might visit us in bed during the night. But this never occurred, although in the daytime he would wander all over the furniture. He particularly liked to stay in the spaces between the wardrobes and the wall.

We could not discount certain manifestations of reason and even of a sense of humor. For instance, Father never failed to appear in the dining room during mealtimes, although his participation in them was purely symbolic. If the dining-room door was by chance closed during dinner and he had been left in the next room, he scratched at the bottom of the door, running up and down along the crack, until we opened it for him. In time, he learned how to insert his pincers and legs under the door, and after some elaborate maneuvers he finally succeeded in insinuating his body through it sideways into the dining room. This seemed to give him pleasure. He would then stop under the table, lying quite still, his abdomen slightly pulsating. What the meaning of these rhythmic pulsations was, we could not imagine. They seemed obscene and malicious, but at the same time expressed a rather gross and lustful satisfaction. Our dog, Nimrod, would approach him slowly and, without conviction, sniff at him cautiously, sneeze, and turn away indifferently, not having reached any conclusions.

Meanwhile, the demoralization in our household was increasing. Genya slept all day long, her slim body bonelessly undulating with her deep breaths. We often found in the soup reels of cotton, which she had thrown in unthinkingly with the vegetables. Our shop was open non-stop, day and night. A continuous sale took place amid complicated bargainings and discussions. To crown it all, Uncle Charles came to stay.

He was strangely depressed and silent. He declared with a sigh that after his recent unfortunate experiences he had decided to change his way of life and devote himself to the study of languages. He never went out but remained locked in the most remote room—from which Genya had removed all the carpets and curtains, as she did not approve of our visitor. There he spent his time, reading old price lists. Several times, he tried viciously to step on Father. Screaming with horror, we told him to stop it. Afterward he only smiled wryly to himself, while Father, not realizing the danger he had been in, hung around and studied some spots on the floor.

My father, quick and mobile as long as he was on his feet, shared with all crustaceans the characteristic that when turned on his back he became largely immobile. It was sad and pitiful to see him desperately moving all his limbs and rotating helplessly around his own axis. We could hardly force ourselves to look at the conspicuous, almost shameless mechanism of his anatomy, completely exposed under the bare articulated belly. At such moments, Uncle Charles could hardly restrain himself from stamping on Father. We ran to his rescue with some object at hand, which he caught tightly with his pincers, quickly regaining his normal position; then at once he started a lightning, zigzag run at double speed, as if wanting to obliterate the memory of his unsightly fall.

I must force myself to report truthfully the unbelievable deed, from which my memory recoils even now. To this day I cannot understand how we became the conscious perpetrators of it. A strange fatality must have been driving us to it; for fate does not evade consciousness or will but engulfs them in its mechanism, so that we are able to admit and accept, as in a hypnotic trance, things that under normal circumstances would fill us with horror.

Shaken badly, I asked my mother in despair, again and again, "How could you have done it? If it were Genya who had done it—but you yourself?" Mother cried, wrung her hands, and could find no answer. Had she thought that Father would be better off? Had she seen in that act the only solution to a hopeless situation, or did she do it out of inconceivable thoughtlessness and frivolity? Fate has a thousand wiles when it chooses to impose on us its incomprehensible whims. A temporary blackout, a moment of inattention or blindness is enough to insinuate an act between the Scylla and Charybdis of decision. Afterward, with hindsight, we may endlessly ponder that act, explain our motives, try to discover our true intentions; but the act remains irrevocable.

When Father was brought in on a dish, we came to our senses and understood fully what had happened. He lay large and swollen from the boiling, pale gray and jellified. We sat in silence, dumbfounded. Only Uncle Charles lifted his fork toward the dish, but at once he put it down uncertainly, looking at us askance. Mother ordered it to be taken to the sitting room. It stood there afterward on a table covered with a velvet cloth, next to the album of family photographs and a musical cigarette box. Avoided by us all, it just stood there.

But my father's earthly wanderings were not yet at an end, and the next installment—the extension of the story beyond permissible limits—is the most painful of all. Why didn't he give up, why didn't he admit that he was beaten when there was every reason to do so and when even fate could go no farther in utterly confounding him? After several weeks of immobility in the sitting room, he somehow rallied and seemed to be slowly recovering. One morning, we found the plate empty. One leg lay on the edge of the dish, in some congealed tomato sauce and aspic that bore the traces of his escape. Although boiled and shedding his legs on the way, with his remaining strength he had dragged himself somewhere to begin a homeless wandering, and we never saw him again.

Translated, from the Polish, by Celina Wieniewska

THE BURNING HOUSE

BY ANN BEATTIE (1979)

Freddy Fox is in the kitchen with me. He has just washed and dried an avocado seed I don't want, and he is leaning against the wall, rolling a joint. In five minutes, I will not be able to count on him. However: he started late in the day, and he has already brought in wood for the fire, gone to the store down the road for matches, and set the table. "You mean you'd know this stuff was Limoges even if you didn't turn the plate over?" he called from the dining room. He pretended to be about to throw one of the plates into the kitchen, like a Frisbee. Sam, the dog, believed him and shot up, kicking the rug out behind him and skidding forward before he realized his error; it was like the Road Runner tricking Wile E. Coyote into going over the cliff for the millionth time. His jowls sank in disappointment.

"I see there's a full moon," Freddy says. "There's just nothing that can hold a candle to nature. The moon and the stars, the tides and the sunshine—and we just don't stop for long enough to wonder at it all. We're so engrossed in ourselves." He takes a very long drag on the joint. "We stand and stir the sauce in the pot instead of going to the window and gazing at the moon."

"You don't mean anything personal by that, I assume."

"I love the way you pour cream in a pan. I like to come up behind you and watch the sauce bubble."

"No, thank you," I say. "You're starting late in the day."

"My responsibilities have ended. You don't trust me to help with the cooking, and I've already brought in firewood and run an errand, and this very morning I exhausted myself by taking Mr. Sam jogging with me, down at Putnam Park. You're sure you won't?"

"No, thanks," I say. "Not now, anyway."

"I love it when you stand over the steam coming out of a pan and the hairs around your forehead curl into damp little curls."

My husband, Frank Wayne, is Freddy's half brother. Frank is an accountant. Freddy is closer to me than to Frank. Since Frank talks to Freddy more than he talks to me, however, and since Freddy is totally loyal, Freddy always knows more than I know. It pleases me that he does not know how to stir sauce; he will start talking, his mind will drift, and when next you look the sauce will be lumpy, or boiling away.

Freddy's criticism of Frank is only implied. "What a gracious gesture to entertain his friends on the weekend," he says.

"Male friends," I say.

"I didn't mean that you're the sort of lady who doesn't draw the line. I most certainly did not mean that," Freddy says. "I would even have been surprised if you had taken a toke of this deadly stuff while you were at the stove."

"O.K.," I say, and take the joint from him. Half of it is left when I take it. Half an inch is left after I've taken two drags and given it back.

"More surprised still if you'd shaken the ashes into the saucepan."

"You'd tell people I'd done it when they'd finished eating, and I'd be embarrassed. You can do it, though. I wouldn't be embarrassed if it was a story you told on yourself."

"You really understand me," Freddy says. "It's moon-madness, but I have to shake just this little bit in the sauce. I have to do it."

He does it.

Frank and Tucker are in the living room. Just a few minutes ago, Frank returned from getting Tucker at the train. Tucker loves to visit. To him, Fairfield County is as mysterious as Alaska. He brought with him from New York a crock of mustard, a jeroboam of champagne, cocktail napkins with a picture of a plane flying over a building on them, twenty egret feathers ("You cannot get them anymore—strictly illegal," Tucker whispered to me), and, under his black cowboy hat with the rhinestone-studded chin strap, a toy frog that hopped when wound. Tucker owns a gallery in SoHo, and Frank keeps his books. Tucker is now stretched out in the living room, visiting with Frank, and Freddy and I are both listening.

". . . so everything I've been told indicates that he lives a purely Jekyll-and-Hyde existence. He's twenty years old, and I can see that since he's still living at home he might not want to flaunt his gayness. When he came into the gallery, he had his hair slicked back—just with water; I got close enough to sniff—and his mother was all but holding his hand. So fresh scrubbed. The stories I'd heard. Anyway, when I called, his father started looking for the number where he could be reached on the Vineyard—very irritated, because I didn't know James, and if I'd just phoned James I could have found him in a flash. He's talking to himself, looking for the number, and I say, 'Oh, did he go to visit friends or—' and his father interrupts and says, 'He was going to a gay pig roast. He's been gone since Monday.' *Just like that.*"

Freddy helps me carry the food out to the table. When we are all at the table, I mention the young artist Tucker was talking about. "Frank says his paintings are really incredible," I say to Tucker.

"Makes Estes look like an Abstract Expressionist," Tucker says. "I want that boy. I really want that boy."

"You'll get him," Frank says. "You get everybody you go after."

Tucker cuts a small piece of meat. He cuts it small so that he can talk while chewing. "Do I?" he says.

Freddy is smoking at the table, gazing dazedly at the moon centered in the window. "After dinner," he says, putting the back of his hand against his forehead when he sees that I am looking at him, "we must all go to the lighthouse."

"If only *you* painted," Tucker says. "I'd want you."

"You couldn't have me," Freddy snaps. He reconsiders. "That sounded halfhearted, didn't it? Anybody who wants me can have me. This is the only place I can be on Saturday night where somebody isn't hustling me."

"Wear looser pants," Frank says to Freddy.

"This is so much better than some bar that stinks of cigarette smoke and leather. Why do I do it?" Freddy says. "Seriously—do you think I'll ever stop?"

"Let's not be serious," Tucker says.

"I keep thinking of this table as a big boat, with dishes and glasses rocking on it," Freddy says.

He takes the bone from his plate and walks out to the kitchen, dripping sauce on the floor. He walks as though he's on the deck of a wave-tossed ship. "Mr. Sam!" he calls, and the dog springs up from the living-room floor, where he had been sleeping; his toenails on the bare wood floor sound like a wheel spinning in gravel. "You don't have to beg," Freddy says. "Jesus, Sammy—I'm just giving it to you."

"I hope there's a bone involved," Tucker says, rolling his eyes to Frank. He cuts another tiny piece of meat. "I hope your brother does understand why I couldn't keep him on. He was good at what he did, but he also might say just *anything* to a customer. You have to believe me that if I hadn't been extremely embarrassed more than once I never would have let him go."

"He should have finished school," Frank says, sopping up sauce on his bread. "He'll knock around a while longer, then get tired of it and settle down to something."

"You think I died out here?" Freddy calls. "You think I can't hear you?"

"I'm not saying anything I wouldn't say to your face," Frank says.

"I'll tell you what I wouldn't say to your face," Freddy says. "You've got a swell wife and kid and dog, and you're a snob, and you take it all for granted."

Frank puts down his fork, completely exasperated. He looks at me.

"He came to work once this stoned," Tucker says. "*Comprenez-vous?*"

"You like me because you feel sorry for me," Freddy says.

He is sitting on the concrete bench outdoors, in the area that's a garden in the springtime. It is early April now—not quite spring. It's very foggy out. It rained while we were eating, and now it has turned mild. I'm leaning against a tree, across from him, glad it's so dark and misty that I can't look down and see the damage the mud is doing to my boots.

"Who's his girlfriend?" Freddy says.

"If I told you her name, you'd tell him I told you."

"Slow down. What?"

"I won't tell you, because you'll tell him that I know."

"He knows you know."

"I don't think so."

"How did you find out?"

"He talked about her. I kept hearing her name for months, and then we went to a party at Andy's, and she was there, and when I said something about her later he said, 'Natalie who?' It was much too casual. It gave the whole thing away."

He sighs. "I just did something very optimistic," he says. "I came out here with Mr. Sam and he dug up a rock and I put the avocado seed in the hole and packed dirt on top of it. Don't say it—I know: can't grow outside, we'll still have another snow, even if it grew, the next year's frost would kill it."

"He's embarrassed," I say. "When he's home, he avoids me. But it's rotten to avoid Mark, too. Six years old, and he calls up his friend Neal to hint that he wants to go over there. He doesn't do that when we're here alone."

Freddy picks up a stick and pokes around in the mud with it. "I'll bet Tucker's after that painter personally, not because he's the hottest thing since pancakes. That expression of his—it's always the same. Maybe Nixon really loved his mother, but with that expression who could believe him? It's a curse to have a face that won't express what you mean."

"Amy!" Tucker calls. "Telephone."

Freddy waves goodbye to me with the muddy stick. "'I am not a crook,'" Freddy says. "Jesus Christ."

Sam bounds halfway toward the house with me, then turns and goes back to Freddy.

It's Marilyn, Neal's mother, on the phone.

"Hi," Marilyn says. "He's afraid to spend the night."

"Oh, no," I say. "He said he wouldn't be."

She lowers her voice. "We can try it out, but I think he'll start crying."

"I'll come get him."

"I can bring him home. You're having a dinner party, aren't you?"

I lower my voice. "Some party. Tucker's here. J.D. never showed up."

"Well," she says. "I'm sure that what you cooked was good."

"It's so foggy out, Marilyn. I'll come get Mark."

"He can stay. I'll be a martyr," she says, and hangs up before I can object.

Freddy comes into the house, tracking in mud. Sam lies in the kitchen, waiting for his paws to be cleaned. "Come on," Freddy says, hitting his hand against his thigh, having no idea what Sam is doing. Sam gets up and runs after him. They go into the small downstairs bathroom together. Sam loves to watch people urinate. Sometimes he sings, to harmonize with the sound of the urine going into the water. There are footprints and pawprints everywhere. Tucker is shrieking with laughter in the living room. ". . . he says, he says to the other one, 'Then, dearie, have you ever played *spin* the bottle?'" Frank's and Tucker's laughter drowns out the sound of Freddy peeing in the bathroom. I turn on the water in the kitchen sink, and it drowns out all the noise. I begin to scrape the dishes. Tucker is telling another story when I turn off the water: ". . . that it was Onassis in the Anvil, and nothing would talk him out of it. They told him Onassis was dead, and he thought they were trying to make him think he was crazy. There was nothing to do but go along with him, but, God—he was trying to goad this poor old fag into fighting about Stavros Niarchos. You know—Onassis's *enemy*. He thought it was *Onassis*. In the *Anvil*." There is a sound of a glass breaking. Frank or Tucker puts "John Coltrane Live in Seattle" on the stereo and turns the volume down low. The bathroom door opens. Sam runs into the kitchen and begins to lap water from his dish. Freddy takes his little silver case and his rolling papers out of his shirt pocket. He puts a piece of paper on the kitchen table and is about to sprinkle grass on it, but realizes just in time that the paper has absorbed water from a puddle. He balls it up with his thumb, flicks it to the floor, puts a piece of rolling paper where the table's dry and shakes a line of grass down it. "You smoke this," he says to me. "I'll do the dishes."

"We'll both smoke it. I'll wash and you can wipe."

"I forgot to tell them I put ashes in the sauce," he says.

"I wouldn't interrupt."

"At least he pays Frank ten times what any other accountant for an art gallery would make," Freddy says.

Tucker is beating his hand on the arm of the sofa as he talks, stomping his feet. ". . . so he's trying to feel him out, to see if this old guy with the dyed hair knew *Maria Callas*. Jesus! And he's so out of it he's trying to think what opera singers are called, and instead of coming up with '*diva*' he comes up with '*duenna*.' At this point, Larry Betwell went up to him and tried to calm him down, and he breaks into song—some aria or something that Maria Callas was famous for. Larry told him he was going to lose his *teeth* if he didn't get it together, and . . ."

"He spends a lot of time in gay hangouts, for not being gay," Freddy says.

I scream and jump back from the sink, hitting the glass I'm rinsing against the faucet, shattering green glass everywhere.

"What?" Freddy says. "Jesus Christ, what is it?"

Too late, I realize what it must have been that I saw: J.D. in a goat mask, the puckered pink plastic lips against the window beside the kitchen sink.

"I'm sorry," J.D. says, coming through the door and nearly colliding with Frank, who has rushed into the kitchen. Tucker is right behind him.

"Ooh," Tucker says, feigning disappointment, "I thought Freddy smooched her."

"I'm sorry," J.D. says again. "I thought you'd know it was me."

The rain must have started again, because J.D. is soaking wet. He has turned the mask around so that the goat's head stares out from the back of his head. "I got lost," J.D. says. He has a farmhouse upstate. "I missed the turn. I went miles. I missed the whole dinner, didn't I?"

"What did you do wrong?" Frank asks.

"I didn't turn left onto 58. I don't know why I didn't realize my mistake, but I went *miles*. It was raining so hard I couldn't go over twenty-five miles an hour. Your driveway is all mud. You're going to have to push me out."

"There's some roast left over. And salad, if you want it," I say.

"Bring it in the living room," Frank says to J.D. Freddy is holding out a plate to him. J.D. reaches for the plate. Freddy pulls it back. J.D. reaches again, and Freddy is so stoned that he isn't quick enough this time—J.D. grabs it.

"I thought you'd know it was me," J.D. says. "I apologize." He dishes salad onto the plate. "You'll be rid of me for six months, in the morning."

"Where does your plane leave from?" Freddy says.

"Kennedy."

"Come in here!" Tucker calls. "I've got a story for you about Perry Dwyer down at the Anvil last week, when he thought he saw Aristotle Onassis."

"Who's Perry Dwyer?" J.D. says.

"That is not the point of the story, dear man. And when you're in Cassis, I want you to look up an American painter over there. Will you? He doesn't have a phone. Anyway—I've been tracking him, and I know where he is now, and I am *very* interested, if you would stress that with him, to do a show in June that will be *only* him. He doesn't answer my letters."

"Your hand is cut," J.D. says to me.

"Forget it," I say. "Go ahead."

"I'm sorry," he says. "Did I make you do that?"

"Yes, you did."

"Don't keep your finger under the water. Put pressure on it to stop the bleeding."

He puts the plate on the table. Freddy is leaning against the counter, staring at the blood swirling in the sink, and smoking the joint all by himself. I can feel the little curls on my forehead that Freddy was talking about. They feel heavy on my skin. I hate to see my own blood. I'm sweating. I let J.D. do what he does; he turns off the water and wraps his hand around my second finger, squeezing. Water runs down our wrists.

Freddy jumps to answer the phone when it rings, as though a siren just went off behind him. He calls me to the phone, but J.D. steps in front of me, shakes his head no, and takes the dish towel and wraps it around my hand before he lets me go.

"Well," Marilyn says. "I had the best of intentions, but my battery's dead."

J.D. is standing behind me, with his hand on my shoulder.

"I'll be right over," I say. "He's not upset now, is he?"

"No, but he's dropped enough hints that he doesn't think he can make it through the night."

"O.K.," I say. "I'm sorry about all of this."

"Six years old," Marilyn says. "Wait till he grows up and gets that feeling."

I hang up.

"Let me see your hand," J.D. says.

"I don't want to look at it. Just go get me a Band-Aid, please."

He turns and goes upstairs. I unwrap the towel and look at it. It's pretty deep, but no glass is in my finger. I feel funny; the outlines of things are turning yellow. I sit in the chair by the phone. Sam comes and lies beside me, and I stare at his black-and-yellow tail, beating. I reach down with my good hand and pat him, breathing deeply in time with every second pat.

"*Rothko?*" Tucker says bitterly, in the living room. "Nothing is great that can appear on greeting cards. Wyeth is that way. Would 'Christina's World' look bad on a cocktail napkin? You know it wouldn't."

I jump as the phone rings again. "Hello?" I say, wedging the phone against my shoulder with my ear, wrapping the dish towel tighter around my hand.

"Tell them it's a crank call, tell them anything," Johnny says. "I miss you. How's Saturday night at your house?"

"All right," I say. I catch my breath.

"Everything's all right here, too. Yes indeed. Roast rack of lamb. Friend of Nicole's who's going to Key West tomorrow had too much to drink and got depressed because he thought it was raining in Key West, and I said I'd go in my study and call the National Weather Service. Hello, Weather Service. How are you?"

J.D. comes down from upstairs with two Band-Aids and stands beside me, unwrapping one. I want to say to Johnny, "I'm cut. I'm bleeding. It's no joke."

It's all right to talk in front of J.D., but I don't know who else might overhear me.

"I'd say they made the delivery about four this afternoon," I say.

"This is the church, this is the steeple. Open the door, and see all the people," Johnny says. "Take care of yourself. I'll hang up and find out if it's raining in Key West."

"Late in the afternoon," I say. "Everything is fine."

"Nothing is fine," Johnny says. "Take care of yourself."

He hangs up. I put the phone down, and realize that I'm still having trouble focussing, the sight of my cut finger made me so light-headed. I don't look at the finger again as J.D. undoes the towel and wraps the Band-Aids around my finger.

"What's going on in here?" Frank says, coming into the dining room.

"I cut my finger," I say. "It's O.K."

"You did?" he says. He looks woozy—a little drunk. "Who keeps calling?"

"Marilyn. Mark changed his mind about staying all night. She was going to bring him home, but her battery's dead. You'll have to get him. Or I will."

"Who called the second time?" he says.

"The oil company. They wanted to know if we got our delivery today."

He nods. "I'll go get him, if you want," he says. He lowers his voice. "Tucker's probably going to whirl himself into a tornado for an encore," he says, nodding toward the living room. "I'll take him with me."

"Do you want me to go get him?" J.D. says.

"I don't mind getting some air," Frank says. "Thanks, though. Why don't you go in the living room and eat your dinner?"

"You forgive me?" J.D. says.

"Sure," I say. "It wasn't your fault. Where did you get that mask?"

"I found it on top of a Goodwill box in Manchester. There was also a beautiful old birdcage—solid brass."

The phone rings again. I pick it up. "Wouldn't I love to be in Key West with you," Johnny says. He makes a sound as though he's kissing me and hangs up.

"Wrong number," I say.

Frank feels in his pants pocket for the car keys.

J.D. knows about Johnny. He introduced me, in the faculty lounge, where J.D. and I had gone to get a cup of coffee after I registered for classes. After being gone for nearly two years, J.D. still gets mail at the department—he said he had to stop by for the mail anyway, so he'd drive me to campus and point me toward the registrar's. J.D. taught English; now he does nothing. J.D. is glad that I've gone back to college to study art again, now that Mark is in school. I'm six credits away from an M.A. in art history. He wants me to think about myself, instead of thinking about Mark all the time. He talks as though I could roll Mark out on a string and let him fly off, high above me. J.D.'s wife and son died in a car crash. His son was Mark's age. "I wasn't prepared," J.D. said when we were driving over that day. He always says this when he talks about it. "How could you be prepared for such a thing?" I asked him. "I am now," he said. Then, realizing he was acting very hardboiled, made fun of himself. "Go on," he said, "punch me in the stomach. Hit me as hard as you can." We both knew he isn't prepared for anything. When he couldn't find a parking place that day, his hands were wrapped around the wheel so tightly that his knuckles turned white.

Johnny came in as we were drinking coffee. J.D. was looking at his junk mail—publishers wanting him to order anthologies, ways to get free dictionaries.

"You are so lucky to be out of it," Johnny said, by way of greeting. "What do you do when you've spent two weeks on 'Hamlet' and the student writes about Hamlet's good friend Horchow?"

He threw a blue book into J.D.'s lap. J.D. sailed it back.

"Johnny," he said, "this is Amy."

"Hi, Amy," Johnny said.

"You remember when Frank Wayne was in graduate school here? Amy's Frank's wife."

"Hi, Amy," Johnny said.

J.D. told me he knew it the instant Johnny walked into the room—he knew that second that he should introduce me as somebody's wife. He could have predicted it all from the way Johnny looked at me.

For a long time J.D. gloated that he had been prepared for what happened next—that Johnny and I were going to get together. It took me to disturb his pleasure in himself—me, crying hysterically on the phone last month, not knowing what to do, what move to make next.

"Don't do anything for a while. I guess that's my advice," J.D. said. "But you probably shouldn't listen to me. All I can do myself is run away, hide out. I'm not the learned professor. You know what I believe. I believe all that wicked fairy-tale crap: your heart will break, your house will burn."

Tonight, because he doesn't have a garage at his farm, J.D. has come to leave his car in the empty half of our two-car garage while he's in France. I look out the window and see his old Saab, glowing in the moonlight. J.D. has brought his favorite book, "A Vision," to read on the plane. He says his suitcase contains only a spare pair of jeans, cigarettes, and underwear. He is going to buy a leather jacket in France, at a store where he almost bought a leather jacket two years ago.

In our bedroom there are about twenty small glass prisms hung with fishing line from one of the exposed beams; they catch the morning light, and we stare at them like a cat eying catnip held above its head. Just now, it is 2 A.M. At six-thirty, they will be filled with dazzling color. At four or five, Mark will come into the bedroom and get in bed with us. Sam will wake up, stretch, and shake, and the tags on his collar will clink, and he will yawn and shake again and go downstairs, where J.D. is asleep in his sleeping bag and Tucker is asleep on the sofa, and get a drink of water from his dish. Mark has been coming into our bedroom for about a year. He gets onto the bed by climbing up on a footstool that horrified me when I first saw it—a gift from Frank's mother: a footstool that says "Today Is the First Day of the Rest of Your Life" in needlepoint. I kept it in a closet for years, but it occurred to me that it would help Mark get up onto the bed, so he would not have to make a little leap and possibly skin his shin again. Now Mark does not disturb us when he comes into the bedroom, except that it bothers me that he has reverted to sucking his thumb. Sometimes he lies in bed with his cold feet against my leg. Sometimes, small as he is, he snores.

Somebody is playing a record downstairs. It's the Velvet Underground—Nico, in a dream or swoon, singing "Sunday Morning." I can barely hear the whispering and tinkling of the record. I can only follow it because I've heard it a hundred times.

I am lying in bed, waiting for Frank to get out of the bathroom.

My cut finger throbs. Things are going on in the house even though I have gone to bed; water runs, the record plays, Sam is still downstairs, so there must be some action.

I have known everybody in the house for years, and as time goes by I know them all less and less. J.D. was Frank's adviser in college. Frank was his best student, and they started to see each other outside of class. They played handball. J.D. and his family came to dinner. We went there. That summer—the summer Frank decided to go to graduate school in business instead of English—J.D.'s wife and son deserted him in a more horrible way, in that car crash. J.D. has quit his job. He has been to Las Vegas, to Colorado, New Orleans, Los Angeles, Paris twice; he tapes postcards to the walls of his living room. A lot of the time, on the weekends, he shows up at our house with his sleeping bag. Sometimes he brings a girl. Lately, not. Years ago, Tucker was in Frank's therapy group in New York, and ended up hiring Frank to work as the accountant for his gallery. Tucker was in therapy at the time because he was obsessed with foreigners. Now he is also obsessed with homosexuals. He gives fashionable parties to which he invites many foreigners and homosexuals. Before the parties he does TM and yoga, and during the parties he does Seconals and isometrics. When I first met him, he was living for the summer in his sister's house in Vermont while she was in Europe, and he called us one night, in New York, in a real panic because there were wasps all over. They were "hatching," he said—big, sleepy wasps that were everywhere. We said we'd come; we drove all through the night to get to Brattleboro. It was true: there were wasps on the undersides of plates, in the plants, in the folds of curtains. Tucker was so upset that he was out behind the house, in the cold Vermont morning, wrapped like an Indian in a blanket, with only his pajamas on underneath. He was sitting in a lawn chair, hiding behind a bush, waiting for us to come.

And Freddy—"Reddy Fox," when Frank is feeling affectionate toward him. When we first met, I taught him to ice-skate and he taught me to waltz; in the summer, at Atlantic City, he'd go with me on a roller coaster that curved high over the waves. I was the one—not Frank—who would get out of bed in the middle of the night and meet him at an all-night deli and put my arm around his shoulders, the way he put his arm around my shoulders on the roller coaster, and talk quietly to him until he got over his latest anxiety attack. Now he tests me, and I retreat: this man he picked up, this man who picked him up, how it feels to have forgotten somebody's name when your hand is in the back pocket of his jeans and you're not even halfway to your apartment. Reddy Fox—admiring my new red silk blouse, stroking his fingertips down the front, and my eyes wide, because I could feel his fingers on my chest, even though I was holding the blouse in front of me on a hanger to be admired. All those moments, and all they meant was that I was fooled into thinking I knew these people because I knew the small things, the personal things.

Freddy will always be more stoned than I am, because he feels comfortable getting stoned with me and I'll always be reminded that he's more lost. Tucker knows he can come to the house and be the center of attention; he can tell all the stories he knows, and we'll never tell the story we know about him hiding in the bushes like a frightened dog. J.D. comes back from his trips with boxes full of postcards, and I look at all of them as though they're photographs taken by him, and I know, and he knows, that what he likes about them is their flatness—the unreality of them, the unreality of what he does.

Last summer, I read "The Metamorphosis" and said to J.D., "Why did Gregor Samsa wake up a cockroach?" His answer (which he would have toyed over with his students forever) was "Because that's what people expected of him."

They make the illogical logical. I don't do anything, because I'm waiting, I'm on hold (J.D.); I stay stoned because I know it's better to be out of it (Freddy); I love art because I myself am a work of art (Tucker).

Frank is harder to understand. One night a week or so ago, I thought we were really attuned to each other, communicating by telepathic waves, and as I lay in bed about to speak I realized that the vibrations really existed: they were him, snoring.

Now he's coming into the bedroom, and I'm trying again to think what to say. Or ask. Or do.

"Be glad you're not in Key West," he says. He climbs into bed.

I raise myself up on one elbow and stare at him.

"There's a hurricane about to hit," he says.

"What?" I say. "Where did you hear that?"

"When Reddy Fox and I were putting the dishes away. We had the radio on." He doubles up his pillow, pushes it under his neck. "Boom goes everything," he says, "Bam. Crash. Poof." He looks at me. "You look shocked." He closes his eyes. Then, after a minute or two, he murmurs, "Hurricanes upset you? I'll try to think of something nice."

He is quiet for so long that I think he has fallen asleep, Then he says, "Cars that run on water. A field of flowers, none alike. A shooting star that goes slow enough for you to watch. Your life to do over again."

He has been whispering in my ear, and when he takes his mouth away I shiver. He slides lower in the bed for sleep. "I'll tell you something really amazing," he says. "Tucker told me he went into a travel agency on Park Avenue last week and asked the travel agent where he should go to pan for gold, and she told him."

"Where did she tell him to go?"

"I think somewhere in Peru. The banks of some river in Peru."

"Did you decide what you're going to do after Mark's birthday?" I say.

He doesn't answer me. I touch him on the side, finally.

"It's two o'clock in the morning. Let's talk about it another time."

"You picked the house, Frank. They're your friends downstairs. I used to be what you wanted me to be."

"They're your friends, too," he says. "Don't be paranoid."

"I want to know if you're staying or going."

He takes a deep breath, lets it out, and continues to lie very still.

"Everything you've done is commendable," he says. "You did the right thing to go back to school. You tried to do the right thing by finding yourself a normal friend like Marilyn. But your whole life you've made one mistake—you've surrounded yourself with men. Let me tell you something. All men—if they're crazy, like Tucker, if they're gay as the Queen of the May, like Reddy Fox, even if they're just six years old—I'm going to tell you something about them. Men think they're Spider-Man and Buck Rogers and Superman. You know what we all feel inside that you don't feel? That we're going to the stars."

He takes my hand. "I'm looking down on all of this from space," he whispers. "I'm already gone."

THE SHAWL

BY CYNTHIA OZICK (1980)

Stella, cold, cold, the coldness of hell. How they walked on the roads together, Rosa with Magda curled up between sore breasts, Magda wound up in the shawl. Sometimes Stella carried Magda. But she was jealous of Magda. A thin girl of fourteen, too small, with thin breasts of her own, Stella wanted to be wrapped in a shawl, hidden away, asleep, rocked by the march, a baby, a round infant in arms. Magda took Rosa's nipple, and Rosa never stopped walking, a walking cradle. There was not enough milk; sometimes Magda sucked air; then she screamed. Stella was ravenous. Her knees were tumors on sticks, her elbows chicken bones.

Rosa did not feel hunger; she felt light, not like someone walking but like someone in a faint, in trance, arrested in a fit, someone who is already a floating angel, alert and seeing everything, but in the air, not there, not touching the road. As if teetering on the tips of her fingernails. She looked into Magda's face through a gap in the shawl: a squirrel in a nest, safe, no one could reach her inside the little house of the shawl's windings. The face, very round, a pocket mirror of a face: but it was not Rosa's bleak complexion, dark like cholera, it was another kind of face altogether, eyes blue as air, smooth feathers of hair nearly as yellow as the Star sewn in to Rosa's coat. You could think she was one of *their* babies.

Rosa, floating, dreamed of giving Magda away in one of the villages. She could leave the line for a minute and push Magda into the hands of any woman on the side of the road. But if she moved out of line they might shoot. And even if she fled the line for half a second and pushed the shawl-bundle at a stranger, would the woman take it? She might be surprised, or afraid; she might drop the shawl, and Magda would fall out and strike her head and die. The little round head. Such a good child, she gave up screaming, and sucked now only for the taste of the drying nipple itself. The neat grip of the tiny gums. One mite of a tooth tip sticking up in the bottom gum, how shining, an elfin tombstone of white marble gleaming there. Without complaining, Magda relinquished Rosa's teats, first the left, then the right; both were cracked, not a sniff of milk. The duct-crevice extinct, a dead volcano, blind eye, chill hole, so Magda took the corner of the shawl and milked it instead. She sucked and sucked, flooding the threads with wetness. The shawl's good flavor, milk of linen.

It was a magic shawl, it could nourish an infant for three days and three nights. Magda did not die, she stayed alive, although very quiet. A peculiar smell, of cinnamon and almonds, lifted out of her mouth. She held her eyes open every moment, forgetting how to blink or nap, and Rosa and sometimes Stella studied their blueness. On the road they raised one burden of a leg after another and studied Magda's face. "Aryan," Stella said, in a voice grown as thin as a string; and Rosa thought how Stella gazed at Magda like a young cannibal. And the time that Stella said "Aryan," it sounded to Rosa as if Stella had really said "Let us devour her."

But Magda lived to walk. She lived that long, but she did not walk very well, partly because she was only fifteen months old, and partly because the spindles of her legs could not hold up her fat belly. It was fat with air, full and round. Rosa gave almost all her food to Magda, Stella gave nothing; Stella was ravenous, a growing child herself, but not growing much. Stella did not menstruate. Rosa did not menstruate. Rosa was ravenous, but also not; she learned from Magda how to drink the taste of a finger in one's mouth. They were in a place without pity, all pity was annihilated in Rosa, she looked at Stella's bones without pity. She was sure that Stella was waiting for Magda to die so she could put her teeth into the little thighs.

Rosa knew Magda was going to die very soon; she should have been dead already, but she had been buried away deep inside the magic shawl, mistaken there for the shivering mound of Rosa's breasts; Rosa clung to the shawl as if it covered only herself. No one took it away from her. Magda was mute. She never cried. Rosa hid her in the barracks, under the shawl, but she knew that one day someone would inform; or one day someone, not even Stella, would steal Magda to eat her. When Magda began to walk Rosa knew that Magda was going to die very soon, something would happen. She was afraid to fall asleep; she slept with the weight of her thigh on Magda's body; she was afraid she would smother Magda under her thigh. The weight of Rosa was becoming less and less; Rosa and Stella were slowly turning into air.

Magda was quiet, but her eyes were horribly alive, like blue tigers. She watched. Sometimes she laughed—it seemed a laugh, but how could it be? Magda had never seen anyone laugh. Still, Magda laughed at her shawl when the wind blew its corners, the bad wind with pieces of black in it, that made Stella's and Rosa's eyes tear. Magda's eyes were always clear and tearless. She watched like a tiger. She guarded her shawl. No one could touch it; only Rosa could touch it. Stella was not allowed. The shawl was Magda's own baby, her pet, her little sister. She tangled herself up in it and sucked on one of the corners when she wanted to be very still.

Then Stella took the shawl away and made Magda die.

Afterward Stella said: "I was cold." And afterward she was always cold, always. The cold went into her heart: Rosa saw that Stella's heart was cold. Magda flopped onward with her little pencil legs scribbling this way and that, in search of the shawl; the pencils faltered at the barracks opening, where the light began. Rosa saw and pursued. But already Magda was in the square outside the barracks, in the jolly light. It was the roll-call arena. Every morning Rosa had to conceal Magda under the shawl against a wall of the barracks and go out and stand in the arena with Stella and hundreds of others, sometimes for hours, and Magda, deserted, was quiet under the shawl, sucking on her corner. Every day Magda was silent, and so she did not die. Rosa saw that today Magda was going to die, and at the same time a fearful joy ran in Rosa's two palms, her fingers were on fire, she was astonished, febrile: Magda, in the sunlight, swaying on her pencil legs, was howling. Ever since the drying up of Rosa's nipples, ever since Magda's last scream on the road, Magda had been devoid of any syllable; Magda was a mute. Rosa believed that something had gone wrong with her vocal cords, with her windpipe, with the cave of her larynx; Magda was defective, without a voice; perhaps she was deaf; there might be something amiss with her intelligence; Magda was dumb. Even the laugh that came when the ash-stippled wind made a clown out of Magda's shawl was only the air-blown showing of her teeth. Even when the lice, head lice and body lice, crazed her so that she became as wild as one of the big rats that plundered the barracks at daybreak looking for carrion, she rubbed and scratched and kicked and bit and rolled without a whimper. But now Magda's mouth was spilling a long viscous rope of clamor.

"Maaaa—"

It was the first noise Magda had ever sent out from her throat since the drying up of Rosa's nipples.

"Maaaa . . . aaa!"

Again! Magda was wavering in the perilous sunlight of the arena, scribbling on such pitiful little bent shins. Rosa saw. She saw that Magda was grieving for the loss of her shawl, she saw that Magda was going to die. A tide of commands hammered in Rosa's nipples: Fetch, get, bring! But she did not know which to go after first, Magda or the shawl. If she jumped out into the arena to snatch Magda up, the howling would not stop, because Magda would still not have the shawl; but if she ran back into the barracks to find the shawl, and if she found it, and if she came after Magda holding it and shaking it, then she would get Magda back, Magda would put the shawl in her mouth and turn dumb again.

Rosa entered the dark. It was easy to discover the shawl. Stella was heaped under it, asleep in her thin bones. Rosa tore the shawl free and flew—she could fly, she was only air—into the arena. The sunheat murmured of another life, of butterflies in summer. The light was placid, mellow. On the other side of the steel fence, far away, there were green meadows speckled with dandelions and deep-colored violets; beyond them, even farther, innocent tiger lilies, tall, lifting their orange bonnets. In the barracks they spoke of "flowers," of "rain": excrement, thick turd-braids, and the slow stinking maroon waterfall that slunk down from the upper bunks, the stink mixed with a bitter fatty floating smoke that greased Rosa's skin. She stood for an instant at the margin of the arena. Sometimes the electricity inside the fence would seem to hum; even Stella said it was only an imagining, but Rosa heard real sounds in the wire: grainy sad voices. The farther she was from the fence, the more clearly the voices crowded at her. The lamenting voices strummed so convincingly, so passionately, it was impossible to suspect them of being phantoms. The voices told her to hold up the shawl, high; the voices told her to shake it, to whip with it, to unfurl it like a flag. Rosa lifted, shook, whipped, unfurled. Far off, very far, Magda leaned across her air-fed belly, reaching out with the rods of her arms. She was high up, elevated, riding someone's shoulder. But the shoulder that carried Magda was not coming toward Rosa and the shawl, it was drifting away, the speck of Magda was moving more and more into the smoky distance. Above the shoulder a helmet glinted. The light tapped the helmet and sparkled it into a goblet. Below the helmet a black body like a domino and a pair of black boots hurled themselves in the direction of the electrified fence. The electric voices began to chatter wildly. "Maamaa, maaamaaa," they all hummed together. How far Magda was from Rosa now, across the whole square, past a dozen barracks, all the way on the other side! She was no bigger than a moth.

All at once Magda was swimming through the air. The whole of Magda travelled through loftiness. She looked like a butterfly touching a silver vine. And the moment Magda's feathered round head and her pencil legs and balloonish belly and zigzag arms splashed against the fence, the steel voices went mad in their growling, urging Rosa to run and run to the spot where Magda had fallen from her flight against the electrified fence; but of course Rosa did not obey them. She only stood, because if she ran they would shoot, and if she tried to pick up the sticks of Magda's body they would shoot, and if she let the wolf's screech ascending now through the ladder of her skeleton break out, they would shoot; so she took Magda's shawl and filled her own mouth with it, stuffed it in and stuffed it in, until she was swallowing up the wolf's screech and tasting the cinnamon and almond depth of Magda's saliva; and Rosa drank Magda's shawl until it dried.

THE BOOKSELLER

BY ELIZABETH HARDWICK (1980)

Saturday, November. Winter, thank heaven. Everyone is wearing something new in the fall line. Skirts are shorter and heels are, thereby, lower. Quite old ladies are in schoolgirl sweaters and men far from young are on silent roller skates—curving backward, slowly spinning around to make a deft, brilliant, soundless stop on the sidewalk.

November. People have stopped going to their country places for the weekend, because, it is said, there is too much going on in the city. How true that is. At the opera, machines float swans across the back of the stage and hurl swords through the air; ballet fans are gossiping on the mezzanine; the hardy are standing in fur or in fat jackets of spring-garden pinks and purples in the long lines outside the movie houses. The city people are as strong as athletes and in elevated spiritual condition, too. Happy hours inside the darkened halls, with so many performing up front in a flood of light. Creamy faces on the screen; thin chiffons and heavy velvets on the stage. He leaping, leaping, and she folding her arms in dejection, like the wings of a bird; another reaching so high, up, up, singing of her lover's treachery to the cause of her father. Saturday night, sold out.

The cafés are steaming, and from the restaurant doors garlic floats toward the hoods of cars waiting for the light. The newspaper kiosks have tomorrow's papers stacked outside and, as always, Roger's secondhand bookstore on Columbus Avenue is open for business. The store is called The Pleiade, but Roger likes to refer to it as the "play aid." He says he has learned to watch out for strangers who can pronounce the name properly, because they know what they are doing and are sure to steal him blind. This caution is not, in fact, Roger's way at all. He approaches theft—the thin volumes hiding in overcoats and the large volumes in shopping bags—with a short cry of pain and a long journey into his imagination, where he finds some poor truant, beaten down by self-awareness like the man in "Notes from Underground," poring with fevered eyes over his treasure.

It is almost eleven when we stop at the shop. Roger says: The overflow from "The Marriage of Maria Braun" is terrific.

Roger is a large man, with sand-colored skin and hair of a curious tan shade, and he is dressed in a sand-colored corduroy jacket with leather patches on the elbows. The elbow patches and the pipe he sometimes smokes do not give him the air of a professor or of a sportsman. He is too seedy and rumpled and sand-strewn for that. He is just the benign, beaming, outsized owner of The Pleiade, and he and his shop are rooted like cabbages in the mixed sod of Columbus Avenue.

Yes, a lot is going on, but Roger never goes to the opera, never goes to the ballet, seldom goes to the movies. He is stuck in his shop, like a flagpole on the village green. He is a man with a single overwhelming passion out of which his being flows. The modernist classics are his passion. Reverence, the tensions of love, the restlessness of pursuit inflect his utterance of the sacred names. Photographs of Frenchmen, Russians, Americans, Italians, martyrs of inspiration, are in frames on the walls of The Pleiade, and their mostly sombre images, caught in the youth of radical invention, are lit like icons by the candle of Roger's beaming eyes. He is haunted by memories. Where, oh where, is his lost copy of "A Barbarian in Asia" with the luck of Michaux's signature circled by cryptic drawings?

Roger and his books. His old friends are aware that he does not *quite* read them and that there is no word accurate for his curious taking in. He flips through the volumes delicately, carefully, and in some agitation of mind and spirit. His classics, with their almost constitutional authority, live under a kind of glass in his admiration. New books, not quite yesterday's or even of the last few years, he receives kindly and with generous hope, and he is quick to sort out those that have about them certain whisperings of futurity, of longevity. But it is not true that Roger has no knowledge of his books. The truth is that he knows them in an intimate, peculiar fashion. He knows well each flavor, each *spécialité*, each domain, and the very quality of the aspiration. In his cheerful heart all the ironies, overturnings, dissonances of modern art ring out their sad notes and fill him with happiness.

If one were to say: Roger, do you admire Bruno Schulz?, he would answer: Oh, yes, oh, yes. And then, reflecting, he might add: But I like "Crocodile Street" better than "Sanatorium." He has made a judgment, reached into the bibliophile quarry that is his head, and brought to life the elusive pages with their type, their chapter headings, their beginnings and endings, their place-names that sparkle with fresh consonants and vowels. And he knows what there is to know of lives—the terrible struggles of authorship that have undone so many.

At The Pleiade, a thin young woman, with hair cold and shiny like a wet cap, set over large, steady eyes, is drinking coffee at a long table at the back. Lois, Roger says.

Up front, there stands on tiptoe a not unusual bookshop scarecrow in black trousers, frayed jacket, and painful shoes long worn by feet much larger than the feet currently trying to find a grounding in them. This pitiful person is holding a book some distance from his eyes. Crazy, Roger says.

A very large dog, like a huge ball of dust, sleeps in the middle of the shop and must be circled by the customers. So it is, with small variations, seven nights a week at The Pleiade. Now a young couple, whispering, examine the titles on the shelves. Roger's eagerness follows their glances. He is in search of essence, the young couple's essence, to be revealed to him as a hand pulls a volume forward and then slowly pushes it back into place. Roger sees the light of recognition and the blankness of ignorance.

Pound's "ABC," the young man whispers to the girl. Twenty-five dollars. The expensive jewel lies in the young man's palm for a moment and then is returned to its alphabetical resting place.

Roger watches the unrolling, as it seems to him, of their biography. He is deeply interested, although the couple do not reveal any eccentricity and their passage through poetry, criticism, art, and fiction is unremarkable. But there is a longing, perhaps, a tenderness and wonder, before first American edition and original English edition, before the contemplation of the out-of-print, the signed, and the limited.

At last, the girl buys a paperback for two dollars and fifty cents. "Kafka's Diaries," Volume I. Roger's smile seems to fade a bit, although not in dishonor to Kafka, for whom he feels a love almost criminal. The fading seems to be a disappointment that the young couple had been thus far deprived of the volume.

They go out in their matching ski jackets, jog down the avenue with their blond hair flying behind. Roger collects his decisions about them. Poets, he says. I think they live downtown, but not in the East Village. Something like West Tenth Street. Respectable types, Amherst and Wellesley. Those two are spacing lines on a page.

Roger. I can see again his large head bowed, as if in grief, in the Milton seminar at Columbia some years ago. He brought to graduate studies his pen and his notebook and the steady downward tug of his dilatory, procrastinating nature. It was the modernist T. S. Eliot and his resurrection of the metaphysical poets that had led Roger disastrously to the seventeenth century. By the perverse authority of institutions he was brutally dragged by his light curls into the study of Milton, a poet not even very high in the regard of Eliot at the time. Roger endured for a few months. He wrote in the margins of "The Student's Milton": "Cf. Virgil," after one line; and "See Pliny the Elder," after another; and at the top of a page "Pythagoras was the only one who had heard the spheres' music."

But his head was too big and his eyes were too small for the peering at lines, and he shuffled about in the text like a melancholy sheep in a pen. At last, he gave up and went cheerfully loping off into the meadow of upper Broadway, and came to a stop some years later as the proprietor of The Pleiade. And yet, even now, Roger can sometimes be heard in the doorway of his shop, greeting a friend with "Hail, holy light!," the only phrase from "Paradise Lost" sequestered in his memory.

Roger knows well a number of regular visitors to The Pleiade and he has friends, themselves a miscellaneous collection, from his Columbia undergraduate days. He knows a French-literature scholar, a Socialist, a Catholic poet, and a lawyer who plays the violin and reads Kleist and Novalis in German.

The night is ending and Lois is nodding at the table. Before Lois, Maureen was for some months sitting at the table, sitting there silent and beautiful and abstracted—very, very much in the Lois manner.

Where is Maureen?

Gone for a spell to the topless towers, Roger says. Is there regret in his tone? No, not exactly. It is Roger's way to meet fate with the sweetest accommodation of the trivial or the violent alteration. Profound passivity, a little wonder, and a flash of puzzlement here and there, and the flux of his domestic arrangements serenely made its way to sea. For this, the troubled people who floated down on him, as if he were a pier for a sudden anchorage, were perhaps grateful.

The topless towers was his designation of Maureen's home town, Troy, New York. And it was there she would go when the peaceful vacancy of her nature took a little turn to the left or right and she had to be got back on the road again.

Lois is a friend of Maureen's, Roger explains. She's looking for work.

Lois nods, and her meditative gaze is so untroubled that it has the effect of a signal of trouble itself.

From time to time, the iron gates over the front of The Pleiade remained closed past noon, and some of Roger's commercial neighbors were taken by curiosity. The cook from the Chinese restaurant often walked out in his apron and peered through the gated windows into the impatient jaws of the dog. The fat palmist, awaiting the evacuation sure to arrive when the landlord, stuck with the derelict for so many years, could decide to what brilliant, prosperous use the palmist's street-front broom closet might be put, glared with deep intention at the locked gates, as if she had at last accomplished a predicted malediction. There was no cordiality between Roger and the palmist, because he detested the occult and the pornographic and, to him, the palmist united the two in her black coils of hair and in the beseeching, whimpering noises directed at passersby.

But soon there would come Roger in a taxi, and out of the taxi came shopping bags filled with more books bought from a bankrupt hole-in-the-wall competitor. The gates rolled back, the cut-rate bin was trundled to the pavement, and the luckless, sneering palmist saw The Pleiade's Mostly Mozart poster return to life. The slim volumes again dozed in the afternoon light. The large volumes of the "High Renaissance" and "The History of Egyptian Art" listened once more to the gassy braking of the No. 11 bus. All was well, except that Roger was undergoing a brief sinking spell because of the new burden of his infatuated buying.

Roger does not drink, but he eats quite a lot of apples, pizzas, and hamburgers, and makes many cups of coffee in his electric pot. He lives in the large, decaying building over the shop. He is one of those brought up by well-to-do parents, sent to good schools, to France for a summer—who, on their own, show no more memory of physical comforts than a prairie dog.

Once, in the bookstore, the lawyer friend spoke about a visit to the apartment to look at a violin Roger had bought. Lethal squalor, he kept repeating, lethal squalor. Yet he found in this jumbled, tumbled theatre of belligerent disorder a fine violin, old paintings of curious interest, fine brasses black with tarnish, rare books, carved wood: twenty-five years of desultory buying in junk shops, elephantine carting, and, at last, forgetful dumping. The lawyer observed that Roger would never starve but he might die from stepping on a rusty nail.

Roger has his dog, with its concentrated sleepy look, and his Maureens and Loises with their unconcentrated, dream-heavy eyes. He has his shop, where he spends his waking hours, and when that is over he goes upstairs to rest, like a peasant returning to his hut at sundown. Perhaps he sleeps on a pallet, wrapped in his winter sheepskin in the unthinkable darkness in which one imagines his bright, daylight smile there someplace in the clutter, beaming away like a night lamp. No matter—the patrician in him is not entirely erased and lingers on in an amiable displacement, remaining in his contentment to keep pace with just where he is, to raise prices as the rent rises, to keep out the street winds, to fill the shopping bags with new loot, and to feel a certain discomfort and confusion when he makes a sale. His father left a good deal of money, but Roger does no resentful bookkeeping. Instead, he shows a flare of pride that his mother is in her ninety-sixth year, consuming the real estate, the insurance, the stocks like an admirable, slowly grazing animal.

The wind from the river comes up suddenly to disperse the Saturday-night rubbish. Into the air go newspapers, candy wrappers, loose tobacco, and the sluggish waters at the curb stir under the tidal moon. The bookstore empties and Roger sighs in the mixed feelings of the end of another day of his long, long celebration. He directs Lois to go across the street to the all-night Puerto Rican grocery store to buy cornflakes. She looks uncertain of this journey but takes the five-dollar bill, scurries away among the cars, looking like a small, blackened crossing sweeper of a century ago.

Majored in fine arts, Roger says. And then, looking up into the sky in which lights from so many rooms flicker like yellow stars, Roger drifts for a moment into a mesmerized, speculative mode. In the rooms, he says, he imagines miserable calculations in every head nodding off to sleep, figures added and subtracted, dreams of selling the very space that held the bed upon which the sleeper's head restlessly lay in its blur of arithmetic. On the street, he has noticed that people keep turning around suddenly, as if future income taxes were brushing by, grazing coats like a pickpocket.

Lois returns, the gates clang before the darkened window, and as they start up the stairs of the tenement Roger ends his historical reverie. Those that are not inside counting up, he says, are outside making marks in indelible ink on every clean wall. Good night, good night.

Some days after, there is Roger at noon explaining things to the Hungarian woman who has for twenty-two years managed alone her dry-cleaning establishment and is now to be evicted in an imaginative glassy renovation which will add its signature to the old avenue's petition of hope. Roger is saying: Landless peasants, that is what we are. Till the soil for centuries and then the messenger comes from St. Petersburg to say the master wants his hectares for an iron foundry.

The dry-cleaning woman says: Mr. Spiegel does not live in St. Petersburg but in Bay Ridge.

. . .

Roger, gregarious as a housefly, is not one asked to dinner at the home of his friends, although he presents a respectable bohemian appearance. He has not accumulated anything for social use and is no more fit for the inside of things than a flowering bush. The byways of life have captured him, even *captivated* his mind, and it is possible to think that his contentment comes from never having to set out the dishes, watch the oven, make drinks, freeze ice, have coffee cups ready and table chairs assembled. And his curiosity is disarming—harmless, quickly satisfied, unassuming, wide rather than deep. It is a sort of credulous, favorable curiosity and surrounds him like heat.

His memory for names is extraordinary. It is names he stores up out of the daily *Times*. Names of painters, names of sopranos, names of leftists and rightists, of murderers, of architects, of film directors, and, above all, the names of writers to go with their titles. These names lie on his brain, smothering it, like the blanketing of the acquisitions in his apartment. His cumulative index of dead and live souls, jangling bits of change with the pennies, nickels, and dimes of celebrity, often has a dampening effect on conversation and, being all-identifying information as it is, the terms of exchange cannot be agreed upon.

Obscure persons, those of some past accomplishment lying under the settled dust, are alarmed by Roger's mysterious recognitions. They start in embarrassment, seeming to fear they have been picked out of the heap by mistake.

Aren't you ——, author of ——? Roger asks with perfect courtesy.

How did you recognize me?

To this Roger can only reply that in truth he does not know. And he is unprepared for the burden his keen eye, his genial salute represented to the modest, the shy, and also to the arrogant.

What is the noise in the back of The Pleiade? Like the sound of some smoothly running machine pleased to be doing its part. It is Roger and the great energy of his friendly, healthy, untroubled ways. Unaccountable exertions at the table in the back of the shop. Roger is typing away at an impressive speed, racing along as confidently as an alert stenographer in court. Behind him, stacked in neat black binders, are the thirteen novels he has written on the typewriter. During the slowness just before the dinner hour, there he is, sitting straight and tall for the protection of his back during his labors. Coffee cools beside him, a cheeseburger waits in its wrapping paper. Clang, clang, clang! Loud, joyful clangs from his thick, strong fingers. In goes a sheet of paper to be greeted by the happy rhythmical clatter and soon with a quick, practiced twist out it comes with a very pleasant zing, and another page rolls in. Pure pleasure rattles through Roger's body as the neat, perfectly typed pages pile up. What gladness in numbers: Chapter 7, page 210.

The pages arrive as if telephoned by the stack of index cards on the right, which contain, sketched in Roger's fine script, the characters who are sending the messages.

From an early work: Desmond, thirty-two, in the O.S.S. on the European front, World War II. English by birth but American citizen after marriage to Melissa, proper Bostonian background. These two were to be involved in a tangle of unbelievable but nevertheless predictable complication.

The gathering ledgers—for that is what they appear to be—ledgers with indecipherable figures noting some forgotten transaction, have seen the creation of disaster plots, cancer plots, celebrity-scandal plots, regional plots, international plots. But there is nothing at all in the stacks of black binders of the avant-garde, nothing of the beloved discordance of modernism, that is the pride of the bookshelves, the consolation of the proprietor. The violent, ecstatic typing—so like a fantastic, rejuvenating regime of arcane exercises. The pile of crisp pages sometimes goes out to the world in envelopes, and the return causes no discouragement.

The French scholar, a lonely man and a terrible snob with an almost paranoid resentment of certain French works in current esteem, among them the poetry of Francis Ponge and the essays of Cioran, often says: I do not understand this deranged typing. It is not hope of fame, of money, or even of publication. It is not anything that can be known.

And he tells of seeing Roger once in a mood of despair as he sat ready to attack the keys. A work in the autobiographical mode was planned, but a painful interruption, a stiffening, a paralysis struck Roger after only a dozen or so pages. Mournfully, he appealed to his reliable fingers, the faithful engines, but they could not be urged to move along. At last, he said: The "I" is not for me. The sheet came out, the black leather cover was placed over the typewriter with the solemnity of defeat—a burial.

Disquieting events at The Pleiade, in December. Maureen returns suddenly from Troy, looking beautiful, with her tranquil eyes, her short curls, and wearing a graceful skirt of Indian cotton.

Sprung, Roger says.

Now Maureen sits at the back of the shop with Lois, also in her full beauty, if somehow edging into dishevelment, save for a new pair of expensive light-blue leather boots, stitched with patterns of pink roses.

They might be Roger's daughters. And what are they? Mistresses? They and the sulky despot, Jenny, whose reign, before Maureen, tormented the walls, accused the shelves, menaced with frowns the old New Directions paperbacks and the first hundred titles of Anchor Books, which Roger, knight of perfect faith, had assembled.

Jenny, in her forties, had come to Roger like a message in a bottle, floating from Yugoslavia, where she was born, to London, where she was briefly married to a second cousin of Roger's, and on to New York with the address of The Pleiade in her hand.

Where indeed is Jenny?

New Jersey, Roger says. Relatives. Serbs chanting folktales from the old oral tradition.

Not one of his friends thinks Maureen or Lois is a mistress. It is unimaginable because of the presence of some cheerful absence in Roger, his blameless peculiarity of not seeming to have an interior. For all his curiosity, he is not inclined to analysis and detail, and those about whom he is curious come into his view as travelling objects. It is as if he were to look up and say: That one is blue with yellow stripes and this one is red and black. Except for the tyrannical Jenny. The violinist believes there might have been an affair in that corner.

And why does he think so? Her deprecating ill-humor, for one thing, he answers.

The two girls, Maureen and Lois, were not altogether friendly and took up more room than the shop could bear. They did not make change, did not advise about the existence of a title, never opened the interesting pages of *Books in Print*. Roger himself swept out in the morning, and at night, often the wrong one, took his huge plastic bags of rubbish to the curb for collection. Two girls might have been six girls, and the multiplication sent Roger into a state of mind unusual for him, a state of unhappiness and vexation. The unbalancing scheme seemed to demand something from him, but he was not clear just what that something might be.

It is not as if they were down and out, he would say with a sigh. He repeated this again and again, and although the girls were only a few feet away they did not appear to be listening.

Both girls were indeed cherished by their confused families. They received money and mail, letters filled with encouragement, letters grateful that they were in beguiling, promising New York City in order to get on with their lives. Their home towns, scenes of disappointment and constriction, were not suitable for advancement. Lois had found early that in her own Pittsburgh there was nothing happening. The two had met in a private sanatorium and each had made her way to therapeutic New York and to the Pleiade hospice. And here they were, in a state of becoming.

The overpopulation left Roger gasping for air, unable to recover his stolen placid breathing. The unmoving freight, stalled, lay in his path, defying all the tools his accepting nature had at hand. He would find the two silently gazing at the store's landscape and limply he would suggest: Shoo! Take a walk.

We are not twins, Maureen would answer. Let Lois take the walk.

The Pleiade is downed by melancholy until Christmas, when Lois is lifted up by holiday sentiment and one morning abandons the bookshop and the apartment for the despised Pittsburgh.

She will not be back, Maureen says. It turns out that Lois's brother walked up and down in front of The Pleiade, entered the challenging stairway of the old tenement, looked in wonder like a detective on a case at Roger, Maureen, the dog, the unkempt and the fashionable customers, and decided that the setting was not promising for Lois's career. With the help of Christmas he led her to take up the trail back home.

The empty chair reassured, space opened up in Roger's heart

once more and its steady, comfortable beating returned. The type-writer clanged from four until six in the afternoon. New classics were magically restored after the cruelty of time had spent itself. The tides flowed and Roger swam.

It is Christmas at The Pleiade. Roger's days soar as he dispenses, in the spirit of charity baskets, the gifts of the world. Storytellers from Africa, epics from Latin America, painful gutting rituals from Japan, women poets from the Russia of the twenties—the nineteen-twenties, the period of his first passions, now a hallowed battlefield filled with noble headstones. Suicides, early death, transfiguration, words, words, words, in all the tongues of the earth. Roger's head, with its wrinkled sandy waves lapping on the shore of his brow, bobs up and down in time to the sacred music.

On the block, the sepulchre of the old fruit market is now a mausoleum of oak cabinets and kitchen tables from the back porches of the Middle West. Taste itself seems to be laughing in the street.

In January, Maureen dimmed and faded away. The dark star of Jenny, with her glimmering scowl, ascended without notice. Remarks burst from her like bullets. He is a toadstool, she would say of Roger in a loud gunfire.

After a pause of shock, Roger found his aim. You see, I am a *cavaliere servente*, he cried out gaily, calling upon page 1 of "The Charterhouse of Parma."

Jenny gradually displayed a few marks of chastening. An unwholesome strain of choleric domesticity invaded her thoughts, a lesson learned. She had turned a corner, but not the one that led to cooking and housekeeping. She was making her way, as if by a private radar, to the interests of ownership. Swift, proprietary gleamings, a sense of things. Her eyes surveyed the books, the collections, like a guard with his flashlight making the midnight rounds. Stirrings in the blood, storage plans for winter, gathering potatoes in the cellar; she was getting older.

Sometimes one would see her studying a piece of brass or old silver brought down from the apartment. A pawnbroker's stare, cynical smile, and shrug of feigned indifference. Roger did not speak of this alteration in her attention, but found relief in the fact that she stayed upstairs a good deal, pushing objects from one corner to another, making promising groupings, looking for the right screw for a hole, an old curve that would welcome a stray rosette of gold leaf. No mending, no polishing. In her fitful accounting all was equal and she might have been engaged in a nightmare dialogue between buyer and seller. Here is the missing leg, in perfect shape; here is the piece that completes the red tail of the dragon on the green china plate; here is Volume IV. Sorting out, Roger said.

In the middle of March, our lawyer friend who played the violin and read Kleist and Novalis died. The death dug its teeth into Roger's soft heart and he looked backward to remember that the friend had not been in The Pleiade for a few months and had for the past year appeared frail and thin. At the Riverside Chapel, we mourned this death of a hero, with his antique passions, as they seemed, his poets known by heart and whose lives were shorter than his own.

He has gone their way early, Roger said in a throttle of tears.

Nothing in the memorial of all this. Instead, accomplishments unknown to us, the accretion of a short, handsome wife and the production of two tall daughters. They haven't got him right, Roger grieved as the tributes went on with their office jokes, mishaps on the tennis court, charitable contributions, and helping hands for the young.

The Pleiade has lost a star and yet, diminished, it faces another spring. Roger himself seems to be adorned with fresh innocence as he watches the begonias and forced gardenias expel the potted chrysanthemums and Jerusalem cherries from the sidewalk outside the florist's. The heavens are clear for a whole week. There is ballet at the State Theatre and yet another at the opera house. Hardly a night passes without an author to be recognized and to receive a murmured approbation, as if a breeze has passed the ear whispering, beloved, here you are at last.

The pleasing winds came one day, drifted away the next, and came once more. The dollar bin at The Pleiade now has a two-dollar sign on it. When the talk turns to unemployment and inflation, Jenny can be heard to say: There is a lot of money in pockets. The Chinese build a glass extension for their restaurant and fill it with smart blue chairs and white tables. In the antique shop a large

Art Deco bar of black glass and chrome humbles the lowly, stripped oak.

So the coming of another spring still finds Roger ruling in the heavens like Zeus. And his great stars, Kafka, Beckett, Walter Benjamin, Joyce, Akhmatova, and old men from Japan with their whores in the snow mountains—all of these shine on and on and on.

WHERE I'M CALLING FROM

BY RAYMOND CARVER (1982)

We are on the front porch at Frank Martin's drying-out facility. Like the rest of us at Frank Martin's, J.P. is first and foremost a drunk. But he's also a chimney sweep. It's his first time here, and he's scared. I've been here once before. What's to say? I'm back. J.P.'s real name is Joe Penny, but he says I should call him J.P. He's about thirty years old. Younger than I am. Not much younger, but a little. He's telling me how he decided to go into his line of work, and he wants to use his hands when he talks. But his hands tremble. I mean, they won't keep still. "This has never happened to me before," he says. He means the trembling. I tell him I sympathize. I tell him the shakes will idle down. And they will. But it takes time.

We've only been in here a couple of days. We're not out of the woods yet. J.P. has these shakes, and every so often a nerve—maybe it isn't a nerve, but it's something—begins to jerk in my shoulder. Sometimes it's at the side of my neck. When this happens my mouth dries up. It's an effort just to swallow then. I know something's about to happen and I want to head it off. I want to hide from it, that's what I want to do. Just close my eyes and let it pass by, let it take the next man. J.P. can wait a minute.

I saw a seizure yesterday morning. A guy they call Tiny. A big fat guy, an electrician from Santa Rosa. They said he'd been in here for nearly two weeks and that he was over the hump. He was going home in a day or two and would spend New Year's Eve with his wife in front of the TV. On New Year's Eve, Tiny planned to drink hot chocolate and eat cookies. Yesterday morning he seemed just fine when he came down for breakfast. He was letting out with quacking noises, showing some guy how he called ducks right down onto his head. "Blam. Blam," said Tiny, picking off a couple. Tiny's hair was damp and was slicked back along the sides of his head. He'd just come out of the shower. He'd also nicked himself on the chin with his razor. But so what? Just about everybody at Frank Martin's has nicks on his face. It's something that happens. Tiny edged in at the head of the table and began telling about something that had happened on one of his drinking bouts. People at the table laughed and shook their heads as they shovelled up their eggs. Tiny would say something, grin, then look around the table for a sign of recognition. We'd all done things just as bad and crazy, so, sure, that's why we laughed. Tiny had scrambled eggs on his plate, and some biscuits and honey. I was at the table but I wasn't hungry. I had some coffee in front of me. Suddenly Tiny wasn't there anymore. He'd gone over in his chair with a big clatter. He was on his back on the floor with his eyes closed, his heels drumming the linoleum. People hollered for Frank Martin. But he was right there. A couple of guys got down on the floor beside Tiny. One of the guys put his fingers inside Tiny's mouth and tried to hold his tongue. Frank Martin yelled, "Everybody stand back!" Then I noticed that the bunch of us were leaning over Tiny, just looking at him, not able to take our eyes off him. "Give him air!" Frank Martin said. Then he ran into the office and called the ambulance.

Tiny is on board again today. Talk about bouncing back. This morning Frank Martin drove the station wagon to the hospital to get him. Tiny got back too late for his eggs, but he took some coffee into the dining room and sat down at the table anyway. Somebody in the kitchen made toast for him, but Tiny didn't eat it. He just sat with his coffee and looked into his cup. Every now and then he moved his cup back and forth in front of him.

I'd like to ask him if he had any signal just before it happened. I'd like to know if he felt his ticker skip a beat, or else begin to race. Did his eyelid twitch? But I'm not about to say anything. He doesn't look like he's hot to talk about it anyway. But what happened to Tiny is something I won't ever forget. Old Tiny flat on the floor, kicking his heels. So every time this little flitter starts up anywhere, I draw some breath and wait to find myself on my back, looking up, somebody's fingers in my mouth.

In his chair on the front porch, J.P. keeps his hands in his lap. I smoke cigarettes and use an old coal bucket for an ashtray. I listen to J.P. ramble on. It's eleven o'clock in the morning—an hour and a half until lunch. Neither one of us is hungry. But just the same we look forward to going inside and sitting down at the table. Maybe we'll get hungry.

What's J.P. talking about, anyway? He's saying how when he was twelve years old he fell into a well in the vicinity of the farm he grew up on. It was a dry well, lucky for him. "Or unlucky," he says, looking around him and shaking his head. He says how late that afternoon, after he'd been located, his dad hauled him out with a rope. J.P. had wet his pants down there. He'd suffered all kinds of terror in that well, hollering for help, waiting, and then hollering some more. He hollered himself hoarse before it was over. But he told me that being at the bottom of that well had made a lasting impression. He'd sat there and looked up at the well mouth. Way up at the top he could see a circle of blue sky. Every once in a while a white cloud passed over. A flock of birds flew across, and it seemed to J.P. their wingbeats set up this odd commotion. He heard other things. He heard tiny rustlings above him in the well, which made him wonder if things might fall down into his hair. He was thinking of insects. He heard wind blow over the well mouth, and that sound made an impression on him, too. In short, everything about his life was different for him at the bottom of that well. But nothing fell on him and nothing closed off that little circle of blue. Then his dad came along with the rope, and it wasn't long before J.P. was back in the world he'd always lived in.

"Keep talking, J.P. Then what?" I say.

When he was eighteen or nineteen years old and out of high school and had nothing whatsoever he wanted to do with his life, he went across town one afternoon to visit a friend. This friend lived in a house with a fireplace. J.P. and his friend sat around drinking beer and batting the breeze. They played some records. Then the doorbell rings. The friend goes to the door. This young woman chimney sweep is there with her cleaning things. She's wearing a top hat, the sight of which knocked J.P. for a loop. She tells J.P.'s friend that she has an appointment to clean the fireplace. The friend lets her in and bows. The young woman doesn't pay him any mind. She spreads a blanket on the hearth and lays out her gear. She's wearing these black pants, black shirt, black shoes and socks. Of course by now she's taken her hat off. J.P. says it nearly drove him nuts to look at her. She does the work, she cleans the chimney, while J.P. and his friend play records and drink beer. But they watch her and they watch what she does. Now and then J.P. and his friend look at each other and grin, or else they wink. They raise their eyebrows when the upper half of the young woman disappears into the chimney. She was all-right-looking, too, J.P. said. She was about his age.

When she'd finished her work, she rolled her things up in the blanket. From J.P.'s friend she took a check that had been made out to her by his parents. And then she asks the friend if he wants to kiss her. "It's supposed to bring good luck," she says. That does it for J.P. The friend rolls his eyes. He clowns some more. Then, probably blushing, he kisses her on the cheek. At this minute J.P. made his mind up about something. He put his beer down. He got up from the sofa. He went over to the young woman as she was starting to go out the door.

"Me, too?" J.P. said to her. She swept her eyes over him. J.P. says he could feel his heart knocking. The young woman's name, it turns out, was Roxy.

"Sure," Roxy says. "Why not? I've got some extra kisses." And she kissed him a good one right on the lips and then turned to go.

Like that, quick as a wink, J.P. followed her onto the porch. He held the porch screen door for her. He went down the steps with her and out to the drive, where she'd parked her panel truck. It was something that was out of his hands. Nothing else in the world counted for anything. He knew he'd met somebody who could set his legs atremble. He could feel her kiss still burning on his lips, etc. At that minute J.P. couldn't begin to sort anything out. He was filled with sensations that were carrying him every which way.

He opened the rear door of the panel truck for her. He helped her store her things inside. "Thanks," she told him. Then he blurted it out—that he'd like to see her again. Would she go to a movie with him sometime? He'd realized, too, what he wanted to do with his life. He wanted to do what she did. He wanted to be a chimney sweep. But he didn't tell her that then.

J.P. says she put her hands on her hips and looked him over. Then she found a business card in the front seat of her truck. She gave it to him. She said, "Call this number after ten o'clock tonight. The answering machine will be turned off then. We can talk. I have to go now." She put the top hat on and then took it off. She looked at J.P. once more. She must have liked what she saw, because this time she grinned. He told her there was a smudge near her mouth. Then she got into her truck, tooted the horn, and drove away.

"Then what?" I say. "Don't stop now, J.P." I was interested. But I would have listened if he'd been going on about how one day he'd decided to start pitching horseshoes.

It rained last night. The clouds are banked up against the hills across the valley. J.P. clears his throat and looks at the hills and the clouds. He pulls his chin. Then he goes on with what he was saying.

Roxy starts going out with him on dates. And little by little he talks her into letting him go along on jobs with her. But Roxy's in business with her father and brother and they've got just the right amount of work. They don't need anybody else. Besides, who was this guy J.P.? J.P. what? Watch out, they warned her.

So she and J.P. saw some movies together. They went to a few dances. But mainly the courtship revolved around their cleaning chimneys together. Before you know it, J.P. says, they're talking about tying the knot. And after a while they do it, they get married. J.P.'s new father-in-law takes him in as a full partner. In a year or so, Roxy has a kid. She's quit being a chimney sweep. At any rate, she's quit doing the work. Pretty soon she has another kid. J.P.'s in his mid-twenties by now. He's buying a house. He says he was happy with his life. "I was happy with the way things were going," he says. "I had everything I wanted. I had a wife and kids I loved, and I was doing what I wanted to do with my life." But for some reason—who knows why we do what we do?—his drinking picks up. For a long time he drinks beer and beer only. Any kind of beer—it didn't matter. He says he could drink beer twenty-four hours a day. He'd drink beer at night while he watched TV. Sure, once in a while he drank hard stuff. But that was only if they went out on the town, which was not often, or else when they had company over. Then a time comes, he doesn't know why, when he makes the switch from beer to gin-and-tonic. And he'd have more gin-and-tonic after dinner, sitting in front of the TV. There was always a glass of gin-and tonic in his hand. He says he actually liked the taste of it. He began stopping off after work for drinks before he went home to have more drinks. Then he began missing some dinners. He just wouldn't show up. Or else he'd show up but he wouldn't want anything to eat. He'd filled up on snacks at the bar. Sometimes he'd walk in the door and for no good reason throw his lunch pail across the living room. When Roxy yelled at him, he'd turn around and go out again. He moved his drinking time up to early afternoon, while he was still supposed to be working. He tells me that he was starting off the morning with a couple of drinks. He'd have a belt of the stuff before he brushed his teeth. Then he'd have his coffee. He'd go to work with a thermos bottle of vodka in his lunch pail.

J.P. quits talking. He just clams up. What's going on? I'm listening. It's helping me relax, for one thing. It's taking me away from my own situation. After a minute, I say, "What the hell? Go on, J.P." He's pulling his chin. But pretty soon he starts talking again.

J.P. and Roxy are having some real fights now. I mean *fights*. J.P. says that one time she hit him in the face with her fist and broke his nose. "Look at this," he says. "Right here." He shows me a line across the bridge of his nose. "That's a broken nose." He returned the favor. He dislocated her shoulder for her on that occasion. Another time he split her lip. They beat on each other in front of the kids. Things got out of hand. But he kept on drinking. He couldn't stop. And nothing could make him stop. Not even with Roxy's dad and her brother threatening to beat hell out of him. They told Roxy she should take the kids and clear out. But Roxy said it was her problem. She got herself into it, and she'd solve it.

Now J.P. gets real quiet again. He hunches his shoulders and pulls down in his chair. He watches a car driving down the road between this place and the hills.

I say, "I want to hear the rest of this, J.P. You better keep talking."

"I just don't know," he says. He shrugs.

"It's all right," I say. And I mean it's O.K. for him to tell it. "Go on, J.P."

One way she tried to solve things, J.P. says, was by finding a boyfriend. J.P. would like to know how she found the time with the house and kids.

I look at him and I'm surprised. He's a grown man. "If you want to do that," I say, "you find the time. You make the time."

J.P. shakes his head. "I guess so," he says.

Anyway, he found out about it—about Roxy's boyfriend—and he went wild. He manages to get Roxy's wedding ring off her finger. And when he does he cuts it into several pieces with a pair of wire cutters. Good solid fun. They'd already gone a couple of rounds on this occasion. On his way to work the next morning he gets arrested on a drunk-driving charge. He loses his driver's license. He can't drive the truck to work anymore. Just as well, he says. He'd already fallen off a roof the week before and broken his thumb. It was just a matter of time until he broke his God-damned neck, he says.

He was here at Frank Martin's to dry out and to figure how to get his life back on track. But he wasn't here against his will, any more than I was. We weren't locked up. We could leave anytime we wanted. But a minimum stay of a week was recommended, and two weeks or a month was, as they put it, "strongly advised."

As I said, this is my second time at Frank Martin's. When I was trying to sign a check to pay in advance for a week's stay, Frank Martin said, "The holidays are always a bad time. Maybe you should think of sticking around a little longer this time? Think in terms of a couple of weeks. Can you do a couple of weeks? Think about it, anyway. You don't have to decide anything right now," he said. He held his thumb on the check and I signed my name. Then I walked my girlfriend to the front door and said goodbye. "Goodbye," she said, and she lurched into the doorjamb and then onto the porch. It's late afternoon. It's raining. I go from the door to the window. I move the curtain and watch her drive away. She's in my car. She's drunk. But I'm drunk, too, and there's nothing I can do. I make it to a big old chair that's close to the radiator, and I sit down. Some guys look up from their TV. Then slowly they shift back to what they were watching. I just sit there. Now and then I look up at something that's happening on the screen.

Later that afternoon the front door banged open and J.P. was brought in between these two big guys—his father-in-law and brother-in-law I find out afterward. They steered J.P. across the room. The old guy signed him in and gave Frank Martin a check. Then these two guys helped J.P. upstairs. I guess they put him to bed. Pretty soon the old guy and the other guy came downstairs and headed for the front door. They couldn't seem to get out of this place fast enough. It was as if they couldn't wait to wash their hands of all this. I didn't blame them. Hell, no. I don't know how I'd act if I was in their shoes.

A day and a half later J.P. and I meet up on the front porch. We shake hands and comment on the weather. J.P. has a case of the shakes. We sit down and prop our feet on the railing. We lean back in our chairs as if we're just out there taking our ease, as if we might be getting ready to talk about our bird dogs. That's when J.P. gets going with his story.

It's cold out, but not too cold. It's a little overcast. At one point Frank Martin comes outside to finish his cigar. He has on a sweater buttoned up to his Adam's apple. Frank Martin is short and heavyset. He has curly gray hair and a small head. His head is out of proportion with the rest of his body. Frank Martin puts the cigar in his mouth and stands with his arms crossed over his chest. He works that cigar in his mouth and looks across the valley. He stands there like a prizefighter, like somebody who knows the score.

J.P. gets real quiet again. I mean, he's hardly breathing. I toss my cigarette into the coal bucket and look hard at J.P., who scoots farther down in his chair. J.P. pulls up his collar. What the hell's going on, I wonder. Frank Martin uncrosses his arms and takes a puff on the cigar. He lets the smoke carry out of his mouth. Then he raises his chin toward the hills and says, "Jack London used to have a big place on the other side of this valley. Right over there behind that green hill you're looking at. But alcohol killed him. Let that be a lesson. He was a better man than any of us. But he couldn't handle the stuff, either." He looks at what's left of his cigar. It's gone out. He tosses it into the bucket. "You guys want to read something while you're here, read that book of his 'The Call of the Wild.' You know the one I'm talking about? We have it inside, if you want to read something. It's about this animal that's half dog and half wolf. They don't write books like that anymore. But we could have helped Jack

London, if we'd been here in those days. And if he'd let us. If he'd asked for our help. Hear me? Like we can help you. *If. If* you ask for it and *if* you listen. End of sermon. But don't forget it. If," he says again. Then he hitches his pants and tugs his sweater down. "I'm going inside," he says. "See you at lunch."

"I feel like a bug when he's around," J.P. says. "He makes me feel like a bug. Something you could step on." J.P. shakes his head. Then he says, "Jack London. What a name! I wish I had me a name like that. Instead of the name I got."

Frank Martin talked about that "if" the first time I was here. My wife brought me up here that time. That's when we were still living together, trying to make things work out. She brought me here and she stayed around for an hour or two, talking to Frank Martin in private. Then she left. The next morning Frank Martin got me aside and said, "We can help you. If you want help and want to listen to what we say." But I didn't know if they could help me or not. Part of me wanted help. But there was another part. All said, it was a very big if.

This time around, six months after my first stay, it was my girlfriend who drove me here. She was driving my car. She drove us through a rainstorm. We drank champagne all the way. We were both drunk when she pulled up in the drive. She intended to drop me off, turn around, and drive home again. She had things to do. One thing she had to do was to go to work the next day. She was a secretary. She had an O.K. job with this electronic-parts firm. She also had this mouthy teen-age son. I wanted her to get a motel room in town, spend the night, and then drive home. I don't know if she got the room or not. I haven't heard from her since she led me up the front steps the other day and walked me into Frank Martin's office and said, "Guess who's here."

But I wasn't mad at her. In the first place she didn't have any idea what she was letting herself in for when she said I could stay with her after my wife asked me to leave. I felt sorry for her. The reason I felt sorry for her was that on the day before Christmas her Pap smear came back from the lab, and the news was not cheery. She'd have to go back to the doctor, and real soon. That kind of news was reason enough for both of us to start drinking. So what we did was get ourselves good and drunk. And on Christmas Day we were still drunk. We had to go out to a restaurant to eat, because she didn't feel anything like cooking. The two of us and her mouthy teen-age son opened some presents, and then we went to this steak house near her apartment. I wasn't hungry. I had some soup and a hot roll. I drank a bottle of wine with the soup. She drank some wine, too. Then we started in on Bloody Marys. For the next couple of days I didn't eat anything except cashew nuts. But I drank a lot of bourbon. On the morning of the twenty-eighth I said to her, "Sugar, I think I'd better pack up. I better go back to Frank Martin's. I need to try that place on again. Hey, how about you driving me?"

She tried to explain to her son that she was going to be gone that afternoon and evening, and he'd have to get his own dinner. But right as we were going out the door this God-damned kid screamed at us. He screamed, "You call this love? The hell with you both! I hope you never come back. I hope you kill yourselves!" Imagine this kid!

Before we left town I had her stop at the liquor store, where I bought us three bottles of champagne. Quality stuff—Piper. We stopped someplace else for plastic glasses. Then we picked up a bucket of fried chicken. We set out for Frank Martin's in this rainstorm, drinking champagne and listening to music on the radio. She drove. I looked after the radio and poured champagne. We tried to make a little party out of it. But we were sad, too. There was that fried chicken, but we didn't eat any of it.

I guess she got home O.K. I think I would have heard something if she hadn't made it back. But she hasn't called me, and I haven't called her. Maybe she's had some news about herself by now. Then again, maybe she hasn't heard anything. Maybe it was all a mistake. Maybe it was somebody else's test. But she has my car, and I have things at her house. I know we'll be seeing each other again.

They clang an old farm bell here to signal mealtime. J.P. and I get out of our chairs slowly, like old geezers, and we go inside. It's starting to get too cold on the porch anyway. We can see our breath drifting out from us as we talk.

New Year's Eve morning I try to call my wife. There's no answer. It's O.K. But even if it wasn't O.K., what am I supposed to do? The last time we talked on the phone, a couple of weeks ago, we screamed at each other. I hung a few names on her. "Wet brain!" she said, and put the phone back where it belonged.

But I wanted to talk to her now. Something had to be done about my stuff. I still had things at her house, too.

One of the guys here is a guy who travels. He goes to Europe and the Middle East. That's what he says, anyway. Business, he says. He also says he has his drinking under control and doesn't have any idea why he's here at Frank Martin's. But he doesn't remember getting here. He laughs about it, about his not remembering. "Anyone can have a blackout," he says. "That doesn't prove a thing." He's not a drunk—he tells us this and we listen. "That's a serious charge to make," he says. "That kind of talk can ruin a good man's prospects." He further says that if he'd only stick to whiskey and water, no ice, he'd never get "intoxicated"—his word—and have these blackouts. It's the ice they put into your drink that does it. "Who do you know in Egypt?" he asks me. "I can use a few names over there."

For New Year's Eve dinner Frank Martin serves steak and baked potato. A green salad. My appetite's coming back. I eat the salad. I clean up everything on my plate and I could eat more. I look over at Tiny's plate. Hell, he's hardly touched anything. His steak is just sitting there getting cold. Tiny is not the same old Tiny. The poor bastard had planned to be at home tonight. He'd planned to be in his robe and slippers in front of the TV, holding hands with his wife. Now he's afraid to leave. I can understand. One seizure means you're a candidate for another. Tiny hasn't told any more nutty stories on himself since it happened. He's stayed quiet and kept to himself. Pretty soon I ask him if I can have his steak, and he pushes his plate over to me.

They let us keep the TV on until the New Year has been rung in at Times Square. Some of us are still up, sitting around the TV, watching the crowds on the screen, when Frank Martin comes in to show us his cake. He brings it around and shows it to each of us. I know he didn't make it. It's a God-damned bakery cake. But still it's a cake. It's a big white cake. Across the top of the cake there's writing in pink letters. The writing says "Happy New Year—1 Day At A Time."

"I don't want any stupid cake," says the guy who goes to Europe and the Middle East. "Where's the champagne?" he says, and laughs.

We all go into the dining room. Frank Martin cuts the cake. I sit next to J.P. J.P. eats two pieces and drinks a Coke. I eat a piece and wrap another piece in a napkin, thinking of later.

J.P. lights a cigarette—his hands are steady now—and he tells me his wife is coming to visit him in the morning. The first day of the New Year.

"That's great," I say. I nod. I lick the frosting off my finger. "That's good news, J.P."

"I'll introduce you," he says.

"I look forward to it," I say.

We say good night. We say Happy New Year. Sleep well. I use a napkin on my fingers. We shake hands.

I go to the pay phone once more, put in a dime, and call my wife collect. But nobody answers this time, either. I think about calling my girlfriend, and I'm dialling her number when I realize I don't want to talk to her. She's probably at home watching the same thing on TV that I've been watching. But maybe she isn't. Maybe she's out. Why shouldn't she be? Anyway, I don't want to talk to her. I hope she's O.K. But if she has something wrong with her I don't want to know about it. Not now. In any case, I won't talk to her tonight.

After breakfast J.P. and I take coffee out to the porch, where we plan to wait for his wife. The sky is clear, but it's cold enough so we're wearing our sweaters and jackets.

"She asked me if she should bring the kids," J.P. says. "I told her she should keep the kids at home. Can you imagine? My God, I don't want my kids up here."

We use the coal bucket for an ashtray. We look across the valley to where Jack London used to live. We're drinking more coffee, when this car turns off the road and comes down the drive.

"That's her!" J.P. says. He puts his cup next to his chair. He gets up and goes down the steps to the drive.

I see this woman stop the car and set the brake. I see J.P. open the car door. I watch her get out, and I see them embrace. They hug each other. I look away. Then I look back. J.P. takes the woman's arm and they come up the stairs. This woman has crawled into chimneys. This woman broke a man's nose once. She has had two kids, and much trouble, but she loves this man who has her by the arm. I get up from the chair.

"This is my friend," J.P. says to his wife. "Hey, this is Roxy."

Roxy takes my hand. She's a tall, good-looking woman in a blue knit cap. She has on a coat, a heavy white sweater, and dark slacks. I recall what J.P. told me about the boyfriend and the wire cutters—all that—and I glance at her hands. Right. I don't see any wedding ring. That's in pieces somewhere. Her hands are broad and the fingers have these big knuckles. This is a woman who can make fists if she has to.

"I've heard about you," I say. "J.P. told me how you got acquainted. Something about a chimney, J.P. said."

"Yes, a chimney," she says. Her eyes move away from my face, then return. She nods. She's anxious to be alone with J.P., which I can understand. "There's probably a lot else he didn't tell you," she says. "I bet he didn't tell you everything," she says, and laughs. Then—she can't wait any longer—she slips her arm around J.P.'s waist and kisses him on the cheek. They start to move toward the door. "Nice meeting you," she says over her shoulder. "Hey, did he tell you he's the best sweep in the business?" She lets her hand slide down from J.P.'s waist onto his hip.

"Come on now, Roxy," J.P. says. He has his hand on the doorknob.

"He told me he learned everything he knew from you," I say.

"Well, that much is sure true," she says. She laughs again. But it's as if she's thinking about something else. J.P. turns the doorknob. Roxy lays her hand over his hand. "Joe, can't we go into town for lunch? Can't I take you someplace for lunch?"

J.P. clears his throat. He says, "It hasn't been a week yet." He takes his hand off the doorknob and brings his fingers to his chin. "I think they'd like it, you know, if I didn't leave the place for a little while yet. We can have some coffee inside," he says.

"That's fine," she says. Her eyes light on me once more. "I'm glad Joe's made a friend here. Nice to meet you," she says again.

They start to go inside. I know it's a foolish thing to do, but I do it anyway. "Roxy," I say. And they stop in the doorway and look at me. "I need some luck," I say. "No kidding. I could do with a kiss myself."

J.P. looks down. He's still holding the doorknob, even though the door is open. He turns the doorknob back and forth. He's embarrassed. I'm embarrassed, too. But I keep looking at her. Roxy doesn't know what to make of it. She grins. "I'm not a sweep anymore," she says. "Not for years. Didn't Joe tell you? What the hell. Sure, I'll kiss you. Sure. For luck."

She moves over, she takes me by the shoulders—I'm a big man—and she plants this kiss on my lips. "How's that?" she says.

"That's fine," I say.

"Nothing to it," she says. She's still holding me by the shoulders. She's looking me right in the eyes. "Good luck," she says, and then she lets go of me.

"See you later, pal," J.P. says. He opens the door all the way, and they go inside.

I sit down on the front steps and light a cigarette. I watch what my hand does, then I blow out the match. I've got a case of the shakes. I started out with them this morning. This morning I wanted something to drink. It's depressing, and I didn't say anything about it to J.P. I try to put my mind on something else and for once it works.

I'm thinking about chimney sweeps—all that stuff I heard from J.P—when for some reason I start to think about the house my wife and I lived in just after we were married. That house didn't have a chimney—hell, no—so I don't know what makes me remember it now. But I remember the house and how we'd only been in there a few weeks when I heard a noise outside one morning and woke up. It was Sunday morning and so early it was still dark in the bedroom. But there was this pale light coming in from the bedroom window. I listened. I could hear something scrape against the side of the house. I jumped out of bed and went to the window.

"My God!" my wife says, sitting up in bed and shaking the hair away from her face. Then she starts to laugh. "It's Mr. Venturini," she says. "The landlord. I forgot to tell you. He said he was coming to paint the house today. Early. Before it gets too hot. I forgot all about it," she says, and laughs some more. "Come on back to bed, honey. It's just the landlord."

"In a minute," I say.

I push the curtain away from the window. Outside, this old guy in white coveralls is standing next to his ladder. The sun is just starting to break above the mountains. The old guy and I look each other over. It's the landlord, all right—this old guy in coveralls. But his coveralls are too big for him. He needs a shave, too. And he's wearing this baseball cap to cover his bald head. God damn it, I think, if he isn't a weird old hombre, then I've never seen one. And at that minute a wave of happiness comes over me that I'm not him—that I'm me and that I'm inside this bedroom with my wife. He jerks his thumb toward the sun. He pretends to wipe his forehead. He's letting me know he doesn't have all that much time. The old duffer breaks into a grin. It's then I realize I'm naked. I look down at myself. I look at him again and shrug. I'm smiling. What'd he expect?

My wife laughs. "Come *on*," she says. "Get back in this bed. Right now. This minute. Come on back to bed."

I let go of the curtain. But I keep standing there at the window. I can see the landlord nod to himself as if to say, "Go on, sonny, go back to bed. I understand," as if he'd heard my wife calling me. He tugs the bill of his cap. Then he sets about his business. He picks up his bucket. He starts climbing the ladder.

I lean back into the step behind me now and cross one leg over the other. Maybe later this afternoon I'll try calling my wife again. And then I'll call to see what's happening with my girlfriend. But I don't want to get her mouthy son on the line. If I do call, I hope he'll be out somewhere doing whatever he does when he's not hanging around the house. I try to remember if I ever read any Jack London books. I can't remember. But there was a story of his I read in high school. "To Build a Fire" it was called. This guy in the Yukon is freezing. Imagine it—he's actually going to freeze to death if he can't get a fire going. With a fire he can dry his socks and clothing and warm himself. He gets his fire going, but then something happens to it. A branchful of snow drops on it. It goes out. Meanwhile, the temperature is falling. Night is coming on.

I bring some change out of my pocket. I'll try my wife first. If she answers, I'll wish her a Happy New Year. But that's it. I won't bring up business. I won't raise my voice. Not even if she starts something. She'll ask me where I'm calling from, and I'll have to tell her. I won't say anything about New Year's resolutions. There's no way to make a joke out of this. After I talk to her, I'll call my girlfriend. Maybe I'll call her first. I'll just have to hope I don't get her son on the line. "Hello, sugar," I'll say when she answers. "It's me."

THE FIRST AMERICAN

BY LORE SEGAL (1983)

Ilka Weissnix had been three months in this country when she went West and discovered her first American sitting on a stool in a bar in the desert, across from the railroad. He bought her a whiskey and asked her what in the name of the blessed Jehoshaphat she was doing in Cowtown, Nevada.

"Nevada!" Ilka said. "I have believed I am being in Utah, isn't it?"

"Utah!" The face of the big American turned a sick, gray color. "Where the hell am I?" he asked the barman.

"Hagen," replied the barman, swiping a dish towel at a glass beer mug, "ass end of Noplace, Nevada."

"Aha! So!" Ilka sipped her whiskey and, hiding her smile inside her glass, said, "I do not believe."

"What don't you believe?" asked the American.

"That I sit in Utah."

"Nevada," the man said.

"I do not believe Nevada, Utah, America."

Ilka was twenty-one. It had taken her more than a decade to get from Vienna to New York. She had left in 1938, when Hitler came. The Austrian Weissnixes had known so little of their relations, the Litvak Fishgoppels, Ilka had been unaware that she had an American cousin until some time after the end of the war, when the cousin traced Ilka's whereabouts and sent her a visa and an air ticket.

Fishgoppel had come into New York to meet the new refugee at Idlewild. "*Ich muss nemen ein examen. Ich muss gein back to school,*" shouted Fishgoppel across the roar and shriek of the subway that was carrying them uptown. "*Ihr will stay in mein apartment in New York, O.K.?*"

"Excuse, please?" Ilka had shouted back.

"I'm sorry! My horrible Yiddish!" yelled Fishgoppel and hit herself in the head.

"Yiddish!" shouted Ilka, lighting on the only word she understood. "By us in Vienna has nobody speaken Yiddish outside the Polischen!"

"What?" hollered Fishgoppel, and they laughed and turned out both palms of their hands, understanding each other to mean, "Too noisy. One can't even talk!"

Fishgoppel's small upper-West Side apartment had the simple layout of a dumbbell. The front door opened into the middle of a narrow foyer with a room at each end.

"One for you," said Fishgoppel, "and one for your mother, when we get her to America."

"I don't know where my mother is. I don't know if she lives," said Ilka. She looked around at Fishgoppel's possessions; each object was out of harmony with every other in a way for which the laws of probability did not account. Ilka looked at Fishgoppel: only a persevering spirit could have parlayed that pure skin and wonderful black hair and those sweet, clever eyes into such dowdiness.

"Look at the time!" cried Fishgoppel. "Here is a dictionary. Here is the map of the subway. This is where you get off for the employment agency. Here's where they give English classes. . . . Are you going to manage?"

"Thanks!" said Ilka.

"The butcher on the corner of Broadway speaks German. The shul is two blocks that way."

"Excuse me?"

"Here is my number. Call me. I'll call you. I'll come in for the day as soon as my exams are over. Will you be all right?"

"Yes. Thanks," said Ilka.

"*Don't!*" cried Fishgoppel. "Don't *thank* me!"

. . .

Minutes after Fishgoppel had run to catch the train back to New Haven, Ilka took the elevator down and burst into the streets of New York, which looked like the streets of Ilka's childhood Vienna—the same flat, staid, gray façades except that here, right in front of her, walked a real American couple, having an American conversation. Ilka ran to catch up, and walked close behind them. She understood the old man saying, "Because I wear proper shoes in which a person can walk." The old woman said, "Because you don't have bunions." The man said, "Because I wear proper shoes," and Ilka recognized that it was German they were speaking, with the round Viennese vowels cushioned between relaxed Viennese consonants.

When Ilka got back to the apartment the telephone was ringing for Fishgoppel: Would Fishgoppel collect on the sixth floor for the United Negro College Fund?

"I will collect. I am the cousin from Fishgoppel," said Ilka, who wanted to get a look into—to *get* inside—American homes.

The nameplate outside Apartment 6-A said "Wolfgang Placzek." He handed her fifty cents through the cracked door. While 6-B went to look for change, Ilka put her head inside the foyer and saw the little green marble boy extracting the same splinter from his foot, on the same tree stump, on the same round lace doily on which he had sat in Ilka's mother's foyer in Vienna. The woman came back. "Nix! Nothing," she said. It did her grief but her man was not to house. 6-C was Fishgoppel, and 6-D would not open; the voice through the peephole came from Berlin. It did her grief also but her sister had a stroke and was to bed.

"*How?*" Ilka asked the woman at the employment agency when she told Ilka to go away and practice her English. "With *whom* shall I praxis, when *you* are the only American I met in New York? The onlies others that I met in my English class are yet other outlanders, which know always only yet other outlanders, which know yet lesser English as I!"

The woman on the other side of the desk drew her head back from the assault of Ilka's complaining. She was a fat woman with a lot of corseted and useless bosom. She looked as if there was some complaining *she* might do, give her half a chance. "New York," she finally said to Ilka, "is not America, like all you people always think."

The next time Fishgoppel came in to see how Ilka was managing, Ilka complained to her that New York was not America.

Fishgoppel frowned, did some mental arithmetic, and offered Ilka the week's trip West.

Fishgoppel returned to New Haven and Ilka went West. She practiced her English with the train conductor. He leaned over the back of the seat in front of Ilka and asked her to guess how long he had been on this Denver–Los Angeles run.

"Excuse me?" Ilka smiled the self-conscious smile she knew from her mirror, and regretted. It exposed her two long front teeth with the little gap between and made her look, she believed, like a friendly village simpleton. She was a thin girl. In certain lights her hair matched the color of her eyes, which Ilka thought of as khaki. She smiled apologetically and sweetly at the round, red-faced conductor; he looked like a healthy old baby. He held up three left and two right fingers. "Thirty-two years!"

"Aha!" said Ilka.

"Know it like"—he pointed to the inside of his pocket, "like the"—and he held up the palm of his hand and pointed at it. "I'll be back," he promised.

Ilka looked out at land as level as the primordial water before the creation of breath disturbed its surface, uninterrupted by any object, man-made or natural, as far as the ruler-straight horizon, except outside the window on her left, where a grid of apartment buildings formed a small, square city whose near perimeter coincided with the railroad platform. The train stopped when it had aligned Ilka with Main Street, at the far end of which stood a mountain, like a giant purple ice-cream cone turned upside down on the perfectly flat world. Ilka wanted somebody to laugh with, to turn to and say, "I don't believe this!" She might have imagined that she had imagined this Atlantis onto the desert floor but for the details, which were not in her experience to engender: bars, bowling alleys, barbershops, numberless eating places with neon signs that ran and jumped and stopped, and switched from pastel greens to pale yellows to pinks leached out by the tail end of daylight.

Ilka's conductor returned. He multiplied his ten fingers by thrusting them into Ilka's face nine separate times: "A ninety-minute stopover." He handed her down the steps.

And that was how Ilka Weissnix from Vienna came to stand in the middle of the New World. Ilka thought she was in Utah, and she thought Utah was dead in the heart of America.

Ilka was very excited. She ran up the platform until it stopped across from the long, low building which formed the northwest corner of the square little town. The building was made of a rosy, luminescent brick and quivered in the blue haze of the oncoming night—it levitated. Its classic windows and square white letters saying "AMERICAN GLUE INC" moved Ilka with a sense of beauty so out of proportion with its object she recognized euphoria. It knocked out her common sense of time. Afraid of being left behind, but more afraid that she might miss what more there might be to be seen, Ilka turned and ran close alongside the train until the platform stopped across from the shack which held the northeast end of town down upon the desert the way one of those little gummed corners fixes your snapshot in place on the page of a photograph album. The shack had a roof like a cocked hat slipped down over one eye. A neon sign said "Larr 's B r nd Eats."

With the reluctance of someone who sticks a foot into an alien element, Ilka stepped off the platform onto the dirt road, crossed to the other side, and with a palpitating heart depressed the handle of the door.

The thin man behind the bar went on wiping a glass with an agitated white dishcloth, but the elderly American swivelled on his barstool to see who had come in. He was a very large, very stout man with grizzled hair, cut peculiarly short, and flattened against the big skull in a way the girl did not understand. His skin had a yellow hue. The nose was flat, the mouth wide—like a frog's, Ilka would have thought, if it had not been for a look about him of weight, of weightiness. Like a Roman senator, thought Ilka.

Feeling herself looked at, Ilka had ducked into the booth nearest the door. By the time she raised her self-conscious smile, the big American had returned to his conversation with the barman. There were women who got looked at longer—Ilka knew that. Anyway, he was an older man, and what Ilka had come West for was American conversation.

Ilka listened and thought the barman said, "Coming down cats and dogs but I mean something fierce," and, thinking she hadn't been listening properly, she listened harder.

The barman said, "This kid I knew in high school's dad is in a cab coming down Lex I think it was."

The man on the barstool said, "This is in New York?," which Ilka understood. She felt encouraged and leaned closer and listened.

The barman said, "Where else is there? Guess the brakes quit on the guy. This kid's dad. He lost his thumb, busted both legs, left side of his face is all chewed up, and this pip of a shyster out of nowhere is running alongside the stretcher, says he can get him a lump sum in compensation, which is what I'm telling you is what you have to have, once in your lifetime, give you an opportunity."

Ilka was trying to connect "shyster" (the English cognate, presumably, of the German "*scheissen*") and "lump" (as in a mattress) plus "sum" (the mathematical result of totting up), and she had missed everything the barman said after that. She forgot to listen and studied the red plastic booth she sat in. Ilka thought that the back seats of two automobiles had been taken out and placed face to face; three booths times two back seats in each made—six red automobiles!

The barman said, "Got the wife to sue for deprivation of sexual excess or whatever—"

"Access?" suggested the older man on the stool.

"You name it, he sued for it." The barman was coming around the bar and walking toward Ilka saying, "Physicaltormentalanguish-diminishedreproductivity . . . What'll it be?" he asked Ilka.

"Excuse, please?" said Ilka and smiled at him with her apologetic teeth and shook her head. "I cannot yet so well English."

The barman, who seemed worn to bone and nerve by a chronic high of exasperation, picked a shred of plastic off the flaking red seat while his foot kicked the center leg to see if the table held. He raised his chin like a dog about to howl and said, "You want a drink?"

"Please, coffee," said Ilka.

"Coffee!" howled the barman in a voice outside the human range of sound. He walked back around the bar and disappeared through a door into a region beyond Ilka's sight and outside the range of her imagination. She pictured a blackness, out of which the barman's voice went on with what he had been telling the man on the barstool: "This kid's dad comes out the hospital, has lost his hearing in one ear—or *wishes* he lost it, is what he used to tell us kids, so he wouldn't hear this noise all the time like someone pissing inside his ear, loud, like Niagara."

"Jesus!" the man on the stool said. "That could drive a man to drink."

"Only thing could drown it out was trumpets turned with the volume all the way up. See," said the barman, "this is hi-fi coming in. This guy, he buys every damn book, reads up in the magazines, and goes into audio with his lump sum in compensation, and makes a mint. Owns his own home in Bayshead! But you don't get a lump sum," said the barman, coming out with Ilka's cup of coffee, "you don't got a opportunity, I don't care what anybody is going to tell you."

"And that's true, too," said the stout older man. He raised his voice to the tenor pitch that best carried it into the booth by the door, where the young blonde sat and watched him. "The problem, as I see it, is how you're going to put your idea over."

"My idea?" said the barman.

"You want me to introduce it in the United Nations for you?"

Ilka was surprised at the high, hilarious note coming from the weighty-looking older man.

"Or were you thinking in terms of an amendment to the Bill of Rights?"

"Was I thinking . . ."

"We hold these truths to be self-evident, that all men have the unalienable right to a lump sum?"

"Once in your lifetime," said the barman, "is all I'm saying to you."

"See if I understand you, now, is this for white only, or Negro as well?"

"Listen! I ain't prejudiced like your local cowboys. I'm from New York!" said the barman. "Ain't I standing here talking to you like a person? You want, I'll make you a sandwich?"

"Jesus God!" the man on the stool said gaily. "Imagine every one of us black sons of a gun going to have an equal opportunity to get our thumbs, legs, and eardrums busted, same as any white man in the land! Let me check *this* out with you: Everybody has to first get pretty much chewed up is what you're saying?"

"That's what it's compensation *for!* The way I figure it you don't get something for nothing, but how it is now you get nothing period."

"It's an idea," said the man on the stool, "that will revolutionize the economy!"

"It is? It will?" The barman looked nervous.

"Sure!" the man on the stool said. He crossed one ankle over the other, effecting a quarter turn in Ilka's direction. "Say you take the Social Security money for the year X and, instead of pissing it away on the poor, the old, and the sick, you divvy it up—let's say three thousand bucks apiece, to every baby born that same year, black *and* white—and—stick with me here—the government invests each baby's three thousand at, say, five per cent, till the babies get to be twenty-nine. Or would you say thirty-five?"

"Thirty-five has more horse sense," said the barman.

"O.K. Now," said the man on the stool, "when the babies are thirty-five they cut off their thumbs, break their legs, pierce their eardrums, and give each and every one of them the lump sum of . . ." He patted his breast pocket, took out an envelope, and said, "You got a pencil there? Thank you. Three thousand at five per cent times thirty-five compounded"—the man on the stool did arithmetic for a while—"dollars fifteen thousand seven hundred and sixty!" he said triumphantly.

The barman looked agitated. "And the poor, old, sick folks?"

"*What* poor, old, sick folks!" cried the man on the stool. "*They* got *their* lumps when *they* were thirty-five and made a mint! They own their own homes—Negroes, whites, everybody! In Bayshead!"

"I guess," said the barman.

Ilka had stopped listening. She studied the expanse of the older man's tweed back. It was an autumnal mixture of heather flecked with rust, mauve, green. . . . Ilka had observed that same easy angle of the wrist of the hand which held the cigarette in other men, and women, too. She thought it connoted the carnal know-how she despaired of for herself. Ilka could see the man's tongue laughing inside his enormous mouth. She had never seen a grown person laugh so loudly for such a long time, with the mouth so wide open. Now he raised his eloquent right hand; he beckoned. Ilka turned to see who might have come in the door behind her, but there was no one to claim the gesture and she turned back with a conscious smile, trusting it to double for an acknowledgment, in case he meant her, and a general complaisance if he hadn't.

"You ever get yours?" the man asked the barman.

"Worse luck," said the barman. "I was in construction, damn near killed in a cave-in. Man, what a mess! See now, here's what I'm telling you. When they used to give me my thirty bucks Saturday night, by Monday morning—like you said—I pissed it away, what else is there? But you put five thousand smackeroos *into* my hand, I'm a capitalist! I'm going to hang on to every lousy buck! I'm going to *make* something out of myself."

"What did you do?"

"I read where they were building this four-lane highway, and I come out here, I see the surveyors with my own eyes! Outside this window! I figure I buy this place cheap—the big money wants to be *on* Main—and do it up nice, like New York. You can't tell anymore now, but ten years ago this place was, I mean sharp! I figure every one of the fellers be coming in here for his breakfast, lunch, a home away from home, and booze it up nights for the three or whatever years it's going to take them to build me a highway up to my front door, I sell out at a price, go back, and open a classy place on Third Avenue—how can I lose?"

"What happened?" the man on the stool asked.

"They built the highway four miles the other side of town is what happened."

"You going to sell out, then?"

"To who? You going to be fool enough to take my monkey and put it on your back? Are you? No, you are not!"

"You got the custom from the railroad," the man said.

"Oh, right!" the barman said. "There's the 10:45 A.M. Denver–L.A. and the 12:15 L.A.–Denver, and the 5:40 you got off of, and the 8 P.M. the lady came on"—he indicated Ilka, listening in her booth—

"maybe a couple rednecks drop in for a beer and put two nickels in the juke. You want another bourbon?"

"Maybe the lady will join me?"

He did mean me, thought Ilka, gratified. It was me he beckoned.

"Will you have a drink?"

"Thanks, no," said Ilka. "I must soon back in the train. Thanks!"

But the man had risen and was standing, with a nice formality, next to his stool. It took Ilka time to extricate her feet from under the table and walk across the floor. The man waited until she had seated herself before resuming his own stool. He offered her a cigarette. "Thanks, no." Ilka did not smoke. What would she like to drink? Ilka did not drink.

"No, thanks. *Likör* makes me—how do you say it in English '*sich übergeben*'? To overgive the self . . . You can maybe German?"

"A little Swahili?" the man offered.

"Excuse, please?"

"I don't know German. I'm sorry."

Ilka did a charade, and he said, "Liquor makes you throw up! No it doesn't." To the barman he said, "The lady will have a Black & White diluted with a little water, start her off nice and easy. I'll teach you how to drink," he told Ilka.

"You are living here?" Ilka asked him.

"Christ, no!" the man said. He told Ilka that he was en route from California to New York for a brand-new start and had stopped off to have himself one, last big bender.

"Speak, please, slower," said Ilka.

"I'm going to tie one on," explained the man, and it was here he had asked Ilka what in the name of the blessed Jehoshaphat she was doing in Cowtown, Nevada, which Ilka had mistaken, and was, for the years to come, to persist in mistaking, for Utah.

Ilka said, "I search for Americans. Except the woman from the employment office, you are my first real."

"Real . . . ?" The man leaned his ear toward her.

"A real American," said Ilka.

"Of the second class," said the big man.

Ilka shook her head and said, "I think every moment I am understanding lesser and lesser."

It was here that Carter Bayoux introduced himself. He said, "I'm a wonderful teacher."

"My name is Ilonka Weissnix," said Ilka. "And I want to learn"—she made a large, inclusive gesture—"this all."

They shook hands. He said, "Let me buy you a sandwich. What do you like?"

Ilka smiled inside her glass and said, "I cannot the names of the American sandwich."

"You make Reubens?" the man asked the barman.

"Do fish swim?" is what Ilka thought the barman replied before he disappeared back into his private darkness.

"You don't look like a teacher," said Ilka and blushed: she thought she was flirting.

The man regarded Ilka with his bright brown stare and asked, "Like what do I look?"

"That," said Ilka, "is what I am not understanding. When I walk on Broadway and see an old Viennese pair I can understand already from behind what the man has worked in Vienna, how it looked in their room . . ." Ilka stopped, appalled at the number and complication of the English sentences ahead.

"Go on," the man said.

She shook her head. Ilka meant that she recognized the proportions, height by width, of the old man's Jewish back, which fit and failed to fit, in the same places, into the same suit Ilka's father wore to the shop. The fabric that upholstered the fat old wife was the navy cotton, patterned with the same full-blown roses, bows, garlands, and violins, of Great-Aunt Mali's Sunday dresses. Those German pre-war cottons wore like iron and had outlasted Great-Aunt Mali, as well as Ilka's father and three aunts, five uncles, and two of the cousins who used to gather for Aunt Mali's afternoons of *Kaffee und Gugelhupf*. Aunt Mali's oversize table had stood square in the middle of the room; the tile stove in the left corner gave off too much heat. The walls were dark and striped, the curtains lace, and the drapes flowered and fringed with black wooden beads, which little Ilka, lying on the Turkey carpet—cozy, too hot, bored, more than half asleep—had pulled off one after the other. Aunt Mali had sat drinking coffee, and watched Ilka.

Ilka shook her head and said, "It is too complicate to tell it. But I look at you and . . ."

"Yes?"

Ilka shook her head. She meant that she did not understand his hair; that the size of his mouth and his laughter did not go with the urbane bend of his wrist and the way he crossed his ankles; that the luxurious tweed of his jacket contradicted his wide nose and mouth.

Ilka said, "Take for an example these two Americans which are coming in by the door." She swivelled on her stool and watched the newcomers settle into the booth she had recently vacated. They called for Larry. "Couple beers, Larry!" One was a little shorter, with a big chest, the other a few years younger perhaps. Both were in their thirties, of middling height, and wore, it seemed to Ilka, their undershirts. They had ruddy arms and blunt, round heads and they looked underdone, as if they had been taken out prematurely and put down in the world.

Ilka said, "I look, and I am seeing two men, but I cannot imagine what they are making for a living, or how dress their wives, or how it looks in their rooms . . ."

The one who was perhaps younger shouted, "Larry? What's with Larry?" and stuck his head out of the booth; he looked around the room, and the American on the stool said, "Keep talking," in a different, high voice Ilka had not heard before. She turned to see what had happened. Nothing had happened. There was nothing different in the way he sat, with his ankles crossed, his right hand around the glass on the bar; he had not moved so much as his eyes to take in the newcomers, but sat very still; only his left arm, pivoting at the shoulder, brought the cigarette to his mouth and took it away again. In his new voice, pitched in the high, thin register of the castrato, he said, "I'll buy you dinner on Main Street."

"Oh! But," said Ilka, "Larry makes already our sandwich, isn't it?"

And here came Larry with two foaming mugs, which he carried around the bar and across the floor. He set them on the table between the two men and slid into the booth, next to the one with the big chest. (This aborted and unexplained sandwich Ilka laid away in the patient back part of the mind where a child keeps things it doesn't know what to make of, and other things it doesn't know it doesn't understand; there they lie forgotten, but available to join with future information that will elucidate some but not all.)

The man on the stool smoked his cigarette down to a nubbin, then took his wallet from his breast pocket. He said, "We leave separately."

"Excuse me?"

"Go out the door, turn left, walk to Main Street, and wait for me."

"I can wait in here," said Ilka.

The man did not say anything. Ilka looked at him. Was it that his neck had thickened—or shortened? Or withdrawn into his shoulders? Had the ears retracted? The head and shoulders had streamlined; some outside pressure, failing to eliminate his person, had compacted it, and reduced its size without affecting its bulk. He looked like a high-calibre torpedo. Ilka saw what she saw and stored it away in her mind. She said, "Yes, so then, I will wait at the corner."

He did not raise his head; he was busy with his wallet. Ilka collected her things and rose.

"We are not all white" was what she thought one of the men in the booth had said. She stopped and looked in and the man with the chest was looking her straight in the eye. It was to her he was talking.

Ilka said, "Excuse me?" The other, younger man, too, was looking at her. Ilka said, "I am new in America, and cannot so well understand." She smiled her sweet, apologetic smile, and leaned closer to listen harder, and the man, looking her in the eye and enunciating very clearly, said it again: "We are not all white."

Ilka smiled. She shook her head.

"Either one of you fellows once in your lifetime got a lump sum? Did *you* ever have a opportunity?" the barman was asking the two men as Ilka walked out of the door.

This end of town was deserted and dark, the way the blacked-out wartime cities of Europe had been dark, except for that same curious pink glow Ilka had observed in the night sky over Manhattan. She imagined that it emanated from the noisy neon lights of every Times Square or Main Street, floated upward and spread like a comforter of rosy and possibly noxious haze over America.

Ilka walked to Main Street and waited. Presently the big American from the bar stood at the curb beside her. He kept a slice of the night air between them. The purple mountain had been assumed into the blackness, which had pepped up the colored lights. Over the restaurant across the street a blue cow blinked glamorous Disney lashes once, twice, and went out. "THE BLUE COW" spelled itself in yellow capitals. Ilka felt excited and hilarious. On both thronging sidewalks everyone was male and young.

"I don't *believe!* I think this I have imagined!" Ilka laughed. She turned to the American.

He was looking at her; he looked deliberately across the street, and back at Ilka, and said, "We're standing here, side by side, but how do I know what you see?"

"This," Ilka said with a sensation of bliss, "is what I am meaning." She was afterward to identify it as the moment in which she fell in love; it coincided with a break in the traffic and his first, slight touch under her elbow—an anachronistic courtesy that assumes the woman cannot step down into the street or make it safely to the other side without the man's supporting hand. He withdrew it as soon as he had helped her up the curb.

"Where would you like to eat?"

"I would like that you are choosing."

"Right," he said. He walked her past "THE BLUE COW" and past the "Bar and Beef." "Are you afraid?" he asked her.

"No," said Ilka, "because I am with you."

"With me. Ah," the big American said, walking past the "Steak and Swill" and past "Harry's Hash," but at "The Versailles"—no better, it seemed to Ilka, and no worse than the others—he opened and held the door.

"Here by the window is good for looking," said the insatiable Ilka, but the man walked her past the window table, walked past a second and a third empty table, and made a U-turn around a table from which three men had raised their eyes. The three men watched a large middle-aged yellow-skinned Negro march out the door, followed by a thin young blonde.

Back in the street, he asked Ilka if she was hungry.

"Not so hungry," said Ilka.

They walked past Harry's Hash, and he turned and looked

behind him. Ilka turned also. She said, "I don't understand what for men are all these . . ."

"Men!" said the man. They passed the Steak and Swill. "Good enough fellows, as fellows go—care for their kids, satisfy their wives some of the time, do their work well as can be expected, and pay their taxes, mostly, go to church, or not, and will string me up as soon as look at me."

"String you?" Ilka did not understand him. She said, "I think soon I must again instep in the train, isn't it?"

"I'll wait with you," said the man. They walked past the Bar and Beef, past the Blue Cow. He held her elbow across the dirt road and assisted her up onto the platform.

"Aren't you afraid of me?" the big American asked Ilka as they walked alongside the empty, darkened train.

Ilka thought about this, and said, "No."

They sat down on a bench underneath one of the half-dozen lamps, weak and unsteady as gaslight, that made no inroads upon the darkness.

"I would have liked to make love to you," said the American gloomily.

Ilka, who was not in the habit of receiving propositions, understood this one as a courtesy, intended as a compliment. The man said, "When a man hasn't so much as managed to buy a woman dinner, it's not conducive."

"I'm not so hungry," said Ilka.

"Well well well well well," the American said. "I owe you."

They exchanged addresses. He wrote Fishgoppel's telephone number into a well-worn leather-bound address book. On the corner of an envelope he wrote the name of the hotel in New York where, he said, he used to live and might take a room, if they had one, until he figured out what the hell he was doing.

"There is my conductor," said Ilka.

"When do you get back to town?"

"Sunday," said Ilka. "Monday I must go again to—I call it the agency of unemployment."

"Ah, yes, indeed," the man said. He handed her up the steps, into the train.

When Ilka turned to say goodbye she saw the droop of his face, and the sad expanse of his cheek grew large, larger, blurred; it filled Ilka's eyes, and Ilka's lips touched and depressed the male softness of his flesh, while her mind went scampering after something funny, in English, with which to unsay what she was doing here. Ilka laughed and said, "This also I do not believe! You, I know, I imagined!" and withdrew her head to the distance at which the features of his face resumed their surface and outline with a difference: his wide-open, unblinking eyes looked without a hint of irony, and shameless with emotion, full into Ilka's face.

Ilka ducked up the stairs, found her seat, and let the window down. When had the platform filled with so many people saying their goodbyes and getting onto the train? It took her a moment to identify the back of the American from the barstool, already walking away.

THE RED GIRL

BY JAMAICA KINCAID (1983)

I always slammed the gate to our yard behind me when I was up to something. If I was leaving the house—we lived on the island of Antigua—the slam was to let my mother know that I had left, so she could stop worrying about me and put her mind on something else. Then, after a proper time had passed, I would quietly unlatch the gate, creep back into the yard, and dive under the house to extract or hide some object that was forbidden me—usually some object that had come into my possession through my expert stealing. If I was returning home, I would reverse this procedure, first being very quiet, checking my things under the house, making sure that everything was still in place, often adding a new treasure; then the loud bang of the gate to announce to my mother that I had only just then returned home. My mother would usually say, "How many times do I have to tell you not to slam the gate?"

I had under the house almost all the books I had ever read. After reading a book, whether I liked it or not, I couldn't bear to part with it. I would then steal it. I was always successful, because casting suspicion away from me and putting on an innocent face had become a specialty of mine. I had a few books that I had received in the usual straightforward way, for birthdays and Christmas, and as prizes in school; these were all displayed on a little shelf my father had built for me, and whenever I felt I was falling out of my mother's good graces I would let her see me absorbed in these books. She would come over and caress my forehead, kiss me, and say, "I know how you like to read, but you mustn't strain your eyes." Feeling the slate wiped clean, I would then plot something new.

It was my mother who gave me my first marbles. They had come, a pair of them, as a bonus in a box of oats, and she thought that their unusual size—they were as big as plums—and their color would amuse me. One was white with blue, the other white with a brownish yellow. They looked to me like miniature globes, the white representing the seas, the colors representing land masses. I didn't think very much of them as I rolled them around in my palms, but my mother, taking the brownish-yellow one in her hand and holding it up in the air, said, "What a nice color! Amber." Amber! Needless to say, when I showed the marbles to my friends at school I said, "Such a nice color, amber," causing the desired effect among them, for on hearing me say the word "amber" they widened their eyes and shaped their mouths into tiny "o"s.

One day, I was throwing stones at the guava tree, trying to knock down a ripe guava, when the Red Girl came along and said, "Which one do you want?" After I pointed it out, she climbed up the tree, picked the one I wanted off its branch, climbed down, and presented it to me. How my eyes did widen and my mouth form an "o" at this. I had never seen a girl do this before. All the boys climbed trees for the fruit they wanted, and all the girls threw stones to knock the fruit off the trees. But look at the way she climbed that tree: better than any boy.

Polishing off the delicious ripe-to-perfection guava in two bites, I took a good look at the Red Girl. How right I had been to take some special notice of her the first time I had seen her. She was holding on to her mother's skirt; I was holding on to my mother's. Our mothers waved to each other as they passed, calling out the usual greetings, making the usual inquiries. I noticed that the girl's hair was the color of a penny fresh from the mint, and that it was so unruly it had to be forcibly twisted into corkscrews, the ends tied tightly with white thread. The corkscrews didn't lie flat on her head, they stood straight up, and when she walked they bounced up and down as if they were something amphibian and alive. Right away to myself I called her the Red Girl. For as she passed, in my mind's eye I could see her surrounded by flames, the house she lived in on fire, and she could not escape. I rescued her, and after that she followed me around worshipfully and took with great forbearance any and every abuse I heaped on her. I would have gone on like that for a while, but my mother tugged at me, claiming my attention; I heard her say, "Such a nice woman, to keep that girl so dirty."

The Red Girl and I stood under the guava tree looking each other up and down. What a beautiful thing I saw standing before me. Her face was big and round and red, like a moon—a red moon. She had big, broad, flat feet, and they were naked to the bare ground; her dress was dirty, the skirt and blouse tearing away from each other at one side; the red hair that I had first seen standing up on her head was matted and tangled; her hands were big and fat, and her fingernails held at least ten anthills of dirt under them. And on top of that she had such an unbelievable, wonderful smell, as if she had never taken a bath in her whole life.

I soon learned this about her: She took a bath only once a week, and that was only so that she could be admitted to her grandmother's presence. She didn't like to bathe, and her mother didn't force her. She changed her dress once a week for the same reason. She preferred to wear a dress until it just couldn't be worn anymore. Her mother didn't mind that, either. She didn't like to comb her hair, though on the first day of school she could put herself out for that. She didn't like to go to Sunday school, and her mother didn't force her. She didn't like to brush her teeth, but occasionally her mother said it was necessary. She loved to play marbles, and was so good that only Skerritt boys now played against her. Oh, what an angel she was, and what a heaven she lived in! I, on the other hand, took a full bath every morning and a sponge bath every night. I could hardly go out on my doorstep without putting my shoes on. I was not allowed to play in the sun without a hat on my head. My mother paid a woman who lived five houses away from us sevenpence a week—a penny for each school day and two pence for Sunday—to comb my hair. On Saturday, my mother washed my hair. Before I went to sleep at night, I had to make sure my uniform was clean and creaseless and all laid out for the next day. I had to make sure that my shoes were clean and polished to a nice shine. I went to Sunday school every Sunday unless I was sick. I was not allowed to play marbles, and, as for Skerritt boys, that was hardly mentionable.

By the time the Red Girl and I had told each other all this, we had walked to the top of the hill behind my house. At the top of the hill was an old lighthouse. It must have been a useful lighthouse at one time, but now it was just there for mothers to say to their children, "Don't play at the lighthouse," my own mother leading the chorus, I am sure. Whenever I did go to the lighthouse behind my mother's back, I would have to gather up all my courage to go to the top, the height made me so dizzy. But now I marched boldly up behind the Red Girl as if at the top were my own room, with all my familiar comforts waiting for me. At the top, we stood on the balcony and looked out toward the sea. We could see some boats coming and going; we could see some children our own age coming home from games; we could see some sheep being driven home from pasture; we could see my father coming home from work.

It went without saying between us that my mother should never know that we had become friends, that we planned to meet at the lighthouse in this way every day for the rest of our lives and beyond, that I now worshipped the ground her unwashed feet walked on. Just before we parted, she gave me three marbles; they were an ordinary kind, the kind you could buy three for a penny—glass orbs with a tear-shaped drop suspended in the center. Another secret to keep from my mother!

And now I started a new series of betrayals of people and things I would have sworn only minutes before to die for. There was Gweneth, whom I loved so, and who was my dearest friend in spite of the fact that she met with my mother's complete approval, but she had such slyness and so many pleasing, to me, ways that my mother could never have imagined. There she was, waiting for me in our usual spot behind the cistern. "Oh, Gwen, wait until I tell you this," I would begin after we had embraced and exchanged kisses. We would then bring each other up to date on all our latest triumphs and disappointments. But now, as my head rested on her shoulder, I thought how dull was the fresh pressedness of her uniform, the cleanness of her neck, the neatness of her just combed plaits. We walked into our classroom in the usual way, arm in arm—her head on *my* shoulder, since I was the taller—identical smiles on our faces. The Little Lovebirds, our friends called us. Who could have guessed that I no longer felt the same? Certainly not Gwen. For, of course, in bringing her up to date I never mentioned the Red Girl.

As for the marbles! Quite by accident, in a moment when I was just fooling about, I discovered that I had a talent for playing marbles. I played a game and I won. I played another game and I won. I took winning for a sign of the perfection of my new union with the Red Girl. I devoted my spare time to playing and winning marbles. No longer could I head a side for a game of rounders; no longer could I, during a break for recess, walk over from our schoolyard into the neighboring churchyard to sit on tombstones and gather important information from the other girls on what exactly it was I should do to make my breasts begin growing. We were at that moment in the stage where we regarded our breasts as treasured shrubs, needing only the proper combination of water and sunlight to make them delicately sprout. All my free time was devoted to games of marbles. And how I won! From the day I went to school with the three gifts from the Red Girl and came home that same day with twenty—enough to fill an old one-pound tin. Everyone attributed my talent to my long arms and my steady gaze. What a surprise it was to me—something about myself I had not known. Perhaps it had stuck in my mind that once my mother said to me, "I am so glad you are not one of those girls who like to play marbles." I soon had so many marbles that I had to store them in old containers, hiding them under the house in places where they would not be readily visible if my mother should just one day stoop down and make a sweeping search with her ever-inquisitive, ever-sharp eyes. If I had not yet come up with the trick of slamming the gate, I would surely have come up with it now. Sometimes I slammed the gate so hard that even I began to be afraid it would come off its hinges.

At first, the Red Girl and I met every day. Every day after I finished my chores, each chore being a small rehearsal for that faraway day, thank God, when I would be the mistress of my own house, that faraway day when I would have to abandon Gwen, the Red Girl, meetings behind cistern and at lighthouse, marbles, places under the house, and every other secret pleasure. I would say to my mother, "I think I will just go and stretch my legs a bit." It didn't take her very long to wonder why, after all my daily activities, I should suddenly have an urge to stretch my legs. She said to me, "Why, after all the things you do every day, the sudden urge to have your legs stretched?" I had always been extremely lazy, enjoying nothing so much as lying under the house, my legs sticking out to catch the hot sun, reading one of my stolen books or just toying with another stolen treasure. After my mother said this, I stopped going to the lighthouse for a few days, and I worried about how to explain this interference to the Red Girl. How convenient for me it would be, I thought, to have a mother to whom I was not a prime interest. But I found a new tack. A few days later, I told my mother that for my drawing class I had been asked to observe a field at sunset, so that in class I could reproduce it in watercolors; would it be all right, then, if I just went for a small walk up and over the hill? The question was framed in just the way it would appeal to her, so eager was she to contribute to my scholarship. Of course she agreed. My feet must have had wings; in minutes, I was at the top of the lighthouse.

All the time I had been kept prisoner by the watchful gaze of my mother, the Red Girl had faithfully gone to our meeting place every day. Every day, she went and waited for me, and every day I failed to show up. What could I say to her now? "My mother, the Nosy Parker, would kill me—or, worse, not speak to me for at least a few hours—if she knew that I met you in a secret place," I said. For a while after that, we said nothing, only staring out to sea, watching the boats coming and going, watching the children our own age coming home from games, watching the sheep being driven home from pasture. Then, still without saying a word, the Red Girl began to pinch me. She pinched hard, picking up pieces of my almost non-existent flesh and twisting it around. At first, I vowed not to cry, but it went on for so long that tears I could not control streamed down my face. I cried so much that my small chest began to heave, and then, as if my heaving chest caused her to have some pity on me, she stopped pinching and began to kiss me on the same spots where shortly before I felt the pain of her pinch. Oh, the sensation was delicious—the combination of pinches and kisses. And so wonderful we found it that, almost every time we met, pinching by her, followed by tears from me, followed by kisses from her were the order of the day. I stopped wondering why all the girls whom I had mistreated and abandoned followed me around with looks of love and adoration on their faces.

I now quite regularly had to observe a field or something for drawing class; collect specimens of leaves, flowers, or whole plants for botany class; gather specimens of rocks for geology class. In other words, my untruthfulness apparatus was now in full gear. My mother, keeping the usual close tabs, marvelled at my industriousness and ambition. I was already first in my class, and I was first without ever really trying hard, so I had nothing much to worry about. I was such a good liar that, almost as if to prove all too true my mother's saying "Where there's a liar, there's a thief," I began to steal. But how could I not? I had no money of my own. And what a pleasure it was to bring a gift and see that red face, on receiving it, grow even redder in the light of the setting sun on the balcony at the top of the lighthouse. Reaching into my mother's purse for the odd penny or so was easy enough to do, I had had so much practice at it. But that wasn't enough to buy two yards of multicolored grosgrain ribbon, or a pair of ring combs studded with rhinestones, or a pair of artificial rosebuds suitable for wearing at the waist of a nice dress. I hardly asked myself what use the Red Girl could really have for these gifts; I hardly cared that she only glanced at them for a moment and then placed them in a pocket of her dirty dress. I simply loved giving her things. But where did I get the money for them? I knew where my parents stored a key to a safe in which they kept what was to me a lot of money. It wasn't long before I could get the key, unlock the safe, and remove some money, and I am sure I could have done this blindfolded. If they missed it, they must have chalked it up to a mistake. It was a pleasure to see that they didn't know everything.

One afternoon, after making some outlandish claim of devotion to my work at school, I told my mother that I was going off to observe or collect—it was all the same to me—one ridiculous thing or other. I was off to see the Red Girl, of course, and I was especially happy to be going on that day because my gift was an unusually beautiful marble—a marble of blue porcelain. I had never seen a marble like it before, and from the time I first saw it I wanted very much to possess it. I had played against the girl to whom it belonged for three days in a row until finally I won all her marbles—thirty-three—except for that one. Then I had to play her and win six games in a row to get the prize—the marble made of blue porcelain. Using the usual slamming-the gate-and-quietly-creeping-back technique, I dived under the house to retrieve the marble from the special place where I had hidden it. As I came out from under the house, what should I see before me but my mother's two enormous, canvas-clad feet. From the look on my face, she guessed immediately that I was up to something; from the look on her face, I guessed immediately that everything was over. "What do you have in your hand?" she asked, and I had no choice but to open my hand, revealing the hard-earned prize to her angrier and angrier eyes.

My mother said, "Marbles? I had heard you played marbles, but I just couldn't believe it. You were not off to look for plants at all, you were off to play marbles."

"Oh, no," I said. "Oh, no."

"Where are your other marbles?" said my mother. "If you have one, you have many."

"Oh, no," I said. "Oh, no. I don't have marbles, because I don't play marbles."

"You keep them under the house," said my mother, completely ignoring everything I said.

"Oh, no."

"I am going to find them and throw them into the bottom of the sea," she said.

My mother now crawled under the house and began a furious and incredible search for my marbles. If she and I had been taking a walk in the Amazon forest, two of my steps equalling one of her strides, and after a while she noticed that I was no longer at her side, her search for me then would have equalled her search for my marbles now. On and on went her search—behind some planks my father had stored years ago for some long-forgotten use; behind some hatboxes that held old Christmas and birthday cards and old letters from my mother's family; tearing apart my neat pile of books, which, if she had opened any one of them, would have revealed to her, stamped on the title page, these words: "Public Library, Antigua." Of course, that would have been a whole other story, and I can't say which would have been worse, the stolen books or playing marbles. On it went.

"Where are the marbles?" she asked.

"I don't have any marbles," I would reply. "Only this one I found one day as I was crossing the street to school."

Of course I thought, At any minute I am going to die. For there were the marbles staring right at me, staring right at her. Sometimes her hand was actually resting on them. I had stored them in old cans, though my most valued ones were in an old red leather handbag of hers. There they were at her feet, as she rested for a moment, her heel actually digging into the handbag. My heart could have stopped.

My father came home. My mother postponed the rest of the search. Over supper, which, in spite of everything, I was allowed to eat with them, she told him about the marbles, adding a list of things that seemed as long as two chapters from the Old Testament. I could hardly recognize myself from this list—how horrible I was—though all of it was true. But still. They talked about me as if I weren't there sitting in front of them, as if I had boarded a boat for South America without so much as a goodbye. I couldn't remember my mother's being so angry with me ever before; in the meantime all thoughts of the Red Girl vanished from my mind. Trying then to swallow a piece of bread that I had first softened in my gravy, I thought, Well, that's the end of that; if tomorrow I saw that girl on the street, I would just act as if we had never met before, as if her very presence at any time was only an annoyance. As my mother went on to my father in her angry vein, I rearranged my life: Thank God I hadn't abandoned Gwen completely, thank God I was so good at rounders that the girls would be glad to have me head a side again, thank God my breasts hadn't grown and I still needed some tips about them.

Days went by. My mother kept up the search for the marbles. How she would torment me! When I left for school, she saw me out the gate, then watched me until I was a pin on the horizon. When I came home, there she was waiting for me. Of course, there was no longer any question of going off in the late afternoon for observations and gatherings. Not that I wanted to anyway—all that was finished. But on it would go. She would ask me for the marbles, and in my sweetest voice I would say I didn't have any. Each of us must have secretly vowed to herself not to give in to the other. But then she tried this new tack. She told me this: When she was a girl, it was her duty to accompany her father up to ground on Saturdays. When they got there, her father would check on the plantain and banana trees, the grapefruit and lime and lemon trees, and check the mongoose traps. Before returning, they would harvest some food for the family to eat in the coming week: plantains, green figs, grapefruit, limes, lemons, coffee beans, cocoa beans, almonds, nutmegs, cloves, dasheen, cassavas, all depending on what was ripe to be harvested. On one particular day, after they had loaded up the donkeys with the provisions, there was an extra bunch of green figs, and my mother was to carry it on her head. She and her father started off for their home, and as they walked my mother noticed that the bunch of figs grew heavier and heavier—much heavier than any bunch of figs she had ever carried before. She ached, from the top of her neck to the base of her spine. The weight of the green figs caused her to walk slowly, and sometimes she lost sight of her father. She was all alone on the road, and she heard all sorts of sounds that she had never heard before and sounds that she could not account for. Full of fright and in pain, she walked into her yard, very glad to get rid of the green figs. She no sooner had taken the load from her head when out of it crawled a very long black snake. She didn't have time to shout, it crawled away so quickly into the bushes. Perhaps from fright, perhaps from the weight of the load she had just gotten rid of, she collapsed.

When my mother came to the end of this story, I thought my heart would break. Here was my mother, a girl then, certainly no older than I, travelling up that road from the ground to her house with a snake on her head. I had seen pictures of her at that age. What a beautiful girl she was! So tall and thin. Long, thick black hair, which she wore in two plaits that hung down past her shoulders. Her back was already curved from not ever standing up straight, even though she got repeated warnings. She was so shy that she never smiled enough for you to see her teeth, and if she ever burst out laughing she would instantly cover her mouth with her hands. She always obeyed her mother, and her sister worshipped her. She, in turn, worshipped her brother, Joseph, and when he died of something the doctor knew nothing about, of something the obeah woman knew everything about, my mother refused food for a week. Oh, to think of a dangerous, horrible black snake on top of that beautiful head; to think of those beautifully arched, pink-soled feet (the feet of which mine were an exact replica, as hers were an exact replica of her mother's) stumbling on the stony, uneven road, the weight of snake and green figs too much for that small back. If only I had been there, I would not have hesitated for even a part of a second to take her place. How I would have loved my mother if I had known her then. To have been the same age as someone so beautiful, someone who even then loved books, someone who threw stones at monkeys in the forest! What I wouldn't have done for her. Nothing would ever be too much. And so, feeling such love and such pity for this girl standing in front of me, I was on the verge of giving to my mother my entire collection of marbles. She wanted them so badly. What could some marbles matter? Already a snake had sat on her head for miles. The words "The marbles are in the corner over there" were on the very tip of my tongue, when I heard my mother, her voice warm and soft and treacherous, say to me, "Well, Little Miss, where are your marbles?" Summoning my own warm, soft, and newly acquired treacherous voice, I said, "I don't have any marbles. I have never played marbles, you know."

Soon after, I started to menstruate, and I stopped playing marbles. I was ashamed to be menstruating. It meant the end of everything. My mother even said so. On giving me my little cloths and the instructions on how to use them, she laughed her triumphant laugh and said, "You are just like me. I was your age when I started."

I never saw the Red Girl again. For a reason not having to do with me, she had been sent to Anguilla to live with her grandparents and finish her schooling. The night of the day I heard about it, I dreamt of her. I dreamt that the boat on which she had been travelling suddenly splintered in the middle of the sea, causing all the passengers to drown except for her, whom I rescued in a small boat. I took her to an island, where we lived together forever, I suppose, and fed on wild pigs and sea grapes. At night, we would sit on the sand and watch ships filled with people on a cruise steam by. We sent confusing signals to the ships, causing them to crash on some nearby rocks. We laughed as their cries of joy turned to cries of sorrow.

LOVE

BY WILLIAM MAXWELL (1983)

M*iss Vera Brown*, she wrote on the blackboard, letter by letter in flawlessly oval Palmer method. Our teacher for the fifth grade. The name might as well have been graven in stone.

As she called the roll, her voice was as gentle as the expression in her beautiful dark brown eyes. She reminded me of pansies. When she called on Alvin Ahrens to recite and he said, "I know but I can't say," the class snickered but she said, "Try," encouragingly, and waited, to be sure that he didn't know the answer, and then said, to one of the hands waving in the air, "Tell Alvin what one-fifth of three-eighths is." If we arrived late to school, red-faced and out of breath and bursting with the excuse we had thought up on the way, before we could speak she said, "I'm sure you couldn't help it. Close the door, please, and take your seat." If she kept us after school it was not to scold us but to help us past the hard part.

Somebody left a big red apple on her desk for her to find when she came into the classroom, and she smiled and put it in her desk, out of sight. Somebody else left some purple asters, which she put in her drinking glass. After that the presents kept coming. She was the only pretty teacher in the school. She never had to ask us to be quiet or to stop throwing erasers. We would not have dreamed of doing anything that would displease her.

Somebody wormed it out of her when her birthday was. While she was out of the room the class voted to present her with flowers from the greenhouse. Then they took another vote and sweet peas won. When she saw the florist's box waiting on her desk, she said, "Oh?"

"Look inside," we all said.

Her delicate fingers seemed to take forever to remove the ribbon. In the end, she raised the lid of the box and exclaimed.

"Read the card!" we shouted.

Many Happy Returns to Miss Vera Brown, from the Fifth Grade, it said.

She put her nose in the flowers and said, "Thank you all very, very much," and then turned our minds to the spelling lesson for the day.

After school we escorted her downtown in a body to a special matinée of D. W. Griffith's "Hearts of the World." She was not allowed to buy her ticket. We paid for everything.

We meant to have her for our teacher forever. We intended to pass right up through the sixth, seventh, and eighth grades and on into high school taking her with us. But that isn't what happened. One day there was a substitute teacher. We expected our real teacher to be back the next day but she wasn't. Week after week passed, and the substitute continued to sit at Miss Brown's desk, calling on us to recite and giving out tests and handing them back with grades on them, and we went on acting the way we had when Miss Brown was there because we didn't want her to come back and find we hadn't been nice to the substitute. One Monday morning she cleared her throat and said that Miss Brown was sick and not coming back for the rest of the term.

In the fall we had passed on into the sixth grade and she was still not back. Benny Irish's mother found out that she was living with an aunt and uncle on a farm a mile or so beyond the edge of town, and told my mother, who told somebody in my hearing. One afternoon after school Benny and I got on our bikes and rode out to see her. At the place where the road turned off to go to the cemetery and the Chautauqua grounds, there was a red barn with a huge circus poster on it, showing the entire inside of the Sells-Floto Circus tent and everything that was going on in all three rings. In the summertime, riding in the back seat of my father's open Chalmers, I used to crane my neck as we passed that turn, hoping to see every last tiger and flying-trapeze artist, but it was never possible. The poster was weather-beaten now, with loose strips of paper hanging down.

It was getting dark when we wheeled our bikes up the lane of the farmhouse where Miss Brown lived.

"You knock," Benny said as we started up on the porch.

"No, you do it," I said.

We hadn't thought ahead to what it would be like to see her. We wouldn't have been surprised if she had come to the door herself and thrown up her hands in astonishment when she saw who it was, but instead a much older woman opened the door and said, "What do you want?"

"We came to see Miss Brown," I said.

"We're in her class at school," Benny explained.

I could see that the woman was trying to decide whether she should tell us to go away, but she said, "I'll find out if she wants to see you," and left us standing on the porch for what seemed like a long time. Then she appeared again and said, "You can come in now."

As we followed her through the front parlor I could make out in the dim light that there was an old-fashioned organ like the kind you used to see in country churches, and linoleum on the floor, and stiff uncomfortable chairs, and family portraits behind curved glass in big oval frames.

The room beyond it was lighted by a coal-oil lamp but seemed ever so much darker than the unlighted room we had just passed through. Propped up on pillows in a big double bed was our teacher, but so changed. Her arms were like sticks, and all the life in her seemed concentrated in her eyes, which had dark circles around them and were enormous. She managed a flicker of recognition but I was struck dumb by the fact that she didn't seem glad to see us. She didn't belong to us anymore. She belonged to her illness.

Benny said, "I hope you get well soon."

The angel who watches over little boys who know but they can't say it saw to it that we didn't touch anything. And in a minute we were outside, on our bicycles, riding through the dusk toward the turn in the road and town.

A few weeks later I read in the Lincoln *Evening Courier* that Miss

Vera Brown, who taught the fifth grade in Central School, had died of tuberculosis, aged twenty-three years and seven months.

Sometimes I went with my mother when she put flowers on the graves of my grandparents. The cinder roads wound through the cemetery in ways she understood and I didn't, and I would read the names on the monuments: Brower, Cadwallader, Andrews, Bates, Mitchell. In loving memory of. Infant daughter of. Beloved wife of. The cemetery was so large and so many people were buried there, it would have taken a long time to locate a particular grave if you didn't know where it was already. But I know, the way I sometimes know what is in wrapped packages, that the elderly woman who let us in and who took care of Miss Brown during her last illness went to the cemetery regularly and poured the rancid water out of the tin receptacle that was sunk below the level of the grass at the foot of her grave, and filled it with fresh water from a nearby faucet and arranged the flowers she had brought in such a way as to please the eye of the living and the closed eyes of the dead.

THE WAY WE LIVE NOW

BY SUSAN SONTAG (1986)

At first he was just losing weight, he felt only a little ill, Max said to Ellen, and he didn't call for an appointment with his doctor, according to Greg, because he was managing to keep on working at more or less the same rhythm, but he did stop smoking, Tanya pointed out, which suggests he was frightened, but also that he wanted, even more than he knew, to be healthy, or healthier, or maybe just to gain back a few pounds, said Orson, for he told her, Tanya went on, that he expected to be climbing the walls (isn't that what people say?) and found, to his surprise, that he didn't miss cigarettes at all and revelled in the sensation of his lungs' being ache-free for the first time in years. But did he have a good doctor, Stephen wanted to know, since it would have been crazy not to go for a checkup after the pressure was off and he was back from the conference in Helsinki, even if by then he was feeling better. And he said, to Frank, that he would go, even though he was indeed frightened, as he admitted to Jan, but who wouldn't be frightened now, though, odd as that might seem, he hadn't been worrying until recently, he avowed to Quentin, it was only in the last six months that he had the metallic taste of panic in his mouth, because becoming seriously ill was something that happened to other people, a normal delusion, he observed to Paolo, if one was thirty-eight and had never had a serious illness; he wasn't, as Jan confirmed, a hypochondriac. Of course, it was hard not to worry, everyone was worried, but it wouldn't do to panic, because, as Max pointed out to Quentin, there wasn't anything one could do except wait and hope, wait and start being careful, be careful, and hope. And even if one did prove to be ill, one shouldn't give up, they had new treatments that promised an arrest of the disease's inexorable course, research was progressing. It seemed that everyone was in touch with everyone else several times a week, checking in, I've never spent so many hours at a time on the phone, Stephen said to Kate, and when I'm exhausted after the two or three calls made to me, giving me the latest, instead of switching off the phone to give myself a respite I tap out the number of another friend or acquaintance, to pass on the news I'm not sure I can afford to think so much about it, Ellen said, and I suspect my own motives, there's something morbid I'm getting used to, getting excited by, this must be like what people felt in London during the Blitz. As far as I know, I'm not at risk, but you never know, said Aileen. This thing is totally unprecedented, said Frank. But don't you think he ought to see a doctor, Stephen insisted. Listen, said Orson, you can't force people to take care of themselves, and what makes you think the worst, he could be just run down, people still do get ordinary illnesses, awful ones, why are you assuming it has to be *that*. But all I want to be sure, said Stephen, is that he understands the options, because most people don't, that's why they won't see a doctor or have the test, they think there's nothing one can do. But is there anything one can do, he said to Tanya (according to Greg), I mean what do I gain if I go to the doctor; if I'm really ill, he's reported to have said, I'll find out soon enough.

And when he was in the hospital, his spirits seemed to lighten, according to Donny. He seemed more cheerful than he had been in the last months, Ursula said, and the bad news seemed to come almost as a relief, according to Ira, as a truly unexpected blow, according to Quentin, but you'd hardly expect him to have said the same thing to all his friends, because his relation to Ira was so different from his relation to Quentin (this according to Quentin, who was proud of their friendship), and perhaps he thought Quentin wouldn't be undone by seeing him weep, but Ira insisted that couldn't be the reason he behaved so differently with each, and that maybe he was feeling less shocked, mobilizing his strength to fight for his life, at the moment he saw Ira but overcome by feelings of hopelessness when Quentin arrived with flowers, because anyway the flowers threw him into a bad mood, as Quentin told Kate, since the hospital room was choked with flowers, you couldn't have crammed another flower into that room, but surely you're exaggerating, Kate said, smiling, everybody likes flowers. Well, who wouldn't exaggerate at a time like this, Quentin said sharply. Don't you think *this* is an exaggeration. Of course I do, said Kate gently, I was only teasing, I mean I didn't mean to tease. I know that, Quentin said, with tears in his eyes, and Kate hugged him and said well, when I go this evening I guess I won't bring flowers, what does he want, and Quentin said, according to Max, what he likes best is chocolate. Is there anything else, asked Kate, I mean like chocolate but not chocolate. Licorice, said Quentin, blowing his nose. And besides that. Aren't *you* exaggerating now, Quentin said, smiling. Right, said Kate, so if I want to bring him a whole raft of stuff, besides chocolate and licorice, what else. Jelly beans, Quentin said.

He didn't want to be alone, according to Paolo, and lots of people came in the first week, and the Jamaican nurse said there were other patients on the floor who would be glad to have the surplus flowers, and people weren't afraid to visit, it wasn't like the old days, as Kate pointed out to Aileen, they're not even segregated in the hospital anymore, as Hilda observed, there's nothing on the door of his room warning visitors of the possibility of contagion, as there was a few years ago; in fact, he's in a double room and, as he told Orson, the old guy on the far side of the curtain (who's clearly on the way out, said Stephen) doesn't even have the disease, so, as Kate went on, you really should go and see him, he'd be happy to see you, he likes having people visit, you aren't not going because you're afraid, are you. Of course not, Aileen said, but I don't know what to say, I think I'll feel awkward, which he's bound to notice, and that will make him feel worse, so I won't be doing him any good, will I. But he won't notice anything, Kate said, patting Aileen's hand, it's not like that, it's not the way you imagine, he's not judging people or wondering about their motives, he's just happy to see his friends. But I never was really a friend of his, Aileen said, you're a friend, he's always liked you, you told me he talks about Nora with you, I know he likes me, he's even attracted to me, but he respects you. But, according to Wesley, the reason Aileen was so stingy with her visits was that she could never have him to herself, there were always others there already and by the time they left still others had arrived, she'd been in love with him for years, and I can understand, said Donny, that Aileen should feel bitter that if there could have been a woman friend he did more than occasionally bed, a woman he really loved, and my God, Victor said, who had known him in those years, he was crazy about Nora, what a heartrending couple they were, two surly angels, then it couldn't have been she.

And when some of the friends, the ones who came every day, waylaid the doctor in the corridor, Stephen was the one who asked the most informed questions, who'd been keeping up not just with the stories that appeared several times a week in the *Times* (which Greg confessed to have stopped reading, unable to stand it anymore) but with articles in the medical journals published here and in England and France, and who knew socially one of the principal doctors in Paris who was doing some much-publicized research on the disease, but his doctor said little more than that the pneumonia was not life-threatening, the fever was subsiding, of course he was still weak but he was responding well to the antibiotics, that he'd have to complete his stay in the hospital, which entailed a minimum of twenty-one days on the I.V., before she could start him on the new drug, for she was optimistic about the possibility of getting him into the protocol; and when Victor said that if he had so much trouble eating (he'd say to everyone, when they coaxed him to eat some of the hospital meals, that food didn't taste right, that he had a funny metallic taste in his mouth) it couldn't be good that friends were bringing him all that chocolate, the doctor just smiled and said that in these cases the patient's morale was also an important factor, and if chocolate made him feel better she saw no harm in it, which worried Stephen, as Stephen said later to Donny, because they wanted to believe in the promises and taboos of today's high-tech medicine but here this reassuringly curt and silver-haired specialist in the disease, someone quoted frequently in the papers, was talking like some oldfangled country G.P. who tells the family that tea with honey or chicken soup may do as much for the patient as penicillin, which might mean, as Max said, that they were just going through the motions of treating him, that they were not sure about what to do, or rather, as Xavier interjected, that they didn't know what the hell they were doing, that the truth, the real truth, as Hilda said, upping the ante, was that they didn't, the doctors, really have any hope.

Oh, no, said Lewis, I can't stand it, wait a minute, I can't believe it, are you sure, I mean are they sure, have they done all the tests, it's getting so when the phone rings I'm scared to answer because I think it will be someone telling me someone else is ill; but did Lewis really not know until yesterday, Robert said testily, I find that hard to believe, everybody is talking about it, it seems impossible that someone wouldn't have called Lewis; and perhaps Lewis did know, was for some reason pretending not to know already, because, Jan recalled, didn't Lewis say something months ago to Greg, and not only to Greg, about his not looking well, losing weight, and being worried about him and wishing he'd see a doctor, so it couldn't come as a total surprise. Well, everybody is worried about everybody now, said Betsy, that seems to be the way we live, the way we live now. And, after all, they were once very close, doesn't Lewis still have the keys to his apartment, you know the way you let someone keep the keys after you've broken up, only a little because you hope the person might just saunter in, drunk or high, late some evening, but mainly because it's wise to have a few sets of keys strewn around town, if you live alone, at the top of a former commercial building that, pretentious as it is, will never acquire a doorman or even a resident superintendent, someone whom you can call on for the keys late one night if you find you've lost yours or have locked yourself out. Who else has keys, Tanya inquired, I was thinking somebody might drop by tomorrow before coming to the hospital and bring some treasures, because the other day, Ira said, he was complaining about how dreary the hospital room was, and how it was like being locked up in a motel room, which got everybody started telling funny stories about motel rooms they'd known, and at Ursula's story, about the Luxury Budget Inn in Schenectady, there was an uproar of laughter around his bed, while he watched them in silence, eyes bright with fever, all the while, as Victor recalled, gobbling that damned chocolate. But, according to Jan, whom Lewis's keys enabled to tour the swank of his bachelor lair with an eye to bringing over some art consolation to brighten up the hospital room, the Byzantine icon wasn't on the wall over his bed, and that was a puzzle until Orson remembered that he'd recounted without seeming upset (this disputed by Greg) that the boy he'd recently gotten rid of had stolen it, along with four of the *maki-e* lacquer boxes, as if these were objects as easy to sell on the street as a TV or a stereo. But he's always been very generous, Kate said quietly, and though he loves beautiful things isn't really attached to them, to things, as Orson said, which is unusual in a collector, as Frank commented, and when Kate shuddered and tears sprang to her eyes and Orson inquired anxiously if he, Orson, had said something wrong, she pointed out that they'd begun talking about him in a retrospective mode, summing up what he was like, what made them fond of him, as if he were finished, completed, already a part of the past.

Perhaps he was getting tired of having so many visitors, said Robert, who was, as Ellen couldn't help mentioning, someone who had come only twice and was probably looking for a reason not to be in regular attendance, but there could be no doubt, according to Ursula, that his spirits had dipped, not that there was any discouraging news from the doctors, and he seemed now to prefer being alone a few hours of the day; and he told Donny that he'd begun keeping a diary for the first time in his life, because he wanted to record the course of his mental reactions to this astonishing turn of events, to do something parallel to what the doctors were doing, who came every morning and conferred at his bedside about his body, and that perhaps it wasn't so important what he wrote in it, which amounted, as he said wryly to Quentin, to little more than the usual banalities about terror and amazement that this was happening to him, to him also, plus the usual remorseful assessments of his past life, his pardonable superficialities, capped by resolves to live better, more deeply, more in touch with his work and his friends, and not to care so passionately about what people thought of him, interspersed with admonitions to himself that in this situation his will to live counted more than anything else and that if he really wanted to live, and trusted life, and liked himself well enough (down, ol' debbil Thanatos!), he *would* live, he would be an exception; but perhaps all this, as Quentin ruminated, talking on the phone to Kate, wasn't the point, the point was that by the very keeping of the diary he was accumulating something to reread one day, slyly staking out his claim to a future time, in which the diary would be an object, a relic, in which he might not actually reread it, because he would want to have put this ordeal behind him, but the diary would be there in the drawer of his stupendous Majorelle desk, and he could already, he did actually say to Quentin one late sunny afternoon, propped up in the hospital bed, with the stain of chocolate framing one corner of a heartbreaking smile, see himself in the penthouse, the October sun streaming through those clear windows instead of this streaked one, and the diary, the pathetic diary, safe inside the drawer.

It doesn't matter about the treatment's side effects, Stephen said (when talking to Max), I don't know why you're so worried about that, every strong treatment has some dangerous side effects, it's inevitable, you mean otherwise the treatment wouldn't be effective, Hilda interjected, and anyway, Stephen went on doggedly, just because there *are* side effects it doesn't mean he has to get them, or all of them, each one, or even some of them. That's just a list of all the possible things that could go wrong, because the doctors have to cover themselves, so they make up a worst-case scenario, but isn't what's happening to him, and to so many other people, Tanya interrupted, a worst-case scenario, a catastrophe no one could have imagined, it's too cruel, and isn't everything a side effect, quipped Ira, even *we* are all side effects, but we're not bad side effects, Frank said, he likes having his friends around, and we're helping each other, too; because his illness sticks us all in the same glue, mused Xavier, and, whatever the jealousies and grievances from the past that have made us wary and cranky with each other, when something like this happens (the sky is falling, the sky is falling!) you understand what's really important. I agree, Chicken Little, he is reported to have said. But don't you think, Quentin observed to Max, that being as close to him as we are, making time to drop by the hospital every day, is a way of our trying to define ourselves more firmly and irrevocably as the well, those who aren't ill, who aren't going to fall ill, as if what's happened to him couldn't happen to us, when in fact the chances are that before long one of us will end up where he is, which is probably what he felt when he was one of the cohort visiting Zack in the spring (you never knew Zack, did you?), and, according to Clarice, Zack's widow, he didn't come very often, he said he hated hospitals, and didn't feel he was doing Zack any good, that Zack would see on his face how uncomfortable he was. Oh, he was one of those, Aileen said. A coward. Like me.

And after he was sent home from the hospital, and Quentin had volunteered to move in and was cooking meals and taking telephone messages and keeping the mother in Mississippi informed, well, mainly keeping her from flying to New York and heaping her grief on her son and confusing the household routine with her oppressive ministrations, he was able to work an hour or two in his study, on days he didn't insist on going out, for a meal or a movie, which tired him. He seemed optimistic, Kate thought, his appetite was good, and what he said, Orson reported, was that he agreed when Stephen advised him that the main thing was to keep in shape, he was a fighter, right, he wouldn't be who he was if he weren't, and was he ready for the big fight, Stephen asked rhetorically (as Max told it to Donny), and he said you bet, and Stephen added it could be a lot worse, you could have gotten the disease two years ago, but now so many scientists are working on it, the American team and the French team, everyone bucking for that Nobel Prize a few years down the road, that all you have to do is stay healthy for another year or two and then there will be good treatment, real treatment. Yes, he said, Stephen said, my timing is good. And Betsy, who had been climbing on and rolling off macrobiotic diets for a decade, came up with a Japanese specialist she wanted him to see but thank God, Donny reported, he'd had the sense to refuse, but he did agree to see Victor's visualization therapist, although what could one possibly visualize, said Hilda, when the point of visualizing disease was to see it as an entity with contours, borders, here rather than there, something limited, something you were the host of, in the sense that you could disinvite the disease, while this was so total; or would be, Max said. But the main thing, said Greg, was to see that he didn't go the macrobiotic route, which might be harmless for plump Betsy but could only be devastating for him, lean as he'd always been, with all the cigarettes and other appetite-suppressing chemicals he'd been welcoming into his body for years; and now was hardly the time, as Stephen pointed out, to be worried about cleaning up his act, and eliminating the chemical additives and other pollutants that we're all blithely or not so blithely feasting on, blithely since we're healthy, healthy as we can be; so far, Ira said. Meat and potatoes is what I'd be happy to see him eating, Ursula said wistfully. And spaghetti and clam sauce, Greg added. And thick cholesterol-rich omelettes with smoked mozzarella, suggested Yvonne, who had flown from London for the weekend to see him. Chocolate cake, said Frank. Maybe not chocolate cake, Ursula said, he's already eating so much chocolate.

And when, not right away but still only three weeks later, he was accepted into the protocol for the new drug, which took considerable behind-the-scenes lobbying with the doctors, he talked less about being ill, according to Donny, which seemed like a good sign, Kate felt, a sign that he was not feeling like a victim, feeling not that he *had* a disease but, rather, was living *with* a disease (that was the right cliché, wasn't it?), a more hospitable arrangement, said Jan, a kind of cohabitation which implied that it was something temporary, that it could be terminated, but terminated how, said Hilda, and when you say hospitable, Jan, I hear hospital. And it was encouraging, Stephen insisted, that from the start, at least from the time he was finally persuaded to make the telephone call to his doctor, he was willing to say the name of the disease, pronounce it often and easily, as if it were just another word, like boy or gallery or cigarette or money or deal, as in no big deal, Paolo interjected, because, as Stephen continued, to utter the name is a sign of health, a sign that one has accepted being who one is, mortal, vulnerable, not exempt, not an exception after all, it's a sign that one is willing, truly willing, to fight for one's life. And we must say the name, too, and often, Tanya added, we mustn't lag behind him in honesty, or let him feel that, the effort of honesty having been made, it's something done with and he can go on to other things. One is so much better prepared to help him, Wesley replied. In a way he's fortunate, said Yvonne, who had taken care of a problem at the New York store and was flying back to London this evening, sure, fortunate, said Wesley, no one is shunning him, Yvonne went on, no one's afraid to hug him or kiss him lightly on the mouth, in London we are, as usual, a few years behind you, people I know, people who would seem to be not even remotely at risk, are just terrified, but I'm impressed by how cool and rational you all are; you find us cool, asked Quentin. But I have to say, he's reported to have said, I'm terrified, I find it very hard to read (and you know how he loves to read, said Greg; yes, reading is his television, said Paolo) or to think, but I don't feel hysterical. I feel quite hysterical, Lewis said to Yvonne. But you're able to *do* something for him, that's wonderful, how I wish I could stay longer, Yvonne answered, it's rather beautiful, I can't help thinking, this utopia of friendship you've assembled around him (this pathetic utopia, said Kate), so that the disease, Yvonne concluded, is not, anymore, out there. Yes, don't you think we're more at home here, with him, with the disease, said Tanya, because the imagined disease is so much worse than the reality of him, whom we all love, each in our fashion, having it. I know for me his getting it has quite demystified the disease, said Jan, I don't feel afraid, spooked, as I did before he became ill, when it was only news about remote acquaintances, whom I never saw again after they became ill. But you know you're not going to come down with the disease, Quentin said, to which Ellen replied, on her behalf, that's not the point, and possibly untrue, my gynecologist says that everyone is at risk, everyone who has a sexual life, because sexuality is a chain that links each of us to many others, unknown others, and now the great chain of being has become a chain of death as well. It's not the same for you, Quentin insisted, it's not the same for you as it is for me or Lewis or Frank or Paolo or Max, I'm more and more frightened, and I have every reason to be. I don't think about whether I'm at risk or not, said Hilda, I know that I was afraid to know someone with the disease, afraid of what I'd see, what I'd feel, and after the first day I came to the hospital I felt so relieved. I'll never feel that way, that fear, again; he doesn't seem different from me. He's not, Quentin said.

According to Lewis, he talked more often about those who visited more often, which is natural, said Betsy, I think he's even keeping a tally. And among those who came or checked in by phone every day, the inner circle as it were, those who were getting more points, there was still a further competition, which was what was getting on Betsy's nerves, she confessed to Jan; there's always that vulgar jockeying for position around the bedside of the gravely ill, and though we all feel suffused with virtue at our loyalty to him (speak for yourself, said Jan), to the extent that we're carving time out of every day, or almost every day, though some of us are dropping out, as Xavier pointed out, aren't we getting at least as much out of this as he is. Are we, said Jan. We're rivals for a sign from him of special pleasure over a visit, each stretching for the brass ring of his favor, wanting to feel the most wanted, the true nearest and dearest, which is inevitable with someone who doesn't have a spouse and children or an official in-house lover, hierarchies that no one would dare contest, Betsy went on, so we are the family he's founded, without meaning to, without official titles and ranks (we, we, snarled Quentin); and is it so clear, though some of us, Lewis and Quentin and Tanya and Paolo, among others, are ex-lovers and all of us more or less than friends, which one of us he prefers, Victor said (now it's us, raged Quentin), because sometimes I think he looks forward more to seeing Aileen, who has visited only three times, twice at the hospital and once since he's been home, than he does you or me; but, according to Tanya, after being very disappointed that Aileen hadn't come, now he was angry, while, according to Xavier, he was not really hurt but touchingly passive, accepting Aileen's absence as something he somehow deserved. But he's happy to have people around, said Lewis; he says when he doesn't have company he gets very sleepy, he sleeps (according to Quentin), and then perks up when someone arrives, it's important that he not feel ever alone. But, said Victor, there's one person he hasn't heard from, whom he'd probably like to hear from more than most of us; but she didn't just vanish, even right after she broke away from him, and he knows exactly where she lives now, said Kate, he told me he put in a call to her last Christmas Eve, and she said it's nice to hear from you and Merry Christmas, and he was shattered, according to Orson, and furious and disdainful, according to Ellen (what do you expect of her, said Wesley, she was burned out), but Kate wondered if maybe he hadn't phoned Nora in the middle of a sleepless night, what's the time difference, and Quentin said no, I don't think so, I think he wouldn't want her to know.

. . .

And when he was feeling even better and had regained the pounds he'd shed right away in the hospital, though the refrigerator started to fill up with organic wheat germ and grapefruit and skimmed milk (he's worried about his cholesterol count, Stephen lamented), and told Quentin he could manage by himself now, and did, he started asking everyone who visited how he looked, and everyone said he looked great, so much better than a few weeks ago, which didn't jibe with what anyone had told him at that time; but then it was getting harder and harder to know how he looked, to answer such a question honestly when among themselves they wanted to be honest, both for honesty's sake and (as Donny thought) to prepare for the worst, because he'd been looking like this for so long, at least it seemed so long, that it was as if he'd always been like this, how did he look before, but it was only a few months, and those words, pale and wan-looking and fragile, hadn't they always applied? And one Thursday Ellen, meeting Lewis at the door of the building, said, as they rode up together in the elevator, how is he really? But you see how he is, Lewis said tartly, he's fine, he's perfectly healthy, and Ellen understood that of course Lewis didn't think he was perfectly healthy but that he wasn't worse, and that was true, but wasn't it, well, almost heartless to talk like that. Seems inoffensive to me, Quentin said, but I know what you mean, I remember once talking to Frank, somebody, after all, who has volunteered to do five hours a week of office work at the Crisis Center (I know, said Ellen), and Frank was going on about this guy, diagnosed almost a year ago, and so much further along, who'd been complaining to Frank on the phone about the indifference of some doctor, and had gotten quite abusive about the doctor, and Frank was saying there was no reason to be so upset, the implication being that he, Frank, wouldn't behave so irrationally, and I said, barely able to control my scorn, but Frank, Frank, he has every reason to be upset, he's dying, and Frank said, said according to Quentin, oh, I don't like to think about it that way.

And it was while he was still home, recuperating, getting his weekly treatment, still not able to do much work, he complained, but, according to Quentin, up and about most of the time and turning up at the office several days a week, that bad news came about two remote acquaintances, one in Houston and one in Paris, news that was intercepted by Quentin on the ground that it could only depress him, but Stephen contended that it was wrong to lie to him, it was so important for him to live in the truth; that had been one of his first victories, that he was candid, that he was even willing to crack jokes about the disease, but Ellen said it wasn't good to give him this end-of-the-world feeling, too many people were getting ill, it was becoming such a common destiny that maybe some of the will to fight for his life would be drained out of him if it seemed to be as natural as, well, death. Oh, Hilda said, who didn't know personally either the one in Houston or the one in Paris, but knew *of* the one in Paris, a pianist who specialized in twentieth-century Czech and Polish music, I have his records, he's such a valuable person, and, when Kate glared at her, continued defensively, I know every life is equally sacred, but that *is* a thought, another thought, I mean, all these valuable people who aren't going to have their normal four-score as it is now, these people aren't going to be replaced, and it's such a loss to the culture. But this isn't going to go on forever, Wesley said, it can't, they're bound to come up with something (they, they, muttered Stephen), but did you ever think, Greg said, that if some people don't die, I mean even if they can keep them alive (they, they, muttered Kate), they continue to be carriers, and that means, if you have a conscience, that you can never make love, make love fully, as you'd been wont—wantonly, Ira said—to do. But it's better than dying, said Frank. And in all his talk about the future, when he allowed himself to be hopeful, according to Quentin, he never mentioned the prospect that even if he didn't die, if he were so fortunate as to be among the first generation of the disease's survivors, never mentioned, Kate confirmed, that whatever happened it was over, the way he had lived until now, but, according to Ira, he did think about it, the end of bravado, the end of folly, the end of trusting life, the end of taking life for granted, and of treating life as something that, samurai-like, he thought himself ready to throw away lightly, impudently; and Kate recalled, sighing, a brief exchange she'd insisted on having as long as two years ago, huddling on a banquette covered with steel-gray industrial carpet on an upper level of The Prophet and toking up for their next foray onto the dance floor: she'd said hesitantly, for it felt foolish asking a prince of debauchery to, well, take it easy, and she wasn't keen on playing big sister, a role, as Hilda confirmed, he inspired in many women, are you being careful, honey, you know what I mean. And he replied, Kate went on, no, I'm not, listen, I can't, I just can't, sex is too important to me, always has been (he started talking like that, according to Victor, after Nora left him), and if I get it, well, I get it. But he wouldn't talk like that now, would he, said Greg; he must feel awfully foolish now, said Betsy, like someone who went on smoking, saying I can't give up cigarettes, but when the bad X-ray is taken even the most besotted nicotine addict can stop on a dime. But sex isn't like cigarettes, is it, said Frank, and, besides, what good does it do to remember that he was reckless, said Lewis angrily, the appalling thing is that you just have to be unlucky once, and wouldn't he feel even worse if he'd stopped three years ago and had come down with it anyway, since one of the most terrifying features of the disease is that you don't know when you contracted it, it could have been ten years ago, because surely this disease has existed for years and years, long before it was recognized; that is, named. Who knows how long (I think a lot about that, said Max) and who knows (I know what you're going to say, Stephen interrupted) how many are going to get it.

I'm feeling fine, he's reported to have said whenever someone asked him how he was, which was almost always the first question anyone asked. Or: I'm feeling better, how are you? But he said other things, too. I'm playing leapfrog with myself, he is reported to have said, according to Victor. And: There must be a way to get something positive out of this situation, he's reported to have said to Kate. How American of him, said Paolo. Well, said Betsy, you know the old American adage: When you've got a lemon, make lemonade. The one thing I'm sure I couldn't take, Jan said he said to her, is becoming disfigured, but Stephen hastened to point out the disease doesn't take that form very often anymore, its profile is mutating, and, in conversation with Ellen, wheeled up words like blood-brain barrier, I never thought there was a barrier *there*, said Jan. But he mustn't know about Max, Ellen said, that would really depress him, please don't tell him, he'll have to know, Quentin said grimly, and he'll be furious not to have been told. But there's time for that, when they take Max off the respirator, said Ellen; but isn't it incredible, Frank said, Max was fine, not feeling ill at all, and then to wake up with a fever of a hundred and five, unable to breathe, but that's the way it often starts, with absolutely no warning, Stephen said, the disease has so many forms. And when, after another week had gone by, he asked Quentin where Max was, he didn't question Quentin's account of a spree in the Bahamas, but then the number of people who visited regularly was thinning out, partly because the old feuds that had been put aside through the first hospitalization and the return home had resurfaced, and the flickering enmity between Lewis and Frank exploded, even though Kate did her best to mediate between them, and also because he himself had done something to loosen the bonds of love that united the friends around him, by seeming to take them all for granted, as if it were perfectly normal for so many people to carve out so much time and attention for him, visit him every few days, talk about him incessantly on the phone with each other; but, according to Paolo, it wasn't that he was less grateful, it was just something he was getting used to, the visits. It had become, with time, a more ordinary kind of situation, a kind of ongoing party, first at the hospital and now since he was home, barely on his feet again, it being clear, said Robert, that I'm on the B list; but Kate said, that's absurd, there's no list; and Victor said, but there is, only it's not he, it's Quentin who's drawing it up. He wants to see us, we're helping him, we have to do it the way he wants, he fell down yesterday on the way to the bathroom, he mustn't be told about Max (but he already knew, according to Donny), it's getting worse.

When I was home, he is reported to have said, I was afraid to sleep, as I was dropping off each night it felt like just that, as if I were falling down a black hole, to sleep felt like giving in to death, I slept every night with the light on; but here, in the hospital, I'm less afraid. And to Quentin he said, one morning, the fear rips through me, it tears me open; and, to Ira, it presses me together, squeezes me toward myself. Fear gives everything its hue, its high. I feel *so*, I don't know how to say it, exalted, he said to Quentin. Calamity is an amazing high, too. Sometimes I feel so well, so powerful, it's as if I could jump out of my skin. Am I going crazy, or what? Is it all this attention and coddling I'm getting from everybody, like a child's dream of being loved? Is it the drugs? I know it sounds crazy but sometimes I think this is a *fantastic* experience, he said shyly; but there was also the bad taste in the mouth, the pressure in the head and at the back of the neck, the red, bleeding gums, the painful, if pink-lobed, breathing, and his ivory pallor, color of white chocolate. Among those who wept when told over the phone that he was back in the hospital were Kate and Stephen (who'd been called by Quentin), and Ellen, Victor, Aileen, and Lewis (who were called by Kate), and Xavier and Ursula (who were called by Stephen). Among those who didn't weep were Hilda, who said that she'd just learned that her seventy-five-year-old aunt was dying of the disease, which she'd contracted from a transfusion given during her successful double bypass of five years ago, and Frank and Donny and Betsy, but this didn't mean, according to Tanya, that they weren't moved and appalled, and Quentin thought they might not be coming soon to the hospital but would send presents; the room, he was in a private room this time, was filling up with flowers, and plants, and books, and tapes. The high tide of barely suppressed acrimony of the last weeks at home subsided into the routines of hospital visiting, though more than a few resented Quentin's having charge of the visiting book (but it was Quentin who had the idea, Lewis pointed out); now, to insure a steady stream of visitors, preferably no more than two at a time (this, the rule in all hospitals, wasn't enforced here, at least on his floor; whether out of kindness or inefficiency, no one could decide), Quentin had to be called first, to get one's time slot, there was no more casual dropping by. And his mother could no longer be prevented from taking a plane and installing herself in a hotel near the hospital; but he seemed to mind her daily presence less than expected, Quentin said; said Ellen it's we who mind, do you suppose she'll stay long. It was easier to be generous with each other visiting him here in the hospital, as Donny pointed out, than at home, where one minded never being alone with him; coming here, in our twos and twos, there's no doubt about what our role is, how we should be, collective, funny, distracting, undemanding, light, it's important to be light, for in all this dread there is gaiety, too, as the poet said, said Kate. (His eyes, his glittering eyes, said

Lewis.) His eyes looked dull, extinguished, Wesley said to Xavier, but Betsy said his face, not just his eyes, looked soulful, warm; whatever is there, said Kate, I've never been so aware of his eyes; and Stephen said, I'm afraid of what my eyes show, the way I watch him, with too much intensity, or a phony kind of casualness, said Victor. And, unlike at home, he was clean-shaven each morning, at whatever hour they visited him; his curly hair was always combed; but he complained that the nurses had changed since he was here the last time, and that he didn't like the change, he wanted everyone to be the same. The room was furnished now with some of his personal effects (odd word for one's things, said Ellen), and Tanya brought drawings and a letter from her nine-year-old dyslexic son, who was writing now, since she'd purchased a computer; and Donny brought champagne and some helium balloons, which were anchored to the foot of his bed; tell me about something that's going on, he said, waking up from a nap to find Donny and Kate at the side of his bed, beaming at him; tell me a story, he said wistfully, said Donny, who couldn't think of anything to say; *you're* the story, Kate said. And Xavier brought an eighteenth-century Guatemalan wooden statue of St. Sebastian with upcast eyes and open mouth, and when Tanya said what's that, a tribute to eros past, Xavier said where I come from Sebastian is venerated as a protector against pestilence. Pestilence symbolized by arrows? Symbolized by arrows. All people remember is the body of a beautiful youth bound to a tree, pierced by arrows (of which he always seems oblivious, Tanya interjected), people forget that the story continues, Xavier continued, that when the Christian women came to bury the martyr they found him still alive and nursed him back to health. And he said, according to Stephen, I didn't know St. Sebastian didn't die. It's undeniable, isn't it, said Kate on the phone to Stephen, the fascination of the dying. It makes me ashamed. We're learning how to die, said Hilda, I'm not ready to learn, said Aileen; and Lewis, who was coming straight from the other hospital, the hospital where Max was still being kept in I.C.U., met Tanya getting out of the elevator on the tenth floor, and as they walked together down the shiny corridor past the open doors, averting their eyes from the other patients sunk in their beds, with tubes in their noses, irradiated by the bluish light from the television sets, the thing I can't bear to think about, Tanya said to Lewis, is someone dying with the TV on.

He has that strange, unnerving detachment now, said Ellen, that's what upsets me, even though it makes it easier to be with him. Sometimes he was querulous. I can't stand them coming in here taking my blood every morning, what are they doing with all that blood, he is reported to have said; but where was his anger, Jan wondered. Mostly he was lovely to be with, always saying how are *you*, how are you feeling. He's so sweet now, said Aileen. He's so nice, said Tanya. (Nice, nice, groaned Paolo.) At first he was very ill, but he was rallying, according to Stephen's best information, there was no fear of his not recovering this time, and the doctor spoke of his being discharged from the hospital in another ten days if all went well, and the mother was persuaded to fly back to Mississippi, and Quentin was readying the penthouse for his return. And he was still writing his diary, not showing it to anyone, though Tanya, first to arrive one late-winter morning, and finding him dozing, peeked, and was horrified, according to Greg, not by anything she read but by a progressive change in his handwriting: in the recent pages, it was becoming spidery, less legible, and some lines of script wandered and tilted about the page. I was thinking, Ursula said to Quentin, that the difference between a story and a painting or photograph is that in a story you can write, He's still alive. But in a painting or a photo you can't show "still." You can just show him being alive. He's still alive, Stephen said.

EMERGENCY

BY DENIS JOHNSON (1991)

I'd been working in the emergency room for about three weeks, I guess. This was in 1973, before the summer ended. With nothing to do on the overnight shift but batch the insurance reports from the daytime shifts, I just started wandering around, over to the coronary-care unit, down to the cafeteria, et cetera, looking for Georgie, the orderly, a pretty good friend of mine. He often stole pills from the cabinets.

He was running over the tiled floor of the operating room with a mop. "Are you still doing that?" I said.

"Jesus, there's a lot of blood here," he complained.

"Where?" The floor looked clean enough to me.

"What the hell were they doing in here?" he asked me.

"They were performing surgery, Georgie," I told him.

"There's so much goop inside of us, man," he said, "and it all wants to get out." He leaned his mop against a cabinet.

"What are you crying for?" I didn't understand.

He stood still, raised both arms slowly behind his head, and tightened his ponytail. Then he grabbed the mop and started making broad random arcs with it, trembling and weeping and moving all around the place really fast. "What am I *crying* for?" he said. "Jesus. Wow, oh boy, perfect."

I was hanging out in the E.R. with fat, quivering Nurse. One of the

Family Service doctors that nobody liked came in looking for Georgie to wipe up after him. "Where's Georgie?" this guy asked.

"Georgie's in O.R.," Nurse said.

"Again?"

"No," Nurse said. "Still."

"Still? Doing what?"

"Cleaning the floor."

"Again?"

"No," Nurse said again. "Still."

Back in O.R., Georgie dropped his mop and bent over in the posture of a child soiling its diapers. He stared down with his mouth open in terror.

He said, "What am I going to do about these fucking *shoes*, man?"

"Whatever you stole," I said, "I guess you already ate it all, right?"

"Listen to how they squish," he said, walking around carefully on his heels.

"Let me check your pockets, man."

He stood still a minute, and I found his stash. I left him two of each, whatever they were. "Shift is about half over," I told him.

"Good. Because I really, really, really need a drink," he said. "Will you please help me get this blood mopped *up*?"

Around 3:30 A.M. a guy with a knife in his eye came in, led by Georgie.

"I hope *you* didn't do that to him," Nurse said.

"Me?" Georgie said. "No. He was like this."

"My wife did it," the man said. The blade was buried to the hilt in the outside corner of his left eye. It was a hunting knife kind of thing.

"Who brought you in?" Nurse said.

"Nobody. I just walked down. It's only three blocks," the man said.

Nurse peered at him. "We'd better get you lying down."

"O.K., I'm certainly ready for something like that," the man said.

She peered a bit longer into his face. "Is your other eye," she said, "a glass eye?"

"It's plastic, or something artificial like that," he said.

"And you can see out of *this* eye?" she asked, meaning the wounded one.

"I can see. But I can't make a fist out of my left hand because this knife is doing something to my brain."

"My God," Nurse said.

"I guess I'd better get the doctor," I said.

"There you go," Nurse agreed.

They got him lying down, and Georgie says to the patient, "Name?"

"Terrence Weber."

"Your face is dark. I can't see what you're saying."

"Georgie," I said.

"What are you saying, man? I can't see."

Nurse came over, and Georgie said to her, "His face is dark."

She leaned over the patient. "How long ago did this happen, Terry?" she shouted down into his face.

"Just a while ago. My wife did it. I was asleep," the patient said.

"Do you want the police?"

He thought about it and finally said, "Not unless I die."

Nurse went to the wall intercom and buzzed the doctor on duty, the Family Service person. "Got a surprise for you," she said over the intercom. He took his time getting down the hall to her, because he knew she hated Family Service and her happy tone of voice could only mean something beyond his competence and potentially humiliating.

He peeked into the trauma room and saw the situation: the clerk—that is, me—standing next to the orderly, Georgie, both of us on drugs, looking down at a patient with a knife sticking up out of his face.

"What seems to be the trouble?" he said.

The doctor gathered the three of us around him in the office and said, "Here's the situation. We've got to get a team here, an entire team. I want a good eye man. A great eye man. The best eye man. I want a brain surgeon. And I want a really good gas man, get me a genius. I'm not touching that head. I'm just going to watch this one. I know my limits. We'll just get him prepped and sit tight. Orderly!"

"Do you mean me?" Georgie said. "Should I get him prepped?"

"Is this a hospital?" the doctor asked. "Is this the emergency room? Is that a patient? Are you the orderly?"

I dialled the hospital operator and told her to get me the eye man and the brain man and the gas man.

Georgie could be heard across the hall, washing his hands and singing a Neil Young song that went "Hello cowgirl in the sand. Is this place at your command?"

"That person is not right, not at all, not one bit," the doctor said.

"As long as my instructions are audible to him it doesn't concern me," Nurse insisted, spooning stuff up out of a little Dixie cup. "I've got my own life and the protection of my family to think of."

"Well, O.K., O.K. Don't chew my head off," the doctor said.

The eye man was on vacation or something. While the hospital's operator called around to find someone else just as good, the other specialists were hurrying through the night to join us. I stood around looking at charts and chewing up more of Georgie's pills. Some of them tasted the way urine smells, some of them burned, some of them tasted like chalk. Various nurses, and two physicians who'd been tending somebody in I.C.U., were hanging out down here with us now.

Everybody had a different idea about exactly how to approach the problem of removing the knife from Terrence Weber's brain. But when Georgie came in from prepping the patient—from shaving the patient's eyebrow and disinfecting the area around the wound, and so on—he seemed to be holding the hunting knife in his left hand.

The talk just dropped off a cliff.

"Where," the doctor asked finally, "did you get that?"

Nobody said one thing more, not for quite a long time.

After a while, one of the I.C.U. nurses said, "Your shoelace is untied." Georgie laid the knife on a chart and bent down to fix his shoe.

There were twenty more minutes left to get through.

"How's the guy doing?" I asked.

"Who?" Georgie said.

It turned out that Terrence Weber still had excellent vision in the one good eye, and acceptable motor and reflex, despite his earlier motor complaint. "His vitals are normal," Nurse said. "There's nothing wrong with the guy. It's one of those things."

After a while you forget it's summer. You don't remember what the morning is. I'd worked two doubles with eight hours off in between, which I'd spent sleeping on a gurney in the nurses' station. Georgie's pills were making me feel like a giant helium-filled balloon, but I was wide awake. Georgie and I went out to the lot, to his orange pickup.

We lay down on a stretch of dusty plywood in the back of the truck with the daylight knocking against our eyelids and the fragrance of alfalfa thickening on our tongues.

"I want to go to church," Georgie said.

"Let's go to the county fair."

"I'd like to worship. I would."

"They have these injured hawks and eagles there. From the Humane Society," I said.

"I need a quiet chapel about now."

Georgie and I had a terrific time driving around. For a while the day was clear and peaceful. It was one of the moments you stay in, to hell with all the troubles of before and after. The sky is blue, and the dead are coming back. Later in the afternoon, with sad resignation, the county fair bares its breasts. A champion of the drug LSD, a very famous guru of the love generation, is being interviewed amid a TV crew off to the left of the poultry cages. His eyeballs look like he bought them in a joke shop. It doesn't occur to me, as I pity this extraterrestrial, that in my life I've taken as much acid as he has.

After that, we got lost. We drove for hours, literally hours, but we couldn't find the road back to town.

Georgie started to complain. "That was the worst fair I've been to. Where were the rides?"

"They had rides," I said.

"I didn't see one ride."

A jackrabbit scurried out in front of us, and we hit it.

"There was a merry-go-round, a Ferris wheel, and a thing called the Hammer that people were bent over vomiting from after they got off," I said. "Are you completely blind?"

"What was that?"

"A rabbit."

"Something thumped."

"You hit him. *He* thumped."

Georgie stood on the brake pedal. "Rabbit stew."

He threw the truck in reverse and zigzagged back toward the rabbit. "Where's my hunting knife?" He almost ran over the poor animal a second time.

"We'll camp in the wilderness," he said. "In the morning we'll breakfast on its haunches." He was waving Terrence Weber's hunting knife around in what I was sure was a dangerous way.

In a minute he was standing at the edge of the fields, cutting the scrawny little thing up, tossing away its organs. "I should have been a doctor," he cried.

A family in a big Dodge, the only car we'd seen for a long time, slowed down and gawked out the windows as they passed by. The father said, "What is it, a snake?"

"No, it's not a snake," Georgie said. "It's a rabbit with babies inside it."

"Babies!" the mother said, and the father sped the car forward, over the protests of several little kids in the back.

Georgie came back to my side of the truck with his shirtfront stretched out in front of him as if he were carrying apples in it, or some such, but they were, in fact, slimy miniature bunnies. "No way I'm eating those things," I told him.

"Take them, take them. I gotta drive, take them," he said, dumping them in my lap and getting in on his side of the truck. He started driving along faster and faster, with a look of glory on his face. "We killed the mother and saved the children," he said.

"It's getting late," I said. "Let's get back to town."

"You bet." Sixty, seventy, eighty-five, just topping ninety.

"These rabbits better be kept warm." One at a time I slid the little things in between my shirt buttons and nestled them against my belly. "They're hardly moving," I told Georgie.

"We'll get some milk and sugar and all that, and we'll raise them up ourselves. They'll get as big as gorillas."

The road we were lost on cut straight through the middle of the world. It was still daytime, but the sun had no more power than an ornament or a sponge. In this light the truck's hood, which had been bright orange, had turned a deep blue.

Georgie let us drift to the shoulder of the road, slowly, slowly, as if he'd fallen asleep or given up trying to find his way.

"What is it?"

"We can't go on. I don't have any headlights," Georgie said.

We parked under a strange sky with a faint image of a quarter-moon superimposed on it.

There was a little woods beside us. This day had been dry and hot, the buck pines and what all simmering patiently, but as we sat there smoking cigarettes it started to get very cold.

"The summer's over," I said.

That was the year when arctic clouds moved down over the Midwest, and we had two weeks of winter in September.

"Do you realize it's going to snow?" Georgie asked me.

He was right, a gun-blue storm was shaping up. We got out and walked around idiotically. The beautiful chill! That sudden crispness, and the tang of evergreen stabbing us!

The gusts of snow twisted themselves around our heads while the night fell. I couldn't find the truck. We just kept getting more and more lost. I kept calling, "Georgie, can you see?" and he kept saying, "See what? See what?"

The only light visible was a streak of sunset flickering below the hem of the clouds. We headed that way.

We bumped softly down a hill toward an open field that seemed to be a military graveyard, filled with rows and rows of austere, identical markers over soldiers' graves. I'd never before come across this cemetery. On the farther side of the field, just beyond the curtains of snow, the sky was torn away and the angels were descending out of a brilliant blue summer, their huge faces streaked with light and full of pity. The sight of them cut through my heart and down the knuckles of my spine, and if there'd been anything in my bowels I would have messed my pants from fear.

Georgie opened his arms and cried out, "It's the drive-in, man!"

"The drive-in . . ." I wasn't sure what these words meant.

"They're showing movies in a fucking blizzard!" Georgie screamed.

"I see. I thought it was something else," I said.

We walked carefully down there and climbed through the busted fence and stood in the very back. The speakers, which I'd mistaken for grave markers, muttered in unison. Then there was tinkly music, of which I could very nearly make out the tune. Famous movie stars rode bicycles beside a river, laughing out of their gigantic lovely mouths. If anybody had come to see this show, they'd left when the weather started. Not one car remained, not even a broken-down one from last week, or one left here because it was out of gas. In a couple of minutes, in the middle of a whirling square dance, the screen turned black, the cinematic summer ended, the snow went dark, there was nothing but my breath.

"I'm starting to get my eyes back," Georgie said in another minute.

A general grayness was giving birth to various shapes, it was true. "But which ones are close and which ones are far off?" I begged him to tell me.

By trial and error, with a lot of walking back and forth in wet shoes, we found the truck and sat inside it, shivering.

"Let's get out of here," I said.

"We can't go anywhere without headlights."

"We've gotta get back. We're a long way from home."

"No, we're not."

"We must have come three hundred miles."

"We're right outside town, Fuckhead. We've just been driving around and around."

"This is no place to camp. I hear the interstate over there."

"We'll just stay here till it gets late. We can drive home late. We'll be invisible."

We listened to the big rigs going from San Francisco to Pennsylvania along the interstate, like shudders down a long hacksaw blade, while the snow buried us.

Eventually Georgie said, "We better get some milk for those bunnies."

"We don't have *milk*," I said.

"We'll mix sugar up with it."

"Will you forget about this milk all of a sudden?"

"They're mammals, man."

"Forget about those rabbits."

"Where are they, anyway?"

"You're not listening to me. I said, 'Forget the rabbits.' "

"Where are they?"

The truth was I'd forgotten all about them, and they were dead.

"They slid around behind me and got squashed," I said tearfully.

"They slid around *behind*?"

He watched while I pried them out from behind my back.

I picked them out one at a time and held them in my hands and we looked at them. There were eight. They weren't any bigger than my fingers, but everything was there.

Little feet! Eyelids! Even whiskers! "Deceased," I said.

Georgie asked, "Does everything you touch turn to shit? Does this happen to you every time?"

"No wonder they call me Fuckhead."

"It's a name that's going to stick."

"I realize that."

" 'Fuckhead' is gonna ride you to your grave."

"I just said so. I agreed with you in advance," I said.

Or maybe that wasn't the time it snowed. Maybe it was the time we slept in the truck and I rolled over on the bunnies and flattened them. It doesn't matter. What's important for me to remember now is that early the next morning the snow was melted off the windshield and the daylight woke me up. A mist covered everything and, with the sunshine, was beginning to grow sharp and strange. The bunnies weren't a problem yet, or they'd already been a problem and were already forgotten, and there was nothing on my mind. I felt the beauty of the morning. I could understand how a drowning man might suddenly feel a deep thirst being quenched. Or how the slave might become a friend to his master. Georgie slept with his face right on the steering wheel.

I saw bits of snow resembling an abundance of blossoms on the stems of the drive-in speakers—no, revealing the blossoms that were always there. A bull elk stood still in the pasture beyond the fence giving off an air of authority and stupidity. And a coyote jogged across the pasture and faded away among the saplings.

That afternoon we got back to work in time to resume everything as if it had never stopped happening and we'd never been anywhere else.

"The Lord," the intercom said, "is my shepherd." It did that each evening because this was a Catholic hospital. "Our Father, who art in Heaven," and so on.

"Yeah, yeah," Nurse said.

The man with the knife in his head, Terrence Weber, was released around suppertime. They'd kept him overnight and given him an eyepatch—all for no reason, really.

He stopped off at E.R. to say goodbye. "Well, those pills they gave me make everything taste terrible," he said.

"It could have been worse," Nurse said.

"Even my tongue."

"It's just a miracle you didn't end up sightless or at least dead," she reminded him.

The patient recognized me. He acknowledged me with a smile. "I was peeping on the lady next door while she was out there sunbathing," he said. "My wife decided to blind me."

He shook Georgie's hand. Georgie didn't know him. "Who are you supposed to be?" he asked Terrence Weber.

Some hours before that, Georgie had said something that had suddenly and completely explained the difference between us. We'd been driving back toward town, along the Old Highway, through the flatness. We picked up a hitchhiker, a boy I knew. We stopped the truck and the boy climbed slowly up out of the fields as out of the mouth of a volcano. His name was Hardee. He looked even worse than we probably did.

"We got messed up and slept in the truck all night," I told Hardee.

"I had a feeling," Hardee said. "Either that or, you know, driving a thousand miles."

"That, too," I said.

"Or you're sick or diseased or something."

"Who's this guy?" Georgie asked.

"This is Hardee. He lived with me last summer. I found him on the doorstep. What happened to your dog?" I asked Hardee.

"He's still down there."

"Yeah, I heard you went to Texas."

"I was working on a bee farm," Hardee said.

"Wow. Do those things sting you?"

"Not like you'd think," Hardee said. "You're part of their daily drill. It's all part of a harmony."

Outside, the same identical stretch of ground repeatedly rolled past our faces. The day was cloudless, blinding. But Georgie said, "Look at that," pointing straight ahead of us.

One star was so hot it showed, bright and blue, in the empty sky.

"I recognized you right away," I told Hardee. "But what happened to your hair? Who chopped it off?"

"I hate to say."

"Don't tell me."

"They drafted me."

"Oh no."

"Oh yeah. I'm AWOL. I'm bad AWOL. I got to get to Canada."

"Oh, that's terrible," I said to Hardee.

"Don't worry," Georgie said. "We'll get you there."

"How?"

"Somehow. I think I know some people. Don't worry. You're on your way to Canada."

That world! These days it's all been erased and they've rolled it up like a scroll and put it away somewhere. Yes, I can touch it with my fingers. But where is it?

After a while Hardee asked Georgie, "What do you do for a job?," and Georgie said, "I save lives."

THE PUGILIST AT REST

BY THOM JONES (1991)

Hey Baby got caught writing a letter to his girl when he was supposed to be taking notes on the specs of the M-14 rifle. We were sitting in a stifling hot Quonset hut during the first weeks of boot camp, August, 1966, at the Marine Corps Recruit Depot in San Diego. Sergeant Wright snatched the letter out of Hey Baby's hand, and later that night in the squad bay he read the letter to the Marine recruits of Platoon 263, his voice laden with sarcasm. "*Hey, Baby!*" he began, and then as he went into the body of the letter he worked himself into a state of outrage and disgust. It was a letter to *Rosie Rottencrotch*, he said at the end, and what really mattered, what was really at issue and what was of utter importance was not *Rosie Rottencrotch* and her steaming-hot panties but rather the muzzle velocity of the M-14 rifle.

Hey Baby paid for the letter by doing a hundred squat thrusts on the concrete floor of the squad bay, but the main prize he won that night was that he became forever known as Hey Baby to the recruits of Platoon 263—in addition to being a shitbird, a faggot, a turd, a maggot, and other such standard appellations. To top it all off, shortly after the incident, Hey Baby got a Dear John from this girl back in Chicago, of whom Sergeant Wright, myself, and seventy-eight other Marine recruits had come to know just a little.

Hey Baby was not in the Marine Corps for very long. The reason for this was that he started in on my buddy, Jorgeson. Jorgeson was my main man, and Hey Baby started calling him Jorgepussy and began harassing him and pushing him around. He was down on Jorgeson because whenever we were taught some sort of combat maneuver or tactic, Jorgeson would say, under his breath, "You could get *killed* if you try that." Or, "Your ass is *had*, if you do that." You got the feeling that Jorgeson didn't think loving the American flag and defending democratic ideals in Southeast Asia were all that important. He told me that what he really wanted to do was have an artist's loft in the SoHo district of New York City, wear a beret, eat liver-sausage sandwiches made with stale baguettes, drink Tokay wine, smoke dope, paint pictures, and listen to the wailing, sorrowful songs of that French singer Edith Piaf, otherwise known as "The Little Sparrow."

After the first half hour of boot camp most of the other recruits wanted to get out, too, but they nourished dreams of surfboards, Corvettes, and blond babes. Jorgeson wanted to be a beatnik and hang out with Jack Kerouac and Neal Cassady, slam down burning shots of amber whiskey, and hear Charles Mingus play real cool jazz on the bass fiddle. He wanted to practice Zen Buddhism, throw the I Ching, eat couscous, and study astrology charts. All of this was foreign territory to me. I had grown up in Aurora, Illinois, and had never heard of such things. Jorgeson had a sharp tongue and was so supercilious in his remarks that I didn't know quite how seriously I should take this talk, but I enjoyed his humor and I did believe he had the sensibilities of an artist. It was not some vague yearning. I believed very much that he could become a painter of pictures. At that point he wasn't putting his heart and soul into becoming a Marine. He wasn't a true believer like me.

Some weeks after Hey Baby began hassling Jorgeson, Sergeant Wright gave us his best speech: "You men are going off to war, and it's not a pretty thing," etc. & etc., "and if Luke the Gook knocks down one of your buddies, a fellow-Marine, you are going to risk your life and go in and get that Marine and you are going to bring him out. Not because I said so. No! You are going after that Marine because you are a Marine, a member of the most élite fighting force in the world, and that man out there who's gone down is a Marine, and he's your *buddy*. He is your brother! Once you are a Marine, you are *always* a Marine and you will never let another Marine down."

Etc. & etc. "You can take a Marine out of the Corps but you can't take the Corps out of a Marine." Etc. & etc. At the time it seemed to me a very good speech, and it stirred me deeply. Sergeant Wright was no candy ass. He was one squared-away dude, and he could call cadence. Man, it puts a lump in my throat when I remember how that man could sing cadence. Apart from Jorgeson, I think all of the recruits in Platoon 263 were proud of Sergeant Wright. He was the real thing, the genuine article. He was a crackerjack Marine.

In the course of training, lots of the recruits dropped out of the original platoon. Some couldn't pass the physical-fitness tests and had to go to a special camp for pussies. This was a particularly shameful shortcoming, the most humiliating apart from bed-wetting. Other recruits would get pneumonia, strep throat, infected foot blisters, or whatever, and lose time that way. Some didn't qualify at the rifle range. One would break a leg. Another would have a nervous breakdown (and this was also deplorable). People dropped out right and left. When the recruit corrected whatever deficiency he had, or when he got better, he would be picked up by another platoon that was in the stage of basic training that he had been in when his training was interrupted. Platoon 263 picked up dozens of recruits in this fashion. If everything went well, however, you got through with the whole business in twelve weeks. That's not a long time, but it seemed like a long time. You did not see a female in all that time. You did not see a newspaper or a television set. You did not eat a candy bar. Another thing was the fact that you had someone on top of you, watching every move you made. When it was time to "shit, shower, and shave," you were given just ten minutes, and had to confront lines and so on to complete the entire affair. Head calls were so infrequent that I spent a lot of time that might otherwise have been neutral or painless in the eye-watering anxiety that I was going to piss my pants. We ran to chow, where we were faced with enormous steam vents that spewed out a sickening smell of rancid, superheated grease. Still, we entered the mess hall with ravenous appetites, ate a huge tray of food in just a few minutes, and then *ran* back to our company area in formation, choking back the burning bile of a meal too big to be eaten so fast. God forbid that you would lose control and vomit.

If all had gone well in the preceding hours, Sergeant Wright would permit us to smoke one cigarette after each meal. Jorgeson had shown me the wisdom of switching from Camels to Pall Malls—they were much longer, packed a pretty good jolt, and when we snapped open our brushed-chrome Zippos, torched up, and inhaled the first few drags, we shared the overmastering pleasure that tobacco can bring if you use it seldom and judiciously. These were always the best moments of the day—brief respites from the tyrannical repression of recruit training. As we got close to the end of it all Jorgeson liked to play a little game. He used to say to me (with fragrant blue smoke curling out of his nostrils), "If someone said, 'I'll give you ten thousand dollars to do all of this again,' what would you say?" "No way, Jack!" He would keep on upping it until he had John Beresford Tipton, the guy from "The Millionaire," offering me a check for a million bucks. "Not for any money," I'd say.

While they were all smoldering under various pressures, the recruits were also getting pretty "salty"—they were beginning to believe. They were beginning to think of themselves as Marines. If you could make it through this, the reasoning went, you wouldn't crack in combat. So I remember that I had tears in my eyes when Sergeant Wright gave us the spiel about how a Marine would charge a machine-gun nest to save his buddies, dive on a hand grenade, do whatever it takes—and yet I was ashamed when Jorgeson caught me wiping them away. All of the recruits were teary except Jorgeson. He had these very clear cobalt-blue eyes. They were so remarkable that they caused you to notice Jorgeson in a crowd. There was unusual beauty in these eyes, and there was an extraordinary power in them. Apart from having a pleasant enough face, Jorgeson was small and unassuming except for these eyes. Anyhow, when he caught me getting sentimental he gave me this look that penetrated to the core of my being. It was the icy look of absolute contempt, and it caused me to doubt myself. I said, "Man! Can't you get into it? For Christ's sake!"

"I'm not like you," he said. "But I am into it, more than you could ever know. I never told you this before, but I am Kal-El, born on the planet Krypton and rocketed to Earth as an infant, moments before my world exploded. Disguised as a mild-mannered Marine, I have resolved to use my powers for the good of mankind. Whenever danger appears on the scene, truth and justice will be served as

I slip into the green U.S.M.C. utility uniform and become Earth's greatest hero."

I got highly pissed and didn't talk to him for a couple of days after this. Then, about two weeks before boot camp was over, when we were running out to the parade field for drill with our rifles at port arms, all assholes and elbows, I saw Hey Baby give Jorgeson a nasty shove with his M-14. Hey Baby was a large and fairly tough young man who liked to displace his aggressive impulses on Jorgeson, but he wasn't as big or as tough as I.

Jorgeson nearly fell down as the other recruits scrambled out to the parade field, and Hey Baby gave a short, malicious laugh. I ran past Jorgeson and caught up to Hey Baby; he picked me up in his peripheral vision, but by then it was too late. I set my body so that I could put everything into it, and with one deft stroke I hammered him in the temple with the sharp edge of the steel butt plate of my M-14. It was not exactly a premeditated crime, although I had been laying to get him. My idea before this had simply been to lay my hands on him, but now I had blood in my eye. I was a skilled boxer, and I knew the temple was a vulnerable spot; the human skull is otherwise hard and durable, except at its base. There was a sickening crunch, and Hey Baby dropped into the ice plants along the side of the company street.

The entire platoon was out on the parade field when the house mouse screamed at the assistant D.I., who rushed back to the scene of the crime to find Hey Baby crumpled in a fetal position in the ice plants with blood all over the place. There was blood from the scalp wound as well as a froth of blood emitting from his nostrils and his mouth. Blood was leaking from his right ear. Did I see skull fragments and brain tissue? It seemed that I did. To tell you the truth, I wouldn't have cared in the least if I had killed him, but like most criminals I was very much afraid of getting caught. It suddenly occurred to me that I could be headed for the brig for a long time. My heart was pounding out of my chest. Yet the larger part of me didn't care. Jorgeson was my buddy, and I wasn't going to stand still and let someone fuck him over.

The platoon waited at parade rest while Sergeant Wright came out of the duty hut and took command of the situation. An ambulance was called, and it came almost immediately. A number of corpsmen squatted down alongside the fallen man for what seemed an eternity. Eventually they took Hey Baby off with a fractured skull. It would be the last we ever saw of him. Three evenings later, in the squad bay, the assistant D.I. told us rather ominously that Hey Baby had recovered consciousness. That's all he said. What did *that* mean? I was worried, because Hey Baby had seen me make my move, but, as it turned out, when he came to he had forgotten the incident and all events of the preceding two weeks. Retrograde amnesia. Lucky for me. I also knew that at least three other recruits had seen what I did, but none of them reported me. Every member of the platoon was called in and grilled by a team of hard-ass captains and a light colonel from the Criminal Investigation Detachment. It took a certain amount of balls to lie to them, yet none of my fellow-jarheads reported me. I was well liked and Hey Baby was not. Indeed, many felt that he got exactly what was coming to him.

The other day—Memorial Day, as it happened—I was cleaning some stuff out of the attic when I came upon my old dress-blue uniform. It's a beautiful uniform, easily the most handsome worn by any of the U.S. armed forces. The rich color recalled Jorgeson's eyes for me—not that the color matched, but in the sense that the color of each was so startling. The tunic does not have lapels, of course, but a high collar with red piping and the traditional golden eagle, globe, and anchor insignia on either side of the neck clasp. The tunic buttons are not brassy—although they are in fact made of brass—but are a delicate gold in color, like Florentine gold. On the sleeves of the tunic my staff-sergeant's chevrons are gold on red. High on the left breast is a rainbow display of fruit salad representing my various combat citations. Just below these are my marksmanship badges; I shot Expert in rifle as well as pistol.

I opened a sandalwood box and took my various medals out of the large plastic bag I had packed them in to prevent them from tarnishing. The Navy Cross and the two Silver Stars are the best; they are such pretty things they dazzle you. I found a couple of Thai sticks in the sandalwood box as well. I took a whiff of the box and smelled the smells of Saigon—the whores, the dope, the saffron, cloves, jasmine, and patchouli oil. I put the Thai sticks back, recalling the three-day hangover that particular batch of dope had given me more than twenty-three years before. Again I looked at my dress-blue tunic. My most distinctive badge, the crowning glory, and the one of which I am most proud, is the set of Airborne wings. I remember how it was, walking around Oceanside, California—the Airborne wings and the high-and-tight haircut were recognized by all the Marines; they meant you were the crème de la crème, you were a recon Marine.

Recon was all Jorgeson's idea. We had lost touch with each other after boot camp. I was sent to com school in San Diego, where I had to sit in a hot Class A wool uniform all day and learn the Morse code. I deliberately flunked out, and when I was given the perfunctory option for a second shot, I told the colonel, "Hell no, sir. I want to go 003—infantry. I want to be a ground-pounder. I didn't join the service to sit at a desk all day."

I was on a bus to Camp Pendleton three days later, and when I got there I ran into Jorgeson. I had been thinking of him a lot. He was a clerk in headquarters company. Much to my astonishment, he was fifteen pounds heavier, and had grown two inches, and he told me he was hitting the weight pile every night after running seven miles up and down the foothills of Pendleton in combat boots, carrying a rifle and a full field pack. After the usual what's-been-happening? b.s., he got down to business and said, "They need people in Force Recon, what do you think? Headquarters is one boring motherfucker."

I said, "Recon? Paratrooper? You got to be shittin' me! When did you get so gung-ho, man?"

He said, "Hey, you were the one who *bought* the program. Don't fade on me now, God damn it! Look, we pass the physical fitness test and then they send us to jump school at Benning. If we pass that, we're in. And we'll pass. Those doggies ain't got jack. Semper fi, motherfucker! Let's do it."

There was no more talk of Neal Cassady, Edith Piaf, or the artist's loft in SoHo. I said, "If Sergeant Wright could only see you now!"

We were just three days in country when we got dropped in somewhere in the western highlands of the Quang Tri province. It was a routine reconnaissance patrol. It was not supposed to be any kind of big deal at all—just acclimation. The morning after our drop we approached a clear field. I recall that it gave me a funny feeling, but I was too new to fully trust my instincts. *Everything* was spooky; I was fresh meat, F.N.G.—a Fucking New Guy.

Before moving into the field, our team leader sent Hanes—a lance corporal, a short-timer, with only twelve days left before his rotation was over—across the field as a point man. This was a bad omen and everyone knew it. Hanes had two Purple Hearts. He followed the order with no hesitation and crossed the field without drawing fire. The team leader signalled for us to fan out and told me to circumvent the field and hump through the jungle to investigate a small mound of loose red dirt that I had missed completely but that he had picked up with his trained eye. I remember I kept saying, "Where?" He pointed to a heap of earth about thirty yards along the tree line and about ten feet back in the bushes. Most likely it was an anthill, but you never knew—it could have been an N.V.A. tunnel. "Over there," he hissed. "God damn it, do I have to draw pictures for you?"

I moved smartly in the direction of the mound while the rest of the team reconverged to discuss something. As I approached the mound I saw that it was in fact an anthill, and I looked back at the team and saw they were already halfway across the field, moving very fast.

Suddenly there were several loud hollow pops and the cry "Incoming!" Seconds later the first of a half-dozen mortar rounds landed in the loose earth surrounding the anthill. For a millisecond, everything went black. I was blown back and lifted up on a cushion of warm air. At first it was like the thrill of a carnival ride, but it was quickly followed by that stunned, jangly, electric feeling you get when you hit your crazy bone. Like that, but not confined to a small area like the elbow. I felt it shoot through my spine and into all four limbs. A thick plaster of sand and red clay plugged up my nostrils and ears. Grit was blown in between my teeth. If I hadn't been wearing a pair of Ray-Ban aviator shades, I would certainly have been blinded permanently—as it was, my eyes were loaded with grit. (I later discovered that fine red earth was somehow blown in behind the crystal of my pressure-tested Rolex Submariner, underneath my fingernails and toenails, and deep into the pores of my skin.) When

I was able to, I pulled out a canteen filled with lemon-lime Kool-Aid and tried to flood my eyes clean. This helped a little, but my eyes still felt like they were on fire. I rinsed them again and blinked furiously.

I rolled over on my stomach in the prone position and levelled my field-issue M-16. A company of screaming N.V.A. soldiers ran into the field, firing as they came—I saw their green tracer rounds blanket the position where the team had quickly congregated to lay out a perimeter, but none of our own red tracers were going out. Several of the Marines had been killed outright by the mortar rounds. Jorgeson was all right, and I saw him cast a nervous glance in my direction. Then he turned to the enemy and began to fire his M-16. I clicked my rifle on to automatic and pulled the trigger, but the gun was loaded with dirt and it wouldn't fire.

Apart from Jorgeson, the only other American putting out any fire was Second Lieutenant Milton, also a fairly new guy, a "cherry," who was down on one knee firing his .45, an exercise in almost complete futility. I assumed that Milton's 16 had jammed, like mine, and watched as AK-47 rounds, having penetrated his flak jacket and then his chest, ripped through the back of his field pack and buzzed into the jungle beyond like a deadly swarm of bees. A few seconds later, I heard the swoosh of an R.P.G. rocket, a dud round that dinged the lieutenant's left shoulder before it flew off in the bush behind him. It took off his whole arm, and for an instant I could see the white bone and ligaments of his shoulder, and the red flesh of muscle tissue, looking very much like fresh prime beef, well marbled and encased in a thin layer of yellowish-white adipose tissue that quickly became saturated with dark-red blood. What a lot of blood there was. Still, Milton continued to fire his .45. When he emptied his clip, I watched him remove a fresh one from his web gear and attempt to load the pistol with one hand. He seemed to fumble with the fresh clip for a long time, until at last he dropped it, along with his .45. The lieutenant's head slowly sagged forward, but he stayed up on one knee with his remaining arm extended out to the enemy, palm upward in the soulful, heartrending gesture of Al Jolson doing a rendition of "Mammy."

A hail of green tracer rounds buzzed past Jorgeson, but he coolly returned fire in short, controlled bursts. The light, tinny pops from his M-16 did not sound very reassuring, but I saw several N.V.A. go down. AK-47 fire kicked up red dust all around Jorgeson's feet. He was basically out in the open, and if ever a man was totally alone it was Jorgeson. He was dead meat and he had to know it. It was very strange that he wasn't hit immediately.

Jorgeson zigged his way over to the body of a large black Marine who carried an M-60 machine gun. Most of the recon Marines carried grease guns or Swedish Ks; an M-60 was too heavy for travelling light and fast, but this Marine had been big and he had been paranoid. I had known him least of anyone in the squad. In three days he had said nothing to me, I suppose because I was F.N.G., and had spooked him. Indeed, now he was dead. That august seeker of truth, Schopenhauer, was correct: *We are like lambs in a field, disporting themselves under the eye of the butcher, who chooses out first one and then another for his prey. So it is that in our good days we are all unconscious of the evil Fate may have presently in store for us—sickness, poverty, mutilation, loss of sight or reason.*

It was difficult to judge how quickly time was moving. Although my senses had been stunned by the concussion of the mortar rounds, they were, however paradoxical this may seem, more acute than ever before. I watched Jorgeson pick up the machine gun and begin to spread an impressive field of fire back at the enemy. Thuk thuk thuk, thuk thuk thuk, thuk thuk thuk! I saw several more bodies fall, and began to think that things might turn out all right after all. The N.V.A. dropped for cover, and many of them turned back and headed for the tree line. Jorgeson fired off a couple of bandoliers, and after he stopped to load another, he turned back and looked at me with those blue eyes and a smile like "How am I doing?" Then I heard the steel-cork pop of an M-79 launcher and saw a rocket grenade explode through Jorgeson's upper abdomen, causing him to do something like a back flip. His M-60 machine gun flew straight up into the air. The barrel was glowing red like a hot poker, and continued to fire in a "cook off" until the entire bandolier had run through.

In the meantime I had pulled a cleaning rod out of my pack and worked it through the barrel of my M-16. When I next tried to shoot, the Tonka-toy son of a bitch remained jammed, and at last I frantically broke it down to find the source of the problem. I had a dirty bolt. Fucking dirt everywhere. With numbed fingers I removed the firing pin and worked it over with a toothbrush, dropping it in the red dirt, picking it up, cleaning it, and dropping it again. My fingers felt like Novocain, and while I could see far away, I was unable to see up close. I poured some more Kool-Aid over my eyes. It was impossible for me to get my weapon clean. Lucky for me, ultimately.

Suddenly N.V.A. soldiers were running through the field shoving bayonets into the bodies of the downed Marines. It was not until an N.V.A. trooper kicked Lieutenant Milton out of his tripod position that he finally fell to the ground. Then the soldiers started going through the dead Marines' gear. I was still frantically struggling with my weapon when it began to dawn on me that the enemy had forgotten me in the excitement of the firefight. I wondered what had happened to Hanes and if he had gotten clear. I doubted it, and hopped on my survival radio to call in an air strike when finally a canny N.V.A. trooper did remember me and headed in my direction most ricky-tick.

With a tight grip on the spoon, I pulled the pin on a fragmentation grenade and then unsheathed my K-bar. About this time Jorgeson let off a horrendous shriek—a gut shot is worse than anything. Or did Jorgeson scream to save my life? The N.V.A. moving in my direction turned back to him, studied him for a moment, and then thrust a bayonet into his heart. As badly as my own eyes hurt, I was able to see Jorgeson's eyes—a final flash of glorious azure before they faded into the unfocussed and glazed gray of death. I repinned the grenade, got up on my knees, and scrambled away until finally I was on my feet with a useless and incomplete handful of M-16 parts, and I was running as fast and as hard as I have ever run in my life. A pair of Phantom F-4s came in very low with delayed-action high-explosive rounds and napalm. I could feel the almost unbearable heat waves of the latter, volley after volley. I can still feel it and smell it to this day.

Concerning Lance Corporal Hanes: they found him later, fried to a crisp by the napalm, but it was nonetheless ascertained that he had been mutilated while alive. He was like the rest of us—eighteen, nineteen, twenty years old. What did we know of life? Before Vietnam, Hanes didn't think he would ever die. I mean, yes, he knew that in theory he would die, but he *felt* like he was going to live forever. I know that I felt that way. Hanes was down to twelve days and a wake-up. When other Marines saw a short-timer get greased, it devastated their morale. However, when I saw them zip up the body bag on Hanes I became incensed. Why hadn't Milton sent him back to the rear to burn shit or something when he got so short? Twelve days to go and then mutilated. Fucking Milton! Fucking Second Lieutenant!

Theogenes was the greatest of gladiators. He was a boxer who served under the patronage of a cruel nobleman, a prince who took great delight in bloody spectacles. Although this was several hundred years before the times of those most enlightened of men, Socrates, Plato, and Aristotle, and well after the Minoans of Crete, it still remains a high point in the history of Western civilization and culture. It was the approximate time of Homer, the greatest poet who ever lived. Then, as now, violence, suffering, and the cheapness of life were the rule.

The sort of boxing Theogenes practiced was not like modern-day boxing with those kindergarten Queensberry Rules. The two contestants were not permitted the freedom of a ring. Instead, they were strapped to flat stones, facing each other nose-to-nose. When the signal was given they would begin hammering each other with fists encased in heavy leather thongs. It was a fight to the death. Fourteen hundred and twenty-five times Theogenes was strapped to the stone and fourteen hundred and twenty-five times he emerged a victor.

Perhaps it is Theogenes who is depicted in the famous Roman statue (based on the earlier Greek original) of "The Pugilist at Rest." I keep a grainy black-and-white photograph of it in my room. The statue depicts a muscular athlete approaching his middle age. He has a thick beard and a full head of curly hair. In addition to the telltale broken nose and cauliflower ears of a boxer, the pugilist has the slanted, drooping brows that bespeak torn nerves. Also, the forehead is piled with scar tissue. As may be expected, the pugilist has the musculature of a fighter. His neck and trapezius muscles are well developed. His shoulders are enormous; his chest is thick and flat, without the bulging pectorals of the bodybuilder. His back, oblique, and abdominal muscles are highly pronounced, and he has that greatest asset of the modern boxer—sturdy legs. The arms are large, particularly the forearms, which are reinforced with the leather wrappings of the cestus. It is the body of a small heavyweight—lithe rather than bulky, but by no means lacking in power: a Jack Johnson or a Dempsey, say. If you see the authentic statue at the Terme Museum, in Rome, you will see that the seated boxer is really not much more than a light heavyweight. People were small in those days. The important thing was that he was perfectly proportioned.

The pugilist is sitting on a rock with his forearms balanced on his thighs. That he is seated and not pacing implies that he has been through all this many times before. It appears that he is conserving his strength. His head is turned as if he were looking over his shoulder—as if someone had just whispered something to him. It is in this that the "art" of the sculpture is conveyed to the viewer. Could it be that someone has just summoned him to the arena? There is a slight look of befuddlement on his face, but there is no trace of fear. There is an air about him that suggests that he is eager to proceed and does not wish to cause anyone any trouble or to create a delay, even though his life will soon be on the line. Besides the deformities on his noble face, there is also the suggestion of weariness and philosophical resignation. *All the world's a stage, and all the men and women merely players.* Exactly! He knew this more than two thousand years before Shakespeare penned the line. How did he come to be at this place in space and time? Would he rather be safely removed to the countryside—an obscure, stinking peasant shoving a plow behind a mule? Would that be better? Or does he revel in his role? Perhaps he once did, but surely not now. Is this the great Theogenes or merely a journeyman fighter, a former slave or criminal bought by one of the many contractors who for months trained the condemned for their brief moment in the arena? I wonder if Marcus Aurelius loved the "Pugilist" as I do, and came to study it and to meditate before it?

I cut and ran from that field in Southeast Asia. I've read that Davy Crockett, hero of the American frontier, was cowering under a bed when Santa Anna and his soldiers stormed into the Alamo. What is the truth? Jack Dempsey used to get so scared before his fights that he sometimes wet his pants. But look what he did to Willard and to Luis Firpo, the Wild Bull of the Pampas! It was something close to homicide. What is courage? What is cowardice? The magnificent Roberto Duran gave us "*No más*," but who had a greater fighting heart than Duran?

I got over that first scare and saw that I was something quite other than that which I had known myself to be. Hey Baby proved only my warm-up act. There was a reservoir of malice, poison, and vicious sadism in my soul, and it poured forth freely in the jungles and rice paddies of Vietnam. I pulled three tours. I wanted some payback for Jorgeson. I grieved for Lance Corporal Hanes. I grieved for myself and what I had lost. I committed unspeakable crimes and got medals for it.

It was only fair that I got a head injury myself. I never got a scratch in Vietnam, but I got tagged in a boxing smoker at Pendleton. Fought a bad-ass light heavyweight from artillery. Nobody would fight this guy. He could box. He had all the moves. But mainly he was a puncher—it was said that he could punch with either hand. It was said that his hand speed was superb. I had finished off at least a half rack of Hamm's before I went in with him and started getting hit with head shots I didn't even see coming. They were right. His hand speed *was* superb.

I was twenty-seven years old, smoked two packs a day, was a borderline alcoholic. I shouldn't have fought him—I knew that—but he had been making noise. A very long time before, I had been the middleweight champion of the 1st Marine Division. I had been a so-called war hero. I had been a recon Marine. But now I was a garrison Marine and in no kind of shape.

He put me down almost immediately, and when I got up I was terribly afraid. I was tight and I could not breathe. It felt like he was hitting me in the face with a ball-peen hammer. It felt like he was busting light bulbs in my face. Rather than one opponent, I saw three. I was convinced his gloves were loaded, and a wave of self-pity ran through me.

I began to move. He made a mistake by expending a lot of energy trying to put me away quickly. I had no intention of going down again, and I knew I wouldn't. My buddies were watching, and I had to give them a good show. While I was afraid, I was also exhilarated; I had not felt this alive since Vietnam. I began to score with my left jab, and because of this I was able to withstand his bull charges and divert them. I thought he would throw his bolt, but in the beginning he was tireless. I must have hit him with four hundred left jabs. It got so that I could score at will, with either hand, but he would counter, trap me on the ropes, and pound. He was the better puncher and was truly hurting me, but I was scoring, and as the fight went on the momentum shifted and I took over. I staggered him again and again. The Marines at ringside were screaming for me to put him away, but however much I tried, I could not. Although I could barely stand by the end, I was sorry that the fight was over. Who had won? The referee raised my arm in victory, but I think it was pretty much a draw. Judging a prizefight is a very subjective thing.

About an hour after the bout, when the adrenaline had subsided, I realized I had a terrible headache. It kept getting worse, and I rushed out of the N.C.O. Club, where I had gone with my buddies to get loaded.

I stumbled outside, struggling to breathe, and I headed away from the company area toward Sheepshit Hill, one of the many low brown foothills in the vicinity. Like a dog who wants to die alone, so it was with me. Everything got swirly, and I dropped in the bushes.

I was unconscious for nearly an hour, and for the next two weeks I walked around like I was drunk, with double vision. I had constant headaches and seemed to have grown old overnight. My health was gone.

I became a very timid individual. I became introspective. I wondered what had made me act the way I had acted. Why had I killed my fellow-men in war, without any feeling, remorse, or regret? And when the war was over, why did I continue to drink and swagger around and get into fistfights? Why did I like to dish out pain, and why did I take positive delight in the suffering of others? Was I insane? Was it too much testosterone? Women don't do things like that. The rapacious Will to Power lost its hold on me. Suddenly I began to feel sympathetic to the cares and sufferings of all living creatures. You lose your health and you start thinking this way.

Has man become any better since the times of Theogenes? The world is replete with badness. I'm not talking about that old routine where you drag out the Spanish Inquisition, the Holocaust, Joseph Stalin, the Khmer Rouge, etc. It happens in our own back yard.

Twentieth-century America is one of the most materially prosperous nations in history. But take a walk through an American prison, a nursing home, the slums where the homeless live in cardboard boxes, a cancer ward. Go to a Vietnam vets' meeting, or an A.A. meeting, or an Overeaters Anonymous meeting. *How hollow and unreal a thing is life, how deceitful are its pleasures, what horrible aspects it possesses.* Is the world not rather like a hell, as Schopenhauer, that clearheaded seer—who has helped me transform my suffering into an object of understanding—was so quick to point out? They called him a pessimist and dismissed him with a word, but it is peace and self-renewal that I have found in his pages.

About a year after my fight with the guy from artillery I started having seizures. I suffered from a form of left-temporal-lobe seizure which is sometimes called Dostoyevski's epilepsy. It's so rare as to be almost unknown. Freud, himself a neurologist, speculated that Dostoyevski was a hysterical epileptic, and that his fits were unrelated to brain damage—psychogenic in origin. Dostoyevski did not have his first attack until the age of twenty-five, when he was imprisoned in Siberia and received fifty lashes after complaining about the food. Freud figured that after Dostoyevski's mock execution, the four years' imprisonment in Siberia, the tormented childhood, the murder of his tyrannical father, etc. & etc.—he had all the earmarks of hysteria, of grave psychological trauma. And Dostoyevski had displayed the trademark features of the psychomotor epileptic long before his first attack. These days physicians insist there is no such thing as the "epileptic personality." I think they say this because they do not want to add to the burden of the epileptic's suffering with an extra stigma. Privately they do believe in these traits. Dostoyevski was nervous and depressed, a tormented hypochondriac, a compulsive writer obsessed with religious and philosophic themes. He was hyperloquacious, raving, etc. & etc. His gambling addiction is well known. By most accounts he was a sick soul.

The peculiar and most distinctive thing about his epilepsy was that in the split second before his fit—in the aura, which is in fact officially a part of the attack—Dostoyevski experienced a sense of felicity, of ecstatic well-being unlike anything an ordinary mortal could hope to imagine. It was the experience of satori. Not the nickel-and-dime satori of Abraham Maslow, but the Supreme. He said that he wouldn't trade ten years of life for this feeling, and I, who have had it, too, would have to agree. I can't explain it, I don't understand it—it becomes slippery and elusive when it gets any distance on you—but I have felt this down to the core of my being. Yes, God exists! But then it slides away and I lose it. I become a doubter. Even Dostoyevski, the fervent Christian, makes an almost airtight case against the possibility of the existence of God in the Grand Inquisitor digression in "The Brothers Karamazov." It is probably the greatest passage in all of world literature, and it tilts you to the court of the atheist. This is what happens when you approach Him with the intellect.

It is thought that St. Paul had a temporal-lobe fit on the road to Damascus. Paul warns us in First Corinthians that God will confound the intellectuals. It is known that Muhammad composed the Koran after attacks of epilepsy. Black Elk experienced fits before his grand "buffalo" vision. Joan of Arc is thought to have been a left-temporal-lobe epileptic. Each of these in a terrible flash of brain lightning was able to pierce the murky veil of illusion which is spread over all things. Just so did the scales fall from my eyes. It is called the "sacred disease."

But what a price. I rarely leave the house anymore. To avoid falling injuries, I always wear my old boxer's headgear, and I always carry my mouthpiece. Rather more often than the aura where "every common bush is afire with God," I have the typical epileptic aura, which is that of terror and impending doom. If I can keep my head and think of it, and if there is time, I slip the mouthpiece in and thus avoid biting my tongue. I bit it in half once, and when they sewed it back together it swelled enormously, like a huge red-and-black sausage. I was unable to close my mouth for more than two weeks.

The fits are coming more and more. I'm loaded on Depakene, phenobarbital, Tegretol, Dilantin—the whole shitload. A nurse from the V.A. bought a pair of Staffordshire terriers for me and trained them to watch me as I sleep, in case I have a fit and smother face down in my bedding. What delightful companions these dogs are! One of them, Gloria, is especially intrepid and clever. Inevitably, when I come to I find that the dogs have dragged me into the kitchen, away from blankets and pillows, rugs, and objects that might suffocate me, and that they have turned me on my back. There's Gloria, barking in my face. Isn't this incredible?

My sister brought a neurosurgeon over to my place around Christmas—not some V.A. butcher but a guy from the university hospital. He was a slick dude in a nine-hundred-dollar suit. He came down on me hard, like a used-car salesman. He wants to cauterize a small spot in a nerve bundle in my brain. "It's not a lobotomy, it's a *cingulotomy*," he said.

Reckless, desperate, last-ditch psychosurgery is still pretty much unthinkable in the conservative medical establishment. That's why he made a personal visit to my place. A house call. Drumming up some action to make himself a name. "See that bottle of Thorazine?" he said. "You can throw that poison away," he said. "All that amitriptyline. That's garbage, you can toss that, too." He said, "Tell me something. How can you take all of that shit and still walk?" He said, "You take enough drugs to drop an elephant."

He wants to cut me. He said that the feelings of guilt and worthlessness, and the heaviness of a heart blackened by sin, will go away. "It is *not* a lobotomy," he said.

I don't like the guy. I don't trust him. I'm not convinced, but I can't go on like this. If I am not having a panic attack I am engulfed in tedious, unrelenting depression. I am overcome with a deadening sense of languor; I can't *do* anything. I wanted to give my buddies a good show! What a goddam fool. I am a goddam fool!

It has taken me six months to put my thoughts in order, but I wanted to do it in case I am a vegetable after the operation. I know that my buddy Jorgeson was a real American hero. I wish that he had lived to be something else, if not a painter of pictures then even some kind of fuckup with a factory job and four divorces, bankruptcy petitions, in and out of jail. I wish he had been that. I wish he had been *anything* rather than a real American hero. So, then, if I am to feel somewhat *indifferent* to life after the operation, all the better. If not, not.

If I had a more conventional sense of morality I would shitcan those dress blues, and I'd send that Navy Cross to Jorgeson's brother. Jorgeson was the one who won it, who pulled the John Wayne number up there near Khe Sanh and saved my life, although

I lied and took the credit for all of those dead N.V.A. He had created a stunning body count—nothing like Theogenes, but Jorgesen only had something like twelve minutes total in the theatre of war.

The high command almost awarded me the Medal of Honor, but of course there were no witnesses to what I claimed I had done, and I had saved no one's life. When I think back on it, my tale probably did not sound as credible as I thought it had at the time. I was only nineteen years old and not all that practiced a liar. I figure if they *had* given me the Medal of Honor, I would have stood in the ring up at Camp Las Pulgas in Pendleton and let that light heavyweight from artillery fucking kill me.

Now I'm thinking I might call Hey Baby and ask how he's doing. No shit, a couple of neuro/psyches—we probably have a lot in common. I could apologize to him. But I learned from my fits that you don't have to do that. Good and evil are only illusions. Still, I cannot help but wonder sometimes if my vision of the Supreme Reality was any more real than the demons visited upon schizophrenics and madmen. Has it all been just a stupid neurochemical event? Is there no God at all? The human heart rebels against this.

If they fuck up the operation, I hope I get to keep my dogs somehow—maybe stay at my sister's place. If they send me to the nuthouse I lose the dogs for sure.

BULLET IN THE BRAIN

BY TOBIAS WOLFF (1995)

The line was endless. Anders couldn't get to the bank until just before it closed and now he was stuck behind two women whose loud, stupid conversation put him in a murderous temper. He was never in the best of tempers anyway, Anders—a book critic known for the weary, elegant savagery with which he dispatched almost everything he reviewed.

With the line still doubled around the rope, one of the tellers stuck a Position Closed sign in her window and walked to the back of the bank, where she leaned against a desk and began to pass the time with a man shuffling papers. The women in front of Anders broke off their conversation and watched the teller with hatred. "Oh, that's nice," one of them said. She turned to Anders and added, confident of his accord, "One of those little human touches that keep us coming back."

Anders had conceived his own towering hatred of the teller, but he immediately turned it on the presumptuous crybaby in front of him. "Damned unfair," he said. "Tragic, really. If they're not chopping off the wrong leg, or bombing your ancestral village, they're closing their positions."

She stood her ground. "I didn't say it was tragic," she said. "I just think it's a pretty lousy way to treat your customers."

"Unforgivable," Anders said. "Heaven will take note."

She sucked in her cheeks but stared past him and said nothing. Anders saw that the other woman, her friend, was looking in the same direction. And then the tellers stopped what they were doing, and the customers slowly turned, and silence came over the bank. Two men wearing black ski masks and blue business suits were standing to the side of the door. One of them had a pistol pressed against the guard's neck. The guard's eyes were closed, and his lips were moving. The other man had a sawed-off shotgun. "Keep your big mouth shut!" the man with the pistol said, though no one had spoken a word. "One of you tellers hits the alarm, you're all dead meat. Got it?"

The tellers nodded.

"Oh, bravo," Anders said. "Dead meat." He turned to the woman in front of him. "Great script, eh? The stern, brass-knuckled poetry of the dangerous classes."

She looked at him with drowning eyes.

The man with the shotgun pushed the guard to his knees. He handed the shotgun to his partner and yanked the guard's wrists up behind his back and locked them together with a pair of handcuffs. He then toppled him onto the floor with a kick between the shoulder blades. He took his shotgun back and went over to the security gate at the end of the counter. He was short and heavy and moved with peculiar slowness, even torpor. "Buzz him in," his partner said. The man with the shotgun sauntered along the line of tellers, handing each of them a Hefty bag. When he came to the empty position he looked over at the man with the pistol, who said, "Whose slot is that?"

Anders watched the teller. She put her hand to her throat and turned to the man she'd been talking to. He nodded. "Mine," she said.

"Then get your ugly ass in gear and fill that bag."

"There you go," Anders said to the woman in front of him. "Justice is done."

"Hey! Bright boy! Did I tell you to talk?"

"No," Anders said.

"Then shut your trap."

"Did you hear that?" Anders said. "'Bright boy.' Right out of 'The Killers.'"

"Please be quiet," the woman said.

"Hey, you deaf or what?" The man with the pistol walked over to Anders. He poked the weapon into Anders' gut. "You think I'm playing games?"

"No," Anders said, but the barrel tickled like a stiff finger and he had to fight back the titters. He did this by making himself stare into the man's eyes, which were clearly visible behind the holes in the mask: pale-blue and rawly red-rimmed. The man's left eyelid kept twitching. He breathed out a piercing, ammoniac smell that shocked Anders more than anything that had happened, and he was beginning to develop a sense of unease when the man prodded him again with the pistol.

"You like me, bright boy?" he said. "You want to suck my dick?"

"No," Anders said.

"Then stop looking at me."

Anders fixed his gaze on the man's shiny wing-tip shoes.

"Not down there. Up there." He stuck the pistol under Anders' chin and pushed it upward until Anders was looking at the ceiling.

Anders had never paid much attention to that part of the bank, a pompous old building with marble floors and counters and pillars and gilt scrollwork over the tellers' cages. The domed ceiling had been decorated with mythological figures whose fleshy, toga-draped ugliness Anders had taken in at a glance many years earlier and afterward declined to notice. Now he had no choice but to scrutinize the painter's work. It was worse than he remembered, and all of it executed with the utmost gravity. The artist had a few tricks up his sleeve and used them again and again—a certain rosy blush on the underside of the clouds, a coy backward glance on the faces of the cupids and fauns. The ceiling was crowded with various dramas, but the one that caught Anders' eye was Zeus and Europa—portrayed, in this rendition, as a bull ogling a cow from behind a haystack. To make the cow sexy, the painter had canted her hips suggestively and given her long, droopy eyelashes, through which she gazed back at the bull with sultry welcome. The bull wore a smirk and his eyebrows were arched. If there'd been a bubble coming out of his mouth, it would have said, "Hubba hubba."

"What's so funny, bright boy?"

"Nothing."

"You think I'm comical? You think I'm some kind of clown?"

"No."

"You think you can fuck with me?"

"No."

"Fuck with me again, you're history. *Capeesh?*"

Anders burst out laughing. He covered his mouth with both hands and said, "I'm sorry, I'm sorry," then snorted helplessly through his fingers and said, "*Capeesh*, oh, God, *capeesh*," and at that the man with the pistol raised the pistol and shot Anders right in the head.

The bullet smashed Anders' skull and plowed through his brain and exited behind his right ear, scattering shards of bone into the cerebral cortex, the corpus callosum, back toward the basal ganglia, and down into the thalamus. But before all this occurred, the first appearance of the bullet in the cerebrum set off a crackling chain of ion transports and neurotransmissions. Because of their peculiar origin, these traced a peculiar pattern, flukishly calling to life a summer afternoon some forty years past, and long since lost to memory. After striking the cranium, the bullet was moving at nine hundred feet per second, a pathetically sluggish, glacial pace compared with the synaptic lightning that flashed around it. Once in the brain, that is, the bullet came under the mediation of brain time, which gave Anders plenty of leisure to contemplate the scene that, in a phrase he would have abhorred, "passed before his eyes."

It is worth noting what Anders did not remember, given what he did remember. He did not remember his first lover, Sherry, or what he had most madly loved about her, before it came to irritate him—her unembarrassed carnality, and especially the cordial way she had with his unit, which she called Mr. Mole, as in "Uh-oh, looks like Mr. Mole wants to play," and "Let's hide Mr. Mole!" Anders did not remember his wife, whom he had also loved, before she exhausted him with her predictability, or his daughter, now a sullen professor of economics at Dartmouth. He did not remember standing just outside his daughter's door as she lectured her bear about his naughtiness and described the truly appalling punishments Paws would receive unless he changed his ways. He did not remember a single line of the hundreds of poems he had committed to memory in his youth so that he could give himself the shivers at will—not "Silent, upon a peak in Darien," or "My God, I heard this day," or "All my pretty ones? Did you say all? O hell-kite! All?" None of these did he remember; not one. Anders did not remember his dying mother saying of his father, "I should have stabbed him in his sleep."

He did not remember Professor Josephs telling his class how the Spartans had released Athenian prisoners from their mines if they could recite Aeschylus, and then reciting Aeschylus himself, right there, in the Greek. Anders did not remember how his eyes had burned at those sounds. He did not remember the surprise of seeing a college classmate's name on the jacket of a novel not long after they graduated, or the respect he had felt after reading the book. He did not remember the pleasure of giving respect.

Nor did Anders remember seeing a woman leap to her death from the building opposite his own, just days after his daughter was born. He did not remember shouting, "Lord have mercy!" He did not remember deliberately crashing his father's car into a tree, or having his ribs kicked in by three policemen at an antiwar rally, or waking himself up with laughter. He did not remember when he began to regard the heap of books on his desk with boredom and dread, or when he grew angry at writers for writing them. He did not remember when everything began to remind him of something else.

This is what he remembered. Heat. A baseball field. Yellow grass, the whirr of insects, himself leaning against a tree as the boys of the neighborhood gather for a pickup game. The captains, precociously large boys named Burns and Darsch, argue the relative genius of Mantle and Mays. They have been worrying this subject all summer, and it has become tedious to Anders; an oppression, like the heat.

Then the last two boys arrive, Coyle and a cousin of his from Mississippi. Anders has never met Coyle's cousin before and will never see him again. He says hi with the rest but takes no further notice of him until they've chosen sides and Darsch asks the cousin what position he wants to play. "Shortstop," the boy says. "Short's the best position they is." Anders turns and looks at him. He wants to hear Coyle's cousin repeat what he's just said, but he knows better than to ask. The others will think he's being a jerk, ragging the kid for his grammar. But that isn't it, not at all—it's that Anders is strangely roused, elated, by those final two words, their pure unexpectedness and their music. He takes the field in a trance, repeating them to himself.

The bullet is already in the brain; it won't be outrun forever, or charmed to a halt. In the end, it will do its work and leave the troubled skull behind, dragging its comet's tail of memory and hope and talent and love into the marble hall of commerce. That can't be helped. But for now Anders can still make time. Time for the shadows to lengthen on the grass, time for the tethered dog to bark at the flying ball, time for the boy in right field to smack his sweat-blackened mitt and softly chant, *They is, they is, they is.*

HOW TO DATE A BROWN GIRL (BLACK GIRL, WHITE GIRL, OR HALFIE)

BY JUNOT DÍAZ (1995)

Wait until your brother, your sisters, and your mother leave the apartment. You've already told them that you were feeling too sick to go to Union City to visit that *tía* who likes to squeeze your nuts. (He's gotten big, she'll say.) And even though your moms knew you weren't sick you stuck to your story until finally she said, Go ahead and stay, *malcriado*.

Clear the government cheese from the refrigerator. If the girl's from the Terrace, stack the boxes in the crisper. If she's from the Park or Society Hill, then hide the cheese in the cabinet above the oven, where she'll never see it. Leave a reminder under your pillow to get out the cheese before morning or your moms will kick your ass. Take down any embarrassing photos of your family in the *campo*, especially, that one with the half-naked kids dragging a goat on a rope. Hide the picture of yourself with an Afro. Make sure the bathroom is presentable. Since your toilet can't flush toilet paper, put the bucket with all the crapped-on toilet paper under the sink. Spray the bucket with Lysol, then close the lid.

Shower, comb, dress. Sit on the couch and watch TV. If she's an outsider her father will bring her, maybe her mother. Her parents won't want her seeing a boy from the Terrace—people get stabbed in the Terrace—but she's strong-headed and this time will get her way. If she's a white girl, you're sure you'll at least get a hand job.

The directions you gave her were in your best handwriting, so her parents won't think you're an idiot. Get up from the couch and check the parking lot. Nothing. If the girl's local, don't sweat. She'll flow over when she's good and ready. Sometimes she'll run into her friends and a whole crowd will show up, and even though that means you ain't getting shit it will be fun anyway and you'll wish these people would come over more often. Sometimes the girl won't flow over at all and the next day in school she'll say, Sorry, and smile, and you'll believe her and be stupid enough to ask her out again.

You wait, and after an hour you go out to your corner. The neighborhood is full of traffic—commuters now cut through the neighborhood—making it hard on the kids and the *viejas*, who are used to empty streets. Give one of your friends a shout and when he says, Still waiting on that bitch? say, Hell, yeah.

Get back inside. Call her house and when her father picks up ask if she's there. If he sounds like a principal or a police chief, a dude with a big neck, someone who never has to watch his back, then hang up. Sit and wait. And wait. Until finally, just as your stomach is about to give out on you, a Honda, or maybe a Cherokee, will pull in and out she'll come.

Hey, she'll say.

Come on in, you'll say.

Look, she'll say. My mom wants to meet you. She's got herself all worried about nothing.

Don't panic. Say, Hey, no problem. Run a hand through your hair like the white boys do, even though the only thing that runs easily through your hair is Africa. She will look good. White girls are the ones you want most, aren't they? But the out-of-towners are usually black—black girls who grew up with ballet and Girl Scouts, and have three cars in their driveway. If she's a halfie don't be surprised that her mother is the white one. Say, Hi. She'll say, Hi, and you'll see that you don't scare her, not really. She will say that she needs easier directions to get out, and even though she already has the best directions on her lap, give her new ones. Make her happy.

If the girl's from the Terrace, none of this will happen.

You have choices. If the girl's from around the way, take her to El Cibao for dinner. Order everything in your busted-up Spanish. Amaze her if she's black, let her correct you if she's Latina. If she's not from around the way, Wendy's will do. As you walk to the restaurant, talk about school. A local girl won't need stories about the neighborhood, but the others might. Tell her about the *pendejo* who stored cannisters of Army tear gas in his basement for years until one day they all cracked and the neighborhood got a dose of military-strength stuff. Don't tell her that your moms knew right away what it was, that she recognized the smell from the year the United States invaded your island.

Hope that you don't run into your nemesis, Howie, the Puerto Rican kid with the two killer mutts. He walks them all over the neighborhood, and every now and then the mutts corner a cat and tear it to shreds, as Howie laughs and the cat flips up in the air, its neck twisted around like an owl's, red meat showing through the soft fur. And if his dogs haven't cornered a cat, then he'll be behind you, asking, Is that your new fuckbuddy?

Let him talk. Howie weighs two hundred pounds and could eat you if he wanted. But at the field he'll turn away. He has new sneakers and doesn't want them muddy. If the girl's an outsider, that's when she'll hiss, What a fucking asshole. A homegirl would have been yelling back at him the whole time, unless she was shy. Either way, don't feel bad that you didn't do anything. Never lose a fight on a first date.

Dinner will be tense. You are not good at talking to people you don't know.

A halfie will tell you that her parents met in the Movement. Back then, she'll say, people thought it was a radical thing to do. It will sound like something her parents made her memorize. Your brother heard that one, too, and said, Sounds like a whole lot of Uncle Tomming to me. Don't repeat this.

Put down your hamburger and say, It must have been hard.

It was, she will say.

She'll appreciate your interest. She'll tell you more. Black people, she will say, treat me real bad. That's why I don't like them. You'll wonder how she feels about Dominicans. Don't ask. Let her speak on it and when you've finished eating, walk back through the neighborhood. The skies will be magnificent. Pollutants have made Jersey sunsets one of the wonders of the world. Point it out. Touch her shoulder and say, Isn't that nice?

Get serious. Watch TV, but stay alert. Sip some of the Bermudez your father left in the cabinet, which nobody touches. She'll drink enough to make her brave. A local girl will have hips and a nice ass but won't be quick about letting you touch her. She has to live in the same neighborhood as you do. She might just chill with you and then go home. She might kiss you and then leave. Or she might, if she's reckless, give it up, but that's rare. Kissing will suffice. A white girl might give it up right then. Don't stop her. She'll take her gum out of her mouth, stick it to the plastic sofa covers, and then move close to you. You have nice eyes, she might say.

Tell her that you love her hair, her skin, her lips, because, in truth, you love them more than you love your own.

She'll say, I like Spanish guys, and even though you've never been to Spain, say, I like you. You'll sound smooth.

You'll be with her until about eight-thirty, and then she'll want to wash up. In the bathroom, she'll hum a song from the radio and her waist will keep the beat against the lip of the sink. Think of her old lady coming to get her, and imagine what she would say if she knew that her daughter had just lain under you and blown your name into your ear. While she's in the bathroom, you might call one of your boys and say, *Ya lo hice, cabrón.* Or sit back on the couch and smile.

But usually it won't work this way. Be prepared. She will not want to kiss you. Just cool it, she'll say. The halfie might lean back and push you away. She will cross her arms and say, I hate my tits. Pretend to watch the TV, and then turn to her to stroke her hair, even though you know she'll pull away again. I don't like anybody to touch my hair, she will say. She will act like somebody you don't know. In school, she is known for her attention-grabbing laugh, high and far-ranging like a gull's, but here she will worry you. You will not know what to say.

You're the only kind of guy who asks me out, she will say. Your neighbors will start their hyena calls, now that the alcohol is in them. She will say, You and the black boys.

You want to say, Who do you want to ask you out? But you already know. Let her button her shirt and comb her hair, the sound of it like a crackling fire between you. When her father pulls in and beeps, let her go without too much of a goodbye. She won't want it. During the next hour, the phone will ring. You will be tempted to pick it up. Don't. Watch the shows you want to watch, without a family around to argue with you. Don't go downstairs. Don't fall asleep. It won't help. Put the government cheese back in its place before your moms kills you.

PEOPLE LIKE THAT ARE THE ONLY PEOPLE HERE

BY LORRIE MOORE (1997)

A beginning, an end: there seems to be neither. The whole thing is like a cloud that just lands, and everywhere inside it is full of rain. A start: the Mother finds a blood clot in the Baby's diaper. What is the story? Who put this here? It is big and bright, with a broken, khaki-colored vein in it. Over the weekend, the Baby had looked listless and spacey, clayey and grim. But today he looks fine—so what is this thing, startling against the white diaper, like a tiny mouse heart packed in snow? Perhaps it belongs to someone else. Perhaps it is something menstrual, something belonging to the Mother or to the Babysitter, something the Baby has found in a wastebasket and for his own demented baby reasons stowed away here. (Babies—they're crazy! What can you do?) In her mind, the Mother takes this away from his body and attaches it to someone else's. There. Doesn't that make more sense?

Still, she phones the children's-hospital clinic. Blood in the diaper, she says, and, sounding alarmed and perplexed, the woman on the other end says, "Come in now."

Such pleasingly instant service! Just say "blood." Just say "diaper." Look what you get!

In the examination room, the pediatrician, the nurse, and the head resident all seem less alarmed and perplexed than simply perplexed. At first, stupidly, the Mother is calmed by this. But soon, besides peering and saying "Hmm," the doctor, the nurse, and the head resident are all drawing their mouths in, bluish and tight—morning glories sensing noon. They fold their arms across their white-coated chests, unfold them again, and jot things down. They order an ultrasound. Bladder and kidneys. Here's the card. Go downstairs, turn left.

In Radiology, the Baby stands anxiously on the table, naked against the Mother, as she holds him still against her legs and waist, the Radiologist's cold scanning disk moving about the Baby's back. The Baby whimpers, looks up at the Mother. *Let's get out of here*, his eyes beg. *Pick me up!* The Radiologist stops, freezes one of the many swirls of oceanic gray, and clicks repeatedly, a single moment within the long, cavernous weather map that is the Baby's insides.

"Are you finding something?" asks the Mother. Last year, her Uncle Larry had a kidney removed for something that turned out to be benign. These imaging machines! They are like dogs, or metal detectors: they find everything but don't know what they've found. That's where the surgeons come in. They're like the owners of the dogs. *Give me that*, they say to the dog. *What the heck is that?*

"The surgeon will speak to you," says the Radiologist.

"Are you finding something?"

"The surgeon will speak to you," the Radiologist says again. "There seems to be something there, but the surgeon will talk to you about it."

"My uncle once had something on his kidney," says the Mother. "So they removed the kidney and it turned out the something was benign."

The Radiologist smiles a broad, ominous smile. "That's always the way it is," he says. "You don't know exactly what it is until it's in the bucket."

"In the bucket," the Mother repeats.

"That's doctor talk," the Radiologist says.

"It's very appealing," says the Mother. "It's a very appealing way to talk." Swirls of bile and blood, mustard and maroon in a pail, the colors of an African flag or some exuberant salad bar: *in the bucket*—she imagines it all.

"The surgeon will see you soon," he says again. He tousles the Baby's ringlety hair. "Cute kid," he says.

. . .

"Let's see now," says the Surgeon, in one of his examining rooms. He has stepped in, then stepped out, then come back in again. He has crisp, frowning features, sharp bones, and a tennis-in-Bermuda tan. He crosses his blue-cottoned legs. He is wearing clogs.

The Mother knows her own face is a big white dumpling of worry. She is still wearing her long, dark parka, holding the Baby, who has pulled the hood up over her head because he always thinks it's funny to do that. Though on certain windy mornings she would like to think she could look vaguely romantic like this, like some French Lieutenant's Woman of the Prairie, in all her saner moments she knows she doesn't. She knows she looks ridiculous—like one of those animals made out of twisted party balloons. She lowers the hood and slips one arm out of the sleeve. The Baby wants to get up and play with the light switch. He fidgets, fusses, and points.

"He's big on lights these days," explains the Mother.

"That's O.K.," says the Surgeon, nodding toward the light switch. "Let him play with it." The Mother goes and stands by it, and the Baby begins turning the lights off and on, off and on.

"What we have here is a Wilms' tumor," says the Surgeon, suddenly plunged into darkness. He says "tumor" as if it were the most normal thing in the world.

"Wilms'?" repeats the Mother. The room is quickly on fire again with light, then wiped dark again. Among the three of them here there is a long silence, as if it were suddenly the middle of the night. "Is that apostrophe 's' or 's' apostrophe?" the Mother says finally. She is a writer and a teacher. Spelling can be important—perhaps even at a time like this, though she has never before been at a time like this, so there are barbarisms she could easily commit without knowing.

The lights come on; the world is doused and exposed.

" 'S' apostrophe," says the Surgeon. "I think." The lights go back out, but the Surgeon continues speaking in the dark. "A malignant tumor of the left kidney."

Wait a minute. Hold on here. The Baby is only a baby, fed on organic applesauce and soy milk—a little prince!—and he was standing so close to her during the ultrasound. How could he have this terrible thing? It must have been *her* kidney. A fifties kidney. A DDT kidney. The Mother clears her throat. "Is it possible it was my kidney on the scan? I mean, I've never heard of a baby with a tumor, and, frankly, I was standing very close." She would make the blood hers, the tumor hers; it would all be some treacherous, farcical mistake.

"No, that's not possible," says the Surgeon. The light goes back on.

"It's not?" says the Mother. Wait until it's *in the bucket*, she thinks. Don't be so sure. *Do we have to wait until it's in the bucket to find out a mistake has been made?*

"We will start with a radical nephrectomy," says the Surgeon, instantly thrown into darkness again. His voice comes from nowhere and everywhere at once. "And then we'll begin with chemotherapy after that. These tumors usually respond very well to chemo."

"I've never heard of a baby having chemo," the Mother says. Baby and Chemo, she thinks: they should never even appear in the same sentence together, let alone the same life. In her other life, her life before this day, she was a believer in alternative medicine. Chemotherapy? Unthinkable. Now, suddenly, alternative medicine seems the wacko maiden aunt to the Nice Big Daddy of Conventional Treatment. How quickly the old girl faints and gives way, leaves one just standing there. Chemo? Of course: chemo! Why, by all means: chemo. Absolutely! Chemo!

The Baby flicks the switch back on, and the walls reappear, big wedges of light checkered with small framed watercolors of the local lake. The Mother has begun to cry: all of life has led her here, to this moment. After this there is no more life. There is something else, something stumbling and unlivable, something mechanical, something for robots, but not life. Life has been taken and broken, quickly, like a stick. The room goes dark again, so that the Mother can cry more freely. How can a baby's body be stolen so fast? How much can one heaven-sent and unsuspecting child endure? Why has he not been spared this inconceivable fate?

Perhaps, she thinks, she is being punished: too many babysitters too early on. ("Come to Mommy! Come to Mommy-Babysitter!" she used to say. But it was a joke!) Her life, perhaps, bore too openly the marks and wigs of deepest drag. Her unmotherly thoughts had all been noted: the panicky hope that his nap would last just a little longer than it did; her occasional desire to kiss him passionately on the mouth (to make out with her baby!); her ongoing complaints about the very vocabulary of motherhood, how it degraded the speaker. ("Is this a poopie onesie? Yes, it's a very poopie onesie!") She had, moreover, on three occasions used the formula bottles as flower vases. She twice let the Baby's ears get fudgy with wax. A few afternoons last month, at snack time, she placed a bowl of Cheerios on the floor for him to eat, like a dog. She let him play with the Dustbuster. Just once, before he was born, she said, "Healthy? I just want the kid to be rich." A joke, for God's sake. After he was born, she announced that her life had become a daily sequence of mind-wrecking chores, the same ones over and over again, like a novel by Mrs. Camus. Another joke! These jokes will kill you. She had told too often, and with too much enjoyment, the story of how the Baby had said "Hi" to his high chair, waved at the lake waves, shouted "Goody-goody-goody" in what seemed to be a Russian accent, pointed at his eyes and said "Ice." And all that nonsensical baby talk: wasn't it a stitch? *Canonical babbling*, the language experts called it. He recounted whole stories in it, totally made up, she could tell; he embroidered, he fished, he exaggerated. What a card! To friends she spoke of his eating habits (carrots yes, tuna no). She mentioned, too much, his sidesplitting giggle. Did she have to be so boring? Did she have no consideration for others, for the intellectual demands and courtesies of human society? Would she not even attempt to be more interesting? It was a crime against the human mind not even to try.

Now her baby, for all these reasons—lack of motherly gratitude, motherly judgment, motherly proportion—will be taken away.

The room is fluorescently ablaze again. The Mother digs around in her parka pocket and comes up with a Kleenex. It is old and thin, like a mashed flower saved from a dance; she dabs it at her eyes and nose.

"The baby won't suffer as much as you," says the Surgeon.

And who can contradict? Not the Baby, who in his Slavic Betty Boop voice can say only *mama*, *dada*, *cheese*, *ice*, *bye-bye*, *outside*, *boogie-boogie*, *goody-goody*, *eddy-eddy*, and *car*. (Who is Eddy? They have no idea.) This will not suffice to express his mortal suffering. Who can say what babies do with their agony and shock? Not they themselves. (Baby talk: isn't it a stitch?) They put it all no place anyone can really see. They are like a different race, a different species: they seem not to experience pain the way we do. Yeah, that's it: their nervous systems are not as fully formed, and *they just don't experience pain the way we do.* A tune to keep one humming through the war. "You'll get through it," the Surgeon says.

"How?" asks the Mother. "How does one get through it?"

"You just put your head down and go," says the Surgeon. He picks up his file folder. He is a skilled manual laborer. The tricky emotional stuff is not to his liking. The babies. The babies! What can be said to console the parents about the babies? "I'll go phone the oncologist on duty to let him know," he says, and leaves the room.

"Come here, sweetie," the Mother says to the Baby, who has toddled off toward a gum wrapper on the floor. "We've got to put your jacket on." She picks him up and he reaches for the light switch again. Light, dark. Peekaboo: Where's baby? Where did baby go?

At home, she leaves a message—Urgent! Call me!—for the Husband on his voice mail. Then she takes the Baby upstairs for his nap, rocks him in the rocker. The Baby waves goodbye to his little bears, then looks toward the window and says, "Bye-bye, outside." He has, lately, the habit of waving goodbye to everything, and now it seems as if he sensed some imminent departure, and it breaks her heart to hear him. *Bye-bye!* She sings low and monotonously, like a small appliance, which is how he likes it. He is drowsy, dozy, drifting off. He has grown so much in the last year he hardly fits in her lap anymore; his limbs dangle off like a Pietà. His head rolls slightly inside the crook of her arm. She can feel him falling backward into sleep, his mouth round and open like the sweetest of poppies. All the lullabies in the world, all the melodies threaded through with maternal melancholy now become for her—abandoned as mothers can be by working men and napping babies—the songs of hard, hard grief. Sitting there, bowed and bobbing, the Mother feels the entirety of her love as worry and heartbreak. A quick and irrevocable alchemy: there is no longer one unworried scrap left for happiness. "If you go," she keens low into his soapy neck, into the ranunculus coil of his ear, "we are going with you. We are nothing without you. Without you, we are a heap of rocks. Without you, we are two stumps, with nothing any longer in our hearts. Wherever this takes you, we are following; we will be there. Don't be scared. We are going, too, wherever you go. That is that. That is that."

"Take notes," says the Husband, after coming straight home from work, midafternoon, hearing the news, and saying all the words out loud—*surgery*, *metastasis*, *dialysis*, *transplant*—then collapsing in a chair in tears. "Take notes. We are going to need the money."

"Good God," cries the Mother. Everything inside her suddenly begins to cower and shrink, a thinning of bones. Perhaps this is a soldier's readiness, but it has the whiff of death and defeat. It feels like a heart attack, a failure of will and courage, a power failure: a failure of everything. Her face, when she glimpses it in a mirror, is cold and bloated with shock, her eyes scarlet and shrunk. She has already started to wear sunglasses indoors, like a celebrity widow. From where will her own strength come? From some philosophy? From some frigid little philosophy? She is neither stalwart nor realistic and has trouble with basic concepts, such as the one that says events move in one direction only and do not jump up, turn around, and take themselves back.

The Husband begins too many of his sentences with "What if." He is trying to piece everything together, like a train wreck. He is trying to get the train to town.

"We'll just take all the steps, move through all the stages. We'll go where we have to go, we'll hunt, we'll find, we'll pay what we have to pay. What if we can't pay?"

"Sounds like shopping."

"I cannot believe this is happening to our little boy," he says, and starts to sob again.

What is to be said? You turn just slightly and there it is: the death of your child. It is part symbol, part devil, and in your blind spot all along, until it is upon you. Then it is a fierce little country abducting you; it holds you squarely inside itself like a cellar room, the best boundaries of you are the boundaries of it. Are there windows? Sometimes aren't there windows?

The Mother is not a shopper. She hates to shop, is generally bad at it, though she does like a good sale. She cannot stroll meaningfully through anger, denial, grief, and acceptance. She goes straight to bargaining and stays there. How much? She calls out to the ceiling, to some makeshift construction of holiness she has desperately though not uncreatively assembled in her mind and prayed to; a doubter, never before given to prayer, she must now reap what she has not sown; she must reassemble an entire altar of worship and begging. She tries for noble abstractions, nothing too anthropomorphic, just some Higher Morality, though if this particular Highness looks something like the Manager at Marshall Field's, sucking a Frango mint, so be it. Amen. Just tell me what you want, requests the Mother. And how do you want it? More charitable acts? A billion, starting now. Charitable thoughts? Harder, but of course! Of course! I'll do the cooking, honey, I'll pay the rent. Just tell me. *Excuse me?* Well, if not to you, to whom do I speak? Hello? To whom do I have to speak around here? A higher-up? A superior? Wait? I can wait. I've got the whole damn day.

The Husband now lies next to her on their bed, sighing. "Poor little guy could survive all this only to be killed in a car crash at the age of sixteen," he says.

The Mother, bargaining, considers this. "We'll take the car crash," she says.

"What?"

"Let's Make a Deal! Sixteen is a full life! We'll take the car crash. We'll take the car crash in front of which Carol Merrill is now standing."

Now the Manager of Marshall Field's reappears. "To take the surprises out is to take the life out of life," he says.

The phone rings. The Husband leaves the room.

"But I don't want these surprises," says the Mother. "Here! You take these surprises!"

"To know the narrative in advance is to turn yourself into a machine," the Manager continues. "What makes humans human is precisely that they do not know the future. That is why they do the fateful and amusing things they do: who can say how anything will turn out? Therein lies the only hope for redemption, discovery, and—let's be frank—fun, fun, fun! There might be things people will get away with. And not just motel towels. There might be great illicit loves, enduring joy—or faith-shaking accidents with farm machinery. But you have to not know in order to see what stories your life's efforts bring you. The mystery is all."

The Mother, though shy, has grown confrontational. "Is this the kind of bogus, random crap they teach at merchandising school? We would like fewer surprises, fewer efforts and mysteries, thank you. K through 8; can we just get K through 8?" It now seems like the luckiest, most beautiful, most musical phrase she's ever heard: K through 8—the very lilt. The very thought.

The Manager continues, trying things out. "I mean, the whole conception of 'the story,' of cause and effect, the whole idea that people have a clue as to how the world works, is just a piece of laughable metaphysical colonialism perpetrated upon the wild country of time."

Did they own a gun? The Mother begins looking through drawers.

The Husband comes back in the room and observes her. "Ha! The Great Havoc That Is the Puzzle of All Life!" he says of the Marshall Field's management policy. He has just gotten off a conference call with the insurance company and the hospital. The surgery will be Friday. "It's all just some dirty capitalist's idea of a philosophy."

"Maybe it's just a fact of narrative, and you really can't politicize it," says the Mother. It is now only the two of them.

"Whose side are you on?"

"I'm on the Baby's side."

"Are you taking notes for this?"

"No."

"You're not?"

"No. I can't. Not this! I write fiction. This isn't fiction."

"Then write nonfiction. Do a piece of journalism. Get two dollars a word."

"Then it has to be true and full of information. I'm not trained. I'm not that skilled. Plus, I have a convenient personal principle about artists' not abandoning art. One should never turn one's back on a vivid imagination. Even the whole memoir thing annoys me."

"Well, make things up but pretend they're real."

"I'm not that insured."

"You're making me nervous."

"Sweetie, darling, I'm not that good. I can't *do this.* I can do—what can I do? I can do quasi-amusing phone dialogue. I can do succinct descriptions of weather. I can do screwball outings with the family pet. Sometimes I can do those. Honey, I only do what I can. I do *the careful ironies of daydream.* I do *the marshy ideas upon which intimate life is built.* But this? Our baby with cancer? I'm sorry. My stop was two stations back. This is irony at its most gaudy and careless. This is a Hieronymus Bosch of facts and figures and blood and graphs. This is a nightmare of narrative slop. This cannot be designed. This cannot even be noted in preparation for a design—"

"We're going to need the money."

"To say nothing of the moral boundaries of pecuniary recompense in a situation such as this—"

"What if the other kidney goes? What if he needs a transplant? Where are the moral boundaries there? What are we going to do, have bake sales?"

"We can sell the house. I hate this house. It makes me crazy."

"And we'll live—where, again?"

"The Ronald McDonald place. I hear it's nice. It's the least McDonald's can do."

"You have a keen sense of justice."

"I try. What can I say?"

The Husband buries his face in his hands: "Our poor baby. How did this happen to him?" He looks over and stares at the bookcase that serves as their nightstand. "And is any one of these baby books a help?" He picks up the Leach, the Spock, the "What to Expect." "Where in the pages or index of any of these does it say 'chemotherapy' or 'Hickman catheter' or 'renal sarcoma'? Where does it say 'carcinogenesis' or 'metastasis'? You know what these books are obsessed with? *Holding a fucking spoon.*" He begins hurling the books off the nightstand and against the far wall.

"Hey," says the Mother, trying to soothe. "Hey, hey, hey." But, compared with his stormy roar, her words are those of a backup singer—a Shondell, a Pip—a doo-wop ditty. Books, and now more books, continue to fly.

. . .

Take Notes.

Is "fainthearted" one word or two? Student prose has wrecked her spelling.

It's one word. Two words—faint hearted—what would that be? The name of a drag queen.

Take Notes.

In the end you suffer alone. But at the beginning you suffer with a whole lot of others. When your child has cancer you are instantly whisked away to another planet: one of bald-headed little boys. Pediatric Oncology. Peed-Onk. You wash your hands for thirty seconds in antibacterial soap before you are allowed to enter through the swinging doors. You put paper slippers on your shoes. You keep your voice down. "Almost all the children are boys," one of the nurses says. "No one knows why. It's been documented, but a lot of people out there still don't realize it." The little boys are all from sweet-sounding places, Janesville and Appleton—little heartland towns with giant landfills, agricultural runoff, paper factories, Joe McCarthy's grave. (Alone a site of great toxicity, thinks the Mother. The soil should be tested.)

All the bald little boys look like brothers. They wheel their I.V.s up and down the single corridor of Peed-Onk. Some of the lively ones, feeling good for a day, ride the lower bars of their I.V.s while their large, cheerful mothers whizz them along the halls. *Wheee!*

The Mother does not feel large and cheerful. In her mind she is scathing, acid-tongued, wraith-thin, and chain-smoking out on a fire escape somewhere. Below her lie the gentle undulations of the Midwest, with all its aspirations to be—to be what? To be Long Island. How it has succeeded! Strip mall upon strip mall. Lurid water, poisoned potatoes. The Mother drags deeply, blowing clouds of smoke out over the disfigured cornfields. When a baby gets cancer, it seems stupid ever to have given up smoking. When a baby gets cancer, you think, Whom are we kidding? Let's all light up. When a baby gets cancer, you think, Who came up with *this* idea? What celestial abandon gave rise to *this*? Pour me a drink, so I can refuse to toast.

The Mother does not know how to be one of these other mothers, with their blond hair and sweatpants and sneakers and determined pleasantness. She does not think that she can be anything similar. She does not feel remotely like them. She knows, for instance, too many people in Greenwich Village. She mail-orders oysters and tiramisù from a shop in SoHo. She is close friends with four actual homosexuals. Her husband is asking her to Take Notes.

Where do these women get their sweatpants? She will find out.

She will start, perhaps, with the costume and work from there.

She will live according to the bromides: Take one day at a time. Take a positive attitude. *Take a hike!* She wishes that there were more interesting things that were useful and true, but it seems now that it's only the boring things that are useful and true. *One day at a time.* And *At least we have our health.* How ordinary. How obvious. One day at a time: you need a brain for that?

While the Surgeon is fine-boned, regal, and laconic—they have correctly guessed his game to be doubles—there is a bit of the mad, overcaffeinated scientist to the Oncologist. He speaks quickly. He knows a lot of studies and numbers. He can do the math. Good! Someone should be able to do the math! "It's a fast but wimpy tumor," he explains. "It typically metastasizes to the lung." He rattles off some numbers, time frames, risk statistics. Fast but wimpy: the Mother tries to imagine this combination of traits, tries to think and think, and can only come up with Claudia Osk from the fourth grade, who blushed and almost wept when called on in class but in gym could outrun everyone in the quarter-mile, fire-door-to-fence dash. The Mother thinks now of this tumor as Claudia Osk. They are going to get Claudia Osk, make her sorry. All right! Claudia Osk must die. Though it has never been mentioned before, it now seems clear that Claudia Osk should have died long ago. Who was she, anyway? So conceited, not letting anyone beat her in a race. Well, hey, hey, hey—don't look now, Claudia!

The Husband nudges her. "Are you listening?"

"The chances of this happening even just to one kidney are one in fifteen thousand. Now, given all these other factors, the chances on the second kidney are about one in eight."

"One in eight," says the Husband. "Not bad. As long as it's not one in fifteen thousand."

The Mother studies the trees and fish along the ceiling's edge in the Save the Planet wallpaper border. Save the Planet. Yes! But the windows in this very building don't open, and diesel fumes are leaking into the ventilating system, near which, outside, a delivery truck is parked. The air is nauseous and stale.

"Really," the Oncologist is saying, "of all the cancers he could get, this is probably one of the best."

"We win," says the Mother.

"'Best,' I know, hardly seems the right word. Look, you two probably need to get some rest. We'll see how the surgery and histology go. Then we'll start with chemo the week following. A little light chemo: vincristine and—"

"Vincristine?" interrupts the Mother. "Wine of Christ?"

"The names are strange, I know. The other one we use is actinomycin-D. Sometimes called dactinomycin. People move the 'D' around to the front."

"They move the 'D' around to the front," repeats the Mother.

"Yup," the Oncologist says. "I don't know why, they just do!"

"Christ didn't survive his wine," says the Husband.

"But of course he did," says the Oncologist and nods toward the Baby, who has now found a cupboard full of hospital linens and bandages and is yanking them all out onto the floor. "I'll see you guys tomorrow, after the surgery." And with that the Oncologist leaves.

"Or, rather, Christ was his wine," mumbles the Husband. Everything he knows about the New Testament he has gleaned from the soundtrack of "Godspell." "His blood was the wine. What a great beverage idea."

"A little light chemo. Don't you like that one?" says the Mother. "*Eine kleine* dactinomycin. I'd like to see Mozart write that one up for a big wad o' cash."

"Come here, honey," the Husband says to the Baby, who has now pulled off both his shoes.

"It's bad enough when they refer to medical science as an inexact science," says the Mother. "But when they start referring to it as an art I get extremely nervous."

"Yeah. If we wanted art, Doc, we'd go to an art museum." The Husband picks up the Baby. "You're an artist," he says to the Mother with the taint of accusation in his voice. "They probably think you find creativity reassuring."

The Mother sighs. "I just find it inevitable. Let's go get something to eat." And so they take the elevator to the cafeteria, where there is a high chair, and where, not noticing, they all eat a lot of apples with the price tags still on them.

Because his surgery is not until tomorrow, the Baby likes the hospital. He likes the long corridors, down which he can run. He likes everything on wheels. The flower carts in the lobby! ("Please keep your boy away from the flowers," says the vender. "We'll buy the whole display," snaps the Mother, adding, "Actual children in a children's hospital—unbelievable, isn't it?") The Baby likes the other little boys. Places to go! People to see! Rooms to wander into! There is Intensive Care. There is the Trauma Unit. The Baby smiles and waves. What a little Cancer Personality! Bandaged citizens smile and wave back. In Peed-Onk there are the bald little boys to play with. Joey, Eric, Tim, Mort, and Tod. (Mort! Tod!) There is the four-year-old, Ned, holding his little deflated rubber ball, the one with the intriguing curling hose. The Baby wants to play with it. "It's mine, leave it alone," says Ned. "Tell the baby to leave it alone."

"Baby, you've got to share," says the Mother from a chair some feet away.

Suddenly, from down near the Tiny Tim Lounge, comes Ned's mother, large and blond and sweatpanted. "Stop that! Stop it!" she cries out, dashing toward the Baby and Ned and pushing the Baby away. "Don't touch that!" she barks at the Baby, who is only a baby and bursts into tears because he has never been yelled at like this before.

Ned's mom glares at everyone. "This is drawing fluid from Neddy's liver!" She pats at the rubber thing and starts to cry a little.

"Oh, my God," says the Mother. She comforts the Baby, who is also crying. She and Ned, the only dry-eyed people, look at each other. "I'm so sorry," she says to Ned and then to his mother. "I'm so stupid. I thought they were squabbling over a toy."

"It does look like a toy," agrees Ned. He smiles. He is an angel.

All the little boys are angels. Total, sweet, bald little angels, and now God is trying to get them back for himself. Who are they, mere mortal women, in the face of this, this powerful and overwhelming and inscrutable thing, God's will? They are the mothers, that's who. You can't have him! they shout every day. You dirty old man! *Get out of here! Hands off!*

"I'm so sorry," says the Mother again. "I didn't know."

Ned's mother smiles vaguely. "Of course you didn't know," she says, and walks back to the Tiny Tim Lounge.

The Tiny Tim Lounge is a little sitting area at the end of the Peed-Onk corridor. There are two small sofas, a table, a rocking chair, a television, and a VCR. There are various videos: "Speed," "Dune," "Star Wars." On one of the lounge walls there is a gold plaque with the musician Tiny Tim's name on it: years ago, his son was treated at this hospital, and so he donated money for this lounge. It is a cramped little lounge, which one suspects would be larger if Tiny Tim's son had actually lived. Instead, he died here, at this hospital, and now there is this tiny room which is part gratitude, part generosity, part *Fuck you.*

Sifting through the videocassettes, the Mother wonders what science fiction could begin to compete with the science fiction of cancer itself: a tumor, with its differentiated muscle and bone cells, a clump of wild nothing and its mad, ambitious desire to be something—something inside you, instead of you, another organism but with a monster's architecture, a demon's sabotage and chaos. Think of leukemia, a tumor diabolically taking liquid form, the better to swim about incognito in the blood. George Lucas, direct that!

Sitting with the other parents in the Tiny Tim Lounge, the night before the surgery, having put the Baby to bed in his high steel crib two rooms down, the Mother begins to hear the stories: leukemia in kindergarten, sarcomas in Little League, neuroblastomas discovered at summer camp. *Eric slid into third base, but then the scrape didn't heal.* The parents pat one another's forearms and speak of other children's hospitals as if they were resorts. "You were at St. Jude's last winter? So were we. What did you think of it? We loved the staff." Jobs have been quit, marriages hacked up, bank accounts ravaged; the parents have seemingly endured the unendurable. They speak not of the *possibility* of comas brought on by the chemo but of the *number* of them. "He was in his first coma last July," says Ned's mother. "It was a scary time, but we pulled through."

Pulling through is what people do around here. There is a kind of bravery in their lives that isn't bravery at all. It is automatic, unflinching, a mix of man and machine, consuming and unquestionable obligation meeting illness move for move in a giant, even-Steven game of chess: an unending round of something that looks like shadowboxing—though between love and death, which is the shadow? "Everyone admires us for our courage," says one man. "They have no idea what they're talking about."

I could get out of here, thinks the Mother. I could just get on a bus and go, never come back. Change my name. A kind of witness-relocation thing.

"Courage requires options," the man adds.

The Baby might be better off.

"There are options," says a woman with a thick suède headband. "You could give up. You could fall apart."

"No, you can't. Nobody does. I've never seen it," says the man. "Well, not *really* fall apart." Then the lounge is quiet. Over the VCR someone has taped the fortune from a fortune cookie. *Optimism,* it says, *is what allows a teakettle to sing though up to its neck in hot water.* Underneath, someone else has taped a clipping from a summer horoscope. *Cancer rules!* it says. Who would tape this up? Somebody's twelve-year-old brother. One of the fathers—Joey's father—gets up and tears them both off, makes a small wad in his fist.

There is some rustling of magazine pages.

The Mother clears her throat. "Tiny Tim forgot the wet bar," she says.

Ned, who is still up, comes out of his room and down the corridor, whose lights dim at nine. Standing next to the Mother's chair, he says to her, "Where are you from? What is wrong with your baby?"

In the little room that is theirs, she sleeps fitfully in her sweatpants, occasionally leaping up to check on the Baby. This is what the sweatpants are for: leaping. In case of fire. In case of anything. In case the difference between day and night starts to dissolve and there is no difference at all so why pretend. In the cot beside her the Husband, who has taken a sleeping pill, is snoring loudly, his arms folded about his head in a kind of origami. How could either of them have stayed back at the house, with its empty high chair and empty crib? Occasionally the Baby wakes and cries out, and she bolts up, goes to him, rubs his back, rearranges the linens. The clock on the metal dresser shows that it is five after three. Then twenty to five. And then it is really morning, the beginning of this day, Nephrectomy Day. Will she be glad when it's over, or barely alive, or both? Each day of this week has arrived huge, empty, and unknown, like a spaceship, and this one especially is lit an incandescent gray.

"He'll need to put this on," says John, one of the nurses, bright and early, handing the Mother a thin greenish garment with roses and Teddy bears printed on it. A wave of nausea hits her: this smock, she thinks, will soon be splattered with—with what?

The Baby is awake but drowsy. She lifts off his pajamas. "Don't forget, *bubeleh*," she whispers, undressing and dressing him. "We will be with you every moment, every step. When you think you are asleep and floating off far away from everybody, Mommy will still be there." If she hasn't fled on a bus. "Mommy will take care of you. And Daddy, too." She hopes the Baby does not detect her own fear and uncertainty, which she must hide from him, like a limp. He is hungry, not having been allowed to eat, and he is no longer amused by this new place but worried about its hardships. Oh, my baby, she thinks. And the room starts to swim a little. The Husband comes in to take over. "Take a break," he says to her. "I'll walk him around for five minutes."

She leaves but doesn't know where to go. In the hallway she is approached by a kind of social worker, a customer-relations person, who had given them a video to watch about the anesthesia: how the parent accompanies the child into the operating room, and how gently, nicely the drugs are administered.

"Did you watch the video?"

"Yes," says the Mother.

"Wasn't it helpful?"

"I don't know," says the Mother.

"Do you have any questions?" asks the video woman. *Do you have any questions?* asked of someone who has recently landed in this fearful, alien place seems to the Mother an absurd and amazing little courtesy. The very specificity of a question would give the lie to the overwhelming strangeness of everything around her.

"Not right now," says the Mother. "Right now I think I'm just going to go to the bathroom."

When she comes back to the Baby's room, everyone is there: the Surgeon, the Anesthesiologist, all the nurses, the social worker. In their blue caps and scrubs they look like a clutch of forget-me-nots, and forget them who could? The Baby, in his little Teddy-bear smock, seems cold and scared. He reaches out and the Mother lifts him from the Husband's arms, rubs his back to warm him.

"Well, it's time!" says the Surgeon, forcing a smile.

"Shall we go?" says the Anesthesiologist.

What follows is a blur of obedience and bright lights. They take an elevator down to a big concrete room, the anteroom, the greenroom, the backstage of the operating room. Lining the walls are long shelves full of blue surgical outfits. "Children often become afraid of the color blue," one of the nurses says. But of course. Of course! "Now, which one of you would like to come into the operating room for the anesthesia?"

"I will," says the Mother.

"Are you sure?" says the Husband.

"Yup." She kisses the Baby's hair. Mr. Curlyhead people keep calling him here, and it seems both rude and nice. Women look admiringly at his long lashes and exclaim, "Always the boys! Always the boys!"

Two surgical nurses put a blue smock and a blue cotton cap on the Mother. The Baby finds this funny and keeps pulling at the cap. "This way," says another nurse, and the Mother follows. "Just put the Baby down on the table."

In the video, the mother holds the baby and fumes from the mask are gently waved under the baby's nose until he falls asleep. Now, out of view of camera or social worker, the Anesthesiologist is anxious to get this under way and not let too much gas leak out into the room generally. The occupational hazard of this, his chosen profession, is gas exposure and nerve damage, and it has started to worry him. No doubt he frets about it to his wife every night. Now he turns the gas on and quickly clamps the plastic mouthpiece over the Baby's cheeks and lips.

The Baby is startled. The Mother is startled. The Baby starts to scream and redden behind the plastic, but he cannot be heard. He thrashes. "Tell him it's O.K.," says the nurse to the Mother.

O.K.? "It's O.K.," repeats the Mother, holding his hand, but she knows he can tell it's not O.K., because he can see that not only is she still wearing that stupid paper cap but her words are mechanical and swallowed, and she is biting her lips to keep them from trembling. Panicked, he attempts to sit, he cannot breathe, his arms reach up. *Bye-bye, outside.* And then, quite quickly, his eyes shut, he untenses and has fallen not into sleep but aside to sleep, an odd, kidnapping kind of sleep, his terror now hidden someplace deep inside him.

"How did it go?" asks the social worker, waiting in the concrete outer room. The Mother is hysterical. A nurse has ushered her out.

"It wasn't at all like the film strip!" she cries. "It wasn't like the film strip at all!"

"The film strip? You mean the video?" asks the social worker.

"It wasn't like that at all! It was brutal and unforgivable."

"Why, that's terrible," she says, her role now no longer misinformational but janitorial, and she touches the Mother's arm. The Mother shakes her off and goes to find the Husband.

She finds him in the large mulberry Surgery Lounge, where he has been taken and where there is free hot chocolate in small plastic-foam cups. Red cellophane garlands festoon the doorways. She has totally forgotten it is as close to Christmas as this. A pianist in the corner is playing "Carol of the Bells," and it sounds not only unfestive but scary, like the theme from "The Exorcist."

There is a giant clock on the far wall. It is a kind of porthole into the operating room, a way of assessing the Baby's ordeal: forty-five minutes for the Hickman implant; two and a half hours for the nephrectomy. And then, after that, three months of chemotherapy. The magazine on her lap stays open at a ruby-hued perfume ad.

"Still not taking notes," says the Husband.

"Nope."

"You know, in a way, this is the kind of thing you've *always* written about."

"You are really something, you know that? This is life. This isn't a 'kind of thing.'"

"But this is the kind of thing that fiction is: it's the unlivable life, the strange room tacked on to the house, the extra moon that is circling the earth unbeknownst to science."

"I told you that."

"I'm quoting you."

She looks at her watch, thinking of the Baby. "How long has it been?"

"Not long. Too long. In the end, those're the same things."

"What do you suppose is happening to him right this second?"

Infection? Slipping knives? "I don't know. But you know what? I've gotta go. I've gotta just walk a bit." The Husband gets up, walks around the lounge, then comes back and sits down.

The synapses between the minutes are unswimmable. An hour is thick as fudge. The Mother feels depleted; she is a string of empty tin cans attached by wire, something a goat would sniff and chew, something now and then enlivened by a jolt of electricity.

She hears their names being called over the intercom. "Yes? Yes?" She stands up quickly. Her voice has flown out before her, an exhalation of birds. The piano music has stopped. The pianist is gone. She and the Husband approach the main desk, where a man looks up at them and smiles. Before him is a Xeroxed list of patients' names. "That's our little boy right there," says the Mother, seeing the Baby's name on the list and pointing at it. "Is there some word? Is everything O.K.?"

"Yes," says the man. "Your boy is doing fine. They've just finished with the catheter and they are moving on to the kidney."

"But it's been two hours already! Oh, my God, did something go wrong, what happened, what went wrong?"

"Did something go wrong?" The Husband tugs at his collar.

"Not really. It just took longer than they expected. I'm told everything is fine. They wanted you to know."

"Thank you," says the Husband. They turn and walk back toward where they were sitting.

"I'm not going to make it," sighs the Mother, sinking into a fake-leather chair shaped somewhat like a baseball mitt. "But before I go I'm taking half this hospital out with me."

"Do you want some coffee?" asks the Husband.

"I don't know," says the Mother. "No, I guess not. No. Do you?"

"Nah, I don't, either, I guess," he says.

"Would you like part of an orange?"

"Oh, maybe, I guess, if you're having one." She takes a temple orange from her purse and just sits there peeling its difficult skin, the flesh rupturing beneath her fingers, the juice trickling down her hands, stinging the hangnails. She and the Husband chew and swallow, discreetly spit the seeds into Kleenex, and read from photocopies of the latest medical research which they begged from the interne. They read, and underline, and sigh and close their eyes, and after some time the surgery is over. A nurse from Peed-Onk comes down to tell them.

"Your little boy's in recovery right now. He's doing well. You can see him in about fifteen minutes."

How can it be described? How can any of it be described? The trip and the story of the trip are always two different things. The narrator is the one who has stayed home but then, afterward, presses her mouth upon the traveller's mouth, in order to make the mouth work, to make the mouth say, say, say. One cannot go to a place and speak of it, one cannot both see and say, not really. One can go, and upon returning make a lot of hand motions and indications with the arms. The mouth itself, working at the speed of light, at the eye's instructions, is necessarily struck still; so fast, so much to report, it hangs open and dumb as a gutted bell. All that unsayable life! That's where the narrator comes in. The narrator comes with her kisses and mimicry and tidying up. The narrator comes and makes a slow, fake song of the mouth's eager devastation.

It is a horror and a miracle to see him. He is lying in his crib in his room, tubed up, splayed like a boy on a cross, his arms stiffened into cardboard "no-no"s so that he cannot yank out the tubes. There is the bladder catheter, the nasal-gastric tube, and the Hickman, which, beneath the skin, is plugged into his jugular, then popped out his chest wall and capped with a long plastic cap. There is a large bandage taped over his abdomen. Groggy, on a morphine drip, still he is able to look at her when, maneuvering through all the vinyl wiring, she leans to hold him, and when she does he begins to cry, but cry silently, without motion or noise. She has never seen a baby cry without motion or noise. It is the crying of an old person: silent, beyond opinion, shattered. In someone so tiny, it is frightening and unnatural. She wants to pick up the Baby and run—out of there, out of there. She wants to whip out a gun: *No-nos, eh? This whole thing is what I call a no-no.* "Don't you touch him!" she wants to shout at the surgeons and the needle nurses. "Not anymore! No more! No more!" She would crawl up and lie beside him in the crib if she could. But instead, because of all his intricate wiring, she must lean and cuddle, sing to him, songs of peril and flight: "We gotta get out of this place, if it's the last thing we ever do. We gotta get out of this place. Baby, there's a better life for me and for you."

Very 1967. She was eleven then, and impressionable.

The Baby looks at her, pleadingly, his arms outstretched in surrender. To where? Where is there to go? Take me! Take me!

That night, post-op night, the Mother and the Husband lie afloat in their cots. A fluorescent lamp near the crib is kept on in the dark. The Baby breathes evenly but thinly in his drugged sleep. The morphine in its first flooding doses apparently makes him feel as if he were falling backward—or so the Mother has been told—and it causes the Baby to jerk, to catch himself over and over, as if he were being dropped from a tree. "Is this right? Isn't there something that should be done?" The nurses come in hourly, different ones—the night shifts seem strangely short and frequent. If the Baby stirs or frets, the nurses give him more morphine through the Hickman catheter, then leave to tend to other patients. The Mother rises to check on him herself in the low light. There is gurgling from the clear plastic suction tube coming out of his mouth. Brownish clumps have collected in the tube. What is going on? The Mother rings for the nurse. Is it Renee or Sarah or Darcy? She's forgotten.

"What, what is it?" murmurs the Husband, waking up.

"Something is wrong," says the Mother. "It looks like blood in his N-G tube."

"What?" The Husband gets out of bed. He, too, is wearing sweatpants.

The nurse—Valerie—pushes open the heavy door to the room and enters quietly. "Everything O.K.?"

"There's something wrong here. The tube is sucking blood out of his stomach. It looks like it may have perforated his stomach and now he's bleeding internally. Look!"

Valerie is a saint, but her voice is the standard hospital saint voice: an infuriating, pharmaceutical calm. It says, *Everything is normal here. Death is normal. Pain is normal. Nothing is abnormal. So there is nothing to get excited about.* "Well, now, let's see." She holds up the plastic tube and tries to see inside it. "Hmm," she says. "I'll call the attending physician."

Because this is a research and teaching hospital, all the regular doctors are at home sleeping in their Mission-style beds. Tonight, as is apparently the case every weekend night, the attending physician is a medical student. He looks fifteen. The authority he attempts to convey he cannot remotely inhabit. He is not even in the same building with it. He shakes everyone's hand, then strokes his chin, a gesture no doubt gleaned from some piece of dinner theatre his parents took him to once. As if there were an actual beard on that chin! As if beard growth on that chin were even possible! "Our Town"! "Kiss Me Kate"! "Barefoot in the Park"! He is attempting to convince if not to impress.

"We're in trouble," the Mother whispers to the Husband. She is tired, tired of young people grubbing for grades. "We've got Dr. 'Kiss Me Kate' here."

The Husband looks at her blankly, a mixture of disorientation and divorce.

The medical student holds the tubing in his hands. "I don't really see anything," he says.

He flunks! "You don't?" The Mother shoves her way in, holds the clear tubing in both hands. "That," she says. "Right here and here." Just this past semester she said to one of her own students, "If you don't see how this essay is better than that one, then I want you to just go out into the hallway and stand there until you do." Is it important to keep one's voice down? The Baby stays asleep. He is drugged and dreaming, far away.

"Hmm," says the medical student. "Perhaps there's a little irritation in the stomach."

"A little irritation?" The Mother grows furious. "This is blood. These are clumps and clots. This stupid thing is sucking the life right out of him!" Life! She is starting to cry.

They turn off the suction and bring in antacids, which they feed into the Baby through the tube. Then they turn the suction on again. This time on "low."

"What was it on before?" asks the Husband.

"High," says Valerie. "Doctor's orders, though I don't know why. I don't know why these doctors do a lot of the things they do."

"Maybe they're—not all that bright?" suggests the Mother. She is feeling relief and rage simultaneously: there is a feeling of prayer and litigation in the air. Yet essentially she is grateful. Isn't she? She thinks she is. And still, and still: look at all the things you have to do to protect a child, a hospital merely an intensification of life's cruel obstacle course.

The Surgeon comes to visit on Saturday morning. He steps in and nods at the Baby, who is awake but glazed from the morphine, his eyes two dark, unseeing grapes. "The boy looks fine," he announces. He peeks under the Baby's bandage. "The stitches look good," he says. The Baby's abdomen is stitched all the way across, like a baseball. "And the other kidney, when we looked at it yesterday face to face, looked fine. We'll try to wean him off the morphine a little, and see how he's doing on Monday."

"Is he going to be O.K.?"

"The boy? The boy is going to be fine," he says, then taps her stiffly on the shoulder. "Now, you take care. It's Saturday. Drink a little wine."

Over the weekend, while the Baby sleeps, the Mother and the Husband sit together in the Tiny Tim Lounge. The Husband is restless and makes cafeteria and sundry runs, running errands for everyone. In his absence, the other parents regale her further with their sagas. Pediatric cancer and chemo stories: the children's amputations, blood poisoning, teeth flaking like shale, the learning delays and disabilities caused by chemo frying the young, budding brain. But strangely optimistic codas are tacked on: endings as stiff and loopy as carpenter's lace, crisp and empty as lettuce, reticulate as a net—ah, words. "After all that business with the tutor, he's better now, and fitted with new incisors by my wife's cousin's husband, who did dental school in two and a half years, if you can believe that. We hope for the best. We take things as they come. Life is hard."

"Life's a big problem," agrees the Mother. Part of her welcomes and invites all their tales. In the few long days since this nightmare began, part of her has become addicted to disaster and war stories. She only wants to hear about the sadness and emergencies of others. They are the only situations that can join hands with her own; everything else bounces off her shiny shield of resentment and unsympathy. Nothing else can even stay in her brain. From this, no doubt, the philistine world is made, or should one say recruited? Together the parents huddle all day in the Tiny Tim Lounge—no need to watch "Oprah." They leave "Oprah" in the dust. "Oprah" has nothing on them. They chat matter-of-factly, then fall silent and watch "Dune" or "Star Wars," in which there are bright and shiny robots, whom the Mother now sees not as robots at all but as human beings who have had terrible things happen to them.

Some of their friends visit with stuffed animals and soft "Looking good"s for the dozing baby, though the room is way past the stuffed-animal limit. The Mother arranges, once more, a plateful of Mint Milano cookies and cups of takeout coffee for guests. All her nutso pals stop by—the two on Prozac, the one obsessed with the word "penis" in the word "happiness," the one who recently had her hair foiled green. "Your friends put the *de* in *fin de siècle*," says the Husband. Overheard, or recorded, all marital conversation sounds as if someone must be joking, though usually no one is.

She loves her friends, especially loves them for coming, since there are times they all fight and don't speak for weeks. Is this friendship? For now and here, it must do and is, and is, she swears it is. For one, they never offer impromptu spiritual lectures about death, how it is part of life, its natural ebb and flow, how we all must accept that, or other such utterances that make her want to scratch out somebody's eyes. Like true friends, they take no hardy or elegant stance loosely choreographed from some broad perspective. They get right in there and mutter "Jesus Christ!" and shake their heads. Plus, they are the only people who will not only laugh at her stupid jokes but offer up stupid ones of their own. *What do you get when you cross Tiny Tim with a pit bull?* A child's illness is a strain on the mind. They know how to laugh in a flutey, desperate way—unlike the people who are more her husband's friends and who seem just to deepen their sorrowful gazes, nodding their heads in Sympathy. How Exiling and Estranging are everybody's Sympathetic Expressions! When anyone laughs, she thinks, O.K. Hooray! A buddy. In disaster as in show business.

Nurses come and go; their chirpy voices both startle and soothe. Some of the other Peed-Onk parents stick their heads in to see how the Baby is and offer encouragement.

Green Hair scratches her head: "Everyone's so friendly here. Is there someone in this place who isn't doing all this airy, scripted optimism—or are people like that the only people here?"

"It's Modern Middle Medicine meets the Modern Middle Family," says the Husband. "In the Modern Middle West."

Someone has brought in takeout lo mein, and they all eat it out in the hall by the elevators.

Parents are allowed use of the Courtesy Line.

"You've got to have a second child," says a friend on the phone, a friend from out of town. "An heir and a spare. That's what we did. We had another child to insure we wouldn't off ourselves if we lost our first."

"Really?"

"I'm serious."

"A formal suicide? Wouldn't you just drink yourself into a lifelong stupor and let it go at that?"

"Nope. I knew how I would do it even. For a while, until our second came along, I had it all planned."

"You did? What did you plan?"

"I can't go into too much detail, because—hi, honey!—the kids are here now in the room. But I'll spell out the general idea: R-O-P-E."

Sunday evening she goes and sinks down on the sofa in the Tiny Tim Lounge next to Frank, Joey's father. He is a short, stocky man with the currentless, flat-lined look behind the eyes that all the parents eventually get here. He has shaved his head bald in solidarity with his son. His little boy has been battling cancer for five years. It is now in the liver, and the rumor around the corridor is that Joey has three weeks to live. She knows that Joey's mother, Roseanne, left Frank years ago, two years into the cancer, and has remarried and had another child, a girl named Brittany. The Mother sees Roseanne here sometimes with her new life—the cute little girl and the new full-haired husband, who will never be so maniacally and debilitatingly obsessed with Joey's illness the way Frank, her first husband, is. Roseanne comes to visit Joey, to say hello and now goodbye, but she is not Joey's main man. Frank is.

Frank is full of stories—about the doctors, about the food, about the nurses, about Joey. Joey, affectless from his meds, sometimes leaves his room and comes out to watch TV in his bathrobe. He is jaundiced and bald, and though he is nine he looks no older than six. Frank has devoted the last four and a half years to saving Joey's life. When the cancer was first diagnosed, the doctors gave Joey a twenty-per-cent chance of living six more months. Now here it is almost five years later, and Joey's still here. It is all due to Frank, who, early on, quit his job as vice-president of a consulting firm in order to commit himself totally to his son. He is proud of everything he's given up and done, but he is tired. Part of him now really believes that things are coming to a close, that this is the end. He says this without tears. There are no more tears.

"You have probably been through more than anyone else on this corridor," says the Mother.

"I could tell you stories," he says. There is a sour odor between them, and she realizes that neither of them has bathed for days.

"Tell me one. Tell me the worst one." She knows he hates his ex-wife and hates her new husband even more.

"The worst? They're all the worst. Here's one: one morning I went out for breakfast with my buddy—it was the only time I'd left Joey alone ever, left him for two hours is all—and when I came back his N-G tube was full of blood. They had the suction on too high, and it was sucking the guts right out of him."

"Oh, my God. That just happened to us," said the Mother.

"It did?"

"Friday night."

"You're kidding. They let that happen again? I gave them such a chewing out about that!"

"I guess our luck is not so good. We get your very worst story on the second night we're here."

"It's not a bad place, though."

"It's not?"

"Naw. I've seen worse. I've taken Joey everywhere."

"He seems very strong." Truth is, at this point Joey seems like a zombie and frightens her.

"Joey's a fucking genius. A biological genius. They'd given him six months, remember."

The Mother nods.

"Six months is not very long," says Frank. "Six months is nothing. He was four and a half years old."

All the words are like blows. She feels flooded with affection and mourning for this man. She looks away, out the window, out past the hospital parking lot, up toward the black marbled sky and the electric eyelash of the moon. "And now he's nine," she says. "You're his hero."

"And he's mine," says Frank, though the fatigue in his voice seems to overwhelm him. "He'll be that forever. Excuse me," he says. "I've got to go check. His breathing hasn't been good. Excuse me."

"Good news and bad," says the Oncologist on Monday. He has knocked, entered the room, and now stands there. Their cots are unmade. One wastebasket is overflowing with coffee cups. "We've got the pathologist's report. The bad news is that the kidney they removed had certain lesions, called 'rests,' which are associated with a higher risk for disease in the other kidney. The good news is that the tumor is Stage I, regular cell structure, and under five hundred grams, which qualifies you for a national experiment in which chemotherapy isn't done but your boy is simply monitored with ultrasound. It's not all that risky, given that the patient's watched closely, but here is the literature on it. There are forms to sign, if you decide to do that. Read all this and we can discuss it further. You have to decide within four days."

Lesions? Rests? They dry up and scatter like M&M's on the

floor. All she hears is the part about no chemo. Another sigh of relief rises up in her and spills out. In a life where there is only the bearable and the unbearable, a sigh of relief is an ecstasy.

"No chemo?" says the husband. "Do you recommend that?"

The Oncologist shrugs. What casual gestures these doctors are permitted! "I know chemo. I like chemo," says the Oncologist. "But this is for you to decide. It depends how you feel."

The Husband leans forward. "But don't you think that now that we have the upper hand with this thing we should keep going? Shouldn't we stomp on it, beat it, smash it to death with the chemo?"

The Mother swats him angrily and hard. "Honey, you're delirious!" She whispers, but it comes out as a hiss. "This is our lucky break." Then she adds gently, "We don't want the Baby to have chemo."

The Husband turns back to the Oncologist. "What do you think?"

"It could be," he says, shrugging. "It could be that this is your lucky break. But you won't know for sure for five years."

The Husband turns back to the Mother. "O.K.," he says. "O.K."

The Baby grows happier and strong. He begins to move and sit and eat. Wednesday morning they are allowed to leave, and to leave without chemo. The Oncologist looks a little nervous. "Are you nervous about this?" asks the Mother.

"Of course I'm nervous." But he shrugs and doesn't look that nervous. "See you in six weeks for the ultrasound," he says, then he waves and leaves, looking at his big black shoes.

The Baby smiles, even toddles around a little, the sun bursting through the clouds, an angel chorus crescendoing. Nurses arrive. The Hickman is taken out of the Baby's neck and chest, antibiotic lotion is dispensed. The Mother packs up their bags. The baby sucks on a bottle of juice and does not cry.

"No chemo?" says one of the nurses. "Not even a little chemo?"

"We're doing watch-and-wait," says the Mother.

The other parents look envious but concerned. They have never seen any child get out of there with his hair and white blood cells intact.

"Will you be O.K.?" says Ned's mother.

"The worry's going to kill us," says the Husband.

"But if all we have to do is worry," chides the Mother, "every day for a hundred years, it'll be easy. It'll be nothing. I'll take all the worry in the world if it wards off the thing itself."

"That's right," says Ned's mother. "Compared to everything else, compared to all the actual events, the worry is nothing."

The Husband shakes his head. "I'm such an amateur," he moans.

"You're both doing admirably," says the other mother. "Your baby's lucky, and I wish you all the best."

The Husband shakes her hand warmly. "Thank you," he says. "You've been wonderful."

Another mother, the mother of Eric, comes up to them. "It's all very hard," she says, her head cocked to one side. "But there's a lot of collateral beauty along the way."

Collateral beauty? Who is entitled to such a thing? A child is ill. No one is entitled to any collateral beauty.

"Thank you," says the Husband.

Joey's father, Frank, comes up and embraces them both. "It's a journey," he says. He chucks the Baby on the chin. "Good luck, little man."

"Yes, thank you so much," says the Mother. "We hope things go well with Joey." She knows that Joey had a hard, terrible night.

Frank shrugs and steps back. "Gotta go," he says. "Goodbye!"

"Bye," she says, and then he is gone. She bites the inside of her lip, a bit tearily, then bends down to pick up the diaper bag, which is now stuffed with little animals; helium balloons are tied to its zipper. Shouldering the thing, the Mother feels she has just won a prize. All the parents have now vanished down the hall in the opposite direction. The Husband moves close. With one arm he takes the Baby from her; with the other he rubs her back. He can see she is starting to get weepy.

"Aren't these people nice? Don't you feel better hearing about their lives?" he asks.

Why does he do this, form clubs all the time—why does even this society of suffering soothe him? When it comes to death and dying, perhaps someone in this family ought to be more of a snob.

"All these nice people with their brave stories," he continues as they make their way toward the elevator bank, waving goodbye to the nursing staff as they go, even the Baby waving shyly. *Bye-bye! Bye-bye!* "Don't you feel consoled, knowing we're all in the same boat, that we're all in this together?"

But who on earth would want to be in this boat? the Mother thinks. This boat is a nightmare boat. Look where it goes: to a silver-and-white room, where, just before your eyesight and hearing and your ability to touch or be touched disappear entirely, you must watch your child die.

Rope! Bring on the rope.

"Let's make our own way," says the Mother, "and not in this boat."

Woman Overboard! She takes the Baby back from the Husband, cups the Baby's cheek in her hand, kisses his brow and then, quickly, his flowery mouth. The Baby's heart—she can hear it—drums with life. "For as long as I live," says the Mother, pressing the elevator button—up or down, everyone in the end has to leave this way—"I never want to see any of these people again."

There are the notes.

Now, where is the money?

BROKEBACK MOUNTAIN

BY ANNIE PROULX (1997)

They were raised on small, poor ranches in opposite corners of the state, Jack Twist in Lightning Flat, up on the Montana border, Ennis del Mar from around Sage, near the Utah line, both high-school drop-out country boys with no prospects, brought up to hard work and privation, both rough-mannered, rough-spoken, inured to the stoic life. Ennis, reared by his older brother and sister after their parents drove off the only curve on Dead Horse Road, leaving them twenty-four dollars in cash and a two-mortgage ranch, applied at age fourteen for a hardship license that let him make the hour-long trip from the ranch to the high school. The pickup was old, no heater, one windshield wiper, and bad tires; when the transmission went, there was no money to fix it. He had wanted to be a sophomore, felt the word carried a kind of distinction, but the truck broke down short of it, pitching him directly into ranch work.

In 1963, when he met Jack Twist, Ennis was engaged to Alma Beers. Both Jack and Ennis claimed to be saving money for a small spread; in Ennis's case that meant a tobacco can with two five-dollar bills inside. That spring, hungry for any job, each had signed up with Farm and Ranch Employment—they came together on paper as herder and camp tender for the same sheep operation north of Signal. The summer range lay above the tree line on Forest Service land on Brokeback Mountain. It would be Jack Twist's second summer on the mountain, Ennis's first. Neither of them was twenty.

They shook hands in the choky little trailer office in front of a table littered with scribbled papers, a Bakelite ashtray brimming with stubs. The venetian blinds hung askew and admitted a triangle of white light, the shadow of the foreman's hand moving into it. Joe Aguirre, wavy hair the color of cigarette ash and parted down the middle, gave them his point of view.

"Forest Service got designated campsites on the allotments. Them camps can be a couple a miles from where we pasture the sheep. Bad predator loss, nobody near lookin after em at night. What I want—camp tender in the main camp where the Forest Service says, but the *herder*"—pointing at Jack with a chop of his hand—"pitch a pup tent on the Q.T. with the sheep, out a sight, and he's goin a *sleep* there. Eat supper, breakfast in camp, but *sleep with the sheep*, hundred percent, *no fire*, don't leave *no sign*. Roll up that tent every mornin case Forest Service snoops around. Got the dogs, your .30-.30, sleep there. Last summer had goddam near twenty-five-percent loss. I don't want that again. *You*," he said to Ennis, taking in the ragged hair, the big nicked hands, the jeans torn, button-gaping shirt, "Fridays twelve noon be down at the bridge with your next-week list and mules. Somebody with supplies'll be there in a pickup." He didn't ask if Ennis had a watch but took a cheap round ticker on a braided cord from a box on a high shelf, wound and set it, tossed it to him as if he weren't worth the reach. "*Tomorrow mornin* we'll truck you up the jump-off." Pair of deuces going nowhere.

They found a bar and drank beer through the afternoon, Jack telling Ennis about a lightning storm on the mountain the year before that killed forty-two sheep, the peculiar stink of them and the way they bloated, the need for plenty of whiskey up there. At first glance Jack seemed fair enough, with his curly hair and quick laugh, but for a small man he carried some weight in the haunch and his smile disclosed buckteeth, not pronounced enough to let him eat popcorn out of the neck of a jug, but noticeable. He was infatuated with the rodeo life and fastened his belt with a minor bull-riding buckle, but his boots were worn to the quick, holed beyond repair, and he was crazy to be somewhere, anywhere, else than Lightning Flat.

Ennis, high-arched nose and narrow face, was scruffy and a little cave-chested, balanced a small torso on long, caliper legs, and possessed a muscular and supple body made for the horse and for fighting. His reflexes were uncommonly quick, and he was far-sighted enough to dislike reading anything except Hamley's saddle catalogue.

The sheep trucks and horse trailers unloaded at the trailhead, and a bandy-legged Basque showed Ennis how to pack the mules—two packs and a riding load on each animal, ring-lashed with double diamonds and secured with half hitches—telling him, "Don't never order soup. Them boxes a soup are real bad to pack." Three puppies belonging to one of the blue heelers went in a pack basket, the runt inside Jack's coat, for he loved a little dog. Ennis picked out a big chestnut called Cigar Butt to ride, Jack a bay mare that turned out to have a low startle point. The string of spare horses included a mouse-colored grullo whose looks Ennis liked. Ennis and Jack, the dogs, the horses and mules, a thousand ewes and their lambs flowed up the trail like dirty water through the timber and out above the tree line into the great flowery meadows and the coursing, endless wind.

They got the big tent up on the Forest Service's platform, the kitchen and grub boxes secured. Both slept in camp that first night, Jack already bitching about Joe Aguirre's sleep-with-the-sheep-and-no-fire order, though he saddled the bay mare in the dark morning without saying much. Dawn came glassy-orange, stained from below by a gelatinous band of pale green. The sooty bulk of the mountain paled slowly until it was the same color as the smoke from Ennis's breakfast fire. The cold air sweetened, banded pebbles and crumbs of soil cast sudden pencil-long shadows, and the rearing lodgepole pines below them massed in slabs of somber malachite.

During the day Ennis looked across a great gulf and sometimes saw Jack, a small dot moving across a high meadow, as an insect moves across a tablecloth; Jack, in his dark camp, saw Ennis as night fire, a red spark on the huge black mass of mountain.

Jack came lagging in late one afternoon, drank his two bottles of beer cooled in a wet sack on the shady side of the tent, ate two bowls of stew, four of Ennis's stone biscuits, a can of peaches, rolled a smoke, watched the sun drop.

"I'm commutin four hours a day," he said morosely. "Come in for breakfast, go back to the sheep, evenin get em bedded down, come in for supper, go back to the sheep, spend half the night jumpin up and checkin for coyotes. By rights I should be spendin the night here. Aguirre got no right a make me do this."

"You want a switch?" said Ennis. "I wouldn't mind herdin. I wouldn't mind sleepin out there."

"That ain't the point. Point is, we both should be in this camp. And that goddam pup tent smells like cat piss or worse."

"Wouldn't mind bein out there."

"Tell you what, you got a get up a dozen times in the night out there over them coyotes. Happy to switch but give you warnin I can't cook worth a shit. Pretty good with a can opener."

"Can't be no worse than me, then. Sure, I wouldn't mind a do it."

They fended off the night for an hour with the yellow kerosene lamp, and around ten Ennis rode Cigar Butt, a good night horse, through the glimmering frost back to the sheep, carrying leftover biscuits, a jar of jam, and a jar of coffee with him for the next day, saying he'd save a trip, stay out until supper.

"Shot a coyote just first light," he told Jack the next evening, sloshing his face with hot water, lathering up soap, and hoping his razor had some cut left in it, while Jack peeled potatoes. "Big son of a bitch. Balls on him size a apples. I bet he'd took a few lambs. Looked like he could a eat a camel. You want some a this hot water? There's plenty."

"It's all yours."

"Well, I'm goin a warsh everthing I can reach," he said, pulling off his boots and jeans (no drawers, no socks, Jack noticed), slopping the green washcloth around until the fire spat.

They had a high-time supper by the fire, a can of beans each, fried potatoes, and a quart of whiskey on shares, sat with their backs against a log, boot soles and copper jeans rivets hot, swapping the bottle while the lavender sky emptied of color and the chill air drained down, drinking, smoking cigarettes, getting up every now and then to piss, firelight throwing a sparkle in the arched stream, tossing sticks on the fire to keep the talk going, talking horses and rodeo, roughstock events, wrecks and injuries sustained, the submarine Thresher lost two months earlier with all hands and how it must have been in the last doomed minutes, dogs each had owned and known, the military service, Jack's home ranch, where his father and mother held on, Ennis's family place, folded years ago after his folks died, the older brother in Signal and a married sister in Casper. Jack said his father had been a pretty well-known bull rider years back but kept his secrets to himself, never gave Jack a word of advice, never came once to see Jack ride, though he had put him on the woollies when he was a little kid. Ennis said the kind of riding that interested him lasted longer than eight seconds and had some point to it. Money's a good point, said Jack, and Ennis had to agree. They were respectful of each other's opinions, each glad to have a companion where none had been expected. Ennis, riding against the wind back to the sheep in the treacherous, drunken light, thought he'd never had such a good time, felt he could paw the white out of the moon.

The summer went on and they moved the herd to new pasture, shifted the camp; the distance between the sheep and the new camp was greater and the night ride longer. Ennis rode easy, sleeping with his eyes open, but the hours he was away from the sheep stretched out and out. Jack pulled a squalling burr out of the harmonica, flattened a little from a fall off the skittish bay mare, and Ennis had a good raspy voice; a few nights they mangled their way through some songs. Ennis knew the salty words to "Strawberry Roan." Jack tried a Carl Perkins song, bawling "What I say-ay-ay," but he favored a sad hymn, "Water-Walking Jesus," learned from his mother, who believed in the Pentecost, and that he sang at dirge slowness, setting off distant coyote yips.

"Too late to go out to them damn sheep," said Ennis, dizzy drunk on all fours one cold hour when the moon had notched past two. The meadow stones glowed white-green and a flinty wind worked over the meadow, scraped the fire low, then ruffled it into yellow silk sashes. "Got you a extra blanket I'll roll up out here and grab forty winks, ride out at first light."

"Freeze your ass off when that fire dies down. Better off sleepin in the tent."

"Doubt I'll feel nothin." But he staggered under canvas, pulled his boots off, snored on the ground cloth for a while, woke Jack with the clacking of his jaw.

"Jesus Christ, quit hammerin and get over here. Bedroll's big enough," said Jack in an irritable sleep-clogged voice. It was big enough, warm enough, and in a little while they deepened their intimacy considerably. Ennis ran full throttle on all roads whether fence mending or money spending, and he wanted none of it when Jack seized his left hand and brought it to his erect cock. Ennis jerked his hand away as though he'd touched fire, got to his knees, unbuckled his belt, shoved his pants down, hauled Jack onto all fours, and, with the help of the clear slick and a little spit, entered him, nothing he'd done before but no instruction manual needed. They went at it in silence except for a few sharp intakes of breath and Jack's choked "Gun's goin *off*," then out, down, and asleep.

Ennis woke in red dawn with his pants around his knees, a top-grade headache, and Jack butted against him; without saying anything about it, both knew how it would go for the rest of the summer, sheep be damned.

As it did go. They never talked about the sex, let it happen, at first only in the tent at night, then in the full daylight with the hot sun striking down, and at evening in the fire glow, quick, rough, laughing and snorting, no lack of noises, but saying not a goddam word except once Ennis said, "I'm not no queer," and Jack jumped in with "Me neither. A one-shot thing. Nobody's business but ours." There were only the two of them on the mountain, flying in the euphoric, bitter air, looking down on the hawk's back and the crawling lights of vehicles on the plain below, suspended above ordinary affairs and distant from tame ranch dogs barking in the dark hours. They believed themselves invisible, not knowing Joe Aguirre had watched them through his 10x42 binoculars for ten minutes one day, waiting until they'd buttoned up their jeans, waiting until Ennis rode back to the sheep, before bringing up the message that Jack's people had sent word that his uncle Harold was in the hospital with pneumonia and expected not to make it. Though he did, and Aguirre came up again to say so, fixing Jack with his bold stare, not bothering to dismount.

In August Ennis spent the whole night with Jack in the main camp, and in a blowy hailstorm the sheep took off west and got among a herd in another allotment. There was a damn miserable time for five days, Ennis and a Chilean herder with no English trying to sort them out, the task almost impossible as the paint brands were worn and faint at this late season. Even when the numbers were right Ennis knew the sheep were mixed. In a disquieting way everything seemed mixed.

The first snow came early, on August 13th, piling up a foot, but was followed by a quick melt. The next week Joe Aguirre sent word to bring them down, another, bigger storm was moving in from the Pacific, and they packed in the game and moved off the mountain with the sheep, stones rolling at their heels, purple cloud crowding in from the west and the metal smell of coming snow pressing them on. The mountain boiled with demonic energy, glazed with flickering broken-cloud light; the wind combed the grass and drew from the damaged krummholz and slit rock a bestial drone. As they descended the slope Ennis felt he was in a slow-motion, but headlong, irreversible fall.

Joe Aguirre paid them, said little. He had looked at the milling sheep with a sour expression, said, "Some a these never went up there with you." The count was not what he'd hoped for, either. Ranch stiffs never did much of a job.

"You goin a do this next summer?" said Jack to Ennis in the street, one leg already up in his green pickup. The wind was gusting hard and cold.

"Maybe not." A dust plume rose and hazed the air with fine grit and he squinted against it. "Like I said, Alma and me's gettin married in December. Try to get somethin on a ranch. You?" He looked away from Jack's jaw, bruised blue from the hard punch Ennis had thrown him on the last day.

"If nothin better comes along. Thought some about going back up to my daddy's place, give him a hand over the winter, then maybe head out for Texas in the spring. If the draft don't get me."

"Well, see you around, I guess." The wind tumbled an empty feed bag down the street until it fetched up under the truck.

"Right," said Jack, and they shook hands, hit each other on the shoulder; then there was forty feet of distance between them and nothing to do but drive away in opposite directions. Within a mile Ennis felt like someone was pulling his guts out hand over hand a yard at a time. He stopped at the side of the road and, in the whirling new snow, tried to puke but nothing came up. He felt about as bad as he ever had and it took a long time for the feeling to wear off.

In December Ennis married Alma Beers and had her pregnant by mid-January. He picked up a few short-lived ranch jobs, then settled in as a wrangler on the old Elwood Hi-Top place, north of Lost Cabin, in Washakie County. He was still working there in September when Alma, Jr., as he called his daughter, was born and their bedroom was full of the smell of old blood and milk and baby shit, and the sounds were of squalling and sucking and Alma's sleepy groans, all reassuring of fecundity and life's continuance to one who worked with livestock.

When the Hi-Top folded they moved to a small apartment in Riverton, up over a laundry. Ennis got on the highway crew, tolerating it but working weekends at the Rafter B in exchange for keeping his horses out there. A second girl was born and Alma wanted to stay in town near the clinic because the child had an asthmatic wheeze.

"Ennis, please, no more damn lonesome ranches for us," she said, sitting on his lap, wrapping her thin, freckled arms around him. "Let's get a place here in town."

"I guess," said Ennis, slipping his hand up her blouse sleeve and stirring the silky armpit hair, fingers moving down her ribs to the jelly breast, the round belly and knee and up into the wet gap all the way to the north pole or the equator depending which way you thought you were sailing, working at it until she shuddered and bucked against his hand and he rolled her over, did quickly what she hated. They stayed in the little apartment, which he favored because it could be left at any time.

The fourth summer since Brokeback Mountain came on and in June Ennis had a general-delivery letter from Jack Twist, the first sign of life in all that time.

> Friend this letter is a long time over due. Hope you get it. Heard you was in Riverton. I'm coming thru on the 24th, thought I'd stop and buy you a beer. Drop me a line if you can, say if your there.

The return address was Childress, Texas. Ennis wrote back, "You bet," gave the Riverton address.

The day was hot and clear in the morning, but by noon the clouds had pushed up out of the west rolling a little sultry air before them. Ennis, wearing his best shirt, white with wide black stripes, didn't know what time Jack would get there and so had taken the day off, paced back and forth, looking down into a street pale with dust. Alma was saying something about taking his friend to the Knife & Fork for supper instead of cooking it was so hot, if they could get a babysitter, but Ennis said more likely he'd just go out with Jack and get drunk. Jack was not a restaurant type, he said, thinking of the dirty spoons sticking out of the cans of cold beans balanced on the log.

Late in the afternoon, thunder growling, that same old green pickup rolled in and he saw Jack get out of the truck, beat-up Resistol tilted back. A hot jolt scalded Ennis and he was out on the landing pulling the door closed behind him. Jack took the stairs two and two. They seized each other by the shoulders, hugged mightily, squeezing the breath out of each other, saying son of a bitch, son of a bitch; then, and as easily as the right key turns the lock tumblers, their mouths came together, and hard, Jack's big teeth bringing blood, his hat falling to the floor, stubble rasping, wet saliva welling, and the door opening and Alma looking out for a few seconds at Ennis's straining shoulders and shutting the door again and still they clinched, pressing chest and groin and thigh and leg together, treading on each other's toes until they pulled apart to breathe and Ennis, not big on endearments, said what he said to his horses and daughters, "Little darlin."

The door opened again a few inches and Alma stood in the narrow light.

What could he say? "Alma, this is Jack Twist. Jack, my wife, Alma." His chest was heaving. He could smell Jack—the intensely familiar odor of cigarettes, musky sweat, and a faint sweetness like grass, and with it the rushing cold of the mountain. "Alma," he said, "Jack and me ain't seen each other in four years." As if it were a reason. He was glad the light was dim on the landing but did not turn away from her.

"Sure enough," said Alma in a low voice. She had seen what she had seen. Behind her in the room, lightning lit the window like a white sheet waving and the baby cried.

"You got a kid?" said Jack. His shaking hand grazed Ennis's hand, electrical current snapped between them.

"Two little girls," Ennis said. "Alma, Jr., and Francine. Love them to pieces." Alma's mouth twitched.

"I got a boy," said Jack. "Eight months old. Tell you what, I married a cute little old Texas girl down in Childress—Lureen." From the vibration of the floorboard on which they both stood Ennis could feel how hard Jack was shaking.

"Alma," he said. "Jack and me is goin out and get a drink. Might not get back tonight, we get drinkin and talkin."

"Sure enough," Alma said, taking a dollar bill from her pocket. Ennis guessed she was going to ask him to get her a pack of cigarettes, bring him back sooner.

"Please to meet you," said Jack, trembling like a run-out horse.

"Ennis—" said Alma in her misery voice, but that didn't slow him down on the stairs and he called back, "Alma, you want smokes there's some in the pocket a my blue shirt in the bedroom."

They went off in Jack's truck, bought a bottle of whiskey, and within twenty minutes were in the Motel Siesta jouncing a bed. A few handfuls of hail rattled against the window, followed by rain and a slippery wind banging the unsecured door of the next room then and through the night.

The room stank of semen and smoke and sweat and whiskey, of old carpet and sour hay, saddle leather, shit and cheap soap. Ennis lay spread-eagled, spent and wet, breathing deep, still half tumescent; Jack blew forceful cigarette clouds like whale spouts, and said, "Christ, it got to be all that time a yours a-horseback makes it so goddam good. We got to talk about this. Swear to God I didn't know we was goin a get into this again—yeah, I did. Why I'm here. I fuckin knew it. Red-lined all the way, couldn't get here fast enough."

"I didn't know where in the *hell* you was," said Ennis. "Four years. I about give up on you. I figured you was sore about that punch."

"Friend," said Jack, "I was in Texas rodeoin. How I met Lureen. Look over on that chair."

On the back of a soiled orange chair he saw the shine of a buckle. "Bull ridin?"

"Yeah. I made three fuckin thousand dollars that year. Fuckin starved. Had to borrow everthing but a toothbrush from other guys. Drove grooves across Texas. Half the time under that cunt truck fixin it. Anyway, I didn't never think about losin. Lureen? There's some serious money there. Her old man's got it. Got this farm-machinery business. Course he don't let her have none a the money, and he hates my fuckin guts, so it's a hard go now but one a these days—"

"Well, you're goin a go where you look. Army didn't get you?" The thunder sounded far to the east, moving from them in its red wreaths of light.

"They can't get no use out a me. Got some crushed vertebrates. And a stress fracture, the arm bone here, you know how bull ridin you're always leverin it off your thigh?—she gives a little ever time you do it. Even if you tape it good you break it a little goddam bit at a time. Tell you what, hurts like a bitch afterward. Had a busted leg. Busted in three places. Come off the bull and it was a big bull with a lot a drop, he got rid a me in about three flat and he come after me and he was sure faster. Lucky enough. Friend a mine got his oil checked with a horn dipstick and that was all she wrote. Bunch a other things, fuckin busted ribs, sprains and pains, torn ligaments. See, it ain't like it was in my daddy's time. It's guys with money go to college, trained athaletes. You got to have some money to rodeo now. Lureen's old man wouldn't give me a dime if I dropped it, except one way. And I know enough about the game now so I see that I ain't never goin a be on the bubble. Other reasons. I'm gettin out while I still can walk."

Ennis pulled Jack's hand to his mouth, took a hit from the cigarette, exhaled. "Sure as hell seem in one piece to me. You know, I was sittin up here all that time tryin to figure out if I was—? I know I ain't. I mean, here we both got wives and kids, right? I like doin it with women, yeah, but Jesus H., ain't nothin like this. I never had no thoughts a doin it with another guy except I sure wrang it out a hunderd times thinkin about you. You do it with other guys, Jack?"

"Shit no," said Jack, who had been riding more than bulls, not rolling his own. "You know that. Old Brokeback got us good and it sure ain't over. We got to work out what the fuck we're goin a do now."

"That summer," said Ennis. "When we split up after we got paid out I had gut cramps so bad I pulled over and tried to puke, thought I ate somethin bad at that place in Dubois. Took me about a year to figure out it was that I shouldn't a let you out a my sights. Too late then by a long, long while."

"Friend," said Jack. "We got us a fuckin situation here. Got a figure out what to do."

"I doubt there's nothin now we can do," said Ennis. "What I'm sayin, Jack, I built a life up in them years. Love my little girls. Alma? It ain't her fault. You got your baby and wife, that place in Texas. You and me can't hardly be decent together if what happened back there"—he jerked his head in the direction of the apartment—"grabs on us like that. We do that in the wrong place we'll be dead. There's no reins on this one. It scares the piss out a me."

"Got to tell you, friend, maybe somebody seen us that summer. I was back there the next June, thinkin about goin back—I didn't, lit out for Texas instead—and Joe Aguirre's in the office and he says to me, he says, 'You boys found a way to make the time pass up there, didn't you,' and I gave him a look but when I went out I seen he had a big-ass pair a binoculars hangin off his rearview." He neglected to add that the foreman had leaned back in his squeaky wooden tilt chair and said, "Twist, you guys wasn't gettin paid to leave the dogs baby-sit the sheep while you stemmed the rose," and declined to rehire him. Jack went on, "Yeah, that little punch a yours surprised me. I never figured you to throw a dirty punch."

"I come up under my brother K.E., three years older'n me, slugged me silly every day. Dad got tired a me come bawlin in the house and when I was about six he set me down and says, Ennis, you got a problem and you got a fix it or it's goin a be with you until you're ninety and K.E.'s ninety-three. Well, I says, he's bigger'n me. Dad says, You got a take him unawares, don't say nothin to him, make him feel some pain, get out fast and keep doin it until he takes the message. Nothin like hurtin somebody to make him hear good. So I did. I got him in the outhouse, jumped him on the stairs, come over to his pillow in the night while he was sleepin and pasted him damn good. Took about two days. Never had trouble with K.E. since. The lesson was, Don't say nothin and get it over with quick." A telephone rang in the next room, rang on and on, stopped abruptly in mid-peal.

"You won't catch me again," said Jack. "Listen. I'm thinkin, tell you what, if you and me had a little ranch together, little cow-and-calf operation, your horses, it'd be some sweet life. Like I said, I'm gettin out a rodeo. I ain't no broke dick rider but I don't got the bucks a ride out this slump I'm in and I don't got the bones a keep gettin wrecked. I got it figured, got this plan, Ennis, how we can do it, you and me. Lureen's old man, you bet he'd give me a bunch if I'd get lost. Already more or less said it—"

"Whoa, whoa, whoa. It ain't goin a be that way. We can't. I'm stuck with what I got, caught in my own loop. Can't get out of it. Jack, I don't want a be like them guys you see around sometimes. And I don't want a be dead. There was these two old guys ranched together down home, Earl and Rich—Dad would pass a remark when he seen them. They was a joke even though they was pretty tough old birds. I was what, nine years old, and they found Earl dead in a irrigation ditch. They'd took a tire iron to him, spurred him up, drug him around by his dick until it pulled off, just bloody pulp. What the tire iron done looked like pieces a burned tomatoes all over him, nose tore down from skiddin on gravel."

"You seen that?"

"Dad made sure I seen it. Took me to see it. Me and K.E. Dad laughed about it. Hell, for all I know he done the job. If he was alive and was to put his head in that door right now you bet he'd go get his tire iron. Two guys livin together? No. All I can see is we get together once in a while way the hell out in the back a nowhere—"

"How much is once in a while?" said Jack. "Once in a while ever four fuckin years?"

"No," said Ennis, forbearing to ask whose fault that was. "I goddam hate it that you're goin a drive away in the mornin and I'm goin back to work. But if you can't fix it you got a stand it," he said. "Shit. I been lookin at people on the street. This happen a other people? What the hell do they do?"

"It don't happen in Wyomin and if it does I don't know what

they do, maybe go to Denver," said Jack, sitting up, turning away from him, "and I don't give a flyin fuck. Son of a bitch, Ennis, take a couple days off. Right now. Get us out a here. Throw your stuff in the back a my truck and let's get up in the mountains. Couple a days. Call Alma up and tell her you're goin. Come on, Ennis, you just shot my airplane out a the sky—give me somethin a go on. This ain't no little thing that's happenin here."

The hollow ringing began again in the next room, and as if he were answering it Ennis picked up the phone on the bedside table, dialled his own number.

A slow corrosion worked between Ennis and Alma, no real trouble, just widening water. She was working at a grocery-store clerk job, saw she'd always have to work to keep ahead of the bills on what Ennis made. Alma asked Ennis to use rubbers because she dreaded another pregnancy. He said no to that, said he would be happy to leave her alone if she didn't want any more of his kids. Under her breath she said, "I'd have em if you'd support em." And under that thought, Anyway, what you like to do don't make too many babies.

Her resentment opened out a little every year: the embrace she had glimpsed, Ennis's fishing trips once or twice a year with Jack Twist and never a vacation with her and the girls, his disinclination to step out and have any fun, his yearning for low-paid, long-houred ranch work, his propensity to roll to the wall and sleep as soon as he hit the bed, his failure to look for a decent permanent job with the county or the power company put her in a long, slow dive, and when Alma, Jr., was nine and Francine seven she said, What am I doin, hangin around with him, divorced Ennis, and married the Riverton grocer.

Ennis went back to ranch work, hired on here and there, not getting much ahead but glad enough to be around stock again, free to drop things, quit if he had to, and go into the mountains at short notice. He had no serious hard feelings, just a vague sense of getting short-changed, and showed it was all right by taking Thanksgiving dinner with Alma and her grocer and the kids, sitting between his girls and talking horses to them, telling jokes, trying not to be a sad daddy. After the pie Alma got him off in the kitchen, scraped the plates and said she worried about him and he ought to get married again. He saw she was pregnant, about four, five months, he guessed.

"Once burned," he said, leaning against the counter, feeling too big for the room.

"You still go fishin with that Jack Twist?"

"Some." He thought she'd take the pattern off the plate with the scraping.

"You know," she said, and from her tone he knew something was coming, "I used to wonder how come you never brought any trouts home. Always said you caught plenty. So one time I got your creel case open the night before you went on one a your little trips—price tag still on it after five years—and I tied a note on the end of the line. It said, 'Hello, Ennis, bring some fish home, love, Alma.' And then you come back and said you'd caught a bunch a browns and ate them up. Remember? I looked in the case when I got a chance and there was my note still tied there and that line hadn't touched water in its life." As though the word "water" had called out its domestic cousin, she twisted the faucet, sluiced the plates.

"That don't mean nothin."

"Don't lie, don't try to fool me, Ennis. I know what it means. Jack Twist? Jack Nasty. You and him—"

She'd overstepped his line. He seized her wrist and twisted; tears sprang and rolled, a dish clattered.

"Shut up," he said. "Mind your own business. You don't know nothin about it."

"I'm goin a yell for Bill."

"You fuckin go right ahead. Go on and fuckin yell. I'll make him eat the fuckin floor and you too." He gave another wrench that left her with a burning bracelet, shoved his hat on backward and slammed out. He went to the Black and Blue Eagle bar that night, got drunk, had a short dirty fight, and left. He didn't try to see his girls for a long time, figuring they would look him up when they got the sense and years to move out from Alma.

They were no longer young men with all of it before them. Jack had filled out through the shoulders and hams; Ennis stayed as lean as a clothespole, stepped around in worn boots, jeans, and shirts summer and winter, added a canvas coat in cold weather. A benign growth appeared on his eyelid and gave it a drooping appearance; a broken nose healed crooked.

Years on years they worked their way through the high meadows and mountain drainages, horse-packing into the Big Horns, the Medicine Bows, the south end of the Gallatins, the Absarokas, the Granites, the Owl Creeks, the Bridger-Teton Range, the Freezeouts and the Shirleys, the Ferrrises and the Rattlesnakes, the Salt River range, into the Wind Rivers over and again, the Sierra Madres, the Gros Ventres, the Washakies, the Laramies, but never returning to Brokeback.

Down in Texas Jack's father-in-law died and Lureen, who inherited the farm-equipment business, showed a skill for management and hard deals. Jack found himself with a vague managerial title, travelling to stock and agricultural machinery shows. He had some money now and found ways to spend it on his buying trips. A little Texas accent flavored his sentences, "cow" twisted into "kyow" and "wife" coming out as "waf." He'd had his front teeth filed down, set with steel plugs, and capped, said he'd felt no pain, wore Texas suits and a tall white hat.

In May of 1983 they spent a few cold days at a series of little icebound, no-name high lakes, then worked across into the Hail Strew River drainage.

Going up, the day was fine, but the trail deep-drifted and slopping wet at the margins. They left it to wind through a slashy cut, leading the horses through brittle branch wood, Jack lifting his head in the heated noon to take the air scented with resinous lodgepole, the dry needle duff and hot rock, bitter juniper crushed beneath the horses' hooves. Ennis, weather-eyed, looked west for the heated cumulus that might come up on such a day, but the boneless blue was so deep, said Jack, that he might drown looking up.

Around three they swung through a narrow pass to a southeast slope where the strong spring sun had had a chance to work, dropped down to the trail again, which lay snowless below them. They could hear the river muttering and making a distant train sound a long way off. Twenty minutes on they surprised a black bear on the bank above them rolling a log over for grubs, and Jack's horse shied and reared, Jack saying "Wo! Wo!" and Ennis's bay dancing and snorting but holding. Jack reached for the .30-.06 but there was no need; the startled bear galloped into the trees with the lumpish gait that made it seem it was falling apart.

The tea-colored river ran fast with snowmelt, a scarf of bubbles at every high rock, pools and setbacks streaming. The ochre-branched willows swayed stiffly, pollened catkins like yellow thumbprints. The horses drank and Jack dismounted, scooped icy water up in his hand, crystalline drops falling from his fingers, his mouth and chin glistening with wet.

"Get beaver fever doin that," said Ennis, then, "Good enough place," looking at the level bench above the river, two or three fire rings from old hunting camps. A sloping meadow rose behind the bench, protected by a stand of lodgepole. There was plenty of dry wood. They set up camp without saying much, picketed the horses in the meadow. Jack broke the seal on a bottle of whiskey, took a long, hot swallow, exhaled forcefully, said, "That's one a the two things I need right now," capped it and tossed it to Ennis.

On the third morning there were the clouds Ennis had expected, a gray racer out of the West, a bar of darkness driving wind before it and small flakes. It faded after an hour into tender spring snow that heaped wet and heavy. By nightfall it had turned colder. Jack and Ennis passed a joint back and forth, the fire burning late, Jack restless and bitching about the cold, poking the flames with a stick, twisting the dial of the transistor radio until the batteries died.

Ennis said he'd been putting the blocks to a woman who worked part-time at the Wolf Ears bar in Signal where he was working now for Car Scrope's cow-and-calf outfit, but it wasn't going anywhere and she had some problems he didn't want. Jack said he'd had a thing going with the wife of a rancher down the road in Childress and for the last few months he'd slank around expecting to get shot by Lureen or the husband, one. Ennis laughed a little and said he probably deserved it. Jack said he was doing all right but he missed Ennis bad enough sometimes to make him whip babies.

The horses nickered in the darkness beyond the fire's circle of light. Ennis put his arm around Jack, pulled him close, said he saw his girls about once a month, Alma, Jr., a shy seventeen-year-old with his beanpole length, Francine a little live wire. Jack slid his cold hand between Ennis's legs, said he was worried about his boy who was, no doubt about it, dyslexic or something, couldn't get anything right, fifteen years old and couldn't hardly read, *he* could see it though goddam Lureen wouldn't admit to it and pretended the kid was O.K., refused to get any bitchin kind a help about it. He didn't know what the fuck the answer was. Lureen had the money and called the shots.

"I used a want a boy for a kid," said Ennis, undoing buttons, "but just got little girls."

"I didn't want none a either kind," said Jack. "But fuck-all has worked the way I wanted. Nothin never come to my hand the right way." Without getting up he threw deadwood on the fire, the sparks flying up with their truths and lies, a few hot points of fire landing on their hands and faces, not for the first time, and they rolled down into the dirt. One thing never changed: the brilliant charge of their infrequent couplings was darkened by the sense of time flying, never enough time, never enough.

A day or two later in the trailhead parking lot, horses loaded into the trailer, Ennis was ready to head back to Signal, Jack up to Lightning Flat to see the old man. Ennis leaned into Jack's window, said what he'd been putting off the whole week, that likely he couldn't get away again until November, after they'd shipped stock and before winter feeding started.

"November. What in hell happened a August? Tell you what, we said August, nine, ten days. Christ, Ennis! Whyn't you tell me this before? You had a fuckin week to say some little word about it. And why's it we're always in the friggin cold weather? We ought a do somethin. We ought a go South. We ought a go to Mexico one day."

"Mexico? Jack, you know me. All the travellin I ever done is goin around the coffeepot lookin for the handle. And I'll be runnin the baler all August, that's what's the matter with August. Lighten up, Jack. We can hunt in November, kill a nice elk. Try if I can get Don Wroe's cabin again. We had a good time that year."

"You know, friend, this is a goddam bitch of a unsatisfactory situation. You used a come away easy. It's like seein the Pope now."

"Jack, I got a work. Them earlier days I used a quit the jobs. You got a wife with money, a good job. You forget how it is bein broke all the time. You ever hear a child support? I been payin out for years and got more to go. Let me tell you, I can't quit this one. And

I can't get the time off. It was tough gettin this time—some a them late heifers is still calvin. You don't leave then. You don't. Scrope is a hell-raiser and he raised hell about me takin the week. I don't blame him. He probly ain't got a night's sleep since I left. The trade-off was August. You got a better idea?"

"I did once." The tone was bitter and accusatory.

Ennis said nothing, straightened up slowly, rubbed at his forehead; a horse stamped inside the trailer. He walked to his truck, put his hand on the trailer, said something that only the horses could hear, turned and walked back at a deliberate pace.

"You been a Mexico, Jack?" Mexico was the place. He'd heard. He was cutting fence now, trespassing in the shoot-em zone.

"Hell yes, I been. Where's the fuckin problem?" Braced for it all these years and here it came, late and unexpected.

"I got a say this to you one time, Jack, and I ain't foolin. What I don't know," said Ennis, "all them things I don't know could get you killed if I should come to know them."

"Try this one," said Jack, "and *I'll* say it just one time. Tell you what, we could a had a good life together, a fuckin real good life. You wouldn't do it, Ennis, so what we got now is Brokeback Mountain. Everything built on that. It's all we got, boy, fuckin all, so I hope you know that if you don't never know the rest. Count the damn few times we been together in twenty years. Measure the fuckin short leash you keep me on, then ask me about Mexico and then tell me you'll kill me for needin it and not hardly never gettin it. You got no fuckin idea how bad it gets. I'm not you. I can't make it on a couple a high-altitude fucks once or twice a year. You're too much for me, Ennis, you son of a whoreson bitch. I wish I knew how to quit you."

Like vast clouds of steam from thermal springs in winter the years of things unsaid and now unsayable—admissions, declarations, shames, guilts, fears—rose around them. Ennis stood as if heart-shot, face gray and deep-lined, grimacing, eyes screwed shut, fists clenched, legs caving, hit the ground on his knees.

"Jesus," said Jack. "Ennis?" But before he was out of the truck, trying to guess if it was a heart attack or the overflow of an incendiary rage, Ennis was back on his feet, and somehow, as a coat hanger is straightened to open a locked car and then bent again to its original shape, they torqued things almost to where they had been, for what they'd said was no news. Nothing ended, nothing begun, nothing resolved.

What Jack remembered and craved in a way he could neither help nor understand was the time that distant summer on Brokeback when Ennis had come up behind him and pulled him close, the silent embrace satisfying some shared and sexless hunger.

They had stood that way for a long time in front of the fire, its burning tossing ruddy chunks of light, the shadow of their bodies a single column against the rock. The minutes ticked by from the round watch in Ennis's pocket, from the sticks in the fire settling into coals. Stars bit through the wavy heat layers above the fire. Ennis's breath came slow and quiet, he hummed, rocked a little in the sparklight, and Jack leaned against the steady heartbeat, the vibrations of the humming like faint electricity and, standing, he fell into sleep that was not sleep but something else drowsy and tranced until Ennis, dredging up a rusty but still usable phrase from the childhood time before his mother died, said, "Time to hit the hay, cowboy. I got a go. Come on, you're sleepin on your feet like a horse," and gave Jack a shake, a push, and went off in the darkness. Jack heard his spurs tremble as he mounted, the words "See you tomorrow," and the horse's shuddering snort, grind of hoof on stone.

Later, that dozy embrace solidified in his memory as the single moment of artless, charmed happiness in their separate and difficult lives. Nothing marred it, even the knowledge that Ennis would not then embrace him face to face because he did not want to see or feel that it was Jack he held. And maybe, he thought, they'd never got much farther than that. Let be, let be.

Ennis didn't know about the accident for months until his postcard to Jack saying that November still looked like the first chance came back stamped "DECEASED." He called Jack's number in Childress, something he had done only once before, when Alma divorced him, and Jack had misunderstood the reason for the call, had driven twelve hundred miles north for nothing. This would be all right; Jack would answer, had to answer. But he did not. It was Lureen and she said who? who is this? and when he told her again she said in a level voice yes, Jack was pumping up a flat on the truck out on a back road when the tire blew up. The bead was damaged somehow and the force of the explosion slammed the rim into his face, broke his nose and jaw and knocked him unconscious on his back. By the time someone came along he had drowned in his own blood.

No, he thought, they got him with the tire iron.

"Jack used to mention you," she said. "You're the fishing buddy or the hunting buddy, I know that. Would have let you know," she said, "but I wasn't sure about your name and address. Jack kept most a his friends' addresses in his head. It was a terrible thing. He was only thirty-nine years old."

The huge sadness of the Northern plains rolled down on him. He didn't know which way it was, the tire iron or a real accident, blood choking down Jack's throat and nobody to turn him over. Under the wind drone he heard steel slamming off bone, the hollow chatter of a settling tire rim.

"He buried down there?" He wanted to curse her for letting Jack die on the dirt road.

The little Texas voice came slip-sliding down the wire, "We put a stone up. He use to say he wanted to be cremated, ashes scattered on Brokeback Mountain. I didn't know where that was. So he was cremated, like he wanted, and, like I say, half his ashes was interred here, and the rest I sent up to his folks. I thought Brokeback Mountain was around where he grew up. But knowing Jack, it might be some pretend place where the bluebirds sing and there's a whiskey spring."

"We herded sheep on Brokeback one summer," said Ennis. He could hardly speak.

"Well, he said it was his place. I thought he meant to get drunk. Drink whiskey up there. He drank a lot."

"His folks still up in Lightnin Flat?"

"Oh yeah. They'll be there until they die. I never met them. They didn't come down for the funeral. You get in touch with them. I suppose they'd appreciate it if his wishes was carried out."

No doubt about it, she was polite but the little voice was as cold as snow.

. . .

The road to Lightning Flat went through desolate country past a dozen abandoned ranches distributed over the plain at eight- and ten-mile intervals, houses sitting blank-eyed in the weeds, corral fences down. The mailbox read "John C. Twist." The ranch was a meagre little place, leafy spurge taking over. The stock was too far distant for him to see their condition, only that they were black baldies. A porch stretched across the front of the tiny brown stucco house, four rooms, two down, two up.

Ennis sat at the kitchen table with Jack's father. Jack's mother, stout and careful in her movements as though recovering from an operation, said, "Want some coffee, don't you? Piece a cherry cake?"

"Thank you, Ma'am, I'll take a cup a coffee but I can't eat no cake just now."

The old man sat silent, his hands folded on the plastic tablecloth, staring at Ennis with an angry, knowing expression. Ennis recognized in him a not uncommon type with the hard need to be the stud duck in the pond. He couldn't see much of Jack in either one of them, took a breath.

"I feel awful bad about Jack. Can't begin to say how bad I feel. I knew him a long time. I come by to tell you that if you want me to take his ashes up there on Brokeback like his wife says he wanted I'd be proud to."

There was a silence. Ennis cleared his throat but said nothing more.

The old man said, "Tell you what, I know where Brokeback Mountain is. He thought he was too goddam special to be buried in the family plot."

Jack's mother ignored this, said, "He used a come home every year, even after he was married and down in Texas, and help his daddy on the ranch for a week, fix the gates and mow and all. I kept his room like it was when he was a boy and I think he appreciated that. You are welcome to go up in his room if you want."

The old man spoke angrily. "I can't get no help out here. Jack used a say, 'Ennis del Mar,' he used a say, 'I'm goin a bring him up here one a these days and we'll lick this damn ranch into shape.' He had some half-baked idea the two a you was goin a move up here, build a log cabin, and help me run this ranch and bring it up. Then this spring he's got another one's goin a come up here with him and build a place and help run the ranch, some ranch neighbor a his from down in Texas. He's goin a split up with his wife and come back here. So he says. But like most a Jack's ideas it never come to pass."

So now he knew it had been the tire iron. He stood up, said you bet he'd like to see Jack's room, recalled one of Jack's stories about this old man. Jack was dick-clipped and the old man was not; it bothered the son, who had discovered the anatomical disconformity during a hard scene. He had been about three or four, he said, always late getting to the toilet, struggling with buttons, the seat, the height of the thing, and often as not left the surroundings sprinkled down. The old man blew up about it and this one time worked into a crazy rage. "Christ, he licked the stuffin out a me, knocked me down on the bathroom floor, whipped me with his belt. I thought he was killin me. Then he says, 'You want a know what it's like with piss all over the place? I'll learn you,' and he pulls it out and lets go all over me, soaked me, then he throws a towel at me and makes me mop up the floor, take my clothes off and warsh them in the bathtub, warsh out the towel, I'm bawlin and blubberin. But while he was hosin me down I seen he had some extra material that I was missin. I seen they'd cut me different like you'd crop a ear or scorch a brand. No way to get it right with him after that."

The bedroom, at the top of a steep stair that had its own climbing rhythm, was tiny and hot, afternoon sun pounding through the west window, hitting the narrow boy's bed against the wall, an ink-stained desk and wooden chair, a B.B. gun in a hand-whittled rack over the bed. The window looked down on the gravel road stretching south and it occurred to him that for Jack's growing-up years that was the only road he knew. An ancient magazine photograph of some dark-haired movie star was taped to the wall beside the bed, the skin tone gone magenta. He could hear Jack's mother downstairs running water, filling the kettle and setting it back on the stove, asking the old man a muffled question.

The closet was a shallow cavity with a wooden rod braced across, a faded cretonne curtain on a string closing it off from the rest of the room. In the closet hung two pairs of jeans crease-ironed and folded neatly over wire hangers, on the floor a pair of worn packer boots he thought he remembered. At the north end of the closet a tiny jog in the wall made a slight hiding place and here, stiff with long suspension from a nail, hung a shirt. He lifted it off the nail. Jack's old shirt from Brokeback days. The dried blood on the sleeve was his own blood, a gushing nosebleed on the last afternoon on the mountain when Jack, in their contortionistic grappling and wrestling, had slammed Ennis's nose hard with his knee. He had stanched the blood, which was everywhere, all over both of them, with his shirtsleeve, but the stanching hadn't held, because Ennis had suddenly swung from the deck and laid the ministering angel out in the wild columbine, wings folded.

The shirt seemed heavy until he saw there was another shirt inside it, the sleeves carefully worked down inside Jack's sleeves. It was his own plaid shirt, lost, he'd thought, long ago in some damn laundry, his dirty shirt, the pocket ripped, buttons missing, stolen by Jack and hidden here inside Jack's own shirt, the pair like two skins, one inside the other, two in one. He pressed his face into the fabric and breathed in slowly through his mouth and nose, hoping for the faintest smoke and mountain sage and salty sweet stink of Jack, but there was no real scent, only the memory of it, the imagined power of Brokeback Mountain of which nothing was left but what he held in his hands.

In the end the stud duck refused to let Jack's ashes go. "Tell you what, we got a family plot and he's goin in it." Jack's mother stood at the table coring apples with a sharp, serrated instrument. "You come again," she said.

Bumping down the washboard road Ennis passed the country cemetery fenced with sagging sheep wire, a tiny fenced square on the welling prairie, a few graves bright with plastic flowers, and didn't want to know Jack was going in there, to be buried on the grieving plain.

A few weeks later, on the Saturday, he threw all the Coffeepot's dirty horse blankets into the back of his pickup and took them down to the Quik Stop Car Wash to turn the high-pressure spray on them. When the wet clean blankets were stowed in the truck bed he stepped into Higgins' gift shop and busied himself with the postcard rack.

"Ennis, what are you lookin for, rootin through them postcards?"

said Linda Higgins, throwing a sopping brown coffee filter into the garbage can.

"Scene a Brokeback Mountain."

"Over in Fremont County?"

"No, north a here."

"I didn't order none a them. Let me get the order list. They got it I can get you a hunderd. I got a order some more cards anyway."

"One's enough," said Ennis.

When it came—thirty cents—he pinned it up in his trailer, brass-headed tack in each corner. Below it he drove a nail and on the nail he hung a wire hanger and the two old shirts suspended from it. He stepped back and looked at the ensemble through a few stinging tears.

"Jack, I swear—" he said, though Jack had never asked him to swear anything and was himself not the swearing kind.

Around that time Jack began to appear in his dreams, Jack as he had first seen him, curly-headed and smiling and buck-toothed, talking about getting up off his pockets and into the control zone, but the can of beans with the spoon handle jutting out and balanced on the log was there as well, in a cartoon shape and lurid colors that gave the dreams a flavor of comic obscenity. The spoon handle was the kind that could be used as a tire iron. And he would wake sometimes in grief, sometimes with the old sense of joy and release; the pillow sometimes wet, sometimes the sheets.

There was some open space between what he knew and what he tried to believe, but nothing could be done about it, and if you can't fix it you've got to stand it.

THE TELEPHONE GAME

BY WILLIAM TREVOR (1998)

Since the conventional separation of the sexes on the evening before a wedding did not appeal to Liese, Tony agreed that there should be a party to which both sides of the wedding came instead. A party was necessary because the formalities of the day would not allow for much of a reunion with friends they had not seen for some time, but they did not wish the reception to be an occasion that went on and on: they wanted to be in Venice in time for the first dinner of their marriage. So in Tony's flat, already rearranged for married life, his friends and Liese's mixed jollily in advance, while wine flowed generously and there was background music that was danced to, while tomorrow's bride and groom learned a little more about one another from what was said; friendships here were longer than their own.

Tonight, there was a solemnity about Liese's manner which softened further the beauty of her features: her mind was on her marriage. Smooth, pale as wheat, her hair fell to her shoulders; her light-blue eyes were a degree less tranquil than usually they were, but when she smiled all that tranquillity came back. "Oh Tony, you are lucky," a cousin who had not met Liese before remarked, and Tony said he knew it. He was fair-haired, too, by nature insouciant and humorous, handsome in his way.

In Germany, Liese's father was a manufacturer of gloves. In England, Tony had been looked after by an aunt ever since his parents died in the worst air disaster of 1977—the runway collision of two jumbo jets—when Tony was six, an only child. Nineteen years later he and Liese had met by chance, in a bustling lunchtime restaurant, not far from Victoria Station. "D'you think we could see each other again?" he had pleaded, while a tubby, middle-aged waitress, bringing their coffee in that moment, approved of his boldness and let it show. 00178 was the number on the back of the driver's seat in the first taxi they sat in together, black digits on an oval of white enamel. Afterward, romantically, they both remembered that, and the taxi driver's conversation and the tubby waitress.

Already in love, Liese was told about the tragedy in 1977, Tony about the gloves that had been the source of livelihood in Liese's family for generations. Driven by love, Tony played the part required of him in Schelesnau, asking questions about lambskin and pigskin and doeskin, showing an interest in hand-stitching and dyeing skills and thonging. Liese was nervous in anticipation before meeting Tony's aunt, who was getting on a bit now, in a small South Coast resort with a distant view of the ferries plying back and forth to France. But Liese needn't have been apprehensive. "She's lovely," Tony's aunt said, while in Schelesnau—where there were Liese's two younger sisters and a busy family life—Tony was considered charming. In Schelesnau and in England there was at first a faint concern that the marriage was taking on a burden that marriage did not always have to, that would have been avoided if Liese had chosen to marry a German or Tony an English girl: after all, there had been enmity in two terrible wars. It was a vague feeling, very much at odds with the sentiments of the time, and although it hovered like some old, long-discredited ghost, it failed in the end to gain a place in the scheme of things. What did, instead, was the telephone game.

On the night before the wedding it was Tony who suggested playing it. Afterward, he hardly knew why he did, why he had imagined that Germans would understand the humor of the game, but of course he'd had a certain amount to drink. For her part, Liese wished she had insisted that her wedding party wasn't an occasion for this kind of diversion. "Oh, Tony!" was her single, halfhearted protest, and Tony didn't hear it.

Already he had explained to Liese's sisters—both of whom were to be bridesmaids—that strangers were telephoned, that you won if you held a stranger in conversation longer than anyone else could with their random calls. The information was passed around among the bewildered Germans, who politely wondered what was coming next.

"I am in engine boats," a man who had been a classmate of Liese's in Fräulein Groenewold's kindergarten was saying when the music was turned off. " 'Outboards,' you say?"

He, and all the others—more than thirty were still left at the party—were asked to be silent then. A number was dialled by Tony's best man and the first of the strangers informed that there was a gas leak in the street, asked to check the rooms of his house for a telltale smell, then to return to the phone with information as to that. The next was told that an external fuse had blown, that all electrical connections should be unplugged or turned off to obviate danger. The next was advised to close and lock his windows against a roving polecat.

"The Water Board here," Tony said when his turn came. "We're extremely sorry to call you out so late. We have an emergency."

Some of the German visitors were still perplexed. "So they are all your friends?" a girl with a plait asked, in spite of what had been said. "This is a joke with friends?"

Liese explained again that the people who were telephoned were just anyone. She whispered, in case her voice should carry to Tony's victim. "*Was? Stimmt irgendwas nicht?*" her friend whispered back, and Liese said it was all just for fun.

"What we would like you to do," Tony said, "is to make your way to the water tanks in your loft and turn off the inlet tap. This tap is usually red, Madam, but of course the color may have worn off. What we're endeavoring to do is to prevent the flooding of your house."

"Flooding?" the woman he spoke to repeated, her voice drowsy with sleep. "Eh?"

"One of our transformer valves has failed. Dangerously high pressure level."

"I can't go up into the lofts at this hour" came the voice again. "It's the middle of the night."

"We're having to ask everyone in the area, Madam. Perhaps your husband—"

"I ain't got no husband. I ain't got no one here. I'm seventy-three years of age. How d'you think I'd know about a tap?"

"We're sorry for the inconvenience, Madam. We naturally would not ask you to do this if it were not necessary. When a transformer valve goes it is a vital matter. The main articulated valve may go next and then of course it is too late. When the articulated valve goes the floodwater could rise to sixteen feet within minutes. In which case I would advise you to keep to the upstairs rooms."

Tony put the palm of his hand over the mouthpiece. She had beetled off to get a stepladder, he whispered, and a flashlight. He listened again and said there was the mewing of a cat.

"It'll be all right now?" another German girl leaned forward to ask Liese, and the German who was in outboard motors, who perfectly understood the game, gestured with a smile that it would be. The game was amusing, he considered, but not a game to play in Schelesnau. It was sophisticated. It was the famous English sense of humor.

Tony heard the shuffle of footsteps, a door closing in the distance, and in the distance also the mewing of the cat again. Then there was silence.

Tony looked round his guests, some of them, as he was, a little drunk. He laughed, careless now of allowing the sound to pass to the other house, since its lone occupant was presumably already in her loft. He put the receiver down beside the directories on the narrow telephone table, and reached out with a bottle of Sancerre to attend to a couple of empty glasses. A friend he'd been at school with began to tell of a time when a man in Hoxton was sent out onto the streets to see if a stolen blue van had just been parked there. Some of the Germans said they must be going now.

"Sh-h-h." Listening again, Tony held up a hand. But there was no sound from the other end. "She's still aloft," he said, and put the receiver down beside the directories again.

"In Germany," it was explained by the man in outboard motors, "we might say this was *Ärgernis*."

"Oh, here, too," an English girl who did not approve of the telephone game said. "If that means 'harassment.'"

Those who remained left in a bunch at last, the Germans telling about *Wasservexierungsport*, a practical joke involving jets of water.

You put your ten pfennigs into a slot machine to bring the lights on in a grotto and found yourself drenched instead. "Watervexing," the outboard-motors man translated.

"You could stay here, you know," Tony said when he and Liese had collected the glasses and the ashtrays, when everything had been washed and dried, the cushions plumped up, a window opened to let in a stream of cold night air.

"But I have yet to finish packing up my things. The morning will be busy."

They walked about the flat that soon would be their home, going from room to room, although they knew the rooms well. Softly, the music still played, and they danced a little in the small hall, happy to be alone now. The day they'd met there had been an office party in the busy lunchtime restaurant, a lot of noise, and a woman in a red-dotted dress quarrelling with her friend at the table next to theirs. How cautious Liese had been that day was afterward remembered, and how cautious she'd been much later when Tony said he loved her. Remembered, too, with that same fondness was how both of them had wanted marriage, not some substitute, how they had wanted the binding of its demands and vows and rigors. London was the city of their romance and it was in London—to the discomfort and annoyance of her parents, defying all convention—that Liese had insisted the marriage should take place.

While they danced, Tony noticed that his telephone receiver was still lying beside the directories. Half an hour ago he had forgotten about it. He reached to pick it up, bringing their dance to an end.

"She hasn't put hers back," he said.

Liese took the receiver from him. She listened, too, and heard the empty sound of a connected line. "Hullo," she said. "Hullo."

"She forgot. She went to bed."

"Would she forget, Tony?"

"Well, something like it."

"Did she give a name? You have the number still?"

Tony shook his head. "She didn't give a name." He had forgotten the number; he'd simply made it up as he dialled, he said.

"What did she say, Tony?"

"Only that she was without a husband."

"Her husband was out? At this time?"

They had drawn away from one another. Tony turned the music off.

"She meant she was widowed," he said. "She wasn't young. Seventy, or something like that."

"This old woman goes to her loft—"

"Well, I mean, she said she would. More likely, she didn't believe a word I said."

"She went to look for a stepladder and a flashlight. You told us."

"I think she said she was cold in her nightdress. More likely, she just went back to bed. I don't blame her."

Listening again, Liese said, "I can hear the cat."

But when she passed the receiver over, Tony said he couldn't hear anything. Nothing at all, he said.

"Very far away. The cat was mewing, and suddenly it stopped. Don't put it back!" Liese cried when Tony was about to return the receiver to its cradle. "She is there in her loft, Tony."

"Oh, honestly, I don't think so. Why should she be? It doesn't take an hour and a quarter to turn a stopcock off."

"What is a stopcock?"

"Just a way of controlling the water."

The mewing of the cat came faintly to him, a single mew and then another. Not knowing why he did so, Tony shook his head again, silently denying this sound.

"She could have fallen down," Liese said. "It would be hard to see with her flashlight and she could have fallen down."

"No, I don't think so."

For the first time in the year and a half she had known him Liese heard a testiness in Tony's voice. There was no point in not replacing the receiver, he said. "Look, let's forget it, Liese."

Solemnly, but in distress, Liese gazed into the features of the man she was to marry in just over twelve hours' time. He smiled a familiar, easy smile. No point, he said again, more softly. No point in going on about this.

"Honestly, Liese."

They had walked about, that first afternoon. He had taken her through Green Park, then down to the river. She was in London to perfect her English; that afternoon she should have been at another class. And it was a quarter past five before Tony explained, untruthfully, his absence from his desk. The next day they met again.

"Nothing has happened, Liese."

"She could be dead."

"Oh, Liese, don't be silly."

At once, having said that, Tony apologized. Of course she wasn't silly. That game was silly. He was sorry they'd played it tonight.

"But, Tony—"

"Of course she isn't dead."

"Why do you think you can be sure?"

He shook his head, meaning to indicate that he wasn't claiming to be sure, only that reason implied what he suggested. During the months they were getting to know one another he had learned that Liese's imagination was sometimes a nuisance; she had said so herself. Purposeless and dispensable, she said—a quirk of nature that caused her, too often, to doubt the surface of things. Well, you could call music purposeless, he had replied, the petal of a flower dispensable: what failed the marketplace was often what should be treasured most. But Liese called her quirk of nature a pest; and experiencing an instance of it for the first time now, Tony understood.

"Let's not quarrel, Liese."

But the quarrel—begun already while neither noticed—spread, insidious in the stillness that the silent telephone, once more passed from hand to hand, seemed to inspire. Neither heard the mewing of the cat again, and Tony said, "Look, in the morning she'll see that receiver hanging there and she'll remember she forgot to put it back."

"It is morning now. Tony, we could go to the police."

"The *police*? What on earth for?"

"They could find out where that house is."

"Oh, none of this makes sense!" And Tony, who happened just then to be holding the telephone receiver, would again have replaced it.

Liese snatched it, anger flushing through her cheeks. She asked him why he'd wanted to do that, and he shrugged and didn't answer. He didn't because all this was ridiculous, because he didn't trust himself to say anything.

"The police couldn't find out," he said after a silence had gone on. The police wouldn't have a telephone number to go on. All they could tell the police was that in a house somewhere in London there was an old woman and a cat. All over London, Tony said, there were old women and cats.

"Tony, try to remember the number."

"Oh, for God's sake! How can I remember the bloody number when I didn't even know it in the first place?"

"Well, then it will be in the computers."

"What computers?"

"In Germany all calls go into the computers."

"Look, we can't just walk round to a police station at nearly three o'clock in the morning to report that an old woman has gone up to her loft. It was a harmless game, Liese."

She tried to say nothing, but did not succeed. The words came anyway, unchosen, ignoring her will.

"It is a horrible game. How can it not be horrible when it ends like this?"

The old woman lies there, Liese heard her own voice insist. And light comes up through the open trapdoor, and the stepladder is below. There are the dusty boards, the water pipes. The cat's eyes are pinpricks in the gloom.

"Has she struck her head, Tony? And bones go brittle when you're old. I'm saying what could be true."

"We have no reason whatsoever to believe any of this has happened."

"The telephone left hanging—"

"She did not replace the telephone because she forgot to."

"You asked her to come back. You said to do what you asked and to tell you if it was done."

"Sometimes people can tell immediately that it's a put-up thing."

"Hullo! Hullo!" Liese agitatedly shouted into the receiver. "Hullo . . . Please."

"Liese, we have to wait until she wakes up again."

"At least the cat will keep the mice away."

Other people will see the lights left on. Other people will come to the house and find the dangling telephone. Why should an old woman in her nightclothes set a stepladder under a trapdoor? The people who come will ask that. They'll give the cat a plate of milk and then they'll put the telephone back, and one of them will climb up the ladder.

"I wish it had happened some other night."

"Liese—"

"You wanted to put the receiver back. You wanted not to know. You wanted us forever not to know, to make a darkness of it."

"No, of course I didn't."

"Sometimes a person doesn't realize. A person acts in some way and doesn't realize."

"Please," Tony begged again and Liese felt his arms around her. Tears for a moment smudged away the room they were in, softly he stroked her hair. When she could speak she whispered through his murmured consolation, repeating that she wished all this had happened sooner, not tonight. As though some illness had struck her, she experienced a throbbing ache, somewhere in her body, she didn't know where. That came from muddle and confusion was what she thought, or else from being torn apart, as if she possessed two selves. There was not room for quarrels between them. There had not been, there was not still. Why had it happened tonight, why now? Imagining was Gothic castles and the fairy tales she made up when she was in Fräulein Groenewold's kindergarten, and fantasies with favorite film stars later on. It became a silliness when reality was distorted. Of course he was right.

"I can't help thinking of her," Liese whispered nonetheless. "I cannot help it."

Tony turned away, and slowly crossed to the window. He wanted to be outside, to walk about the streets, to have a chance to think. He had been asked to reason with Liese when she wanted her wedding to be in London. A longish letter had come from Schelesnau, pleading with him to intervene, to make her see sense. It was inconvenient for everyone; it was an added and unnecessary expense; it was *exzentrisch* of her.

Tonight Liese had learned that Tony had been daring as a boy, that he had walked along a ledge from one dormitory window to another, eighteen feet above the ground. She had delighted in that—that he had not told her himself, that he was courageous and did not boast of it. Yet everything seemed different now.

"It is a feeling," Liese said.

At the window, Tony stared down into the empty street. The artificial light had not yet been extinguished and would not be for hours. Yet dawn had already crept in, among the parked cars, the plastic sacks brought up from basements the night before, bicycles chained to railings. What did she mean, a feeling?

"Honestly, there is no reason to be upset."

As he spoke, Tony turned from the window. Liese's face was tight and nervous now, for a moment not beautiful. The air that came into the room was refreshingly cold, and again he wanted to be walking in it, alone somewhere. She did not love him was what she meant, she had been taken from him. He said so, staring down into the street again, his back to her.

"Oh no, I love you, Tony."

All over London, sleeping now, were tomorrow's wedding guests—her mother and her father, her friends come all the way from Schelesnau. Her sisters' bridesmaids' dresses were laid out. Flowers had been ordered, and a beribboned car. The grass of the hotel lawns was trimmed for the reception. In her house by the sea Tony's aunt had ironed the clothes she'd chosen, and Liese imagined them waiting on their hangers. The morning flights would bring more guests from Germany. She had been stubborn about the city of their romance. There would have been no old woman's sleep disturbed in Schelesnau, no ugly unintended incident. Why did she know that the dead were carried from a house in a plain long box, not a coffin?

"We are different kinds of people, Tony."

"Because you are German and I am English? Is that it? That history means something after all?"

She shook her head. Why did he think that? Why did he seize such a useful cliché?

"We are not enemies, we are friends." She said a little more, trying to explain what did not seem to her to be complicated. Yet she felt she made it so, for the response was bewilderment. And Tony said, "Remember that office party? The quarrelling woman in red? The waitress smiling when we went off together? 00178. Remember that?"

She tried to, but the images would not come as clearly as they usually did. "Yes, I remember," she said.

The doubt in their exchanges brought hesitation, was an inflection that could not be disguised. Silences came, chasms that each time were wider.

"This has to do with us, not with the past we did not know." Liese shook her head, firm in her emphasis.

Tony nodded and, saying nothing, felt the weight of patience. He wondered about it in a silence that went on for minutes, before there was the far-off rattle of a human voice, faint and small. He looked from the window to where Liese had laid the receiver on the table. He watched her move to pick it up, and saw, an instant later, the glow of relief spreading in her face.

The wedding guests strolled on tidy hotel lawns. A photographer fussed beneath a bright blue sky. "You are more beautiful than I ever knew," Tony whispered while more champagne was drunk and there was talk in German and in English. "And I love you more."

Liese smiled in the moment they had purloined, before another speech was called for, before her father expressed his particular joy that the union of two families brought with it today the union of two nations. "We are two foolish people," Tony had said when at last the telephone receiver was replaced, after the journey to the loft had been retailed in detail, an apology offered because carrying out the instructions had taken so long. They had embraced, clinging to one another tightly, gratefully delivered from their territory of unease. And the shadow of truth that had come was lost in the euphoria.

"I'm sorry," Liese said in the next day's sunshine. "I'm sorry I was a nuisance."

Glasses were raised to greater happiness than the happiness of the day. Together they smiled and waved from the car when it came to take them away. Then private at last, they let their tiredness show, each reaching for a hand. Their thoughts were different. He had been right. Yet again, for Tony, that conclusion repeated itself: not once in the night had he doubted that he'd been right. And Liese wondered why it was that passing incidents seemed more significant in people's lives and their relationships than the enmity or amity of nations. For a moment she wanted to speak of that, and almost did before deciding not to.

THE THIRD AND FINAL CONTINENT

BY JHUMPA LAHIRI (1999)

I left India in 1964 with a certificate in commerce and the equivalent, in those days, of ten dollars to my name. For three weeks I sailed on the S.S. Roma, an Italian cargo vessel, in a cabin next to the ship's engine, across the Arabian Sea, the Red Sea, the Mediterranean, and finally to England. I lived in London, in Finsbury Park, in a house occupied entirely by penniless Bengali bachelors like myself, at least a dozen and sometimes more, all struggling to educate and establish ourselves abroad.

I attended lectures at L.S.E. and worked at the university library to get by. We lived three or four to a room, shared a single, icy toilet, and took turns cooking pots of egg curry, which we ate with our hands on a table covered with newspapers. Apart from our jobs we had few responsibilities. On weekends we lounged barefoot in drawstring pajamas, drinking tea and smoking Rothmans, or set out to watch cricket at Lord's. Some weekends the house was crammed with still more Bengalis, to whom we had introduced ourselves at the greengrocer, or on the Tube, and we made yet more egg curry, and played Mukesh on a Grundig reel-to-reel, and soaked our dirty dishes in the bathtub. Every now and then someone in the house moved out, to live with a woman whom his family back in Calcutta had determined he was to wed. In 1969, when I was thirty-six years old, my own marriage was arranged. Around the same time, I was offered a full-time job in America, in the processing department of a library at M.I.T. The salary was generous enough to support a wife, and I was honored to be hired by a world-famous university, and so I obtained a green card, and prepared to travel farther still.

By then I had enough money to go by plane. I flew first to Calcutta, to attend my wedding, and a week later to Boston, to begin my new job. During the flight I read "The Student Guide to North America," for although I was no longer a student, I was on a budget all the same. I learned that Americans drove on the right side of the road, not the left, and that they called a lift an elevator and an engaged phone busy. "The pace of life in North America is different from Britain, as you will soon discover," the guidebook informed me. "Everybody feels he must get to the top. Don't expect an English cup of tea." As the plane began its descent over Boston Harbor, the pilot announced the weather and the time, and that President Nixon had declared a national holiday: two American men had landed on the moon. Several passengers cheered. "God bless America!" one of them hollered. Across the aisle, I saw a woman praying.

I spent my first night at the Y.M.C.A. in Central Square, Cambridge, an inexpensive accommodation recommended by my guidebook which was within walking distance of M.I.T. The room contained a cot, a desk, and a small wooden cross on one wall. A sign on the door said that cooking was strictly forbidden. A bare window overlooked Massachusetts Avenue. Car horns, shrill and prolonged, blared one after another. Sirens and flashing lights heralded endless emergencies, and a succession of buses rumbled past, their doors opening and closing with a powerful hiss, throughout the night. The noise was constantly distracting, at times suffocating. I felt it deep in my ribs, just as I had felt the furious drone of the engine on the S.S. Roma. But there was no ship's deck to escape to, no glittering ocean to thrill my soul, no breeze to cool my face, no one to talk to. I was too tired to pace the gloomy corridors of the Y.M.C.A. in my pajamas. Instead I sat at the desk and stared out the window. In the morning I reported to my job at the Dewey Library, a beige fortlike building by Memorial Drive. I also opened a bank account, rented a post-office box, and bought a plastic bowl and a spoon. I went to a supermarket called Purity Supreme, wandering up and down the aisles, comparing prices with those in England. In the end I bought a carton of milk and a box of cornflakes. This was my first meal in America. Even the simple chore of buying milk was new to me; in London we'd had bottles delivered each morning to our door.

In a week I had adjusted, more or less. I ate cornflakes and milk morning and night, and bought some bananas for variety, slicing them into the bowl with the edge of my spoon. I left my carton of milk on the shaded part of the windowsill, as I had seen other residents at the Y.M.C.A. do. To pass the time in the evenings I read the Boston *Globe* downstairs, in a spacious room with stained-glass windows. I read every article and advertisement, so that I would grow familiar with things, and when my eyes grew tired I slept. Only I did not sleep well. Each night I had to keep the window wide open; it was the only source of air in the stifling room, and the noise was intolerable. I would lie on the cot with my fingers pressed into my ears, but when I drifted off to sleep my hands fell away, and the noise of the traffic would wake me up again. Pigeon feathers drifted onto the windowsill, and one evening, when I poured milk over my cornflakes, I saw that it had soured. Nevertheless I resolved to stay at the Y.M.C.A. for six weeks, until my wife's passport and green card were ready. Once she arrived I would have to rent a proper apartment, and from time to time I studied the classified section of the newspaper, or stopped in at the housing office at M.I.T. during my lunch break to see what was available. It was in this manner that I discovered a room for immediate occupancy, in a house on a quiet street, the listing said, for eight dollars per week. I dialled the number from a pay telephone, sorting through the coins, with which I was still unfamiliar, smaller and lighter than shillings, heavier and brighter than paisas.

"Who is speaking?" a woman demanded. Her voice was bold and clamorous.

"Yes, good afternoon, Madam. I am calling about the room for rent."

"Harvard or Tech?"

"I beg your pardon?"

"Are you from Harvard or Tech?"

Gathering that Tech referred to the Massachusetts Institute of Technology, I replied, "I work at Dewey Library," adding tentatively, "at Tech."

"I only rent rooms to boys from Harvard or Tech!"

"Yes, Madam."

I was given an address and an appointment for seven o'clock that evening. Thirty minutes before the hour I set out, my guidebook in my pocket, my breath fresh with Listerine. I turned down a street shaded with trees, perpendicular to Massachusetts Avenue. In spite of the heat I wore a coat and tie, regarding the event as I would any other interview; I had never lived in the home of a person who was not Indian. The house, surrounded by a chain-link fence, was off-white with dark-brown trim, with a tangle of forsythia bushes plastered against its front and sides. When I pressed the bell, the woman with whom I had spoken on the phone hollered from what seemed to be just the other side of the door, "One minute, please!"

Several minutes later the door was opened by a tiny, extremely old woman. A mass of snowy hair was arranged like a small sack on top of her head. As I stepped into the house she sat down on a wooden bench positioned at the bottom of a narrow carpeted staircase. Once she was settled on the bench, in a small pool of light, she peered up at me, giving me her undivided attention. She wore a long black skirt that spread like a stiff tent to the floor, and a starched white shirt edged with ruffles at the throat and cuffs. Her hands, folded together in her lap, had long pallid fingers, with swollen knuckles and tough yellow nails. Age had battered her features so that she almost resembled a man, with sharp, shrunken eyes and prominent creases on either side of her nose. Her lips, chapped and faded, had nearly disappeared, and her eyebrows were missing altogether. Nevertheless she looked fierce.

"Lock up!" she commanded. She shouted even though I stood only a few feet away. "Fasten the chain and firmly press that button on the knob! This is the first thing you shall do when you enter, is that clear?"

I locked the door as directed and examined the house. Next to the bench was a small round table, its legs fully concealed, much like the woman's, by a skirt of lace. The table held a lamp, a transistor radio, a leather change purse with a silver clasp, and a telephone. A thick wooden cane was propped against one side. There was a parlor to my right, lined with bookcases and filled with shabby claw-footed furniture. In the corner of the parlor I saw a grand piano with its top down, piled with papers. The piano's bench was missing; it seemed to be the one on which the woman was sitting. Somewhere in the house a clock chimed seven times.

"You're punctual!" the woman proclaimed. "I expect you shall be so with the rent!"

"I have a letter, Madam." In my jacket pocket was a letter from M.I.T. confirming my employment, which I had brought along to prove that I was indeed from Tech.

She stared at the letter, then handed it back to me carefully, gripping it with her fingers as if it were a plate heaped with food. She did not wear glasses, and I wondered if she'd read a word of it. "The last boy was always late! Still owes me eight dollars! Harvard boys aren't what they used to be! Only Harvard and Tech in this house! How's Tech, boy?"

"It is very well."

"You checked the lock?"

"Yes, Madam."

She unclasped her fingers, slapped the space beside her on the bench with one hand, and told me to sit down. For a moment she was silent. Then she intoned, as if she alone possessed this knowledge: "There is an American flag on the moon!"

"Yes, Madam." Until then I had not thought very much about the moon shot. It was in the newspaper, of course, article upon article. The astronauts had landed on the shores of the Sea of Tranquillity, I had read, travelling farther than anyone in the history of civilization. For a few hours they explored the moon's surface. They gathered rocks in their pockets, described their surroundings (a magnificent desolation, according to one astronaut), spoke by phone to the President, and planted a flag in lunar soil. The voyage was hailed as man's most awesome achievement.

The woman bellowed, "A flag on the moon, boy! I heard it on the radio! Isn't that splendid?"

"Yes, Madam."

But she was not satisfied with my reply. Instead she commanded, "Say 'Splendid!'"

I was both baffled and somewhat insulted by the request. It reminded me of the way I was taught multiplication tables as a child, repeating after the master, sitting cross-legged on the floor of my one-room Tollygunge school. It also reminded me of my wedding, when I had repeated endless Sanskrit verses after the priest, verses I barely understood, which joined me to my wife. I said nothing.

"Say 'Splendid!'" the woman bellowed once again.

"Splendid," I murmured. I had to repeat the word a second time at the top of my lungs, so she could hear. I was reluctant to raise my voice to an elderly woman, but she did not appear to be offended. If anything the reply pleased her, because her next command was:

"Go see the room!"

I rose from the bench and mounted the narrow staircase. There were five doors, two on either side of an equally narrow hallway, and one at the opposite end. Only one door was open. The room contained a twin bed under a sloping ceiling, a brown oval rug, a basin with an exposed pipe, and a chest of drawers. One door led to a closet, another to a toilet and a tub. The window was open; net curtains stirred in the breeze. I lifted them away and inspected the view: a small back yard, with a few fruit trees and an empty clothesline. I was satisfied.

When I returned to the foyer the woman picked up the leather change purse on the table, opened the clasp, fished about with her fingers, and produced a key on a thin wire hoop. She informed me that there was a kitchen at the back of the house, accessible through the parlor. I was welcome to use the stove as long as I left it as I found it. Sheets and towels were provided, but keeping them clean was my own responsibility. The rent was due Friday mornings on the ledge above the piano keys. "And no lady visitors!"

"I am a married man, Madam." It was the first time I had announced this fact to anyone.

But she had not heard. "No lady visitors!" she insisted. She introduced herself as Mrs. Croft.

My wife's name was Mala. The marriage had been arranged by my older brother and his wife. I regarded the proposition with neither objection nor enthusiasm. It was a duty expected of me, as it was expected of every man. She was the daughter of a schoolteacher in Beleghata. I was told that she could cook, knit, embroider, sketch landscapes, and recite poems by Tagore, but these talents could not make up for the fact that she did not possess a fair complexion, and so a string of men had rejected her to her face. She was twenty-seven, an age when her parents had begun to fear that she would never marry, and so they were willing to ship their only child halfway across the world in order to save her from spinsterhood.

For five nights we shared a bed. Each of those nights, after applying cold cream and braiding her hair, she turned from me and wept; she missed her parents. Although I would be leaving the country in a few days, custom dictated that she was now a part of my household, and for the next six weeks she was to live with my brother and his wife, cooking, cleaning, serving tea and sweets to guests. I did nothing to console her. I lay on my own side of the bed, reading my guidebook by flashlight. At times I thought of the tiny room on the other side of the wall which had belonged to my mother. Now the room was practically empty; the wooden pallet on which she'd once slept was piled with trunks and old bedding. Nearly six years ago, before leaving for London, I had watched her die on that bed, had found her playing with her excrement in her final days. Before we cremated her I had cleaned each of her fingernails with a hairpin, and then, because my brother could not bear it, I had assumed the role of eldest son, and had touched the flame to her temple, to release her tormented soul to heaven.

The next morning I moved into Mrs. Croft's house. When I unlocked the door I saw that she was sitting on the piano bench, on the same side as the previous evening. She wore the same black skirt, the same starched white blouse, and had her hands folded together the same way in her lap. She looked so much the same that I wondered if she'd spent the whole night on the bench. I put my suitcase upstairs and then headed off to work. That evening when I came home from the university, she was still there.

"Sit down, boy!" She slapped the space beside her.

I perched on the bench. I had a bag of groceries with me—more milk, more cornflakes, and more bananas, for my inspection of the kitchen earlier in the day had revealed no spare pots or pans. There were only two saucepans in the refrigerator, both containing some orange broth, and a copper kettle on the stove.

"Good evening, Madam."

She asked me if I had checked the lock. I told her I had.

For a moment she was silent. Then suddenly she declared, with the equal measures of disbelief and delight as the night before, "There's an American flag on the moon, boy!"

"Yes, Madam."

"A flag on the moon! Isn't that splendid?"

I nodded, dreading what I knew was coming. "Yes, Madam."

"Say 'Splendid!' "

This time I paused, looking to either side in case anyone was there to overhear me, though I knew perfectly well that the house was empty. I felt like an idiot. But it was a small enough thing to ask. "Splendid!" I cried out.

Within days it became our routine. In the mornings when I left for the library Mrs. Croft was either hidden away in her bedroom, on the other side of the staircase, or sitting on the bench, oblivious of my presence, listening to the news or classical music on the radio. But each evening when I returned the same thing happened: she slapped the bench, ordered me to sit down, declared that there was a flag on the moon, and declared that it was splendid. I said it was splendid, too, and then we sat in silence. As awkward as it was, and as endless as it felt to me then, the nightly encounter lasted only about ten minutes; inevitably she would drift off to sleep, her head falling abruptly toward her chest, leaving me free to retire to my room. By then, of course, there was no flag standing on the moon. The astronauts, I read in the paper, had seen it fall before they flew back to Earth. But I did not have the heart to tell her.

Friday morning, when my first week's rent was due, I went to the piano in the parlor to place my money on the ledge. The piano keys were dull and discolored. When I pressed one, it made no sound at all. I had put eight dollar bills in an envelope and written Mrs. Croft's name on the front of it. I was not in the habit of leaving money unmarked and unattended. From where I stood I could see the profile of her tent-shaped skirt in the hall. It seemed unnecessary to make her get up and walk all the way to the piano. I never saw her walking about, and assumed, from the cane propped against the round table, that she did so with difficulty. When I approached the bench she peered up at me and demanded:

"What is your business?"

"The rent, Madam."

"On the ledge above the piano keys!"

"I have it here." I extended the envelope toward her, but her fingers, folded together in her lap, did not budge. I bowed slightly and lowered the envelope, so that it hovered just above her hands. After a moment she accepted it, and nodded her head.

That night when I came home, she did not slap the bench, but out of habit I sat beside her as usual. She asked me if I had checked the lock, but she mentioned nothing about the flag on the moon. Instead she said:

"It was very kind of you!"

"I beg your pardon, Madam?"

"Very kind of you!"

She was still holding the envelope in her hands.

On Sunday there was a knock on my door. An elderly woman introduced herself: she was Mrs. Croft's daughter, Helen. She walked into the room and looked at each of the walls as if for signs of change, glancing at the shirts that hung in the closet, the neckties draped over the doorknob, the box of cornflakes on the chest of drawers, the dirty bowl and spoon in the basin. She was short and thick-waisted, with cropped silver hair and bright pink lipstick. She wore a sleeveless summer dress, a necklace of white plastic beads, and spectacles on a chain that hung like a swing against her chest. The backs of her legs were mapped with dark-blue veins, and her upper arms sagged like the flesh of a roasted eggplant. She told me she lived in Arlington, a town farther up Massachusetts Avenue. "I come once a week to bring Mother groceries. Has she sent you packing yet?"

"It is very well, Madam."

"Some of the boys run screaming. But I think she likes you. You're the first boarder she's ever referred to as a gentleman."

She looked at me, noticing my bare feet. (I still felt strange wearing shoes indoors, and always removed them before entering my room.) "Are you new to Boston?"

"New to America, Madam."

"From?" She raised her eyebrows.

"I am from Calcutta, India."

"Is that right? We had a Brazilian fellow, about a year ago. You'll find Cambridge a very international city."

I nodded, and began to wonder how long our conversation would last. But at that moment we heard Mrs. Croft's electrifying voice rising up the stairs.

"You are to come downstairs immediately!"

"What is it?" Helen cried back.

"Immediately!"

I put on my shoes. Helen sighed.

I followed Helen down the staircase.

She seemed to be in no hurry, and complained at one point that she had a bad knee. "Have you been walking without your cane?" Helen called out. "You know you're not supposed to walk without that cane." She paused, resting her hand on the bannister, and looked back at me. "She slips sometimes."

For the first time Mrs. Croft seemed vulnerable. I pictured her on the floor in front of the bench, flat on her back, staring at the ceiling, her feet pointing in opposite directions. But when we reached the bottom of the staircase she was sitting there as usual, her hands folded together in her lap. Two grocery bags were at her feet. She did not slap the bench, or ask us to sit down. She glared.

"What is it, Mother?"

"It's improper!"

"What's improper?"

"It is improper for a lady and gentleman who are not married to one another to hold a private conversation without a chaperone!"

Helen said she was sixty-eight years old, old enough to be my mother, but Mrs. Croft insisted that Helen and I speak to each other downstairs, in the parlor. She added that it was also improper for a lady of Helen's station to reveal her age, and to wear a dress so high above the ankle.

"For your information, Mother, it's 1969. What would you do if you actually left the house one day and saw a girl in a miniskirt?"

Mrs. Croft sniffed. "I'd have her arrested."

Helen shook her head and picked up one of the grocery bags. I picked up the other one, and followed her through the parlor and into the kitchen. The bags were filled with cans of soup, which

Helen opened up one by one with a few cranks of a can opener. She tossed the old soup into the sink, rinsed the saucepans under the tap, filled them with soup from the newly opened cans, and put them back in the refrigerator. "A few years ago she could still open the cans herself," Helen said. "She hates that I do it for her now. But the piano killed her hands." She put on her spectacles, glanced at the cupboards, and spotted my tea bags. "Shall we have a cup?"

I filled the kettle on the stove. "I beg your pardon, Madam. The piano?"

"She used to give lessons. For forty years. It was how she raised us after my father died." Helen put her hands on her hips, staring at the open refrigerator. She reached into the back, pulled out a wrapped stick of butter, frowned, and tossed it into the garbage. "That ought to do it," she said, and put the unopened cans of soup in the cupboard. I sat at the table and watched as Helen washed the dirty dishes, tied up the garbage bag, and poured boiling water into two cups. She handed one to me without milk, and sat down at the table.

"Excuse me, Madam, but is it enough?"

Helen took a sip of her tea. Her lipstick left a smiling pink stain on the rim of the cup. "Is what enough?"

"The soup in the pans. Is it enough food for Mrs. Croft?"

"She won't eat anything else. She stopped eating solids after she turned one hundred. That was, let's see, three years ago."

I was mortified. I had assumed Mrs. Croft was in her eighties, perhaps as old as ninety. I had never known a person who had lived for over a century. That this person was a widow who lived alone mortified me further still. Widowhood had driven my own mother insane. My father, who worked as a clerk at the General Post Office of Calcutta, died of encephalitis when I was sixteen. My mother refused to adjust to life without him; instead she sank deeper into a world of darkness from which neither I, nor my brother, nor concerned relatives, nor psychiatric clinics on Rash Behari Avenue could save her. What pained me most was to see her so unguarded, to hear her burp after meals or expel gas in front of company without the slightest embarrassment. After my father's death my brother abandoned his schooling and began to work in the jute mill he would eventually manage, in order to keep the household running. And so it was my job to sit by my mother's feet and study for my exams as she counted and recounted the bracelets on her arm as if they were the beads of an abacus. We tried to keep an eye on her. Once she had wandered half naked to the tram depot before we were able to bring her inside again.

"I am happy to warm Mrs. Croft's soup in the evenings," I suggested. "It is no trouble."

Helen looked at her watch, stood up, and poured the rest of her tea into the sink. "I wouldn't if I were you. That's the sort of thing that would kill her altogether."

That evening, when Helen had gone and Mrs. Croft and I were alone again, I began to worry. Now that I knew how very old she was, I worried that something would happen to her in the middle of the night, or when I was out during the day. As vigorous as her voice was, and imperious as she seemed, I knew that even a scratch or a cough could kill a person that old; each day she lived, I knew, was something of a miracle. Helen didn't seem concerned. She came and went, bringing soup for Mrs. Croft, one Sunday after the next.

In this manner the six weeks of that summer passed. I came home each evening, after my hours at the library, and spent a few minutes on the piano bench with Mrs. Croft. Some evenings I sat beside her long after she had drifted off to sleep, still in awe of how many years she had spent on this earth. At times I tried to picture the world she had been born into, in 1866—a world, I imagined, filled with women in long black skirts, and chaste conversations in the parlor. Now, when I looked at her hands with their swollen knuckles folded together in her lap, I imagined them smooth and slim, striking the piano keys. At times I came downstairs before going to sleep, to make sure she was sitting upright on the bench, or was safe in her bedroom. On Fridays I put the rent in her hands. There was nothing I could do for her beyond these simple gestures. I was not her son, and, apart from those eight dollars, I owed her nothing.

At the end of August, Mala's passport and green card were ready. I received a telegram with her flight information; my brother's house in Calcutta had no telephone. Around that time I also received a letter from her, written only a few days after we had parted. There was no salutation; addressing me by name would have assumed an intimacy we had not yet discovered. It contained only a few lines. "I write in English in preparation for the journey. Here I am very much lonely. Is it very cold there. Is there snow. Yours, Mala."

I was not touched by her words. We had spent only a handful of days in each other's company. And yet we were bound together; for six weeks she had worn an iron bangle on her wrist, and applied vermillion powder to the part in her hair, to signify to the world that she was a bride. In those six weeks I regarded her arrival as I would the arrival of a coming month, or season—something inevitable, but meaningless at the time. So little did I know her that, while details of her face sometimes rose to my memory, I could not conjure up the whole of it.

A few days after receiving the letter, as I was walking to work in the morning, I saw an Indian woman on Massachusetts Avenue, wearing a sari with its free end nearly dragging on the footpath, and pushing a child in a stroller. An American woman with a small black dog on a leash was walking to one side of her. Suddenly the dog began barking. I watched as the Indian woman, startled, stopped in her path, at which point the dog leaped up and seized the end of the sari between its teeth. The American woman scolded the dog, appeared to apologize, and walked quickly away, leaving the Indian woman to fix her sari, and quiet her crying child. She did not see me standing there, and eventually she continued on her way. Such a mishap, I realized that morning, would soon be my concern. It was my duty to take care of Mala, to welcome her and protect her. I would have to buy her her first pair of snow boots, her first winter coat. I would have to tell her which streets to avoid, which way the traffic came, tell her to wear her sari so that the free end did not drag on the footpath. A five-mile separation from her parents, I recalled with some irritation, had caused her to weep.

Unlike Mala, I was used to it all by then: used to cornflakes and milk, used to Helen's visits, used to sitting on the bench with Mrs. Croft. The only thing I was not used to was Mala. Nevertheless I did what I had to do. I went to the housing office at M.I.T. and found a furnished apartment a few blocks away, with a double bed and a private kitchen and bath, for forty dollars a week. One last Friday I handed Mrs. Croft eight dollar bills in an envelope, brought my suitcase downstairs, and informed her that I was moving. She put my key into her change purse. The last thing she asked me to do was hand her the cane propped against the table, so that she could walk to the door and lock it behind me. "Goodbye, then," she said, and retreated back into the house. I did not expect any display of emotion, but I was disappointed all the same. I was only a boarder, a man who paid her a bit of money and passed in and out of her home for six weeks. Compared with a century, it was no time at all.

At the airport I recognized Mala immediately. The free end of her sari did not drag on the floor, but was draped in a sign of bridal modesty over her head, just as it had draped my mother until the day my father died. Her thin brown arms were stacked with gold bracelets, a small red circle was painted on her forehead, and the edges of her feet were tinted with a decorative red dye. I did not embrace her, or kiss her, or take her hand. Instead I asked her, speaking Bengali for the first time in America, if she was hungry.

She hesitated, then nodded yes.

I told her I had prepared some egg curry at home. "What did they give you to eat on the plane?"

"I didn't eat."

"All the way from Calcutta?"

"The menu said oxtail soup."

"But surely there were other items."

"The thought of eating an ox's tail made me lose my appetite."

When we arrived home, Mala opened up one of her suitcases, and presented me with two pullover sweaters, both made with bright-blue wool, which she had knitted in the course of our separation, one with a V neck, the other covered with cables. I tried them on; both were tight under the arms. She had also brought me two new pairs of drawstring pajamas, a letter from my brother, and a packet of loose Darjeeling tea. I had no present for her apart from the egg curry. We sat at a bare table, staring at our plates. We ate with our hands, another thing I had not yet done in America.

"The house is nice," she said. "Also the egg curry." With her left hand she held the end of her sari to her chest, so it would not slip off her head.

"I don't know many recipes."

She nodded, peeling the skin off each of her potatoes before eating them. At one point the sari slipped to her shoulders. She readjusted it at once.

"There is no need to cover your head," I said. "I don't mind. It doesn't matter here."

She kept it covered anyway.

I waited to get used to her, to her presence at my side, at my table and in my bed, but a week later we were still strangers. I still was not used to coming home to an apartment that smelled of steamed rice, and finding that the basin in the bathroom was always wiped clean, our two toothbrushes lying side by side, a cake of Pears soap residing in the soap dish. I was not used to the fragrance of the coconut oil she rubbed every other night into her scalp, or the delicate sound her bracelets made as she moved about the apartment. In the mornings she was always awake before I was. The first morning when I came into the kitchen she had heated up the leftovers and set a plate with a spoonful of salt on its edge, assuming I would eat rice for breakfast, as most Bengali husbands did. I told her cereal would do, and the next morning when I came into the kitchen she had already poured the cornflakes into my bowl. One morning she walked with me to M.I.T., where I gave her a short tour of the campus. The next morning before I left for work she asked me for a few dollars. I parted with them reluctantly, but I knew that this, too, was now normal. When I came home from work there was a potato peeler in the kitchen drawer, and a tablecloth on the table, and chicken curry made with fresh garlic and ginger on the stove. After dinner I read the newspaper, while Mala sat at the kitchen table, working on a cardigan for herself with more of the blue wool, or writing letters home.

On Friday, I suggested going out. Mala set down her knitting and disappeared into the bathroom. When she emerged I regretted the suggestion; she had put on a silk sari and extra bracelets, and coiled her hair with a flattering side part on top of her head. She was prepared as if for a party, or at the very least for the cinema, but I had no such destination in mind. The evening was balmy. We walked several blocks down Massachusetts Avenue, looking into the windows of restaurants and shops. Then, without thinking, I led her down the quiet street where for so many nights I had walked alone.

"This is where I lived before you came," I said, stopping at Mrs. Croft's chain-link fence.

"In such a big house?"

"I had a small room upstairs. At the back."

"Who else lives there?"

"A very old woman."

"With her family?"

"Alone."

"But who takes care of her?"

I opened the gate. "For the most part she takes care of herself."

I wondered if Mrs. Croft would remember me; I wondered if she had a new boarder to sit with her each evening. When I pressed the bell I expected the same long wait as that day of our first meeting, when I did not have a key. But this time the door was opened almost immediately, by Helen. Mrs. Croft was not sitting on the bench. The bench was gone.

"Hello there," Helen said, smiling with her bright pink lips at Mala. "Mother's in the parlor. Will you be visiting awhile?"

"As you wish, Madam."

"Then I think I'll run to the store, if you don't mind. She had a little accident. We can't leave her alone these days, not even for a minute."

I locked the door after Helen and walked into the parlor. Mrs. Croft was lying flat on her back, her head on a peach-colored cushion, a thin white quilt spread over her body. Her hands were folded together on her chest. When she saw me she pointed at the sofa, and told me to sit down. I took my place as directed, but Mala wandered over to the piano and sat on the bench, which was now positioned where it belonged.

"I broke my hip!" Mrs. Croft announced, as if no time had passed.

"Oh dear, Madam."

"I fell off the bench!"

"I am so sorry, Madam."

"It was the middle of the night! Do you know what I did, boy?"

I shook my head.

"I called the police!"

She stared up at the ceiling and grinned sedately, exposing a crowded row of long gray teeth. "What do you say to that, boy?"

As stunned as I was, I knew what I had to say. With no hesitation at all, I cried out, "Splendid!"

Mala laughed then. Her voice was full of kindness, her eyes bright with amusement. I had never heard her laugh before, and it was loud enough so that Mrs. Croft heard, too. She turned to Mala and glared.

"Who is she, boy?"

"She is my wife, Madam."

Mrs. Croft pressed her head at an angle against the cushion to get a better look. "Can you play the piano?"

"No, Madam," Mala replied.

"Then stand up!"

Mala rose to her feet, adjusting the end of her sari over her head and holding it to her chest, and, for the first time since her arrival, I felt sympathy. I remembered my first days in London, learning how to take the Tube to Russell Square, riding an escalator for the first time, unable to understand that when the man cried "piper" it meant "paper," unable to decipher, for a whole year, that the conductor said "Mind the gap" as the train pulled away from each station. Like me, Mala had travelled far from home, not knowing where she was going, or what she would find, for no reason other than to be my wife. As strange as it seemed, I knew in my heart that one day her death would affect me, and stranger still, that mine would affect her. I wanted somehow to explain this to Mrs. Croft, who was still scrutinizing Mala from top to toe with what seemed to be placid disdain. I wondered if Mrs. Croft had ever seen a woman in a sari, with a dot painted on her forehead and bracelets stacked on her wrists. I wondered what she would object to. I wondered if she could see the red dye still vivid on Mala's feet, all but obscured by the bottom edge of her sari. At last Mrs. Croft declared, with the equal measures of disbelief and delight I knew well:

"She is a perfect lady!"

Now it was I who laughed. I did so quietly, and Mrs. Croft did not hear me. But Mala had heard, and, for the first time, we looked at each other and smiled.

I like to think of that moment in Mrs. Croft's parlor as the moment when the distance between Mala and me began to lessen. Although we were not yet fully in love, I like to think of the months that followed as a honeymoon of sorts. Together we explored the city and met other Bengalis, some of whom are still friends today. We discovered that a man named Bill sold fresh fish on Prospect Street, and that a shop in Harvard Square called Cardullo's sold bay leaves and cloves. In the evenings we walked to the Charles River to watch sailboats drift across the water, or had ice-cream cones in Harvard Yard. We bought a camera with which to document our life together, and I took pictures of her posing in front of the Prudential Building, so that she could send them to her parents. At night we kissed, shy at first but quickly bold, and discovered pleasure and solace in each other's arms. I told her about my voyage on the S.S. Roma, and about Finsbury Park and the Y.M.C.A., and my evenings on the bench with Mrs. Croft. When I told her stories about my mother, she wept. It was Mala who consoled me when, reading the *Globe* one evening, I came across Mrs. Croft's obituary. I had not thought of her in several months—by then those six weeks of the summer were already a remote interlude in my past—but when I learned of her death I was stricken, so much so that when Mala looked up from her knitting she found me staring at the wall, unable to speak. Mrs. Croft's was the first death I mourned in America, for hers was the first life I had admired; she had left this world at last, ancient and alone, never to return.

As for me, I have not strayed much farther. Mala and I live in a town about twenty miles from Boston, on a tree-lined street much like Mrs. Croft's, in a house we own, with room for guests, and a garden that saves us from buying tomatoes in summer. We are American citizens now, so that we can collect Social Security when it is time. Though we visit Calcutta every few years, we have decided to grow old here. I work in a small college library. We have a son who attends Harvard University. Mala no longer drapes the end of her sari over her head, or weeps at night for her parents, but occasionally she weeps for our son. So we drive to Cambridge to visit him, or bring him home for a weekend, so that he can eat rice with us with his hands, and speak in Bengali, things we sometimes worry he will no longer do after we die.

Whenever we make that drive, I always take Massachusetts Avenue, in spite of the traffic. I barely recognize the buildings now, but each time I am there I return instantly to those six weeks as if they were only the other day, and I slow down and point to Mrs. Croft's street, saying to my son, Here was my first home in America, where I lived with a woman who was a hundred and three. "Remember?" Mala says, and smiles, amazed, as I am, that there was ever a time that we were strangers. My son always expresses his astonishment, not at Mrs. Croft's age but at how little I paid in rent, a fact nearly as inconceivable to him as a flag on the moon was to a woman born in 1866. In my son's eyes I see the ambition that had first hurled me across the world. In a few years he will graduate and pave his own way, alone and unprotected. But I remind myself that he has a father who is still living, a mother who is happy and strong. Whenever he is discouraged, I tell him that if I can survive on three continents, then there is no obstacle he cannot conquer. While the astronauts, heroes forever, spent mere hours on the moon, I have remained in this new world for nearly thirty years. I know that my achievement is quite ordinary. I am not the only man to seek his fortune far from home, and certainly I am not the first. Still, there are times I am bewildered by each mile I have travelled, each meal I have eaten, each person I have known, each room in which I have slept. As ordinary as it all appears, there are times when it is beyond my imagination.

DRINKING COFFEE ELSEWHERE

BY ZZ PACKER (2000)

Orientation games began the day I arrived at Yale from Baltimore. In my group we played heady, frustrating games for smart people. One game appeared to be charades reinterpreted by existentialists; another involved listening to rocks. Then a freshman counsellor made everyone play Trust. The idea was that if you had the faith to fall backward and wait for four scrawny former high-school geniuses to catch you, just before your head cracked on the slate sidewalk, then you might learn to trust your fellow-students. Russian roulette sounded like a better game.

"No way," I said. The white boys were waiting for me to fall, holding their arms out for me, sincerely, gallantly. "No fucking way."

"It's all cool, it's all cool," the counsellor said. Her hair was a shade of blond I'd seen only on *Playboy* covers, and she raised her hands as though backing away from a growling dog. "Sister," she said, in an I'm-down-with-the-struggle voice, "you don't have to play this game. As a person of color, you shouldn't have to fit into any white, patriarchal system."

I said, "It's a bit too late for that."

In the next game, all I had to do was wait in a circle until it was my turn to say what inanimate object I wanted to be. One guy said he'd like to be a gadfly, like Socrates. "Stop me if I wax Platonic," he said. The girl next to him was eating a rice cake. She wanted to be the Earth, she said. Earth with a capital "E."

There was one other black person in the circle. He wore an Exeter T-shirt and his overly elastic expressions resembled a series of facial exercises. At the end of each person's turn, he smiled and bobbed his head with unfettered enthusiasm. "Oh, that was good," he said, as if the game were an experiment he'd set up and the results were turning out better than he'd expected. "Good, good, good!"

When it was my turn I said, "My name is Dina, and if I had to be any object, I guess I'd be a revolver." The sunlight dulled as if on cue. Clouds passed rapidly overhead, presaging rain. I don't know why I said it. Until that moment I'd been good in all the ways that were meant to matter. I was an honor-roll student—though I'd learned long ago not to mention it in the part of Baltimore where I lived. Suddenly I was hard-bitten and recalcitrant, the kind of kid who took pleasure in sticking pins into cats; the kind who chased down smart kids to spray them with mace.

"A revolver," a counsellor said, stroking his chin, as if it had grown a rabbinical beard. "Could you please elaborate?"

The black guy cocked his head and frowned, as if the beakers and Erlenmeyer flasks of his experiment had grown legs and scurried off.

"You were just kidding," the dean said, "about wiping out all of mankind. That, I suppose, was a joke." She squinted at me. One of her hands curved atop the other to form a pink, freckled molehill on her desk.

"Well," I said, "maybe I meant it at the time." I quickly saw that that was not the answer she wanted. "I don't know. I think it's the architecture."

Through the dimming light of the dean's-office window, I could see the fortress of the old campus. On my ride from the bus station to the campus, I'd barely glimpsed New Haven—a flash of crumpled building here, a trio of straggly kids there. A lot like Baltimore. But everything had changed when we reached those streets hooded by the gothic buildings. I imagined how the college must have looked when it was founded, when most of the students owned slaves. I pictured men wearing tights and knickers, smoking pipes.

"The architecture," the dean repeated. She bit her lip and seemed to be making a calculation of some sort. I noticed that she blinked less often than most people. I sat there, waiting to see how long it would be before she blinked again.

My revolver comment won me a year's worth of psychiatric counselling, weekly meetings with Dean Guest, and—since the parents of the roommate I'd never met weren't too hip on the idea of their Amy sharing a bunk bed with a budding homicidal loony—my very own room.

Shortly after getting my first D, I also received the first knock on my door. The female counsellors never knocked. The dean had spoken to them; I was a priority. Every other day, right before dinnertime, they'd look in on me, unannounced. "Just checking up," a counsellor would say. It was the voice of a suburban mother in training. By the second week, I had made a point of sitting in a chair in front of the door, just when I expected a counsellor to pop her head around. This was intended to startle them. I also made a point of being naked. The unannounced visits ended.

The knocking persisted. Through the peephole I saw a white face, distorted and balloonish.

"Let me in." The person looked like a boy but sounded like a girl. "Let me in," the voice repeated.

"Not a chance," I said.

Then the person began to sob, and I heard a back slump against the door. If I hadn't known the person was white from the peephole, I'd have known it from a display like this. Black people didn't knock on strangers' doors, crying. Not that I understood the black people at Yale. There was something pitiful in how cool they were. Occasionally one would reach out to me with missionary zeal, but I'd rebuff that person with haughty silence.

"I don't have anyone to talk to!" the person on the other side of the door cried.

"That is correct."

"When I was a child," the person said, "I played by myself in a corner of the schoolyard all alone. I hated dolls and I hated games, animals were not friendly and birds flew away. If anyone was looking for me I hid behind a tree and cried out 'I am an orphan—' "

I opened the door. It was a she.

"Plagiarist!" I yelled. She had just recited a Frank O'Hara poem as though she'd thought it up herself. I knew the poem because it was one of the few things I'd been forced to read that I wished I'd written myself.

The girl turned to face me, smiling weakly, as though her triumph were not in getting me to open the door but in the fact that she was able to smile at all when she was so accustomed to crying. She was large but not obese, and crying had turned her face the color of raw chicken. She blew her nose into the waist end of her T-shirt, revealing a pale belly.

"How do you know that poem?"

She sniffed. "I'm in your Contemporary Poetry class."

She was Canadian and her name was Heidi, although she said she wanted people to call her Henrik. "That's a guy's name," I said. "What do you want? A sex change?"

She looked at me with so little surprise that I suspected she hadn't discounted this as an option. Then her story came out in teary, hiccup-like bursts. She had sucked some "cute guy's dick" and he'd told everybody and now people thought she was "a slut."

"Why'd you suck his dick? Aren't you a lesbian?"

She fit the bill. Short hair, hard, roach-stomping shoes. Dressed like an aspiring plumber. The lesbians I'd seen on TV were wiry, thin strips of muscle, but Heidi was round and soft and had a moon-like face. Drab mud-colored hair. And lesbians had cats. "Do you have a cat?" I asked.

Her eyes turned glossy with new tears. "No," she said, her voice wavering, "and I'm not a lesbian. Are you?"

"Do I look like one?" I said.

She didn't answer.

"O.K.," I said. "I could suck a guy's dick, too, if I wanted. But I don't. The human penis is one of the most germ-ridden objects there is." Heidi looked at me, unconvinced. "What I meant to say," I began again, "is that I don't like anybody. Period. Guys or girls. I'm a misanthrope."

"I am, too."

"No," I said, guiding her back through my door and out into the hallway. "You're not."

"Have you had dinner?" she asked. "Let's go to Commons."

I pointed to a pyramid of ramen-noodle packages on my windowsill. "See that? That means I never have to go to Commons. Aside from class, I have contact with no one."

"I hate it here, too," she said. "I should have gone to McGill, eh."

"The way to feel better," I said, "is to get some ramen and lock yourself in your room. Everyone will forget about you and that guy's dick and you won't have to see anyone ever again. If anyone looks for you—"

"I'll hide behind a tree."

"A revolver?" Dr. Raeburn said, flipping through a manila folder. He looked up at me as if to ask another question, but he didn't.

Dr. Raeburn was the psychiatrist. He had the gray hair and whiskers of a Civil War general. He was also a chain smoker with beige teeth and a navy wool jacket smeared with ash. He asked about the revolver at the beginning of my first visit. When I was unable to explain myself he smiled, as if this were perfectly respectable.

"Tell me about your parents."

I wondered what he already had on file. The folder was thick, though I hadn't said a thing of significance since Day One.

"My father was a dick and my mother seemed to like him."

He patted his pockets for his cigarettes. "That's some heavy stuff," he said. "How do you feel about Dad?" The man couldn't say the word "father." "Is Dad someone you see often?"

"I hate my father almost as much as I hate the word 'Dad.'"

He started tapping his cigarette.

"You can't smoke in here."

"That's right," he said, and slipped the cigarette back into the packet. He smiled, widening his eyes brightly. "Don't ever start."

I thought that that first encounter would be the last of Heidi, but then her head appeared in a window of Linsly-Chit during my Chaucer class. Next, she swooped down a flight of stairs in Harkness. She hailed me from across Elm Street and found me in the Sterling Library stacks. After one of my meetings with Dr. Raeburn, she was waiting for me outside Health Services, legs crossed, cleaning her fingernails.

"You know," she said, as we walked through Old Campus, "you've got to stop eating ramen. Not only does it lack a single nutrient but it's full of MSG."

"I like eating chemicals," I said. "It keeps the skin radiant."

"There's also hepatitis." She already knew how to get my attention—mention a disease.

"You get hepatitis from unwashed lettuce," I said. "If there's anything safe from the perils of the food chain, it's ramen."

"But you refrigerate what you don't eat. Each time you reheat it, you're killing good bacteria, which then can't keep the bad bacteria in check. A guy got sick from reheating Chinese noodles, and his son died from it. I read it in the *Times*." With this, she put a jovial arm around my neck. I continued walking, a little stunned. Then, just as quickly, she dropped her arm and stopped walking. I stopped, too.

"Did you notice that I put my arm around you?"

"Yes," I said. "Next time, I'll have to chop it off."

"I don't want you to get sick," she said. "Let's eat at Commons."

In the cold air, her arm had felt good.

The problem with Commons was that it was too big; its ceiling was as high as a cathedral's, but below it there were no awestruck worshippers, only eighteen-year-olds at heavy wooden tables, chatting over veal patties and Jell-O.

We got our food, tacos stuffed with meat substitute, and made our way through the maze of tables. The Koreans had a table. Each singing group had a table. The crew team sat at a long table of its own. We passed the black table. The sheer quantity of Heidi's flesh accentuated just how white she was.

"How you doing, sista?" a guy asked, his voice full of accusation, eyeballing me as though I were clad in a Klansman's sheet and hood. "I guess we won't see you till graduation."

"If," I said, "you graduate."

The remark was not well received. As I walked past, I heard protests, angry and loud, as if they'd discovered a cheat at their poker game. Heidi and I found an unoccupied table along the periphery, which was isolated and dark. We sat down. Heidi prayed over her tacos.

"I thought you didn't believe in God," I said.

"Not in the God depicted in the Judeo-Christian Bible, but I do believe that nature's essence is a spirit that—"

"All right," I said. I had begun to eat, and cubes of diced tomato fell from my mouth when I spoke. "Stop right there. Tacos and spirits don't mix."

"You've always got to be so flip," she said. "I'm going to apply for another friend."

"There's always Mr. Dick," I said. "Slurp, slurp."

"You are so lame. So unbelievably lame. I'm going out with Mr. Dick. Thursday night at Atticus. His name is Keith."

Heidi hadn't mentioned Mr. Dick since the day I'd met her. That was more than a month ago and we'd spent a lot of that time together. I checked for signs that she was lying; her habit of smiling too much, her eyes bright and cheeks full, so that she looked like a chipmunk. But she looked normal. Pleased, even, to see me so flustered.

"You're insane! What are you going to do this time?" I asked. "Sleep with him? Then when he makes fun of you, what? Come pound your head on my door reciting the 'Collected Poems of Sylvia Plath'?"

"He's going to apologize for before. And don't call me insane. You're the one going to the psychiatrist."

"Well, I'm not going to suck his dick, that's for sure."

She put her arm around me in mock comfort, but I pushed it off, and ignored her. She touched my shoulder again, and I turned, annoyed, but it wasn't Heidi after all; a sepia-toned boy dressed in khakis and a crisp plaid shirt was standing behind me. He handed me a hot-pink square of paper without a word, then briskly made his way toward the other end of Commons, where the crowds blossomed. Heidi leaned over and read it: "Wear Black Leather—the Less, the Better."

"It's a gay party," I said, crumpling the card. "He thinks we're fucking gay."

Heidi and I signed on to work at the Saybrook Dining Hall as dishwashers. The job consisted of dumping food from plates and trays into a vat of rushing water. It seemed straightforward, but then I learned better. You wouldn't believe what people could do with food until you worked in a dish room. Lettuce and crackers and soup would be bullied into a pulp in the bowl of some bored anorexic; ziti would be mixed with honey and granola; trays would appear heaped with mashed-potato snow women with melted chocolate ice cream for hair. Frat boys arrived at the dish-room window, en masse. They liked to fill glasses with food, then seal them, airtight, onto their trays. If you tried to prize them off, milk, Worcestershire sauce, peas, chunks of bread vomited onto your dish-room uniform.

When this happened one day in the middle of the lunch rush, for what seemed like the hundredth time, I tipped the tray toward one of the frat boys, popping the glasses off so that the mess spurted onto his Shetland sweater.

He looked down at his sweater. "Lesbo bitch!"

"No," I said, "that would be your mother."

Heidi, next to me, clenched my arm in support, but I remained motionless, waiting to see what the frat boy would do. He glared at me for a minute, then walked away.

"Let's take a smoke break," Heidi said.

I didn't smoke, but Heidi had begun to, because she thought it would help her lose weight. As I hefted a stack of glasses through the steamer, she lit up.

"Soft packs remind me of you," she said. "Just when you've smoked them all and you think there's none left, there's always one more, hiding in that little crushed corner." Before I could respond she said, "Oh, God. Not another mouse. You know whose job that is."

By the end of the rush, the floor mats got full and slippery with food. This was when mice tended to appear, scurrying over our shoes; more often than not, a mouse got caught in the grating that covered the drains in the floor. Sometimes the mouse was already dead by the time we noticed it. This one was alive.

"No way," I said. "This time you're going to help. Get some gloves and a trash bag."

"That's all I'm getting. I'm not getting that mouse out of there."

"Put on the gloves," I ordered. She winced, but put them on. "Reach down," I said. "At an angle, so you get at its middle. Otherwise, if you try to get it by its tail, the tail will break off."

"This is filthy, eh."

"That's why we're here," I said. "To clean up filth. Eh."

She reached down, but would not touch the mouse. I put my hand around her arm and pushed it till her hand made contact. The cries from the mouse were soft, songlike. "Oh, my God," she said. "Oh, my God, ohmigod." She wrestled it out of the grating and turned her head away.

"Don't you let it go," I said.

"Where's the food bag? It'll smother itself if I drop it in the food bag. Quick," she said, her head still turned away, her eyes closed, "lead me to it."

"No. We are not going to smother this mouse. We've got to break its neck."

"You're one heartless bitch."

I wondered how to explain that if death is unavoidable it should be quick and painless. My mother had died slowly. At the hospital, they'd said it was kidney failure, but I knew that, in the end, it was my father. He made her scared to live in her own home, until she was finally driven away from it in an ambulance.

"Breaking its neck will save it the pain of smothering," I said. "Breaking its neck is more humane. Take the trash bag and cover it so you won't get any blood on you, then crush."

The loud jets of the steamer had shut off automatically and the dish room grew quiet. Heidi breathed in deeply, then crushed the mouse. She shuddered, disgusted. "Now what?"

"What do you mean, 'Now what?' Throw the little bastard in the trash."

At our third session, I told Dr. Raeburn I didn't mind if he smoked. He sat on the sill of his open window, smoking behind a jungle screen of office plants.

We spent the first ten minutes discussing the Iliad, and whether or not the text actually states that Achilles had been dipped in the River Styx. He said it did, and I said it didn't. After we'd finished with the Iliad, and with my new job in what he called "the scullery," he asked more questions about my parents. I told him nothing. It was none of his business. Instead, I talked about Heidi. I told him about that day in Commons, Heidi's plan to go on a date with Mr. Dick, and the invitation we'd been given to the gay party.

"You seem preoccupied by this soirée." He arched his eyebrows at the word "soirée."

"Wouldn't you be?"

"Dina," he said slowly, in a way that made my name seem like a song title, "have you ever had a romantic interest?"

"You want to know if I've ever had a boyfriend?" I said. "Just go ahead and ask if I've ever fucked anybody."

This appeared to surprise him. "I think that you are having a crisis of identity," he said.

"Oh, is that what this is?"

His profession had taught him not to roll his eyes. Instead, his exasperation revealed itself with a tiny pursing of his lips, as though he'd just tasted something awful and were trying very hard not to offend the cook.

"It doesn't have to be, as you say, someone you've fucked, it doesn't have to be a boyfriend," he said.

"Well, what are you trying to say? If it's not a boy, then you're saying it's a girl—"

"Calm down. It could be a crush, Dina." He lit one cigarette off another. "A crush on a male teacher, a crush on a dog, for heaven's sake. An interest. Not necessarily a relationship."

It was sacrifice time. If I could spend the next half hour talking about some boy, then I'd have given him what he wanted.

So I told him about the boy with the nice shoes.

I was sixteen and had spent the last few coins in my pocket on bus fare to buy groceries. I didn't like going to the Super Fresh two blocks away from my house, plunking government food stamps into the hands of the cashiers.

"There she go reading," one of them once said, even though I was only carrying a book. "Don't your eyes get tired?"

On Greenmount Avenue you could read schoolbooks—that was understandable. The government and your teachers forced you to read them. But anything else was anti-social. It meant you'd rather submit to the words of some white dude than shoot the breeze with your neighbors.

I hated those cashiers, and I hated them seeing me with food stamps, so I took the bus and shopped elsewhere. That day, I got off the bus at Govans, and though the neighborhood was black like my own—hair salon after hair salon of airbrushed signs promising arabesque hair styles and inch-long fingernails—the houses were neat and orderly, nothing at all like Greenmount, where every other house had at least one shattered window. The store was well swept, and people quietly checked long grocery lists—no screaming kids, no loud cashier-customer altercations. I got the groceries and left the store.

I decided to walk back. It was a fall day, and I walked for blocks. Then I sensed someone following me. I walked more quickly, my arms around the sack, the leafy lettuce tickling my nose. I didn't want to hold the sack so close that it would break the eggs or squash the hamburger buns, but it was slipping, and as I looked behind a boy my age, maybe older, rushed toward me.

"Let me help you," he said.

"That's all right." I set the bag on the sidewalk. Maybe I saw his face, maybe it was handsome enough, but what I noticed first, splayed on either side of the bag, were his shoes. They were nice shoes, real leather, a stitched design like a widow's peak on each one, or like birds' wings, and for the first time in my life I understood what people meant when they said "wing-tip shoes."

"I watched you carry them groceries out that store, then you look around, like you're lost, but like you liked being lost, then you walk down the sidewalk for blocks and blocks. Rearranging that bag, it almost gone to slip, then hefting it back up again."

"Huh, huh," I said.

"And then I passed my own house and was still following you. And then your bag really look like it was gone crash and everything. So I just thought I'd help." He sucked in his bottom lip, as if to keep it from making a smile. "What's your name?" When I told him, he said, "Dina, my name is Cecil." Then he said, "'D' comes right after 'C.'"

"Yes," I said, "it does, doesn't it."

Then, half question, half statement, he said, "I could carry your groceries for you? And walk you home?"

I stopped the story there. Dr. Raeburn kept looking at me. "Then what happened?"

I couldn't tell him the rest: that I had not wanted the boy to walk me home, that I didn't want someone with such nice shoes to see where I lived.

Dr. Raeburn would only have pitied me if I'd told him that I ran down the sidewalk after I told the boy no, that I fell, the bag slipped, and the eggs cracked, their yolks running all over the lettuce. Clear amniotic fluid coated the can of cinnamon rolls. I left the bag there on the sidewalk, the groceries spilled out randomly like cards loosed from a deck. When I returned home, I told my mother that I'd lost the food stamps.

"Lost?" she said. I'd expected her to get angry, I'd wanted her to get angry, but she hadn't. "Lost?" she repeated. Why had I been so clumsy and nervous around a harmless boy? I could have brought the groceries home and washed off the egg yolk, but, instead, I'd just left them there. "Come on," Mama said, snuffing her tears, pulling my arm, trying to get me to join her and start yanking cushions off the couch. "We'll find enough change here. We got to get something for dinner before your father gets back."

We'd already searched the couch for money the previous week, and I knew there'd be nothing now, but I began to push my fingers into the couch's boniest corners, pretending that it was only a matter of time before I'd find some change or a lost watch or an earring. Something pawnable, perhaps.

"What happened next?" Dr. Raeburn asked again. "Did you let the boy walk you home?"

"My house was far, so we went to his house instead." Though I was sure Dr. Raeburn knew that I was making this part up, I continued. "We made out on his sofa. He kissed me."

Dr. Raeburn lit his next cigarette like a detective. Cool, suspicious. "How did it feel?"

"You know," I said. "Like a kiss feels. It felt nice. The kiss felt very, very nice."

Raeburn smiled gently, though he seemed unconvinced. When he called time on our session his cigarette had become one long pole of ash. I left his office, walking quickly down the corridor, afraid to look back. It would be like him to trot after me, his navy blazer flapping, just to eke the truth out of me. *You never kissed anyone.* The words slid from my brain, and knotted in my stomach.

When I reached my dorm, I found an old record player blocking my door and a Charles Mingus LP propped beside it. I carried them inside and then, lying on the floor, I played the Mingus over and over again until I fell asleep. I slept feeling as though Dr. Raeburn had attached electrodes to my head, willing into my mind a dream about my mother. I saw the lemon meringue of her skin, the long bone of her arm as she reached down to clip her toenails. I'd come home from a school trip to an aquarium, and I was explaining the differences between baleen and sperm whales according to the size of their heads, the range of their habitats, their feeding patterns.

I awoke remembering the expression on her face after I'd finished my dizzying whale lecture. She looked like a tourist who'd asked for directions to a place she thought was simple enough to get to only to hear a series of hypothetical turns, alleys, one-way streets. Her response was to nod politely at the perilous elaborateness of it all; to nod in the knowledge that she would never be able to get where she wanted to go.

The dishwashers always closed down the dining hall. One night, after everyone else had punched out, Heidi and I took a break, and though I wasn't a smoker, we set two milk crates upside down on the floor and smoked cigarettes.

The dishwashing machines were off, but steam still rose from them like a jungle mist. Outside in the winter air, students were singing carols in their groomed and tailored singing-group voices. The Whiffenpoofs were back in New Haven after a tour around the world, and I guess their return was a huge deal. Heidi and I craned our necks to watch the year's first snow through an open window.

"What are you going to do when you're finished?" Heidi asked. Sexy question marks of smoke drifted up to the windows before vanishing.

"Take a bath."

She swatted me with her free hand. "No, silly. Three years from now. When you leave Yale."

"I don't know. Open up a library. Somewhere where no one comes in for books. A library in a desert."

She looked at me as though she'd expected this sort of answer and didn't know why she'd asked in the first place.

“What are you going to do?” I asked her.

“Open up a psych clinic. In a desert. And my only patient will be some wacko who runs a library.”

“Ha,” I said. “Whatever you do, don’t work in a dish room ever again. You’re no good.” I got up from the crate. “C’mon. Let’s hose the place down.”

We put out our cigarettes on the floor, since it was our job to clean it, anyway. We held squirt guns in one hand and used the other to douse the floors with the standard-issue, eye-burning cleaning solution. We hosed the dish room, the kitchen, the serving line, sending the water and crud and suds into the drains. Then we hosed them again so the solution wouldn’t eat holes in our shoes as we left. Then I had an idea. I unbuckled my belt.

“What the hell are you doing?” Heidi said.

“Listen, it’s too cold to go outside with our uniforms all wet. We could just take a shower right here. There’s nobody but us.”

“What the fuck, eh?”

I let my pants drop, then took off my shirt and panties. I didn’t wear a bra, since I didn’t have much to fill one. I took off my shoes and hung my clothes on the stepladder.

“You’ve flipped,” Heidi said. “I mean, really, psych-ward flipped.”

I soaped up with the liquid hand soap until I felt as glazed as a ham. “Stand back and spray me.”

“Oh, my God,” she said. I didn’t know whether she was confused or delighted, but she picked up the squirt gun and sprayed me. She was laughing. Then she got too close and the water started to sting.

“God damn it!” I said. “That hurt!”

“I was wondering what it would take to make you say that.”

When all the soap had been rinsed off, I put on my regular clothes and said, “O.K. You’re up next.”

“No way,” she said.

“Yes way.”

She started to take off her uniform shirt, then stopped.

“What?”

“I’m too fat.”

“You goddam right.” She always said she was fat. One time, I’d told her that she should shut up about it, that large black women wore their fat like mink coats. “You’re big as a house,” I said now.

"Frozen yogurt may be low in calories but not if you eat five tubs of it. Take your clothes off. I want to get out of here."

She began taking off her uniform, then stood there, hands cupped over her breasts, crouching at the pubic bone.

"Open up," I said, "or we'll never get done."

Her hands remained where they were. I threw the bottle of liquid soap at her, and she had to catch it, revealing herself as she did.

I turned on the squirt gun, and she stood there, stiff, arms at her sides, eyes closed, as though awaiting mummification. I began with the water on low, and she turned around in a full circle, hesitantly, letting the droplets from the spray fall on her as if she were submitting to a death by stoning.

When I increased the water pressure, she slipped and fell on the sudsy floor. She stood up and then slipped again. This time she laughed and remained on the floor, rolling around on it as I sprayed.

I think I began to love Heidi that night in the dish room, but who is to say that I hadn't begun to love her the first time I met her? I sprayed her and sprayed her, and she turned over and over like a large beautiful dolphin, lolling about in the sun.

Heidi started sleeping at my place. Sometimes she slept on the floor; sometimes we slept sardinelike, my feet at her head, until she complained that my feet were "taunting" her. When we finally slept head to head, she said, "Much better." She was so close I could smell her toothpaste. "I like your hair," she told me, touching it through the darkness. "You should wear it out more often."

"White people always say that about black people's hair. The worse it looks, the more they say they like it."

I'd expected her to disagree, but she kept touching my hair, her hands passing through it till my scalp tingled. When she began to touch the hair around the edge of my face, I felt myself quake. Her fingertips stopped for a moment, as if checking my pulse, then resumed.

"I like how it feels right here. See, mine just starts with the same old texture as the rest of my hair." She found my hand under the blanket and brought it to her hairline. "See," she said.

It was dark. As I touched her hair, it seemed as though I could smell it, too. Not a shampoo smell. Something richer, murkier. A bit dead, but sweet, like the decaying wood of a ship. She guided my hand.

"I see," I said. The record she'd given me was playing in my mind, and I kept trying to shut it off. I could also hear my mother saying that this is what happens when you've been around white people: things get weird. So weird I could hear the stylus etching its way into the flat vinyl of the record. "Listen," I said finally, when the bass and saxes started up. I heard Heidi breathe deeply, but she said nothing.

We spent the winter and some of the spring in my room—never hers—missing tests, listening to music, looking out my window to comment on people who wouldn't have given us a second thought. We read books related to none of our classes. I got riled up by "The Autobiography of Malcolm X" and "The Chomsky Reader"; Heidi read aloud passages from "The Anxiety of Influence." We guiltily read mysteries and "Clan of the Cave Bear," then immediately threw them away. Once, we looked up from our books at exactly the same moment, as though trapped at a dinner table with nothing to say. A pleasant trap of silence.

Then one weekend I went back to Baltimore. When I returned, to a sleepy, tree-scented spring, a group of students were holding what was called "Coming Out Day." I watched it from my room.

The m.c. was the sepia boy who'd invited us to that party months back. His speech was strident but still smooth, and peppered with jokes. There was a speech about AIDS, with lots of statistics: nothing that seemed to make "coming out" worth it. Then the women spoke. One girl pronounced herself "out" as casually as if she'd announced the time. Another said nothing at all: she appeared at the microphone accompanied by a woman who began cutting off her waist-length, bleached-blond hair. The woman doing the cutting tossed the shorn hair in every direction as she cut. People were clapping and cheering and catching the locks of hair.

And then there was Heidi. She was proud that she liked girls, she said when she reached the microphone. She loved them, wanted to sleep with them. She was a dyke, she said repeatedly, stabbing her finger to her chest in case anyone was unsure to whom she was referring. She could not have seen me. I was across the street, three stories up. And yet, when everyone clapped for her, she seemed to be looking straight at me.

Heidi knocked. "Let me in." It was like the first time I met her. The tears, the raw pink of her face.

We hadn't spoken in weeks. Outside, pink-and-white blossoms hung from the Old Campus trees. Students played hackeysack in T-shirts and shorts. Though I was the one who'd broken away after she went up to that podium, I still half expected her to poke her head out a window in Linsly-Chit, or tap on my back in Harkness, or even join me in the Commons dining hall, where I'd asked for my dish-room shift to be transferred. She did none of these.

"Well," I said, "what is it?"

She looked at me. "My mother," she said.

She continued to cry, but it seemed to have grown so silent in my room I wondered if I could hear the numbers change on my digital clock.

"When my parents were getting divorced," she said, "my mother bought a car. A used one. An El Dorado. It was filthy. It looked like a huge crushed can coming up the street. She kept trying to clean it out. I mean—"

I nodded and tried to think what to say in the pause she left behind. Finally I said, "We had one of those," though I was sure ours was an Impala.

She looked at me, eyes steely from trying not to cry. "Anyway, she'd drive me around in it and although she didn't like me to eat in it, I always did. One day, I was eating cantaloupe slices, spitting the seeds on the floor. Maybe a month later, I saw this little sprout, growing right up from the car floor. I just started laughing and she kept saying what, what? I was laughing and then I saw she was so—"

She didn't finish. So what? So sad? So awful? Heidi looked at me with what seemed to be a renewed vigor. "We could have gotten a better car, eh?"

"It's all right. It's not a big deal," I said.

Of course, that was the wrong thing to say. And I really didn't mean it to sound the way it had come out.

. . .

I told Dr. Raeburn about Heidi's mother having cancer and how I'd said it wasn't a big deal, though I'd wanted to say exactly the opposite. I meant that I knew what it was like to have a parent die. My mother had died. I knew how eventually one accustoms oneself to the physical world's lack of sympathy: the buses that still run on time, the kids who still play in the street, the clocks that won't stop ticking for the person who's gone.

"You're pretending," Dr. Raeburn said, not sage or professional but a little shocked by the discovery, as if I'd been trying to hide a pack of his cigarettes behind my back.

"I'm pretending?" I shook my head. "All those years of psych grad," I said. "And to tell me *that*?"

"You construct stories about yourself and dish them out—one for you, one for you—" Here he reënacted the process, showing me handing out lies as if they were apples.

"Pretending. I believe the professional name for it might be denial," I said. "Are you calling me gay?"

He pursed his lips noncommittally. "No, Dina. I don't think you're gay."

I checked his eyes. I couldn't read them.

"No. Not at all," he said, sounding as if he were telling a subtle joke. "But maybe you'll finally understand."

"Understand what?"

"That constantly saying what one doesn't mean accustoms the mouth to meaningless phrases." His eyes narrowed. "Maybe you'll understand that when you need to express something truly significant, your mouth will revert to the insignificant nonsense it knows so well." He looked at me, his hands sputtering in the air in a gesture of defeat. "Who knows?" he asked, with a glib, psychiatric smile I'd never seen before. "Maybe it's your survival mechanism. Black living in a white world."

I heard him, but only vaguely. I'd hooked on to that one word, pretending. What Dr. Raeburn would never understand was that pretending was what had got me this far. I remembered the morning of my mother's funeral. I'd been given milk to settle my stomach; I'd pretended it was coffee. I imagined I was drinking coffee elsewhere. Some Arabic-speaking country where the thick coffee served in little cups was so strong it could keep you awake for days. Some Arabic country where I'd sit in a tented café and be more than happy to don a veil.

Heidi wanted me to go with her to the funeral. She'd sent this message through the dean. "We'll pay for your ticket to Vancouver," the dean said.

"What about my ticket back?" I asked. "Maybe the shrink will pay for that."

The dean looked at me as though I were an insect she'd like to squash. "We'll pay for the whole thing. We might even pay for some lessons in manners."

So I packed my suitcase and walked from my suicide-single dorm to Heidi's room. A thin wispy girl in ragged cutoffs and a shirt that read "LSBN!" answered the door. A group of short-haired girls in thick black leather jackets, bundled up despite the summer heat, encircled Heidi in a protective fairy ring. They looked at me critically, clearly wondering if Heidi was too fragile for my company.

"You've got our numbers," one said, holding on to Heidi's shoulder. "And Vancouver's got a great gay community."

"Oh God," I said. "She's going to a funeral, not a 'Save the Dykes' rally."

One of the girls stepped in front of me.

"It's O.K., Cynthia," Heidi said. Then she ushered me into her bedroom and closed the door. A suitcase was on her bed, half packed. She folded a polka-dotted T-shirt that was wrong for any occasion. "Why haven't you talked to me?" she said. "Why haven't you talked to me in two months?"

"I don't know," I said.

"You don't know," she said, each syllable seeped in sarcasm. "You don't know. Well, I know. You thought I was going to try to sleep with you."

"Try to? We slept together all winter!"

"Smelling your feet is not 'sleeping together.' You've got a lot to learn." She seemed thinner and meaner.

"So tell me," I said. "What can you show me that I need to learn?" But as soon as I said it I somehow knew that she still hadn't slept with anyone.

"Am I supposed to come over there and sweep your enraged self into my arms?" I said. "Like in the movies? Is this the part where we're both so mad we kiss each other?"

She shook her head and smiled weakly. "You don't get it," she said. "My mother is dead." She closed her suitcase, clicking shut the old-fashioned locks. "My mother is dead," she said again, this time reminding herself. She set the suitcase upright on the floor and sat on it. She looked like someone waiting for a train.

"Fine," I said. "And she's going to be dead for a long time." Though it sounded stupid, I felt good saying it. As though I had my own locks to click shut.

Heidi went to Vancouver for her mother's funeral. I didn't go. Instead, I went back to Baltimore and moved in with an aunt I barely knew. Every day was the same: I read and smoked outside my aunt's apartment, studying the row of hair salons across the street, where girls in denim cutoffs and tank tops would troop in and come out hours later, a flash of neon nails, coifs the color and sheen of patent leather. And every day I imagined visiting Heidi in Vancouver. Her house would not be large, but it would be clean. Flowery shrubs would line the walks. The Canadian wind would whip us about like pennants. I'd be visiting her at some vague time in the future, deliberately vague, for people like me, who realign past events to suit themselves. In that future time, you always have a chance to catch the groceries before they fall, your words can always be rewound and erased, rewritten and revised.

But once I imagined Heidi visiting me. There would be no psychiatrists or deans. No boys with nice shoes or flip cashiers. Just me in my single room. She would knock on the door and say, "Open up."

U.F.O. IN KUSHIRO

BY HARUKI MURAKAMI (2001)

Five straight days she spent in front of the television, staring at crumbled banks and hospitals, whole blocks of stores in flames, severed rail lines and expressways. She never said a word. Sunk deep in the cushions of the sofa, her mouth clamped shut, she wouldn't answer when Komura spoke to her. She wouldn't shake her head or nod. Komura could not be sure that the sound of his voice was even getting through to her.

Komura's wife came from way up north in Yamagata, and, as far as he knew, she had no friends or relatives who could have been hurt in Kobe. Yet she stayed planted in front of the television from morning to night. When he got up, Komura would make his own toast and coffee, and head off to work. When he came home in the evening, he'd fix himself a snack with whatever he found in the refrigerator and eat it by himself. She'd still be glaring at the late news when he dropped off to sleep. In his presence, at least, she ate nothing and drank nothing and never went to the toilet. A stone wall of silence surrounded her. Komura gave up trying to break through.

And when he came home from work on Sunday, the sixth day, his wife had disappeared.

Komura was a salesman at one of the oldest audio-equipment stores in Tokyo's Akihabara "Electronics Town." He handled high-end stuff and earned a sizable commission whenever he made a sale.

Most of his clients were doctors, wealthy independent businessmen, and rich provincials. He had been doing this for eight years and had earned a decent income right from the start. The economy was healthy, real-estate prices were rising, and Japan was overflowing with money. Wallets were bursting with ten-thousand-yen bills, and everyone was dying to spend them. The most expensive items were often the first to sell out.

Komura was tall and slim and a stylish dresser. He was good with people. In his bachelor days, he had dated a lot of women. But after getting married, at twenty-six, he found that his desire for sexual adventures simply—and mysteriously—vanished. He hadn't slept with any woman but his wife during the five years of their marriage. Not that the opportunity had never presented itself—but he had lost all interest in fleeting affairs and one-night stands. He much preferred to come home early, have a relaxed meal with his wife, talk with her awhile on the sofa, then go to bed and make love. This was everything he wanted.

Komura's friends were puzzled by his marriage. Next to his clean, classic looks, his wife could not have seemed more ordinary. She was short, with thick arms, and she had a dull, even stolid, appearance. And it wasn't just physical: there was nothing attractive about her personality, either. She rarely spoke, and her expression was often sullen.

Still, though he himself did not quite understand why, Komura always felt his tension dissipate when he and his wife were together under one roof; it was the only time he could truly relax. He slept well with her, undisturbed by the strange dreams that had troubled him in the past. His erections were hard; his sex life was warm. He no longer had to worry about death or venereal disease or the vastness of the universe.

His wife, on the other hand, disliked Tokyo's crowded urban life style and longed for Yamagata. She missed her parents and her two older sisters, and she would go home to see them whenever she felt the need. Her parents operated a successful inn, which kept them financially comfortable. Her father was crazy about his youngest daughter and happily paid her round-trip fares. Several times, Komura had come home from work to find his wife gone and a note on the kitchen table telling him that she would be visiting her parents for a while. He never objected. He just waited for her to come back, and she always did, after a week or ten days, in a good mood.

But the letter his wife had left for him five days after the earthquake was different: "I am never coming back," she had written, and gone on to explain simply but clearly why she no longer wanted to live with Komura. "The problem is that you never give me anything," she wrote. "Or, to put it more precisely, you have nothing inside you that you can give me. You are good and kind and handsome, but living with you is like living with a chunk of air. It's not your fault. There are lots of women who will fall in love with you. But please don't call me. Just get rid of the stuff I'm leaving behind."

Not that she had left much of anything behind. Her clothes, her shoes, her umbrella, her coffee mug, her hair dryer: all were gone. She must have packed them in boxes and shipped them out after he left for work that morning. The only things still in the house that could be called "her stuff" were the bicycle she used for shopping and a few books. The Beatles and Bill Evans CDs that Komura had been collecting since his bachelor days had also vanished.

The next day, he tried calling his wife's parents' house in Yamagata. His mother-in-law answered the phone and told him that his wife didn't want to talk to him. She sounded somewhat apologetic. She also told him that his wife would be sending him the necessary divorce forms soon and that he should sign them and send them back right away.

Komura answered that he might not be able to send them back right away. This was an important matter, and he wanted time to think it over.

"You can think it over all you want, but I don't think that'll change anything," his mother-in-law said.

She was probably right, Komura thought. No matter how long he waited, things would never be the same. He was sure of that.

Shortly after he sent the papers back, Komura asked for a week off from work. February was a slow month, and he had already told his boss what was going on in his life. He had no trouble getting permission.

A colleague of Komura's named Sasaki came over to him at lunch and said, "I hear you're taking time off. Are you planning to do something?"

"I don't know," Komura said. "What *should* I do?"

Sasaki was a bachelor, three years younger than Komura. He had a delicate build and short hair, and he wore round, gold-rimmed glasses. He talked too much and had a certain overconfident air about him, which a lot of people disliked, but he got along well enough with the easygoing Komura.

"What the hell—as long as you're taking the time off, why not travel somewhere nice?"

"Not a bad idea," Komura said.

Wiping his glasses with his handkerchief, Sasaki peered at Komura as if examining him for some kind of clue.

"Have you ever been to Hokkaido?" he asked.

"Never," Komura said.

"Would you like to go?"

"Why do you ask?"

Sasaki narrowed his eyes and cleared his throat. "To tell the truth, I've got a small package I'd like to send to Kushiro, and I'm hoping you'll take it there for me. You'd be doing me a big favor, and I'd be glad to pay for the ticket. I could cover your hotel in Kushiro, too."

"A small package?"

"Like this," Sasaki said, shaping a four-inch cube with his hands. "Nothing heavy."

"Something to do with work?"

Sasaki shook his head. "Not at all," he said. "Strictly personal. I just don't want it to get knocked around, which is why I can't mail it. I'd like you to deliver it by hand, if possible. I really ought to do it myself, but I haven't had the time to fly all the way to Hokkaido."

"Is it something important?"

His closed lips curling slightly, Sasaki nodded. "It's nothing fragile, and there are no 'hazardous materials.' There's no need to worry about it. They're not going to stop you when they X-ray it at the airport. I promise I'm not going to get you in trouble. The only reason I'm not mailing it is I just don't *feel* like mailing it."

Hokkaido in February would be freezing cold, Komura knew, but cold or hot it was all the same to him.

"So who do I give the package to?"

"My sister. My younger sister. She lives up there."

Komura decided to accept Sasaki's offer. Thinking it over would have been too much trouble. He had no reason to refuse, and nothing else to do. Sasaki called the airline immediately and reserved a ticket for two days later.

At work the next day, he handed Komura a box like the ones used for human ashes, only smaller, wrapped in manila paper. Judging from the feel, it was made of wood. It weighed almost nothing. Broad strips of transparent tape were wrapped around the package, over the paper. Komura held it in his hands and studied it for a few seconds. He gave it a little shake, but he couldn't feel or hear anything moving inside.

"My sister will pick you up at the airport," Sasaki said. "She'll be arranging a room for you. All you have to do is meet her at the gate."

Komura left home with the box in his suitcase, wrapped in a thick shirt. The plane was far more crowded than he had imagined it would be. Why were all these people going from Tokyo to Kushiro in the middle of winter? he wondered.

The morning paper was full of earthquake reports. He read it from beginning to end on the plane. The number of dead was rising. Many areas were still without water and electricity, and countless people had lost their homes. Each article contained some new tragedy, but to Komura those tragedies registered as oddly lacking in depth. The aftermath of the earthquake was like a distant monotonous echo to him. The only thing he could give any serious thought to was his wife's drawing ever further away.

When he grew tired of thinking about his wife and of following the lines of type, he closed his eyes and napped. When he woke, he thought about his wife again. Why had she followed the earthquake reports with such intensity, from morning to night, without eating or sleeping? What had she seen that he didn't see?

Two young women wearing overcoats of similar design and color approached Komura at the airport. One was fair-skinned and maybe five feet six, with short hair. The area from her nose to her full upper lip was oddly extended, in a way that made Komura think of short-haired hoofed animals. The other woman was closer to five feet one and would have been quite pretty if her nose hadn't been so small. Her long hair fell straight to her shoulders. Her ears were exposed, and there were two moles on her right earlobe which were emphasized by the earrings she wore. Both women looked to be in their mid-twenties. They took Komura to a café in the airport.

"I'm Keiko Sasaki," the taller woman said. "My brother told me how helpful you have been to him. This is my friend Shimao."

"Nice to meet you," Komura said.

"Hi," Shimao said.

"My brother tells me that your wife recently passed away," Keiko Sasaki said, with a respectful expression.

Komura waited a moment before answering, "No, she didn't die."

"I just talked to my brother the day before yesterday. I'm sure he said quite clearly that you had lost your wife."

"I did. She left me. But, as far as I know, she's alive and well."

"That's strange. I couldn't possibly have misheard something so important." She gave him an injured look. Komura put a small amount of sugar in his coffee and stirred it gently before taking a sip. The liquid was thin, with no taste to speak of. What the hell am I doing here? he wondered.

"Well, I guess I did mishear it. I can't imagine how else to explain the mistake," Keiko Sasaki said, apparently satisfied now. She drew in a deep breath and bit her lower lip. "Please forgive me. I was very rude."

"Don't worry about it. Either way, she's gone."

Shimao said nothing while Komura and Keiko spoke, but she smiled and kept her eyes on Komura. She seemed to like him. He could tell from her expression and her subtle body language. A short silence fell over the three of them.

"Anyway, let me give you the important package I brought," Komura said. He unzipped his suitcase and pulled the box out of the folds of the thick shirt he had wrapped it in.

Keiko stretched her hands across the table, her expressionless eyes fixed on the package. After testing its weight, she did the same thing Komura had and gave it a few shakes by her ear. She flashed him a smile as if to signal that everything was fine, and slipped the box into her oversized shoulder bag.

"I have to make a call," she said. "Do you mind if I excuse myself for a moment?"

"Not at all," Komura said. "Feel free."

Keiko slung the bag over her shoulder and walked off toward a distant phone booth. Komura studied the way she walked. The upper half of her body was still, while everything from the hips down made large, smooth, mechanical movements. He had the impression that he was witnessing some moment from the past, shoved with random suddenness into the present.

"Have you been to Hokkaido before?" Shimao asked.

Komura shook his head.

"Yeah, I know. It's a long way to come."

Komura nodded. Then he turned to survey his surroundings. "Strange, though," he said, "sitting here like this, it doesn't feel as if I've come all that far."

"Because you flew. Those planes are too damn fast. Your mind can't keep up with your body."

"You may be right."

"Did you want to make such a long trip?"

"I guess so," Komura said.

"Because your wife left?"

Komura nodded.

"No matter how far you travel, you can never get away from yourself," Shimao said.

Komura was staring at the sugar bowl on the table as she spoke, but then he raised his eyes to hers.

"It's true," he said. "No matter how far you travel, you can never get away from yourself. It's like your shadow. It follows you everywhere."

Shimao looked hard at Komura. "I bet you loved her, didn't you?"

Komura dodged the question. "You're a friend of Keiko Sasaki's?"

"Right. We do stuff together."

"What kind of stuff?"

Instead of answering him, Shimao asked, "Are you hungry?"

"I don't know," Komura said. "I feel kind of hungry and kind of not."

"Let's go and have something warm, the three of us. Eating something warm will help you relax."

Shimao drove a small four-wheel-drive Subaru. Keiko Sasaki sat next to Shimao, and Komura had the cramped rear seat to himself. There was nothing particularly wrong with Shimao's driving, but the noise in the back was terrible, and the suspension was nearly shot. The car had to have more than a hundred thousand miles on it. The automatic transmission slammed into gear whenever it downshifted, and the heater blew hot and cold. Shutting his eyes, Komura imagined that he had been imprisoned in a washing machine.

No snow had been allowed to accumulate on the streets in Kushiro, but dirty, icy mounds stood at random intervals on both sides of the road. Dense clouds hung low, and, although it was not yet sunset, everything was dark and desolate. The wind tore through the city in sharp squeals. There were no people out walking. Even the traffic lights looked frozen.

"This is one part of Hokkaido that doesn't get much snow," Keiko explained in a loud voice, looking back at Komura. "We're on the coast, and the wind is strong, so whatever piles up gets blown away. It's cold, though, *freezing* cold. Sometimes it feels like it's taking your ears off."

"You hear about drunks who freeze to death sleeping on the street," Shimao said.

"Do you get bears around here?" Komura asked.

Keiko giggled and turned to Shimao. "Bears!"

Shimao gave the same kind of giggle.

"I don't know much about Hokkaido," Komura said by way of excuse.

"I know a good story about bears," Keiko said. "Right, Shimao?"

"A *great* story!" Shimao said.

But their talk broke off at that point, and neither of them told the bear story. Komura didn't ask to hear it. Soon they reached their destination, a big noodle shop on the highway. They parked in the lot and went inside.

Komura had a beer and a hot bowl of ramen noodles. The place was dirty and empty, and the chairs and tables were rickety, but the ramen was terrific, and when he had finished eating Komura did, in fact, feel more relaxed.

"Tell me, Mr. Komura," Keiko said, "do you have something you want to do in Hokkaido? My brother says you're going to spend a week here."

Komura thought about it for a moment but couldn't come up with anything that he wanted to do.

"How about a hot spring? I know a little country place not far from here."

"Not a bad idea," Komura said.

"I'm sure you'd like it. It's really nice. No bears or anything."

The two women looked at each other and laughed again.

"Do you mind if I ask you about your wife?" Keiko asked.

"I don't mind."

"When did she leave?"

"Hmm . . . five days after the earthquake, so that's more than two weeks ago now."

"Did it have something to do with the earthquake?"

Komura shook his head. "Probably not. I don't think so."

"Still, I wonder if things like that aren't connected somehow," Shimao said with a tilt of her head.

"Yeah," Keiko said. "It's just that you can't see how."

"Right," Shimao said. "Stuff like that happens all the time."

"Stuff like what?" Komura asked.

"Like, say, what happened with somebody I know," Keiko said.

"You mean Mr. Saeki?" Shimao asked.

"Exactly," Keiko said. "There's this guy—Saeki. He lives in Kushiro. He's about forty years old. A hair stylist. His wife saw a U.F.O. last year. She was driving on the edge of town all by herself in the middle of the night and she saw a huge U.F.O. land in a field. *Whoosh!* Like in 'Close Encounters.' A week later, she left home. Just disappeared and never came back. They weren't having any domestic problems or anything."

"And it was because of the U.F.O.?" Komura asked.

"I don't know why. She just up and left. No note or anything. She had two kids in elementary school, and she just walked out. Not a word from her since," Keiko said. "The whole week before she left, all she'd do was tell people about the U.F.O. You couldn't get her to stop. She'd just go on and on about how big and beautiful it was."

She paused to let the story sink in.

"My wife left a note," Komura said. "And we don't have any kids."

"So your situation's a little better than Saeki's," Keiko said.

"Yeah. Kids make a big difference," Shimao said, nodding.

"Shimao's father left home when she was seven," Keiko explained with a frown. "Ran off with his wife's younger sister."

A silence settled over the group.

"Maybe Mr. Saeki's wife didn't run away but was captured by an alien from the U.F.O.," Komura said, to change the subject.

"It's possible," Shimao said with a sombre expression. "You hear stories like that all the time."

"You mean like you're-walking-along-the-street-and-a-bear-eats-you kind of thing?" Keiko asked. The two women laughed.

The three of them left the noodle shop and went to a nearby love hotel. It was on the edge of town, on a strange street where love hotels alternated with gravestone dealers. The hotel Shimao had chosen was an odd building, constructed to look like a European castle. A triangular red flag flew on its highest tower.

Keiko got the key at the front desk, and they took the elevator to the room. The windows were tiny, compared with the absurdly big bed. Komura hung his down jacket on a hanger and went into the toilet. During the few minutes that he was gone, the two women managed to run a bath, dim the lights, turn up the heat, turn on the television, examine the delivery menus from local restaurants, test the light switches at the head of the bed, and check the contents of the minibar.

"The owners are friends of mine," Keiko said. "I had them get a big room ready. It's a love hotel, but don't let that bother you. You're not bothered, are you?"

"Not at all," Komura said.

"I thought this would make a lot more sense than sticking you in a cramped little room in some cut-rate business hotel by the station."

"I'm sure you're right," Komura said.

"Why don't you take a bath? I filled the tub."

Komura did as he was told. The tub was huge. Komura felt almost uneasy soaking in it alone. The couples who came to this hotel probably took baths together.

When he emerged from the bathroom, Komura was surprised to see that Keiko Sasaki had left. Shimao was still there, drinking beer and watching TV.

"Keiko went home," Shimao said. "She wanted me to apologize and tell you that she'll be back tomorrow morning. Do you mind if I stay here a little while and have a beer?"

"No," Komura said.

"You're sure it's no problem? Like, you want to be alone, or you can't relax if somebody else is around or something?"

Komura insisted that it was no problem. Drinking his beer and drying his hair with a towel, he watched TV with Shimao. It was a news special on the Kobe earthquake. The same images appeared again and again: tilted buildings, buckled streets, tearful old women, confusion, and aimless anger. When a commercial came on, Shimao used the remote to switch off the TV.

"Let's talk," she said, "as long as we're here."

"Fine," Komura said.

"What should we talk about?"

"In the car, you and Keiko said something about a bear, remember? You said it was a great story."

"Oh, yeah," she said, nodding. "The bear story."

"You want to tell it to me?"

"Sure, why not?"

Shimao got a fresh beer from the refrigerator and filled both their glasses.

"It's a little raunchy," she said. "You don't mind?"

Komura shook his head. "No, go ahead."

"I mean, some men don't like hearing a woman tell certain kinds of stories."

"I'm not like that."

"It's something that actually happened to me, so it's a little embarrassing."

"I'd like to hear it if you're O.K. with it."

"I'm O.K.," Shimao said, "if you're O.K."

"I'm O.K.," Komura said.

"Three years ago—back around the time I started college—I was dating this guy. He was a year older than me, and he was the first guy I had sex with. One day, the two of us were out hiking—in the mountains way up north." Shimao took a sip of beer. "It was fall, and the hills were full of bears. That's the time of year when the bears are getting ready to hibernate, so they're out looking for food and they're really dangerous. Sometimes they attack people. They'd done an awful job on a hiker three days before we went out. So somebody gave us a bell to carry with us. We were supposed to shake it while we walked to warn the bears that there were people around. Bears don't attack people on purpose. I mean, they're pretty much vegetarians. They don't have to attack people. What happens is they suddenly bump into people in their territory and they get surprised or angry and they attack out of reflex. If you walk along ringing your bell, they'll avoid you. Get it?"

"I get it."

"So that's what we were doing, walking along and ringing the bell. We got to this place where there was nobody else around, and all of a sudden he said he wanted to . . . do it. I kind of liked the idea, too, so I said O.K., and we went into this bushy place off the trail where nobody could see us, and we spread out a piece of plastic. But I was afraid of the bears. I mean, think how awful it would be to have some bear attack you from behind and kill you while you're having sex! I would never want to die that way. Would you?"

Komura agreed that he would not want to die that way.

"So there we were, shaking the bell with one hand and having sex. Kept it up from start to finish. *Ding-a-ling! Ding-a-ling!*"

"Which one of you shook the bell?"

"We took turns. We'd trade off when our hands got tired. It was so weird, shaking this bell the whole time we were doing it! I think about it sometimes even now, when I'm having sex, and I start laughing."

Komura gave a little laugh, too.

Shimao clapped her hands. "Oh, that's wonderful," she said. "You can laugh, after all!"

"Of course I can laugh," Komura said, but, come to think of it, this was the first time he had laughed in quite a while. When was the last time?

"Do you mind if I take a bath, too?" Shimao asked.

"No," Komura said.

While she was bathing, Komura watched a variety show m.c.'d by a comedian with a loud voice. He didn't find it the least bit funny, but he couldn't tell whether that was the show's fault or his own. He drank a beer and opened a packet of nuts from the minibar. Shimao stayed in the bath for a very long time. Finally, she came out wearing nothing but a towel and sat on the edge of the bed. Dropping the towel, she slid between the sheets like a cat and lay there staring at Komura.

"When was the last time you did it with your wife?" she asked.

"At the end of December, I think."

"And nothing since?"

"Nothing."

"Not with anybody?"

Komura closed his eyes and nodded.

"You know what I think," Shimao said. "You need to lighten up and learn to enjoy life a little more. I mean, think about it: tomorrow there could be an earthquake; you could be kidnapped by aliens; you could be eaten by a bear. Nobody knows what's going to happen."

"Nobody knows what's going to happen," Komura echoed.

"*Ding-a-ling*," Shimao said.

After several failed attempts to have sex with Shimao, Komura gave up. This had never happened to him before.

"You must have been thinking about your wife," Shimao said.

"Yup," Komura said, but in fact what he had been thinking about was the earthquake. Images of it had come to him one after another, as if in a slide show, flashing on the screen and fading away. Highways, flames, smoke, piles of rubble. He couldn't break the chain of silent images.

Shimao pressed her ear against his naked chest.

"These things happen," she said.

"Uh-huh."

"You shouldn't let it bother you."

"I'll try not to," Komura said.

"Men always let it bother them, though."

Komura said nothing.

Shimao played with his nipple.

"You said your wife left a note, didn't you?"

"I did."

"What did it say?"

"That living with me was like living with a chunk of air."

"A chunk of air?" Shimao tilted her head back to look up at Komura. "What does that mean?"

"That there's nothing inside me, I guess."

"Is it true?"

"Could be," Komura said. "I'm not sure, though. I may have nothing inside me, but what would *something* be?"

"Yeah, really, come to think of it. What *would* something be? My mother was crazy about salmon skin. She always used to wish that there were a kind of salmon that was made of nothing but skin. So there may be some cases when it's better to have nothing inside. Don't you think?"

Komura tried to imagine what a salmon made of nothing but skin would be like. But even supposing there were such a thing, wouldn't the skin itself be the something inside? Komura took a deep breath, raising and then lowering Shimao's head on his chest.

"I'll tell you this, though," Shimao said. "I don't know whether you've got nothing or something inside you, but I think you're terrific. I'll bet the world is full of women who would understand you and fall in love with you."

"It said that, too."

"What? Your wife's note?"

"Uh-huh."

"No kidding," Shimao said. Her earring rubbed against the skin of his chest.

"Come to think of it," Komura said, "what's the something inside that box I brought up here?"

"Is that bothering you?"

"It wasn't bothering me before. But now, I don't know, it's starting to."

"Since when?"

"Just now."

"All of a sudden?"

"Yeah, once I started thinking about it, all of a sudden."

"I wonder why it's started to bother you now, all of a sudden."

Komura stared at the ceiling for a minute. "I wonder."

The two listened to the moaning of the wind. The wind came from someplace unknown to Komura, and it blew past, to another place unknown to him.

"I'll tell you why," Shimao said in a low voice. "It's because that box contains the something that was inside you. You didn't know that when you carried it here and gave it to Keiko with your own hands. Now you'll never get it back."

Komura lifted himself from the mattress and looked down at the woman. Tiny nose, moles on her earlobe. In the room's silence, his heart beat with a loud, dry sound. His bones cracked as he leaned forward. For a split second, Komura felt as if he were on the verge of committing an act of incredible violence.

"Just kidding," Shimao said, when she saw the look on his face. "I said the first thing that popped into my head. It was a lousy joke. I'm sorry. Don't take it personally. I didn't mean to hurt you."

Komura forced himself to calm down and sank his head into his pillow again. He closed his eyes and took a deep breath. The huge bed stretched out around him like a nocturnal sea. His heart was still pounding.

"Are you starting to feel a little as if you've come a long way?" Shimao asked.

"Hmm. Now I feel as if I've come a very long way," Komura answered honestly.

Shimao traced a complicated design on Komura's chest with her fingertip, as if casting a magic spell.

"But really," she said, "you're just at the beginning."

Translated, from the Japanese, by Jay Rubin

SEVEN

BY EDWIDGE DANTICAT (2001)

Next month would make it seven years since he'd last seen his wife. Seven, a number he despised but had discovered was a useful marker. There were seven days between paychecks, seven hours, not counting lunch, spent each day at his day job, seven at his night job. Seven was the last number in his age—thirty-seven. And now there were seven hours left before his wife was due to arrive. Maybe it would be more, with her having to wait for her luggage and then make it through the long immigration line and past customs to look for him in the crowd of welcoming faces on the other side of the sliding doors at J.F.K. That is, if the flight from Port-au-Prince wasn't delayed, as it often was, or cancelled altogether.

He shared an apartment in the basement of a house in East Flatbush, Brooklyn, with two other men. To prepare for the reunion, he had cleaned his room. He had thrown out some cherry-red rayon shirts that he knew she would hate. And then he had climbed the splintered steps to the first floor to tell the landlady that his wife was coming. His landlady was also Haitian, a self-employed accountant. "I don't have a problem with your wife coming," she had told him. She was microwaving a frozen dessert. "I just hope she is clean."

"She is clean," he said.

The kitchen was the only room in the main part of the house that he'd ever seen. It was spotless, and the dishes were neatly organized in glass cabinets. It smelled of pine-scented air freshener.

"Did you tell the men?" she asked. She opened the microwave and removed two small plastic plates of something that vaguely resembled strawberry cheesecake.

"I told them," he said.

He was waiting for her to announce that she would have to charge him extra. She had agreed to rent the room to one person, not two—a man she'd probably taken for a bachelor.

"I don't know if I can keep this arrangement if everyone's wife starts coming," she said.

He could not speak for the two other men. Michel and Dany had wives, too, but he had no idea if or when those wives would be joining them.

"A woman living down there with three men," the landlady said. "Maybe your wife will be uncomfortable."

He wanted to tell her that it was not up to her to decide whether or not his wife would be comfortable. But he had been prepared for this, too, for some unpleasant remark about his wife. Actually, he was up there as much to give notice that he was looking for an apartment as to announce that his wife was coming. As soon as he found one, he would be moving.

"O.K., then," she said, opening her silverware drawer. "Just remember, you start the month, you pay the whole thing."

"Thank you very much, Madame," he said.

As he walked back downstairs, he scolded himself for calling her Madame. Why had he acted like a servant who had been dismissed? It was one of those class things from home that he couldn't shake. On the other hand, if he had addressed the woman respectfully, it wasn't because she was so-called upper class, or because she spoke French (though never to him), or even because after five years in the same room he was still paying only three hundred and fifty dollars a month. If he had addressed the woman politely that day, it was because he was making a sacrifice for his wife.

After his conversation with the landlady, he decided to have a more thorough one with the men who occupied the other two rooms in the basement. The day before his wife was to arrive, he went into the kitchen to see them. The fact that they were wearing only white, rather sheer, loose boxers, as they stumbled about bleary-eyed, concerned him.

"You understand, she's a woman," he told them. He wasn't worried that she'd be tempted—they were skin and bones—but if she was still as sensitive as he remembered, their near-nakedness might embarrass her.

The men understood.

"If it were my wife," Michel said, "I would feel the same."

Dany simply nodded.

They had robes, Michel declared after a while. They would wear them.

They didn't have robes—all three men knew this—but Michel would buy some, out of respect for the wife. Michel, at forty, the oldest of the three, had advised him to pretty up his room—to buy some silk roses, some decorative prints for the walls (no naked girls), and some vanilla incense, which would be more pleasing than the air fresheners the woman upstairs liked so much.

Dany told him that he would miss their evenings out together. In the old days, they had often gone dancing at the Rendez-Vous, which was now the Cenegal night club. But they hadn't gone much since the place had become famous—Abner Louima was arrested there, then beaten and sodomized at a nearby police station.

He told Dany not to mention those nights out again. His wife wasn't to know that he had ever done anything but work his jobs—as a day janitor at Medgar Evers College and as a night janitor at King's County Hospital. And he wasn't going to tell her about those women who had occasionally come home with him in the early-morning hours. Those women, most of whom had husbands, boyfriends, fiancés, and lovers in other parts of the world, had never meant much to him anyway.

Michel, who had become a lay minister at a small Baptist church near the Rendez-Vous and never danced there, laughed as he listened. "The cock can no longer crow," he said. "You might as well give the rest to Jesus."

"Jesus wouldn't know what to do with what's left of this man," Dany said.

Gone were the late-night domino games. Gone was the phone number he'd had for the past five years, ever since he'd had a phone. (He didn't need other women calling him now.) And it was only as he stood in the crowd of people waiting to meet the flights arriving simultaneously from Kingston, Santo Domingo, and Port-au-Prince that he stopped worrying that he might not see any delight or recognition in his wife's face. There, he began to feel some actual joy, even exhilaration, which made him want to leap forward and grab every woman who vaguely resembled the latest pictures she had sent him, all of which he had neatly framed and hung on the walls of his room.

They were searching her suitcase. Why were they searching her suitcase? One meagre bag, which, aside from some gifts for her husband, contained the few things she'd been unable to part with, the things her relatives hadn't nabbed from her, telling her that she could get more, and better, where she was going. She had kept only her undergarments, a nightgown, and two outfits: the green princess dress she was wearing and a red jumper that she'd gift wrapped before packing so that no one would take it. People in her neighborhood who had travelled before had told her to gift wrap everything so that it wouldn't be opened at the airport in New York. Now the customs man was tearing her careful wrapping to shreds as he barked questions at her in mangled Creole.

"*Ki sa l ye?*" He held a package out in front of her before opening it.

What was it? She didn't know anymore. She could only guess by the shapes and sizes.

He unwrapped all her gifts—the mangoes, sugarcane, avocados, the orange- and grapefruit-peel preserves, the peanut, cashew, and coconut confections, the coffee beans, which he threw into a green bin decorated with drawings of fruits and vegetables with red lines across them. The only thing that seemed as though it might escape disposal was a small packet of trimmed chicken feathers, which her husband used to enjoy twirling in his ear cavity. In the early days, soon after he'd left, she had spun the tips of the feathers inside her ears, too, and discovered that from them she could get *jwisans*, pleasure, an orgasm. She had thought to herself then that maybe the foreign television programs were right: sex was mostly between the ears.

When the customs man came across the small package of feathers, he stared down at it, then looked up at her, letting his eyes linger on her face, mostly, it seemed to her, on her ears. Obviously, he had seen feathers like these before. Into the trash they went, along with the rest of her offerings.

By the time he was done with her luggage, she had little left. The suitcase was so light now that she could walk very quickly as she carried it in her left hand. She followed a man pushing a cart, which tipped and swerved under the weight of three large boxes. And suddenly she found herself before a door that slid open by itself, parting like a glass sea, and as she was standing there the door closed again, and when she moved a few steps forward it opened, and then she saw him. He charged at her and wrapped both his arms around her. And as he held her she felt her feet leave the ground. It was when he put her back down that she finally believed she was really somewhere else, on another soil, in another country.

He could tell she was happy that so many of her pictures were displayed on the wall facing his bed. During the ride home, he had nearly crashed the car twice. He wasn't sure why he was driving so fast. They dashed through the small talk, the inventory of friends and family members and the state of their health. She had no detailed anecdotes about anyone in particular. Some had died and some were still living; he couldn't even remember which. She was bigger than she had been when he left her, what people here might call chubby. It was obvious that she had been to a professional hairdresser, because she was elegantly coiffed with her short hair gelled down to her scalp and a fake bun bulging in the back. She smelled good—a mixture of lavender and lime. He had simply wanted to get her home, if home it was, to that room, and to reduce the space between them until there was no air for her to breathe that he wasn't breathing, too.

The drive had reminded him of the one they had taken to their one-night honeymoon at the Ifé Hotel, when he had begged the uncle who was driving them to go faster, because the next morning he would be on a plane for New York. That night, he'd had no idea that it would be seven years before he would see her again. He'd had it all planned. He knew that he couldn't send for her right away, since he would be overstaying a tourist visa. But he was going to work hard, to find a lawyer and get himself a green card, and then send for his wife. The green card had taken six years and nine months. But now she was here with him, staring at the pictures on his wall as though they were of someone else.

"Do you remember that one?" he asked, to reassure her. He was pointing at a framed eight-by-twelve of her lying on a red mat by a tiny Christmas tree in a photographer's studio. "You sent it last Noël?"

She remembered, she said. It was just that she looked so desperate, as if she were trying to force *him* to remember *her*.

"I never forgot you for an instant," he said.

She said that she was thirsty.

"What do you want to drink?" He listed the juices he had purchased from the Cuban grocer down the street, the combinations he was sure she'd be craving, papaya and mango, guava and pineapple, cherimoya and passion fruit.

"Just a little water," she said. "Cold."

He didn't want to leave her alone while he went to the kitchen. He would have called through the walls for one of the men to get some water, if they were not doing such a good job of hiding behind the closed doors of their rooms to give him some privacy.

When he came back with the glass, she examined it, as if for dirt, and then gulped it down. It was as though she hadn't drunk anything since the morning he'd got on the plane and left her behind.

"Do you want more?" he asked.

She shook her head.

It's too bad, he thought, that in Creole the word for love, *renmen*, is also the word for like, so that as he told her he loved her he had to embellish it with phrases that illustrated the degree of that love. He loved her more than there were seconds in the years they'd been apart, he babbled. He loved her more than the size of the ocean she had just crossed. To keep himself from saying more insipid things, he jumped on top of her and pinned her down on the bed. She was not as timid as she had been on their wedding night. She tugged at his black tie so fiercely that he was sure his neck was bruised. He yanked a few buttons off her dress and threw them aside as she unbuttoned his starched and ironed white shirt, and though in the rehearsals in past daydreams he had gently placed a cupped hand over her mouth, he didn't think to do it now. He didn't care that the other men could hear her, or him. Only for a moment did he think to feel sorry that it might be years before the others could experience the same thing.

He was exhausted when she grabbed the top sheet from the bed, wrapped it around her, and announced that she was going to the bathroom.

"Let me take you," he said.

"*Non non,*" she said. "I can find it."

He couldn't stand to watch her turn away and disappear.

He heard voices in the kitchen, her talking to the men, introducing herself. He bolted right up from the bed when he remembered that all she had on was the sheet. As he raced to the door, he collided with her coming back.

There were two men playing dominoes in the kitchen, she told him, dressed in identical pink satin robes.

He left early for work the next day, along with the other men, but not before handing her a set of keys and instructing her not to let anyone in. He showed her how to work the stove and how to find all the Haitian stations on the AM/FM dial of his night-table radio. She slept late, reliving the night, their laughter after she'd seen the men, who, he explained, had hurried to buy those robes for her benefit. They had made love again and again, forcing themselves to do so more quietly each time. Seven times, by his count—once for each year they'd been apart—but fewer by hers. He had assured her that there was no need to be embarrassed. They were married, before God and a priest. This was crucial for her to remember. That's why he had seen to it on the night before he left. So that something more judicial and committing than a mere promise would bind them. So that even if their union had become a victim of distance and time, it could not have been easily dissolved. They would have had to sign papers to come apart, write letters, speak on the phone about it. He told her that he didn't want to leave her again, not for one second. But he had asked for the day off and his boss had refused. At least they would have the weekends, Saturdays and Sundays, to do with as they wished—to go dancing, sightseeing, shopping, and apartment-hunting. Wouldn't she like to have her own apartment?

To make love as much as they wanted and not worry that some men in women's robes had heard them?

At noon, the phone rang. It was him. He asked her what she was doing. She lied and told him that she was cooking, making herself something to eat. He asked what. She said eggs, guessing that there must be eggs in the refrigerator. He asked if she was bored. She said no. She was going to listen to the radio and write letters home.

When she hung up, she turned on the radio. She scrolled between the stations he had pointed out to her and was glad to hear people speaking Creole. There was music playing, too—*konpa* by a group named Top Vice. She switched to a station with a talk show. She sat up to listen as some callers talked about a Haitian-American named Patrick Dorismond who had been killed. He had been shot by a policeman in a place called Manhattan. She wanted to call her husband back, but he hadn't left a number. Lying back, she raised the sheet over her head and through it listened to the callers, each one angrier than the last.

When he came home, he saw that she had used what she had found in the refrigerator and the kitchen cabinets to cook a large meal for all four of them. She insisted that they wait for the other men to drift in before they ate, even though he had only a few hours before he had to leave for his night job.

The men complimented her enthusiastically on her cooking, and he could tell that this meal made them feel as though they were part of a family, something they had not experienced in years. They seemed to be happy, eating for pleasure as well as sustenance, chewing more slowly than they ever had before. Usually they ate standing up, Chinese or Jamaican takeout from places down the street. Tonight there was little conversation, beyond praise for the food. The men offered to clean the pots and dishes once they were done, and he suspected that they wanted to lick them before washing them.

He and his wife went to the room and lay on their backs on the bed. He explained why he had two jobs. It had been partly to fill the hours away from her, but also partly because he had needed to support both himself here and her in Port-au-Prince. And now he was saving up for an apartment and, ultimately, a house. She said that she, too, wanted to work. She had finished a secretarial course; perhaps that would be helpful here. He warned her that, because she didn't speak English, she might have to start as a cook in a restaurant or as a seamstress in a factory. He fell asleep mid-thought. She woke him up at nine o'clock, when he was supposed to start work. He rushed to the bathroom to wash his face, came back, and changed his overalls, all the while cursing himself. He was stupid to have overslept, and now he was late. He kissed her goodbye and ran out. He hated being late, being lectured by the night manager, whose favorite reprimand was "There's tons of people like you in this city. Half of them need a job."

She spent the whole week inside, worried that she'd get lost if she ventured out alone, that she might not be able to retrace her steps. Her days fell into a routine. She'd wake up and listen to the radio for news of what was happening both here and back home. Somewhere, not far from where she was, people were in the streets, marching, protesting Dorismond's death, their outrage made even greater by the fact that the Dorismond boy was the American-born son of a well-known singer, whose voice they had heard on the radio back in Haiti. "No justice, no peace!" she chanted while stewing chicken and frying fish. In the afternoons, she wrote letters home. She wrote of the meals that she had made, of the pictures of her on the wall, of the songs and protest chants on the radio. She wrote to family members, and to childhood girlfriends who had been so happy that she was finally going to be with her husband, and to newer acquaintances from the secretarial school who had been jealous. She also wrote to a male friend, a neighbor who had come to her house three days after her husband had left to see why she had locked herself inside.

He had knocked for so long that she'd had no choice but to open the door. She was still wearing the dress she'd worn to see her husband off. When she collapsed in his arms, he had put a cold compress on her forehead and offered her some water. She had swallowed so much water so quickly that she'd vomited. That night, he had lain down next to her, and in the dark had told her that this was love, if love there was—having the courage to abandon the present for a future that one could only imagine. He had assured her that her husband loved her.

In the afternoons, while she was writing her letters, she would hear someone walking back and forth on the floor above. She took to pacing as well, as she waited for the men to come home. She wanted to tell her husband about that neighbor who had slept next to her for those days after he'd left and in whose bed she had spent many nights after that. Only then would she feel that their future would be true. Someone had said that people lie only at the beginning of relationships. The middle is where the truth resides. But there had been no middle for her husband and herself, just a beginning and many dream-rehearsed endings.

He had first met his wife during carnival in the mountains in Jacmel. His favorite part of the festivities was the finale, on the day before Ash Wednesday, when a crowd of tired revellers would gather on the beach to burn their carnival masks and costumes and feign weeping, symbolically purging themselves of the carousing of the preceding days and nights. She had volunteered to be one of the official weepers—one of those who wailed convincingly as the carnival relics turned to ashes in the bonfire.

"*Papa Kanaval ou ale?*" "Where have you gone, Father Carnival?" she had howled, with real tears running down her face.

If she could grieve so passionately on demand, he thought, perhaps she could love even more. After the other weepers had left, she stayed behind until the last embers of the bonfire had dimmed. It was impossible to distract her, to make her laugh. She could never fake weeping, she told him. Every time she cried for anything, she cried for everything else that had ever hurt her.

He had travelled between Jacmel and Port-au-Prince while he was waiting for his visa to come through. And when he finally had a travel date he had asked her to marry him.

One afternoon, when he came home from work, he found her sitting on the edge of the bed in that small room, staring at the pictures of herself on the opposite wall. She did not move as he kissed the top of her head. He said nothing, simply slipped out of his clothes and lay down on the bed, pressing his face against her back. He did not want to trespass on her secrets. He simply wanted to extinguish the carnivals burning in her head.

. . .

She was happy when the weekend finally came. Though he slept until noon, she woke up at dawn, rushed to the bathroom before the men could, put on her red jumper and one of his T-shirts, then sat staring down at him on the bed, waiting for his eyes to open.

"What plan do we have for today?" she asked when they finally did.

The plan, he said, was whatever she wanted.

She wanted to walk down a street with him and see faces. She wanted to eat something, an apple or a chicken leg, out in the open with the sun beating down on her face.

As they were leaving the house, they ran into the woman whose footsteps she had been hearing all week long above her head. The woman smiled coyly and said, "*Bienvenue.*" She nodded politely, then pulled her husband away by the hand.

They walked down a street filled with people doing their Saturday food shopping at outside stalls stacked with fruits and vegetables.

He asked if she wanted to take the bus.

"Where to?"

"Anywhere," he said.

From the bus, she counted the frame and row houses, beauty-shop signs, church steeples, and gas stations. She pressed her face against the window, and her breath occasionally blocked her view of the streets speeding by. She turned back now and then to look at him, sitting next to her. There was still a trace of sleepiness in his eyes. He watched her as though he were trying to put himself in her place, to see it all as if for the first time, but could not.

He took her to a park in the middle of Brooklyn, Prospect Park, a vast stretch of land, trees, and trails. They strolled deep into the park, until they could see only a few of the surrounding buildings, which towered like mountains above the landscape. In all her day-dreams, she had never imagined that there would be a place like this here. This immense garden, he told her, was where he came to ponder the passing seasons, lost time, and interminable distances.

It was past seven o'clock when they emerged from the park and headed down Parkside Avenue. She had reached for his hand at 5:10 P.M., he had noted, and had not released it since. And now, as they were walking down a dimly lit side street, she kept her eyes upward, looking into the windows of apartments lit by the indigo glow of television screens. When she said she was hungry, they turned onto Flatbush Avenue in search of something to eat.

Walking hand in hand with her through crowds of strangers made him long for his other favorite piece of carnival theatre. A bride and groom, in their most lavish wedding clothing, would wander the streets. Scanning a crowd of revellers, they would pick the most stony-faced person and ask, "Would you marry us?" Over the course of several days, for variety, they would modify this request. "Would you couple us?" "Would you make us one?" "Would you tie the noose of love around our necks?" The joke was that when the person took the bait and looked closely, he or she might discover that the bride was a man and the groom a woman. The couple's makeup was so skillfully applied that only the most observant could detect this.

On the nearly empty bus on the way home, he sat across the aisle from her, not next to her as he had that morning. She pretended to keep her eyes on the night racing past the window behind him. He was watching her again. This time he seemed to be trying to see *her* as if for the first time, but could not.

She, too, was thinking of carnival, and of how, the year after they'd met, they had dressed as a bride and groom looking for someone to marry them. She had disguised herself as the bride and he as the groom, forgoing the traditional puzzle.

At the end of the celebrations, she had burned her wedding dress in the bonfire and he had burned his suit. She wished now that they had kept them. They could have walked these foreign streets in them, performing their own carnival. Since she didn't know the language, they wouldn't have to speak or ask any questions of the stony-faced people around them. They could perform their public wedding march in silence, a silence like the one that had come over them now.

THE COURTESY

BY JOHN BERGER (2002)

In a square in Lisboa, there is a tree called a Lusitanian cypress. Its branches, instead of pointing up to the sky, have been trained to grow outward, horizontally, so that they form a gigantic, impenetrable low umbrella. A hundred people could easily shelter under it. The branches are supported by metal props, arranged in circles around the twisted massive trunk; the tree is at least two hundred years old. Beside it stands a formal notice board with a poem. I paused to try to decipher a few lines: "I am the handle of your hoe, the gate of your house, the wood of your cradle and of your own coffin."

Nearby, chickens were pecking on unkempt grass. Men were playing *sueca*, each one selecting and then placing his card on the table with an expression that combined wisdom and resignation. Winning was a quiet pleasure.

It was the end of May. In a week or two, Africa, which begins—in a manner of speaking—on the far bank of the Tagus, would start to impose its distant yet tangible presence. A man carrying a suitcase crossed the square with the air of someone going to a rendezvous that he kept every day. A woman holding a little dog in her arms walked past on her way toward the Avenida da Liberdade. There was an old woman with an umbrella, sitting very still on one of the park benches. She had the kind of stillness that draws attention to itself—she seemed to want her presence to be noticed. But by whom?

Abruptly, she got to her feet, turned, and, using her umbrella like a walking stick, came toward me.

I recognized her walk long before I could see her face. The walk of somebody already looking forward to arriving and sitting down. It was my mother.

It happens sometimes in my dreams that I have to phone my parents' flat, in order to tell them—or to ask them to tell somebody else—that I'm likely to be late, because I've missed a connection. I want to warn them that I'm not where I'm meant to be. But I don't have my address book with me, and although I attempt to remember their telephone number and I try out several variations, I never find the right one. This corresponds with the truth that in my waking life I have forgotten the telephone number of the flat where my parents lived for twenty years. But what I forget in my dreams is that my parents are dead. My father died twenty-five years ago and my mother ten years later.

In the square, she took my arm and we walked slowly toward the Mãe d'Água staircase.

There's something, John, you shouldn't forget. And it's this: the dead don't stay where they are buried.

As she spoke, she looked concentratedly at the ground a few metres ahead of us, as if she were worried about tripping.

I'm not talking about Heaven, she said. Heaven is all very well, but I happen to be talking about something different. She paused and chewed as if one of the words had gristle on it and needed more chewing before being swallowed. Then she went on. The dead when they're dead can choose where they want to live on earth, always supposing they decide to stay on the earth.

We were at the top of the stairway. She took hold of the rail, and we walked three steps down.

How do the dead choose where they want to stay?

She didn't answer; instead, she gathered up her skirt and sat down on the next step of the staircase.

I've chosen Lisboa! she said, as if repeating something very obvious.

Did you ever come here—I hesitated, for I didn't want to make the distinction too blatant—*before*?

Again she ignored the question.

Is Father here?

She shook her head.

Where is he?

I don't know and I don't ask him. I fancy he may be in Rome.

Because of the Holy See?

For the first time, she looked at me, a little triumph of a joke in her eyes.

Not at all—because of the tablecloths!

I put my arm around her. Gently she removed my hand from her arm, and, still holding it, placed it on the stone step.

Don't you remember my warning you? I told you it would be like this. Beyond days or months or hundreds of years, beyond time.

She was peering toward Africa.

So time doesn't count and place does? I said this to tease her. I had liked teasing her, and she went along with it.

When I was a child, her sureness enraged me. It was a sureness that revealed a vulnerability behind the bravura, a hesitancy, whereas I wanted her to be invincible. Consequently, I would contradict whatever it was that she was being so certain about. Yet my counterattacks made her even more frail.

So time doesn't count and place does? I asked again.

It's not just any place, my boy. There aren't many cities left with trams, are there? Here you can hear them all the while—except for a few hours during the night. There's hardly a street in the center of Lisboa where you can't hear trams.

It was a No. 194, wasn't it? We took it every Wednesday from East to South Croydon and back. First we shopped in Surrey Street market, then we went to the Davies Picture Palace, with an electric organ changing color when the man played it.

I knew the organist, she said. I bought celery for him in the market.

You also bought kidneys.

Your father enjoyed them for breakfast.

Like Leopold Bloom.

Don't show off! There's nobody here to notice. You always wanted to sit in the front of the tram upstairs. Yes, it was a 194.

And climbing up the stairs of the tram, you complained, Ah, my legs, my poor legs!

You wanted to be up in front because there you could drive and wanted me to watch you drive.

I loved the corners! Do you remember the sparks?

In the damn rain, yes.

Driving after the cinema was best.

I never saw anyone look as hard as you did, sitting on the edge of your seat.

In the tram?

In the tram and in the cinema, too.

You often cried in the cinema, I told her. You had a way of dabbing at your eyes.

Shall I tell you something? I don't suppose you've noticed the tower of Santa Justa, just down there? It's owned by the Lisboa Tramway Company. There's a lift in it, and the lift goes nowhere, really. It takes people up, they take a look around from the platform, and then it brings the same people down. Now, a film, John, can do the same thing. It takes you up and brings you back to the same place. That's one of the reasons people cry in the cinema.

She licked her lower lip, with a gesture she once used after applying lipstick. On one of the roofs above the Mãe d'Água staircase a woman was singing as she pegged out sheets on a line to dry. Her voice was plaintive, and the sheets were very white.

When I first came to Lisboa, my mother said, I came down in that lift of the Santa Justa. I have never been up in it—you understand? I came down in it. As we all do. That's why it was built. And do you know the first thing I saw, when I stepped out of the lift? A shop for digital photography!

She got to her feet and started climbing back up the staircase. She had difficulty breathing, and so, to make it easier, to encourage herself, she blew out long hisses between her lips, pursed as if for whistling. It was she who first taught me to whistle.

I am not leaving this place, she said when we reached the top. For the moment, I'm waiting. Whereupon she turned around and walked back to the bench she had been sitting on, and the square became demonstrably still, so still that she eventually vanished.

. . .

During the next few days, she kept herself hidden. I wandered around the city. I wasn't looking for her. But from time to time something reminded me of her—usually something only half seen.

Lisboa is a hiding place. It has a relationship with the visible world like no other city's. It plays games. Its squares and streets are paved with patterns of white and colored stones, and its walls are covered with the famous *azulejo* tiles. The tiles depict fabulous things: a monkey playing pipes, a woman picking grapes, saints, whales, crusaders in their boats, basil plants, magpies, lovers embracing, a lion, a *moreia* fish with spots like a leopard. The tiles draw attention to what can be seen.

At the same time, the tiles are saying something different—in fact, the opposite. They are everywhere, and everywhere something is being covered by their crackly white surfaces, their vivacious colors and patterns: what's behind them is hidden and will remain hidden forever.

Perhaps Lisboa is a stopover for the dead. Perhaps here the dead show themselves more than in any other city. The Italian novelist Antonio Tabucchi, who loves Lisboa deeply, spent a whole day with the dead here.

As I wandered around Lisboa, I got lost several times.

Once, we were trying to get out of London and had taken the wrong road. Father stopped the car and unfolded a map. We are going far, too far to the west, Mother said. I have a good bump for direction, a phrenologist told me so more than once. He could feel it here. She was touching the back of her head. She had very fine hair. He said my bump for places was here.

Nobody, I retorted from the back seat, takes phrenologists seriously. They are a bunch of crypto-Fascists.

Why do you say that?

You can't measure a person's gifts with a pair of calipers. And, anyway, where did they get their norms? From the Greeks, of course. Narrowly European. Racist.

The one who felt my head was Chinese, she muttered, and, anyway, he was right about me. I have a good bump for places. We've come too far—we should have turned left miles back, where we saw that poor man without any legs. Now we may as well go on, no point in turning back now, it's too late!

"It's too late!"—one of her favorite phrases. And, hearing it, I was invariably filled with fury. She would pronounce the three words lightly, without pathos, almost as if she were quoting a price: some things are savable and others are not. My fury was directed partly at this calm.

I thought of this while I drank a small cup of sharp coffee in an Alfama bar. I looked at the faces of the other men, all over fifty and weathered in the same way. Lisboetas often talk of a feeling, a mood, which they call *saudade*. It is usually translated as "nostalgia." Nostalgia implies a comfort, even an indolence, such as Lisboa has never enjoyed.

Saudade, I decided as I drank a second coffee and watched a drunk's hands carefully arranging the story he was telling, as if it were a pile of envelopes, was a mood of fury at having to hear the words "too late" pronounced too calmly. And *fado* is the unmistakable music of this fury.

On Sunday, I was in the Baixa district, crossing the immense Square of Commerce. The Baixa is the only part of the old city that is flat and low. Lisboa is surrounded on three sides by its famous hills; its fourth side is the estuary of the Tagus, known as the Sea of Straw, because its waters, in a certain light, have a golden sheen. Lisboa was once the richest capital of Europe, trading in everything that defied the Atlantic: gold, slaves from the Congo, silks, diamonds, spices. From the fifteenth century, Lisboa's navigators, merchants, and slave traders set out for Africa, the Orient, and, later, Brazil.

Stick two cloves into each apple, she always instructed me, and then we'll bake them with brown sugar.

When she wasn't looking, I'd stick in a third, in the conviction that this would make the apple taste finer. If she spotted the third one, she'd take it out and put it back in the jar. They come from Madagascar, she explained. Waste not, want not!

This was another phrase that was dear to her. Yet, unlike "It's too late," "Waste not, want not!" was a warning rather than a lament. A warning that somehow applied to the Square of Commerce, I thought as I walked across it. All its dimensions, its projected geometries, were those of an unrealizable dream.

During the first week of November, 1755, an earthquake, and the tidal wave that followed it, and the fires that came after devastated a third of Lisboa and killed tens of thousands. While the fires were still burning, and people had only the tattered clothes they stood up in, men bought and sold looted diamonds among ashes and rubble. There was the blue sky above and the golden tan of the Sea of Straw, and everywhere there was famine and disease, punishment and retribution.

The next year, the Marquês de Pombal, dreaming of a new city of reason and symmetry, began to rebuild Lisboa. He had a banker's vision of regular streets, perfectly kept accounts, and an immense Square of Commerce that would be open to the trade of the entire world. But Lisboa was neither Manchester nor Birmingham, and the industrial revolution occurred elsewhere. Portugal would become the poorest nation in Western Europe.

No matter how many people there are in the Praça do Comércio, it always looks half empty.

She kept little in her purse. Her gestures when handling cash were neat and precise. She hid small sums, earmarked for certain projects, in different envelopes or in the drawers of her dressing table, so that she wouldn't be tempted to spend them. Once, she lost a ten-shilling note, which represented a third of a working woman's monthly wage. It's gone! she sobbed. It's gone! She said this as if the note were an animal that had ungratefully run away after being given a good home. Gone!

When she wept, she turned away from me. This may have been to spare me, but it was also because her tears took her back to other times, before I had been thought of. While she was crying, I waited, as you wait for a long train to pass at a level crossing.

After a while, she wiped her eyes and said, We'll manage. All we have to do is make a little go a long way.

By now, I was in the Rua Augusta, one of the straight streets of the banker's dream. Because it was Sunday, the opticians and hairdressers, the travel agencies and maritime-insurance offices were shut.

People were on their way to have lunch with family or friends. Many were carrying little packages of sweetmeats, Sunday gifts, elaborately folded and knotted with their ribbons tied in bows.

On the corner of the Rua da Conceição, a crowd waited, peering toward the Madalena church. I decided to wait, too. There was no traffic. Even the trams had been stopped.

I heard people cheering farther down the street. Then a hundred and fifty runners appeared. They were moving steadily, keeping together in a bunch, encouraging one another, with no bravura or overt competitiveness. Men and women, teen-agers and seventy-year-olds, all with their heads held high, some snorting like horses when they breathed out. Their long strides beat a slow regular rhythm on the cobbles between the tram lines.

A child who wanted to see better pushed me in the back, and I stepped a little to one side. It turned out to be her. She took my hand. All her life she had had cold hands.

Do you see that man's face, she whispered. See how his face is stretched by the effort he's making?

It's stretched into a kind of smile.

And the smile is acknowledging his own name!

What's his name?

Costa. Bravo, Costa! she called.

And her?

Madalena!

You know all their names?

Madalena is smiling! Bravo, Madalena!

One man had Luiz written on his T-shirt. Luiz! I shouted, not to be outdone.

José and Dominique! she screamed.

Smiling every one! I said.

This is not a city, my boy, that fucks itself up. That's why I'm here.

I glanced at her. She, too, was smiling, and there were many folds around her eyes, and her old woman's face looked like crumpled paper. But her voice had changed. It had become the voice of a seventeen-year-old. It had the somatic assurance, the impudence of that age.

A century had passed since she was seventeen.

We walked in the direction of the Chiado, and, on the spur of the moment, I found myself entering a bakery to ask whether it had a certain dessert, a kind of custard flan with almonds called Bacon from Heaven. *Toicinho do céu.* It tastes like marzipan, and has nothing to do with bacon. My mother stayed outside. I bought two portions, and the baker's wife made a package with a ribbon the color of the Sea of Straw. I stepped out into the street.

It's what I like best. How on earth did you know? she asked me.

We found a café near the Praça de Luiz de Camões, decorated with blue-and-white *azulejo* tiles.

The blue on these tiles is the same as Reckitt's Blue soap, she said. Every little square packet was wrapped in this blue.

I remember wringing the water out of the sheets for you.

There was water everywhere.

There were mops.

You helped a lot in the mornings before you started going to school.

Before I went to school, Mother, nothing we did ever stopped. Can you guess what the fabulous object in my childhood was?

You sound like somebody writing an autobiography. Don't!

Don't what?

You're bound to get it wrong.

Don't you want to guess what the most fabulous object in my childhood was?

Tell me.

Your barometer.

The one beside your father's desk? We took it with us whenever we moved. And your father got out his toolbox and screwed it to the wall. I forget how many times. Many, many times. It was a wedding present.

There's a metal plaque pinned to it that says so. You were married on the sixth of February, 1926, and I was born on the fifth of November the same year.

It doesn't say that! How could they know? Though I knew the very second you were conceived.

I must have been conceived on your wedding night in Paris. That makes exactly nine months.

Paris. I loved Paris. The pillowcases and the statue of Molière!

Why aren't you there now, then? You could have chosen Paris.

You can't live a honeymoon all your life.

No, Mama, but perhaps all your death!

This made her laugh until she had to dab her eyes.

Every day you went to the barometer, I said, and tapped the glass with your knuckles. Then you looked at it again and announced, It's going up! Or, the next day, It's coming down! I watched you when you polished it, and I saw the secret smile on your face and knew that you had changed what was going to happen! The needle would shift, the prophesy would be different. It would be closer to FAIR, leaving CHANGE farther behind. On other days, if you were anxious, you tapped hard on the glass, and the needle shifted closer to STORMY. And it was never wrong. If it pointed to STORMY, stormy it would be.

So you believed I was in control?

I did.

I kept many things under control.

Never me!

I never tried with you.

No?

People try to control what risks getting out of control. I left you alone from the beginning.

I felt alone.

To my great surprise, my boy, you were free.

I was scared by one thing after another. I still am.

Naturally. How could it be otherwise? You can be fearless or you can be free. You can't be both.

To know how to be both is surely the aim of all philosophy, Mother.

It's not philosophy that takes you there, although love can for a few moments. She started to nibble her favorite flan.

Were you there often?

Once or twice. When she said this she smiled.

You know, don't you, I said, that after your funeral we learned, to our considerable surprise, that you'd been married long before you met Father?

Everything comes out in the wash! she said. We loved each other a lot, the first husband and I.

So what made you get divorced?

Because I wanted to have children. She pointed at me with a finger that had custard on it.

And he didn't?

He and I looked at the stars together. In the beginning, I wasn't in a hurry. I was only seventeen. To tell the truth, I was sixteen when I met him—1909, the year I read Maeterlinck's "Blue Bird." I met him in the Tate Gallery. I went there every Sunday to look at Turner's paintings. He invited me to have a cup of tea—there wasn't much coffee in those days—and he told me all about Turner's double life as an old man. I thought *he* was an old man—though he was only half as old as you are today And I remember wondering whether he had a double life, too.

He was the first person ever to call me Miriam. At home, I'd always been Mim. I left the stables and the warehouse horses my father looked after, and I was Mim. I walked across the Vauxhall Bridge, and on the other side of the Thames, where he greeted me, I was suddenly Miriam.

You married him when?

He'd come back from India, and I thought that if I married him it would be a way of keeping him, and I kept him for nine years. For nine years he was happy with his wife.

He didn't work?

He wondered about things, he asked questions. And I learned and I read, so I could talk with him. Sometimes we talked all night. He'd wake me up and take me out into the garden; we had a big garden, and at the bottom of it was a bust of Seneca, and nobody could see us, and we'd stand there like Adam and Eve watching the sun come up.

Like Adam and Eve?

Naked.

The house was where?

Croydon.

Croydon! I shouted in surprise.

Sh-h-h! Don't shout, people don't shout in this city. And I still remember the words I learned by heart sitting under that statue. "You must want nothing if you wish to challenge Jupiter, who himself wants nothing!"

But by now you wanted children and Jupiter didn't!

Don't be vulgar. Alfred worshipped me. Do you understand? He made me feel very beautiful. Your father was a more manly man. Alfred worshipped me.

Did Father meet Alfred?

After the divorce, he became a tramp.

That must have been hard on you.

It was what he wanted.

I think I saw him once.

You couldn't have!

One day in Croydon you left me in a big store.

Kennards!

You left me in the toy department.

You loved watching the trains. The new electric trains.

You took me to the toy department and said, Wait here, John, I won't be gone long. I waited. The trains seemed to go slower and slower. I wasn't worried, but it was a long while. I watched the signals change color a thousand times. When you came back, you looked very flushed, as if you'd been running. We took the lift straight down to the ground floor. Outside, behind the store, in a back street, a man blocked our way, and you put your handkerchief up to your face. His clothes were held together with string. He had a straggling beard. And his expression! I couldn't take my eyes off his face.

Alfred! my mother whispered.

He was large, I said, and his decrepitude made him look larger still. You remember what happened next? He gave you something in a packet.

It was some letters. He said he didn't have anyplace to keep them now that he was on the street, and he couldn't bring himself to destroy them, so he wanted to give them back.

They still exist?

She shook her head.

I burned them, burned them as soon as we got home.

Then he put out a filthy hand and ruffled my hair and he said to you, He needs taking care of.

My mother started to cry in the café with the blue-and-white *azulejos*.

You were still in love with him?

He had eyes that burned through you.

The moment I saw him I knew you'd been with him that afternoon, I said.

He died soon after. He was knocked down by a car.

She put her hands up to her face to hide it.

It's dangerous, she muttered, to live on just virtue, or what Seneca called wisdom. It leads to addiction, like drink. I've seen it.

Why did he say I needed taking care of?

She lowered her hands.

He could tell by looking at you. You were ten, and you had a mouth that was always hanging open.

Did he know that you had children?

I hid nothing from him.

A face so full of pain, I said.

There followed a long silence and we both looked out the window and watched the white of the buildings and the blue of the sky.

Then she said, Alfred taught me and I taught you and I'm telling you that what you saw in his face wasn't only pain. Not only pain. I'm going to take a little rest now.

She got to her feet and walked slowly toward the toilets.

She is serving mashed potatoes. Nice and fluffy, she says, still stirring them with a fork. She wears a kerchief over her hair. She worked all day in the kitchen of the teahouse in which we lived. She suffered from the heat of the stoves, yet when she sucked her fingers because they had icing sugar or homemade custard on them she couldn't help smiling: she was a good cook. I see her writing in her diary. She bought herself one every year, often waiting until February, when they were cheaper. The diaries she chose invariably had a small thin pencil attached to them. The pencil slipped through a loop and lay along the golden edges of the pages. Smaller and thinner than a cigarette—she smoked a brand of cigarettes called Dumaurier—it was often the only pencil we could find to write something down with. Sometimes I drew with it. Be sure to give it back to me. It was always carefully reinserted into its loop. And with it she makes her diary entries, noting her rare appointments and, each day, systematically, the weather. Morning: rain. Afternoon: bright patches.

The trams in the center of Lisboa are very different from the red double-decker ones that used to run in Croydon; they are as cramped as small fishing boats and they are lemon-yellow. Their drivers, as they negotiate the steep one-way streets and nose their way around blind jetties, give the impression of hauling in ropes and holding rudders rather than turning wheels and operating levers. Yet, despite the sudden descents, the lurches, the choppiness, the passengers, mostly elderly, remain contemplative and calm—as if they were sitting in their living rooms. And, indeed, in places the trams, with their open windows, sway so close to these rooms that it would be easy with one's hand to touch a birdcage hanging from a balcony and with a little push set it swinging.

I had caught the No. 28. It goes to the old cemetery, the Prazeres (the Pleasures), where the mausoleums have front doors with windowpanes and you can look at the abodes of the departed. Many are furnished with low tables, chairs, bunks with bedspreads, rugs, photographs. One has a pair of dancing shoes. Another has a bicycle and a fishing rod.

As the tram was passing through the district of Bairro Alto, I saw my mother. Like other pedestrians on the narrow street, she was flattening herself against a shop front to let the tram pass. She spotted me, and, at the next corner where the tram stopped and its two sets of doors unfolded noisily like wooden curtains, she climbed aboard, took a ticket out of her purse, and, using her umbrella as a stick, as usual, came to stand beside me and slip her arm through mine.

At the next stop, she said, we're going to the market, I take it?

Yes, that was my idea.

We get off, she said, in one minute and it's downhill all the way to the Mercado da Ribeira.

She led me, tripping light-footedly, umbrella scarcely touching the flagstones, past the vegetables and fruit, to the avenues of fish. It crossed my mind that the Mercado da Ribeira was why she had chosen to come to Lisboa.

Large fish markets are strange places. Entering one, you enter another kingdom. The stony sea urchins, the locust lobsters, the lampreys, the squids, the rings, the turbots insist that here the measures of time and space are different. There are forty-five thousand species of shellfish, all of them eaters, all of them constituting food for others.

She bent over a basket of lady crabs. Their dark shells were like brown velvet, soft to the touch, and their legs were smeared with blue, as if they had sidled their way through oil.

The choicest of all crabs, she said. Here they call them *naralheira felpuda*. *Felpuda* means "hairy."

I've learned a lot since my death. You should use me while you're here. You can look things up in a dead person the way you can in a dictionary. She straightened her back and looked into my eyes with an expression I hadn't seen before. It was one of happy impertinence.

We walked down one of the aisles, past flounders, tuna, John Dories, mackerels, sardines, anchovies, sabre fish.

The sabre, she said, comes up from his depths only on nights with a full moon.

The fishmongers were women. Women with strong shoulders, hefty forearms, wearing rubber boots, handling the ice as if it were hot metal. Their tied scarves and their eyes were very feminine. They treated the fish as they might treat distant, mildly irritating members of their families. We walked down another aisle and passed a slab on which there were a dozen of the reddest fish I've seen—a scarlet fire-red, such as no flower has, even a tropical one.

Atlantic redfish, she murmured.

I've always put life before writing, I said.

Don't boast.

It's true.

Then pass over it in silence.

We stopped before a bank of salmon.

Salmon was Father's favorite dish, wasn't it?

Yes, she said, but since his death he prefers swordfish. The *espadarte!* The *espadarte* with its upper beak, like a blade, slashes out left and right, to kill the fish it is hunting. It was a swordfish—wasn't it?—that the old man of the sea wrestled with in Hemingway's story. The book made me think of your father and of life in the trenches during the Great War. What's the connection? I can't explain everything. The story made me think of your father and the war. I can't explain why.

A connection of courage?

She nodded.

I never saw a man who wept as often as your father and I never knew a man who was half as brave.

I took her arm.

The strangest thing of all is that the flesh of the *espadarte*, this huge fish, when it is marinated and cooked, is the most delicate. It dissolves in the mouth like a soufflé. Each time, after I've cooked it, I place it on his plate like a kiss.

He comes to eat it here?

Of course not. He'll eat it, wherever he is, when he happens to think of me. Just as I think of him, when I'm preparing it.

Do we have to find an *espadarte*, I asked, or can we just think of one, as we're doing now?

What are you saying? I told you it has to be marinated in lemon juice and olive oil! So we have to find lemons and a green pepper and a yellow pepper and a red one. You cut up the peppers and put them in the pan so they give off their liquid, then you pop in the fish. Takes very little time to cook—it must never be overcooked. Best to put a lid on the pan. Some serve it with capers. I don't. I'll get the fish. You go and find the lemon and peppers.

She didn't turn up again for several days.

The weather was gusty with squalls of Atlantic rain. I had an anorak pulled over my head, and I was crossing another square, the Campo dos Mártires da Pátria, named after the martyrs of the fatherland. They were executed by hanging, in 1817. All twelve of them were Freemasons, accused of being conspirators against the monarchy. The English were governing the country, and the execution was ordered by Marshal Beresford. As the twelve were being blindfolded, they prayed for the city. They were killed here, exactly where a roundabout now is.

The square, with its trams and unending traffic, is still full of prayers. You edge your way among prayers, as among cattle in a livestock market—the prayers for the martyrs or for the dead, lying in the morgue, just north of the square, or the prayers of those who have come here to be blessed by the man whose statue is in the middle of the roundabout, Dr. José Thomas de Sousa Martins. Around the statue stand stone tablets, which look like headstones for graves—some leaning against the plinth of the statue, others against one another. But they are not tombstones; what is written on them is prayers of thanks to the doctor who once cured a cirrhosis, or a bronchitis, or hemorrhoids, a case of impotence, a child's asthma, or a woman's stress. Some of the cures were performed after his death.

Dr. Sousa looked somewhat like my Uncle Edgar, my father's elder brother, a man of learning who never stopped learning. He was a man of ideals who never despaired. He was also a man whom everyone, including my mother, treated as a failure. He had a wart on the middle finger of his right hand where he held his pen, writing hundreds of pages of a book that nobody published or even read. What the two faces had in common was an unusual looseness about the mouth, indicating not weakness but a desire to kiss rather than to bite. They also had similar foreheads—not of imposing intelligence but of immense, inspiring calm. Today, a century after his death, Dr. Sousa is referred to in Lisboa as Doctor of the Heavens and of the Earth. And my Uncle Edgar still demonstrates to me the power of reticent love.

The wind was smacking wet, and the gulls were flying very low over the roofs. It was a day when people turned their backs to the sea if they had no one out on it.

Women, crouched under dark umbrellas, were selling candles. Three sizes of candle, priced accordingly, though no price was marked. The largest were thirty centimetres tall, their wax the color of parchment. Near the statue of the doctor, candles were burning on two metal tables. The tabletops, encrusted with old melted wax, had spikes for impaling the new candles, and a tall metal sheet behind to cut the wind. I watched the flames. They flickered, they guttered, they were blown sideways as from a toy dragon's mouth.

Slowly the idea came to me to buy and light some candles myself. I was thinking of a friend who, at that moment, felt lost.

I bought three of the tallest candles, which would burn the longest, and I walked over to one of the tables and impaled them, one after the other. Only then did it occur to me that I should have lit one first from a burning candle. Now it would be difficult in the wind to light them with a match, and anyway I didn't have any matches.

As I realized my mistake, a woman behind me offered me a

small candle. I took it, without looking around, not doubting for a moment who had offered it to me. Then I stood there, mesmerized by the three new, flickering flames.

When I did at last turn, I was amazed to discover that the woman behind me was not my mother.

I'm so sorry, I blurted out, I thought you were my mother! I spoke in French, which is the language I fall back on when I'm confused.

I think I'm almost young enough to be your daughter, she replied lightly, speaking French with a Portuguese accent. I gave her back her candle, which was still burning, and I bowed.

She had blue eyes. Her face was strong but unprotected. Senhora, can I offer you a coffee out of the rain? I asked.

No, I'll place my candle and then I must get home. It's for my husband.

He's ill?

No, he's not ill. He had an accident—fell off the roof he was working on.

Is he badly hurt?

She stared at my chest, as if it were the distant Sea of Straw. I knew then that he was dead.

You should have brought an umbrella like me, she said. Our candles will go on burning, doing whatever they can without us.

I stepped off the roundabout and found a café. I went inside and took off my soaked anorak. The café was full of people, and many of them were particularly well dressed. I heard German and English. The clientele, I concluded, were probably from the nearby embassies.

So this morning you went to see Dr. Sousa. There was a good man! Some of us still go to consult him.

I heard her say this, yet I couldn't see her. I was sitting alone.

What do they complain of, I whisper—your friends who consult him?

Many suffer from hopefulness. Among us hopefulness is as common as depression among the living.

You see hopefulness as an illness?

One of its terminal symptoms is a desire to intervene again in life.

Is there a cure?

Dr. Sousa prescribes a spell with the martyrs!

It seems he loved women, I told her, and sometimes he prescribed himself as the cure.

She laughed. A crystalline laugh, as if all the people in the café were clinking glasses. Nobody else gave any sign of hearing it.

If they made a film about him, he'd be played by Groucho Marx, she said.

In the Davies Picture Palace, the two of us saw "A Night at the Opera" and "Duck Soup." Her laughter in the cinema had been muffled, as if she didn't want to draw attention to our presence, which bordered on being illicit—because neither of us had mentioned our visit to the Picture Palace to anybody else, and, in a more direct sense, because she had contrived to get us in without paying. A question of narrow uncarpeted stairs and safety exits.

All my books have been about you, I suddenly said.

Nonsense! Maybe you wrote them so I should be there, keeping you company. And I was. Yet they were about everything in the world but me! I've had to wait until now, until you are an old man in Lisboa, for you to be writing this very short story about me.

Books are also about language, and language for me is inseparable from your voice.

You're trying to be clever. Don't. Just think of me. Then you'll learn endurance. Something that can be learned only from a woman, never from a man.

Scott in the Antarctic?

Think of Scott's wife. Her name was Kathleen. I regret, Kathleen said, nothing but his suffering.

Why did you never read any of my books?

I liked books that took me to another life—a life I might have lived. That's why I read the books I did. Many. When I read them, I lost all sense of time. Your books, I hoped, were about another life but one I wanted only to imagine. So it was better that I didn't read them. I could see them through the glass door of the bookcase. That was enough for me.

I risk writing nonsense these days.

You put something down and you don't immediately know what it is. It has always been like that, she said. All you need to know is whether you're lying or telling the truth. You can't afford to make a mistake about that distinction any longer.

I was thirteen when she had to have all her teeth pulled. She was brought back home in a taxi. I stood at the door of her bedroom. She lay on her back, chin protruding, cheeks hollow through the new lack of teeth. I knew I had to choose between two things. I could scream or I could go and lie beside her. So I lay beside her. She was too artful to show her pleasure immediately. We both had to wait. After several minutes, she pulled an arm out from under the bedclothes and held my wrist in her cold hand. She kept her eyes shut. Most people, she said, can't stand the truth. It's too bad but there it is, most people can't stand it. You, John, I think you can bear the truth, we'll see. Time will tell.

Where do I see you again? I asked.

On the aqueduct. The Águas Livres Aqueduct.

It's very long—fourteen kilometres, I think.

Where it crosses the Alcântara Valley. The arches are sixty metres high there. From up there, you can almost see America! I'll be waiting for you by the sixteenth arch.

The sixteenth counting which way?

What do you think? From the Mãe d'Água. I'll meet you there on Tuesday morning.

As soon as I started asking how to get up on to the aqueduct, I understood why she had slyly made the rendezvous for the following Tuesday. It was going to take some time. All the entrances were locked, and one had to apply for permission from the Water Company. Even supposing that one had a persuasive reason, there was bound to be a bureaucratic delay. I decided I would claim that I was writing a story about Lisbon.

Do you know the city well? the publicist asked me. She looked worried, as if she had to correct too many exam papers.

No, I replied, I love the city but I don't know it well. That's why I need your help.

As you are probably aware, the Águas Livres supplied water to the city until a very few years ago. Now it doesn't, but we keep it running as—how do you say?—as a kind of homage. You could go up on Monday morning with Fernando. He's the maintenance inspector.

Could it be Tuesday?

I thought you said it was urgent.

Tuesday would be better.

Then come Tuesday.

Fernando turned out to be a man in his mid-sixties, awaiting retirement. He had worked all his life for the Empresa Portuguesa das Águas Livres. He held himself very upright for his age, and he had the air of a man used to being alone—like a shepherd or a steeplejack. His private passion was for the water on its long, solitary, unnatural, improbable journey from its sources. A journey underground, overground, and through the sky. Up there, in its ducts, the water had to be kept cool—tranquil and transparent.

The aqueduct at its top is only about five metres wide and consists of an apparently endless stone tunnel and an open, very straight path on either side. Fernando considered the water something alive, which had to be protected, fed, cleaned up after—almost like an animal in a zoo. Once a week, he walked the fourteen kilometres to the water's sources in Belas. I think he had the impression that the water, when he approached, recognized him.

I told him that I wanted to see the view, and he nodded and unlocked a door that led into the tunnel, saying that when I was finished I could come and find him.

I started walking fast down the outside path, enticed by the aqueduct's straightness. When I reached the far side of the valley, I turned back and counted the arches until I found the sixteenth, which was not far from Fernando's open door. Later, while leaning against the parapet opposite, I thought I heard him talking—brief sentences, as if making notes. Yet there was nobody with him.

Below, there were unfinished streets and houses. A poor suburb rather than a *favela*. I could see a car without wheels, a balcony the size of a kitchen chair, a child's swing with only one rope attached to a tree, red tiles with concrete blocks on them to prevent them being blown away by the Atlantic winds, a window without a frame and with a double mattress hanging out of it, a dog on a chain, barking in the sun.

Do you see? she suddenly said. Everything is broken, slightly broken, like factory rejects sold at half price. Not really damaged, only rejects. Everything—the hills, the Sea of Straw, the child's swing, the car, everything is a reject, and has been so since the beginning.

She was sitting on a portable stool. It had three folding legs and was very light, and she used to carry it with her so she could sit down in public places. She was wearing a cloche hat.

Everything in the universe, she said, began sour, then went sweet, and afterward became bitter.

Did Father enjoy his swordfish? I asked.

I'm talking about life, not about details, she said. There was a mistake at the beginning.

I don't understand.

One day, when you're in my situation, you will. The Creation, she continued, began with a death.

Two white butterflies were circling above her hat. Perhaps they had come with her, for there was little on the aqueduct at that height to attract butterflies.

Surely, I asked, the Creation would begin with a birth?

You'd think so, but now I see it wasn't like that. The births came later. Precisely because they offered the chance of repairing some of what was damaged after the death. That's why we are here, John. To repair.

Yet you are not really here, are you?

How stupid can you get! We—us—we are all here. Just as you and the living are here—to repair a little of what was broken. This is why we occurred.

Occurred?

Came to be. Don't forget, she said, one thing repaired changes a thousand others!

At this point, she got up from her stool.

The dog down there, she remarked, is on too short a chain. Change it, lengthen it. Then he'll be able to reach the shade, and he'll lie down and stop barking. And the silence will remind the mother that she wanted a canary in a cage in the kitchen. And when the canary sings she'll do more ironing. And the father's shoulders in a freshly ironed shirt will ache less when he goes to work. And so when he comes home he'll sometimes joke, as he once did, with his teen-age daughter. And the daughter will change her mind and decide, exceptionally, to bring her lover home one evening. And on another evening the father will propose to the young man that they go fishing together.

The dog was still barking.

Write down whatever you find, and do us the courtesy of noticing us.

You *are* no longer here!

Hence the courtesy, John!

After saying this, she handed me the folding stool, and proceeded to the door that Fernando had left unlocked. She tugged it open and stepped—as if she had done the same thing every morning of her life—over the water duct, up onto the narrow flagged walkway.

Inside, the air was cooler, as if we were underground instead of in the sky. Every fifty metres, the vaulted roof opened out into a small tower, which was built so that daylight could enter through it. The daylight fell like a golden curtain. In the quiet, we heard the lapping—as discreet as a cat's tongue when drinking—of water flowing down the channels on its way to the Mãe d'Água.

I don't know how long we stood there facing each other—perhaps we had been there for the fifteen years since her death. After the death of a mother, time often accelerates, no?

Eventually, she turned, bit her lower lip, and began to walk away. The courtesy, John! she said, without looking back.

She approached the first cascade of light. On either side, the water reflected sparks that bobbed up and down like floating candles. When she entered the light, it hid her like a curtain, and I did not see her again until she came out on the far side. She seemed to be walking with increasing ease; the farther away she got, the more sprightly she became. She was small because of the distance. She disappeared into the next golden curtain and when she reëmerged I could scarcely see her.

I bent down, and I let my hand trail in the water that was flowing after her.

MY FATHER ADDRESSES ME ON THE FACTS OF OLD AGE

BY GRACE PALEY (2002)

My father had decided to teach me how to grow old. I said O.K. My children didn't think it was such a great idea. If I knew how, they thought, I might do so too easily. No, no, I said, it's for later, years from now. And, besides, if I get it right it might be helpful to you kids in time to come.

They said, Really?

My father wanted to begin as soon as possible. For God's sake, he said, you can talk to the kids later. Now, listen to me, send them out to play. You are so distractable.

We should probably begin at the beginning, he said. Change. First there is change, which nobody likes—even men. You'd be surprised. You can do little things—putting cream on the corners of your mouth, also the heels of your feet. But here is the main thing. Oh, I wish your mother was alive—not that she had time—

But Pa, I said, Mama never knew anything about cream. I did not say she was famous for not taking care.

Forget it, he said sadly. But I must mention squinting. DON'T SQUINT. Wear your glasses. Look at your aunt, so beautiful once. I know someone has said men don't make passes at girls who wear glasses, but that's an idea for a foolish person. There are many handsome women who are not exactly twenty-twenty.

Please sit down, he said. Be patient. The main thing is this—

when you get up in the morning you must take your heart in your two hands. You must do this every morning.

That's a metaphor, right?

Metaphor? No, no, you can do this. In the morning, do a few little exercises for the joints, not too much. Then put your hands like a cup over and under the heart. Under the breast, he said tactfully. It's probably easier for a man. Then talk softly, don't yell. Under your ribs, push a little. When you wake up, you must do this massage. I mean pat, stroke a little, don't be ashamed. Very likely no one will be watching. Then you must talk to your heart.

Talk? What?

Say anything, but be respectful. Say—maybe say, Heart, little heart, beat softly but never forget your job, the blood. You can whisper also, Remember, remember. For instance, I said to it yesterday, Heart, heart, do you remember my brother, Grisha, how he made work for you that day when he came to the store and he said, Your boss's money, Zenya, right now? How he put a gun in my face and I said, Grisha, are you crazy? Why don't you ask me at home? I would give you. We were in this America not more than two years. He was only a kid. And he said, he said, Who needs your worker's money? For the movement—only from your boss. O little heart, you worked like a bastard, like a dog, like a crazy slave, bang, bang, bang that day, remember? That's the story I told my heart yesterday, my father said. What a racket it made to answer me, I remember, I remember, till I was dizzy with the thumping.

Why'd you do that, Pa? I don't get it.

Don't you see? This is good for the old heart—to get excited—just as good as for the person. Some people go running till late in life—for the muscles, they say, but the heart knows the real purpose. The purpose is the expansion of the arteries, a river of blood, it cleans off the banks, carries junk out of the system. I myself would rather remind the heart how frightened I was by my brother than go running in a strange neighborhood, miles and miles, with the city so dangerous these days.

I said, Oh, but then I said, Well, thanks.

I don't think you listened, he said. As usual—probably worried about the kids. They're not babies, you know. If you were better organized you wouldn't have so many worries.

. . .

I stopped by a couple of weeks later. This time he was annoyed.

Why did you leave the kids home? If you keep doing this, they'll forget who I am. Children are like old people in that respect.

They won't forget you, Pa, never in a million years.

You think so? God has not been so good about a million years. His main interest in us began—actually, he put it down in writing fifty-six, fifty-seven hundred years ago. In the Book. You know our Book, I suppose.

O.K. Yes.

Probably a million years is too close to his lifetime, if you could call it life, what he goes through. I believe he said several times—when he was still in contact with us—I am a jealous God. Here and there he makes an exception. I read there are three-thousand-year-old trees somewhere in some godforsaken place. Of course, that's how come they're still alive. We should all be so godforsaken.

But no more joking around. I have been thinking what to tell you now. First of all, soon, maybe in twenty, thirty years, you'll begin to get up in the morning—4, 5 A.M. In a farmer that's O.K., but for us—you'll remember everything you did, didn't, what you omitted, whom you insulted, betrayed—betrayed, that is the worst. Do you remember, you didn't go see your aunt, she was dying? That will be on your mind like a stone. Of course, I myself did not behave so well. Still, I was so busy those days, long office hours, remember it was usual in those days for doctors to make house calls. No elevators, fourth floor, fifth floor, even in a nice Bronx tenement. But this morning, I mean *this* morning, a few hours ago, my mother, your babushka, came into my mind, looked at me.

Have I told you I was arrested? Of course I did. I was arrested a few times, but this time for some reason the policeman walked me past the office of the local jail. My mama was there. I saw her through the window. She was bringing me a bundle of clean clothes. She put it on the officer's table. She turned. She saw me. She looked at me through the glass with such a face, eye-to-eye. Despair. No hope. This morning, 4 A.M., I saw once more how she sat there, very straight. Her eyes. Because of that look, I did my term, my sentence, the best I could. I finished up six months in Arkhangel'sk, where they finally sent me. Then no more, no more,

I said to myself, no more saving Imperial Russia, the great pogrom-maker, from itself.

Oh, Pa.

Don't make too much out of everything. Well, anyway, I want to tell you also how the body is your enemy. I must warn you it is not your friend the way it was when you were a youngster. For example. Greens—believe me—are overrated. Some people believe they will cure cancer. It's the style. My experience with maybe a hundred patients proves otherwise. Greens are helpful to God. That fellow Sandburg, the poet—I believe from Chicago—explained it. Grass tiptoes over the whole world, holds it in place—except the desert, of course, everything there is loose, flying around.

How come you bring up God so much? When I was a kid you were a strict atheist, you even spit on the steps of the synagogue.

Well, God is very good for conversation, he said. By the way, I believe I have to tell you a few words about the stock market. Your brother-in-law is always talking about how brilliant he is, investing, investing. My advice to you: Stay out of it.

But people *are* making money. A lot. Read the paper. Even kids are becoming millionaires.

But what of tomorrow? he asked.

Tomorrow, I said, they'll make another million.

No, no, no, I mean TOMORROW. I was there when TOMORROW came in 1929. So I say to them and their millions, HA HA HA, TOMORROW will come. Go home now, I have a great deal more to tell you. Somehow, I'm always tired.

I'll go in a minute—but I have to tell you something, Pa. I had to tell him that my husband and I were separating. Maybe even divorce, the first in the family.

What? What? Are you crazy? I don't understand you people nowadays. I married your mother when I was a boy. It's true I had a first-class mustache, but I was a kid, and you know I stayed married till the end. Once or twice, she wanted to part company, but not me. The reason, of course, she was inclined to be jealous.

He then gave me the example I'd heard five or six times before. What it was, one time two couples went to the movies. Arzemich and his wife, you remember. Well, I sat next to his wife, the lady of the couple, by the way a very attractive woman, and during the show, which wasn't so great, we talked about this and that, laughed a couple times. When we got home, your mother said, O.K. Anytime you want, right now, I'll give you a divorce. We will go our separate ways. Naturally, I said, What? Are you ridiculous?

My advice to you—stick it out. It's true your husband, he's a peculiar fellow, but think it over. Go home. Maybe you can manage at least till old age. Then, if you still don't get along, you can go to separate old-age homes.

Pa, it's no joke. It's my life.

It is a joke. A joke is necessary at this time. But I'm tired.

You'll see, in thirty, forty years from now, you'll get tired often. It doesn't mean you're sick. This is something important that I'm telling you. Listen. To live a long time, long years, you've got to sleep a certain extra percentage away. It's a shame.

It was at least three weeks before I saw him again. He was drinking tea, eating a baked apple, one of twelve my sister baked for him every ten days. I took another one out of the refrigerator. "Fathers and Sons" was on the kitchen table. Most of the time he read history. He kept Gibbon and Prescott on the lamp stand next to his resting chair. But this time, thinking about Russia for some reason in a kindly way, he was reading Turgenev.

You were probably pretty busy, he said. Where are the kids? With the father? He looked at me hopefully.

No hope, Pa.

By the way, you know, this fellow Turgenev? He wasn't a showoff. He wrote a certain book, and he became famous right away. One day he went to Paris, and in the evening he went to the opera. He stepped into his box, and just as he was sitting down the people began to applaud. The whole opera house was clapping. He was known. Everybody knew his book. He said, I see Russia is known in France.

You're a lucky girl that these books are in the living room, more on the table than on the shelf.

Yes.

Excuse me, also about Turgenev, I don't believe he was an anti-Semite. Of course, most of them were, even if they had brains. I don't think Gorky was, Gogol probably. Tolstoy, no, Tolstoy had an opinion about the Mexican-American War. Did you know? Of course, most were anti-Semites. Dostoyevsky. It was natural, it seems. Ach, why is it we read them with such interest and they don't return the favor?

That's what women writers say about men writers.

Please don't start in. I'm in the middle of telling you some things you don't know. Well, I suppose you do know a number of Gentiles, you're more in the American world. I know very few. Still, I was telling you—Jews were not allowed to travel in Russia. I told you that. But a Jewish girl if she was a prostitute could go anywhere throughout all Russia. Also a Jew if he was a merchant first class. Even people with big stores were only second class. Who else? A soldier who had a medal, I think St. George. Do you know nobody could arrest him? Even if he was a Jew. If he killed someone a policeman could not arrest him. He wore a certain hat. Why am I telling you all this?

Well, it is interesting.

Yes, but I'm supposed to tell you a few things, give advice, a few last words. Of course, the fact is I am obliged because you are always getting yourself mixed up in politics. Because your mother and I were such radical kids—socialists—in constant trouble with the police—it was 1904, 5. You have the idea it's O.K. for you and it is not O.K. in this country, which is a democracy. And you're running in the street like a fool. Your cousin saw you a few years ago in school, suspended. Sitting with other children in the auditorium, not allowed to go to class. You thought Mama and I didn't know.

Pa, that was thirty-five years ago, in high school. Anyway, what *about* Mama? You mentioned the Arzemich family. She was a dentist, wasn't she?

Right, a very capable woman.

Well, Mama probably felt bad about not getting to school and, you know, becoming something, having a profession like Mrs. What's-Her-Name. I mean, she did run the whole house and family and the office and people coming to live with us, but she was sad about that, surely.

He was quiet. Then he said, You're right. It was a shame, everything went into me, so I should go to school, I should graduate, I should be the doctor, I should have the profession. Poor woman, she was extremely smart. At least as smart as me. In Russia, in the movement, you know, when we were youngsters, she was considered the more valuable person. Very steady, honest. Made first-class contact with the workers, a real organizer. I could be only an intellectual. But maybe if life didn't pass so quick, speedy, like a winter day—short. You know, also, she was very musical, she had perfect pitch. A few years ago your sister made similar remarks to me about Mama. Questioning me, like history is my fault. Your brother only looked at me the way he does—not with complete approval.

Then one day my father surprised me. He said he wanted to talk a little, but not too much, about love or sex or whatever it's called—its troubling persistence. He said that might happen to me, too, eventually. It should not be such a surprise. Then, a little accusingly, After all, I have been a man alone for many years. Did you ever think about that? Maybe I suffered. Did it even enter your mind? You're a grownup woman, after all.

But Pa, I wouldn't ever have thought of bringing up anything like that—you and Mama were so damn puritanical. I never heard you say the word "sex" till this day—either of you.

We were serious Socialists, he said. So? He looked at me, raising one nice thick eyebrow. You don't understand politics too well, do you?

Actually, I had thought of it now and then, his sexual aloneness. I was a grownup woman. But I turned it into a tactful question: Aren't you sometimes lonely, Pa?

I have a nice apartment.

Then he closed his eyes. He rested his talking self. I decided to water the plants. He opened one eye. Take it easy. Don't overwater.

Anyway, he said, only your mother, a person like her, could put up with me. Her patience—you know, I was always losing my temper. But finally with us everything was all right, ALL right, accomplished. Do you understand? Your brother and sister finished college, married. We had a beautiful grandchild. I was working very hard, like a dog. We were only fifty years old then, but, look, we bought the place in the country. Your sister and brother came often. You yourself were running around with a dozen kids in bathing suits all day. Your mama was planting all kinds of flowers every minute. Trees were growing. Your grandma, your babushka, sat on a good chair on the lawn. In back of her were birch trees. I put in a nice row of spruce. Then one day in the morning she comes to me, my wife. She shows me a spot over her left breast. I know right away. I don't touch it. I see it. In my mind I turn it this way and that. But I know in that minute, in one minute, everything is finished, finished—happiness, pleasure, finished, years ahead black.

No. That minute had been told to me a couple of years ago, maybe twice in ten years. Each time it nearly stopped my heart. No.

He recovered from the telling. Now, listen, this means, of course, that you should take care of yourself. I don't mean eat vegetables. I mean go to the doctor on time. Nowadays a woman as sick as your mama could live many years. Your sister, for example, after terrible operations—heart bypass, colon cancer—more she probably hides from me. She is running around to theatre, concerts, probably supports Lincoln Center. Ballet, chamber, symphony—three, four times a week. But you must pay attention. One good thing, don't laugh, is bananas. Really. Potassium. I myself eat one every day.

But, seriously, I'm running out of advice. It's too late to beg you to finish school, get a couple of degrees, a decent profession, be a little more strict with the children. They should be prepared for the future. Maybe they won't be as lucky as you. Well, no more advice. I restrain myself.

Now I'm changing the whole subject. I will ask you a favor. You have many friends—teachers, writers, intelligent people. Jews, non-Jews. These days I think often, especially after telling you the story a couple of months ago, about my brother Grisha. I want to know what happened to him.

I guess we know he was deported around 1922, right?

Yes, yes, but why did they go after him? The last ten years before that, he calmed down quite a bit, had a nice job, I think. But that's what they did—did you know? Even after the Palmer raids—that was maybe 1919—they kept deporting people. They picked them up at home, at the Russian Artists' Club, at meetings. Of course, you weren't even around yet, maybe just born. They thought that these kids had in mind a big revolution—like in Russia. Some joke. Ignorance. Grisha and his friends didn't like Lenin from the beginning. More Bakunin. Emma Goldman, her boyfriend, I forgot his name.

Berkman.

Right. They were shipped, I believe, to Vladivostok. There must be a file somewhere. Archives salted away. Why did they go after him? Maybe they were mostly Jews. Anti-Semitism in the American blood from Europe—a little thinner, I suppose. But why didn't we talk? All the years not talking. Me seeing sick people day and night. Strangers. And not talking to my brother till all of a sudden he's on a ship. Gone.

Go home now. I don't have much more to tell you. Anyway, it's late. I have to prepare now all of my courage, not for sleep, for waking in the early morning, maybe 3 or 4 A.M. I have to be ready for them, my morning visitors—your babushka, your mama, most of all, to tell the truth, it's for your aunt, my sister, the youngest. She said to me, that day in the hospital, Don't leave me here, take me home to die. And I didn't. And her face looked at me that day and many, many mornings looks at me still.

I stood near the door holding my coat. A space at last for me to say something. My mouth open.

Enough, already, he said. I had the job to tell you how to take care of yourself, what to expect. About the heart—you know it was not a metaphor. But in the end a great thing, a really interesting thing, would be to find out what happened to our Grisha. You're smart. You can do it. Also, you'll see, you'll be lucky in this life to have something you must do to take your mind off all the things you didn't do.

Then he said, I suppose that is something like a joke. But, my dear girl, very serious.

GALLATIN CANYON

BY THOMAS MCGUANE (2003)

The day we planned the trip, I told Louise that I didn't like going to Idaho via the Gallatin Canyon. It's too narrow, and while trucks don't belong on this road, there they are, lots of them. Tourist pulloffs and wild animals on the highway complete the picture. We could have gone by way of Ennis, but Louise had learned that there were road repairs on Montana Highway 84—twelve miles of torn-up asphalt—in addition to its being rodeo weekend, and "Do we have to go to Idaho?" she asked.

I said that I thought it was obvious. A lot rode on the success of our little jaunt, which was ostensibly to close the sale of a small car dealership I owned in the sleepy town of Rigby. But, since accepting the offer of a local buyer, I had received a far better one from elsewhere, which, my attorney said, I couldn't take unless my original buyer backed out—and he would only back out if he got sufficiently angry at me. Said my attorney: Make him mad. So I was headed to Rigby, Idaho, expressly to piss off a small-town businessman, who was trying to give me American money for a going concern on the strip east of town, and thereby make room for a rich Atlanta investor, new to our landscapes, who needed this dealership as a kind of flagship for his other intentions. The question was how to provoke Rigby without arousing his suspicions, and I might have collected my thoughts a little better had I not had to battle trucks and tourists in the Gallatin Canyon.

Louise and I had spent a lot of time together in recent years, and we were both probably wondering where things would go from here. She had been married, briefly, long ago, and that fact, together with the relatively peaceful intervening years, gave a pleasant detachment to most of her relationships, including the one she had with me. In the past, that would have suited me perfectly; but it did not seem to suit me now, and I was so powerfully attached to her it made me uncomfortable that she wasn't interested in discussing our mutual future, though at least she had never suggested that we wouldn't *have* one. With her thick blond hair pulled back in a barrette, her strong, shapely figure, and the direct fullness of her mouth, she was often noticed by other men. After ten years in Montana, she still had a strong Massachusetts accent. Louise was a lawyer, specializing in the adjudication of water rights between agricultural and municipal interests. In our rapidly changing world, she was much in demand. Though I wished we could spend more time together, Louise had taught me not to challenge her on this.

No longer the country crossroads of recent memory, Four Corners was filled with dentists' offices, fast-food and espresso shops, large and somehow foreboding filling stations that looked, at night, like colonies in space; nevertheless, the intersection was true to its name, sending you north to a transcontinental interstate, east into town, west to the ranches of Madison County, and south, my reluctant choice, up the Gallatin Canyon to Yellowstone and the towns of southeast Idaho, one of which contained property with my name on the deed.

We joined the stream of traffic heading south, the Gallatin River alongside and usually much below the roadway, a dashing high-gradient river with anglers in reflective stillness at the edges of its pools, and bright rafts full of delighted tourists in flotation jackets and crash helmets sweeping through its white water. Gradually, the mountains pressed in on all this humanity, and I found myself behind a long line of cars trailing a cattle truck at well below the speed limit. This combination of cumbersome commercial traffic and impatient private cars was a lethal mixture that kept our canyon in the papers, as it regularly spat out corpses. In my rearview mirror, I could see a line behind me that was just as long as the one ahead, stretching back, thinning, and vanishing around a green bend. There was no passing lane for several miles. A single amorous elk could have turned us all into twisted, smoking metal.

"You might have been right," Louise said. "It doesn't look good."

She almost certainly had better things to do. But, looking down the line of cars, I felt my blood pressure rising. Her hands rested quietly in her lap. I couldn't possibly have rivalled such serenity.

"How do you plan to anger this guy in Rigby?" she asked.

"I'm going to try haughtiness. If I suggest that he bought the dealership cheap, he might tell me to keep the damn thing. The Atlanta guy just wants to start *somewhere*. All these people have a sort of parlay mentality and they need to get on the playing field before they can start running it up. I'm a trader. It all happens for me in the transition. The moment of liquidation is the essence of capitalism."

"What about the man in Rigby?"

"He's an end user. He wants to keep it."

I reflected on the pathos of ownership and the way it could bog you down.

"You should be in my world," Louise said. "According to the law, water has no reality except its use. In Montana, water isn't even wet. Every time some misguided soul suggests that fish need it, it ends up in the state supreme court."

Birds were fleeing the advance of automobiles. I was elsewhere, trying to imagine my buyer, red-faced, storming out of the closing. I'd offer to let bygones be bygones, I'd take him to dinner, I'd throw a steak into him, for Christ's sake. In the end, he'd be glad he wasn't stuck with the lot.

Traffic headed toward us, far down the road. We were all packed together to make sure no one tried to pass. The rules had to be enforced. Occasionally, someone drifted out for a better look, but not far enough that someone else could close his space and possibly seal his fate.

This trip had its risks. I had only recently admitted to myself that I would like to make more of my situation with Louise than currently existed. Though ours was hardly a chaste relationship, real intimacy was relatively scarce. People in relationships nowadays seemed to retain their secrets like bank deposits—they always set some aside, in case they might need them to spend on someone new. I found it unpleasant to think that Louise could be withholding anything.

But I thought I was more presentable than I had been. When Louise and I first met, I was just coming off two and a half years of peddling satellite dishes in towns where a couple of dogs doing the wild thing in the middle of the road amounted to the high point of a year, and the highest-grossing business was a methamphetamine tent camp out in the sagebrush. Now I had caught the upswing in our local economy—cars, storage, tool rental, and mortgage-discounting. I had a pretty home, debt-free, out on Sourdough. I owned a few things. I could be O.K. I asked Louise what she thought of the new prosperity around us. She said, wearily, "I'm not sure it's such a good thing, living in a boomtown. It's basically a high-end carny atmosphere."

We were just passing Storm Castle and Garnet Mountain. When I glanced in the mirror, I saw a low red car with a scoop in its hood pull out to pass. I must have reacted somehow, because Louise asked me if I would like her to drive.

"No, that's fine. Things are getting a bit lively back there."

"Drive defensively."

"Not much choice, is there?"

I had been mentally rehearsing the closing in Rigby, and I wasn't getting anywhere. I had this sort of absurd picture of myself strutting into the meeting. I tried again to picture the buyer looking seriously annoyed, but I'd met him before and he seemed pretty levelheaded. I suspected I'd have to be really outlandish to get a rise out of him. He was a fourth-generation resident of Rigby, so I could always urge him to get to know his neighbors, I decided. Or, since he had come up through the service department, I could try emphasizing the need to study how the cars actually ran. I'd use hand signals to fend off objections. I felt more secure.

Some elk had wandered into the parking lot at Buck's T4 and were grazing indifferently as people pulled off the highway to admire them. I don't know if it was the great unmarred blue sky overhead or the balsamic zephyr that poured down the mountainside, but I found myself momentarily buoyed by all this idleness, people out of their cars. I am always encouraged when I see animals doing something other than running for their lives. In any case, the stream of traffic ahead of us had been much reduced by the pedestrian rubbernecking.

"My husband lived here one winter," Louise said. "He sold his pharmacy after we divorced, not that he had to, and set out to change his life. He became a mountain man, wore buckskin clothes. He tried living off the land one day a week, with the idea that he would build up. But then he just stuck with one day a week—he'd shoot a rabbit or something, more of a diet, really. He's a real-estate agent now, at Big Sky. I think he's doing well. At least he's quit killing rabbits."

"Remarried?"

"Yes."

As soon as we hit the open country around West Yellowstone, Louise called her office. When her secretary put her on hold, Louise covered the mouthpiece and said, "He married a super gal. Minnesota, I think. She should be good for Bob, and he's not easy. Bob's from the South. For men, it's a full-time job being Southern. It just wears them out. It wore me out, too. I developed doubtful behaviors. I pulled out my eyelashes, and ate twenty-eight hundred dollars' worth of macadamia nuts."

Her secretary came back on the line, and Louise began editing her schedule with impressive precision, mouthing the word "sorry" to me when the conversation dragged on. I began musing about my capacity to live successfully with someone as competent as Louise. There was no implied hierarchy of status between us, but I wondered if, in the long run, something would have to give.

West Yellowstone seemed entirely given over to the well-being of the snowmobile, and the billboards dedicated to it were anomalous on a sunny day like today. By winter, schoolchildren would be petitioning futilely to control the noise at night so that they could do their schoolwork, and the town would turn a blind eye as a cloud of smoke arose to gas residents, travellers, and park rangers alike. It seemed incredible to me that recreation could acquire this level of social momentum, that it could be seen as an inalienable right.

We came down Targhee Pass and into Idaho, into a wasteland of spindly pines that had replaced the former forest, and Louise gave voice to the thoughts she'd been having for the past few miles.

"Why don't you just let this deal close? You really have no guarantees from the man from Atlanta. And there's a good-faith issue here, too, I think."

"A lawyerly notation."

"So be it, but it's true. Are you trying to get every last cent out of this sale?"

"That's second. The first priority is to be done with it. It was meant to be a passive investment, and it has turned out not to be. I get twenty calls a day from the dealership, most with questions I can't answer. It's turning me into a giant bullshit machine."

"No investments are really passive."

"Mutual funds are close."

"That's why they don't pay."

"Some of them pay, or they would cease to exist."

"You make a poor libertarian, my darling. You sound like that little puke David Stockman."

"Stockman was right about everything. Reagan just didn't have the guts to take his advice."

"*Reagan*. Give me a break."

I didn't mind equal billing in a relationship, but I did dread the idea of parties speaking strictly from their entitlements across a chasm. Inevitably, sex would make chaos of much of this, but you couldn't, despite Benjamin Franklin's suggestion, "use venery" as a management tool.

Louise adjusted her seat back and folded her arms, gazing at the sunny side of the road. The light through the windshield accentuated the shape of her face, now in repose. I found her beautiful. I adored her when she was a noun and was alarmed when she was a verb, which was usually the case. I understood that this was not the best thing I could say about myself. When her hand drifted over to my leg, I hardly knew what to do with this reference to the other life we led. I knew that it was an excellent thing to be reminded of how inconsequential my worldly concerns were, but one warm hand, rested casually, and my interest travelled to the basics of the species.

Ashton, St. Anthony, Sugar City: Mormon hamlets, small farms, and the furious reordering of watersheds into industrial canals. Irrigation haze hung over the valley of the Snake, and the skies were less bright than they had been just a few miles back, in Montana. Many locals had been killed when the Teton Dam burst, and despite that they wanted to build it again: the relationship to water here was like a war, and in war lives are lost. These were the folk to whom I'd sold many a plain car; ostentation was thoroughly unacceptable hereabouts. The four-door sedan with a six-cylinder engine was the desired item, an identical one with a hundred and fifty thousand miles on it generally taken in trade at zero value, thanks to the manipulation of rebates against the manufacturer's suggested retail. Appearances were foremost, and the salesman who could leave a customer's smugness undisturbed flourished in this atmosphere. I had two of them, potato-fattened, bland opportunists with nine kids between them. They were the asset I was selling; the rest was little more than bricks and mortar.

We pressed on toward Rexburg, and amid the turnoffs for Wilford, Newdale, Hibbard, and Moody the only thing that had any flavor was Hog Hollow Road, which was a shortcut to France—not the one in Europe but the one just a hop, skip, and a jump south of Squirrel, Idaho. There were license-plate holders with my name on them in Squirrel, and I was oddly vain about that.

"Sure seems lonesome around here," Louise said.

"Oh, boy."

"The houses are like little forts."

"The winters are hard." But it was less that the small neat dwellings around us appeared defensive than that they seemed to be trying to avoid attracting the wrath of some inattentive god.

"It looks like government housing for Eskimos. They just sit inside waiting for a whale, or something."

This banter had the peculiar effect of making me want to cleave to Louise, and desperately, too—to build a warm new civilization, possibly in a foolish house with turrets. The road stretched before me like an arrow. There was only enough of it left before Rigby for me to say, perhaps involuntarily, "I wonder if we shouldn't just get married."

Louise quickly looked away. Her silence conferred a certain seriousness on my question.

. . .

But there was Rigby, and, in the parlance of all who have extracted funds from locals, Rigby had been good to me. Main Street was lined with ambitious and beautiful stone buildings, old for this part of the world. Their second and third floors were now affordable housing, and their street levels were occupied by businesses hanging on by their fingernails. You could still detect the hopes of the dead, their dreams, even, though it seemed to be only a matter of time before the wind carried them away, once and for all.

I drove past the car lot at 200 East Fremont without comment and—considering the amount of difficulty it had caused me in the years before I got it stabilized and began to enjoy its very modest yields—without much feeling. I remembered the day, sometime earlier, when I had tried to help park the cars in the front row and got everything so crooked that the salesmen, not concealing their contempt, had to do it all over again. The title company where we were heading was on the same street, and it was a livelier place, from the row of perky evergreens out front to the merry receptionist who greeted us, a handsome young woman, probably a farm girl only moments before, enjoying the clothes, makeup, and perquisites of the new world that her firm was helping to build.

We were shown into a spacious conference room with a long table and chairs, freshly sharpened pencils, and crisp notepads bearing the company letterhead. "Shall I stay?" Louise asked, the first thing she'd said since my earlier inadvertent remark, which I intuited had not been altogether rejected.

"Please," I said, gesturing toward a chair next to the one I meant to take. At that moment, the escrow agent entered and, standing very close to us, introduced himself as Brent Colby. Then he went to the far end of the table, where he spread his documents around in an orderly fan. Colby was around fifty, with iron-gray hair and a deeply lined face. He wore pressed jeans, a brilliant-white snap-button shirt, cowboy boots, and a belt buckle with a steer head on it. He had thick, hairy hands and a gleaming wedding band. Just as he raised his left wrist to check his watch, the door opened and Oren Johnson, the buyer, entered. He went straight to Louise and, taking her hand in both of his, introduced himself. It occurred to me that, in trying to be suave, Oren Johnson had revealed himself to be a clodhopper, but I was probably just experiencing the mild hostility that emanates from every sale of property. Oren wore a suit, though it suggested less a costume for business than one for church. He had a gold tooth and a cautious pompadour. He, too, bore an investment-grade wedding band, and I noted that there was plenty of room in his black-laced shoes for his toes. He turned and said that it was good to see me again after so long. The time had come for me to go into my act. With grotesque hauteur, I said that I didn't realize we had ever met. This was work.

Oren Johnson bustled with inchoate energy; he was the kind of small-town leader who sets an example by silently getting things done. He suggested this just by arranging his pencils and notepad and repositioning his chair with rough precision. Locking eyes with me, he stated that he was a man of his word. I didn't know what he was getting at, but took it to mean that the formalities of a closing were superfluous to the old-time handshake with which Oren Johnson customarily did business. I smiled and quizzically cocked my head as if to say that the newfangled arrangements with well-attested documents promptly conveyed to the courthouse suited me just fine, that deals made on handshakes were strictly for the pious or the picturesque. My message was clear enough that Louise shifted uncomfortably in her chair, and Brent Colby knocked his documents edgewise on the desk to align them. As far as Oren Johnson was concerned, I was beginning to feel that anyone who strayed from the basic patterns of farm life to sell cars bore watching. Like a Method actor, I already believed my part.

"You're an awfully lucky man, Oren Johnson," I said to him, leaning back in my chair. I could see Louise openmouthed two seats away from Brent Colby, and observing myself through her eyes gave me a sudden burst of panic.

"Oh?" Oren Johnson said. "How's that?"

"*How's that?*" I did a precise job of replicating his inflection. "I am permitting you to purchase my car lot. You've seen the books: how often does a man get a shot at a business where all the work's been done for him?"

Brent Colby was doing an incomplete job of concealing his distaste; he was enough of a tinhorn to clear his throat theatrically. But Oren Johnson treated this as a colossal interruption and cast a firm glance his way.

"It doesn't look all that automatic to me," he said.

"Aw, hell, you're just going to coin it. Pull the lever and relax!"

"What about the illegal oil dump? I wish I had a nickel for every crankcaseful that went into that hole. Then I wouldn't worry about what's going to happen when the D.E.Q. lowers the boom."

"Maybe you ought to ride your potato harvester another year or two, if you're so risk-averse. Cars are the future. They're not for everybody."

Oren Johnson's face reddened. He pushed his pencils and notepad almost out of reach in the middle of the conference table. He contemplated these supplies a moment before raising his eyes to mine. "I suppose you could put this car lot where the sun don't shine, if that suits you."

Johnson having taken a stand, I immediately felt unsure that I even had another buyer. Had I ever acknowledged how much I longed to get rid of this business and put an end to all those embarrassing phone calls? I wanted to hand the moment off to someone else while I collected my thoughts, but as I looked around the room I found no one who was interested in rescuing me—least of all Louise, who had raised one eyebrow at the vast peculiarity of my performance. Suddenly, I was desperate to keep the deal from falling apart. I gave my head a little twist to free my neck from the constrictions of my collar. I performed this gesture too vigorously, and I had the feeling that it might seem like the first movement of some sort of dance filled with sensual flourishes and bordering on the moronic. I had lost my grip.

"Oren," I said, and the familiarity seemed inappropriate. "I was attached to this little enterprise. I wanted to be sure you valued it."

The deal closed, and I had my check. I tipped back in my chair to think of a few commemorative words for the new owner, but the two men left the room without giving me the chance to speak. I shrugged at Louise, and she, too, rose to go, pausing a moment beneath an enormous Kodachrome of a bugling elk. I was aware of her distance, and I sensed that my waffling hadn't gone over particularly well. I concluded that at no time in the future would I act out a role to accomplish anything. This decision quickly evaporated with the realization that that is practically all we do in life. Comedy failed, too. When I told Louise that I had been within an inch of opening a can of whup-ass on the buyer, I barely got a smile. There's nothing more desolating than having a phrase like that die on your lips.

It was dark when we got back to Targhee Pass. Leaving town, we passed the Beehive assisted-living facility and the Riot Zone, a "family fun park." Most of the citizens we spotted there seemed unlikely rioters. I drove past a huge neon steak, its blue T-bone flashing above a restaurant that was closed and dark. There were deer on the road, and once, as we passed through a murky section of forest, we saw the pale faces of children waiting to cross.

"What are they doing out at this hour?"

"I don't know," Louise said.

I made good time on the pine flats north of the Snowmobile Capital of the World, and I wondered what it would be like to live in a town that was the world capital of a mechanical gadget. In Rigby, we had seen a homely museum dedicated to Philo T. Farnsworth, the inventor of television, which featured displays of Farnsworth's funky assemblages of tubes and wire and, apparently, coat hangers—stuff his wife was probably always attempting to throw out, a goal Louise supported. "Too bad Mama Farnsworth didn't take all that stuff to the dump," she said.

We had the highway to ourselves, and clouds of stars seemed to rise up from the wilderness, lighting the treetops in a cool fire. Slowly, the canyon closed in around us, and we entered its flowing, dark space.

The idyll ended just past the ranger station at Black Butte, when a car pulled in behind us abruptly enough that I checked my speed to see if I was violating the limit, but I wasn't. Then the car was very close, and the driver shifted his lights to a high beam so intense that I could see our shadows on the dashboard, my knuckles on the steering wheel glaringly white. I was nearly blinded by my own mirrors, which I hastily adjusted.

I said, "What's with this guy?"

"Just let him pass."

"I don't know that he wants to."

I softened my pressure on the gas pedal. I thought that by easing my already moderate speed I would politely suggest that he might go by me. I even hugged the shoulder, but he remained glued to our bumper. There was something about this that reminded me strongly of my feeling of failure back in Rigby, but I was unable to put my finger on it. Maybe it was the hot light of liquidation, in the glare of which all motives seem laid bare. I slowed down even more without managing to persuade my tormentor to pass. "Jesus," Louise said. "Pull over." In her accent, it came out as "pull ovah."

I moved off to the side of the road slowly and predictably, but although I had stopped, the incandescent globes persisted in our rearview mirror. "This is very strange," Louise said.

"Shall I go back and speak to him?"

After considering for a moment, she said, "No."

"Why?"

"Because this is not normal."

I put the car in gear again and pulled back onto the highway. The last reasonable thought I had was that I would proceed to Bozeman as though nothing were going on, and once I was back in civilization my tormentor's behavior would be visible to all, and I could, if necessary, simply drive to the police station with him in tow.

Our blinding, syncopated journey continued another mile before we reached a sweeping eastward bend, closely guarded by the canyon walls. I knew that just beyond the bend there was a scenic pull-off, and that the approaching curve was acute enough for a small lead to put me out of sight. Whether or not this was plausible, I had no idea: I was exhilarated to be taking a firm hand in my own affairs. And a firm foot! As we entered the narrows, I pinned the accelerator, and we shot into the dark. Louise grabbed the front edges of her seat and stared at the road twisting in front of us. She emitted something like a moan, which I had heard before in a very different context. Halfway around the curve, my tormentor vanished behind us, and although my car seemed only marginally under control, the absence of blinding light was a relief as we fled into darkness.

When we emerged and the road straightened, I turned off my lights. I was going so fast I felt light-headed, but the road was visible under the stars, and I was able to brake hard and drop down into the scenic turnoff. Seconds later, our new friend shot past, lights blazing into nowhere. He was clearly determined to catch us: his progress up the canyon was rapid and increasingly erratic. We watched in fascination until the lights suddenly jerked sideways, shining in white cones across the river, turned downward, then disappeared.

I heard Louise say, in a tone of reasonable observation, "He went in."

I had an urgent feeling that took a long time to turn into words. "Did I do that?"

She shook her head, and I pulled out onto the highway, my own headlights on once more. I drove in an odd, measured way, as if bound for an undesired destination, pulled along by something outside myself, thinking: Liquidation. We could see where he'd gone through the guardrail. We pulled over and got out. Any hope we might have had for the driver—and we shall be a long time determining if we had any—was gone the minute we looked down from the riverbank. The car was submerged, its lights still burning freakishly, illuminating a bulge of crystalline water, a boulder in the exuberance of a mountain watershed. Presently, the lights sank into blackness, and only the silver sheen of river in starlight remained.

Louise cried, "I wish I could *feel* something!" And when I reached to comfort her she shoved me away. I had no choice but to climb back up to the roadway.

After that, I could encounter Louise only by telephone. I told her that he'd had a record as long as your arm. "It's not enough!" she said. I called later to say that he was of German and Italian extraction. That proved equally unsatisfactory, and when I called to inform her that he hailed from Wisconsin she just hung up on me, this time for good.

WHAT YOU PAWN I WILL REDEEM

BY SHERMAN ALEXIE (2003)

NOON

One day you have a home and the next you don't, but I'm not going to tell you my particular reasons for being homeless, because it's my secret story, and Indians have to work hard to keep secrets from hungry white folks.

I'm a Spokane Indian boy, an Interior Salish, and my people have lived within a hundred-mile radius of Spokane, Washington, for at least ten thousand years. I grew up in Spokane, moved to Seattle twenty-three years ago for college, flunked out after two semesters, worked various blue- and bluer-collar jobs, married two or three times, fathered two or three kids, and then went crazy. Of course, crazy is not the official definition of my mental problem, but I don't think asocial disorder fits it, either, because that makes me sound like I'm a serial killer or something. I've never hurt another human being, or, at least, not physically. I've broken a few hearts in my time, but we've all done that, so I'm nothing special in that regard. I'm a boring heartbreaker, too. I never dated or married more than one woman at a time. I didn't break hearts into pieces overnight. I broke them slowly and carefully. And I didn't set any land-speed records running out the door. Piece by piece, I disappeared. I've been disappearing ever since.

I've been homeless for six years now. If there's such a thing as an effective homeless man, then I suppose I'm effective. Being homeless is probably the only thing I've ever been good at. I know where to get the best free food. I've made friends with restaurant and convenience-store managers who let me use their bathrooms. And I don't mean the public bathrooms, either. I mean the employees' bathrooms, the clean ones hidden behind the kitchen or the pantry or the cooler. I know it sounds strange to be proud of this, but it means a lot to me, being trustworthy enough to piss in somebody else's clean bathroom. Maybe you don't understand the value of a clean bathroom, but I do.

Probably none of this interests you. Homeless Indians are everywhere in Seattle. We're common and boring, and you walk right on by us, with maybe a look of anger or disgust or even sadness at the terrible fate of the noble savage. But we have dreams and families. I'm friends with a homeless Plains Indian man whose son is the editor of a big-time newspaper back East. Of course, that's his story, but we Indians are great storytellers and liars and mythmakers, so maybe that Plains Indian hobo is just a plain old everyday Indian. I'm kind of suspicious of him, because he identifies himself only as Plains Indian, a generic term, and not by a specific tribe. When I asked him why he wouldn't tell me exactly what he is, he said, "Do any of us know exactly what we are?" Yeah, great, a philosophizing Indian. "Hey," I said, "you got to have a home to be that homely." He just laughed and flipped me the eagle and walked away.

I wander the streets with a regular crew—my teammates, my defenders, my posse. It's Rose of Sharon, Junior, and me. We matter to each other if we don't matter to anybody else. Rose of Sharon is a big woman, about seven feet tall if you're measuring over-all effect and about five feet tall if you're only talking about the physical. She's a Yakama Indian of the Wishram variety. Junior is a Colville, but there are about a hundred and ninety-nine tribes that make up the Colville, so he could be anything. He's good-looking, though, like he just stepped out of some "Don't Litter the Earth" public-service advertisement. He's got those great big cheekbones that are like planets, you know, with little moons orbiting them. He gets me jealous, jealous, and jealous. If you put Junior and me next to each other, he's the Before Columbus Arrived Indian and I'm the After

Columbus Arrived Indian. I am living proof of the horrible damage that colonialism has done to us Skins. But I'm not going to let you know how scared I sometimes get of history and its ways. I'm a strong man, and I know that silence is the best method of dealing with white folks.

This whole story really started at lunchtime, when Rose of Sharon, Junior, and I were panning the handle down at Pike Place Market. After about two hours of negotiating, we earned five dollars—good enough for a bottle of fortified courage from the most beautiful 7-Eleven in the world. So we headed over that way, feeling like warrior drunks, and we walked past this pawnshop I'd never noticed before. And that was strange, because we Indians have built-in pawnshop radar. But the strangest thing of all was the old powwow-dance regalia I saw hanging in the window.

"That's my grandmother's regalia," I said to Rose of Sharon and Junior.

"How you know for sure?" Junior asked.

I didn't know for sure, because I hadn't seen that regalia in person ever. I'd only seen photographs of my grandmother dancing in it. And those were taken before somebody stole it from her, fifty years ago. But it sure looked like my memory of it, and it had all the same color feathers and beads that my family sewed into our powwow regalia.

"There's only one way to know for sure," I said.

So Rose of Sharon, Junior, and I walked into the pawnshop and greeted the old white man working behind the counter.

"How can I help you?" he asked.

"That's my grandmother's powwow regalia in your window," I said. "Somebody stole it from her fifty years ago, and my family has been searching for it ever since."

The pawnbroker looked at me like I was a liar. I understood. Pawnshops are filled with liars.

"I'm not lying," I said. "Ask my friends here. They'll tell you."

"He's the most honest Indian I know," Rose of Sharon said.

"All right, honest Indian," the pawnbroker said. "I'll give you the benefit of the doubt. Can you prove it's your grandmother's regalia?"

Because they don't want to be perfect, because only God is perfect, Indian people sew flaws into their powwow regalia. My family always sewed one yellow bead somewhere on our regalia. But we always hid it so that you had to search really hard to find it.

"If it really is my grandmother's," I said, "there will be one yellow bead hidden somewhere on it."

"All right, then," the pawnbroker said. "Let's take a look."

He pulled the regalia out of the window, laid it down on the glass counter, and we searched for that yellow bead and found it hidden beneath the armpit.

"There it is," the pawnbroker said. He didn't sound surprised. "You were right. This is your grandmother's regalia."

"It's been missing for fifty years," Junior said.

"Hey, Junior," I said. "It's my family's story. Let me tell it."

"All right," he said. "I apologize. You go ahead."

"It's been missing for fifty years," I said.

"That's his family's sad story," Rose of Sharon said. "Are you going to give it back to him?"

"That would be the right thing to do," the pawnbroker said. "But I can't afford to do the right thing. I paid a thousand dollars for this. I can't just give away a thousand dollars."

"We could go to the cops and tell them it was stolen," Rose of Sharon said.

"Hey," I said to her. "Don't go threatening people."

The pawnbroker sighed. He was thinking about the possibilities.

"Well, I suppose you could go to the cops," he said. "But I don't think they'd believe a word you said."

He sounded sad about that. As if he was sorry for taking advantage of our disadvantages.

"What's your name?" the pawnbroker asked me.

"Jackson," I said.

"Is that first or last?"

"Both," I said.

"Are you serious?"

"Yes, it's true. My mother and father named me Jackson Jackson. My family nickname is Jackson Squared. My family is funny."

"All right, Jackson Jackson," the pawnbroker said. "You wouldn't happen to have a thousand dollars, would you?"

"We've got five dollars total," I said.

"That's too bad," he said, and thought hard about the possibilities. "I'd sell it to you for a thousand dollars if you had it. Heck, to make it fair, I'd sell it to you for nine hundred and ninety-nine dollars. I'd lose a dollar. That would be the moral thing to do in this case. To lose a dollar would be the right thing."

"We've got five dollars total," I said again.

"That's too bad," he said once more, and thought harder about the possibilities. "How about this? I'll give you twenty-four hours to come up with nine hundred and ninety-nine dollars. You come back here at lunchtime tomorrow with the money and I'll sell it back to you. How does that sound?"

"It sounds all right," I said.

"All right, then," he said. "We have a deal. And I'll get you started. Here's twenty bucks."

He opened up his wallet and pulled out a crisp twenty-dollar bill and gave it to me. And Rose of Sharon, Junior, and I walked out into the daylight to search for nine hundred and seventy-four more dollars.

1 P.M.

Rose of Sharon, Junior, and I carried our twenty-dollar bill and our five dollars in loose change over to the 7-Eleven and bought three bottles of imagination. We needed to figure out how to raise all that money in only one day. Thinking hard, we huddled in an alley beneath the Alaska Way Viaduct and finished off those bottles—one, two, and three.

2 P.M.

Rose of Sharon was gone when I woke up. I heard later that she had hitchhiked back to Toppenish and was living with her sister on the reservation.

Junior had passed out beside me and was covered in his own vomit, or maybe somebody else's vomit, and my head hurt from thinking, so I left him alone and walked down to the water. I love the smell of ocean water. Salt always smells like memory.

When I got to the wharf, I ran into three Aleut cousins, who sat on a wooden bench and stared out at the bay and cried. Most of the homeless Indians in Seattle come from Alaska. One by one, each of them hopped a big working boat in Anchorage or Barrow or Juneau, fished his way south to Seattle, jumped off the boat with a pocketful of cash to party hard at one of the highly sacred and traditional Indian bars, went broke and broker, and has been trying to find his way back to the boat and the frozen North ever since.

These Aleuts smelled like salmon, I thought, and they told me they were going to sit on that wooden bench until their boat came back.

"How long has your boat been gone?" I asked.

"Eleven years," the elder Aleut said.

I cried with them for a while.

"Hey," I said. "Do you guys have any money I can borrow?"

They didn't.

3 P.M.

I walked back to Junior. He was still out cold. I put my face down near his mouth to make sure he was breathing. He was alive, so I dug around in his bluejeans pockets and found half a cigarette. I smoked it all the way down and thought about my grandmother.

Her name was Agnes, and she died of breast cancer when I was fourteen. My father always thought Agnes caught her tumors from the uranium mine on the reservation. But my mother said the disease started when Agnes was walking back from a powwow one night and got run over by a motorcycle. She broke three ribs, and my mother always said those ribs never healed right, and tumors take over when you don't heal right.

Sitting beside Junior, smelling the smoke and the salt and the vomit, I wondered if my grandmother's cancer started when somebody stole her powwow regalia. Maybe the cancer started in her broken heart and then leaked out into her breasts. I know it's crazy, but I wondered whether I could bring my grandmother back to life if I bought back her regalia.

I needed money, big money, so I left Junior and walked over to the Real Change office.

4 P.M.

Real Change is a multifaceted organization that publishes a newspaper, supports cultural projects that empower the poor and the homeless, and mobilizes the public around poverty issues. Real Change's mission is to organize, educate, and build alliances to create solutions to homelessness and poverty. It exists to provide a voice for poor people in our community.

I memorized Real Change's mission statement because I sometimes sell the newspaper on the streets. But you have to stay sober to sell it, and I'm not always good at staying sober. Anybody can sell the paper. You buy each copy for thirty cents and sell it for a dollar, and you keep the profit.

"I need one thousand four hundred and thirty papers," I said to the Big Boss.

"That's a strange number," he said. "And that's a lot of papers."

"I need them."

The Big Boss pulled out his calculator and did the math.

"It will cost you four hundred and twenty-nine dollars for that many," he said.

"If I had that kind of money, I wouldn't need to sell the papers."

"What's going on, Jackson-to-the-Second-Power?" he asked. He is the only person who calls me that. He's a funny and kind man.

I told him about my grandmother's powwow regalia and how much money I needed in order to buy it back.

"We should call the police," he said.

"I don't want to do that," I said. "It's a quest now. I need to win it back by myself."

"I understand," he said. "And, to be honest, I'd give you the papers to sell if I thought it would work. But the record for the most papers sold in one day by one vender is only three hundred and two."

"That would net me about two hundred bucks," I said.

The Big Boss used his calculator. "Two hundred and eleven dollars and forty cents," he said.

"That's not enough," I said.

"And the most money anybody has made in one day is five hundred and twenty-five. And that's because somebody gave Old Blue five hundred-dollar bills for some dang reason. The average daily net is about thirty dollars."

"This isn't going to work."

"No."

"Can you lend me some money?"

"I can't do that," he said. "If I lend you money, I have to lend money to everybody."

"What can you do?"

"I'll give you fifty papers for free. But don't tell anybody I did it."

"O.K.," I said.

He gathered up the newspapers and handed them to me. I held them to my chest. He hugged me. I carried the newspapers back toward the water.

5 P.M.

Back on the wharf, I stood near the Bainbridge Island Terminal and tried to sell papers to business commuters boarding the ferry.

I sold five in one hour, dumped the other forty-five in a garbage can, and walked into McDonald's, ordered four cheeseburgers for a dollar each, and slowly ate them.

After eating, I walked outside and vomited on the sidewalk. I hated to lose my food so soon after eating it. As an alcoholic Indian with a busted stomach, I always hope I can keep enough food in me to stay alive.

6 P.M.

With one dollar in my pocket, I walked back to Junior. He was still passed out, and I put my ear to his chest and listened for his heartbeat. He was alive, so I took off his shoes and socks and found one dollar in his left sock and fifty cents in his right sock.

With two dollars and fifty cents in my hand, I sat beside Junior and thought about my grandmother and her stories.

When I was thirteen, my grandmother told me a story about the Second World War. She was a nurse at a military hospital in Sydney,

Australia. For two years, she healed and comforted American and Australian soldiers.

One day, she tended to a wounded Maori soldier, who had lost his legs to an artillery attack. He was very dark-skinned. His hair was black and curly and his eyes were black and warm. His face was covered with bright tattoos.

"Are you Maori?" he asked my grandmother.

"No," she said. "I'm Spokane Indian. From the United States."

"Ah, yes," he said. "I have heard of your tribes. But you are the first American Indian I have ever met."

"There's a lot of Indian soldiers fighting for the United States," she said. "I have a brother fighting in Germany, and I lost another brother on Okinawa."

"I am sorry," he said. "I was on Okinawa as well. It was terrible."

"I am sorry about your legs," my grandmother said.

"It's funny, isn't it?" he said.

"What's funny?"

"How we brown people are killing other brown people so white people will remain free."

"I hadn't thought of it that way."

"Well, sometimes I think of it that way. And other times I think of it the way they want me to think of it. I get confused."

She fed him morphine.

"Do you believe in Heaven?" he asked.

"Which Heaven?" she asked.

"I'm talking about the Heaven where my legs are waiting for me."

They laughed.

"Of course," he said, "my legs will probably run away from me when I get to Heaven. And how will I ever catch them?"

"You have to get your arms strong," my grandmother said. "So you can run on your hands."

They laughed again.

Sitting beside Junior, I laughed at the memory of my grandmother's story. I put my hand close to Junior's mouth to make sure he was still breathing. Yes, Junior was alive, so I took my two dollars and fifty cents and walked to the Korean grocery store in Pioneer Square.

7 P.M.

At the Korean grocery store, I bought a fifty-cent cigar and two scratch lottery tickets for a dollar each. The maximum cash prize was five hundred dollars a ticket. If I won both, I would have enough money to buy back the regalia.

I loved Mary, the young Korean woman who worked the register. She was the daughter of the owners, and she sang all day.

"I love you," I said when I handed her the money.

"You always say you love me," she said.

"That's because I will always love you."

"You are a sentimental fool."

"I'm a romantic old man."

"Too old for me."

"I know I'm too old for you, but I can dream."

"O.K.," she said. "I agree to be a part of your dreams, but I will only hold your hand in your dreams. No kissing and no sex. Not even in your dreams."

"O.K.," I said. "No sex. Just romance."

"Goodbye, Jackson Jackson, my love. I will see you soon."

I left the store, walked over to Occidental Park, sat on a bench, and smoked my cigar all the way down.

Ten minutes after I finished the cigar, I scratched my first lottery ticket and won nothing. I could only win five hundred dollars now, and that would only be half of what I needed.

Ten minutes after I lost, I scratched the other ticket and won a free ticket—a small consolation and one more chance to win some money.

I walked back to Mary.

"Jackson Jackson," she said. "Have you come back to claim my heart?"

"I won a free ticket," I said.

"Just like a man," she said. "You love money and power more than you love me."

"It's true," I said. "And I'm sorry it's true."

She gave me another scratch ticket, and I took it outside. I like to scratch my tickets in private. Hopeful and sad, I scratched that third ticket and won real money. I carried it back inside to Mary.

"I won a hundred dollars," I said.

She examined the ticket and laughed.

"That's a fortune," she said, and counted out five twenties. Our fingertips touched as she handed me the money. I felt electric and constant.

"Thank you," I said, and gave her one of the bills.

"I can't take that," she said. "It's your money."

"No, it's tribal. It's an Indian thing. When you win, you're supposed to share with your family."

"I'm not your family."

"Yes, you are."

She smiled. She kept the money. With eighty dollars in my pocket, I said goodbye to my dear Mary and walked out into the cold night air.

8 P.M.

I wanted to share the good news with Junior. I walked back to him, but he was gone. I heard later that he had hitchhiked down to Portland, Oregon, and died of exposure in an alley behind the Hilton Hotel.

9 P.M.

Lonesome for Indians, I carried my eighty dollars over to Big Heart's in South Downtown. Big Heart's is an all-Indian bar. Nobody knows how or why Indians migrate to one bar and turn it into an official Indian bar. But Big Heart's has been an Indian bar for twenty-three years. It used to be way up on Aurora Avenue, but a crazy Lummi Indian burned that one down, and the owners moved to the new location, a few blocks south of Safeco Field.

I walked into Big Heart's and counted fifteen Indians—eight men and seven women. I didn't know any of them, but Indians like to belong, so we all pretended to be cousins.

"How much for whiskey shots?" I asked the bartender, a fat white guy.

"You want the bad stuff or the badder stuff?"

"As bad as you got."

"One dollar a shot."

I laid my eighty dollars on the bar top.

"All right," I said. "Me and all my cousins here are going to be drinking eighty shots. How many is that apiece?"

"Counting you," a woman shouted from behind me, "that's five shots for everybody."

I turned to look at her. She was a chubby and pale Indian woman, sitting with a tall and skinny Indian man.

"All right, math genius," I said to her, and then shouted for the whole bar to hear. "Five drinks for everybody!"

All the other Indians rushed the bar, but I sat with the mathematician and her skinny friend. We took our time with our whiskey shots.

"What's your tribe?" I asked.

"I'm Duwamish," she said. "And he's Crow."

"You're a long way from Montana," I said to him.

"I'm Crow," he said. "I flew here."

"What's your name?" I asked them.

"I'm Irene Muse," she said. "And this is Honey Boy."

She shook my hand hard, but he offered his hand as if I was supposed to kiss it. So I did. He giggled and blushed, as much as a dark-skinned Crow can blush.

"You're one of them two-spirits, aren't you?" I asked him.

"I love women," he said. "And I love men."

"Sometimes both at the same time," Irene said.

We laughed.

"Man," I said to Honey Boy. "So you must have about eight or nine spirits going on inside you, enit?"

"Sweetie," he said. "I'll be whatever you want me to be."

"Oh, no," Irene said. "Honey Boy is falling in love."

"It has nothing to do with love," he said.

We laughed.

"Wow," I said. "I'm flattered, Honey Boy, but I don't play on your team."

"Never say never," he said.

"You better be careful," Irene said. "Honey Boy knows all sorts of magic."

"Honey Boy," I said, "you can try to seduce me, but my heart belongs to a woman named Mary."

"Is your Mary a virgin?" Honey Boy asked.

We laughed.

And we drank our whiskey shots until they were gone. But the other Indians bought me more whiskey shots, because I'd been so generous with my money. And Honey Boy pulled out his credit card, and I drank and sailed on that plastic boat.

After a dozen shots, I asked Irene to dance. She refused. But Honey Boy shuffled over to the jukebox, dropped in a quarter, and selected Willie Nelson's "Help Me Make It Through the Night." As Irene and I sat at the table and laughed and drank more whiskey, Honey Boy danced a slow circle around us and sang along with Willie.

"Are you serenading me?" I asked him.

He kept singing and dancing.

"Are you serenading me?" I asked him again.

"He's going to put a spell on you," Irene said.

I leaned over the table, spilling a few drinks, and kissed Irene hard. She kissed me back.

10 P.M.

Irene pushed me into the women's bathroom, into a stall, shut the door behind us, and shoved her hand down my pants. She was short, so I had to lean over to kiss her. I grabbed and squeezed her everywhere I could reach, and she was wonderfully fat, and every part of her body felt like a large, warm, soft breast.

MIDNIGHT

Nearly blind with alcohol, I stood alone at the bar and swore I had been standing in the bathroom with Irene only a minute ago.

"One more shot!" I yelled at the bartender.

"You've got no more money!" he yelled back.

"Somebody buy me a drink!" I shouted.

"They've got no more money!"

"Where are Irene and Honey Boy?"
"Long gone!"

2 A.M.

"Closing time!" the bartender shouted at the three or four Indians who were still drinking hard after a long, hard day of drinking. Indian alcoholics are either sprinters or marathoners.

"Where are Irene and Honey Boy?" I asked.

"They've been gone for hours," the bartender said.

"Where'd they go?"

"I told you a hundred times, I don't know."

"What am I supposed to do?"

"It's closing time. I don't care where you go, but you're not staying here."

"You are an ungrateful bastard. I've been good to you."

"You don't leave right now, I'm going to kick your ass."

"Come on, I know how to fight."

He came at me. I don't remember what happened after that.

4 A.M.

I emerged from the blackness and discovered myself walking behind a big warehouse. I didn't know where I was. My face hurt. I felt my nose and decided that it might be broken. Exhausted and cold, I pulled a plastic tarp from a truck bed, wrapped it around me like a faithful lover, and fell asleep in the dirt.

6 A.M.

Somebody kicked me in the ribs. I opened my eyes and looked up at a white cop.

"Jackson," the cop said. "Is that you?"

"Officer Williams," I said. He was a good cop with a sweet tooth. He'd given me hundreds of candy bars over the years. I wonder if he knew I was diabetic.

"What the hell are you doing here?" he asked.

"I was cold and sleepy," I said. "So I lay down."

"You dumb-ass, you passed out on the railroad tracks."

I sat up and looked around. I was lying on the railroad tracks. Dockworkers stared at me. I should have been a railroad-track pizza, a double Indian pepperoni with extra cheese. Sick and scared, I leaned over and puked whiskey.

"What the hell's wrong with you?" Officer Williams asked. "You've never been this stupid."

"It's my grandmother," I said. "She died."

"I'm sorry, man. When did she die?"

"Nineteen seventy-two."

"And you're killing yourself now?"

"I've been killing myself ever since she died."

He shook his head. He was sad for me. Like I said, he was a good cop.

"And somebody beat the hell out of you," he said. "You remember who?"

"Mr. Grief and I went a few rounds."

"It looks like Mr. Grief knocked you out."

"Mr. Grief always wins."

"Come on," he said. "Let's get you out of here."

He helped me up and led me over to his squad car. He put me in the back. "You throw up in there and you're cleaning it up," he said.

"That's fair."

He walked around the car and sat in the driver's seat. "I'm taking you over to detox," he said.

"No, man, that place is awful," I said. "It's full of drunk Indians."

We laughed. He drove away from the docks.

"I don't know how you guys do it," he said.

"What guys?" I asked.

"You Indians. How the hell do you laugh so much? I just picked your ass off the railroad tracks, and you're making jokes. Why the hell do you do that?"

"The two funniest tribes I've ever been around are Indians and Jews, so I guess that says something about the inherent humor of genocide."

We laughed.

"Listen to you, Jackson. You're so smart. Why the hell are you on the street?"

"Give me a thousand dollars and I'll tell you."

"You bet I'd give you a thousand dollars if I knew you'd straighten up your life."

He meant it. He was the second-best cop I'd ever known.

"You're a good cop," I said.

"Come on, Jackson," he said. "Don't blow smoke up my ass."

"No, really, you remind me of my grandfather."

"Yeah, that's what you Indians always tell me."

"No, man, my grandfather was a tribal cop. He was a good cop. He never arrested people. He took care of them. Just like you."

"I've arrested hundreds of scumbags, Jackson. And I've shot a couple in the ass."

"It don't matter. You're not a killer."

"I didn't kill them. I killed their asses. I'm an ass-killer."

We drove through downtown. The missions and shelters had already released their overnighters. Sleepy homeless men and women stood on street corners and stared up at a gray sky. It was the morning after the night of the living dead.

"Do you ever get scared?" I asked Officer Williams.

"What do you mean?"

"I mean, being a cop, is it scary?"

He thought about that for a while. He contemplated it. I liked that about him.

"I guess I try not to think too much about being afraid," he said. "If you think about fear, then you'll be afraid. The job is boring most of the time. Just driving and looking into dark corners, you know, and seeing nothing. But then things get heavy. You're chasing somebody, or fighting them or walking around a dark house, and you just know some crazy guy is hiding around a corner, and hell, yes, it's scary."

"My grandfather was killed in the line of duty," I said.

"I'm sorry. How'd it happen?"

I knew he'd listen closely to my story.

"He worked on the reservation. Everybody knew everybody. It was safe. We aren't like those crazy Sioux or Apache or any of those other warrior tribes. There've only been three murders on my reservation in the last hundred years."

"That is safe."

"Yeah, we Spokane, we're passive, you know. We're mean with words. And we'll cuss out anybody. But we don't shoot people. Or stab them. Not much, anyway."

"So what happened to your grandfather?"

"This man and his girlfriend were fighting down by Little Falls."

"Domestic dispute. Those are the worst."

"Yeah, but this guy was my grandfather's brother. My great-uncle."

"Oh, no."

"Yeah, it was awful. My grandfather just strolled into the house. He'd been there a thousand times. And his brother and his girlfriend were drunk and beating on each other. And my grandfather stepped between them, just as he'd done a hundred times before. And the girlfriend tripped or something. She fell down and hit her head and started crying. And my grandfather kneeled down beside her to make sure she was all right. And for some reason my great-uncle reached down, pulled my grandfather's pistol out of the holster, and shot him in the head."

"That's terrible. I'm sorry."

"Yeah, my great-uncle could never figure out why he did it. He went to prison forever, you know, and he always wrote these long letters. Like fifty pages of tiny little handwriting. And he was always trying to figure out why he did it. He'd write and write and write and try to figure it out. He never did. It's a great big mystery."

"Do you remember your grandfather?"

"A little bit. I remember the funeral. My grandmother wouldn't let them bury him. My father had to drag her away from the grave."

"I don't know what to say."

"I don't, either."

We stopped in front of the detox center.

"We're here," Officer Williams said.

"I can't go in there," I said.

"You have to."

"Please, no. They'll keep me for twenty-four hours. And then it will be too late."

"Too late for what?"

I told him about my grandmother's regalia and the deadline for buying it back.

"If it was stolen, you need to file a report," he said. "I'll investigate it myself. If that thing is really your grandmother's, I'll get it back for you. Legally."

"No," I said. "That's not fair. The pawnbroker didn't know it was stolen. And, besides, I'm on a mission here. I want to be a hero, you know? I want to win it back, like a knight."

"That's romantic crap."

"That may be. But I care about it. It's been a long time since I really cared about something."

Officer Williams turned around in his seat and stared at me. He studied me.

"I'll give you some money," he said. "I don't have much. Only thirty bucks. I'm short until payday. And it's not enough to get back the regalia. But it's something."

"I'll take it," I said.

"I'm giving it to you because I believe in what you believe. I'm hoping, and I don't know why I'm hoping it, but I hope you can turn thirty bucks into a thousand somehow."

"I believe in magic."

"I believe you'll take my money and get drunk on it."

"Then why are you giving it to me?"

"There ain't no such thing as an atheist cop."

"Sure, there is."

"Yeah, well, I'm not an atheist cop."

He let me out of the car, handed me two fivers and a twenty, and shook my hand.

"Take care of yourself, Jackson," he said. "Stay off the railroad tracks."

"I'll try," I said.

He drove away. Carrying my money, I headed back toward the water.

8 A.M.

On the wharf, those three Aleuts still waited on the wooden bench.

"Have you seen your ship?" I asked.

"Seen a lot of ships," the elder Aleut said. "But not our ship."

I sat on the bench with them. We sat in silence for a long time. I wondered if we would fossilize if we sat there long enough.

I thought about my grandmother. I'd never seen her dance in her regalia. And, more than anything, I wished I'd seen her dance at a powwow.

"Do you guys know any songs?" I asked the Aleuts.

"I know all of Hank Williams," the elder Aleut said.

"How about Indian songs?"

"Hank Williams is Indian."

"How about sacred songs?"

"Hank Williams is sacred."

"I'm talking about ceremonial songs. You know, religious ones. The songs you sing back home when you're wishing and hoping."

"What are you wishing and hoping for?"

"I'm wishing my grandmother was still alive."

"Every song I know is about that."

"Well, sing me as many as you can."

The Aleuts sang their strange and beautiful songs. I listened. They sang about my grandmother and about their grandmothers. They were lonesome for the cold and the snow. I was lonesome for everything.

10 A.M.

After the Aleuts finished their last song, we sat in silence for a while. Indians are good at silence.

"Was that the last song?" I asked.

"We sang all the ones we could," the elder Aleut said. "The others are just for our people."

I understood. We Indians have to keep our secrets. And these Aleuts were so secretive they didn't refer to themselves as Indians.

"Are you guys hungry?" I asked.

They looked at one another and communicated without talking.

"We could eat," the elder Aleut said.

11 A.M.

The Aleuts and I walked over to the Big Kitchen, a greasy diner in the International District. I knew they served homeless Indians who'd lucked into money.

"Four for breakfast?" the waitress asked when we stepped inside.

"Yes, we're very hungry," the elder Aleut said.

She took us to a booth near the kitchen. I could smell the food cooking. My stomach growled.

"You guys want separate checks?" the waitress asked.

"No, I'm paying," I said.

"Aren't you the generous one," she said.

"Don't do that," I said.

"Do what?" she asked.

"Don't ask me rhetorical questions. They scare me."

She looked puzzled, and then she laughed.

"O.K., Professor," she said. "I'll only ask you real questions from now on."

"Thank you."

"What do you guys want to eat?"

"That's the best question anybody can ask anybody," I said. "What have you got?"

"How much money you got?" she asked.

"Another good question," I said. "I've got twenty-five dollars I can spend. Bring us all the breakfast you can, plus your tip."

She knew the math.

"All right, that's four specials and four coffees and fifteen per cent for me."

The Aleuts and I waited in silence. Soon enough, the waitress returned and poured us four coffees, and we sipped at them until she returned again, with four plates of food. Eggs, bacon, toast, hash-brown potatoes. It's amazing how much food you can buy for so little money.

Grateful, we feasted.

NOON

I said farewell to the Aleuts and walked toward the pawnshop. I heard later that the Aleuts had waded into the salt water near Dock 47 and disappeared. Some Indians swore they had walked on the water and headed north. Other Indians saw the Aleuts drown. I don't know what happened to them.

I looked for the pawnshop and couldn't find it. I swear it wasn't in the place where it had been before. I walked twenty or thirty blocks looking for the pawnshop, turned corners and bisected intersections, and looked up its name in the phone books and asked people walking past me if they'd ever heard of it. But that pawnshop seemed to have sailed away like a ghost ship. I wanted to cry. And just when I'd given up, when I turned one last corner and thought I might die if I didn't find that pawnshop, there it was, in a space I swear it hadn't occupied a few minutes ago.

I walked inside and greeted the pawnbroker, who looked a little younger than he had before.

"It's you," he said.

"Yes, it's me," I said.

"Jackson Jackson."

"That is my name."

"Where are your friends?"

"They went travelling. But it's O.K. Indians are everywhere."

"Do you have the money?"

"How much do you need again?" I asked, and hoped the price had changed.

"Nine hundred and ninety-nine dollars."

It was still the same price. Of course, it was the same price. Why would it change?

"I don't have that," I said.

"What do you have?"

"Five dollars."

I set the crumpled Lincoln on the countertop. The pawnbroker studied it.

"Is that the same five dollars from yesterday?"

"No, it's different."

He thought about the possibilities.

"Did you work hard for this money?" he asked.

"Yes," I said.

He closed his eyes and thought harder about the possibilities. Then he stepped into the back room and returned with my grandmother's regalia.

"Take it," he said, and held it out to me.

"I don't have the money."

"I don't want your money."

"But I wanted to win it."

"You did win it. Now take it before I change my mind."

Do you know how many good men live in this world? Too many to count!

I took my grandmother's regalia and walked outside. I knew that solitary yellow bead was part of me. I knew I was that yellow bead in part. Outside, I wrapped myself in my grandmother's regalia and breathed her in. I stepped off the sidewalk and into the intersection. Pedestrians stopped. Cars stopped. The city stopped. They all watched me dance with my grandmother. I was my grandmother, dancing.

A RICH MAN

BY EDWARD P. JONES (2003)

Horace and Loneese Perkins—one child, one grandchild—lived most unhappily together for more than twelve years in Apartment 230 at Sunset House, a building for senior citizens at 1202 Thirteenth Street NW. They moved there in 1977, the year they celebrated forty years of marriage, the year they made love for the last time—Loneese kept a diary of sorts, and that fact was noted on one day of a week when she noted nothing else. "He touched me," she wrote, which had always been her diary euphemism for sex. That was also the year they retired, she as a pool secretary at the Commerce Department, where she had known one lover, and he as a civilian employee at the Pentagon, as the head of veteran records. He had been an Army sergeant for ten years before becoming head of records; the Secretary of Defense gave him a plaque as big as his chest on the day he retired, and he and the Secretary of Defense and Loneese had their picture taken, a picture that hung for all those twelve years in the living room of Apartment 230, on the wall just to the right of the heating-and-air-conditioning unit.

A month before they moved in, they drove in their burgundy-and-gold Cadillac from their small house on Chesapeake Street in Southeast to a Union Station restaurant and promised each other that Sunset House would be a new beginning for them. Over blackened catfish and a peach cobbler that they both agreed could have been better, they vowed to devote themselves to each other and become even better grandparents. Horace had long known about the Commerce Department lover. Loneese had told him about the man two months after she had ended the relationship, in 1969. "He worked in the mail room," she told her husband over a spaghetti supper she had cooked in the Chesapeake Street home. "He touched me in the motel room," she wrote in her diary, "and after it was over he begged me to go away to Florida with him. All I could think about was that Florida was for old people."

At that spaghetti supper, Horace did not mention the dozens of lovers he had had in his time as her husband. She knew there had been many, knew it because they were written on his face in the early years of their marriage, and because he had never bothered to hide what he was doing in the later years. "I be back in a while. I got some business to do," he would say. He did not even mention the lover he had slept with just the day before the spaghetti supper, the one he bid goodbye to with a "Be good and be sweet" after telling her he planned to become a new man and respect his marriage vows. The woman, a thin school-bus driver with clanking bracelets up to her elbows on both arms, snorted a laugh, which made Horace want to slap her, because he was used to people taking him seriously. "Forget you, then," Horace said on the way out the door. "I was just tryin to let you down easy."

Over another spaghetti supper two weeks before moving, they reiterated what had been said at the blackened-catfish supper and did the dishes together and went to bed as man and wife, and over the next days sold almost all the Chesapeake Street furniture. What they kept belonged primarily to Horace, starting with a collection of six hundred and thirty-nine record albums, many of them his "sweet babies," the 78s. If a band worth anything had recorded between 1915 and 1950, he bragged, he had the record; after 1950, he said, the bands got sloppy and he had to back away. Horace also kept the Cadillac he had painted to honor a football team, paid to park the car in the underground garage. Sunset had once been intended as a luxury place, but the builders, two friends of the city commissioners, ran out of money in the middle and the commissioners had the city-government people buy it off them. The city-government people completed Sunset, with its tiny rooms, and then, after one commissioner gave a speech in Southwest about looking out for old people, some city-government people in Northeast came up with the idea that old people might like to live in Sunset, in Northwest.

Three weeks after Horace and Loneese moved in, Horace went down to the lobby one Saturday afternoon to get their mail and happened to see Clara Knightley getting her mail. She lived in Apartment 512. "You got this fixed up real nice," Horace said of Apartment 512 a little less than an hour after meeting her. "But I could see just in the way that you carry yourself that you got good taste. I could tell that about you right off." "You swellin my head with all that talk, Mr. Perkins," Clara said, offering him coffee, which he rejected, because such moments always called for something stronger. "Whas a woman's head for if a man can't swell it up from time to time. Huh? Answer me that, Clara. You just answer me that." Clara was fifty-five, a bit younger than most of the residents of Sunset House, though she was much older than all Horace's other lovers. She did not fit the city people's definition of a senior citizen, but she had a host of ailments, from high blood pressure to diabetes, and so the city people had let her in.

Despite the promises, the marriage, what little there had been of it, came to an end. "I will make myself happy," Loneese told the diary a month after he last touched her. Loneese and Horace had fixed up their apartment nicely, and neither of them wanted to give the place up to the other. She wanted to make a final stand with the man who had given her so much heartache, the man who had told her, six months after her confession, what a whore she had been to sleep with the Commerce Department mail-room man. Horace, at sixty, had never thought much of women over fifty, but Clara—and, after her, Willa, of Apartment 1001, and Miriam, of Apartment 109—had awakened something in him, and he began to think that women over fifty weren't such a bad deal after all. Sunset House had dozens of such women, many of them attractive widows, many of them eager for a kind word from a retired Army sergeant who had so many medals and ribbons that his uniform could not carry them. As far as he could see, he was cock of the walk: many of the men in Sunset suffered from diseases that Horace had so far escaped, or they were not as good-looking or as thin, or they were encumbered by wives they loved. In Sunset House he was a rich man. So why move and give that whore the satisfaction?

They lived separate lives in a space that was only a fourth as large as the Chesapeake Street house. The building came to know them as the man and wife in 230 who couldn't stand each other. People talked about the Perkinses more than they did about anyone else, which was particularly upsetting to Loneese, who had been raised to believe family business should stay in the family. "Oh, Lord, what them two been up to now?" "Fight like cats and dogs, they do." "Who he seein now?" They each bought their own food from the Richfood on Eleventh Street or from the little store on Thirteenth Street, and they could be vile to each other if what one bought was disturbed or eaten by the other. Loneese stopped speaking to Horace for nine months in 1984 and 1985, when she saw that her pumpkin pie was a bit smaller than when she last cut a slice from it. "I ain't touch your damn pie, you crazy woman," he said when she accused him. "How long you been married to me? You know I've never been partial to pumpkin pie." "That's fine for you to say, Horace, but why is some missing? You might not be partial to it, but I know you. I know you'll eat anything in a pinch. That's just your dirty nature." "My nature ain't no more dirty than yours."

After that, she bought a small icebox for the bedroom where she slept, though she continued to keep the larger items in the kitchen refrigerator. He bought a separate telephone, because he complained that she wasn't giving him his messages from his "associates." "I have never been a secretary for whores," she said, watching him set up an answering machine next to the hide-a-bed couch where he slept. "Oh, don't get me started bout whores. I'd say you wrote the damn book." "It was dictated by you."

Their one child, Alonzo, lived with his wife and son in Baltimore. He had not been close to his parents for a long time, and he could not put the why of it into words for his wife. Their boy, Alonzo, Jr., who was twelve when his grandparents moved into Sunset, loved to visit them. Horace would unplug and put away his telephone when the boy visited. And Loneese and Horace would sleep together in the bedroom. She'd put a pillow between them in the double bed to remind herself not to roll toward him.

Their grandson visited less and less as he moved into his teenage years, and then, after he went away to college, in Ohio, he just called them every few weeks, on the phone they had had installed in the name of Horace and Loneese Perkins.

In 1987, Loneese's heart began the countdown to its last beat and she started spending more time at George Washington University Hospital than she did in the apartment. Horace never visited her. She died two years later. She woke up that last night in the hospital and went out into the hall and then to the nurses' station but could not find a nurse anywhere to tell her where she was or why she was there. "Why do the patients have to run this place alone?" she said to the walls. She returned to her room and it came to her why she was there. It was nearing three in the morning, but she called her own telephone first, then she dialled Horace's. He answered, but she never said a word. "Who's this playin on my phone?" Horace kept asking. "Who's this? I don't allow no playin on my phone." She hung up and lay down and said her prayers. After moving into Sunset, she had taken one more lover, a man at Vermont Avenue Baptist Church, where she went from time to time. He was retired, too. She wrote in her diary that he was not a big eater and that "down there, his vitals were missing."

Loneese Perkins was buried in a plot at Harmony Cemetery that she and Horace had bought when they were younger. There was a spot for Horace and there was one for their son, but Alonzo had long since made plans to be buried in a cemetery just outside Baltimore.

Horace kept the apartment more or less the way it was on the last day she was there. His son and daughter-in-law and grandson took some of her clothes to the Goodwill and the rest they gave to other women in the building. There were souvenirs from countries that Loneese and Horace had visited as man and wife—a Ghanaian carving of men surrounding a leopard they had killed, a brass menorah from Israel, a snow globe of Mt. Fuji with some of the snow stuck forever to the top of the globe. They were things that did not mean very much to Alonzo, but he knew his child, and he knew that one day Alonzo, Jr., would cherish them.

Horace tried sleeping in the bed, but he had been not unhappy in his twelve years on the hide-a-bed. He got rid of the bed and moved the couch into the bedroom and kept it open all the time.

He realized two things after Loneese's death: His own "vitals" had rejuvenated. He had never had the problems other men had, though he had failed a few times along the way, but that was to be expected. Now, as he moved closer to his seventy-third birthday, he felt himself becoming ever stronger, ever more potent. God is a strange one, he thought, sipping Chivas Regal one night before he went out: he takes a man's wife and gives him a new penis in her place.

The other thing he realized was that he was more and more attracted to younger women. When Loneese died, he had been keeping company with a woman of sixty-one, Sandy Carlin, in Apartment 907. One day in February, nine months after Loneese's death, one of Sandy's daughters, Jill, came to visit, along with one of Jill's friends, Elaine Cunningham. They were both twenty-five years old. From the moment they walked through Sandy's door, Horace began to compliment them—on their hair, the color of their fingernail polish, the sharp crease in Jill's pants ("You iron that yourself?"), even "that sophisticated way" Elaine crossed her legs. The young women giggled, which made him happy, pleased with himself, and Sandy sat in her place on the couch. As the ice in the Pepsi-Cola in her left hand melted, she realized all over again that God had never promised her a man until her dying day.

When the girls left, about three in the afternoon, Horace offered to accompany them downstairs, "to keep all them bad men away." In the lobby, as the security guard at her desk strained to hear, he made it known that he wouldn't mind if they came by to see him sometime. The women looked at each other and giggled some more. They had been planning to go to a club in Southwest that evening, but they were amused by the old man, by the way he had his rap together and put them on some sort of big pedestal and shit, as Jill would tell another friend weeks later. And when he saw how receptive they were he said why not come on up tonight, shucks, ain't no time like the present. Jill said he musta got that from a song, but he said no, he'd been sayin that since before they were born, and Elaine said thas the truth, and the women giggled again. He said I ain't gonna lie bout bein a seasoned man, and then he joined in the giggling. Jill looked at Elaine and said want to? And Elaine said what about your mom? And Jill shrugged her shoulders and Elaine said O.K. She had just broken up with a man she had met at another club and needed something to make the pain go away until there was another man, maybe from a better club.

At about eleven-thirty, Jill wandered off into the night, her head liquored up, and Elaine stayed and got weepy—about the man from the not-so-good club, about the two abortions, about running away from home at seventeen after a fight with her father. "I just left him nappin on the couch," she said, stretched out on Horace's new living-room couch, her shoes off and one of Loneese's throws over her feet. Horace was in the chair across from her. "For all I know, he's still on that couch." Even before she got to her father, even before the abortions, he knew that he would sleep with her that night. He did not even need to fill her glass a third time. "He was a fat man," she said of her father. "And there ain't a whole lot more I remember."

"Listen," he said as she talked about her father, "everything's gonna work out right for you." He knew that, at such times in a seduction, the more positive a man was the better things went. It would not have done to tell her to forget her daddy, that she had done the right thing by running out on that fat so-and-so; it was best to focus on tomorrow and tell her that the world would be brighter in the morning. He came over to the couch, and before he sat down on the edge of the coffee table he hiked up his pants just a bit with his fingertips, and seeing him do that reminded her vaguely of something wonderful. The boys in the club sure didn't do it that way. He took her hand and kissed her palm. "Everything's gonna work out to the good," he said.

Elaine Cunningham woke in the morning with Horace sleeping quietly beside her. She did not rebuke herself and did not look over at him with horror at what she had done. She sighed and laid her head back on the pillow and thought how much she still loved the man from the club, but there was nothing more she could do: not even the five-hundred-dollar leather jacket she had purchased for the man had brought him around. Two years after running away, she had gone back to where she had lived with her parents, but they had moved and no one in the building knew where they had gone. But everyone remembered her. "You sure done growed up, Elaine," one old woman said. "I wouldna knowed if you hadn't told me who you was." "Fuck em," Elaine said to the friends who had given her a ride there. "Fuck em all to hell." Then, in the car, heading out to Capitol Heights, where she was staying, "Well, maybe not fuck my mother. She was good." "Just fuck your daddy then?" the girl in the back seat said. Elaine thought about it as they went down Rhode Island Avenue, and just before they turned onto New Jersey Avenue she said, "Yes, just fuck my daddy. The fat fuck."

She got out of Horace's bed and tried to wet the desert in her mouth as she looked in his closet for a bathrobe. She rejected the blue and the paisley ones for a dark-green one that reminded her of something wonderful, just as Horace's hiking up his pants had. She smelled the sleeves once she had it on, but there was only the strong scent of detergent.

In the half room that passed for a kitchen, she stood and drank most of the orange juice in the gallon carton. "Now, that was stupid, girl," she said. "You know you shoulda drunk water. Better for the thirst." She returned the carton to the refrigerator and marvelled at all the food. "Damn!" she said. With the refrigerator door still open, she stepped out into the living room and took note of all that Horace had, thinking, A girl could live large here if she did things right. She had been crashing at a friend's place in Northeast, and the friend's mother had begun to hint that it was time for her to move on. Even when she had a job, she rarely had a place of her own. "Hmm," she said, looking through the refrigerator for what she wanted to eat. "Boody for home and food. Food, home. Boody. You shoulda stayed in school, girl. They give courses on this. Food and Home the first semester. Boody Givin the second semester."

But, as she ate her eggs and bacon and Hungry Man biscuits, she knew that she did not want to sleep with Horace too many more times, even if he did have his little castle. He was too tall, and she had never been attracted to tall men, old or otherwise. "Damn! Why couldn't he be what I wanted and have a nice place, too?" Then, as she sopped up the last of the yolk with the last half of the last biscuit, she thought of her best friend, Catrina, the woman she was crashing with. Catrina Stockton was twenty-eight, and though she had once been a heroin addict, she was one year clean and had a face and a body that testified not to a woman who had lived a bad life on the streets but to a nice-looking Virginia woman who had married at seventeen, had had three children by a truck-driving husband, and had met a man in a Fredericksburg McDonald's who had said that women like her could be queens in D.C.

Yes, Elaine thought as she leaned over the couch and stared at the photograph of Horace and Loneese and the Secretary of Defense, Catrina was always saying how much she wanted love, how it didn't matter what a man looked like, as long as he was good to her and loved her morning, noon, and night. The Secretary of Defense was in the middle of the couple. She did not know who he was, just that she had seen him somewhere, maybe on the television. Horace was holding the plaque just to the left, away from the Secretary. Elaine reached over and removed a spot of dust from the picture with her fingertip, and before she could flick it away a woman said her name and she looked around, chilled.

She went into the bedroom to make sure that the voice had not been death telling her to check on Horace. She found him sitting up in the bed, yawning and stretching. "You sleep good, honey bunch?" he said. "I sure did, sweetie pie," she said and bounded across the room to hug him. A breakfast like the one she'd had would cost at least four dollars anywhere in D.C. or Maryland. "Oh, but Papa likes that," Horace said. And even the cheapest motels out on New York Avenue, the ones catering to the junkies and prostitutes, charged at least twenty-five dollars a night. What's a hug compared with that? And, besides, she liked him more than she had thought, and the issue of Catrina and her moving in had to be done delicately. "Well, just let me give you a little bit mo, then."

Young stuff is young stuff, Horace thought the first time Elaine brought Catrina by and Catrina gave him a peck on the cheek and said, "I feel like I know you from all that Elaine told me." That was in early March.

In early April, Elaine met another man at a new club on F Street Northwest and fell in love, and so did Horace with Catrina, though Catrina, after several years on the street, knew what she was feeling might be in the neighborhood of love but it was nowhere near the right house. She and Elaine told Horace the saddest of stories about the man Elaine had met in the club, and before the end of April he was sleeping on Horace's living-room floor. It helped that the man, Darnell Mudd, knew the way to anyone's heart, man or woman, and that he claimed to have a father who had been a hero in the Korean War. He even knew the name of the Secretary of Defense in the photograph and how long he had served in the Cabinet.

By the middle of May, there were as many as five other people, friends of the three young people, hanging out at any one time in Horace's place. He was giddy with Catrina, with the blunts, with the other women who snuck out with him to a room at the motel across Thirteenth Street. By early June, more than a hundred of his old records had been stolen and pawned. "Leave his stuff alone," Elaine said to Darnell and his friends as they were going out the door with ten records apiece. "Don't take his stuff. He loves that stuff." It was eleven in the morning and everyone else in the apartment, including Horace, was asleep. "Sh-h-h," Darnell said. "He got so many he won't notice." And that was true. Horace hadn't played records in many months. He had two swords that were originally on the wall opposite the heating-and-air-conditioning unit. Both had belonged to German officers killed in the Second World War. Horace, high on the blunts, liked to see the young men sword fight with them. But the next day, sober, he would hide them in the bottom of the closet, only to pull them out again when the partying started, at about four in the afternoon.

His neighbors, especially the neighbors who considered that Loneese had been the long-suffering one in the marriage, complained to the management about the noise, but the city-government people read in his rental record that he had lost his wife not long ago and told the neighbors that he was probably doing some kind of grieving. The city-government people never went above the first floor in Sunset. "He's a veteran who just lost his wife," they would say to those who came to the glass office on the first floor. "Why don't you cut him some slack?" But Horace tried to get a grip on things after a maintenance man told him to be careful. That was about the time one of the swords was broken and he could not for the life of him remember how it had happened. He just found it one afternoon in two pieces in the refrigerator's vegetable bin.

Things toned down a little, but the young women continued to come by and Horace went on being happy with them and with

Catrina, who called him Papa and pretended to be upset when she saw him kissing another girl. "Papa, what am I gonna do with you and all your hussies?" "Papa, promise you'll only love me." "Papa, I need a new outfit. Help me out, willya please?"

Elaine had become pregnant not long after meeting Darnell, who told her to have the baby, that he had always wanted a son to carry on his name. "We can call him Junior," he said. "Or Little Darnell," she said. As she began showing, Horace and Catrina became increasingly concerned about her. Horace remembered how solicitous he had been when Loneese had been pregnant. He had not taken the first lover yet, had not even thought about anyone else as she grew and grew. He told Elaine no drugs or alcohol until the baby was born, and he tried to get her to go to bed at a decent hour, but that was often difficult with a small crowd in the living room.

Horace's grandson called in December, wanting to come by to see him, but Horace told him it would be best to meet someplace downtown, because his place was a mess. He didn't do much cleaning since Loneese died. "I don't care about that," Alonzo, Jr., said. "Well, I do," Horace said. "You know how I can be bout these things."

In late December, Elaine gave birth to a boy, several weeks early. They gave him the middle name Horace. "See," Darnell said one day, holding the baby on the couch. "Thas your grandpa. You don't mind me callin you his granddad, Mr. Perkins? You don't mind, do you?" The city-government people in the rental office, led by someone new, someone who took the rules seriously, took note that the old man in Apartment 230 had a baby and his mama and daddy in the place and not a single one of them was even related to him, though if one had been it still would have been against the rules as laid down in the rule book of apartment living.

By late February, an undercover policeman had bought two packets of crack from someone in the apartment. It was a woman, he told his superiors at first, and that's what he wrote in his report, but in a subsequent report he wrote that he had bought the rocks from a man. "Start over," said one of his superiors, who supped monthly with the new mayor, who lived for numbers, and in March the undercover man went back to buy more.

It was late on a warm Saturday night in April when Elaine woke to the crackle of walkie-talkies outside the door. She had not seen Darnell in more than a month, and something told her that she should get out of there because there might not be any more good times. She thought of Horace and Catrina asleep in the bedroom. Two men and two women she did not know very well were asleep in various places around the living room, but she had dated the brother of one of the women some three years ago. One of the men claimed to be Darnell's cousin, and, to prove it to her, when he knocked at the door that night he showed her a Polaroid of him and Darnell at a club, their arms around each other and their eyes red, because the camera had been cheap and the picture cost only two dollars.

She got up from the couch and looked into the crib. In the darkness she could make out that her son was awake, his little legs kicking and no sound from him but a happy gurgle. The sound of the walkie-talkie outside the door came and went. She could see it all on the television news—"Drug Dealing Mama in Jail. Baby Put in Foster Care." She stepped over the man who said he was Darnell's cousin and pushed the door to the bedroom all the way open. Catrina was getting out of bed. Horace was snoring. He had never snored before in his life, but the drugs and alcohol together had done bad things to his airway.

"You hear anything?" Elaine whispered as Catrina tiptoed to her.

"I sure did," Catrina said. Sleeping on the streets required keeping one eye and both ears open. "I don't wanna go back to jail."

"Shit. Me, neither," Elaine said. "What about the window?"

"Go out and down two floors? With a baby? Damn!"

"We can do it," Elaine said, looking over Catrina's shoulder to the dark lump that was Horace mumbling in his sleep. "What about him?"

Catrina turned her head. "He old. They ain't gonna do anything to him. I'm just worried bout makin it with that baby."

"Well, I sure as hell ain't gonna go without my child."

"I ain't said we was," Catrina hissed. "Down two floors just ain't gonna be easy, is all."

"We can do it," Elaine said.

"We can do it," Catrina said. She tiptoed to the chair at the foot of the bed and went through Horace's pants pockets. "Maybe fifty dollars here," she whispered after returning. "I already got about three hundred."

"You been stealin from him?" Elaine said. The lump in the bed turned over and moaned, then settled back to snoring.

"God helps them that helps themselves, Elaine. Les go." Catrina had her clothes in her hands and went on by Elaine, who watched as the lump in the bed turned again, snoring all the while. Bye, Horace. Bye. I be seein you.

The policeman in the unmarked car parked across Thirteenth Street watched as Elaine stood on the edge of the balcony and jumped. She passed for a second in front of the feeble light over the entrance and landed on the sloping entrance of the underground parking garage. The policeman was five years from retirement and he did not move, because he could see quite well from where he sat. His partner, only three years on the job, was asleep in the passenger seat. The veteran thought the woman jumping might have hurt herself, because he did not see her rise from the ground for several minutes. I wouldn't do it, the man thought, not for all a rich man's money. The woman did rise, but before she did he saw another woman lean over the balcony dangling a bundle. Drugs? he thought. Nah. Clothes? Yeah, clothes more like it. The bundle was on a long rope or string—it was too far for the man to make out. The woman on the balcony leaned over very far and the woman on the ground reached up as far as she could, but still the bundle was a good two feet from her hands.

Just let them clothes drop, the policeman thought. Then Catrina released the bundle and Elaine caught it. Good catch. I wonder what she looks like in the light. Catrina jumped, and the policeman watched her pass momentarily in front of the light, and then he looked over at his partner. He himself didn't mind filling out the forms so much, but his partner did, so he let him sleep on. I'll be on a lake fishin my behind off and you'll still be doin this. When he looked back, the first woman was coming up the slope of the entrance with the bundle in her arms and the second one was limping after her. I wonder what that one looks like in a good light. Once on the sidewalk, both women looked left, then right, and headed down Thirteenth Street. The policeman yawned and watched through his sideview mirror as the women crossed M Street. He yawned again. Even at three o'clock in the morning people still jaywalked.

The man who was a cousin of Darnell's was on his way back from the bathroom when the police broke through the door. He frightened easily, and though he had just emptied his bladder, he peed again as the door came open and the light of the hallway and the loud men came spilling in on him and his sleeping companions.

Horace began asking about Catrina and Elaine and the baby as soon as they put him in a cell. It took him that long to clear his head and understand what was happening to him. He pressed his face against the bars, trying to get his bearings and ignoring everything behind him in the cell. He stuck his mouth as far out of the bars as he could and shouted for someone to tell him whether they knew if the young women and the baby were all right. "They just women, y'all," he kept saying for some five minutes. "They wouldn't hurt a flea. Officers, please. Please, Officers. What's done happened to them? And that baby . . . That baby is so innocent." It was a little after six in the morning, and men up and down the line started hollering for him to shut up or they would stick the biggest dick he ever saw in his mouth. Stunned, he did quiet down, because, while he was used to street language coming from the young men who came and went in his apartment, no bad words had ever been directed at him. They talked trash with the filthiest language he had ever heard but they always invited him to join in and "talk about how it really is," talk about his knowing the Secretary of Defense and the Mayor. Usually, after the second blunt, he was floating along with them. Now someone had threatened to do to him what he and the young men said they would do to any woman that crossed them.

Then he turned from the bars and considered the three men he was sharing the two-man cell with. The city-jail people liked to make as little work for themselves as possible, and filling cells beyond their capacity meant having to deal with fewer locks. One man was cocooned in blankets on the floor beside the tiered metal beds. The man sleeping on the top bunk had a leg over the side, and because he was a tall man the leg came down to within six inches of the face of the man lying on the bottom bunk. That man was awake and on his back and picking his nose and staring at Horace. His other hand was under his blanket, in the crotch of his pants. What the man got out of his nose he would flick up at the bottom of the bunk above him. Watching him, Horace remembered that a very long time ago, even before the Chesapeake Street house, Loneese would iron his handkerchiefs and fold them into four perfect squares.

"Daddy," the man said, "you got my smokes?"

"What?" Horace said. He recalled doing it to Catrina about two or three in the morning and then rolling over and going to sleep. He also remembered slapping flies away in his dreams, flies that were as big as the hands of policemen.

The man seemed to have an infinite supply of boogers, and the more he picked the more Horace's stomach churned. He used to think it was such a shame to unfold the handkerchiefs, so wondrous were the squares. The man sighed at Horace's question and put something from his nose on the big toe of the sleeping man above him. "I said do you got my smokes?"

"I don't have my cigarettes with me," Horace said. He tried the best white man's English he knew, having been told by a friend who was serving with him in the Army in Germany that it impressed not only white people but black people who weren't going anywhere in life. "I left my cigarettes at home." His legs were aching and he wanted to sit on the floor, but the only available space was in the general area of where he was standing and something adhered to his shoes every time he lifted his feet. "I wish I did have my cigarettes to give you."

"I didn't ask you bout *your* cigarettes. I don't wanna smoke them. I ask you bout *my* cigarettes. I wanna know if you brought *my* cigarettes."

Someone four cells down screamed and called out in his sleep: "Irene, why did you do this to me? Irene, ain't love worth a damn anymore?" Someone else told him to shut up or he would get a king-sized dick in his mouth.

"I told you I do not have any cigarettes," Horace said.

"You know, you ain't worth shit," the man said. "You take the cake and mess it all up. You really do. Now, you know you was comin to jail, so why didn't you bring my goddam smokes? What kinda fuckin consideration is that?"

Horace decided to say nothing. He raised first one leg and then the other and shook them, hoping that would relieve the aches. Slowly, he turned around to face the bars. No one had told him what was going to happen to him. He knew a lawyer, but he did not know if he was still practicing. He had friends, but he did not want any of them to see him in jail. He hoped the man would go to sleep.

"Don't turn your fuckin back on me after all we meant to each other," the man said. "We have this long relationship and you do this to me. Whas wrong with you, Daddy?"

"Look," Horace said, turning back to the man. "I done told you I ain't got no smokes. I ain't got your smokes. I ain't got my smokes. I ain't got nobody's smokes. Why can't you understand that?" He was aware that he was veering away from the white man's English, but he knew that his friend from Germany was probably home asleep safely in his bed. "I can't give you what I don't have." Men were murdered in the D.C. jail, or so the Washington *Post* told him. "Can't you understand what I'm sayin?" His back stayed as close to the bars as he could manage. Who was this Irene, he thought, and what had she done to steal into a man's dreams that way?

"So, Daddy, it's gonna be like that, huh?" the man said, raising his head and pushing the foot of the upper-bunk man out of the way so he could see Horace better. He took his hand out of his crotch and pointed at Horace. "You gon pull a Peter-and-Jesus thing on me and deny you ever knew me, huh? Thas your plan, Daddy?" He lowered his head back to the black-and-white striped pillow. "I've seen some low-down dirty shit in my day, but you the lowest. After our long relationship and everything."

"I never met you in my life," Horace said, grabbing the bars behind him with both hands, hoping, again, for relief.

"I won't forget this, and you know how long my memory is. First, you don't bring me my smokes, like you know you should. Then you deny all that we had. Don't go to sleep in here, Daddy, thas all I gotta say."

He thought of Reilly Johnson, a man he had worked with in the Pentagon. Reilly considered himself something of a photographer. He had taken the picture of Horace with the Secretary of Defense. What would the bail be? Would Reilly be at home to receive his call on a Sunday morning? Would they give him bail? The policemen who pulled him from his bed had tsk-tsked in his face. "Sellin drugs and corruptin young people like that?" "I didn't know nothin about that, Officer. Please." "Tsk tsk. An old man like you."

"The world ain't big enough for you to hide from my righteous wrath, Daddy. And you know how righteous I can be when I get started. The world ain't big enough, so you know this jail ain't big enough."

Horace turned back to the bars. Was something in the back as painful as something in the stomach? He touched his face. Rarely, even in the lost months with Catrina, had he failed to shave each morning. A man's capable demeanor started with a shave each morning, his sergeant in boot camp had told him a thousand years ago.

The man down the way began calling for Irene again. Irene, Horace called in his mind. Irene, are you out there? No one told the man to be quiet. It was about seven and the whole building was waking up and the man calling Irene was not the loudest sound in the world anymore.

"Daddy, you got my smokes? Could use my smokes right about now."

Horace, unable to stand anymore, slowly sank to the floor. There he found some relief. The more he sat, the more he began to play over the arrest. He had had money in his pocket when he took off his pants the night before, but there was no money when they booked him. And where had Catrina and Elaine been when the police marched him out of the apartment and down to the paddy wagon, with the Sunset's female security guard standing behind her desk with an "Oh, yes, I told you so" look? Where had they been? He had not seen them. He stretched out his legs and they touched the feet of the sleeping man on the floor. The man roused. "Love don't mean shit anymore," the man on the lower bunk said. It was loud enough to wake the man on the floor all the way, and that man sat up and covered his chest with his blanket and looked at Horace, blinking and blinking and getting a clearer picture of Horace the more he blinked.

Reilly did not come for him until the middle of Monday afternoon. Somebody opened the cell door and at first Horace thought the policeman was coming to get one of his cellmates.

"Homer Parkins," the man with the keys said. The doors were

supposed to open electronically, but that system had not worked in a long time.

"Thas me," Horace said and got to his feet. As he and the man with the keys walked past the other cells, someone said to Horace, "Hey, Pops, you ain't too old to learn to suck dick." "Keep moving," the man with the keys said. "Pops, I'll give you a lesson when you come back."

As they poured his things out of a large manila envelope, the two guards behind the desk whispered and laughed. "Everything there?" one of them asked Horace. "Yes." "Well, good," the guard said. "I guess we'll be seein you on your next trip here." "Oh, leave that old man alone. He's somebody's grandfather." "When they start that old," the first man said, "it gets in their system and they can't stop. Ain't that right, Pops?"

He and Reilly did not say very much after Reilly said he had been surprised to hear from Horace and that he had wondered what had happened to him since Loneese died. Horace said he was eternally grateful to Reilly for bailing him out and that it was all a mistake as well as a long story that he would soon share with him. At Sunset, Reilly offered to take him out for a meal, but Horace said he would have to take a rain check. "Rain check?" Reilly said, smiling. "I didn't think they said that anymore."

The key to the apartment worked the way it always had, but something was blocking the door, and he had to force it open. Inside, he found destruction everywhere. On top of the clothes and the mementos of his life, strewn across the table and the couch and the floor were hundreds and hundreds of broken records. He took three steps into the room and began to cry. He turned around and around, hoping for something that would tell him it was not as bad as his eyes first reported. But there was little hope—the salt and pepper shakers had not been touched, the curtains covering the glass door were intact. There was not much beyond that for him to cling to.

He thought immediately of Catrina and Elaine. What had he done to deserve this? Had he not always shown them a good and kind heart? He covered his eyes, but that seemed only to produce more tears, and when he lowered his hands the room danced before him through the tears. To steady himself, he put both hands on the table, which was covered in instant coffee and sugar. He brushed broken glass off the chair nearest him and sat down. He had not got it all off, and he felt what was left through his pants and underwear.

He tried to look around but got no farther than the picture with the Secretary of Defense. It had two cracks in it, one running north to south and the other going northwest to southeast. The photograph was tilting, too, and something told him that if he could straighten the picture it all might not be so bad. He reached out a hand, still crying, but he could not move from the chair.

He stayed as he was through the afternoon and late into the evening, not once moving from the chair, though the tears did stop around five o'clock. Night came and he still did not move. My name is Horace Perkins, he thought just as the sun set. My name is Horace Perkins and I worked many a year at the Pentagon. The apartment became dark, but he did not have it in him to turn on the lights.

The knocking had been going on for more than ten minutes when he finally heard it. He got up, stumbling over debris, and opened the door. Elaine stood there with Darnell, Jr., in her arms.

"Horace, you O.K.? I been comin by. I been worried about you, Horace."

He said nothing but opened the door enough for her and the baby to enter.

"It's dark, Horace. What about some light?"

He righted the lamp on the table and turned it on.

"Jesus in Heaven, Horace! What happened! My Lord Jesus! I can't believe this." The baby, startled by his mother's words, began to cry. "It's O.K.," she said to him, "It's O.K.," and gradually the baby calmed down. "Oh, Horace, I'm so sorry. I really am. This is the worst thing I've ever seen in my life." She touched his shoulder with her free hand, but he shrugged it off. "Oh, my dear God! Who could do this?"

She went to the couch and moved enough trash aside for the baby. She pulled a pacifier from her sweater pocket, put it momentarily in her mouth to remove the lint, then put it in the baby's mouth. He appeared satisfied and leaned back on the couch.

She went to Horace, and right away he grabbed her throat. "I'm gonna kill you tonight!" he shouted. "I just wish that bitch Catrina was here so I could kill her, too." Elaine struggled and sputtered out one "please" before he gripped her tighter. She beat his arms but that seemed to give him more strength. She began to cry. "I'm gonna kill you tonight, girl, if it's the last thing I do."

The baby began to cry, and she turned her head as much as she could to look at him. This made him slap her twice, and she started to fall, and he pulled her up and, as he did, went for a better grip, which was time enough for her to say, "Don't kill me in front of my son, Horace." He loosened his hands. "Don't kill me in front of my boy, Horace." Her tears ran down her face and over and into his hands. "He don't deserve to see me die. You know that, Horace."

"Where, then!"

"Anywhere but in front of him. He's innocent of everything."

He let her go and backed away.

"I did nothin, Horace," she whispered. "I give you my word, I did nothin." The baby screamed, and she went to him and took him in her arms.

Horace sat down in the same chair he had been in.

"I would not do this to you, Horace."

He looked at her and at the baby, who could not take his eyes off Horace, even through his tears.

One of the baby's cries seemed to get stuck in his throat, and to release it the baby raised a fist and punched the air, and finally the cry came free. How does a man start over with nothing? Horace thought. Elaine came near him, and the baby still watched him as his crying lessened. How does a man start from scratch?

He leaned down and picked up a few of the broken albums from the floor and read the labels. "I would not hurt you for anything in the world, Horace," Elaine said. Okeh Phonograph Corporation. Domino Record Co. RCA Victor. Darnell, Jr.,'s crying stopped, but he continued to look down at the top of Horace's head. Cameo Record Corporation, N.Y. "You been too good to me for me to hurt you like this, Horace." He dropped the records one at a time: "It Takes an Irishman to Make Love." "I'm Gonna Pin a Medal on the Girl I Left Behind." "Ragtime Soldier Man." "Whose Little Heart Are You Breaking Now." "The Syncopated Walk."

CHICXULUB

BY T. CORAGHESSAN BOYLE (2004)

My daughter is walking along the roadside late at night—too late, really, for a seventeen-year-old to be out alone, even in a town as safe as this—and it is raining, the first rain of the season, the streets slick with a fine immiscible glaze of water and petrochemicals, so that even a driver in full possession of her faculties, a driver who hadn't consumed two apple Martinis and three glasses of Hitching Post pinot noir before she got behind the wheel of her car, would have trouble keeping the thing out of the gutters and the shrubbery, off the sidewalk and *the highway median*, for Christ's sake. . . . But that's not really what I want to talk about, or not yet, anyway.

Have you heard of Tunguska? In Russia?

This was the site of the last known large-body impact on the Earth's surface, nearly a hundred years ago. Or that's not strictly accurate—the meteor, which was an estimated sixty yards across, never actually touched down. The force of its entry—the compression and superheating of the air beneath it—caused it to explode some twenty-five thousand feet above the ground, but then the term "explode" hardly does justice to the event. There was a detonation—a flash, a thunderclap—with the combustive power of eight hundred Hiroshima bombs. Thirty miles away, reindeer in their loping herds were struck dead by the blast wave, and the clothes of a hunter another thirty miles beyond that burst into flame even as he was poleaxed to the ground. Seven hundred square miles of Siberian forest were levelled in an instant. If the meteor had struck just five hours later, it would have exploded over St. Petersburg and annihilated every living thing in that glorious, baroque city. And this was only a rock. And it was only sixty yards across.

My point? You'd better get down on your knees and pray to your gods, because each year this big spinning globe we ride intersects the orbits of some twenty million asteroids, at least a thousand of which are more than half a mile in diameter.

But my daughter. She's out there in the dark and the rain, walking home. Maureen and I bought her a car, a Honda Civic, the safest thing on four wheels, but the car was used—pre-owned, in dealerspeak—and as it happens it's in the shop with transmission problems and, because she just had to see her friends and gossip and giggle and balance slick multicolored clumps of raw fish and pickled ginger on conjoined chopsticks at the mall, Kimberly picked her up and Kimberly will bring her home. Maddy has a cell phone and theoretically she could have called us, but she didn't—or that's how it appears. And so she's walking. In the rain. And Alice K. Petermann, of 16 Briar Lane, white, divorced, a Realtor with Hyperion, who has picked at a salad and left her glasses on the bar, loses control of her vehicle.

It is just past midnight. I am in bed with a book, naked, and hardly able to focus on the clustered words and rigid descending paragraphs, because Maureen is in the bathroom slipping into the sheer black negligee I bought her at Victoria's Secret for her birthday, and her every sound—the creak of the medicine cabinet on its hinges, the tap running, the susurrus of the brush at her teeth—electrifies me. I've lit a candle and am waiting for Maureen to step into the room so that I can flick off the light. We had cocktails earlier, and a bottle of wine with dinner, and we sat close on the couch and shared a joint in front of the fire, because our daughter was out and we could do that with no one the wiser. I listen to the little sounds from the bathroom, seductive sounds, maddening. I am ready. More than ready. "Hey," I call, pitching my voice low, "are you coming or not? You don't expect me to wait all night, do you?"

Her face appears in the doorway, the pale lobes of her breasts and the dark nipples visible through the clinging black silk. "Oh, are you waiting for me?" she says, making a game of it. She hovers at the door, and I can see the smile creep across her lips, the pleasure of the moment, drawing it out. "Because I thought I might go down and work in the garden for a while—it won't take long, a couple hours, maybe. You know, spread a little manure, bank up some of the mulch on the roses. You'll wait for me, won't you?"

Then the phone rings.

We stare blankly at each other through the first two rings and then Maureen says, "I'd better get it," and I say, "No, no, forget it—it's nothing. It's nobody."

But she's already moving.

"Forget it!" I shout, and her voice drifts back to me—"What if it's Maddy?"—then I watch her put her lips to the receiver and whisper, "Hello?"

The night of the Tunguska explosion the skies were unnaturally bright across Europe—as far away as London people strolled in the parks past midnight and read novels out of doors while the sheep kept right on grazing and the birds stirred uneasily in the trees. There were no stars visible, no moon—just a pale, quivering light, as if all the color had been bleached out of the sky. But, of course, that midnight glow and the fate of those unhappy Siberian reindeer were nothing at all compared to what would have happened if a larger object had invaded the Earth's atmosphere. On average, objects greater than a hundred yards in diameter strike the planet once every five thousand years, and asteroids half a mile across thunder down at intervals of three hundred thousand years. Three hundred thousand years is a long time in anybody's book. But if—when—such a collision occurs, the explosion will be in the million-megaton range and will cloak the atmosphere in dust, thrusting the entire planet into a deep freeze and effectively stifling all plant growth for a period of a year or more. There will be no crops. No forage. No sun.

There has been an accident, that is what the voice on the other end of the line is telling my wife, and the victim is Madeline Biehn, of 1337 Laurel Drive, according to the I.D. the paramedics found in her purse. (The purse, with a silver clasp that has been driven half an inch into the flesh under her arm by the force of the impact, is a little thing, no bigger than a hardcover book, with a ribbon-thin strap, the same purse all the girls carry, as if it were part of a uniform.) Is this her parent or guardian speaking?

I hear my wife say, "This is her mother." And then, the bottom dropping out of her voice, "Is she—?"

Is she? They don't answer such questions, don't volunteer information, not over the phone. The next ten seconds are thunderous, cataclysmic, my wife standing there numbly with the phone in her hand as if it were some unidentifiable object she'd found in the street while I fumble out of bed to search for my pants—and my shoes, where are my shoes? The car keys? My wallet? This is the true panic, the loss of faith and control, the punch to the heart, and the struggle for breath. I say the only thing I can think to say, just to hear my own voice, just to get things straight: "She was in an accident. Is that what they said?"

"She was hit by a car. She's—they don't know. In surgery."

"What hospital? Did they say what hospital?"

My wife is in motion now, too, the negligee ridiculous, unequal to the task, and she jerks it over her head and flings it to the floor even as she snatches up a blouse, shorts, flip-flops—anything, anything to cover her nakedness and get her out the door. The dog is whining in the kitchen. There is the sound of rain on the roof, intensifying, hammering at the gutters. I don't bother with shoes—there are no shoes, shoes do not exist—and my shirt hangs limply from my shoulders, misbuttoned, sagging, tails hanging loose, and we're in the car now and the driver's-side wiper is beating out of synch and the night closing on us like a fist.

And then there's Chicxulub. Sixty-five million years ago, an asteroid (or perhaps a comet—no one is quite certain) collided with the Earth on what is now the Yucatán Peninsula. Judging from the impact crater, which is a hundred and twenty miles wide, the object—this big flaming ball—was some six miles across. When it came down, day became night and that night extended so far into the future that at least seventy-five per cent of all known species were extinguished, including the dinosaurs in nearly all their forms and array and some ninety per cent of the oceans' plankton, which in turn devastated the pelagic food chain. How fast was it travelling? The nearest estimates put it at fifty-four thousand miles an hour, more than sixty times the speed of a bullet. Astrophysicists call such objects "civilization enders," and calculate the chances that a disaster of this magnitude will occur during any individual's lifetime at roughly one in ten thousand, the same odds as dying in an auto accident in the next six months—or, more tellingly, living to be a hundred in the company of your spouse.

All I see is windows, an endless grid of lit windows climbing one above the other into the night, as the car shoots into the Emergency Vehicles Only lane and slides in hard against the curb. Both doors fling open simultaneously. Maureen is already out on the sidewalk, already slamming the door behind her and breaking into a trot, and I'm right on her heels, the keys still in the ignition and the lights stabbing at the pale underbelly of a diagonally parked ambulance—and they can have the car, anybody can have it and keep it forever, if they'll just tell me that my daughter is all right. "Just tell me," I mutter, out of breath, "just tell me and it's yours," and this is a prayer, the first in a long discontinuous string, addressed to whoever or whatever may be listening. Overhead, the sky is having a seizure, black above, quicksilver below, the rain coming down in windblown arcs, and I wouldn't even notice but for the fact that we are suddenly—instantly—wet, our hair knotted and clinging and our clothes stuck like flypaper to the slick tegument of our skin.

In we come, side by side, through the doors that jolt back from us in alarm, and all I can think is that the hospital is a death factory and that we have come to it like the walking dead, haggard, sallow, shoeless. "My daughter," I say to the nurse at the admittance desk, "she's—they called. You called. She's been in an accident."

Maureen is at my side, tugging at the fingers of one hand as if she were trying to remove an invisible glove. "A car. A car accident."

"Name?" the nurse asks. About this nurse: she's young, Filipina, with opaque eyes and the bone structure of a cadaver; every day she sees death and it blinds her. She doesn't see us. She sees a computer screen; she sees the TV monitor mounted in the corner and the shadows that pass there; she sees the walls, the floor, the naked light of the fluorescent tube. But not us. Not us.

For one resounding moment that thumps in my ears and then thumps again, I can't remember my daughter's name—I can picture her leaning into the mound of textbooks spread out on the dining-room table, the glow of the overhead light making a nimbus of her hair as she glances up at me with a glum look and half a rueful smile, as if to say, *It's all in a day's work for a teen-ager, Dad, and you're lucky you're not in high school anymore*, but her name is gone.

"Maddy," my wife says. "Madeline Biehn."

I watch, mesmerized, as the nurse's fleshless fingers maneuver the mouse, her eyes locked on the screen before her. A click. Another click. The eyes lift to take us in, even as they dodge away again. "She's still in surgery," she says.

"Where is it?" I demand. "What room? Where do we go?"

Maureen's voice cuts in then, elemental, chilling, and it's not a question she's posing, not a statement or demand, but a plea: "What's wrong with her?"

Another click, but this one is just for show, and the eyes never move from the screen. "There was an accident," the nurse says. "She was brought in by the paramedics. That's all I can tell you."

It is then that I become aware that we are not alone, that there are others milling around the room—other zombies like us, hurriedly dressed and streaming water till the beige carpet is black with it—and why, I wonder, do I despise this nurse more than any human being I've ever encountered, this young woman not much older than my daughter, with her hair pulled back in a bun and a white cap like a party favor perched atop it, *who is just doing her job?* Why do I want to reach across the counter that separates us and awaken her to a swift, sure knowledge of hate and fear and pain? Why?

"Ted," Maureen says, and I feel her grip at my elbow, and then we're moving again—hurrying, sweeping, practically running—out of this place, down a corridor under the glare of the lights that are a kind of death in themselves, and into a worse place, a far worse place.

The thing that disturbs me about Chicxulub, aside from the fact that it erased the dinosaurs and wrought catastrophic and irreversible change, is the deeper implication that we, and all our works and worries and attachments, are so utterly inconsequential. Death cancels our individuality, we know that, yes, but ontogeny recapitulates phylogeny, and the kind goes on, human life and culture succeed us. That, in the absence of God, is what allows us to accept the death of the individual. But when you throw Chicxulub into the mix—or the next Chicxulub, the Chicxulub that could come howling down to obliterate all and everything even as your eyes skim the lines of this page—where does that leave us?

"You're the parents?" We are in another room, gone deeper now, the loudspeakers murmuring their eternal incantations—*Dr. Chandrasoma to Emergency, Dr. Bell, Paging Dr. Bell*—and here is another nurse, grimmer, older, with lines like the strings of a tobacco pouch pulled tight around her lips. She's addressing us, me and my wife, but I have nothing to say, either in denial or affirmation. If I claim Maddy as my own—and I'm making deals again—then I'm sure to jinx her, because those powers that might or might not be, those gods of the infinite and the minute, will see how desperately I love her and they'll take her away just to spite me for refusing to believe in them. *Voodoo, Hoodoo, Santería, Bless me, Father, for I have sinned.* I hear Maureen's voice, emerging from a locked vault, the single whispered monosyllable, and then: "Is she going to be all right?"

"I don't have that information," the nurse says, and her voice is neutral, robotic even. This is not her daughter. Her daughter's at home, asleep in a pile of Teddy bears, pink sheets, fluffy pillows, the night-light glowing like the all-seeing eye of a sentinel.

I can't help myself. It's that neutrality, that maddening clinical neutrality, and can't anybody take any responsibility for anything? "What information *do* you have?" I say, and maybe I'm too loud, maybe I am. "Isn't that your job, for Christ's sake—to know what's going on here? You call us up in the middle of the night—our daughter's hurt, she's been in an accident, and you tell me you don't have *any fucking information*?"

People turn their heads, eyes burn into us. They're slouched in orange plastic chairs, stretched out on the floor, praying, pacing, their lips moving in silence. They want information, too. We all want information. We want news, good news: it was all a mistake, minor cuts and bruises—contusions, that's the word—and your daughter, son, husband, grandmother, first cousin twice removed will be walking through that door over there any minute. . . .

The nurse drills me with a look, and then she's coming out from behind the desk, a short woman, dumpy—almost a dwarf—and striding briskly to a door, which swings open on another room, deeper yet. "If you'll just follow me, please," she says.

Suddenly sheepish, I duck my head and comply, two steps behind Maureen. This room is smaller, an examining room, with a set of scales and charts on the walls and its slab of a table covered with a sheet of antiseptic paper. "Wait here," the nurse tells us, already shifting her weight to make her escape. "The doctor will be in in a minute."

"What doctor?" I want to know. "What for? What does he want?"

But the door has already drawn closed.

I turn to Maureen. She's standing there in the middle of the room, afraid to touch anything or to sit down or even to move for fear of breaking the spell. She's listening for footsteps, her eyes fixed on the door. I hear myself murmur her name, and then she's in my arms, sobbing, and I know I should hold her, know that we both need it, the human contact, the love and support, but all I feel is the burden of her—there is nothing and no one that can make this better, can't she see that? I don't want to console or be consoled. I don't want to be touched. I just want my daughter back.

Maureen's voice comes from so deep in her throat I can barely make out what she's saying. It takes a second to register, even as she pulls away from me, her face crumpled and red, and this is her prayer, whispered aloud: "She's going to be all right, isn't she?"

"Sure," I say, "sure she is. She'll be fine. She'll have some bruises, that's for sure, maybe a couple broken bones even . . ." and I trail off, trying to picture it, the crutches, the cast, the Band-Aids, the gauze: our daughter returned to us in a halo of shimmering light.

"Maybe she broke her arm—she could break her arm. That would— Or her leg, even her leg. But why would she be in surgery? Why would she be in surgery so long? Why? Why would that be?"

I don't have an answer to that. I don't want to have an answer.

"It was a car," Maureen says. "A car, Ted. A car hit her."

The room seems to tick and buzz with the fading energy of the larger edifice, and I can't help thinking of the congeries of wires strung inside the walls, the cables bringing power to the X-ray lab, the EKG and EEG machines, the life-support systems, and of the myriad pipes and the fluids that they drain.

A car. Three thousand pounds of steel, chrome, glass, iron.

"What was she even doing walking like that? She knows better than that."

My wife nods, the wet ropes of her hair beating at her shoulders like the flails of the penitents. "She probably had a fight with Kimberly—I'll bet that's it. I'll bet anything."

"Where is the son of a bitch?" I snarl. "This doctor—where is he?"

We are in that room, in that purgatory of a room, for a good hour or more. Twice I thrust my head out the door to give the nurse an annihilating look, but there is no news, no doctor, nothing. And then, at quarter past two, the inner door swings open, and there he is, a man too young to be a doctor, an infant with a smooth bland face and hair that rides a wave up off his brow, and he doesn't have to say a thing, not a word, because I can see what he's bringing us and my heart seizes with the shock of it. He looks to Maureen, looks to me, then drops his eyes. "I'm sorry," he says.

When it comes, the meteor will punch through the atmosphere and strike the Earth in the space of a single second, vaporizing on impact and creating a fireball that will in that moment achieve temperatures of sixty thousand degrees Kelvin, or ten times the surface reading of the sun. If it is Chicxulub-size and it hits one of our landmasses, some two hundred thousand cubic kilometres of the Earth's surface will be thrust up into the atmosphere, even as the thermal radiation of the blast sets fire to the Earth's cities and forests. This will be succeeded by seismic and volcanic activity on a scale unknown in human history, and then the dark night of cosmic winter. If it should land in the sea, as the Chicxulub meteor did, it would spew superheated water into the atmosphere, instead, extinguishing the light of the sun and triggering the same scenario of seismic catastrophe and eternal winter, while simultaneously sending out a rippling ring of water three miles high to rock the continents as if they were saucers in a dishpan.

So what does it matter? What does anything matter? We are powerless. We are bereft. And the gods—all the gods of all the ages combined—are nothing but a rumor.

The gurney is the focal point in a room of gurneys, people laid out as if there'd been a war, the beaked noses of the victims poking up out of the maze of sheets like a series of topographic blips on a glaciated plain. These people are alive still, fluids dripping into their veins, machines monitoring their vital signs, nurses hovering over them like ghouls, but they'll be dead soon, all of them. That much is clear. But *the* gurney, the one against the back wall with the sheet pulled up over the impossibly small and reduced form—this is all that matters. The doctor leads us across the room, speaking in a low voice of internal injuries, a ruptured spleen, trauma, the brain stem, and I can barely control my feet.

Can I tell you how hard it is to lift this sheet? Thin percale, and it might as well be made of lead, iron, iridium, might as well be the repository of all the dark matter in the universe. The doctor steps back, hands folded before him. The entire room or triage ward or whatever it is holds its breath. Maureen moves in beside me till our shoulders are touching, till I can feel the flesh and the heat of her pressing into me, and I think of this child we made together, this thing under the sheet, and the hand clenches at the end of my arm, the fingers there, prehensile, taking hold. The sheet draws back millimetre by millimetre, the slow striptease of death—and I can't do this, I can't—until Maureen lunges forward and jerks the thing off in a single violent motion.

It takes us a moment—the shock of the bloated and discolored flesh, the crusted mat of blood at the temple and the rag of the hair, this obscene violation of everything we know and expect and love—before the surge of joy hits us. Maddy is a redhead, like her mother, and though she's seventeen, she's as rangy and thin as a child, with oversized hands and feet, and she never did pierce that smooth sweet run of flesh beneath her lower lip. I can't speak. I'm rushing still with the euphoria of this new mainline drug I've discovered, soaring over the room, the hospital, the whole planet. Maureen says it for me: "This is not our daughter."

Our daughter is not in the hospital. Our daughter is asleep in her room beneath the benevolent gaze of the posters on the wall—Britney and Brad and Justin—her things scattered around her as if laid out for a rummage sale. Our daughter has in fact gone to Hana Sushi at the mall, as planned, and Kimberly has driven her home. Our daughter has, unbeknownst to us or anyone else, fudged the rules a bit—the smallest thing in the world, nothing really, the sort of thing every teen-ager does without thinking twice. She has loaned her I.D. to her second-best friend, Kristi Cherwin, because Kristi is sixteen and Kristi wants to see—is dying to see—the movie at the Cineplex with Brad Pitt in it, the one rated NC-17. Our daughter doesn't know that we've been to the hospital, doesn't know about Alice K. Petermann and the pinot noir and the glasses left on the bar, doesn't know that even now the phone is ringing at the Cherwins'.

I am sitting on the couch with a drink, staring into the ashes of the fire. Maureen is in the kitchen with a mug of Ovaltine, gazing vacantly out the window where the first streaks of light have begun to limn the trunks of the trees. I try to picture the Cherwins—they've been to the house a few times, Ed and Lucinda—and I draw a blank until a backlit scene from the past presents itself, a cookout at their place, the adults gathered around the grill with gin-and-tonics, the radio playing some forgotten song, the children, our daughters, riding their bikes up and down the cobbled drive, making a game of it, spinning, dodging, lifting the front wheels from the ground even as their hair fans out behind them and the sun crashes through the trees. Flip a coin ten times and it could turn up heads ten times in a row—or not once. The rock is coming, the new Chicxulub, hurtling through the dark and the cold to remake our fate. But not tonight. Not for me.

For the Cherwins, it's already here.

THE PLAGUE OF DOVES

BY LOUISE ERDRICH (2004)

Some years before the turn of the last century, my great-uncle, one of the first Catholic priests of aboriginal blood, put the call out to his congregation, telling everyone to gather at St. Gabriel's, wearing scapulars and holding missals. From that place, they would proceed to walk the fields in a long, sweeping row, and with each step loudly pray away the doves. My great-uncle's human flock had taken up the plow and farmed among Norwegian settlers. Unlike the French, who mingled with my ancestors, the Norwegians took little interest in the women native to the land and did not intermarry. In fact, they disregarded everybody but themselves and were quite clannish. But the doves ate their crops just the same. They ate the wheat seedlings and the rye and started on the corn. They ate the sprouts of new flowers and the buds of apples and the tough leaves of oak trees and even last year's chaff. The doves were plump, and delicious smoked, but one could wring the necks of hundreds or even thousands and effect no visible diminishment of their number. The pole-and-mud houses of the mixed-bloods and the skin tents of the blanket Indians were crushed by the weight of the birds. When they descended, both Indians and whites set up great bonfires and tried to drive them into nets. The birds were burned, roasted, baked in pies, stewed, salted down in barrels, or clubbed to death with sticks and left to rot. But the dead only fed the living, and each morning when the people woke it was to the scraping and beating of wings, the murmurous susurration, the awful cooing babble, and the sight of the curious and gentle faces of those creatures.

My great-uncle had hastily constructed crisscrossed racks of sticks to protect the rare glass windows of what was grandly called the rectory. In a corner of that one-room cabin, his twelve-year-old brother, whom he had saved from a life of excessive freedom, slept on a pallet of cottonwood branches and a mattress stuffed with grass. This was the softest bed the boy had ever had, and he did not want to leave it, but my great-uncle thrust a choirboy surplice at him and ordered him to polish up the candelabra that he would carry in the procession.

This boy would be my grandfather's father, my Mooshum, and since he lived to be over a hundred I was able to hear him tell and retell the story of the most momentous day of his life—which began with this attempt to vanquish the plague of doves. Sitting on a hard chair, between our first television and the small alcove of bookshelves set into the wall of our government-owned house on the Bureau of Indian Affairs school campus, he told us how he'd heard the scratching of the doves' feet as they climbed all over the screens of sticks that his brother had made. He dreaded going to the outhouse, because some of the birds had got mired in the filth beneath the hole and set up a screeching clamor of despair that caused others of their kind to throw themselves against the hut in rescue attempts. But he did not dare relieve himself anywhere else. So through a flurry of wings, shuffling so as not to step on the birds, he made his way to the outhouse and completed the necessary actions with his eyes shut. Leaving, he tied the door closed so that no other doves would be trapped.

The outhouse drama, always the first scene in Mooshum's story of that momentous day, was filled with the sort of details that my brother and I found interesting; the outhouse—which was an exotic but not unfamiliar feature—and the horror of the birds' death by excrement gripped our attention. Mooshum was our second-favorite indoor entertainment. Television was the first. But our father had removed the television's knobs and hidden them. Despite constant efforts, we couldn't find the knobs, and we came to believe that he carried them on his person at all times. So instead we listened to our

Mooshum. While he talked, we sat on kitchen chairs and twisted our hair. Our mother had given him a red Folgers coffee can for spitting snoose. He wore soft, worn green Sears work clothes, a pair of battered brown lace-up boots, and a twill cap, even in the house. His eyes shone from slits cut deep into his face. He was hunched and dried-out, with random wisps of white hair falling over his ears and neck. From time to time, as he spoke, we glimpsed the murky scraggle of his teeth. Still, such was his conviction in the telling of this story that it wasn't hard at all to imagine him at twelve.

My great-uncle put on his vestments, hand-me-downs from a Minneapolis parish. Since real incense was impossible to obtain, he stuffed the censer with dry sage rolled up in balls. Then he wet a comb at the cabin's iron hand pump and slicked back his hair and his little brother's hair. The church cabin was just across the yard, and wagons had been pulling up for the past hour or so, each with a dog or two tied in the box to keep the birds and their droppings off the piled hay where people would sit. The constant movement of the birds made some of the horses skittish. Many wore blinders and had bouquets of calming chamomile tied to their harnesses. As our Mooshum walked across the yard, he saw that the roof of the church was covered with birds that repeatedly—in play, it seemed—flew up and knocked one another off the holy cross that marked the cabin as a church. Great-Uncle was more than six feet tall, an imposing man, whose melodious voice carried over the confusion of sounds as he organized his parishioners into a line. The two brothers stood at the center, and with the faithful congregants spread out on either side they made their way slowly down the hill toward the first of the fields they hoped to clear.

The sun was dull that day, thickly clouded over, and the air was oppressively still, so that pungent clouds of sage smoke hung all around the metal basket on its chain as it swung in each direction. In the first field, the doves were packed so tightly on the ground that there was a sudden agitation among the women, who could not move forward without sweeping the birds into their skirts. In panic, the birds tangled themselves in the cloth. The line halted suddenly as the women erupted in a raging dance, each twirling, stamping, beating, and flapping her skirts. So vehement was the dance that the birds all around them popped into flight, frightening other birds, and within moments the entire field was a storm of birds that roared and blasted down upon the people, who nonetheless stood firm with splayed missals on their heads. To move forward, the women forsook their modesty. They knotted their skirts up around their thighs, held out their rosaries or scapulars, and chanted the Hail Mary into the wind of beating wings. Mooshum, who had rarely seen a woman's lower limbs, dropped behind, delighted. As he watched the women's naked round brown legs thrash through the field, he lowered the candelabra that his brother had given him to protect his face. Instantly, he was struck on the forehead by a bird that hurtled from the sky with such force that it seemed to have been flung directly by God, to smite and blind him before he carried his sin of appreciation any further.

At this point in the story, Mooshum often became so agitated that he acted out the smiting and, to our pleasure, mimed his collapse, throwing himself upon the floor. Then he opened his eyes and lifted his head and stared into space, clearly seeing, even now, the vision of the Holy Spirit, which appeared to him not in the form of a white bird among the brown doves but as the earthly body of a girl.

Our family has something of a historical reputation for romantic encounters. My aunt Philomena, struck by the smile of a man on a passenger train, raised her hand from the ditch where she stood picking berries, and was unable to see his hand wave in return. But something made her stay there until nightfall and then camp there overnight, and wait quietly for another whole day until the man came walking back to her from the next stop, sixty miles ahead. My oldest cousin, Curtis, dated the Haskell Indian Princess, who cut her braids off and gave them to him the night she died of tuberculosis. He remained a bachelor, in her memory, until his fifties. My aunt Agathe left the convent for a priest. My cousin Eugene reformed a small-town stripper. Even my sedate-looking father was swept through the Second World War by one promising glance from my mother. And so on.

These tales of extravagant encounter contrasted with the modesty of the subsequent marriages and occupations of my relatives. We are a tribe of office workers, bank tellers, booksellers, and bureaucrats. The wildest of us (Eugene) owns a restaurant, and the most heroic of us (my father) teaches seventh grade. Yet this current of drama holds together the generations, I think, and my brother and I listened to Mooshum not only to find out what had happened but also because we hoped for instructions on how to behave when our own moment of recognition, or romantic trial, should arrive.

In truth, I thought that mine had probably already come, for even as I sat there listening to Mooshum my fingers obsessively spelled out the name of my beloved on my arm or in my hand or on my knee. I believed that if I wrote his name on my body a million times he would kiss me. I knew that he loved me, and he was safe in the knowledge that I loved him, but we attended a Roman Catholic grade school in the early nineteen-sixties, when boys and girls who were known to be in love hardly talked to each other and certainly never touched. We played softball and kickball together, and acted and spoke through other children who were eager to deliver messages. I had copied a series of these secondhand love statements into my tiny leopard-print diary, which had a golden lock. The key was hidden in the hollow knob of my bedstead. Also, I had written the name of my beloved, in blood from a scratched mosquito bite, along the inner wall of my closet. His name held for me the sacred resonance of those Old Testament words written in fire by an invisible hand. *Mene, mene, tekel, upharsin.* I could not say his name aloud. I could only write it with my fingers on my skin, until my mother feared I'd got lice and coated my hair with mayonnaise, covered my head with a shower cap, and told me to sit in a bath that was as hot as I could stand until my condition should satisfy her.

I locked the bathroom door, controlled the hot water with my toe, and, since I had nothing else to do, decided to advance my name-writing total by several thousand. As I wrote, I found places on myself that changed and warmed in response to the repetition of those letters, and without an idea in the world what I was doing I gave myself successive alphabetical orgasms so shocking in their intensity and delicacy that the mayonnaise must have melted off my head. I then stopped writing on myself. I believed that I had reached the million mark, and didn't dare try the same thing again.

Ash Wednesday passed, and I was reminded that I was made of dust only and would return to dust as soon as life was done with me.

My body, inscribed everywhere with the holy name Merlin Koppin (I can say it now), was only a temporary surface, soon to crumble like a leaf. As always, we entered the Lenten season aware that our hunger for sweets or salted pretzels or whatever we had given up was only a phantom craving. The hunger of the spirit alone was real. It was my good fortune not to understand that writing my boyfriend's name on myself had been an impure act, so I felt that I had nothing worse to atone for than my collaboration with my brother's discovery that pliers from the toolbox worked as well as knobs on the television. As soon as my parents were gone, we could watch "The Three Stooges"—our and Mooshum's favorite, and a show that my parents thought abominable. It was Palm Sunday before my father happened to come home from an errand and rest his hand on the hot surface of the television and then fix us with the fox-like suspicion that his students surely dreaded. He got the truth out of us quickly. The pliers were hidden, along with the knobs, and Mooshum's story resumed.

The girl who would become my great-grandmother had fallen behind the other women in the field, because she was too shy to knot up her skirts. Her name was Junesse, and she, too, was twelve years old. The trick, she found, was to walk very slowly so that the birds had time to move politely aside instead of starting upward. Junesse wore a long white Communion dress made of layers of filmy muslin. She had insisted on wearing this dress, and the aunt who cared for her had given in but had promised to beat her if she returned with a rip or a stain. This threat, too, had deterred Junesse from joining in the other women's wild dance. But now, finding herself alone with the felled candelabra-bearer, she perhaps forced their fate in the world by kneeling in a patch of bird slime to revive him, and then sealed it by using her sash to blot away the wash of blood from his forehead, where the bird had wounded him.

And there she was! Mooshum paused in his story. His hands opened and the hundreds of wrinkles in his face folded into a mask of unsurpassable happiness. Her black hair was tied with a white ribbon. Her white dress had a bodice embroidered with white flower petals and white leaves. And she had the pale, heavy skin and slanting black eyes of the Métis women in whose honor a bishop of that diocese had written a warning to his priests, advising them to pray hard and to remember that although women's forms could be inordinately fair, they were also savage and permeable. The Devil came and went in them at will. Of course, Junesse Malaterre was innocent, but she was also sharp of mind. Her last name, which came down to us from some French *voyageur*, refers to the cleft furrows of godless rock, the barren valleys, striped outcrops, and mazelike configurations of rose, gray, tan, and purple stone that characterize the Badlands of North Dakota. To this place Mooshum and Junesse eventually made their way.

"We seen into each udder's dept'" was how my Mooshum put it, in his gentle reservation accent. There was always a moment of silence among the three of us as the scene played out. Mooshum saw what he described. I don't know what my brother saw—perhaps another boy. (He eventually came out to everyone at my parents' silver-anniversary dinner party.) Or perhaps he saw that, after a whirl of experience and a minor car accident, he, too, would settle into the dull happiness of routine with his insurance-claims adjuster. As for me, I saw two beings—the boy shaken, frowning, the girl in white kneeling over him pressing the sash of her dress to the wound on his head, stanching the flow of blood. Most important, I saw their dark, mutual gaze. The Holy Spirit hovered between them. Her sash reddened. His blood defied gravity and flowed up her arm. Then her mouth opened. Did they kiss? I couldn't ask Mooshum. She hadn't had time to write his name on her body even once, and, besides, she didn't know his name. They had seen into each other's being, therefore names were irrelevant. They ran away together, Mooshum said, before either had thought to ask what the other was called. And then they decided not to have names for a while—all that mattered was that they had escaped, slipped their knots, cut the harnesses that their relatives had tightened. Junesse fled her aunt's beating and the endless drudgery of caring for six younger cousins, who would all die the following winter of a choking cough. Mooshum fled the sanctified future that his brother had picked out for him.

The two children in white clothes melted into the wall of birds. Their robes soon became as dark as the soil, and so they blended into the earth as they made their way along the edges of fields, through open country, to where the farmable land stopped and the ground split open and the beautifully abraded knobs and canyons of the Badlands began. Although it took them several years to physically consummate their feelings (Mooshum hinted at this but never came right out and said it), they were in love. And they were survivors. They knew how to make a fire from scratch, and for the first few days they were able to live on the roasted meat of doves. It was too early in the year for there to be much else to gather in the way of food, but they stole birds' eggs and dug up weeds. They snared rabbits, and begged what they could from isolated homesteads.

On the Monday that we braided our blessed palms in school, braces were put on my teeth. Unlike now, when every other child undergoes some sort of orthodonture, braces were rare then. It is really extraordinary that my parents, in such modest circumstances, decided to correct my teeth at all. Our dentist was old-fashioned, and believed that to protect the enamel of my front teeth from the wires he should cap them in gold. So one day I appeared in school with two long, resplendent front teeth and a mouth full of hardware. It hadn't occurred to me that I'd be teased, but then somebody whispered, "Easter Bunny!" By noon recess, boys swirled around me, poking, trying to get me to smile. Suddenly, as if a great wind had blown everyone else off the bare gravel yard, there was Merlin Koppin. He shoved me and laughed right in my face. Then the other boys swept him away. I took refuge in the only sheltered spot on the playground, an alcove in the brick on the southern side facing the littered hulks of cars behind a gas station. I stood in a silent bubble, rubbing my collarbone where his hands had pushed, wondering. What had happened to our love? It was in danger, maybe finished. Because of golden teeth. Even then, such a radical change in feeling seemed impossible to bear. Remembering our family history, though, I rallied myself to the challenge. Included in the romantic tales were episodes of reversals. I had justice on my side, and, besides, when my braces came off I would be beautiful. Of this I had been assured by my parents. So as we were entering the classroom in our usual parallel lines, me in the girls' line, he in the boys', I maneuvered myself across from Merlin, punched him in the arm, hard, and said, "Love me or leave me." Then I marched away. My knees were weak, my heart pounded. My act had been wild and unprecedented.

Soon everyone had heard about it, and I was famous, even among the eighth-grade girls, one of whom, Tenny McElwayne, offered to beat Merlin up for me. Power was mine, and it was Holy Week.

The statues were shrouded in purple except for our church's exceptionally graphic Stations of the Cross. Nowadays, the Stations of the Cross are carved in tasteful wood or otherwise abstracted. But our church's version was molded of plaster and painted with bloody relish. Eyes rolled to the whites. Mouths contorted. Limbs flailed. It was all there. The side aisles of the church were wide, and there was plenty of room for schoolchildren to kneel on the aggregate stone floor and contemplate the hard truths of torture. The most sensitive of the girls, and one boy, destined not for the priesthood but for a spectacular musical career, wept openly and luxuriantly. The rest of us, soaked in guilt or secretly admiring the gore, tried to sit back unobtrusively on our bottoms and spare our kneecaps. At some point, we were allowed into the pews, where, during the three holiest hours of the afternoon on Good Friday, with Christ slowly dying underneath his purple cape, we were supposed to maintain silence. During that time, I decided to begin erasing Merlin's name from my body by writing it backward a million times: Nippok Nilrem. I began my task in the palm of my hand, then moved to my knee. I'd managed only a hundred when I was thrilled to realize that Merlin was trying frantically to catch my eye, a thing that had never happened before. As I've said, our love affair had been carried out by intermediaries. But my fierce punch seemed to have hot-wired his emotions. That he should be so impetuous, so desperate, as to seek me out directly! I was overcome with a wash of shyness and terror. I wanted to acknowledge Merlin, but I couldn't now. I stayed frozen in place until we were dismissed.

Easter Sunday. I am dressed in blue dotted nylon swiss. The seams prickle and the neck itches, but the over-all effect, I think, is glorious. I own a hat that has fake lilies of the valley on it and a stretchy band that digs into my chin. At the last moment, I beg to wear my mother's lace mantilla instead, the one like Jackie Kennedy's, headgear that only the most fashionable older girls wear. Nevertheless, I am completely unprepared for what happens when I return from taking Holy Communion. I am kneeling at the end of the pew. We are instructed to remain silent and to allow Christ's presence to diffuse in us. I do my best. But then I see Merlin in the line for Communion on my side of the church, which means that on the way back to his seat he will pass only inches from me. I can keep my head demurely down, or I can look up. The choice dizzies me. And I do look up. He rounds the first pew. I hold my gaze steady. He sees that I am looking at him—freckles, dark slicked-back hair, narrow brown eyes—and he does not look away. With the Host of the Resurrection in his mouth, my first love gives me a glare of anguished passion that suddenly ignites the million invisible names.

For one whole summer, my great-grandparents lived off a bag of contraband pinto beans. They killed the rattlesnakes that came down to the streambed to hunt, roasted them, used salt from a little mineral wash to season the meat. They managed to find some berry bushes and to snare a few gophers and rabbits. But the taste of freedom was eclipsed now by their longing for a good, hot dinner. Though desolate, the Badlands were far from empty; they were peopled in Mooshum's time by unpurposed miscreants and outlaws as well as by honest ranchers. One day, Mooshum and Junesse heard an inhuman shrieking from some bushes deep in a draw where they'd set snares. Upon cautiously investigating, they found that they had snared a pig by its hind leg. While they were debating how to kill it, there appeared on a rise the silhouette of an immense person wearing a wide fedora and seated on a horse. They could have run, but as the rider approached them they were too amazed to move, or didn't want to, for the light now caught the features of a giant woman dressed in the clothing of a man. Her eyes were small and shrewd, her nose and cheeks pudgy, her lip a narrow curl of flesh. One long braid hung down beside a large and motherly breast. She wore twill trousers, boots, chaps, leather gauntlets, and a cowhide belt with silver conchas. Her wide-brimmed hat was banded with the skin of a snake. Her brown bloodstock horse stopped short, polite and obedient. The woman spat a stream of tobacco juice at a quiet lizard, laughed when it jumped and skittered, then ordered the two children to stand still while she roped her hog. With swift and expert motions, she dismounted and tied the pig to the pommel of her saddle, then released its hind leg.

"Climb on," she commanded, gesturing at the horse, and when

the children did she grasped the halter and started walking. The roped pig trotted along behind. By the time they reached the woman's ranch, which was miles off, the two had fallen asleep. The woman had a ranch hand take them down, still sleeping, and lay them in a bedroom in her house, which was large and ramshackle, partly sod and partly framed. There were two little beds in the room, plus a trundle where she herself sometimes slept, snoring like an engine, when she was angry with her husband, the notorious Ott Black. In this place my Mooshum and his bride-to-be would live until they turned sixteen.

In Erling Nicolai Rolfsrud's compendium of memorable women and men from North Dakota, "Mustache" Maude Black is described as not unwomanly, though she smoked, drank, was a crack shot and a hard-assed camp boss. These things, my Mooshum said, were all true, as was the mention of both her kind ways and her habit of casual rustling. The last was just a sport to her, Mooshum said; she never meant any harm by it. Mustache Maude sometimes had a mustache, and sometimes, when she plucked it out, she didn't. She kept a neat henhouse and a tidy kitchen. She grew very fond of Mooshum and Junesse, taught them to rope, ride, shoot, and make an unbeatable chicken-and-dumpling stew. Divining their love, she quickly banished Mooshum to the men's bunkhouse, where he soon learned the many ways in which he could make children in the future with Junesse. He practiced in his mind, and could hardly wait. But Maude forbade their marriage until both were sixteen. When that day came, she threw a wedding supper that was talked about for years, featuring several delectably roasted animals that seemed to be the same size and type as those which had gone missing from the farms of the dinner guests. This caused a stir, but Maude kept the liquor flowing, and most of the ranchers shrugged it off.

What was not shrugged off, what was truly resented, was the fact that Maude had thrown an elaborate shindig for a couple of Indians. Or half-breeds. It didn't matter which. These were uncertain times in North Dakota. People's nerves were still shot over what had happened to Custer, and every few years there occurred a lynching. Just a few years before, the remains of five men had been found, still strung from trees, supposedly the victims of a vigilante party led by Flopping Bill Cantrell. Some time later, an entire family was murdered and three Indians were caught by a mob and hanged for maybe doing it, including a boy named Paul Holy Track, who was only thirteen.

The foul murder of a woman on a farm just to the west of Maude's place caused the neighbors to disregard, in their need for immediate revenge, the sudden absence of that woman's husband and to turn their thoughts to the nearest available Indian. There I was, Mooshum said. One night, the yard of pounded dirt between the bunkhouse and Maude's sleeping quarters filled with men hoisting torches of flaring pitch. Their howls rousted Maude from her bed. As a precaution, she had sent Mooshum down to her kitchen cellar to sleep the night. So he knew what happened only through the memory of his wife, for he heard nothing and dreamed his way through the danger.

"Send him out to us," they bawled, "or we will take him ourselves."

Maude stood in the doorway in her nightgown, her holster belted on, a cocked pistol in either hand. She never liked to be woken from sleep.

"I'll shoot the first two of youse that climbs down off his horse," she said, then gestured to the sleepy man beside her, "and Ott Black will plug the next!"

The men were very drunk and could hardly control their horses. One fell off, and Maude shot him in the leg. He started screaming worse than the snared pig.

"Which one of you boys is next?" Maude roared.

"Send out the goddam Indian!" they called. But the yell had less conviction, punctuated, as it was, by the shot man's hoarse shrieks.

"What Indian?"

"That boy!"

"He ain't no Indian," Maude said. "He's a Jew from the land of Galilee! One of the lost tribe of Israel!"

Ott Black nearly choked at his wife's wit.

The men laughed nervously, and called for the boy again.

"I was just having fun with you," Maude said. "Fact is, he's Ott Black's trueborn son."

This threw the men back in their saddles. Ott blinked, then caught on and bellowed, "You men never knowed a woman till you knowed Maude Black!"

The men fell back into the night and left their fallen would-be lyncher kicking in the dirt and pleading to God for mercy. Maybe Maude's bullet had hit a nerve or a bone, for the man seemed to be in an unusual amount of pain for just a gunshot wound to the leg. He began to rave and foam at the mouth, so Maude tied him to his saddle and set out for the doctor's. He died on the way from loss of blood. Before dawn, Maude came back, gave my great-grandparents her two best horses, and told them to ride hard back the way they had come. Which was how they ended up on their home reservation in time to receive their allotments, where they farmed using government-issue seed and plows and reared their six children, one of whom was my grandfather, and where my parents took us every summer just after the wood ticks had settled down.

The story may have been true, for, as I have said, there really was a Mustache Maude Black who had a husband named Ott. Only the story changed. Sometimes Maude was the one to claim Mooshum as her son in the story and sometimes she went on to claim that she'd had an affair with Chief Gall. And sometimes she plugged the man in the gut. But if there was embellishment it had to do only with facts. St. Gabriel's Church was named for God's messenger, the archangel who currently serves as the patron saint of telecommunications workers. Those doves were surely the passenger pigeons of legend and truth, whose numbers were such that nobody thought they could ever be wiped from the earth.

As Mooshum grew frailer and had trouble getting out of his chair, our parents relaxed their television boycott. More often now, our father fixed the magic circles of plastic onto their metal posts and twiddled them until the picture cleared. We sometimes all watched "The Three Stooges" together. The black-haired one looked a lot like the woman who had saved his life, Mooshum said, nodding and pointing at the set. I remember imagining his gnarled brown finger as the hand of a strong young man gripping the candelabra, which, by the way, my great-grandparents had lugged all the way down to the Badlands, where it had come in handy for killing snakes and gophers. They had given their only possession to Maude as a gesture of their gratitude. She had thrust it back at them the night they escaped.

That tall, seven-branched silver-plated instrument, with its finish worn down to tin in some spots, now stood in a place of honor in the center of our dining-room table. It held beeswax tapers, which had been lit during Easter dinner. A month later, in the little alcove on the school playground, I kissed Merlin Koppin. Our kiss was hard, passionate, strangely mature. Afterward, I walked home alone. I walked very slowly. Halfway there, I stopped and stared at a piece of the sidewalk that I'd crossed a thousand times and knew intimately. There was a crack in it—deep, long, jagged, and dark. It was the day when the huge old cottonwood trees shed cotton. Their heart-shaped leaves ticked and hissed high above me. The air was filled with falling down, and the gutters were plump with a snow of light. I had expected to feel joy, but instead I felt a confusion of sorrow, or maybe fear, for it suddenly seemed that my life was a hungry story and I its source and with this kiss I had begun to deliver myself to the words.

LAST EVENINGS ON EARTH

BY ROBERTO BOLAÑO (2005)

This is the situation: B and his father are going on vacation to Acapulco. They are planning to leave very early, at six in the morning. B spends the night at his father's house. He doesn't dream, or, if he does, he forgets his dreams as soon as he opens his eyes. He hears his father in the bathroom. He looks out the window; it is still dark. He gets dressed without switching on the light. When he comes out of his room, his father is sitting at the table, reading the sports section from the day before, and breakfast is ready. Coffee and huevos rancheros. B says hello to his father and goes into the bathroom.

His father's car is a 1970 Ford Mustang. At six-thirty, they get into the car and head out of the city. The city is Mexico City, and the year in which B and his father leave Mexico City for a short vacation is 1975.

Over all, the trip goes smoothly. Driving out of the city, both father and son feel cold, but as they leave the high valley behind and descend into the state of Guerrero the temperature climbs and they have to take off their sweaters and roll down the windows. B, who is inclined to melancholy (or so he likes to think), is at first completely absorbed in contemplating the landscape, but after a few hours the mountains and forests become monotonous and he starts reading a book instead.

Before they get to Acapulco, B's father pulls up in front of a roadside café. The café serves iguana. Shall we try it? he suggests. The iguanas are alive and they hardly move when B's father goes over to look at them. B leans against the mudguard of the Mustang, watching him. Without waiting for an answer, B's father orders a portion of iguana for himself and one for his son. Only then does B move away from the car. He approaches the open-air eating area—four tables under a canvas awning that is swaying slightly in the breeze—and sits down at the table farthest from the highway. B's father orders two beers. Father and son have unbuttoned their shirts and rolled up their sleeves. Both are wearing light-colored shirts. The waiter, by contrast, is wearing a black long-sleeved shirt and doesn't seem bothered by the heat.

Going to Acapulco? the waiter asks. B's father nods. They are the only customers at the café. Cars whiz past on the bright highway. B's father gets up and goes out the back. For a moment, B thinks his father is going to the bathroom, but then he realizes that he has gone to the kitchen to see how they cook the iguanas. The waiter follows him without a word. B hears them talking. First his father, then the man's voice, and finally the voice of a woman B can't see. B's forehead is beaded with sweat. His glasses are misted and dirty. He takes them off and cleans them with his shirttail. When he puts them back on, he sees his father watching him from the kitchen. He can see only his father's face and part of his shoulder; the rest is hidden behind a red curtain with black dots, and B has the fleeting impression that this curtain separates not only the kitchen from the eating area but also one time from another.

Then B looks away and his gaze falls on the book lying on the table. It is a book of poetry, an anthology of French Surrealist poets, translated into Spanish by the Argentinean Surrealist Aldo Pellegrini. B has been reading this book for two days. He likes it. He likes the photos of the poets. The photo of Unik, the one of Desnos, the photos of Artaud and Crevel. The book is thick and covered with transparent plastic. It was covered not by B (who never covers his books) but by a particularly fastidious friend. B opens the book at random and comes face to face with Gui Rosey—the photo of Gui Rosey and his poems—and when he looks up again his father's head has disappeared.

The heat is stifling. B would be more than happy to go back

to Mexico City, but he isn't going back, at least not yet; he knows that. Soon, his father is sitting next to him and they are both eating iguana with chili sauce and drinking more beer. The waiter in the black shirt has turned on a transistor radio and now some vaguely tropical music is blending with the noises of the jungle and the noise of the cars passing on the highway. The iguana tastes like chicken. It's tougher than chicken, B says, not entirely convinced. It's tasty, his father says, and orders another portion. They have cinnamon coffee. The man in the black shirt serves the iguana, but the woman from the kitchen brings out the coffee. She is young, almost as young as B; she is wearing white shorts and a yellow blouse with white flowers printed on it, flowers B doesn't recognize, perhaps because they don't exist. As they drink their coffee, B feels nauseous, but he doesn't say anything. He smokes and looks at the canvas awning, which is barely moving, as if weighed down by a narrow puddle of rainwater. But it can't be that, B thinks. What are you looking at? his father asks. The awning, B says. It's like a vein. But he doesn't say the bit about the vein; he only thinks it.

They arrive in Acapulco as night is falling. For a while, they drive up and down the avenues by the sea with the windows wide open and the breeze ruffling their hair. They stop at a bar and go in for a drink. This time, B's father orders tequila. B thinks for a moment. Then he orders tequila, too. The bar is modern and has air-conditioning. B's father talks with the waiter and asks him about hotels near the beach. By the time they get back to the Mustang, a few stars are visible, and for the first time that day B's father looks tired. Even so, they visit a couple of hotels, which for one reason or another are found unsatisfactory, before finding one that will do. The hotel is called La Brisa; it's small, a stone's throw from the beach, and has a swimming pool. B's father likes it. So does B. It's the off-season, so the hotel is almost empty and the prices are reasonable. The room they are given has two twin beds and a small bathroom with a shower. The only window looks onto the hotel's terrace, where the swimming pool is. B's father would have preferred a sea view. The air-conditioning, they soon discover, is out of order. But the room is fairly cool, so they don't complain. They make themselves at home: each opens up his suitcase and puts his clothes in the wardrobe. B puts his books on the bedside table. They change their shirts. B's father takes a cold shower while B just washes his face, and when they are ready they go out to dinner.

The reception desk is manned by a short guy with teeth like a rabbit's. He's young and seems friendly. He recommends a restaurant near the hotel. B's father asks if there's somewhere lively nearby. B understands what his father means. The receptionist doesn't. A place with a bit of action, B's father says. A place where you can find girls, B says. Ah, the receptionist says. For a moment, B and his father stand there, without speaking. The receptionist crouches down, disappearing behind the counter, and reappears with a card, which he holds out. B's father looks at the card, asks if the establishment is reliable, then extracts a bill from his wallet, which the receptionist catches on the fly.

But after dinner they go straight back to the hotel.

The next day, B wakes up very early. As quietly as possible, he takes a shower, brushes his teeth, puts on his bathing suit, and leaves the room. The hotel is on a street that runs straight down to the beach, which is empty except for a boy renting out surfboards. B asks him how much it costs for an hour. The boy quotes a price that sounds reasonable, so B rents a board and pushes off into the sea. Out a ways is a little island, toward which he steers the board. At first, he has some trouble, but soon he gets the hang of it. At this time of day, the sea is crystal clear, and B thinks he can see red fish under the board, about a foot and a half long, swimming toward the beach as he paddles toward the island.

It takes exactly fifteen minutes for him to get from the beach to the island. B doesn't know this, because he isn't wearing a watch, and for him time slows down. The crossing seems to last an eternity. At the last minute, waves rear unexpectedly, impeding his approach. The sand on the island is noticeably different from that of the beach by the hotel; back there it was a golden, tawny color, perhaps because of the time of day (though B doesn't think so), while here it is a dazzling white, so bright it hurts his eyes to look at it.

B stops paddling and just sits there, at the mercy of the waves, which begin to carry him slowly away from the island. By the time he finally reacts, he has drifted halfway back. B decides to turn around. The return is calm and uneventful. When he gets to the beach, the boy who rents out the boards comes up and asks if he had a problem. Not at all, B says. An hour later, B returns to the hotel without having had breakfast and finds his father sitting in the dining room with a cup of coffee and a plate in front of him on which are scattered the remains of toast and eggs.

The following hours are hazy. They drive around aimlessly, watching people from the car. Sometimes they get out to have a cold drink or an ice cream. In the afternoon, on the beach, while his father is stretched out asleep in a deck chair, B rereads Gui Rosey's poems and the brief story of his life or his death:

One day, a group of Surrealists arrives in the South of France, from Paris. The north and the west of the country are occupied by the Germans. The south is under the control of Pétain. They try to get visas to go to the United States. Day after day, the U.S. consulate delays its decision. Among the members of the group are Breton, Tzara, and Péret, but there are also less famous figures. Gui Rosey is one of them. In the photo, he has the look of a minor poet, B thinks. He is ugly; he is impeccably dressed; he looks like an unimportant civil servant or a bank teller. Up to this point, a few disagreements, but nothing out of the ordinary, B thinks. The Surrealists gather every afternoon at a café by the port. They make plans and chat; Rosey is always there. But one afternoon he fails to appear. At first, he isn't missed. He is a minor poet and no one pays much attention to minor poets. After a few days, however, the others start to worry. At the pension where he is staying, no one knows what has happened; his suitcases and books are there, undisturbed, so he clearly hasn't tried to leave without paying (as guests at pensions on the Côte d'Azur are prone to do). His friends try to find him. They visit all the hospitals and police stations in the area. No one can tell them anything. One morning, the visas arrive. Most of the group boards a ship and sets off for the United States. Those who remain, who will never get visas, soon forget about Rosey and his disappearance; people are disappearing all the time, in large numbers, and they have to look out for themselves.

That night, after dinner at the hotel, B's father suggests they go and find a bit of action. B looks at his father. He is blond (B is dark), his eyes are gray, and he is still in good shape. He looks happy and ready to have a good time. What sort of action? asks B, who knows perfectly well what his father is referring to. The usual kind, B's father says. Drinking and women. For a while, B says nothing, as if he were pondering a reply. His father looks at him. The look might seem inquisitive, but in fact it is only affectionate. Finally, B says he's not in the mood for sex. It's not just about getting laid, his father says. We'll go and see, have a few drinks, and enjoy ourselves with some friends. What friends? B says. We don't know anyone here. You always make friends when you're out for a ride. The expression makes B think of horses. When he was seven, his father bought him a horse. Where did my horse come from? B asks now. This takes his father by surprise. Horse? he asks. The one you bought me when I was a kid, B says, in Chile. Ah, Hullabaloo, his father says, smiling. He was from the island of Chiloé, he says, then after a moment's reflection he starts talking about brothels again. The way he talks about them, they could be dance halls, B thinks. Then both of them fall silent.

That night they don't go anywhere.

While his father is sleeping, B goes out to the terrace to read by the swimming pool. The terrace is empty except for him. From his table, B can see part of the reception area, where the receptionist from the night before is standing at the counter reading something or doing the accounts. B reads the French Surrealists; he reads Gui Rosey. To tell the truth, Gui Rosey doesn't interest him much. He is far more interested in Desnos and Éluard, and yet he always ends up coming back to Rosey's poems and looking at his photo, a studio portrait, in which he has the air of a solitary, wretched soul, with large, glassy eyes and a dark tie that seems to be strangling him.

He must have committed suicide, B thinks. He knew he was never going to get a visa, so he decided to end it there and then. B imagines or tries to imagine a town on the Mediterranean coast of France. He has been all over Latin America, or almost, but he still hasn't set foot in Europe. So his image of a Mediterranean town is derived from his image of Acapulco. Heat; a small, cheap hotel; beaches of golden sand and beaches of white sand. And the distant sound of music. B doesn't realize that there is a crucial element missing from the soundtrack of this scene: the clanging rigging of the small boats that throng the ports of all the towns on the Mediterranean coast. The sound of the rigging at night, when the sea is as still as a millpond.

Someone comes out to the terrace. The silhouette of a woman. She sits down at the farthest table, in a corner, near two large urns. A moment later, the receptionist appears, bringing her a drink. Then, instead of going back to the counter, he comes over to B, who is sitting by the edge of the pool, and asks if he and his father are having a good time. Very good, B says. Do you like Acapulco? the receptionist asks. Very much, B says. How was the San Diego? the receptionist asks. B doesn't understand the question. The San Diego? For a moment, he thinks the receptionist is referring to the hotel, but then he remembers that the hotel is called something else. Which San Diego? B asks. The receptionist smiles. The club with the hookers. Then B remembers the card the receptionist gave his father. We haven't gone yet, he says. It's a reliable place, the receptionist says. B moves his head in a way that could mean almost anything. It's on Constituyentes, the receptionist says. There's another club on that avenue, the Ramada, but I wouldn't recommend it. The Ramada, B says, watching the woman's motionless silhouette in the corner of the terrace and the apparently untouched glass in front of her, between the enormous urns, whose shadows stretch and taper off under the neighboring tables. Best to steer clear of the Ramada, the receptionist says. Why? B asks, for something to say, although he has no intention of visiting either place. It's not reliable, the receptionist says, and his bright little rabbit teeth shine in the semidarkness that has suddenly submerged the terrace, as if someone at reception had switched off half of the lights.

When the receptionist goes away, B opens his book of poetry again, but the words are illegible now, so he leaves the book open on the table, shuts his eyes, and, instead of the faint chimes of rigging, he hears an atmospheric sound, the sound of enormous layers of hot air descending on the hotel and the surrounding trees. He feels like getting into the pool. For a moment, he thinks he might.

Then the woman in the corner stands up and begins to walk toward the stairs that lead from the terrace up to the reception area, but midway she stops, as if she felt ill, resting one hand on the edge of a planter in which there are no longer flowers, only weeds.

B watches her. The woman is wearing a loose, light-colored summer dress, cut low, leaving her shoulders bare. He expects her to start walking again, but she stands still, her hand fixed to the planter, looking down, so B gets up with the book in his hand and goes over to her. The first thing that surprises him is her face. She's about sixty years old, B guesses, although from a distance he wouldn't have said she was more than thirty. She is North American, and when he approaches she looks up and smiles at him. Good night, she says, rather incongruously, in Spanish. Are you all right? B asks. The woman doesn't understand, and B has to ask again, in English. I'm just thinking, the woman says, smiling at him fixedly. For a few seconds, B considers what she has said to him. Thinking, thinking, thinking. And suddenly it seems to him that this declaration conceals a threat. Something approaching over the sea. Something advancing in the wake of the dark clouds crossing the Bay of Acapulco. But he doesn't move or make any attempt to break the spell that seems to be holding him captive. Then the woman looks at the book in B's left hand and asks him what he is reading, and B says, Poetry. I'm reading poems. The woman looks him in the eyes, with the same smile on her face (a smile that is at once bright and faded, B thinks, feeling more uneasy by the moment), and says that she used to like poetry, at one time. Which poets? B asks, keeping absolutely still. I can't remember them now, the woman says, and again she seems to lose herself in the contemplation of something visible only to her. B assumes she is making an effort to remember, and waits in silence. After a while, she looks at him again and says, Longfellow. And straightaway she starts reciting lines with a monotonous rhythm which sound to B like a nursery rhyme, a far cry, in any case, from the poets he is reading. Do you know Longfellow? the woman asks. B shakes his head, although in fact he has read some Longfellow. We did it in school, the woman says, with her invariable smile. And then she adds, It's too hot, don't you think? It is very hot, B whispers. There could be a storm coming, the woman says. There is something very definite about her tone. At this point, B looks up: he can't see a single star. But he can see lights in the hotel. And, at the window of his room, the shape of someone watching them makes him start, as if he had just been struck by the first, sudden drops of a tropical downpour.

For a moment, he is bewildered.

It is his father, on the other side of the glass, wrapped in a blue bathrobe that he must have brought with him (B hasn't seen it before and it certainly doesn't belong to the hotel), staring at them, although when B notices him his father steps back, recoiling as if bitten by a snake, lifts his hand in a shy wave, and disappears behind the curtains.

The Song of Hiawatha, the woman says. B looks at her. The Song of Hiawatha, the poem by Longfellow. Ah, yes, B says.

Then the woman says good night, again, and makes a gradual exit: first she goes up the stairs to reception, where she spends a few moments chatting with someone B can't see, then she sets off across the hotel lobby, her slim figure framed by successive windows, until she turns into the corridor that leads to the inside stairs.

Half an hour later, B goes to their room and finds his father asleep again. For a few seconds, before going to the bathroom to brush his teeth, B stands very straight at the foot of the bed, gazing at him, as if steeling himself for a fight. Good night, Dad, he says. His father gives not the slightest indication that he has heard.

On the second full day of their stay in Acapulco, B and his father go to see the cliff divers. They have two options: they can watch the show from an open-air platform or go to the bar restaurant of the hotel that overlooks the cliff. B's father asks about the prices. The first person he asks doesn't know. He persists. Finally, an old ex-diver who is hanging around doing nothing tells him what it costs: six times more to watch from the hotel bar. Let's go to the bar, B's father says without hesitating. We'll be more comfortable. B follows him. The other people in the bar are North American or Mexican tourists wearing what are obviously vacation clothes; B and his father stand out. They are dressed as people dress in Mexico City, in clothes that seem to belong to some endless dream. The waiters notice. They know the sort—no chance of a big tip—so they make no effort to serve them promptly. To top it off, B and his father can hardly see the show from where they are sitting. We would have been better off on the platform, B's father says. Although it's not bad here, either, he adds. B nods. When the diving is over, having drunk two cocktails each, they go outside and start making plans for the rest of the day. Hardly anyone is left on the platform, but B's father recognizes the old ex-diver sitting on a railing and goes over to him.

The ex-diver is short and has a very broad back. He is reading a cowboy novel and doesn't look up until B and his father are at his side. He recognizes them and asks what they thought of the show. Not bad, B's father says, although in precision sports you need experience to judge properly. Would I be right in guessing that you were a sportsman yourself? the ex-diver asks. B's father looks at him for a moment and then says, You could say that. The ex-diver gets to his feet with an energetic movement, as if he were back on the edge of the cliff. He must be about fifty, B thinks, so he's not much older than my father, but the wrinkles on his face, like scars, make him look much older. Are you gentlemen on vacation? the ex-diver asks. B's father nods and smiles. And what was your sport, sir, if I might ask? Boxing, B's father says. How about that, the ex-diver says. So you must have been a heavyweight? B's father smiles broadly and says yes.

Before he knows what is going on, B finds himself walking toward the Mustang with his father and the ex-diver and then all three get into the car and B listens to the ex-diver giving his father instructions as if he were listening to the radio. For a while, the car glides along the Avenida Costera Miguel Alemán, but then they turn and head inland, and soon the tourist hotels and restaurants give way to an ordinary cityscape with tropical touches. The car keeps climbing, heading away from the golden horseshoe of Acapulco, driving along badly paved or unpaved roads, until it pulls up beside the dusty sidewalk in front of a cheap restaurant, a fixed-price place. The ex-diver and B's father get out of the car immediately. They have been talking all the way, and while they wait for B on the sidewalk they continue their conversation, gesturing incomprehensibly. B takes his time getting out of the car. We're going in to eat, his father says. So it seems, B says.

The place is dark inside and only a quarter of the space is occupied by tables. The rest looks like a dance floor, with a stage for the band, surrounded by a long balustrade made of rough wood. At first, B can't see a thing, but then his eyes adjust to the darkness and he sees a man coming over to the ex-diver. They look alike. The stranger listens attentively to an introduction that B doesn't catch, shakes hands with his father, and a few seconds later turns to B. B reaches out to shake his hand. The stranger says a name, and his handshake, which is no doubt meant to be friendly, is not so much firm as violent. He does not smile. B decides not to smile, either. B's father and the ex-diver are already sitting at a table. B sits down next to them. The stranger, who turns out to be the ex-diver's younger brother, stands beside them, waiting for instructions. The gentleman here, the ex-diver says, was heavyweight champion of his country. So you're foreigners? his brother asks. Chileans, B's father says. Do you have red snapper? the ex-diver says. We do, his brother says. Bring us one, then, a red snapper Guerrero style, the ex-diver says. And beers all around, B's father says, for you, too. Thank you, the brother murmurs, taking a notebook from his pocket and painstakingly writing down an order that, in B's opinion, a child could remember.

Along with the beers, the brother brings them some savory crackers to nibble and three rather small glasses of oysters. They're fresh, the ex-diver says, putting chili sauce on all three. Funny, isn't it. This stuff's called chili and so's your country, he says, pointing to the bottle full of bright-red chili sauce. Yes, intriguing, isn't it. Like the way the sauce is the opposite of chilly, he adds. B looks at his father with barely veiled incredulity. The conversation revolves around boxing and diving until the red snapper arrives.

Later, B and his father leave. The hours have flown by without their noticing and by the time they climb into the Mustang it is already seven in the evening. The ex-diver comes with them. For a moment, B thinks they'll never get rid of him, but when they reach the center of Acapulco the ex-diver gets out in front of a billiard hall. When he has gone, B's father comments favorably on the service at the restaurant and the price they paid for the red snapper. If we'd had it here, he says, pointing to the hotels along the beachfront, it would have cost an arm and a leg. When they get back to their room, B puts on his bathing suit and goes to the beach. He swims for a while and then tries to read in the fading light. He reads the Surrealist poets and is completely bewildered. A peaceful, solitary man, on the brink of death. Images, wounds. That is all he can see. And the images are dissolving little by little, like the setting sun, leaving only the wounds. A minor poet disappears while waiting for a visa to admit him to the New World. A minor poet disappears without a trace, hopelessly stranded in some town on the Mediterranean coast of France. There is no investigation. There is no corpse. By the time B turns to Daumal, night has already fallen on the beach; he shuts the book and slowly makes his way back to the hotel.

After dinner, his father proposes that they go out and have some fun. B declines this invitation. He suggests to his father that he go alone, and says that he's not in the mood for fun; he'd prefer to stay in the room and watch a film on TV. I can't believe it, his father says. You're behaving like an old man, at your age! B looks at his father, who is putting on clean clothes after a shower, and laughs.

Before his father goes out, B tells him to take care. His father looks at him from the doorway and says he's only going to have a couple of drinks. You take care yourself, he says, and gently shuts the door.

Once he's on his own, B takes off his shoes, looks for his cigarettes, turns on the TV, and collapses onto the bed. Without intending to, he falls asleep. He dreams that he is living in (or visiting) the city of the Titans. The dream is an endless wandering through vast dark streets that recall other dreams. And in the dream his attitude is one that he knows he doesn't have in waking life. Faced with buildings whose voluminous shadows seem to be knocking against one another, he is, if not exactly courageous, unworried or indifferent.

A while later, B wakes up with a jolt, and, as if responding to a summons, turns off the TV and goes to the window. On the terrace, half-hidden in the same corner as the night before, the North American woman is sitting with a cocktail or a glass of fruit juice in front of her. B observes her indifferently, then goes back and sits on the bed, opens his book of Surrealist poets, and tries to read. But he can't. So he tries to think, and to that end he lies down on the bed again, with his arms outstretched, and shuts his eyes. For a moment, he thinks he is on the point of falling asleep. He even catches an oblique glimpse of a street from the dream city. But soon he realizes that he is only remembering the dream; he opens his eyes and lies there for a while, contemplating the ceiling. Then he switches off the bedside lamp and goes back over to the window.

The North American woman is still there, motionless. The shadows of the urns stretch out and touch the shadows of the neighboring tables. The reception area, fully lit, unlike the terrace, is reflected in the swimming pool. Suddenly, a car pulls up a few yards from the entrance of the hotel. His father's Mustang, B thinks. But no one appears at the hotel gate for a long time, and B thinks he must have been mistaken. Then he makes out his father's silhouette climbing the stairs. First his head, then his broad shoulders, then the rest of his body, and finally the shoes, a pair of white moccasins that B, as a rule, finds profoundly disgusting, but the feeling they provoke in him now is something like tenderness. The way he came into the hotel, he thinks, it was like he was dancing. The way he made his entrance, it was as if he had come back from a wake, unconsciously glad to be alive. But the strangest thing is that, after appearing briefly in the reception area, his father turns around and heads toward the terrace; he goes down the stairs, walks around the pool, and sits at a table near the North American woman. And when the guy from reception finally appears with a glass, his father pays and, without even waiting for him to be gone, gets up, glass in hand, goes over to the table where the North American woman is sitting, and stands there for a while, gesticulating and drinking, until, apparently at the woman's invitation, he takes a seat beside her.

She's too old for him, B thinks. Then he goes back to his bed, lies down, and soon realizes that all the sleepiness that was weighing him down before has evaporated. Still, he doesn't want to turn on the light (although he feels like reading); he doesn't want his father to think (even for a moment) that B is spying on him. He thinks about women; he thinks about travel. Finally, he goes to sleep.

Twice during the night, he wakes up with a start and sees that his father's bed is empty. The third time, day is already dawning and he sees his father's back: he is sleeping deeply. B turns on the light and stays in bed for a while, smoking and reading.

Later that morning, B goes to the beach and hires a surfboard. This time, he has no trouble reaching the island. There he has a mango juice and swims for a while in the sea, alone. Then he goes back to the beach by the hotel, returns the board to the boy, who smiles at him, and takes a roundabout way back to the hotel. He finds his father in the dining room drinking coffee. He sits down beside him. His father has just shaved and gives off an odor of cheap aftershave that B finds pleasant. On his right cheek there is a scratch from ear to chin. B considers asking him what happened last night, but decides not to.

The rest of the day goes by in a blur. At some point, B and his father walk along a beach near the airport. The beach is vast and lined with wattle-roofed shacks where the fishermen keep their gear. The sea is choppy; for a while B and his father watch the waves breaking in the bay of Puerto Marqués. A fisherman tells them that it's not a good day for swimming. You're right, B says. His father goes in for a swim anyway. B sits down on the sand, with his knees up, and watches him advance to meet the waves. The fisherman shades his eyes and says something that B doesn't catch. For a moment, he loses sight of his father's head, and his arms stroking seaward. Now there are two boys with the fisherman. They are all standing, looking out to sea, except for B, who is still sitting down. A plane appears in the sky, curiously inaudible. B stops looking at the sea and watches the plane until it disappears behind a rounded hill covered with vegetation. He remembers waking up, exactly a year before, at the Acapulco airport. He was returning from Chile, on his own, and the plane stopped in Acapulco. He remembers opening his eyes and seeing an orange light with blue and pink overtones, like the fading colors of an old film, and knowing then that he was back in Mexico and safe at last, in a sense. That was in 1974, and B had not yet turned twenty-one. Now he is twenty-two and his father must be about forty-nine. B closes his eyes. Because of the wind, the fisherman's and the boys' cries of alarm are unintelligible. The sand is cold. When he opens his eyes, he sees his father coming out of the sea.

He shuts his eyes and doesn't open them again until he feels a large wet hand grip his shoulder and hears his father's voice proposing that they go eat turtle eggs.

There are things you can tell people and things you just can't, B thinks disconsolately. From this moment on, he knows the disaster is approaching.

In spite of which, the next forty-eight hours go by in a placid sort of daze, which B's father associates with what he calls "the Idea of the Holiday." (B can't tell whether his father is serious or pulling his leg.) They go to the beach; they eat at the hotel or at a moderately priced restaurant on the Avenida López Mateos. One afternoon, they rent a boat, a small plastic rowboat, and follow the coastline near their hotel, along with the trinket venders who peddle their wares from beach to beach, travelling upright on surfboards or in very shallow-bottomed boats, like tightrope walkers or the ghosts of drowned sailors. On the way back, B and his father even have an accident.

B's father steers the boat too close to the rocks and it capsizes. In itself, this is not dramatic. Both of them can swim reasonably well and the boat is made to float when upside down; it isn't hard to right it and climb in again. And that is what B and his father do. Not the slightest danger at any point, B thinks. But when both of them have climbed back into the boat, B's father realizes that he has lost his wallet. Tapping his chest, he says, My wallet, and without hesitation he dives back into the water. B can't help laughing, but then, stretched out in the boat, he looks over the side, sees no sign of his father, and for a moment imagines him diving, or, worse, sinking like a stone, open-eyed, into a deep trench, above which, on the surface, in a rocking boat, his son has stopped laughing and begun to worry. Then B sits up and, having looked over the other side of the boat and seen no sign of his father there, either, jumps into the water, and this is what happens: as B goes down with his eyes open, his father is coming up (they almost touch), holding his wallet in his right hand. They look at each other as they pass, but can't alter their trajectories, or at least not right away, so B's father keeps ascending silently while B continues his silent descent.

For sharks—for most fish, in fact (flying fish excepted)—hell is the surface of the sea. For B (and many, perhaps most, young men of his age), it sometimes takes the form of the seafloor. As he follows in his father's wake, but heading in the opposite direction, the situation strikes him as particularly absurd. The bottom isn't sandy, as he had for some reason imagined it would be; there are only rocks piled on top of one another, as if this part of the coast were a submerged mountain range and he were near a high peak, having hardly begun the descent. Then he starts to rise again, and looks up at the boat, which seems to be levitating one moment and about to sink the next; he finds his father sitting right in the middle, attempting to light a wet cigarette.

. . .

Then the lull comes to an end, the days of grace in the course of which B and his father have visited various bars in Acapulco, lain on the beach, and slept, eaten, and even laughed, and an icy phase begins, a phase that appears to be normal but is ruled by deities of ice (who do not, however, offer any relief from the heat that reigns in Acapulco); hours of what, in former days, when he was an adolescent, perhaps, B would have called boredom, although he would certainly not use that word now—disaster, he would call it, a private disaster whose main effect is to drive a wedge between B and his father, part of the price they must pay for existing.

It all begins with the reappearance of the ex-diver, who, as B realizes straightaway, has come looking for his father, and not for the family unit constituted by father and son. B's father invites the ex-diver to have a drink on the hotel terrace. The ex-diver says that he knows a better place. B's father looks at him, smiles, and says, O.K. As they go out into the street, the light is beginning to fade. B feels an inexplicable stab of pain and thinks that perhaps it would have been better to stay at the hotel and leave his father to his own devices. But it's already too late. The Mustang is heading up the Avenida Constituyentes, and from his pocket B's father takes the card that the receptionist gave him days ago. The night spot is called the San Diego, he says. In the ex-diver's opinion, it's too expensive. I've got money, B's father says. I've been living in Mexico since 1968, and this is the first time I've taken a vacation. B, who is sitting next to his father, tries to see the ex-diver's face in the rearview mirror, but can't. So first they go to the San Diego and for a while they drink and dance with the girls. For each dance, they have to give the girl a ticket bought beforehand at the bar. To begin with, B's father buys only three tickets. There's something unreal about this system, he says to the ex-diver. But then he starts enjoying himself and buys a whole bundle. B dances, too. His first dance partner is a slim girl with Indian features. The second is a woman with big breasts who seems to be preoccupied or angry for a reason that B will never discover. The third is fat and happy, and, after dancing for a little while, she whispers into B's ear that she's high. On what? B asks. Mushrooms, the woman says, and B laughs. Meanwhile, B's father is dancing with a girl who looks like an Indian and B is glancing across at him from time to time. Actually, all the girls look like Indians. The one dancing with his father has a pretty smile. They are talking (they haven't stopped talking, in fact), although B can't hear what they are saying. Then his father disappears and B goes to the bar with the ex-diver. They start talking, too. About the old days. About courage. About the cliffs where the ocean waves break. About women. Subjects that don't interest B, or at least not at the moment. But they talk anyway.

Half an hour later, his father comes back to the bar. His blond hair is wet and freshly combed (B's father combs his hair back), and his face is red. He smiles and says nothing; B observes him and says nothing. Time for dinner, B's father says. B and the ex-diver follow him back to the Mustang. They eat an assortment of shellfish in a place that's long and narrow, like a coffin. As they eat, B's father watches B as if he were searching for an answer. B looks back at him. He is sending a telepathic message: there is no answer, because it's not a valid question. It's an idiotic question. Then, before he knows what is going on, B is back in the car with his father and the ex-diver, who talk about boxing all the way to a place on the outskirts of Acapulco. It's a brick-and-wood building with no windows, and inside there's a jukebox with songs by Lucha Villa and Lola Beltrán. Suddenly, B feels nauseous. He leaves his father and the ex-diver and looks for the toilet or the back yard or the door to the street, belatedly realizing that he has had too much to drink. He also realizes that apparently well-meaning hands have prevented him from going out into the street. They don't want me to get away, B thinks. Then he vomits several times in the yard, among stacks of beer boxes, under the eye of a chained dog; having relieved himself, he looks up at the stars. A woman soon appears beside him. Her shadow is darker than the darkness of the night. If it weren't for her white dress, B could hardly have made her out. You want a blow job? she asks. Her voice is young and husky. B looks at her, uncomprehending. The whore kneels down beside him and undoes his fly. Then B understands and lets her proceed. When it's over, he feels cold. The whore stands up and B hugs her. Together they gaze at the night sky. When B says he's going back to his father's table, the woman doesn't follow him. Let's go, B says, but she resists. Then B realizes that he has hardly seen her face. It's better that way. I hugged her, he thinks, but I don't even know what she looks like. Before he goes in, he turns around and sees her walking over to pet the dog.

Inside, his father is sitting at a table with the ex-diver and two other guys. B comes up behind him and whispers in his ear: Let's go. His father is playing cards. I'm winning, he says, I can't leave now. They're going to steal all our money, B thinks. Then he looks at the women, who are looking at him and his father with commiseration in their eyes. They know what's going to happen to us, B thinks. Are you drunk? his father asks him, taking a card. No, B says, not anymore. Have you taken any drugs? his father asks. No, B says. Then his father smiles and orders a tequila. B gets up and goes to the bar, and from there he surveys the scene of the crime with manic eyes. It is clear to B now that he will never travel with his father again. He shuts his eyes; he opens his eyes. The whores watch him curiously; one offers him a drink, which B declines with a gesture. When he shuts his eyes, he keeps seeing his father with a pistol in each hand, entering through an impossibly situated door. In he comes, impossibly, urgently, with his gray eyes shining and his hair ruffled. This is the last time we'll travel together, B thinks. That's all there is to it. The jukebox is playing a Lucha Villa song and B thinks of Gui Rosey, a minor poet who disappeared in the South of France. His father deals the cards, laughs, tells stories, and listens to those of his companions, each more sordid than the last. B remembers going to his father's house when he returned from Chile in 1974. His father had broken his foot and was in bed reading a sports magazine. What was it like? he asked, and B recounted his adventures. An episode from the chronicle of Latin America's doomed revolutions. I almost got killed, he said. His father looked at him and smiled. How many times? he asked. Twice, at least, B replied. Now B's father is roaring with laughter and B is trying to think clearly. Gui Rosey committed suicide, he thinks, or got killed. His corpse is at the bottom of the sea.

A tequila, B says. A woman hands him a half-full glass. Don't get drunk again, kid, she says. No, I'm all right now, B says, feeling perfectly lucid. Then two other women approach him. What would you like to drink? B asks. Your father's really nice, says the younger one, who has long black hair. Maybe she's the one who gave me the blow job, B thinks. And he remembers (or tries to remember) apparently disconnected scenes. The first time he smoked in front of his father: he was fourteen; it was a Viceroy cigarette; they were waiting in his father's truck for a freight train and it was a very cold morning. Stories of guns and knives, family stories. The whores are drinking tequila with Coca-Cola. How long was I outside vomiting? B asks himself. You were kind of jumpy before, one of the whores says. You want some? Some what? B says. He is shaking and his skin is cold as ice. Some weed, says the woman, who is about thirty years old and has long hair like the other one, but dyed blond. Acapulco Gold? B asks, taking a gulp of tequila, while the two women come a little closer and start stroking his back and his legs. Yup, calms you down, the blonde says. B nods, and the next thing he knows there is a cloud of smoke between him and his father. You really love your dad, don't you? one of the women says. Well, I wouldn't go that far, B says. What do you mean? the dark woman says. The woman serving at the bar laughs. Through the smoke, B sees his father turn his head and look at him for a moment. A deadly serious look, he thinks. Do you like Acapulco? the blonde asks. Only at this point does he realize that the bar is almost empty. At one table there are two men drinking in silence; at another, his father, the ex-diver, and the two strangers playing cards. All the other tables are empty.

The door to the yard opens and a woman in a white dress appears. She's the one who gave me the blow job, B thinks. She looks about twenty-five, but is probably much younger, maybe sixteen or seventeen. Like almost all the others, she has long hair, and is wearing shoes with very high heels. As she walks through the bar (toward the bathroom), B looks carefully at her shoes: they are white and smeared with mud on the sides. His father also looks up and examines her for a moment. B watches the whore opening the bathroom door, then he looks at his father. He shuts his eyes and when he opens them again the whore is gone and his father has turned his attention back to the game. The best thing for you to do would be to get your father out of this place, one of the women whispers in his ear. B orders another tequila. I can't, he says. The woman slides her hand up under his loose-fitting Hawaiian shirt. She's checking to see if I have a weapon, B thinks. The woman's fingers climb up his chest and close on his left nipple. She squeezes it. Hey, B says. Don't you believe me? the woman asks. What's going to happen? B asks. Something bad, the woman says. How bad? I don't know, but if I was you I'd get out of here. B smiles and looks into her eyes for the first time: Come with us, he says, taking a gulp of tequila. Not in a million years, the woman says. Then B remembers his father saying to him, before he left for Chile, "You're an artist and I'm a worker." What did he mean by that? he wonders. The bathroom door opens and the whore in the white dress comes out again, her shoes immaculate now, goes across to the table where the card game is happening, and stands there next to one of the strangers. Why? B asks. Why do we have to go? The woman looks at him out of the corner of her eye and says nothing. There are things you can tell people, B thinks, and things you just can't. He shuts his eyes.

As if in a dream, he goes back out to the yard. The woman with the dyed-blond hair leads him by the hand. I have already done this, B thinks; I'm drunk; I'll never get out of here. Certain gestures are repeated: the woman sits on a rickety chair and opens his fly, the night seems to float like a lethal gas among the empty beer boxes. But some things are missing: the dog has gone, for one, and in the sky, to the east, where the moon hung before, a few filaments of light herald dawn. When they finish, the dog appears, perhaps attracted by B's groans. He doesn't bite, the woman says, while the dog stands a few yards away, baring its teeth. The woman gets up and smoothes her dress. The fur on the dog's back is standing up and a string of translucent saliva hangs from his muzzle. Stay, Fang, stay, the woman says. He's going to bite us, B thinks as they retreat toward the door. What happens next is confused: At his father's table, all the card players are standing up. One of the strangers is shouting at the top of his voice. B soon realizes that the man is insulting his father. As a precaution, he orders a bottle of beer at the bar, which he drinks in long gulps, almost choking, before going over to the table. His father seems calm. In front of him are a considerable number of bills, which he is picking up one by one and putting in his pocket. You're not leaving here with that money, the stranger shouts. B looks at the ex-diver, trying to tell from his face which side he will take. The stranger's, probably, B thinks. The beer runs down his neck and only then does he realize that he is burning hot.

B's father finishes counting his money and looks at the three men standing in front of him and at the woman in white. Well, gentlemen, he says, we're leaving. Come over here, son. B pours what is left of his beer onto the floor and grips the bottle by the neck. What are you doing, son? B's father says. B can hear the tone of reproach in his voice. We're going to leave calmly, B's father says, then he turns around and asks the women how much they owe. The woman at the bar looks at a piece of paper and reads out a sizable sum. The blond woman, who is standing halfway between the table and the bar, says another figure. B's father adds them up, takes out the money and hands it to the blonde: What we owe you and the drinks. Then he gives her a couple more bills: the tip. Now we're going to leave, B thinks. The two strangers block their exit. B doesn't want to look at her, but he does: the woman in white has sat down in one of the vacant chairs and is examining the cards scattered on the table, touching them with her fingertips. Don't get in my way, his father whispers, and it takes a while for B to realize that he is speaking to him. The ex-diver puts his hands in his pockets. The one who was shouting before starts insulting B's father again, telling him to come back to the table and keep playing. The game's over, B's father says. For a moment, looking at the woman in white (who strikes him now, for the first time, as very beautiful), B thinks of Gui Rosey, who disappeared off the face of the earth, quiet as a lamb, without a trace, while Nazi hymns rose into a blood-red sky, and he sees himself buried in some vacant lot in Acapulco, vanished forever, but then he hears his father, who is accusing the ex-diver of something, and he realizes that unlike Gui Rosey he is not alone.

Then his father walks toward the door stooping slightly and B stands aside to give him room to move. Tomorrow we'll leave, tomorrow we'll go back to Mexico City, B thinks joyfully. And then the fight begins.

Translated, from the Spanish, by Chris Andrews

DIMENSION

BY ALICE MUNRO (2006)

Doree had to take three buses—one to Kincardine, where she waited for one to London, where she waited again, for the city bus out to the facility. She started the trip on a Sunday at nine in the morning. Because of the waiting times between buses, it took her until about two in the afternoon to travel the hundred-odd miles. All that sitting, either on buses or in the depots, was not a thing she should have minded. Her daily work was not of the sitting-down kind.

She was a chambermaid at the Comfort Inn. She scrubbed bathrooms and stripped and made beds and vacuumed rugs and wiped mirrors. She liked the work—it occupied her thoughts to a certain extent and tired her out so that she could sleep at night. She was seldom faced with a really bad mess, though some of the women she worked with could tell stories to make your hair curl. These women were older than her, and they all thought that she should try to work her way up. They told her that she should get trained for a job behind the desk, while she was still young and decent-looking. But she was content to do what she did. She didn't want to have to talk to people.

None of the people she worked with knew what had happened. Or, if they did, they didn't let on. Her picture had been in the paper—they'd used the photo he took of her with all three kids, the new baby, Dimitri, in her arms, and Barbara Ann and Sasha on either side, looking on. Her hair had been long and wavy and brown then, natural in curl and color, as he liked it, and her face bashful and soft—a reflection less of the way she was than of the way he wanted to see her.

Since then, she had cut her hair short and bleached and spiked it, and she had lost a lot of weight. And she went by her second name now: Fleur. Also, the job they had found for her was in a town a good distance away from where she used to live.

This was the third time she had made the trip. The first two times he had refused to see her. If he did that again she would just quit trying. Even if he did see her, she might not come again for a while. She was not going to go overboard. She didn't really know what she was going to do.

On the first bus she was not too troubled. Just riding along and looking at the scenery. She had grown up on the coast, where there was such a thing as spring, but here winter jumped almost directly into summer. A month ago there had been snow, and now it was hot enough to go bare-armed. Dazzling patches of water lay in the fields, and the sunlight was pouring down through naked branches.

On the second bus she began to feel jittery, and she couldn't help trying to guess which of the women around her might be going to the same place. They were women alone, usually dressed with some care, maybe to make themselves look as if they were going to church. The older ones looked as if they were going to strict old-fashioned churches where you had to wear a skirt and stockings and some sort of hat, while the younger ones might have belonged to a livelier congregation, which accepted pants suits, bright scarves, earrings, and puffy hairdos. When you took a second look, you saw that some of the pants-suit women were quite as old as the others.

Doree didn't fit into either category. In the whole year and a half that she had been working she had not bought herself a single new piece of clothing. She wore her uniform at work and her jeans everywhere else. She had got out of the way of wearing makeup because he hadn't allowed it, and now, though she could have, she didn't. Her spikes of corn-colored hair didn't suit her bony bare face, but it didn't matter.

On the third bus she got a seat by the window, and tried to keep herself calm by reading the signs—both the advertising and the street signs. There was a certain trick she had picked up, to keep her mind occupied. She took the letters of whatever word her eyes lit on, and she tried to see how many new words she could make out of them. "Coffee," for instance, would give you "fee," and then "foe," and "off" and "of," and "shop" would provide "hop" and "sop" and "so" and—wait a minute—"posh." Words were more than plentiful on the way out of the city, as they passed billboards, monster stores, car lots, even balloons moored on roofs to advertise sales.

Doree had not told Mrs. Sands about her last two attempts, and probably wouldn't tell her about this one, either. Mrs. Sands, whom she saw on Monday afternoons, spoke of moving on, though she always said that it would take time, that things could not be hurried. She told Doree that she was doing fine, that she was gradually discovering her own strength.

"I know those words have been done to death," she said. "But they're still true."

She blushed at what she heard herself say—*death*—but did not make it worse by apologizing.

When Doree was sixteen—that was seven years ago—she'd gone to visit her mother in the hospital every day after school. Her mother was recovering from an operation on her back, which was said to have been serious but not dangerous. Lloyd was an orderly. He and Doree's mother had in common the fact that they were both old hippies—though Lloyd was actually a few years the younger—and whenever he had time he'd come in and chat with her about the concerts and protest marches they'd both attended, the outrageous people they'd known, drug trips that had knocked them out, that sort of thing.

Lloyd was popular with the patients, because of his jokes and his sure, strong touch. He was stocky and broad-shouldered and authoritative enough to be sometimes taken for a doctor. (Not that he was pleased by that—he held the opinion that a lot of medicine was a fraud and a lot of doctors were jerks.) He had sensitive reddish skin and light hair and bold eyes.

He kissed Doree in the elevator and told her that she was a flower in the desert. Then he laughed at himself, and said, "How original can you get?"

"You're a poet and don't know it," she said, to be kind.

One night her mother died suddenly, of an embolism. Doree's mother had a lot of women friends who would have taken Doree in—and she stayed with one of them for a time—but the new friend Lloyd was the one Doree preferred. By her next birthday she was pregnant, then married. Lloyd had never been married before, though he had at least two children whose whereabouts he was not certain of. They would have been grown up by then, anyway. His philosophy of life had changed as he got older—he believed now in marriage, constancy, and no birth control. And he found the Sechelt Peninsula, where he and Doree lived, too full of people these days—old friends, old ways of life, old lovers. Soon he and Doree moved across the country to a town they picked from a name on the map: Mildmay. They didn't live in town; they rented a place in the country. Lloyd got a job in an ice-cream factory. They planted a garden. Lloyd knew a lot about gardening, just as he did about house carpentry, managing a woodstove, and keeping an old car running.

Sasha was born.

"Perfectly natural," Mrs. Sands said.

Doree said, "Is it?"

Doree always sat on a straight-backed chair in front of the desk, not on the sofa, which had a flowery pattern and cushions. Mrs. Sands moved her own chair to the side of the desk, so that they could talk without any kind of barrier between them.

"I've sort've been expecting you would," she said. "I think it's what I might have done, in your place."

Mrs. Sands would not have said that in the beginning. A year ago, even, she'd have been more cautious, knowing how Doree would have revolted, then, at the idea that anybody, any living soul, could be in her place. Now she knew that Doree would just take it as a way, even a humble way, of trying to understand.

Mrs. Sands was not like some of them. She was not brisk, not thin, not pretty. Not too old, either. She was about the age that Doree's mother would have been, though she did not look as if she'd ever been a hippie. Her graying hair was cut short and she had a mole riding on one cheekbone. She wore flat shoes and loose pants and flowered tops. Even when they were of a raspberry or turquoise color these tops did not make her look as if she really cared what she put on—it was more as if somebody had told her she needed to smarten herself up and she had obediently gone shopping for something she thought might do that. Her large, kind, impersonal sobriety drained all assaulting cheerfulness, all insult, out of those clothes.

"Well, the first two times I never saw him," Doree said. "He wouldn't come out."

"But this time he did? He did come out?"

"Yes, he did. But I wouldn't hardly have known him."

"He'd aged?"

"I guess so. I guess he's lost some weight. And those clothes. Uniforms. I never saw him in anything like that."

"Wasn't he once an orderly?"

"It wasn't the same."

"He looked to you like a different person?"

"No." Doree caught at her upper lip, trying to think what the difference was. He'd been so still. She had never seen him so still. He hadn't even seemed to know that he should sit down opposite her. Her first words to him had been "Aren't you going to sit down?" And he had said, "Is it all right?"

"He looked sort of vacant," she said. "I wondered if they had him on drugs?"

"Maybe something to keep him on an even keel. Mind you, I don't know. Did you have a conversation?"

Doree wondered if it could be called that. She had asked him some stupid ordinary questions. How was he feeling? (O.K.) Did he get enough to eat? (He thought so.) Was there any place where he could walk if he wanted to? (Under supervision, yes. He guessed you could call it a place. He guessed you could call it walking.)

She'd said, "You have to get fresh air."

He'd said, "That's true."

She'd nearly asked him if he had made any friends. The way you ask your kid about school. The way, if your kids went to school, you would ask them.

"Yes. Yes," Mrs. Sands said, nudging the ready box of Kleenex forward. Doree didn't need it; her eyes were dry. The trouble was in the bottom of her stomach. The heaves.

Mrs. Sands just waited, knowing enough to keep her hands off.

And, as if he'd detected what she was on the verge of saying, Lloyd had told her that there was a psychiatrist who came and talked to him every so often.

"I tell him he's wasting his time," Lloyd said. "I know as much as he does."

That was the only time that he had sounded to Doree anything like himself.

All through the visit her heart had kept thumping. She'd thought she might faint or die. It cost her such an effort to look at him, to get him into her vision as this thin and gray, diffident yet cold, mechanically moving yet uncoördinated man.

She had not said any of this to Mrs. Sands. Mrs. Sands might have asked—tactfully—whom she was afraid of. Herself or him? But she wasn't *afraid*.

When Sasha was one and a half, Barbara Ann was born, and, when Barbara Ann was two, they had Dimitri. They had named Sasha together, and then they made a pact that he would name the boys and she would name the girls.

Dimitri was the first one to be colicky. Doree thought that he was maybe not getting enough milk, or that her milk was not rich enough. Or too rich? Not right, anyway. Lloyd had a lady from the La Leche League come and talk to her. Whatever you do, the lady said, you must not put him on a supplementary bottle. That would be the thin edge of the wedge, she said, and pretty soon you would have him rejecting the breast altogether. She spoke as if that would be a major tragedy.

Little did she know that Doree had been giving him a supplement already. And it seemed to be true that he preferred that—he fussed more and more at the breast. By three months he was entirely bottle-fed, and then there was no way to keep it from Lloyd. She told him that her milk had dried up, and she'd had to start supplementing. Lloyd squeezed one breast after the other with frantic determination and succeeded in getting a couple of drops of miserable-looking milk out. He called her a liar. They fought. He said that she was a whore like her mother.

All those hippies were whores, he said.

Soon they made up. But whenever Dimitri was fretful, whenever he had a cold, or was afraid of the older children's pet rabbit, or still hung on to chairs at the age when his brother and sister had been walking unsupported, the failure to breast-feed was recalled.

The first time Doree had gone to Mrs. Sands's office, one of the other women there had given her a pamphlet. On the front of it was a gold cross and words made up of gold and purple letters: "When Your Loss Seems Unbearable . . ." Inside, there was a softly colored picture of Jesus and some finer print that Doree did not read.

In her chair in front of the desk, still clutching the pamphlet, Doree began to shake. Mrs. Sands had to pry it out of her hand.

"Did somebody give you this?" Mrs. Sands said.

Doree said, "Her," and jerked her head at the closed door.

"You don't want it?"

"When you're down is when they'll try and get at you," Doree said, and then realized that this was something her mother had said, when some ladies with a similar message came to visit her in the hospital. "They think you'll fall on your knees and then it'll be all right."

Mrs. Sands sighed.

"Well," she said. "It's certainly not that simple."

"Not even possible," Doree said.

"Maybe not."

They never spoke of Lloyd, in those days. Doree never thought of him if she could help it, and then only as if he were some terrible accident of nature.

"Even if I believed in that stuff," she said—meaning what was in the pamphlet—"it would only be so that . . ." She meant to say that such a belief would be convenient because she could then think of Lloyd burning in Hell, or something of that sort, but she was unable to go on, because it was just too stupid to talk about. And because of a familiar impediment, that was like a hammer hitting her in the belly.

. . .

Lloyd thought that their children should be educated at home. This was not for religious reasons—going against dinosaurs and cavemen and monkeys and all that—but because he wanted them to be close to their parents and to be introduced to the world carefully and gradually, rather than thrown into it all at once. "I just happen to think they are my kids," he said. "I mean they are our kids, not the Department of Education's kids."

Doree wasn't sure that she could handle this, but it turned out that the Department of Education had guidelines, and lesson plans that you could get from your local school. Sasha was a bright boy who practically taught himself to read, and the other two were still too little to learn much yet. In the evenings and on weekends Lloyd taught Sasha about geography and the solar system and the hibernation of animals and how a car runs, covering each subject as the questions came up. Pretty soon Sasha was ahead of the school plans, but Doree picked them up anyway and put him through the exercises right on time so that the law would be satisfied.

There was another mother in the district doing homeschooling. Her name was Maggie and she had a minivan. Lloyd needed his car to get to work, and Doree had not learned to drive, so she was glad when Maggie offered her a ride to the school once a week to turn in the finished exercises and pick up the new ones. Of course they took all the children along. Maggie had two boys. The older one had so many allergies that she had to keep a strict eye on everything he ate—that was why she taught him at home. And then it seemed that she might as well keep the younger one there as well. He wanted to stay with his brother and he had a problem with asthma, anyway.

How grateful Doree was then, comparing her healthy three. Lloyd said that it was because she'd had her children when she was still young, while Maggie had waited until she was on the verge of menopause. He was exaggerating how old Maggie was, but it was true that she had waited. She was an optometrist. She and her husband had been partners, and they hadn't started their family until she could leave the practice and they had a house in the country.

Maggie's hair was pepper-and-salt, cropped close to her head. She was tall, flat-chested, cheerful, and opinionated. Lloyd called her the Lezzie. Only behind her back, of course. He kidded with her on the phone but mouthed at Doree, "It's the Lezzie." That didn't really bother Doree—he called lots of women Lezzies. But she was afraid that the kidding would seem overly friendly to Maggie, an intrusion, or at least a waste of time.

"You want to speak to the ole lady. Yeah, I got her right here. She's rubbing my work pants up and down the scrub board. See, I only got the one pair of pants. Anyway, I believe in keeping her busy."

Doree and Maggie got into the habit of shopping for groceries together, after they'd picked up the papers at the school. Then sometimes they got take-out coffees at Tim Horton's and took the children to Riverside Park. They sat on a bench while Sasha and Maggie's boys raced around or hung from the climbing contraptions, and Barbara Ann pumped on the swing and Dimitri played in the sandbox. Or they sat in the mini, if it was cold. They talked mostly about the children, and things they cooked, but somehow Doree found out about how Maggie had trekked around Europe before training as an optometrist and Maggie found out how young Doree had been when she got married. Also about how easily she had become pregnant at first, and how she didn't so easily anymore, and how that made Lloyd suspicious, so that he went through her dresser drawers looking for birth-control pills—thinking she must be taking them on the sly.

"And are you?" Maggie asked.

Doree was shocked. She said she wouldn't dare.

"I mean, I'd think that was awful to do, without telling him. It's just kind of a joke when he goes looking for them."

"Oh," Maggie said.

And one time Maggie said, "Is everything all right with you? I mean in your marriage? You're happy?"

Doree said yes, without hesitation. After that she was more careful about what she said. She saw that there were things that she was used to that another person might not understand. Lloyd had a certain way of looking at things; that was just how he was. Even when she'd first met him, in the hospital, he'd been like that. The head nurse was a starchy sort of person, so he'd called her Mrs. Bitch-out-of-hell, instead of her name, which was Mrs. Mitchell. He said it so fast that you could barely catch on. He'd thought that she picked favorites, and he wasn't one of them. Now there was somebody he detested at the ice-cream factory, somebody he called Suck-stick Louie. Doree didn't know the man's real name. But at least that proved that it wasn't only women who provoked him.

Doree was pretty sure that these people weren't as bad as Lloyd thought, but it was no use contradicting him. Perhaps men just had to have enemies, the way they had to have their jokes. And sometimes Lloyd did make the enemies into jokes, just as if he were laughing at himself. She was even allowed to laugh with him, as long as she wasn't the one who started the laughing.

She hoped that he wouldn't get that way about Maggie. At times she was afraid she saw something of the sort coming. If he prevented her from riding to the school and the grocery store with Maggie it would be a big inconvenience. But worse would be the shame. She would have to make up some stupid lie, to explain things. But Maggie would know—at least she would know that Doree was lying, and she would interpret that, probably, as meaning that Doree was in a worse situation than she really was. Maggie had her own sharp no-nonsense way of looking at things.

Then Doree asked herself why she should care, anyway, what Maggie might think. Maggie was an outsider, not even somebody Doree felt particularly comfortable with. It was Lloyd and Doree and their family that mattered. Lloyd said that, and he was right. The truth of things between them, the bond, was not something that anybody else could understand and it was not anybody else's business. If Doree could watch her own loyalty it would be all right.

It got worse, gradually. No direct forbidding, but more criticism. Lloyd coming up with the theory that Maggie's boys' allergies and asthma might be Maggie's fault. The reason was often the mother, he said. He used to see it at the hospital all the time. The overcontrolling, usually overeducated mother.

"Some of the time kids are just born with something," Doree said, unwisely. "You can't say it's the mother every time."

"Oh. Why can't I?"

"I didn't mean you. I didn't mean you can't. I meant couldn't they be born—"

"Since when are you such a medical authority?"

"I didn't say I was."

"No. And you're not."

Bad to worse. He wanted to know what they talked about, she and Maggie.

"I don't know. Nothing, really."

"That's funny. Two women riding in a car. First I heard of it. Two women talking about nothing. She is out to break us up."

"Who is? *Maggie?*"

"I've got experience of her kind of woman."

"What kind?"

"Her kind."

"Don't be silly."

"Careful. Don't call me silly."

"What would she want to do that for?"

"How am I supposed to know? She just wants to do it. You wait. You'll see. She'll get you over there bawling and whining about what a bastard I am."

And in fact it turned out as he had said. At least it would certainly have looked that way, to Lloyd. She did find herself at around ten o'clock one night in Maggie's kitchen, sniffling back her tears and drinking herbal tea. Maggie's husband had said, "What the hell?" when she knocked—she heard him through the door. He hadn't known who she was. She'd said, "I'm really sorry to bother you—" while he stared at her with lifted eyebrows and a tight mouth. And then Maggie had come.

Doree had walked all the way there in the dark, first along the gravel road that she and Lloyd lived on, then on the highway. She headed for the ditch every time a car came, and that slowed her down considerably. She did take a look at the cars that passed, thinking that one of them might be Lloyd. She didn't want him to find her, not yet, not till he was scared out of his craziness. Other times she had been able to scare him out of it herself, by weeping and howling and even banging her head on the floor, chanting, "It's not true, it's not true, it's not true," over and over. Finally he would back down. He would say, "O.K., O.K. I'll believe you. Honey, be quiet. Think of the kids. I'll believe you, honest. Just stop."

But tonight she had pulled herself together just as she was about to start that performance. She had put on her coat and walked out the door, with him calling after her, "Don't do this. I warn you!"

Maggie's husband had gone to bed, not looking any better pleased about things, while Doree kept saying, "I'm sorry. I'm so sorry, barging in on you at this time of the night."

"Oh, shut up," Maggie said, kind and businesslike. "Do you want a glass of wine?"

"I don't drink."

"Then you'd better not start now. I'll get you some tea. It's very soothing. Raspberry-camomile. It's not the kids, is it?"

"No."

Maggie took her coat and handed her a wad of Kleenex for her eyes and nose. "Don't try to tell me yet. We'll soon get you settled down."

Even when she was partway settled down Doree didn't want to blurt out the whole truth, and let Maggie know that she herself was at the heart of the problem. More than that, she didn't want to have to explain Lloyd. No matter how worn out she got with him, he was still the closest person in the world to her, and she felt that everything would collapse if she were to bring herself to tell someone exactly how he was, if she were to be entirely disloyal.

She said that she and Lloyd had got into an old argument and she was so sick and tired of it that all she'd wanted was to get out. But she would get over it, she said. They would.

"Happens to every couple sometime," Maggie said.

The phone rang then, and Maggie answered.

"Yes. She's O.K. She just needed to walk something out of her system. Fine. O.K. then, I'll deliver her home in the morning. No trouble. O.K. Good night.

"That was him," she said. "I guess you heard."

"How did he sound? Did he sound normal?"

Maggie laughed. "Well, I don't know how he sounds when he's normal, do I? He didn't sound drunk."

"He doesn't drink, either. We don't even have coffee in the house."

"Want some toast?"

. . .

In the morning, early, Maggie drove her home. Maggie's husband hadn't left for work yet, and he stayed with the boys.

Maggie was in a hurry to get back, so she just said, "Bye-bye. Phone me if you need to talk," as she turned the minivan around in the yard.

It was a cold morning in early spring, snow still on the ground, but there was Lloyd sitting on the steps without a jacket on.

"Good morning," he said, in a loud, sarcastically polite voice. And she said good morning, in a voice that pretended not to notice his.

He did not move aside to let her up the steps.

"You can't go in there," he said.

She decided to take this lightly.

"Not even if I say please? Please."

He looked at her but did not answer. He smiled with his lips held together.

"Lloyd?" she said. "Lloyd?"

"You better not go in."

"I didn't tell her anything, Lloyd. I'm sorry I walked out. I just needed a breathing space, I guess."

"Better not go in."

"What's the matter with you? Where are the kids?"

He shook his head, as he did when she said something he didn't like to hear. Something mildly rude, like "holy shit."

"*Lloyd*. Where are the kids?"

He shifted just a little, so that she could pass if she liked.

Dimitri still in his crib, lying sideways. Barbara Ann on the floor beside her bed, as if she'd got out or been pulled out. Sasha by the kitchen door—he had tried to get away. He was the only one with bruises on his throat. The pillow had done for the others.

"When I phoned last night?" Lloyd said. "When I phoned, it had already happened.

"You brought it all on yourself," he said.

The verdict was that he was insane, he couldn't be tried. He was criminally insane—he had to be put in a secure institution.

Doree had run out of the house and was stumbling around the

yard, holding her arms tight across her stomach as if she had been sliced open and was trying to keep herself together. This was the scene that Maggie saw, when she came back. She had had a premonition, and had turned the minivan around in the road. Her first thought was that Doree had been hit or kicked in the stomach by her husband. She could make nothing out of the noises Doree was making. But Lloyd, who was still sitting on the steps, moved aside courteously for her, without a word, and she went into the house and found what she was now expecting to find. She phoned the police.

For some time Doree kept stuffing whatever she could grab into her mouth. After the dirt and grass it was sheets or towels or her own clothing. As if she were trying to stifle not just the howls that rose up but the scene in her head. She was given a shot of something, regularly, to quiet her down, and this worked. In fact she became very quiet, though not catatonic. She was said to be stabilized. When she got out of the hospital and the social worker brought her to this new place, Mrs. Sands took over, found her somewhere to live, found her a job, established the routine of talking with her once a week. Maggie would have come to see her, but she was the one person Doree could not stand to see. Mrs. Sands said that that feeling was natural—it was the association. She said that Maggie would understand.

Mrs. Sands said that whether or not Doree continued to visit Lloyd was up to her. "I'm not here to approve or disapprove, you know. Did it make you feel good to see him? Or bad?"

"I don't know."

Doree could not explain that it had not really seemed to be him she was seeing. It was almost like seeing a ghost. So pale. Pale loose clothes on him, shoes that didn't make any noise—probably slippers—on his feet. She had the impression that some of his hair had fallen out. His thick and wavy, honey-colored hair. There seemed to be no breadth to his shoulders, no hollow in his collarbone where she used to rest her head.

What he had said, afterward, to the police—and it was quoted in the newspapers—was "I did it to save them the misery."

What misery?

"The misery of knowing that their mother had walked out on them," he said.

That was burned into Doree's brain and maybe when she decided to try to see him it had been with the idea of making him take it back. Making him see, and admit, how things had really gone.

"You told me to stop contradicting you or get out of the house. So I got out of the house."

"I only went to Maggie's for one night. I fully intended to come back. I wasn't walking out on anybody."

She remembered perfectly how the argument had started. She had bought a tin of spaghetti that had a very slight dent in it. Because of that it had been on sale and she had been pleased with her thriftiness. She had thought that she was doing something smart. But she didn't tell him that, once he had begun questioning her about it. For some reason she'd thought it better to pretend that she hadn't noticed.

Anybody would notice, he said. We could have all been poisoned. What was the matter with her? Or was that what she had in mind? Was she planning to try it out on the kids or on him?

She had told him not to be crazy.

He had said that it wasn't him who was crazy. Who but a crazy woman would buy poison for her family?

The children had been watching from the doorway of the front room. That was the last time she'd seen them alive.

So was that what she had been thinking—that she could make him see, finally, who it was that was crazy?

When she realized what was in her head, she should have got off the bus. She could have got off even at the gates, with the few other women who plodded up the drive. She could have crossed the road and waited for the bus back to the city. Probably some people did that. They were going to make a visit and then decided not to. People probably did that all the time.

But maybe it was better that she had gone on, and seen him so strange and wasted. Not a person worth blaming for anything. Not a person. He was like a character in a dream.

She had dreams. In one dream she had run out of the house after finding them, and Lloyd had started to laugh in his old easy way, and then she had heard Sasha laughing behind her and it had dawned on her, wonderfully, that they were all playing a joke.

. . .

"You asked me if it made me feel good or bad when I saw him? Last time, you asked me?"

"Yes, I did," Mrs. Sands said.

"I had to think about it."

"Yes."

"I decided it made me feel bad. So I haven't gone again."

It was hard to tell with Mrs. Sands, but the nod she gave seemed to show some satisfaction or approval.

So when Doree decided that she would go again, after all, she thought that it was better not to mention it. And since it was hard not to mention whatever happened to her—there being so little, most of the time—she phoned and cancelled her appointment. She said that she was going on a holiday. They were getting into summer, when holidays were the usual thing. With a friend, she said.

"You aren't wearing the jacket you had on last week."

"That wasn't last week."

"Wasn't it?"

"It was three weeks ago. The weather's hot now. This is lighter but I don't really need it. You don't need a jacket at all."

He asked about her trip, what buses she'd had to take from Mildmay.

She told him that she wasn't living there anymore. She told him where she lived, and about the three buses.

"That's quite a trek for you. Do you like living in a bigger place?"

"It's easier to get work there."

"So you work?"

She had told him last time about where she lived, the buses, where she worked.

"I clean rooms in a motel," she said. "I told you."

"Yes. Yes. I forgot. I'm sorry. Do you ever think about going back to school? Night school?"

She said that she did think about it but never seriously enough to do anything. She said that she didn't mind the work she was doing.

Then it seemed as if they could not think of anything more to say.

He sighed. He said, "Sorry. Sorry. I guess I'm not so used to conversation."

"So what do you do all the time?"

"I guess I read quite a bit. Kind of meditate. Informally."

"Oh."

"I appreciate you coming here. It means a lot to me. But don't think you have to keep it up. I mean, just when you want to. Just come when you want to. If something comes up, or if you don't feel like it—What I'm trying to say is, just the fact that you could come at all, that you even came once, that's a bonus for me. Do you get what I mean?"

She said yes, she thought so.

He said that he didn't want to interfere with her life.

"You're not," she said.

"Was that what you were going to say? I thought you were going to say something else."

In fact, she had almost said, What life?

No, she said, not really, nothing else.

"Good."

Three more weeks and she got a phone call. It was Mrs. Sands herself on the line, not one of the women in the office.

"Oh, Doree. I thought you might not be back yet. From your holiday. So you are back?"

"Yes," Doree said, trying to think where she could say she had been.

"But you hadn't got around to arranging another appointment?"

"No. Not yet."

"That's O.K. I was just checking. You are all right?"

"I'm all right."

"Fine. Fine. You know where I am if you ever need me. Ever just want to have a talk."

"Yes."

"So take care."

She hadn't mentioned Lloyd, hadn't asked if the visits had continued. Well, of course, Doree had said that they weren't going to. But Mrs. Sands was pretty good, usually, about sensing what was going on. Pretty good at holding off, too, when she understood that a question might not get her anywhere. Doree didn't know what she would have said, if asked—whether she would have backtracked and told a lie or come out with the truth. She had gone back, in fact, the very next Sunday after he more or less told her that it didn't matter whether she came or not.

He had a cold. He didn't know how he'd got it.

Maybe he had been coming down with it, he said, the last time he saw her, and that was why he'd been morose.

Morose. She seldom had anything to do, nowadays, with anyone who used a word like that, and it sounded strange to her. But he had always had a habit of using such words, and of course at one time they hadn't struck her as they did now.

"Do I seem like a different person to you?" he asked.

"Well, you look different," she said cautiously. "Don't I?"

"You look beautiful," he said sadly.

Something softened in her. But she fought against it.

"Do you feel different?" he asked. "Do you feel like a different person?"

She said she didn't know. "Do you?"

He said, "Altogether."

Later in the week a large envelope was given to her at work. It had been addressed to her care of the motel. It contained several sheets of paper, with writing on both sides. She didn't think at first of its being from him—she somehow had the idea that people in prison were not allowed to write letters. But, of course, he was a different sort of prisoner. He was not a criminal. He was only criminally insane.

There was no date on the document and not even a "Dear Doree." It just started talking to her in such a way that she thought it had to be some sort of religious invitation:

> People are looking all over for the solution. Their minds are sore (from looking). So many things jostling around and hurting them. You can see in their faces all their bruises and pains. They are troubled. They rush around. They have to shop and go to the laundromat and get their hair cut and earn a living or pick up their welfare checks. The poor ones have to do that and the rich ones have to look hard for the best ways to spend their money. That is work too. They have to build the best houses

with gold faucets for their hot and cold water. And their Audis and magical toothbrushes and all possible contraptions and then burglar alarms to protect against slaughter and all neigh neither rich nor poor have any peace in their souls. I was going to write "neighbor" instead of "neither," why was that? I have not got any neighbor here. Where I am at least people have got beyond a lot of confusion. They know what their possessions are and always will be and they don't even have to buy or cook their own food. Or choose it. Choices are eliminated.

All we that are here can get is what we can get out of our own minds.

At the beginning all in my head was purturbation (Sp?). There was everlasting storm, and I would knock my head against cement in the hope of getting rid of it. Stopping my agony and my life. So punishments were meted. I got hosed down and tied up and drugs introduced in my bloodstream. I am not complaining either, because I had to learn there is no profit in that. Nor is it any different from the so-called real world, in which people drink and carry on and commit crimes to eliminate their thoughts which are painful. And often they get hauled off and incarcerated but it is not long enough for them to come out on the other side. And what is that? It is either total insanity or peace.

Peace. I arrived at peace and am still sane. I imagine reading this now you are thinking I am going to say something about God Jesus or at any rate Buddha as if I had arrived at a religious conversion. No. I do not close my eyes and get lifted up by any specific Higher Power. I do not really know what is meant by any of that. What I do is Know Myself. Know Thyself is some kind of Commandment from somewhere, probably the Bible so at least in that I may have followed Christianity. Also, To Thy Own Self Be True—I have attempted that if it is in the Bible also. It does not say which parts—the bad or the good—to be true to so it is not intended as a guide to morality. Also Know Thyself does not relate either to morality as we know it in Behavior. But Behavior is not really my concern because I have been judged quite correctly as a person who cannot be trusted to judge how he should behave and that is the reason I am here.

Back to the Know part in Know Thyself. I can say perfectly soberly that I know myself and I know the worst I am capable of and I know that I have done it. I am judged by the World as a Monster and I have no quarrel with that, even though I might say in passing that people who rain down bombs or burn cities or starve and murder hundreds of thousands of people are not generally considered Monsters but are showered with medals and honors, only acts against small numbers being considered shocking and evil. This being not meant as an excuse but just observation.

What I Know in Myself is my own Evil. That is the secret of my comfort. I mean I know my Worst. It may be worse than other people's worst but in fact I do not have to think or worry about that. No excuses. I am at peace. Am I a Monster? The World says so and if it is said so then I agree. But then I say, the World does not have any real meaning for me. I am My Self and have no chance to be any other Self. I could say that I was crazy then but what does that mean? Crazy. Sane. I am I. I could not change my I then and I cannot change it now.

Doree, if you have read this far, there is one special thing I want to tell you about but cannot write it down. If you ever think of coming back here then maybe I can tell you. Do not think I am heartless. It isn't that I wouldn't change things if I could but I can't.

I am sending this to your place of work which I remember and the name of the town so my brain is working fine in some respects.

She thought that they would have to discuss this piece of writing at their next meeting and she read it over several times, but she could not think of anything to say. What she really wanted to talk about was whatever he had said was impossible to put in writing. But when she saw him again he behaved as if he had never written to her at all. She searched for a topic and told him about a once famous folksinger who had stayed at the motel that week. To her surprise he knew more than she did about the singer's career. It turned out that he had a television, or at least access to one, and watched some shows and, of course, the news, regularly. That gave them a bit more to talk about, until she could not help herself.

"What was the thing you couldn't tell me except in person?"

He said that he wished she hadn't asked him. He didn't know if they were ready to discuss it.

Then she was afraid that it would be something she really could not handle, something unbearable, such as that he still loved her. "Love" was a word she could not stand to hear.

"O.K.," she said. "Maybe we're not."

Then she said, "Still, you better tell me. If I walked out of here and was struck down by a car then I would never know, and you would never have the chance to tell me again."

"True," he said.

"So what is it?"

"Next time. Next time. Sometimes I can't talk anymore. I want to but I just dry up, talking."

> I have been thinking of you Doree ever since you left and regret I disappointed you. When you are sitting opposite me I tend to get more emotional than perhaps I show. It is not my right to go emotional in front of you, since you certainly have the right more than me and you are always very controlled. So I am going to reverse what I said before because I have come to the conclusion I can write to you after all better than I can talk.
>
> Now where do I start?
>
> Heaven exists.
>
> That is one way but not right because I never believed in Heaven and Hell, etc. As far as I was concerned that was always a pile of crap. So it must sound pretty weird of me to bring up the subject now.
>
> I will just say then: I have seen the children.
>
> I have seen them and talked to them.
>
> There. What are you thinking at the moment? You are thinking well, now he is really round the bend. Or, it's a dream and he can't distinguish a dream, he doesn't know the difference between a dream and awake. But I want to tell you I do know the difference and what I know is, they exist. I say they exist, not they are alive, because alive means in our particular Dimension, and I am not saying that is where they are. In fact I think they are not. But they do exist and it must be that there is another

Dimension or maybe innumerable Dimensions, but what I know is that I have got access to whatever one they are in. Possibly I got hold of this from being so much on my own and having to think and think and with such as I have to think about. So after such suffering and solitude there is a Grace that has seen the way to giving me this reward. Me the very one that deserves it the least to the world's way of thinking.

Well if you have kept reading this far and not torn this to pieces you must want to know something. Such as how they are. They are fine. Really happy and smart. They don't seem to have any memory of anything bad. They are maybe a little older than they were but that is hard to say. They seem to understand at different levels. Yes. You can notice with Dimitri that he has learned to talk which he was not able to do. They are in a room I can partly recognize. It's like our house but more spacious and nicer. I asked them how they were being looked after and they just laughed at me and said something like they were able to look after themselves. I think Sasha was the one who said that. Sometimes they don't talk separately or at least I can't separate their voices but their identities are quite clear and I must say, joyful.

Please don't conclude that I am crazy. That is the fear that made me not want to tell you about this. I was crazy at one time but believe me I have shed all my old craziness like the bear sheds his coat. Or maybe I should say the snake sheds his skin. I know that if I had not done that I would never have been given this ability to reconnect with Sasha and Barbara Ann and Dimitri. Now I wish that you could be granted this chance as well because if it is a matter of deserving then you are way ahead of me. It may be harder for you to do because you live in the world so much more than I do but at least I can give you this information—the Truth—and in telling you I have seen them hope that it will make your heart lighter.

Doree wondered what Mrs. Sands would say or think, if she read this letter. Mrs. Sands would be careful, of course. She would be careful not to pass any outright verdict of craziness but she would carefully, kindly, steer Doree around in that direction. Or you might say she wouldn't steer—she would just pull the confusion away so that Doree would have to face what would then seem to have been her own conclusion all along. She would have to put the whole dangerous nonsense—this was Mrs. Sands speaking—out of her mind.

That was why Doree was not going anywhere near her.

Doree did think that he was crazy. And in what he had written there seemed to be some trace of the old bragging. She didn't write back. Days went by. Weeks. She didn't alter her opinion but she still held on to what he'd written, like a secret. And from time to time, when she was in the middle of spraying a bathroom mirror or tightening a sheet, a feeling came over her. For almost two years she had not taken any notice of the things that generally made people happy, such as nice weather or flowers in bloom or the smell of a bakery. She still did not have that spontaneous sense of happiness, exactly, but she had a reminder of what it was like. It had nothing to do with the weather or flowers. It was the idea of the children in what he had called their Dimension that came sneaking up on her in this way, and for the first time brought a light feeling to her, not pain.

In all the time since what had happened had happened, any thought of the children had been something she had to get rid of, pull out immediately like a knife in her throat. She could not think their names, and if she heard a name that sounded like one of theirs she had to pull that out, too. Even children's voices, their shrieks and slapping feet as they ran to and from the motel swimming pool, had to be banished by a sort of gate that she could slam down behind her ears. What was different now was that she had a refuge she could go to as soon as such dangers rose anywhere around her.

And who had given it to her? Not Mrs. Sands—that was for sure. Not in all those hours sitting by the desk with the Kleenex discreetly handy.

Lloyd had given it to her. Lloyd, that terrible person, that isolated and insane person.

Insane if you wanted to call it that. But wasn't it possible that what he said was true—that he had come out on the other side? And who was to say that the visions of a person who had done such a thing and made such a journey might not mean something?

This notion wormed its way into her head and stayed there.

Along with the thought that Lloyd, of all people, might be the person she should be with now. What other use could she be in the world—she seemed to be saying this to somebody, probably to Mrs. Sands—what was she here for if not at least to listen to him?

I didn't say "forgive," she said to Mrs. Sands in her head. I would never say that. I would never do it.

But think. Aren't I just as cut off by what happened as he is? Nobody who knew about it would want me around. All I can do is remind people of what nobody can stand to be reminded of.

Disguise wasn't possible, not really. That crown of yellow spikes was pathetic.

So she found herself travelling on the bus again, heading down the highway. She remembered those nights right after her mother had died, when she would sneak out to meet Lloyd, lying to her mother's friend, the woman she was staying with, about where she was going. She remembered the friend's name, her mother's friend's name. Laurie.

Who but Lloyd would remember the children's names now, or the color of their eyes? Mrs. Sands, when she had to mention them, did not even call them children, but "your family," putting them in one clump together.

Going to meet Lloyd in those days, lying to Laurie, she had felt no guilt, only a sense of destiny, submission. She had felt that she was put on earth for no reason other than to be with him and try to understand him.

Well, it wasn't like that now. It was not the same.

She was sitting on the front seat across from the driver. She had a clear view through the windshield. And that was why she was the only passenger on the bus, the only person other than the driver, to see a pickup truck pull out from a side road without even slowing down, to see it rock across the empty Sunday-morning highway in front of them and plunge into the ditch. And to see something even stranger: the driver of the truck flying through the air in a manner that seemed both swift and slow, absurd and graceful. He landed in the gravel at the edge of the pavement, on the opposite side of the highway.

The other passengers didn't know why the driver had put on the brakes and brought them to a sudden uncomfortable stop. And at first all that Doree thought was, How did he get out? That young man or boy, who must have fallen asleep at the wheel. How did he fly out of the truck and launch himself so elegantly into the air?

"Fellow right in front of us," the driver said to his passengers. He was trying to speak loudly and calmly, but there was a tremor of amazement, something like awe, in his voice. "Just plowed across the road and into the ditch. We'll be on our way again as soon as we can and in the meantime please don't get out of the bus."

As if she had not heard that, or had some special right to be useful, Doree got out behind him. He did not reprimand her.

"Goddam asshole," he said as they crossed the road and there was nothing in his voice now but anger and exasperation. "Goddam asshole kid, can you believe it?"

The boy was lying on his back, arms and legs flung out, like somebody making an angel in the snow. Only there was gravel around him, not snow. His eyes were not quite closed. He was so young, a boy who had shot up tall before he even needed to shave. Possibly without a driver's license.

The driver was talking on his phone.

"Mile or so south of Bayfield, on 21, east side of the road."

A trickle of pink foam came out from under the boy's head, near the ear. It did not look like blood at all, but like the stuff you skim off the strawberries when you're making jam.

Doree crouched down beside him. She laid a hand on his chest. It was still. She bent her ear close. Somebody had ironed his shirt recently—it had that smell.

No breathing.

But her fingers on his smooth neck found a pulse.

She remembered something she'd been told. It was Lloyd who had told her, in case one of the children had an accident and he wasn't there. The tongue. The tongue can block the breathing, if it has fallen into the back of the throat. She laid the fingers of one hand on the boy's forehead and two fingers of the other hand under his chin. Press down on the forehead, press up on the chin, to clear the airway. A slight firm tilt.

If he still didn't breathe she would have to breathe into him.

She pinches the nostrils, takes a deep breath, seals his mouth with her lips, and breathes. Two breaths and check. Two breaths and check.

Another male voice, not the driver's. A motorist must have

stopped. "You want this blanket under his head?" She shook her head tightly. She had remembered something else, about not moving the victim, so that you would not injure the spinal cord. She enveloped his mouth. She pressed his warm fresh skin. She breathed and waited. She breathed and waited again. And a faint moisture seemed to rise against her face.

The driver said something but she could not look up. Then she felt it for sure. A breath out of the boy's mouth. She spread her hand on the skin of his chest and at first she could not tell if it was rising and falling, because of her own trembling.

Yes. Yes.

It was a true breath. The airway was open. He was breathing on his own. He was breathing.

"Just lay it over him," she said to the man with the blanket. "To keep him warm."

"Is he alive?" the driver said, bending over her.

She nodded. Her fingers found the pulse again. The horrible pink stuff had not continued to flow. Maybe it was nothing important. Not from his brain.

"I can't hold the bus for you," the driver said. "We're behind schedule as it is."

The motorist said, "That's O.K. I can take over."

Be quiet, be quiet, she wanted to tell them. It seemed to her that silence was necessary, that everything in the world outside the boy's body had to concentrate, help it not to lose track of its duty to breathe.

Shy but steady whiffs now, a sweet obedience in the chest. Keep on, keep on.

"You hear that? This guy says he'll stay and watch out for him," the driver said. "Ambulance is coming as fast as they can."

"Go on," Doree said. "I'll hitch a ride to town with them and catch you on your way back tonight."

He had to bend to hear her. She spoke dismissively, without raising her head, as if she were the one whose breath was precious.

"You sure?" he said.

Sure.

"You don't have to get to London?"

No.

GOOD PEOPLE

BY DAVID FOSTER WALLACE (2007)

They were up on a picnic table at that park by the lake, by the edge of the lake, with part of a downed tree in the shallows half hidden by the bank. Lane A. Dean, Jr., and his girlfriend, both in bluejeans and button-up shirts. They sat up on the table's top portion and had their shoes on the bench part that people sat on to picnic or fellowship together in carefree times. They'd gone to different high schools but the same junior college, where they had met in campus ministries. It was springtime, and the park's grass was very green and the air suffused with honeysuckle and lilacs both, which was almost too much. There were bees, and the angle of the sun made the water of the shallows look dark. There had been more storms that week, with some downed trees and the sound of chainsaws all up and down his parents' street. Their postures on the picnic table were both the same forward kind with their shoulders rounded and elbows on their knees. In this position the girl rocked slightly and once put her face in her hands, but she was not crying. Lane was very still and immobile and looking past the bank at the downed tree in the shallows and its ball of exposed roots going all directions and the tree's cloud of branches all half in the water. The only other individual nearby was a dozen spaced tables away, by himself, standing upright. Looking at the torn-up hole in the ground there where the tree had gone over. It was still early yet and all the shadows wheeling right and shortening. The girl wore a thin old checked cotton shirt with pearl-colored snaps with the long sleeves down and always smelled very good and clean, like someone you could trust and care about even if you weren't in love. Lane Dean had liked the smell of her right away. His mother called her *down to earth* and liked her, thought she was good people, you could tell—she made this evident in little ways. The shallows lapped from different directions at the tree as if almost teething on it. Sometimes when alone and thinking or struggling to turn a matter over to Jesus Christ in prayer, he would find himself putting his fist in his palm and turning it slightly as if still playing and pounding his glove to stay sharp and alert in center. He did not do this now; it would be cruel and indecent to do this now. The older individual stood beside his picnic table—he was at it but not sitting—and looked also out of place in a suit coat or jacket and the kind of men's hat Lane's grandfather wore in photos as a young insurance man. He appeared to be looking across the lake. If he moved, Lane didn't see it. He looked more like a picture than a man. There were not any ducks in view.

One thing Lane Dean did was reassure her again that he'd go with her and be there with her. It was one of the few safe or decent things he could really say. The second time he said it again now she shook her head and laughed in an unhappy way that was more just air out her nose. Her real laugh was different. Where he'd be was the waiting room, she said. That he'd be thinking about her and feeling bad for her, she knew, but he couldn't be in there with her. This was so obviously true that he felt like a ninny that he'd kept on about it and now knew what she had thought every time he went and said it—it hadn't brought her comfort or eased the burden at all. The worse he felt, the stiller he sat. The whole thing felt balanced on a knife or wire; if he moved to put his arm up or touch her the whole thing could tip over. He hated himself for sitting so frozen. He could almost visualize himself tiptoeing past something explosive. A big stupid-looking tiptoe, like in a cartoon. The whole last black week had been this way and it was wrong. He knew it was wrong, knew something was required of him that was not this terrible frozen care and caution, but he pretended to himself he did not know what it was that was required. He pretended it had no name. He pretended that not saying aloud what he knew to be right and true was for her sake, was for the sake of her needs and feelings. He also worked dock and routing at UPS, on top of school, but had traded to get the day off after they'd decided together. Two days before, he had awakened very early and tried to pray but could not. He was freezing more and more solid, he felt like, but he had not thought of his father or the blank frozenness of his father, even in church, which had once filled him with such pity. This was the truth. Lane Dean, Jr., felt sun on one arm as he pictured in his mind an image of himself on a train, waving mechanically to something that got smaller and smaller as the train pulled away. His father and his mother's father had the same birthday, a Cancer. Sheri's hair was colored an almost corn blond, very clean, the skin through her central part pink in the sunlight. They'd sat here long enough that only their right side was shaded now. He could look at her head, but not at her. Different parts of him felt unconnected to each other. She was smarter than him and they both knew it. It wasn't just school—Lane Dean was in accounting and business and did all right; he was hanging in there. She was a year older, twenty, but it was also more—she had always seemed to Lane to be on good terms with her life in a way that age could not account for. His mother had put it that she *knew what it is she wanted*, which was nursing and not an easy program at Peoria Junior College, and plus she worked hostessing at the Embers and had bought her own car. She was serious in a way Lane liked. She had a cousin that died when she was thirteen, fourteen, that she'd loved and been close with. She only talked about it that once. He liked her smell and her downy arms and the way she exclaimed when something made her laugh. He had liked just being with her and talking to her. She was serious in her faith and values in a way that Lane had liked and now, sitting here with her on the table, found himself afraid of. This was an awful thing. He was starting to believe that he might not be serious in his faith. He might be somewhat of a hypocrite, like the Assyrians in Isaiah, which would be a far graver sin than the appointment—he had decided he believed this. He was desperate to be good people, to still be able to feel he was good. He rarely before now had thought of damnation and Hell—that part of it didn't speak to his spirit—and in worship services he more just tuned himself out and tolerated Hell when it came up, the same way you tolerate the job you've got to have to save up for what it is you want. Her tennis shoes had little things doodled on them from sitting in her class lectures. She stayed looking down like that. Little notes or reading assignments in Bic in her neat round hand on the rubber elements around the sneaker's rim. Lane A. Dean, looking now at her inclined head's side's barrettes in the shape of blue ladybugs. The appointment was for afternoon, but when the doorbell had rung so early and his mother'd called to him up the stairs, he had known, and a terrible kind of blankness had commenced falling through him.

He told her that he did not know what to do. That he knew if he was the salesman of it and forced it upon her that was awful and wrong. But he was trying to understand—they'd prayed on it and talked it through from every different angle. Lane said how sorry she knew he was, and that if he was wrong in believing they'd truly decided together when they decided to make the appointment she should please tell him, because he thought he knew how she must have felt as it got closer and closer and how she must be so scared, but that what he couldn't tell was if it was more than that. He was totally still except for moving his mouth, it felt like. She did not reply. That if they needed to pray on it more and talk it through, then he was here, he was ready, he said. The appointment could get moved back; if she just said the word they could call and push it back to take more time to be sure in the decision. It was still so early in it—they both knew that, he said. This was true, that he felt this way, and yet he also knew he was also trying to say things that would get her to open up and say enough back that he could see her and read her heart and know what to say to get her to go through with it. He knew this without admitting to himself that this was what he wanted, for it would make him a hypocrite and liar. He knew, in some locked-up little part of him, why it was that he'd gone to no one to open up and seek their life counsel, not Pastor Steve or the prayer partners at campus ministries, not his UPS friends or the spiritual counselling available through his parents' old church. But he did not know why Sheri herself had not gone to Pastor Steve—he could not read her heart. She was blank and hidden. He so fervently wished it never happened. He felt like he knew now why it was a true sin and not just a leftover rule from past society. He felt like he had been brought low by it and humbled and now did believe that the rules were there for a reason. That the rules were concerned with him personally, as an individual. He promised God he had learned his lesson. But what if that, too, was a hollow promise, from a hypocrite who repented only after, who promised submission but really only wanted a reprieve? He might not even know his own heart or be able to read and know himself. He kept thinking also of 1 Timothy and the hypocrite therein who *disputeth over words*. He felt a terrible inner resistance but could not feel what it was that it resisted. This was the truth. All the different angles and ways they had come at the decision together did not ever include it—the word—for had he once said it, avowed that he did love her, loved Sheri Fisher, then it all would have been transformed. It would not be a different stance or angle, but a difference in the very thing they were praying and deciding on together. Sometimes they had prayed together over the phone, in a kind of half code in case anybody accidentally picked up the extension. She continued to sit as if thinking, in the pose of thinking, like that one statue. They were right up next to each other on the table. He was looking over past her at the tree in the water. But he could not say he did: it was not true.

But neither did he ever open up and tell her straight out he did not love her. This might be his *lie by omission*. This might be the frozen resistance—were he to look right at her and tell her he didn't, she would keep the appointment and go. He knew this. Something in him, though, some terrible weakness or lack of values, could not tell her. It felt like a muscle he did not have. He didn't know why; he just could not do it, or even pray to do it. She believed he was good, serious in his values. Part of him seemed willing to more or less just about lie to someone with that kind of faith and trust, and what did that make him? How could such a type of individual even pray? What it really felt like was a taste of the reality of what might be meant by Hell. Lane Dean had never believed in Hell as a lake of fire or a loving God consigning folks to a burning lake of fire—he knew in his heart this was not true. What he believed in was a living God of compassion and love and the possibility of a personal relationship with Jesus Christ through whom this love was enacted in human time. But sitting here beside this girl as unknown to him now as outer space, waiting for whatever she might say to unfreeze him, now he felt like he could see the edge or outline of what a real vision of Hell might be. It was of two great and terrible armies within himself, opposed and facing each other, silent. There would be battle but no victor. Or never a battle—the armies would stay like that, motionless, looking across at each other, and seeing therein something so different and alien from themselves that they could not understand, could not hear each other's speech as even words or read anything from what their face looked like, frozen like that, opposed and uncomprehending, for all human time. Two-hearted, a hypocrite to yourself either way.

When he moved his head, a part of the lake further out flashed with sun—the water up close wasn't black now, and you could see into the shallows and see that all the water was moving but gently, this way and that—and in this same way he besought to return to himself as Sheri moved her leg and started to turn beside him. He could see the man in the suit and gray hat standing motionless now at the lake's rim, holding something under one arm and looking across at the opposite side where a row of little forms on camp chairs sat in a way that meant they had lines in the water for crappie—which mostly only your blacks from the East Side ever did—and the little white shape at the row's end a Styrofoam creel. In his moment or time at the lake now just to come, Lane Dean first felt he could take this all in whole: everything seemed distinctly lit, for the circle of the pin oak's shade had rotated off all the way, and they sat now in sun with their shadow a two-headed thing in the grass before them. He was looking or gazing again at where the downed tree's branches seemed to all bend so sharply just under the shallows' surface when he was given to know that through all this frozen silence he'd despised he had, in truth, been praying, or some little part of his heart he could not hear had, for he was answered now with a type of vision, what he would later call within his own mind a vision or *moment of grace*. He was not a hypocrite, just broken and split off like all men. Later on, he believed that what happened was he'd had a moment of almost seeing them both as Jesus saw them—as blind but groping, wanting to please God despite their inborn fallen nature. For in that same given moment he saw, quick as light, into Sheri's heart, and was made to know what would occur here as she finished turning to him and the man in the hat watched the fishing and the downed elm shed cells into the water. This down-to-earth girl that smelled good and wanted to be a nurse would take and hold one of his hands in both of hers to unfreeze him and make him look at her, and she would say that she cannot do it. That she is sorry she did not know this sooner, that she hadn't meant to lie—she agreed because she'd wanted to believe that she could, but she cannot. That she will carry this and have it; she has to. With her gaze clear and steady. That all night last night she prayed and searched inside herself and decided this is what love commands of her. That Lane should please please sweetie let her finish. That listen—this is her own decision and obliges him to nothing. That she knows he does not love her, not that way, has known it all this time, and that it's all right. That it is as it is and it's all right. She will carry this, and have it, and love it and make no claim on Lane except his good wishes and respecting what she has to do. That she releases him, all claim, and hopes he finishes up at P.J.C. and does so good in his life and has all joy and good things. Her voice will be clear and steady, and she will be lying, for Lane has been given to read her heart. To see through her. One of the opposite side's blacks raises his arm in what may be greeting, or waving off a bee. There is a mower cutting grass someplace off behind them. It will be a terrible, last-ditch gamble born out of the desperation in Sheri Fisher's soul, the knowledge that she can neither do this thing today nor carry a child alone and shame her family. Her values blocked the way either way, Lane could see, and she has no other options or choice—this lie is not a sin. Galatians 4:16, *Have I then become your enemy?* She is gambling that he is good. There on the table, neither frozen nor yet moving, Lane Dean, Jr., sees all this, and is moved with pity, and also with something more, something without any name he knows, that is given to him in the form of a question that never once in all the long week's thinking and division had even so much as occurred—why is he so sure he doesn't love her? Why is one kind of love any different? What if he has no earthly idea what love is? What would even Jesus do? For it was just now he felt her two small strong soft hands on his, to turn him. What if he was just afraid, if the truth was no more than this, and if what to pray for was not even love but simple courage, to meet both her eyes as she says it and trust his heart?

ANOTHER MANHATTAN

BY DONALD ANTRIM (2008)

They had lied to each other so many times, over so many years, that deceptions between them had become commonplace, practically repertoire. Everyone knew this about them—it wasn't news among their friends. That night, they had dinner reservations with Elliot and Susan, who were accustomed to following the shifts in attitude and tone—Kate's theatrical sighs, for instance, in reaction to Jim's mournful looks across the table at her—brought on by the strain of living in an atmosphere of worry and betrayal. It was winter, and dark, and the air in their little apartment was dry and nauseatingly warm; and yet what they needed, it seemed to Jim, was not to flee their home for another night of exciting conversational pauses and sly four-way flirting. They needed to sit down together, no matter how stuffy it got in the living room, no matter how loudly the radiators hissed and banged, and take turns speaking their minds. They had to talk. But first he would stop at the florist's on his way home from the outpatient clinic. If he walked through the door carrying a bouquet, there was a chance that Kate might smile.

There was a chance also that it wouldn't look awkward or strange when, at the end of the evening—he didn't really believe that he and Kate would be staying in—he paired with Susan for the walk through the cold, from the restaurant to Elliot's car. It might look, in other words, as if he were not bothered by Kate's whispering to another man. (She had a way, with Elliot, of bowing her head and mumbling furiously through the strands of hair that fell across the side of her face, so that, in order to make out her words, Elliot was forced to stoop and lean into the fog of her breath.) Jim's own affair, his affair with Susan, had been over for almost five months, long enough, he thought, as he approached the florist's on the corner by his and Kate's building, for him to begin experimenting—later that same night, if the mood was right—with innocently putting his arm around Susan's shoulder while she and he and Kate and Elliot walked in two sets of two toward the parking garage.

Of course, he wanted to be careful not to punish Kate, or, at least, not to seem to punish her, for her success in adultery. Elliot made her laugh—in a sweet way. Anyone meeting them for the first time would think they were a new couple.

It was wrong to hate her.

He'd arrived at the florist's. Inside, he went straight over to the roses in their refrigerated case. Though it was a cold day, cold and very windy, and he'd come in chilled, the short walk across the heated space warmed him, and he could feel the frigid air hit him in the face when he yanked open the glass door. He leaned in and peered at the flowers. He asked the girl, "Do you have yellow roses that haven't already bloomed and, you know, opened?"

Yellow roses, signifying friendship more than eros, seemed right, given the complex potentials of the evening.

"We only have these."

"They're pretty, but they're not going to last."

She was pretty as well, the girl showing him roses. Had he seen her in here before and somehow not noticed? How old was she? Should he risk looking into her eyes? Was she wearing a ring? What about her ass? And what had he said to her just now? Blooming and opening meant the same thing in relation to flowers. He'd become inarticulate in her presence.

Kate, in the meantime, was upstairs in the apartment, talking on the phone to Elliot. The call had gone on for more than five hours. Kate had had to use all available phones: her cell phone and, before the cell, the apartment's two cheap cordless handsets, one in the kitchen and one in the bedroom. "Can you hear beeping? I've got to switch phones. Hang on," she'd exclaimed when the kitchen phone's battery began dying. Carrying that phone (her first of the call), she'd gone into the bedroom, picked up its brother from the night table, and said, into this new phone, "Are you there? Can you hear me? Hold on while I hang up the other phone," after which she'd taken both phones to the kitchen and dropped the dead one into its cradle on the wall. A small cabinet door beside this phone opened onto a narrow and dark airshaft that had once housed a dumbwaiter. Kate opened and closed this empty cabinet several times while explaining, on the bedroom phone, why Elliot's being married and her being married shouldn't necessarily be considered something they had in common. That they were both childless could stand as an area of emotional parity, she felt, considering the fact that they both remained unsure as to whether to have children, while their spouses frequently made it clear that, in their opinions—Susan's specifically regarding Elliot, Jim's specifically regarding Kate, and neither Susan nor Jim meaning to suggest a marital reconfiguration—they'd make "a great dad" or "a great mom."

Elliot interrupted: "Don't you get tired of hearing that?"

"It's beside the point," Kate answered, and went on, "Oh, Elliot, why is talking to you so damn fucking difficult?"

"Do you need an answer?"

"You know me, always curious." How stupid was that? She'd been trying, not for the first time, to lovingly make clear to Elliot why she could no longer sleep with him. During the first hours of the conversation she'd been able to control the impulse to bait and flirt. But the business of swapping phones, the walking from room to room in the stuffy apartment, had, as it were, weakened her. It was as if, in losing that first phone, she'd lost a line of defense, however symbolic, against Elliot's desire. Or maybe, she thought as she stood in the kitchen, opening and closing the dumbwaiter door with one hand, the necessary act of sacrificing one phone for another could be read as a veiled enactment of the sort of ambivalence required for alternating between lovers in the first place. Or was that too absurd?

"Say that once more. I didn't hear what you were saying," she said to Elliot. The heating pipes banged; day was turning to dusk. She listened to the hiss of steam escaping from the radiator beneath the kitchen window. Elliot began again, "I was saying that I sometimes think that you think that because I'm a psychiatrist I can automatically see all the different sides of a situation. But I'm not that kind of psychiatrist."

"Please don't talk to me like I'm one of your postdocs," she said, and he took a long breath.

He said, "Kate, we're involved with each other, Kate."

"Jim's your friend."

"And so are you my friend."

"Your wife is my friend, too." She continued, "Fuck, I hate this. Now *this* motherfucking phone is beeping. Hold on. Elliot, can you hold on?" She swapped the bedroom phone for the insufficiently charged kitchen phone, went with that phone back into the bedroom, and sat on the edge of the bed.

"Kate, why are you bringing up Susan? I need to know what your point is. We agreed that we weren't going to talk about Susan. So where are you going with this? Kate? Are you there?"

He waited.

"Will you talk to me? Please, don't do this. Don't do this, Kate. All right, fuck this, fuck this, fuck—"

His phone was beeping. It wasn't the battery. It was another call. He said, "Kate, hang on a minute. Hang on, Kate."

He took the call. "Hello?"

"It's me," she said, and then informed him in a miserable voice that both her home phones were dead, and that she was on her cell phone and just wanted to say that she didn't much enjoy dishonesty.

"You'll have to speak up," he said.

"Can you hear me? Tell me when the signal is clear." She pressed the cell phone against her ear and walked from the bedroom to the living room, then into the kitchen, then straight down the hall, passing the tiny second bathroom, with the broken, unusable toilet, to the apartment's miniature front foyer.

"Here?" she said. "Here?"

"I'm losing you," he said. And so she retraced her route, winding up back in the living room, where she turned on a lamp. The sky was dark. Everywhere on the city's horizon she saw other people's lit windows. Once again, Elliot had bullied her—or she'd *let* him bully her—into leaving open the question of their affair. What was the use in arguing, anyway? Jim would come home any minute, and, a little later, the two of them would go out and meet Elliot and Susan for dinner. How crazy was that? She still had to shower and dress. She conceded to Elliot, "All right, I'll think about it."

"Tomorrow, then?" Elliot said, and added, "I knew you'd come to your senses." He joked that if he didn't get out of his office in the next few minutes he'd be forced to show up at the restaurant in his white coat. They said goodbye, and she put down the phone and wept for a quarter of an hour.

Downstairs at the florist's, Jim's bouquet for Kate was growing and growing. It featured not only yellow roses but red and pink solitaires, along with sprigs of heather, freesia, and alstroemeria; green and white calla lilies; blue irises; mums; and some other things the girl had plucked from buckets and waved in the air for him to see and approve. "What else? What does she like?" she'd asked him, as she leaned into the refrigerator and reached for more.

"That looks so nice. I think she'll like just what you like," he said, and wondered whether it was O.K. for him to have said it. Was it provocative? There were no other customers in the shop. Staying close but keeping his distance, he followed the girl from one display case to another. He might as well have been buying lingerie, he felt; and, in fact, it seemed to him that the bouquet was somehow intended for the girl, as much as for Kate, who would've been, well, not exactly mortified to know that her husband was downstairs using a shopgirl as a proxy to get himself worked up for sex later that night.

"Baby's breath," the girl said to him.

"Excuse me?"

"I love baby's breath."

"In that case, we'll have to have a bunch," Jim said.

"Good."

She turned away, laid the unfinished bouquet on its side on the countertop beside the cash register, and, with her back to him, said, "We have a *lot* to work with here." She glanced back over her shoulder (did she want him to come closer?), then, quickly—what a great flirt, he thought—turned away again and set to work breaking down the bouquet and separating the flowers into groups, a variegated series of stacks that she arranged not by color or type (except in the case of the combined red, pink, and yellow roses) but, as became clear, by stem length. When she had her piles, she picked up clippers.

"This will take a minute," she said.

He watched her snip the stems. He said, "Take your time."

But there was a problem: what were these flowers going to cost? The bouquet as she assembled it—as it came to *be*, in her hands—was broader and taller by far than what he'd come into the florist's wanting. It was less a bouquet than a proper arrangement, a centerpiece, thanks in part to the leafy green branches the girl stuffed between blossoms, and the pale-white baby's breath, which she didn't so much layer as clump into the globular mass.

"Can we take some out?" he asked, and wished he hadn't. What kind of man courts a woman by letting her make an enormous bouquet for his wife, then asks her to pare back?

"What would you like me to take out?" the girl asked. Was she annoyed? She had her back to him. Did she think less of him? Did she think he was a cheap bastard who cheats on his wife?

"It's just that I was hoping to use a particular Arts and Crafts vase on the mantel, which, in my opinion, these would look lovely in," he elaborately lied. (Actually, there was a vase on the mantel—but so what?) He went on, "What I mean to say is that the vase I have in mind isn't very big."

Did he need excuses? Did he need to bring up his home life?

He went into reverse. "Come to think of it, never mind about that vase on the mantel. It would be a shame to wreck such a nice bouquet."

"I'm not going to wreck anything."

Was she scolding him? Were things heating up between them? He waited for her next move.

"I can give you a bigger vase," she proposed, finally.

He held his breath. She had to be at least twenty years younger than he. But it wasn't their age difference, nor the fact that he was married, that made him feel uncertain of himself. The problem was his thought process: the lithium he was taking in small doses brought a slower speed to reality. It was the lithium or the antidepressant cocktail or all of it in concert. At times, when he spoke, he felt as if a kind of mental wind were blowing his thoughts back at him, forcing him to self-consciously order his syntax as he pushed words out.

"I just got—I just got out of the hospital!" he blurted.

He watched her as she turned to face him; in her hands she held white lilies and a red satin bow, and her eyes looked left, right, left.

"I shouldn't've said that! Forget I said that! I didn't mean to say that! Give me the vase. I want a vase."

"Oh!" she said, as if startled to realize that she was still clutching pieces of the bouquet. "Let me run in the back and get one."

While Jim and the girl sorted themselves out downstairs, Kate was marching around the apartment in her red platform heels, shoving items into her purse and looking in the usual places for her keys. She had to flee before Jim walked in. She could phone him from the street and tell him that she'd meet him at the restaurant. Going from Elliot to Jim to Elliot *and* Jim *and* Susan without a break was bullshit. But, seriously, where was she going to go? It was too cold out to sit on a bench. The bar next door to the restaurant was bleak and depressing, an old men's dive, and the bar inside the restaurant would be a mob scene of people pushing for tables. She could stand idly flipping through magazines at the newsstand across Broadway, but that would mean accommodating the line of men squeezing past her to look at porn at the rear of the store. She slammed the apartment door behind her and started down the five flights of stairs. Too often in winter she failed to leave the apartment before sunset. It worked hell on her mood.

Outside, the wind was blowing hard. She wasn't wearing a hat. She tightened her scarf around her neck, tugged up her coat collar, lowered her head, and walked toward Broadway with her fists punched down into her pockets and her purse clinched under her arm. If only it would snow. But when did it ever snow anymore? Hat or no hat, she wouldn't've minded a few snowflakes swirling down through the city light to settle on her head. When she'd been a girl, snow had lain on the ground all winter. That was what she remembered. Of course, she was thinking of the farm, of New England, not New York. So what was her point? These days, it rarely snowed the way it had back in the years before her parents died. The snowfalls she remembered from her childhood seemed lost to time and, she supposed, the changing climate.

She hurried along as quickly as she could in her high heels. At Broadway, she turned uptown and passed the florist's, where the pretty shop assistant had just come out from the back with the flowers—flowers for *her*, for Kate—in their vase.

"Here we are," the girl announced to Jim. She extended her arms and held the flowers out in front of her, presenting them. Before he could move to take them from her, however—it was the medication, warping his mind and delaying his reaction—she heaved the arrangement onto the counter and explained that she'd had to search high and low for an extra-heavy vase, one that was not only broad enough but also deep enough to properly anchor the bouquet.

Jim and the girl admired her creation. With its stalks vertical and free to fan out or droop down, the bouquet's real immensity became apparent. Roses with their thorns stuck out everywhere, and the lilies, whose columnar stalks the girl had bunched at the center, shot up through the top of the bouquet like, like, like—like insane trees towering above some insane world, he thought. He was light-headed when he spoke. "I love the way you've used ribbons and bows to tie the blossoms into clusters. It looks like a bouquet made of little bouquets! There's so much to see! I can smell the lilies. Don't you want to inhale that scent? Do you know the painter Fragonard? Do you know Boucher? Look at Boucher's flowers. They're practically obscene. There might be a Boucher hanging at the Frick."

He went for it. "Do you like museums?"

"When I have time."

"I could show you the Frick!" He grinned widely and shrugged his shoulders and tipped his head, and she mirrored him, shrugging her own shoulders and making a funny face.

"You're very good at what you do," he added, and she said, "Thank you," then asked him, "How would you like to pay?"

He tried to imagine what he'd be forced to spend. Whatever the amount, it would be too great. The bills from his recent hospitalizations were mainly covered by Kate's insurance—the policy was hers; they'd gone ahead and got married in order for him to take advantage of it during this protracted (Kate's word, sometimes used sarcastically) time of crisis in his life—but there were nevertheless many outstanding fees, brand-new bills arriving every other week, plus the only partly reimbursable expense of the aftercare program he attended across town, on the Upper East Side.

"Let's charge it." He handed the girl his debit card.

She swiped the card. "It's not going through," she said. After passing the card through the machine a second time, she apologized. "This doesn't automatically mean that there's a problem with the account," she said. "You'll have to contact your bank. Would you like to try another account?"

"I don't have another. Tell me the total?"

"Three hundred and forty-one dollars and sixty cents."

His anxiety spiked and he took a breath. How could a bouquet of flowers be that much?

He put his hand in his pocket and felt around for cash, but what was the point?

"Hold on a minute," he said.

What to do, what to do? He was going to have to call his wife. Was he going to have to call her? He was going to have to call her. He took out his phone and dialled—in that moment he was glad that he had his meds on board—and right away Kate picked up and hollered, "Where *are* you? I'm at the restaurant with Susan! Elliot is out parking the car. Did you go to your *therapy*?"

"Could you not shout, Kate?"

"It's goddam packed in here!"

"I need to talk to you, privately," he said, and turned away from the shopgirl. But there was no way, in the small space, to keep the girl from overhearing, so he put his hand over the phone, leaned toward her, and whispered, "I'll be right back," then stepped out of the shop, stood on the sidewalk in the freezing wind, and slowly, deliberately humiliated himself, saying to Kate, "I stopped on my way home and bought you flowers, but the bank account isn't coöperating with my card for some reason and now I'm stuck at the florist's because I don't have enough cash on me, and I think the problem is simply that—shit, I don't know what the problem is, I must not have kept my eye on the balance, and it's possible that we're overdrawn. I know we've talked about this. But it's not a serious problem, I promise."

"Oh, Jim. Are you *spending*? How much have you *spent*?" Kate cried, and he winced.

He said, "Is Susan there?"

"Do you not hear a word I say? She's right here! We're drinking Manhattans. Are you coming? We're waiting for you. Why do you want to talk to Susan? Jim, are you spending our money?"

"I don't want to talk to Susan. I'd just prefer that this conversation be private between the two of us."

"Please, Jim, as if everyone we know doesn't already know everything there is to know?"

"I'm not—I am not spending our money."

"You're agitated."

"Why are you diagnosing me? I'm not agitated. I wanted to surprise you with flowers. But clearly it was just another of my many mistakes. I'll think twice next time. Everything I do is unwanted."

"Stop it," Kate said to him then.

Through the phone he could hear sounds from the restaurant bar, voices and other noises in the after-work crush. Then the wind came up, and the only sound he heard was the phone's own static. The wind died, and Kate's voice was saying, "Elliot is here now, and Lorenzo is clearing us a table. Let me talk to someone about the flowers."

In this way he was forced to trudge back into the shop, hold the phone out, and say to the girl, "She wants to talk to you."

The girl hesitated, then reached out and let him pass the phone into her hand.

"Hello?" she said into his phone.

He retreated to a corner of the store. Joking aside, he didn't care to loiter about, smelling the flowers, while the girl wrote down his wife's American Express number. He would never learn the girl's name, not now, Kate would see to that, he told himself as he peered out from his hiding place behind a leafy potted tree. He saw the shop's buckets of flowers and the refrigerators in a row, and the door leading to the back, but where was the girl? He heard her laugh in response to some remark Kate must've made, and realized that she was standing behind the bouquet. "Oh, don't I just know that about men and their important purchases!" she exclaimed.

What was Kate saying to her? Was he being made fun of, as usual? Was she calling him bipolar?

He had a problem with anxiety and suicidality, and, as Kate

had reminded him in their conversation a moment earlier, everyone knew about his previous autumn's sojourns on the Fifty-ninth Street Bridge and his games of chicken—no, not games, not at all, really—on the fire escape outside their bedroom window.

He didn't want to think about any of that. Yet it was the reason he was now crouched behind a ficus, eavesdropping while a girl he wanted to fuck got treated to an earful of Kate—on *his* phone! And what was the big problem, anyway, if, a handful of times on his way home from day care, as he sometimes called his ongoing treatment, he'd got excited about life and jumped off the crosstown bus at Fifth Avenue and run into Bergdorf Goodman and ridden the elevator to the second floor and tried on clothes until closing? Was that unhealthy? His doctors didn't think he was manic-depressive; in fact, they'd ruled it out. Kate had been reading the clinical literature, though, and felt autodidactically certain that the Payne Whitney professionals were minimizing something in plain sight: his death-trip history, considered alongside the "conspicuous" spending on coats, ties, shirts, and shoes, represented, at the least, she thought, a mixed-state depression. "Why don't they have you on Olanzapine?" she'd got in the habit of asking him. He begged her not to interfere with his treatment, and suggested—thinking of her father's death and the forfeiture of the family farm in Massachusetts, when she was a teen-ager—that her consuming anxiety about bankruptcy, her emphasis on this as a potentially mortal trauma, might have less to do with his new handmade suits than with the ways in which his almost dying had reactivated an old mourning in her.

He peered from behind the ficus. He was wearing a ridiculous cashmere overcoat, and his suit today was a medium-gray flannel herringbone. It featured, on the jacket, minimal shoulder padding, dual vents, and a graceful, three-rolled-to-two-button stance (his current favorite lapel style), and, on the pants, single-reverse pleats and one-and-a-quarter-inch-cuffed trouser legs. Why would a man ever not cuff his trousers? He kept a single jacket-sleeve button open on the left, another open on the right. He didn't look like blown credit. Did he?

Kate was going to kill him. She was mad enough to kill him. That was a fact. What was he doing, charging expensive flowers for no reason on an average night in the middle of the week when they were already committed to a crippling tab—it was sure to be a huge bar bill, by evening's close—for dinner with Elliot and Susan? But, Kate thought, as she sat with their friends, waiting for him at a tiny table near the back of the restaurant, this was how it went with her husband: he made the gestures; she absorbed the costs. "How awful this all is," she sighed. She was on the phone to the girl at the florist's. Kate hadn't meant to be audible, not to the girl, and certainly not to Elliot, who would take her vexation over Jim as a cue to call her up the next day and argue for more afternoons at the hotel.

She'd been going once or sometimes twice a week to the East Side to meet Elliot at the Lowell Hotel, on Sixty-third Street between Madison and Park. She rode the bus. Typically, she arrived first. She got the room key, went up, and showered; if Elliot was held up at the lab and the day was growing dark, she might unlock the minibar and concoct a Manhattan or an approximation of a Manhattan, then recline naked by the window and look north toward the East Nineties, Carnegie Hill, where her mother, an only child, like Kate, had lived before marrying her father and moving to the farm.

Manhattans had been her mother's drink. Unlike her mother, Kate tried to keep herself to three an evening. At Lorenzo's that night, she was ahead of pace, finishing her second before having eaten a bite. She held her glass in one hand and her phone in the other, listening hard through the restaurant noise as the girl at the florist's recited back her AmEx number. Elliot sat quietly beside her. He had his arms crossed, and his chair pushed back at an angle to make room for his legs. Susan had got up from the table; she'd announced to Kate—sounding well on the way to being tight—"Kate, you're my best friend, but I don't know how you drink such a strong drink." To Kate and Elliot together, she'd added, "Will you two do me a big giant favor? Will you snag Lorenzo and ask him to bring me a Cosmo?"

"Don't utter a word to me about my husband," Kate warned Elliot, once Susan had gone to the bathroom.

Into the phone, to the girl, she said, "I'm sorry, I didn't mean you. I was talking to somebody else."

Meanwhile, in the women's room, Susan was on her own phone, calling Jim's number from a stall.

It was the girl who answered, of course.

"Hello, can you hold?" the girl said. The line went briefly dead. After a pause, the girl came back and said, "May I ask who is calling?"

"May I ask who's answering?"

"Hold, please."

"Sir?" the girl called out to Jim. She looked this way and that for him. Where had he gone? The shop closed at eight. It was nearly closing time. "A woman is calling you!"

"I'm here! I'm right here!" he answered from behind his tree.

"He'll be with you in one second," he heard her promise the caller. After that, there was a pause, before, in a businesslike tone, the girl resumed with Kate. "I'm sorry to have to ask you this again. Would you mind verifying the last five digits and the expiration date?"

Back when he was in the hospital—in the past six months, there had been three emergency-room visits and two locked-ward admissions—he had spent day after day lying on a mattress, crying. His doctors (along with the psychiatric nurses and the social workers who led the daily therapy groups) had encouraged him to uncurl himself from the fetal position and try, at least try, to watch television or play a board game with the other patients, but this had mostly proved too great a challenge. There had been times when, walking to or from the bathroom or the water fountain or the patients' common room, or standing in line to receive his medications at the nurses' station, or even simply sitting upright on the table in the examining room, he'd had the strong sensation that the air through which he moved was gathering around him and becoming—really, no word was sufficient to name it—substantive. Its weight pressed in on him. This hurt, it hurt terribly, yet when he tried to locate the source of the pain he could not: it came, as he knew, only from himself. On the mattress, shattered and sobbing over, say, Kate and their messed-up love, he'd lain crushed, as if by atmospheres.

"Sir?"

The girl's voice seemed to echo through the shop. He peeked up. When had she come out from behind the bouquet? He could see her standing on the other side of the tree. She was looking at him through the leaves.

"Are you all right, sir?"

"I maybe—I need a minute." His mouth was dry and his heart was beating fast. That could be his meds, of course.

"There's someone who wants to talk to you. Do you think you can take the call? Would you like to try?" She held his phone out with one hand, reaching toward him through the branches.

He had to reach into the tree to meet her hand. He was sweating.

"Hello?" he said into the phone.

"What the hell, Jim?" Susan said to him from the women's-room toilet at Lorenzo's.

"Susan, how are you?" he said.

"I've been better."

"I'm sorry."

"We're all here, Jim. We're waiting and waiting for you."

"I'm doing my best to get there. Have you ordered yet? What are the specials? What looks good?"

"Kate is beside herself. She says the two of you are bankrupt. She says you've spent all the money."

"I haven't."

"Don't lie to me, Jim. Please, don't lie to me." She was sniffling, beginning to weep, lightly.

"Stop crying, stop crying, baby," he whispered into the phone. Then he laid his hand over the receiver and said to the girl, who was still peering down at him through the leaves of the tree, "You'll have to excuse me one more time." With a powerful effort of will, he stood upright and came out from behind the ficus. He didn't dare look at the girl, but he heard her telling him, as he pushed painfully past her toward the door, that it looked like his wife's American Express card wasn't working, either—and was there any way for him to pay for the flowers?

He waved his hand, motioning that he'd return. He stepped out into the cold on Broadway. He pulled up his overcoat's shawl collar. The door to the florist's closed behind him.

Back at their table for four, Kate and Elliot had hit a snag.

"Let me talk to him," Elliot said. He had his elbows on the table. He'd drunk almost none of his Scotch.

"That's not a good idea."

"Give me your phone." He held out his hand.

"I'm on hold."

"Kate," he said.

"Leave me alone."

"As you wish," he said, leaning back in his chair, and she burst out at him, "How can you act like this? You're a doctor. How can you be so unfeeling?"

He said, "What does my being a doctor have to do with my feelings?" (She rolled her eyes at this, but he didn't appear to notice.) He went on, "I may be a doctor, but I'm not your husband's doctor."

"His name is Jim, remember?"

"I think you're drunk. That's what I think."

He got up from the table, patted his pockets—checking for his own phone—and said, "God damn it, I do research. I don't treat patients. He has excellent doctors. I'll call him myself."

When he'd gone and Kate was alone, Lorenzo arrived with Susan's Cosmopolitan.

"Everybody has gone away and left you," Lorenzo said, and Kate chirped back, "Everybody's gone!"

"Let me bring you another Manhattan." Lorenzo placed Susan's cocktail on the table and picked up Kate's empty glass. Kate managed a little smile. She held her phone to her ear. "Jim? Jim, are you there?" she whispered.

Six blocks downtown, Jim was on the line to Susan. "I'm here, I'm here with you, baby," he assured her. In fact, he wasn't thinking of sleeping with her again. Oh, he'd loved sleeping with Susan—that wasn't the problem. But that evening his body was compressing: the weight of the air was on him, flattening his libido and his trust in humankind.

"Susan," he said. "Susan."

"What is it?" she said. Her voice filled the stall. "What is happening? Is it happening? Is it happening to you now? I'm so scared. What do I *do*?"

"Susan," he said. "Susan."

He explained to her that in a few minutes he was going to calmly walk back inside the florist's and steal a mysterious and beautiful bouquet that he and an angel had made for Kate. He'd helped the angel, he pointed out. He was feeling honest. He acknowledged to Susan that he was speaking metaphorically when it came to angels—in order to seem aboveboard and keep her trust. He needed her to be cool when he entered the restaurant, he told her. Then he ended the call and switched over to Kate.

"I'm coming," he said.

"I'm glad," she said.

"I love you," he said.

"I love you, I love you," she said. She was alone at their table.

She said, "Have you talked to Elliot?"

He said, "I haven't heard from him."

Elliot, in the meantime, had been unable to get through, Jim's phone lines having been taken up by both their wives. He'd left two messages already, one saying, "Jim, call me, all right?," the other, "Jim, will you call me?" His third attempt got through, but Jim didn't answer. He heard the beeping, plucked the phone away from his ear, glanced at it, saw who was calling, and said, to Kate, "It's him. There is no way that I want to speak to him right now."

"I understand," she said. Then she said, "Just get here, dear, and have dinner with us. We all need food. We need to eat."

He said, "Has he taken care with you, since I've been gone?"

"Gone?" she said.

"I don't know how else to put it."

She asked, "Will you stay where you are, until people come?"

"Don't send an ambulance," he said to her.

He put his phone in his pocket. He turned and faced the door to the flower shop. A few people swept past him on the windy avenue—or so it seemed; his thoughts were with the pain that was coalescing beneath his temple. He wanted to put it out. He could imagine different ways to do this. This was how it was when his mind turned to high open windows or unlocked rooftop fire doors or breaks in the chain-link fences lining bridge walkways.

He took a step forward. The door was made partly of glass, and he could see into the shop. It occurred to him that it would be easy to break the window with his fist and deliberately cut up the veins in his arms. Instead, he put his hand on the doorframe and pushed. He stuck his head inside. He was acting guiltily, though he knew there was no reason to, not at the florist's—he hadn't done anything yet. Still, he snuck in, ashamed.

The girl was nowhere in sight. The bouquet looked bigger than it had the last time he'd sized it up. How would he manage to get it up Broadway in his trembling hands? Beside it on the table—careful, he had to be careful—were the girl's pruning shears, as well as regular scissors and a small sharp knife.

He told himself to let those things lie.

Uptown at the restaurant, Lorenzo brought Kate her drink. She asked for bread, and apologized to him for taking so long to order dinner. "We'll all be here together soon," she sighed.

She was right about that. Elliot had given up trying to reach Jim, and the cold had driven him back inside. He was threading his way down the aisle to their table. Susan, too, would return, as soon as she had peed. Pride had made her unable to, while on the phone.

And that left Jim, who had no desire to become a thief. Might he, instead, offer something in barter for the flowers? His wristwatch wasn't worth much. His overcoat was brand-new, and cost well more than the watch and the bouquet combined. He decided to leave an I.O.U., promising to come back another day with money, or, if not with actual money, then with a clear idea of when one or another of his or his wife's credit cards might again be active and usable.

But when he tried to hold a pen in his hand, he could not; and when he tried to focus his eyes on the piece of paper lying beside the cash register—it was the scrap of a receipt on which the girl had pencilled Kate's American Express information—he found that his mind was frantic. This was his disorder. This was the descent. He crumpled the receipt and shoved it into his pocket. He reached for the bouquet. The girl had put water in the vase.

Had you been walking downtown on Broadway that February night at a little past eight, you might have seen a man hurrying toward you with a great concrescence of blooms. You might have noticed that he did not even pause for traffic signals, but charged across streets against the lights; and so you might rightly have supposed that he could not see through the floral arrangement that he held (doing what he could to keep clear of thorns) at arm's length before him. Whenever a siren sounded in the distance—and, once, beating helicopter blades in the night sky caused him to sprint up a side street—he dropped into a furtive, crouching gait. His balance was off; he was paranoid about police. Windblown flowers lashed at his head. Seen from a distance, he might have brought to mind an old, out-of-favor stereotype: the savage in a headdress. But as he came closer, you would have noticed his European clothes, his stylish haircut; and you might have asked yourself, "What's wrong with that man?"

Had you stepped to the side as he hurtled past, tightened your scarf securely around your neck, and continued on your way, you might next have encountered a young woman on a street corner, distraught and coatless. "Did you happen to see a man carrying a bouquet of flowers?" she might have asked in a startled voice, and you would have looked away from her bare, pale legs, pointed upwind, and told her, "He went that way." By then, the first snowflakes would have been swirling through the caverns between the apartment buildings, down onto the thoroughfare.

Jim looked up and saw the snow on his way into Lorenzo's. For an instant, he took it as an omen—of what, though? He pulled hard on the restaurant door, forcing it open, and stumbled with his tattered flowers into the dark realm between the door and the velvet drapes that had been hung to keep the cold from sweeping in over diners at the front of the room.

He parted the curtains. "Pardon me," he said to the people seated near the entrance. Long- and short-stemmed flowers alike had snagged on the drapes. Now a waiter approached—and here came Lorenzo, too, calling, in his soft, *ristoratore's* voice, "*Ciao*, James. *Ciao*. I cannot call you Jim, you know."

"Lorenzo, *ciao*," Jim said. The waiter was busy tugging on the curtains. Lorenzo lent a hand. "This way, try this way," Lorenzo instructed. Jim spun left then right, enshrouding himself—and the bouquet—within the folds of drapery fabric. There followed a flurry of petals. The rose thorns came loose; the bouquet's topmost stems sprung free. He tumbled out into the room.

"I'm good, I'm fine," he said, nodding reassuringly (he hoped) to Lorenzo, the waiter, the people who'd turned in their seats to stare.

"What has happened to you, James?" Lorenzo pulled his white silk pocket square from his breast pocket and reached around the yellow and pink and blue and white flowers to dab at Jim's forehead.

"I ran all the way here," Jim said.

"You're bleeding," Lorenzo told him. Jim saw the blood spotting Lorenzo's handkerchief.

Lorenzo said, "You have a lot of scratches. You look like you've been in a fight with some squirrels or something." He laughed, nicely.

"I've—I have been fighting, Lorenzo. Not with squirrels. Roses," Jim specified, and Lorenzo said, "Ah, of course. Let me take them."

He spoke to the waiter. "Paul, will you please take these from James?" To Jim, he added, "We will bring them to your table."

"No, no," Jim said. He explained to Lorenzo that the flowers were a gift for Kate, and that he needed to present them himself. This was crucial, he informed Lorenzo. He clutched the vase. His pants were wet from water that had sloshed over the rim. Water stained his shoes. He could see tiny snags marking the sleeves of his overcoat and the front of his suit. How frustrating, after having labored so hard to avoid the thorns. His clothes would have to go to a reweaver, he thought. Then his thinking disintegrated into bitter resignation. Everything he touched was ruined. The flowers were almost destroyed.

Nonetheless, he bore them down the aisle. Here and there, people ducked forward in their chairs, or to the side, letting him through. As he progressed toward the back, the room quieted. People put down their silverware, their wineglasses; Jim felt eyes watching him.

"Eat! Live while you can!" he wanted to proclaim to the crowd. But what did he have to teach anyone? He was a thief, a common criminal—worse. He'd stolen a bouquet to give to the love of his life.

When she saw him, she was filled with happiness. She'd had a lot to drink—but, well, it wasn't that alone.

"Kate," he said. She stood, and he lurched toward her. Elliot and Susan stood as well. They flanked Kate, who came out from between them—not unlike Jim, she was unsteady on her feet—saying, "I'm sorry, excuse me," as she tacked her way through the sea of tables.

They met near the bathrooms. The bar was to their right. Kate raised her open hands to wipe the blood from his face. Blood had run down his neck, and stained the collar of his shirt. "These are for you," he told her.

She was quietly crying, whispering, "They're beautiful, beautiful." Then her crying began in force, and she wailed, "You made it, oh, you *made* it, we were all so scared, and I felt so lost."

"I'm here," he said, and his own tears started. He wanted to tell her that everything would be better, that *he* would be better, that one day soon he would work again, and start paying some bills, and take the burden off her shoulders; that they would be able, at last, to leave the little apartment with the busted plumbing. He wanted to tell her how much he needed her.

But he could see, out of the corner of his eye, his horrid reflection in the mirror behind the bar. He looked down at Kate's hands, the blood smeared across her palms. And he saw the restaurant-goers and the waiters and waitresses and busboys, who, not knowing what to make of the bleeding and the crying and the broken lilies arcing over Jim and Kate's heads like some insane wedding canopy, had come from the kitchen or the bar to stand mutely around them. The pain in his body grew, and the words that spilled out of him were not words of love. Or they were. He spoke to his wife, as he spoke to the people gathered.

"Don't you see, Kate? Don't you *see*? It's time for me to go. I can't do this anymore. I have no place here. I don't belong. I hurt so. You can live and be happy. That will never be for me."

"No, no, baby," she wept at him.

Someone touched his arm. It was Elliot, who'd come up behind him. He said to Jim, "Let's get in the car."

Lorenzo was there, too. Kate said to Jim, "Honey, let Lorenzo take the flowers. Just for now," and he did.

A moment later, Lorenzo came back with a wet cloth. Kate used it to wipe her eyes and to clean Jim's face and her hands. She tied the belt around his overcoat. She said, "There."

They went out of the restaurant, the four of them. Susan let Jim lean on her, and Elliot steadied Kate. On the way out the door, they heard Lorenzo, behind them, telling his patrons, "Everything is all right. Our friend has had a bad time. Please, let me buy everyone a drink."

On Broadway, the wind had died, and the air seemed to have warmed. They walked out into new snow. And, wouldn't you know, Jim did wrap his arm around Susan's shoulders, and Elliot ducked down close to Kate, listening to her mumble whatever it was she had to say to him.

At the garage, Jim and Kate got into the back seat of Elliot's car. Susan sat beside Elliot. Elliot started the engine, turned on the headlights and the windshield wipers. *Thump, thump, thump.* He steered east. During the trip, Jim took his belt from around his waist. He gave Kate his scarf and his phone and his keys and all his money, which amounted to about thirty dollars.

Later, she would get on her knees on the emergency-room floor and extract the laces from his shoes. A nurse would come, then another, and a doctor promising sleeping pills.

By that time, after midnight, Elliot and Susan would have driven up the F.D.R. Drive and out of Manhattan, through the Bronx, and into Westchester County.

"You can go home now, if you'd like," the doctor said to Kate. "We won't let anything happen to him."

He gave Kate a plastic garbage bag, into which she put Jim's overcoat and his suit jacket. She would use the last of his money for her crosstown taxi, and for milk and cereal at the Korean market near the apartment.

In the deep of the night, they came for him. A male nurse helped him into a wheelchair, and then pushed him through the white labyrinth of hallways and waited for the elevator.

Margaret, one of the night nurses, met him on the ward. She said, "Hello, Mr. Davis. You're back with us again, I see." She asked, "Do you think you can walk?" She gave him Ativan and a paper cup of water, and watched while he swallowed. Then she showed him to a room of his own.

IN THE SOUTH

BY SALMAN RUSHDIE (2009)

The day that Junior fell down began like any other day: the explosion of heat rippling the air, the trumpeting sunlight, the traffic's tidal surges, the prayer chants in the distance, the cheap film music rising from the floor below, the loud pelvic thrusts of an "item number" dancing across a neighbor's TV, a child's cry, a mother's rebuke, unexplained laughter, scarlet expectorations, bicycles, the newly plaited hair of schoolgirls, the smell of strong sweet coffee, a green wing flashing in a tree. Senior and Junior, two very old men, opened their eyes in their bedrooms on the fourth floor of a sea-green building on a leafy lane, just out of sight of Elliot's Beach, where, that evening, the young would congregate, as they always did, to perform the rites of youth, not far from the village of the fisherfolk, who had no time for such frivolity. The poor were puritans by night and day. As for the old, they had rites of their own and did not need to wait for evening. With the sun stabbing at them through their window blinds, the two old men struggled to their feet and lurched out onto their adjacent verandas, emerging at almost the same moment, like characters in an ancient tale, trapped in fateful coincidences, unable to escape the consequences of chance.

Almost at once they began to speak. Their words were not new. These were ritual speeches, obeisances to the new day, offered in call-and-response format, like the rhythmic dialogues or "duels" of the virtuosos of Carnatic music during the annual December festival.

"Be thankful we are men of the south," Junior said, stretching and yawning. "Southerners are we, in the south of our city in the south of our country in the south of our continent. God be praised. We are warm, slow, and sensual guys, not like the cold fishes of the north." Senior, scratching first his belly and then the back of his neck, contradicted him at once. "In the first place," Senior said, "the south is a fiction, existing only because men have agreed to call it that. Suppose men had imagined the earth the other way up! We would be the northerners then. The universe does not understand up and down; neither does a dog. To a dog, there is no north or south. In this regard, the points of the compass are like money, which has value only because men say that it does. And in the second place you're not that warm a character, and a woman would laugh to hear you call yourself sensual. But you are slow—that is beyond a doubt."

This was how they were: they fought, going at each other like ancient wrestlers whose left feet were tied together at the ankles. The rope that bound them so tightly was their name. By a curious chance—which they had come to think of as "destiny" or, as they more often called it, "a curse"—they shared a name, a long name like so many names of the south, a name that neither of them cared to speak. By banishing the name, by reducing it to its initial letter, "V," they made the rope invisible, which did not mean that it did not exist. They echoed each other in other ways—their voices were high, they were of a similarly wiry build and medium height, they were both nearsighted, and, after a lifetime of priding themselves on the quality of their teeth, they had both surrendered to the humiliating inevitability of dentures—but it was the unused name, that symmetrical V., the Name That Could Not Be Spoken, that had joined them together, like Siamese twins, for decades. The two old men did not share a birthday, however. One was seventeen days older than the other. That must have been how "Senior" and "Junior" got started, though the nicknames had been in use so long now that nobody could remember who had originally thought them up. V. Senior and V. Junior they had become, Junior V. and Senior V. forevermore, quarrelling to the death. They were eighty-one years old.

"You look terrible," Junior told Senior, as he did every morning. "You look like a man who is only waiting to die."

Senior—nodding gravely, and also speaking in accordance with their private tradition—responded, "That is better than looking, as you do, like a man who is still waiting to live."

Neither man slept well anymore. At night they lay on hard beds without pillows and, behind their closed eyelids, their unsettled thoughts ran in opposite directions. Of the two men, V. Senior had lived by far the fuller life. He had been the youngest of ten brothers, all of whom had excelled in their chosen fields—as athletes, scientists, teachers, soldiers, priests. He himself had begun his career as a college-champion long-distance runner, had then risen to a senior position with the railway company, and for years had travelled the railroads, covering tens of thousands of miles to assure himself and the authorities that the proper safety levels were being maintained. He had married a kind woman and fathered six daughters and three sons, each of whom had proved fertile in his or her turn, providing him with a haul of thirty-three grandchildren. His nine brothers had sired a total of thirty-three more children, his nephews and nieces, who had inflicted upon him no fewer than a hundred and eleven further relatives. To many this would have been proof of his good fortune, for a man blessed with two hundred and four family members was a rich man indeed, but abundance gave the ascetically inclined Senior a permanent low-level headache. "If I had been sterile," he told Junior frequently, "how peaceful life would be."

After his retirement, Senior had been one of a group of ten friends who met every day to discuss politics, chess, poetry, and music at a local Besant Nagar coffeehouse, and several of his commentaries on these topics had been published in the excellent daily newspaper based in the city. Among his friends was the editor of that newspaper, and also one of the editor's employees—a celebrated local figure, a bit of a firebrand and too much of a boozer, but the creator of wonderfully grotesque political cartoons. Then there was the city's finest astrologer, who had been trained as an astronomer but had come to believe that the true messages of the stars could not be received through a telescope; and a fellow who for many years had fired the starting pistol at the racetrack's well-attended meets; and so on. Senior had revelled in the company of these men, telling his wife that it was a grand thing for a man to have friends from whom he could learn something new every day. But now they were all dead. His friends had gone up in flames one by one, and the coffeehouse that might have preserved their memory had been torn down, too. Of the ten brothers only he remained, and the brothers' wives, too, were long departed. Even his own kindly wife was dead, and he had remarried, finding himself a woman with a wooden leg, toward whom he behaved with an irritability that surprised his children and grandchildren. "Not having much choice at my age," he would say to her, hurtfully, "I chose you." She retaliated by ignoring his simplest demands, even requests for water, which no civilized person should ever refuse. Her name was Aarthi, but he never used it. Nor did he call her by a diminutive or an endearment. To him she was always "Woman" or "Wife."

Senior endured the multiple health problems of the very old, the daily penances of bowel and urethra, of back and knee, the milkiness climbing in his eyes, the breathing troubles, the nightmares, the slow failing of the soft machine. His days emptied out into tedious inaction. Once, he had given lessons in mathematics, singing, and the Vedas to pass the time. But his pupils had all gone away. There remained the wife with the wooden leg, the blurry television set, and Junior. It was not, by a long chalk, enough. Each morning he regretted that he had not died in the night. Of his two hundred and four family members, quite a few had already gone to their fiery rest. He forgot exactly how many, and their names, inevitably, eluded him. Many of the survivors came to see him and treated him with gentleness and care. When he said that he was ready to die, which was often, their faces took on hurt expressions and their bodies sagged or stiffened, depending on their nature, and they spoke to him reassuringly, encouragingly, and, of course, in injured tones, of the value of a life so full of love. But love had begun to annoy him, like everything else. His was a family of mosquitoes, he thought, a buzzing swarm, and love was their itchy bite. "If only there were a coil one could light to keep one's relations away," he told Junior. "If only there were a net around one's cot that kept them out."

Junior's life had been a disappointment to him. He had not expected to be ordinary. He had been reared by doting parents who had instilled in him a sense of destiny and entitlement, but he had turned out to be an average sort of fellow, doomed by average academic achievement to a life of clerical work in the offices of the municipal water board. His above-average dreams—of road travel, rail travel, air travel, perhaps even space travel—had long since been abandoned. Yet he was not an unhappy man. The discovery of his affliction with the incurable disease of mediocrity might have cowed a less ebullient spirit, but he remained bright-eyed, with a ready smile for the world. Still, in spite of his apparent enthusiasm for life, there was a certain deficiency in the energy department. He did not run but walked, and walked slowly—had done so even in the distant years of his youth. He abhorred exercise and had a way of poking gentle fun at those who took it. Nor did he interest himself in politics, or the all-pervasive popular culture of the cinema and the music that it spawned. In all significant particulars, he had failed to be a participant in the parade of life. He had not married. The great events of eight decades had managed to occur without any effort on his part to help them along. He had stood by and watched as an empire fell and a nation rose, and avoided expressing an opinion on the matter. He had been a man at a desk. Maintaining the flow of the municipality's water had been a sufficient challenge for him. Yet he gave every appearance of being a man for whom living was still a joy. He had been an only child, so there were few relatives to look out for him in his advanced years. Senior's immense family had adopted him long ago and brought him tiffin and attended to his needs.

The question of the dividing wall between Senior's and Junior's adjoining apartments was sometimes raised by the visiting hordes of Senior's blood kin: whether it should be taken down so that the two old men could share their lives more easily. On this matter, however, Junior and Senior spoke with one voice.

"No!" Junior said.

"Over my dead body," Senior clarified.

"Which would make the whole exercise pointless, anyhow," Junior said, as if that settled things.

The wall remained in place.

Junior had one friend, D'Mello, a man twenty years younger than him, an old colleague from his water-board days. D'Mello had grown up in another city, Mumbai, the legendary bitch-city, *urbs prima in Indis*, and had to be spoken to in English. Whenever D'Mello visited Junior, Senior sulked and refused to speak, even though, secretly, he was proud of his prowess in what he called "the world's No. 1 tongue." Junior tried to hide from Senior how much he looked forward to D'Mello's comings; the younger man bubbled with a kind of cosmopolitan brio that Junior found inspirational. D'Mello always arrived with stories—sometimes angry accounts of injustices against the poor in a Mumbai slum, sometimes funny anecdotes about the characters who took their ease at the Wayside Inn, the famous Mumbai café in the Kala Ghoda area, named for a no longer present equestrian statue, "the Black Horse district from which the black horse has been exiled." D'Mello fell in love with movie stars (from a distance, of course), and provided gory details of the killing spree of a not-yet-arrested madman in the district of Trombay. "The miscreant is still at large!" he cried gaily. His conversation was littered with wonderful names: Worli Sea Face, Bandra, Hornby Vellard, Breach Candy, Pali Hill. These places sounded altogether more exotic than the prosaic localities to which Junior was accustomed: Besant Nagar, Adyar, Mylapore.

D'Mello's most heartbreaking Mumbai story was his tale of the great poet of the city, who had surrendered to Alzheimer's disease. The poet still walked to his small magazine-infested office every day, without knowing why he went there. His feet knew the way, and so he went and sat looking into space until it was time to go home again and his feet walked him back to his shabby residence, through the evening crowds massing outside Churchgate station—the jasmine sellers, the hustling urchins, the roar of the B.E.S.T. buses, the girls on their Vespas, the sniffing, hungry dogs.

When D'Mello was present and talking, Junior had the sense that he was living another, very different life, a life of action and color; that he was becoming, vicariously, the type of man he had never been—dynamic, passionate, engaged with the world. Senior, observing the light in Junior's eyes, inevitably became cross. One day, when D'Mello was speaking of Mumbai and its people with his habitual, gesticulating fervor, Senior, breaking his rule of silence, snapped at him in English, "Why your body doesn't return there only since your head has already gone?" But D'Mello shook his head sadly. He no longer had a foothold in his city of origin. Only in his dreams and conversations was it still his home. "I will die here," he answered Senior. "In the south, among sour fruits like you."

. . .

Senior's wife, the lady with the wooden leg, increasingly took her revenge upon her unloving husband by filling their apartment with family members. She, too, came from a large family, of hundreds of persons, and she began most particularly to invite her younger relations, the great-nephews and great-nieces, with their wives and husbands and, especially, their babies in tow. The presence in the small apartment of large numbers of babies, toddlers, high-speed pigtailed girls, and slow plump boys fulfilled her own matriarchal ambitions, and also, very satisfyingly, drove Senior wild. It was the babies-in-law that really got his goat. The babies-in-law rattled their rattles and giggled their giggles and screamed their baby screams. They slept, and then Senior had to be quiet, or they woke up, and then Senior could not hear himself think. They ate and defecated and puked, and the smell of excrement and vomit remained in the apartment, even when the babies-in-law had gone, mingling with a smell that Senior disliked even more: that of talcum powder. "At the end of life," he complained to Junior, in whose apartment he often took refuge from the squalling hordes of his and his wife's blood kin, "nothing stinks worse than the smells of life's sweet beginning—bibs and ribbons and warm bottled milk and formula, and farting, talcumed behinds." Junior could not help replying, "Soon you also will be helpless and need someone to tend to your natural functions. Babydom is not only our past but our future, too." The thunderous expression on Senior's face revealed that the words had hit their mark.

For, it's true, they were both fortunate men. They were neither wholly blind nor wholly deaf, and their minds had not betrayed them like the Mumbai poet's. The food they ate was soft and easily digestible, but it was not old buggers' mush. Above all they were still ambulatory, still able, once a week, to climb slowly down their building's stairs to street level, and then to shuffle along, helped by walking sticks and frequent little rest stops, to the local post office, where they cashed their pension slips. They did not need to do this. Many of the young who thronged Senior's apartment, driving him next door to quarrel with Junior, would readily have dashed down the street to cash the checks for the frail old gentlemen. But the gentlemen did not care to allow the young to dash for them. It was a point of pride to cash one's own pension slip—on this, if on nothing else, they agreed—to travel under one's own steam to the counter where, behind a metal grille, a postal-services operative waited to dispense the weekly sum that was their return for a lifetime's service. "You can see the respect in the fellow's expression," Senior said loudly to Junior, who kept mum, because what he saw behind the grille was something more like boredom, or contempt.

To Senior the pension trip was an act of validation; the weekly sum, small as it was, honored his deeds, transmuting into banknotes society's gratitude for his life. Junior thought of the journey more as an act of defiance. "You care nothing for me," he once said flatly to the face behind the grille. "It means nothing to you to count out the cash. But, when your turn comes to stand where I stand, then you will comprehend." One of the few privileges of very old age was that you were allowed to say exactly what you thought, even to strangers. Nobody told you to keep your mouth shut, and few people had the guts to answer back. They think we will soon be dead, Junior thought, so there's no point getting into a fight with us. He understood the nature of the contempt in the eyes of the post-office employee. It was the scorn of life for death.

On the day that Junior fell down, he and Senior set forth on their errand at their customary midmorning hour. It was late in the year. The local Christians, D'Mello included, had just finished celebrating their Savior's birth, and the consequent proximity of New Year's Eve—with its promise of a future, of, indeed, an interminable future in which a sequence of such Eves stretched out at their predetermined intervals toward infinity—was bothering Senior. "Either I will die in the next five days, meaning that there will be no new year for me," he told Junior, "or else a year will begin in which my end will surely come, which is hardly a thing to look forward to." Junior sighed. "Your gloom and doom," he moaned, "will be the death of me." This sentence struck them both as so funny that they laughed heartily, and then for a while they had to huff and puff for breath. They were descending their building's staircase at this point, so the laughter was not without danger. They clung to the bannisters and panted. Junior was lower down than Senior, past the second-floor landing. This was how they customarily descended, some distance apart, so that if one of them should fall he would not drag the other down with him. They were too unsteady to trust each other. Trust, too, was a casualty of age.

In the front yard they paused briefly by the golden-shower tree that stood there. They had watched it grow from a tiny shoot to its present sixty-foot grandeur. It had grown quickly, and, though they did not say so, this rapid growth had disturbed them, suggesting, as it did, the speed of the passing of the years. The Indian laburnum: that was another name for it, a name among many names. It was *konrai* in their own, southern language, *amaltas* in the tongue of the north, *Cassia fistula* in the language of flowers and trees. "It has stopped growing now," Junior said, approvingly, "having understood that eternity is better than progress. In the eye of God, time is eternal. This even animals and trees can comprehend. Only men have the illusion that time moves." Senior snorted. "The tree has stopped," he said, "because that is in its nature, just as it is in ours. We, too, will stop soon enough." He placed his gray trilby on his head and moved through the gate into the lane. Junior was bareheaded and traditionally dressed in a white *veshti* and a long blue checked shirt and sandals, but Senior liked to go to the post office in the guise of a European gentleman, wearing a suit and hat and twirling a silver-handled walking stick, like that Beau-somebody of Piccadilly of whom he had read, or the man in the old song he liked, *who walked along the Bois de Boulogne with an independent air*, the Man That Broke the Bank at Monte Caaar-lo.

The shady lane gave way to the brilliant sun-soaked street, where the noise of traffic drowned out the softer music of the sea. The beach was just four blocks away, but the city didn't care. Junior and Senior shuffled slowly past the homeopathy shop, the pharmacy where prescription drugs could easily be bought without troubling any doctor, the general store, with its jars of nuts and chilies, its tins of clarified butter and its imported cheese, and the sidewalk bookstall, with its many pirated editions of popular books brazenly on display, and set their sights on the traffic lights a hundred yards ahead. There they would have to cross the lawless main road, where a dozen forms of transport battled for space. After that a left turn, and another hundred yards of walking, and then they would be at the post office. A five-minute journey for the young, half an hour each way, minimum, for the two old men. The sun was behind them, and both men, inching slowly forward, were looking down at their shadows, which lay side by side upon the dusty pavement. Like lovers, they both thought, but neither of them spoke, their habit of opposition being too ingrained to permit them to express so fond an idea.

Afterward, Senior regretted that he had not spoken. "He was my shadow," he said to the woman with the wooden leg, "and I was his. Two shadows, each shadowing the other, to that we were reduced, that is so. The old move through the world of the young like shades, unseen, of no concern. But the shadows see each other and know who they are. So it was with us. We knew, let me say this, who we were. And now I am a shadow without a shadow to shadow. He who knew me knows nothing now, and therefore I am not known. What else, woman, is death?"

"The day you stop talking," she replied. "The day these tomfool notions stop dropping from your mouth. When your mouth itself has been eaten by the fire. That will be the day." It was the most she had said to him in more than a year, and he understood from it that she hated him, and was sorry that Junior was the one who had fallen.

It happened because of the girls on the Vespa, the girls on their new Vespa making their way to college, pigtails horizontal behind them as, giggling, they rode toward murder. Their faces were vivid in Senior's mind, the long thin one driving the scooter and her chubbier friend behind her, holding on *for dear life*. But life was not dear to such persons. Life was cheap, like a garment idly flung away after a single use, like their music, like their thoughts. This was how he judged them, and when he discovered afterward that they were not at all like his unjust characterization it was too late to change his mind. They were serious students, the thin one of electrical engineering and the other of architecture, and, far from being unaffected by the accident, they both went into dreadful, guilt-ridden shock, and for weeks afterward they could be seen almost every day standing silently with lowered heads across the lane from Junior's home, just standing there, heads bowed in expiation, waiting for forgiveness. But there was nobody to forgive them; the one who would have done so had died, and the one who could have done so would not. Haughty Senior looked down upon them with disdain. What did they think a human life was? Could it be so cheaply bought off? No, it could not. Let them stand there for a thousand years, it would not be long enough.

The Vespa had wobbled, no doubt about that; its young driver was inexperienced and it had wobbled too close to where Junior stood, waiting to cross the road. Of late he had been complaining of a weakness in his ankles. He had said, "Sometimes when I get out of bed I do not think that they will bear my weight." He had also said, "Sometimes when I go down the stairs I worry that an ankle will turn. I never used to worry about my ankles, but now I do." Senior had responded adversarially, as was customary. "Worry about your interior," he had said. "Your kidneys or your liver will fail long before your ankle does." However, he had been wrong. The Vespa had come too close and Junior had leaped back. When he landed on his left foot, his ankle had indeed turned, and that had induced a second half-leap, as Junior tried to save himself. So it had been a strange fall, more like a hop and a skip, but at the end there was the tumble, and Junior, toppling backward to the sidewalk, had bumped his head, not hard enough to be knocked out, but, still, hard enough. He was winded, too. Air left him in a great *whoosh* as he clattered down.

Senior was too busy shouting at the terrified girls on the Vespa, calling them assassins and worse things, to notice the moment when the thing happened that must happen to us all in the end, when the last little puff of vapor pops out of our mouths and dissolves into fetid air. "The spirit, whatever it is," Junior used to say. "I do not believe in an immortal soul, but I also do not believe that we are only flesh and bone. I believe in a mortal soul, the non-corporeal essence of ourselves, lurking within our flesh like a parasite, flourishing when we flourish, and dying when we die." Senior was more formal in his religious beliefs. He read the ancient texts often, and the sound of Sanskrit was for him akin to the music of the spheres—the subtlety and profundity of those texts, which were capable of questioning whether even the creative entity itself understood its creation. Once, he had discussed these texts with his students, but there had not been any students for a long time, and he had been obliged to keep his own counsel on the grand matters of being. The ancient ambiguities gave him joy; Junior's lay-philosophical invention of a soul that died was banal by comparison.

So Senior thought, and, ranting as he was, he missed the telltale little puff of air that might have persuaded him to think again. An instant later there was no Junior anymore, just a body on the sidewalk, a thing to be disposed of before the heat of the tropics did its malodorous worst. There was only one thing to be done. Senior reached into his friend's pocket and took out the pension slip. Then, sending the Vespa girls to his apartment to speak to his wife and relations, he set off on his mission alone. There would be time for death to be respected. In the traditions of the Palakkad Aiyars or Iyers, from whom both he and Junior were descended, the rites in honor of the dead lasted for thirteen days.

The next morning, in the south of the planet, far away from Senior's home town, but not far enough, there was a great earthquake under the ocean's surface, and the mighty water, answering the agony of the land beneath it with an agony of its own, gathered itself up into a series of waves and hurled its pain across the globe. Two such waves travelled across the Indian Ocean and, at a quarter to seven in the morning, Senior felt his bed begin to shake. It was a violent and puzzling vibration, because there had never been an earthquake in this city. Senior got up and went out onto his veranda. The veranda next door was empty, of course. Junior was gone. Junior was ashes now. The neighbors were all out in the lane, improperly dressed, hugging blankets around their shoulders. Everyone had a radio on. The earthquake's epicenter had been near the distant island of Sumatra. The tremors stopped and people went on with their day. Two and a quarter hours later, the first giant wave arrived.

The coastal areas were smashed. Elliot's Beach, Marina Beach, the beachfront houses, the cars, the Vespas, the people. At ten o'clock in the morning, the sea made a second such assault. The numbers of the dead grew: the lost dead, taken by the sea, the marooned dead, washed up on the remnants of the sands, the broken dead, everywhere the dead. The waves did not get as far as Senior's house. Senior's lane was undamaged. Everybody lived.

Except Junior.

It was fortunate that the waves arrived at Elliot's Beach in the morning. The romantic young who laughed and flirted there in the evenings would all have been slain if the waves had come at night. So young friends and lovers survived. The fishermen were not so lucky. The nearby fishing village—its name was Nochikuppam—ceased to exist. A seaside temple remained standing, but the fishermen's huts and catamarans and many of the fisherfolk themselves were lost. After that day the fishermen who survived said that they hated the sea and refused to return to it. For a long time it was hard to buy fish in the markets.

Senior did not like the Japanese word everyone used to name the waters of death. To him the waves were Death itself and needed no other name. Death had come to his city, had come a-harvesting and had taken Junior and many strangers away. In the aftermath of the waves, there grew up all around him, like a forest, the noises and actions that inevitably follow on calamity—the good behavior of the kind, the bad behavior of the desperate and the powerful, the surging aimless crowds. He was lost in the forest of the aftermath and saw nothing except the empty veranda next to his own and, in the lane below, the girls with the lowered heads. News came that D'Mello was among the lost. D'Mello, too, was gone. Perhaps he was not dead. Perhaps he had simply gone home, at last, to his storied city of Mumbai, on the country's other coast, that city which was neither of the north nor of the south but a frontierville, the greatest, most wondrous, and most dreadful of all such places, the megalopolis of the borderlands, the place of in-between. Or, on the other hand, perhaps D'Mello had drowned and Death, swallowing him, had denied his body the Christian dignity of a grave.

He, Senior, was the one who had asked for death. Yet Death had left him alive, had taken so many others, had taken even Junior and D'Mello, but left him untouched. The world was meaningless. There was no meaning to be found in it, he thought. The texts were empty and his eyes were blind. Perhaps he said some of this aloud. He may even have shouted it out. The girls in the lane below were looking up at him, and the green birds in the golden-shower tree were disturbed. Then, all of a sudden, he imagined that across the way, on the empty adjacent veranda, he saw a shadow move. He had cried out, "Why not me?," and in response a shadow had flickered where Junior used to stand. Death and life were just adjacent verandas. Senior stood on one of them as he always had, and on the other, continuing their tradition of many years, was Junior, his shadow, his namesake, arguing.

OLD WOUNDS

BY EDNA O'BRIEN (2009)

We didn't have a flower garden. There were a few clumps of devil's pokers—spears of smoldering crimson when in bloom, and milky yellow when not. But my mother's sister and her family, who lived closer to the mountain, had a ravishing garden: tall festoons of pinkish-white roses, a long low border of glorious golden tulips, and red dahlias that, even in hot sun, exuded the coolness of velvet. When the wind blew in a certain direction, the perfume of the roses vanquished the smell of dung from the yard, where the sow and her young pigs spent their days foraging and snortling. My aunt was so fond of the piglets that she gave each litter pet names, sometimes the same pet names, which she appropriated from the romance novels she borrowed from the library and read by the light of a paraffin lamp, well into the night.

Our families had a falling out. For several years there was no communication between us at all, and, when the elders met at funerals, they did not acknowledge one another and studiously looked the other way. Yet we were still intimately bound up with each other and any news of one family was of interest to the other, even if that news was disconcerting.

When the older and possibly more begrudging people had died off, and my cousin, Edward, and I were both past middle age—as he kept reminding me, he was twelve years older than I was and had been fitted with a pacemaker—we met again and set aside the lingering hostilities. About a year later, we paid a visit to the family graveyard, which was on an island in the broad stretch of the Shannon River. It was a balmy day in autumn, the graveyard spacious, uncluttered, the weathered tombs far more imposing than those in the graveyard close to the town. They were limestone tombs, blotched with white lichen, great splashes of it, which added an improvised gaiety to the scene. Swallows were swooping and scudding in and out of the several sacred churches, once the abode of monks but long since uninhabited, the roofs gone but the walls and ornamental doorways still standing, gray and sturdy, with their own mosaics of lichen. The swallows did not so much sing as caw and gabble, their circuits a marvel of speed and ingenuity.

Now I was seeing the graveyard in daylight with my cousin, but once, a few years before, I had gone there surreptitiously. The youngster who rowed me across worked for a German man who bred pheasants on one of the other islands and was able to procure a boat. We set out just before dark. The boy couldn't stop talking or singing. And he smoked like a chimney.

"Didn't yer families fight?" he asked, when I trained a torch on the names of my ancestors carved on a tall headstone. Undaunted by my silence, the boy kept prying and then, with a certain insouciance, informed me that the family fight had come about because of what Edward had done to his widowed mother, flinging her out once she had signed the place over to him.

"That's all in the past," I said curtly, and recited the names, including those of a great-grandmother and a great-grandfather, a Bridget and a Thomas, of whom I knew nothing. Others I had random remembrances of. In our house, preserved in a china cabinet, on frayed purple braid, were the medals of an uncle who had been a soldier of the Irish Free State and had met with a violent death, aged twenty-eight. I remembered my grandfather falling into a puddle in the yard, when he came home drunk from a fair, and laughing jovially. My grandmother was stern and made me drink hot milk with pepper before sending me up to bed early. She was forever dinning into me the stories of our forebears and how they had suffered, our people driven from their holdings and their cabins down the years. She said that the knowledge of eviction and the fear of the poorhouse ran in our blood. I must have been seven or eight at the time. For Sunday Mass, she wore a bonnet made of black satin, with little felt bobbins that hopped against her cheek in the judder, as my grandfather drove helter-skelter so as not to be late. The traps and the sidecars were tethered outside the chapel gates, and the horses seemed to know one another and to nod lazily. As a treat, my grandmother let me smell a ball of nutmeg, which was kept in a round tin that had once held cough pastilles. The feather bed, which I shared with her, sagged almost to the floor and the pillow slips smelled of flour, because they were made from flour bags that she had bleached and sewn. My grandfather, who snored, slept in a settle bed down in the kitchen, near the fire.

About two years after my clandestine visit to the graveyard, Edward and I met by chance at a garden center. I was home on holiday and had gone to buy broom shrubs for my nephew. As we approached each other on a pathway between a line of funereal yew trees, my cousin saw me, then pretended not to and feigned interest in a huge tropical plant, which bore a resemblance to rhubarb. Deciding to brave it, I said his name, and, turning, he asked with a puzzled look, "Who do I have here?," although he well knew. And so the ice was broken. Yes, his eyes were bad, as he later told me, but he had indeed recognized me and felt awkward. As we got to be friends, I learned of the journeys to the eye doctor in Dublin, of the treatments required before the doctor could operate, and when I sent him flowers at the hospital the nurse, bearing them to his bedside, said, "Well, someone loves you," and he was proud to tell her that it was me.

We corresponded. His letters were so immediate. They brought that mountain terrain to life, along with the unvarying routine of his days: out to the fields straight after breakfast, herding, mending fences, fixing gates, clearing drains, and often, as he said, sitting on a wall for a smoke, to drink in his surroundings. He loved the place. He said that people who did not know the country—did not know nature and did not stay close to it—could never understand the loss that they were feeling. I felt that, in an oblique way, he was referring to me. He wrote these letters at night by the fire, after his wife had gone up to bed. Her health was poor, her sleep fitful, so she went to bed early to get as many hours as she could. He sometimes, while writing, took a sup of whiskey, but he said he was careful not to get too fond of it.

He knew the lake almost as well as he knew the mountain, and, through his binoculars, from his front porch he watched the arrival of the dappers in the month of May, a whole fleet of boats from all over the country and even from foreign parts. They arrived as the hatched mayflies came out of the nearby bushes and floated above the water, in bacchanalian swarms, so that the fishermen were easily able to catch them and fix them to the hooks of their long rods. He himself had fished there every Sunday of his life, trolling from his boat with wet or dry bait, and so canny was he that the neighbors were quite spiteful, saying that he knew exactly where the fish lay hiding, and, hence, there was not a pike or a perch or a trout left for anyone else.

He was a frugal man. In Dublin, he would walk miles from the railway station to the eye hospital, often having to ask the way and frequently going astray because of his ailing sight. His wife and son would scold him for not taking a taxi, to which he always said, "I could if I wanted to." Yet I recalled that time when, young, he had brought my sister and me a gift, the same gift, a red glassy bracelet on an elasticated band. The raised red beads were so beautiful that I licked them as I would jellies. My sister was older than me, and it was for her that he had a particular fondness. They flirted, though I did not know then that it was called that. They teased each other, and then ran around the four walls of our sandstone house, and eventually fell into an embrace, breathless from their hectic exertions. I was wild with jealousy and snapped on the band of my new bracelet. They aped dancing, as if in a ballroom, she swooning, her upper back reclining on the curve of his forearm as he sang, "You'll be lonely, little sweetheart, in the spring," and she gazed up at him, daring him to kiss her. He was handsome then, not countrified, like most of the farmers or their grown sons, and he wore a long white belted motor coat. He had a mop of silky brown hair, and his skin was sallow.

I met Grania, the woman to whom he got engaged some two or three years later, on the way home from school one day. She stopped me and asked if I was his cousin, though she knew well who I was and pointedly ignored the two girls who were with me. She asked me jokingly if she was making the right choice, as someone had warned her that my cousin was "bad news." She repeated the words "bad news" with a particular relish. She was wearing a wrap-around red dress and red high-heeled toeless sandals, which looked incongruous but utterly beautiful on that dusty godforsaken road. She was like flame, a flame in love with my cousin, and her eyes danced with mischief. It was not long after they got married that he called his mother out into the hay shed and informed her that his wife felt unwanted in the house and that, for the sake of his marriage, he had to ask her to leave. Thus the coolness from our side of the family. There was general outrage in the parish that an only son had pitched his mother out, and pity for the mother, who had to walk down that road, carrying her few belongings and her one heirloom, a brass lamp with a china shade, woebegone, like a woman in a ballad. She stayed with us for a time, and did obliging things for my mother, being, as she was, in her own eyes, a mendicant, and once, when she let fall a tray of good china cups and saucers, she knelt down and said, "I'll replace these," even though we knew she couldn't. In the evenings, she often withdrew from the kitchen fire to sit alone in our cold vacant room, with a knitted shawl over her shoulders, brooding. Eventually, she rented a room in the town, and my mother gave her cane chairs, cushions, and a pale-green candlewick bedspread, to give the room a semblance of home.

But, with so many dead, there was no need for estrangement anymore.

Edward sent me a photograph of a double rainbow, arcing from the sky above his house across a patchwork of small green fields and over the lake toward the hill that contained the graves of the Leinster men. On the back of the photograph he had written the hour of evening at which the rainbow had appeared and lasted for about ten minutes, before eking its watery way back into the sky. I put it on the mantelpiece for luck. The rainbow, with its seven bands of glorious color, always presaged happiness. In his next letter and in answer to my question, he said that the Leinster men were ancient chieftains who had come for a banquet in Munster, where they were insulted and subsequently murdered, but that someone had thought to bury them facing their own province.

Each summer, when I went back to Ireland, we had outings, outings that he had been planning all year. One year, mysteriously, I found that we were driving far from his farm, up an isolated road, with nothing in sight except clumps of wretched rushes and the abandoned ruins from famine times. Then, almost at the peak, he parked the jeep and took two shotguns out of the boot. He had dreamed all year of teaching me to shoot and he set about it with a zest. He loved shooting. As a youngster, unbeknownst to his mother, he had cycled to Limerick two nights a week to learn marksmanship in a gallery. With different gundogs, he shot pheasants, grouse, ducks, and snipe, but his particular favorites were the woodcock, which came all the way from Siberia or Chernobyl. He described them to me, silhouetted against an evening sky—they disliked light—their beaks like crochet hooks, then furtively landing in a swamp or on a cowpat to catch insects or partake of the succulence of the water. Yet he could not forgo the thrill of shooting them, then picking them up, feeling the scant flesh on the bone, and snapping off a side feather to post to an ornithologist in England. September 1st, he said, was the opening of duck shooting on the lake, a hundred guns or more out there, *bang-bang*-ing in all directions. Later, adjourning to the pub, the sportsmen swapped stories of the day's adventure, comparing what they'd shot and how they'd shot and what they'd missed—a camaraderie such as he was not used to.

For a target, he affixed a saucepan lid to a wooden post. Then, taking the lighter of the two guns, he loaded it with brass bullets, handed it to me, and taught me to steady it, to put my finger on the trigger and look down through the nozzle of the long blue-black barrel.

"Now shoot," he said in a belligerent voice, and I shot so fearfully and, at the same time, so rapidly that I believed I was levitating. The whole thing felt unreal, bullets bursting and zapping through the air, some occasionally clattering off the side of the tin lid and my aim so awry that even to him it began to be funny. He had started to lay out a picnic on a tartan rug—milky tea in a bottle, hard-boiled eggs, slices of brown bread already buttered—when out of thin air a huge black dog appeared, like a phantom or an animal from the underworld, its snarls strange and spiteful. Its splayed paws were enormous and mud-spattered, its eyes bloodshot, the sockets bruised, as if it were fresh from battle.

"He'll smell your fear," my cousin said.

"I can't help it," I said and lowered the gun, thinking that this might, in some way, appease the animal. There wasn't a stone or a stick to throw at it. There was nothing up there, only the fearsome dog and us and the saucepan lid rattling like billio.

Edward knew every dog for miles around, and every breed of dog, and said that this freak was a "blow-in." Eventually, he sacrificed every bit of food in order to get the animal to run, throwing each piece farther and farther, as, matador-like, he followed bearing the stake on which the lid was nailed, shouting in a voice that I could not believe was his, so barbaric and inhuman did it sound. The dog, wearying of the futility of this, decided to gallop off over the edge of the mountain and disappear from sight.

"Jesus," my cousin said.

We sat in the jeep because, as he said, we were in no hurry to get home. We didn't talk about family things, his wife or my ex-husband, my mother or his mother, possibly fearing that it would open up old wounds. There had been so many differences between the two families—over greyhounds, over horses, over some rotten bag of seed potatoes—and always with money at the root of it. My father, in his wild tempers, would claim that my mother's father had not paid her dowry and would go to his house in the dead of night, shouting up at a window to demand it.

Instead, we talked of dogs.

Having been a huntsman all his life, Edward had several dogs, good dogs, faithful dogs, retrievers, pointers, setters, and springers. His favorite was an Irish red setter, which he called Maire Ruadh, for a red-haired noblewoman who had her husbands pitched into the Atlantic once she tired of them. He had driven all the way to Kildare, in answer to an advertisement, to vet this pedigree dog, and his wife had decided to come along. Straightaway they had liked the look of her; they had studied the pedigree papers, paid out a hefty sum, and there and then given her her imperious name. On the way back, they'd had high tea at a hotel in Roscrea, and, what with the price he'd paid for Maire Ruadh and the tea and the cost of the petrol, it had proved to be an expensive day.

I told him the story of an early morning in a café in Paris, a straggle of people—two men, each with a bottle of pale-amber beer, and a youngish woman, writing in a ruled copybook, her dog at her feet, quiet, suppliant. When she finished her essay, or whatever it was that she had been writing, she groped in her purse and all of a sudden the obedient dog reared to get away. She pulled on the lead, dragging it back beside her, the dog resistant and down on its haunches. Grasping the animal by the crown of its head, she opened its mouth very wide and with her other hand dispatched some powdered medicine from a sachet onto its tongue. Pinned as it was, the dog could vent its fury only by kicking, which got it nowhere. Once the dog had downed the powder, she patted it lovingly and it answered in kind, with soft whimpers.

"Man's best friend," my cousin said, a touch dolefully.

We came back by a different route because he wanted me to see the ruin of a cottage where a workman of ours had lived. As a child, I had been dotingly in love with the man and had intended to elope with him, when I came of age. The house itself was gone and all that remained was a tumbledown porch with some overgrown stalks of geranium, their scarlet blooms prodigal in that godforsaken place. We didn't even get out of the car. Yet nearby we came upon a scene of such gaiety that it might have been a wedding party. Twenty or so people sitting out of doors at a long table strewn with lanterns, eating, drinking, and calling for toasts in different tongues. Behind the cacophony of voices we could hear the strains of music from a melodeon. It was the hippies who had come to the district, the "blow-ins," as Edward called them, giving them the same scathing name as the fearsome dog. They had made Ireland their chosen destination when the British government, in order to avoid paying them social benefits, gave them a lump sum to scoot it. They crossed the Irish Sea and found ideal havens by streams and small rivers, building houses, growing their own vegetables and their own marijuana, and, he had been told on good authority, taking up wife-swapping. He had the native's mistrust of the outsider. We had to come to a stop because some of their ducks were waddling across the road. We couldn't see them in the dusk but heard their quacking, and then some children with their faces painted puce came to the open window of the jeep, holding lighted sods of turf, serenading us.

"Hi, guv," one of the men at the table called out, but my cousin did not answer.

It was in his back yard, still sitting in the jeep, that he began to cry. As we drove in, he could see by the light in the upstairs room that his wife had gone to bed early, so I declined his invitation to have a cup of tea. He cried for a long time. The stars were of the same brightness and fervor as the stars I had seen in childhood and, though distant, seemed to have been put there for us, as if someone in the great house called Heaven had gone from room to room, turning on this constellation of lamps. He was crying, he said, because the families had been divided for so long. He had even tried to find me in England, had written to some priest who served in a parish in Kilburn, because, according to legend, Kilburn was where Irish people flocked and had fights on Saturday nights outside pubs and pool halls. The priest couldn't trace me but suggested a parish in Wimbledon, where I had indeed lived for a time, before fleeing from bondage. What hurt my cousin most was the fact that his wife's cousins, as she frequently reminded him, had kept in touch, had sent Christmas cards and visited in the summer, each of them rewarded with a gift of a pair of fresh trout. In his wife's estimation, his cousins, meaning my family, were heartless. It took him a while to calm down. The tissues that he took from his pockets were damp shreds. Eventually, somewhat abashed, he said, "Normally, I am not an emotional man," then, backing the car toward the open gate, he drove down the mountain road to the small town where my nephew lived.

One evening soon after that, when I telephoned him from London, he said that he had known it would be me; he had come in from the fields ten minutes before the Angelus tolled, because of this hunch he had that I would be ringing. We talked at our ease: the cornea transplant he had recently undergone, the weather as ever wet and squally. He told me that it was unlikely he would make silage anymore and therefore intended to sell the cattle that he had fattened all summer. He might, he said, buy yearlings the following May, if his health held up. He did not say how happy the call had made him, but I could feel the pitch of excitement in his voice as he told me again that he had come in early from the fields because he knew that I would ring.

We took to talking on the phone about once a month. When his wife went to Spain with their son, from whom he was estranged, he wrote to tell me that he would phone me on a particular evening at seven o'clock. I knew then that these conversations buoyed him up.

It was the third summer of our reunion, and he had the boat both tarred and painted a Prussian blue. We were bound for the graveyard. The day could not have been more perfect: sunshine, a soft breeze, Edward slipping the boat out with one oar through a thicket of lush bamboo and reeds, a scene that could easily have taken place somewhere in the East. He took a loop away from the direction of the island, in order to get the wind at our backs, then turned on the engine and, despite his worsening sight, steered with unfailing instinct, because he had, he said, a map of the entire lake inside his head. The water was a plateau of dazzling silver, waves barely nudging the boat. We couldn't hear each other because of the noise of the engine but sat quiet, content, the hills all around us sloping toward us, enfolding us in their friendliness. It was only when we reached the pier that I realized how poor his sight was—by the difficulty he had tying the rope to its ballast and reading the handwritten sign that said "Bull on island."

"We'll have to brave it," he said. Our headway was cautious, what with the steep climb, the fear of the bull, and, presently, a herd of bullocks fixing us with their stupid glare, and a few of them making abortive attempts to charge at us. Once through the lych-gate that led to the graveyard, we sat and availed ourselves of the port wine that I had brought in a hip flask. Sitting on the low wall opposite the resting place of our ancestors, he said what a pity it was that my mother had chosen not to be buried there. Her explanation was that she wished to be near a roadside so that passersby might bless themselves for the repose of her soul, but I had always felt that there was another reason, a hesitation in her heart.

"I came here twice since I last saw you . . . to think," he said.

"To think?"

"I was feeling rotten. . . . I came here and talked to them." He did not elaborate, but I imagined that he might have been brooding over unfinished business with his mother, or maybe his marriage, which had grown bleaker amid the desolations of age. It was not money he was worried about, because, as he told me, he had been offered princely sums for fields of his that bordered the lake; people were pestering him, developers and engaged couples, to sell them sites, and he had refused resolutely.

"My wants are few," he said and rolled a cigarette, regaining his good humor and rejoicing at the fact that we had picked such a great day for our visit. He surprised me by telling a story of how, after my mother died, my father had gone to the house of Grania's older sister, Oonagh, recently returned from Australia, and had proposed to her. Without any pretense at courtship, he had simply asked her to marry him. He had needed a wife. He had even pressed her to think it over, been narked at her refusal, and gone on the batter for several weeks. I could not imagine anyone other than my mother in our kitchen, in our upstairs or downstairs rooms; she was the presiding spirit of the place.

He then said that Grania had also expressed a wish to be buried in a grave near the town and he could not understand why anyone would want to be in a place where the remains were squeezed in like sardines.

Birds whirled in and out, such a freedom to their movements, such an airiness, as if the whole place belonged to them and we were the intruders. He spoke of souls buried there in pagan times, then Christian times, the monks in the monasteries fasting, praying, and most likely having to fend off invaders. It was a place of pilgrimage, where all-night Masses were celebrated; he pointed to boulders with little cavities, where the pilgrims had dipped their hands and their feet in the blessed water.

"Hallowed ground," I said. The grassy mound that covered our family grave was a rich warm green strewn with speckled wildflowers.

"You have as much right to be there as I have," he said suddenly, and my heart leaped with a childish joy.

"Do I really?"

"I'm telling you . . . you'll be right beside me," he said, and he stood up and took my hand, and we walked over the mound, measuring it, as it were, hands held in solidarity. It meant everything to me. I would be the only one from our branch of the family to lie with relatives whom I had always admired as being more stoic than us and truer to the hardships of the land.

When his wife got sick the next winter, his letters became infrequent. He rarely went out to the fields, having to tend her, and the only help was a twice-weekly visit from a jubilee nurse, who came to change her dressings. They could not tell whether it was the cancer causing all the wounds down her spine or whether she was allergic to the medicines that she had been prescribed. Sometimes, he wrote, she roared with pain, said that the pain was hammering against her chest, and begged to be dead. I was abroad when she died and he telephoned to let me know. A message was passed on to me and I was able to send roses by Interflora. To my surprise, I learned that she had been buried on the island after all, and on the phone, when I later spoke to him, he described the crossing of the funeral procession, the first boat for the flowers, as was the custom, then himself and his son in the next boat, and the mourners following behind.

"A grand crowd . . . good people," he said, and I realized that he was vexed with me for not having been there. I asked whether she had died suddenly, and he answered that he would rather not describe the manner of her passing. Nor did he say why she had changed her mind about being buried in the family plot.

I could not tell what had caused it, but a chasm had sprung up between us. The friendliness had gone from his voice when I rang, and his letters were formal now. I wondered if he felt that his friendship with me had somehow compromised his love for his wife, or if he was in the grip of that contrariness which comes, or so I feared, with advancing years. A home help, a very young girl, visited him three days a week, put groceries in the fridge, cooked his dinner, and occasionally went upstairs to hoover and change the sheets.

"Maybe you should give her a bonus," I said, suggesting that she would then come every day.

"The state pays her plenty," he said, disgruntled by my remark.

I got out of the habit of phoning him, but one Christmas morning, in a burst of sentiment, I rang, hoping that things might be smoothed over. Over-politely, he answered a few questions about the weather, his health, a large magnifying machine that he had got for reading, and then quite suddenly he blurted it out. He had been looking into the cost of a tombstone for his wife and himself and had found that it was going to be very expensive.

"Have you thought of what you intend to do?" he asked.

"I haven't," I said flatly.

"Maybe you would like to purchase yours now," he said.

"I don't understand the question," I said, although I understood it all too clearly and a river of outrage ran through me. I felt that he had violated kinship and decency. The idea of being interred in the graveyard beside him seemed suddenly odious to me. Yet, perversely, I was determined not to surrender my place under the grassy slope.

There were a few seconds of wordless confrontation and then the line went dead. He had hung up. I rang back, but the telephone was off the hook, and that night, when I called again, there was no answer; he probably guessed that it was me.

It was August and pouring rain when I travelled to the local hospital to see him. A nurse, with her name tag, "M. Gleeson," met me in the hallway. She was a stout woman with short bobbed hair and extremely affable. She eyed me up and down, guessed correctly whom I had come to see, and said that her mother had known me well, but, of course, I wouldn't remember, being citified. If my cousin had come in at Easter, things might have been different now, she said, but, as it was, the news was not promising.

"How's the humor?" I asked tentatively.

"Cantankerous," she said, adding that most patients knew their onions, knew how to play up to her, realizing that she would be the one to wash them, feed them, and bring them cups of tea at all hours, but not cousin Edward.

"I should have brought flowers," I said.

"Ah, aren't you flower enough!" she said and herded me toward the open door of his little room, announcing me bluffly.

He was in an armchair with a fawn dressing gown over his pajamas, as thin as a rake, his whole body drooping, and when he looked up and saw me, or perhaps only barely saw me, but heard my name, his eyes narrowed with hatred. I saw that I should not have come.

"I couldn't find anywhere to buy you a flower," I said.

"A flower?" he said with disdain.

"They don't sell them in the garden center anymore—only trees and plants," I explained, and the words hung in the air. The rain sloshed down the narrow windowpane as if it couldn't reach the sill quickly enough, then overflowed onto a patch of ground that was rife with nettle and dock.

"How are you?" I asked after some time.

He pondered the question and then replied, coldly, "That's what I keep asking myself—how am I?"

I wanted to put things right. I wanted to say, "Let's talk about the tombstone and then forget about it forever," but I couldn't. The way he glared at me was beginning to make me angry. I felt the urge to shake him. On the bedside table there was a peeled mandarin orange that had been halved but left untouched. There will be another time, I kept telling myself. Except that I knew he was dying. He had that aghastness which shows itself, months, often a year, before the actual death. We were getting nowhere. The tension was unbearable, rain splashing down, and he with his head lowered, having a colloquy with himself. I reminded myself how hardworking, how frugal, he had been all his life, never admitting to the loneliness that he must have felt, and I thought, Why don't I throw my arms around him and say something? But I couldn't. I simply couldn't. It wouldn't have been true. It would have been false. I knew that he despised me for the falsity of my coming and the falsity of my not bringing the matter up, and that he despised himself equally for having done something irreparable.

"Have you been to the grave?" he asked sharply.

"No, but I'm going this afternoon. I've booked the boatman," I said.

"You'll find Grania's name and mine on my grandfather's tomb . . . chiselled," he said.

"Chiselled." The word seemed to cut through the shafts of suffocating air between us.

I knew that he wanted me to leave.

As it turned out, the trip across the lake was cancelled because the weather was so foul. The boatman deemed it too rough and too dangerous. It was the day of a big horse race and he and his wife were in their front room with the fire lit, the television on, and an open bottle of Tia Maria on a little brass table.

Strange to say, neither Edward's name nor Grania's was on the tombstone when I went to his funeral, on a drizzling wet day that November. The grave had already been dug. "Ten fellas," as Jacksie the boatman said, had turned up to do the job. Buckets of water had been bailed out of it, but the clay itself was still wet, with a dark boggy seepage. His coffin would rest on his wife's, hers still new-looking, its varnish undimmed, and, in an exchange of maudlin condolences, women remarked that most likely Grania was in there still, waiting to welcome him.

Underneath his wife's remains were those of his mother, the woman she had quarrelled with and driven out of her home, and down in succession were others—husbands, wives, children, all with their differences silenced. When my turn came, I would rest on Edward's coffin, with runners underneath to cushion the weight. These thoughts were passing through my mind as the priest shook holy water over the grave and three young girls threw in red roses. I did not recognize them. Neighbors' children, I assumed. They threw the roses with a certain theatricality, and one of them blushed a fierce crimson. Death had not yet touched them.

When the priest started the Rosary, there were nudges and blatant sighs, as it became clear that he was going to recite the full five decades, and not just one decade, as some priests did. He was in a wheelchair and had to have a boat all to himself. Men had had to support him up the gravel path to the graveyard. Despite his condition, his voice boomed out onto the lake, where the water birds shivered in the rushes, and over it to the main road, where crows had perched in a neat sepulchral line on the telephone wires as the coffin was being removed from the hearse. The mourners answered the Our Fathers and the Hail Marys with a routine solemnity, and the gravediggers stood by their shovels, expressionless, witnessing a scene such as they witnessed every other day.

At the end of the prayers, a purple cloth was laid over Edward's coffin, the undertaker tucking it in as if it were a living person that he was putting down to bed. I felt no sorrow, or, to be more precise, I felt nothing, only numbness. I watched a single flake of snow drift through the cold air, discolored and lonesome-looking.

Most of the people ambled down toward the pier, but a few stayed behind to watch as the men closed the grave. The wreaths and artificial flowers in their glass domes were lifted off the strip of green plastic carpet, which had been temporarily placed over the grave to lessen the sense of grimness. The gravediggers shovelled hurriedly, gravel and small stones hopping off the coffins and the purple sheath, and finally they unrolled the piece of turf and laid it back where it belonged. Wildflowers of a darkish purple bloomed on graves nearby, but on the strip that had been dug up they had expired. The undertaker, who was full of cheer, said that they would grow again, as the birds scattered seeds all over and flowers of every description sprouted up.

On the way down the steep path, Nurse Gleeson tugged at my arm as if we were old friends. First it was a slew of compliments about the tweed suit I was wearing, singling out the heather flecks in it, and she said what a pity it was that she was size 18, as I could not pass it on to her when I grew tired of it. Then it was my head scarf, an emerald green with an assortment of other garish colors, quite inappropriate for a funeral, except that it was the only one I had thrown into my suitcase. She remembered my flying visit to the hospital, had, in fact, gone to get a tray of tea and biscuits, when, holy cripes, on returning to the room, she saw that I had vanished.

"Did he say anything?" I asked.

"Oh, he sang dumb," she said, then, gripping my arm even tighter, she indicated that there was something important that she needed to impart to me.

A few days before the end, my cousin had asked her for a sheet of notepaper in order to write me a letter. There was a cranberry bowl in the kitchen at home, which he wished me to have, he had said. As it happened, she had found the sheet of paper in the top pocket of his pajamas after he died, but with nothing written on it.

"The strength gave out," she said and asked if I knew which bowl it was. I could see it quite clearly, as I had seen it one day, while waiting in his kitchen for a sun shower to pass, rays of sun alighting on it, divesting it of its sheath of brown dust, the red ripples flowing through it, so that it seemed to liquefy, as if it were being newly blown. It had been full of things—screwdrivers, a tiny torch, receipts, and pills for pain. When I admired it, he turned the contents out onto the table and held it in the palm of his hand, proudly, like a chalice of warm wine.

I hoped that the unwritten letter had been an attempt at reconciliation.

Sitting in the boat with a group of friendly people, I could still see the island, shrouded in a veil of thin gray rain. Why, I asked myself, did I want to be buried there? Why, given the different and gnawing perplexities? It was not love and it was not hate but something for which there is no name, because to name it would be to deprive it of its truth.

MIDNIGHT IN DOSTOEVSKY

BY DON DELILLO (2009)

We were two sombre boys hunched in our coats, grim winter settling in. The college was at the edge of a small town way upstate, barely a town, maybe a hamlet, we said, or just a whistle stop, and we took walks all the time, getting out, going nowhere, low skies and bare trees, hardly a soul to be seen. This was how we spoke of the local people: they were souls, they were transient spirits, a face in the window of a passing car, runny with reflected light, or a long street with a shovel jutting from a snowbank, no one in sight.

We were walking parallel to the tracks when an old freight train approached and we stopped and watched. It seemed the kind of history that passes mostly unobserved, a diesel engine and a hundred boxcars rolling over remote country, and we shared an unspoken moment of respect, Todd and I, for times past, frontiers gone, and then walked on, talking about nothing much but making something of it. We heard the whistle sound as the train disappeared into late afternoon.

This was the day we saw the man in the hooded coat. We argued about the coat—loden coat, anorak, parka. It was our routine; we were ever ready to find a matter to contest. This was why the man had been born, to end up in this town wearing that coat. He was well ahead of us and walking slowly, hands clasped behind his back, a smallish figure turning now to enter a residential street and fade from view.

"A loden coat doesn't have a hood. A hood isn't part of the context," Todd said. "It's a parka or an anorak."

"There's others. There's always others."

"Name one."

"Duffel coat."

"There's duffel bag."

"There's duffel coat."

"Does the word imply a hood?"

"The word implies toggles."

"The coat had a hood. We don't know if the coat had toggles."

"Doesn't matter," I said. "Because the guy was wearing a parka."

" 'Anorak' is an Inuit word."

"So what."

"I say it's an anorak," he said.

I tried to invent an etymology for the word "parka" but couldn't think fast enough. Todd was on another subject—the freight train, laws of motion, effects of force, sneaking in a question about the number of boxcars that trailed the locomotive. We hadn't stated in advance that a tally would be taken, but each of us had known that the other would be counting, even as we spoke about other things. When I told him now what my number was, he did not respond, and I knew what this meant. It meant that he'd arrived at the same number. This was not supposed to happen—it unsettled us, it made the world flat—and we walked for a time in chagrined silence. Even in matters of pure physical reality, we depended on a friction between our basic faculties of sensation, his and mine, and we understood now that the rest of the afternoon would be spent in the marking of differences.

We headed back for a late class.

"An anorak is substantial. The thing he was wearing looked pretty flimsy," I said. "And an anorak would have a fur-lined hood. Consider the origin of the word. You're the one who brought up the Inuits. Wouldn't an Inuit use fur to line his hood? They have polar bear. They have walrus. They need coats with bulk and substance top to bottom."

"We saw the guy from behind," he said. "How do you know what kind of hood it was? From behind and from a distance."

Consider the origin of the word. I was using his Inuit lore against him, forcing him to respond reasonably, a rare sign of weakness on his part. Todd was a determined thinker who liked to work a fact or an idea to the seventh level of interpretation. He was tall and sprawling, all bony framework, the kind of body not always in synch with its hinges and joints. Somebody said that he seemed the love child of storks, others thought ostriches. He did not seem to taste food; he consumed it, absorbed it, ingestible matter of plant or animal origin. He spoke of distances in metres and kilometres, and it took me a while to understand that this was not an affectation so much as a driving need to convert units of measurement more or less instantaneously. He liked to test himself on what he knew. He liked to stop walking to emphasize a point as I walked on. This was my counterpoint, to let him stand there talking to a tree. The shallower our arguments, the more intense we became.

I wanted to keep this one going, to stay in control, to press him hard. Did it matter what I said?

"Even from a distance the hood looked too small to be fur-lined. The hood was snug," I said. "A true anorak would have a hood that's roomy enough to fit a woollen cap underneath. Isn't that what the Inuits do?"

The campus appeared in fragments, through ranks of tall trees on the other side of a country road. We lived in a series of energy-efficient structures with solar panels, turfed rooftops, and red cedar walls. Classes were held in the original buildings, several massive concrete units known collectively as the Cellblock, a bike ride or long walk away from the dorms, and the flow of students back and forth in tribal swarms seemed part of the architecture of the place. This was my first year here, and I was still trying to interpret the signs and adapt to the patterns.

"They have caribou," I said. "They have seal meat and ice floes."

At times, abandon meaning to impulse. Let the words be the facts. This was the nature of our walks—to register what was out there, all the scattered rhythms of circumstance and occurrence, and to reconstruct it as human noise.

. . .

The class was Logic, in Cellblock 2, thirteen of us seated along both sides of a long table, with Ilgauskas at the head, a stocky man, late forties, beset this day by periodic coughing. He spoke from a standing position, bent forward, hands set on the table, and often stared for long moments into the blank wall at the other end of the room.

"The causal nexus," he said, and stared into the wall.

He stared; we glanced. We exchanged glances frequently, one side of the table with the other. We were fascinated by Ilgauskas. He seemed a man in a trance state. But he wasn't simply absent from his remarks, another drained voice echoing down the tunnel of teaching years. We'd decided, some of us, that he was suffering from a neurological condition. He was not bored but simply unbound, speaking freely and erratically out of a kind of stricken insight. It was a question of neurochemistry. We'd decided that the condition was not understood well enough to have been given a name. And if it did not have a name, we said, paraphrasing a proposition in logic, then it could not be treated.

"The atomic fact," he said.

Then he elaborated for ten minutes while we listened, glanced, made notes, riffled the textbook to find refuge in print, some semblance of meaning that might be roughly equivalent to what he was saying. There were no laptops or handheld devices in class. Ilgauskas didn't exclude them; we did, sort of, unspokenly. Some of us could barely complete a thought without touch pads or scroll buttons, but we understood that high-speed data systems did not belong here. They were an assault on the environment, which was defined by length, width, and depth, with time drawn out, computed in heartbeats. We sat and listened or sat and waited. We wrote with pens or pencils. Our notebooks had pages made of flexible sheets of paper.

I tried to exchange glances with the girl across the table. This was the first time we'd been seated face to face, but she kept looking down at her notes, her hands, maybe the grain of the wood along the edge of the table. I told myself that she was averting her eyes not from me but from Ilgauskas.

"*F* and not-*F*," he said.

He made her shy, the blunt impact of the man, thick body, strong voice, staccato cough, even the old dark suit he wore, unpressed, to every class, his chest hair curling up out of the open shirt collar.

He used German and Latin terms without defining them. I tried to insert myself into the girl's line of sight, scrunching down and peering up. We listened earnestly, all of us, hoping to understand and to transcend the need to understand.

Sometimes he coughed into his cupped hand, other times into the table, and we imagined microscopic life forms teeming toward the tabletop and ricocheting into breathable space. Those seated nearest him ducked away with a wince that was also a smile, half apologetic. The shy girl's shoulders quivered, even though she was sitting at some distance from the man. We didn't expect Ilgauskas to excuse himself. He was Ilgauskas. We were the ones at fault, for being there to witness the coughing, or for not being adequate to the seismic scale of it, or for other reasons not yet known to us.

"Can we ask this question?" he said.

We waited for the question. We wondered whether the question he'd asked was the question we were waiting for him to ask. In other words, could he ask the question he was asking? It was not a trick, not a game or a logical puzzle. Ilgauskas didn't do that. We sat and waited. He stared into the wall at the far end of the room.

It felt good to be out in the weather, that wintry sting of approaching snow. I was walking down a street of older houses, some in serious need of repair, sad and handsome, bay window here, curved porch there, when he turned the corner and came toward me, slightly crouched, same coat, face nearly lost inside the hood. He was walking slowly, as before, hands behind his back, as before, and he seemed to pause when he saw me, almost imperceptibly, head lowered now, path not quite steady.

There was no one else on the street. As we approached each other, he veered away, and then so did I, just slightly, to reassure him, but I also sent a stealthy look his way. The face inside the hood was stubbled—gray old man, I thought, large nose, eyes on the sidewalk but also noting my presence. After we'd passed each other, I waited a moment and then turned and looked. He wasn't wearing gloves, and this seemed fitting, I'm not sure why, no gloves, despite the unrelenting cold.

About an hour later, I was part of the mass movement of students going in opposite directions, in wind-whipped snow, two roughly parallel columns moving from old campus to new and vice versa, faces in ski masks, bodies shouldering into the wind or pushed along by it. I saw Todd, long-striding, and pointed. This was our standard sign of greeting or approval—we pointed. I shouted into the weather as he went by.

"Saw him again. Same coat, same hood, different street."

He nodded and pointed back, and two days later we were walking in the outlying parts of town. I gestured toward a pair of large trees, bare branches forking up fifty or sixty feet.

"Norway maple," I said.

He said nothing. They meant nothing to him, trees, birds, baseball teams. He knew music, classical to serial, and the history of mathematics, and a hundred other things. I knew trees from summer camp, when I was twelve, and I was pretty sure the trees were maples. Norway was another matter. I could have said red maple or sugar maple, but Norway sounded stronger, more informed.

We both played chess. We both believed in God.

Houses here loomed over the street, and we saw a middle-aged woman get out of her car and take a baby stroller from the rear seat and unfold it. Then she took four grocery bags from the car, one at a time, and placed each in the stroller. We were talking and watching. We were talking about epidemics, pandemics, and plagues, but we were watching the woman. She shut the car door and pulled the stroller backward over the hard-packed snow on the sidewalk and up the long flight of steps to her porch.

"What's her name?"

"Isabel," I said.

"Be serious. We're serious people. What's her name?"

"O.K., what's her name?"

"Her name is Mary Frances. Listen to me," he whispered. "*Mar-y Fran-ces*. Never just Mary."

"O.K., maybe."

"Where the hell do you get Isabel?"

He showed mock concern, placing a hand on my shoulder.

"I don't know. Isabel's her sister. They're identical twins. Isabel's the alcoholic twin. But you're missing the central questions."

"No, I'm not. Where's the baby that goes with the stroller? Whose baby is it?" he said. "What's the baby's name?"

We started down the street that led out of town and heard aircraft from the military base. I turned and looked up and they were there and gone, three fighter jets wheeling to the east, and then I saw the hooded man a hundred yards away, coming over the crest of a steep street, headed in our direction.

I said, "Don't look now."

Todd turned and looked. I talked him into crossing the street to put some space between the man and us. We watched from a driveway, standing under a weathered backboard-and-rim fastened to the ridge beam above the garage door. A pickup went by, and the man stopped briefly, then walked on.

"See the coat. No toggles," I said.

"Because it's an anorak."

"It's a parka—it was always a parka. Hard to tell from here, but I think he shaved. Or someone shaved him. Whoever he lives with. A son or daughter, grandkids."

He was directly across the street from us now, moving cautiously to avoid stretches of unshovelled snow.

"He's not from here," Todd said. "He's from somewhere in Europe. They brought him over. He couldn't take care of himself anymore. His wife died. They wanted to stay where they were, the two elderly people. But then she died."

He was speaking distantly, Todd was, watching the man but talking through him, finding his shadow somewhere on the other side of the world. The man did not see us, I was sure of this. He reached the corner, one of his hands behind his back, the other making small conversational gestures, and then he turned onto the next street and was gone.

"Did you see his shoes?"

"They weren't boots."

"They were shoes that reach to the ankle."

"High shoes."

"Old World."

"No gloves."

"Jacket below the knees."

"Possibly not his."

"A hand-me-down or hand-me-up."

"Think of the hat he'd be wearing if he was wearing a hat," I said.

"He's not wearing a hat."

"But if he was wearing a hat, what kind of hat?"

"He's wearing a hood."

"But what kind of hat, if he was wearing a hat?"

"He's wearing a hood," Todd said.

We walked down to the corner now and started across the street. He spoke an instant before I did.

"There's only one kind of hat he could conceivably wear. A hat with an earflap that reaches from one ear around the back of the head to the other ear. An old soiled cap. A peaked cap with a flap for the ears."

I said nothing. I had nothing to say to this.

There was no sign of the man along the street he'd entered. For a couple of seconds, an aura of mystery hovered over the scene. But his disappearance simply meant that he lived in one of the houses on the street. Did it matter which house? I didn't think it mattered, but Todd disagreed. He wanted a house that matched the man.

We walked slowly down the middle of the street, six feet apart, using rutted car tracks in the snow to make the going easier. He took off a glove and extended his hand, fingers spread and flexing.

"Feel the air. I say minus nine Celsius."

"We're not Celsius."

"But he is, where he's from, that's Celsius."

"Where *is* he from? There's something not too totally white about him. He's not Scandinavian."

"Not Dutch or Irish."

I wondered about Andalusian. Where was Andalusia exactly? I didn't think I knew. Or an Uzbek, a Kazakh. But these seemed irresponsible.

"Middle Europe," Todd said. "Eastern Europe."

He pointed to a gray frame house, an ordinary two-story, with a shingled roof and no sign of the fallen grace that defined some of the houses elsewhere in town.

"Could be that one. His family allows him to take a walk now and then, provided he stays within a limited area."

"The cold doesn't bother him much."

"He's used to colder."

"Plus, he has very little feeling in his extremities," I said.

There was no Christmas wreath on the front door, no holiday lights. I didn't see anything about the property that might suggest who lived there, from what background, speaking which language. We approached the point where the street ended in a patch of woods, and we turned and headed back.

We had class in half an hour, and I wanted to speed up the pace. Todd was still looking at houses. I thought of the Baltic states and the Balkan states, briefly confused—which was which and which was where.

I spoke before he did.

"I see him as a figure who escaped the war in the nineteen-nineties. Croatia, Serbia, Bosnia. Or who didn't leave until recently."

"I don't feel that here," he said. "It's not the right model."

"Or he's Greek, and his name is Spyros."

"I wish you a painless death," he said, not bothering to look my way.

"German names. Names with umlauts."

This last had nothing but nuisance value. I knew that. I tried walking faster, but he paused a moment, standing in his skewed way to look at the gray house.

"In a few hours, think of it, dinner's over, the others are watching TV, he's in his little room sitting on the edge of a narrow bed in his long johns, staring into space."

I wondered if this was a space that Todd expected us to fill.

We waited through the long silences and then nodded when he coughed, in collegial approval. He'd coughed only twice so far today. There was a small puckered bandage at the edge of his jaw. He shaves, we thought. He cuts himself and says shit. He wads up a sheet of toilet paper and holds it to the cut. Then he leans into the mirror, seeing himself clearly for the first time in years. Ilgauskas, he thinks.

We never took the same seats, class after class. We weren't sure how this had started. One of us, in a spirit of offhand mischief, may have spread the word that Ilgauskas preferred it this way. In fact the idea had substance. He didn't want to know who we were. We were passersby to him, smeary faces, we were roadkill. It was an aspect of his neurological condition, we thought, to regard others as displaceable, and this seemed interesting, seemed part of the course, displaceability, one of the truth functions that he referred to now and then.

But we were violating the code, the shy girl and I, seated face to face once again. This happened because I had entered the room after she did and had simply fallen into the empty chair directly across from her. She knew I was there, knew it was me, same gaping lad, eager to make eye contact.

"Imagine a surface of no color whatsoever," he said.

We sat there and imagined. He ran a hand through his dark hair, a shaggy mass that flopped in several directions. He did not bring books to class, never a sign of the textbook or a sheaf of notes, and his shambling discourses made us feel that we were becoming what he saw before him, an amorphous entity. We were basically stateless. He could have been speaking to political prisoners in orange jumpsuits. We admired this. We were in the Cellblock, after all. We exchanged glances, she and I, tentatively. Ilgauskas leaned toward the table, eyes swimming with neurochemical life. He looked at the wall, talked to the wall.

"Logic ends where the world ends," he said.

The world, yes. But he seemed to be speaking with his back to the world. Then again the subject was not history or geography. He was instructing us in the principles of pure reason. We listened intently. One remark dissolved into the next. He was an artist, an abstract artist. He asked a series of questions, and we made earnest notes. The questions he asked were unanswerable, at least by us, and he was not expecting answers, in any case. We did not speak in class; no one ever spoke. There were never any questions, student to professor. That steadfast tradition was dead here.

He said, "Facts, pictures, things."

What did he mean by "things"? We would probably never know. Were we too passive, too accepting of the man? Did we see dysfunction and call it an inspired form of intellect? We didn't want to like him, only to believe in him. We tendered our deepest trust to the stark nature of his methodology. Of course, there was no methodology. There was only Ilgauskas. He challenged our reason for being, what we thought, how we lived, the truth or falsity of what we believed to be true or false. Isn't this what great teachers do, the Zen masters and Brahman scholars?

He leaned toward the table and spoke about meanings fixed in advance. We listened hard and tried to understand. But to understand at this point in our study, months along, would have been confusing, even a kind of disillusionment. He said something in Latin, hands pressed flat to the tabletop, and then he did a strange thing. He looked at us, eyes gliding up one row of faces, down the other. We were all there, we were always there, our usual shrouded selves. Finally, he raised his hand and looked at his watch. It didn't matter what time it was. The gesture itself meant that class was over.

A meaning fixed in advance, we thought.

We sat there, she and I, while the others gathered books and papers and lifted coats off chair backs. She was pale and thin, hair pinned back, and I had an idea that she wanted to look neutral, seem neutral in order to challenge people to notice her. She placed her textbook on top of her notebook, centering it precisely, then raised her head and waited for me to say something.

"O.K., what's your name?"

"Jenna. What's yours?"

"I want to say Lars-Magnus just to see if you believe me."

"I don't."

"It's Robby," I said.

"I saw you working out in the fitness center."

"I was on the elliptical. Where were you?"

"Just passing by, I guess."

"Is that what you do?"

"Pretty much all the time," she said.

The last to leave were shuffling out now. She stood and dropped her books into her backpack, which dangled from the chair. I remained where I was, watching.

"I'm curious to know what you have to say about this man."

"The professor."

"Do you have insights to offer?"

"I talked to him once," she said. "Person to person."

"Are you serious? Where?"

"At the diner in town."

"You talked to him?"

"I get off-campus urges. I have to go somewhere."

"I know the feeling."

"It's the only place to eat, other than here, so I walked in and sat down and there he was in the booth across the aisle."

"That's incredible."

"I sat there and thought, It's him."

"It's him."

"There was a big foldout menu that I hid behind while I kept sneaking looks. He was eating a full meal, something slopped in brown gravy from the center of the earth. And he had a Coke with a straw bending out of the can."

"You talked to him."

"I said something not too original, and we talked off and on. He had his coat thrown onto the seat opposite him, and I was eating a salad, and there was a book lying on top of his coat, and I asked him what he was reading."

"You talked to him. The man who makes you lower your eyes in primitive fear and dread."

"It was a diner. He was drinking Coke through a straw," she said.

"Fantastic. What was he reading?"

"He said he was reading Dostoevsky. I'll tell you exactly what he said. He said, 'Dostoevsky day and night.' "

"Fantastic."

"And I told him my coincidence, that I'd been reading a lot of poetry and I'd read a poem just a couple of days earlier with a phrase I recalled. 'Like midnight in Dostoevsky.' "

"What did he say?"

"Nothing."

"Does he read Dostoevsky in the original?"

"I didn't ask."

"I wonder if he does. I have a feeling he does."

There was a pause, and then she said that she was leaving school. I was thinking about Ilgauskas in the diner. She told me that she wasn't happy here, that her mother always said how accomplished she was at being unhappy. She was heading west, she said, to Idaho. I didn't say anything. I sat there with my hands folded at my belt line. She left without a coat. Her coat was probably in the coatrack on the first floor.

At the winter break I stayed on campus, one of the few. We called ourselves the Left Behind and spoke in broken English. The routine included zombie body posture and blurred vision, lasting half a day before we'd all had enough.

At the gym I did my dumb struts on the elliptical and lapsed into spells of lost thought. Idaho, I thought. Idaho, the word, so vowelled and obscure. Wasn't where we were, right here, obscure enough for her?

The library was deserted during the break. I entered with a key card and took a novel by Dostoevsky down from the shelves. I placed the book on a table and opened it and then leaned down into the splayed pages, reading and breathing. We seemed to assimilate each other, the characters and I, and when I raised my head I had to tell myself where I was.

I knew where my father was—in Beijing, trying to wedge his securities firm into the Chinese century. My mother was adrift, possibly in the Florida Keys with a former boyfriend named Raúl. My father pronounced it *raw-eel*, like a thing you eat with your eyes closed.

In snowfall, the town looked ghosted over, dead still at times. I took walks nearly every afternoon, and the man in the hooded coat was never far from my mind. I walked up and down the street where he lived, and it seemed only fitting that he was not to be seen. This was an essential quality of the place. I began to feel intimate with these streets. I was myself here, able to see things singly and plainly, away from the only life I'd known, the city, stacked and layered, a thousand meanings a minute.

On the stunted commercial street in town, there were three places still open for business, one of them the diner, and I ate there once and stuck my head in the door two or three times, scanning the booths. The sidewalk was old, pocked bluestone. In the convenience store, I bought a fudge bar and talked to the woman behind the counter about her son's wife's kidney infection.

At the library, I devoured about a hundred pages a sitting, small cramped type. When I left the building the book remained on the table, open to the page where I'd stopped reading. I returned the next day, and the book was still there, open to the same page.

Why did this seem magical? Why did I sometimes lie in bed, moments from sleep, and think of the book in the empty room, open to the page where I'd stopped reading?

On one of those midnights, just before classes resumed, I got out of bed and went down the hall to the sun parlor. The area was enclosed by a slanted canopy of partitioned glass, and I unlatched a panel and swung it open. My pajamas seemed to evaporate. I felt the cold in my pores, my teeth. I thought my teeth were ringing. I stood and looked, I was always looking. I felt like a child now, responding to a dare. How long could I take it? I peered into the northern sky, the living sky, my breath turning to little bursts of smoke, as if I were separating from my body. I'd come to love the cold, but this was idiotic, and I closed the panel and went back to my room. I paced awhile, swinging my arms across my chest, trying to roil the blood, warm the body, and twenty minutes after I was back in bed, wide awake, the idea came to mind. It came from nowhere, from the night, fully formed, extending in several directions, and when I opened my eyes in the morning it was all around me, filling the room.

Those afternoons the light died quickly and we talked nearly nonstop, race-walking into the wind. Every topic had spectral connections, Todd's congenital liver condition shading into my ambition to run a marathon, this leading to that, the theory of prime numbers to the living sight of rural mailboxes set along a lost road, eleven standing units, rusted over and near collapse, a prime number, Todd announced, using his cell phone to take a picture.

One day, we approached the street where the hooded man lived. This was when I told Todd about the idea I'd had, the revelation in the icy night. I knew who the man was, I said. Everything fit, every element, the man's origins, his family ties, his presence in this town.

He said, "O.K."

"First, he's a Russian."

"A Russian."

"He's here because his son is here."

"He doesn't have the bearing of a Russian."

"The bearing? What's the bearing? His name could easily be Pavel."

"No, it couldn't."

"Great name possibilities. Pavel, Mikhail, Aleksei. Viktor with a 'k.' His late wife was Tatiana."

We stopped and looked down the street toward the gray frame house designated as the place where the man lived.

"Listen to me," I said. "His son lives in this town because he teaches at the college. His name is Ilgauskas."

I waited for him to be stunned.

"Ilgauskas is the son of the man in the hooded coat," I said. "Our Ilgauskas. They're Russian, father and son."

I pointed at him and waited for him to point back.

He said, "Ilgauskas is too old to be the man's son."

"He's not even fifty. The man is in his seventies, easy. Mid-seventies, most likely. It fits, it works."

"Is Ilgauskas a Russian name?"

"Why wouldn't it be?"

"Somewhere else, somewhere nearby, but not necessarily Russian," he said.

We stood there looking toward the house. I should have anticipated this kind of resistance, but the idea had been so striking that it had overwhelmed my cautious instincts.

"There's something you don't know about Ilgauskas."

He said, "O.K."

"He reads Dostoevsky day and night."

I knew that he would not ask how I'd come upon this detail. It was a fascinating detail, and it was mine, not his, which meant that he would let it pass without comment. But the silence was a brief one.

"Does he have to be Russian to read Dostoevsky?"

"That's not the point. The point is that it all fits together. It's a formulation, it's artful, it's structured."

"He's American, Ilgauskas, same as we are."

"A Russian is always Russian. He even speaks with a slight accent."

"I don't hear an accent."

"You have to listen. It's there," I said.

I didn't know whether it was there or not. The Norway maple didn't have to be Norway. We worked spontaneous variations on the source material of our surroundings.

"You say the man lives in that house. I accept this," I said. "I say he lives there with his son and his son's wife. Her name is Irina."

"And the son. Ilgauskas, so called. His first name?"

"We don't need a first name. He's Ilgauskas. That's all we need," I said.

His hair was mussed, suit jacket dusty and stained, ready to come apart at the shoulder seams. He leaned into the table, square-jawed, sleepy-looking.

"If we isolate the stray thought, the passing thought," he said, "the thought whose origin is unfathomable, then we begin to understand that we are routinely deranged, everyday crazy."

We loved the idea of being everyday crazy. It rang so true, so real.

"In our privatest mind," he said, "there is only chaos and blur. We invented logic to beat back our creatural selves. We assert or deny. We follow 'M' with 'N.'"

Our privatest mind, we thought. Did he really say that?

"The only laws that matter are laws of thought."

His fists were clenched on the tabletop, knuckles white.

"The rest is devil worship," he said.

We went walking but did not see the man. The wreaths were mostly gone from the front doors and the occasional bundled figure scraped snow off a car's windshield. Over time, we began to understand that these walks were not casual off-campus rambles. We were not looking at trees or boxcars, as we normally did, naming, counting, categorizing. This was different. There was a measure to the man in the hooded coat, old stooped body, face framed in monkish cloth, a history, a faded drama. We wanted to see him one more time.

We agreed on this, Todd and I, and collaborated, in the meantime, on describing his day.

He drinks coffee black, from a small cup, and spoons cereal out of a child's bowl. His head practically rests in the bowl when he bends to eat. He never looks at a newspaper. He goes back to his room after breakfast, where he sits and thinks. His daughter-in-law comes in and makes the bed, Irina.

Although Todd did not concede the binding nature of the name.

Some days we had to wrap scarves around our faces and speak in muffled voices, only our eyes exposed to the street and the weather.

There are two schoolchildren and one smaller girl, Irina's sister's child, here for reasons not yet determined, and the old man often passes the morning fitfully watching TV cartoons with the child, though not seated beside her. He occupies an armchair well away from the TV set, dozing now and then. Mouth open, we said. Head tilted and mouth hanging open.

We weren't sure why we were doing this. But we tried to be scrupulous, adding new elements every day, making adjustments and refinements, and all the while scanning the streets, trying to induce an appearance through joint force of will.

Soup for lunch, every day it's soup, homemade, and he holds his big spoon over the soup bowl, the old-country bowl, in a manner not unlike the child's, ready to plant a trowel and scoop.

Todd said that Russia was too big for the man. He'd get lost in the vast expanse. Think about Romania, Bulgaria. Better yet, Albania. Is he a Christian, a Muslim? With Albania, he said, we deepen the cultural context. "Context" was his fallback word.

When he is ready for his walk, Irina tries to help him button his parka, his anorak, but he shakes her off with a few brusque words. She shrugs and replies in kind.

I realized I'd forgotten to tell Todd that Ilgauskas read Dostoevsky in the original. This was a feasible truth, a usable truth. It made Ilgauskas, in context, a Russian.

He wears trousers with suspenders.

Until we decided that he didn't; it was too close to stereotype. Who shaved the old man? Did he do it himself? We didn't want him to. But who did it and how often?

This was my crystalline link: the old man to Ilgauskas to Dostoevsky to Russia. I thought about it all the time. Todd said it would become my life's work. I would spend my life in a thought bubble, purifying the link.

He doesn't have a private toilet. He shares a toilet with the children but never seems to use it. He is as close to being invisible as a man can get in a household of six. Sitting, thinking, disappearing on his walk.

We shared a vision of the man in his bed, at night, mind roaming back—the village, the hills, the family dead. We walked the same streets every day, obsessively, and we spoke in subdued tones even when we disagreed. It was part of the dialectic, our looks of thoughtful disapproval.

He probably smells bad, but the only one who seems to notice is the oldest child, a girl, thirteen. She makes faces now and then, passing behind his chair at the dinner table.

It was the tenth straight sunless day. The number was arbitrary, but the mood was beginning to bear down, not the cold or the wind but the missing light, the missing man. Our voices took on an anxious cadence. It occurred to us that he might be dead.

We talked about this all the way back to campus.

Do we make him dead? Do we keep assembling the life posthumously? Or do we end it now, tomorrow, the next day, stop coming to town, stop looking for him? One thing I knew: he does not die Albanian.

The next day, we stood at the end of the street where the designated house was located. We were there for an hour, barely speaking. Were we waiting for him to appear? I don't think we knew. What if he came out of the wrong house? What would this mean? What if someone else came out of the designated house, a young couple carrying ski equipment toward the car in the driveway? Maybe we were there simply to show deferential regard, standing quietly in the presence of the dead.

No one emerged, no one went in, and we left feeling unsure of ourselves.

Minutes later, approaching the railroad tracks, we saw him. We stopped and pointed at each other, holding the pose a moment. It was enormously satisfying, it was thrilling, to see the thing happen, see it become three-dimensional. He made a turn into a street at a right angle to the one we were on. Todd hit me on the arm, turned, and started jogging. Then I started jogging. We were going back in the direction we'd just come from. We went around one corner, ran down the street, went around another corner, and waited. In time, he appeared, walking now in our direction.

This was what Todd wanted, to see him head on. We moved

toward him. He seemed to walk a sort of pensive route, meandering with his thoughts. I pulled Todd toward the curb with me so that the man would not have to pass between us. We waited for him to see us. We could almost count off the footsteps to the instant when he would raise his head. It was an interval drawn taut with detail. We were close enough to see the sunken face, heavily stubbled, pinched in around the mouth, jaw sagging. He saw us now and paused, one hand gripping a button at the front of his coat. He looked haunted inside the shabby hood. He looked misplaced, isolated, someone who could easily be the man we were in the process of imagining.

We walked on past and continued for eight or nine paces, then turned and watched.

"That was good," Todd said. "That was totally worthwhile. Now we're ready to take the next step."

"There is no next step. We got our close look," I said. "We know who he is."

"We don't know anything."

"We wanted to see him one more time."

"Lasted only seconds."

"What do you want to do, take a picture?"

"My cell phone needs recharging," he said seriously. "The coat is an anorak, by the way, definitely, up close."

"The coat is a parka."

The man was two and a half blocks from the left turn that would put him on the street where he lived.

"I think we need to take the next step."

"You said that."

"I think we need to talk to him."

I looked at Todd. He wore a fixed smile, grafted on.

"That's crazy."

"It's completely reasonable," he said.

"We do that, we kill the idea, we kill everything we've done. We can't talk to him."

"We'll ask a few questions, that's all. Quiet, low key. Find out a few things."

"It's never been a matter of literal answers."

"I counted eighty-seven boxcars. You counted eighty-seven boxcars. Remember."

"This is different, and we both know it."

"I can't believe you're not curious. All we're doing is searching out the parallel life," he said. "It doesn't affect what we've been saying all this time."

"It affects everything. It's a violation. It's crazy."

I looked down the street toward the man in question. He was still moving slowly, a little erratically, hands folded behind his back now, where they belonged.

"If you're sensitive about approaching him, I'll do it," he said.

"No, you won't."

"Why not?"

"Because he's old and frail. Because he won't understand what you want."

"What do I want? A few words of conversation. If he shies away, I'm out of there in an instant."

"Because he doesn't even speak English."

"You don't know that. You don't know anything."

He started to move away, and I clutched his arm and turned him toward me.

"Because you'll scare him," I said. "Just the sight of you. Freak of nature."

He looked straight into me. It took time, this look. Then he pulled his arm away, and I shoved him into the street. He turned and started walking, and I caught up with him and spun him around and struck him in the chest with the heel of my hand. It was a sample blow, an introduction. A car came toward us and veered away, faces in windows. We began to grapple. He was too awkward to be contained, all angles, a mess of elbows and knees, and deceptively strong. I had trouble getting a firm grip and lost a glove. I wanted to hit him in the liver but didn't know where it was. He began flailing in slow motion. I moved in and punched him on the side of the head with my bare hand. It hurt us both, and he made a sound and went into a fetal crouch. I snatched his cap and tossed it. I wanted to wrestle him down and pound his head into the asphalt, but he was too firmly set, still making the sound, a determined hum, science fiction. He unfolded then, flushed and wild-eyed, and started swinging blind. I stepped back and half circled, waiting for an opening, but he fell before I could hit him, scrambling up at once and starting to run.

The hooded man was about to move out of sight, turning into his street. I watched Todd run, long, slack, bouncy strides. He would have to go faster if he expected to reach the man before he disappeared into the gray frame house, the designated house.

I saw my lost glove lying in the middle of the street. Then Todd running, bareheaded, trying to skirt areas of frozen snow. The scene empty everywhere around him. I couldn't make sense of it. I felt completely detached. His breath visible, streams of trailing vapor. I wondered what it was that had caused this thing to happen. He only wanted to talk to the man.

THE OTHER PLACE

BY MARY GAITSKILL (2011)

My son, Douglas, loves to play with toy guns. He is thirteen. He loves video games in which people get killed. He loves violence on TV, especially if it's funny. How did this happen? The way everything does, of course. One thing follows another, naturally.

Naturally, he looks like me: shorter than average, with a fine build, hazel eyes, and light-brown hair. Like me, he has a speech impediment and a condition called "essential tremor" that causes involuntary hand movements, which make him look more fragile than he is. He hates reading, but he is bright. He is interested in crows because he heard on a nature show that they are one of the only species that are more intelligent than they need to be to survive. He does beautiful, precise drawings of crows.

Mostly, though, he draws pictures of men holding guns. Or men hanging from nooses. Or men cutting up other men with chainsaws—in these pictures there are no faces, just figures holding chainsaws and figures being cut in two, with blood spraying out.

My wife, Marla, says that this is fine, as long as we balance it out with other things—family dinners, discussions of current events, sports, exposure to art and nature. But I don't know. Douglas and I were sitting together in the living room last week, half watching the TV and checking e-mail, when an advertisement for a movie flashed across the screen: it was called "Captivity" and the ad showed a terrified blond girl in a cage, a tear running down her face. Doug didn't speak or move. But I could feel his fascination, the suddenly deepening quality of it. And I don't doubt that he could feel mine. We sat there and felt it together.

And then she was there, the woman in the car. In the room with my son, her black hair, her hard laugh, the wrinkled skin under her hard eyes, the sudden blood filling the white of her blue eye. There was excited music on the TV and then the ad ended. My son's attention went elsewhere; she lingered.

When I was a kid, I liked walking through neighborhoods alone, looking at houses, seeing what people did to make them homes: the gardens, the statuary, the potted plants, the wind chimes. Late at night, if I couldn't sleep, I would sometimes slip out my bedroom window and just spend an hour or so walking around. I loved it, especially in late spring, when it was starting to be warm and there were night sounds—crickets, birds, the whirring of bats, the occasional whooshing car, some lonely person's TV. I loved the mysterious darkness of the trees, the way they moved against the sky if there was wind—big and heavy movements, but delicate, too, in all the subtle, reactive leaves. In that soft, blurry weather, people slept with their windows open; it was a small town and they weren't afraid. Some houses—I'm thinking of two in particular, where the Legges and the Myers lived—had yards that I would actually hang around in at night. Once, when I was sitting on the Legges' front porch, thinking about stealing a piece of their garden statuary, their cat came and sat with me. I petted him and when I got up and went for the statuary he followed me with his tail up. The Legges' statues were elves, not corny, cute elves but sinister, wicked-looking elves, and I thought that one would look good in my room. But they were too heavy, so I just moved them around the yard.

I did things like that, dumb pranks that could only irritate those who noticed them: rearranging statuary, leaving weird stuff in mailboxes, looking into windows to see where people had dinner or left their personal things—or, in the case of the Legges, where their daughter, Jenna, slept. She was on the ground floor, her bed so close to the window that I could watch her chest rise and fall the way I watched the grass on their lawn stirring in the wind. The worst thing I did, probably, was put a giant marble in the Myers' gas tank, which could've really caused a problem if it had rolled over the gas hole while one of the Myers was driving on the highway, but I guess it never did.

Mostly, though, I wasn't interested in causing that kind of problem. I just wanted to sit and watch, to touch other people's things, to drink in their lives. I suspect that it's some version of these impulses that makes me the most successful real-estate agent in the Hudson Valley now: the ability to know what physical objects and surroundings will most please a person's sense of identity and make him feel at home.

I wish that Doug had this sensitivity to the physical world, and the ability to drink from it. I've tried different things with him: I used to throw the ball with him out in the yard, but he got tired of that; he hates hiking and likes biking only if he has to get someplace. What's working now a little bit is fishing, fly-fishing hip deep in the Hudson. An ideal picture of normal childhood.

I believe I had a normal childhood. But you have to go pretty far afield to find something people would call abnormal these days. My parents were divorced, and then my mother had boyfriends—but this was true of about half the kids I knew. She and my father fought, in the house, when they were together, and they went on fighting, on the phone, after they separated—loud, screaming fights sometimes. I didn't love it, but I understood it; people fight. I was never afraid that my father was going to hurt her, or me. I had nightmares occasionally, in which he turned into a murderer and came after me, chasing me, getting closer, until I fell down, unable to make my legs move right. But I've read that this is one of those primitive fears which everybody secretly has; it bears little relation to what actually happens.

What actually happened: he forced me to play golf with him for hours when I visited on Saturdays, even though it seemed only to make him miserable. He'd curse himself if he missed a shot and then that would make him miss another one and he'd curse himself more. He'd whisper, "Oh, God," and wipe his face if anything went wrong, or even if it didn't, as if just being there were an ordeal, and then I had to feel sorry for him. He'd make these noises sometimes, painful grunts when he picked up the sack of clubs, and it put me on edge and even disgusted me.

Now, of course, I see it differently. I remembered those Saturdays when I was first teaching Doug how to cast, out in the back yard. I wasn't much good myself yet, and I got tangled up in the bushes a couple of times. I could feel the boy's flashing impatience; I felt my age, too. Then we went to work disentangling and he came closer to help me. We linked in concentration, and it occurred to me that the delicacy of the line and the fine movements needed to free it appealed to him the way drawing appealed to him, because of their beauty and precision.

Besides, he was a natural. When it was his turn to try, he kept his wrist stiff and gave the air a perfect little punch and *zip*—great cast. The next time, he got tangled up, but he was speedy about getting unstuck so that he could do it again. Even when the tremor acted up. Even when I lectured him on the laws of physics. It was a good day.

There is one not-normal thing you could point to in my childhood, which is that my mother, earlier in her life, before I was born, had occasionally worked as a prostitute. But I don't think that counts, because I didn't know about it as a child. I didn't learn about it until six years ago, when I was thirty-eight and my mother was sick with a strain of flu that had killed a lot of people, most of them around her age. She was in the hospital and she was feverish and thought she was dying. She held my hand as she told me, her eyes sad half-moons, her lips still full and provocative. She said that she wanted me to know because she thought it might help me to understand some of the terrible things I'd heard my father say to her—things I mostly hadn't even listened to. "It wasn't anything really bad," she said. "I just needed the money sometimes, between jobs. It's not like I was a drug addict—it was just hard to make it in Manhattan. I only worked for good escort places. I never had a pimp or went out on the street. I never did anything perverted—I didn't have to. I was beautiful. They'd pay just to be with me."

Later, when she didn't die, she was embarrassed that she'd told me. She laughed that raucous laugh of hers and said, "Way to go, Marcy! On your deathbed, tell your son you're a whore and then don't die!"

"It's O.K.," I said.

And it was. It frankly was not really even much of a surprise. It was her vanity that disgusted me, the way she undercut the confession with a preening, maudlin joke. I could not respect that even then.

I don't think that my mom's confession, or whatever it may have implied, had anything to do with what I think of as "it." When I was growing up, there was, after all, no evidence of her past, nothing that could have affected me. But suddenly, when I was about fourteen, I started getting excited by the thought of girls being hurt. Or killed. A horror movie would be on TV, a girl in shorts would be running and screaming with some guy chasing her, and to me it was like porn. Even a scene where a sexy girl was getting her legs torn off by a shark—bingo. It was like pushing a button. My mom would be in the kitchen making dinner and talking on the phone, stirring and striding around with the phone tucked between her shoulder and her chin. Outside, cars would go by, or a dog would run across the lawn. My homework would be slowly getting done in my lap while this sexy girl was screaming "God help me!" and having her legs torn off. And I would go invisibly into an invisible world that I called "the other place." Where I sometimes passively watched a killer and other times became one.

It's true that I started drinking and drugging right about then. All my friends did. My mom tried to lay down the law, but I found ways around her. We'd go into the woods, me and usually Chet Wotazak and Jim Bonham, and we'd smoke weed we'd got from Chet's brother, a local dealer named Dan, and drink cheap wine. We could sometimes get Chet's dad to lend us a gun—in my memory he had an AK-47, though I don't know how that's possible—and we'd go out to a local junk yard and take turns shooting up toilets, the long tubes of fluorescent lights, whatever was there. Then we'd go to Chet's house, up to his room, where we'd play loud music and tell dumb jokes and watch music videos in which disgusting things happened: snakes crawled over a little boy's sleeping face and he woke up being chased by a psychopath in a huge truck; a girl was turned into a pig and then a cake and then the lead singer bit off her head.

You might think that the videos and the guns were part of it, that they encouraged my violent thoughts. But Chet and Jim were watching and doing the same things and they were not like me. They said mean things about girls, and they were disrespectful sometimes, but they didn't want to hurt them, not really. They wanted to touch them and be touched by them; they wanted that more than anything. You could hear it in their voices and see it in their eyes, no matter what they said.

So I would sit with them and yet be completely apart from them, talking and laughing about normal things in a dark mash of music and snakes and children running from psychos and girls being eaten—images that took me someplace my friends couldn't see, although it was right there in the room with us.

It was the same at home. My mother made dinner, talked on the phone, fought with my dad, had guys over. Our cat licked itself and ate from its dish. Around us, people cared about one another. Jenna Legge slept peacefully. But in the other place sexy girls—and sometimes ugly girls or older women—ran and screamed for help as an unstoppable, all-powerful killer came closer and closer. There was no school or sports or mom or dad or caring, and it was great.

I've told my wife about most of this, the drinking, the drugs, the murder fantasies. She understands, because she has her past, too: extreme sex, vandalizing cars, talking vulnerable girls into getting more drunk than they should on behalf of some guy. There's a picture of her and another girl in bathing suits, the other girl chugging a beer that is being held by a guy so that it goes straight down her throat as her head is tipped way back. Another guy is watching, and my smiling wife is holding the girl's hand. It's a picture that foreshadows some kind of cruelty or misery, or maybe just a funny story to tell about throwing up in the bathroom later. Privately, I see no similarity between it and my death obsession. For my wife, the connection is drugs and alcohol; she believes that we were that way because we were both addicts expressing our pain and anger through violent fantasies and blind actions.

. . .

The first time I took Doug out to fish, it was me on the hot golf course all over again. As we walked to the lake in our heavy boots and clothes, I could feel his irritation at the bugs and the brightness, the squalor of nature in his fastidious eyes. I told him that fly-fishing was like driving a sports car, as opposed to the Subaru of rod and reel. I went on about how anything beautiful had to be conquered. He just turned down his mouth.

He got interested, though, in tying on the fly; the simple elegance of the knot (the "fish-killer") intrigued him. He laid it down the first time, too, placing the backcast perfectly in a space between trees. He gazed at the brown, light-wrinkled water with satisfaction. But when I put my hand on his shoulder I could feel him inwardly pull away.

As I got older, my night walks became rarer, with a different, sadder feeling to them. I would go out when I was not drunk or high but in a quiet mood, wanting to be somewhere that was neither the normal social world nor the other place. A world where I could sit and feel the power of nature come up through my feet, and be near other people without them being near me. Where I could believe in and for a moment possess the goodness of their lives. Jenna Legge still slept on the ground floor and sometimes I would look in her window and watch her breathe, and, if I was lucky, see one of her developing breasts swell out of her nightgown.

I never thought of killing Jenna. I didn't think about killing anyone I actually knew—not the girls I didn't like at school or the few I had sex with. The first times I had sex, I was so caught up in the feeling of it that I didn't even think about killing—I didn't think about anything at all. But I didn't have sex much. I was small, awkward, too quiet; I had that tremor. My expression must've been strange as I sat in class, feeling hidden in my other place, but outwardly visible to whoever looked—not that many did.

Then one day I was with Chet's brother, Dan, on a drug drop; he happened to be giving me a ride because his drop, at the local college, was on the way to wherever I was going. It was a guy buying, but, when we arrived, a girl opened the door. She was pretty and she knew it, but whatever confidence that knowledge gave her was superficial. We stayed for a while and smoked the product with her and her boyfriend. The girl sat very erect and talked too much, as if she were smart, but there was a question at the end of everything she said. When we left, Dan said, "That's the kind of lady I'd like to slap in the face." I asked, "Why?" But I knew. I don't remember what he said, because it didn't matter. I already knew. And later, instead of making up a girl, I thought of that one.

I forgot to mention: one night when I was outside Jenna's window, she opened her eyes and looked right at me. I was stunned, so stunned that I couldn't move. There was nothing between us but a screen with a hole in it. She looked at me and blinked. I said, "Hi." I held my breath; I had not spoken to her since third grade. But she just sighed, rolled over, and lay still. I stood there trembling for a long moment. And then, slowly and carefully, I walked through the yard and onto the sidewalk, back to my house.

I cut school the next day and the next, because I was scared that Jenna had told everybody and that I would be mocked. But eventually it became clear that nobody was saying anything, so I went back. In class, I looked at Jenna cautiously, then gratefully. But she did not return my look. At first, this moved me, made me consider her powerful. I tried insistently to catch her eye, to let her know what I felt. Finally our eyes met, and I realized that she didn't understand why I was looking at her. I realized that although her eyes had been open that night, she had still been asleep. She had looked right at me, but she had not seen me at all.

And so one night, or early morning, really, I got out of bed, into my mother's car, and drove to the campus to look for her—the college girl.

The campus was in a heavily wooded area bordering a nature preserve. The dorms were widely scattered, though some, resembling midsized family homes, were clustered together. The girl lived in one of those, but while I remembered the general location I couldn't be sure which one it was. I couldn't see into any of the windows, because even the open ones had blinds pulled down. While I was standing indecisively on a paved path between dorms, I saw two guys coming toward me. Quickly, I walked off into a section of trees and underbrush. I moved carefully through the thicket, coming to a wide field that led toward the nature preserve. The darkness deepened as I got farther from the dorms. I could feel things coming up from the ground—teeth and claws, eyes, crawling legs, and brainless eating mouths. A song played in my head, an enormously popular, romantic song about love and death that had supposedly made a bunch of teen-agers kill themselves.

Kids still listen to that song. I once heard it coming from the computer in our family room. When I went in and looked over Doug's hunched shoulder, I realized that the song was being used as the soundtrack for a graphic video about a little boy in a mask murdering people. It was spellbinding, the yearning, eerie harmony of the song juxtaposed with terrified screaming; I told Doug to turn it off. He looked pissed, but he did it and went slumping out the door. I found it and watched it by myself later.

I went back to the campus many times. I went to avoid my mother as much as anything. Her new boyfriend was an asshole, and she whined when he was around. When he wasn't around, she whined about him on the phone. Sometimes she called two people in a row to whine about exactly the same things that he'd said or done. Even when I played music loud so I couldn't hear her, I could *feel* her. When that happened, I'd leave my music on so that she'd think I was still in my room and I'd go to the campus. I'd follow lone female students as closely as I could, and I'd feel the other place running against the membrane of the world, almost touching it.

Why does it make sense to put romantic music together with a story about a little boy murdering people? Because it does make sense—only I don't know how. It seems dimly to have to do with justice, with some wrong being avenged, but what? The hurts of childhood? The stupidity of life? The kid doesn't seem to be having fun. Random murder just seems like a job he has to do. But why?

Soon enough I realized that the college campus was the wrong place to think about making it real. It wasn't an environment I could control; there were too many variables. I needed to get the girl someplace private. I needed to have certain things there. I needed to have a gun. I could find a place; there were deserted places. I could get a gun from Chet's house; I knew where his father kept his. But the girl?

Then, while I was in the car with my mom one day, we saw a guy hitchhiking. He was middle-aged and fucked-up-looking, and my mom—we were stopped at a light—remarked that nobody in their right mind would pick him up. Two seconds later, somebody pulled over for him. My mom laughed.

I started hitchhiking. Most of the people who picked me up were men, but there were women, too. No one was scared of me. I was almost eighteen by then, but I was still small and quiet-looking. Women picked me up because they were concerned about me.

I didn't really plan to do it. I just wanted to feel the gun in my pocket and look at the woman and know that I *could* do it. There was this one—a thirtyish blonde with breasts that I could see through her open coat. But then she said that she was pregnant and I started thinking about what if I was killing the baby?

Doug had a lot of nightmares when he was a baby, by which I mean between the ages of two and four. When he cried out in his sleep, it was usually Marla who went to him. But one night she was sick and I told her to stay in bed while I went to comfort the boy. He was still crying "Mommy!" when I sat on the bed, and I felt his anxiety at seeing me instead of his mother, felt the moment of hesitation in his body before he came into my arms, vibrating rather than trembling, sweating and fragrant with emotion. He had dreamed that he was home alone and it was dark, and he was calling for his mother, but she wasn't there. "Daddy, Daddy," he wept, "there was a sick lady with red eyes and Mommy wouldn't come. Where is Mommy?"

That may've been the first time I truly remembered her, the woman in the car. It was so intense a moment that in a bizarre intersection of impossible feelings I got an erection with my crying child in my arms. But it lasted only a moment. I picked Doug up and carried him into our bedroom so that he could see his mother and nestle against her. I stayed awake nearly all night watching them.

The day it happened was a bright day, but windy and cold, and my mom would not shut up. I just wanted to watch a movie, but even with the TV turned up loud—I guess that's why she kept talking; she didn't think I could hear her—I couldn't blot out the sound of her yakking about how ashamed this asshole made her feel. I whispered, "If you're so ashamed, why do you talk about it?" She said, "It all goes back to being fucking molested." She lowered her voice; the only words I caught were "fucking corny." I went out into the hallway to listen. "The worst of it was that he wouldn't look at me," she said. I could almost hear her pacing around, the phone tucked against her shoulder. "That's why I fall for these passive-aggressive types who turn me on and then make me feel ashamed." Whoever she was talking to must have said something funny then, because she laughed. I left the TV on and walked out. I took the gun, but more for protection against perverts than the other thing.

I gave my boy that dream as surely as if I'd handed it to him. But I've given him a lot of other things, too. The first time he caught a fish he responded to my encouraging words with a bright glance that I will never forget. We let that one go, but only after he had held it in his hands, cold and quick, muscle with eyes and a heart, scales specked with yellow and red, and one tiny orange fin. Then the next one, bigger, leaping to break the rippling murk—I said, "Don't point the rod at the fish. Keep the tip up, keep it up"—and he listened to me and he brought it in. There is a picture of it on the corkboard in his room, the fish in the net, the lure bristling in its crude mouth. I have another picture, too, of him smiling triumphantly, holding it in his hands, its shining, still living body fully extended.

She was older than I'd wanted, forty or so, but still good-looking. She had a voice that was strong and lifeless at the same time. She had black hair and she wore tight black pants. She did not have a wedding ring, which meant that maybe no one would miss her. She picked me up on a lightly travelled forty-five-mile-an-hour road. She was listening to a talk show on the radio and she asked if I wanted to hear music instead. I said no, I liked talk shows.

"Yeah?" she said. "Why?"

"Because I'm interested in current events."

"I'm not," she said. "I just listen to this shit because the voices relax me. I don't really care what they're talking about."

They were talking about a war somewhere. Bombs were exploding in markets where people bought vegetables; somebody's legs had been blown off. We turned onto a road with a few cars, but none close to us.

"You don't care?"

"No, why should I? Oh, about this?" She paused. There was something about a little boy being rushed to an overcrowded hospital. "Yeah, that's bad. But it's not like we can do anything about it." On the radio, foreign people cried.

I took the gun out of my pocket.

I said, "Do you have kids?"

"No," she said. "Why?"

"Take me to Old Post Road. I'm going to the abandoned house there."

"I'm not going by there, but I can get you pretty close. So why do you care about current events? I didn't give a shit at your age."

"Take me there or I'll kill you."

She cocked her head and wrinkled her brow, as if she were trying to be sure she'd heard right. Then she looked down at the gun, and cut her eyes up at me; quickly, she looked back at the road. The car picked up speed.

"Take the next right or you'll die." My voice at that moment came not from me but from the other place. My whole body felt like an erection. She hit the right-turn signal. There was a long moment as we approached the crucial road. The voices on the radio roared ecstatically.

She pulled over to the shoulder.

"What are you doing?"

She put the car in park.

"Turn right or you die!"

She unbuckled her seat belt and turned to face me. "I'm ready," she said. She leaned back and gripped the steering wheel with one hand, as if to steady herself. With her free hand, she tapped herself between the eyes—bright, hot blue, rimmed with red. "Put it here," she said. "Go for it."

A car went by. Somebody in the passenger seat glanced at us blankly. "I don't want to do it here. There's witnesses. You need to take me to the place."

"What witnesses? That car's not stopping—nobody's going to stop unless the emergency lights are on and they're not, look."

"But if I shoot you in the head the blood will spray on the window and somebody could see." It was my own voice again: the power was gone. The people on the radio kept talking. Suddenly I felt my heart beating.

"O.K., then do it here." She opened her jacket to show me her chest. "Nobody'll hear. When you're done you can move me to the passenger seat and drive the car wherever."

"Get into the passenger seat now and I'll do it."

She laughed, hard. Her eyes were crazy. They were crazy the way an animal can be crazy in a tiny cage. "Hell, no. I'm not going to your place with you. You do it here, motherfucker."

I realized then that her hair was a wig, and a cheap one. For some reason, that made her seem even crazier. I held my gun hand against my body to hide the tremor.

"Come on, honey," she said. "Go for it."

Like a star, a red dot appeared in the white of her left eye. The normal place and the other place were turning into the same place, quick but slow, the way a car accident is quick but slow. I stared. The blood spread raggedly across her eye. She shifted her eyes from my face to a spot somewhere outside the car and fixed them there. I fought the urge to turn and see what she was looking at. She shifted her eyes again. She looked me deep in the face.

"Well?" she said. "Are you going to do it or not?"

Words appeared in my head, like a sign reading "I Don't Want To."

She leaned forward and turned on the emergency lights. "Get out of my car," she said quietly. "You're wasting my time."

As soon as I got out, she hit the gas and burned rubber. I walked into the field next to the road, without an idea of where I might go. I realized after she was gone that she might call the police, but I felt in my gut that she would not—in the other place there are no police, and she was from the other place.

Still, as I walked I took the bullets out of the gun and scattered them, kicking snow over them and stamping it down. I walked a long time, shivering horribly. I came across a drainage pipe and threw the empty gun into it. I thought, I should've gut-shot her—that's what I should've done. And then got her to the abandoned house. I should've gut-shot the bitch. But I knew why I hadn't. She'd been shot already, from the inside. If she had been somebody different I might actually have done it. But somehow the wig-haired woman had changed the channel and I don't even know if she'd meant to.

The fly bobbing on the brown, gentle water. The long grasses so green that they cast a fine, bright green on the brown water. The primitive fish mouth straining for water and finding it as my son releases it in the shallows. Its murky vanishing.

The blood bursting in her eye, poor woman, poor mother. My mother died of colon cancer just nine months ago. Shortly after that, it occurred to me that the woman had been wearing that awful wig because she was sick and undergoing chemo. Though of course I don't know.

The hurts of childhood that must be avenged: so small and so huge. Before I grew up and stopped thinking about her, I thought about that woman a lot. About what would've happened if I'd got her there, to the abandoned house. I don't remember anymore the details of these thoughts, only that they were distorted, swollen, blurred: broken face, broken voice, broken body left dying on the floor, watching me go with dimming, despairing eyes.

These pictures are faded now and far away. But they can still make me feel something.

The second time I put my hand on Doug's shoulder, he didn't move away inside; he was too busy tuning in to the line and the lure. Somewhere in him is the other place. It's quiet now, but I know it's there. I also know that he won't be alone with it. He won't know that I'm there with him, because we will never speak of it. But I will be there. He will not be alone with that.

GOING FOR A BEER

BY ROBERT COOVER (2011)

He finds himself sitting in the neighborhood bar drinking a beer at about the same time that he began to think about going there for one. In fact, he has finished it. Perhaps he'll have a second one, he thinks, as he downs it and asks for a third. There is a young woman sitting not far from him who is not exactly good-looking but good-looking enough, and probably good in bed, as indeed she is. Did he finish his beer? Can't remember. What really matters is: Did he enjoy his orgasm? Or even have one? This he is wondering on his way home through the foggy night streets from the young woman's apartment. Which was full of Kewpie dolls, the sort won at carnivals, and they made a date, as he recalls, to go to one. Where she wins another—she has a knack for it. Whereupon they're in her apartment again, taking their clothes off, she excitedly cuddling her new doll in a bed heaped with them. He can't remember when he last slept, and he's no longer sure, as he staggers through the night streets, still foggy, where his own apartment is, his orgasm, if he had one, already fading from memory. Maybe he should take her back to the carnival, he thinks, where she wins another Kewpie doll (this is at least their second date, maybe their fourth), and this time they go for a romantic nightcap at the bar where they first met. Where a brawny dude starts hassling her. He intervenes and she turns up at his hospital bed, bringing him one of her Kewpie dolls to keep him company. Which is her way of expressing the bond between them, or so he supposes, as he leaves the hospital on crutches, uncertain what part of town he is in. Or what part of the year. He decides that it's time to call the affair off—she's driving him crazy—but then the brawny dude turns up at their wedding and apologizes for the pounding he gave him. He didn't realize, he says, how serious they were. The guy's wedding present is a gift certificate for two free drinks at the bar where they met and a pair of white satin ribbons for his crutches. During the ceremony, they both carry Kewpie dolls that probably have some barely hidden significance, and indeed do. The child she bears him, his or another's, reminds him, as if he needed reminding, that time is fast moving on. He has responsibilities now and he decides to check whether he still has the job that he had when he first met her. He does. His absence, if he has been absent, is not remarked on, but he is not congratulated on his marriage, either, no doubt because—it comes back to him now—before he met his wife he was engaged to one of his colleagues and their co-workers had already thrown them an engagement party, so they must resent the money they spent on gifts. It's embarrassing and the atmosphere is somewhat hostile, but he has a child in kindergarten and another on the way, so what can he do? Well, he still hasn't cashed in the gift certificate, so, for one thing, what the hell, he can go for a beer, two, in fact, and he can afford a third. There's a young woman sitting near him who looks like she's probably good in bed, but she's not his wife and he has no desire to commit adultery, or so he tells himself, as he sits on the edge of her bed with his pants around his ankles. Is he taking them off or putting them on? He's not sure, but now he pulls them on and limps home, having left his beribboned crutches somewhere. On arrival, he finds all the Kewpie dolls, which were put on a shelf when the babies started coming, now scattered about the apartment, beheaded and with their limbs amputated. One of the babies is crying, so, while he warms up a bottle of milk on the stove, he goes into its room to give it a pacifier and discovers a note from his wife pinned to its pajamas, which says that she has gone off to the hospital to have another baby and she'd better not find him here when she gets back, because if she does she'll kill him. He believes her, so he's soon out on the streets again, wondering if he ever gave that bottle to the baby, or if it's still boiling away on the stove. He passes the old neighborhood bar and is tempted but decides that he has had enough trouble for one lifetime and is about to walk on when he is stopped by that hulk who beat him up and who now gives him a cigar because he's just become a father and drags him into the bar for a celebratory drink, or, rather, several, he has lost count. The celebrations are already over, however, and the new father, who has married the same woman who threw him out, is crying in his beer about the miseries of married life and congratulating him on being well out of it, a lucky man. But he doesn't feel lucky, especially when he sees a young woman sitting near them who looks like she's probably good in bed and decides to suggest that they go to her place, but too late—she's already out the door with the guy who beat him up and stole his wife. So he has another beer, wondering where he's supposed to live now, and realizing—it's the bartender who so remarks while offering him another on the house—that life is short and brutal and before he knows it he'll be dead. He's right. After a few more beers and orgasms, some vaguely remembered, most not, one of his sons, now a race-car driver and the president of the company he used to work for, comes to visit him on his deathbed and, apologizing for arriving so late (I went for a beer, Dad, things happened), says he's going to miss him but it's probably for the best. For the best what? he asks, but his son is gone, if he was ever there in the first place. Well . . . you know . . . life, he says to the nurse who has come to pull the sheet over his face and wheel him away.

TENTH OF DECEMBER

BY GEORGE SAUNDERS (2011)

The pale boy with unfortunate Prince Valiant bangs and cublike mannerisms hulked to the mudroom closet and requisitioned Dad's white coat. Then requisitioned the boots he'd spray-painted white. Painting the pellet gun white had been a no. That was a gift from Aunt Chloe. Every time she came over he had to haul it out so she could make a big stink about the woodgrain.

Today's assignation: walk to pond, ascertain beaver dam. Likely he would be detained. By that species that lived amongst the old rock wall. They were small but, upon emerging, assumed certain proportions. And gave chase. This was just their methodology. His aplomb threw them loops. He knew that. And revelled it. He would turn, level the pellet gun, intone: Are you aware of the usage of this human implement?

Blam!

They were Netherworlders. Or Nethers. They had a strange bond with him. Sometimes for whole days he would just nurse their wounds. Occasionally, for a joke, he would shoot one in the butt as it fled. Who henceforth would limp for the rest of its days. Which could be as long as an additional nine million years.

Safe inside the rock wall, the shot one would go, Guys, look at my butt.

As a group, all would look at Gzeemon's butt, exchanging sullen glances of: Gzeemon shall indeed be limping for the next nine million years, poor bloke.

Because yes: Nethers tended to talk like that guy in "Mary Poppins."

Which naturally raised some mysteries as to their origin here on Earth.

Detaining him was problematic for the Nethers. He was wily. Plus could not fit through their rock-wall opening. When they tied him up and went inside to brew their special miniaturizing potion—*Wham!*—he would snap their antiquated rope with a move from his self-invented martial-arts system, Toi Foi, a.k.a. Deadly Forearms. And place at their doorway an implacable rock of suffocation, trapping them inside.

Later, imagining them in their death throes, taking pity on them, he would come back, move the rock.

Blimey, one of them might say from withal. Thanks, guv'nor. You are indeed a worthy adversary.

Sometimes there would be torture. They would make him lie on his back looking up at the racing clouds while they tortured him in ways he could actually take. They tended to leave his teeth alone. Which was lucky. He didn't even like to get a cleaning. They were dunderheads in that manner. They never messed with his peen and never messed with his fingernails. He'd just abide there, infuriating them with his snow angels. Sometimes, believing it their coup de grâce, not realizing he'd heard this since time in memorial from certain in-school cretins, they'd go, Wow, we didn't even know Robin could be a boy's name. And chortle their Nether laughs.

Today he had a feeling that the Nethers might kidnap Suzanne Bledsoe, the new girl in homeroom. She was from Montreal. He just loved the way she talked. So, apparently, did the Nethers, who planned to use her to repopulate their depleted numbers and bake various things they did not know how to bake.

All suited up now, NASA. Turning awkwardly to go out door.

Affirmative. We have your coördinates. Be careful out there, Robin.

Whoa, cold, dang.

Duck thermometer read ten. And that was without windchill. That made it fun. That made it real. A green Nissan was parked where Poole dead-ended into the soccer field. Hopefully the owner was not some perv he would have to outwit.

Or a Nether in the human guise.

Bright, bright blue and cold. Crunch went the snow as he crossed the soccer field. Why did cold such as this give a running guy a headache? Likely it was due to Prominent Windspeed Velocity.

The path into the woods was as wide as one human. It seemed the Nether had indeed kidnapped Suzanne Bledsoe. Damn him! And his ilk. Judging by the single set of tracks, the Nether appeared to be carrying her. Foul cad. He'd better not be touching Suzanne inappropriately while carrying her. If so, Suzanne would no doubt be resisting with untamable fury.

This was concerning, this was very concerning.

When he caught up to them, he would say, Look, Suzanne, I know you don't know my name, having misaddressed me as Roger that time you asked me to scoot over, but nevertheless I must confess I feel there is something to us. Do you feel the same?

Suzanne had the most amazing brown eyes. They were wet now, with fear and sudden reality.

Stop talking to her, mate, the Nether said.

I won't, he said. And, Suzanne? Even if you don't feel there is something to us, rest assured I will still slay this fellow and return you home. Where do you live again? Over in El Cirro? By the water tower? Those are some nice houses back there.

Yes, Suzanne said. We also have a pool. You should come over next summer. It's cool if you swim with your shirt on. And also, yes to there being something to us. You are by far the most insightful boy in our class. Even when I take into consideration the boys I knew in Montreal, I am just like: no one can compare.

Well, that's nice to hear, he said. Thank you for saying that. I know I'm not the thinnest.

The thing about girls? Suzanne said. Is we are more content-driven.

Will you two stop already? the Nether said. Because now is the time for your death. Deaths.

Well, now is certainly the time for somebody's death, Robin said.

The twerpy thing was you never really got to save anyone. Last summer there'd been a dying raccoon out here. He'd thought of lugging it home so Mom could call the vet. But up close it was too scary. Raccoons being actually bigger than they appear in cartoons. And this one looked like a potential biter. So he ran home to get it some water at least. Upon his return, he saw where the raccoon had done some apparent last-minute thrashing. That was sad. He didn't do well with sad. There had perchance been some pre-weeping, by him, in the woods.

That just means you have a big heart, Suzanne said.

Well, I don't know, he said modestly.

Here was the old truck tire. Where the high-school kids partied. Inside the tire, frosted with snow, were three beer cans and a wadded-up blanket.

You probably like to party, the Nether had cracked to Suzanne moments earlier as they passed this very spot.

No, I don't, Suzanne said. I like to play. And I like to hug.

Hoo boy, the Nether said. Sounds like Dullsville.

Somewhere there is a man who likes to play and hug, Suzanne said.

He came out of the woods now to the prettiest vista he knew. The pond was a pure frozen white. It struck him as somewhat Switzerlandish. Someday he would know for sure. When the Swiss threw him a parade or whatnot.

Here the Nether's tracks departed from the path, as if he had contemplatively taken a moment to gaze at the pond. Perhaps this Nether was not all bad. Perhaps he was having a debilitating conscience attack vis-à-vis the valiantly struggling Suzanne atop his back. At least he seemed to somewhat love nature.

Then the tracks returned to the path, wound around the pond, and headed up Lexow Hill.

What was this strange object? A coat? On the bench? The bench the Nethers used for their human sacrifices?

No accumulated snow on coat. Inside of coat still slightly warm.

Ergo: the recently discarded coat of the Nether.

This was some strange juju. This was an intriguing conundrum, if he had ever encountered one. Which he had. Once, he'd found a bra on the handlebars of a bike. Once, he'd found an entire untouched steak dinner on a plate behind Fresno's. And hadn't eaten it. Though it had looked pretty good.

Something was afoot.

Then he beheld, halfway up Lexow Hill, a man.

Coatless, bald-headed man. Super skinny. In what looked like pajamas. Climbing plodfully, with tortoise patience, bare white arms sticking out of his p.j. shirt like two bare white branches sticking out of a p.j. shirt. Or grave.

What kind of person leaves his coat behind on a day like this? The mental kind, that was who. This guy looked sort of mental. Like an Auschwitz dude or sad confused grandpa.

Dad had once said, Trust your mind, Rob. If it smells like shit but has writing across it that says Happy Birthday and a candle stuck down in it, what is it?

Is there icing on it? he'd said.

Dad had done that thing of squinting his eyes when an answer was not quite there yet.

What was his mind telling him now?

Something was wrong here. A person needed a coat. Even if the person was a grownup. The pond was frozen. The duck thermometer said ten. If the person was mental, all the more reason to come to his aid, as had not Jesus said, Blessed are those who help those who cannot help themselves, but are too mental, doddering, or have a disability?

He snagged the coat off the bench.

It was a rescue. A real rescue, at last, sort of.

Ten minutes earlier, Don Eber had paused at the pond to catch his breath.

He was so tired. What a thing. Holy moly. When he used to walk Sasquatch out here they'd do six times around the pond, jog up the hill, tag the boulder on top, sprint back down.

Better get moving, said one of two guys who'd been in discussion in his head all morning.

That is, if you're still set on the boulder idea, the other said.

Which still strikes us as kind of fancy-pants.

Seemed like one guy was Dad and the other Kip Flemish.

Stupid cheaters. They'd switched spouses, abandoned the

switched spouses, fled together to California. Had they been gay? Or just swingers? Gay swingers? The Dad and Kip in his head had acknowledged their sins and the three of them had struck a deal: he would forgive them for being possible gay swingers and leaving him to do Soap Box Derby alone, with just Mom, and they would consent to giving him some solid manly advice.

He wants it to be nice.

This was Dad now. It seemed Dad was somewhat on his side.

Nice? Kip said. *That is not the word I would use.*

A cardinal zinged across the day.

It was amazing. Amazing, really. He was young. He was fifty-three. Now he'd never deliver his major national speech on compassion. What about going down the Mississippi in a canoe? What about living in an A-frame near a shady creek with the two hippie girls he'd met in 1968 in that souvenir shop in the Ozarks, when Allen, his stepfather, wearing those crazy aviators, had bought him a bag of fossil rocks? One of the hippie girls had said that he, Eber, would be a fox when he grew up, and would he please be sure to call her at that time? Then the hippie girls had put their tawny heads together and giggled at his prospective foxiness. And that had never—

That had somehow never—

Sister Val had said, Why not shoot for being the next J.F.K.? So he had run for class president. Allen had bought him a Styrofoam straw boater. They'd sat together, decorating the hatband with Magic Markers. WIN WITH EBER! On the back: GROOVY! Allen had helped him record a tape. Of a little speech. Allen had taken that tape somewhere and come back with thirty copies, "to pass around."

"Your message is good," Allen had said. "And you are incredibly well spoken. You can do this thing."

And he'd done it. He'd won. Allen had thrown him a victory party. A pizza party. All the kids had come.

Oh, Allen.

Kindest man ever. Had taken him swimming. Had taken him to découpage. Had combed out his hair so patiently that time he came home with lice. Never a harsh, etc., etc.

Not so once the suffering begat. Began. God damn it. More and more his words. Askew. More and more his words were not what he would hoped.

Hope.

Once the suffering began, Allen had raged. Said things no one should say. To Mom, to Eber, to the guy delivering water. Went from a shy man, always placing a reassuring hand on your back, to a diminished pale figure in a bed, shouting CUNT!

Except with some weird New England accent, so it came out KANT!

The first time Allen had shouted KANT! there followed a funny moment during which he and Mom looked at each other to see which of them was being called KANT. But then Allen amended, for clarity: KANTS!

So it was clear he meant both of them. What a relief.

They'd cracked up.

Jeez, how long had he been standing here? Daylight was waiting.

Wasting.

I honestly didn't know what to do. But he made it so simple.

Took it all on himself.

So what else is new?

Exactly.

This was Jodi and Tommy now.

Hi, kids.

Big day today.

I mean, sure, it would have been nice to have a chance to say a proper goodbye.

But at what cost?

Exactly. And see—he knew that.

He was a father. That's what a father does.

Eases the burdens of those he loves.

Saves the ones he loves from painful last images that might endure for a lifetime.

Soon Allen had become THAT. And no one was going to fault anybody for avoiding THAT. Sometimes he and Mom would huddle in the kitchen. Rather than risk incurring the wrath of THAT. Even THAT understood the deal. You'd trot in a glass of water, set it down, say, very politely, Anything else, Allen? And you'd see THAT thinking, All these years I was so good to you people and now I am merely

THAT? Sometimes the gentle Allen would be inside there, too, indicating, with his eyes, Look, go away, please go away, I am trying so hard not to call you KANT!

Rail-thin, ribs sticking out.

Catheter taped to dick.

Waft of shit smell.

You are not Allen and Allen is not you.

So Molly had said.

As for Dr. Spivey, he couldn't say. Wouldn't say. Was busy drawing a daisy on a Post-it. Then finally said, Well, honestly? As these things grow, they can tend to do weird things. But it doesn't necessarily have to be terrible. Had one guy? Just always craved him a Sprite.

And Eber had thought, Did you, dear doctor/savior/lifeline, just say *craved him a Sprite*?

That's how they got you. You thought, Maybe I'll just crave me a Sprite. Next thing you knew, you were THAT, shouting KANT!, shitting your bed, swatting at the people who were scrambling to clean you.

No, sir.

No sirree bob.

Wednesday he'd fallen out of the med-bed again. There on the floor in the dark it had come to him: I could spare them.

Spare us? Or spare you?

Get thee behind me.

Get thee behind me, sweetie.

A breeze sent down a sequence of linear snow puffs from somewhere above. Beautiful. Why were we made just so, to find so many things that happened every day pretty?

He took off his coat.

Good Christ.

Took off his hat and gloves, stuffed the hat and gloves in a sleeve of the coat, left the coat on the bench.

This way they'd know. They'd find the car, walk up the path, find the coat.

It was a miracle. That he'd got this far. Well, he'd always been strong. Once, he'd run a half-marathon with a broken foot. After his vasectomy he'd cleaned the garage, no problem.

He'd waited in the med-bed for Molly to go off to the pharmacy. That was the toughest part. Just calling out a normal goodbye.

His mind veered toward her now, and he jerked it back with a prayer: Let me pull this off. Lord, let me not fuck it up. Let me bring no dishonor. Leg me do it cling.

Let. Let me do it cling.

Clean.

Cleanly.

Estimated time of overtaking the Nether, handing him his coat? Approximately nine minutes. Six minutes to follow the path around the pond, an additional three minutes to fly up the hillside like a delivering wraith or mercy-angel, bearing the simple gift of a coat.

That is just an estimate, NASA. I pretty much made that up.

We know that, Robin. We know very well by now how irreverent you work.

Like that time you cut a fart on the moon.

Or the time you tricked Mel into saying, "Mr. President, what a delightful surprise it was to find an asteroid circling Uranus."

That estimate was particularly iffy. This Nether being surprisingly brisk. Robin himself was not the fastest wicket in the stick. He had a certain girth. Which Dad prognosticated would soon triumphantly congeal into linebackerish solidity. He hoped so. For now he just had the slight man-boobs.

Robin, hurry, Suzanne said. I feel so sorry for that poor old guy.

He's a fool, Robin said, because Suzanne was young, and did not yet understand that when a man was a fool he made hardships for the other men, who were less foolish than he.

He doesn't have much time, Suzanne said, bordering on the hysterical.

There, there, he said, comforting her.

I'm just so frightened, she said.

And yet he is fortunate to have one such as I to hump his coat up that big-ass hill, which, due to its steepness, is not exactly my cup of tea, Robin said.

I guess that's the definition of "hero," Suzanne said.

I guess so, he said.

I don't mean to continue being insolent, she said. But he seems to be pulling away.

What would you suggest? he said.

With all due respect, she said, and because I know you consider us as equals but different, with me covering the brainy angle and special inventions and whatnot?

Yes, yes, go ahead, he said.

Well, just working through the math in terms of simple geometry—

He saw where she was going with this. And she was quite right. No wonder he loved her. He must cut across the pond, thereby decreasing the ambient angle, ergo trimming valuable seconds off his catchup time.

Wait, Suzanne said. Is that dangerous?

It is not, he said. I have done it numerous times.

Please be careful, Suzanne implored.

Well, once, he said.

You have such aplomb, Suzanne demurred.

Actually never, he said softly, not wishing to alarm her.

Your bravery is irascible, Suzanne said.

He started across the pond.

It was actually pretty cool walking on water. In summer, canoes floated here. If Mom could see him, she'd have a conniption. Mom treated him like a piece of glass. Due to his alleged infant surgeries. She went on full alert if he so much as used a stapler.

But Mom was a good egg. A reliable counsellor and steady hand of guidance. She had a munificent splay of long silver hair and a raspy voice, though she didn't smoke and was even a vegan. She'd never been a biker chick, although some of the in-school cretins claimed she resembled one.

He was actually quite fond of Mom.

He was now approximately three-quarters, or that would be sixty per cent, across.

Between him and the shore lay a grayish patch. Here in summer a stream ran in. Looked a tad iffy. At the edge of the grayish patch he gave the ice a bonk with the butt of his gun. Solid as anything.

Here he went. Ice rolled a bit underfoot. Probably it was shallow here. Anyways he hoped so. Yikes.

How's it going? Suzanne said, trepidly.

Could be better, he said.

Maybe you should turn back, Suzanne said.

But wasn't this feeling of fear the exact feeling all heroes had to confront early in life? Wasn't overcoming this feeling of fear what truly distinguished the brave?

There could be no turning back.

Or could there? Maybe there could. Actually there should.

The ice gave way and the boy fell through.

Nausea had not been mentioned in "The Humbling Steppe."

A blissful feeling overtook me as I drifted off to sleep at the base of the crevasse. No fear, no discomfort, only a vague sadness at the thought of all that remained undone. This is death? I thought. It is but nothing.

Author, whose name I cannot remember, I would like a word with you.

A-hole.

The shivering was insane. Like a tremor. His head was shaking on his neck. He paused to puke a bit in the snow, white-yellow against the white-blue.

This was scary. This was scary now.

Every step was a victory. He had to remember that. With every step he was fleeing father and father. Farther from father. Stepfarther. What a victory he was wresting. From the jaws of the feet.

He felt a need at the back of his throat to say it right.

From the jaws of defeat. From the jaws of defeat.

Oh, Allen.

Even when you were THAT you were still Allen to me.

Please know that.

Falling, Dad said.

For some definite time he waited to see where he would land and how much it would hurt. Then there was a tree in his gut. He found himself wrapped fetally around some tree.

Fucksake.

Ouch, ouch. This was too much. He hadn't cried after the surgeries or during the chemo, but he felt like crying now. It wasn't fair. It happened to everyone supposedly but now it was happening specifically to him. He'd kept waiting for some special dispensation. But no. Something/someone bigger than him kept refusing. You were told the big something/someone loved you especially but in the end you saw it was otherwise. The big something/someone was neutral. Unconcerned. When it innocently moved, it crushed people.

Years ago at "The Illuminated Body" he and Molly had seen this brain slice. Marring the brain slice had been a nickel-size brown spot. That brown spot was all it had taken to kill the guy. Guy must have had his hopes and dreams, closet full of pants, and so on, some treasured childhood memories: a mob of koi in the willow shade at Gage Park, say, Gram searching in her Wrigley's-smelling purse for a tissue—like that. If not for that brown spot, the guy might have been one of the people walking by on the way to lunch in the atrium. But no. He was defunct now, off rotting somewhere, no brain in his head.

Looking down at the brain slice Eber had felt a sense of superiority. Poor guy. It was pretty unlucky, what had happened to him.

He and Molly had fled to the atrium, had hot scones, watched a squirrel mess with a plastic cup.

Wrapped fetally around the tree Eber traced the scar on his head. Tried to sit. No dice. Tried to use the tree to sit up. His hand wouldn't close. Reaching around the tree with both hands, joining his hands at the wrists, he sat himself up, leaned back against the tree.

How was that?

Fine.

Good, actually.

Maybe this was it. Maybe this was as far as he got. He'd had it in mind to sit cross-legged against the boulder at the top of the hill, but really what difference did it make?

All he had to do now was stay put. Stay put by force-thinking the same thoughts he'd used to propel himself out of the med-bed and into the car and across the soccer field and through the woods: MollyTommyJodi huddling in the kitchen filled with pity/loathing, MollyTommyJodi recoiling at something cruel he'd said, Tommy hefting his thin torso up in his arms so that MollyJodi could get under there with a wash—

Then it would be done. He would have preëmpted all future debasement. All his fears about the coming months would be mute.

Moot.

This was it. Was it? Not yet. Soon, though. An hour? Forty minutes? Was he doing this? Really? He was. Was he? Would he be able to make it back to the car even if he changed his mind? He thought not. Here he was. He was here. This incredible opportunity to end things with dignity was right in his hands.

All he had to do was stay put.

I will fight no more forever.

Concentrate on the beauty of the pond, the beauty of the woods, the beauty you are returning to, the beauty that is everywhere as far as you can—

Oh, for shitsake.

Oh, for crying out loud.

Some kid was on the pond.

Chubby kid in white. With a gun. Carrying Eber's coat.

You little fart, put that coat down, get your ass home, mind your own—

Damn. Damn it.

Kid tapped the ice with the butt of his gun.

You wouldn't want some kid finding you. That could scar a kid. Although kids found freaky things all the time. Once, he'd found a naked photo of Dad and Mrs. Flemish. That had been freaky. Of course, not as freaky as a grimacing cross-legged—

Kid was swimming.

Swimming was not allowed. That was clearly posted. *No Swimming.*

Kid was a bad swimmer. Real thrashfest down there. Kid was creating with his thrashing a rapidly expanding black pool. With each thrash the kid incrementally expanded the boundary of the black—

He was on his way down before he knew he'd started. *Kid in the pond, kid in the pond*, ran repetitively through his head as he minced. Progress was tree-to-tree. Standing there panting, you got to know a tree well. This one had three knots: eye, eye, nose. This started out as one tree and became two.

Suddenly he was not purely the dying guy who woke nights in the med-bed thinking, Make this not true make this not true, but again, partly, the guy who used to put bananas in the freezer, then crack them on the counter and pour chocolate over the broken chunks, the guy who'd once stood outside a classroom window in a rainstorm to see how Jodi was faring with that little red-headed shit who wouldn't give her a chance at the book table, the guy who used to hand-paint bird feeders in college and sell them on weekends in Boulder, wearing a jester hat and doing a little juggling routine he'd—

He started to fall again, caught himself, froze in a hunched-over position, hurtled forward, fell flat on his face, chucked his chin on a root.

You had to laugh.

You almost had to laugh.

He got up. Got doggedly up. His right hand presented as a bloody glove. Tough nuts, too bad. Once, in football, a tooth had come out. Later in the half, Eddie Blandik had found it. He'd taken it from Eddie, flung it away. That had also been him.

Here was the switchbank. It wasn't far now. Switchback.

What to do? When he got there? Get kid out of pond. Get kid moving. Force-walk kid through woods, across soccer field, to one of the houses on Poole. If nobody home, pile kid into Nissan, crank up heater, drive to— Our Lady of Sorrows? UrgentCare? Fastest route to UrgentCare?

Fifty yards to the trailhead.

Twenty yards to the trailhead.

Thank you, God, for my strength.

In the pond, he was all animal-thought, no words, no self, blind panic. He resolved to really try. He grabbed for the edge. The edge broke away. Down he went. He hit mud and pushed up. He grabbed for the edge. The edge broke away. Down he went. It seemed like it should be easy, getting out. But he just couldn't do it. It was like at the carnival. It should be easy to knock three sawdust dogs off a ledge. And it was easy. It just wasn't easy with the number of balls they gave you.

He wanted the shore. He knew that was the right place for him. But the pond kept saying no.

Then it said maybe.

The ice edge broke again, but, breaking it, he pulled himself infinitesimally toward shore, so that, when he went down, his feet found mud sooner. The bank was sloped. Suddenly there was hope.

He went nuts. He went total spaz. Then he was out, water streaming off him, a piece of ice like a tiny pane of glass in the cuff of his coat sleeve.

Trapezoidal, he thought.

In his mind, the pond was not finite, circular, and behind him but infinite and all around.

He felt he'd better lie still or whatever had just tried to kill him would try again. What had tried to kill him was not just in the pond but out here, too, in every natural thing, and there was no him, no Suzanne, no Mom, no nothing, just the sound of some kid crying like a terrified baby.

Eber jog-hobbled out of the woods and found: no kid. Just black water. And a green coat. His coat. His former coat, out there on the ice. The water was calming already.

Oh, shit.

Your fault.

Kid was only out there because of—

Down on the beach near an overturned boat was some ignoramus. Lying face down. On the job. Lying down on the job. Must have been lying there even as that poor kid—

Wait, rewind.

It was the kid. Oh, thank Christ. Face down like a corpse in a Brady photo. Legs still in the pond. Like he'd lost steam crawling out. Kid was soaked through, the white coat gone gray with wet.

Eber dragged the kid out. It took four distinct pulls. He didn't have the strength to flip him over, but, turning the head, at least got the mouth out of the snow.

Kid was in trouble.

Soaking wet, ten degrees.

Doom.

Eber went down on one knee and told the kid in a grave fatherly way that he had to get up, had to get moving or he could lose his legs, he could die.

The kid looked at Eber, blinked, stayed where he was.

He grabbed the kid by the coat, rolled him over, roughly sat him up. The kid's shivers made his shivers look like nothing. Kid seemed to be holding a jackhammer. He had to get the kid warmed up. How to do it? Hug him, lie on top of him? That would be like Popsicle-on-Popsicle.

Eber remembered his coat, out on the ice, at the edge of the black water.

Ugh.

Find a branch. No branches anywhere. Where the heck was a good fallen branch when you—

All right, all right, he'd do it without a branch.

He walked fifty feet downshore, stepped onto the pond, walked a wide loop on the solid stuff, turned to shore, started toward the black water. His knees were shaking. Why? He was afraid he might fall in. Ha. Dope. Poser. The coat was fifteen feet away. His legs were in revolt. His legs were revolting.

Doctor, my legs are revolting.

You're telling me.

He tiny-stepped up. The coat was ten feet away. He went down on his knees, knee-walked slightly up. Went down on his belly. Stretched out an arm.

Slid forward on his belly.

Bit more.

Bit more.

Then had a tiny corner by two fingers. He hauled it in, slid himself back via something like a reverse breaststroke, got to his knees, stood, retreated a few steps, and was once again fifteen feet away and safe.

Then it was like the old days, getting Tommy or Jodi ready for bed when they were zonked. You said, "Arm," the kid lifted an arm. You said, "Other arm," the kid lifted the other arm. With the coat off, Eber could see that the boy's shirt was turning to ice. Eber peeled the shirt off. Poor little guy. A person was just some meat on a frame. Little guy wouldn't last long in this cold. Eber took off his pajama shirt, put it on the kid, slid the kid's arm into the arm of the coat. In the arm were Eber's hat and gloves. He put the hat and gloves on the kid, zipped the coat up.

The kid's pants were frozen solid. His boots were ice sculptures of boots.

You had to do things right. Eber sat on the boat, took off his boots and socks, peeled off his pajama pants, made the kid sit on the boat, knelt before the kid, got the kid's boots off. He loosened the pants up with little punches and soon had one leg partly out. He was stripping off a kid in ten-degree weather. Maybe this was exactly the wrong thing. Maybe he'd kill the kid. He didn't know. He just didn't know. Desperately, he gave the pants a few more punches. Then the kid was stepping out.

Eber put the pajama pants on him, then the socks, then the boots.

The kid was standing there in Eber's clothes, swaying, eyes closed.

We're going to walk now, O.K.? Eber said.

Nothing.

Eber gave the kid an encouraging pop in the shoulders. Like a football thing.

We're going to walk you home, he said. Do you live near here?

Nothing.

He gave a harder pop.

The kid gaped at him, baffled.

Pop.

Kid started walking.

Pop-pop.

Like fleeing.

Eber drove the kid out ahead of him. Like cowboy and cow. At first, fear of the popping seemed to be motivating the kid, but then good old panic kicked in and he started running. Soon Eber couldn't keep up.

Kid was at the bench. Kid was at the trailhead.

Good boy, get home.

Kid disappeared into the woods.

Eber came back to himself.

Oh, boy. Oh, wow.

He had never known cold. Had never known tired.

He was standing in the snow in his underwear near an overturned boat.

He hobbled to the boat and sat in the snow.

. . .

Robin ran.

Past the bench and the trailhead and into the woods on the old familiar path.

What the heck? What the heck had just happened? He'd fallen into the pond? His jeans had frozen solid? Had ceased being bluejeans. Were whitejeans. He looked down to see if his jeans were still whitejeans.

He had on pajama pants that, tucked into some tremendoid boots, looked like clown pants.

Had he been crying just now?

I think crying is healthy, Suzanne said. It means you're in touch with your feelings.

Ugh. That was done, that was stupid, talking in your head to some girl who in real life called you Roger.

Dang.

So tired.

Here was a stump.

He sat. It felt good to rest. He wasn't going to lose his legs. They didn't even hurt. He couldn't even feel them. He wasn't going to die. Dying was not something he had in mind at this early an age. To rest more efficiently, he lay down. The sky was blue. The pines swayed. Not all at the same rate. He raised one gloved hand and watched it tremor.

He might close his eyes for a bit. Sometimes in life one felt a feeling of wanting to quit. Then everyone would see. Everyone would see that teasing wasn't nice. Sometimes with all the teasing his days were subtenable. Sometimes he felt he couldn't take even one more lunchtime of meekly eating on that rolled-up wrestling mat in the cafeteria corner near the snapped parallel bars. He did not have to sit there. But preferred to. If he sat anywhere else, there was the chance of a comment or two. Upon which he would then have the rest of the day to reflect. Sometimes comments were made on the clutter of his home. Thanks to Bryce, who had once come over. Sometimes comments were made on his manner of speaking. Sometimes comments were made on the style faux pas of Mom. Who was, it must be said, a real eighties gal.

Mom.

He did not like it when they teased about Mom. Mom had no idea of his lowly school status. Mom seeing him more as the paragon or golden-boy type.

Once, he'd done a secret rendezvous of recording Mom's phone calls, just for the reconnaissance aspect. Mostly they were dull, mundane, not about him at all.

Except for this one with her friend Liz.

I never dreamed I could love someone so much, Mom had said. I just worry I might not be able to live up to him, you know? He's so *good*, so *grateful*. That kid deserves—that kid deserves it all. Better school, which we cannot afford, some trips, like abroad, but that is also, uh, out of our price range. I just don't want to *fail* him, you know? That's all I want from my life, you know? Liz? To feel, at the end, like I did right by that magnificent little dude.

At that point it seemed like Liz had maybe started vacuuming.

Magnificent little dude.

He should probably get going.

Magnificent Little Dude was like his Indian name.

He got to his feet and, gathering his massive amount of clothes up like some sort of encumbering royal train, started toward home.

Here was the truck tire, here the place where the trail briefly widened, here the place where the trees crossed overhead like reaching for one another. Weave-ceiling, Mom called it.

Here was the soccer field. Across the field, his house sat like a big sweet animal. It was amazing. He'd made it. He'd fallen into the pond and lived to tell the tale. He had somewhat cried, yes, but had then simply laughed off this moment of mortal weakness and made his way home, look of wry bemusement on his face, having, it must be acknowledged, benefitted from the much appreciated assistance of a certain aged—

With a shock he remembered the old guy. What the heck? An image flashed of the old guy standing bereft and blue-skinned in his tighty-whities like a P.O.W. abandoned at the barbed wire due to no room on the truck. Or a sad traumatized stork bidding farewell to its young.

He'd bolted. He'd bolted on the old guy. Hadn't even given him a thought.

Blimey.

What a chickenshittish thing to do.

He had to go back. Right now. Help the old guy hobble out. But he was so tired. He wasn't sure he could do it. Probably the old guy was fine. Probably he had some sort of old-guy plan.

But he'd bolted. He couldn't live with that. His mind was telling him that the only way to undo the bolting was to go back now, save the day. His body was saying something else: It's too far, you're just a kid, get Mom, Mom will know what to do.

He stood paralyzed at the edge of the soccer field like a scarecrow in huge flowing clothes.

Eber sat slumped against the boat.

What a change in the weather. People were going around with parasols and so forth in the open part of the park. There was a merry-go-round and a band and a gazebo. People were frying food on the backs of certain merry-go-round horses. And yet, on others, kids were riding. How did they know? Which horses were hot? For now there was still snow, but snow couldn't last long in this bomb.

Balm.

If you close your eyes, that's the end. You know that, right?

Hilarious.

Allen.

His exact voice. After all these years.

Where was he? The duck pond. So many times he'd come out here with the kids. He should go now. Goodbye, duck pond. Although hang on. He couldn't seem to stand. Plus you couldn't leave a couple of little kids behind. Not this close to water. They were four and six. For God's sake. What had he been thinking? Leaving those two little dears by the pond. They were good kids, they'd wait, but wouldn't they get bored? And swim? Without life jackets? No, no, no. It made him sick. He had to stay. Poor kids. Poor abandoned—

Wait, rewind.

His kids were excellent swimmers.

His kids had never come close to being abandoned.

His kids were grown.

Tom was thirty. Tall drink of water. Tried so hard to know things. But even when he thought he knew a thing (fighting kites, breeding rabbits) Tom would soon be shown for what he was: the dearest, most agreeable young man ever, who knew no more about fighting kites/breeding rabbits than the average person could pick up from ten minutes on the Internet. Not that Tom wasn't smart. Tom was smart. Tom was a damn quick study. Oh, Tom, Tommy, Tommikins! The heart in that kid! He just worked and worked. For the love of his dad. Oh, kid, you had it, you have it, Tom, Tommy, even now I am thinking of you, you are very much on my mind.

And Jodi, Jodi was out there in Santa Fe. She'd said she'd take off work and fly home. As needed. But there was no need. He didn't like to impose. The kids had their own lives. Jodi-Jode. Little freckle-face. Pregnant now. Not married. Not even dating. Stupid Lars. What kind of man deserted a beautiful girl like that? A total dear. Just starting to make some progress in her job. You couldn't take that kind of time off when you'd only just started—

Reconstructing the kids in this way was having the effect of making them real to him again. Which—you didn't want to get that ball roiling. Jodi was having a baby. Rolling. He could have lasted long enough to see the baby. Hold the baby. It was sad, yes. That was a sacrifice he'd had to make. He'd explained it in the note. Hadn't he? No. Hadn't left a note. Couldn't. There'd been some reason he couldn't. Hadn't there? He was pretty sure there'd been some—

Insurance. It couldn't seem like he'd done it on purpose.

Little panic.

Little panic here.

He was offing himself. Offing himself, he'd involved a kid. Who was wandering the woods hypothermic. Offing himself two weeks before Christmas. Molly's favorite holiday. Molly had a valve thing, a panic thing, this business might—

This was not—this was not him. This was not something he would have done. Not something he would ever do. Except he—he'd done it. He was doing it. It was in progress. If he didn't get moving, it would—it would be accomplished. It would be done.

This very day you will be with me in the kingdom of—

He had to fight.

But couldn't seem to keep his eyes open.

He tried to send some last thoughts to Molly. Sweetie, forgive me. Biggest fuckup ever. Forget this part. Forget I ended this thisly. You know me. You know I didn't mean this.

He was at his house. He wasn't at his house. He knew that. But could see every detail. Here was the empty med-bed, the studio portrait of HimMollyTommyJodi posed around that fake rodeo fence. Here was the little bedside table. His meds in the pillbox. The bell he rang to call Molly. What a thing. What a cruel thing. Suddenly he saw clearly how cruel it was. And selfish. Oh, God. Who was he? The front door swung open. Molly called his name. He'd hide in the sunroom. Jump out, surprise her. Somehow they'd remodelled. Their sunroom was now the sunroom of Mrs. Kendall, his childhood piano teacher. That would be fun for the kids, to take piano lessons in the same room where he'd—

Hello? Mrs. Kendall said.

What she meant was: Don't die yet. There are many of us who wish to judge you harshly in the sunroom.

Hello, hello! she shouted.

Coming around the pond was a silver-haired woman.

All he had to do was call out.

He called out.

To keep him alive she started piling on him various things from life, things smelling of a home—coats, sweaters, a rain of flowers, a hat, socks, sneakers—and with amazing strength had him on his feet and was maneuvering him into a maze of trees, a wonderland of trees, trees hung with ice. He was piled high with clothes. He was like the bed at a party on which they pile the coats. She had all the answers: where to step, when to rest. She was strong as a bull. He was on her hip now like a baby; she had both arms around his waist, lifting him over a root.

They walked for hours, seemed like. She sang. Cajoled. She hissed at him, reminding him, with pokes in the forehead (right in his forehead), that her freaking *kid* was at *home*, near-*frozen*, so they had to *book it*.

Good God, there was so much to do. If he made it. He'd make it. This gal wouldn't let him not make it. He'd have to try to get Molly to see—see why he'd done it. *I was scared, I was scared, Mol.* Maybe Molly would agree not to tell Tommy and Jodi. He didn't like the thought of them knowing he'd been scared. Didn't like the thought of them knowing what a fool he'd been. Oh, to hell with that! Tell everyone! He'd done it! He'd been driven to do it and he'd done it and that was it. That was him. That was part of who he was. No more lies, no more silence, it was going to be a new and different life, if only he—

They were crossing the soccer field.

Here was the Nissan.

His first thought was: Get in, drive it home.

Oh, no, you don't, she said with that smoky laugh and guided him into a house. A house on the park. He'd seen it a million times. And now was in it. It smelled of man-sweat and spaghetti sauce and old books. Like a library where sweaty men went to cook spaghetti. She sat him in front of a woodstove, brought him a brown blanket that smelled of medicine. Didn't talk but in directives: Drink this, let me take that, wrap up, what's your name, what's your number?

What a thing! To go from dying in your underwear in the snow to this! Warmth, colors, antlers on the walls, an old-time crank phone like you saw in silent movies. It was something. Every second was something. He hadn't died in his shorts by a pond in the snow. The kid wasn't dead. He'd killed no one. Ha! Somehow he'd got it all back. Everything was good now, everything was—

The woman reached down, touched his scar.

Oh, wow, ouch, she said. You didn't do that out there, did you?

At this he remembered that the brown spot was as much in his head as ever.

Oh, Lord, there was still all that to go through.

Did he still want it? Did he still want to live?

Yes, yes, oh, God, yes, please.

Because, O.K., the thing was—he saw it now, was starting to see it—if some guy, at the end, fell apart, and said or did bad things, or had to be helped, helped to quite a considerable extent? So what? What of it? Why should he not do or say weird things or look strange or disgusting? Why should the shit not run down his legs? Why should those he loved not lift and bend and feed and wipe him, when he would gladly do the same for them? He'd been afraid to be lessened by the lifting and bending and feeding and wiping, and was still afraid of that, and yet, at the same time, now saw that there could still be many—many drops of goodness, is how it came to him—many drops of happy—of good fellowship—ahead, and those drops of fellowship were not—had never been—his to withheld.

Withhold.

The kid came out of the kitchen, lost in Eber's big coat, pajama pants pooling around his feet with the boots now off. He took Eber's bloody hand gently. Said he was sorry. Sorry for being such a dope in the woods. Sorry for running off. He'd just been out of it. Kind of scared and all.

Listen, Eber said hoarsely. You did amazing. You did perfect. I'm here. Who did that?

There. That was something you could do. The kid maybe felt better now? He'd given the kid that? That was a reason. To stay around. Wasn't it? Can't console anyone if not around? Can't do squat if gone?

When Allen was close to the end, Eber had done a presentation at school on the manatee. Got an A from Sister Eustace. Who could be quite tough. She was missing two fingers on her right hand from a lawnmower incident and sometimes used that hand to scare a kid silent.

He hadn't thought of this in years.

She'd put that hand on his shoulder not to scare him but as a form of praise. *That was just terrific. Everyone should take their work as seriously as Donald here. Donald, I hope you'll go home and share this with your parents.* He'd gone home and shared it with Mom. Who suggested he share it with Allen. Who, on that day, had been more Allen than THAT. And Allen—

Ha, wow, Allen. There was a man.

Tears sprang into his eyes as he sat by the woodstove.

Allen had—Allen had said it was great. Asked a few questions. About the manatee. What did they eat again? Did he think they could effectively communicate with one another? What a trial that must have been! In his condition. Forty minutes on the manatee? Including a poem Eber had composed? A sonnet? On the manatee?

He'd felt so happy to have Allen back.

I'll be like him, he thought. I'll try to be like him.

The voice in his head was shaky, hollow, unconvinced.

Then: sirens.

Somehow: Molly.

He heard her in the entryway. Mol, Molly, oh, boy. When they were first married they used to fight. Say the most insane things. Afterward, sometimes there would be tears. Tears in bed? Somewhere. And then they would—Molly pressing her hot wet face against his hot wet face. They were sorry, they were saying with their bodies, they were accepting each other back, and that feeling, that feeling of being accepted back again and again, of someone's affection for you always expanding to encompass whatever new flawed thing had just manifested in you, that was the deepest, dearest thing he'd ever—

She came in flustered and apologetic, a touch of anger in her face. He'd embarrassed her. He saw that. He'd embarrassed her by doing something that showed she hadn't sufficiently noticed him needing her. She'd been too busy nursing him to notice how scared he was. She was angry at him for pulling this stunt and ashamed of herself for feeling angry at him in his hour of need, and was trying to put the shame and anger behind her now so she could do what might be needed.

All of this was in her face. He knew her so well.

Also concern.

Overriding everything else in that lovely face was concern.

She came to him now, stumbling a bit on a swell in the floor of this stranger's house.

WHAT WE TALK ABOUT WHEN WE TALK ABOUT ANNE FRANK

BY NATHAN ENGLANDER (2011)

They're in our house maybe ten minutes and already Mark's lecturing us on the Israeli occupation. Mark and Lauren live in Jerusalem, and people from there think it gives them the right.

Mark is looking all stoic and nodding his head. "If we had what you have down here in South Florida," he says, and trails off. "Yup," he says, and he's nodding again. "We'd have no troubles at all."

"You do have what we have," I tell him. "All of it. Sun and palm trees. Old Jews and oranges and the worst drivers around. At this point, we've probably got more Israelis than you." Debbie, my wife, puts a hand on my arm—her signal that I'm either taking a tone, interrupting someone's story, sharing something private, or making an inappropriate joke. That's my cue, and I'm surprised, considering how often I get it, that she ever lets go of my arm.

"Yes, you've got everything now," Mark says. "Even terrorists."

I look at Lauren. She's the one my wife has the relationship with—the one who should take charge. But Lauren isn't going to give her husband any signal. She and Mark ran off to Israel twenty years ago and turned Hasidic, and neither of them will put a hand on the other in public. Not for this. Not to put out a fire.

"Wasn't Mohamed Atta living right here before 9/11?" Mark says, and now he pantomimes pointing out houses. "Goldberg, Goldberg, Goldberg—Atta. How'd you miss him in this place?"

"Other side of town," I say.

"That's what I'm talking about. That's what you have that we don't. Other sides of town. Wrong sides of the tracks. Space upon space." And now he's fingering the granite countertop in our kitchen, looking out into the living room and the dining room, staring through the kitchen windows at the pool. "All this house," he says, "and one son? Can you imagine?"

"No," Lauren says. And then she turns to us, backing him up. "You should see how we live with ten."

"Ten kids," I say. "We could get you a reality show with that here in the States. Help you get a bigger place."

The hand is back pulling at my sleeve. "Pictures," Debbie says. "I want to see the girls." We all follow Lauren into the den for her purse.

"Do you believe it?" Mark says. "Ten girls!" And the way it comes out of his mouth, it's the first time I like the guy. The first time I think about giving him a chance.

Facebook and Skype brought Deb and Lauren back together. They were glued at the hip growing up. Went all the way through school together. Yeshiva school. All girls. Out in Queens till high school and then riding the subway together to one called Central in Manhattan. They stayed best friends until I married Deb and turned her secular, and soon after that Lauren met Mark and they went off to the Holy Land and shifted from Orthodox to *ultra*-Orthodox, which to me sounds like a repackaged detergent—ORTHODOXULTRA®, now with more deep-healing power. Because of that, we're supposed to call them Shoshana and Yerucham now. Deb's been doing it. I'm just not saying their names.

"You want some water?" I offer. "Coke in the can?"

"'You'—which of us?" Mark says.

"You both," I say. "Or I've got whiskey. Whiskey's kosher, too, right?"

"If it's not, I'll kosher it up real fast," he says, pretending to be easygoing. And right then he takes off that big black hat and plops down on the couch in the den.

Lauren's holding the verticals aside and looking out at the yard. "Two girls from Forest Hills," she says. "Who ever thought we'd be the mothers of grownups?"

"Trevor's sixteen," Deb says. "You may think he's a grownup, and he may think he's a grownup—but we are not convinced."

Right then is when Trev comes padding into the den, all six feet of him, plaid pajama bottoms dragging on the floor and T-shirt full of holes. He's just woken up, and you can tell he's not sure if he's still dreaming. We told him we had guests. But there's Trev, staring at this man in the black suit, a beard resting on his belly. And Lauren, I met her once before, right when Deb and I got married, but ten girls and a thousand Shabbos dinners later—well, she's a big woman, in a bad dress and a giant blond Marilyn Monroe wig. Seeing them at the door, I can't say I wasn't shocked myself.

"Hey," he says.

And then Deb's on him, preening and fixing his hair and hugging him. "Trevy, this is my best friend from childhood," she says. "This is Shoshana, and this is—"

"Mark," I say.

"Yerucham," Mark says, and sticks out a hand. Trev shakes it. Then Trev sticks out his hand, polite, to Lauren. She looks at it, just hanging there in the air.

"I don't shake," she says. "But I'm so happy to see you. Like meeting my own son. I mean it." And here she starts to cry, and then she and Deb are hugging. And the boys, we just stand there until Mark looks at his watch and gets himself a good manly grip on Trev's shoulder.

"Sleeping until three on a Sunday? Man, those were the days," Mark says. "A regular little Rumpleforeskin." Trev looks at me, and I want to shrug, but Mark's also looking, so I don't move. Trev just gives us both his best teen-age glare and edges out of the room. As he does, he says, "Baseball practice," and takes my car keys off the hook by the door to the garage.

"There's gas," I say.

"They let them drive here at sixteen?" Mark says. "Insane."

"So what brings you here after all these years?" I say.

"My mother," Mark says. "She's failing, and my father's getting old—and they come to us for Sukkot every year. You know?"

"I know the holidays."

"They used to fly out to us. For Sukkot and Pesach, both. But they can't fly now, and I just wanted to get over while things are still good. We haven't been in America—"

"Oh, gosh," Lauren says. "I'm afraid to think how long it's been. More than ten years. Twelve," she says. "With the kids, it's just impossible until enough of them are big."

"How do you do it?" Deb says. "Ten kids? I really do want to hear."

That's when I remember. "I forgot your drink," I say to Mark.

"Yes, his drink. That's how," Lauren says. "That's how we cope."

And that's how the four of us end up back at the kitchen table with a bottle of vodka between us. I'm not one to get drunk on a Sunday afternoon, but, I tell you, when the plan is to spend the day with Mark I jump at the chance. Deb's drinking, too, but not for the same reason. I think she and Lauren are reliving a little bit of the wild times. The very small window when they were together, barely grown up, two young women living in New York on the edge of two worlds.

Deb says, "This is really racy for us. I mean, *really* racy. We try not to drink much at all these days. We think it sets a bad example for Trevor. It's not good to drink in front of them right at this age when they're all transgressive. He's suddenly so interested in that kind of thing."

"I'm just happy when he's interested in something," I say.

Deb slaps at the air. "I just don't think it's good to make drinking look like it's fun with a teen-ager around."

Lauren smiles and straightens her wig. "Does anything we do look fun to our kids?"

I laugh at that. Honestly, I'm liking her more and more.

"It's the age limit that does it," Mark says. "It's the whole American puritanical thing, the twenty-one-year-old drinking age and all that. We don't make a big deal about it in Israel, and so the kids, they don't even notice alcohol. Except for the foreign workers on Fridays, you hardly see anyone drunk at all."

"The workers and the Russians," Lauren says.

"The Russian immigrants," he says, "that's a whole separate matter. Most of them, you know, not even Jews."

"What does that mean?" I say.

"It means matrilineal descent, is what it means," Mark says. "With the Ethiopians there were conversions."

But Deb wants to keep us away from politics, and the way we're arranged, me in between them and Deb opposite (it's a round table, our kitchen table), she practically has to throw herself across to grab hold of my arm. "Fix me another," she says.

And here she switches the subject to Mark's parents. "How's the visit been going?" she says, her face all sombre. "How are your folks holding up?"

Deb is very interested in Mark's parents. They're Holocaust survivors. And Deb has what can only be called an unhealthy obsession with the idea of that generation being gone. Don't get me wrong. It's important to me, too. All I'm saying is there's healthy and unhealthy, and my wife, she gives the subject a *lot* of time.

"What can I say?" Mark says. "My mother's a very sick woman. And my father, he tries to keep his spirits up. He's a tough guy."

"I'm sure," I say. Then I look down at my drink, all serious, and give a shake of my head. "They really are amazing."

"Who?" Mark says. "Fathers?"

I look back up and they're all staring at me. "Survivors," I say, realizing I jumped the gun.

"There's good and bad," Mark says. "Like anyone else."

Lauren says, "The whole of Carmel Lake Village, it's like a D.P. camp with a billiards room."

"One tells the other, and they follow," Mark says. "From Europe to New York, and now, for the end of their lives, again the same place."

"Tell them that crazy story, Yuri," Lauren says.

"Tell us," Deb says.

"So you can picture my father," Mark says. "In the old country, he went to *heder*, had the *peyes* and all that. But in America a classic *galusmonger*. He looks more like you than me. It's not from him that I get this," he says, pointing at his beard. "Shoshana and I—"

"We know," I say.

"So my father. They've got a nice nine-hole course, a driving range, some greens for the practice putting. And my dad's at the clubhouse. I go with him. He wants to work out in the gym, he says.

Tells me I should come. Get some exercise. And he tells me"—and here Mark points at his feet, sliding a leg out from under the table so we can see his big black clodhoppers—"'You can't wear those Shabbos shoes on the treadmill. You need the sneakers. You know, sports shoes?' And I tell him, 'I know what sneakers are. I didn't forget my English any more than your Yiddish is gone.' So he says, '*Ah shaynem dank dir in pupik.*' Just to show me who's who."

"Tell them the point," Lauren says.

"He's sitting in the locker room, trying to pull a sock on, which is, at that age, basically the whole workout in itself. It's no quick business. And I see, while I'm waiting, and I can't believe it—I nearly pass out. The guy next to him, the number on his arm, it's three before my father's number. You know, in sequence."

"What do you mean?" Deb says.

"I mean the number tattooed. It's the same as my father's camp number, digit for digit, but my father's ends in an eight. And this guy's, it ends in a five. That's the only difference. I mean, they're separated by two people. So I say, 'Excuse me, sir.' And the guy just says, 'You with the Chabad? I don't want anything but to be left alone. I already got candles at home.' I tell him, 'No. I'm not. I'm here visiting my father.' And to my father I say, 'Do you know this gentleman? Have you two met? I'd really like to introduce you, if you haven't.' And they look each other over for what, I promise you, is minutes. Actual minutes. It is—with *kavod* I say this, with respect for my father—but it is like watching a pair of big beige manatees sitting on a bench, each with one sock on. They're just looking each other up and down, everything slow. And then my father says, 'I seen him. Seen him around.' The other guy, he says, 'Yes, I've seen.' 'You're both survivors,' I tell them. 'Look. The numbers.' And they look. 'They're the same,' I say. And they both hold out their arms to look at the little ashen tattoos. To my father I say, 'Do you get it? The same, except his—it's right ahead of yours. Look! Compare.' So they look. They compare." Mark's eyes are popping out of his head. "Think about it," he says. "Around the world, surviving the unsurvivable, these two old guys end up with enough money to retire to Carmel Lake and play golf every day. So I say to my dad, 'He's right ahead of you. Look, a five,' I say. 'And yours is an eight.' And my father says, 'All that means is he cut ahead of me in line. There same as here. This guy's a cutter. I just didn't want to say.' 'Blow it out your ear,' the other guy says. And that's it. Then they get back to putting on socks."

Deb looks crestfallen. She was expecting something empowering. Some story with which to educate Trevor, to reaffirm her belief in the humanity that, from inhumanity, forms.

But me, I love that kind of story. I'm starting to take a real shine to these two, and not just because I'm suddenly feeling sloshed.

"Good story, Yuri," I say, copying his wife. "Yerucham, that one's got zing."

Yerucham hoists himself up from the table, looking proud. He checks the label of our white bread on the counter, making sure it's kosher. He takes a slice, pulls off the crust, and rolls the white part against the countertop with the palm of his hand, making a little ball. He comes over and pours himself a shot and throws it back. Then he eats that crazy dough ball. Just tosses it in his mouth, as if it's the bottom of his own personal punctuation mark—you know, to underline his story.

"Is that good?" I say.

"Try it," he says. He goes to the counter and pitches me a slice of white bread, and says, "But first pour yourself a shot."

I reach for the bottle and find that Deb's got her hands around it, and her head's bowed down, like the bottle is anchoring her, keeping her from tipping back.

"Are you O.K., Deb?" Lauren says.

"It's because it was funny," I say.

"Honey!" Deb says.

"She won't tell you, but she's a little obsessed with the Holocaust. That story—no offense, Mark—it's not what she had in mind."

I should leave it be, I know. But it's not like someone from Deb's high school is around every day offering insights.

"It's like she's a survivor's kid, my wife. It's crazy, that education they give them. Her grandparents were all born in the Bronx, and here we are twenty minutes from downtown Miami but it's like it's 1937 and we live on the edge of Berlin."

"That's not it!" Deb says, openly defensive, her voice super high up in the register. "I'm not upset about that. It's the alcohol. All this alcohol. It's that and seeing Lauren. Seeing Shoshana, after all this time."

"Oh, she was always like this in high school," Shoshana says. "Sneak one drink, and she started to cry. You want to know what used to get her going, what would make her truly happy?" Shoshana says. "It was getting high. That's what always did it. Smoking up. It would make her laugh for hours and hours."

And, I tell you, I didn't see it coming. I'm as blindsided as Deb was by that numbers story.

"Oh, my God," Deb says, and she's pointing at me. "Look at my big bad secular husband. He really can't handle it. He can't handle his wife's having any history of naughtiness at all—Mr. Liberal Open-Minded." To me she says, "How much more chaste a wife can you dream of than a modern-day yeshiva girl who stayed a virgin until twenty-one? Honestly. What did you think Shoshana was going to say was so much fun?"

"Honestly-honestly?" I say. "I don't want to. It's embarrassing."

"Say it!" Deb says, positively glowing.

"Honestly, I thought you were going to say it was something like competing in the Passover Nut Roll, or making sponge cake. Something like that." I hang my head. And Shoshana and Deb are laughing so hard they can't breathe. They're grabbing at each other so that I can't tell if they're holding each other up or pulling each other down.

"I can't believe you told him about the nut roll," Shoshana says.

"And I can't believe," Deb says, "you just told my husband of twenty-two years how much we used to get high. I haven't touched a joint since before we were married," she says. "Have we, honey? Have we smoked since we got married?"

"No," I say. "It's been a very long time."

"So come on, Shosh. When was it? When was the last time you smoked?"

Now, I know I mentioned the beard on Mark. But I don't know if I mentioned how hairy a guy he is. That thing grows right up to his eyeballs. Like having eyebrows on top and bottom both. So when Deb asks the question, the two of them, Shosh and Yuri, are basically giggling like children, and I can tell, in the little part that shows, in the bit of skin I can see, that Mark's eyelids and earlobes are in full blush.

"When Shoshana said we drink to get through the days," Mark says, "she was kidding about the drinking."

"We don't drink much," Shoshana says.

"It's smoking that she means," he says.

"We still get high," Shoshana says. "I mean, all the time."

"Hasidim!" Deb screams. "You're not allowed!"

"Everyone does in Israel. It's like the sixties there," Mark says. "It's the highest country in the world. Worse than Holland and India and Thailand put together. Worse than anywhere, even Argentina—though they may have us tied."

"Well, maybe that's why the kids aren't interested in alcohol," I say.

"Do you want to get high now?" Deb says. And we all three look at her. Me, with surprise. And those two with straight longing.

"We didn't bring," Shoshana says. "Though it's pretty rare anyone at customs peeks under the wig."

"Maybe you guys can find your way into the glaucoma underground over at Carmel Lake," I say. "I'm sure that place is rife with it."

"That's funny," Mark says.

"I'm funny," I say, now that we're all getting on.

"We've got pot," Deb says.

"We do?" I say. "I don't think we do."

Deb looks at me and bites at the cuticle on her pinkie.

"You're not secretly getting high all these years?" I say. I really don't feel well at all.

"Our son," Deb says. "He has pot."

"Our son?"

"Trevor," she says.

"Yes," I say. "I know which one."

It's a lot for one day, that kind of news. And it feels to me a lot like betrayal. Like my wife's old secret and my son's new secret are bound up together, and I've somehow been wronged. Also, I'm not one to recover quickly from any kind of slight from Deb—not when there are people around. I really need to talk stuff out. Some time alone, even five minutes, would fix it. But it's super apparent that Deb doesn't need any time alone with me. She doesn't seem troubled at all. What she seems is focussed. She's busy at the counter, using a paper tampon wrapper to roll a joint.

"It's an emergency-preparedness method we came up with in high school," Shoshana says. "The things teen-age girls will do when they're desperate."

"Do you remember that nice boy that we used to smoke in front of?" Deb says. "He'd just watch us. There'd be six or seven of us in a circle, girls and boys not touching—we were so religious. Isn't that crazy?" Deb is talking to me, as Shoshana and Mark don't think it's crazy at all. "The only place we touched was passing the joint, at the thumbs. And this boy, we had a nickname for him."

"Passover!" Shoshana yells.

"Yes," Deb says, "that's it. All we ever called him was Passover. Because every time the joint got to him he'd just pass it over to the next one of us. Passover Rand."

Shoshana takes the joint and lights it with a match, sucking deep. "It's a miracle when I remember anything these days," she says. "After my first was born, I forgot half of everything I knew. And then half again with each one after. Just last night, I woke up in a panic. I couldn't remember if there were fifty-two cards in a deck or fifty-two weeks in a year. The recall errors—I'm up all night worrying over them, just waiting for the Alzheimer's to kick in."

"It's not that bad," Mark tells her. "It's only everyone on one side of your family that has it."

"That's true," she says, passing her husband the joint. "The other side is blessed only with dementia. Anyway, which is it? Weeks or cards?"

"Same, same," Mark says, taking a hit.

When it's Deb's turn, she holds the joint and looks at me, like I'm supposed to nod or give her permission in some husbandly anxiety-absolving way. But instead of saying, "Go ahead," I pretty much bark at Deb. "When were you going to tell me about our son?"

At that, Deb takes a long hit, holding it deep, like an old pro.

"Really, Deb. How could you not tell me you knew?"

Deb walks over and hands me the joint. She blows the smoke in my face, not aggressive, just blowing.

"I've only known five days," she says. "I was going to tell you. I just wasn't sure how, or if I should talk to Trevy first, maybe give him a chance," she says.

"A chance to what?" I ask.

"To let him keep it as a secret between us. To let him know he could have my trust if he promised to stop."

"But he's the son," I say. "I'm the father. Even if it's a secret with him, it should be a double secret between me and you. I should always get to know—even if I pretend not to know—any secret with him."

"Do that double part again," Mark says. But I ignore him.

"That's how it's always been," I say to Deb. And, because I'm desperate and unsure, I follow it up with "Hasn't it?"

I mean, we really trust each other, Deb and I. And I can't remember feeling like so much has hung on one question in a long time. I'm trying to read her face, and something complex is going on, some formulation. And then she sits right there on the floor, at my feet.

"Oh, my God," she says. "I'm so fucking high. Like instantly. Like, like," and then she starts laughing. "Like, Mike," she says. "Like, kike," she says, turning completely serious. "Oh, my God, I'm really messed up."

"We should have warned you," Shoshana says.

As she says this, I'm holding my first hit in, and already trying to fight off the paranoia that comes rushing behind that statement.

"Warned us what?" I say, my voice high, and the smoke still sweet in my nose.

"This isn't your father's marijuana," Mark says. "The THC levels. One hit of this new hydroponic stuff, it's like if maybe you smoked a pound of the stuff we had when we were kids."

"I feel it," I say. And I do. I sit down with Deb on the floor and take her hands. I feel nice. Though I'm not sure if I thought that or said it, so I try it again, making sure it's out loud. "I feel nice," I say.

"I found the pot in the laundry hamper," Deb says. "Leave it to a teen-age boy to think that's the best place to hide something. His clean clothes show up folded in his room, and it never occurs to him that someone empties that hamper. To him, it's the loneliest, most forgotten space in the world. Point is I found an Altoids tin at the bottom, stuffed full." Deb gives my hands a squeeze. "Are we good now?"

"We're good," I say. And it feels like we're a team again, like it's us against them. Because Deb says, "Are you sure you guys are allowed to smoke pot that comes out of a tin that held non-kosher candy? I really don't know if that's O.K." And it's just exactly the kind of thing I'm thinking.

"First of all, we're not eating it. We're smoking it," Shoshana says. "And even so, it's cold contact, so it's probably all right either way."

"'Cold contact'?" I say.

"It's a thing," Shoshana says. "Just forget about it and get up off the floor. Chop-chop." And they each offer us a hand and get us standing. "Come, sit back at the table," Shoshana says.

"I'll tell you," Mark says. "That's got to be the No. 1 most annoying thing about being Hasidic in the outside world. Worse than the rude stuff that gets said is the constant policing by civilians. Everywhere we go, people are checking on us. Ready to make some sort of liturgical citizen's arrest."

"Strangers!" Shoshana says. "Just the other day, on the way in from the airport. Yuri pulled into a McDonald's to pee, and some guy in a trucker hat came up to him as he went in and said, 'You allowed to go in there, brother?' Just like that."

"Not true!" Deb says.

"It's not that I don't see the fun in that," Mark says. "The allure. You know, we've got Mormons in Jerusalem. They've got a base there. A seminary. The rule is—the deal with the government—they can have their place, but they can't do outreach. No proselytizing. Anyway, I do some business with one of their guys."

"From Utah?" Deb says.

"From Idaho. His name is Jebediah, for real—do you believe it?"

"No, Yerucham and Shoshana," I say. "Jebediah is a very strange name." Mark rolls his eyes at that, handing me what's left of the joint. Without even asking, he gets up and gets the tin and reaches into his wife's purse for another tampon. And I'm a little less comfortable with this than with the white bread, with a guest coming into the house and smoking up all our son's pot. Deb must be thinking something similar, as she says, "After this story, I'm going to text Trev and make sure he's not coming back anytime soon."

"So when Jeb's at our house," Mark says, "when he comes by to eat and pours himself a Coke, I do that same religious-police thing. I can't resist. I say, 'Hey, Jeb, you allowed to have that?' People don't mind breaking their own rules, but they're real strict about someone else's."

"So are they allowed to have Coke?" Deb says.

"I don't know," Mark says. "All Jeb ever says back is 'You're thinking of coffee, and mind your own business, either way.' "

And then my Deb. She just can't help herself. "You heard about the scandal? The Mormons going through the Holocaust list."

"Like in 'Dead Souls,' " I say, explaining. "Like in the Gogol book, but real."

"Do you think we read that?" Mark says. "As Hasidim, or before?"

"They took the records of the dead," Deb says, "and they started running through them. They took these people who died as Jews and started converting them into Mormons. Converting the six million against their will."

"And this is what keeps an American Jew up at night?" Mark says.

"What does that mean?" Deb says.

"It means—" Mark says.

But Shoshana interrupts him. "Don't tell them what it means, Yuri. Just leave it unmeant."

"We can handle it," I say. "We are interested, even, in handling it."

"Your son, he seems like a nice boy."

"Do not talk about their son," Shoshana says.

"Do not talk about our son," Deb says. This time I reach across and lay a hand on her elbow.

"Talk," I say.

"He does not," Mark says, "seem Jewish to me."

"How can you say that?" Deb says. "What is wrong with you?" But Deb's upset draws less attention than my response. I'm laughing so hard that everyone turns toward me.

"What?" Mark says.

"Jewish to you?" I say. "The hat, the beard, the blocky shoes. A lot of pressure, I'd venture, to look Jewish to you. Like, say, maybe Ozzy Osbourne, or the guys from Kiss, like them telling Paul Simon, 'You do not look like a musician to me.'"

"It is not about the outfit," Mark says. "It's about building life in a vacuum. Do you know what I saw on the drive over here? Supermarket, supermarket, adult bookstore, supermarket, supermarket, firing range."

"Floridians do like their guns and porn," I say. "And their supermarkets."

"What I'm trying to say, whether you want to take it seriously or not, is that you can't build Judaism only on the foundation of one terrible crime," Mark says. "It's about this obsession with the Holocaust as a necessary sign of identity. As your only educational tool. Because for the children there is no connection otherwise. Nothing Jewish that binds."

"Wow, that's offensive," Deb says. "And close-minded. There is such a thing as Jewish culture. One can live a culturally rich life."

"Not if it's supposed to be a Jewish life. Judaism is a religion. And with religion comes ritual. Culture is nothing. Culture is some construction of the modern world. It is not fixed; it is ever changing, and a weak way to bind generations. It's like taking two pieces of metal, and instead of making a nice weld you hold them together with glue."

"What does that even mean?" Deb says. "Practically."

Mark raises a finger to make his point, to educate. "In Jerusalem we don't need to busy ourselves with symbolic efforts to keep our memories in place. Because we live exactly as our parents lived before the war. And this serves us in all things, in our relationships, too, in our marriages and parenting."

"Are you saying your marriage is better than ours?" Deb says. "Really? Just because of the rules you live by?"

"I'm saying your husband would not have the long face, worried his wife is keeping secrets. And your son, he would not get into the business of smoking without first coming to you. Because the relationships, they are defined. They are clear."

"Because they are welded together," I say, "and not glued."

"Yes," he says. "And I bet Shoshana agrees." But Shoshana is distracted. She is working carefully with an apple and a knife. She is making a little apple pipe, all the tampons gone.

"Did your daughters?" Deb says. "If they tell you everything, did they come to you first, before they smoked?"

"Our daughters do not have the taint of the world we grew up in. They have no interest in such things."

"So you think," I say.

"So I know," he says. "Our concerns are different, our worries."

"Let's hear 'em," Deb says.

"Let's not," Shoshana says. "Honestly, we're drunk, we're high, we are having a lovely reunion."

"Every time you tell him not to talk," I say, "it makes me want to hear what he's got to say even more."

"Our concern," Mark says, "is not the past Holocaust. It is the current one. The one that takes more than fifty per cent of the Jews of this generation. Our concern is intermarriage. It's the Holocaust that's happening now. You don't need to be worrying about some Mormons doing hocus-pocus on the murdered six million. You need to worry that your son marries a Jew."

"Oh, my God," Deb says. "Are you calling intermarriage a Holocaust?"

"You ask my feeling, that's my feeling. But this, no, it does not exactly apply to you, except in the example you set for the boy. Because you're Jewish, your son, he is as Jewish as me. No more, no less."

"I went to yeshiva, too, Born-Again Harry! You don't need to explain the rules to me."

"Did you just call me 'Born-Again Harry'?" Mark asks.

"I did," Deb says. And she and he, they start to laugh at that. They think 'Born-Again Harry' is the funniest thing they've heard in a while. And Shoshana laughs, and then I laugh, because laughter is infectious—and it is doubly so when you're high.

"You don't really think our family, my lovely, beautiful son, is headed for a Holocaust, do you?" Deb says. "Because that would really cast a pall on this beautiful day."

"No, I don't," Mark says. "It's a lovely house and a lovely family, a beautiful home that you've made for that strapping young man. You're a real *balabusta*," Mark says.

"That makes me happy," Deb says. And she tilts her head nearly ninety degrees to show her happy, sweet smile. "Can I hug you? I'd really like to give you a hug."

"No," Mark says, though he says it really politely. "But you can hug my wife. How about that?"

"That's a great idea," Deb says. Shoshana gets up and hands the loaded apple to me, and I smoke from the apple as the two women hug a tight, deep, dancing-back-and-forth hug, tilting this way and that, so, once again, I'm afraid they might fall.

"It is a beautiful day," I say.

"It is," Mark says. And both of us look out the window, and both of us watch the perfect clouds in a perfect sky, so that we're both staring out as the sky suddenly darkens. It is a change so abrupt that the ladies undo their hug to watch.

"It's like that here," Deb says. And the clouds open up and torrential tropical rain drops straight down, battering. It is loud against the roof, and loud against the windows, and the fronds of the palm trees bend, and the floaties in the pool jump as the water boils.

Shoshana goes to the window. And Mark passes Deb the apple and goes to the window. "Really, it's always like this here?" Shoshana says.

"Sure," I say. "Every day. Stops as quick as it starts."

And both of them have their hands pressed up against the window. And they stay like that for some time, and when Mark turns around, harsh guy, tough guy, we see that he is weeping.

"You do not know," he says. "I forget what it's like to live in a place rich with water. This is a blessing above all others."

"If you had what we had," I say.

"Yes," he says, wiping his eyes.

"Can we go out?" Shoshana says. "In the rain?"

"Of course," Deb says. Then Shoshana tells me to close my eyes. Only me. And I swear I think she's going to be stark naked when she calls, "Open up."

She's taken off her wig is all, and she's wearing one of Trev's baseball caps in its place.

"I've only got the one wig this trip," she says. "If Trev won't mind."

"He won't mind," Deb says. And this is how the four of us find ourselves in the back yard, on a searingly hot day, getting pounded by all this cool, cool rain. It's just about the best feeling in the world. And, I have to say, Shoshana looks twenty years younger in that hat.

We do not talk in the rain. We are too busy frolicking and laughing and jumping around. And that's how it happens that I'm holding Mark's hand and sort of dancing, and Deb is holding Shoshana's hand, and they're doing their own kind of jig. And when I take Deb's hand, though neither Mark nor Shoshana is touching the other, somehow we've formed a broken circle. We've started dancing our own kind of hora in the rain.

It is the silliest and freest and most glorious I can remember feeling in years. Who would think that's what I'd be saying with these strict, suffocatingly austere people visiting our house? And then my Deb, my love, once again she is thinking what I'm thinking, and she says, face up into the rain, all of us spinning, "Are you sure this is O.K., Shoshana? That it's not mixed dancing? I don't want anyone feeling bad after."

"We'll be just fine," Shoshana says. "We will live with the consequences." The question slows us, and stops us, though no one has yet let go.

"It's like the old joke," I say. Without waiting for anyone to ask which one, I say, "Why don't Hasidim have sex standing up?"

"Why?" Shoshana says.

"Because it might lead to mixed dancing."

Deb and Shoshana pretend to be horrified as we let go of hands, as we recognize that the moment is over, the rain disappearing as quickly as it came. Mark stands there staring into the sky, lips pressed tight. "That joke is very, very old," he says. "And mixed dancing makes me think of mixed nuts, and mixed grill, and *insalata mista*. The sound of 'mixed dancing' has made me wildly hungry. And I'm going to panic if the only kosher thing in the house is that loaf of bleached American bread."

"You have the munchies," I say.

"Diagnosis correct," he says.

Deb starts clapping at that, tiny claps, her hands held to her chest in prayer. She says to him, absolutely beaming, "You will not even believe what riches await."

. . .

The four of us stand in the pantry, soaking wet, hunting through the shelves and dripping on the floor. "Have you ever seen such a pantry?" Shoshana says, reaching her arms out. "It's gigantic." It is indeed large, and it is indeed stocked, an enormous amount of food, and an enormous selection of sweets, befitting a home that is often host to a swarm of teen-age boys.

"Are you expecting a nuclear winter?" Shoshana says.

"I'll tell you what she's expecting," I say. "You want to know how Holocaust-obsessed she really is? I mean, to what degree?"

"To no degree," Deb says. "We are done with the Holocaust."

"Tell us," Shoshana says.

"She's always plotting our secret hiding place," I say.

"No kidding," Shoshana says.

"Like, look at this. At the pantry, with a bathroom next to it, and the door to the garage. If you sealed it all up—like put drywall at the entrance to the den—you'd never suspect. If you covered that door inside the garage up good with, I don't know—if you hung your tools in front of it and hid hinges behind, maybe leaned the bikes and the mower against it, you'd have this closed area, with running water and a toilet and all this food. I mean, if someone sneaked into the garage to replenish things, you could rent out the house. Put in another family without their having any idea."

"Oh, my God," Shoshana says. "My short-term memory may be gone from having all those children—"

"And from the smoking," I say.

"And from that, too. But I remember from when we were kids," Shoshana says, turning to Deb. "You were always getting me to play games like that. To pick out spaces. And even worse, even darker—"

"Don't," Deb says.

"I know what you're going to say," I tell her, and I'm honestly excited. "The game, yes? She played that crazy game with you?"

"No," Deb says. "Enough. Let it go."

And Mark—who is utterly absorbed in studying kosher certifications, who is tearing through hundred-calorie snack packs and eating handfuls of roasted peanuts, and who has said nothing since we entered the pantry except "What's a Fig Newman?"—he stops and says, "I want to play this game."

"It's not a game," Deb says.

And I'm happy to hear her say that, as it's just what I've been trying to get her to admit for years. That it's not a game. That it's dead serious, and a kind of preparation, and an active pathology that I prefer not to indulge.

"It's the Anne Frank game," Shoshana says. "Right?"

Seeing how upset my wife is, I do my best to defend her. I say, "No, it's not a game. It's just what we talk about when we talk about Anne Frank."

"How do we play this non-game?" Mark says. "What do we do?"

"It's the Righteous Gentile game," Shoshana says.

"It's Who Will Hide Me?" I say.

"In the event of a second Holocaust," Deb says, giving in. "It's a serious exploration, a thought experiment that we engage in."

"That you play," Shoshana says.

"That, in the event of an American Holocaust, we sometimes talk about which of our Christian friends would hide us."

"I don't get it," Mark says.

"Of course you do," Shoshana says. "It's like this. If there was a Shoah, if it happened again—say we were in Jerusalem, and it's 1941 and the Grand Mufti got his way, what would Jebediah do?"

"What could he do?" Mark says.

"He could hide us. He could risk his life and his family's and everyone's around him. That's what the game is: would he—for real—would he do that for you?"

"He'd be good for that, a Mormon," Mark says. "Forget this pantry. They have to keep a year of food stored in case of the Rapture, or something like that. Water, too. A year of supplies. Or maybe it's that they have sex through a sheet. No, wait. I think that's supposed to be us."

"All right," Deb says. "Let's not play. Really, let's go back to the kitchen. I can order in from the glatt kosher place. We can eat outside, have a real dinner and not just junk."

"No, no," Mark says. "I'll play. I'll take it seriously."

"So would the guy hide you?" I say.

"The kids, too?" Mark says. "I'm supposed to pretend that in Jerusalem he's got a hidden motel or something where he can put the twelve of us?"

"Yes," Shoshana says. "In their seminary or something. Sure."

Mark thinks about this for a long, long time. He eats Fig Newmans and considers, and you can tell that he's taking it seriously—serious to the extreme.

"Yes," Mark says, looking choked up. "Jeb would do that for us. He would risk it all."

Shoshana nods. "Now you go," she says to us. "You take a turn."

"But we don't know any of the same people anymore," Deb says. "We usually just talk about the neighbors."

"Our across-the-street neighbors," I tell them. "They're the perfect example. Because the husband, Mitch, he would hide us. I know it. He'd lay down his life for what's right. But that wife of his."

"Yes," Deb says. "Mitch would hide us, but Gloria, she'd buckle. When he was at work one day, she'd turn us in."

"You could play against yourselves," Shoshana says. "What if one of you wasn't Jewish? Would you hide the other?"

"I'll do it," I say. "I'll be the Gentile, because I could pass best. A grown woman with an ankle-length denim skirt in her closet—they'd catch you in a flash."

"Fine," Deb says. And I stand up straight, put my shoulders back, like maybe I'm in a lineup. I stand there with my chin raised so my wife can study me. So she can decide if her husband really has what it takes. Would I have the strength, would I care enough—and it is not a light question, not a throwaway question—to risk my life to save her and our son?

Deb stares, and Deb smiles, and gives me a little push to my chest. "Of course he would," Deb says. She takes the half stride that's between us and gives me a tight hug that she doesn't release. "Now you," Deb says. "You and Yuri go."

"How does that even make sense?" Mark says. "Even for imagining."

"Sh-h-h," Shoshana says. "Just stand over there and be a good Gentile while I look."

"But if I weren't Jewish I wouldn't be me."

"That's for sure," I say.

"He agrees," Mark says. "We wouldn't even be married. We wouldn't have kids."

"Of course you can imagine it," Shoshana says. "Look," she says, and goes over and closes the pantry door. "Here we are, caught in

South Florida for the second Holocaust. You're not Jewish, and you've got the three of us hiding in your pantry."

"But look at me!" he says.

"I've got a fix," I say. "You're a background singer for ZZ Top. You know that band?"

Deb lets go of me so she can give my arm a slap.

"Really," Shoshana says. "Look at the three of us like it's your house and we're your charges, locked up in this room."

"And what're you going to do while I do that?" Mark says.

"I'm going to look at you looking at us. I'm going to imagine."

"O.K.," he says. "*Nu*, get to it. I will stand, you imagine."

And that's what we do, the four of us. We stand there playing our roles, and we really get into it. I can see Deb seeing him, and him seeing us, and Shoshana just staring at her husband.

We stand there so long I can't tell how much time has passed, though the light changes ever so slightly—the sun outside again dimming—in the crack under the pantry door.

"So would I hide you?" he says. And for the first time that day he reaches out, as my Deb would, and puts his hand to his wife's hand. "Would I, Shoshi?"

And you can tell that Shoshana is thinking of her kids, though that's not part of the scenario. You can tell that she's changed part of the imagining. And she says, after a pause, yes, but she's not laughing. She says yes, but to him it sounds as it does to us, so that he is now asking and asking. But wouldn't I? Wouldn't I hide you? Even if it was life and death—if it would spare you, and they'd kill me alone for doing it? Wouldn't I?

Shoshana pulls back her hand.

She does not say it. And he does not say it. And of the four of us no one will say what cannot be said—that this wife believes her husband would not hide her. What to do? What will come of it? And so we stand like that, the four of us trapped in that pantry. Afraid to open the door and let out what we've locked inside.

BLACK BOX

BY JENNIFER EGAN (2012)

1

People rarely look the way you expect them to, even when you've seen pictures.

The first thirty seconds in a person's presence are the most important.

If you're having trouble perceiving and projecting, focus on projecting.

Necessary ingredients for a successful projection: giggles; bare legs; shyness.

The goal is to be both irresistible and invisible.

When you succeed, a certain sharpness will go out of his eyes.

2

Some powerful men actually call their beauties "Beauty."

Counter to reputation, there is a deep camaraderie among beauties.

If your Designated Mate is widely feared, the beauties at the house party where you've gone undercover to meet him will be especially kind.

Kindness feels good, even when it's based on a false notion of your identity and purpose.

3

Posing as a beauty means not reading what you would like to read on a rocky shore in the South of France.

Sunlight on bare skin can be as nourishing as food.

Even a powerful man will be briefly self-conscious when he first disrobes to his bathing suit.

It is technically impossible for a man to look better in a Speedo than in swim trunks.

If you love someone with dark skin, white skin looks drained of something vital.

4

When you know that a person is violent and ruthless, you will see violent ruthlessness in such basic things as his swim stroke.

"What are you doing?" from your Designated Mate amid choppy waves after he has followed you into the sea may or may not betray suspicion.

Your reply—"Swimming"—may or may not be perceived as sarcasm.

"Shall we swim together toward those rocks?" may or may not be a question.

"All that way?" will, if spoken correctly, sound ingenuous.

"We'll have privacy there" may sound unexpectedly ominous.

5

A hundred feet of blue-black Mediterranean will allow you ample time to deliver a strong self-lecture.

At such moments, it may be useful to explicitly recall your training:

"You will be infiltrating the lives of criminals.

"You will be in constant danger.

"Some of you will not survive, but those who do will be heroes.

"A few of you will save lives and even change the course of history.

"We ask of you an impossible combination of traits: ironclad scruples and a willingness to violate them;

"An abiding love for your country and a willingness to consort with individuals who are working actively to destroy it;

"The instincts and intuition of experts, and the blank records and true freshness of ingénues.

"You will each perform this service only once, after which you will return to your lives.

"We cannot promise that your lives will be exactly the same when you go back to them."

6

Eagerness and pliability can be expressed even in the way you climb from the sea onto chalky yellow rocks.

"You're a very fast swimmer," uttered by a man who is still submerged, may not be intended as praise.

Giggling is sometimes better than answering.

"You are a lovely girl" may be meant straightforwardly.

Ditto "I want to fuck you now."

"Well? What do you think about that?" suggests a preference for direct verbal responses over giggling.

"I like it" must be uttered with enough gusto to compensate for a lack of declarative color.

"You don't sound sure" indicates insufficient gusto.

"I'm not sure" is acceptable only when followed, coyly, with "You'll have to convince me."

Throwing back your head and closing your eyes allows you to give the appearance of sexual readiness while concealing revulsion.

7

Being alone with a violent and ruthless man, surrounded by water, can make the shore seem very far away.

You may feel solidarity, at such a time, with the beauties just visible there in their bright bikinis.

You may appreciate, at such a time, why you aren't being paid for this work.

Your voluntary service is the highest form of patriotism.

Remind yourself that you aren't being paid when he climbs out of the water and lumbers toward you.

Remind yourself that you aren't being paid when he leads you behind a boulder and pulls you onto his lap.

The Dissociation Technique is like a parachute—you must pull the cord at the correct time.

Too soon, and you may hinder your ability to function at a crucial moment;

Too late, and you will be lodged too deeply inside the action to wriggle free.

You will be tempted to pull the cord when he surrounds you with arms whose bulky strength reminds you, fleetingly, of your husband's.

You will be tempted to pull it when you feel him start to move against you from below.

You will be tempted to pull it when his smell envelops you: metallic, like a warm hand clutching pennies.

The directive "Relax" suggests that your discomfort is palpable.

"No one can see us" suggests that your discomfort has been understood as fear of physical exposure.

"Relax, relax," uttered in rhythmic, throaty tones, suggests that your discomfort is not unwelcome.

8

Begin the Dissociation Technique only when physical violation is imminent.

Close your eyes and slowly count backward from ten.

With each number, imagine yourself rising out of your body and moving one step farther away from it.

By eight, you should be hovering just outside your skin.

By five, you should be floating a foot or two above your body, feeling only vague anxiety over what is about to happen to it.

By three, you should feel fully detached from your physical self.

By two, your body should be able to act and react without your participation.

By one, your mind should drift so free that you lose track of what is happening below.

White clouds spin and curl.

A blue sky is as depthless as the sea.

The sound of waves against rocks existed millennia before there were creatures who could hear it.

Spurs and gashes of stone narrate a violence that the earth itself has long forgotten.

Your mind will rejoin your body when it is safe to do so.

9

Return to your body carefully, as if you were reëntering your home after a hurricane.

Resist the impulse to reconstruct what has just happened.

Focus instead on gauging your Designated Mate's reaction to the new intimacy between you.

In some men, intimacy will prompt a more callous, indifferent attitude.

In others, intimacy may awaken problematic curiosity about you.

"Where did you learn to swim like that?," uttered lazily, while supine, with two fingers in your hair, indicates curiosity.

Tell the truth without precision.

"I grew up near a lake" is both true and vague.

"Where was the lake?" conveys dissatisfaction with your vagueness.

"Columbia County, New York" suggests precision while avoiding it.

"Manhattan?" betrays unfamiliarity with the geography of New York State.

Never contradict your Designated Mate.

"Where did *you* grow up?," asked of a man who has just asked you the same thing, is known as "mirroring."

Mirror your Designated Mate's attitudes, interests, desires, and tastes.

Your goal is to become part of his atmosphere: a source of comfort and ease.

Only then will he drop his guard when you are near.

Only then will he have significant conversations within your earshot.

Only then will he leave his possessions in a porous and unattended state.

Only then can you begin to gather information systematically.

10

"Come. Let's go back," uttered brusquely, suggests that your Designated Mate has no more wish to talk about himself than you do.

Avoid the temptation to analyze his moods and whims.

Salt water has a cleansing effect.

11

You will see knowledge of your new intimacy with your Designated Mate in the eyes of every beauty on shore.

"We saved lunch for you" may or may not be an allusion to the reason for your absence.

Cold fish is unappealing, even when served in a good lemon sauce.

Be friendly to other beauties, but not solicitous.

When you are in conversation with a beauty, it is essential that you be perceived as no more or less than she is.

Be truthful about every aspect of your life except marriage (if any).

If married, say that you and your spouse have divorced, to give an impression of unfettered freedom.

"Oh, that's sad!" suggests that the beauty you're chatting with would like to marry.

12

If your Designated Mate abruptly veers toward the villa, follow him.

Taking his hand and smiling congenially can create a sense of low-key accompaniment.

An abstracted smile in return, as if he'd forgotten who you are, may be a sign of pressing concerns.

The concerns of your Designated Mate are your concerns.

The room assigned to a powerful man will be more lavish than the one you slept in while awaiting his arrival.

Never look for hidden cameras: the fact that you're looking will give you away.

Determine whether your Designated Mate seeks physical intimacy; if not, feign the wish for a nap.

Your pretense of sleep will allow him to feel that he is alone.

Curling up under bedclothes, even those belonging to an enemy subject, may be soothing.

You're more likely to hear his handset vibrate if your eyes are closed.

13

A door sliding open signals his wish to take the call on the balcony.

Your Designated Mate's important conversations will take place outdoors.

If you are within earshot of his conversation, record it.

Since beauties carry neither pocketbooks nor timepieces, you cannot credibly transport recording devices.

A microphone has been implanted just beyond the first turn of your right ear canal.

Activate the microphone by pressing the triangle of cartilage across your ear opening.

You will hear a faint whine as recording begins.

In extreme quiet, or to a person whose head is adjacent to yours, this whine may be audible.

Should the whine be detected, swat your ear as if to deflect a mosquito, hitting the on/off cartilage to deactivate the mike.

You need not identify or comprehend the language your subject is using.

Your job is proximity; if you are near your Designated Mate, recording his private speech, you are succeeding.

Profanity sounds the same in every language.

An angry subject will guard his words less carefully.

14

If your subject is angry, you may leave your camouflage position and move as close to him as possible to improve recording quality.

You may feel afraid as you do this.

Your pounding heartbeat will not be recorded.

If your Designated Mate is standing on a balcony, hover in the doorway just behind him.

If he pivots and discovers you, pretend that you were on the verge of approaching him.

Anger usually trumps suspicion.

If your subject brushes past you and storms out of the room, slamming the door, you have eluded detection.

15

If your Designated Mate leaves your company a second time, don't follow him again.

Deactivate your ear mike and resume your "nap."

A moment of repose may be a good time to reassure your loved ones.

Nuanced communication is too easily monitored by the enemy.

Your Subcutaneous Pulse System issues pings so generic that detection would reveal neither source nor intent.

A button is embedded behind the inside ligament of your right knee (if right-handed).

Depress twice to indicate to loved ones that you are well and thinking of them.

You may send this signal only once each day.

A continuous depression of the button indicates an emergency.

You will debate, each day, the best time to send your signal.

You will reflect on the fact that your husband, coming from a culture of tribal allegiance, understands and applauds your patriotism.

You will reflect on the enclosed and joyful life that the two of you have shared since graduate school.

You will reflect on the fact that America is your husband's chosen country, and that he loves it.

You will reflect on the fact that your husband's rise to prominence would have been unimaginable in any other nation.

You will reflect on your joint conviction that your service had to be undertaken before you had children.

You will reflect on the fact that you are thirty-three, and have spent your professional life fomenting musical trends.

You will reflect on the fact that you must return home the same person you were when you left.

You will reflect on the fact that you've been guaranteed you will *not* be the same person.

You will reflect on the fact that you had stopped being that person even before leaving.

You will reflect on the fact that too much reflection is pointless.

You will reflect on the fact that these "instructions" are becoming less and less instructive.

Your Field Instructions, stored in a chip beneath your hairline, will serve as both a mission log and a guide for others undertaking this work.

Pressing your left thumb (if right-handed) against your left middle fingertip begins recording.

For clearest results, mentally speak the thought, as if talking to yourself.

Always filter your observations and experience through the lens of their didactic value.

Your training is ongoing; you must learn from each step you take.

When your mission is complete, you may view the results of the download before adding your Field Instructions to your mission file.

Where stray or personal thoughts have intruded, you may delete them.

16

Pretend sleep can lead to actual sleep.

Sleep is restorative in almost every circumstance.

The sound of showering likely indicates the return of your Designated Mate.

As a beauty, you will be expected to return to your room and change clothes often; a fresh appearance at mealtimes is essential.

The goal is to be a lovely, innocuous, evolving surprise.

A crisp white sundress against tanned skin is widely viewed as attractive.

Avoid overbright colors; they are attention-seeking and hinder camouflage.

White is not, technically speaking, a bright color.

White is, nevertheless, bright.

Gold spike-heeled sandals may compromise your ability to run or jump, but they look good on tanned feet.

Thirty-three is still young enough to register as "young."

Registering as "young" is especially welcome to those who may not register as "young" much longer.

If your Designated Mate leads you to dinner with an arm at your waist, assume that your attire change was successful.

17

When men begin serious talk, beauties are left to themselves.

"How long have you been divorced?" suggests the wish to resume a prior conversation.

"A few months," when untrue, should be uttered without eye contact.

"What was he like, your husband?" may be answered honestly.

"From Africa. Kenya" will satisfy your wish to talk about your husband.

"Black?," with eyebrows raised, may indicate racism.

"Yes. Black," in measured tones, should deliver a gentle reprimand.

"How black?" suggests that it did not.

"Very black" is somewhat less gentle, especially when accompanied by a pointed stare.

"Nice" hints at personal experience.

"Yes. It is nice" contradicts one's alleged divorce. "Was nice" is a reasonable correction.

"But not nice enough?," with laughter, indicates friendly intimacy. Especially when followed by "Or too nice!"

18

House-party hosts are universally eager to make guests eat.

For most beauties, the lure of food is a hazard; as a beauty of limited tenure, you may eat what you want.

Squab can be consumed by ripping the bird apart with your hands and sucking the meat from the bones.

A stunned expression reveals that your host expected the use of utensils.

A host who caters to violent guests will understand implicitly the need for discretion.

The adjacency of your host's chair to your own may presage a confidence.

If your job is to appear simpleminded, a confidence may mean that you have failed.

Everyone should brush his teeth before dinner.

Turning your ear toward your host's mouth will prevent you from having to smell the breath coming from it.

Ears must be kept clean at all times.

If your host warns you that your Designated Mate may pose an immediate danger to you, assume that your Designated Mate has left the room.

19

Going to the rest room is the most efficient means of self-jettisoning.

Never betray urgency, not even in an empty hallway.

If you have no idea in which direction your Designated Mate has gone, hold still.

If you find yourself hovering beside a pair of glass doors, you may open them and step outside.

Nights in the South of France are a strange, dark, piercing blue.

A bright moon can astonish, no matter how many times you have seen it.

If you were a child who loved the moon, looking at the moon will forever remind you of childhood.

Fatherless girls may invest the moon with a certain paternal promise.

Everyone has a father.

A vague story like "Your father died before you were born" may satisfy a curious child for an unlikely number of years.

The truth of your paternity, discovered in adulthood, will make the lie seem retroactively ludicrous.

Publicists occasionally have flings with their movie-star clients.

Discovering that you are a movie star's daughter is not necessarily a comfort.

It is especially not a comfort when the star in question has seven other children from three different marriages.

Discovering that you are a movie star's daughter may prompt you to watch upward of sixty movies, dating from the beginning of his career.

You may think, watching said movies, You don't know about me, but I am here.

You may think, watching said movies, I'm invisible to you, but I am here.

A sudden reconfiguration of your past can change the fit and feel of your adulthood.

It may cleave you, irreparably, from the mother whose single goal has been your happiness.

If your husband has transformed greatly in his own life, he will understand your transformation.

Avoid excessive self-reflection; your job is to look out, not in.

20

"There you are," whispered from behind by your Designated Mate, suggests that he has been looking for you.

Holding still can sometimes prove more effective than actively searching.

"Come," uttered softly, may communicate a renewed wish for intimate contact.

The moon's calm face can make you feel, in advance, that you are understood and forgiven.

The sea is audible against the rocks well before you see it.

Even at night, the Mediterranean is more blue than black.

If you wish to avoid physical intimacy, the sight of a speedboat will bring relief, despite the myriad new problems it presents.

If no words are exchanged between your Designated Mate and the speedboat's captain, their meeting was likely prearranged.

A man known for his cruelty may still show great care in guiding his beauty into a rocking speedboat.

He may interpret her hesitation to board as a fear of falling in.

Resist the impulse to ask where you are going.

Try, when anxious, to summon up a goofy giggle.

Locate your Personal Calming Source and use it.

If your Personal Calming Source is the moon, be grateful that it is dark and that the moon is especially bright.

Reflect on the many reasons you can't yet die:

You need to see your husband.

You need to have children.

You need to tell the movie star that he has an eighth child, and that she is a hero.

21

The moon may appear to move, but really it is you who are moving.

At high velocity, a speedboat slams along the tops of waves.

Fear and excitement are sometimes indistinguishable.

When the captain of a boat adjusts his course in response to commands from your Designated Mate, he may not know where he is taking you.

If your Designated Mate keeps looking up, he's probably using the stars for navigation.

The Mediterranean is vast enough to have once seemed infinite.

A beauty should require no more context than the presence of her Designated Mate.

A beauty must appear to enjoy any journey he initiates.

Simulate said enjoyment by putting an affectionate arm around him and nestling your head close to his.

A beauty whose head is aligned with her Designated Mate's can share in his navigation and thus calculate the route.

At night, far from shore, stars pulse with a strength that is impossible to conceive of in the proximity of light.

Your whereabouts will never be a mystery; you will be visible at all times as a dot of light on the screens of those watching over you.

You are one of hundreds, each a potential hero.

Technology has afforded ordinary people a chance to glow in the cosmos of human achievement.

Your lack of espionage and language training is what makes your record clean and neutral.

You are an ordinary person undertaking an extraordinary task.

You need not be remarkable for your credentials or skill sets, only for your bravery and equilibrium.

Knowing that you are one of hundreds shouldn't feel belittling.

In the new heroism, the goal is to merge with something larger than yourself.

In the new heroism, the goal is to throw off generations of self-involvement.

In the new heroism, the goal is to renounce the American fixation with being seen and recognized.

In the new heroism, the goal is to dig beneath your shiny persona.

You'll be surprised by what lies under it: a rich, deep crawl space of possibilities.

Some liken this discovery to a dream in which a familiar home acquires new wings and rooms.

The power of individual magnetism is nothing against the power of combined selfless effort.

You may accomplish astonishing personal feats, but citizen agents rarely seek individual credit.

They liken the need for personal glory to cigarette addiction: a habit that feels life-sustaining even as it kills you.

Childish attention-seeking is usually satisfied at the expense of real power.

An enemy of the state could not have connived a better way to declaw and distract us.

Now our notorious narcissism is our camouflage.

22

After a juddering ride of several hours, you may not notice at first that the boat is approaching a shore.

A single lighted structure stands out strongly on a deserted coastline.

Silence after a roaring motor is a sound of its own.

The speedboat's immediate departure signals that you won't be making a return trip anytime soon.

Knowing your latitude and longitude is not the same as knowing where you are.

A new remote and unfamiliar place can make the prior remote and unfamiliar place seem like home.

Imagining yourself as a dot of light on a screen is oddly reassuring.

Because your husband is a visionary in the realm of national security, he occasionally has access to that screen.

If it calms you to imagine your husband tracking your dot of light, then imagine it.

Do not, however, close your eyes while ascending a rocky path in darkness.

At Latitude X, Longitude Y, the flora is dry and crumbles under your feet.

A voice overhead suggests that your arrival was expected and observed.

An empty shore is not necessarily unpatrolled.

The best patrols are imperceptible.

23

A formal handshake between your new host and your Designated Mate implies that this is their first meeting.

A formal handshake followed by a complex and stylized hand gesture implies a shared allegiance.

So does the immediate use of a language you don't recognize.

In certain rich, powerful men, physical slightness will seem a source of strength.

The failure of your new host to acknowledge you may indicate that women do not register in his field of vision.

Being invisible means that you won't be closely watched.

Your job is to be forgotten yet still present.

A white, sparkling villa amid so much scrabbly darkness will appear miragelike.

A man to whom women are invisible may still have many beauties in his domain.

These neglected beauties will vie for his scant attention.

Among neglected beauties, there is often an alpha beauty who assumes leadership.

As you enter the house, her cool scrutiny will ripple through the other beauties and surround you.

The sensation will remind you of going as a child with your mother to visit families with two parents and multiple children.

At first, the knot of unfamiliar kids would seem impenetrable.

You would wish, keenly, that you had a sibling who could be your ally.

Feeling at the mercy of those around you prompted a seismic internal response.

The will to dominate was deeper than yourself.

You were never childish, even as a child.

Your unchildishness is something your husband has always loved in you.

Once the new children were under your control, it was crushing to leave their midst.

24

A small table and chairs carved into a spindly clifftop promontory are doubtless designed for private conversation.

If your Designated Mate brings you with him to this place, it may mean that he feels less than perfectly at ease with your new host.

When your new host dismisses his own alpha beauty, important business may be under way.

An alpha beauty will not tolerate her own exclusion if another beauty is included.

If your new host makes a motion of dismissal at you, look to your Designated Mate.

Take orders from no one but your Designated Mate.

If your Designated Mate keeps an arm around you in the face of your new host's dismissal, you have become the object of a power play.

If your new host moves close to your face and speaks directly into it, he is likely testing your ignorance of his language.

If your Designated Mate stiffens beside you, your new host's words are probably offensive.

When you become an object of contention, try to neutralize the conflict.

A giggle and a look of incomprehension are a beauty's most reliable tools.

If the men relax into their chairs, neutralization has been successful.

Your new host has insulted you and, by extension, your Designated Mate.

Your Designated Mate has prevailed in his claim that you're too harmless to bother sending away.

Congratulate yourself on preserving your adjacency and activate your ear mike.

25

In the presence of business conversation, project an utter lack of interest or curiosity.

Notice where you are at all times.

On a high, narrow promontory at Latitude X, Longitude Y, the ocean and heavens shimmer in all directions.

There will be moments in your mission, perhaps very few, when you'll sense the imminence of critical information.

It may come in the form of a rush of joy.

This joy may arise from your discovery that the moon, hard and radiant, is still aloft.

It may arise from the knowledge that, when your task is complete, you will return to the husband you adore.

It may arise from the extremity of the natural beauty around you, and the recognition that you are alive in this moment.

It may arise from your knowledge that you have accomplished every goal you've set for yourself since childhood.

It may arise from the knowledge that at long last you've found a goal worthy of your considerable energies.

It may arise from the knowledge that, by accomplishing this goal, you'll have helped to perpetuate American life as you know it.

A wave of joy can make it difficult to sit still.

Beware of internal states—positive or negative—that obscure what is happening around you.

When two subjects begin making sketches, concrete planning may have commenced.

The camera implanted in your left eye is operated by pressing your left tear duct.

In poor light, a flash may be activated by pressing the outside tip of your left eyebrow.

When using the flash, always cover your non-camera eye to shield it from temporary blindness occasioned by the flash.

Never deploy flash photography in the presence of other people.

26

Springing from your seat with a gasp and peering toward the house will focus the attention of others in that direction.

Having heard something inaudible to others puts you in an immediate position of authority.

"What? What did you hear?," uttered close to your face by your Designated Mate, means that your diversion was successful.

Wait until their eagerness to know verges on anger, evidenced by the shaking of your shoulders.

Then tell them, faintly, "I heard screaming."

Men with a history of violence live in fear of retribution.

Your new host will be the first to depart in the direction of alleged screaming.

Your Designated Mate's glance toward the dock, far below, may reveal that his interests are not fully aligned with your new host's.

His attention to his handset may portend that your diversion has run amok, undermining the transaction you meant to capture.

Among the violent, there is always a plan for escape.

27

It is reasonable to hope that a backlit screen will distract its user from a camera flash at some slight distance.

Move close to the sketches you wish to photograph, allowing them to fill your field of vision.

Hold very still.

A flash is far more dramatic in total darkness.

An epithet in another language, followed by "What the fuck was that?," means you overestimated your Designated Mate's handset absorption.

A bright, throbbing total blindness means that you neglected to cover your non-camera eye.

Distance yourself from agency in the flash by crying out, truthfully, "I can't see!"

It is hard to safely navigate a clifftop promontory at high speed while blind.

It is hard to defer said navigation when your Designated Mate is forcefully yanking your hand.

A distant buzz presages an approaching speedboat.

Cooler air and a downward slope indicate that you are now below the cliff's edge.

Trying to negotiate a crumbling wooded path in a state of blindness (and heels) will soon lead to tripping and collapsing.

Receding downhill footfalls indicate that you've overtaxed your limited value to your Designated Mate.

A sense of helpless disorientation may prevent you from doing much more than sitting there in the dirt.

28

Variegation in the textures around you is a first sign that your temporary blindness has begun to fade.

Temporary blindness sharpens one's appreciation for not being blind.

In the aftermath of blindness, the accretion of objects around you may have an almost sensual quality.

A boat departing at high speed will send a vibration trembling up through the soil.

The knowledge that you are alone, without your Designated Mate, will settle upon you slowly and coldly.

Each new phase of aloneness reveals that you were previously less alone than you thought.

This more profound isolation may register, at first, as paralysis.

If it soothes you to lie back in the dirt, then lie back.

The moon shines everywhere.

The moon can seem as expressive as a face.

Human beings are fiercely, primordially resilient.

In uneasy times, draw on the resilience you carry inside you.

Recall that the mythical feats you loved to read about as a child are puny beside the accomplishments of human beings on earth.

29

The presence of another person can be sensed, even when not directly perceived.

The discovery of another person at close range, when you thought you were alone, may occasion fear.

Leaping from a supine into a standing posture will induce a head rush.

"I see you. Come out" must be uttered calmly, from the Readiness Position.

If you show fear, make sure that it isn't the fear you actually feel.

When you've expected a man, the appearance of a woman may be shocking.

Despite all that you know and are, you may experience that shock as a relief.

"Why are you here?," uttered by your new host's alpha beauty, is likely hostile.

Respond to abstract questions on the most literal level: "He left without me."

"Bastard," muttered bitterly, suggests familiarity with the phenomenon of being left behind.

Sympathy from an unexpected source can prompt a swell of emotion.

Measure the potential liability of shedding tears before you let them fall.

The perfumed arm of a beauty may pour strength and hope directly into your skin.

30

A lavish clifftop villa may look even more miragelike on a second approach.

Sustaining an atmosphere of luxury in a remote place requires an enormous amount of money.

So does coördinated violence.

Your job is to follow money to its source.

A powerful man whose associate has fled the premises after a false alarm is unlikely to be cheerful.

The reappearance of the vanished associate's stranded beauty will likely startle him.

Astonishment is satisfying to witness on any face.

"Where the fuck did he go?" is remarkably easy to decipher, even in a language you don't recognize.

A shrug is comprehensible to everyone.

An alpha beauty's complete indifference to the consternation of her mate may mean that he's easily moved to consternation.

It may also mean that he's not her mate.

As a beauty, you will sometimes be expected to change hands.

Generally, you will pass from the hands of a less powerful man to those of a more powerful man.

Greater proximity to the source of money and control is progress.

Your job is identical regardless of whose hands you are in.

If your vulnerability and helplessness have drawn the interest of an enemy subject, accentuate them.

Scraped and dirty legs may accentuate your vulnerability to the point of disgust.

They might get you a hot shower, though.

31

Homes of the violent rich have excellent first-aid cabinets.

If, after tending to your scrapes, you are shown to a bathing area with a stone-encrusted waterfall, assume you won't be alone for long.

The fact that a man has ignored and then insulted you does not mean that he won't want to fuck you.

Slim, powerful men often move with catlike swiftness.

Begin your countdown early—as he lowers himself into the tub.

By the time he seizes your arm, you should be at five.

By the time your forehead is jammed against a rock, you should perceive your body only vaguely, from above.

32

If you feel, on returning to your body, that much time has passed, don't dwell on how much.

If your limbs are sore and your forehead scraped and raw, don't dwell on why.

When you emerge from a warm, churning bath where you've spent an indeterminate period of time, expect to feel shaky and weak.

Remind yourself that you are receiving no payment, in currency or kind, for this or any act you have engaged in.

These acts are forms of sacrifice.

An abundance of diaphanous bathrobes suggests that the occupants of this bathroom are often female.

A soiled and tattered white sundress can seem oddly precious when it's all you have.

Keep with you the things that matter—you won't come back for them later.

The stationing of a male attendant outside the bathroom means that you haven't been forgotten.

If he shows you to a tiny room containing a very large bed, your utility to your new host may not have been exhausted.

A tray containing a meat pie, grapes, and a pitcher of water suggests that visits such as yours are routine.

At times, you may wish to avoid the moon.

At times, the moon may appear like a surveillance device, tracking your movements.

The ability to sleep in stressful conditions is essential to this work.

Sleep whenever you can safely do so.

33

Your abrupt awakening may feel like a reaction to a sound.

In moments of extreme solitude, you may believe you've heard your name.

We reassure ourselves by summoning, in our dreams, those we love and miss.

Having awakened to find them absent, we may be left with a sense of having spoken with them.

Even the most secure houses achieve, in deep night, a state of relative unconsciousness.

A beauty in a diaphanous lavender bathrobe can go anywhere, as long as she appears to be delivering herself to someone.

34

A universal principle of home construction makes it possible to guess which door will lead to the master bedroom.

Linen closets, with doors closed, can resemble master bedrooms.

So can bathrooms.

Bare feet are virtually soundless on a stone floor.

Even a slim, catlike man may snore.

When trespassing in a sleeping man's bedroom, go straight to his bed, as if you were seeking him out.

An alpha beauty who has appeared to have no tie to your new host may turn out to be his intimate, after all.

Their sleeping entanglement may contradict everything you have witnessed between them.

A small crib near the bed may indicate the presence of a baby.

Avoid indulging your own amazement; it wastes time.

Master bedrooms in lavish homes often divide into "his" and "hers" areas.

A beauty's closet is unmistakable, like a quiver of bright arrows.

The closet of a slight, catlike man will usually be compact.

Having penetrated a man's personal space, immediately seek out his Sweet Spot.

The Sweet Spot is where he empties his pockets at the end of the day and stores the essentials he needs to begin the next.

The Sweet Spot of a secretive, catlike man will most often be inside a cupboard or a drawer.

When you find it, consider using a Data Surge to capture the contents of his handset.

A Data Surge must be deployed with extreme caution, and only if you feel confident of an exceptional yield.

The quantity of information captured will require an enormous amount of manpower to tease apart.

Its transmission will register on any monitoring device.

We can guarantee its effectiveness only once.

35

Reach between your right fourth and pinky toes (if right-handed) and remove the Data Plug from your Universal Port.

Attached to the plug is a cable with a connection pin at one end for insertion into the handset's data port.

Sit on the floor, away from sharp surfaces, and brace your back against a wall.

A red ribbon has been tucked inside your Universal Port; enclose this in one of your palms.

Spread apart your toes and gently reinsert the plug, now fused to your subject's handset, into your Universal Port.

You will feel the surge as the data flood your body.

The surge may contain feeling, memory, heat, cold, longing, pain, even joy.

Although the data are alien, the memories dislodged will be your own:

Peeling an orange for your husband in bed on a Sunday, sunlight splashing the sheets;

The smoky earthen smell of the fur of your childhood cat;

The flavor of the peppermints your mother kept for you inside her desk.

The impact of a Data Surge may prompt unconsciousness or short-term memory loss.

The purpose of the red ribbon is to orient you; if you awaken to find yourself clutching one, look to your foot.

When your body is quiet, unplug the handset and return it to its original location.

36

A Data Surge leaves a ringing in your ears that may obscure the sound of another person's arrival.

A face that brought you relief once may trigger relief a second time.

When an alpha beauty accosts you at high volume in an unfamiliar language, it may mean she's too sleepy to remember who you are.

It may also mean she's calling someone else.

Beauty status will not excuse, for another beauty, your appearance where you are not supposed to be.

Should you be perceived as an enemy, prepare to defend yourself at the first sign of physical encroachment.

Your new host lunging at you, shouting, "What the fuck are you doing?," constitutes physical encroachment.

Thrust your elbow upward into the tender socket underneath his jaw, sending him backward onto the floor.

The wails of a newborn will lure its mother away from almost anything, including the physical travails of her mate.

A man disabled by an elbow blow will have little reaction to infant cries.

37

At the revelation of martial-arts expertise, a man who has perceived you as merely a beauty will recalculate your identity and purpose.

Watch his eyes: he'll be measuring the distance to his nearest firearm.

An immediate exit is advisable.

A slim, catlike man may well rebound before a hasty exit can be made.

Obstructing the path of a violent man to his firearm will nearly always result in another encroachment.

Kicking him in the foreneck, even barefoot, will temporarily occlude his windpipe.

The alpha beauty of a violent man will know where his firearm is kept, and how to use it.

A woman holding a gun and a baby no longer qualifies as a beauty.

No beauty is really a beauty.

Disabling a gun holder is likely to hurt the baby she is holding, too.

When self-preservation requires that you harm the innocent, we can provide no more than guidelines.

As Americans, we value human rights above all else and cannot sanction their violation.

When someone threatens our human rights, however, a wider leeway becomes necessary.

Follow your instincts while bearing in mind that we must, and will, hew to our principles.

A woman holding a thrashing baby in one arm may have trouble aiming a firearm with the other.

Bullets do actually whistle in an enclosed space.

If a person has shot at you and missed, incapacitate her before she can fire again.

We are most reluctant to hurt those who remind us of ourselves.

38

A lag time exists between getting shot and knowing that you have been shot.

Assuming there is no artery involvement, wounds to the upper limbs are preferable.

Bony, tendony body parts bleed less, but are harder to reconstruct if shattered.

The right shoulder is a bony, tendony part.

When shots have been fired in a powerful man's home, you have minutes, if not seconds, before the arrival of security.

Your physical person is our Black Box; without it, we have no record of what has happened on your mission.

It is imperative that you remove yourself from enemy possession.

When you find yourself cornered and outnumbered, you may unleash, as a last resort, your Primal Roar.

The Primal Roar is the human equivalent of an explosion, a sound that combines screaming, shrieking, and howling.

The Roar must be accompanied by facial contortions and frenetic body movement, suggesting a feral, unhinged state.

The Primal Roar must transform you from a beauty into a monster.

The goal is to horrify your opponent, the way trusted figures, turned evil, are horrifying in movies and in nightmares.

Deploy your camera flash repeatedly while Roaring.

When approached by a howling, spasmodic, flashing monster, most women holding newborns will step aside.

Discontinue Roaring the instant you're free from immediate danger.

Those stampeding to the aid of a powerful man will barely notice a dishevelled beauty they pass in a hallway.

If you're lucky, this will buy you time to flee his house.

Resume your beauty role while running: smooth your hair and cover your bleeding wound with the sundress scrunched in your pocket.

The fact that you can't hear alarms doesn't mean you haven't set them off.

39

After violence in a closed room, cool night air will have a clarifying effect.

Get to the bottom of a hill any way you can, including sliding and rolling.

In residences of the violent rich, there will be at least one guard at each port of egress.

In deep night, if you are extremely lucky (and quiet), that guard will be asleep.

Assume, as well as you can, the air of a beauty larkishly gambolling.

If running barefoot onto a dock transports you back to your childhood, pain may be making you hallucinate.

Lying with girlfriends on a still-warm dock in upstate New York, watching shooting stars, is a sensation you remember after many years.

Hindsight creates the illusion that your life has led you inevitably to the present moment.

It's easier to believe in a foregone conclusion than to accept that our lives are governed by chance.

Showing up for a robotics course by accident, because of a classroom mix-up, is chance.

Finding an empty seat beside a boy with very dark skin and beautiful hands is chance.

When someone has become essential to you, you will marvel that you could have lain on a warm dock and not have known him yet.

Expect reimmersion in your old life to be difficult.

Experience leaves a mark, regardless of the reasons and principles behind it.

What our citizen agents most often require is simply for time to pass.

Our counsellors are available around the clock for the first two weeks of your reimmersion and during business hours thereafter.

We ask that you allow our Therapeutic Agents, rather than those in the general population, to address your needs.

Secrecy is the basis of what we do, and we require your extreme discretion.

40

Even preternatural swimming strength cannot propel you across a blue-black sea.

Staring with yearning ferocity from the end of a dock cannot propel you across a blue-black sea.

When your body has been granted exceptional powers, it is jarring to encounter a gulf between your desires and your abilities.

For millennia, engineers have empowered human beings to accomplish mythical feats.

Your husband is an engineer.

Children raised among wild animals learn to detect irregular movements in their landscape.

That particular awareness, coupled with scientific genius, has made your husband a national-security hero.

Intimacy with another human can allow you to scrutinize your surroundings as he would.

Along a rocky, moonlit shore, the irregular movement is the one that is lurching in time with the water beneath an overhang of brush.

A speedboat has most likely been hidden by your new host as a means of emergency escape.

The key will be inside it.

41

Slither between branches and board the boat; untie it and lower its motor into the water.

Be grateful for the lakes in upstate New York where you learned to pilot motorboats.

Fluff up your hair with your functional arm and essay a wide, carefree smile.

A smile is like a shield; it freezes your face into a mask of muscle that you can hide behind.

A smile is like a door that is both open and closed.

Turn the key and gun the motor once before aiming into the blue-black sea and jamming the accelerator.

Wave and giggle loudly at the stunned, sleepy guard.

Steer in a zigzag motion until you are out of gunshot range.

42

The exultation of escape will be followed almost immediately by a crushing onslaught of pain.

The house, its occupants, even the gunshots will seem like phantoms beside this clanging immediacy.

If the pain makes thought impossible, concentrate solely on navigation.

Only in specific Geographic Hotspots can we intervene.

While navigating toward a Hotspot, indicate an emergency by pressing the button behind your knee for sixty continuous seconds.

You must remain conscious.

If it helps, imagine yourself in the arms of your husband.

If it helps, imagine yourself in your apartment, where his grandfather's hunting knife is displayed inside a Plexiglas box.

If it helps, imagine harvesting the small tomatoes you grow on your fire escape in summer.

If it helps, imagine that the contents of the Data Surge will help thwart an attack in which thousands of American lives would have been lost.

Even without enhancements, you can pilot a boat in a semi-conscious state.

Human beings are superhuman.

Let the moon and the stars direct you.

43

When you reach the approximate location of a Hotspot, cut the engine.

You will be in total darkness, in total silence.

If you wish, you may lie down at the bottom of the boat.

The fact that you feel like you're dying doesn't mean that you will die.

Remember that, should you die, your body will yield a crucial trove of information.

Remember that, should you die, your Field Instructions will provide a record of your mission and lessons for those who follow.

Remember that, should you die, you will have triumphed merely by delivering your physical person into our hands.

The boat's movement on the sea will remind you of a cradle.

You'll recall your mother rocking you in her arms when you were a baby.

You'll recall that she has always loved you fiercely and entirely.

You'll discover that you have forgiven her.

You'll understand that she concealed your paternity out of faith that her own inexhaustible love would be enough.

The wish to tell your mother that you forgive her is yet another reason you must make it home alive.

You will not be able to wait, but you will have to wait.

We can't tell you in advance what direction relief will come from.

We can only reassure you that we have never yet failed to recover a citizen agent, dead or alive, who managed to reach a Hotspot.

44

Hotspots are not hot.

Even a warm night turns frigid at the bottom of a wet boat.

The stars are always there, scattered and blinking.

Looking up at the sky from below can feel like floating, suspended, and looking down.

The universe will seem to hang beneath you in its milky glittering mystery.

Only when you notice a woman like yourself, crumpled and bleeding at the bottom of a boat, will you realize what has happened.

You've deployed the Dissociation Technique without meaning to.

There is no harm in this.

Released from pain, you can waft free in the night sky.

Released from pain, you can enact the fantasy of flying that you nurtured as a child.

Keep your body in view at all times; if your mind loses track of your body, it may be hard—even impossible—to reunite the two.

As you waft free in the night sky, you may notice a steady rhythmic churning in the gusting wind.

Helicopter noise is inherently menacing.

A helicopter without lights is like a mixture of bat, bird, and monstrous insect.

Resist the urge to flee this apparition; it has come to save you.

45

Know that in returning to your body you are consenting to be racked, once again, by physical pain.

Know that in returning to your body you are consenting to undertake a jarring reimmersion into an altered life.

Some citizen agents have chosen not to return.

They have left their bodies behind, and now they shimmer sublimely in the heavens.

In the new heroism, the goal is to transcend individual life, with its petty pains and loves, in favor of the dazzling collective.

You may picture the pulsing stars as the heroic spirits of former agent beauties.

You may imagine Heaven as a vast screen crowded with their dots of light.

46

If you wish to return to your body, it is essential that you reach it before the helicopter does.

If it helps, count backward.

By eight, you should be close enough to see your bare and dirty feet.

By five, you should be close enough to see the bloody dress wrapped around your shoulder.

By three, you should be close enough to see the dimples you were praised for as a child.

By two, you should hear the shallow bleating of your breath.

47

Having returned to your body, witness the chopper's slow, throbbing descent.

It may appear to be the instrument of a purely mechanical realm.

It may look as if it had come to wipe you out.

It may be hard to believe that there are human beings inside it.

You won't know for sure until you see them crouching above you, their faces taut with hope, ready to jump.

AN ABDUCTION

BY TESSA HADLEY (2012)

Jane Allsop was abducted when she was fifteen, and nobody noticed. This happened a long time ago, in Surrey, in the nineteen-sixties, when parents were more careless. She was home from boarding school for the summer, and day after day the sun rose into a cloudless sky, from which Jane couldn't unfix the word "cerulean," which she'd learned in the art room. (She wasn't clever or literary, and was nervous of new words, which seemed to stick to her.) "Cerulean" was more of a blank, baking glare than mere merry blue. It prised its way each morning like a chisel through the crack between Jane's flowered bedroom curtains and between the eyelids she squeezed tightly shut in an effort to stay inside her dreams. It wasn't acceptable in Jane's kind of family to complain about good weather, yet the strain of it told on them, parents and children: they were remorselessly cheerful, while secretly they longed for rain. Jane imagined herself curled up with a bag of licorice beside a streaming windowpane, reading about the Chalet School. But her mother said it was a crime to stay indoors while the sun shone, and Jane couldn't read outside with the same absorption; there was always some strikingly perfect speckled insect falling onto your page like a reminder (of what? of itself), or a root nudging into your back, or stinging ants inside your shorts.

The morning of the abduction, Mrs. Allsop—dishevelled in a limp linen shirtdress—was wielding her secateurs up a ladder, pruning the climbing roses. She was immensely capable; tall and big-boned with a pink, pleasant face and dry yellow hair chopped sensibly short. Jane admired her mother greatly, especially when she transformed herself at night, for a concert in London or a Rotary Club dinner, with clip-on pearl earrings and lipstick and scent, a frilled taupe satin stole. Jane coveted this stole and tried it on when her mother was at the shops, making sultry faces at herself in the mirror—although sultry was the last thing her mother was, and everyone told Jane that she looked just like her. She certainly seemed to have her mother's figure, with not much bust, no waist to speak of, and a broad flat behind.

"Why don't you call up some of your old friends?" Mrs. Allsop suggested from the ladder top. "Invite them round to play Ping-Pong."

Jane responded with evasive enthusiasm. (She didn't know her old friends anymore; that was what happened when you were sent away to boarding school.) She said she was heading inside to find her Jokari set (a rubber ball attached by a long elastic string to a wooden base—you could hit the ball back and forth with a paddle all by yourself for hours on end). It was part of the family code that sport and physical exercise were meaningful ways of passing leisure time; without them, you risked dissipation, letting value slip away. Only Jane's brother, Robin, was allowed a special dispensation, because he was studying to get into Oxford—it was all right for him to have his head stuck in a book all day and to go around scowling, complaining that the sun gave him headaches. When Jane strayed into Robin's room ("Buzz off, shrimp, you're not permitted across my threshold"), he was curled up on his side on the bed, his clasped hands between his drawn-up knees, his glasses off, and his book propped across his face, Pink Floyd playing subduedly on the stereo. It was obvious that he'd been smoking. Mrs. Allsop smoked, with a casual elegance that startled Jane, but only on the silk-stole evenings, or if she had women friends around for tea. (For Robin, blind on his bed with a headache and sex fantasies and short-circuiting flashes of insane ambition, his sister, mutely protesting—she simply stood there till he got up and pushed her out and locked the door behind her—was a visitant from his insipid past, when they'd been friends.)

Jane was listless, her mind a blank with vivid little jets of dissatisfaction firing off in it. Real children, somewhere, were wholesomely intent on untying boats or building dams or collecting butterflies to asphyxiate in jars (as she and Robin had done one summer). She should be like them, she reproached herself; or she should be more thoroughly embarked on her teen-age self, like some of the girls at school, painting on makeup, then scrubbing it off, nurturing crushes on friends' brothers she'd only ever seen from a distance, cutting out pictures of pop stars from *Jackie* magazine. Jane knew that these girls were ahead of her in the fated trek toward adulthood, which she had half learned about in certain coy biology lessons. Yet theirs seemed also a backward step into triviality, away from the thing that this cerulean day—munificent, broiling, burning across her freckled shoulders, hanging so heavily on her hands—ought to become, if only she knew better how to use it.

She carried the Jokari set down through the patch of woodland toward the bottom of the garden. Her sister, Frances, dark-skinned and fey, not at all like their mother and not yet old enough for boarding school, had chums around to play with. They were supposed to be clearing the drive of rabbit droppings with spoons and plastic bags, for money, but they were all four hunkered in a semicircle under the pine trees, where they had set out tea things for their dolls, a pinecone on each tiny plate, a rabbit dropping in each tiny cup. Jane heard Frances chanting in two alternating voices while the others watched, in thrall to her.

"Don't want it! Don't want it!" Frances said in her whiny voice.

"Eat it *up*," her vicious voice replied. "*Take* your nasty medicine."

When Jane came near, the little girls melted into the undergrowth with hostile backward looks. She kicked their dolls over and hurled the pinecones as far as she could toward the flaunting patches of sky between the treetops (she had a strong throw, her father always said, better than Robin's); but she lacked conviction even in her malevolence. "We hate her! She's so ugly," the witch-children hummed, drifting between the bald pine trunks, keeping out of sight. Jane remembered, as she often did, how once at a friend's house she had overheard the dotty grandmother asking too loudly who the "plain" one was. The witches didn't even bother to follow her, to spy on her, which would at least have been some kind of game. She set up her Jokari on a scorched patch of grass beside where their chalky drive debouched onto the road. No cars passed. The road was a dead end, leading only to more big houses like theirs, secretive behind their screens of trees, some atmospheric with the half-timbering that Jane didn't yet know was a badge of inauthenticity, some with tennis courts from which the thwack of balls didn't often come.

Kicking off her flip-flops, she settled resignedly into her game. The pock and thud of the Jokari ball on the baked ground soothed her, and she started to care about whether she could break her own record of consecutive hits. (She had passed Robin's record long ago.) Rapt, she didn't notice her father steering the Rover down the drive, on his way out to pick up the Saturday paper; to save petrol, he liked to roll down with the hand brake off, starting the engine only when he turned into the road. Jane scooped low to the ground under an awkward shot, getting it up with too much force just as the sleek black of the car eased into the edge of her vision; the ball on its elastic must have seemed smashed deliberately and vindictively against the car's side window (which luckily was not open). Assaulted amid his reverie, Mr. Allsop was outraged out of all proportion to the offense—nothing was broken. He stopped the car and half stood up out of it to rant across its roof at Jane: Stupid girl! Didn't she have anything better to do? Then the car rolled on, ominously firing to life when it felt the road, and Jane was left wounded, staring after it. The wings of her spirit, which had been beginning to soar, faltered and flung her to earth, because, after all, she had been doing her best, nothing else; and also because her father was supposed to be her ally in the family, though they weren't at all alike. Mr. Allsop was small and dark, like Frances, easily bored, and clever with figures. He thought about Jane vaguely, through a fog of fond concern, fearing that she had her mother's flat, bland surface without Mrs. Allsop's force of conviction—or whatever it was that kept her impermeable, buoyant.

Jane dropped her paddle in an uncharacteristic gesture of despair. Tears stung her eyes; she stood with her hands by her sides, palms outward, in a kind of resigned openness. What next, then, if even her attempt at virtue had failed?

And that was how they first saw her. They passed Mr. Allsop in the Rover; he was turning out of the un-made-up road just as they turned into it. Mr. Allsop noticed them, because he knew most of the cars that visited the road, and he didn't recognize or much like the look of this one: an expensive dark-green sporty two-seater convertible, with one long-haired youth in a sloppy vest lolling in each seat, and one—smoking something that might have been more sinister than a cigarette—squeezed into the little luggage space behind, craning forward, as he was bound to, between his friends. The driver, who had one languid hand on the wheel, cornered carelessly in a puff of chalk dust, tires spitting loose stones. (If they were my kids, Mr. Allsop thought, catch me allowing them anywhere near my car. It's not all bad that Robin's such a drip.) Had the family ever realized that Jane had been abducted, her father would probably have remembered and suspected these visiting aliens.

The boys were drunk and stoned, and hadn't been to bed at all the night before (but then they hadn't got out of bed until four the previous afternoon). They were out looking for girls, in Nigel's father's car. (Nigel was the one squeezed into the luggage space.) They'd finished their second year at Oxford and were staying at Nigel's house, about a twenty-minute drive from the Allsops', while his parents were away in France. After sagging at dawn, dozing in the angular Swedish armchairs in the lounge, and filling Nigel's mother's fashionable ashtrays while listening to the Grateful Dead, all three had found a second wind, swimming several thrashing lengths in Nigel's pool. The loveliness of the morning had then seemed their own fresh discovery: the light as limpid as the water, birdsong skimming the flat echoless air, the sun's touch intricate on their skin. They had decided that they needed to find girls to crown the day. That was a few hours ago. It had taken them a while to get started; and then there'd been a striking absence, everywhere they'd driven, of available girls.

"She'll do," one of them called out when they saw Jane, loud enough for her to hear. It was Paddy (not Irish at all), the bulky, clever-looking one in the passenger seat, with small eyes like chinks of bright glass and greasy hair the color and texture of old rope, pushed behind pink ears. He took the joint from Nigel and blinked at Jane through its smoke with a sort of appraising impartial severity, not lascivious.

"But where will we put these girls?" Nigel asked facetiously, after one glance at Jane: he didn't fancy sharing his small space (and wasn't, in fact, much interested in girls). Paddy explained that they'd have to collect them one at a time.

Jane stood barefoot, hands still open in that gesture of self-relinquishment. She wasn't plain in that moment, though she didn't know it. Something was revealed in her that was normally hidden: an auburn light in her face, her freckles startling as the camouflage of an animal, blotting up against her lips and eyelids. There were ginger glints, too, in her hair, which she wore in two bunches, fastened with different-colored elastic bands. Her eyes with their pale lashes, because she was unhappy, communicated keenly. Her family called her pudgy, but she just looked soft, as if she were longing to nestle. Her jawline was pure, the pale lips rather full, cracked, parted. She seemed not fake or stuck up—and, just then in the dappled light, not a child, either. None of this was wasted on the boys.

It didn't occur to Jane that the car would stop for her; she watched it hungrily, sifting the silky dust between her toes. Daniel, the driver, Jane saw at once, was the best-looking of the three; in fact, he was crushingly beautiful—his features smudged and vivid at once, as if sketched in black ink—and her heart fastened on him. When he had stopped the car, he asked her what her name was and she told him. "Want to come for a ride?" he said kindly.

She hesitated only for a moment.

"Not in the back," she said, quite clear about it. Already, she didn't care for Nigel.

"Between us in the front," Paddy said, squeezing over.

And so she climbed in, carrying her flip-flops in her hand. On a whim, she had decided against shorts that morning; she was wearing a washed-out old dress in flowered cotton, with a Peter Pan collar.

On their way back to Nigel's house, Jane was an accomplice in an episode of shoplifting—which fortunately went undetected, or at least unreported. She had never stolen anything before; the possibility hadn't crossed her mind. But she was disoriented: as they drove along, Paddy had pulled the elastic bands off her two bunches so that her hair blew crazily into all their faces. Whipping across her vision, the strands of it were like a hallucination, distracting her from her larger bewilderment at half sitting on Paddy's knee, feeling

Daniel ease his arm around her once, on a straight stretch when he wasn't changing gears. (Nigel's father had chosen a manual gearbox on the M.G.C.) "It's all right," Daniel had said. "Don't worry about us. We're not all bad."

"I like her," Paddy commented. "She doesn't talk too much."

The oddest thing was that she wasn't worrying, although she knew she ought to be; especially when they made plans to keep the shopkeeper talking while she, Jane, slipped bottles of whatever alcohol she could get into their canvas haversack. "He keeps it in a little side room," Daniel said. "You don't look as if you drink, so no one will suspect you. If they do, you can cry and say that we kidnapped you and made you do it."

Jane didn't recognize the shop, though it was only a few miles from her home; her mother had most of their groceries delivered, and, anyway, Mrs. Allsop would never have shopped in such a dimly lit, cellar-smelling place, its windows hung with conflicting advertisements for cigarettes and tea, its shelves crowded promiscuously with faded tins, china souvenirs, regiments of sweet jars. A naked fat ham in orange bread crumbs jostled for space on the counter with packets of parsley sauce and marked-down broken biscuits. Repulsion at the ham's sickly flesh smell fuelled Jane's impossible swift acts. She chose the cool bottles by feel in the dark little off-license nook, beyond a curtain of plastic strips, because she could hardly see in there; her eyes were dazzled from the light outside. Her heart thudded as violently as an engine stalling, but her hands were sure. The boys paid for the sliced bread and tomatoes and tin of tuna they bought, thanking the shopkeeper loftily as they left. Jane sat in the car again between them, her trophies chinking on her knee.

"Isn't she good?" Paddy said when they'd driven on and he'd excavated in the haversack, finding dusty Mateus rosé and Johnnie Walker and several bottles of barley wine.

"She's a natural," Daniel said.

"Now she belongs to us," Paddy said. "We've got the dirt on her."

Jane sought in the recesses of her consciousness the remorse that she knew ought to be lying in wait—that poor honest shopkeeper, struggling to make a living! But it was as if all recesses had flattened out for the moment, into a balmy infinite present amid the sunshine and the gusts and swirls of wind as the M.G.C. swerved around bends. Her consciousness was filled to the brim with her contact—astonishing because she was so virgin in contacts—with the boys' warm bodies, lapping against her; she didn't even much mind Nigel's chin resting showily on her shoulder, when he leaned over from his perch in the back. It had never occurred to her, until now, that the masculine—a suspect realm of deep-voiced otherness, beard growth, fact-authority, and bathroom smells—could be so intimately important, in relation to herself; it seemed as improbable as two planets colliding.

Now, below the surface of the moment, she began to wait in secret—patiently, because her self-discoveries were very new—for Daniel's hand to jostle her thigh when he changed gears. She stole long gazes at him from behind the blinding strands of her hair, drinking in whatever it was in his looks that tugged at her so exquisitely. His head was poised on his slight frame in a way that reminded her of the poet's bust (she couldn't remember which poet) on the piano at home, which nobody played; his dark hair fell in floppy curls like the poet's sculpted ones, and his face had the same keen, forward-slanting lines. A fine dimple of skin, puckering beside his mouth when he gave one of his rare quick smiles, was a fatal last touch: Jane thought he was as handsome as a rock star or a film star—only more so, because they flaunted crudely from their posters, whereas Daniel held something back.

Nigel had a bottle opener on his key ring, and they started on the barley wine, after a discussion with Jane over whether she drank alcohol or not. "I don't," she owned up candidly. "But I might start." Daniel, solicitous, said that they mustn't give her too much, just a little sip at a time. They watched her face to see whether she liked the taste and laughed delightedly when it was obvious that she didn't, although she bravely insisted ("I do! I do quite like it!"), as entertained as if they were feeding beer to a puppy.

If Nigel's parents' house had been anything like Jane's, she might have felt a pang of recollection when they arrived, but although it was secluded behind trees like hers, and with the same defensive air of privilege, it was modern—all glass rectangles and slats of unpainted reddish wood. Somehow it explained Nigel, Jane thought:

his angular unease and his gape, as if he were blinking in reflected light. Daniel braked on the gravel with a flourish, and they got out of the car, straggling in through the front of the house and then out again at the back almost immediately, as if the bright indoors were an optical trick, not absorbent like the gloomy interiors Jane knew, which were dense with family history. A terrace at the back overlooked a garden landscaped in Japanese style, with artful quartz boulders and ginkgo and Japanese maple trees. The boys seemed unsure for a moment what to do next; Jane knew from observing her mother that it was her role to fill awkward silences.

"What a shame I didn't bring my costume," she remarked conversationally, looking at the pool, which Nigel was supposed to skim of its flotsam of twigs and leaves and dead insects every day, but hadn't.

"What costume, Bo Peep?" Nigel said. "This isn't a fancy-dress party."

He'd become waspish at the sight of the awful mess in the house, torn between bravado and responsibility (he thought about his mother); toying with the idea of washing dishes, he put it aside for later.

"My *swimming* costume," Jane explained.

Transplanted out of her familiar world, she seemed to find it easier to be dignified, as if she were moving inside a different skin, sleeker. Perhaps it was partly the barley wine. She was able to penetrate, too, into the others' motives and relations—grown-up insight seemed to come not through gradual accretion but all at once. Daniel had power over the other two, she saw, just as he had power over her, though not through any conscious exertion of his will. They tracked his movements and his moods: if he was at ease, then they could be, too. And yet he wasn't tyrannical, was only either pleasant or absent; if he was abstracted, you felt the curse of your failure to interest him. (Paddy, who picked up a book to read as soon as he sat down on the terrace, didn't care as much as she and Nigel did. Because he was cleverer, he was more detached, with reserves of irony.) Now Daniel suggested coffee and sandwiches, as if this were a summer lunch party and not the tail end of an all-nighter. The idea made everyone carefree; they discovered they were starving. Nigel hunted in the fridge for butter. If Jane had been older, she might have taken the opportunity to parade her femininity in the kitchen, but it didn't occur to her. Daniel and Nigel made tuna-and-salad-cream sandwiches; she waited with an air of calm entitlement for hers to be brought to her.

While they ate, they catechized her on her opinions, and were delighted to find that she believed in God and expected to vote Conservative when she was twenty-one. ("Not just because my parents do," she insisted. "I shall read the newspapers and make up my own mind.") They were sitting on the terrace in Nigel's mother's striking wicker chairs; Jane's was a shallow cone set in a cast-iron frame. Daniel was cross-legged on the terrace beside her. She said that it was only fair for everyone to do a day's hard work, and that people who criticized England all the time should try going to live somewhere else, and that she hated cruelty to animals. All the time she was talking, Daniel was doing something to her feet, which dangled from the rim of the wicker cone: tickling them with a grass seed head, pulling the grass backward and forward between her toes where they were calloused from the thong on her flip-flops. Jane was suffused with a sensation that was mingled ecstasy and shame: shame because she hated her feet, prosaic flat slabs that took an extra-wide fitting. Daniel's feet (he had been barefoot even when he was driving and in the shop—the shopkeeper had stared) were brown and finely complex, high-arched with wire-taut tendons, curling dark hairs tufting each toe.

"D'you think we're layabouts and social parasites?" Paddy asked her.

"I thought that perhaps you were students," she said shyly. "I sort of know the type, because my brother's trying for Oxford."

Daniel said that he'd rather not talk about Oxford. "His career there hangs in the balance between brilliance and disaster," Paddy explained on his behalf. (Daniel's senior tutor had warned that after certain brushes with the drug squad he might not be allowed to sit his finals.) "And he doesn't know whether he cares."

"I think we should swim," Daniel suggested. "It's just too fucking hot."

Jane blushed: his word was so forbidden that she hardly knew how she knew it—the girls never used it at school. It was an entrance, glowering with darkness, into the cave of things unknown to her.

"But I haven't got a costume," she said.

"Bo Peep's lost her sheep," Nigel mocked.

"Swim nude," Daniel suggested. "No one can see—except us, and we like you."

She looked around at them all to see if they were joking, then drew her breath in testingly as you did on the brink of plunging into water. Inspired (and she had been sipping barley wine again, with her sandwich), just then she was capable of anything. Tipping herself out of the cone chair, she took hold of the hem of her dress, to pull it up over her head while the boys watched. (It was as easy as playing with Robin in the old days, she thought, in the garden with the paddling pool.) She was aware uninhibitedly of her young body beneath the dress, in its knickers and bra (she would keep those on, perhaps). But at that very moment another girl appeared from inside the house, astonishing them all: she came through the sliding doors, carrying a glass of fizzing drink ceremoniously, stirring the ice cubes and sucking at it through a plastic bendy straw. Slender and disdainful, with a long narrow nose and slightly squinting eyes, she was wrapped in a sarong. Her chestnut-dark hair fell well below her waist in symmetrical waves, as if it had been tied in plaits and then undone.

"She can borrow my old swimsuit if she wants," the girl said, with an air of unmasking male proceedings beneath her dignity.

Nigel had leaped out of his chair, a suspended wicker basket, which went swinging wildly. "Fiona! When did you get here? How did you get in? What on earth are you drinking?"

"Vodka," Fiona said. "And I got in while you were *out*, because you actually failed to lock anything up behind you, you idiot. I mean, God, Nige, what if I'd been a burglar or something? Then I was fast asleep, until you lot started banging around down here. And this pool's a disgusting swamp—weren't you supposed to do something about it? Hi, Daniel and Paddy. Hi, what's-your-name. My cozzy's in a drawer in the chest in my bedroom, if you want it."

Fiona was Nigel's younger sister, aged eighteen and returned by herself from the South of France on her way to drama school. She chose to sit with her drink under an orange umbrella at the far end of the terrace, as if she were semidetached from her brother and his friends. But Jane, with her new intuitiveness, guessed that she sat there because it meant that she was in Daniel's sight lines the whole time she was yawning and stretching and pretending to sunbathe, showing off her legs through the slit in her sarong.

Jane borrowed Fiona's swimming costume (which was tight on her) and powered up and down the short pool with her strong crawl, face turning into the water then out to breathe, as she'd been taught, all the accumulated rubbish (leathery wet leaves, sodden drowned butterflies and daddy longlegs, an empty cigarette pack) bobbing against her breasts and lips and knees as she swam. No one joined her in the pool. Jane had hardly expected them to; she had accepted immediately the justice of her defeat—right at the moment that she'd had all the boys' eyes on her—by the older, prettier, more sophisticated girl. (Still, the word "woebegone" nudged at her, from a poem she'd read at school.) When she got out, she would ask Paddy to drive her to a bus stop, then to lend her the money for her bus fare home. She would ask for his address, so that she could repay him: out of her pocket money, because she could never tell her parents where she'd been.

Heaving herself out at the side of the pool, she stood streaming water, too shy to ask for a towel. The others were planning a visit to the pub in the nearest village. Jane had never been inside a pub in her life, but she thought there was bound to be a bus stop somewhere in the village.

"Come on, let's *go*," Fiona said impatiently. There was only half an hour until afternoon closing time.

"We can't all get in the car," Nigel said, worrying.

"We can if we hold on tight. It'll be a scream. Paddy, come on."

Obediently, Paddy stood up, stuffing his book into his back pocket. (It was Herman Hesse's "Steppenwolf.") He went to look for shoes. Fiona was aware suddenly of Jane. "Oh, God, she's still got that costume on. Can't you just put your dress on over the top?"

Jane looked down mutely at herself, still dripping.

Daniel hadn't moved from where he was spread-eagled now in a deck chair. He'd been watching Jane's steady stroke in the pool, how she submitted to the rhythm of it and forgot herself, forgot to wonder whether they were looking at her or not. He had felt, while he watched, that he was seeing deeply into her raw sensibility: fatalistic, acutely responsive, open to anything. He was aware all the time, of course, of Fiona's maneuvering to make him notice her—there was a bit of past history between them, which he was wary of reviving, not wanting her to get it into her head that she had any rights of possession over him. Anyway, her blasé, bossy voice was grating on him this afternoon. Her displays of sophistication seemed childish, and he was unmoved by the skinny brown stomach flashing at him so insistently from above the sarong.

"You go ahead," he said. "Jane has to change. I'll wait and walk down with her. We'll catch up."

Fiona couldn't hide the sour disappointment in her face, but she had staked too much, too noisily, on her desperate need for the pub to back down now. Jane looked anxiously from one to the other. "I don't mind," she said. "You don't have to wait for me."

"What are you *up* to, Daniel?" Fiona laughed ungraciously.

Daniel kept his eyes closed against the sun while the others quarrelled, getting ready; Jane went inside to change. When he heard the car receding on the road, he followed her in, confused at first in the interior patchwork of light and shadows, after the glare outdoors. He stood listening at the bottom of the open-tread staircase, his breath barely stirring the bright dust motes in their circling. The house was as perfectly quiet as if it were empty, yet he was aware of the girl standing somewhere upstairs, equally still, listening for him. The moment seemed eloquent, as he put his foot on the bottom step and started up, breaking into the peace.

He found Jane in Fiona's room, where she'd left her dress; she was still in the wet costume, although she'd pulled down the blind out of modesty, so that he saw her waiting in a pink half-light. (She'd been afraid, suddenly, to be naked, in case he came looking for her.) His mouth when he kissed her (her first-ever kiss) seemed scalding, because her mouth was cold from the water and from fear. She was cold and clammy all over. When Daniel tried to peel off the sodden swimming costume it knotted itself around her in a rubbery clinging rope and she had to help, rolling it and dragging at it. They left it where it lay when she kicked it off, and its wetness soaked into Fiona's red rug.

. . .

Fiona found the wet patch on her rug later and guessed immediately (she had intuitions, too) the story behind it; she thought for one outraged moment that they'd actually done it *on her bed*. But her bed was intact—thank God for that, at least. Daniel must have taken Jane into the spare room, where he and Paddy were staying. By now it was late afternoon, and Jane was in a phone box in the village, ringing home. (Nigel didn't want them using the phone at the house, in case his parents complained about the bill.) Daniel waited for her, not interested in her difficulties over what to say. He was smoking, leaning back against the phone box, head tilted to look up at the sky, which was still immaculately blue, just beginning to pale. Even while Jane spoke to her mother in the ordinary words that seemed to flow convincingly, as if from her old self, her new self pressed her free palm on the rectangle of thick glass against which, on the other side, Daniel in his blue shirt was also miraculously pressed, oblivious of her touch. (And she knew now the long brown nakedness of his back under the shirt, with its ripple of vertebrae.) Forever afterward, the smell inside one of those old red phone boxes—dank and mushroomy and faintly urinous—could turn Jane's heart over in erotic excitement.

Her mother's mild voice was in her ear, incurious: they had begun to wonder where she was. "I told Daddy you'd probably gone off to play Ping-Pong somewhere."

"I'm at Alison's," Jane said. "Alison Lefanu. You remember, from Junior Orchestra? French horn. Can I stay the night? It doesn't matter about toothbrush and pajamas. Her mum says I can borrow them."

Mrs. Allsop, blessedly vague, sent her love to Mrs. Lefanu. "The Lefanus live out at Headley, don't they? You didn't walk all that way?"

"I was on my way down to the village, and they drove past. I just got in."

Jane was thinking, Will I ever see my home again? It seemed unlikely.

"Don't be a nuisance," her mother said. "Eat whatever they put in front of you, even if it's cauliflower."

. . .

Now they all sat talking on the terrace in an evening light as thick as syrup; clouds of insects swarmed above the Japanese water features, swallows slipped close along the earth, a blackbird sang. They were drinking Jane's shoplifted wine and her whiskey; then the boys started messing around with a needle and little glass vials of methedrine, which Paddy fetched from his room. "Don't look, it's not for nice girls," Daniel said to Jane, and so, obediently, she closed her eyes. The boys' huddle over this ceremony—so intimate, taken so seriously—frightened Fiona and made her even more furious than the wet patch on her rug. She went inside and crashed around the house, effecting a transformation: washing dishes, scrubbing the stove and the kitchen floor, throwing the windows wide open, emptying ashtrays with a clang of the dustbin lid. She shook out the mats from the sitting room, cracking them like whips over the boys' heads on the terrace. Gradually, as she worked, the resentment slipped out of her and her mood changed. She began to enjoy her own strength and to feel serenely indifferent to the others. If her brother's friends wanted to get doped up, why should she care? She started to think about drama school. Later, she warmed up some tinned soup, and brought out cheese and crackers for them all. By this time it was dark and the only light came from the lamps she'd turned on inside.

Daniel was trying to explain the idea of the soul as it was understood in the Hindu Vedanta. His words were punctuated by the clonk of the bamboo shishi-odoshi in the garden, which filled up with water then tipped and emptied, falling back against its rock. What he wanted to describe was how the soul's origins were in wholeness and light, but on its entry into the world it took on the filth of violence and corruption. The soul trapped in the individual forgot its home and despaired; but despair was only another illusion to be stripped away. He wanted to say that revolution was a kind of cleansing that conferred its own immortality in a perpetual present. Art had to be revolutionary or it would die in time. He believed as he spoke that he was brilliantly eloquent, but in truth he was rambling incoherently.

Paddy, getting the gist of it, quoted poetry in an ironic voice: "'Heard melodies are sweet, but those unheard are sweeter.'"

"Signor Keats, I do believe," Nigel said.

“Oh, *that’s* the poet,” Jane said. “We have his bust at home, on the piano.”

Cross-legged on a cushion at Daniel’s feet, she was leaning lightly against him, as if she could ground the tension quivering in his right foot, which was balanced across his left knee. His intelligence seemed as ceaseless as an engine working. She felt exceptionally attuned to the boys’ voices rising through earnestness to mockery and back again, although she hardly heard their words, only what ran underneath: a current of strain, a jostling of contest and display. She saw how Nigel tried to match the other two and failed, and how he suffered, yearning for Daniel’s approval. Meanwhile, her own new knowledge filled her up, not in the form of thoughts but as sensations, overwhelming. Her experience in the strange bed that afternoon hadn’t been joyous: there’d been some swooning, obliterating pleasure in the preliminaries, but then too much anxiety in the clumsy arrangements, which she had known (from her biology lessons) would follow. Remembering it all now, though, she was sick with desire and longed for the time to come when Daniel would touch her again.

When they did go to bed, however, Daniel was suddenly exhausted; stoop-backed, he crawled between the sheets in his underpants, turning away from Jane, toward the window. “Watch over me” was the last thing he mumbled.

And so she kept vigil faithfully for hours in the quiet of the night, presiding over the mystery of her changed life, adjusting her body against the peremptory curve of his turned back and legs in the narrow single bed. But at last she couldn’t help it—she fell asleep herself. And when she awoke in the morning Daniel was gone. After a while, when he didn’t come back, she put on her underclothes and her dress, and set off around the house in search of him. Downstairs, she smelled Paddy’s sweat and saw the tousled mess of his hair, poking from the top of a sleeping bag on the sofa in the lounge. Nigel was making a racket outside with the sliding door of the garage, in search of the net for the swimming pool. Jane climbed upstairs again. Nigel’s parents’ bedroom was at the front of the house, opening off the landing ahead of her; the door was ajar, and Jane stepped soundlessly inside.

It was a beautiful room, like nothing she'd ever seen before, with a pale wood floor and plain white walls, creamy sheepskin rugs. Fresh sunlight, pouring through windows all along its length, was reflected in the mirrored doors of the built-in wardrobes; the curtains, in some kind of rough white translucent linen, were cut too long for the windows, and the cloth fell in heaps on the floor. A huge bed seemed to be all white sheets and no blankets. (Jane had never seen a duvet before.) In the bed, with the duvet kicked to their feet, Daniel and Fiona lay naked and asleep, facing away from each other, their slim tanned legs tangled together. Jane, who had done the Greeks in history, thought that they looked like young warriors in a classical scene, fallen in the place where they had been wrestling. She withdrew from the room without waking them, as quietly as she had come in.

Nigel, rather the worse for wear, in his pajama bottoms, was smoking and skimming the pool, dumping the rubbish in a soaking heap beside him. He watched when Jane came to stand at the pool's brink; she stared in with dry, hot eyes.

"So now you know," he said.

But she repudiated his offer of companionship in her unrequited love. Her experience was not like anyone else's. She asked only if he would drive her home, and he said he'd get the car out as soon as he'd finished with the pool.

"I'd like to go now," she said crisply, sounding like her mother. "If you don't mind."

On the way back, they hardly spoke, except when Nigel asked for directions as they drew near the house. Jane forgot, in her absorption, to notice the way they'd come, so that she never afterward knew where she'd been. And she never saw Nigel's house again, or any of the boys (Fiona once, perhaps, at a party).

He dropped her off at the bottom of the drive. It was still quite early in the morning—only nine o'clock. Jane stared around her as if she'd never seen the place before, as if it were more mysterious than anywhere she'd been—the scuffed dirt at the edge of the road, the old mossy gateposts, blackbirds flitting in the dead leaves at the bottom of the hedge, the hard lime-yellow fruits in the hedge apple tree, her own footprints from the day before intact in the dust, the Jokari paddle left where she had dropped it.

. . .

Her mother didn't seem surprised to see her so early.

"Did you have a nice time, dear?"

Jane said that she'd had fun. But that afternoon she suffered with pain in her stomach and bloating ("What exactly did you eat at the Lefanus?"). And the next day her period came rather copiously and early—which ought to have been a relief but wasn't, because it hadn't occurred to her until then (despite the biology lessons) that she could be pregnant. The weather changed, too. So it was all right for her to curl up under her eiderdown, hugging a hot-water bottle to her stomach, reading her Chalet School books and looking up from time to time at the rain running down the window. Her mother brought her tea with two sugars, and aspirin.

Jane never told anyone what had happened to her (not even, years later, the boyfriend who became her husband, and who might have wondered). And in a way she never assimilated the experience, though she didn't forget it, either. As an adult, she took on board all the usual Tory disapproval toward drugs and juvenile delinquency and underage sex, and never saw any implications for her own case. She was fearful for her own daughters, as normal mothers were, without connecting her fears to anything that had happened to her. Her early initiation stayed in a sealed compartment in her thoughts and seemed to have no effects, no consequences.

Jane and her husband divorced in their mid-fifties, and her friends advised her to have counselling. The counsellor was a nice, intelligent woman. (Actually, she couldn't help feeling exasperated by Jane and her heavy, patient sorrows: her expensive clothes, her lack of imagination, the silk scarf thrown girlishly over one shoulder. Of course, she was much too professional to let this show.) Jane confessed that she had always felt as if she were on the wrong side of a barrier, cutting her off from the real life she was meant to be living.

"What's it like, then, real life on the other side?"

Haltingly, Jane described a summer day beside a swimming pool. A long sunlit room with white walls and a white bed. A breeze is blowing; long white curtains are dragged sluggishly backward and forward on a pale wood floor. (These women's fantasies, the counsellor thought, have more to do with interior décor than with repressed desires.) Then Jane got into her stride, and the narrative became more interesting. "A boy and a girl," she said, "are naked, asleep in the bed. I am curled on a rug on the floor beside them. The boy turns over in his sleep, flings out his arm, and his hand dangles to the floor. I think he's seeking out the cool, down there under the bed. I move carefully on my rug, so as not to wake him. I move so that his hand is touching me."

That's more like it, the counsellor thought. That's something.

As for Daniel, well, he trained as a lawyer after he'd finished his literature degree. He got out of the drink and the drugs not long after university. (Paddy never did; he died.) Daniel lives in Zurich now, with his second wife, whom he loves very much, and occasionally, when he's bored with his respectable Swiss friends and wants to shock them, he tells stories about his wild youth. He is in international human-rights law; he's a force for good. He's a good husband and father, too (more dedicated, because of the wildness in his past). Of course, he's ambitious and likes power.

He can just about remember Nigel, and Nigel's parents' house that summer, and Fiona (they were together off and on for a few months afterward). But he has no memory at all of Jane. Even if by some miracle he ever met her, and she recognized him and told him the whole story (which she would never do), it wouldn't bring anything back. It isn't only that the drink and the drugs made him forget. He's had too much happiness in his life since, too much experience; he's lost that fine-tuning that could hold on to the smell of the ham in the off-license, the wetness of the swimming costume, the girl's cold skin and her naïveté, her extraordinary offer of herself without reserve, the curtains sweeping the floor in the morning light. It's all just gone.

A VOICE IN THE NIGHT

BY STEVEN MILLHAUSER (2012)

The boy Samuel wakes in the dark. Something's not right. Most commentators agree that the incident takes place inside the temple, rather than in a tent outside the temple doors, under the stars. Less certain is whether Samuel's bed is in the sanctuary itself, where the Ark of the Covenant stands before a seven-branched oil lamp that is kept burning through the night, or in an adjoining chamber. Let's say that he is lying in an inner chamber, close to the sanctuary, perhaps adjacent to it. A curtained doorway leads to the chamber of Eli, the high priest of the temple of Shiloh. We like such details, but they do not matter. What matters is that Samuel wakes suddenly in the night. He is twelve years old, according to Flavius Josephus, or he may be a year or two younger. Something has startled him awake. He hears it again, clearly this time: "Samuel!" Eli is calling his name. What's wrong? Eli never calls his name in the middle of the night. Did Samuel forget to close the temple doors at sunset, did he allow one of the seven flames of the lamp to go out? But he remembers it well: pushing shut the heavy doors of cedar, visiting the sanctuary and replenishing the seven gold branches with consecrated olive oil so that the flames will burn brightly all night long. "Samuel!" He flings aside his goat's-hair blanket and hurries, almost runs, through the dark. He pushes through the curtain and enters Eli's chamber. The old man is lying on his back. Because he is the high priest of the temple of Shiloh, his mattress on the wooden platform is stuffed with wool, not straw. Eli's head rests on a pillow of goat's hair and his long-fingered hands lie crossed on his chest, beneath his white beard. His eyes are closed. "You called me," Samuel says, or perhaps his words are "Here am I; for thou calledst me." Eli opens his eyes. He seems a little confused, like a man roused from sleep. "I didn't call you," he answers. Or perhaps, with a touch of gruffness, since he doesn't like being awakened in the night: "I called not; lie down again." Samuel turns obediently away. He walks back to his chamber, where he lies down but doesn't close his eyes. In his years of attending Eli he's come to understand a great deal about the temple and its rules, and he tries to understand this night as well. Is it possible that Eli called his name without knowing it? The priest is old, sometimes he makes noises with his lips in his sleep, or mutters strange words. But never once has he called Samuel in the night. Has Samuel had a dream, in which a voice called out his name? Only recently he dreamed that he was walking alone through the parted waters of the Red Sea. Shimmering cliffs of water towered up on both sides, and as the watery walls began to plunge down on him he woke with a cry. From outside the walls of the temple he hears the high-pitched wail of a young sheep. Slowly Samuel closes his eyes.

II

It's a summer night in Stratford, Connecticut, 1950. The boy, seven years old, lies awake in his bed on the second floor, under the two screened windows that look down on his back yard. Through the windows he can hear the sound of summer: the *chk chk chk* of crickets from the vacant lot on the other side of the back-yard hedge. For donkeys it's hee-haw, for roosters it's cock-a-doodle-doo, but for crickets you have to make up your own sound. Sometimes a car passes on the street alongside the yard, throwing two rectangles of light across the dark ceiling. The boy thinks the rectangles are the shapes of the open windows under the partially raised blinds, but he isn't sure. He's listening: hard. That afternoon in his Sunday-school class at the Jewish Community Center, Mrs. Kraus read the story of the boy Samuel. In the middle of the night a voice called out his name: "Samuel! Samuel!" He was an attendant of the high priest and lived in the temple of Shiloh, without his parents. When he heard his name, Samuel thought the high priest was calling him. Three times in the night he heard his name, three times he went to the bedside of Eli. But it was the voice of the Lord calling him. The boy in Stratford is listening for his name in the night. The story of Samuel has made him nervous, tense as a cat. The slightest sound stiffens his whole body. He never thinks about the old man with a beard on the front of his "Child's Illustrated Old Testament," but now he's wondering. What would his voice be like? His father says God is a story that people made up to explain things they don't understand. When his father speaks about God to company at dinner, his eyes grow angry and gleeful behind his glasses. But the voice in the night is scary as witches. The voice in the night knows you're there, even though you're hidden in the dark. If the voice calls your name, you have to answer. The boy imagines the voice calling his name. It comes from the ceiling, it comes from the walls. It's like a terrible touch, all over his body. He doesn't want to hear the voice, but if he hears it he'll have to answer. You can't get out of it. He pulls the covers up to his chin and thinks of the walls of water crashing down on the Egyptians, on their chariots and horses. Through the window screens the crickets seem to be growing louder.

III

The Author is sixty-eight years old, in good health, most of his teeth, half his hair, not dead yet, though lately he hasn't been sleeping well. He's always been a light sleeper, the slightest sound jostles him awake, but this is different: he falls asleep with a book on his chest, then wakes up for no damn reason and strains his neck to look at the green glow of his digital clock, where it's always some soul-crushing time like 2:16 or 3:04 in the miserable morning. Hell time, abyss time, the hour of no return. He wonders whether he should turn on his bedside lamp, try to read a little, relax, but he knows the act of switching on the light will wake him up even more, and besides, there's the problem of what to read when you wake up at two or three in the godforsaken morning. If he reads something that interests him he'll excite his mind and ruin his chance for sleep, but if he reads something that bores him he'll become impatient, restless, and incapable of sleep. Better to lie there and curse his fate, like a man with a broken leg lying in a ditch. He listens to the sounds of the dark: *hsssh* of a passing car, *mmmm* of a neighbor's air-conditioner, *skriiik* of a floorboard in the attic—a resident ghost. Things drift through your mind at doom-time in the morning, and as he listens he thinks of the boy in the house in Stratford, the bed by the two windows, the voice in the night. He thinks of the boy a lot these days, sometimes with irritation, sometimes with a fierce love that feels like sorrow. The boy tense, whipped up, listening for a voice in the night. He feels like shouting at the boy, driving some sense into that head of his. Oil your baseball glove! Jump on your bike! Do chin-ups on the swing set! Make yourself strong! But why yell at the boy? What'd he ever do to you? Better to imagine the voice calling right here, right now: Hello, old atheist, have I got news for you. Sorry, pal. Don't waste your time. You should've made your pitch when I was seven. Had the boy really expected to hear his name in the night? So long ago: Bobby Benson and the B-Bar-B Riders on the radio, his father at dinner attacking McCarthy. War in Korea, the push to Pusan. Those old stories got to you: Joseph in the pit, the parting of the Red Sea, David soothing the soul of Saul with his harp. In Catholic working-class Stratford, he was the only boy who didn't make the sign of the cross when they passed Holy Name Church on the way to school. Girls with smudges of ash on their foreheads. His God-scorning father driving him to Sunday school but taking him home when the others went to Hebrew class. No bar mitzvah for him. His father mocking his own rabbi for making boys jabber words they didn't understand. "Pure gibberish." A new word: gibberish. He liked it: gibberish. Still: Sunday school, "Rock of Ages," the story of Samuel, why is this night different from all other nights. The boy lying there listening, wanting his name to be called. Had he wanted his name to be called? Through the window the Author hears the sound of a distant car, the cry of the crickets. Sixty years later, upstate New York, and still the cry of the crickets in the summer in Stratford. Time to sleep, old man.

I

Samuel wakes again. This time he's sure: Eli has called his name. The voice stands out sharply, like a name written on a wall. "Samuel!" He throws off the goat's-hair blanket and steps onto the straw mat on the floor by his bed. He has lived with Eli in the temple of Shiloh for as long as he can remember. Once a year his mother and father visit him, when they come up from Ramah to offer the annual sacrifice. When he was born, his mother gave him to the Lord. She had asked the Lord for a son, and that's why his name is Asked-of-the-Lord. That's why he wears a linen ephod, that's why his hair flows down below his shoulders: no razor shall ever come upon his head. Samuel: Asked of the Lord. He enters Eli's chamber, where he expects to find Eli sitting up in bed, waiting impatiently for him. Instead, Eli is lying on his back with his eyes closed, like a man asleep. Should he wake Eli? Did Eli call Samuel's name and then fall back to sleep? Samuel hesitates to wake a man who's old and filled with worries. Though Eli is the high priest of the temple, his sons are wicked. They are priests who do not obey. When flesh is offered for sacrifice, they take the best part for themselves. They practice iniquities with women who come to the doors of the temple. "Here am I!" Samuel says, in a voice a little louder than he intended. Eli stirs and opens his eyes. "For thou didst call me," Samuel says, more softly. The old priest raises his head with difficulty. "I called not, my son; lie down again." Samuel doesn't protest, but lowers his eyes and turns away with the uneasy sense of having disturbed an old man's sleep. As he enters his own chamber, he tries to understand. Why has Eli called his name twice in the night? He called out in a loud, clear voice, a voice that could not be mistaken for some other sound. But Eli, who speaks only truth, has denied it. Samuel lies down on his bed and pulls the blanket up to his shoulders. Eli is very old. Does he call out Samuel's name and then, when Samuel appears beside him, forget that he has called? Old men are forgetful. The other day, when Eli spoke to Samuel of his own childhood, he could not remember a name he was searching for and grew troubled. Samuel has seen an old man at the temple whose body trembles like well water in a goatskin bucket. His eyes are unlit lamps. Eli is old, his eyesight is growing dim, but his body doesn't tremble and his voice is still strong. On the shoulders of his purple-and-scarlet ephod are two onyx stones, each engraved with the names of six tribes of Israel. When he stands in sunlight, the stones shine like fire. Slowly Samuel drifts into sleep.

II

It's the next night, and the boy in Stratford again lies awake, listening. He doesn't really believe he'll hear his name, but he wants to be awake in case it happens. He doesn't like to miss things. If he knows something important is coming, like a trip to the merry-go-round and the Whip at Pleasure Beach, he'll wait for it minute by minute, day after day, as if by taking his attention away from it for even a second he might cause it not to happen. But this is different. He doesn't know it's going to happen. It probably won't happen, how could it happen, but there's a chance, who knows. What he really needs to figure out is how to answer, if his name is called. In the story, Samuel was told to answer "Speak, Lord; for thy servant heareth." He tries to imagine it: "Speak, Lord; for thy servant heareth." It sounds like a boy in a play. Better to say "Yes?," which is what he'd say if his father called his name. But the Lord is not his father. The Lord is more powerful than his powerful father. He's more like the policeman in front of the school on Barnum Avenue, with his dangerous stick hanging from his belt. Better to say "Yes, sir," as he'd say if the policeman called his name. If he hears his name, that's what he'll say: "Yes, sir." Don't shout it: say it. Yes, sir. A voice in the dark, calling his name. The thought stirs him up again. He's too old to be scared of the dark, but the fear still comes on him sometimes. He likes to play a scare-game with his sister, the way they did when he was four and she was two. She lies in her dark room pretending to be asleep and he whispers, "Booooo haunt moan. Booooo haunt moan." Then they both burst into wild, scared laughter. But a voice in the night is not funny. He's through with witches, ghosts, monsters, isn't he, they're not real, so why is he scaring himself with the story of Samuel? It's only a story. His father has explained it to him: the Bible is stories. Like "Tootle" or "The Story of Dr. Dolittle." Trains don't leave the tracks to chase butterflies, the pushmi-pullyu with a head at each end isn't an animal you'll ever find in the zoo, and the Lord doesn't call your name in the night. Stories are about things that don't happen. They could happen, but they don't. But they could. What if his name was called? He would want to be there. He'd want to know what comes next. What did the Lord say to Samuel? He can't remember. The most important part, and he can't remember. That's one thing about him: he can't remember the important things. He can remember the prince climbing the hair to the top of the tower but he can't remember the capital of Connecticut. Is it Bridgeport? The library in Bridgeport has long stone steps and high pillars. It's what he first thought of when he heard that Samuel was serving the Lord in the temple of Shiloh. A temple is different from a church. Jews go to temple and Christians go to church. But Catholics go to Catholic church. And everybody goes to the library. He's getting tired. At the backyard hedge, Billy turned to him and said, "Do you believe in Jesus?" His eyes were hard. There're two answers to that question. One is "No." The other's what his father said to him: "Jesus was a great teacher." But he was a coward and looked down. A door opens and he hears footsteps in the hall. Do his parents know he's lying awake, listening for his name? He hears the door to the bathroom open and close. Sometimes his father is up in the night. If he opens his door and waits for his father? Tell me about Samuel. Tell me. Tell me about the voice in the night. If you heard that voice, nothing would ever be the same. He pushes the thought away. Tomorrow they're going to drive out past the Sikorsky plant to Short Beach, where he can wade out to the sandbar.

III

One-fifty-four in the morning. The gods are out to get him. Sleep for an hour, wake for no reason, stare like a madman, waiting for sleep. Dragging himself through the day like a stepped-on snail. Won't take a pill, they leave him groggy. Sloggy and boggy. That all you've got? Draggy and saggy. Baggy and shaggy. Like a hag, haggy. Now he's alert, full of useless energy. In the old days he'd recite fistfuls of sonnets. My mistress' eyes are nothing like the sun. Three things there be that prosper up apace. Now all he can do is lie there thinking about things, far-off things, high school, grade school, the boy in the room in Stratford, listening for the voice in the night. Did it really happen that way, or is he embellishing? Habit of the trade. But no, he lay there waiting for his name. The two windows, the two bookcases his father had made from orange crates, the bed against the other wall for his sister to sleep in when one of the grandmothers came to stay. One grandma from West 110th Street, one from Washington Heights. Father's mother, mother's mother, first one, then the other, never together. Waiting for the train at the Bridgeport station, with long dark benches and the row of hand-cranked picture machines. The something-scopes. Turning the handles, making the pictures move. The grandmother with crooked fingers who brought packs of playing cards and dyed her hair orange and wore lots of rattly bracelets, the grandmother with the accent who made cold red soup with sour cream. Mutoscopes. Two women born in the nineteenth century, who can grasp it, one in New York, one in Minsk, before skyscrapers, before horseless carriages, before the extinction of the dinosaurs. His own mother growing up with Russian Jewish parents on the Lower East Side. Her father escaping the tsar, embracing America, naming his first son Abraham, middle name Lincoln. Moving them to a new apartment every few months, skipping out on the rent. She said he sat reading Dostoyevsky in Russian while his sons waited on customers in the store. The Stratford boy's own early childhood in Brooklyn, all there in the photo albums: pretty mother with flower in her hair on a bench in Prospect Park, pretty mother in wide-brimmed hat standing with little son in sailor suit on the Coney Island boardwalk. The two of them riding the trolley. Trolley tracks in the street, wires in the sky, the grooved wheel at the top of the trolley pole: a forgotten world. His invisible father holding up the light meter, adjusting the f-number, staring down into the ground-glass screen of the twin-lens reflex. Then Stratford, working-class neighborhood, where else can a professor afford to live. Milk delivered in glass bottles to the back porch each morning. Italians and Eastern Europeans, Zielski and Stoccatore and Saksa and Mancini. Riccio's drugstore. Ciccarelli's lot. Ralph Politano. Tommy Pavluvcik. Mario Recupido. What is a Jew? A Jew is someone who doesn't cross himself in front of Holy Name Church. A Jew is someone who stays indoors practicing the piano on bright summer mornings while everyone else is outside playing baseball. His mother playing Chopin nocturnes and waltzes, DEE dah-dah-dah, DEE dah-dah-dah, teaching him scales, reading on the couch with her legs tucked under her. The mahogany bookcase by the staircase, the wall bookcase by the fireplace. His father driving them home one night: "Did you see that? Not a book in the house!" What is a Jew? A Jew is someone who has books in the house. His father demolishing an argument for the existence of God, his lips twisted in scorn. Jewish Community Center but no bar mitzvah. A tree every Christmas, a menorah once or twice. No baby Jesuses, no Marys or mangers. A package of matzo once a year: like big saltines. The strange word: unleavened. Dyeing Easter eggs, walking under the roof of cornstalks and branches at Sukkoth, biting into hollow crumbly chocolate bunnies, lighting the yahrzeit candle for the grandmother from Minsk. What is a Jew? A Jew is someone who thinks of Easter as a holiday celebrating rabbits. His mother a first-grade teacher, his father a teacher at the university. The grandmother with crooked fingers, once a piano teacher. The whole family teaching up a storm. A tutor who tooted the flute. Tried to tutor two tooters to toot. What is a Jew? A Jew is someone who comes from people who teach. Erleen, from the project in Bridgeport, watching gently over him each day when he came home from school. The rhyme in the street: Eenie meenie miney mo, catch a nigger by the toe. His father serious, quiet-voiced, his mouth tight: "People use that word, but not in this house. It is disgusting." Negro: a word of respect. Respect people. His all-Jewish Cub Scout troop. "You don't look for trouble," the Scoutmaster said. "But you don't let anyone call you a kike." Not in this house. A new word: kike. He tried to imagine it: kike. Hey, kike! Hit him, kill him. Did he really lie awake night after night, listening for his name? The child Samuel. All about obedience. Saul's flaw: disobedience. Samuel thrusting his sword into the belly of the King of the Amalekites. That's what happens when your name is called in the night. The righteous life, the life of moral ferocity. His father and Samuel, two of a kind. Samuel: "Thou art wicked." His father: "You are ignorant." A special sect: the Jewish atheist. The thirteenth tribe. And you? Who are you? I am the one whose name was not called in the night.

I

The voice calls again. This time Samuel doesn't hesitate. He swings his legs out of bed and rushes through the dark to Eli's side. "Here am I," he cries, impatient now, "for thou didst call me." Eli is lying on his back, his eyes closed, his hands crossed on his chest. All at once he's leaning up on an elbow, searching Samuel's face. Samuel feels aggrieved, anxious, expectant. What is happening? Something is happening. He doesn't know what. The long hand of the priest rests on Samuel's arm. Samuel suddenly understands two things: Eli did not call his name, and Eli knows who did. Does Samuel know? He almost knows. He knows and doesn't dare to know. But Eli is speaking, Eli is telling him who it is that has called his name. It is the Lord. "Go, lie down: and it shall be, if he call thee, that thou shalt say, Speak, Lord; for thy servant heareth." The searching look, the hand on his arm: Samuel understands that he must ask no more questions. He returns to his bed and lies down on his back with his eyes open. He wants to hear with both ears. One hand is pressed against his chest. His heart is like a fist beating against the inside of the bone. What if his name isn't called again? Eli said, "If he call thee." Three times, and he failed to answer. Should he have known? He knew, he almost knew, he was about to know. Now he knows. What he doesn't know is whether he will hear the voice again. If his name is not called, he will never forgive himself. And if his name is called? Then what? What should he say? Oh, don't you remember? Speak, Lord; for thy servant heareth. Speak, Lord; for thy servant heareth. He remembers the first time he saw Eli, the high priest of the temple. A powerful man, with shining gems on the shoulders of his ephod. His legs were like tall columns of stone. His hands the size of oil jars. Now Eli's beard is white, he mutters in his sleep. Difficult sons, wicked sons he cannot restrain. Calm yourself. Stop trembling. Listen.

II

The third night, and the boy in his bed in Stratford still hasn't heard his name. He's not really listening, is he? He thought he heard it once, a distant call, fooling him for a second, that cat cry or whatever it was. He no longer expects to hear anything, so why's he still waiting? By now there's a spirit of stubbornness in it: he's waited this long, might as well wait some more. But that isn't it. What *it* is, he doesn't believe the voice in the night will come, but his unbelief upsets him as much as belief would, if he believed. If the voice doesn't come, it means he hasn't been chosen. He likes being chosen. He was chosen to represent his class in the school spelling bee. It's easy to spell, he doesn't know how to spell words wrong, but it still feels good to be chosen. He's not so good on the playground, can't kick the ball as hard as most of them, lucky if he gets to first. He wants the voice to call him in the night, even though it won't happen. He doesn't believe those old stories, doesn't believe the prince climbing the hair or the thorns growing up and covering the castle, so why should he believe the story of the voice in the night? His father doesn't believe those stories. His father doesn't believe in God. But when the boy asked, his father didn't get the angry look, he got the serious quiet look. He said you have to think about it yourself and make up your mind when you're older. The boy wonders how old is older. When is when? If he hears the voice now, he'll know. But he already knows. He knows he won't hear the voice. Why should he be chosen? He's no Samuel. He's a good speller. He plays the piano with two hands, he can write a poem about George Washington and draw a picture of a kingfisher or a red-winged blackbird. But Samuel opens the doors to the temple when the sun comes up, Samuel fills the lamp with oil so that it burns all night. Down below he hears a car going by. It's passing his yard and the vacant lot, the two bars of light sliding across the ceiling, now it's passing the bakery down by the stream, he loves the bakery, smell of hot rye, the gingerbread men and the muffins with raisins, now it's climbing the hill, sound of tires like the waterfall in the park earlier this summer, over the hill toward Bridgeport. He feels old, very old, older than Eli, he wishes he were young again, a child. He wishes he'd never heard that stupid story. Sh-h-h. Sleep now.

III

Another night, another waking. Not a good sign. Death by insomnia at sixty-eight. All Samuel's fault, keeping everybody up when they ought to be snoring away. The boy in Stratford battling it out at the age of seven. By high school, no tolerance for the once-a-week churchgoers. Priest or atheist: choose one. The move to Fairfield, the beach, Protestant churches galore. Presbyterian, First Congregational, Episcopalian. Roper. Warren. Kane. No Jews allowed in the beach club. Who'd want to join a beach club? Reading the five arguments for the existence of God and their rebuttals. The ontological argument. The teleological argument. Walking along the beach at night, the deserted lifeguard stands, the lights of Long Island. Challenge to a friend: Why do you go to church? Why only on Sunday? He knew what he knew: always or never. If the voice calls your name, your other life is over. No going back. Short of that, sorry, please pass the ketchup. By the age of fifteen, done with religion, like the baseball books of his childhood. No regrets. Girls in tight skirts reaching up into lockers, girls in tight blouses hugging books to their chests as they hip-swing down the halls. Let me touch! Let me see! The house for sale on his friend's street out near the junior high. "They'll never sell to Jews." "Why not?" "You know how those people are." "How are they?" "They take over the neighborhood." "You're talking to one." "Oh, you're not *that* kind of Jew." At age eleven, the talk with his father: "We don't do anything in Sunday school. Just play games and fool around. I don't want to go anymore." His father taking his pipe out of his mouth, looking at him gravely: "You don't have to go." He'd expected resistance, a look of reproach. Might as well blame it all on Jehovah. Could have called his name in the night. The boy in Stratford, listening. Something extreme in his temperament, even then. Shy and extreme. Stubborn. You don't call my name, I won't call yours. Even Steven. Dr. Dolittle and Pecos Bill instead of Samuel and King Saul. Don't have to go. The neighborhood goes to church, the family stays home and reads. In high school, asking his father whether he liked teaching. His father's pause, his grave look, his utter attention: "If I were a millionaire, I would pay for the privilege of teaching." The son knows he's heard something important. He is moved, he is proud of his father, he's envious. He thinks, I want to say that someday. They call it a calling. Samuel's call in the night. His father's calling. Lying awake remembering these things. Walking in his bathing suit, towel around his neck, to the beach in Fairfield with his parents' friends from the city. Janey with her long black hair and tight white one-piece, waving her arm at the street of ranch houses: "Suburbia." Her voice mocking, disdainful. New York judging Connecticut. Jews moving out of New York: abandoning the tribe. Always the connection to the city. The four years in Brooklyn, corner of Clinton and Joralemon, the grandmother on West 110th Street and the grandmother in Washington Heights, mother growing up on the

Lower East Side, father on the Upper West Side. Childhood trips to the city, the stone bridges of the Merritt Parkway. The Museum of Natural History with dinosaur skeletons like gigantic fishbones, lunch at the Automat: the sandwiches behind the little glass windows. Horn & Hardart. Early admission to Oberlin, but he chooses Columbia. Walking along the eighth floor of John Jay Hall, the thrilling sound of violins and cellos behind closed doors: the good Jewish boys practicing their instruments. Weinstein, or was it Marinoff: "What kind of Jew are you?" A Jew from suburbia. A nothing Jew, a secular Jew, an unjewish Jew. A Jew without a bar mitzvah, a Jew without a bump in his nose. Later he develops the idea of the Negative Jew. A Negative Jew is a Jew about whom another Jew says, "You don't *look* Jewish." A Negative Jew is a Jew who says to another Jew, "Judaism is a superstition that I reject," and to an anti-Semite, "I have Jewish blood." A Negative Jew is a Jew who says, "I don't believe in Judaism," while being herded into a cattle car. Hitler, the great clarifier. His father's German Jewish colleague, Dr. What's-Her-Name, one of the first women admitted to a German university, her passion for Kant, for all things German. Stayed put till 1939. Blamed it all on the Polish Jews. "They gave us a bad name." The boy in Stratford, lying awake at night. Hard to remember how it was. A game, was it? Scare yourself with witches, scare yourself with Jehovah. A shudder of delight. All those old stories, wonderful and terrible: the voice in the night, the parting of the Red Sea, Hansel in the cage, the children following the piper into the mountain. "Hamlet" and "Oedipus Rex" as pale reflections of the nightmare tales of childhood. Everything connected: David playing the harp for Saul, the boy in Stratford practicing the piano, the cellos and violins behind the closed doors. The boy listening for his name, the man waiting for the rush of inspiration. Where do you get your ideas? A voice in the night. When did you decide to become a writer? Three thousand years ago, in the temple of Shiloh.

I

And the Lord came, and stood, and called as at other times, Samuel, Samuel. Commentators disagree about the meaning of the word "stood." Some say that the Lord assumes a bodily presence before

Samuel. Others argue that the Lord never takes on a bodily form and that therefore the voice has drawn closer to Samuel, so that the effect is of a person drawing closer in the dark. In one version of this argument, the boy hears the voice and imagines a form standing beside him. All this, the Author thinks, can be left to the interpreters. What matters to us is that the voice of the Lord calls Samuel's name. After all, Eli had said, "If he call thee." For it was not inevitable that the voice, which had called three times and not received an answer, would call again. Now the boy Samuel has heard the voice a fourth time and knows who is calling him. He doesn't yet know why the Lord is calling him, but he knows how to answer, for Eli has told him exactly what to say: "Speak, Lord; for thy servant heareth." Samuel resists, the words refuse to come, then he says it aloud: "Speak; for thy servant heareth." He hears his words clearly in the dark: "Speak; for thy servant heareth." There is no doubt: he has said "Speak" and not "Speak, Lord," as he was instructed to do. Was he so frightened of uttering the sacred name? He feels a rush of self-reproach, before commanding himself to be still and listen. He lies motionless, alert all over his body, fiercely calm. He has served in the temple of Shiloh ever since early childhood, but nothing has prepared him for this moment. He does not try to imagine what the Lord will tell him, but he readies himself to remember every word, in the order of speaking. Eli is awake, waiting in the next chamber. Eli will ask him what the Lord has said. Though the voice of the Lord is strong, Samuel knows it cannot be heard by Eli, and not because Eli is too far away to hear. The voice is for him alone. He knows this without arrogance. And he will remember. He has a good memory, he's proud of his memory, though he watches over his pride so that it doesn't become vanity. Words read to him or heard by him remain unchanged inside him. It has always been that way. Now the Lord speaks, and Samuel listens. There is nothing in the world but these words. The words are harsh. The house of Eli will be judged for its iniquity. The sons of Eli are wicked and Eli has not restrained them. Therefore the Lord will perform against Eli all things which he has spoken concerning his house. The sons of Eli will die on the same day. The House of Eli will come to an end. When the Lord departs, it is like the silence after thunder. Samuel lies awake in the dark. It seems to him that the dark has become darker, a dark so dark that it is like the darkness upon the face of the deep, before the Lord moved upon the face of the waters. The words have shaken him like a wind. He can feel Eli lying awake in his chamber, waiting for Samuel to tell him what the Lord has said. But Samuel cannot bring himself to leave his bed and go to Eli's chamber. If Eli asks him, and Eli will certainly ask him, he will speak the truth, but he does not want to speak the truth unbidden. Samuel lies in the dark a long time, listening for the Lord, listening for Eli, but all is silent. Has the darkness become less dark? Can darkness be less dark and still be dark? The darkness is growing lighter. Soon it will be time to open the temple doors. Eli will ask what the Lord has said, and Samuel will repeat the terrible words. Samuel understands that nothing will ever be the same. But now, as the darkness is fading, without yet losing its quality of darkness, he wants to lie in his bed as if he could be a child forever, he wants to lie there as if his name had not been called in the night.

II

It's the fourth night, and by now the boy in Stratford knows he'll never hear his name. Still, he's awake, and in case he's wrong he's still listening, no harm in that, though at the same time he makes fun of himself for lying there, waiting, and for what? His name? It's only a story in a book. You might as well lie awake waiting for a genie to rise up out of a lamp. And even if it isn't only a story, why would the Lord call his name? Samuel was an attendant of the high priest of the temple, Samuel was already favored by the Lord. The boy in Stratford goes to the Jewish Community Center on Sunday for two hours and skips Hebrew lessons. He doesn't make the sign of the cross in front of Holy Name Church, but he looks forward to Christmas as if it's the greatest day of winter. No crosses or angels on his tree, no lit-up statues of Mary blinking on the front lawn, but still, stockings, colored tree-lights, glittery tinsel, presents piled high. Christmas: a holiday celebrating the end of the year. Rosh Hashanah: a holiday he can't pronounce, celebrating something he can't remember. The Lord, if he's even up there, shouldn't call his name. And that's fine with him. He doesn't want his name to be called. If your name is called, everything changes. It would be like going to Sunday school all week long. He likes the way things are: catching fly balls and grounders in the back yard, walking in the hot sand at Short Beach, firecrackers on the Fourth of July, sitting in front of the fireplace in winter reading a book while his father grades papers at one end of the couch and his mother reads at the other end, birthday parties, reading "The 500 Hats of Bartholomew Cubbins" to his sister, playing double solitaire with Grandma Lena, watching the black-and-white pictures rise into the white paper in the developing tray in his father's darkroom, riding slowly in the boat through the Old Mill at Pleasure Beach. He doesn't want to leave his family, doesn't want to leave his room with the two windows looking down at the back yard, the big record-player in the living room, where he and his sister listen to "Peter and the Wolf." His mother looking at him one day, touching him, her eyes shining: "Oh, my firstborn." His father answering all his questions with that serious look, as if nothing is more important than those questions. What happens when you die? What is God? What is the most important thing in the world? He doesn't want to leave it all for the temple of Shiloh. School starts in a few weeks, he's still got lots of summer left, picnics by the river, drives into Bridgeport, the smell of hot roasted nuts in Morrow's Nut House, the elevator operators in their maroon jackets and white gloves in Read's department store, the wooden ships with rigging in the window of Blinn's. He's done with Samuel, done with the voice in the night, but now, as he feels sleep coming on, he gives a final listen, just in case, straining his ears, holding his breath, listening for the voice that came to Samuel in that old story that's only a story but one he knows he'll never forget, no matter how hard he tries.

III

Again. Enough already. But hey, look on the bright side: four in the morning, three hours of sleep instead of one. The long walk after dinner, more than an hour, hoping to outwit insomnia. Walk for one hour, wake up at four. Walk for two hours, wake up at five. Walk for three hours, wake up at six. Walk for four hours, drop dead of a heart attack. His flab-armed father's muscular calves. Walked all over Manhattan in his City College days, late nineteen-twenties,

Harlem to the Battery. A safe city. The boy in Stratford walking up Canaan Road to the White Walk Market, walking to school along Franklin Avenue and Collins Street and the street that led past Holy Name. Calves skinny as forearms. His father walking a mile to the bus stop each morning to catch the bus to Bridgeport, no car till the boy is in second grade: city people don't drive. No television till fifth grade: TV is for people who don't read. Last in the neighborhood. Back from Manhattan with a ten-inch box, an Air King, set up on a table next to the piano. The feverish pleasure of black-and-white cartoons. Czerny exercises and Farmer Al Falfa. Mozart and Mighty Mouse. His mother playing Schumann and laughing with him at "The Merry Mailman." His grave father bent over the Scrooge McDuck comic, praising the diving board in the money bin. Reading "Tootle" to him, telling him how good the first sentence is. "Far, far to the west of everywhere is the village of Lower Trainswitch." Far, far to the west of everywhere. His father said, "There are three great opening sentences in all of literature. The first is 'In the beginning God created the heaven and the earth.' The second is 'Call me Ishmael.' The third is 'Far, far to the west of everywhere is the village of Lower Trainswitch.'" A father who's serious and funny: you have to watch his face carefully. The book about the whale: he knows where it is on the shelf, he's held it in his hands, thinking, When I'm older. The whale, God: when he's older. Books, always books. Ten years old: his father lashing out at Eisenhower. "He doesn't open a book!" The trip to Spain after Columbia, one-way ticket, two pieces of luggage: one for clothes, one for books. The boy in Stratford lying awake at night because of a story in a book. What's a story? A demon in the night. He wants to protect the boy, warn him before it's too late. Don't listen to stories! They'll keep you awake at night, suck out your blood, leave teeth marks in your skin. Let him sleep! Let him live! His New York Jew parents in working-class Stratford, with their books and their piano. The professor who doesn't do work with his hands. Joey's father a machinist at the helicopter plant, Mike's father a carpenter who builds his own house in the vacant lot on the other side of the hedge. Joey turning to him with a fighting look: "Can your father make a wheel?" The old sun-browned Italian men working in their gardens. The grapevines growing all over Jimmy Stoccatore's high fence, the bunches of purple grapes, heavy in the hand. Old man Ciccarelli chasing kids out of his lot. Eenie meenie miney mo, catch a tiger by the toe. Not in this house. The Jewish Boy Scout troop, where he learned to tie a sheepshank but never could identify poison sumac. His refusal to be Jesus in the Sunday-school play. Mrs. Kraus's shocked surprise. "But why?" "Because Jesus betrayed the Jews." Her confusion, fear. "I never taught you that!" His father: "Jesus was a great teacher." Sixty years later, awake at night, at the mercy of memory. Rapunzel! Rapunzel! Let down your hair! And the Lord came, and stood, and called as at other times, Samuel, Samuel. The boy in Stratford, listening. Thank you, Old Man of the Sky, for not calling his name. Better for all concerned. He can't really have believed it, can he? Working himself up into a temporary blaze of half-belief, a possibility: a ghost in the dark. Better for him to stay out of the temple of Shiloh, better to go play in the green back yards of Stratford, grow up in a world of family excursions and shelves of books until the writing fever seized him and claimed him for life. A calling. Not Samuel's call but another. Not that way but this way. Samuel ministering unto the Lord, his teacher-father ministering unto the generations. And the son? What about him? Far, far to the west of everywhere, ministering unto the Muse. Thanks, Old Sea-Parter, for leaving me be. Tired now. Soon we'll all sleep.

THE EMBASSY OF CAMBODIA

BY ZADIE SMITH (2013)

0–1

Who would expect the Embassy of Cambodia? Nobody. Nobody could have expected it, or be expecting it. It's a surprise, to us all. The Embassy of Cambodia!

Next door to the embassy is a health center. On the other side, a row of private residences, most of them belonging to wealthy Arabs (or so we, the people of Willesden, contend). They have Corinthian pillars on either side of their front doors, and—it's widely believed—swimming pools out back. The embassy, by contrast, is not very grand. It is only a four- or five-bedroom North London suburban villa, built at some point in the thirties, surrounded by a red brick wall, about eight feet high. And back and forth, cresting this wall horizontally, flies a shuttlecock. They are playing badminton in the Embassy of Cambodia. Pock, smash. Pock, smash.

The only real sign that the embassy is an embassy at all is the little brass plaque on the door (which reads, "THE EMBASSY OF CAMBODIA") and the national flag of Cambodia (we assume that's what it is—what else could it be?) flying from the red tiled roof. Some say, "Oh, but it has a high wall around it, and this is what signifies that it is not a private residence, like the other houses on the street but, rather, an embassy." The people who say so are foolish. Many of the private houses have high walls, quite as high as the Embassy of Cambodia's—but they are not embassies.

0-2

On the sixth of August, Fatou walked past the embassy for the first time, on her way to a swimming pool. It is a large pool, although not quite Olympic size. To swim a mile you must complete eighty-two lengths, which, in its very tedium, often feels as much a mental exercise as a physical one. The water is kept unusually warm, to please the majority of people who patronize the health center, the kind who come not so much to swim as to lounge poolside or rest their bodies in the sauna. Fatou has swum here five or six times now, and she is often the youngest person in the pool by several decades. Generally, the clientele are white, or else South Asian or from the Middle East, but now and then Fatou finds herself in the water with fellow-Africans. When she spots these big men, paddling frantically like babies, struggling simply to stay afloat, she prides herself on her own abilities, having taught herself to swim, several years earlier, at the Carib Beach Resort, in Accra. Not in the hotel pool—no employees were allowed in the pool. No, she learned by struggling through the rough gray sea, on the other side of the resort walls. Rising and sinking, rising and sinking, on the dirty foam. No tourist ever stepped onto the beach (it was covered with trash), much less into the cold and treacherous sea. Nor did any of the other chambermaids. Only some reckless teen-age boys, late at night, and Fatou, early in the morning. There is almost no way to compare swimming at Carib Beach and swimming in the health center, warm as it is, tranquil as a bath. And, as Fatou passes the Embassy of Cambodia, on her way to the pool, over the high wall she sees a shuttlecock, passed back and forth between two unseen players. The shuttlecock floats in a wide arc softly rightward, and is smashed back, and this happens again and again, the first player always somehow able to retrieve the smash and transform it, once more, into a gentle, floating arc. High above, the sun tries to force its way through a cloud ceiling, gray and filled with water. Pock, smash. Pock, smash.

0-3

When the Embassy of Cambodia first appeared in our midst, a few years ago, some of us said, "Well, if we were poets perhaps we could have written some sort of an ode about this surprising appearance of the embassy." (For embassies are usually to be found in the center of the city. This was the first one we had seen in the suburbs.) But we are not really a poetic people. We are from Willesden. Our minds tend toward the prosaic. I doubt there is a man or woman among us, for example, who—upon passing the Embassy of Cambodia for the first time—did not immediately think: "genocide."

0-4

Pock, smash. Pock, smash. This summer we watched the Olympics, becoming well attuned to grunting, and to the many other human sounds associated with effort and the triumph of the will. But the players in the garden of the Embassy of Cambodia are silent. (We can't say for sure that it is a garden—we have a limited view over the wall. It may well be a paved area, reserved for badminton.) The only sign that a game of badminton is under way at all is the motion of the shuttlecock itself, alternately being lobbed and smashed, lobbed and smashed, and always at the hour that Fatou passes on her way to the health center to swim (just after ten in the morning on Mondays). It should be explained that it is Fatou's employers—and not Fatou—who are the true members of this health club; they have no idea that she uses their guest passes in this way. (Mr. and Mrs. Derawal and their three children—aged seventeen, fifteen, and ten—live on the same street as the embassy, but the road is almost a mile long, with the embassy at one end and the Derawals at the other.) Fatou's deception is possible only because on Mondays Mr. Derawal drives to Eltham to visit his mini-market there, and Mrs. Derawal works the counter in the family's second mini-mart, in Kensal Rise. In the slim drawer of a faux-Louis XVI console, in the entrance hall of the Derawals' primary residence, one can find a stockpile of guest passes. Nobody besides Fatou seems to remember that they are there.

Since August 6th (the first occasion on which she noticed the badminton), Fatou has made a point of pausing by the bus stop opposite the embassy for five or ten minutes before she goes in to swim, idle minutes she can hardly afford (Mrs. Derawal returns to the house at lunchtime) and yet seems unable to forgo. Such is the strangely compelling aura of the embassy. Usually, Fatou gains nothing from this waiting and observing, but on a few occasions she has seen people arrive at the embassy and watched as they are buzzed through the gate. Young white people carrying rucksacks. Often they are scruffy, and wearing sandals, despite the cool weather. None of the visitors so far have been visibly Cambodian. These young people are likely looking for visas. They are buzzed in and then pass through the gate, although Fatou would really have to stand on top of the bus stop to get a view of whoever it is that lets them in. What she can say with certainty is that these occasional arrivals have absolutely no effect on the badminton, which continues in its steady pattern, first gentle, then fast, first soft and high, then hard and low.

0–5

On the twentieth of August, long after the Olympians had returned to their respective countries, Fatou noticed that a basketball hoop had appeared in the far corner of the garden, its net of synthetic white rope rising high enough to be seen over the wall. But no basketball was ever played—at least not when Fatou was passing. The following week it had been moved closer to Fatou's side of the wall. (It must be a mobile hoop, on casters.) Fatou waited a week, two weeks, but still no basketball game replaced the badminton, which carried on as before.

0-6

When I say that we were surprised by the appearance of the Embassy of Cambodia, I don't mean to suggest that the embassy is in any way unique in its peculiarity. In fact, this long, wide street is notable for a number of curious buildings, in the context of which the Embassy of Cambodia does not seem especially strange. There is a mansion called GARYLAND, with something else in Arabic engraved below GARYLAND, and both the English and the Arabic text are inlaid in pink-and-green marble pillars that bookend a gigantic fence, far higher than the embassy's, better suited to a fortress. Dramatic golden gates open automatically to let vehicles in and out. At any one time, GARYLAND has five to seven cars parked in its driveway.

There is a house with a huge pink elephant on the doorstep, apparently made of mosaic tiles.

There is a Catholic nunnery with a single red Ford Focus parked in front. There is a Sikh institute. There is a faux-Tudor house with a pool that Mickey Rooney rented for a season, while he was performing in the West End fifteen summers ago. That house sits opposite a dingy retirement home, where one sometimes sees distressed souls, barely covered by their dressing gowns, standing on their tiny balconies, staring into the tops of the chestnut trees.

So we are hardly strangers to curious buildings, here in Willesden & Brondesbury. And yet still we find the Embassy of Cambodia a little surprising. It is not the right sort of surprise, somehow.

0–7

In a discarded *Metro* found on the floor of the Derawal kitchen, Fatou read with interest a story about a Sudanese "slave" living in a rich man's house in London. It was not the first time that Fatou had wondered if she herself was a slave, but this story, brief as it was, confirmed in her own mind that she was not. After all, it was her father, and not a kidnapper, who had taken her from Ivory Coast to Ghana, and when they reached Accra they had both found employment in the same hotel. Two years later, when she was eighteen, it was her father again who had organized her difficult passage to Libya and then on to Italy—a not insignificant financial sacrifice on his part. Also, Fatou could read English—and speak a little Italian—and this girl in the paper could not read or speak anything except the language of her tribe. And nobody beat Fatou, although Mrs. Derawal had twice slapped her in the face, and the two older children spoke to her with no respect at all and thanked her for nothing. (Sometimes she heard her name used as a term of abuse between them. "You're as black as Fatou." Or "You're as stupid as Fatou.") On the other hand, just like the girl in the newspaper, she had not seen her passport with her own eyes since she arrived at the Derawals', and she had been told from the start that her wages were to be retained by the Derawals to pay for the food and water and heat she would require during her stay, as well as to cover the rent for the room she slept in. In the final analysis, however, Fatou was not confined to the house. She had an Oyster Card, given to her by the Derawals, and was trusted to do the food shopping and other outside tasks for which she was given cash and told to return with change and receipts for everything. If she did not go out in the evenings that was only because she had no money with which to go out, and anyway knew very few people in London. Whereas the girl in the paper was not allowed to leave her employers' premises, not ever—she was a prisoner.

On Sunday mornings, for example, Fatou regularly left the house to meet her church friend Andrew Okonkwo at the 98 bus stop and go with him to worship at the Sacred Heart of Jesus, just off the Kilburn High Road. Afterward Andrew always took her to a Tunisian café, where they had coffee and cake, which Andrew, who worked as a night guard in the City, always paid for. And on Mondays Fatou swam. In very warm water, and thankful for the semi-darkness in which the health club, for some reason, kept its clientele, as if the place were a night club, or a midnight Mass. The darkness helped disguise the fact that her swimming costume was in fact a sturdy black bra and a pair of plain black cotton knickers. No, on balance she did not think she was a slave.

0–8

The woman exiting the Embassy of Cambodia did not look especially like a New Person or an Old Person—neither clearly of the city nor of the country—and of course it is a long time since this division meant anything in Cambodia. Nor did these terms mean anything to Fatou, who was curious only to catch her first sighting of a possible Cambodian anywhere near the Embassy of Cambodia. She was particularly interested in the woman's clothes, which were precise and utilitarian—a gray shirt tucked tightly into a pair of tan slacks, a blue mackintosh, a droopy rain hat—just as if she were a man, or no different from a man. Her straight black hair was cut short. She had in her hands many bags from Sainsbury's, and this Fatou found a little mysterious: where was she taking all that shopping? It also surprised her that the woman from the Embassy of Cambodia should shop in the same Willesden branch of Sainsbury's where Fatou shopped for the Derawals. She had an idea that Oriental people had their own, secret establishments. (She believed the Jews did, too.) She both admired and slightly resented this self-reliance, but had no doubt that it was the secret to holding great power, as a people. For example, when the Chinese had come to Fatou's village to take over the mine, an abiding local mystery had been: what did they eat and where did they eat it? They certainly did not buy food in the market, or from the Lebanese traders along the main road. They made their own arrangements. (Whether back home or here, the key to surviving as a people, in Fatou's opinion, was to make your own arrangements.)

But, looking again at the bags the Cambodian woman carried, Fatou wondered whether they weren't in fact very old bags—hadn't their design changed? The more she looked at them the more convinced she became that they contained not food but clothes or something else again, the outline of each bag being a little too rounded and smooth. Maybe she was simply taking out the rubbish. Fatou stood at the bus stop and watched until the Cambodian woman reached the corner, crossed, and turned left toward the high road. Meanwhile, back at the embassy the badminton continued to be played, though with a little more effort now because of a wayward wind. At one point it seemed to Fatou that the next lob would blow southward, sending the shuttlecock over the wall to land lightly in her own hands. Instead the other player, with his vicious reliability (Fatou had long ago decided that both players were men), caught the shuttlecock as it began to drift and sent it back to his opponent—another deathly, downward smash.

0–9

No doubt there are those who will be critical of the narrow, essentially local scope of Fatou's interest in the Cambodian woman from the Embassy of Cambodia, but we, the people of Willesden, have some sympathy with her attitude. The fact is if we followed the history of every little country in this world—in its dramatic as well as its quiet times—we would have no space left in which to live our own lives or to apply ourselves to our necessary tasks, never mind indulge in occasional pleasures, like swimming. Surely there is something to be said for drawing a circle around our attention and remaining within that circle. But how large should this circle be?

0–10

It was the Sunday after Fatou saw the Cambodian that she decided to put a version of this question to Andrew, as they sat in the Tunisian café eating two large fingers of dough stuffed with cream and custard and topped with a strip of chocolate icing. Specifically, she began a conversation with Andrew about the Holocaust, as Andrew was the only person she had found in London with whom she could have these deep conversations, partly because he was patient and sympathetic to her, but also because he was an educated person, currently studying for a part-time business degree at the College of North West London. With his student card he had been given free, twenty-four-hour access to the Internet.

"But more people died in Rwanda," Fatou argued. "And nobody speaks about that! Nobody!"

"Yes, I think that's true," Andrew conceded, and put the first of four sugars in his coffee. "I have to check. But, yes, millions and millions. They hide the true numbers, but you can see them online. There's always a lot of hiding; it's the same all over. It's like this bureaucratic Nigerian government—they are the greatest at numerology, hiding figures, changing them to suit their purposes. I have a name for it: I call it 'demonology.' Not 'numerology'—'demonology.'"

"Yes, but what I am saying is like this," Fatou pressed, wary of the conversation's drifting back, as it usually did, to the financial corruption of the Nigerian government. "Are we born to suffer? Sometimes I think we were born to suffer more than all the rest."

Andrew pushed his professorial glasses up his nose. "But, Fatou, you're forgetting the most important thing. Who cried most for Jesus? His mother. Who cries most for you? Your father. It's very logical, when you break it down. The Jews cry for the Jews. The

Russians cry for the Russians. We cry for Africa, because we are Africans, and, even then, I'm sorry, Fatou"—Andrew's chubby face creased up in a smile—"if Nigeria plays Ivory Coast and we beat you into the ground, I'm laughing, man! I can't lie. I'm celebrating. Stomp! Stomp!" He did a little dance with his upper body, and Fatou tried, not for the first time, to imagine what he might be like as a husband, but could see only herself as the wife, and Andrew as a teen-age son of hers, bright and helpful, to be sure, but a son all the same—though in reality he was three years older than she. Surely it was wrong to find his baby fat and struggling mustache so off-putting. Here was a good man! She knew that he cared for her, was clean, and had given his life to Christ. Still, some part of her rebelled against him, some unholy part.

"Hush your mouth," she said, trying to sound more playful than disgusted, and was relieved when he stopped jiggling and laid both his hands on the table, his face suddenly quite solemn.

"Believe me, that's a natural law, Fatou, pure and simple. Only God cries for us all, because we are *all* his children. It's very, very logical. You just have to think about it for a moment."

Fatou sighed, and spooned some coffee foam into her mouth. "But I still think we have more pain. I've seen it myself. Chinese people have never been slaves. They are always protected from the worst."

Andrew took off his glasses and rubbed them on the end of his shirt. Fatou could tell that he was preparing to lay knowledge upon her.

"Fatou, think about it for a moment, please: what about Hiroshima?"

It was a name Fatou had heard before, but sometimes Andrew's superior knowledge made her nervous. She would find herself struggling to remember even the things she had believed she already knew.

"The big wave . . ." she began, uncertainly—it was the wrong answer. He laughed mightily and shook his head at her.

"No, man! Big bomb. Biggest bomb in the world, made by the U.S.A., of course. They killed five million people in one second. Can you imagine that? You think just because your eyes are like this"—he tugged the skin at both temples—"you're always protected? Think again. This bomb, even if it didn't blow you up, a week later it melted the skin off your bones."

Fatou realized that she had heard this story before, or some version of it. But she felt the same vague impatience with it as she did with all accounts of suffering in the distant past. For what could be done about the suffering of the past?

"O.K.," she said. "Maybe all people have their hard times, in the past of history, but I still say—"

"Here is a counterpoint," Andrew said, reaching out and gripping her shoulder. "Let me ask you, Fatou, seriously, think about this. I'm sorry to interrupt you, but I have thought a lot about this and I want to pass it on to you, because I know you care about things seriously, not like these people." He waved a hand at the assortment of cake eaters at other tables. "You're not like the other girls I know, just thinking about the club and their hair. You're a person who thinks. I told you before, anything you want to know about, ask me—I'll look it up, I'll do the research. I have access. Then I'll bring it to you."

"You're a very good friend to me, Andrew, I know that."

"Listen, we are friends to each other. In this world you need friends. But, Fatou, listen to my question. It's a counterpoint to what you have been saying. Tell me, why would God choose us especially for suffering when we, above all others, praise his name? Africa is the fastest-growing Christian continent! Just think about it for a minute! It doesn't even make sense!"

"But it's not him," Fatou said quietly, looking over Andrew's shoulder at the rain beating on the window. "It's the Devil."

O–II

Andrew and Fatou sat in the Tunisian coffee shop, waiting for it to stop raining, but it did not stop raining, and at 3 P.M. Fatou said she would just have to get wet. She shared Andrew's umbrella as far as the Overground, letting him pull her into his clammy, high-smelling body as they walked. At Brondesbury station Andrew had to get the train, and so they said goodbye. Several times he tried to press his umbrella on her, but Fatou knew the walk from Acton

Central to Andrew's bed-sit was long and she refused to let him suffer on her account.

"Big woman. Won't let anybody protect you."

"Rain doesn't scare me."

Fatou took from her pocket a swimming cap she had found on the floor of the health-club changing room. She wound her plaits into a bun and pulled the cap over her head.

"That's a very original idea," Andrew said, laughing. "You should market that! Make your first million!"

"Peace be with you," Fatou said, and kissed him chastely on the cheek. Andrew did the same, lingering a little longer with his kiss than was necessary.

0–12

By the time Fatou reached the Derawals', only her hair was dry, but before going to get changed she rushed to the kitchen to take the lamb out of the freezer, though it was pointless—there were not enough hours before dinner—and then upstairs to collect the dirty clothes from the matching wicker baskets in four different bedrooms. There was no one in the master bedroom, or in Faizul's, or Julie's. Downstairs a television was blaring. Entering Asma's room, hearing nothing, assuming it empty, Fatou headed straight for the laundry bin in the corner. As she opened the lid she felt a hand hit her hard on the back; she turned around.

There was the youngest, Asma, in front of her, her mouth open like a trout fish. Before Fatou could understand, Asma punched the huge pile of clothes out of her hands. Fatou stooped to retrieve them. While she was kneeling on the floor, another strike came, a kick to her arm. She left the clothes where they were and got up, frightened by her own anger. But when she looked at Asma now she saw the girl gesturing frantically at her own throat, then putting her hands together in prayer, and then back to her throat once more. Her eyes were bulging. She veered suddenly to the right; she threw herself over the back of a chair. When she turned back to Fatou her face was gray and Fatou understood finally and ran to her, grabbed her round her waist, and pulled upward as she had been taught in the hotel. A marble—with an iridescent ribbon of blue at its center, like a wave—flew from the child's mouth and landed wetly in the carpet's plush.

Asma wept and drew in frantic gulps of air. Fatou gave her a hug, and worried when the clothes would get done. Together they went down to the den, where the rest of the family was watching "Britain's Got Talent" on a flat-screen TV attached to the wall. Everybody stood at the sight of Asma's wild weeping. Mr. Derawal paused the Sky box. Fatou explained about the marble.

"How many times I tell you not to put things in your mouth?" Mr. Derawal asked, and Mrs. Derawal said something in their language—Fatou heard the name of their God—and pulled Asma onto the sofa and stroked her daughter's silky black hair.

"I couldn't breathe, man! I couldn't call nobody," Asma cried. "I was gonna die!"

"What you putting marbles in your mouth for anyway, you idiot," Faizul said, and un-paused the Sky box. "What kind of chief puts a marble in her mouth? Idiot. Bet you was bricking it."

"Oi, she saved your life," said Julie, the eldest child, whom Fatou generally liked the least. "Fatou saved your life. That's deep."

"I woulda just done this," Faizul said, and performed an especially dramatic Heimlich to his own skinny body. "And if that didn't work I woulda just start pounding myself karate style, bam bam bam bam bam—"

"Faizul!" Mr. Derawal shouted, and then turned stiffly to Fatou, and spoke not to her, exactly, but to a point somewhere between her elbow and the sunburst mirror behind her head. "Thank you, Fatou. It's lucky you were there."

Fatou nodded and moved to leave, but at the doorway to the den Mrs. Derawal asked her if the lamb had defrosted and Fatou had to confess that she had only just taken it out. Mrs. Derawal said something sharply in her language. Fatou waited for something further, but Mr. Derawal only smiled awkwardly at her, and nodded as a sign that she could go now. Fatou went upstairs to collect the clothes.

O-13

"To keep you is no benefit. To destroy you is no loss" was one of the mottoes of the Khmer Rouge. It referred to the New People, those city dwellers who could not be made to give up city life and work on a farm. By returning everybody to the land, the regime hoped to create a society of Old People—that is to say, of agrarian peasants. When a New Person was relocated from the city to the country, it was vital not to show weakness in the fields. Vulnerability was punishable by death.

In Willesden, we are almost all New People, though some of us, like Fatou, were, until quite recently, Old People, working the land in our various countries of origin. Of the Old and New People of Willesden I speak; I have been chosen to speak for them, though they did not choose me and must wonder what gives me the right. I could say, "Because I was born at the crossroads of Willesden, Kilburn, and Queen's Park!" But the reply would be swift and damning: "Oh, don't be foolish, many people were born right there; it doesn't mean anything at all. We are not one people and no one can speak for us. It's all a lot of nonsense. We see you standing on the balcony, overlooking the Embassy of Cambodia, in your dressing gown, staring into the chestnut trees, looking gormless. The real reason you speak in this way is because you can't think of anything better to do."

0–14

On Monday, Fatou went swimming. She paused to watch the badminton. She thought that the arm that delivered the smashes must make a movement similar to the one she made in the pool, with her clumsy yet effective front crawl. She entered the health center and gave a guest pass to the girl behind the desk. In the dimly lit changing room, she put on her sturdy black underwear. As she swam, she thought of Carib Beach. Her father serving snapper to the guests on the deck, his bow tie always a little askew, the ugly tourists, the whole scene there. Of course, it was not surprising in the least to see old white men from Germany with beautiful local girls on their laps, but she would never forget the two old white women from England—red women, really, thanks to the sun—each of them as big as two women put together, with Kweku and Osai lying by their sides, the boys hooking their scrawny black bird-arms round the women's massive red shoulders, dancing with them in the hotel "ballroom," answering to the names Michael and David, and disappearing into the women's cabins at night. She had known the boys' real girlfriends; they were chambermaids like Fatou. Sometimes they cleaned the rooms where Kweku and Osai spent the night with the English women. And the girls themselves had "boyfriends" among the guests. It was not a holy place, that hotel. And the pool was shaped like a kidney bean: nobody could really swim in it, or showed any sign of wanting to. Mostly, they stood in it and drank cocktails. Sometimes they even had their burgers delivered to the pool. Fatou hated to watch her father crouching to hand a burger to a man waist high in water.

The only good thing that happened in Carib Beach was this: once a month, on a Sunday, the congregation of a local church poured out of a coach at the front gates, lined up fully dressed in the courtyard, and then walked into the pool for a mass baptism. The tourists were never warned, and Fatou never understood why the congregants were allowed to do it. But she loved to watch their white shirts bloat and spread across the surface of the water, and to hear the weeping and singing. At the time—though she was not then a member of that church, or of any church except the one in her heart—she had felt that this baptism was for her, too, and that it kept her safe, and that this was somehow the reason she did not become one of the "girls" at the Carib Beach Resort. For almost two years—between her father's efforts and the grace of an unseen and unacknowledged God—she did her work, and swam Sunday mornings at the crack of dawn, and got along all right. But the Devil was waiting.

She had only a month left in Accra when she entered a bedroom to clean it one morning and heard the door shut softly behind her before she could put a hand to it. He came, this time, in Russian form. Afterward, he cried and begged her not to tell anyone: his wife had gone to see the Cape Coast Castle and they were leaving the following morning. Fatou listened to his blubbering and realized that he thought the hotel would punish him for his action, or that the police would be called. That was when she knew that the Devil was stupid as well as evil. She spat in his face and left. Thinking about the Devil now made her swimming fast and angry, and for a while she easily lapped the young white man in the lane next to hers, the faster lane.

0-15

"Don't give the Devil your anger, it is his food," Andrew had said to her, when they first met, a year ago. He handed her a leaflet as she sat eating a sandwich on a bench in Kilburn Park. "Don't make it so easy for him." Without being invited, he took the seat next to hers and began going through the text of his leaflet. It was printed to look like a newspaper, and he started with the headline: "WHY IS THERE PAIN?" She liked him. They began a theological conversation. It continued in the Tunisian café, and every Sunday for several months. A lot of the things he said she had heard before from other people, and they did not succeed in changing her attitude. In the end, it was one thing that he said to her that really made the difference. It was after she'd told him this story:

"One day, at the hotel, I heard a commotion on the beach. It was early morning. I went out and I saw nine children washed up dead on the beach. Ten or eleven years old, boys and girls. They had gone into the water, but they didn't know how to swim. Some people were crying, maybe two people. Everyone else just shook their heads and carried on walking to where they were going. After a long time, the police came. The bodies were taken away. People said, 'Well, they are with God now.' Everybody carried on like before. I went back to work. The next year I arrived in Rome. I saw a boy who was about fifteen years old knocked down on his bike. He was dead. People were screaming and crying in the street. Everybody crying. They were not his family. They were only strangers. The next day, it was in the paper."

And Andrew replied, "A tap runs fast the first time you switch it on."

0-16

Twenty more laps. Fatou tried to think of the last time she had cried. It was in Rome, but it wasn't for the boy on the bike. She was cleaning toilets in a Catholic girls' school. She did not know Jesus then, so it made no difference what kind of school it was—she knew only that she was cleaning toilets. At midday, she had a fifteen-minute break. She would go to the little walled garden across the road to smoke a cigarette. One day, she was sitting on a bench near a fountain, and spotted something odd in the bushes. A tin of green paint. A gold spray can. A Statue of Liberty costume. An identity card with the name Rajib Devanga. One shoe. An empty wallet. A plastic tub with a slit cut in the top meant for coins and euro notes—empty. A little stain of what looked like blood on this tub. Until that point, she had been envious of the Bengali boys on Via Nazionale. She felt that she, too, could paint herself green and stand still for an hour. But when she tried to find out more the Bengalis would not talk to her. It was a closed shop, for brown men only. Her place was in the bathroom stalls. She thought those men had it easy. Then she saw that little sad pile of belongings in the bush and cried; for herself or for Rajib, she wasn't sure.

Now she turned onto her back in the water for the final two laps, relaxed her arms, and kicked her feet out like a frog. Water made her think of more water. "When you're baptized in our church, all sin is wiped, you start again": Andrew's promise. She had never told Andrew of the sin precisely, but she knew that he knew she was not a virgin. The day she finally became a Catholic, February 6, 2011, Andrew had taken her, hair still wet, to the Tunisian café and asked her how it felt.

She was joyful! She said, "I feel like a new person!"

But happiness like that is hard to hold on to. Back at work the next day, picking Julie's dirty underwear up off the floor inches from the wicker basket, she had to keep reminding herself of her new relationship with Jesus and how it changed everything. Didn't it change everything? The following Sunday she expressed some of her doubt, cautiously, to Andrew.

"But did you think you'd never feel sad again? Never angry or tired or just pissed off—sorry about my language. Come on, Fatou! Wise up, man!"

Was it wrong to hope to be happy?

O–17

Lost to these watery thoughts, Fatou got home a little later than usual and was through the door only minutes before Mrs. Derawal.

"How is Asma?" Fatou asked. She had heard the girl cry out in the night.

"My goodness, it was just a little marble," Mrs. Derawal said, and Fatou realized that it was not in her imagination: since Sunday night, neither of the adult Derawals had been able to look her in the eye. "What a fuss everybody is making. I have a list for you—it's on the table."

0–18

Fatou watched Andrew pick his way through the tables in the Tunisian café, holding a tray with a pair of mochas on it and some croissants. He hit the elbow of one man with his backside and then trailed the belt of his long, silly leather coat through the lunch of another, apologizing as he went. You could not say that he was an elegant man. But he was generous, he was thoughtful. She stood up to push a teetering croissant back onto its plate. They sat down at the same time, and smiled at each other.

"Awhile ago you asked me about Cambodia," Andrew said. "Well, it's a very interesting case." He tapped the frame of his glasses. "If you even wore a pair of these? They would kill you. Glasses meant you thought too much. They had very primitive ideas. They were enemies of logic and progress. They wanted everybody to go back to the country and live like simple people."

"But sometimes it's true that things are simpler in the country."

"In some ways. I don't really know. I've never lived in the country."

I don't really know. It was good to hear him say that! It was a good sign. She smiled cheekily at him. "People are less sinful in the country," she said, but he did not seem to see that she was flirting with him, and embarked on another lecture:

"That's true. But you can't force people to live in the country. That's what I call a Big Man Policy. I invented this phrase for my dissertation. We know all about Big Man Policies in Nigeria. They come from the top, and they crush you. There's always somebody who wants to be the Big Man, and take everything for himself, and tell everybody how to think and what to do. When, actually, it's he who is weak. But if the Big Men see that *you* see that *they* are weak they have no choice but to destroy you. That is the real tragedy."

Fatou sighed. "I never met a man who didn't want to tell everybody how to think and what to do," she said.

Andrew laughed. "Fatou, you include me? Are you a feminist now, too?"

Fatou brought her mug up to her lips and looked penetratingly at Andrew. There were good and bad kinds of weakness in men, and she had come to the conclusion that the key was to know which kind you were dealing with.

"Andrew," she said, putting her hand on his, "would you like to come swimming with me?"

0–19

Because Fatou believed that the Derawals' neighbors had been instructed to spy on her, she would not let Andrew come to the house to pick her up on Monday, instead leaving as she always did, just before ten, carrying misleading Sainsbury's bags and walking toward the health center. She spotted him from a long way off—the road was so straight and he had arrived early. He stood shivering in the drizzle. She felt sorry, but also a little prideful: it was the prospect of seeing her body that had raised this big man from his bed. Still, it was a sacrifice, she knew, for her friend to come out to meet her on a weekday morning. He worked all night long and kept the daytime for sleeping. She watched him waving at her from their agreed meeting spot, just on the corner, in front of the Embassy of Cambodia. After a while, he stopped waving—because she was still so far away—and then, a little later, he began waving again. She waved back, and when she finally reached him they surprised each other by holding hands. "I'm an excellent badminton player," Andrew said, as they passed the Embassy of Cambodia. "I would make you weep for mercy! Next time, instead of swimming we should play badminton somewhere." Next time, we should go to Paris. Next time, we should go to the moon. He was a dreamer. But there are worse things, Fatou thought, than being a dreamer.

0-20

"So you're a guest and this is your guest?" the girl behind the desk asked.

"I am a guest and this is another guest," Fatou replied.

"Yeah . . . that's not really how it works?"

"Please," Fatou said. "We've come from a long way."

"I appreciate that," the girl said. "But I really shouldn't let you in, to be honest."

"Please," Fatou said again. She could think of no other argument.

The girl took out a pen and made a mark on Fatou's guest pass.

"This one time. Don't tell no one I did this, please. One time only! I'll need to cross off two separate visits."

For one time only, then, Andrew and Fatou approached the changing rooms together and parted at the doors that led to the men's and the women's. In her changing room, Fatou got ready with lightning speed. Yet somehow he was already there on a lounger when she came out, eyes trained on the women's changing-room door, waiting for her to emerge.

"Man, this is the life!" he said, putting his arms behind his head.

"Are you getting in?" Fatou asked, and tried to place her hands, casually, in front of her groin.

"Not yet, man, I'm just taking it all in, taking it all in. You go in. I'll come in a moment."

Fatou climbed down the steps and began to swim. Not elegant, not especially fast, but consistent and determined. Every now and then she would angle her head to try to see if Andrew was still on his chair, smiling to himself. After twenty laps, she swam to where he lay and put her elbows on the tiles.

"You're not coming in? It's so warm. Like a bath."

"Sure, sure," he said. "I'll try it."

As he sat up his stomach folded in on itself, and Fatou wondered whether he had spent all that time on the lounger to avoid her seeing its precise bulk and wobble. He came toward the stairs; Fatou held out a hand to him, but he pushed it away. He made his way down and stood in the shallow end, splashing water over his shoulders like a prince fanning himself, and then crouching down into it.

"It is warm! Very nice. This is the life, man! You go, swim—I'll follow you."

Fatou kicked off, creating so much splash that she heard someone in the adjacent lane complain. At the wall, she turned and looked for Andrew. His method, such as it was, involved dipping deep under the water and hanging there like a hippo, then batting his arms till he crested for air, and then diving down again and hanging. It was a lot of energy to expend on such a short distance, and by the time he reached the wall he was panting like a maniac. His eyes—he had no goggles—were painfully red.

"It's O.K.," Fatou said, trying to take his hand again. "If you let me, I'll show you how." But he shrugged her off, and rubbed at his eyes.

"There's too much bloody chlorine in this pool."

"You want to leave?"

Andrew turned back to look at Fatou. His eyes were streaming. He looked, to Fatou, like a little boy trying to disguise the fact he had been crying. But then he held her hand, under the water.

"No. I'm just going to take it easy right here."

"O.K.," Fatou said.

"You swim. You're good. You swim."

"O.K.," Fatou said, and set off, and found that each lap was more distracted and rhythmless than the last. She was not used to being watched while she swam. Ten laps later, she suddenly stood up halfway down the lane and walked the rest of the distance to the wall.

"You want to go in the Jacuzzi?" she asked him, pointing to it. In the hot tub sat a woman dressed in a soaking tracksuit, her head covered with a head scarf. A man next to the woman, perhaps her husband, stared at Fatou and said something to her. He was so hairy he was almost as covered as she was. Together they rose up out of the water and left. He was wearing the tiniest of Speedos, the kind Fatou had feared Andrew might wear, and was grateful he had not. Andrew's shorts were perfectly nice, knee length, red and solid, and looked good against his skin.

"No," Andrew said. "It's great just to be here with you, watching the world go by."

0-21

That same evening, Fatou was fired. Not for the guest passes—the Derawals never found out how many miles Fatou had travelled on their membership. In fact, it was hard for Fatou to understand exactly why she was being fired, as Mrs. Derawal herself did not seem able to explain it very precisely.

"What you don't understand is that we have no need for a nanny," she said, standing in the doorway of Fatou's room—there was not really enough space in there for two people to stand without one of them being practically on the bed. "The children are grown. We need a housekeeper, one who cleans properly. These days, you care more about the children than the cleaning," Mrs. Derawal added, though Fatou had never cared for the children, not even slightly. "And that is of no use to us."

Fatou said nothing. She was thinking that she did not have a proper suitcase and would have to take her things from Mrs. Derawal's house in plastic bags.

"And so you will want to find somewhere else to live as soon as possible," Mrs. Derawal said. "My husband's cousin is coming to stay in this room on Friday—this Friday."

Fatou thought about that for a moment. Then she said, "Can I please use the phone for one call?"

Mrs. Derawal inspected a piece of wood that had flaked from the doorframe. But she nodded.

"And I would like to have my passport, please."

"Excuse me?"

"My passport, please."

At last Mrs. Derawal looked at Fatou, right into her eyes, but her face was twisted, as if Fatou had just reached over and slapped her. Anyone could see the Devil had climbed inside poor Mrs. Derawal. He was lighting her up with a pure fury.

"For goodness' sake, girl, I don't have your passport! What would I want with your passport? It's probably in a drawer in the kitchen somewhere. Is that my job now, too, to look for your things?"

Fatou was left alone. She packed her things into the decoy shopping bags she usually took to the swimming pool. While she was doing this, someone pushed her passport under the door. An hour later, she carried her bags downstairs and went directly to the phone in the hall. Faizul walked by and lifted his hand for a high-five. Fatou ignored him and dialled Andrew's number. From her friend's voice she knew that she had woken him, but he was not even the slightest bit angry. He listened to all she had to say and seemed to understand, too, without her having to say so, that at this moment she could not speak freely. After she had said her part, he asked a few quick technical questions and then explained clearly and carefully what was to happen.

"It will all be O.K. They need cleaners in my offices—I will ask for you. In the meantime, you come here. We'll sleep in shifts. You can trust me. I respect you, Fatou."

But she did not have her Oyster Card; it was in the kitchen, on the fridge under a magnet of Florida, and she would rather die than go in there. Fine: he could meet her at 6 P.M., at the Brondesbury Overground station. Fatou looked at the grandfather clock in front of her: she had four hours to kill.

"Six o' clock," she repeated. She put the phone down, took the rest of the guest passes from the drawer of the Louis XVI console, and left the house.

"Weighed down a bit today," the girl at the desk of the health club said, nodding at Fatou's collection of plastic bags. Fatou held out a guest pass for a stamp and did not smile. "See you next time," this same girl said, an hour and a half later, as Fatou strode past, still weighed down and still unwilling to be grateful for past favors. Gratitude was just another kind of servitude. Better to make your own arrangements.

Walking out into the cold gray, Fatou felt a sense of brightness, of being washed clean, that neither the weather nor her new circumstance could dim. Still, her limbs were weary and her hair was wet; she would probably catch a cold, waiting out here. It was only four-thirty. She put her bags on the pavement and sat down next to them, just by the bus stop opposite the Embassy of Cambodia. Buses came and went, slowing down for her and then jerking forward when they realized that she had no interest in getting up and on. Many of us walked past her that afternoon, or spotted her as we rode the bus, or through the windscreens of our cars, or from our balconies.

Naturally, we wondered what this girl was doing, sitting on damp pavement in the middle of the day. We worried for her. We tend to assume the worst, here in Willesden. We watched her watching the shuttlecock. Pock, smash. Pock, smash. As if one player could imagine only a violent conclusion and the other only a hopeful return.

THE CHRISTMAS MIRACLE

BY REBECCA CURTIS (2013)

Cats were dying. This happens, of course. But in this case they were dying in a gory way, one after another, and my nieces, who were six and seven years old, were witnessing the deaths, and it was Christmas, the most magical, horrible, spiritual, dark, and stressful time of the year, so we—my older sister and her husband, my younger twin brothers, my sister's in-laws, our mother and our uncle, and the other relatives who were gathered at my sister's house in Revelstoke for the holiday—were trying to prevent more cat deaths. My sister had had five cats. She'd adopted them from the pound, because they were going to be killed. She wanted every living being to be happy. I am telling this story to you, K, even though you are a Russian Communist and a Jewish person who doesn't believe Jesus was the son of God, and even though Christmas is an obnoxious holiday when millions of people decapitate pine trees and watch them slowly die in their living rooms, because miracles can happen on any day, and as long as man has existed he's celebrated this weirdest time of year, the shortest stretch of sunlight, the winter solstice, as a time of fear, change, courage, and passion. I'm going to tell you the story of a miracle that happened at Christmas.

I was not at a great point in my life leading up to the miracle. I was teaching creative-writing classes, but I hadn't managed to think clearly enough to write and publish anything in years. I had Lyme disease and some co-infections that I was treating with intravenous antibiotics: babesiosis, a malaria-like virus that drains red blood cells and causes fatigue; and bartonellosis, a bacterial infection common among homeless men, which causes vascular inflammation in the brain and bouts of madness, fantastical visions, and frank or rude speech, usually set off by eating carbohydrates. I'd completed my degree in nutrition, and had luck helping clients overcome ailments, especially infertile women who wanted to conceive, so I knew which foods I *should* eat and which I *shouldn't*. But if cake was nearby I wasn't always able to prevent myself from having one bite; then the sugar fed the Bartonella bacteria, which *commanded* me to eat more, and I would, and then I'd go insane.

With this in mind, I'd asked my sister to cancel the traditions of: 1) baking, frosting, and decorating forty dozen sugar cookies; 2) constructing a ginger-bread mansion; 3) baking eight pecan pies; 4) stuffing everyone's stocking full of milk chocolate. My sister had replied that these traditions were integral to the joy of Christmas. I knew that her response was reasonable. But I was literally unable to control myself around sugar, and I worried about containing my fits of madness. I was also concerned about our family's ability to prevent the remaining cats from dying, though my sister assured me she'd implemented a system to achieve this; I was worried, too, that no one would like the cheap, ugly Christmas presents I'd got them; I'd also become aware of my strong urge to inform my sister's sister-in-law Kunda, a shy, forty-four-year-old neurosurgeon and Canadian Medical Officer of Health, that I knew she'd been trying to get pregnant, and that if she'd accept my help I could make it happen, despite my sister's warning that no one was supposed to know Kunda was "trying" and that I must not accost her; finally, I was concerned, as always during family visits, about the safety and comfort of my nieces around our uncle, who was a pedophile, especially since the previous Christmas, when my sister and I weren't vigilant enough, I'd caught him rubbing the butt of the elder girl, then six years old, in a dark, empty room. That, too, my sister assured me, was under control: the girls would never be left alone with him, and at night they'd sleep on cots in her room. Everyone in our family meant well and wanted to be a family.

I know too, K, that you cringe whenever I mention the pedophile thing, and feel that it should not be placed in any story, because it overwhelms it and is too terrible for words. But I'd like to point out that my nieces are two beautiful, talented, and privileged girls, who see their grand-uncle only a few days a year; and that our uncle is not a bad man, just a sick one. So please quell any squeamishness or horror and bear in mind that it could be worse.

I'd also like to say—regarding the Christmas miracle—that it was my elder niece who instigated the Kamikaze Cat Training, not me. I have two nieces but only one goddaughter. And though I've abandoned Catholicism, the cult that I was born into, and am one of about eight godmothers, I take my duty seriously. Perhaps I can be forgiven at least one mistake I made that holiday.

Clara died first. She was eaten by a coyote. She was a nice cat. I don't expect you to care about the cats. Clara was a long-haired Maine coon mix who loved to be petted. She went outside to use the bathroom, or frolic, or whatever cats do, around sunset, and never came back.

The problem was an influx of hungry coyotes into the development where my sister lived. As the town crawled up the mountain, coyotes, bears, and lynxes were displaced from their habitats and wandered down the mountain, where they discovered the delicious new food, cat. In September, when my sister's family barbecued on their back deck, they saw coyotes trot through the pines at their yard's edge.

Clara was eaten in October. Afterward, my nieces cried, blahblahblah. My sister, too; Clara had been her first cat. And through the years, whenever my sister felt sad about anything—fight, failed test, car accident, etc.—Clara sensed it, came to her, and sat in her lap.

My sister instituted a lockdown. The cats got one outing, at dusk, to use the bathroom in the yard. They were let out for five minutes, watched, and lured back in with cooked shrimp.

The other cats were Chocolate, a diabetic brown male with postnasal drip who made stinky farts and loved all people, but especially loved to sit on the chest of my brother-in-law (who once spent five thousand dollars on an operation to save Chocolate's pancreas and life); Patches, a brindle who loved playing in the bathroom sink; Simmy, a bony Siamese loner who fought other cats and never purred; and Crow, a black cat. Crow was fit, above average size, and a mouser. She left dead mice in my sister's bed, which displeased my sister, because Crow first bit out the eyes. Crow did not curl up in anyone's lap. But she slept on my elder niece's bed most nights.

Wildfires burned throughout the Monashee Mountains that fall; though it was now December, there'd been no snow. Rather than disappearing, bears, lynxes, and coyotes foraged in the developments, thinking it still time to fatten up. Patches was eaten next. One evening, she sneaked past the yard's edge when no one was looking, probably to investigate a mouse smell, and never came back.

My sister made a new rule: no cats outside.

But two weeks later Simmy, the Siamese who fought other cats, sped past my brother-in-law one night as he opened the door to the deck. When he lunged for her, she slipped into the forest. My sister's family walked the woods until midnight, calling her name.

When I arrived in Revelstoke for the holiday, everyone was still shell-shocked about the cat deaths. My elder niece, Adira, a pale, black-haired tomboy, would occasionally mutter, "We shouldn't have let her out"—about Clara or Patches, I guess—and my sister would say that if she hadn't been able to go out at *all* she wouldn't have been happy; and my niece would say, "But she'd be *alive*"; and so forth.

My sister's house was large—its kitchen opened to a dining area and a "circle room" with a fifty-foot solar-panelled glass dome—but contained few rooms. So I was given my elder niece's second-floor bedroom, my brothers shared my younger niece's room, and our mother and our uncle took the sleeper couch in the library, on whose carpet Crow often peed.

Because we were aware of the traumatic cat deaths, we all behaved well, even me, and when our uncle knelt down and spread his arms wide and said to my nieces, "Come give Uncle D a kiss!" and I had to watch my nieces tense up, walk stiffly toward him, and let him grab their faces and kiss their lips, I didn't say anything. I just smiled widely and continued to behave, that afternoon, by not eating any gumdrops while my family spent several hours baking and constructing the gingerbread mansion, and we all felt, I think, good after the mansion was completed. It was late afternoon on December 23rd, and I probably never would have instituted the Kamikaze Training if it hadn't been for what happened *after* the gingerbread mansion was finished, which was that we all went for a walk in the woods.

The fires hadn't reached Revelstoke. The ground in the forest was a soft red-and-bronze carpet of pine needles, and the fields around the forest were gold brush. Revelstoke is set beside a river formed by glaciers circled by six-thousand-foot-high craggy mountains, and the sky above was velveteen blue. We were all breathing hard, laughing, running along the forest path when my younger niece giggled, pointed to an opening in the pines, and said, "What's that thing?" and ran off the path, and my mother said, "Lily, be careful, don't touch it," but she was touching it, and it turned out to be Simmy. The cat's mouth was open, her gums shrunk, her teeth exposed, her tan torso gutted. My brother-in-law wrapped the cat remainder in dead leaves and carried it home, and then he and my uncle worked for an hour to dig a hole in the frozen back yard.

We all felt, I think, eager to bring calm back to Christmas, so after dinner my brother-in-law went to bathe, as did my mother; my sister took refuge in doing dishes; my brothers and my younger niece played Super Mario Kart together on one living-room couch; and, on the other, my elder niece, Adira, read a book, one of her easy-readers, "Ramona Quimby, Age 8." My uncle entered the room, still dirty from digging the cat-hole, and said kindly, "Adira, would you like a foot rub?" and the girl tensed and a small "Nnnneh" sound came out of her mouth, and my uncle sat down next to her and began rubbing her feet.

I felt the Bartonella bacteria in my head move. They had been fed when I ate my dinner of chicken and broccoli. I'd been careful not to eat a speck of sugar, but even the carbohydrates in broccoli could feed them. I felt them grow strong and say to me, "There's a gingerbread house on the counter. Its frosting is sugar and cream, it's soft and warm, you can eat some!"

Meanwhile, Adira sat stiffly, staring at her book but not reading; my uncle had pulled her legs onto his lap and was kneading her calves. I sat in a leather chair nearby, not reading, either, because I heard the Bartonella bacteria yelling, "Sugar! Sugar!" I don't know how many minutes passed before my sister asked our uncle, from the kitchen, whether Adira had said that she wanted a foot rub. Our uncle answered, in a soothing, asset-management-specialist's voice, Yes, she had; my sister responded in a clipped voice that she thought she'd heard my niece say, "Nnnneh." Our uncle continued to rub my niece's feet, and then my sister said angrily to my niece that she needed help in the kitchen, and Adira put her book down and walked into the kitchen without looking right or left and said quietly, "What do you want me to do?"

My sister said, "Dry these dishes."

Our uncle went downstairs to shower, and I helped do dishes, too, because sugar was in the kitchen—and not just the gingerbread house. In the cupboards, I knew, there were Mint Milano cookies. Full dark pulsed outside the sliding glass doors to the deck, and a coyote yip-yip-yip-yipped in the woods. When my sister looked over her shoulder through the dark glass, I just dipped my finger into the gingerbread mansion's white trim. From the living room, my brothers saw me do it, and one told me loudly not to eat the mansion with my fingers, because that was gross and others would get my germs, but Bartonella said, "Ignore him. Do again." And so I finger-dipped again, and the other twin yelled that I was disgusting and was destroying the mansion, and that hurt my feelings and made me angry, so that before my sister went to bed I cornered her in the empty kitchen and told her that I did not think my nieces felt comfortable when our uncle kissed their lips, and that we should stop it. My sister, in a stretched voice, reminded me that grand-uncles kissing grand-nieces was normal, and that she'd spoken to a professional family counsellor about correct procedures in these cases, and the real me said, "O.K.," but Bartonella me, who was larger than me and lived outside me, said, "Not O.K."

My sister added that she was the mother.

The real me said, "I know."

But Bartonella me said, "You are the mother. Big deal. I am the godmother!"

The counsellor had warned her, my sister said, that telling her daughters our concerns would damage their psychological development, and that the issue must never be addressed.

My sister said, "*Promise* you won't say anything about Uncle D to the girls," and the real me said, "O.K.," and she said, "*Also*, don't bring up the fact that Kunda's trying to conceive when Kunda comes over—it's *secret*," and I said, "I won't," but Bartonella said, "Eat sugar."

The only notable thing about Kunda, besides that she was a hot, nice, Hindi immigrant who had put herself through college by waitressing, is that she worshipped her husband, a pimply blond government secretary in her department. She met him when she was thirty-seven, and after they started dating she told me, "I love him." I said, "Really? He's so ugly, pink-faced, and blond," and she said, "He's a good one, a keeper." She always worked the same schedule as he, so that no other female official could "get him." For the past five years, apparently, she'd been failing to have his baby, owing to "mystery infertility," and was racked by shame.

At 3 A.M. I woke and ate half the gingerbread mansion. I'm not proud of that, but I do blame it for the rest of the story.

At 7 A.M., I awakened dizzy, wanting more sugar, already tasting it in my mouth. When I entered the barely lit circle room and found Adira alone, playing Super Mario Kart on a couch, it was Bartonella who said, "Kamikaze Training."

On the loft stairs, the large black cat, Crow, curled and watched. Beside my niece, the fat brown cat, Chocolate, licked its rear.

My niece paused her game and said, "What?" and Bartonella explained that I'd pay her to say a few phrases. The real me remembered my sister's warning, but Bartonella said, "The therapist's wrong."

Bartonella felt that our difference of opinion stemmed from the previous holiday, at our uncle's Texas ranch, when my sister hadn't seen what I had. Christmas night, she'd played backgammon with most of our family in the living room; I'd wandered the house looking for a quiet place to read, and gone into the dark den, where we'd all watched a movie earlier. She hadn't seen my elder niece asleep on her belly on the couch—or feigning sleep—and our uncle seated behind her, massaging her ass. She hadn't had to think, Christ, why me? or notice that my niece's tiny hands were clenched. I'd told my niece I had a present for her upstairs, and she'd vaulted up and run with me to my bedroom, where I gave her an old rubber eraser; I'd got her out of there, but like a thousand-per-cent wuss I said nothing to my uncle. Later I told my sister what had happened, said we should do something, and she said we'd be more vigilant. But she hadn't seen what I had.

So, about fifteen feet from the couch, I squatted down in the posture that our uncle always adopted when he spread his arms and said, "Come give Uncle D a kiss," and I informed my niece that I was going to tell her to give me a kiss, and that she should respond by saying she didn't feel like giving me one, and that if she followed my instructions I'd pay her a dollar.

My niece started playing her game again.

I said, "I'll pay you a dollar!"

She smiled a little. She said, "Aunt D, do you know what my allowance is?"

I said, "Five dollars?"

She shook her head.

Her hand waved upward.

I said, "Is your allowance *ten* dollars?"

Guiltily, she nodded.

On the screen, she leaped over a mushroom.

She whispered, "I don't want to say it."

I knelt in his posture, I opened my arms the way he did, and I growled in his voice, being careful not to be so loud I'd wake everybody, "Come give me a kiss!"

Her eyes were wide.

I said, "Now you say, 'I don't feel kissy.' I'll pay you ten dollars."

On the stairs, Crow got up. Her black pupils went large.

On the couch, my niece shook her head.

Bartonella exhorted my niece to say it. If she can't say it she's a sucker, Bartonella said. If she can't say it she's doomed.

My niece said she didn't want to say it.

I kept exhorting. I offered her the choice of two phrases—"I don't feel kissy right now" or "No thanks, I must go clean my room"—and was telling her again that I'd pay her ten dollars, when my niece started breathing as if she couldn't get enough air. Her posture wasn't good; she'd hunched.

She whispered, "It's too scary."

My real self said, Stop, you're being a jerk, you made her cry, jerk; but Bartonella said, Someone's gotta train her.

Bartonella said, "Adira, if you say it, I'll buy you a ruby necklace."

She looked at me.

I added, "And matching earrings."

I knew from experience that one could buy a "real" ruby necklace and earrings on eBay for ten dollars.

My niece looked down. Wiped her cheek. Said, "O.K."

Crow licked her right paw. She stared at me.

I squatted down and said in my uncle's voice, "*Come* give me a *kiss*!"

She breathed shallowly, and whispered in a high, artificial voice, "I don't feel—"; Chocolate farted, a smell of cheese/egg filled the room, and at that second my uncle walked in and yelled, "Hellooo! What's everybody doing?"

He paused, sniffed.

Crow's tail whipped.

I said, "Nothing"; Adira said, "Nothing."

My sister entered behind my uncle and announced that she'd found a mouse by her bed. She held it up by the tail. Its paws dangled. Where its eyes had been were deep holes. She stared at Crow and said, "Crow, I *don't* want you to do this again." Crow's head lifted. She closed and reopened her eyes, then stood, stretched, and padded up the loft stairs. My sister watched her go. Then she saw my niece's face. She looked at me. Her brow furrowed. She asked my niece why she was crying. Was it something Aunt D had said? Bartonella said, "Ohnoooyourefucked!!!!!!!!!!!!!!!" and my niece said calmly, "I was remembering Simmy." Then my *sister* started crying, and I did, too—for fun and because I wanted sugar so bad—and my niece re-started her video game and my uncle baked us all cinnamon buns for breakfast.

That afternoon, in preparation for guests, we made forty dozen sugar cookies in the shape of jingle bells, angels, and snowmen. My sister watched me eat three, and said carefully, "Drip your I.V. yet?" and I said, "Yeah," although I had not, and decorating cookies was so much fun that everyone got along well up until the tragedy.

It's hard to describe one family frosting cookies, or maybe not worth the effort, but: picture bowls with colored frosting on a kitchen island. Picture my younger niece, a round-faced, brown-eyed six-year-old in a loose red dress sitting on a stool at the island; across from her was my mother, a plump sixty-something Swede with blond hair and a puffy, sad face, bent over giving directions like "Use pink for the bell, Lily," and "Why don't you put three Red Hots on the holly?" I was also frosting, beside my younger niece, only I was creating, using colored jimmies, bespoke snowmen who resembled family members; I'd secretly frosted an extra bump onto one and given it curly black licorice hair to make it represent a pregnant Kunda. Outside the kitchen's sliding glass doors, the sun shone upon golden-brown grass; it was fifty degrees; everyone was happy. My sister laid wheat noodles in vats for lasagna; her husband dumped sixteen cans of corn syrup into four mixing bowls to make eight pecan pies; my elder niece sat across from me, cutting cookies into squares and icing them yellow to resemble SpongeBob; our uncle, a handsome, red-haired retired asset-management specialist in his mid-sixties who loved to ride horses, build furniture, and collect antique books, sat on my younger niece's other side and frosted cookies as best he could, without particular imagination, slabbing pink on a heart and yellow on a bell, and holding it up for everyone and saying, "Hey, guys. I did a bell. See?" From time to time he dropped his butter knife, and when he did he'd say, "Whoops, I dropped my butter knife," and get down and crawl around underneath my younger niece's stool; at which my niece, whose bare legs dangled from her dress, giggled nervously. Then our uncle would pop over to the sink, near where my sister was working, and say, "Excuse me, my knife's dirty. I'm going to wash it." He dropped his knife five times, I guess.

I know, K, that you'll protest that that's not realistic: how can a man drop a butter knife five times? I'm sorry to say that it's easy—the fingers spread, the knife drops. And you bet that part of me observed the proceedings and thought, This is crazy, I'm going to kill something, I'm gonna tear down *walls* or some shit! But the rational me thought, So he crawls under her stool, maybe sees panties, so what? Respect your sister's wishes. Everybody wants a peaceful Christmas.

Also, I was distracted by the fact that my sister was preparing wheat-based lasagna for dinner: my sister and my elder niece had both had Lyme disease, and were warned by doctors never to eat dairy (mucus-forming), soy (goitrogenic), or wheat, which spiked blood sugar, caused inflammation, and depressed the immune system. I knew that I was not supposed to criticize my sister's food choices, because she'd told me not to, but the third time our uncle dropped his butter knife I felt my frustration surge, and said, "Nina, why can't we make chicken stir-fry? You're not supposed to eat wheat!" and my sister replied that guests were arriving, and everyone liked lasagna, and I said, "They might like *gluten-free* lasagna," and she said that *no one* liked gluten-free lasagna, and added that normally she did not eat lasagna, but today was Christmas Eve, she was making it, and I needed to lay off her food choices, and outside a V of fat geese floated through the slate sky, and I thought wistfully how, if I could muscle-test Kunda to identify the supplements that would best replenish her iodine and support her adrenals, I could get her pregnant, and our uncle's butter knife clattered and he said, "Whoops! I'm clumsy!" and crawled under my younger niece's chair and the kid's legs kicked, and I *knew* I shouldn't say anything, I knew I shouldn't cause trouble, but I felt dizzy. I saw Crow, who was crouched on the loft stairs, shimmer and float above and beside herself, as if she were three cats, and I yelled, "But I see that you have wheat *bread* on your counter!" and my sister said coldly, "That's for the girls," and I said, "But *they* shouldn't eat wheat either—it's a Frankenfood!" and I was describing wheat's thyroid-hampering properties when my sister turned to our mother, who was petting Chocolate, and said, "Mother, I *said* don't pet Chocolate, *stop*!"

Our mother was allergic to most animals. But my sister's reprimand probably hurt her feelings, so she ushered my nieces into the circle room and told them a Jesus story. One about his entering a town and healing a blind man by spitting on his eyes. As our mother spoke, my sister banged pots and pans. Our mother always loved Christ, but she probably loved him more after her husband died and she was left broke, not fully bipolar but not right in the head, with four kids age six and under. She prayed to Jesus for help, and later that week our father's older brother, a confirmed bachelor and an asset-management specialist, offered to let her bring us all to his ranch and live with him, and to send her kids to college. To thank him, our mother cleaned and cooked for our uncle and the arrangement worked out, mostly. To thank God, she attended church twice weekly and spoke with Jesus for an hour every day.

From the kitchen, my sister ordered our mother to stop proselytizing; our mother kept speaking. Her voice was sweet in a way it rarely was. Our mother loved Jesus. I didn't condemn her. Personally, I agreed that many Jewish guys were extra-talented, kind, and good with touch, and I'd had "relationships" with emotionally distant, mostly unavailable Jewish guys myself, so I sympathized; my older sister did not.

When my sister repeated her request, our mother yelled, "*Then* Jesus asked, 'What do you see?' and the blind man said, 'I see *people*! They look like *trees*, walking around!' " and, temper shot, my sister ordered my nieces to play in their rooms.

Everyone slumped in the living room. Our uncle asked who wanted to go for a walk; no one did. Our mother sneezed. Our uncle said, "I guess I'll go by myself, then!" and left. We all read—my siblings books, my mother a magazine called *Real Simple*. The bells' carol played and the tree's lights twinkled. I was reading a biography of my favorite writer, who at forty-five begged Stalin to be allowed to finish his work before he was shot by a firing squad, when we heard a *thump thump thump* in the hall.

"What's that?" one of my brothers said.

"I don't know," my sister said.

We heard shrieks and giggles.

"Jump!" a voice cried.

We entered the hall and saw that my nieces had used their old tights to affix a coyote to the bannister. It was a donkey piñata, really; but they'd glued red-brown felt to it and taped coyote ears to its head. They'd cut holes where the donkey eyes had been, and in the holes they'd taped Doritos. My elder niece dangled a cat toy on a wire and made its attractive end bounce near the Doritos. Chocolate panted and lunged at the toy madly, fatly, his belly heaving. But each time he failed to reach it and fell with a thump. Crow watched from the top of the stairs.

Adira peered at her.

"Crow!" she urged. "Get it! Come!"

My sister asked what they were doing.

Adira muttered.

My sister said, "'Kamikaze Cat Training'???"

"We're teaching them to fight coyotes."

Her blue-black hair flared, tangled, around her shoulders.

"We'd train Crow," Adira said, "but she won't come near Chocolate. He bullies her and she's scared."

"First of all," my sister said, "that's not a coyote. It's a donkey. Chocolate does not see a coyote. He sees Doritos." Cats were not smart, she said. Cats were dumb. Crow was not being trained. She was watching the girls act stupid. No cat could kill a coyote. Furthermore, no cat was in danger, because no cat was ever going outside.

My sister said that she needed help in the kitchen, and told my nieces to clean up their mess.

I'm sure other families have fallen into bad holiday moods over similarly trivial incidents.

But I felt a sadness. I couldn't knock it; I don't know why. At any rate, I had to contemplate the prospect of my family eating wheat lasagna, which had goitrogenic effects; though, regarding that, they didn't believe me. My family found my health ideas absurd. My brothers, both dentists, had told me that my nutritionist work should be illegal, because only doctors are qualified to dispense supplements; my sister said that I'd never make rent as a nutritionist, and that I should give up. I was forbidden to offer Kunda the most commonsense advice. I considered, still with wonder, my clients who'd got pregnant: a dozen women in their mid-forties who had each had three failed I.V.F. treatments before they did protocols with me. Many had had repeat miscarriages, several had ovarian cysts, and all had tried unsuccessfully for years; but once we had replenished their minerals, supported their thyroid and adrenals, used herbs to balance their hormones, and changed their diets, they'd all conceived. They'd all had healthy, non-retarded babies. They'd sent me referrals, but not enough. My sister was right: I couldn't pay my bills. I'd spent a few hundred bucks on Google AdWords, but I made bad ads and they didn't work. My Web site was ugly. I'd had some unsatisfied clients, old ladies who'd gained weight instead of losing it, and they'd Yelped me, calling me a quack. I thought about how, if I helped Kunda, I'd have a district medical officer's Yelp endorsement, and how many clients that'd get me. I didn't give a fig about Kunda's sensitivity; I was dizzy, from actual dizziness or from grandiosity; I thought, So what if my degree's an Internet diploma?

I was slicing onions when I noticed, beyond the kitchen's glass doors, my mother standing in the back yard, staring contemplatively into the distant pines, under that pale vast Shuswap sky.

My sister said, "What's she doing?"

We wandered toward the glass—my sister and I, her husband, my nieces behind him—and saw that my mother was watching Chocolate, who was hunched privately at yard's edge, depositing number twos into the grass; as we observed, a handsome coyote the size of a large dog, but more yellow-gray and with a long narrow snout, strolled into the yard, bent down to Chocolate as if to whisper in his ear, and bit his throat. It pulled, ripping flesh, and the cat convulsed. The coyote plucked up Chocolate's body and trotted into the trees.

All I remember of the ensuing chaos is my sister's husband shouting in a high, almost teen-age voice, "You weren't supposed to let the cat out! Why'd you let the cat out? You weren't supposed to do that!"

Apparently, our mother had thought the cats were still allowed outside to use the bathroom at dusk. She was watching Chocolate, she explained. "I was *right there*," she said.

We had thirty minutes until our guests arrived.

I dripped medicine in my room. I'd put it off because there's a thing called a Herxheimer reaction: when you kill thousands of bacteria the remaining billions heighten their activity. I often hallucinated after dripping. I disliked feeling cold fluid slide through my veins. Also, inserting tubes into my arm-port was embarrassing and I tried to do it privately, so as not to repulse my family. Now I had to make a sixty-minute I.V. drip in thirty, so the pressure was high. I was lying on my bed, feeling logy, when the door swung open. A second later, Crow jumped onto the bed. A minute later, a hand tapped the door; Adira asked to enter.

I said it was her room.

She was wearing her gray track pants and a SpongeBob T-shirt. She hopped onto the bed and lay to my left. She asked what I was doing; I said I was dripping; she nodded. She'd been "tick sick," so she knew what it was. She reached across me to pet Crow; Crow let her. She read her book, then said, "I don't want Crow to die," into the pillow. I told her not to be stupid; she said, "Someone will let her outside, I know it," and I said, "You're being stupid" and she said, "*You're* stupid," and I said, "You're stupid like SpongeBob" and she said, "SpongeBob's awesome, I love SpongeBob!" and I swore that no one would let Crow out. Then I looked to my right and saw an old woman, as dark as night, bent and withered but still strong and smiling grimly. She had sharp teeth and yellow eyes, and was crouching. I jumped. My niece asked why I'd jumped. I explained that I'd dripped too fast. My niece said reasonably, "Why don't you slow it down?" and I said because we had guests coming. I wiped my eyes, gook came out; I looked at my fingers, they'd puffed like sausages. My niece asked what I'd got her for Christmas, and I said something cheap and small, which was true.

She smiled and said, "I bet I like it."

I said, "Listen, tardface, no one's letting Crow outside."

We slept.

The thing with nieces, K, is that they just happen. You may be a broke, semi-jobless loser who's never loved, hates kids, and is repelled by marriage, and suddenly your successful sibling may have these things: babies that look like you and know your name. And there's nothing you can do. I remember this one time, the year I took a job in Vancouver (the worst place on earth) to be near my sister, and she drove down to visit with her husband and my nieces, Lily still a baby, Adira then two, this wild fast skinny thing with an elf face and ebony hair, and we hiked through Lighthouse Park, along a trail that wound two miles through thousand-year-old cedars and descended steeply to an inlet called Starboat Cove, and my niece ran its length but on the way back got tired, and I asked if she wanted a piggy-back ride. I probably said, "Smellface, want a ride?" and she said, "Yes!" and my older sister got an odd look and asked my niece, "Do you want *me* to give you a piggy-back ride?"; there was a pause, these white clouds moved in the perfect sky above the cove, the ocean smacked saltily, fishily on the rocks below our feet, and my niece composed her face as if contemplating how to put things; I knew my sister would always be her one love—we all knew that—but she said, in her breathy two-year-old voice, "Sometimes when your heart is big, all you really want is Aunt D," and I was, like, "Great, I'm fucked, I'm going to like this kid, this niece thing, forever."

We'd slept through dinner. I was glad, because I'd decided to starve myself in order to starve the Bartonella. My sister offered me food and I declined, though ravenous. I saw by the remnants on the counter that my family had consumed ten pans of buttered squash, twelve loaves of bread, and eight vats of lasagna. I was surprised but didn't dwell on it. Holidays make people hungry. My relatives are fit and they exercise and have good metabolisms. However, the sight of ricotta droppings made me nauseous, and when I pulled the trash compactor out from the counter I saw thousands of silverfish sliding atop squash peels. My stomach rolled; they sparkled and slithered. I closed the drawer. My sister asked what was wrong; I said nothing, opened the trash, saw only squash rinds. I helped carry eight pecan pies into the circle room, where relatives were settling into couches, and a strange thing happened, or I guess not so strange, when you consider that I'd dripped my I.V. too fast; instead of my beloved family and pleasant in-laws gathered around the tree, sitting on the circle room's several couches, I saw animals. My sister's father-in-law, a witty, retired postal worker who was now making well-deserved cash selling disaster insurance, was a wily wild boar, wearing plaid pants, a blue polo, and a bow tie, with a bald boar's head and bristles coming out of his large tan ears. He was telling my brother-in-law—a timid giraffe in a blue T-shirt, with two hooves poking out of each jean leg—about some fire/tornado/hurricane packages he'd sold in new developments, and his snout nodded as his maw said, "Went like hotcakes."

My sister's mother-in-law, in real life a beautiful textile designer, was a kangaroo, her soft brown legs splayed on the couch, knitting next to my younger niece, who looked up at her adoringly; my sister, I'm sorry to say—don't think badly of me, blame the Bartonella—was a Chihuahua who went yipping around the room bringing everyone a slice of pie by carrying each plate in her mouth, and whenever her mouth was free she'd yip, "How are you? We have mulled wine!" Everyone was talking happily. The kangaroo told my sister in a warbly voice, while stroking her pelt with one paw, that she and her husband had coyotes in their back yard, too, and had kept their cats inside for years now; she looked over to the boar, who was adjusting his bow tie, and said, "Greg's thinking of shooting some! Good money for the pelts!" and my sister panted and yipped, "Let's not talk about that right now! I don't want to upset the girls! It's Christmas!" and the kangaroo said, "Of course!" and my mother, a flushed potbellied pig who wore a pink velour dress and was seated next to a hairy gentleman with dark fur and a fedora, snorted, "Marianne, how are your fair-trade scarves doing? Are your scarves in a department store?" and all these people—or animals, I have no idea—were eating pecan pie. I knew I was hallucinating, but the part I felt sure was real was that they were consuming eight pies, and the Chihuahua yipped, "Cassandra! Do you want a piece, maybe a small one?"

I shook my head. I knew she didn't want me to eat it, even when she offered me the plate in her mouth, because her tail flattened and her mouth growled, so I declined and the Chihuahua said, "Adira? Pie?" and my niece, beside me on the couch, accepted. As she ate, a hairy orangutan with a big pink nose and beady eyes, who in real life was her uncle, the secretary, gnashed his teeth from across the room and said, "Adira, you've gotten taller! If you eat another bite of pie, you'll be taller than your mother!" and the Chihuahua jumped up and down angrily and said, "Nononono, not yet!" and a beautiful gray-skinned elephant wearing a purple sari, seated on the couch beside the orangutan, touched his shoulder with her trunk, and her gray lips said, "She's got another year before she'll catch her mother," and, beside me, my niece grinned.

I don't know, K, why my inflamed brain turned my district medical officer sister-in-law, a tall Hindi woman with wide cheeks and curly black hair, into an elephant—I think it was the association of elephants and Hinduism, plus I'm racist. At any rate, all was well. I'd accepted that I was hallucinating and decided to retire, pleading illness, when the Chihuahua declared it time for the *most important* Christmas Eve tradition: everyone must open one gift from under the tree; both my nieces exclaimed "Yay!" and in the ensuing pause the hairy gentleman across the room, who wore a fedora and a gray suit and had gray fur on his chin, appraised my elder niece and said, "Adira, you look very attractive this evening."

No one spoke. The kangaroo frowned and her needles paused; the potbellied pig turned pinker. I felt my niece push backward, into the couch. I thought, Ah well, it's *done*. I don't know why I thought that, except that suddenly I tasted corn syrup, lard, and stale pecans in my mouth; I don't know who put them there. The Chihuahua yipped, "Uncle D! You should compliment Lily! *Lily* has a new dress on and a bow in her hair! *Adira's* wearing *old* track pants and a *dirty* T-shirt! Lily is the one who looks pretty!" The distinguished gentleman turned to my younger niece, who was now admiring her own dress, and said, "Lily, you also look very pretty."

Everyone observed my nieces.

As the pie sugar hit my blood I felt a surge of—adrenaline? neuron death? It was true about the track pants—for the last year, my elder niece had worn nothing but nylon track pants, because anything else bothered her skin. The word "skin" flashed through my mind as I considered this, and I felt wired, alert, crazed, and I saw the elephant across the room. Her gray skin was wrinkled, and as she peered at the grandfather clock in the hall I remembered that wrinkles indicate iodine deficiency, and that the elephant was trying to get pregnant, and I yelled, "Kunda, do you think lately you have wrinkles?"

The kangaroo frowned and said, "Everyone has wrinkles!"

The Chihuahua jumped up and down and said, "Yes, that was rude! Everyone has wrinkles!"

I was implementing a business strategy from a book called "How to Master the Art of Selling," whereby you ask your potential clients questions they're bound to say "yes" to. You start with something easy, like "It's a nice day out, isn't it?" and keep going. Once they get in the pattern of saying "Yes," they can't stop—that's the idea. I knew certain things about Kunda, because she was a woman suffering from infertility, plus she was an elephant, so I said, "Kunda, I suspect your body temperature's low. Do you often feel cold?"

The elephant stared at me. Her trunk curled down. She said, "I do feel cold often. Why?"

I looked at her gray, bald head and sad brown eyes. I said, "Kunda, your eyebrows are thinning at the outer edges, aren't they? In fact, I don't think you have eyebrows at all! Are you losing hair in the shower drain?"

The elephant's hooves went to her forehead. Her mouth dropped open.

The orangutan next to her frowned.

Everyone stared at me.

I thought, Yes!

I said, "Kunda, do you crave sugar in the afternoon? Salt? Caffeine?"

The elephant peered at me. Slowly she said, "Yes. Why?"

"Ignore her!" the Chihuahua yipped. "She's tick sick! She has Lyme disease!"

Beside me, my older niece said, "Aunt D, what are you doing?"

The kangaroo said that she didn't think this was a nice conversation.

I peered at the elephant, on the couch. "Kunda," I said. "You look big to me. Do you have belly fat? Are you having trouble losing weight?"

In reality, K, Kunda was slender. But I knew that women in their forties are paranoid about everything, and for no reason that I understand I was intent on showing Kunda that she was suffering from iodine deficiency.

I said, "You're cold and fat around your middle, right?"

The elephant nodded.

The orangutan yelled, "I won't stand for this! You're saying things that are totally inappropriate!" It came at me from across the room; I was afraid, in fact terrified, and my niece whispered, "Aunt D, stop," and I yelled, "Too bad, Kunda. Those are all symptoms of a deficiency in iodine, the mineral most essential for fertility. That's why you can't conceive!"

The orangutan stopped inches from me. "That's enough!" he said.

The elephant turned mauve. She rose clumsily and headed toward the kitchen.

I struggled to frame my closer as a "Yes" question. I yelled, "Kunda, if a cheap nutritionist in-law who charges cheap rates could help you fix these problems cheaply, you'd want help, wouldn't you?"

Suddenly it was done. Instead of an elephant I saw a lithe, forty-something Indian woman striding toward my sister's back door. She opened the door, closed it carefully behind her, and walked into the dark yard. My sister, not a Chihuahua but a tallish blond investment banker with great skin and runner's legs, twisted my right wrist. She said, "Everything you said is unacceptable."

Some of our relatives—our gray-suited uncle, his mouth curled as if a friend had told him a joke; our mother, in her pink velour dress; my sister's husband's parents, the ex-postal worker with his bald head and bristly black brows and his slope-faced, brown-eyed wife—stared at me, appalled, from a couch; on a love seat, one of my brothers leaned toward the other and whispered, "We might commit her; Nina will pay."

Beyond the glass dome of the circle room was clear black sky; under the Christmas tree sat mounds of gifts decked in sparkling gold-and-red paper and tied with organza ribbons.

I said, "I apologize."

I kept saying it.

My sister sighed and said that someone should go to Kunda; her husband said that he would, but my sister said, "No, let me." She walked through the kitchen, slid the heavy glass door open, and strode out. Behind her, the black cat sauntered across the kitchen tiles and out the door and into the grass. It padded left, past the swing set, and headed into the trees.

That's how we reëntered the forest, now frigid and pitch black. Though it was late, all of us lurched through the woods, calling the cat's name. My sister didn't own enough flashlights for everyone, so we searched in clusters and pairs. The trees were dark, still shapes; I heard twigs crack and people in distant places call the cat's name. It was terrible and no one spoke much, but at one point my sister ended up next to me, and said, "I don't want to discuss this evening right now, because I'm too upset, but . . ." She'd worked hard to make the holiday nice for everyone, she said, and to enable everyone to get along. She'd worked hard to make me happy, too, and it seemed that all I wanted to do was criticize her and make people upset; I wasn't myself, and she was curious—what had she done to me, to deserve this? And I was, like, Christ. I felt terrible. I knew she'd spent days shopping for gifts, party favors, groceries, stocking stuffers; she'd bought us all snow boards and ski passes—time she barely had, since she worked eighty hours a week at her banking job. She tried so hard and no one thanked her. "I'm so sorry," I said. "I didn't mean to, I'm sick—" and she said, "Don't use that excuse." She'd had Lyme disease, too, she said. Maybe she hadn't had Bartonella, but she'd had spirochetes in her nervous system, they'd affected her neurologically, and she hadn't acted like I was now; her throat caught. The real me felt ashamed and said, "You're right, I'm so sorry," but Bartonella heard her say, "Bartonella," and awakened. Bartonella me yelled, "You want to know why? Because I'm *pissed* at you, bitch!" and she gasped and asked how *dare* I call her that? And added that, truthfully, she was angry at me, too; I heard branches rustle and, distantly, someone call, "Who's there?" but, out of my head, I said, "Bring it on, bitch! Here's my chin!" I saw my sister frown and rear back. Then an immense fist like a sledgehammer punched my jaw.

I fell on my butt on the trail. An orange pain was my jaw and also the world. I had three faces and saw three sisters. It wasn't she who'd hit me—it was the orangutan. Rather, the secretary, Kunda's husband; I heard him say, "I've never punched anyone before, I was just so mad about what she said to Kunda," and my sister muttered, "Done is done," and the willowy black shadow of one of my brothers said, "She sort of . . ." and the other's said, "Deserved it," and the secretary touched my face and said, "No worries, it's not dislocated"; the others showed up, my nieces asked what happened, my sister's mouth opened and closed, as did the secretary's, and I said, "I fell and hit my jaw on a stone." My sister announced that we weren't finding Crow tonight and should go home. My nieces protested that we couldn't leave Crow, so my sister told them that she was probably hiding in a safe place in the forest, just waiting for daylight to come home.

Adira begged us to leave the sliding door open for the cat. My sister didn't want to wake up to raccoons in the kitchen, but my niece insisted. So my sister—who couldn't deny her daughters anything—said O.K.

. . .

The weird thing about blood-sugar issues is that they don't go away just because you've had a bad Christmas. I woke up at 3 A.M. The house was quiet. I guessed everyone was asleep. I figured I could sneak into the kitchen and eat half a pecan pie and no one would know. I entered the kitchen and found half a pecan pie, covered in foil, on the counter. I unwrapped it. I already tasted it in my mouth, even before eating it; that's the horrible thing. Stale pecans, wheat crust, lard, and corn syrup—I was desperate for it. Outside, it was coal-black. Cold wind blew through the open door. I stuck my finger in the pie and scooped out a big blob. The pecan-syrup blob was moving toward my mouth when I heard a high-pitched cry, outside in the yard. I felt afraid. I put the blob back in the pie tin, and stepped away; a black ball shot into the kitchen, moving toward me fast, uttering a high sound, once-cat, but it moved on its belly, pulled itself forward by using its front paws, which scraped madly, nails clicking, across the floor; it had no legs, only a head and a torso, it seemed to roll past me, it paused between the circle room and the kitchen and looked at me. It was Crow, but her back legs seemed to have disappeared—she was half a cat and her face looked gigantic, puffed to twice its size. I've never been so terrified of anything in my life, and nothing else has ever made me so sad as hearing that pitiful cry and seeing the cat with no hindquarters.

My sister appeared in the hall. "God," she said. "We have to get it out of here. I don't want the girls to see it, it will upset them—"

My elder niece appeared. She said simply, "The coyote ate her legs," and walked toward her cat, and my sister yelled, "Don't touch her! She's hurt, she may bite you," but the kid knelt by the cat and pressed her hand along its back; it didn't move, and my sister rushed forward to pull my niece away, but as soon as she neared the animal it opened its mouth, its enormous swollen face twitched, and it released two gelatinous orbs.

Once they came out, the cat's face became normal-sized. The whitish blobs slid across the floor—golf-ball size, like undercooked eggs with red tendrils. In one I could see the golden disk and the dark pupil.

My sister said, "What are those? Ugh!"

My niece said, "She got them."

. . .

Revelstoke is an unusual town. The veterinary clinic's reception contains Oriental rugs and damask couches, and the clinic stays open all night, even on Christmas. We took the cat in and they operated immediately, saving one hind leg, which had been folded behind her; the technicians weren't certain, but they said that the thighs appeared serrated by coyote's teeth, and all seven of them—there were seven technicians—said they'd never seen a cat get away from a coyote, and that it was a miracle that she was alive. We left the clinic at 6 A.M., the pet's remaining leg in a cast, and I'm sure you saw this coming, K, but the sky had grayed over, and, as we left the clinic and saw the firs on the distant mountains, down came white flakes, huge, far apart, as large as in picture books, the first of the year, and they fell onto our tongues, as if the earth were saying, "Jesus is Lord," or else, "Here is some snow," or just, "Global warming hasn't killed me yet, I'm alive."

A somewhat odd thing happened that morning. My sister, who stuck up for me when she was a kid, but whom no one stuck up for—ever, in any way—thanked our mother and uncle for coming, and told our uncle that he had to go.

Some say that those born between December 22nd and January 19th carry existential sadness within them. They say that Capricorns are at the end of their line; everything they want to do, they have to do within this life. Perhaps that's why they're stubborn plodders who'll trek step by tiny step to reach their goals. I'm a hundred per cent sure that, as a Russian Communist, K, you'll say that that's bunk, and that I should never mention astrology in a story again. For what it's worth, I write to you as one child of winter to another.

APOLLO

BY CHIMAMANDA NGOZI ADICHIE (2015)

Twice a month, like a dutiful son, I visited my parents in Enugu, in their small overfurnished flat that grew dark in the afternoon. Retirement had changed them, shrunk them. They were in their late eighties, both small and mahogany-skinned, with a tendency to stoop. They seemed to look more and more alike, as though all the years together had made their features blend and bleed into one another. They even smelled alike—a menthol scent, from the green vial of Vicks VapoRub they passed to each other, carefully rubbing a little in their nostrils and on aching joints. When I arrived, I would find them either sitting out on the veranda overlooking the road or sunk into the living-room sofa, watching Animal Planet. They had a new, simple sense of wonder. They marvelled at the wiliness of wolves, laughed at the cleverness of apes, and asked each other, "Ifukwa? Did you see that?"

They had, too, a new, baffling patience for incredible stories. Once, my mother told me that a sick neighbor in Abba, our ancestral home town, had vomited a grasshopper—a living, writhing insect, which, she said, was proof that wicked relatives had poisoned him. "Somebody texted us a picture of the grasshopper," my father said. They always supported each other's stories. When my father told me that Chief Okeke's young house help had mysteriously died, and the story around town was that the chief had killed the teen-ager and used her liver for moneymaking rituals, my mother added, "They say he used the heart, too."

Fifteen years earlier, my parents would have scoffed at these stories. My mother, a professor of political science, would have said "Nonsense" in her crisp manner, and my father, a professor of education, would merely have snorted, the stories not worth the effort of speech. It puzzled me that they had shed those old selves, and become the kind of Nigerians who told anecdotes about diabetes cured by drinking holy water.

Still, I humored them and half listened to their stories. It was a kind of innocence, this new childhood of old age. They had grown slower with the passing years, and their faces lit up at the sight of me and even their prying questions—"When will you give us a grandchild? When will you bring a girl to introduce to us?"—no longer made me as tense as before. Each time I drove away, on Sunday afternoons after a big lunch of rice and stew, I wondered if it would be the last time I would see them both alive, if before my next visit I would receive a phone call from one of them telling me to come right away. The thought filled me with a nostalgic sadness that stayed with me until I got back to Port Harcourt. And yet I knew that if I had a family, if I could complain about rising school fees as the children of their friends did, then I would not visit them so regularly. I would have nothing for which to make amends.

During a visit in November, my parents talked about the increase in armed robberies all over the east. Thieves, too, had to prepare for Christmas. My mother told me how a vigilante mob in Onitsha had caught some thieves, beaten them, and torn off their clothes—how old tires had been thrown over their heads like necklaces, amid shouts for petrol and matches, before the police arrived, fired shots in the air to disperse the crowd, and took the robbers away. My mother paused, and I waited for a supernatural detail that would embellish the story. Perhaps, just as they arrived at the police station, the thieves had turned into vultures and flown away.

"Do you know," she continued, "one of the armed robbers, in fact the ring leader, was Raphael? He was our houseboy years ago. I don't think you'll remember him."

I stared at my mother. "Raphael?"

"It's not surprising he ended like this," my father said. "He didn't start well."

My mind had been submerged in the foggy lull of my parents' storytelling, and I struggled now with the sharp awakening of memory.

My mother said again, "You probably won't remember him. There were so many of those houseboys. You were young."

But I remembered. Of course I remembered Raphael.

Nothing changed when Raphael came to live with us, not at first. He seemed like all the others, an ordinary-looking teen from a nearby village. The houseboy before him, Hyginus, had been sent home for insulting my mother. Before Hyginus was John, whom I remembered because he had not been sent away; he had broken a plate while washing it and, fearing my mother's anger, had packed his things and fled before she came home from work. All the houseboys treated me with the contemptuous care of people who disliked my mother. Please come and eat your food, they would say—I don't want trouble from Madam. My mother regularly shouted at them, for being slow, stupid, hard of hearing; even her bell-ringing, her thumb resting on the red knob, the shrillness searing through the house, sounded like shouting. How difficult could it be to remember to fry the eggs differently, my father's plain and hers with onions, or to put the Russian dolls back on the same shelf after dusting, or to iron my school uniform properly?

I was my parents' only child, born late in their lives. "When I got pregnant, I thought it was menopause," my mother told me once. I must have been around eight years old, and did not know what "menopause" meant. She had a brusque manner, as did my father; they had about them the air of people who were quick to dismiss others. They had met at the University of Ibadan, married against their families' wishes—his thought her too educated, while hers preferred a wealthier suitor—and spent their lives in an intense and intimate competition over who published more, who won at badminton, who had the last word in an argument. They often read aloud to each other in the evening, from journals or newspapers, standing rather than sitting in the parlor, sometimes pacing, as though about to spring at a new idea. They drank Mateus rosé—

that dark, shapely bottle always seemed to be resting on a table near them—and left behind glasses faint with reddish dregs. Throughout my childhood, I worried about not being quick enough to respond when they spoke to me.

I worried, too, that I did not care for books. Reading did not do to me what it did to my parents, agitating them or turning them into vague beings lost to time, who did not quite notice when I came and went. I read books only enough to satisfy them, and to answer the kinds of unexpected questions that might come in the middle of a meal—What did I think of Pip? Had Ezeulu done the right thing? I sometimes felt like an interloper in our house. My bedroom had bookshelves, stacked with the overflow books that did not fit in the study and the corridor, and they made my stay feel transient, as though I were not quite where I was supposed to be. I sensed my parents' disappointment in the way they glanced at each other when I spoke about a book, and I knew that what I had said was not incorrect but merely ordinary, uncharged with their brand of originality. Going to the staff club with them was an ordeal: I found badminton boring, the shuttlecock seemed to me an unfinished thing, as though whoever had invented the game had stopped halfway.

What I loved was kung fu. I watched "Enter the Dragon" so often that I knew all the lines, and I longed to wake up and be Bruce Lee. I would kick and strike at the air, at imaginary enemies who had killed my imaginary family. I would pull my mattress onto the floor, stand on two thick books—usually hardcover copies of "Black Beauty" and "The Water-Babies"—and leap onto the mattress, screaming "Haaa!" like Bruce Lee. One day, in the middle of my practice, I looked up to see Raphael standing in the doorway, watching me. I expected a mild reprimand. He had made my bed that morning, and now the room was in disarray. Instead, he smiled, touched his chest, and brought his finger to his tongue, as though tasting his own blood. My favorite scene. I stared at Raphael with the pure thrill of unexpected pleasure. "I watched the film in the other house where I worked," he said. "Look at this."

He pivoted slightly, leaped up, and kicked, his leg straight and high, his body all taut grace. I was twelve years old and had, until then, never felt that I recognized myself in another person.

. . .

Raphael and I practiced in the back yard, leaping from the raised concrete soakaway and landing on the grass. Raphael told me to suck in my belly, to keep my legs straight and my fingers precise. He taught me to breathe. My previous attempts, in the enclosure of my room, had felt stillborn. Now, outside with Raphael, slicing the air with my arms, I could feel my practice become real, with soft grass below and high sky above, and the endless space mine to conquer. This was truly happening. I could become a black belt one day. Outside the kitchen door was a high open veranda, and I wanted to jump off its flight of six steps and try a flying kick. "No," Raphael said. "That veranda is too high."

On weekends, if my parents went to the staff club without me, Raphael and I watched Bruce Lee videotapes, Raphael saying, "Watch it! Watch it!" Through his eyes, I saw the films anew; some moves that I had thought merely competent became luminous when he said, "Watch it!" Raphael knew what really mattered; his wisdom lay easy on his skin. He rewound the sections in which Bruce Lee used a nunchaku, and watched unblinking, gasping at the clean aggression of the metal-and-wood weapon.

"I wish I had a nunchaku," I said.

"It is very difficult to use," Raphael said firmly, and I felt almost sorry to have wanted one.

Not long afterward, I came back from school one day and Raphael said, "See." From the cupboard he took out a nunchaku—two pieces of wood, cut from an old cleaning mop and sanded down, held together by a spiral of metal springs. He must have been making it for at least a week, in his free time after his housework. He showed me how to use it. His moves seemed clumsy, nothing like Bruce Lee's. I took the nunchaku and tried to swing it, but only ended up with a thump on my chest. Raphael laughed. "You think you can just start like that?" he said. "You have to practice for a long time."

At school, I sat through classes thinking of the wood's smoothness in the palm of my hand. It was after school, with Raphael, that my real life began. My parents did not notice how close Raphael and I had become. All they saw was that I now happened to play outside, and Raphael was, of course, part of the landscape of outside: weeding the garden, washing pots at the water tank. One afternoon,

Raphael finished plucking a chicken and interrupted my solo practice on the lawn. "Fight!" he said. A duel began, his hands bare, mine swinging my new weapon. He pushed me hard. One end hit him on the arm, and he looked surprised and then impressed, as if he had not thought me capable. I swung again and again. He feinted and dodged and kicked. Time collapsed. In the end, we were both panting and laughing. I remember, even now, very clearly, the smallness of his shorts that afternoon, and how the muscles ran wiry like ropes down his legs.

On weekends, I ate lunch with my parents. I always ate quickly, dreaming of escape and hoping that they would not turn to me with one of their test questions. At one lunch, Raphael served white disks of boiled yam on a bed of greens, and then cubed pawpaw and pineapple.

"The vegetable was too tough," my mother said. "Are we grass-eating goats?" She glanced at him. "What is wrong with your eyes?"

It took me a moment to realize that this was not her usual figurative lambasting—"What is that big object blocking your nose?" she would ask, if she noticed a smell in the kitchen that he had not. The whites of Raphael's eyes were red. A painful, unnatural red. He mumbled that an insect had flown into them.

"It looks like Apollo," my father said.

My mother pushed back her chair and examined Raphael's face. "Ah-ah! Yes, it is. Go to your room and stay there."

Raphael hesitated, as though wanting to finish clearing the plates.

"Go!" my father said. "Before you infect us all with this thing."

Raphael, looking confused, edged away from the table. My mother called him back. "Have you had this before?"

"No, Madam."

"It's an infection of your conjunctiva, the thing that covers your eyes," she said. In the midst of her Igbo words, "conjunctiva" sounded sharp and dangerous. "We're going to buy medicine for you. Use it three times a day and stay in your room. Don't cook until it clears." Turning to me, she said, "Okenwa, make sure you don't go near him. Apollo is very infectious." From her perfunctory tone, it was clear that she did not imagine I would have any reason to go near Raphael.

Later, my parents drove to the pharmacy in town and came back with a bottle of eye drops, which my father took to Raphael's room in the boys' quarters, at the back of the house, with the air of someone going reluctantly into battle. That evening, I went with my parents to Obollo Road to buy akara for dinner; when we returned, it felt strange not to have Raphael open the front door, not to find him closing the living-room curtains and turning on the lights. In the quiet kitchen, our house seemed emptied of life. As soon as my parents were immersed in themselves, I went out to the boys' quarters and knocked on Raphael's door. It was ajar. He was lying on his back, his narrow bed pushed against the wall, and turned when I came in, surprised, making as if to get up. I had never been in his room before. The exposed light bulb dangling from the ceiling cast sombre shadows.

"What is it?" he asked.

"Nothing. I came to see how you are."

He shrugged and settled back down on the bed. "I don't know how I got this. Don't come close."

But I went close.

"I had Apollo in Primary 3," I said. "It will go quickly, don't worry. Have you used the eye drops this evening?"

He shrugged and said nothing. The bottle of eye drops sat unopened on the table.

"You haven't used them at all?" I asked.

"No."

"Why?"

He avoided looking at me. "I cannot do it."

Raphael, who could disembowel a turkey and lift a full bag of rice, could not drip liquid medicine into his eyes. At first, I was astonished, then amused, and then moved. I looked around his room and was struck by how bare it was—the bed pushed against the wall, a spindly table, a gray metal box in the corner, which I assumed contained all that he owned.

"I will put the drops in for you," I said. I took the bottle and twisted off the cap.

"Don't come close," he said again.

I was already close. I bent over him. He began a frantic blinking.

"Breathe like in kung fu," I said.

I touched his face, gently pulled down his lower left eyelid, and dropped the liquid into his eye. The other lid I pulled more firmly, because he had shut his eyes tight.

"Ndo," I said. "Sorry."

He opened his eyes and looked at me, and on his face shone something wondrous. I had never felt myself the subject of admiration. It made me think of science class, of a new maize shoot growing greenly toward light. He touched my arm. I turned to go.

"I'll come before I go to school," I said.

In the morning, I slipped into his room, put in his eye drops, and slipped out and into my father's car, to be dropped off at school.

By the third day, Raphael's room felt familiar to me, welcoming, uncluttered by objects. As I put in the drops, I discovered things about him that I guarded closely: the early darkening of hair above his upper lip, the ringworm patch in the hollow between his jaw and his neck. I sat on the edge of his bed and we talked about "Snake in the Monkey's Shadow." We had discussed the film many times, and we said things that we had said before, but in the quiet of his room they felt like secrets. Our voices were low, almost hushed. His body's warmth cast warmth over me.

He got up to demonstrate the snake style, and afterward, both of us laughing, he grasped my hand in his. Then he let go and moved slightly away from me.

"This Apollo has gone," he said.

His eyes were clear. I wished he had not healed so quickly.

I dreamed of being with Raphael and Bruce Lee in an open field, practicing for a fight. When I woke up, my eyes refused to open. I pried my lids apart. My eyes burned and itched. Each time I blinked, they seemed to produce more pale ugly fluid that coated my lashes. It felt as if heated grains of sand were under my eyelids. I feared that something inside me was thawing that was not supposed to thaw.

My mother shouted at Raphael, "Why did you bring this thing to my house? Why?" It was as though by catching Apollo he had conspired to infect her son. Raphael did not respond. He never did when she shouted at him. She was standing at the top of the stairs, and Raphael was below her.

"How did he manage to give you Apollo from his room?" my father asked me.

"It wasn't Raphael. I think I got it from somebody in my class," I told my parents.

"Who?" I should have known my mother would ask. At that moment, my mind erased all my classmates' names.

"Who?" she asked again.

"Chidi Obi," I said finally, the first name that came to me. He sat in front of me and smelled like old clothes.

"Do you have a headache?" my mother asked.

"Yes."

My father brought me Panadol. My mother telephoned Dr. Igbokwe. My parents were brisk. They stood by my door, watching me drink a cup of Milo that my father had made. I drank quickly. I hoped that they would not drag an armchair into my room, as they did every time I was sick with malaria, when I would wake up with a bitter tongue to find one parent inches from me, silently reading a book, and I would will myself to get well quickly, to free them.

Dr. Igbokwe arrived and shined a torch in my eyes. His cologne was strong; I could smell it long after he'd gone, a heady scent close to alcohol that I imagined would worsen nausea. After he left, my parents created a patient's altar by my bed—on a table covered with cloth, they put a bottle of orange Lucozade, a blue tin of glucose, and freshly peeled oranges on a plastic tray. They did not bring the armchair, but one of them was home throughout the week that I had Apollo. They took turns putting in my eye drops, my father more clumsily than my mother, leaving sticky liquid running down my face. They did not know how well I could put in the drops myself. Each time they raised the bottle above my face, I remembered the look in Raphael's eyes that first evening in his room, and I felt haunted by happiness.

My parents closed the curtains and kept my room dark. I was sick of lying down. I wanted to see Raphael, but my mother had banned him from my room, as though he could somehow make my condition worse. I wished that he would come and see me. Surely he could pretend to be putting away a bedsheet, or bringing a bucket to the bathroom. Why didn't he come? He had not even said sorry to me. I strained to hear his voice, but the kitchen was too far away and his voice, when he spoke to my mother, was too low.

Once, after going to the toilet, I tried to sneak downstairs to the kitchen, but my father loomed at the bottom of the stairs.

"Kedu?" he asked. "Are you all right?"

"I want water," I said.

"I'll bring it. Go and lie down."

Finally, my parents went out together. I had been sleeping, and woke up to sense the emptiness of the house. I hurried downstairs and to the kitchen. It, too, was empty. I wondered if Raphael was in the boys' quarters; he was not supposed to go to his room during the day, but maybe he had, now that my parents were away. I went out to the open veranda. I heard Raphael's voice before I saw him, standing near the tank, digging his foot into the sand, talking to Josephine, Professor Nwosu's house help. Professor Nwosu sometimes sent eggs from his poultry, and never let my parents pay for them. Had Josephine brought eggs? She was tall and plump; now she had the air of someone who had already said goodbye but was lingering. With her, Raphael was different—the slouch in his back, the agitated foot. He was shy. She was talking to him with a kind of playful power, as though she could see through him to things that amused her. My reason blurred.

"Raphael!" I called out.

He turned. "Oh. Okenwa. Are you allowed to come downstairs?"

He spoke as though I were a child, as though we had not sat together in his dim room.

"I'm hungry! Where is my food?" It was the first thing that came to me, but in trying to be imperious I sounded shrill.

Josephine's face puckered, as though she were about to break into slow, long laughter. Raphael said something that I could not hear, but it had the sound of betrayal. My parents drove up just then, and suddenly Josephine and Raphael were roused. Josephine hurried out of the compound, and Raphael came toward me. His shirt was stained in the front, orangish, like palm oil from soup. Had my parents not come back, he would have stayed there mumbling by the tank; my presence had changed nothing.

"What do you want to eat?" he asked.

"You didn't come to see me."

"You know Madam said I should not go near you."

Why was he making it all so common and ordinary? I, too, had been asked not to go to his room, and yet I had gone, I had put in his eye drops every day.

"After all, you gave me the Apollo," I said.

"Sorry." He said it dully, his mind elsewhere.

I could hear my mother's voice. I was angry that they were back. My time with Raphael was shortened, and I felt the sensation of a widening crack.

"Do you want plantain or yam?" Raphael asked, not to placate me but as if nothing serious had happened. My eyes were burning again. He came up the steps. I moved away from him, too quickly, to the edge of the veranda, and my rubber slippers shifted under me. Unbalanced, I fell. I landed on my hands and knees, startled by the force of my own weight, and I felt the tears coming before I could stop them. Stiff with humiliation, I did not move.

My parents appeared.

"Okenwa!" my father shouted.

I stayed on the ground, a stone sunk in my knee. "Raphael pushed me."

"What?" My parents said it at the same time, in English. "What?"

There was time. Before my father turned to Raphael, and before my mother lunged at him as if to slap him, and before she told him to go pack his things and leave immediately, there was time. I could have spoken. I could have cut into that silence. I could have said that it was an accident. I could have taken back my lie and left my parents merely to wonder.

COLD LITTLE BIRD

BY BEN MARCUS (2015)

It started with bedtime. A coldness. A formality.

Martin and Rachel tucked the boy in, as was their habit, then stooped to kiss him good night.

"Please don't do that," he said, turning to face the wall.

They took it as teasing, flopped onto his bed to nuzzle and tickle him.

The boy turned rigid, endured the cuddle, then barked out at them, "I really don't like that!"

"Jonah?" Martin said, sitting up.

"I don't want your help at bedtime anymore," he said. "I'm not a baby. You have Lester. Go cuddle with him."

"Sweetheart," Rachel said. "We're not helping you. We're just saying good night. You like kisses, right? Don't you like kisses and cuddles? You big silly."

Jonah hid under the blankets. A classic pout. Except that he wasn't a pouter, he wasn't a hider. He was a reserved boy who generally took a scientific interest in the tantrums and emotional extravagances of other children, marvelling at them as though they were some strange form of street theatre.

Martin tried to tickle the blanketed lump of person that was his son. He didn't know what part of Jonah he was touching. He just dug at him with a stiff hand, thinking a laugh would come out, some sound of pleasure. It used to work. One stab of the finger and the kid exploded with giggles. But Jonah didn't speak, didn't move.

"We love you so much. You know?" Martin said. "So we like to show it. It feels good."

"Not to me. I don't feel that way."

"What way? What do you mean?"

They sat with him, perplexed, and tried to rub his back, but he'd rolled to the edge of the bed, nearly flattening himself against the wall.

"I don't love you," Jonah said.

"Oh, now," Martin said. "You're just tired. No need to say that sort of stuff. Get some rest."

"You told me to tell the truth, and I'm telling the truth. I. Don't. Love. You."

This happened. Kids tested their attachments. They tried to push you away to see just how much it would take to really lose you. As a parent, you took the blow, even sharpened the knife yourself before handing it to the little fiends, who stepped right up and plunged. Or so Martin had heard.

They hovered by Jonah's bed, assuring him that it had been a long day—although the day had been entirely unremarkable—and he would feel better in the morning.

Martin felt like a robot saying these things. He felt like a robot thinking them. There was nothing to do but leave the boy there, let him sleep it off.

Downstairs, they cleaned the kitchen in silence. Rachel was troubled or not, he couldn't tell, and it was better not to check. In some way, Martin was captivated. If he were Jonah, ten years old and reasonably smart, starting to sniff out the world and find his angle, this might be something worth exploring. Getting rid of the soft, warm, dumb providers who spun opportunity around you relentlessly, answering your every need. Good play, Jonah. But how do you follow such a strong, definitive opening move? What now?

Over the next few weeks, Jonah stuck by his statement, wandering through their lives like some prisoner of war who'd been trained not to talk. He endured his parents, leaving for school in the morning with scarcely a goodbye. Upon coming home, he put away his coat and shoes, did his homework without prompting. He helped himself to snacks, dragging a chair into the kitchen so that he could climb on the counter. He got his own glass, filling it with water at the sink. When he was done eating, he loaded his dishes in the dishwasher. Martin, working from home in the afternoons, watched all this, impressed but bothered. He kept offering to help, but Jonah always said that he was fine, he could handle it. At bedtime, Martin and Rachel still fussed over Lester, who, at six years old, regressed and babified himself in order to drink up the extra attention. Jonah insisted on saying good night with no kiss, no hug. He shut his door and disappeared every night at 8 P.M.

When Martin or Rachel caught Jonah's eye, the boy forced a smile at them. But it was so obviously fake. Could a boy his age do that?

"Of course," Rachel said. "You think he doesn't know how to pretend?"

"No, I know he can pretend. But this seems different. I mean, to have to pretend that he's happy to see us. First of all, what the fuck is he so upset about? And, second, it just seems so kind of . . . grownup. In the worst possible way. A fake smile. It's a tool one uses with strangers."

"Well, I don't know. He's ten. He has social skills. He can hide his feelings. That's not such an advanced thing to do."

Martin studied his wife.

"O.K., so you think everything's fine?"

"I think maybe he's growing up and you don't like it."

"And you like it? That's what you're saying? You like this?"

His voice had gone up. He had lost control for a minute there, and, as per motherfucking usual, it was a deal-breaker. Rachel put up her hand, and she was gone. From the other room, he heard her say, "I'm not going to talk to you when you're like this."

O.K., he thought. Goodbye. We'll talk some other time when I'm not like this, a.k.a. never.

Jonah, it turned out, reserved this behavior solely for his parents. A probing note to his teacher revealed nothing. He was fine in school, did not act withdrawn, had successfully led a team project on Antarctica, and seemed to run and play with his friends during recess. Run and play? What animal were they discussing here? Everybody loved Jonah was the verdict, along with some bullshit about how happy he seemed. "Seemed" was just the thing. Seemed! If you were an idiot who didn't know the boy, who had no grasp of human behavior.

At home, Jonah doted on his brother, read to him, played with him, even let Lester climb on his back for rides around the house, all fairly verboten in the old days, when Jonah's interest in Lester had only ever been theoretical. Lester was thrilled by it all. He suddenly had a new friend, the older brother he worshipped, who used to ignore him. Life was good. But to Martin it felt like a calculated display. With this performance of tenderness toward his brother, Jonah seemed to be saying, "Look, this is what you no longer get. See? It's over for you. Go fuck yourself."

Martin took it too personally, he knew. Maybe because it was personal.

One night, when Jonah hadn't touched his dinner, they were asking him if he would like something else to eat, and, because he wasn't answering, and really had not been answering for some weeks now, other than in one-word responses, curt and formal, Martin and Rachel abandoned their usual rules, the guideposts of parenting they'd clung to, and moved through a list of bribes. They dangled the promise of ice cream, and then those monstrosities passing for Popsicles, shaped like animals with chocolate faces or hats, which used to turn Jonah craven and desperate. When Jonah remained silent and sort of washed-out looking, Martin offered his son candy. He could have some right now. If only he'd fucking say something.

"It's just that you're all in his face," Rachel said to him later. "How's he supposed to breathe?"

"You think my desire for him to speak is making him silent?"

"It's probably not helping."

"Whereas your approach is so amazing."

"My approach? You mean being his mother? Loving him for who he is? Keeping him safe? Yeah, it is pretty amazing."

He turned over to sleep while Rachel clipped on her book light.

They'd ride this one out in silence, apparently.

Yes, well. They'd written their own vows, promising to be "intensely honest" with each other. They had not specifically said that they would hold up each other's flaws to the most rigorous scrutiny, calling out each other's smallest mistakes, like fact checkers, believing, perhaps, that the marriage would thrive only if all personal errors and misdeeds were rooted out of it. This mission had gone unstated.

In the morning, when Martin got up, Jonah sat reading while Lester played soldiers on the rug. Lester was fully dressed, his backpack near the door. There was no possible way that Lester had done this on his own. Obviously, Jonah had dressed his brother, emptied the boy's backpack of yesterday's crap art from the first-grade praise farm he attended, and readied it for a new day. Months ago, they'd asked Jonah to perform this role in the morning, to dress and prepare his brother, so that they could sleep in, and Jonah had complied a few times, but halfheartedly, with a certain mysterious cost to little Lester, who was often speechless and tear-streaked by the time they found him. The chore had quickly lapsed, and usually Martin awoke to a hungry, half-naked Lester, waiting for his help.

Today, Lester seemed happy. There was no sign of crying.

"Good morning, Daddy," he said.

"Hello there, Les, my friend. Sleep O.K.?"

"Jonah made me breakfast. I had juice and Cheerios. I brought in my own dishes."

"Way to go! Thank you."

Martin figured he'd just play it casual, not draw too much attention to anything.

"Good morning, champ," he said to Jonah. "What are you reading?"

Martin braced himself for silence, for stillness, for a child who hadn't heard or who didn't want to answer. But Jonah looked at him.

"It's a book called 'The Short.' It's a novel," he said, and then he resumed reading.

A fat bolt of lightning filled the cover. A boy ran beneath it. The title lettering was achieved graphically with one long wire, a plug trailing off the cover.

"Oh, yeah?" Martin said. "What's it about? Tell me about it."

There was a long pause this time. Martin went into the kitchen to get his coffee started. He popped back out to the living room and snapped his fingers.

"Jonah, hello. Your book. What's it about?"

Jonah spoke quietly. His little flannel shirt was buttoned up to the collar, as if he were headed out into a blizzard. Martin almost heard a kind of apology in his voice.

"Since I have to leave for school in fifteen minutes, and since I was hoping to get to page 100 this morning, would it be O.K. if I didn't describe it to you? You can look it up on Amazon."

He told Rachel about this later in the morning, the boy's unsettling calm, his odd response.

"Yeah, I don't know," she said. "I mean, good for him, right? He just wanted to read, and he told you that. So what?"

"Huh," Martin said.

Rachel was busy cleaning. She hadn't looked at him. Their argument last night had either been forgotten or stored for later activation. He'd find out. She seemed engrossed by a panicked effort at tidying, as if guests were arriving any second, as if their house were going to be inspected by the fucking U.N. Martin followed her around while they talked, because if he didn't she'd roam out of earshot and the conversation would expire.

"He just seems like a stranger to me," Martin said, trying to add a lightness to his voice so she wouldn't hear it as a complaint.

Rachel stopped cleaning. "Yeah."

For a moment, it seemed that she might agree with him and they'd see this thing similarly.

"But he's not a stranger. I don't know. He's growing up. You should be happy that he's reading. At least he wasn't begging to be on the stupid iPad, and it seems like he's talking again. He wanted to read, and you're freaking out. Honestly."

Yes, well. You had these creatures in your house. You fed them. You cleaned them. And here was the person you'd made them with. She was beautiful, probably. She was smart, probably. It was impossible to know anymore. He looked at her through an unclean filter, for sure. He could indulge a great anger toward her that would suddenly vanish if she touched his hand. What was wrong? He'd done something or he hadn't done something. Figure it the fuck out, Martin thought. Root out the resentment. Apologize so hard it leaks from her body. Then drink the liquid. Or use it in a soup. Whatever.

. . .

Jonah came and went, such a weird bird of a boy, so serious. Martin tried to tread lightly. He tried not to tread at all. Better to float overhead, to allow the cold remoteness of his elder son to freeze their home. He studied Rachel's caution, her distance-giving, her respect, the confidence she possessed that he clearly lacked, even as he saw the toll it took on her, what had become of this person who needed to touch her young son and just couldn't.

Then, one afternoon, he forgot himself. He came home with groceries and saw Jonah down on the rug with Lester, setting up his Lego figures for him, such an impossibly small person, dressed so carefully by his own hand, his son—it still seemed ridiculous and a miracle to Martin that there'd be such a thing as a son, that a little creature in this world would be his to protect and befriend. Without thinking about it, he sat down next to Jonah and took the whole of the boy in his arms. He didn't want to scare him, and he didn't want to hurt him, but he needed this boy to feel what it was like to be held, to really be swallowed up in a father's arms. Maybe he could squeeze all the aloofness out of the boy, just choke it out until it was gone.

Jonah gave nothing back. He went limp, and the hug didn't work the way Martin had hoped. You couldn't do it alone. The person being hugged had to do something, to be something. The person being hugged had to fucking exist. And whoever this was, whoever he was holding, felt like nothing.

Finally, Martin released him, and Jonah straightened his hair. He did not look happy.

"I know that you and Mom are in charge and you make the rules," Jonah said. "But even though I'm only ten, don't I have a right not to be touched?"

The boy sounded so reasonable.

"You do," Martin said. "I apologize."

"I keep asking, but you don't listen."

"I listen."

"You don't. Because you keep doing it. So does Mom. You want to treat me like a stuffed animal, and I don't want to be treated like that."

"No, I don't, buddy."

"I don't want to be called buddy. Or mister. Or champ. I don't do that to you. You wouldn't want me always inventing some new ridiculous name for you."

"O.K." Martin put up his hands in surrender. "No more nicknames. I promise. It's just that you're my son and I like to hug you. We like to hug you."

"I don't want you to anymore. And I've said that."

"Well, too bad," Martin said, laughing, and, as if to prove he was right, he grabbed Lester, and Lester squealed with delight, squirming in his father's arms.

Do you see how this used to work? Martin wanted to say to Jonah. This was you once, this was us.

Jonah seemed genuinely puzzled. "It doesn't matter to you that I don't like it?"

"It matters, but you're wrong. You can be wrong, you know. You'll die, without affection. I'm not kidding. You will actually dry up and die."

Again, he found he had to explain love to this boy, to detail what it was like when you felt a desperate connection with someone else, how you wanted to hold that person and just crush him with hugs. But as Martin fought through the difficult and ridiculous discussion, he felt as if he were having a conversation with a lawyer. A lawyer, a scold, a little prick of a person. Whom he wanted to hug less and less. Maybe it'd be simpler just to give Jonah what he wanted. What he thought he wanted.

Jonah seemed pensive, concerned.

"Does any of that make sense to you?" Martin asked.

"It's just that I'd rather not say things that could hurt someone," Jonah said.

"Well . . . that's good. That's how you should feel."

"I'd rather not have to say anything about you and Mom. At school. To Mr. Fourenay."

Mr. Fourenay was what they called a "feelings doctor." He was paid, certainly not very much, to take the kids and their feelings very, very seriously. Martin and Rachel had trouble taking *him* seriously. He looked like a man who had subsisted, for a very long time, on a strict diet of the feelings of children. Gutted, wasted, and soft.

"Jonah, what are you talking about?"

"About you touching me when I don't want you to. I don't want to have to mention that to anyone at school. I really don't."

Martin stood up. It was as if a hand had moved inside him.

He stared at Jonah, who held his gaze patiently, waiting for an answer.

"Message received. I'll discuss it with Mom."

"Thank you."

Without really thinking about it, Martin had crafted an adulthood that was essentially friendless. There were, of course, the friends of the marriage, who knew him only as part of a couple—the dour, rotten part—and thus they were ruled out for anything remotely candid, like a confession of what the fuck had just gone down in his own home. Before the children came, he'd managed, sometimes erratically, to maintain preposterous phone relationships with several male friends. Deep, searching, facially sweaty conversations on the phone with other semi-articulate, vaguely unhappy men. In general, these friendships had heated up and found their purpose around a courtship or a breakup, when an aria of complaint or desire could be harmonized by some pathetic accomplice. But after Jonah was born, and then Lester, phone calls with friends had become out of the question. There was just never a time when it was O.K., or even appealing, to talk on the phone. When he was home, he was in shark mode, cruising slowly and brutally through the house, cleaning and clearing, scrubbing food from rugs, folding and storing tiny items of clothing, and, if no one was looking, occasionally stopping at his laptop to see if his prospects had suddenly been lifted by some piece of tremendous fortune, delivered via e-mail. When he finally came to rest, in a barf-covered chair, he was done for the night. He poured several beers, in succession, right onto his pleasure center, which could remain dry and withered no matter what came soaking down.

The gamble of a friendless adulthood, whether by accident or design, was that your partner would step up to the role. She for you, and you for her.

But when Martin thought about Jonah's threat—blackmail, really—he knew he couldn't tell Rachel. In a certain light, the only light that mattered, he was in the wrong. The instructions were already out that they were not to get all huggy with Jonah, and here he'd gone and done it anyway. Rachel would just ask him what he had expected and why he was surprised that Jonah had lashed out at him for not respecting his boundaries.

So, yeah, maybe, maybe that was all true. But there was the other part. The threat that came out of the boy. The quiet force of it. To even mention that Jonah had threatened to report them for touching him ghosted an irreversible suspicion into people's minds. You couldn't talk about it. You couldn't mention it. It seemed better to not even think it, to do the work that would begin to block such an event from memory.

The boys were talking quietly on the couch one afternoon a few days later. Martin was in the next room, and he caught the sweet tones, the two voices he loved, that he couldn't even bear. For a minute he forgot what was going on and listened to the life he'd helped make. They were speaking like little people, not kids, back and forth, a real discussion. Jonah was explaining something to Lester, and Lester was asking questions, listening patiently. It was heartbreaking.

He snuck out to see the boys on the couch, Lester cuddled up against his older brother, who had a big book in his hands. A grownup one. On the cover, instead of a boy dashing beneath a bolt of lightning, were the good old Twin Towers. The title, "Lies," was glazed in blood, which dripped down the towers themselves.

Oh, motherfucking hell.

"What's this?" Martin asked. "What are you reading there?"

"A book about 9/11. Who caused it."

Martin grabbed it, thumbed the pages. "Where'd you get it?"

"From Amazon. With my birthday gift card."

"Hmm. Do you believe it?"

"What do you mean? It's true."

"What's true?"

"That the Jews caused 9/11 and they all stayed home that day so they wouldn't get killed."

Martin excused Lester. Told him to skedaddle and, yes, it was O.K. to watch TV, even though watching time hadn't started yet. Just go, go.

"O.K., Jonah," he whispered. "Jonah, stop. This is not O.K. Not at all O.K. First of all, Jonah, you have to listen to me. This is insane. This is a book by an insane person."

"You know him?"

"No, I don't know him. I don't have to. Listen to me, you know that we're Jewish, right? You, me, Mom, Lester. We're Jewish."

"Not really."

"What do you mean, not really?"

"You don't go to synagogue. You don't seem to worship. You never talk about it."

"That's not all that matters."

"Last month was Yom Kippur and you didn't fast. You didn't go to services. You don't ever say Happy New Year on Rosh Hashanah."

"Those are rituals. You don't need to observe them to be part of the faith."

"But do you know anything about it?"

"9/11?"

"No, being Jewish. Do you know what it means and what you're supposed to believe and how you're supposed to act?"

"I do, yes. I have a pretty good idea."

"Then tell me."

"Jonah."

"What? I'm just wondering how you can call yourself Jewish."

"How? Are you fucking kidding me?"

He needed to walk away before he did something.

"O.K., Jonah, it's actually really simple. I'll tell you how. Because everyone else in the world would call me Jewish. With no debate. None. Because of my parents and their parents, and their parents, including whoever got turned to dust in the war. Zayde Anshel's whole family. You walk by their picture every day in the hall. Do you think you're not related to them? And because I was called a kike in junior high school, and high school, and college, and probably beyond that, right up to this fucking day. And because if they started rounding up Jews again they'd take one look at our name and they'd know. And that's you, too, mister. They would come for us and kill us. O.K.? You."

He was shaking his fist in his son's face. Just old-school shouting. He wanted to do more. He wanted to tear something apart. There was no safe way to behave right now.

"They would kill you. And you'd be dead. You'd die."

"Martin?" Rachel said. "What's going on?"

Of course. There she was. Lurking. He had no idea how long she'd been standing there, what she'd heard.

Martin wasn't done. Jonah seemed fascinated, his eyes wide as his father ranted.

"Even if you said that you hated Jews, too, and that Jews were evil and caused all the suffering in the world, they would look at you and know for sure that you were Jewish, for sure! Buddy, champ, mister"—just spitting these names at his son—"because only a Jew, they would say, only a Jew would betray his own people like that."

Jonah looked at him. "I understand," he said. He didn't seem shaken. He didn't seem disturbed. Had he heard? How could he really understand?

The boy picked up the book and thumbed through it.

"This is just a different point of view. You always say that I should have an open mind, that I should think for myself. You say that to me all the time."

"Yes, I do. You're right." Martin was trembling.

"Then do I have your permission to keep reading it?"

"No, you absolutely don't. Not this time. Permission denied."

Rachel was shaking her head.

"Do you see what he's reading? Do you see it?" he shouted.

He waved the book at her, and she just looked at him with no expression at all.

After the kids were in bed, and the house had been quietly put back together, Rachel said they needed to talk.

Yes, we do, he thought, and about fucking time.

"Honestly," she said. "It's upsetting that he had that book, but the way you spoke to him? I don't want you going anywhere near him."

"Yeah, well, that's not for you to say. You're his mom, not mine. You want to file papers? You want to seek custody? Good luck, Mrs. Freeze. I'm his father. And you didn't hear it. You didn't hear it all. You have no fucking idea."

"I heard it, and I heard you. Martin, you need help. You're, I don't know, depressed. You're self-pitying. You think everything is some concerted attack on you. For the record, I am worried about Jonah. Really worried. Something is seriously wrong. There is no debate there. But you're just the worst possible partner in that worry—the fucking worst—because you make everything harder, and we can't discuss it without analyzing your bullshit feelings. You act wounded and hurt, and we're all supposed to feel sorry for you. For you! This isn't about you. So shut down the pity party already."

When this kind of talk came on, Martin knew to listen. This was the scold she'd been winding up for, and if he could endure it, and cop to it, there might be some release and clarity at the other end. A part of him found these outbursts from Rachel thrilling, and in some ways it was possible that he co-engineered them, without really thinking about it. Performed the sullen and narcissistic dance moves that, over time, would yield this kind of eruption from her. His wife was alive. She cared. Even if it seemed that she might sort of hate him.

He circled the house for a while, cooling off, letting the attack—no, no, the truth—settle. Any argument or even discussion to the contrary would just feed her point and read as the defensive bleating of a cornered man. Any speech, that is, except admission, contrition, and apology, the three horsemen.

Which was who he brought back into the room with him.

Rachel was in bed reading, eyes burned onto the page. She didn't seem even remotely ready to surrender her anger.

"Hey, listen," Martin said. "So I know you're mad, but I just want to say that I agree with everything you said. I'm scared and I'm worried and I'm sorry."

He let this settle. It needed to spread, to sink in. She needed to realize that he was agreeing with her.

It was hard to tell, but it seemed that some of her anger, with nothing to meet it, was draining out.

"And," he continued. He waited for her to look up, which she finally did. "You'll think I'm kidding, and I know you don't even want to hear this right now, but it's true, and I have to say it. It made me a little bit horny to hear all that."

She shook her head at the bad joke, which at least meant there was room to move here.

"Shut up," she said.

This was the way in. He took it.

"You shut up."

"Sorry to yell, Martin. I am. I just— This is so hard. I'm sorry."

She probably wasn't. This was simply the script back in, to the two of them united, and they both knew it. One day, one of them would choose not to play. It would be so easy not to say their lines.

"No, it's O.K.," he said to her, climbing onto the bed. "I get it. Listen, let's take the little motherfucker to the shop. Get him fixed. I'll call some doctors in the morning."

They hugged. An actual hug, between two consenting people. A novelty in this house.

"O.K.," she said. "I'm terrified. I don't know what's happening. I look at him and want so much to just grab him, but he's not there anymore. What has he done to himself?"

"Maybe he just needs minor surgery. Does that work on 9/11 truthers?"

"Oh, look," she said to him softly. "You're back. The real you. We missed you."

They talked a little and got up close to each other in bed. For a moment, their good feeling came on them—a version of it, anyway. It felt mild and transitory, but he would take it. It was nice. He was in bed with his wife, and they would figure this out.

"Listen," he said to her. "Do you want to just shag a pony right now, get back on track?"

"I don't know," she said. "I feel gross. I feel depressed."

"I feel gross, too. Let's do it. Two gross people licking each other's buttons."

She went to the bathroom and got the jar of enabler. They took their positions on the bed.

He hoped he could. He hoped he could. He hoped he could.

He was cold and insecure, so he left his shirt on. And his socks.

They used a cream. They used their hands. They used an object or two. During the brief strain of actual fornication they persisted with casual conversation about the next day's errands. In the early days of their marriage, this had seemed wicked and sexy, some ironic ballast against the animal greed. Now it just seemed efficient, and the animal greed no longer appeared. Minus the wet spot at the end, and the minor glow one occasionally felt, their sex wasn't so different from riding the subway.

It turned out that there was a deep arsenal of medical professionals who would be delighted to consult on the problem of a disturbed child. Angry, depressed, anxious, remote, bizarre. Even a Jew-hating Jewish child who might very well be dead inside. Only when his parents looked at him, though. Only when his parents spoke to him. Important parameter for the differential.

They zeroed in on recommendations with the help of a high-level participant in this world, a friend named Maureen, whose three exquisitely exceptional children had consumed, and spat back out, various kinds of psych services ever since they could walk. Each of the kids seemed to romance a different diagnosis every month, so Maureen had a pretty good idea of who fixed what and for how much goddam moolah.

When they told her, in pale terms, about Jonah, she, as a connoisseur of alienating behavior from the young, got excited.

"This is so 'The Fifth Child,'" she said. "Did you guys read that? I mean, you probably shouldn't read that. But did you? It's like a fiction novel. I don't think it really happened. But it's still fascinating."

Rachel had read it. Happy couple with four children and perfect life have fifth child, leading to less perfect life. Much, much, much, much less perfect. Sorrow, sorrow, sorrow, grief, and sorrow. Not really life at all.

"Yeah, but the kid in that book is a monster," Rachel said. "So heartless. He's not real. And he just wants to inflict pain. Jonah wouldn't hurt anyone. He wants to be alone. Or, not that, but. I don't know what Jonah wants. He's not violent, though. Or even mad. I don't think."

"All right, but he is hurting you, right?" Maureen said. "I mean, it seems like this is really causing you guys a lot of pain and suffering."

"I haven't read the book," Martin said. "But this isn't about us. This is about Jonah. His pain, his suffering. We just want to get to the bottom of it. To help him. To give him support."

In Rachel's silence he could feel her agreement and, maybe, her surprise that he would, or even could, think this way. He knew what to say now. He wasn't going to get burned again. But did he believe it? Was it true? He honestly didn't even know, and he wasn't so sure it mattered.

The doctor wanted to see them alone first. He said that it was his job to listen. So they talked, just dumped the thing out on the floor. It was ugly, Martin thought, but it was a rough picture of what was going down. The doctor scribbled away, stopping occasionally to look at them, to really deeply look at them, and nod. Since when had the act of listening turned into such a strange charade?

Then the doctor met with Jonah, to see for himself, pull evidence right from the culprit's mouth. Martin and Rachel sat in the waiting room and stared at the door. What would the doctor see? Which kid would he get? Were they crazy and was this all just some preteen freak-out?

Finally, the whole gang of them—doctor, parents, and child—gathered to go over the plan, Jonah sitting polite and alert while the future of his brain was discussed. They told him the proposal: a slow ramp of antidepressants, along with weekly therapy, and then, depending, some group work, if that all sounded good to Jonah.

Jonah didn't respond.

"What do you think?" the doctor said. "So you can feel better? And things can maybe go back to normal?"

"I told you, I feel fine," Jonah said.

"Yes, good! But sometimes when we're sick we think we're not. That can be a symptom of being sick—to think we are well."

"So all the healthy people are just lying to themselves?"

"Well, no, of course not," the doctor said.

"Right now I never think about hurting myself, but you want to give me a medicine that might make me think about hurting myself?"

The doctor seemed uneasy.

"It's called suicidal ideation," Jonah said.

"And how do you know about that?" the doctor asked.

"The Internet."

The adults all looked at one another.

"How come people are so surprised when someone knows something?" Jonah asked. "Your generation had better get used to how completely unspecial it is that a kid can look up a medicine online and learn about the side effects. That's not me being precocious. It's just me using my stupid computer."

"O.K., good. Well, you're right, you should be informed, and I want to congratulate you on finding that out for yourself. That's great work, Jonah."

Martin watched Jonah. He found himself hoping that the real Jonah would appear, scathing and cold, to show the doctor what they were dealing with.

"Thank you," Jonah said. "I'm really proud of myself. I didn't think I could do it, but I just really stuck with it and I kept trying until I succeeded."

Martin could not tell if the doctor caught the tone of this response.

"But you might have also read that that's a very uncommon symptom. It hardly ever happens. We just have to warn you and your parents about it, to be on the lookout for it."

"Maybe. But I have none of the symptoms of depression, either. So why would you risk making me feel like I want to kill myself if I'm not depressed and feel fine?"

"O.K., Jonah. You know what? I'm going to talk to your parents alone now. Does that sound all right? You can wait outside in the play area. There are books and games."

"O.K.," Jonah said. "I'll just run and play now."

"There," Martin said. "There," after Jonah had closed the door. "That was it. That's what he does."

"Sarcasm? Maybe you don't much like it, but we don't treat sarcasm in young people. I think it's too virulent a strain." The doctor chuckled.

"No offense," Martin said to the doctor, "and I'm sure you know your job and this is your specialty, but I think that way of speaking to him—"

"What way?"

"Just, you know, as if he were much younger. He's just— I don't think that works with him."

"And how do you speak to him?"

"Excuse me?"

"How do you speak to him? I'm curious."

Rachel coughed and seemed uncomfortable. They'd agreed to

be open, to let each other have ideas and opinions without feeling mad or threatened.

"It's true," she said. "I mean, Martin, I think you have been surprised lately that Jonah is as mature as he is. That seems to have really almost upset you. You know, you really have yelled at him a lot. We can't just pretend that hasn't happened." She looked at him apologetically. "Aside," she added, "from the scary things that he's been saying."

"Is it maturity? I don't think so. Have I been upset? Fucking hell, yes. And so have you, Rachel. And not because he thinks the Jews caused 9/11 or because he threatened to report us for sexual abuse for trying to hug him, which, for what it's worth, I spared you from, Rachel. I spared you. Because I didn't think you could bear it."

Rachel just stared at him.

"What you're seeing is a very, very bright boy," the doctor said.

"Too smart to treat?" Martin asked.

"I think family therapy would be productive. Very challenging, but worthwhile, in my opinion. I could get you a referral. What you're upset about, in relation to your son, may not fall under the purview of medicine, though."

"The purview? Really?"

"To be honest, I was on the fence about medication. Whatever is going on with Jonah, it does not present as depression. In my opinion, Jonah does not have a medical condition."

Martin stood up.

"He's not sick, he's just an asshole, is what you're saying?"

"I think that's a very dangerous way for a parent to feel," the doctor said.

"Yeah?" Martin said, standing over the doctor now. "You're right. You got that one right. Because all of a parent's feelings are dangerous, you motherfucker."

At home that night, Martin stuffed a chicken with lemon halves, drenched it in olive oil, scattered a handful of salt over it, and blasted it in the oven until it emerged deeply burnished, with skin as crisp as glass. Rachel poured drinks for the two of them, and they cooked in silence. To Martin, it was a harmless silence. He could trust it, and if he couldn't, then to hell with it. He wasn't going to chase down everything unsaid and shout it into their home, as if all important messages on the planet needed to be shared. He'd said enough, things he believed, things he didn't. Quota achieved. Quota surpassed.

Rachel looked small and tired. Beyond that, he wasn't sure. He was more aware than ever, as she set the table and put out Lester's cup and Jonah's big-kid glass, how impossibly unknowable she would always be—what she thought, what she felt—how what was most special about her was the careful way she guarded it all.

No matter their theories—about Jonah or each other or the larger world—their job was to watch over Jonah on his cold voyage. He had to come back. This kind of controlled solitude was unsustainable. No one could pull it off, especially not someone so young. Except that his reasoning on this, he knew, was wishful parental bullshit. Of course a child could do it. Who else but children to lead the fucking species into darkness? Which meant what for the old-timers left behind?

Dinner was brief, destroyed by the savage appetite of Lester, who engulfed his meal before Rachel had even taken a bite, and begged, begged to be excused so that he could return to the platoon of small plastic men he'd deployed on the rug. According to Lester, his men were waiting to be told what to do. "I need to tell my guys who to kill!" he shouted. "I'm in charge!"

At the height of this tantrum, Jonah, silent since they'd returned from the doctor's office, leaned over to Lester, put a hand on his shoulder, and calmly told him not to whine.

"Don't use that tone of voice," he said. "Mom and Dad will excuse you when they're ready."

"O.K.," Lester said, looking up at his brother with a kind of awe, and for the rest of their wordless dinner he sat there waiting, as patiently as a boy his age ever could, his hands folded in his lap.

At bedtime, Rachel asked Martin if he wouldn't mind letting her sleep alone. She was just very tired. She didn't think she could manage otherwise. She gave him a sort of smile, and he saw the effort behind it. She dragged her pillow and a blanket into a corner of the TV room and made herself a little nest there. He had the bedroom to himself. He crawled onto Rachel's side of the mattress, which was higher, softer, less abused, and fell asleep.

In the morning, Jonah did not say goodbye on his way to school, nor did he greet Martin upon his return home. When Martin asked after his day, Jonah, without looking up, said that it had been fine. Maybe that was all there was to say, and why, really, would you ever shit on such an answer?

Jonah took up his spot on the couch and opened a book, reading quietly until dinner, while Lester played at his feet. Martin watched Jonah. Was that a grin or a grimace on the boy's face? he wondered. And what, finally, was the difference? Why have a face at all if what was inside you was so perfectly hidden? The book Jonah was reading was nothing, some silliness. Make-believe and colorful and harmless. It looked like it belonged to a series, along with that book "The Short." On the cover a boy, arms outspread, was gripping wires in each hand, and his whole body was glowing.

THE MIDNIGHT ZONE

BY LAUREN GROFF (2016)

It was an old hunting camp shipwrecked in twenty miles of scrub. Our friend had seen a Florida panther sliding through the trees there a few days earlier. But things had been fraying in our hands, and the camp was free and silent, so I walked through the resistance of my cautious husband and my small boys, who had wanted hermit crabs and kites and wakeboards and sand for spring break. Instead, they got ancient sinkholes filled with ferns, potential death by cat.

One thing I liked was how the screens at night pulsed with the tender bellies of lizards.

Even in the sleeping bag with my smaller son, the golden one, the March chill seemed to blow through my bones. I loved eating, but I'd lost so much weight by then that I carried myself delicately, as if I'd gone translucent.

There was sparse electricity from a gas-powered generator and no Internet and you had to climb out through the window in the loft and stand on the roof to get a cell signal. On the third day, the boys were asleep and I'd dimmed the lanterns when my husband went up and out and I heard him stepping on the metal roof, a giant brother to the raccoons that woke us thumping around up there at night like burglars.

Then my husband stopped moving, and stood still for so long I forgot where he was. When he came down the ladder from the loft, his face had blanched.

Who died? I said lightly, because if anyone was going to die it was going to be us, our skulls popping in the jaws of an endangered cat. It turned out to be a bad joke, because someone actually had died, that morning, in one of my husband's apartment buildings. A fifth-floor occupant had killed herself, maybe on purpose, with aspirin and vodka and a bathtub. Floors four, three, and two were away somewhere with beaches and alcoholic smoothies, and the first floor had discovered the problem only when the water of death had seeped into the carpet.

My husband had to leave. He'd just fired one handyman and the other was on his own Caribbean adventure, eating buffet food to the sound of cruise-ship calypso. Let's pack, my husband said, but my rebelliousness at the time was like a sticky fog rolling through my body and never burning off, there was no sun inside, and so I said that the boys and I would stay. He looked at me as if I were crazy and asked how we'd manage with no car. I asked if he thought he'd married an incompetent woman, which cut to the bone, because the source of our problems was that, in fact, he had. For years at a time I was good only at the things that interested me, and since all that interested me was my work and my children, the rest of life had sort of inched away. And while it's true that my children were endlessly fascinating, two petri dishes growing human cultures, being a mother never had been, and all that seemed assigned by default of gender I would not do because it felt insulting. I would not buy clothes, I would not make dinner, I would not keep schedules, I would not make playdates, never ever. Motherhood meant, for me, that I would take the boys on monthlong adventures to Europe, teach them to blast off rockets, to swim for glory. I taught them how to read, but they could make their own lunches. I would hug them as long as they wanted to be hugged, but that was just being human. My husband had to be the one to make up for the depths of my lack. It is exhausting, living in debt that increases every day but that you have no intention of repaying.

Two days, he promised. Two days and he'd be back by noon on the third. He bent to kiss me, but I gave him my cheek and rolled over when the headlights blazed then dwindled on the wall. In the banishing of the engine, the night grew bold. The wind was making a low, inhuman muttering in the pines, and, inspired, the animals let loose in call-and-response. Everything kept me alert until shortly before dawn, when I slept for a few minutes until the puppy whined and woke me. My older son was crying because he'd thrown off his sleeping bag in the night and was cold but too sleepy to fix the situation.

I made scrambled eggs with a vengeful amount of butter and Cheddar, also cocoa with an inch of marshmallow, thinking I would stupefy my children with calories, but the calories only made them stronger.

Our friend had treated the perimeter of the clearing with panther deterrent, some kind of synthetic superpredator urine, and we felt safe-ish near the cabin. We ran footraces until the dog went wild and leapt up and bit my children's arms with her puppy teeth, and the boys screamed with pain and frustration and showed me the pink stripes on their skin. I scolded the puppy harshly and she crept off to the porch to watch us with her chin on her paws. The boys and I played soccer. We rocked in the hammock. We watched the circling red-shouldered hawks. I made my older son read "Alice's Adventures in Wonderland" to the little one, which was a disaster, a book so punny and Victorian for modern children. We had lunch, then the older boy tried to make fire by rubbing sticks together, his little brother attending solemnly, and they spent the rest of the day constructing a hut out of branches. Then dinner, singing songs, a bath in the galvanized-steel horse trough someone had converted to a cold-water tub, picking ticks and chiggers off with tweezers, and that was it for the first day.

There had been a weight on us as we played outside, not as if something were actually watching but because of the possibility that something could be watching when we were so far from humanity in all that Florida waste.

The second day should have been like the first. I doubled down on the calories, adding pancakes to breakfast, and succeeded in making the boys lie in pensive digestion out in the hammock for a little while before they ricocheted off the trees.

But in the afternoon the one light bulb sizzled out. The cabin was all dark wood and I couldn't see the patterns on the dishes I was washing. I found a new bulb in a closet, dragged over a stool from the bar area, and made the older boy hold the spinning seat as I climbed aboard. The old bulb was hot, and I was passing it from hand to hand, holding the new bulb under my arm, when the puppy leapt up at my older son's face. He let go of the stool to whack at her, and I did a quarter spin, then fell and hit the floor with my head, and then I surely blacked out.

After a while, I opened my eyes. Two children were looking down at me. They were pale and familiar. One fair, one dark; one small, one big.

Mommy? the little boy said, through water.

I turned my head and threw up on the floor. The bigger boy dragged a puppy, who was snuffling my face, out the door.

I knew very little except that I was in pain and that I shouldn't move. The older boy bent over me, then lifted an intact light bulb from my armpit, triumphantly; I a chicken, the bulb an egg.

The smaller boy had a wet paper towel in his hand and he was patting my cheeks. The pulpy smell made me ill again. I closed my eyes and felt the dabbing on my forehead, on my neck, around my mouth. The small child's voice was high. He was singing a song.

I started to cry with my eyes closed and the tears went hot across my temples and into my ears.

Mommy! the older boy, the solemn dark one, screamed, and when I opened my eyes both of the children were crying, and that was how I knew them to be mine.

Just let me rest here a minute, I said. They took my hands. I could feel the hot hands of my children, which was good. I moved my toes, then my feet. I turned my head back and forth. My neck worked, though fireworks went off in the corners of my eyes.

I can walk to town, the older boy was saying, through wadding, to his brother, but the nearest town was twenty miles away. Safety was twenty miles away and there was a panther between us and there, but also possibly terrible men, sinkholes, alligators, the end of the world. There was no landline, no umbilical cord, and small boys using cell phones would easily fall off such a slick, pitched metal roof.

But what if she's all a sudden dead and I'm all a sudden alone? the little boy was saying.

O.K., I'm sitting up now, I said.

The puppy was howling at the door.

I lifted my body onto my elbows. Gingerly, I sat. The cabin dipped and spun and I vomited again.

The big boy ran out and came back with a broom to clean up. No! I said. I am always too hard on him, this beautiful child who is so brilliant, who has no logic at all.

Sweetness, I said, and couldn't stop crying, because I'd called him Sweetness instead of his name, which I couldn't remember just then. I took five or six deep breaths. Thank you, I said in a calmer voice. Just throw a whole bunch of paper towels on it and drag the rug over it to keep the dog off. The little one did so, methodically, which was not his style; he has always been adept at cheerfully watching other people work for him.

The bigger boy tried to get me to drink water, because this is what we do in our family in lieu of applying Band-Aids, which I refuse to buy because they are just flesh-colored landfill.

Then the little boy screamed, because he'd moved around me and seen the bloody back of my head, and then he dabbed at the cut with the paper towel he had previously dabbed at my pukey mouth. The paper disintegrated in his hands. He crawled into my lap and put his face on my stomach. The bigger boy held something cold on my wound, which I discovered later to be a beer can from the fridge.

They were quiet like this for a very long time. The boys' names came back to me, at first dancing coyly out of reach, then, when I seized them in my hands, mine.

I'd been a soccer player in high school, a speedy and aggressive midfielder, and head trauma was an old friend. I remembered this constant lability from one concussive visit to the emergency room. The confusion and the sense of doom were also familiar. I had a flash of my mother sitting beside my bed for an entire night, shaking me awake whenever I tried to fall asleep, and I now wanted my mother, not in her diminished current state, brittle retiree, but as she had been when I was young, a small person but gigantic, a person who had blocked out the sun.

I sent the little boy off to get a roll of dusty duct tape, the bigger boy to get gauze from my toiletry kit, and when they wandered back

I duct-taped the gauze to my head, already mourning my long hair, which had been my most expensive pet.

I inched myself across the room to the bed and climbed up, despite the sparklers behind my eyeballs. The boys let the forlorn puppy in, and when they opened the door they also let the night in, because my fall had taken hours from our lives.

It was only then, when the night entered, that I understood the depth of time we had yet to face. I had the boys bring me the lanterns, then a can opener and the tuna and the beans, which I opened slowly, because it is not easy, supine, and we made a game out of eating, though the thought of eating anything gave me chills. The older boy brought over Mason jars of milk. I let my children finish the entire half gallon of ice cream, which was my husband's, his one daily reward for being kind and good, but by this point the man deserved our disloyalty, because he was not there.

It had started raining, at first a gentle thrumming on the metal roof.

I tried to tell my children a cautionary tale about a little girl who fell into a well and had to wait a week until firefighters could figure out a way to rescue her, something that maybe actually took place back in the dimness of my childhood, but the story was either too abstract for them or I wasn't making much sense, and they didn't seem to grasp my need for them to stay in the cabin, to not go anywhere, if the very worst happened, the unthinkable that I was skirting, like a pit that opened just in front of each sentence I was about to utter. They kept asking me if the girl got lots of toys when she made it out of the well. This was so against my point that I said, out of spite, Unfortunately, no, she did not.

I made the boys keep me awake with stories. The younger one was into a British television show about marine life, which the older one maintained was babyish until I pretended not to believe what they were telling me. Then they both told me about cookie-cutter sharks, who bore perfect round holes in whales, as if their mouths were cookie cutters. They told me about a fish called the humuhumunukunukuāpua'a, a beautiful name that I couldn't say correctly, even though they sang it to me over and over, laughing, to the tune of "Twinkle Twinkle, Little Star." They told me about the walking catfish, which can stay out of water for days and days, meandering about in the mud. They told me about the sunlight, the twilight, and the midnight zones, the three depths of water, where there is transparent light, then a murky, darkish light, then no light at all. They told me about the world pool, in which one current goes one way, another goes another way, and where they meet they make a tornado of air, which stretches, my little one said, from the midnight zone, where the fish are blind, all the way up up up to the birds.

I had begun shaking very hard, which my children, sudden gentlemen, didn't mention. They piled all the sleeping bags and blankets they could find on me, then climbed under and fell asleep without bathing or toothbrushing or getting out of their dirty clothes, which, anyway, they sweated through within an hour.

The dog did not get dinner but she didn't whine about it, and though she wasn't allowed to, she came up on the bed and slept with her head on my older son's stomach, because he was her favorite, being the biggest puppy of all.

Now I had only myself to sit vigil with me, though it was still early, nine or ten at night.

I had a European novel on the nightstand that filled me with dimness and fret, so I tried to read "Alice's Adventures in Wonderland," but it was incomprehensible with my scrambled brains. Then I looked at a hunting magazine, which made me remember the Florida panther. I hadn't truly forgotten about it, but could manage only a few terrors at a time, and others, when my children had been awake, were more urgent. We had seen some scat in the woods on a walk three days earlier, enormous scat, either a bear's or the panther's, but certainly a giant predator's. The danger had been abstract until we saw this bodily proof of existence, and my husband and I led the children home, singing a round, all four of us holding hands, and we let the dog off the leash to circle us joyously, because, as small as she was, it was bred in her bones that in the face of peril she would sacrifice herself first.

The rain increased until it was deafening and still my sweaty children slept. I thought of the waves of sleep rushing through their brains, washing out the tiny unimportant flotsam of today so that tomorrow's heavier truths could wash in. There was a nice solidity to the rain's pounding on the roof, as if the noise were a barrier that nothing could enter, a stay against the looming night.

I tried to bring back the poems of my youth, and could not remember more than a few floating lines, which I put together into a strange, sad poem, Blake and Dickinson and Frost and Milton and Sexton, a tag-sale poem in clammy meter that nonetheless came alive and held my hand for a little while.

Then the rain diminished until all that was left were scattered clicks from the drops falling from the pines. The batteries of one lantern went out and the light from the remaining lantern was sparse and thwarted. I could hardly see my hand or the shadow it made on the wall when I held it up. This lantern was my sister; at any moment it, too, could go dark. I feasted my eyes on the cabin, which in the oncoming black had turned into a place made of gold, but the shadows seemed too thick now, fizzy at the edges, and they moved when I shifted my eyes away from them. It felt safer to look at the cheeks of my sleeping children, creamy as cheeses.

It was elegiac, that last hour or so of light, and I tried to push my love for my sons into them where their bodies were touching my own skin.

The wind rose again and it had personality; it was in a sharpish, meanish mood. It rubbed itself against the little cabin and played at the corners and broke sticks off the trees and tossed them at the roof so they jigged down like creatures with strange and scrabbling claws. The wind rustled its endless body against the door.

Everything depended on my staying still, but my skin was stuffed with itches. Something terrible in me, the darkest thing, wanted to slam my own head back against the headboard. I imagined it over and over, the sharp backward crack, and the wash and spill of peace.

I counted slow breaths and was not calm by two hundred; I counted to a thousand.

The lantern flicked itself out and the dark poured in.

The moon rose in the skylight and backed itself across the black.

When it was gone and I was alone again, I felt the dissociation, a physical shifting, as if the best of me were detaching from my body and sitting down a few feet distant. It was a great relief.

For a few moments, there was a sense of mutual watching, a wait for something definitive, though nothing definitive came, and then the bodiless me stood and circled the cabin. The dog moved and gave a soft whine through her nose, although she remained asleep. The floors were cool underfoot. My head brushed the beams, though they were ten feet up. Where my body and those of my two sons lay together was a black and pulsing mass, a hole of light.

I passed outside. The path was pale dirt and filled with sandspur and was cold and wet after the rain. The great drops from the tree branches left a pine taste in me. The forest was not dark, because darkness has nothing to do with the forest—the forest is made of life, of light—but the trees moved with wind and subtle creatures. I wasn't in any single place. I was with the raccoons of the rooftop, who were now down fiddling with the bicycle lock on the garbage can at the end of the road, with the red-shouldered hawk chicks breathing alone in the nest, with the armadillo forcing its armored body through the brush. I hadn't realized that I'd lost my sense of smell until it returned hungrily now; I could smell the worms tracing their paths under the pine needles and the mold breathing out new spores, shaken alive by the rain.

I was vigilant, moving softly in the underbrush, and the palmettos' nails scraped down my body.

The cabin was not visible, but it was present, a sore at my side, a feeling of density and airlessness. I couldn't go away from it, I couldn't return, I could only circle the cabin and circle it. With each circle, a terrible, stinging anguish built in me and I had to move faster and faster, each pass bringing up ever more wildness. What had been built to seem so solid was fragile in the face of time because time is impassive, more animal than human. Time would not care if you fell out of it. It would continue on without you. It cannot see you; it has always been blind to the human and the things we do to stave it off, the taxonomies, the cleaning, the arranging, the ordering. Even this cabin with its perfectly considered angles, its veins of pipes and wires, was barely more stable than the rake marks we made in the dust that morning, which time had already scrubbed away.

The self in the woods ran and ran, but the running couldn't hold off the slow shift. A low mist rose from the ground and gradually came clearer. The first birds sent their questions into the chilly air. The sky developed its blue. The sun emerged.

The drawing back was gradual. My older son opened his brown eyes and saw me sitting above him.

You look terrible, he said, patting my face, and my hearing was only half underwater now.

My head ached, so I held my mouth shut and smiled with my eyes and he padded off to the kitchen and came back with peanut-butter-and-jelly sandwiches, with a set of Uno cards, with cold coffee from yesterday's pot for the low and constant thunder of my headache, with the dog whom he'd let out and then fed all by himself.

I watched him. He gleamed. My little son woke but didn't get up, as if his face were attached to my shoulder by the skin. He was rubbing one unbloodied lock of my hair on his lips, the way he did after he nursed when he was a baby.

My boys were not unhappy. I was usually a preoccupied mother, short with them, busy, working, until I burst into fun, then went back to my hole of work; now I could only sit with them, talk to them. I could not even read. They were gentle with me, reminded me of a golden retriever I'd grown up with, a dog with a mouth so soft she would go down to the lake and steal ducklings and hold them intact on her tongue for hours until we noticed her sitting unusually erect in the corner, looking sly. My boys were like their father; they would one day be men who would take care of the people they loved.

I closed my eyes as the boys played game after game after game of Uno.

Noon arrived, noon left, and my husband did not come.

At one point, something passed across the woods outside like a shudder, and a hush fell over everything, and the boys and the dog all looked at me and their faces were like pale birds taking flight, but my hearing had mercifully shut off whatever had occasioned such swift terror over all creatures of the earth, save me.

When we heard the car from afar at four in the afternoon, the boys jumped up. They burst out of the cabin, leaving the door wide open to the blazing light, which hurt my eyes. I heard their father's voice, and then his footsteps, and he was running, and behind him the boys were running, the dog was running. Here were my husband's feet on the dirt drive. Here were his feet heavy on the porch.

For a half-breath, I would have vanished myself. I was everything we had fretted about, this passive Queen of Chaos with her bloody duct-tape crown. My husband filled the door. He is a man born to fill doors. I shut my eyes. When I opened them, he was enormous above me. In his face was a thing that made me go quiet inside, made a long slow sizzle creep up my arms from the fingertips, because the thing I read in his face was the worst, it was fear, and it was vast, it was elemental, like the wind itself, like the cold sun I would soon feel on the silk of my pelt.

CAT PERSON

BY KRISTEN ROUPENIAN (2017)

Margot met Robert on a Wednesday night toward the end of her fall semester. She was working behind the concession stand at the artsy movie theatre downtown when he came in and bought a large popcorn and a box of Red Vines.

"That's an . . . unusual choice," she said. "I don't think I've ever actually sold a box of Red Vines before."

Flirting with her customers was a habit she'd picked up back when she worked as a barista, and it helped with tips. She didn't earn tips at the movie theatre, but the job was boring otherwise, and she did think that Robert was cute. Not so cute that she would have, say, gone up to him at a party, but cute enough that she could have drummed up an imaginary crush on him if he'd sat across from her during a dull class—though she was pretty sure that he was out of college, in his mid-twenties at least. He was tall, which she liked, and she could see the edge of a tattoo peeking out from beneath the rolled-up sleeve of his shirt. But he was on the heavy side, his beard was a little too long, and his shoulders slumped forward slightly, as though he were protecting something.

Robert did not pick up on her flirtation. Or, if he did, he showed it only by stepping back, as though to make her lean toward him, try a little harder. "Well," he said. "O.K., then." He pocketed his change.

But the next week he came into the movie theatre again, and

bought another box of Red Vines. "You're getting better at your job," he told her. "You managed not to insult me this time."

She shrugged. "I'm up for a promotion, so," she said.

After the movie, he came back to her. "Concession-stand girl, give me your phone number," he said, and, surprising herself, she did.

From that small exchange about Red Vines, over the next several weeks they built up an elaborate scaffolding of jokes via text, riffs that unfolded and shifted so quickly that she sometimes had a hard time keeping up. He was very clever, and she found that she had to work to impress him. Soon she noticed that when she texted him he usually texted her back right away, but if she took more than a few hours to respond his next message would always be short and wouldn't include a question, so it was up to her to re-initiate the conversation, which she always did. A few times, she got distracted for a day or so and wondered if the exchange would die out altogether, but then she'd think of something funny to tell him or she'd see a picture on the Internet that was relevant to their conversation, and they'd start up again. She still didn't know much about him, because they never talked about anything personal, but when they landed two or three good jokes in a row there was a kind of exhilaration to it, as if they were dancing.

Then, one night during reading period, she was complaining about how all the dining halls were closed and there was no food in her room because her roommate had raided her care package, and he offered to buy her some Red Vines to sustain her. At first, she deflected this with another joke, because she really did have to study, but he said, "No, I'm serious, stop fooling around and come now," so she put a jacket over her pajamas and met him at the 7-Eleven.

It was about eleven o'clock. He greeted her without ceremony, as though he saw her every day, and took her inside to choose some snacks. The store didn't have Red Vines, so he bought her a Cherry Coke Slurpee and a bag of Doritos and a novelty lighter shaped like a frog with a cigarette in its mouth.

"Thank you for my presents," she said, when they were back outside. Robert was wearing a rabbit-fur hat that came down over his ears and a thick, old-fashioned down jacket. She thought it was a good look for him, if a little dorky; the hat heightened his lumberjack aura, and the heavy coat hid his belly and the slightly sad slump of his shoulders.

"You're welcome, concession-stand girl," he said, though of course he knew her name by then. She thought he was going to go in for a kiss and prepared to duck and offer him her cheek, but instead of kissing her on the mouth he took her by the arm and kissed her gently on the forehead, as though she were something precious. "Study hard, sweetheart," he said. "I will see you soon."

On the walk back to her dorm, she was filled with a sparkly lightness that she recognized as the sign of an incipient crush.

While she was home over break, they texted nearly non-stop, not only jokes but little updates about their days. They started saying good morning and good night, and when she asked him a question and he didn't respond right away she felt a jab of anxious yearning. She learned that Robert had two cats, named Mu and Yan, and together they invented a complicated scenario in which her childhood cat, Pita, would send flirtatious texts to Yan, but whenever Pita talked to Mu she was formal and cold, because she was jealous of Mu's relationship with Yan.

"Why are you texting all the time?" Margot's stepdad asked her at dinner. "Are you having an affair with someone?"

"Yes," Margot said. "His name is Robert, and I met him at the movie theatre. We're in love, and we're probably going to get married."

"Hmm," her stepdad said. "Tell him we have some questions for him."

"My parents are asking about u," Margot texted, and Robert sent her back a smiley-face emoji whose eyes were hearts.

When Margot returned to campus, she was eager to see Robert again, but he turned out to be surprisingly hard to pin down. "Sorry, busy week at work," he replied. "I promise I will c u soon." Margot didn't like this; it felt as if the dynamic had shifted out of her favor, and when eventually he did ask her to go to a movie she agreed right away.

The movie he wanted to see was playing at the theatre where she worked, but she suggested that they see it at the big multiplex just outside town instead; students didn't go there very often, because you needed to drive. Robert came to pick her up in a muddy white Civic with candy wrappers spilling out of the cup holders. On the drive, he was quieter than she'd expected, and he didn't look at her very much. Before five minutes had gone by, she became wildly uncomfortable, and, as they got on the highway, it occurred to her that he could take her someplace and rape and murder her; she hardly knew anything about him, after all.

Just as she thought this, he said, "Don't worry, I'm not going to murder you," and she wondered if the discomfort in the car was her fault, because she was acting jumpy and nervous, like the kind of girl who thought she was going to get murdered every time she went on a date.

"It's O.K.—you can murder me if you want," she said, and he laughed and patted her knee. But he was still disconcertingly quiet, and all her bubbling attempts at making conversation bounced right off him. At the theatre, he made a joke to the cashier at the concession stand about Red Vines, which fell flat in a way that embarrassed everyone involved, but Margot most of all.

During the movie, he didn't hold her hand or put his arm around her, so by the time they were back in the parking lot she was pretty sure that he had changed his mind about liking her. She was wearing leggings and a sweatshirt, and that might have been the problem. When she got into the car, he'd said, "Glad to see you dressed up for me," which she'd assumed was a joke, but maybe she actually had offended him by not seeming to take the date seriously enough, or something. He was wearing khakis and a button-down shirt.

"So, do you want to go get a drink?" he asked when they got back to the car, as if being polite were an obligation that had been imposed on him. It seemed obvious to Margot that he was expecting her to say no and that, when she did, they wouldn't talk again. That made her sad, not so much because she wanted to continue spending time with him as because she'd had such high expectations for him over break, and it didn't seem fair that things had fallen apart so quickly.

"We could go get a drink, I guess?" she said.

"If you want," he said.

"If you want" was such an unpleasant response that she sat

silently in the car until he poked her leg and said, "What are you sulking about?"

"I'm not sulking," she said. "I'm just a little tired."

"I can take you home."

"No, I could use a drink, after that movie." Even though it had been playing at the mainstream theatre, the film he'd chosen was a very depressing drama about the Holocaust, so inappropriate for a first date that when he suggested it she said, "Lol r u serious," and he made some joke about how he was sorry that he'd misjudged her taste and he could take her to a romantic comedy instead.

But now, when she said that about the movie, he winced a little, and a totally different interpretation of the night's events occurred to her. She wondered if perhaps he'd been trying to impress her by suggesting the Holocaust movie, because he didn't understand that a Holocaust movie was the wrong kind of "serious" movie with which to impress the type of person who worked at an artsy movie theatre, the type of person he probably assumed she was. Maybe, she thought, her texting "lol r u serious" had hurt him, had intimidated him and made him feel uncomfortable around her. The thought of this possible vulnerability touched her, and she felt kinder toward him than she had all night.

When he asked her where she wanted to go for a drink, she named the place where she usually hung out, but he made a face and said that it was in the student ghetto and he'd take her somewhere better. They went to a bar she'd never been to, an underground speakeasy type of place, with no sign announcing its presence. There was a line to get inside, and, as they waited, she grew fidgety trying to figure out how to tell him what she needed to tell him, but she couldn't, so when the bouncer asked to see her I.D. she just handed it to him. The bouncer hardly even looked at it; he just smirked and said, "Yeah, no," and waved her to the side, as he gestured toward the next group of people in line.

Robert had gone ahead of her, not noticing what was playing out behind him. "Robert," she said quietly. But he didn't turn around. Finally, someone in line who'd been paying attention tapped him on the shoulder and pointed to her, marooned on the sidewalk.

She stood, abashed, as he came back over to her. "Sorry!" she said. "This is so embarrassing."

"How old *are* you?" he demanded.

"I'm twenty," she said.

"Oh," he said. "I thought you said you were older."

"I told you I was a sophomore!" she said. Standing outside the bar, having been rejected in front of everyone, was humiliating enough, and now Robert was looking at her as if she'd done something wrong.

"But you did that—what do you call it? That gap year," he objected, as though this were an argument he could win.

"I don't know what to tell you," she said helplessly. "I'm twenty." And then, absurdly, she started to feel tears stinging her eyes, because somehow everything had been ruined and she couldn't understand why this was all so hard.

But, when Robert saw her face crumpling, a kind of magic happened. All the tension drained out of his posture; he stood up straight and wrapped his bearlike arms around her. "Oh, sweetheart," he said. "Oh, honey, it's O.K., it's all right. Please don't feel bad." She let herself be folded against him, and she was flooded with the same feeling she'd had outside the 7-Eleven—that she was a delicate, precious thing he was afraid he might break. He kissed the top of her head, and she laughed and wiped her tears away.

"I can't believe I'm crying because I didn't get into a bar," she said. "You must think I'm such an idiot." But she knew he didn't think that, from the way he was gazing at her; in his eyes, she could see how pretty she looked, smiling through her tears in the chalky glow of the streetlight, with a few flakes of snow coming down.

He kissed her then, on the lips, for real; he came for her in a kind of lunging motion and practically poured his tongue down her throat. It was a terrible kiss, shockingly bad; Margot had trouble believing that a grown man could possibly be so bad at kissing. It seemed awful, yet somehow it also gave her that tender feeling toward him again, the sense that even though he was older than her, she knew something he didn't.

When he was done kissing her, he took her hand firmly and led her to a different bar, where there were pool tables and pinball machines and sawdust on the floor and no one checking I.D.s at the door. In one of the booths, she saw the grad student who'd been her English T.A. her freshman year.

"Should I get you a vodka soda?" Robert asked, which she thought was maybe supposed to be a joke about the kind of drink college girls liked, though she'd never had a vodka soda. She actually was a little anxious about what to order; at the places she went to, they only carded people at the bar, so the kids who were twenty-one or had good fake I.D.s usually brought pitchers of P.B.R. or Bud Light back to share with the others. She wasn't sure if those brands were ones that Robert would make fun of, so, instead of specifying, she said, "I'll just have a beer."

With the drinks in front of him and the kiss behind him, and also maybe because she had cried, Robert became much more relaxed, more like the witty person she knew through his texts. As they talked, she became increasingly sure that what she'd interpreted as anger or dissatisfaction with her had, in fact, been nervousness, a fear that she wasn't having a good time. He kept coming back to her initial dismissal of the movie, making jokes that glanced off it and watching her closely to see how she responded. He teased her about her highbrow taste, and said how hard it was to impress her because of all the film classes she'd taken, even though he knew she'd taken only one summer class in film. He joked about how she and the other employees at the artsy theatre probably sat around and made fun of the people who went to the mainstream theatre, where they didn't even serve wine, and some of the movies were in IMAX 3-D.

Margot laughed along with the jokes he was making at the expense of this imaginary film-snob version of her, though nothing he said seemed quite fair, since she was the one who'd actually suggested that they see the movie at the Quality 16. Although now, she realized, maybe that had hurt Robert's feelings, too. She'd thought it was clear that she just didn't want to go on a date where she worked, but maybe he'd taken it more personally than that; maybe he'd suspected that she was ashamed to be seen with him. She was starting to think that she understood him—how sensitive he was, how easily he could be wounded—and that made her feel closer to him, and also powerful, because once she knew how to hurt him she also knew how he could be soothed. She asked him lots of questions about the movies he liked, and she spoke self-deprecatingly about the movies at the artsy theatre that she found boring or incomprehensible; she told him about how much her older co-workers intimidated her, and how she sometimes worried that she wasn't smart enough to form her own opinions on anything. The effect of this on him was palpable and immediate, and she felt as if she were petting a large, skittish animal, like a horse or a bear, skillfully coaxing it to eat from her hand.

By her third beer, she was thinking about what it would be like to have sex with Robert. Probably it would be like that bad kiss, clumsy and excessive, but imagining how excited he would be, how hungry and eager to impress her, she felt a twinge of desire pluck at her belly, as distinct and painful as the snap of an elastic band against her skin.

When they'd finished that round of drinks, she said, boldly, "Should we get out of here, then?," and he seemed briefly hurt, as if he thought she was cutting the date short, but she took his hand and pulled him up, and the look on his face when he realized what she was saying, and the obedient way he trailed her out of the bar, gave her that elastic-band snap again, as did, oddly, the fact that his palm was slick beneath hers.

Outside, she presented herself to him again for kissing, but, to her surprise, he only pecked her on the mouth. "You're drunk," he said, accusingly.

"No, I'm not," she said, though she was. She pushed her body against his, feeling tiny beside him, and he let out a great shuddering sigh, as if she were something too bright and painful to look at, and that was sexy, too, being made to feel like a kind of irresistible temptation.

"I'm taking you home, lightweight," he said, shepherding her to the car. Once they were inside it, though, she leaned into him again, and after a little while, by lightly pulling back when he pushed his tongue too far down her throat, she was able to get him to kiss her in the softer way that she liked, and soon after that she was straddling him, and she could feel the small log of his erection straining against his pants. Whenever it rolled beneath her weight, he let out these fluttery, high-pitched moans that she couldn't help feeling were a little melodramatic, and then suddenly he pushed her off him and turned the key in the ignition.

"Making out in the front seat like a teen-ager," he said, in mock disgust. Then he added, “I’d have thought you’d be too old for that, now that you’re *twenty*.”

She stuck her tongue out at him. “Where do you want to go, then?”

“Your place?”

“Um, that won’t really work. Because of my roommate?”

“Oh, right. You live in the dorms,” he said, as though that were something she should apologize for.

“Where do you live?” she asked.

“I live in a house.”

“Can I . . . come over?”

“You can.”

The house was in a pretty, wooded neighborhood not too far from campus and had a string of cheerful white fairy lights across the doorway. Before he got out of the car, he said, darkly, like a warning, “Just so you know, I have cats.”

“I know,” she said. “We texted about them, remember?”

At the front door, he fumbled with his keys for what seemed a ridiculously long time and swore under his breath. She rubbed his back to try to keep the mood going, but that seemed to fluster him even more, so she stopped.

“Well. This is my house,” he said flatly, pushing the door open.

The room they were in was dimly lit and full of objects, all of which, as her eyes adjusted, resolved into familiarity. He had two large, full bookcases, a shelf of vinyl records, a collection of board games, and a lot of art—or, at least, posters that had been hung in frames, instead of being tacked or taped to the wall.

“I like it,” she said, truthfully, and, as she did, she identified the emotion she was feeling as relief. It occurred to her that she’d never gone to someone’s house to have sex before; because she’d dated only guys her age, there had always been some element of sneaking around, to avoid roommates. It was new, and a little frightening, to be so completely on someone else’s turf, and the fact that Robert’s house gave evidence of his having interests that she shared, if only in their broadest categories—art, games, books, music—struck her as a reassuring endorsement of her choice.

As she thought this, she saw that Robert was watching her closely, observing the impression the room had made. And, as though fear weren't quite ready to release its hold on her, she had the brief wild idea that maybe this was not a room at all but a trap meant to lure her into the false belief that Robert was a normal person, a person like her, when in fact all the other rooms in the house were empty, or full of horrors: corpses or kidnap victims or chains. But then he was kissing her, throwing her bag and their coats on the couch and ushering her into the bedroom, groping her ass and pawing at her chest, with the avid clumsiness of that first kiss.

The bedroom wasn't empty, though it was emptier than the living room; he didn't have a bed frame, just a mattress and a box spring on the floor. There was a bottle of whiskey on his dresser, and he took a swig from it, then handed it to her and kneeled down and opened his laptop, an action that confused her, until she understood that he was putting on music.

Margot sat on the bed while Robert took off his shirt and unbuckled his pants, pulling them down to his ankles before realizing that he was still wearing his shoes and bending over to untie them. Looking at him like that, so awkwardly bent, his belly thick and soft and covered with hair, Margot recoiled. But the thought of what it would take to stop what she had set in motion was overwhelming; it would require an amount of tact and gentleness that she felt was impossible to summon. It wasn't that she was scared he would try to force her to do something against her will but that insisting that they stop now, after everything she'd done to push this forward, would make her seem spoiled and capricious, as if she'd ordered something at a restaurant and then, once the food arrived, had changed her mind and sent it back.

She tried to bludgeon her resistance into submission by taking a sip of the whiskey, but when he fell on top of her with those huge, sloppy kisses, his hand moving mechanically across her breasts and down to her crotch, as if he were making some perverse sign of the cross, she began to have trouble breathing and to feel that she really might not be able to go through with it after all.

Wriggling out from under the weight of him and straddling him helped, as did closing her eyes and remembering him kissing her forehead at the 7-Eleven. Encouraged by her progress, she pulled her shirt up over her head. Robert reached up and scooped her breast out of her bra, so that it jutted half in and half out of the cup, and rolled her nipple between his thumb and forefinger. This was uncomfortable, so she leaned forward, pushing herself into his hand. He got the hint and tried to undo her bra, but he couldn't work the clasp, his evident frustration reminiscent of his struggle with the keys, until at last he said, bossily, "Take that thing off," and she complied.

The way he looked at her then was like an exaggerated version of the expression she'd seen on the faces of all the guys she'd been naked with, not that there were that many—six in total, Robert made seven. He looked stunned and stupid with pleasure, like a milk-drunk baby, and she thought that maybe this was what she loved most about sex—a guy revealed like that. Robert showed her more open need than any of the others, even though he was older, and must have seen more breasts, more bodies, than they had—but maybe that was part of it for him, the fact that he was older, and she was young.

As they kissed, she found herself carried away by a fantasy of such pure ego that she could hardly admit even to herself that she was having it. Look at this beautiful girl, she imagined him thinking. She's so perfect, her body is perfect, everything about her is perfect, she's only twenty years old, her skin is flawless, I want her so badly, I want her more than I've ever wanted anyone else, I want her so bad I might die.

The more she imagined his arousal, the more turned-on she got, and soon they were rocking against each other, getting into a rhythm, and she reached into his underwear and took his penis in her hand and felt the pearled droplet of moisture on its tip. He made that sound again, that high-pitched feminine whine, and she wished there were a way she could ask him not to do that, but she couldn't think of any. Then his hand was inside her underwear, and when he felt that she was wet he visibly relaxed. He fingered her a little, very softly, and she bit her lip and put on a show for him, but then he poked her too hard and she flinched, and he jerked his hand away. "Sorry!" he said.

And then he asked, urgently, "Wait. Have you ever done this before?"

The night did, indeed, feel so odd and unprecedented that her first impulse was to say no, but then she realized what he meant and she laughed out loud.

She didn't mean to laugh; she knew well enough already that, while Robert might enjoy being the subject of gentle, flirtatious teasing, he was not a person who would enjoy being laughed at, not at all. But she couldn't help it. Losing her virginity had been a long, drawn-out affair preceded by several months' worth of intense discussion with her boyfriend of two years, plus a visit to the gynecologist and a horrifically embarrassing but ultimately incredibly meaningful conversation with her mom, who, in the end, had not only reserved her a room at a bed-and-breakfast but, after the event, written her a card. The idea that, instead of that whole involved, emotional process, she might have watched a pretentious Holocaust movie, drunk three beers, and then gone to some random house to lose her virginity to a guy she'd met at a movie theatre was so funny that suddenly she couldn't stop laughing, though the laughter had a slightly hysterical edge.

"I'm sorry," Robert said coldly. "I didn't know."

Abruptly, she stopped giggling.

"No, it was . . . nice of you to check," she said. "I've had sex before, though. I'm sorry I laughed."

"You don't need to apologize," he said, but she could tell by his face, as well as by the fact that he was going soft beneath her, that she did.

"I'm sorry," she said again, reflexively, and then, in a burst of inspiration, "I guess I'm just nervous, or something?"

He narrowed his eyes at her, as though suspicious of this claim, but it seemed to placate him. "You don't have to be nervous," he said. "We'll take it slow."

Yeah, right, she thought, and then he was on top of her again, kissing her and weighing her down, and she knew that her last chance of enjoying this encounter had disappeared, but that she would carry through with it until it was over. When Robert was naked, rolling a condom onto a dick that was only half visible beneath the hairy shelf of his belly, she felt a wave of revulsion that she thought might actually break through her sense of pinned stasis, but then he shoved his finger in her again, not at all gently this time, and she imagined herself from above, naked and spread-eagled with this fat old man's finger inside her, and her revulsion turned to self-disgust and a humiliation that was a kind of perverse cousin to arousal.

During sex, he moved her through a series of positions with brusque efficiency, flipping her over, pushing her around, and she felt like a doll again, as she had outside the 7-Eleven, though not a precious one now—a doll made of rubber, flexible and resilient, a prop for the movie that was playing in his head. When she was on top, he slapped her thigh and said, "Yeah, yeah, you like that," with an intonation that made it impossible to tell whether he meant it as a question, an observation, or an order, and when he turned her over he growled in her ear, "I always wanted to fuck a girl with nice tits," and she had to smother her face in the pillow to keep from laughing again. At the end, when he was on top of her in missionary, he kept losing his erection, and every time he did he would say, aggressively, "You make my dick so hard," as though lying about it could make it true. At last, after a frantic rabbity burst, he shuddered, came, and collapsed on her like a tree falling, and, crushed beneath him, she thought, brightly, This is the worst life decision I have ever made! And she marvelled at herself for a while, at the mystery of this person who'd just done this bizarre, inexplicable thing.

After a short while, Robert got up and hurried to the bathroom in a bow-legged waddle, clutching the condom to keep it from falling off. Margot lay on the bed and stared at the ceiling, noticing for the first time that there were stickers on it, those little stars and moons that were supposed to glow in the dark.

Robert returned from the bathroom and stood silhouetted in the doorway. "What do you want to do now?" he asked her.

"We should probably just kill ourselves," she imagined saying, and then she imagined that somewhere, out there in the universe, there was a boy who would think that this moment was just as awful yet hilarious as she did, and that sometime, far in the future, she would tell the boy this story. She'd say, "And then he said, 'You make my dick so hard,'" and the boy would shriek in agony and grab her leg, saying, "Oh, my God, stop, please, no, I can't take it anymore," and the two of them would collapse into each other's arms and laugh and laugh—but of course there was no such future, because no such boy existed, and never would.

So instead she shrugged, and Robert said, "We could watch a movie," and he went to the computer and downloaded something; she didn't pay attention to what. For some reason, he'd chosen a movie with subtitles, and she kept closing her eyes, so she had no idea what was going on. The whole time, he was stroking her hair and trailing light kisses down her shoulder, as if he'd forgotten that ten minutes ago he'd thrown her around as if they were in a porno and growled, "I always wanted to fuck a girl with nice tits" in her ear.

Then, out of nowhere, he started talking about his feelings for her. He talked about how hard it had been for him when she went away for break, not knowing if she had an old high-school boyfriend she might reconnect with back home. During those two weeks, it turned out, an entire secret drama had played out in his head, one in which she'd left campus committed to him, to Robert, but at home had been drawn back to the high-school guy, who, in Robert's mind, was some kind of brutish, handsome jock, not worthy of her but nonetheless seductive by virtue of his position at the top of the hierarchy back home in Saline. "I was so worried you might, like, make a bad decision and things would be different between us when you got back," he said. "But I should have trusted you." My high-school boyfriend is gay, Margot imagined telling him. We were pretty sure of it in high school, but after a year of sleeping around at college he's definitely figured it out. In fact, he's not even a hundred per cent positive that he identifies as a man anymore; we spent a lot of time over break talking about what it would mean for him to come out as non-binary, so sex with him wasn't going to happen, and you could have asked me about that if you were worried; you could have asked me about a lot of things. But she didn't say any of that; she just lay silently, emanating a black, hateful aura, until finally Robert trailed off. "Are you still awake?" he asked, and she said yes, and he said, "Is everything O.K.?"

"How old are you, exactly?" she asked him.

"I'm thirty-four," he said. "Is that a problem?"

She could sense him in the dark beside her vibrating with fear.

"No," she said. "It's fine."

"Good," he said. "It was something I wanted to bring up with you, but I didn't know how you'd take it." He rolled over and kissed her forehead, and she felt like a slug he'd poured salt on, disintegrating under that kiss.

She looked at the clock; it was nearly three in the morning. "I should go home, probably," she said.

"Really?" he said. "But I thought you'd stay over. I make great scrambled eggs!"

"Thanks," she said, sliding into her leggings. "But I can't. My roommate would be worried. So."

"Gotta get back to the dorm room," he said, voice dripping with sarcasm.

"Yep," she said. "Since that's where I live."

The drive was endless. The snow had turned to rain. They didn't talk. Eventually, Robert switched the radio to late-night NPR. Margot recalled how, when they first got on the highway to go to the movie, she'd imagined that Robert might murder her, and she thought, Maybe he'll murder me now.

He didn't murder her. He drove her to her dorm. "I had a really nice time tonight," he said, unbuckling his seat belt.

"Thanks," she said. She clutched her bag in her hands. "Me, too."

"I'm so glad we finally got to go on a date," he said.

"A *date*," she said to her imaginary boyfriend. "He called that a *date*." And they both laughed and laughed.

"You're welcome," she said. She reached for the door handle. "Thanks for the movie and stuff."

"Wait," he said, and grabbed her arm. "Come here." He dragged her back, wrapped his arms around her, and pushed his tongue down her throat one last time. "Oh, my God, when will it end?" she asked the imaginary boyfriend, but the imaginary boyfriend didn't answer her.

"Good night," she said, and then she opened the door and escaped. By the time she got to her room, she already had a text from him: no words, just hearts and faces with heart eyes and, for some reason, a dolphin.

She slept for twelve hours, and when she woke up she ate waffles in the dining hall and binge-watched detective shows on Netflix and tried to envision the hopeful possibility that he would disappear without her having to do anything, that somehow she could just wish him away. When the next message from him did arrive, just after dinner, it was a harmless joke about Red Vines, but she deleted it immediately, overwhelmed with a skin-crawling loathing that felt vastly disproportionate to anything he had actually done. She told herself that she owed him at least some kind of breakup message, that to ghost on him would be inappropriate, childish, and cruel. And, if she did try to ghost, who knew how long it would take him to get the hint? Maybe the messages would keep coming and coming; maybe they would never end.

She began drafting a message—*Thank you for the nice time but I'm not interested in a relationship right now*—but she kept hedging and apologizing, attempting to close loopholes that she imagined him trying to slip through ("*It's O.K., I'm not interested in a relationship either, something casual is fine!*"), so that the message got longer and longer and even more impossible to send. Meanwhile, his texts kept arriving, none of them saying anything of consequence, each one more earnest than the last. She imagined him lying on his bed that was just a mattress, carefully crafting each one. She remembered that he'd talked a lot about his cats and yet she hadn't seen any cats in the house, and she wondered if he'd made them up.

Every so often, over the next day or so, she would find herself in a gray, daydreamy mood, missing something, and she'd realize that it was Robert she missed, not the real Robert but the Robert she'd imagined on the other end of all those text messages during break.

"Hey, so it seems like you're really busy, huh?" Robert finally wrote, three days after they'd fucked, and she knew that this was the perfect opportunity to send her half-completed breakup text, but instead she wrote back, "Haha sorry yeah" and "I'll text you soon," and then she thought, Why did I do that? And she truly didn't know.

"Just tell him you're not interested!" Margot's roommate, Tamara, screamed in frustration after Margot had spent an hour on her bed, dithering about what to say to Robert.

"I have to say more than that. We had *sex*," Margot said.

"*Do* you?" Tamara said. "I mean, really?"

"He's a nice guy, sort of," Margot said, and she wondered how true that was. Then, abruptly, Tamara lunged, snatching the phone out of Margot's hand and holding it far away from her as her thumbs flew across the screen. Tamara flung the phone onto the bed and Margot scrambled for it, and there it was, what Tamara had written: "Hi im not interested in you stop textng me."

"Oh, my God," Margot said, finding it suddenly hard to breathe.

"What?" Tamara said boldly. "What's the big deal? It's true."

But they both knew that it was a big deal, and Margot had a knot of fear in her stomach so solid that she thought she might retch. She imagined Robert picking up his phone, reading that message, turning to glass, and shattering to pieces.

"Calm down. Let's go get a drink," Tamara said, and they went to a bar and shared a pitcher, and all the while Margot's phone sat between them on the table, and though they tried to ignore it, when it chimed with an incoming message they screamed and clutched each other's arms.

"I can't do it—you read it," Margot said. She pushed the phone toward Tamara. "You did this. It's your fault."

But all the message said was "O.K., Margot, I am sorry to hear that. I hope I did not do anything to upset you. You are a sweet girl and I really enjoyed the time we spent together. Please let me know if you change your mind."

Margot collapsed on the table, laying her head in her hands. She felt as though a leech, grown heavy and swollen with her blood, had at last popped off her skin, leaving a tender, bruised spot behind. But why should she feel that way? Perhaps she was being unfair to Robert, who really had done nothing wrong, except like her, and be bad in bed, and maybe lie about having cats, although probably they had just been in another room.

But then, a month later, she saw him in the bar—her bar, the one in the student ghetto, where, on their date, she'd suggested they go. He was alone, at a table in the back, and he wasn't reading or looking at his phone; he was just sitting there silently, hunched over a beer.

She grabbed the friend she was with, a guy named Albert. "Oh, my God, that's him," she whispered. "The guy from the movie theatre!" By then, Albert had heard a version of the story, though not quite the true one; nearly all her friends had. Albert stepped in front of her, shielding her from Robert's view, as they rushed back to the table where their friends were. When Margot announced that

Robert was there, everyone erupted in astonishment, and then they surrounded her and hustled her out of the bar as if she were the President and they were the Secret Service. It was all so over-the-top that she wondered if she was acting like a mean girl, but, at the same time, she truly did feel sick and scared.

Curled up on her bed with Tamara that night, the glow of the phone like a campfire illuminating their faces, Margot read the messages as they arrived:

"Hi Margot, I saw you out at the bar tonight. I know you said not to text you but I just wanted to say you looked really pretty. I hope you're doing well!"

"I know I shouldnt say this but I really miss you"

"Hey maybe I don't have the right to ask but I just wish youd tell me what it is I did wrog"

"*wrong"

"I felt like we had a real connection did you not feel that way or . . ."

"Maybe I was too old for u or maybe you liked someone else"

"Is that guy you were with tonight your boyfriend"

"???"

"Or is he just some guy you are fucking"

"Sorry"

"When u laguehd when I asked if you were a virgin was it because youd fucked so many guys"

"Are you fucking that guy right now"

"Are you"

"Are you"

"Are you"

"Answer me"

"Whore."

CHAUNT

BY JOY WILLIAMS (2018)

The building was called the Dove. Or Dove. She's out there at Dove, people might say if they wanted to bother. It was eleven stories with a multitude of single rooms, very much like a dovecote, or, as everyone eventually suggested, a columbarium. It was in a windy desert basin with a wonderful view of distant mountains. If you felt that the Dove was the place for you, you gave them all your money and you would be cared for there until the day you died. Should you choose to leave before then, they still kept all your money. Leaving was a poor option and hardly anyone did it.

When the boys died and after she had buried the one who was hers, she moved to Dove. Many days passed—she would be the last to know how many—before anyone spoke to her.

"For beyond the stars' pavilions God shall compensate your grief," the person said.

Jane Click asked him to repeat this.

"For beyond . . ." he began.

"Oh, yes, yes, thank you," she said quickly.

"It's from a poem," he said.

"It sounds like it's from a poem." She had no idea what she was saying. She didn't have to say anything or mean anything. She was at Dove.

The man, who offered his name as Theodore, was extremely dishevelled. He appeared filthy, though he had no odor, none at all.

He wore colorful motley, practically rags, like the professional fool in some decadent court.

Occasionally, there were gatherings on an upper floor at Dove. These gatherings were led, more or less, by visiting youths, who, she suspected, received some sort of credit toward their sentences, though their sentences were never disclosed. Many had tattoos creeping all over their bodies. Obscure, formerly sacred images were popular, also lines of verse. The youths didn't want to wait until they were dead for pretty words to be carved on their gravestones. They wanted the pretty words now. Most of them had shaved their heads as well as their eyebrows. Removing their eyebrows, they explained, eliminated several degrees of expression, producing a cerebral, even mechanical look, a look that appealed to them.

There was no love lost between the youths and the residents of Dove.

The summer had passed, and the great clouds that rise above the desert in that season, towering miles and miles into the sky, so dark and promising, had brought no rain. The waters behind the dams in the vast reservoirs were diminishing. Even when people didn't use the water, which they had every right to use in whatever manner they chose to, it disappeared anyway. Evaporation was a real problem, which officials admitted had to be addressed soon.

"So, how you all doing this evening?" a leader says without a shred of interest. She is a teen-ager, five or six years older than Billy was, with a tattoo of the spider of Nazca on her throat.

After a long silence, someone offers, "I'm good. More and more stuff I'm thinking I can put into words."

"We'd have to challenge you on that one, I'm sure," the leader says mildly.

"But then they belong to others, your thoughts," a woman says cautiously. She is wearing a long, bright canvas coat that looks like a painting torn from its frame.

Many present seem to be crying behind their sunglasses. The light in Dove is almost vindictive. Jane Click feels she will never become used to it and makes no attempt to avoid it. She stares right into it as often as she can.

"Two billion people on this earth less than a hundred years ago," the dishevelled man says. "Now there are seven billion people."

"And you can't love them all is the problem," a woman says, nodding.

No one sits near Theodore. Maybe it's his confusing garments. Maybe they think he's unlucky, though they're all unlucky here, decent enough individuals caught by the mishaps of time in a circumstance of continual, bearable punishment.

Someone mentions that it's her birthday, or will be soon, tomorrow. The others murmur and clap a little.

Jane Click's son, Billy, had a friend, a shy child with a harelip. "Like the rabbit," he'd explained, when Billy first brought him home. He said that on his birthday he always had pie; he didn't care for cake. The driver of the car that struck them as they were on their bicycles, returning on the long, flat road from Chaunt, was a retired thoracic surgeon. He was not without blame, was not guilty, either. He saw the boys only when the situation was upon them all. They had been invisible to him. Invisible in the wolfish dusk.

A group wanted to erect two "ghost bikes" at the spot, bicycles painted a flat and horrid white, but she wouldn't allow it.

"Is your name Jerry or Jerome?" she'd asked when Billy first brought him home.

"Jerome. I don't like my name. I was named for my mother's brother, but I don't know why, because he doesn't like it neither."

"There was a St. Jerome," she told him. "He healed a lion's paw."

"What was wrong with it?"

"It was injured in some way. A thorn."

"That's nice he fixed him."

"So think of the story of Jerome and the lion. They became best friends."

"Billy's my best friend, aren't you, Billy? Are there any pictures of Jerome and the lion?"

"I'll try to find one for you."

The boys were not impressed. St. Jerome was an old man who did not inspire their interest. The lion did not look like a lion.

"It has a face," Jerry said.

"Animals have faces," Billy said.

"It looks like something else's face, though."

"My father had a pet raven once," Billy told him. "He had it for a long time but then it flew away."

"Did it come back?"

"If it came back, why would I be telling you he had one once?"

Jerry shrugged. He was not a boy who took offense. His father wasn't a presence in his life, either, and there were a few stories about him, too. There was a leather jacket that Jerry could wear when he got bigger, but he didn't really want it.

For days after the accident, the authorities chose not to disclose the name of the driver. The way they put it was, "At this time, our intention is not to share."

Eventually, they shared. He was a man of some prominence. He wrote Jane Click a letter expressing sorrow at her loss. Her hands burned holding it. Of course she didn't keep it.

People were not kind to Jane Click after the accident. Jerry's relatives threatened her and threw bags of trash on her doorstep. Billy's father returned for a bit of one day, with a new wife and son, who refused to enter her bright and bookish house or even accept a glass of water. (She hated books now, had not brought a single one to the Dove.) No one could understand why she had allowed two small boys to go to Chaunt again and again. It was twenty miles away, at least, and wasn't even there, a hamlet abandoned long ago, harboring only a few collapsed structures in an exhausted valley.

She doesn't think of the place in terms of distance. If absence becomes great enough, it grows into a genuine apparition, an immediate presence.

When Jane Click still read, she preferred the language of displacement and estrangement that prepared a path to revelation over language that simply refreshed and enlarged upon what she already knew. But if you asked her what was the very last book that she had read—the one that had ultimately led her to the conclusion that books wanted only to expose and destroy you, tear your heart out and leave it in the dust, like the soul of a murdered and soon forgotten little animal—she wouldn't be able to tell you.

Nor would she be able to state with any surety whether it was Billy who had discovered the church at Chaunt or whether the boys had discovered it together. It had been more chapel than church, with a single long rectangular room. And more rubble than chapel now. It took an extravagance of imagination to see it as a house of praise. The roof was gone, though a wheel window remained unbroken, high above the absent door. Inside, a few pews lay scattered, as though smashed with an axe.

The long room was full of animals.

"They weren't made-up animals," Billy said. "They weren't people or statues."

"They weren't zoo animals, exactly, either," Jerry said. "There wasn't an elephant or a lion or a polar bear, not exactly."

"They were waiting," Billy said, "but they weren't waiting for us."

"You know when a dog is lost and he looks at you intently for a minute but . . ."

"Well, less than a minute," Billy said.

"Less than a minute, then, but then he realizes that you aren't the one he needs to find. They looked at us that way and then they went back to waiting."

"There wasn't a sound. You couldn't even hear them breathe, but then you could."

"Once they know you're not who they're waiting for, they don't look at you anymore."

"They become motionless."

"Yes, motionless. But still animals. All the animals you'd ever hope to see," Jerry said with joy.

She tried to get them to describe the animals. Did the boys speak to them or touch them? Were there birds?

There were birds, apparently, but very small ones.

Were there horses there?

When she was a child, she wanted to be a horse. She had a treasured collection of horses—metal, ceramic, plastic, wood. She had never ridden a horse or cared for one, but she had kept pictures of them and much commentary concerning them in a large black notebook for many years, though the book had been missing for just as long.

"Maybe someone's using it as a barn," she said. "A corral."

Her son regarded her with disappointment.

"Maybe. Not really," Jerome said politely.

"When you're there, you know that something is going to happen any moment and you wait with them so you can be there when it happens," Billy said. "You haven't been invited to stay but you're welcome to stay. It's just about to happen."

"But what?" she asked, smiling. "And why?" She remembers smiling. She can feel it still on her lips, the falsity and carelessness of it.

Then they spoke no further of the ruined little building and the animals.

Though sometimes she thinks that they did, that, indeed, that was all they spoke about, but she cannot remember it now, she cannot remember.

The boys continued to travel out there. They would take sandwiches and jars of water and be gone all day. Something extraordinary was about to be known, yet at the same time it would never be known—that was what she thought. That was its disturbing beauty, what made it irresistible. She thought, Soon the children will no longer realize what they understand. They will no longer be at ease with wonder. They will be unable to abide it.

But she is thinking this now. She cannot remember thinking it then.

Sometimes at these get-togethers at Dove, the residents talk about what they miss. Jane Click is not encouraged to speak at these times, which is perfectly understandable. What kind of mother was she, anyway, letting two little boys spend all their time at Chaunt, so far away and not even there.

"I miss the birds," someone says. "They don't come to the feeders. The feeders are always full but no one comes."

"I had a freezer full of elk. I miss having that, the security. Probably all rotten now."

"That's in the very nature of a freezer full of elk."

"So much spoils before it can be utilized. Like certain types of trees, most trees now—they rot before they cure. Don't even burn good."

"I try to eat mostly fruit."

"Yes, but do they have to put those little stickers on everything? On every blueberry, a sticker."

"It's difficult not to just eat those, too. I do."

"But the adhesive . . ."

The dishevelled man sits erect, indignant, shunned, silent. Just that morning, or perhaps it was another morning, he had asked Jane Click if she would like him to drive her out to Chaunt. She was surprised that he had a car.

"I do not have a car," he said. "I have a license. I have the ability to borrow a car."

She had never gone to Chaunt. She had only imagined herself being there, before she came to the Dove. Lying in bed in her silent house, her hair wet with sweat, her body stinking with despair, she was able to travel there. Night was best, for, as everyone knows but does not tell, the sobbing of the earth is most audible at night. You can hear it clearly then, but the sobbing still harbors a little bit of hope, a little bit of promise that the day does not afford. So that was when she went to Chaunt, in her night mind, into the long ruined room full of animals, not analogous to animals, as in a dream, but not quite recognizable as such beings, either. Sometimes, while there, she closed her eyes the better to see them but she could never see them, she could only look.

There was a short, splintered pew that was upright but not steady, a small space, a human space, where she sat awkwardly, feeling the inconsequence of her presence, feeling the sorrowful cataclysm being silently enacted there. She never felt closer to her son or his gentle friend there; she felt closer to the mute enormity of this other absence. It was a place not of solace but of correspondence, a correspondence that might never occur.

Her dream, her access, had gone on for nights. She slept eagerly, desperately, again and again entering the ruined room empty-handed, bearing no offering. She wore a dress that belonged to another season, when she was much younger, a sleeveless, flowered dress, rotting a little along one seam. She found her place, the same small and awkward place, and waited with those other presences. It was never the wrong day, the wrong hour, for waiting knows all days and hours. Soon, something would enter, fearsomely, abruptly, like a judge from the robing room. But before this happened, before it could ever happen, she awoke. It was winter, and snow was falling. The old roads that her mind allowed her to follow reappeared.

She knew that she had to stop going there before she went one night, as always, and found nothing.

Someone addressed Theodore. "Who you going to borrow a car from? No one would lend you a car."

"I'm here now," Jane Click said to Theodore.

For she had made an irrevocable choice, had she not? She could have remained in Chaunt in the manner allowed, in the unfinished masterpiece that was Chaunt, or she could live in a situation like this, with its various services and amenities, where everything was familiar, with the same uselessly familiar panic flowing quietly beneath it.

"Yeah, you are but not," Theodore said. "I escort you to Chaunt, we return the same day, of course, and then you'll be here."

"There's nothing there, dear," Little Betty said. Little Betty, who still used the broom she'd bought years before, which had been advertised to sweep a distance of ninety miles.

"You are beyond the pale, you are," someone said to Theodore. "You shouldn't be borrowing or beseeching no one."

"It's quite all right," Jane Click said. "But thank you, thank you."

"When you first arrived," Theodore persisted, "you said you need no wants. But you do."

"Why this place even tolerates you is beyond me," Dick Ford, the man who missed his freezer, said to Theodore. "Committee must have been drunk when they let you in."

"I believe the qualifications for admission depend upon one's handwriting. . . ."

"I don't think so. It's got to be something else. There are probably any number of . . ."

"You can tell a great deal about what's wrong with a person by his signature."

"It's like I can't imagine you even being born—it's weird," Dick Ford said. He regretted mentioning the freezer; he wasn't sure why.

The dishevelled man shrugged and walked away, gathering his ragged coats around him.

"Do you know what he told me once?" Little Betty asked Jane

Click. "He told me he was a teleologist. I had to look it up. Did he ever tell you?"

"No."

"Do you know what a teleologist is?"

"I don't," Jane Click said.

"I had to look it up. It's a kind of thinking. A belief, even. It sure made him go off the rails."

Jane Click retires to her room, with its view of distant mountains, mountains that are empty, she's been told. No life conceals itself within them anymore. Where was this country she persisted in? It had been vanquished of all but stones.

The leaders stopped coming, but no one missed them. The consensus was that they had not been necessary.

"They may have been here to keep us from feeling sad but I feel sad anyway," Little Betty said. "There's something we should have done and we didn't do it is my suspicion. But life goes its merry way without us. Everything's provisional."

"I disagree," someone said. "I think what's happened is permanent and not provisional at all."

"What I see is a slow and steady profaning of our species out there," someone else said. "Even those so-called leaders kept changing. Did you notice that one boy had a slice of pizza on his head, his shaved head, a tattoo of a slice of pizza, I mean? That kind of attitude belongs out there, so let them finish the job. Theirs is a mop-up operation. They never thought that would be their destiny, I bet, but it is, and nothing will absolve them of it now."

"That's a good way of putting it, Ray. It really is a good way of putting it."

But without the leaders, as indifferent or resentful as they had been, there was little reason for the residents of Dove to congregate. Meetings became more and more infrequent. The only individual Jane Click was now aware of with any regularity was Theodore, who remained dishevelled in a way that seemed unsustainable even here, even within Dove. But he had freed her from his interest.

She did not mind this.

Then even he slipped from her awareness, along with his rags and his beyond-the-stars'-pavilions.

She still heard the boys' soft, precipitate voices, still heard them speaking with that reckless trust she feared she had betrayed. She recognized a rhythm but not words. More and more urgently, their voices addressed her. She longed to return to Chaunt but knew she would not, reasoning that only if she did not witness it again might it endure. In time, she would suffer mere death, as had her child and every mother's child, but those to whom man has awarded extinction surely suffer more than death.

Soon, but still unmercifully long before the Dove released her, the wordless cries would fade to nothing.

ALL WILL BE WELL

BY YIYUN LI (2019)

Once upon a time, I was addicted to a salon. I never called ahead, and rarely had to wait—not everyone went to Lily's for a haircut. The old men Lily called uncles sat at a card table, reading newspapers and magazines in Chinese and Vietnamese. The television above the counter was tuned to a channel based in Riverside, and the aunties—related or not related to the uncles—watched cooking shows and teledramas in Mandarin.

I was the only customer under sixty, and the only one who spoke in English. With others Lily used Vietnamese, Cantonese, or Mandarin. The first time we met, I lied and said that I had been adopted by a couple from Holland when I was a year old and that we moved to America when I was in middle school. Lily forgave me then for not being able to speak one of the languages she preferred. Brought up by foreign devils, she told a nearby auntie in Cantonese. Half foreign, the auntie said; hair still Chinese. Half devil, Lily said; brain not Chinese. Both laughed. I smiled blankly at Lily in the mirror, and she smiled back. What do you do? she asked, and I lied again and said I was a student. She picked up a strand of hair and let it fall. My hair had just begun to show signs of gray. What subject? she asked, and I said I'd gone back to school because I wanted to become a writer. Will you make money being a writer? she asked, and I said not really.

Lily's salon was a few blocks from the high street where armed robberies rarely made even the local news. The salon was caged in metal bars, and there was a chain on the door, which Lily unlocked when she saw her customers coming and locked again right after they entered. If there was a fire, none of us would escape, I had thought when I first started to go there, though that didn't alarm me. I had two small children then, both in preschool, but, despite others' warnings, I did not feel susceptible to the various dangers that the world could dole out. If the world had a mind to harm, it would do so to the prepared and the unprepared equally. Does being a mother give one the right to bluff? If having children is a gamble, one has no choice but to bluff.

We lived on the college campus where I was teaching at the time. Enclosed within the fences was a land of trees and ponds and creeks and fountains. The flowering quinces near our house were said to have been planted by the servants of the founder's family in the eighteen-sixties. The preschool was in a building that, with its white stucco and Spanish tiled roof, looked like an outdated resort in the Mediterranean. America was a young country, California among its youngest states. The college was a mere débutante in a world of grand, old institutes, but all those trees and bushes and buildings gave me the impression that life could be as slowly lived, as long-lasting, as we wanted it to be.

Still, the world was full of perils. Some rather real, some rather close. Once, campus security sent out a warning that an unaccompanied pit bull had been spotted roaming near the swimming pool. Once, an armed man was chased into the cluster of faculty houses on a Saturday night; with police cars and helicopters outside, we turned off our lights and listened to a CD of a French children's drama called "Madame Magic," designed as a language course. Sometimes a drive-by shooting happened on the street corner near the preschool, and on those days the children were deprived of their outdoor time. All these threats, strangely, didn't worry me as much as the eucalyptus trees. A recurring fear I had, during those years, was that on a windy day a eucalyptus branch would fall on our heads. In one of the earliest conversations about nature I had with my children, I pointed out that the settlers had made a mistake introducing eucalyptus trees to California. A fire hazard in the dry season, I said, and in winter storms there was the danger of falling limbs. That didn't scare them, though; on our walks they would sing, "Kookaburra Sits in the Old Gum Tree." Someday, we decided, we would go to Australia and see koala bears and kangaroos and kookaburras.

When I went to Lily's, I wore a dark sweatshirt and bluejeans, with a twenty-dollar bill tucked in the back pocket. Once, returning to campus after a haircut, I ran into a colleague. My goodness, she said, I thought you were a student. I blend in, I replied. I could easily have booked an appointment at a boutique salon in one of the more picturesque suburbs. Lily's was only a few blocks from the college, but was my time so precious that I couldn't drive twenty minutes to a safer neighborhood? Mencius said that a man of wisdom does not stand next to a wall that is about to topple. Even though I wore sneakers and was a fast runner, I should have known that nobody can outrun a bullet.

I went to Lily's more often than was necessary. Had I been superstitious, I would have thought that she had put a spell on me.

Lily liked to chat. There were always dramas in her life. Once, her husband broke a toe when he tripped on the carpet that they had finally installed in their house, after ten years of planning. Once, her youngest son, who went to a state university, overslept on the very same morning that a man hacked at random pedestrians with a knife on their street. "He could've been killed," Lily said. "He's the laziest of the three, but now he says it pays to be lazy." Her father-in-law, just before his death, had made friends with a man whose first name was Casino. "The poor man thought it was a sign that he would win some money," she said. "Turned out Casino was not a true friend. Casino didn't even go gambling with him."

I listened, smiled, and asked questions—these were my most tiresome traits, and I used them tirelessly. Each encounter was a test I set up for myself: How long could I get people to talk about themselves without remembering to ask me a question? I had no stories to share. I had opinions, and yet I was as stubborn as Bartleby. I would prefer not to, I would reply if asked to remark on people's stories. In any case, Lily didn't care about my opinions or my stories—she got plenty of both from the uncles and aunties. I liked to believe that she had waited years for a perfect client like me.

Elsewhere, I wasn't entirely free from the demands of stating my opinions. Once, a student complained about a J. M. Coetzee novel I'd assigned. It's so insulting that this book is all about ideas and offers nothing for the heart, she said, and I snapped, unprofessionally, that in my view bad taste was more insulting. Once, a student called Charles Simic a misogynist because he hadn't written enough about his mother in his memoir. Read a book for what it is, I admonished the student, not for what you want it to be. The student replied that I had only stale ideas of what literature was about. "My goal is to dismantle your canon," she said, pointing to the Tolstoy and Chekhov on my desk. "They're not about real life."

What is life? I wanted to ask. What is real? But right away I felt exhausted. I longed to sit in Lily's chair. She would trim my hair and talk about the bubble-tea-and-frozen-yogurt place her husband had decided to invest in, or her neighbor's new profession as a breeder of rare goldfish, or her oldest son's ridiculous dream of quitting his job at the law firm and attending a culinary institute. Canons did not have a place in Lily's life. If she were to dismantle anything, it would be a house worth buying as a flipper.

So I went to Lily's. To my surprise, that day she did not want to talk about her husband or children or in-laws. Or perhaps it was a different day when she decided to tell me a love story. It didn't matter. All those stories she had told me before had been only a prologue.

It took one haircut for me to get the bare bones of the story, and a few more to gather the details, and still a few more for me to start looking at Lily askance. What was real? What was life? Perhaps we could all make up stories for ourselves when we didn't know the answers.

Here's Lily's story.

She grew up in an ethnic-Chinese family in Vietnam. At sixteen, she fell in love with the Vietnamese boy next door, who was sixteen, too. She was beautiful, he was handsome, but when war broke out between their countries the following year Lily's father decided that it was no longer safe for his family to live in Vietnam.

"Tuan came to my parents," Lily said. "He asked to leave the country with us. He would do anything just to be with me, he told my parents. My father said, 'You're not our son, you're your parents' son.' "

I thought about that war, three weeks and six days long, which was nearly forgotten now. When I was in elementary school in Beijing, my best friend subscribed to a children's magazine that often featured stories set on the border between Vietnam and China, with illustrations of maimed bodies and bombed villages and the heroic faces of intrepid soldiers. But, placed in history, that war was no more than a skinned knee or a sneeze to mankind. When Lily asked me if I knew the history between the two countries, I almost slipped and said yes. Then I remembered: I was supposed to have grown up in a country far from Asia, with an enviable childhood.

Lily's family had become boat people, migrating from Vietnam to Hong Kong to Hawaii and later to California. She had helped her parents in their Chinese takeout, apprenticed with an older cousin who ran a hair salon in Los Angeles, married, and had children. This nondescript life of an immigrant would have continued, if she hadn't recently had news of Tuan, the boy of her girlhood.

"Our story is like a movie," she said.

"Like a play," I said. "'Romeo and Juliet.'"

"Do you know someone who can make our story into a movie?"

For a while, Lily kept asking me that, and each time I replied no, feeling bad for delivering disappointing news, yet not bad enough to stop going to see her. Years of standing in the same spot—cutting and shaving and dyeing and listening to the uncles and aunties—had turned Lily into an unhurried storyteller. She took detours, and, like a verbal magician, offered dazzling distractions and commonplace tricks. "Where does your husband get his hair cut?" she asked once. "Tell him to come here. I'll give him a discount because you're my best client."

More people came into the story, marching in and out like a platoon of extras. Her schoolmates were remembered. Some of them had also had crushes on Tuan. The friendships between the fathers and between the eldest sons of the two families were recollected, but friendships severed by war were hardly worth a movie. Lily's parents had sympathized with their daughter when they first left Vietnam, but soon afterward they had shown impatience when she pined.

"Well, I can't blame them," Lily said. "Love doesn't put rice in the cooker or a roof over our heads."

"What does love do?" I asked.

“Oh, love makes a good movie,” she said. “Without movies, what would we do with ourselves?”

Tuan cried for three days and three nights in front of Lily’s old house after she and her family left. No one could pry his fingers off the chain lock. At the end of the third night, his older brothers were finally able to take him back to their house. Everyone thought he was going to die.

“Three days and three nights,” Lily said. “Never a step away from our door.” She had heard about this from an old friend whom she had seen recently when he and his wife were visiting their children in America.

Could anyone cry non-stop for three days and three nights without food or drink or sleep? But what right did I have to doubt the boy, what right did I have to want him to express his heartbreak more poetically or die more realistically, like Michael Furey? For all I knew, Michael Furey had been a figment of Joyce’s imagination, as perhaps the boy was of Lily’s. I did not know sorrow then, and later, when I did, after my elder son’s death, I thought that Lily’s young lover had been fortunate to have so many tears in him. Sorrow only desiccated me. Tears came to an end. Desiccation persisted.

The boy did not die. He recovered and eventually moved to another province in Vietnam to teach mathematics at a middle school. A woman in town fell in love with him, though he did not reciprocate. “He was waiting for me to come back,” Lily said. “Before we parted, he said he would wait for me all his life.”

A life of waiting was interrupted by a bout of illness, during which the woman took care of Tuan like a good wife. After that, the two were married, and together they raised three daughters.

“Isn’t it interesting that he has three daughters and I have three sons?” Lily said. “Think of where our promises went.”

“Did you promise to return?” I asked.

“Of course I did, but we left as refugees. We knew we wouldn’t go back.”

“But he could’ve kept his promise.”

“Now, that’d be a really good love story,” Lily said. “But I don’t hold it against him that he didn’t. He shouldn’t have.”

. . .

The next time I went to Lily's—after I'd been away for two months for the summer holidays—she looked ruffled. "Where have you been all these weeks?" she asked, and before I could answer she said, "My friends have put me in touch with Tuan."

"Did you see him?"

"No. How can I? We aren't the kind of people who take time off from work, and he lives in Vietnam," Lily said. "But they gave my contact information to him. He wrote and asked about my family, and told me a few things about his wife and daughters."

Everything was fine, then, I thought. A love story had arrived at a tranquil ending.

"He asked me to forgive him," Lily said.

Oh dear, I thought.

A tiny dog rides on a flatbed of a tractor-trailer with a sign reading Undersized Load on its front bumper.

"Do you think I should call him? He asked me if I would be willing to talk on the phone."

"Why not?" I said.

"What if I turn out to be a disappointment? Not the girl he remembered?"

"It's only a phone call. You won't see each other. You'll just hear each other's voice. Say a few nice things. You don't have to talk about the past. The two countries were to blame, not the two of you."

"What if he turns out to be different from the boy I remember?" she said.

"Maybe you shouldn't call him, then," I said. "You don't have to."

"But how can I not? If I miss him this time, we'll miss each other all our lives."

The phone call didn't go the way I had imagined. I had thought that Lily and her former lover would have a bittersweet conversation about their youth, and exchange a few superficial details about their marriages and their children, nothing too concrete, happiness and adversity both withheld. Or that they might be more forthright as adults and take a philosophical view, agreeing that their love might not have weathered the changes as they grew older. They would tell each other that they would remain friends. They might even say that their two families could become friends.

But I'm not a good writer of love stories. There are more things in Heaven and Earth than are dreamt of by my limited imagination.

When Lily finally called, the man had no words but only tears, and she listened to him sob. "He was disturbed," Lily told me. "I almost felt like crying myself, but I kept saying to him, 'Hello, do you have something to say? We've waited for this for so many years. We can't waste our time crying.' "

After a long while, as he was still crying, one of his daughters took the phone away from him. "It's too much for Father," she said to Lily, calling her Auntie. Lily asked the girl about their family life in Vietnam, and she answered with warmth. "Father often talks about you," the girl said. "We all feel you're part of our family."

Lily was working on the nape of my neck when she said this. I couldn't catch her eyes in the mirror. She didn't sound perturbed when she recounted the girl's words, which troubled me. Her voice was dreamy in a menacing way, like a voice-over in a movie. I pictured an actress standing in front of an open window, her back to an unlit room, the moonlight cold in her theatrical eyes. Does he deserve your love, or does he deserve to be killed by you? she asked herself, her face frozen with indecision. Do you have a choice?

"And then," Lily said, "you won't believe this. The daughter said that all three sisters' names have a Chinese character from my name. I never told you. My Chinese name has the character 'blossom' in it. He put the same character in their names."

I shuddered, the way one shudders when stepping out of the hot summer sun and into an abandoned tunnel. Where had that thought of a tunnel come from? And then I remembered. It was an abandoned nuclear shelter next to our apartment building in Beijing. My parents' generation had dug the tunnels when it was feared that a war between China and the Soviet Union was inevitable. In elementary school, I had played truant often and gone into one of the tunnels with a box of matches. The damp and moldy air, the scurrying bugs and rats, the rusty nails I had collected in a box as treasure—I felt terror imagining my children on an exploration like that. Yet I had been happy then.

"And then his daughter said, 'Auntie, I don't think Father can talk with you today. It's too much for him. We worry about his health. But do you want to talk to Mother? She is here. She wants to talk with you, too.' "

"Did you talk to his wife?" I asked, knowing that Lily's pause was a gesture to allow me to be included in her narrative.

She did. I would have, too.

"Do you know anyone who could make this into a movie? I'm telling you, it's a love story, and it's a movie."

"I don't know anyone who makes movies," I said. "But what happened? You talked with his wife, and then what?"

"She came on the phone, and I liked her voice right away. I think he married a good woman. She called me Sister. Like the daughter, she also said he talked about me often. And then she said, 'You don't know how much he loves you. You will never understand.' And all of a sudden I started to cry. Imagine that. I didn't shed a single tear when he was bawling on the phone. His wife said, 'But you shouldn't cry, Sister. You should be happy. You're the only love he's had. All these years he's kept your photo on our nightstand.' "

"In the bedroom the two of them share?" I asked.

"Yes," Lily said.

"Are you serious?"

"Why would I lie?"

Why would anyone lie to anyone? But people do, I thought, all the time.

"I talked with his wife and then with the two other daughters," Lily said. "It was a long phone call. And I didn't hear a single word from him. But you know what made me the saddest? His wife said, 'You're the most beautiful woman I've ever known.' No one has ever said that to me."

We both looked up at the mirror. I had not thought of Lily as a pretty woman. I was an exhausted young mother then, courageously blind to the dangers of the world and stubbornly blind to its beauties. I now studied Lily, and thought that she was indeed pretty. I also started to think that she'd made up the whole story, just as I had invented my upbringing in Holland. We all had our reasons for doing this as long as no harm was done. Even so, I began to resent Lily. She must have put a spell on me, tricking me into her chair, hypnotizing me with girlish dreams that had not been hardened by life.

"Maybe you can write my story, and then someone will make a movie from it," Lily said.

I should have stopped going to Lily's right away. Perhaps she had seen through me. Tell me a story—she must have known that every time I sat down in her chair I was making that request—a real story, Lily.

Let me tell you a story—she agreed—and let me make it unreal for you.

We saw each other one more time after that. She had promised to show me a copy of the photo of her and the boy, the one he kept in his marriage bedroom. A photo would prove nothing, I thought, but where else could I go for a haircut? Finding another salon would be like starting a new relationship, forging a new friendship, while all I wanted was to keep the unknown, good or bad, at a distance. Forget life, real or unreal. What I wanted to do was to raise my children as a good mother should. In those years, the days seemed long, never-ending, and sometimes I felt impatient for my children to grow up, and then felt guilty for my impatience.

The photo that Lily showed me—what can I say? Years later, after my son died, I felt a constant ache, similar to what I had felt for Lily and the boy when I saw them in the photo. The same ache, I imagined, would afflict those who now looked at photos of my son—he died at about the age Lily and Tuan were when they fell in love.

But that ache was still as distant and as theoretical as a nebula when I was sitting in Lily's chair. She opened an envelope in which a sepia-toned black-and-white photo was preserved between two sheets of tissue paper. The girl in the photo was dressed in a white *áo dài*, and the boy in a white silk shirt and a pair of white pants. She was beautiful, he was handsome, but those were not the words I would use to describe them. They were young, their faces cloudless, their bodies insubstantial, closer to childhood than to adulthood. They looked like two lambs, impeccably prepared by their elders as sacrifices to appease a beast or a god. Would anyone have been surprised to hear that they died right after the photo was taken? Some children were born tragedies.

"What do you think?" Lily asked, studying my face.

"Wow," I said.

"Maybe you can write a romantic novel about us."

When tragedies drag on, do they become comedies instead, or grow more tragic?

I could not make a romance out of Lily's story. She was not the first person I had let down with my writing. During those years, when my children were in preschool, at the beginning of each semester we were asked to send a care package that was to be kept at the school in case of a catastrophic earthquake. In the care packages we were to include a few nonperishable snacks, a family photo, a small stuffed animal, and a note to the children, telling them that, if their parents could not make it to the school, there was nothing for them to worry about. Everything would be fine, the note was to say. Everything would be all right in the end.

I had always prepared the snacks and the stuffed animal and the family photo, but I had never been able to write that note to my children. What could I say to them? If your teacher is reading this to you, it means that Mommy and Daddy are late picking you up; it may also mean that we will never come back for you, but all will be well in the end.

We lived through their childhoods without being hit by a deadly earthquake. The care packages were returned to us when the children graduated from preschool. Still, if a writer cannot write a simple note as a parental duty, what meaning is there in the words she does write?

A few days ago, I got an e-mail from my former student who had vowed to dismantle my canon. She said that she was travelling in South America. She mentioned a few things she had learned from our clashes. "I remember that once you said to us: One must want to be great in order to be good. To this day I still wonder why you looked sad when you said that," she wrote.

Under what circumstances had I said that? And sad about what? Had she written to enlighten me about what real life was, I would have applauded her consistency. Instead, in her long e-mail, she talked about what I had taught her. I, too, had been young then; how could I have taught anyone anything? All will be well all will be well and every kind of thing shall be well, yet I could not even write a lying note to console my children.

PLAYING METAL GEAR SOLID V: THE PHANTOM PAIN

BY JAMIL JAN KOCHAI (2020)

First, you have to gather the cash to preorder the game at the local GameStop, where your cousin works, and, even though he hooks it up with the employee discount, the game is still a bit out of your price range because you've been using your Taco Bell paychecks to help your pops, who's been out of work since you were ten, and who makes you feel unbearably guilty about spending money on useless hobbies while kids in Kabul are destroying their bodies to build compounds for white businessmen and warlords—but, shit, it's Kojima, it's Metal Gear, so, after scrimping and saving (like literal dimes you're picking up off the street), you've got the cash, which you give to your cousin, who purchases the game on your behalf, and then, on the day it's released, you just have to find a way to get to the store.

But, because your oldest brother has taken the Civic to Sac State, you're hauling your two-hundred-and-sixty-pound ass on a bicycle you haven't touched since middle school, and thank Allah (if He's up there) that the bike is still rideable, because you're sure there'll be a line if you don't get to GameStop early, so, huffing and puffing, you're regretting all the Taco Bell you've eaten over the past two years, but you ride with such fervor that you end up being only third in line, and it's your cousin himself who hands you the game in a brown paper bag, as if it were something illegal or illicit, which it isn't, of course, it's Metal Gear, it's Kojima, it's the final game in a series so fundamentally a part of your childhood that often, when you hear the Irish Gaelic chorus from "The Best Is Yet to Come," you cannot help weeping softly into your keyboard.

For some reason, riding back home is easier.

You leave the bike behind the trash cans at the side of the house and hop the wooden fence into the back yard and, if the door to the garage is open, you slip in, and if it's not, which it isn't, you've got to take a chance on the screen door in the back yard, but, lo and behold, your father is ankle deep in the dirt, hunched over, yanking at weeds with his bare hands the way he used to as a farmer in Logar, before war and famine forced him to flee to the western coast of the American empire, where he labored for many years until it broke his body for good, and even though his doctor has forbidden him to work in the yard, owing to the torn nerves in his neck and spine—which, you know from your mother, were first damaged when he was tortured by Russians shortly after the murder of his younger brother, Watak, during the Soviet War—he is out here clawing at the earth and its spoils, as if he were digging for treasure or his own grave.

Spotting you only four feet away from the sliding glass door, he gestures for you to come over, and though you are tired and sweaty, with your feet aching and the most important game of the decade hidden inside your underwear, you approach him.

He signals for you to crouch down beside him, then he runs his dirty fingers through his hair until flakes of his scalp fall onto his shoulders and his beard.

This isn't good.

When your father runs his hands through his hair, it is because he has forgotten his terrible, flaking dandruff, which he forgets only during times of severe emotional or physical distress, which means that he is about to tell you a story that is either upsetting or horrifying or both, which isn't fair, because you are a son and not a therapist.

Your father is a dark, sturdy man, and so unlike you that, as a child, you were sure that one day Hagrid would come to your door and inform you of your status as a Mudblood, and then your true life—the life without the weight of your father's history, pain, guilt, hopelessness, helplessness, judgment, and shame—would begin.

Your father asks you where you were.

"The library."

"You have to study?"

You tell him you do, which isn't, technically, a lie.

"All right," he says in English, because he has given up on speaking to you in Pashto, "but, after you finish, come back down. I have something I need to talk to you about."

Hurry.

When you get to your room, you lock the door and turn up MF Doom on your portable speaker to ward off mothers, fathers, grandmothers, sisters, and brothers who want to harp at you about prayer, the Quran, Pashto, Farsi, a new job, new classes, exercise, basketball, jogging, talking, guests, chores, homework help, bathroom help, family time, time, because usually "Madvillainy" does the trick.

Open the brown paper bag and toss the kush your cousin has stashed with your game because he needs a new smoking buddy since his best friend gave up the ganja for God again, and he sees you as a prime target, probably because he thinks you've got nothing better to do with your time or you're not as religious as your brothers or you're desperate to escape the unrelenting nature of a corporeal existence, and, God damn, the physical map of Afghanistan that comes with the game is fucking beautiful.

Not that you're a patriot or a nationalist or one of those Afghans who walk around in a pakol and kameez and play the tabla and claim that their favorite singer is Ahmad Zahir, but the fact that nineteen-eighties Afghanistan is the final setting of the most legendary and artistically significant gaming franchise in the history of time made you all the more excited to get your hands on it, especially since you've been shooting at Afghans in your games (Call of Duty and Battlefield and Splinter Cell) for so long that you've become oddly immune to the self-loathing you felt when you were first massacring wave after wave of militant fighters who looked just like your father.

Now, finally, start the game.

After you escape from the hospital where Big Boss was recovering from the explosion he barely survived in the prequel to the Phantom Pain, you and Revolver Ocelot travel to the brutal scenes of northern Kabul Province—its rocky cliffs, its dirt roads, and its sunlight bleeding off into the dark mountains just the way you remember from all those years ago, when you visited Kabul as a child—and although your initial mission is to locate and extract Kazuhira Miller, the Phantom Pain is the first Metal Gear Solid game to be set in a radically open-world environment, and you decide to postpone the rescue of Kazuhira Miller until after you get some Soviet blood on your hands, a feat you accomplish promptly by locating and massacring an entire base of Russian combatants.

Your father, you know, didn't kill a single Russian during his years as a mujahideen in Logar, but there is something in the act of slaughtering these Soviet N.P.C.s that makes you feel connected to him and his history of warfare.

Thinking of your father and his small village, you head south to explore the outer limits of the open world in the Phantom Pain, crossing trails and deserts and mountain passes, occasionally stopping at a checkpoint or a military barracks to slaughter more Russians, and you find yourself, incredibly, skirting the city of Kabul, still dominated by the Soviets, and continuing on to Logar, to Mohammad Agha, and when you get to Wagh Jan, the roadside-market village that abuts the Kabul-Logar highway, just the way you remember it, you hitch your horse and begin to sneak along the clay compounds and the shops, climbing walls and crawling atop roofs, and, whenever a local Afghan spots you, you knock him out with a tranquillizer, until you make it to the bridge that leads to the inner corridors of your parents' home village, Naw'e Kaleh, which looks so much like the photos and your own blurred memories from the trip when you were a kid that you begin to become uneasy, not yet afraid, but as if consumed by an overwhelming sense of déjà vu.

Sneaking along the dirt roads, past the golden fields and the apple orchards and the mazes of clay compounds, you come upon the house where your father used to reside, and it is there—on the road in front of your father's home—that you spot Watak, your father's sixteen-year-old brother, whom you recognize only because his picture (unsmiling, head shaved, handsome, and sixteen forever) hangs on the wall of the room in your home where your parents pray, but here he is, in your game, and you press Pause and you set down the controller, and now you are afraid.

Sweat is running down your legs in rivulets, in streams, your heart is thumping, and you are wondering if sniffing the kush as you did earlier has got you high.

You look out the window and see your brother walking toward the house in the dark and you realize that you've been playing for too long.

You're blinking a lot.

Too much.

You notice that your room is a mess and that it smells like ass and that you've become so accustomed to its smell and its mess that from the space inside your head, behind your eyes, the space in which your first-person P.O.V. is rooted, you—

Ignore the knock.

It's just your little sister.

Get back to the game.

There is a bearded, heavyset man beside Watak, who, you soon realize, is your father.

You pause the game again and put down the controller.

Doom spits, "His life is like a folklore legend. . . . Why you so stiff, you need to smoke more, bredrin. . . . Instead of trying to riff with the broke war veteran."

It seems to you a sign.

You extract the kush from the trash, and, because you have no matches or lighter, you put hunks of it in your mouth and you chew and nearly vomit twice.

Return to the game.

Hiding in your grandfather's mulberry tree, you listen to your father and his brother discuss what they will eat for suhoor, thereby indicating that it is still Ramadan, that this is just days before Watak's murder.

Then it hits you.

Here is what you're going to do: before your father is tortured and his brother murdered, you are going to tranquillize them both and you are going to carry them to your horse and cross Logar's terrain until you reach a safe spot where you can call a helicopter and fly them back to your offshore platform: Mother Base.

But just as you load your tranquillizers your brother bangs on your door and demands that you come out, and after ignoring him for a bit, which only makes him madder and louder, you shout that you are sick, but the voice that comes out of your mouth is not your own, it is the voice of a faraway man imitating your voice, and your brother can tell.

He leaves, and you return to the game.

From the cover of the mulberry tree, you aim your tranquillizer gun, but you forget that you've got the laser scope activated, and Watak sees the red light flashing on your father's forehead and they're off, running and firing back at your tree with rifles they had hidden underneath their patus, and you are struck twice, so you need a few moments to recover your health and, by the time you do, they're gone.

Your brother is back, and this time he has brought along your oldest brother, who somehow is able to shout louder and bang harder than your second-oldest brother, and they're both asking what you're doing and why you won't come out and why you won't grow up and why you insist on worrying your mother and your father, who you know gets those terrible migraines triggered by stress, and now your oldest brother is banging so hard you're afraid the door will come off its hinges, so you lug your dresser in front of it as a barricade and then you go back to your spot in front of the TV, and you sit on the floor and press Play.

At night, under cover of darkness, you sneak toward your father's compound, and you scale the fifteen-foot-high walls of clay and crawl along the rooftops until you get to the highest point in the compound, where your father stands, on the lookout for incoming jets and firebombs, and you shoot him twice in the back with tranquillizers and, as he is falling, you catch him in your arms, your father, who, at this time, is around the same age that you are now, and in the dark, on the roof of the compound that he will lose to this war, you hold him, his body still strong and well, his heart unbroken, and you set him down gently on the clay so that the sky does not swallow him.

Climbing down into the courtyard, you go from chamber to chamber, spotting uncles and aunts and cousins you've never met in real life, and you find Watak near the cow's shed, sleeping just behind the doorway of a room filled with women, as if to protect them, and, after you aim your tranquillizer gun and send Watak into a deeper sleep, your grandmother, a lifelong insomniac, rises from her toshak and strikes you in the shoulder with a machete and calls for the men in the house, of whom there are many, to awaken and slaughter the Russian who has come to kill us all in our sleep.

The damage from the machete is significant.

Nonetheless, you still have the strength to tranquillize your grandmother, pick up Watak, and climb back onto the roof while all your uncles and cousins and even your grandfather are awakened and armed and begin to fire at your legs as you hustle along, bleeding and weary, to the spot where your father rests.

With your uncle on one shoulder and your father on the other, you leap off the roof into the shadows of an apple orchard.

The men are pouring out onto the roads and the fields, calling upon neighbors and allies, and, because the orchard is soon surrounded on all sides, it seems certain that you will be captured, but you are saved by, of all things, a squadron of Spetsnaz, who begin to fire on the villagers, and in the confusion of the shoot-out, as the entire village is lit up by a hundred gunfights, each fight a microcosm of larger battles and wars and global conflicts strung together by the invisible wires of beloved men who will die peacefully in their sleep, you make your way out of the orchard, passing trails and streams and rivers and mulberry trees, until you reach your horse and ride out of Wagh Jan, toward an extraction point in the nearby Black Mountains.

But now, at the door, is your father.

"Zoya?" he is saying, very gently, the way he used to say it when you were a kid, when you were in Logar, when you got the flu, when the pills and the I.V. and the home remedies weren't working, when there was nothing to do but wait for the aching to ebb, and your father was there, maybe in the orchard, maybe on the veranda, and he was holding you in his lap, running his fingers through your hair, and saying your name, the way he is saying it now, as if it were almost a question.

"Zoya?" he says and, when you do not reply, nothing else.

Keep going.

Russians chase you on the ground and in the air, they fire and you are struck once, twice, three or four times, and there are so many Russians, but your horse is quick and nimble and manages the terrain better than their trucks can, and you make it to the extraction point, in a hollow of the Black Mountains, with enough time to summon the helicopter and to set up a perimeter of mines, and you hide your father and his brother at the mouth of a cave, behind a large boulder the shape of a believer in prostration, where you lie prone with a sniper rifle and begin to pick off Russian paratroopers in the distance, and you fire at the engines of the trucks and ignore the tanks, which will reach you last, and it is mere moments before your helicopter will arrive, and, just as you think you are going to make it, your horse is slaughtered in a flurry of gunfire and your pilot is struck by a single bullet from a lone rifleman, and the helicopter falls to the earth and bursts into flames, killing many Russians, and giving you just enough time to rush into the cave, into the heart of the Black Mountains.

With your father on one shoulder and your uncle on the other, and with the lights of the Soviet gunfire dying away at the outer edges of your vision, you trudge deeper into the darkness of the cave, and though you cannot be sure that your father and his brother are still alive, that they haven't been shot in the chaos, that they are not, now, corpses, you feel compelled to keep moving into a darkness so complete that your reflection becomes visible on the screen of the television in front of you, and it is as if the figures in the image were journeying inside you, delving into your flesh.

To be saved.

VISITOR

BY BRYAN WASHINGTON (2020)

He knocked on my door about a month after the funeral. I almost didn't answer, since I wasn't expecting my fuck buddy. It was entirely too late for anyone to be visiting, but the man in front of me said that he'd been a friend of my father's—and I slipped on the face I wore for those people. It was three or four in the morning. He'd caught a late flight from Kingston to Houston.

Then the man said something else, in a heavy patois. I asked him to repeat it.

His lover, this guy said, rubbing both of his elbows.

I made a new kind of face. Except it couldn't have been a new kind of face. We only get so many.

What, I said.

It's true, he said.

No, I said, and then I laughed.

The man asked to come in. He set his duffel on the carpet, and his jacket beside it, and the doorway was crammed, so we stood, and that's when I got a good look at him: mid-fifties, Asian. Short hair, messy and curly, sloped just below the nape of his neck. His boots were too large. His track pants were too tight. He told me that he'd never flown in a plane before.

The motor, he said, pantomiming the way the engine turned.

He made a circle with his finger, slowly, and then not very slowly at all.

. . .

A few hours later, I found him in the living room, sleeping on the rug. I'd made something like a bed on the sofa, out of some hoodies and a quilt my mom had given me. But I guess it hadn't worked out. He'd folded everything up and placed it on the coffee table.

Hey, I said, toeing him.

The man blinked himself awake, slowly.

Morning, he said. Wah gwan.

No, I said.

No?

No. You got a free night out of me. So tell me who you really are.

I told you, the man said.

You lied, I said.

That's when my visitor sat up, cocking his head at me. He scratched it, mussing his hair even further.

You look just like him, he said.

Stop that, I said.

But you do.

Look, guy.

Completely uncanny, the man said, still scratching, yawning, shaking his ass a little bit.

He stood, arching his back, leaning one way and then the other. We were about the same height.

But you're chubbier, the man said.

Hey, I said.

It's true, he said. Your father could never hold any weight.

The man sat and crossed his legs, slumping with an elbow on the sofa cushion. When he started to yawn, I braced myself, biting my gums, but I couldn't help it—I yawned, too.

The man didn't want me to take him to breakfast, but I'd stopped keeping groceries in the apartment. Everything always rotted.

I drove him to this Jewish deli a few blocks up the road. I'd been living in Bellaire for the past while, just west of the city proper, where it's all Vietnamese coffee shops and Chinese markets and Venezuelan grocery stores and there are loan sharks posted on every corner. No one looks like anyone else, until you drive twenty minutes east, toward midtown, and then everyone's white. My visitor set his ear on the window, and I thought he'd fallen asleep, until he burped and settled his elbows on the dashboard.

At the deli, he ordered one thing from the top of the menu, tentatively, scanning my face. Then he ordered a bagel and some eggs and some potatoes and three biscuits with grits, and also a small plate of lox. Our waiter—some whiteboy—made a funny face and looked from my visitor to me. He wore the same face as he brought our food to the table, juggling three plates with his elbows.

Sorry, my visitor said, when he came up for air. Haven't eaten.

That's fine, I said.

Been about a day.

No worries.

Two days.

You don't have to lie, I said.

You don't have to lie, the man said, grinning, in a voice four octaves higher.

Our waiter stopped by the table again. Lingering. I asked if there was a problem, and he shook his head and stepped away.

So you're from Jamaica, I said.

That's what I told you, the man said.

I opened my mouth, and then I closed it. My visitor tugged on his ear.

I know what's in your head, he said. Plenty of Chinese all over the island. Everywhere. Even if you didn't know that.

I didn't say there weren't, I said, although it's exactly what I'd been thinking.

Eh, the man said.

And then: Your father and I were just kids, he said. Lasted five years, on and off.

Five years, I said.

One, two, five.

And then you stopped?

Stopped? In Jamaica? Of course we stopped.

Did you stay in contact?

Ai-yah, the man said. How would we do that? We stopped. Do they have orange juice?

Maybe, I said. Fuck.

Your father swore, too, the man said.

Fuck, I said again.

Rude boy.

Stop that. How did you two even meet?

He worked in my mother's shop, the man said. At least in the beginning. Short walk from the schoolhouse.

And then what? You just hooked up?

Hooked up?

Never mind, I said. What did y'all do together? How did you two even know?

Know what?

You know what.

This prompted a smile from the man, between mouthfuls of eggs and jelly and bagel. He slid the plate toward me. I tore off a corner of a biscuit.

We just knew, he said. It was obvious. At least to us. Happened how it always happens and then it ended.

I watched this man eat. I tried to think of him with my father. I'd only thought of my dad in the context of my mother, whenever I thought of him at all. His death had felt abrupt—he'd got sick with a brand of illness no one comes back from—and none of our relatives had said much to me, about anything at all, in the years beforehand. We existed on separate planes of reality. But they'd shown out at the funeral. They'd handled all the arrangements. If anything, it seemed like another attempt to push me aside.

Why are you here, I said, and the man looked up.

He grinned again, widely. When he tugged at a napkin from across the table, nearly tipping over the holder, I passed him one of mine.

To meet *you*, he said. You're his son! He had a son!

I knew that my father was born in Jamaica. I knew that he'd lived on the coast. I knew that he'd left the island in his twenties. I knew that he'd met my mother in Toronto, and that they'd moved to New York, and then to Tampa, before tumbling over to Houston. I knew that my father didn't argue, he just made decisions. I knew that, when I was a kid, sometimes my mom would grab my hand, in the middle of the evening, and we'd go for walks around our suburb, leaving my father to himself. I knew that my father played soccer. I knew that he wasn't very good at it. I knew that the day I came out to him, after my mom died, he flipped over the kitchen table, and then a coffee table, and also the dresser sitting under the television. I knew that I slept in the park a few blocks away that night, until my father came looking for me in his pickup, and that when I woke up he was sleeping right next to me, hands tucked under his armpits. I knew that we drove up the road for kolaches the next morning. I knew that we chewed them, sitting across from each other, silent in the diner while high-school girls laughed and poked at their phones behind us. I knew that my father and I didn't talk much after that. I knew that, some days when I was a kid, my mother would look from me to him, shaking her head, smiling.

But I also knew that I couldn't discount my visitor's statements outright. He'd nailed his dates. His geography checked out. Everything was just true enough that I couldn't call bullshit.

My visitor had no itinerary beyond seeing my father's tombstone. His return flight wasn't for another five days. He had, apparently, booked the wrong morning to fly back to Jamaica.

Should've been a shorter trip, he said. Slip of the hand.

That's a pretty big fuckup, I said.

Everything worked out.

What if I'd been out of town? What if I'd told you to fuck off?

You weren't. You didn't.

At least not yet, I said.

You won't, the man said. Everything worked out.

That anyone could be this trusting seemed absurd to me, but my visitor was absurdity incarnate: sometimes, mid-speech, he'd drift off and he wouldn't come back. He fingered the posters—maps of places I'll probably never go—in my apartment. He touched all the cups. He napped, and talked in his sleep, and then he woke up in conversation with himself, cheesing at the punch line.

When my visitor fell asleep, I slipped over to the fuck buddy's apartment. His name was Joel. He stopped me at the door with one kiss, and then another. Before I could say the thing that I came over to tell him, we were on his sofa, out of our hoodies, nearly out of our shorts.

Wait, I said.

You wait, Joel said.

Seriously, I said. I've got this guy staying with me.

This was enough for Joel to look up from what he was doing. His face made something like a smirk. His living room wasn't large, but it was warm, and from the center of it I could smell whatever he'd cooked for dinner—some kind of fish soup, probably, seasoned heavily enough to linger for days. Initially, I couldn't stand that smell. Now I daydreamed about it at work.

Joel blinked. Then he exhaled.

I don't mind, he said.

Good, I said.

Nobody said *we* were anything official, he said.

Correct, I said.

Are you at least being safe, Joel asked.

It's nothing like that, I said. Not a sex thing.

Then he's a roommate?

Hardly.

So it's just an everyday living-with-you-rent-free-with-no-sex thing.

He's a friend of my father's. Maybe more than a friend.

Joel leaned back on the sofa, crossing his arms. He was round, like me. When my father died, he was the first person I told. Joel grew up in Katy, out in the suburbs, and he came from money, through his parents' restaurant on Mason Road, until that restaurant caught on fire one night and both his parents died in it and Joel had to move in with his sister. The money went away.

Now he was a barista. We'd met at a Starbucks, after he fucked up my name. Among other things, Joel was extremely hard to shock.

He said, Did your mystery man say why he's showing up now?

No, I said.

Well, I said, maybe.

Maybe, Joel asked, or no?

He wants to get to know me, I think.

And how's that going?

It isn't.

Sounds about right.

Don't be a dick.

You won't let me, Joel said, brushing mine. Just think about it, he added. If he isn't lying, then this man came back from the dead, too.

I'd hardly call it that.

He came up from Jamaica, right? Where your dad's from?

Was from, I said.

Right, Joel said. So this dude basically split the universe.

That sounds dramatic.

Because it is. You should hear him out.

I am.

In your own way, I'm sure.

Before I could say anything to that, Joel set his head on my chest, hanging halfway off the sofa. Folded his arms into the creases of mine, and just lay there. And I shivered, just a bit, but I didn't get up or anything, and I shut my eyes, and it wasn't entirely unpleasant.

The next morning, my visitor asked me where I went when I left the apartment. I sat cross-legged on the sofa in sweatpants, watching him watch me inhale a bag of shrimp chips. I'd made it back home maybe thirty minutes earlier.

Work, I said. Where else?

Boss man, my visitor said. You have a degree?

Do I look like I have a degree?

Funny guy. How would I know what that looks like?

I went to community college for a while, I said. Shit was expensive. It didn't work out.

So you stopped?

It didn't work out, I said, and the man placed a hand on his chest, and began to hiccup.

What does that mean, he said. You have anything else to eat here?

No, I said. And it means that it didn't work out. Why the fuck do you care?

I'm just trying to figure you out, my visitor said, shrugging and smiling.

I work and I get paid. That's all you need to know.

There's more to life, the man said, and he reached for my chips.

Before I could lift the bag, he'd grabbed four, five, six, dropping crumbs all over the carpet.

. . .

The next day, I told Funke, one of my co-workers at the gas station, about my visitor. We were stacking columns of gum on a shelf, or I was stacking them while she stood beside me, texting.

The man had started folding my clothes, rearranging everything in the drawers. Whenever I left the apartment, he'd stare at my face beforehand, squinting, while I tied my shoes. A layer of fuzz had made its way around his chin.

Bring back some food, he'd said that morning. You hear?

Excuse me? I said. Who the fuck are you talking to?

Fresh food, my visitor said. Something from the earth. Natural.

When I told Funke all this, she made a face.

What's the problem, she said. You don't believe him?

I don't know. It's not like I can ask anyone in my family about this. They wouldn't fucking know.

Well, Funke said.

Right.

Does he have any reason to lie?

Not really. Can you hold these?

Wait a minute, Funke said. I'm talking with my son.

How's he doing?

Don't worry about him. I already tried introducing you.

Fine, I said.

You thought I forgot, Funke said.

I get it. Jesus.

Tell me more about your dead daddy's boyfriend.

It's too soon for you to say that shit.

Wrong, Funke said. Time moves whether we want it to or not.

Fine, I said. This guy knows too much. I guess it's possible that he's not bullshitting.

Stupid, Funke said. Of course it's *possible*. We all live many lives.

She glanced up from her phone while I juggled some Trident. She started to hand me the boxes I'd dropped, and then she dropped them, too.

I don't know, I said.

That's the thing, Funke said. You don't have to know.

Knowing is a *privilege*, she said. The best we can do is brace ourselves.

. . .

My visitor stood over my stove with the groceries I'd bought from the H Mart down the road. He sautéed bell peppers, lightly fried a slab of mackerel, stirred garlic in a pot I'd never seen before. He poured the marinade of garlic and peppers over the fish, dousing everything with red pepper, and slipped the mass from the pan to a bright-blue plate, beside stir-fried spinach and rice.

We ate on the floor, picking at everything with plastic forks. I watched my visitor stuff his face, while buried in one of my oversized flannel shirts.

Your father hated reggae, the man said. He only ever listened to Bob Dylan.

(This was true.)

Your father couldn't cook a lick, the man said. But he loved to eat.

(This was true.)

Your father didn't have a favorite color.

Bullshit, I said. Everyone has a favorite color.

Everyone but your father, the man said. Although he hated purple.

My family flew to Jamaica only once. I was eight, I think, and I spent most of the trip holding my stomach. Everything was too hot for me. Everything tasted too wild. Too fresh. Eventually, my mother and I settled into a circuit between our hotel and a McDonald's, while my father disappeared for hours at a time, meeting us in the lobby after the sun set.

I sat with my mom by the concierge. She read on the floor beside me, my head in her lap.

Once, I asked her where my father went. She looked at me, and closed her book.

After enough time had passed that I'd forgotten the question, she said, Home.

And he can't take us with him?

There's nothing for you to see there.

But I want to see *him.*

I know, my mom said. But his family does, too.

Why can't they come here?

Mmm, my mom said. He's coming back, she said, rubbing my stomach, and then my neck. He's gone, my mom said, but he'll be back.

And she was right. When my father came back to the hotel, he beamed. That smile didn't dim until we'd been back in the States for a couple of months, and then it went out entirely. I never really saw it again.

My visitor wanted to see things.

Everything your father saw, he said. The things he liked.

Impossible, I said.

You're his son. If you don't know, then who does?

So we drove to the Menil. We drove to Buc-ee's. We walked through the Rothko Chapel. We drove to the Children's Museum. We drove up and down Chinatown. We drove to a fish fry on Scott Street, where my visitor got an upset stomach, and I called him a little bitch, until my stomach imploded, too. We made a pit stop at a coffee shop in Montrose, and watched the young men in high heels and trenchcoats order almond lattes. When I asked my visitor if he wanted to see NASA, his eyes lit up, but he declined.

I'd have a heart attack, he said. I'd join your father.

That isn't funny, I said.

No, he said. You're right. Everyone dies. We all go.

Then stop fucking laughing, I said.

I'm sorry, my visitor said.

No, you're not.

No, I'm not.

But by then I was cracking up, too.

Joel and I rarely went out in the world together: I could count the number of times, in two years, on two hands. Once to the CVS behind his place, for lube. Another time to wash his car. A third time for sesame seeds at H-E-B. Once again to the Thai Spice, down the road. Mostly, we were in his apartment: eating or fucking or lying around.

I told him about my customers at the gas station, piss drunk or courteous or stoned beyond all recall. Joel told me about his own customers, inconsolable before caffeine and approachable afterward. Sometimes we watched horror movies. We never finished any of them. Neither of us ever really questioned our routine.

Also: Joel collected facts. Impractical shit that neither of us could use. When I asked him why, Joel blinked and said, Because facts are things that cannot be changed. Facts can't be taken away.

So when, one night, he asked if I'd like to go for a walk, all I could do was stare.

We don't have to, he added.

No, I said. But why not?

So we slipped on our sneakers and walked.

As we rounded the corner of his complex, Joel asked if I knew that less than ten per cent of the world's plastics were actually recycled.

We passed the grocery store by the taquería, and Joel asked if I knew that in 1960 every state in America had antisodomy laws.

We rounded the corner of Walgreens, where I learned that spontaneous yawning is exhibited in all vertebrate mammals.

We jogged across Bellaire Boulevard, and I nearly lost a shoe, and Joel asked if I knew that there are only two distinct seasons in the Philippines.

We turned in to an elementary school's playground, tightroping the length of a sandbox, and I learned that the ring-of-fire eclipse is a semi-regular phenomenon, in which Earth's moon blots out everything but the barest silhouette of the sun.

But mostly we walked in silence. There wasn't really a route. Sometimes Joel led, and sometimes I led. When I took too long to round a corner, Joel stopped; whenever he lingered, I turned around to check on him. Then he'd nod, and I'd nod, and we'd start again.

Whenever the sun set, my visitor asked more questions about my life. I had nothing to tell him. I'd brought some food home from this fusion Caribbean spot by NRG Stadium, and he picked at the beef patties with his fingers, separating his plantains from his rice.

This is how they packed it, the man said.

You don't like it, I said.

Well, the man said. Our food is hard to cook.

Is it?

For the first time, the man gave me a look, a bemused sort of thing, the look you'd give a certain kind of shithead kid. If I'd blinked, I would've missed it.

I'm just saying I wouldn't know, I said.

You'd know better than anyone else, the man said. Your father loved to cook.

You said he sucked at cooking.

Doesn't mean he didn't love it. But I want to hear more about you.

Fine, I said. I work at this gas station. I played football until I fucked up my back. I'm fucking broke.

You work at a store! Like your father.

Sure.

And your mother?

Got sick when I was a kid.

Ai-yah.

Yeah.

She's beautiful.

She's my mom. She was my mom.

She *is* your mother. I always thought he'd end up with someone beautiful.

And what about you, I said. What's your deal?

My deal?

Your life. Your fucking story.

Eh, the man said, and then he didn't say anything else.

He picked a little more at his plate, scooping his peas into piles.

You have anything to drink here, he said. Any beer?

Not really.

A Jamaican with no beer. Glad I lived long enough to see it.

Half, I said. My mom was Canadian.

Is, the man said. And it's all or nothing.

I don't think that's true, I said. And you're changing the subject.

There isn't much to tell, my visitor said. I live on the island. I fish for the market. You really don't have any Red Stripe?

I really don't have any Red Stripe.

Huh, the man said. And no girlfriend, either?

I'm gay.

At this, my visitor covered his mouth. I still don't know whether or not he was feigning it.

And your father? he said. He knew about this, yes?

He did, I said.

Good man. He supported you.

That's one way of putting it.

This made my visitor very quiet. He stood up, and walked into the kitchen. I heard rustling, and then silence, and then more rustling.

In all fairness, my visitor was probably only the third person I'd told whom I wasn't fucking. The second had been Funke, who'd clocked me on sight. What no one tells you is that sometimes, even if you've figured yourself out, you'll have no one around you to share what you've found.

When my visitor came back to the living room, twenty minutes later, I was face down on a pillow.

He sat across from me and put a bowl on the coffee table between us: fried dumplings and avocado slices.

He leaned over, wrapping me in his arms.

Hey, I said.

It's O.K., he said. Relax.

You don't have to do that.

I have to do this.

You don't, I said, but I didn't move, didn't nudge my way out of his arms.

Eventually, my visitor untangled his arms from my body. He motioned toward the food.

Real food, he said. Get it before it gets cold.

My father's death was quick. My mother's was quicker. She caught the flu on a Tuesday. We took her to the hospital on a Thursday. She fell into a coma that Saturday, and she was gone four days later.

I was almost fifteen. The last interaction we had was me tugging at the end of her hospital sheets, and her laughing under her breath, covering her mouth. I don't know why this was hilarious, but it was. So we kept doing it. Eventually, my father walked in, and we tried to keep it going, but he didn't get the joke, and of course we couldn't explain it. So we stopped.

. . .

When I told Joel about this, he sneezed into his elbow. We were eating shabu-shabu at his apartment, in our boxers, and the steam fogged the air between us.

Joel said he knew about the laughter. He'd shared it with his sister.

Sometimes, he said, we'd go on for minutes at a time. I don't think either of us could've said why.

Did you ever talk about it? I asked.

Never, Joel said. We just laughed.

Eventually, I told Funke about the dumplings. She gave me a long look, turning away from her phone.

What, I said.

I could ask you the same thing, she said. It's starting to sound like you're taking advantage of this guy.

You're fucking joking.

I don't joke.

He's living with me! For free!

Funke crossed her arms and leaned against the register.

A grieving man flies into your life from out of the blue, she said. He just found out his lover's died. He's also just found out that the man had a son. How do you think he's feeling? Have you even thought about that?

He's good, I said.

Have you even thought about it?

O.K., I said. You're not even supposed to be on the register.

Don't be mad that I'm right, Funke said, turning back to her phone.

It doesn't even matter, I said. He's leaving in a few days.

It won't hurt you to give a shit about someone else for two minutes, Funke said.

But whatever, she said, and smiled. I guess gay men are still men.

That night, my visitor and I sat in the living room. Out of coffee mugs, we drank the Red Stripe I'd picked up. I'd fried some tortillas alongside eggs and tomatoes—the outer limit of my cooking abilities—and my visitor scarfed two at a time, sprinkling shredded cheese and drenching the paper plates in Cholula.

You're a secret chef, he said.

Hardly, I said.

You should take compliments as they come. It'll clear up your skin.

My skin's fine, I said.

Then I said, Tell me something about him.

My visitor grinned. And then he frowned. For the first time since we'd met, his cheeks turned entirely solemn.

Your father never combed his hair, he said. Your father had the softest skin. Your father hated his brothers, but he loved his sister. He couldn't dribble a soccer ball. He hated the walk to school, but he never missed a day of it. He crossed his eyes when he whistled. He couldn't stomach allspice, but he cooked with a heavy hand. He taught me how to swim.

My dad hated the water, I said.

Correct, the man said. And he still taught me. I asked him to do that and he did.

At that, my visitor turned silent. We both chewed, with our legs crossed. I asked what was wrong.

It's nothing, the man said.

Nothing's nothing.

So you're a sober philosopher, the man said.

I mean that it's nothing to *you*, I said.

Then I asked the man, Were you there when he left Jamaica?

My visitor looked up at me. He looked away.

No, he said. I told your father not to tell me.

Why?

Because that was easier. What could I have done?

And I thought about that. What could he have done? Two boys meet on an island where they shouldn't be meeting at all. They feel things that they shouldn't be feeling at all. They do what they can. One of them leaves. And then he dies.

What *could* he have done?

Later that night, at his place, Joel asked me what we were doing.

We stood barefoot in his kitchen, hunched over his counter, kneading dough. Immediately after fucking, I'd mentioned, offhand, that something sweet wouldn't be a bad idea, and Joel had gone over to the pantry. Now he patted and stirred while I massaged. We dropped globs of sugary dough into the fryer beside us.

Cooking, I said.

I think, Joel said, that we're doing more than that. And I think that you know it. And I think that we should talk about that.

We're talking now, I said.

When Joel went silent, I looked up. The sizzling beside us was all I could hear.

I feel pretty good about you, he said, sighing. All things considered.

Noted, I said.

And I'd like to know if you feel the same. It would mean a lot to me to know that.

But what if I don't feel what you feel, I asked.

Then nothing changes, Joel said. Except that I'd know.

O.K., I said, and what if I do?

Then I don't know, Joel said. But you have to say it. I can't know unless you tell me.

Neither of us said anything to that, until we noticed that the batter was smoking. We lifted three sweet pancakes from the pan to a bowl, and Joel immediately tossed one into his mouth—but not before tearing off a piece for me.

It burned me. It was delicious. We both reached for another.

The night before my visitor flew back to Kingston, I drove him to see my father's tombstone. I smoked by some vending machines instead of wandering the graves beside him, because I'd spent too much time there already. I'll never know if he cried.

Afterward, we sat at Fu Fu Café, a Chinese diner twenty minutes from my apartment. The evening bled through the windows. We settled into chairs at the one empty table. I was friendly with one of the waiters, and he smiled my way, then he said something to my visitor in Mandarin, and my visitor only shook his head, cheesing.

Our waiter looked at me. I shrugged. He shrugged right back. A few minutes later, a spread of chicken and noodles and spinach sat in front of us.

Who was General Tso really, my visitor said.

This is what you want to talk about, I said. Of all the fucking things.

I refuse to believe something so delicious could be the work of a war man.

That's very poetic.

All Jamaicans are poets, my visitor said.

That's bullshit, I said.

It's poetry, my visitor said.

He sipped at a beer, and rubbed his cheeks. In between bites, he looked up and smiled my way.

You should find a boyfriend, he said. Someone steady.

Thank you for your advice.

It's true. I know this. There's some nice boy walking around Houston, with untied shoelaces, waiting to make you happy.

Calm down, I said. And I'm seeing someone.

This made my visitor stand, shaking the table.

Good! the man said.

Can you stop that?

You should've told me! You didn't tell me! What's his name?

I'll tell you if you sit down, I said.

The man settled into his seat. He crossed his legs, stumping his chin in a palm.

Joel, I said.

Joel, my visitor said.

But it probably doesn't matter, I said. I don't even know if it'll work.

Don't take too long to figure it out, the man said.

Well. It's complicated.

Nothing's that complicated.

You wouldn't know. I'm not exactly on top of the sexual pyramid.

Now you're making assumptions about me, my visitor said, smiling.

We looked at the tables beside us—Korean couples and Mexican families and some Nigerian nurses enjoying the end of their workday.

I think you could be more kind to yourself, the man said. And I think you should give this boy a chance. Give yourselves a chance to be happy.

And how exactly would I do that, I said.

Do what?

Make a dude happy. Make someone happy.

Oh, the man said. That's easy. You don't have to do much. A little attention goes a long way. A little bit of food. A fuck from time to time.

This dinner isn't going to end with you teaching me some massive lesson about myself, I said. Life isn't like that.

Sure, my visitor said. But it's not so hard to understand, either.

You get it, though.

I do. Your father did, too.

I opened my mouth, but then I closed it.

I figured I'd let him have that.

And my visitor gave me another one of his long looks, scratching at the hair on his cheeks, chewing his lip. He looked a little different in the lights above us. A little like he was glowing. I wondered if I did, too.

And then my visitor said, Your father told me we'd see each other before we died. That was the promise.

A promise, I said. That's romantic.

He was romantic.

He wasn't that romantic.

Ai-yah, the man said.

The thing on both of our minds hung above us, swaying below the lights.

He did, the man said. If that's what you're thinking.

When I made a face, my visitor shook his head.

Your father held his end of the deal, he said. Even if he didn't come back to the island.

That's bullshit, I said. That's nothing.

And this made the man smile. He took my hand in his.

You don't understand, he said. And that's O.K. I don't expect you to understand.

When our waiter returned, my visitor said something to him, something I couldn't catch. The two of them laughed, rocking the entire table.

A few weeks before my dad's funeral, I'd visited him at his home in Spring. We didn't see each other often. There was always a reason to avoid it. After my mom died, he'd mostly lived by himself. He'd entertain a girlfriend from time to time, but no one ever stuck around, and I wondered whether they grew tired of him, or he grew tired of them, or if the relationships were constructed from the start to fizzle out like matches.

He answered the door with sleep on his face. I had to remind him that he'd called me over to help with some insurance paperwork. It took him a second, but then he nodded, waving me in and wiping his face.

There was luggage in the hallway, but I didn't ask him about it. I didn't want him asking me about my life, either.

He clicked through channels while I typed at his computer in the kitchen. I'd call out for details—an aunt's maiden name, a first childhood pet—and my father yelled them from his perch on the sofa. Then there was another question, your first love, and I typed in my mother's name and that didn't work. I called my dad over, but I didn't tell him why. I told him there was a question I didn't know, could he fill it in.

My father stumbled over to the computer. He typed something in, wordlessly. And I sat down and finished the rest of his paperwork. I put my hand on his shoulder before I left, and I told him I'd see him in a few weeks, but something came up so I didn't go.

CAFÉ LOUP

BY BEN LERNER (2022)

When I became a father, I began to worry not only that I would die and not be able to care for my daughter but that I would die in an embarrassing way, that my death would be an abiding embarrassment for Astra—that in some future world, assuming there is a future, she will be on a date with someone, hard as that is for me to imagine, and her date will ask, "What does your father do?," and she will say, "He died when I was little," and her date will respond, "I'm sorry," hesitate, and then ask, in a bid for intimacy, how I died, and Astra will feel ashamed, will look down into her blue wine, there will be blue wine in the future, and say, "He had an aneurysm on the toilet," which is one of the ways I often fear I might die. (I'm sure she'd withhold the toilet part, at least on a first date, but that would just make it worse, amplify the shame.) If I were to die on the toilet tomorrow, I assume Inma wouldn't share many specifics with Astra—who, like most three-year-olds, finds everything relating to the "potty" fascinating and hilarious—but, as Astra grew older, she would want to know more about the circumstances of my death, at which point Inma would have to either lie or divulge the details ("withholding," "divulging"—all these terms sound scatological). Inma would, I'm confident, eventually tell Astra the truth. In fact, I can imagine a version of the conversation that's tender, sweet: Inma finally tells Astra it happened on the toilet (let's say "while reading on the toilet"), there is an awkward moment of silence, then they both start laughing, then they both start crying, embracing each other, laughing and crying, remembering me as a well-meaning fool who projected or tried to project some seriousness as a poet, as a person, but who in fact met an appropriately ridiculous end, "Silly Dada," as Astra always says.

Maybe it wouldn't be that bad for Astra—to be able to laugh at your father is a kind of gift, perhaps the biggest gift a father can give—but I worried that if I died on the toilet or in some other ignominious way when Astra was still very young, and she had little or no conscious memory of me, then I would, in her mind, be totally identified with the manner of my demise, my entire life, at least for her, would contract to the punch line of my death. "At every point of his life, a man who dies at thirty-five will have been a man who dies at thirty-five," at every point of his life, a man who dies on the toilet will have been a man who was going to die on the toilet, his poems will be the poems of a man who died on the toilet, his loves, his causes, his crises, the loves and causes and crises of the man destined to leave the world on the toilet, and a man who chokes to death at forty on a piece of steak at Café Loup will have been, at every point, that man, and, while choking to death isn't as bad as dying on the toilet, there is still something disgraceful about it, especially if you're a little fat, as I am, if you eat too fast and talk too much, as I do, so that your death is the death of a slob, a word I once—I was nine or ten—heard an elegant aunt of mine use to describe me when she thought I was out of earshot, catalyzing a full-bodied experience of shame that I can feel the echo of now, "slob" less a word you pronounce than a sonic object you disgorge, and to die by choking—especially choking on animal flesh—is linked to the toilet, is involved with digestion and elimination, which is part of the humor and power of the scene in Buñuel's "The Phantom of Liberty," where the guests at a dinner party (if that's what it's called) are seated around a table on toilets and have to discreetly excuse themselves to the "dining room" to eat as quickly as possible in privacy.

When I began to choke, when—maybe because I'd been laughing at something Aaron had said, or because I'd taken too large a bite, or because I'd failed to chew my food sufficiently, which is more likely to happen when you've been drinking—my epiglottis, the flap of cartilage that covers the opening of the trachea when you swallow, failed to close in time, and the piece of steak lodged there, blocking all airflow to my lungs, I felt tremendous shame, shame spread through me as I sat, startled, entirely unable to breathe, the steak having formed a perfect seal as if it had been precisely measured to stop my "windpipe," a word that has always troubled me, that makes it sound as if we were mere instruments, chimes. While Aaron went on talking, I glanced around the packed restaurant to see if anybody else knew my secret: at one table an older couple were reading their menus by the light of their phones; at another a woman with bare shoulders was holding a hand out toward her companion, displaying a ring, maybe I could see a diamond sparkle above the candle. As if to buy time, I took a small sip of my wine—my water glass was empty—but there was nowhere for the wine to go; I let it trickle into my napkin, which I returned to my lap. All the while I was trying to conceal my condition, which was insane, as I should have been alerting Aaron immediately to my choking, but I had the confused if intense sense that if I didn't acknowledge the reality of my choking I'd be fine, and while I was terrified of my shameful secret being discovered (divulged, disgorged), I did not yet register the fear of dying, although I sensed the fear was coming; I sensed a deep ancestral panic was taking form, but it wasn't inside me, it was not yet mine. I pictured—while I sat staring at Aaron without hearing him, as if my ears and not my throat were obstructed—the panic gathering itself in Union Square, on the southeast corner of Union Square, a violently rotating column of air, collecting and scattering leaves and trash, now travelling toward me through the spring night. (Maybe that's what you're seeing whenever you see a little swirling updraft of debris in the city: someone's panic taking shape, someone's death setting out to find their body.)

It was at this point—I'm not sure how many seconds had passed—that I began to write this in my head, by which I mean I started to narrate my choking to myself, as if transforming it into a story would keep me connected to a future in which I might tell it, as if I were a kind of Scheherazade to my own choking, and I started to audition different analogies for that horribly decisive moment when the steak stopped my windpipe, analogies that would emphasize how it felt less like an accident had occurred than like an operation had been successfully performed: a shuttle docking at a space station, a bullet sliding into a chamber, a prophecy being fulfilled. All the analogies were wrong, but that was good, that meant I could go on auditioning them, postponing my death, keeping the tornado of fear from finding the restaurant, my table. "Take all the time you need," a voice said in my head, Mrs. Sackett's voice, my first-grade teacher at Randolph Elementary; she said it each time she gave us a writing prompt.

I'd involuntarily summoned Mrs. Sackett because she was rumored to have once saved a child who was choking on a piece of hard candy by stabbing him in the throat with a pencil, performing an emergency tracheotomy, which had always remained for me a vividly if variously imagined primal scene in which the writing implement is both an instrument of violence and of care, and the teacher both an assailant and a savior; there were also no doubt complex sexual fantasies and fears embedded in this story. I'd read that you're everyone in your dreams, and I'd always imagined myself as both the teacher and the child in this dreamlike scene, my consciousness distributed across the bodies, but also the objects, the pencil, the candy lodged in the child's throat. It was hard to explain, I was going to need a lot of time to tease out the implications, but—miraculously, given that I couldn't breathe—I could take all the time I needed. Part of me was at my table in Café Loup turning pale, staring unseeingly and unhearingly at Aaron, but part of me rose from my desk and walked to the pencil sharpener attached to the wall, and that part of me could smell the cedar shavings as I turned the little crank, could hear the birds in the walnut tree beside the half-open window. I walked back to my desk and sat down and carefully wrote my name in my recently acquired cursive, blowing to disperse the trace amounts of graphite, but when I looked up to check the date—Mrs. Sackett always wrote it on the chalkboard—I saw Aaron's face, saw that Aaron had asked me a question, and now for the first time I tried to speak.

Spinoza wrote that the aleph, the first and silent letter of the Hebrew alphabet, is the sound of "the opening of the throat" as if to speak and not speaking; if the last letter of the alphabet were also silent, it should be assigned to the non-sound I made when I tried to speak, to make any noise at all in response to whatever it was that Aaron had asked; whatever the densest, purest form of silence is, the sound of closing the throat, the black hole of silence that sucks everything you've ever said or might have said into it, that was the non-sound I made when no air escaped through my windpipe, and I no longer felt that I could keep my choking secret, no longer felt that I had time, and that was when the panic entered the restaurant—it wasn't a tornado now, it was spilling across the floor like flame on oil—and touched me.

When I became a father, I secretly gave myself permission to kill myself if anything ever happened to my daughter, and I even selected a spot—"selected" isn't the word; the spot simply started appearing in my mind—near the Brooklyn side of the Manhattan Bridge, where I would jump if something did happen, a place to which I could rush, staying ahead of the pain; I'd hail a cab and run onto the bridge and scale the ineffectual chain-link fence and leap and lose consciousness when I hit the dark water. I would like to think I would not actually kill myself, that I wouldn't do that to Inma, to my family and friends, but it was a definite and comforting image, this particular spot on the bridge; it comforted me to picture it when I couldn't sleep and was ruminating about SIDS or fascists or rising seas, it comforted me during the night we spent in the E.R. because Astra was wheezing or, more recently, when she fell down the stairs in our building (and was fine, but the whole time she was falling, head over heels, eerily silent except for the sound of her body hitting each successive step, I was thinking about jumping). When I tried to speak and could not (this was half a minute into my choking), the image of the water, the moving image, the live stream of that particular patch of black water I'd selected or that had selected me, appeared in my mind and I was internally commanded—as if the father in Kafka's "The Judgment" had screamed "I condemn you to death by drowning," except I was both the father and the son in this version—to flee the restaurant and destroy myself so as to avoid choking to death in front of a hundred people at Café Loup.

How much worse it would be for Astra to have a father who killed himself for no apparent reason than one who died by accident, however embarrassing, but, as adrenaline flooded my body, I no longer felt compelled to keep my secret quietly at the table; instead, I felt compelled to get out of the restaurant as quickly as possible, to die on my own terms, away from the gaze of others; obviously I would not have time to travel the two or three miles to my spot on the bridge, nor would I be able to reach the Hudson, but I could jump in front of a bus or, if there weren't any buses, I could at least expire in the dark, unobserved, as opposed to flailing around and turning purple in Café Loup, where somebody might film my death throes on their phone. This impulse to flight, I would later learn, is common and deadly for people who are choking, and now I stood, I found myself standing, looking across the packed dining room to the door, which seemed to have receded. Aaron thought that I'd stood to greet someone and so he also rose from his chair, turning around to see who had arrived, then turning back to me in confusion. For the first time he now realized that something was wrong, and he asked me if I was O.K. Later he told me that, as I brought my hands to my throat to make the universal sign, I had a slight, apologetic smile. He asked me, "Are you choking?"

I had always been fascinated and slightly disturbed by the question "Are you choking?," the question you are told to ask before rendering assistance. There is something funny or cruel about it, because nothing seems to be less in need of verbal clarification than the fact that somebody is incapable of drawing breath, it's like asking somebody if they're on fire ("No, why do you ask?"), although I understood there must be various conditions that mimic choking in which you don't want somebody doing abdominal thrusts that might break your ribs, and also that the question functions as a request for consent to intervene. Nevertheless, the question—long before Aaron asked it of me that night in Café Loup—haunted me because, paradoxically, the only true way to answer in the affirmative is to be incapable of answering at all. You are taught that if a person who is ostensibly choking says "Yes," they are not really choking; you are supposed to stay with them, monitor them until they swallow or cough or otherwise expel the obstruction. Logicians talk about "the liar paradox." If you say "I am lying" and the statement is true it's false, but if it's false it's true; this is the choker paradox—in which the condition of assent is the incapacity to assent, a yes is a no. Since so much of language is used to obscure the brute reality of bodies and their processes, to cover the real with the symbolic, this scene—where the Good Samaritan asks the choking person if they're choking—became in my mind a ritual acknowledgment of the gap between these two things, the gap but also the interdependence between physical life, respiring and perspiring and chewing and shitting, and the social world of speech, a division unreliably enforced by a leaf-shaped flap of cartilage.

This must be why, ever since Mr. Kessler taught us the steps for "assisting a conscious choking adult" in our eighth-grade health class, and made us rehearse them with one another—without actually performing the "thrusts," which he explained were quite dangerous, leaving us with the sense that we should never actually do what he was supposedly preparing us to do, unless we were trying to inflict harm on an enemy (Mr. Kessler was also the wrestling coach), so that the entire scene became a fraught and confusing mashup of sex ("Assume the position behind your partner") and violence and humiliation that had nothing to do with saving anybody—I have always thought there was sadism haunting the question "Are you choking?," since the one who still draws breath and can form it into speech demands from the person who is choking a response they cannot give. In my mind it also perversely links the emergency protocols for choking with breath play, in which—aside from whatever the physiology of asphyxiation and orgasm might be—there is the erotic drama of being reduced to mere body and then restored to speech. Regardless, choking is a uniquely human drama, a definitional drama for the *homo loquens*, a drama at the heart of the human, or, rather, at the larynx, the voice box, which, as we evolved, moved lower and lower, enabling us to generate a long column of vibrating air we can shape into meaning with our mouthparts, shaped air that might in turn build and shape a world, but this evolutionary "speech advantage" required that the space in our bodies for breathing and swallowing be shared; the formal capacity for speech comes with the risk of choking to death, something only humans frequently do.

Choking and scenes of instruction had always been linked in my mind, not only because of Sackett and Kessler but also because I associated the ritual posing of a question that can't be answered, the addressing of speech to the helpless nonspeaker, with the relation between infant (*in-* "not" + *fant-* "speaking") and parent, the parent who talks to the baby as if she might respond, the very first language lessons, often starting in utero: Hello, little Astra, can you hear me? She wasn't yet named Astra when we attended—a little more than three years before I choked on my steak—the "infant-CPR-and-safety class" Inma's ob-gyn recommended for all new parents. We found ourselves one February night around a table at N.Y.U. Langone with three other couples and one unaccompanied pregnant woman while the instructor, a nurse in light-blue scrubs, circled us with a cart on which were stacked infant CPR manikins, asking each couple to take one. Some of the manikins were brown and some of them were white, and I assumed that the nurse, a white woman, was asking couples to choose their manikin instead of simply distributing them, so that people could select the one whose skin color they believed most closely approximated their future offspring's, although nothing about the plastic tonalities looked human. The man and woman who formed the first couple the cart reached were Black; they selected a brown manikin; the next couple consisted of two white women, and they selected a white "baby"; when it was our turn to choose from the nightmarish cart, I leaned back a little to make it clear to Inma that she should decide. She hesitated, and I assumed she was imagining the future pigmentation of our daughter—would she more closely resemble Inma's coloration or mine, and was Inma's skin color ultimately closer to the brown plastic or the white? It was as if all the future complexity of our interracial family were enfolded in the selection of the dummy, although this might have been only in my mind.

Inma chose a brown one. The woman without a partner—I thought she was white, but I wasn't sure—chose a brown baby, too, and set it down harder than she meant to; the plastic head hit the table with a crack. Once we all had our babies, the nurse sat and began to read from a binder; we were to be congratulated for taking the time to acquire these lifesaving techniques. I'd already decided I'd be unable to assimilate any of the information in real time and would have to catch up later with YouTube tutorials, and, as I expected, everything unfolded for me, once the actual practicing started, in a disordered, disorienting whirl: Lay the infant face down across the arm (you don't have to say "Are you choking" to an infant, but you can), deliver five sharp blows with your palm between the shoulder blades. But how hard? someone asked. Harder than you'd think, the nurse said. Turn your infant over, place two fingers in the center of the doll's chest, quickly compress to at least a third of its depth, approximately an inch and a half. But how fast? someone asked. A rate of around a hundred times a minute, she said; think of the song "Stayin' Alive." I thought the nurse had made a tasteless joke, but she was serious, repeating: "Think of the tempo of 'Stayin' Alive,'" which I would later learn is known as the CPR anthem. I wasn't sure I knew how to "think of a tempo," if I could be confident I hadn't sped it up or slowed it down, but now the song became a mocking soundtrack in my mind: Tilt the baby's head back to open the airway, cover both the child's mouth and nose with your own mouth, and whisper "Stayin' Alive" directly into the infant's brain, inspirit the dummy, its windpipe, then beseech it to stay: Do not leave me; if you do, I'll jump off the Manhattan Bridge, I have a place in mind.

The manikin tasted like rubbing alcohol, I remember pushing it over to Inma, as if it were a strangely shaped bong from which I'd just taken a dizzying hit, but Inma pushed it back. (I'd read that the face of the adult CPR dummy, at least originally, was modelled on the death mask of a teen-age girl found floating in the Seine in the nineteenth century, which made her, in the disturbing formulation I encountered, "the most kissed girl in the world"; I hoped the infant dummies had no particular human source.) Deliver two breaths, the nurse was saying. Each ventilation should last a second. I looked at the couple across the table; they were doing back blows again, so I started doing back blows. The nurse was saying something about the compression-to-ventilation ratio when the woman who didn't have a partner slammed her hands on the table and said, "I killed my baby. My fucking baby is dead, O.K.? I'm the worst. I am the worst mother who ever lived."

In the ensuing silence, I tried to identify her accent. Greek? Israeli? Everyone was staring at the woman or trying not to (she was smiling), or everyone was staring or trying not to stare at the plastic baby she had failed (and now she was crying, but still holding the smile). For a long moment nobody knew what to do. Then Inma and one of the other women pushed back their chairs and went to her as quickly as their pregnant bellies would allow, offering comfort, support, encouragement. ("The worst mother who ever lived" became one of our most enduring jokes, refrains: we were always, especially when Astra was an infant, calling each other "the worst mother who ever lived"; I could also be that mother. We claimed that there were only two kinds of mothers, the "good enough mother" and "the worst mother who ever lived"; if I forgot to buy diapers and I had to go back out, I was the worst mother who ever lived; if Inma nicked Astra while cutting her nails, she was the worst mother who ever lived. It was a useful joke, it helped lighten Inma's tendency toward self-recrimination, it short-circuited the guilt mechanism, laid it bare, and it was good for her to call me a mother, for the impossibly punishing category of mother to be spread around the apartment, so that it lost some of its force, so the Mother in her head would stop saying, "I condemn you to death by drowning," or whatever Inma's equivalent of that condemnation was.) I will never forget that moment of transformation when the sanitized and anxious space of the conference room suddenly became human, how we all scooted our chairs a little closer to the woman, how we all started laughing and joking and talking about how scary and weird this parenting thing was, would be, how the couple forms dissolved into something larger, however briefly, even the nurse joining us, becoming one of us, showing us pictures of her kids on her phone—"This is the troublemaker," "Here's one from Halloween"—before we all returned to our places around the table and the class resumed, infinitely more collaborative now, although I still couldn't keep the emergency protocols straight, couldn't learn anything, except the necessity of repeatedly sweeping your home for choking hazards, as we discussed during the review period, when we'd set our dolls aside. Beware of marbles and Legos your older kids might have left around, beware of screws or washers that might have fallen from your ready-to-assemble furniture, a cashew or a piece of gum a grownup might inadvertently have let fall to the carpet where your child will crawl, and—perhaps most important—you must always remember to properly cut your child's food, to cut round foods like hot dogs and grapes *lengthwise*; the nurse took turns looking us in the eye: "You don't know how many lives would be saved if parents would cut their kids' hot dogs *lengthwise* into strips, then cut them again," and so, in addition to our joke, and the memory of the camaraderie the worst mother enabled, that was what I retained from our child-safety-and-CPR class, that was what I took home, that was what I recalled a year and a half later when Astra began to eat solid food, when we were no longer puréeing what we fed her and/or mixing it with breast milk, and when she would sit in her high chair banging her sippy cup on the tray demanding, *Uvas, uvas*, her favorite food and, according to Inma, her first word, although I think Astra was attempting her mother's name.

When I was a child, somebody gave me a paperweight that contained within it an impossibly detailed forest scene, and when I think of the grapes, of how all the complexity of our family became enfolded in the grapes, I imagine that if I had lifted one of those grapes up to the light and rotated it around I would have perceived within it all of our family histories depicted in miniature, not just me and Inma in our own high chairs at the dawn of the eighties, our parents feeding us, but our own parents being fed in the forties and fifties, all the way back to our respective Old Worlds, Kyiv and San Juan, kasha or plantains, however mouths were sated and policed according to family and cultural custom, and if I kept rotating the grape I'd also see Mrs. Sackett wielding her pencil of life and Mr. Kessler telling us not to practice our thrusts, all of it as intricately rendered as the shield of Achilles, or Zeuxis' grapes, which were so perfectly represented in his paintings that birds tried to eat them, birds, which sing from their syrinx, not their larynx, and cannot to my knowledge choke to death, although some can mimic human speech.

When I was in charge of preparing Astra's food, I chopped everything so finely I admit I might as well have blended it or hit it with a hammer, which is not what I was supposed to be doing, I was supposed to be giving her an experience of texture, as Inma kept pointing out—"She has to learn what she likes; she has to learn to use her teeth"—and since Inma's mother was over many times a week she often witnessed Inma remarking that I'd inadvertently liquefied Astra's food, and of course Inma's mom silently sided with Inma, forming a triangle; I was the neurotic cracker with no experience caring for children who was trying to micromanage the steamed carrots, the hot dogs (which, thankfully, Astra didn't really like), and the grapes. Because Inma's mom had taught kindergarten (she'd recently retired), I'd hoped she might share the intensity of my concern about Astra choking—surely there had been trainings about these things—but although both Inma and her mother were incredibly conscientious caretakers in general, so graceful and competent with Astra that I felt bumbling in comparison, and although they watched her closely when she ate, the fear of her choking quickly became my thing, the worry I carried that carried all of my other worries: I would pulverize the food and they would not quite slice it properly, which is the way of polarization. When Inma's mom was sitting with Astra at the table, it was less that I watched over them than that my effort not to was palpable, and if Inma or her mom was cutting something for Astra I perceived a slight exaggeration in their gestures, a trace of performativity that said, See how tiny these pieces are? Do we have your permission to feed her? It was a cliché, this tension around the child's eating, the triangulation, etc., but I was finding small, mortally uncut grapes in the purple plastic snack container Inma's mom took with Astra to the park, and large grapes on the high chair that were cut in half but never lengthwise (anyway, they should be quartered), and then I'd confront Inma about it, as if it were her fault, demanding she talk to her mom, and before we knew it we would be having a spectacular fight, scaling up from the grapes to questions of power, labor, value, the possibility of love, Astra crying when we yelled (or, worse, taking it all in silently, blinking her large brown eyes). We'd had one such fight only a month or two before I choked.

And it was only when I choked, while I was standing there choking at Café Loup, that I fully realized (although not in these words) that our polarization around the grapes issued from our conflicting but, in fact, equally magical beliefs about the effects of my voicing, again and again, my fear of Astra choking. Inma would of course agree that the food should be cut up, but the intensity of my focus on this particular risk, the repetitive articulation of my concerns—reading statistics off my phone ("Last year alone, every child in America choked to death"), showing with my thumb and index finger the tiny diameter of a child's windpipe—was, in Inma's mind, courting disaster. This was both because talking about it at all invited the evil in and because too much confidence in "risk management," the financialized world view of the privileged, was a kind of hubris, the fantasy that you could halve or quarter the constant threats that attended living; it was asking God, or whatever cosmic force, to cut you lengthwise down to size. Inma, then, did not speak her fears, for fear that speaking them would make them happen (that speaking them would summon one of those little tornadoes of debris); she did not, while pregnant with Astra, ever acknowledge her terror of another late miscarriage, for instance, neither to me nor, I'm sure, to her mother, whereas I told my own mother constantly that the pregnancy wouldn't make it to term, that we were never going to have a child—not because I believed these things with certainty, and not only because I was expressing what Freudians call "signal anxiety" about a prospective trauma, but because I thought, although I would have denied it, that voicing the worst-case scenarios made them at least a little less likely, a kind of negative prayer.

If I survive, I thought as I stood in Café Loup, although not in these words, not in words at all, so "thought" isn't really right—I simply felt, as I stood dying, that if I "lived to tell the tale" of my choking I would not tell it, couldn't tell it, because Inma would believe, or at least half believe, that I was responsible for what had happened (*Ya ves*, I could hear her mom, who would believe it in full, saying), that the steak was my comeuppance for all the worry I'd expressed. That was crazy, and yet it struck me as equally or perhaps even more crazy to think that my choking was entirely random, entirely unrelated to my obsessive worry about Astra's choking and the tension surrounding it. If I didn't accept the idea of mere coincidence, contingency, and I didn't accept that the universe was punishing me, what did I believe? I rejected what I thought of as Inma's Caribbean metaphysics, and yet my substitute religion, the "Jewish Science" of psychoanalysis, would suggest that I'd been unconsciously driven to choke, because I felt unheard about choking, driven to destroy myself over the grapes. And this would really mean that I was responsible for what had happened, that I had quite literally done it to myself, however unconsciously. (Was there a weaker, more plausible version of the psychoanalytic account? Maybe I was more disposed to choke because of all the intensity around choking, maybe I was eating faster or chewing less thoroughly? But this, too, sounded ridiculous, the idea that my throat was primed, that I was just waiting for the right wrong bite.)

Chance, fate, the version of fate the unconscious was—I couldn't accept any of these world views; I had no world view, I'd had forty years to develop one and failed. Again, these were less coherent ideas than waves of feeling issuing from an increasingly unoxygenated brain, but now, out of this metaphysical abyss, I was commanded—just as I'd been commanded at one point to flee the restaurant and destroy myself—never to tell the story of my choking. It felt as if some god or Kafkan father or wrestling coach were making me an offer: If you swear you will not recount your choking, will not turn it into a story, I will allow you to survive, I will break the seal, all of this will have been a warning to shut your mouth, you fucking slob, to stop tempting fate, to learn to withhold, to hold in the sense Inma often ascribed to that term—as when she asked me to "hold" her upset without trying to fix it or explain it or interpret it, or when (I believed) she wanted me to "hold" more of my anxiety without spreading it around in a plume of speech. And what was my problem, exactly—why couldn't I hold a feeling without having to express it, why couldn't I stand to have a thought inside me without having to immediately spit it out, disgorge it, clear the passage? Early in my career as a choker, I believed I would narrate my way back to the world of the breathing, that language would save me, but now I swore, desperately: Yes, if I am allowed to live, I will tell no one what has happened to me, and, starting with that silence, I will learn the way of silence, I will no longer manically ingest and express, will neither tempt fate nor attempt to evade it with talk. Please.

Aaron was behind me, his breath on my neck, trying to figure out where to put his hands. Instead of my life "flashing before my eyes," a series of odors were doing whatever the olfactory equivalent of flashing is, all of them intensified by the fact that I couldn't inhale. Childhood cut grass (nothing is a cliché when you're dying), the sulfur of strike-anywhere matches, asphalt after rain, fresh paint in a room whose windows are open in the spring, movie-theatre popcorn, the sexual smell (that is, the vaginal smell) of a woman who broke my heart in my late twenties, hyacinth, watermelon candy (in the throat of Mrs. Sackett's student?), my first cat (Felix), grilled peaches at my brother's in Seattle—then, as Aaron placed his interlocking hands above my navel, they all started to coalesce around Astra, the odors, the slight soapy smell of Inma's breast milk, of the milk on Astra's infant breath, the milky smell of Astra's shit before she started eating solid foods, the smell of her vomit on the flight back from Ponce, the smell of the baby shampoo on the wisps of her hair mixing with the cherry blossoms when I walked her through the botanical gardens in the carrier, it was all Astra now, as Aaron performed his first ineffectual thrust, tears finally in my eyes, haloing all the tabletop candles, my little aleph, little star, my asterisk, and even as my peripheral vision began to contract and my ears started to ring and I was begging my daughter to forgive me in my mind, I was surprised—and surprised that I was surprised, that in my last moments on earth, as I was flooded with terror and love, I had the mental space to note how the world failed to conform to my expectations of it—that nobody around us in the restaurant seemed aware of what was happening, how was it possible that no waiter had appeared, that people around us were still drinking and laughing and eating and generating columns of vibrating air at their tables while Aaron did it again, how was it possible nobody was answering the phone, it was ringing in our kitchen on Jewell Street, Can someone get that, my mom was yelling, Can someone take a message please, because you are everyone at the tables, the dark splotches in my vision, you are the tables and the candles and clichés.

NARROWING VALLEY

BY JONATHAN LETHEM (2022)

WIDE LOAD / "MR. BLUE SKY"

The characters ride into the story aboard a 1976 Winnebago Minnie Winnie, one driven breakneck across broiling asphalt, overspilling its lane on both sides. Though the story's characters are themselves oblivious, the story acknowledges that it is being written on stolen Tongva land—indeed, the same Tongva land toward which the recreational vehicle now barrels. The story gives respect and reverence to those who came before it, which ought to be absolutely everyone, even you, reader, since the story does not yet and may never exist. Yet here it seems to come—the story, and the recreational vehicle—the Winnebago like a breadbox rumbling westward on fat half-melted tires, a monster's breadbox with its bragging orange stripe, side-view mirrors flying-buttressed a full foot from its cab to make it minimally navigable. The story already occupies too much space, demands too much attention. What the fuck, watch where you're going! Who's driving that thing? A dad in mirrored aviator shades? Why, of course. He's R. Crumb's Whiteman, he's Albert Brooks in "Lost in America," he's the Exhausted Normative Protagonist—our movie's leading man, there's no way to avoid him. Or maybe there is. Maybe one of his kids or his long-suffering wife can provide us with a marginally improved point of view, a parallax position from which to operate. Some fucking oxygen here, though it may be that all the oxygen is recirculated within the tightly sealed Winnebago. They all breathe the same air, surely. At least we can't hear the music that's playing inside: Electric Light Orchestra's "Greatest Hits," on eight-track tape.

THE STORY'S WRITER / "TURN TO STONE"

The alternative is equally unpromising: that we raise up a literary selfie stick and catch a glimpse of the story's writer. We might choose to cast him as the protagonist in a drama of the story's becoming (or, more likely, of the story's failure to launch, burdened as it is with debts and doubts, with qualms and queasy self-loathing). Of course, and it goes without saying, the story's writer is also male and white—another exemplar of the Exhausted Normative. And the project of literary self-consciousness is hardly novel (a pun, there), since it has been indulged in by so many of the writer's immediate and distant influences, from Kurt Vonnegut and Philip K. Dick to Jorge Luis Borges and Laurence Sterne. This model of self-consciousness has lately been renovated, refurbished, under the name "autofiction," yet even so it may once again be an expiring mode. Sure, it offers itself as an exit from the interstate of narrative—the kind of storytelling that doesn't trouble over the existence of the author, just barrels ever forward, claiming the turf of your attention. But perhaps it has proved to be an exit that is closed for repairs, or has simply shut down because no one wishes to go where it leads anymore.

Among those who may wish to avoid self-consciousness: the writer of this story. The writer wants to fight to stay on the interstate of storytelling! He wants to get somewhere! He wants to be aboard the Winnebago!

If so, this is no way to go about it.

FURTHER DISCLAIMERS / "CAN'T GET IT OUT OF MY HEAD"

The story acknowledges borrowing the language of its acknowledgment of its occupation of stolen Tongva land from the Web site of a collective of spirit healers, who will go unnamed in this acknowledgment, for they may not wish to be associated. The story admits that it also depends for its existence on an occupation of the text of R. A. Lafferty's "Narrow Valley," a text that the story's author first encountered in the anthology "Other Dimensions," edited by Robert Silverberg in 1973. The story takes place six years later, in 1979, the year of Three Mile Island, of the Iranian hostage crisis, of the imminence of the Reagan era. The feeling that the Reagan era was coming is a migraine prodrome, a hangover suffered before a decades-long binge on Militarism, Bogus Optimism, and Imperial Fantasy that hasn't abated yet. Since, really, what is the twenty-first century except the endless unspooling of the implications of the Reagan era? But the writer digresses. The clown Emmett Kelly died in 1979, as did John Wayne and Jack Soo and Sid Vicious. Natasha Lyonne and Chris Hayes and Pink were born in 1979. The story now acknowledges consulting Wikipedia's "1979 in the United States" page. But who is R. A. Lafferty? A writer of science fiction and Westerns, Lafferty lived most of his life in Tulsa, Oklahoma. He died at eighty-seven in 2002. He was a Catholic. What's "Narrow Valley"? A short story that is both a science-fiction story and a Western story, as well as a kind of tall tale or parable, typical of Lafferty's eccentric style. In it a white family attempts to homestead on acreage originally given in a land allotment by the U.S. government to a Pawnee Indian named Clarence Big-Saddle, and handed down to his son, Clarence Little-Saddle.

The land appears, from some vantage points, to be a broad and fertile valley, with an alluring topography. However, when the white family attempts to enter the valley, it reveals itself to be a spatial anomaly—a strip of ground between two fences which is too small to enter. Or, more strangely, when outsiders, such as the white family, insist on entering it, it shrinks and flattens them to fit. Lafferty's story, originally published in 1966, still has much to recommend it: a delightful insouciance; admirable ethics (even if expressed in twentieth-century terms); surrealist humor; a winking self-awareness that affiliates it with more labored forms of literary metafiction yet lacks the overt self-consciousness with which the present story is hobbled. The present story now acknowledges that by basing itself on a specific earlier science-fiction story it is also indebted, paradoxically, to another: "The Nine Billion Names of God," by Carter Scholz, which was based on "The Nine Billion Names of God," by

Arthur C. Clarke, and which has amused and obsessed the writer of the present story for decades. The story now acknowledges its utter colonization by its own procedure of serially confessing its sources. The story, which initially believed itself to be operating on a blank page, moving into a horizon of possibility, is dismayed by the likelihood that it has wandered instead into a sucking undertow of bungled authorial good intentions, the pathetic desire to write a story that will acknowledge its colonial crimes and historical debts. The Winnebago, moving with such innocent optimism across deserted Western spaces, may be blundering into a valley of palimpsest. The story is belated.

COLLAPSING FRONTIER / "STRANGE MAGIC"

The man and wife and kids in the Winnebago are moving west. The story moves west with them. All stories around here move west. An exhausting procedure, but necessary. Frederick Jackson Turner made this inevitable with his "frontier thesis." Turner's thesis declares that white people placed their boot prints on the American continent in the name of American democracy. The thesis rationalized their push west as a noble effort to occupy land that was as good as waiting for them, like a medium waiting for the artistry of their realization. It claimed that the land lay as ready as a blank page, one on which new meaning could be sprinkled as easily as tapping at alphabetic keys, as the writer finds himself doing right now. This story has attempted to launch itself on a presumption of innocence: it shouldn't need to push another story off the page in order to be written, should it? It isn't required that the story murder another story! Intertextuality isn't colonization! Reference isn't smallpox! The Winnebago rumbles through open space, not an obstacle in sight. The father has purchased some desert land, sight unseen—acreage described to him by the Realtor as "virgin." He and his family are driving there to claim it. Will they build there? Will they only camp on it? They haven't decided. We have to pretend this might work out, even though we know it doesn't, whether we have read Lafferty's version or not. There are two names for this operation: Suspension of Disbelief and Bad Faith.

The story is headed into crisis, because the white family must—as in Lafferty's original—meet an Indian. A Native American. An Indigenous North American person. The difficulty in producing even a stable term ("These terms have come in and out of favor over the years, and different tribes, not to mention different people, have different preferences. . . . A good rule of thumb for outsiders: Ask the Native people you're talking to what they prefer."—David Treuer, "The Heartbeat of Wounded Knee") shows how unlikely it is that the story's writer will be capable of manifesting such a character, or such a scene, on the page. Should we presume it was simpler for Lafferty? He would at least not have hesitated to call the character an Indian. As a securely twentieth-century human, one who had lived almost his whole life in Oklahoma, Lafferty imparted to characters such as Clarence Little-Saddle an air of fond and easeful familiarity. He employed Clarence Little-Saddle in the cause of "punching up" at the presumptions of the white characters, their avarice and delusions, as well as at the garbled scientific pontification of the characters who are called in as experts to examine the paradox of the mysteriously narrow valley.

It will not be so simple for this story's writer. In his dismay he recalls some astounding advice—a "craft tip"—he absorbed from a talk by the French author Emmanuel Carrère. Carrère had spoken of the difficulty of depicting characters from the legendary past (in his case, a Biblical figure of early Christianity) as if they were human. He said that he'd taken his guidance from early-Renaissance paintings in which the multitude of faces in religious scenes are obviously painted from life—from the fact, that is, that they are clearly portraits of specific people the painter had access to (including, sometimes, self-portraits). Carrère explained that this observation had led him to believe that it would be possible for him to make a literary portrait of someone inaccessible to him only if he decided that it would actually be a likeness of someone from life—and that nearly anyone would do.

The story's writer has seized on this advice in an attempt to rescue his enterprise. If he wishes to avoid caricature or sentimentality in his depiction of the Native person who will intervene in his story, and teach the white family its deserved lesson, he must make that character a portrait of a specific human. He must avoid the generic figure of the benevolent trickster (or "magic Indian") who serves as the projected conscience in so many well-intentioned white narratives, from "One Flew Over the Cuckoo's Nest" to "Dead Man." In this undertaking, he has landed, perhaps perversely, on a recollection of an encounter of his own, with a man named Max Gros-Louis.

MAX GROS-LOUIS / "TELEPHONE LINE"

From Wikipedia:

> Magella Gros-Louis OC [Order of Canada] OQ [Order of Quebec] (6 August 1931-14 November 2020), known as Max Gros-Louis or Oné Onti, was a Canadian politician and businessman in Quebec. For many years, he was Grand Chief of the Huron-Wendat First Nation. . . . Gros-Louis initially made a living by hunting, fishing and trapping. . . . He later opened a small shop "Le Huron" where he sold snowshoes, moccasins and other First Nation crafts, and also managed a dance company. In the course of his business he travelled widely to other indigenous communities and this led to his involvement in politics.

The story's writer met Max Gros-Louis when he was twelve years old, on an anomalous family trip, with his mother and his mother's boyfriend, to Quebec, in midwinter. The boy had never previously been out of the United States. His mother's boyfriend at the time was a younger man, a New York City schoolteacher, but one with a surprising amount of money, perhaps from a family source, and he had swept the boy and his siblings along on an impulsive voyage to French Canada. What the boy remembers of the trip, aside from the encounter with Max Gros-Louis, is French onion soup, buying a French version of a Spider-Man comic book, morning croissants in the Château Frontenac, and warming his frostbitten toes under the radiator at that same hotel after a trudge through slush-crusted streets.

The story's writer had never met a Native tribal chief before, nor has he since. This is a matter not of avoidance but of happenstance.

The story's writer came of age in New York, and has spent his life primarily in cities. He's known Native Americans! ("Some of my best friends are," etc.) The first were the elderly Mohawk women surviving in basement apartments in his childhood neighborhood, widows of the last of the men who built skyscrapers in Manhattan. (These skywalkers and their wives were also from French Canada, though he didn't know that at the time.) He met others, over time, though rarely those who'd been raised on tribal lands, or who'd participated directly in tribal communities. In the life of his family, who were both hippies and Quakers, Native people were also symbolically charged, tragic emblems of some better and nobler existence. That this was a discourse that mixed much that was good with much that was bad he'd understand later. But certainly it was affectionate, and intended to be respectful. The writer's father had copied out lines from "Black Elk Speaks" into the writer's high-school yearbook, for instance. Another example: as a child the writer had practically memorized an LP by a Native folksinger named Floyd Westerman, called "Custer Died for Your Sins." Some of the writer's Midwestern relatives liked to claim a small portion of their lineage as Native. That this was a common fantasy he'd also understand later.

His encounter with Max Gros-Louis, though, was a singular one. The writer's mother and her boyfriend had sought it out, a variation in their Quebec tourism, the majority of which had been in exercise of the fantasy that they'd actually travelled to Paris (croissants, onion soup, etc.). They'd gone to where the city met the reservation to find Max Gros-Louis's business, a shop called the Centre d'Artisanat Le Huron. They'd encouraged the boy to speak with Max Gros-Louis—to meet the chief, who'd dressed for his role in fringed leather and a headband. The boy had come away with the impression of someone kind, and formidable, and quite tall—but also of someone who felt an amused tolerance toward those who'd come to meet him.

The boy and his family didn't buy much, as he recalls. No moccasins, no headdress, no art work. In this they likely represented a disappointment. The boy, however, did purchase a postcard. He was a postcard collector in those days.

It is when the boy becomes the story's writer, nearly fifty years later, that he recognizes that in a semiconscious way he has always associated Max Gros-Louis with the figure in Lafferty's story, Clarence Little-Saddle, the recipient and rebuffer of the white family's attempt to occupy the narrow valley. It is also only when the story's writer conceives this plan to rewrite Lafferty, and connects this to his memory of Max Gros-Louis, that he troubles to Google Max Gros-Louis's name and discovers, from his obituaries, that the Huron-Wendat chief was alive until 2020, and that he was elected and served as the tribal chief in three separate periods across five decades, and that he was regarded as one of the truly great leaders in the First Nations cause in Canada's history.

Had the story's writer imagined that Max Gros-Louis was some kind of trickster or charlatan, a pretend chief who was really a seller of tourist merchandise? No. Yet, in his astonishment at what he learns from the obituaries, the story's writer realizes that he had imagined that Max Gros-Louis was frozen in time—that Max Gros-Louis was a kind of private dream nudging at his awareness. In this, the writer is too typical of himself. That he feels that the past lives in him, and that it stirs him, doesn't mean that the past actually exists inside him. The past, too, is a narrow valley, one refusing occupation. Or no. That's wrong. The past is huge, and real, but you are small. To reënter the valley of the past is, properly, to grow tiny, and to vanish.

WHAT ABOUT THE WINNEBAGO? / "MR. BLUE SKY" (REPRISE)

The Winnebago believes it is moving, but in fact it is parked. The family believes they are rumbling steadily west across the landscape, in pursuit of the valley, the open space, the tabula rasa, but they are mistaken. Such beliefs are belated, lapsed, overdue, like a book checked out from a library and then lost for decades; the story has moved indoors, the frontier has become one of recursion, quotation, paraphrase, allegory. To be specific, the frontier is now an "electronic frontier." The Winnebago is parked in front of a casino, deep in a tribal nation's territory. The family members are shrunken, though they do not suffer from the vertigo that ought to accompany their shrinking; they remain unaware of their tininess, their insignificance. They are inside the casino, together, playing a gambling game that is a video game, designed to separate them from their money. The game is called Win-and-They-Go! The action consists of attempting to place homesteads on every hundred acres of open territory, a frantic effort destined, as in all gambling devices, to tease and entice with sporadic success and to bring in the end total failure and defeat. The soundtrack of the game consists of songs licensed from the band E.L.O.; the design of the "frontier," across which the family navigates, and which repeats like the backdrop in a "Flintstones" cartoon, consists of cacti, distant canyon bluffs, abandoned gold mines, wood-panelled station wagons, and crafty winking trickster Indians selling merchandise at trading posts. All of this is rendered in a nostalgic nineteen-seventies-cartoon style, but the story, it is now apparent, takes place not in 1979 but in the present. The past, even so recent a past as 1979, a time in which a paraphrase of Lafferty's story could still conceivably be written, is unsustainable. The machine is sucking money from the family's coffers. It's O.K., they have a lot of it. The story dollies out now to leave the family there, in the windowless bowels of the casino, to rise up and observe the Winnebago in the parking lot, amid so many other unwieldy vacation vehicles also stilled there. The story climbs ever higher to a wide pan of the surrounding desert, then higher, to find the horizon. The story acknowledges its collapse at this vanishing point, which is not a frontier of any type or variety. The story acknowledges its relief at being over even as it acknowledges the possibility that it never managed to begin. Game over. Thanks for playing.

CROWN HEIGHTS NORTH

BY RIVKA GALCHEN (2024)

The dead man decided to try the running app. He hadn't run for years. Not since his mid-thirties. Now he was in his early fifties. Or he had been in his early fifties, recently enough. Would he be in his early fifties forever? He tapped the gray oblong and waited as the percentage-downloaded dial advanced, slowly. *Much has yet to be revealed*, he whispered to himself, in a tone he had used more often when he was a kid, when he had expected his life to resemble a tale of adventure, or of horror, or one with a mystery to solve, or a magical stone to obtain.

He felt kind of embarrassed—but why, and in front of whom? He had heard good things about the app and he didn't want to run "alone." A voice to keep him company: it was like that Ray Bradbury story he'd read so many times when he was young. Even after he knew its trick, the story was still compelling. In it, an automated voice in a house says things like "Nine-fifteen, time to clean," "Which poem would you like this evening?," and "Since you express no preference, I shall select a poem at random." Eventually, it becomes clear that a nuclear apocalypse, or something of that sort, has wiped out the family and probably humanity, but that the house persists, trying to tend to people who will never return. Did they still teach that story to kids, now that houses really did speak to them, and vice versa? Anyhow, he, the dead man, was up for the companionship of a recorded voice. His wife, through his illness, had said that this running app kept her sane.

The app consisted of a bunch of "Guided Runs," in which various people—coaches, meditation gurus, professional athletes, unappealing artists—talked to you while you ran. At the end of each run, you received data: how far you'd gone, and where, and at what pace. You could earn badges, like a Girl Scout or a soldier, his wife had told him. They just speak cheerful nonsense to you, and it's somehow really reassuring, she said. She sat by his bed in the I.C.U., sharing little thoughts with him, even when he couldn't answer her. She told him about a movie in which one of the main characters wore large headphones in most of the scenes, and you could hear what he was hearing, and not hear what he wasn't hearing, and it had given her a headache. In oases of wellness, when not intubated, he told her about his I.C.U. deliriums. They were hellscapes beyond anything he had ever read or imagined, with horrifying—yet vague and shifting—predicaments, and hostile beings, and also with furniture somehow, of impossible sizes, and the telling failed to communicate the terror, and the only gentle moment he could recall from vision after vision of threat was the feeling, briefly, of a sleepy and benign panther that lived beneath his hospital bed. Why had he never heard or read about this overwhelming phenomenon? He wished it could be transcribed, but it turned as if into lint when he surfaced into full consciousness. Often when he couldn't speak, his wife would read aloud to him, which she knew he perceived, because the measurements of his blood pressure and heart rate on the forever monitors would settle down in response to her ongoing voice. She read Trollope to him, she read the writings of Julian of Norwich. She read "The Lord of the Rings," which his dad had read to him when he was a child, but she decided to stop when the plot moved from parties with hobbits and elves to endless wars. She apologized that she wasn't allowed to bring in their dog, who missed him.

That was then. Now company, even that of a recorded voice, was probably more than a good idea. *This is a necessary part of the adventure*, the dead man said to himself. He scrolled through the Guided Run options. A "Stress-Free" run. A "Running for More Purpose" run. A "Running for Joy" run. A "Menstruation and Training" run, split into two thirty-minute blocks. A "Running for Creativity" run. O.K., so this is not marketed to me, he thought. All the better.

He settled on a "Comeback Run," guided by the app's Global Head Coach. The app asked if he wanted to input which sneakers he was wearing for the run. He did not. Though he felt some sympathy with the practice of hawking wares. It had seemed so tiresome for so long, but now it seemed to him . . . eternal? He hadn't been remembering much, other than the nightmare of the hospital, but now a memory surfaced, asking for his attention. As a young man, he had visited the Sinai Peninsula. He ate cucumbers and sliced Spam in a beach shack near the Red Sea. Later, he had visited a wadi, where he noticed a figure crossing the vast, shadeless sands. What unfathomable intuitions and desires move a person from here to there across a hostile desert, he had wondered. During those travels, he had been reading "The Tale of Genji" and "Moby-Dick" and the works of Thomas Browne, and other things far from his lived experience—but also near, since they were from his roommate's bookshelf. The figure arrived. She unfurled her thin cerulean-blue scarf and laid out bracelets, earrings, a few pins. She was hawking wares.

O.K. Fifteen minutes. He stepped out into his same-old-but-somehow-not neighborhood. The same mixture of Caribbean immigrants and Orthodox Jews and pale youngish people who drank iced coffee with surreal frequency. *You showed up*, the recorded voice said. *Which maybe is something you weren't able to do yesterday!* The dead man started to jog, slowly, with his weak, deconditioned legs. *It's not that I don't care where you were yesterday or the day before—I do care*. But I care more that you're here now. He did not feel like a gazelle, or even like a chubby dog. His arms felt heavy, his fists like clay. *I want to celebrate that you're here. Celebrating starting lines is as important as celebrating finish lines.*

Someone had suggested to his wife that she hire a death doula, but she knew him well enough to know that he did not want a death doula, and he reminded her of the time they visited a friend who had recently given birth and she educated them on the benefits of placenta smoothies and served them cookies with breast milk. Support, coaching, advice, in-touch-ness: it was all adjacent to unbearable. But the Global Head Coach's voice: he didn't turn it off. As he ran, he felt a compression on his calves, not wholly unlike the inflatable cuffs they had put on his legs in the hospital. He listened as the coach chatted about having taught high-school history and coached track for seven years, and how in that time he had seen victories, and defeats, and heartbreak, and tremendous strength. A small harpoon feeling assaulted the dead man's forearm, and a muffled ringing sounded in his head. The Global Head Coach said that he often messed up his own comeback runs, by expecting too much from them. It's very difficult, Coach went on, to go from the state of not running to the state of running, and what's awesome and brave is to run easy, because the best comeback run is one that leaves you feeling ready to come back and run again tomorrow. It's funny, the dead man thought, as he ran around his neighborhood park, listening to Coach, because, if I were to have imagined Hell, it would have a voice-over like Coach, and a landscape in which everything was the same, but also completely wrong, sapped of . . . love? Hell. And yet, since he was running by the same trees and houses and torn plastic bags that he and his wife had again and again walked by, and what with love being a mystery and time a conundrum, this place also converged with a vision of Heaven.

The north side of Crown Heights, maybe because he had lived there when he was ill, was where—sorry, but it was true, he told himself—life had revealed itself to be an abundance, a gift. Mornings, a convention of dogs would manifest in the park. Some dogs dedicated themselves to speed. Others to shade. Or to winning over the affection of strangers. Or to retrieving orange rubber balls or running laps with an impromptu gang of other dogs, whoever had turned up that day. What a just society! The owners were, mostly, weird, sure. The dogs represented an alternative and superior value system, he had decided. Though he wondered if the nearness of death had messed with his perception, like those gas-station sunglasses of childhood road trips. At the courts near the field of dogs, beautiful young men—and occasionally a few women—played basketball. The park had a butterfly garden and skateboarding ramps and ledges and a handball court. There was often a man who knit with yarn the colors of the Jamaican flag, and a cheerful drug dealer with a female bulldog who wore a blue sweater, and there were children on scooters with Orthodox moms who looked like teen-agers and maybe were teen-agers. Unexpected sequel, he thought, for a neighborhood most famous, decades earlier, for the death of a young child hit by a car in a blue-eyed rabbi's motorcade which ran a red light, and then days of angry crowds in the street and the murder of a visiting student. The rabbi, who had since died, still appeared, smiling, on large stickers on the back of most crosswalk lights in the neighborhood, along with the words "Messiah Is Here."

Then the run was over.

He started to run every day, following nearly the same path each time: around the park, then around the park again, maybe inside the park, then around it one more time. It felt good. He didn't want to stray from that loop. He was reluctant to go beyond the familiar space. He got stronger, breathed less heavily, could run more laps. He downloaded in advance the runs that appealed to him, then paged through his "library" of runs. Runs organized by time appealed to him, not those organized by distance. He liked "recovery runs"—the ever-buoyant Global Head Coach, who was the corniest coach but also the one he chose the most often, insisted that most runs should be recovery runs. Sometimes he chose runs with "intervals," where you were asked to run, then rest, then run, then rest, and the whole time you'd be told how strong you were, how good you looked, how proud this person who knew nothing about you was. It was infantile, and it was the result of years of research into how to get a person to push a button and move through space on command. It was a pleasure, which was not what he had spent his life, or most of it, seeking, as his wife had told him when he said he disliked barbecues, picnics, and sunset walks on beaches. It became as if all he was doing was running.

During a run one overcast afternoon, the dead man had the sensation that he could hear his heart beating in his left ear. In his weeks in the I.C.U.—or maybe it was months? Time wasn't a destroyer so much as a whirlpool—he had been convinced that he could feel his pancreas startle and secrete. He could see into his own body, and watch the enzymes, which looked like spilled mercury, asserting themselves, raying out along a confused net of vessels. It was the Edgar Allan Poe story not written, he thought. In moments that resembled clarity, from his hospital bed he composed letters in his mind to the heads of medical-research departments about what he was seeing. There should be interventions to protect people from having to traverse these menacing lands, he thought. At one point, he was being held firmly at the wrist by a woman in a purple cap who informed him that she was bringing him some ice and that his throat might feel sore. He remembered the feeling, as a child, of being inside an adventure, at the mouth of a cave within which dwelled maybe a wizard or an ogre, a false oracle or a real one, and the decision to be made was whether to ask a question, or to knock on the door, or to wield a longbow or a morning star, and then at the periphery his mom saying that she had left a grilled-cheese sandwich on the kitchen counter, and that she had to go, and that she was sorry, they were out of pickles, she would try to get some, but she was very busy, she was gone. The woman in purple told him he would feel more relaxed soon. He worried or hoped for a moment that he was still alive, that his conviction that he had died was only one more hostility, a word he often misread as "hospitality." But who, even in a dream or hallucination, would choose the adventure of dying in a hospital, where the lights were always on, where alarms sounded constantly, where potions moved through you as if through an unrenovated sewage-processing plant? *The run. Is. Done. You were awesome. Now get some fluids.*

He was getting stronger. Fifteen minutes would go by like a coffee, and running now felt like a crossing over from an ordinary life (or death) full of pain and anxiety, into a better life (or death) filled with more bearable kinds of pain, and anxieties that could fit into a pocket. Still, he didn't run out to new neighborhoods, he felt the need to stay close to home, to not fall off into realms beyond his map. Out there, they were probably just hawking wares: incense, hazelnut cookies, button-up dress shirts. He wanted to stay within bounds. It was the opposite of the missions in the stories he had read when he was young: to find a way out of a peril-filled maze, to escape from a place where doors opened on their own when a secret but large metal button on a wall was pushed. Later plots, termed literature, were often still childlike stories about finding a way home or recovering lost time, his wife had pointed out to him during one of their first meals together, when personal conversations were still translated into impersonal observations. He had liked that.

Maybe he was under a spell, and his comrades had been turned into pigs, and he had been lulled into running the same loop, again and again, around the familiar park, so that he wouldn't notice he was captive, and the feat he had to accomplish was to notice and to break his pattern.

And then there they were: traffic cones and security tape. The street in front of the park was blocked off. It was the funeral, a man wearing a tank top and walking a marble-cake-colored dog told him. A line of officers was assembled along the block adjacent to the park and then across the street and on over to the Nazarene church that was previously a synagogue and which still had the Hebrew lettering on its frieze. A bird rested on the small cross atop the building's dome. The dead man asked a man standing in shorts with his arms crossed: Who died? It was an officer who had been shot, off duty. Something random, was the sense. Just outside a deli, killed by a stranger, not something directed at him, or even at the "genre" of him, as a police officer.

"It's an outrage," a voice behind him said. Cars that had been parked along the path of the funeral procession had been towed to God knew where. A row of men in kilts began walking, in tandem, with bagpipes; with them was a line of drummers. "They do whatever they want, they answer to nobody, they're an institution of assholes," was being said, by a guy with an iced drink, to his companion, who wore a jumpsuit. A woman the dead man recognized as active in the church—she ran the Easter-egg hunt, she took care of the plants at the perimeter—was telling another woman that she knew the grieving mother. Her son had been in a coma for nearly three decades. So he had died a long time ago, but was dying only now. "We're all dying," the iced-coffee guy said. "No one's going to tow cars for me."

One disappointment about being dead, so far, was that he had assumed that, in dying, he would learn something. Or: his first assumption was that when he died there wouldn't be anything at all, let alone knowledge. But trailing behind that assumption was a firefly of hope. What was here? There were sparrows and paper clips. There were books, babies, Post-it notes with phone numbers, compost bins with graffiti, ambulance sirens, a statue of a Dalmatian. But as an afterlife was this . . . interesting? Informative? Back in his thirties, when for a spell he had run often, he had enjoyed the way it shook out little unexpected thoughts. Like: tartan plaids make sense, given how weaving works. Or: Thoreau must have had secrets. He had termed these unpursued thoughts "popcorn," a happy word for him, connected to the stovetop popcorn in those disposable aluminum pans with the balloon of thin foil that would pleasingly inflate and fill with popcorn, though sometimes the kernels burned. The "Struggle Run." Why not? The uncertainty of love, the certainty of death—one faced these things. But could he really care? On too many days, in his last months, thinking had lost its allure. He was more interested in watching a kid get frustrated by the difficulty of swimming down to the bottom of the pool to pick up coins; the water kept sending him back up. Boundless blessings was what he was supposed to think about life. He was so angry. The Global Head Coach told him that struggle is about contending with a problem. *Struggle is not about failing but about succeeding in not giving up*. Struggle was a particularly misleading term in relation to illness. He could have altered his outcome in no way. At one point, delirious with what was termed medication, he woke in the middle of the night, gripped his wife's arm, and said, *I have been seduced by the lie of metaphysics*. Later, when his wife told him this, they laughed. But being asleep was a castaway island, with no ships on the horizon. Coach said, *When we struggle, we're never alone. We beat ourselves up because it's easier than picking ourselves up*.

Late in his illness, he had a conversation in his office with Ben, his colleague. Ben had come from an Orthodox family, but had turned away from it—or something. "My father had a lot of medical problems, he really cursed God—but that's because he was like the prophets," Ben was saying to him, or at him. "He struggled with God." Ben could speak unceasingly if not interrupted, and it wasn't easy to interrupt him. Oblivious to the dead man's own "struggle," Ben talked on, hoarding the dead man's time, although his ramblings, which were heartfelt, now and again crossed over into the dead man's own concerns. "You know, the prophets, they struggled with God, too. It's about that struggle." He spoke of how the words Jesus said on the cross were, translated from the Aramaic: Father, why have you forsaken me? "That was my dad, that was his inner life." Ben was struggling, too, having been raised only to be a scholar in an imaginary Messianic landscape, and having left that imaginary landscape for the "real" landscape—what was he supposed to do? "People who think God is a person who gives out candy to some people and not to others—that's so wrong." He explained that it was like the Jews in the desert, complaining, and God said, Come to me, and they said, Why?, and he said, Because I'm God, and they said, It's not a good enough reason. They said, Come to us, and he said, Why?, and they said, Because we've suffered, and he said, That's not a good enough reason.

Even when you were dying, people yammered on about themselves. You could never get that time back. It was returning to him: being alive had become a hell on earth. Had his life been, after all, a tale of adventure? Of horror? Did the ending make any sense? He had felt love in his life and where could it be found now? He saw, at the edge of the familiar park, that mysterious expanse of sand he had visited as a young man. He saw, again, in the distance, a woman, heading toward him. What intuition or desire could be sending her out across that hostile, shadeless expanse? As she neared, it was not without some sense of surprise that the thought arrived that maybe a different kind of story waited for him, one he had never read before, one that he wouldn't have to read alone. *You're awesome*, the Global Head Coach said. *I'm so proud.*

ACKNOWLEDGMENTS

This anthology would not exist without the century of insightful decisions and inspired editorial work put in by *The New Yorker*'s fiction editors. I'd like to acknowledge the enormous contributions of those who served before me: Katharine S. White, Gus Lobrano, Howard Moss, William Maxwell, Robert Henderson, Rachel MacKenzie, Robert Hemenway, Derek Morgan, Frances Kiernan, Charles McGrath, Daniel Menaker, Veronica Geng, Patricia Strachan, Gwyneth Cravens, Linda Asher, and Deborah Garrison, among others. And of those I had or still have the privilege and the pleasure of working alongside: Roger Angell, Bill Buford, Cressida Leyshon, Alice Quinn, Meghan O'Rourke, Sean Wilsey, Carin Besser, and Willing Davidson (as well as the remarkable assistants and assistant editors Field Maloney, Branden Jacobs-Jenkins, Lee Ellis, John McElwee, David S. Wallace, and Dennis Zhou). Since David Remnick became the editor of *The New Yorker* just over a quarter of a century ago, he has happily flown the fiction flag, always ready to take a chance on new voices—and to spend his weekends reading manuscripts. Heartfelt thanks go to him, and to other colleagues at the magazine who helped make this book happen, including Nathan Burstein, Fabio Bertoni, Risa Leibowitz, and Emily Clancy, and to the team at Knopf, including Zuleima Ugalde, Kevin Bourke, Casey Hampton, Chip Kidd, and R. Kikuo Johnson—and, of course, a second tip of the hat to Deborah Garrison, for steering the project there with care and humor and allowing us to make a door-stopper out of it!

INDEX OF CONTRIBUTORS

A NOTE ABOUT THE EDITOR

DEBORAH TREISMAN is *The New Yorker*'s fiction editor and the host of *The New Yorker Fiction Podcast.*

A NOTE ON THE TYPE

This book was set in Janson, a typeface named for the Dutchman Anton Janson but actually the work of Nicholas Kis (1650–1702). The type is an excellent example of the influential and sturdy Dutch types that prevailed in England up to the time William Caslon (1692–1766) developed his own incomparable designs from them.

Composed by North Market Street Graphics,
Lancaster, Pennsylvania

Printed and bound by Friesens Corporation,
Altona, Manitoba, Canada

Designed by Casey Hampton